IRISH GHOST STORIES

Irish Ghost
Stories

Wordsworth Editions

Readers who are interested in other titles from
Wordsworth Editions are invited to visit our website at
www.wordsworth-editions.com

For our latest list and a full mail-order service contact
Bibliophile Books, 5 Thomas Road, London E14 7BN
Tel: +44 0207 515 9222   Fax: +44 0207 538 4115
e-mail: orders@bibliophilebooks.com

This edition published 2005 by Wordsworth Editions Limited
8B East Street, Ware, Hertfordshire SG12 9HJ

ISBN 1 84022 487 8

Typeset by Antony Gray
Printed in Great Britain by
Mackays of Chatham, Chatham, Kent

CONTENTS

SHERIDAN LE FANU

Green Tea

☙❧

PROLOGUE

Martin Hesselius, the German Physician

Though carefully educated in medicine and surgery, I have never practised either. The study of each continues, nevertheless, to interest me profoundly. Neither idleness nor caprice caused my secession from the honourable calling which I had just entered. The cause was a very trifling scratch inflicted by a dissecting knife. This trifle cost me the loss of two fingers, amputated promptly, and the more painful loss of my health, for I have never been quite well since, and have seldom been twelve months together in the same place.

In my wanderings I became acquainted with Dr Martin Hesselius, a wanderer like myself, like me a physician, and like me an enthusiast in his profession. Unlike me in this, that his wanderings were voluntary, and he a man, if not of fortune, as we estimate fortune in England, at least in what our forefathers used to term 'easy circumstances'. He was an old man when I first saw him; nearly five-and-thirty years my senior.

In Dr Martin Hesselius, I found my master. His knowledge was immense, his grasp of a case was an intuition. He was the very man to inspire a young enthusiast like me with awe and delight. My admiration has stood the test of time and survived the separation of death. I am sure it was well founded.

For nearly twenty years I acted as his medical secretary. His immense collection of papers he has left in my care, to be arranged, indexed and bound. His treatment of some of these cases is curious. He writes in two distinct characters. He describes what he saw and heard as an intelligent layman might, and when, in this style of narrative, he had seen the patient either through his own hall-door to the light of day or through the gates of darkness to the caverns of the dead, he returns upon the narrative, and in the terms of his art, and with all the force and originality of genius, proceeds to the work of analysis, diagnosis and illustration.

Here and there a case strikes me as of a kind to amuse or horrify a lay reader with an interest quite different from the peculiar one which it may possess for an expert. With slight modifications, chiefly of language, and of course a change of names, I copy the following. The narrator is Dr Martin Hesselius. I find it among the voluminous notes of cases which he made during a tour in England about sixty-four years ago.

It is related in a series of letters to his friend Professor Van Loo of Leyden. The professor was not a physician, but a chemist, and a man who read history and metaphysics and medicine, and had, in his day, written a play.

The narrative is therefore, if somewhat less valuable as a medical record, necessarily written in a manner more likely to interest an unlearned reader.

These letters, from a memorandum attached, appear to have been returned on the death of the professor, in 1819, to Dr Hesselius. They are written, some in English, some in French, but the greater part in German. I am a faithful though, I am conscious, by no means a graceful translator, and although here and there I omit some passages, and shorten others, and disguise names, I have interpolated nothing.

I

Dr Hesselius Relates How He Met the Reverend Mr Jennings

The Reverend Mr Jennings is tall and thin. He is middle-aged, and dresses with a natty, old-fashioned, high-church precision. He is naturally a little stately, but not at all stiff. His features, without being handsome, are well formed, and their expression extremely kind, but also shy.

I met him one evening at Lady Mary Heyduke's. The modesty and benevolence of his countenance are extremely prepossessing.

We were but a small party, and he joined agreeably enough in the conversation. He seems to enjoy listening very much more than contributing to the talk; but what he says is always to the purpose and well said. He is a great favourite of Lady Mary's, who, it seems, consults him upon many things, and thinks him the most happy and blessed person on earth. Little knows she about him.

The Reverend Mr Jennings is a bachelor, and has, they say, sixty thousand pounds in the funds. He is a charitable man. He is most anxious to be actively employed in his sacred profession, and yet, though always tolerably well elsewhere, when he goes down to his vicarage in Warwickshire, to engage in the actual duties of his sacred calling, his health soon fails him, and in a very strange way. So says Lady Mary.

There is no doubt that Mr Jennings' health does break down in generally a sudden and mysterious way, sometimes in the very act of officiating in his old and pretty church at Kenlis. It may be his heart, it may be his brain. But it has happened three or four times, or oftener, that after proceeding a certain way in the service, he has on a sudden stopped short, and after a silence, apparently quite unable to resume, he has fallen into solitary, inaudible prayer, his hands and his eyes uplifted, and then pale as death, and in the agitation of a strange shame and horror, descended trembling, and got into the vestry-room, leaving his congregation, without explanation, to themselves. This occurred when his curate was absent. When he goes down to Kenlis now, he always takes care to provide a clergyman to share his duty, and to supply his place on the instant should he become thus suddenly incapacitated.

When Mr Jennings breaks down quite, and beats a retreat from the vicarage, and returns to London, where, in a dark street off Piccadilly, he inhabits a very narrow house, Lady Mary says that he is always perfectly well. I have my own opinion about that. There are degrees of course. We shall see.

Mr Jennings is a perfectly gentlemanlike man. People, however, remark something odd. There is an impression a little ambiguous. One thing which certainly contributes to it people, I think, don't remember; or, perhaps, distinctly remark. But I did, almost immediately. Mr Jennings has a way of looking sidelong upon the carpet, as if his eye followed the movements of something there. This, of course, is not always. It occurs only now and then. But often enough to give a certain oddity, as I have said, to his manner, and in this glance travelling along the floor there is something both shy and anxious.

A medical philosopher, as you are good enough to call me, elaborating theories by the aid of cases sought out by himself, and by him watched and scrutinised with more time at command, and consequently infinitely more minuteness than the ordinary practitioner can afford, falls insensibly into habits of observation which accompany him everywhere, and are exercised, as some people would say, impertinently, upon every subject that presents itself with the least likelihood of rewarding enquiry.

There was a promise of this kind in the slight, timid, kindly, but reserved gentleman, whom I met for the first time at this agreeable little evening gathering. I observed, of course, more than I here set down; but I reserve all that borders on the technical for a strictly scientific paper.

I may remark that when I here speak of medical science, I do so, as I hope someday to see it more generally understood, in a much more comprehensive sense than its generally material treatment would warrant. I believe the entire natural world is but the ultimate expression of that spiritual world from which, and in which alone, it has its life. I believe that the essential man is a spirit, that the spirit is an organised substance, but as different in point of material from what we ordinarily understand by matter as light or electricity is; that the material body is, in the most literal sense, a vesture, and death consequently no interruption of the living man's existence, but simply his extrication from the natural body – a process which commences at the moment of what we term death, and the completion of which, at furthest a few days later, is the resurrection 'in power'.

The person who weighs the consequences of these positions will probably see their practical bearing upon medical science. This is, however, by no means the proper place for displaying the proofs and discussing the consequences of this too generally unrecognised state of facts.

In pursuance of my habit, I was covertly observing Mr Jennings – with all my caution, I think he perceived it – and I saw plainly that he was as cautiously observing me. Lady Mary happening to address me by my name, as Dr Hesselius, I saw that he glanced at me more sharply, and then became thoughtful for a few minutes.

After this, as I conversed with a gentleman at the other end of the room, I saw him look at me more steadily, and with an interest which I thought I understood. I then saw him take an opportunity of chatting with Lady Mary, and was, as one always is, perfectly aware of being the subject of a distant enquiry and answer.

This tall clergyman approached me by and by; and in a little time we had got into conversation. When two people who like reading and know books and places, having travelled, wish to discourse, it is very strange if they can't find topics. It was not accident that brought him near me, and led him into conversation. He knew German, and had read my *Essays on Metaphysical Medicine*, which suggest more than they actually say.

This courteous man – gentle, shy, plainly a man of thought and reading, who moving and talking among us, was not altogether of us, and whom I already suspected of leading a life whose transactions and alarms were carefully concealed, with an impenetrable reserve, from not only the world, but from his best beloved friends – was cautiously weighing in his own mind the idea of taking a certain step with regard to me.

I penetrated his thoughts without his being aware of it, and was careful to say nothing which could betray to his sensitive vigilance my suspicions respecting his position, or my surmises about his plans respecting myself.

We chatted upon indifferent subjects for a time but at last he said: 'I was very much interested by some papers of yours, Dr Hesselius, upon what you term metaphysical medicine. I read them in German, ten or twelve years ago – have they been translated?'

'No, I'm sure they have not – I should have heard. They would have asked my leave, I think.'

'I asked the publishers here, a few months ago, to get the book for me in the original German; but they tell me it is out of print.'

'So it is, and has been for some years; but it flatters me as an author to find that you have not forgotten my little book, although,' I added, laughing, 'ten or twelve years is a considerable time to have managed without it; but I suppose you have been turning the subject over again in your mind, or something has happened lately to revive your interest in it.'

At this remark, accompanied by a glance of enquiry, a sudden embarrassment disturbed Mr Jennings, analogous to that which makes a young lady blush and look foolish. He dropped his eyes, and folded his hands together uneasily, and looked oddly, and you would have said, guiltily, for a moment.

I helped him out of his awkwardness in the best way, by appearing not to observe it, and going straight on, I said: 'Those revivals of interest in a subject happen to me often; one book suggests another, and often sends me back on a wild-goose chase over an interval of twenty years. But if you still care to possess a copy, I shall be only too happy to provide you; I have still got two or three by me – and if you allow me to present one, I shall be very much honoured.'

'You are very good indeed,' he said, quite at his ease again, in a moment: 'I almost despaired – I don't know how to thank you.'

'Pray don't say a word; the thing is really of so little worth that I am only ashamed of having offered it, and if you thank me any more I shall throw it into the fire in a fit of modesty.'

Mr Jennings laughed. He enquired where I was staying in London, and after a little more conversation on a variety of subjects, he took his departure.

2

The Doctor Questions Lady Mary, and She Answers

'I like your vicar so much, Lady Mary,' said I, as soon as he was gone. 'He has read, travelled, and thought, and having also suffered, he ought to be an accomplished companion.'

'So he is, and, better still, he is a really good man,' said she. 'His advice is invaluable about my schools, and all my little undertakings at Dawlbridge, and he's so painstaking, he takes so much trouble – you have no idea – wherever he thinks he can be of use: he's so good-natured and so sensible.'

'It is pleasant to hear so good an account of his neighbourly virtues. I can only testify to his being an agreeable and gentle companion, and in addition to what you have told me, I think I can tell you two or three things about him,' said I.

'Really!'

'Yes, to begin with, he's unmarried.'

'Yes, that's right – go on.'

'He has been writing, that is he *was*, but for two or three years perhaps, he has not gone on with his work, and the book was upon some rather abstract subject – perhaps theology.'

'Well, he was writing a book, as you say; I'm not quite sure what it was about, but only that it was nothing that I cared for; very likely you are right, and he certainly did stop – yes.'

'And although he only drank a little coffee here tonight, he likes tea, at least, did like it, extravagantly.'

'Yes, that's quite true.'

'He drank green tea, a good deal, didn't he?' I pursued.

'Well, that's very odd! Green tea was a subject on which we used almost to quarrel.'

'But he has quite given that up,' said I.

'So he has.'

'And, now, one more fact. His mother or his father, did you know them?'

'Yes, both; his father is only ten years dead, and their place is near Dawlbridge. We knew them very well,' she answered.

'Well, either his mother or his father – I should rather think his father, saw a ghost,' said I.

'Well, you really are a conjurer, Dr Hesselius.'

'Conjurer or no, haven't I said right?' I answered merrily.

'You certainly have, and it *was* his father: he was a silent, whimsical man, and he used to bore my father about his dreams, and at last he told him a story about a ghost he had seen and talked with, and a very odd story it was. I remember it particularly, because I was so afraid of him. This story was long before he died – when I was quite a child – and his ways were so silent and moping, and he used to drop in sometimes, in the dusk, when I was alone in the drawing-room, and I used to fancy there were ghosts about him.'

I smiled and nodded.

'And now, having established my character as a conjurer, I think I must say good-night,' said I.

'But how *did* you find it out?'

'By the planets, of course, as the gypsies do,' I answered, and so, gaily, we said good-night.

Next morning I sent the little book he had been enquiring after and a note to Mr Jennings, and on returning late that evening, I found that he had called at my lodgings and left his card. He asked whether I was at home, and asked at what hour he would be most likely to find me.

Does he intend opening his case, and consulting me 'professionally', as they say? I hope so. I have already conceived a theory about him. It is supported by Lady Mary's answers to my parting questions. I should like to ascertain more from his own lips. But what can I do consistent with good breeding to invite a confession? Nothing. I rather think he meditates one. At all events, my dear Van Loo, I shan't make myself difficult of access; I mean to return his visit tomorrow. It will be only civil, in return for his politeness, to ask to see him. Perhaps something may come of it. Whether much, little, or nothing, my dear Van Loo, you shall hear.

3

Dr Hesselius Picks Up Something in Latin Books

Well, I have called at Bolton Street.

On enquiring at the door, I was told by the servant that Mr Jennings was engaged very particularly with a gentleman, a clergyman from Kenlis, his parish in the country. Intending to reserve my privilege and to call again, I merely intimated that I should try another time, and had turned to go when the servant begged my pardon and asked me, looking at me a little more attentively than well-bred persons of his order usually do, whether I was Dr Hesselius; and, on learning that I was, he said, 'Perhaps then, sir, you would allow me to mention it to Mr Jennings, for I am sure he wishes to see you.'

The servant returned in a moment with a message from Mr Jennings asking me to go into his study, which was in effect his back drawing-room, and promising to be with me in a very few minutes.

This was really a study – almost a library. The room was lofty, with two tall slender windows and rich dark curtains. It was much larger than I had expected and stacked with books on every side, from the floor to the ceiling. The upper carpet – for to my tread it felt that there were two or three – was a Turkey carpet. My steps fell noiselessly. The way the bookcases stood out placed the windows, particularly narrow ones, in deep recesses. The effect of the room was, although extremely comfortable, and even luxurious, decidedly gloomy, and aided by the silence, almost oppressive. Perhaps, however, I ought to have allowed something for association. My mind had connected peculiar ideas with Mr Jennings. I stepped into this perfectly silent room, of a very silent house, with a peculiar foreboding; and its darkness, and solemn clothing of books – for except where two narrow looking-glasses were set in the wall, they were everywhere – helped this sombre feeling.

While awaiting Mr Jennings' arrival, I amused myself by looking into some of the books with which his shelves were laden. Not among these, but immediately under them, with their backs upward, on the floor, I lighted upon a complete set of Swedenborg's *Arcana Caelestia*, in the original Latin, a very fine folio set, bound in the natty livery which theology affects, pure vellum, namely, with gold letters and carmine edges. There were paper markers in several of these volumes; I raised and set them, one after the other, upon the table, and opening where these papers were placed, I read in the solemn Latin phraseology a series of sentences indicated by a pencilled line at the margin. Of these I copy here a few, translating them into English.

When man's interior sight is opened, which is that of his spirit, then there appear the things of another life, which cannot possibly be made visible to the bodily sight . . .

By the internal sight it has been granted me to see the things that are in the other life more clearly than I see those that are in the world. From these considerations it is evident that external vision exists from interior vision, and this from a vision still more interior, and so on . . .

There are with every man at least two evil spirits . . .

With wicked genii there is also a fluent speech, but harsh and grating. There is also among them a speech which is not fluent, wherein the dissent of the thoughts is perceived as something secretly creeping along within it.

The evil spirits associated with man are indeed from the hells, but when with man they are not then in hell but are taken out thence. The place where they then are is in the midst between heaven and hell and is called the world of spirits – when the evil spirits who are with man are in that world, they are not in any infernal torment but in every thought and affection of the man, and so, in all that the man himself enjoys. But when they are remitted into their hell, they return to their former state . . .

If evil spirits could perceive that they were associated with man and yet that they were spirits separate from him, and if they could flow into the things of his body, they would attempt by a thousand means to destroy him; for they hate man with a deadly hatred . . .

Knowing, therefore, that I was a man in the body, they were continually striving to destroy me, not as to the body only, but especially as to the soul; for to destroy any man or spirit is the very delight of the life of all who are in hell; but I have been continually protected by the Lord. Hence it appears how dangerous it is for man to be in a living consort with spirits unless he be in the good of faith . . .

Nothing is more carefully guarded from the knowledge of associate spirits than their being thus conjoint with a man, for if they knew it they would speak to him, with the intention to destroy him . . .

The delight of hell is to do evil to man, and to hasten his eternal ruin.

A long note, written with a very sharp and fine pencil, in Mr Jennings' neat hand, at the foot of the page, caught my eye. Expecting his criticism upon the text, I read a word or two, and stopped, for it was something quite different, and began with these words, *Deus misereatur mei* – 'May God compassionate me'. Thus warned of its private nature, I averted my eyes, and shut the book, replacing all the volumes as I had found them, except one which interested me, and in which, as men studious and solitary in their habits will do, I grew so absorbed as to take no cognisance of the outer world, nor to remember where I was.

I was reading some pages which refer to 'representatives' and 'correspondents', in the technical language of Swedenborg, and had arrived at a passage the substance of which is that evil spirits, when seen by other eyes than those of their infernal associates, present themselves, by 'correspondence', in the shape of the beast (*fera*) which represents their particular lust and life, in aspect direful and atrocious. This is a long passage, and particularises a number of those bestial forms.

4

Four Eyes were Reading the Passage

I was running the head of my pencil-case along the line as I read it, and something caused me to raise my eyes.

Directly before me was one of the mirrors I have mentioned, in which I saw reflected the tall shape of my friend, Mr Jennings, leaning over my shoulder, and reading the page at which I was busy, and with a face so dark and wild that I should hardly have known him.

I turned and rose. He stood erect also, and with an effort laughed a little, saying: 'I came in and asked you how you did, but without succeeding in awaking you from your book; so I could not restrain my curiosity, and very impertinently, I'm afraid, peeped over your shoulder. This is not your first time of looking into those pages. You have looked into Swedenborg, no doubt, long ago?'

'Oh dear, yes! I owe Swedenborg a great deal; you will discover traces of him in the little book on metaphysical medicine which you were so good as to remember.'

Although my friend affected a gaiety of manner, there was a slight flush in his face, and I could perceive that he was inwardly much perturbed.

'I'm scarcely yet qualified, I know so little of Swedenborg. I've only had them a fortnight,' he answered, 'and I think they are rather likely to make a solitary man nervous – that is, judging from the very little I have read. I don't say that they have made me so,' he laughed; 'and I'm so very much obliged for the book. I hope you got my note?'

I made all proper acknowledgments and modest disclaimers.

'I never read a book that I go with so entirely as that of yours,' he continued. 'I saw at once there is more in it than is quite unfolded. Do you know Dr Harley?' he asked, rather abruptly.

[In passing, the editor remarks that the physician here named was one of the most eminent who had ever practised in England.]

I did, having exchanged letters with him and experienced from him great courtesy and considerable assistance during my visit to England.

'I think that man one of the very greatest fools I ever met in my life,' said Mr Jennings.

This was the first time I had ever heard him say a sharp thing of anybody, and such a term applied to so high a name a little startled me.

'Really! and in what way?' I asked.

'In his profession,' he answered.

I smiled.

'I mean this,' he said: 'he seems to me one half blind – I mean one half of all he looks at is dark – preternaturally bright and vivid all the rest; and the worst of it is, it seems *wilful*. I can't get him – I mean he won't – I've had some experience of him as a physician, but I look on him as, in that sense, no better than a paralytic mind, an intellect half dead. I'll tell you – I know I shall sometime – all about it,' he said, with a little agitation. 'You stay some months longer in England. If I should be out of town during your stay for a little time, would you allow me to trouble you with a letter?'

'I should be only too happy,' I assured him.

'Very good of you. I am so utterly dissatisfied with Harley.'

'A little leaning to the materialistic school,' I said.

'A *mere* materialist,' he corrected me; 'you can't think how that sort of thing worries one who knows better. You won't tell anyone – any of my friends you know – that I am hippish; now, for instance, no one knows – not even Lady Mary – that I have seen Dr Harley, or any other doctor. So pray don't mention it; and, if I should have any threatening of an attack, you'll kindly let me write, or, should I be in town, have a little talk with you.'

I was full of conjecture, and unconsciously I found I had fixed my eyes gravely on him, for he lowered his for a moment, and he said: 'I see you think I might as well tell you now, or else you are forming a conjecture; but you may as well give it up. If you were guessing all the rest of your life, you would never hit on it.' He shook his head smiling, and over that wintry sunshine a black cloud suddenly came down, and he drew his breath in, through his teeth as men do in pain.

'Sorry, of course, to learn that you apprehend occasion to consult any of us; but, command me when and how you like, and I need not assure you that your confidence is sacred.'

He then talked of quite other things, and in a comparatively cheerful way, and after a little time I took my leave.

5

Dr Hesselius is Summoned to Richmond

We parted cheerfully, but he was not cheerful, nor was I. There are certain expressions of that powerful organ of spirit – the human face – which, although I have seen them often, and possess a doctor's nerve, yet disturb me profoundly. One look of Mr Jennings' haunted me. It had seized my imagination with so dismal a power that I changed my plans for the evening, and went to the opera, feeling that I wanted a change of ideas.

I heard nothing of or from him for two or three days, when a note in his hand reached me. It was cheerful, and full of hope. He said that he had been for some little time so much better – quite well, in fact – that he was going to make a little experiment, and run down for a month or so to his parish, to try whether a little work might not quite set him up. There was in it a fervent religious expression of gratitude for his restoration, as he now almost hoped he might call it.

A day or two later I saw Lady Mary, who repeated what his note had announced, and told me that he was actually in Warwickshire, having resumed his clerical duties at Kenlis; and she added, 'I begin to think that he is really perfectly well, and that there never was anything the matter, more than nerves and fancy; we are all nervous, but I fancy there is nothing like a little hard work for that kind of weakness, and he has made up his mind to try it. I should not be surprised if he did not come back for a year.'

Notwithstanding all this confidence, only two days later I had this note, dated from his house off Piccadilly:

> DEAR SIR – I have returned disappointed. If I should feel at all able to see you, I shall write to ask you kindly to call. At present, I am too low, and, in fact, simply unable to say all I wish to say. Pray don't mention my name to my friends. I can see no one. By and by, please God, you shall hear from me. I mean to take a run into Shropshire, where some of my people are. God bless you! May we, on my return, meet more happily than I can now write.

About a week after this I saw Lady Mary at her own house, the last person, she said, left in town, and just on the wing for Brighton, for the London season was quite over. She told me that she had heard from Mr Jennings' niece Martha, in Shropshire. There was nothing to be gathered from her letter, more than that he was low and nervous. In those words, of which healthy people think so lightly, what a world of suffering is sometimes hidden!

Nearly five weeks had passed without any further news of Mr Jennings. At the end of that time I received a note from him. He wrote:

> I have been in the country, and have had change of air, change of scene, change of faces, change of everything and in everything – but *myself*. I have made up my mind, so far as the most irresolute creature on earth can do it, to tell my case fully to you. If your engagements will permit, pray come to me today, tomorrow or the next day; but, pray defer as little as possible. You know not how much I need help. I have a quiet house at Richmond, where I now am. Perhaps you can manage to come to dinner, or to luncheon, or even to tea. You shall have no trouble in finding me out. The servant at Bolton Street, who takes this note, will have a carriage at your door at any hour you please; and I am always to be found. You will say that I ought not to be alone. I have tried everything. Come and see.

I called up the servant, and decided on going out the same evening, which accordingly I did.

He would have been much better in a lodging-house, or hotel, I thought, as I drove up through a short double row of sombre elms to a very old-fashioned brick house, darkened by the foliage of these trees, which overtopped and nearly surrounded it. It was a perverse choice, for nothing could be imagined more triste and silent. The house, I found, belonged to him. He had stayed for a day or two in town, and, finding it for some cause insupportable, had come out here, probably because being furnished and his own, he was relieved of the thought and delay of selection by coming here.

The sun had already set, and the red reflected light of the western sky illuminated the scene with the peculiar effect with which we are all familiar. The hall seemed very dark, but, getting to the back drawing-room, whose windows command the west, I was again in the same dusky light.

I sat down, looking out upon the richly-wooded landscape that glowed in the grand and melancholy light which was every moment fading. The corners of the room were already dark; all was growing dim, and the gloom was insensibly toning my mind, already prepared for what was sinister. I was waiting alone for his arrival, which soon took place. The door communicating with the front room opened, and the tall figure of Mr Jennings, faintly seen in the ruddy twilight, came, with quiet stealthy steps, into the room.

We shook hands and, taking a chair to the window, where there was still light enough to enable us to see each other's faces, he sat down beside me and, placing his hand upon my arm, with scarcely a word of preface began his narrative.

6

How Mr Jennings Met His Companion

The faint glow of the west, the pomp of the then lonely woods of Richmond, were before us, behind and about us the darkening room, and on the stony face of the sufferer – for the character of his face, though still gentle and sweet, was changed – rested that dim, odd glow which seems to descend and produce, where it touches, lights, sudden though faint, which are lost, almost without gradation, in darkness. The silence, too, was utter; not a distant wheel, or bark, or whistle from without; and within, the depressing stillness of an invalid bachelor's house.

I guessed well the nature, though not even vaguely the particulars, of the revelations I was about to receive from that fixed face of suffering that so oddly flushed stood out, like a portrait of Schalken's, before its background of darkness.

'It began,' he said, 'on the 15th of October, three years and eleven weeks ago, and two days – I keep very accurate count, for every day is torment. If I leave anywhere a chasm in my narrative tell me.

'About four years ago I began a work which had cost me very much thought and reading. It was upon the religious metaphysics of the ancients.'

'I know,' said I; 'the actual religion of educated and thinking paganism, quite apart from symbolic worship. A wide and very interesting field.'

'Yes; but not good for the mind – the Christian mind, I mean. Paganism is all bound together in essential unity, and, with evil sympathy, their religion involves their art, and both their manners, and the subject is a degrading fascination and the Nemesis sure. God forgive me!

'I wrote a great deal; I wrote late at night. I was always thinking on the subject, walking about, wherever I was, everywhere. It thoroughly infected me. You are to remember that all the material ideas connected with it were more or less of the beautiful, the subject itself delightfully interesting, and I, then, without a care.'

He sighed heavily.

'I believe that everyone who sets about writing in earnest does his work, as a friend of mine phrased it, *on* something – tea, or coffee, or tobacco. I suppose there is a material waste that must be hourly supplied in such occupations, or that we should grow too abstracted, and the mind, as it were, pass out of the body, unless it were reminded often of the connection by actual sensation. At all events, I felt the want, and I supplied it. Tea was my companion – at first the ordinary black tea, made in the usual way, not too strong: but I drank a good deal, and increased its strength as I went on. I never experienced an uncomfortable symptom from it. I began to take a little green tea. I found the effect pleasanter, it cleared and intensified the power of thought so. I had come to take it frequently, but not stronger than one might take it for pleasure. I wrote a great deal out here, it was so quiet, and in this room. I used to sit up very late, and it became a habit with me to sip my tea – green tea – every now and then as my work proceeded. I had a little kettle on my table, that swung over a lamp, and made tea two or three times between eleven o'clock and two or three in the morning, my hours of going to bed. I used to go into town every day. I was not a monk, and, although I spent an hour or two in a library, hunting up authorities and looking out lights upon my theme, I was in no morbid state as far as I can judge. I met my friends pretty much as usual and enjoyed their society, and, on the whole, existence had never been, I think, so pleasant before.

'I had met with a man who had some odd old books, German editions in mediaeval Latin, and I was only too happy to be permitted access to them. This obliging person's books were in the City, a very out-of-the-way part of it. I had rather outstayed my intended hour, and, on coming out, seeing no cab near, I was tempted to get into the omnibus which used to drive past this house. It was darker than this by the time the bus had reached an old house you may have remarked, with four poplars at each side of the door, and there the last passenger but myself got out. We drove along rather faster. It was twilight now. I leaned back in my corner next the door, ruminating pleasantly.

'The interior of the omnibus was nearly dark. I had observed in the corner opposite to me at the other side, and at the end next the horses, two small circular reflections, as it seemed to me of a reddish light. They were about two inches apart, and about the size of those small brass buttons that yachting men used to put upon their jackets. I began to speculate, as listless men will, upon this trifle, as it seemed. From what centre did that faint but deep-red light come, and from what – glass beads, buttons, toy decorations – was it reflected? We were lumbering along gently, having nearly a mile still to go. I had not solved the puzzle, and it became in another minute more odd, for these two luminous points, with a sudden jerk, descended nearer the floor, keeping still their relative distance and horizontal position, and then, as suddenly, they rose to the level of the seat on which I was sitting and I saw them no more.

'My curiosity was now really excited, and, before I had time to think, I saw again these two dull lamps, again together near the floor; again they disappeared, and again in their old corner I saw them.

'So, keeping my eyes upon them, I edged quietly up my own side, towards the end at which I still saw these tiny discs of red.

'There was very little light in the bus. It was nearly dark. I leaned forward to aid my endeavour to discover what these little circles really were. They shifted their position a little as I did so. I began now to perceive an outline of something black, and I soon saw, with tolerable distinctness, the outline of a small black monkey, pushing its face forward in mimicry to meet mine; those were its eyes, and I now dimly saw its teeth grinning at me.

'I drew back, not knowing whether it might not meditate a spring. I fancied that one of the passengers had forgot this ugly pet, and wishing to ascertain something of its temper, though not caring to trust my fingers to it, I poked my umbrella softly towards it. It remained immovable – up to it – *through* it. For through it, and back and forward it passed, without the slightest resistance.

'I can't, in the least, convey to you the kind of horror that I felt. When I had ascertained that the thing was an illusion, as I then supposed, there came a misgiving about myself and a terror that fascinated me in impotence to remove my gaze from the eyes of the brute for some moments. As I looked, it made a little skip back, quite into the corner, and I, in a panic, found myself at the door, having put my head out, drawing deep breaths of the outer air, and staring at the lights and trees we were passing, too glad to reassure myself of reality.

'I stopped the bus and got out. I perceived the man look oddly at me as I paid him. I dare say there was something unusual in my looks and manner, for I had never felt so strangely before.'

7

The Journey: First Stage

'When the omnibus drove on, and I was alone upon the road, I looked carefully round to ascertain whether the monkey had followed me. To my indescribable relief I saw it nowhere. I can't describe easily what a shock I had received, and my sense of genuine gratitude on finding myself, as I supposed, quite rid of it.

'I had got out a little before we reached this house, two or three hundred steps. A brick wall runs along the footpath, and inside the wall is a hedge of yew, or some dark evergreen of that kind, and within that again the row of fine trees which you may have remarked as you came.

'This brick wall is about as high as my shoulder, and happening to raise my eyes I saw the monkey, with that stooping gait, on all fours, walking or creeping, close beside me on top of the wall. I stopped, looking at it with a feeling of loathing and horror. As I stopped so did it. It sat up on the wall with its long hands on its knees looking at me. There was not light enough to see it much more than in outline, nor was it dark enough to bring the peculiar light of its eyes into strong relief. I still saw, however, that red foggy light plainly enough. It did not show its teeth, nor exhibit any sign of irritation, but seemed jaded and sulky, and was observing me steadily,

'I drew back into the middle of the road. It was an unconscious recoil, and there I stood, still looking at it. It did not move.

'With an instinctive determination to try something – anything, I turned about and walked briskly towards town with askance look, all the time, watching the movements of the beast. It crept swiftly along the wall, at exactly my pace.

'Where the wall ends, near the turn of the road, it came down, and with a wiry spring or two brought itself close to my feet, and continued to keep up with me as I quickened my pace. It was at my left side, so close to my leg that I felt every moment as if I should tread upon it.

'The road was quite deserted and silent, and it was darker every moment. I stopped, dismayed and bewildered, turning as I did so, the other way – I mean, towards this house, away from which I had been walking. When I stood still, the monkey drew back to a distance of, I suppose, about five or six yards, and remained stationary, watching me.

'I had been more agitated than I have said. I had read, of course, as everyone has, something about "spectral illusions", as you physicians term the phenomena of such cases. I considered my situation, and looked my misfortune in the face.

'These affections, I had read, are sometimes transitory and some-times obstinate. I had read of cases in which the appearance, at first harmless, had, step by step, degenerated into something direful and insupportable, and ended by wearing its victim out. Still as I stood there, but for my bestial companion, quite alone, I tried to comfort myself by repeating again and again the assurance, "the thing is purely disease, a well-known physical affection, as distinct as smallpox or neuralgia. Doctors are all agreed on that, philosophy demonstrates it. I must not be a fool. I've been sitting up too late, and I dare say my digestion is quite wrong, and, with God's help, I shall be all right, and this is but a symptom of nervous dyspepsia." Did I believe all this? Not one word of it, no more than any other miserable being ever did who is once seized and riveted in this satanic captivity. Against my convictions, I might say my knowledge, I was simply bullying myself into a false courage.

'I now walked homeward. I had only a few hundred yards to go. I had forced myself into a sort of resignation, but I had not got over the sickening shock and the flurry of the first certainty of my misfortune.

'I made up my mind to pass the night at home. The brute moved close beside me, and I fancied there was the sort of anxious drawing towards the house which one sees in tired horses or dogs sometimes as they come towards home.

'I was afraid to go into town, I was afraid of anyone's seeing and recognising me. I was conscious of an irrepressible agitation in my manner. Also, I was afraid of any violent change in my habits, such as going to a place of amusement or walking from home in order to fatigue myself. At the hall-door it waited till I mounted the steps, and when the door was opened entered with me.

'I drank no tea that night. I got cigars and some brandy and water. My idea was that I should act upon my material system, and by living for a while in sensation apart from thought, send myself forcibly, as it were, into a new groove. I came up here to this drawing-room. I sat just here. The monkey then got up on a small table that then stood there. It looked dazed and languid. An irrepressible uneasiness as to its movements kept my eyes always upon it. Its eyes were half closed, but I could see them glow. It was looking steadily at me. In all situations, at all hours, it is awake and looking at me. That never changes.

'I shall not continue in detail my narrative of this particular night. I shall describe, rather, the phenomena of the first year, which never varied, essentially. I shall describe the monkey as it appeared in daylight. In the dark, as you shall presently hear, there are peculiarities. It is a small monkey, perfectly black. It has only one peculiarity – a character of malignity – unfathomable malignity. During the first year it looked sullen and sick. But this character of intense malice and vigilance was always underlying that surly languor. During all that time it acted as if on a plan of giving me as little trouble as was consistent with watching me. Its eyes were never off me. I have never lost sight of it, except in my sleep, light or dark, day or night, since it came here, excepting when it withdraws for some weeks at a time, unaccountably.

'In total dark it is visible as in daylight. I do not mean merely its eyes. It is as visible distinctly in a halo that resembles a glow of red embers, and which accompanies it in all its movements.

'When it leaves me for a time, it is always at night, in the dark, and in the same way. It grows at first uneasy, and then furious, and then advances towards me, grinning and shaking, its paws clenched; and, at the same time, there comes the appearance of fire in the grate. I never have any fire – I can't sleep in the room where there is any. It draws nearer and nearer to the chimney, quivering, it seems, with rage, and when its fury rises to the highest pitch, it springs into the grate, and up the chimney, and I see it no more.

'When first this happened, I thought I was released. I was now a new man. A day passed – a night – and no return, and a blessed week – a week – another week. I was always on my knees, Dr Hesselius, always, thanking God and praying. A whole month passed of liberty, but on a sudden, it was with me again.'

8

The Second Stage

'It was with me, and the malice which before was torpid under a sullen exterior, was now active. It was perfectly unchanged in every other respect. This new energy was apparent in its activity and its looks, and soon in other ways.

'For a time, you will understand, the change was shown only in an increased vivacity, and an air of menace, as if it was always brooding over some atrocious plan. Its eyes, as before, were never off me.'

'Is it here now?' I asked.

'No,' he replied, 'it has been absent exactly a fortnight and a day – fifteen days. It has sometimes been away so long as nearly two months, once for three. Its absence always exceeds a fortnight, although it may be by but a single day. Fifteen days having past since I saw it last, it may return now at any moment.'

'Is its return,' I asked, 'accompanied by any peculiar manifestation?'

'Nothing – no,' he said. 'It is simply with me again. On lifting my eyes from a book, or turning my head, I see it, as usual, looking at me, and then it remains, as before, for its appointed time. I have never told so much and so minutely before to anyone.'

I perceived that he was agitated, and looking like death, and he repeatedly applied his handkerchief to his forehead; I suggested that he might be tired, and told him that I would call, with pleasure, in the morning, but he said: 'No, if you don't mind hearing it all now. I have got so far, and I should prefer making one effort of it. When I spoke to Dr Harley, I had nothing like so much to tell. You are a philosophic physician. You give spirit its proper rank. If this thing is real – '

He paused, looking at me with agitated enquiry.

'We can discuss it by and by, and very fully. I will give you all I think,' I answered, after an interval.

'Well – very well. If it is anything real, I say, it is prevailing, little by little, and drawing me more interiorly into hell. Optic nerves, he talked of. Ah! well – there are other nerves of communication. May God Almighty help me! You shall hear.

'Its power of action, I tell you, had increased. Its malice became, in a way aggressive. About two years ago, some questions that were pending between me and the bishop having been settled, I went down to my parish in Warwickshire, anxious to find occupation in my profession. I was not prepared for what happened, although I have since thought I might have apprehended something like it. The reason of my saying so is this – '

He was beginning to speak with a great deal more effort and reluctance, and sighed often, and seemed at times nearly overcome. But at this time his manner was not agitated. It was more like that of a sinking patient who has given himself up.

'Yes, but I will first tell you about Kenlis, my parish.

'It was with me when I left this place for Dawlbridge. It was my silent travelling companion, and it remained with me at the vicarage. When I entered on the discharge of my duties, another change took place. The thing exhibited an atrocious determination to thwart me. It was with me in the church – in the reading-desk – in the pulpit – within the communion rails. At last, it reached this extremity, that while I was reading to the congregation, it would spring upon the open book and squat there, so that I was unable to see the page. This happened more than once.

'I left Dawlbridge for a time. I placed myself in Dr Harley's hands. I did everything he told me. He gave my case a great deal of thought. It interested him, I think. He seemed successful. For nearly three months I was perfectly free from a return. I began to think I was safe. With his full assent I returned to Dawlbridge.

'I travelled in a chaise. I was in good spirits. I was more – I was happy and grateful. I was returning, as I thought, delivered from a dreadful hallucination, to the scene of duties which I longed to enter upon. It was a beautiful sunny evening, everything looked serene and cheerful, and I was delighted. I remember looking out of the window to see the spire of my church at Kenlis among the trees, at the point where one has the earliest view of it. It is exactly where the little stream that bounds the parish passes under the road by a culvert, and where it emerges at the roadside, a stone with an old inscription is placed. As we passed this point, I drew my head in and sat down, and in the corner of the chaise was the monkey.

'For a moment I felt faint, and then quite wild with despair and horror. I called to the driver, and got out, and sat down at the road-side, and prayed to God silently for mercy. A despairing resignation supervened. My companion was with me as I re-entered the vicarage. The same persecution followed. After a short struggle I submitted, and soon I left the place.

'I told you,' he said, 'that the beast has before this become in certain ways aggressive. I will explain a little. It seemed to be actuated by intense and increasing fury whenever I said my prayers, or even meditated prayer. It amounted at last to a dreadful interruption. You will ask, how could a silent immaterial phantom effect that? It was thus, whenever I meditated praying; it was always before me, and nearer and nearer.

'It used to spring on a table, on the back of a chair, on the chimney-piece, and slowly to swing itself from side to side, looking at me all the time. There is in its motion an indefinable power to dissipate thought, and to contract one's attention to that monotony, till the ideas shrink, as it were, to a point, and at last to nothing – and unless I have started up and shaken off the catalepsy, I have felt as if my mind were on the point of losing itself. There are other ways,' he sighed heavily; 'thus, for instance, while I pray with my eyes closed, it comes closer and closer, and I see it. I know it is not to be accounted for physically, but I do actually see it, though my lids are closed, and so it rocks my mind, as it were, and overpowers me, and I am obliged to rise from my knees. If you had ever yourself known this, you would be acquainted with desperation.'

9

The Third Stage

'I see, Dr Hesselius, that you don't lose one word of my statement. I need not ask you to listen specially to what I am now going to tell you. They talk of the optic nerves, and of spectral illusions, as if the organ of sight was the only point assailable by the influences that have fastened upon me – I know better. For two years in my direful case that limitation prevailed. But as food is taken in softly at the lips, and then brought under the teeth, as the tip of the little finger caught in a mill crank will draw in the hand, and the arm, and the whole body, so the miserable mortal who has been once caught firmly by the end of the finest fibre of his nerve, is drawn in and in, by the enormous machinery of hell, until he is as I am. Yes, doctor, as I am, for while I talk to you, and implore relief, I feel that my prayer is for the impossible, and my pleading with the inexorable.'

I endeavoured to calm his visibly increasing agitation, and told him that he must not despair.

While we talked the night had overtaken us. The filmy moonlight was wide over the scene which the window commanded, and I said: 'Perhaps you would prefer having candles. This light, you know, is odd. I should wish you, as much as possible, under your usual conditions while I make my . . . diagnosis, shall I call it? – otherwise I don't care.'

'All lights are the same to me,' he said; 'except when I read or write, I care not if night were perpetual. I am going to tell you what happened about a year ago. The thing began to speak to me.'

'Speak! How do you mean – speak as a man does, do you mean?'

'Yes; speak in words and consecutive sentences, with perfect coherence and articulation; but there is a peculiarity. It is not like the tone of a human voice. It is not by my ears it reaches me – it comes like a singing through my head.

'This faculty, the power of speaking to me, will be my undoing. It won't let me pray, it interrupts me with dreadful blasphemies. I dare not go on, I could not. Oh! doctor, can the skill, and thought, and prayers of man avail me nothing!'

'You must promise me, my dear sir, not to trouble yourself with unnecessarily exciting thoughts; confine yourself strictly to the narrative of *facts*; and recollect, above all, that even if the thing that infests you be, as you seem to suppose, a reality with an actual independent life and will, yet it can have no power to hurt you, unless it be given from above: its access to your senses depends mainly upon your physical condition – this is, under God, your comfort and reliance; we are all alike environed. It is only that in your case, the *paries*, the veil of the flesh, the screen, is a little out of repair, and sights and sounds are transmitted. We must enter on a new course, sir – be encouraged. I'll give tonight to the careful consideration of the whole case.'

'You are very good, sir; you think it worth trying, you don't give me quite up; but, sir, you don't know, it is gaining such an influence over me: it orders me about, it is such a tyrant, and I'm growing so helpless. May God deliver me!'

'It orders you about – of course you mean by speech?'

'Yes, yes; it is always urging me to crimes – to injure others, or myself. You see, doctor, the situation is urgent, it is indeed. When I was in Shropshire, a few weeks ago' (Mr Jennings was speaking rapidly and trembling now, holding my arm with one hand, and looking in my face), 'I went out one day with a party of friends for a walk: my persecutor, I tell you, was with me at the time. I lagged behind the rest: the country near the Dee, you know, is beautiful. Our path happened to lie near a coal mine, and at the verge of the wood is a perpendicular shaft, they say, a hundred and fifty feet deep. My niece had remained behind with me – she knows, of course, nothing of the nature of my sufferings. She knew, however, that I had been ill, and was low, and she remained to prevent my being quite alone. As we loitered slowly on together, the brute that accompanied me was urging me to throw myself down the shaft. I tell you now – oh, sir, think of it! – the one consideration that saved me from that hideous death was the fear lest the shock of witnessing the occurrence should be too much for the poor girl. I asked her to go on and take her walk with her friends, saying that I could go no farther. She made excuses, and the more I urged her the firmer she became. She looked doubtful and frightened. I suppose there was something in my looks or manner that alarmed her; but she would not go, and that literally saved me. You had no idea, sir, that a living man could be made so abject a slave of Satan,' he said, with a ghastly groan and a shudder.

There was a pause here, and I said, 'You were preserved nevertheless. It was the act of God. You are in His hands and in the power of no other being: be therefore confident for the future.'

10

Home

I made him have candles lighted, and saw the room looking cheery and inhabited before I left him. I told him that he must regard his illness strictly as one dependent on physical, though *subtle*, physical causes. I told him that he had evidence of God's care and love in the deliverance which he had just described, and that I had perceived with pain that he seemed to regard its peculiar features as indicating that he had been delivered over to spiritual reprobation. Than such a conclusion nothing could be, I insisted, less warranted; and not only so, but more contrary to facts, as disclosed in his mysterious deliverance from that murderous influence during his Shropshire excursion. First, his niece had been retained by his side without his intending to keep her near him; and, secondly, there had been infused into his mind an irresistible repugnance to execute the dreadful suggestion in her presence.

As I reasoned this point with him, Mr Jennings wept. He seemed comforted. One promise I exacted, which was that should the monkey at any time return, I should be sent for immediately; and, repeating my assurance that I would give neither time nor thought to any other subject until I had thoroughly investigated his case, and that tomorrow he should hear the result, I took my leave.

Before getting into the carriage I told the servant that his master was far from well, and that he should make a point of frequently looking into his room.

My own arrangements I made with a view to being quite secure from interruption.

I merely called at my lodgings, and, with a travelling-desk and carpetbag, set off in a hackney carriage for an inn about two miles out of town called The Horns, a very quiet and comfortable house, with good thick walls. And there I resolved, without the possibility of intrusion or distraction, to devote some hours of the night, in my comfortable sitting-room, to Mr Jennings' case, and so much of the morning as it might require.

[There occurs here a careful note of Dr Hesselius's opinion upon the case, and of the habits, diet and medicines which he prescribed. It is curious – some persons would say mystical. But, on the whole, I doubt whether it would sufficiently interest a reader of the kind I am likely to meet with to warrant its being here reprinted. The whole letter was plainly written at the inn where he had hid himself for the occasion. The next letter is dated from his town lodgings.]

I left town for the inn where I slept last night at half-past nine, and did not arrive at my room in town until one o'clock this afternoon. I found a letter in Mr Jennings' hand upon my table. It had not come by post, and, on enquiry, I learned that Mr Jennings' servant had brought it, and on learning that I was not to return until today, and that no one could tell him my address, he seemed very uncomfortable, and said that his orders from his master were that he was not to return without an answer.

I opened the letter and read:

DEAR DR HESSELIUS – It is here. You had not been an hour gone when it returned. It is speaking. It knows all that has happened. It knows everything – it knows you, and is frantic and atrocious. It reviles. I send you this. It knows every word I have written – I write. This I promised, and I therefore write, but I fear very confusedly, very incoherently. I am so interrupted, disturbed.

Ever yours, sincerely yours,

ROBERT LYNDER JENNINGS

'When did this come?' I asked.

'About eleven last night: the man was here again, and has been here three times today. The last time was about an hour since.'

Thus answered, and with the notes I had made upon his case in my pocket, I was in a few minutes driving towards Richmond, to see Mr Jennings.

I by no means, as you perceive, despaired of Mr Jennings' case. He had himself remembered and applied, though quite in a mistaken way, the principle which I lay down in my *Metaphysical Medicine*, and which governs all such cases. I was about to apply it in earnest. I was profoundly interested, and very anxious to see and examine him while the 'enemy' was actually present.

I drove up to the sombre house and ran up the steps and knocked. The door, in a little time, was opened by a tall woman in black silk. She looked ill, and as if she had been crying. She curtseyed, and heard my question, but she did not answer. She turned her face away, extending her hand towards two men who were coming downstairs; and thus having, as it were, tacitly made me over to them, she passed through a side-door hastily and shut it.

The man who was nearest the hall I at once accosted, but being now close to him, I was shocked to see that both his hands were covered with blood.

I drew back a little, and the man, passing downstairs, merely said in a low tone, 'Here's the servant, sir.'

The servant had stopped on the stairs, confounded and dumb at seeing me. He was rubbing his hands in a handkerchief, and it was steeped in blood.

'Jones, what is it? what has happened?' I asked, while a sickening suspicion overpowered me.

The man asked me to come up to the lobby. I was beside him in a moment and, frowning and pallid, with contracted eyes, he told me the horror which I already half guessed.

His master had made away with himself.

I went upstairs with him to the room – what I saw there I won't tell you. He had cut his throat with his razor. It was a frightful gash. The two men had laid him on the bed, and composed his limbs. It had happened, as the immense pool of blood on the floor declared, at some distance between the bed and the window. There was carpet round his bed, and a carpet under his dressing-table, but none on the rest of the floor, for the man said he did not like a carpet in his bedroom. In this sombre and now terrible room, one of the great elms that darkened the house was slowly moving the shadow of one of its great boughs upon this dreadful floor.

I beckoned to the servant, and we went downstairs together. I turned off the hall into an old-fashioned panelled room, and standing there I heard all the servant had to tell. It was not a great deal.

'I concluded, sir, from your words and looks, sir, as you left last night, that you thought my master seriously ill. I thought it might be that you were afraid of a fit or something. So I attended very close to your directions. He sat up late, till past three o'clock. He was not writing or reading. He was talking a great deal to himself, but that was nothing unusual. At about that hour I assisted him to undress, and left him in his slippers and dressing-gown. I went back softly in about half an hour. He was in his bed, quite undressed, and a pair of candles lighted on the table beside his bed. He was leaning on his elbow, and looking out at the other side of the bed when I came in. I asked him if he wanted anything, and he said no.

'I don't know whether it was what you said to me, sir, or something a little unusual about him, but I was uneasy, uncommon uneasy about him last night.

'In another half-hour, or it might have been a little more, I went up again. I did not hear him talking as before. I opened the door a little. The candles were both out, which was not usual. I had a bedroom candle, and I let the light in, a little bit, looking softly round. I saw him sitting in that chair beside the dressing-table with his clothes on again. He turned round and looked at me. I thought it strange he should get up and dress, and put out the candles to sit in the dark that way. But I only asked him again if I could do anything for him. He said, "No," rather sharp, I thought. I asked if I might light the candles, and he said, "Do as you like, Jones." So I lighted them, and I lingered about the room, and he said, "Tell me the truth, Jones; why did you come again – you did not hear anyone cursing?" "No, sir," I said, wondering what he could mean.

' "No," said he, after me, "of course, no;" and I said to him, "Wouldn't it be well, sir, if you went to bed? It's just five o'clock;" and he said nothing but, "Very likely; good-night, Jones." So I went, sir, but in less than an hour I came again. The door was fast, and he heard me, and called as I thought from the bed to know what I wanted, and he desired me not to disturb him again. I lay down and slept for a little. It must have been between six and seven when I went up again. The door was still fast, and he made no answer, so I did not like to disturb him, and thinking he was asleep, I left him till nine. It was his custom to ring when he wished me to come, and I had no particular hour for calling him. I tapped very gently, and getting no answer, I stayed away a good while, supposing he was getting some rest then. It was not till eleven o'clock I grew really uncomfortable about him – for at the latest he was never, that I could remember, later than half-past ten. I got no answer. I knocked and called, and still no answer. So not being able to force the door, I called Thomas from the stables, and together we forced it, and found him in the shocking way you saw.'

Jones had no more to tell. Poor Mr Jennings was very gentle, and very kind. All his people were fond of him. I could see that the servant was very much moved.

So, dejected and agitated, I passed from that terrible house, and its dark canopy of elms, and I hope I shall never see it more. While I write to you I feel like a man who has but half waked from a frightful and monotonous dream. My memory rejects the picture with incredulity and horror. Yet I know it is true. It is the story of the process of a poison, a poison which excites the reciprocal action of spirit and nerve, and paralyses the tissue that separates those cognate functions of the senses, the external and the interior. Thus we find strange bedfellows, and the mortal and immortal prematurely make acquaintance.

CONCLUSION

A Word for Those Who Suffer

My dear Van Loo, you have suffered from an affliction similar to that which I have just described. You twice complained of a return of it.

Who, under God, cured you? Your humble servant, Martin Hesselius? Let me rather adopt the more emphasised piety of a certain good old French surgeon of three hundred years ago: 'I treated, and God cured you.'

Come, my friend, you are not to be hippish. Let me tell you a fact.

I have met with, and treated, as my book shows, fifty-seven cases of this kind of vision, which I term indifferently 'sublimated', 'precocious' and 'interior'.

There is another class of afflictions which are truly termed – though commonly confounded with those which I describe – spectral illusions. These latter I look upon as being no less simply curable than a cold in the head or a trifling dyspepsia.

It is those which rank in the first category that test our promptitude of thought. Fifty-seven such cases have I encountered, neither more nor less. And in how many of these have I failed? In no one single instance.

There is no one affliction of mortality more easily and certainly reducible, with a little patience, and a rational confidence in the physician. With these simple conditions, I look upon the cure as absolutely certain.

You are to remember that I had not even commenced to treat Mr Jennings' case. I have not any doubt that I should have cured him perfectly in eighteen months, or possibly it might have extended to two years. Some cases are very rapidly curable, others extremely tedious. Every intelligent physician who will give thought and diligence to the task, will effect a cure.

You know my tract on 'The Cardinal Functions of the Brain'. I there, by the evidence of innumerable facts, prove, as I think, the high probability of a circulation, arterial and venous in its mechanism, through the nerves. Of this system, thus considered, the brain is the heart. The fluid, which is propagated hence through one class of nerves, returns in an altered state through another, and the nature of that fluid is spiritual, though not immaterial, any more than, as I before remarked, light or electricity are so.

By various abuses, among which the habitual use of such agents as green tea is one, this fluid may be affected as to its quality, but it is more frequently disturbed as to equilibrium. This fluid being that which we have in common with spirits, a congestion found upon the masses of brain or nerve, connected with the interior sense, forms a surface unduly exposed, on which disembodied spirits may operate: communication is thus more or less effectually established. Between this brain circulation and the heart circulation there is an intimate sympathy. The seat, or rather the instrument, of exterior vision is the eye. The seat of interior vision is the nervous tissue and brain, immediately about and above the eyebrow. You remember how effectually I dissipated your pictures by the simple application of iced eau-de-Cologne. Few cases, however, can be treated exactly alike with anything like rapid success. Cold acts powerfully as a repellent of the nervous fluid. Long enough continued it will even produce that permanent insensibility which we call numbness, and a little longer, muscular as well as sensational paralysis.

I have not, I repeat, the slightest doubt that I should have first dimmed and ultimately sealed that inner eye which Mr Jennings had inadvertently opened. The same senses are opened in delirium tremens, and entirely shut up again when the over-action of the cerebral heart, and the prodigious nervous congestions that attend it, are terminated by a decided change in the state of the body. It is by acting steadily upon the body, by a simple process, that this result is produced – and inevitably produced. I have never yet failed.

Poor Mr Jennings made away with himself. But that catastrophe was the result of a totally different malady, which, as it were, projected itself upon that disease which was established. His case was in the distinctive manner a complication, and the complaint under which he really succumbed, was hereditary suicidal mania. Poor Mr Jennings I cannot call a patient of mine, for I had not even begun to treat his case, and he had not yet given me, I am convinced, his full and unreserved confidence. If the patient does not array himself on the side of the disease, his cure is certain.

SHERIDAN LE FANU

The Familiar

❧

PROLOGUE

Out of about two hundred and thirty cases, more or less nearly akin to that I have entitled 'Green Tea', I select the following, which I call 'The Familiar'.

To this manuscript, Dr Hesselius has, after his wont, attached some sheets of letter-paper, on which are written, in his hand nearly as compact as print, his own remarks upon the case. He says –

In point of conscience, no more unexceptionable narrator than the venerable Irish clergyman who has given me this paper on Mr Barton's case could have been chosen. The statement is, however, medically imperfect. The report of an intelligent physician, who had marked its progress and attended the patient from its earlier stages to its close, would have supplied what is wanting to enable me to pronounce with confidence. I should have been acquainted with Mr Barton's probable hereditary predispositions; I should have known, possibly, by very early indications, something of a remoter origin of the disease than can now be ascertained.

In a rough way, we may reduce all similar cases to three distinct classes. They are founded on the primary distinction between the subjective and the objective. Of those whose senses are alleged to be subject to supernatural impressions some are simply visionaries, and propagate the illusions of which they complain from diseased brain or nerves. Others are, unquestionably, infested by, as we term them, spiritual agencies, exterior to themselves. Others, again, owe their sufferings to a mixed condition. The interior sense, it is true, is opened; but it has been and continues open by the action of disease. This form of disease may, in one sense, be compared to the loss of the scarf-skin, and a consequent exposure of surfaces for whose excessive sensitiveness nature has provided a muffling. The loss of this covering is attended by an habitual assault by influences against which we were intended to be guarded. But in the case of the brain, and the nerves immediately connected with its functions and its sensuous impressions, the cerebral circulation undergoes periodically that vibratory disturbance, which, I believe, I have satisfactorily examined and demonstrated in my manuscript essay, A. 17. This vibratory disturbance differs, as I there prove, essentially from the congestive disturbance, the phenomena of which are examined in A. 19. It is, when excessive, invariably accompanied by *illusions*.

Had I seen Mr Barton, and examined him upon the points in his case which need elucidation, I should have without difficulty referred those phenomena to their proper disease. My diagnosis is now, necessarily, conjectural.

Thus writes Dr Hesselius, adding a great deal which is of interest only to a scientific physician.

The narrative of the Reverend Thomas Herbert, which furnishes all that is known of the case, will be found in the chapters that follow.

I

Footsteps

I was a young man at the time, and intimately acquainted with some of the actors in this strange tale; the impression which its incidents made on me, therefore, were deep and lasting. I shall now endeavour, with precision, to relate them all, combining, of course, in the narrative whatever I have learned from various sources tending, however imperfectly, to illuminate the darkness which involves its progress and termination.

Somewhere about the year 1794, the younger brother of a certain baronet, whom I shall call Sir James Barton, returned to Dublin. He had served in the navy with some distinction, having commanded one of His Majesty's frigates during the greater part of the American War. Captain Barton was apparently some two- or three-and-forty years of age. He was an intelligent and agreeable companion when he chose, though generally reserved, and occasionally even moody.

In society, however, he deported himself as a man of the world, and a gentleman. He had not contracted any of the noisy brusqueness sometimes acquired at sea; on the contrary, his manners were remarkably easy, quiet and even polished. He was in person about the middle size, and somewhat strongly formed; his countenance was marked with the lines of thought, and on the whole wore an expression of gravity and melancholy; being, however, as I have said, a man of perfect breeding, as well as of good family, and in affluent circumstances, he had, of course, ready access to the best society of Dublin, without the necessity of any other credentials.

In his personal habits Mr Barton was inexpensive. He occupied lodgings in one of the *then* fashionable streets on the south side of the town, kept but one horse and one servant and, though a reputed freethinker, yet lived an orderly and moral life, indulging neither in gaming, drinking, nor any other vicious pursuit – living very much to himself, without forming intimacies, or choosing any companions, and appearing to mix in gay society rather for the sake of its bustle and distraction than for any opportunities it offered of interchanging thought or feeling with its votaries.

Barton was, therefore, pronounced a saving, prudent, unsocial sort of fellow, who bid fair to maintain his celibacy alike against stratagem and assault, and was likely to live to a good old age, die rich, and leave his money to a hospital.

It was now apparent, however, that the nature of Mr Barton's plans had been totally misconceived. A young lady, whom I shall call Miss Montague, was at this time introduced into the gay world by her aunt, the Dowager Lady Rochdale. Miss Montague was decidedly pretty and accomplished, and having some natural cleverness, and a great deal of gaiety, became for a while a reigning toast.

Her popularity, however, gained her, for a time, nothing more than that insubstantial admiration which, however pleasant as an incense to vanity, is by no means necessarily antecedent to matrimony – for, unhappily for the young lady in question, it was an understood thing that, beyond her personal attractions, she had no kind of earthly provision. Such being the state of affairs, it will readily be believed that no little surprise was consequent upon the appearance of Captain Barton as the avowed lover of the penniless Miss Montague.

His suit prospered, as might have been expected, and in a short time it was communicated by old Lady Rochdale to each of her hundred-and-fifty particular friends in succession, that Captain Barton had actually tendered proposals of marriage, with her approbation, to her niece, Miss Montague, who had, moreover, accepted the offer of his hand, conditionally upon the consent of her father, who was then upon his homeward voyage from India, and expected in two or three weeks at the furthest.

About this consent there could be no doubt – the delay, therefore, was one merely of form; they were looked upon as absolutely engaged, and Lady Rochdale, with a rigour of old-fashioned decorum with which her niece would, no doubt, gladly have dispensed, withdrew her thenceforward from all further participation in the gaieties of the town.

Captain Barton was a constant visitor as well as a frequent guest at the house, and was permitted all the privileges of intimacy which a betrothed suitor is usually accorded. Such was the relation of parties when the mysterious circumstances which darken this narrative first began to unfold themselves.

Lady Rochdale resided in a handsome mansion on the north side of Dublin, and Captain Barton's lodgings, as we have already said, were situated on the south. The distance intervening was considerable, and it was Captain Barton's habit generally to walk home without an attendant, as often as he passed the evening with the old lady and her fair charge.

His shortest way on such nocturnal walks lay for a considerable space along the line of a street which had as yet merely been laid out, and little more than the foundations of the houses had been constructed.

One night, shortly after his engagement with Miss Montague had commenced, he happened to remain unusually late, in company with her and Lady Rochdale. The conversation had turned upon the evidences of revelation, which he had disputed with the callous scepticism of a confirmed infidel. What were called 'French principles' had in those days found their way a good deal into fashionable society, especially that portion of it which professed allegiance to Whiggism, and neither the old lady nor her charge were so perfectly free from the taint as to look upon Mr Barton's views as any serious objection to the proposed union.

The discussion had degenerated into one upon the supernatural and the marvellous, in which he had pursued precisely the same line of argument and ridicule. In all this, it is but truth to state, Captain Barton was guilty of no affectation – the doctrines upon which he insisted were, in reality, but too truly the basis of his own fixed belief, if so it might be called; and perhaps not the least strange of the many strange circumstances connected with my narrative was the fact that the subject of the fearful influences I am about to describe was himself, from the deliberate conviction of years, an utter disbeliever in what are usually termed preternatural agencies.

It was considerably past midnight when Mr Barton took his leave and set out upon his solitary walk homeward. He in time reached the lonely road, with its unfinished dwarf walls tracing the foundations of the projected rows of houses on either side; the moon was shining mistily, and its imperfect light made the road he trod but additionally dreary; that utter silence which has in it something indefinably exciting reigned there, and made the sound of his steps, which alone broke it, unnaturally loud and distinct.

He had proceeded thus some way when he, on a sudden, heard other footfalls, pattering at a measured pace and, as it seemed, about two score steps behind him.

The suspicion of being dogged is at all times unpleasant: it is, however, especially so in a spot so lonely: and this suspicion became so strong in the mind of Captain Barton, that he abruptly turned about to confront his pursuer; but, though there was quite sufficient moonlight to disclose any object upon the road he had traversed, no form of any kind was visible there.

The steps he had heard could not have been the reverberation of his own, for he stamped his foot upon the ground, and walked briskly up and down, in the vain attempt to awake an echo; though by no means a fanciful person, therefore, he was at last fain to charge the sounds upon his imagination, and treat them as an illusion. Thus satisfying himself, he resumed his walk, but before he had proceeded a dozen paces, the mysterious footfall was again audible from behind, and this time – as if with the special design of showing that the sounds were not the responses of an echo – the steps sometimes slackened nearly to a halt, and sometimes hurried for six or eight strides to a run, and again abated to a walk.

Captain Barton, as before, turned suddenly round, and with the same result – no object was visible above the deserted level of the road. He walked back over the same ground, determined that, whatever might have been the cause of the sounds which had so disconcerted him, it should not escape his search – the endeavour, however, was unrewarded.

In spite of all his scepticism, he felt something like a superstitious fear stealing fast upon him, and with these unwonted and uncomfortable sensations, he once more turned and pursued his way. There was no repetition of these haunting sounds until he had reached the point where he had last stopped to retrace his steps – here they were resumed – and with sudden starts of running, which threatened to bring the unseen pursuer up to the alarmed pedestrian.

Captain Barton arrested his course as formerly – the unaccountable nature of the occurrence filled him with vague and disagreeable sensations – and yielding to the excitement that was gaining upon him, he shouted sternly, 'Who goes there?' The sound of one's own voice, thus exerted, in utter solitude, and followed by total silence, has in it something unpleasantly dismaying, and he felt a degree of nervousness which he had perhaps never known before.

To the very end of this solitary street the steps pursued him – and it required a strong effort of stubborn pride on his part to resist the impulse that prompted him every moment to run for safety at the top of his speed. It was not until he had reached his lodging, and sat by his own fireside, that he felt sufficiently reassured to rearrange and reconsider in his own mind the occurrences which had so discomposed him. So little a matter, after all, is sufficient to upset the pride of scepticism and vindicate the old simple laws of nature within us.

The Watcher

Mr Barton was next morning sitting at a late breakfast, reflecting upon the incidents of the previous night, with more of inquisitiveness than awe – so speedily do gloomy impressions upon the fancy disappear under the cheerful influence of day – when a letter just delivered by the postman was placed upon the table before him.

There was nothing remarkable in the address of this missive, except that it was written in a hand which he did not know – perhaps it was disguised, for the tall narrow characters were sloped backward; with the self-inflicted suspense which we often see practised in such cases, he puzzled over the inscription for a full minute before he broke the seal. When he did so, he read the following words, written in the same hand:

> MR BARTON, late captain of the *Dolphin*, is warned of danger. He will do wisely to avoid — Street [here the locality of his last night's adventure was named]. If he walks there as usual he will meet with something unlucky – let him take warning, once for all, for he has reason to dread
>
> THE WATCHER

Captain Barton read and reread this strange effusion; in every light and in every direction he turned it over and over; he examined the paper on which it was written, and scrutinised the handwriting once more. Defeated here, he turned to the seal; it was nothing but a patch of wax, upon which the accidental impression of a thumb was imperfectly visible.

There was not the slightest mark, or clue of any kind, to lead him to even a guess as to its possible origin. The writer's object seemed a friendly one, and yet he subscribed himself as one whom he had 'reason to dread'. Altogether the letter, its author, and its real purpose were to him an inexplicable puzzle, and one, moreover, unpleasantly suggestive in his mind of other associations connected with his last night's adventure.

In obedience to some feeling – perhaps of pride – Mr Barton did not communicate even to his intended bride the occurrences which I have just detailed. Trifling as they might appear, they had in reality most disagreeably affected his imagination, and he cared not to disclose, even to the young lady in question, what she might possibly look upon as evidences of weakness. The letter might very well be but a hoax and the mysterious footfall but a delusion or a trick. But although he affected to treat the whole affair as unworthy of a thought, it yet haunted him pertinaciously, tormenting him with perplexing doubts, and depressing him with undefined apprehensions. Certain it is that for a considerable time afterwards he carefully avoided the street indicated in the letter as the scene of danger.

It was not until about a week after the receipt of the letter which I have transcribed that anything further occurred to remind Captain Barton of its contents, or to counteract the gradual disappearance from his mind of the disagreeable impressions then received.

He was returning one night, after the interval I have stated, from the theatre, which was then situated in Crow Street, and having there seen Miss Montague and Lady Rochdale into their carriage, he loitered for some time with two or three acquaintances.

With these, however, he parted close to the College, and pursued his way alone. It was now fully one o'clock, and the streets were quite deserted. During the whole of his walk with the companions from whom he had just parted, he had been at times painfully aware of the sound of steps, as it seemed, dogging them on their way.

Once or twice he had looked back, in the uneasy anticipation that he was again about to experience the same mysterious annoyances which had so disconcerted him a week before, and earnestly hoping that he might *see* some form to account naturally for the sounds. But the street was deserted – no one was visible.

Proceeding now quite alone upon his homeward way, he grew really nervous and uncomfortable as he became sensible, with increased distinctness, of the well-known and now absolutely dreaded sounds.

By the side of the blank wall which bounded College Park the sounds followed, recommencing almost simultaneously with his own steps. The same unequal pace – sometimes slow, sometimes for a score yards or so quickened almost to a run – was audible from behind him. Again and again he turned; quickly and stealthily he glanced over his shoulder almost at every half-dozen steps; but no one was visible.

The irritation of this intangible and unseen pursuit became gradually all but intolerable; and when at last he reached his home, his nerves were strung to such a pitch of excitement that he could not rest, and did not attempt even to lie down until after the daylight had broken.

He was awakened by a knock at his chamber-door, and his servant, entering, handed him several letters which had just been received by the penny post. One among them instantly arrested his attention – a single glance at the direction aroused him thoroughly. He at once recognised its character, and read as follows:

You may as well think, Captain Barton, to escape from your own shadow as from me; do what you may, I will see you as often as I please, and you shall see me, for I do not want to hide myself, as you fancy. Do not let it trouble your rest, Captain Barton; for, with a *good conscience*, what need you fear from the eye of

THE WATCHER?

It is scarcely necessary to dwell upon the feelings that accompanied a perusal of this strange communication: Captain Barton was observed to be unusually absent and out of spirits for several days afterwards; but no one divined the cause.

Whatever he might think as to the phantom steps which followed him, there could be no possible illusion about the letters he had received; and, to say the least, their immediate sequence upon the mysterious sounds which had haunted him was an odd coincidence.

The whole circumstance was, in his own mind, vaguely and instinctively connected with certain passages in his past life which of all others he hated to remember.

It happened, however, that in addition to his own approaching nuptials, Captain Barton had just then – fortunately, perhaps, for himself – some business of an engrossing kind connected with the adjustment of a large and long-litigated claim upon certain properties. The hurry and excitement of business had its natural effect in gradually dispelling the gloom which had for a time occasionally oppressed him, and in a little while his spirits had entirely recovered their accustomed tone.

During all this time, however, he was now and then dismayed by indistinct and half-heard repetitions of the same annoyance, and that in lonely places, in the daytime as well as after nightfall. These renewals of the strange impressions from which he had suffered so much were, however, desultory and faint, insomuch that often he really could not, to his own satisfaction, distinguish between them and the mere suggestions of an excited imagination.

One evening he and I walked down to Trinity College with a Mr Norcott, an acquaintance of his and mine. This was one of the few occasions upon which I have been in company with Captain Barton. As we walked down together, I observed that he became absent and silent, and to a degree that seemed to argue the pressure of some urgent and absorbing anxiety. I afterwards learned that during the whole of our walk he had heard the well-known footsteps tracking him as we proceeded.

This, however, was the last time he suffered from this phase of the persecution, of which he was already the anxious victim. A new and a very different one was about to be presented.

3

An Advertisement

Of the new series of impressions which were afterwards gradually to work out his destiny, I that evening witnessed the first; and but for its relation to the train of events which followed, the incident would scarcely have been now remembered by me.

As we were walking in at the passage from College Green, a man, of whom I remember only that he was short in stature, looked like a foreigner and wore a kind of fur travelling-cap, walked very rapidly, and as if under fierce excitement, directly towards us, muttering to himself fast and vehemently the while.

This odd-looking person made straight for Barton, who was foremost of the three, and halted, regarding him for a moment or two with a look of maniacal menace and fury; and then turning about as abruptly, he walked before us at the same agitated pace, and disappeared up a side passage. I do distinctly remember being a good deal shocked at the countenance and bearing of this man, which indeed irresistibly impressed me with an undefined sense of danger such as I have never felt before or since from the presence of anything human; but these sensations were, on my part, far from amounting to anything so disconcerting as to flurry or excite me – I had seen only a singularly evil countenance, agitated, as it seemed, with the excitement of madness.

I was absolutely astonished, however, at the effect of this apparition upon Captain Barton. I knew him to be a man of proud courage and coolness in real danger – a circumstance which made his conduct upon this occasion the more conspicuously odd. He recoiled a step or two as the stranger advanced, and clutched my arm, in silence, with what seemed to be a spasm of agony or terror; and then, as the figure disappeared, shoving me roughly back, he followed it for a few paces, stopped in great disorder, and sat down upon a form. I never beheld a countenance more ghastly and haggard.

'For God's sake, Barton, what is the matter?' said our companion, really alarmed at his appearance. 'You're not hurt, are you? – or unwell? What is it?'

'What did he say? – I did not hear it – what was it?' asked Barton, wholly disregarding the question.

'Nonsense,' said Norcott, greatly surprised; 'who cares what the fellow said. You are unwell, Barton – decidedly unwell; let me call a coach.'

'Unwell! No – not unwell,' he said, evidently making an effort to recover his self-possession; 'but, to say the truth, I am fatigued – a little overworked – and perhaps over-anxious. You know I have been in Chancery, and the winding-up of a suit is always a nervous affair. I have felt uncomfortable all this evening; but I am better now. Come, come – shall we go on?'

'No, no. Take my advice, Barton, and go home; you really do need rest; you are looking quite ill. I really do insist on your allowing me to see you home,' replied his friend.

I seconded Norcott's advice, the more readily as it was obvious that Barton was not himself disinclined to be persuaded. He left us, declining our offered escort. I was not sufficiently intimate with Norcott to discuss the scene we had both just witnessed. I was, however, convinced from his manner in the few commonplace comments and regrets we exchanged, that he was just as little satisfied as I with the extempore plea of illness with which he had accounted for the strange exhibition, and that we were both agreed in suspecting some lurking mystery in the matter.

I called next day at Barton's lodgings, to enquire for him, and learned from the servant that he had not left his room since his return the night before; but that he was not seriously indisposed, and hoped to be out in a few days. That evening he sent for Dr Richards, then in a large and fashionable practice in Dublin, and their interview was, it is said, an odd one.

He entered into a detail of his own symptoms in an abstracted and desultory way, which seemed to argue a strange want of interest in his own cure and at all events made it manifest that there was some topic engaging his mind of more engrossing importance than his present ailment. He complained of occasional palpitations and headache.

Dr Richards asked him, among other questions, whether there was any irritating circumstance or anxiety then occupying his thoughts. This he denied quickly and almost peevishly; the physician thereupon declared his opinion that there was nothing amiss except some slight derangement of the digestion, for which he accordingly wrote a prescription, and was about to withdraw, when Mr Barton, with the air of a man who recollects a topic which had nearly escaped him, recalled him: 'I beg your pardon, doctor, but I really almost forgot; will you permit me to ask you two or three medical questions – rather odd ones, perhaps, but a wager depends upon their solution; you will, I hope, excuse my unreasonableness?'

The physician readily undertook to satisfy the enquirer.

Barton seemed to have some difficulty about opening the proposed interrogatories, for he was silent for a minute, then walked to his bookcase, and returned as he had gone; at last he sat down, and said – 'You'll think them very childish questions, but I can't recover my wager without a decision; so I must put them. I want to know first about lockjaw. If a man actually has had that complaint, and appears to have died of it – so much so, that a physician of average skill pronounces him actually dead – may he, after all, recover?'

The physician smiled, and shook his head.

'But – but a blunder may be made?' resumed Barton. 'Suppose an ignorant pretender to medical skill; may he be so deceived by any stage of the complaint as to mistake what is only a part of the progress of the disease for death itself?'

'No one who had ever seen death,' answered he, 'could mistake it in a case of lockjaw.'

Barton mused for a few minutes. 'I am going to ask you a question perhaps still more childish; but first, tell me, are the regulations of foreign hospitals, such as that of, let us say, Naples, very lax and bungling. May not all kinds of blunders and slips occur in their entries of names, and so forth?'

Dr Richards professed his incompetence to answer that query.

'Well, then, doctor, here is the last of my questions. You will probably laugh at it; but it must out nevertheless. Is there any disease, in all the range of human maladies, which would have the effect of perceptibly contracting the stature, and the whole frame – causing the man to shrink in all his proportions, and yet to preserve his exact resemblance to himself in every particular – with the one exception, his height and bulk; any disease, mark – no matter how rare – how little believed in, generally – which could possibly result in producing such an effect?'

The physician replied with a smile, and a very decided negative.

'Tell me, then,' said Barton, abruptly, 'if a man be in reasonable fear of assault from a lunatic who is at large, can he not procure a warrant for his arrest and detention?'

'Really, that is more a lawyer's question than one in my way,' replied Dr Richards; 'but I believe, on applying to a magistrate, such a course would be directed.'

The physician then took his leave; but, just as he reached the hall-door, remembered that he had left his cane upstairs, and returned. His reappearance was awkward, for a piece of paper, which he recognised as his own prescription, was slowly burning upon the fire, and Barton sitting close by with an expression of settled gloom and dismay.

Dr Richards had too much tact to observe what presented itself; but he had seen quite enough to assure him that the mind, and not the body, of Captain Barton was in reality the seat of suffering.

A few days afterwards, the following advertisement appeared in the Dublin newspapers:

If Sylvester Yelland, formerly a foremast man on board His Majesty's frigate *Dolphin*, or his nearest of kin, will apply to Mr Hubert Smith, attorney, at his office in Dame Street, he or they may hear of something greatly to his or their advantage. Admission may be had at any hour up to twelve o'clock at night, should parties desire to avoid observation; and the strictest secrecy, as to all communications intended to be confidential, shall be honourably observed.

The *Dolphin*, as I have mentioned, was the vessel which Captain Barton had commanded; and this circumstance, connected with the extraordinary exertions made by the circulation of handbills, etc., as well as by repeated advertisements, to secure for this strange notice the utmost possible publicity, suggested to Dr Richards the idea that Captain Barton's extreme uneasiness was somehow connected with the individual to whom the advertisement was addressed, and that he himself was the author of it.

This, however, it is needless to add, was no more than a conjecture. No information whatsoever as to the real purpose of the advertisement was divulged by the agent, nor yet any hint as to who his employer might be.

4

He Talks with a Clergyman

Mr Barton, although he had latterly begun to earn for himself the character of a hypochondriac, was yet very far from deserving it. Though by no means lively, he had yet, naturally, what are termed 'even spirits', and was not subject to undue depressions.

He soon, therefore, began to return to his former habits; and one of the earliest symptoms of this healthier tone of spirits was his appearing at a grand dinner of the Freemasons, of which worthy fraternity he was himself a brother. Barton, who had been at first gloomy and abstracted, drank much more freely than was his wont – possibly with the purpose of dispelling his own secret anxieties – and under the influence of good wine and pleasant company, became gradually (unlike himself) talkative, and even noisy.

It was under this unwonted excitement that he left his company at about half-past ten o'clock; and, as conviviality is a strong incentive to gallantry, it occurred to him to proceed forthwith to Lady Rochdale's, and pass the remainder of the evening with her and his destined bride.

Accordingly, he was soon at Henrietta Street, and chatting gaily with the ladies. It is not to be supposed that Captain Barton had exceeded the limits which propriety prescribes to good fellowship – he had merely taken enough wine to raise his spirits, without however in the least degree unsteadying his mind or affecting his manners.

With this undue elevation of spirits had supervened an entire oblivion or contempt of those undefined apprehensions which had for so long weighed upon his mind, and to a certain extent estranged him from society; but as the night wore away, and his artificial gaiety began to flag, these painful feelings gradually intruded themselves again, and he grew abstracted and anxious as heretofore

He took his leave at length, with an unpleasant foreboding of some coming mischief, and with a mind haunted with a thousand mysterious apprehensions, such as, even while he acutely felt their pressure, he nevertheless inwardly strove, or affected to contemn.

It was this proud defiance of what he regarded as his own weakness which prompted him upon the present occasion to that course which brought about the adventure I am now about to relate.

Mr Barton might have easily called a coach, but he was conscious that his strong inclination to do so proceeded from no cause other than what he desperately persisted in representing to himself to be his own superstitious tremors.

He might also have returned home by a route different from that against which he had been warned by his mysterious correspondent; but for the same reason he dismissed this idea also, and with a dogged and half-desperate resolution to force matters to a crisis of some kind, if there were any reality in the causes of his former suffering, and if not, satisfactorily to bring their delusiveness to the proof, he determined to follow precisely the course which he had trodden upon the night so painfully memorable in his own mind as that on which his strange persecution commenced. Though, sooth to say, the pilot who for the first time steers his vessel under the muzzles of a hostile battery never felt his resolution more severely tasked than did Captain Barton as he breathlessly pursued this solitary path – a path which, spite of every effort of scepticism and reason, he felt to be infested by some (as respected *him*) malignant being.

He pursued his way steadily and rapidly, scarcely breathing from intensity of suspense; he, however, was troubled by no renewal of the dreaded footsteps, and was beginning to feel a return of confidence as, more than three-fourths of the way being accomplished with impunity, he approached the long line of twinkling oil lamps which indicated the frequented streets.

This feeling of self-congratulation was, however, but momentary. The report of a musket at some hundred yards behind him, and the whistle of a bullet close to his head, disagreeably and startlingly dispelled it. His first impulse was to retrace his steps in pursuit of the assassin; but the road on either side was, as we have said, embarrassed by the foundations of a street, beyond which extended waste fields, full of rubbish and neglected lime and brick-kilns, and all now as utterly silent as though no sound had ever disturbed their dark and unsightly solitude. The futility of, single-handedly, attempting under such circumstances a search for the murderer was apparent, especially as no sound, either of retreating steps or any other kind, was audible to direct his pursuit.

With the tumultuous sensations of one whose life has just been exposed to a murderous attempt, and whose escape has been the narrowest possible, Captain Barton turned again; and without, however, quickening his pace actually to a run, hurriedly pursued his way.

He had turned, as I have said, after a pause of a few seconds, and had just commenced his rapid retreat, when on a sudden he met the well-remembered little man in the fur cap. The encounter was but momentary. The figure was walking at the same exaggerated pace, and with the same strange air of menace as before; and as it passed him, he thought he heard it say, in a furious whisper, 'Still alive – still alive!'

The state of Mr Barton's spirits began now to work a corresponding alteration in his health and looks, and to such a degree that it was impossible that the change should escape general remark.

For some reasons, known but to himself, he took no steps whatsoever to bring the attempt upon his life, which he had so narrowly escaped, under the notice of the authorities; on the contrary, he kept it jealously to himself; and it was not for many weeks after the occurrence that he mentioned it, and then in strict confidence, to a gentleman whom the torments of his mind at last compelled him to consult.

Spite of his blue devils, however, poor Barton, having no satisfactory reason to render to the public for any undue remissness in the attentions exacted by the relation existing between him and Miss Montague, was obliged to exert himself, and present to the world a confident and cheerful bearing.

The true source of his sufferings, and every circumstance connected with them, he guarded with a reserve so jealous that it seemed dictated by at least a suspicion that the origin of his strange persecution was known to himself, and that it was of a nature which, upon his own account, he could not or dared not disclose.

The mind thus turned in upon itself, and constantly occupied with a haunting anxiety which it dared not reveal or confide to any human breast, became daily more excited, and, of course, more vividly impressible by a system of attack which operated through the nervous system; and in this state he was destined to sustain, with increasing frequency, the stealthy visitations of that apparition which from the first had seemed to possess so terrible a hold upon his imagination.

It was about this time that Captain Barton called upon the then celebrated preacher, Dr Macklin, with whom he had a slight acquaintance, and an extraordinary conversation ensued.

The divine was seated in his chambers in college, surrounded with works upon his favourite pursuit, and deep in theology, when Barton was announced.

There was something at once embarrassed and excited in his manner, which, along with his wan and haggard countenance, impressed the student with the unpleasant consciousness that his visitor must have recently suffered terribly indeed to account for an alteration so striking – almost shocking.

After the usual interchange of polite greetings, and a few commonplace remarks, Captain Barton, who obviously perceived the surprise which his visit had excited and which Dr Macklin was unable wholly to conceal, interrupted a brief pause by remarking, 'This is a strange call, Dr Macklin, perhaps scarcely warranted by an acquaintance so slight as mine with you. I should not under ordinary circumstances have ventured to disturb you; but my visit is neither an idle nor impertinent intrusion. I am sure you will not so account it when I tell you how afflicted I am.'

Dr Macklin interrupted him with such assurances as good breeding suggested, and Barton resumed, 'I am come to task your patience by asking your advice. When I say your patience, I might, indeed, say more; I might have said your humanity – your compassion; for I have been and am a great sufferer.'

'My dear sir,' replied the churchman, 'it will, indeed, afford me infinite gratification if I can give you comfort in any distress of mind! But – you know – '

'I know what you are about to say,' resumed Barton, quickly; 'I am an unbeliever and therefore incapable of deriving help from religion; but don't take that for granted. At least you must not assume that, however unsettled my convictions may be, I do not feel a deep – a very deep – interest in the subject. Circumstances have lately forced it upon my attention, in such a way as to compel me to review the whole question in a more candid and teachable spirit, I believe, than I ever studied it in before.'

'Your difficulties, I take it for granted, refer to the evidences of revelation,' suggested the clergyman.

'Why – no – not altogether; in fact, I am ashamed to say I have not considered even my objections sufficiently to state them connectedly; but – but there is one subject on which I feel a peculiar interest.'

He paused again, and Dr Macklin pressed him to proceed.

'The fact is,' said Barton, 'whatever may be my uncertainty as to the authenticity of what we are taught to call revelation, of one fact I am deeply and horribly convinced, that there does exist beyond this a spiritual world – a system whose workings are generally in mercy hidden from us, a system which may be, and which is sometimes, partially and terribly revealed. I am sure – I know,' continued Barton, with increasing excitement, 'that there is a God – a dreadful God – and that retribution follows guilt, in ways the most mysterious and stupendous, by agencies the most inexplicable and terrific; there is a spiritual system – great God, how I have been convinced! – a system malignant, and implacable, and omnipotent, under whose persecutions I am, and have been, suffering the torments of the damned! – yes, sir – yes – the fires and frenzy of hell!'

As Barton spoke, his agitation became so vehement that the divine was shocked, and even alarmed. The wild and excited rapidity with which he spoke, and above all the indefinable horror that stamped his features, afforded a contrast to his ordinarily cool and unimpassioned self-possession striking and painful in the last degree.

5

Mr Barton States His Case

'My dear sir,' said Dr Macklin, after a brief pause, 'I fear you have been very unhappy indeed; but I venture to predict that the depression under which you labour will be found to originate in purely physical causes, and that with a change of air, and the aid of a few tonics, your spirits will return, and the tone of your mind be once more cheerful and tranquil as heretofore. There was, after all, more truth than we are quite willing to admit in the classic theories which assigned the undue predominance of any one affection of the mind to the undue action or torpidity of one or other of our bodily organs. Believe me, that a little attention to diet, exercise and the other essentials of health, under competent direction, will make you as much yourself as you can wish.'

'Dr Macklin,' said Barton, with something like a shudder, 'I *cannot* delude myself with such a hope. I have no hope to cling to but one, and that is that by some other spiritual agency more potent than that which tortures me, *it* may be combated and I delivered. If this may not be, I am lost – now and for ever lost.'

'But, Mr Barton, you must remember,' urged his companion, 'that others have suffered as you have done, and –'

'No, no, no,' interrupted he, with irritability – 'no, sir, I am not a credulous and certainly not a superstitious man. I have been, perhaps, too much the reverse – too sceptical, too slow of belief; but unless I were one whom no amount of evidence could convince, unless I were to contemn the repeated, the *perpetual* evidence of my own senses, I am now at last constrained to believe – I have no escape from the conviction, the overwhelming certainty – that I am haunted and dogged, go where I may, by – by a demon!'

There was a preternatural energy of horror in Barton's face, as, with its damp and deathlike lineaments turned towards his companion, he thus delivered himself.

'God help you, my poor friend,' said Dr Macklin, much shocked, 'God help you; for, indeed, you are a sufferer, however your sufferings may have been caused.'

'Ay, ay, God help me,' echoed Barton, sternly; 'but *will* He help me – will He help me?'

'Pray to Him – pray in a humble and trusting spirit,' said he.

'Pray, pray,' echoed he again; 'I can't pray – I could as easily move a mountain by an effort of my will. I have not belief enough to pray; there is something within me that will not pray. You prescribe impossibilities – literal impossibilities.'

'You will not find it so, if you will but try,' said Dr Macklin.

'Try! I *have* tried, and the attempt only fills me with confusion – and sometimes terror. I have tried in vain, and more than in vain. The awful, unutterable idea of eternity and infinity oppresses and maddens my brain whenever my mind approaches the contemplation of the Creator: I recoil from the effort scared. I tell you, Dr Macklin, if I am to be saved, it must be by other means. The idea of an eternal Creator is to me intolerable – my mind cannot support it.'

'Say, then, my dear sir,' urged he, 'say how you would have me serve you – what you would learn of me – what I can do or say to relieve you?'

'Listen to me first,' replied Captain Barton, with a subdued air, and an effort to suppress his excitement, 'listen to me while I detail the circumstances of the persecution under which my life has become all but intolerable – a persecution which has made me fear death and the world beyond the grave as much as I have grown to hate existence.'

Barton then proceeded to relate the circumstances which I have already detailed, and then continued: 'This has now become habitual – an accustomed thing. I do not mean the actual seeing him in the flesh – thank God, *that* at least is not permitted daily. Thank God, from the ineffable horrors of that visitation I have been mercifully allowed intervals of repose, though none of security; but from the consciousness that a malignant spirit is following and watching me wherever I go, I have never, for a single instant, a temporary respite. I am pursued with blasphemies, cries of despair, and appalling hatred. I hear those dreadful sounds called after me as I turn the corners of the streets; they come in the night-time, while I sit in my chamber alone; they haunt me everywhere, charging me with hideous crimes, and – great God! – threatening me with coming vengeance and eternal misery. Hush! do you hear *that*?' he cried, with a horrible smile of triumph; 'there – there, will that convince you?'

The clergyman felt a chill of horror steal over him as, during the wail of a sudden gust of wind, he heard, or fancied he heard, half-articulate sounds of rage and derision mingling in the sough.

'Well, what do you think of *that*? at length Barton cried, drawing a long breath through his teeth.

'I heard the wind,' said Dr Macklin. 'What should I think of it – what is there remarkable about it?'

'The prince of the powers of the air,' muttered Barton, with a shudder.

'Tut, tut! my dear sir,' said the student, with an effort to reassure himself; for though it was broad daylight, there was nevertheless something disagreeably contagious in the nervous excitement under which his visitor so miserably suffered. 'You must not give way to those wild fancies; you must resist these impulses of the imagination.'

'Ay, ay; "Resist the devil and he will flee from thee," ' said Barton, in the same tone; 'but *how* resist him? ay, there it is – there is the rub. What – *what* am I to do? what *can* I do?'

'My dear sir, this is fancy,' said the man of folios; 'you are your own tormentor.'

'No, no, sir – fancy has no part in it,' answered Barton, somewhat sternly. 'Fancy! was it fancy made you, as well as me, hear, but this moment, those accents of hell? Fancy, indeed! No, no.'

'But you have seen this person frequently,' said the ecclesiastic; 'why have you not accosted or secured him? Is it not a little precipitate, to say no more, to assume, as you have done, the existence of a preternatural agency; when, after all, everything may be easily accountable if only proper means were taken to sift the matter.'

'There are circumstances connected with this – this appearance,' said Barton, 'which it is needless to disclose, but which to me are proofs of its horrible nature. I know that the being that follows me is not human – I say I know this; I could prove it to your own conviction.' He paused for a minute, and then added, 'And as to accosting it, I dare not, I could not; when I see it, I am powerless; I stand in the gaze of death, in the triumphant presence of infernal power and malignity. My strength, and faculties, and memory, all forsake me. O God, I fear, sir, you know not what you speak of. Mercy, mercy; heaven have pity on me!'

He leaned his elbow on the table, and passed his hand across his eyes as if to exclude some image of horror, muttering the last words of the sentence he had just concluded again and again.

'Dr Macklin,' he said, abruptly raising himself and looking full upon the clergyman with an imploring eye, 'I know you will do for me whatever may be done. You know now fully the circumstances and the nature of my affliction. I tell you I cannot help myself; I cannot hope to escape; I am utterly passive. I conjure you then to weigh my case well, and if anything may be done for me by vicarious supplication – by the intercession of the good – or by any aid or influence what-soever, I implore of you, I adjure you in the name of the Most High, give me the benefit of that influence – deliver me from the body of this death. Strive for me, pity me; I know you will; you cannot refuse this; it is the purpose and object of my visit. Send me away with some hope – however little – some faint hope of ultimate deliverance, and I will nerve myself to endure, from hour to hour, the hideous dream into which my existence has been transformed.

Dr Macklin assured him that all he could do was to pray earnestly for him, and that so much he would not fail to do. They parted with a hurried and melancholy valediction. Barton hastened to the carriage that awaited him at the door, drew down the blinds, and drove away, while Dr Macklin returned to his chamber to ruminate at leisure upon the strange interview which had just interrupted his studies.

6

Seen Again

It was not to be expected that Captain Barton's changed and eccentric habits should long escape remark and discussion. Various were the theories suggested to account for it. Some attributed the alteration to the pressure of secret pecuniary embarrassments; others to a repug-nance to fulfil an engagement into which he was presumed to have too precipitately entered; and others, again, to the supposed incipiency of mental disease, which latter, indeed, was the most plausible, as well as the most generally received, of the hypotheses circulated in the gossip of the day.

From the very commencement of this change, at first so gradual in its advances, Miss Montague had of course been aware of it. The intimacy involved in their peculiar relation as well as the near interest which it inspired afforded, in her case, a like opportunity and motive for the successful exercise of that keen and penetrating observation peculiar to her sex.

His visits became, at length, so interrupted, and his manner, while they lasted, so abstracted, strange and agitated, that Lady Rochdale, after hinting her anxiety and her suspicions more than once, at length distinctly stated her anxiety, and pressed for an explanation.

The explanation was given, and although its nature at first relieved the worst solicitudes of the old lady and her niece, yet the circumstances which attended it, and the really dreadful consequences which it obviously indicated as regarded the spirits and indeed the reason of the now wretched man who made the strange declaration, were enough, upon little reflection, to fill their minds with perturbation and alarm.

General Montague, the young lady's father, at length arrived. He had himself slightly known Barton some ten or twelve years previously, and being aware of his fortune and connections, was disposed to regard him as an unexceptionable and indeed a most desirable match for his daughter. He laughed at the story of Barton's supernatural visitations, and lost no time in calling upon his intended son-in-law.

'My dear Barton,' he continued, gaily, after a little conversation, 'my sister tells me that you are a victim of blue devils, in quite a new and original shape.'

Barton changed countenance, and sighed profoundly.

'Come, come; I protest this will never do,' continued the general; 'you are more like a man on his way to the gallows than to the altar. These devils have made quite a saint of you.'

Barton made an effort to change the conversation.

'No, no, it won't do,' said his visitor laughing; 'I am resolved to say what I have to say upon this magnificent mock mystery of yours. You must not be angry, but really it is too bad to see you at your time of life, absolutely frightened into good behaviour, like a naughty child by a bugaboo, and as far as I can learn, a very contemptible one. Seriously, I have been a good deal annoyed at what they tell me; but at the same time thoroughly convinced that there is nothing in the matter that may not be cleared up, with a little attention and management, within a week at furthest.'

'Ah, general, you do not know – ' Barton began.

'Yes, but I do know quite enough to warrant my confidence,' interrupted the soldier; 'don't I know that all your annoyance proceeds from the occasional appearance of a certain little man in a cap and greatcoat, with a red vest and a bad face, who follows you about, and pops upon you at corners of lanes and throws you into ague fits? Now, my dear fellow, I'll make it my business to *catch* this mischievous little mountebank, and either beat him to a jelly with my own hands, or have him whipped through the town, at the cart's tail, before a month passes.'

'If *you* knew what *I* knew,' said Barton, with gloomy agitation, 'you would speak very differently. Don't imagine that I am so weak as to assume, without proof the most overwhelming, the conclusion to which I have been forced; the proofs are here, locked up here.' As he spoke he tapped upon his breast, and with an anxious sigh continued to walk up and down the room.

'Well, well, Barton,' said his visitor, 'I'll wager a rump and a dozen I collar the ghost, and convince even you before many days are over.'

He was running on in the same strain when he was suddenly arrested, and not a little shocked, by observing Barton, who had approached the window, stagger slowly back, like one who had received a stunning blow; his arm extended towards the street, his face and his very lips white as ashes, he muttered, 'There – by heaven! – there – there!'

General Montague started mechanically to his feet, and from the window of the drawing-room, saw a figure corresponding, as well as his hurry would permit him to discern, with the description of the person whose appearance so persistently disturbed the repose of his friend.

The figure was just turning from the area rails upon which it had been leaning, and, without waiting to see more, the old gentleman snatched his cane and hat and rushed down the stairs and into the street, in the furious hope of securing the person and punishing the audacity of the mysterious stranger.

He looked round him – but in vain – for any trace of the person he had himself distinctly seen. He ran breathlessly to the nearest corner, expecting to see from thence the retiring figure, but no such form was visible. Back and forth, from crossing to crossing, he ran, at full tilt, and it was not until the curious gaze and laughing countenances of the passers-by reminded him of the absurdity of his pursuit that he checked his hurried pace, lowered his walking cane from the menacing altitude which he had mechanically given it, adjusted his hat and walked composedly back again, inwardly vexed and flurried. He found Barton pale and trembling in every joint; they both remained silent, though under emotions very different. At last Barton whispered, 'You saw it?'

'*It* – him – someone – you mean – to be sure I did,' replied Montague, testily. 'But where is the good or the harm of seeing him? The fellow runs like a lamplighter. I wanted to catch him, but he had stolen away before I could reach the hall-door. However, it is no great matter; next time, I dare say, I'll do better; and, egad, if I once come within reach of him, I'll introduce his shoulders to the weight of my cane.'

Notwithstanding General Montague's undertakings and exhortations, however, Barton continued to suffer from the selfsame unexplained cause; go how, when, or where he would, he was still constantly dogged or confronted by the being who had established over him so horrible an influence.

Nowhere and at no time was he secure against the odious appearance which haunted him with such diabolic perseverance. His depression, misery and excitement became more settled and alarming every day, and the mental agonies that ceaselessly prayed upon him began at last so sensibly to affect his health that Lady Rochdale and General Montague succeeded, without indeed much difficulty, in persuading him to try a short tour on the Continent, in the hope that an entire change of scene would, at all events, have the effect of breaking through the influences of local association, which the more sceptical of his friends assumed to be by no means inoperative in suggesting and perpetuating what they conceived to be a mere form of nervous illusion.

General Montague indeed was persuaded that the figure which haunted his intended son-in-law was by no means the creation of his imagination but, on the contrary, a substantial form of flesh and blood, animated by a resolution, perhaps with some murderous object in perspective, to watch and follow the unfortunate gentleman.

Even this hypothesis was not a very pleasant one; yet it was plain that if Barton could ever be convinced that there was nothing preternatural in the phenomenon which he had hitherto regarded in that light, the affair would lose all its terrors in his eyes and wholly cease to exercise upon his health and spirits the baleful influence which it had hitherto done. He therefore reasoned that if the annoyance were actually escaped by mere locomotion and change of scene, it obviously could not have originated in any supernatural agency.

7

Flight

Yielding to their persuasions, Barton left Dublin for England, accompanied by General Montague. They posted rapidly to London, and thence to Dover, whence they took the packet with a fair wind for Calais. The general's confidence in the result of the expedition on Barton's spirits had risen day by day since their departure from the shores of Ireland; for to the inexpressible relief and delight of the latter, he had not since then so much as even once fancied a repetition of those impressions which had, when at home, drawn him gradually down to the very depths of despair.

This exemption from what he had begun to regard as the inevitable condition of his existence, and the sense of security which began to pervade his mind, were inexpressibly delightful; and in the exultation of what he considered his deliverance, he indulged in a thousand happy anticipations for a future into which so lately he had hardly dared to look; and, in short, both he and his companion secretly congratulated themselves upon the termination of that persecution which had been to its immediate victim a source of such unspeakable agony.

It was a beautiful day, and a crowd of idlers stood upon the jetty to receive the packet, and enjoy the bustle of the new arrivals. Montague walked a few paces in advance of his friend, and as he made his way through the crowd, a little man touched his arm, and said to him, in a broad provincial *patois*, 'Monsieur is walking too fast; he will lose his sick comrade in the throng, for, by my faith, the poor gentleman seems to be fainting.'

Montague turned quickly, and observed that Barton did indeed look deadly pale. He hastened to his side.

'My dear fellow, are you ill,' he asked anxiously.

The question was unheeded, and twice repeated, ere Barton stammered, 'I saw him – by God, I saw him!'

'*Him!* – the wretch who . . . ? – where now? – where is he?' cried Montague, looking around him.

'I saw him – but he is gone,' repeated Barton, faintly.

'But where – where? For God's sake speak,' urged Montague, vehemently.

'It was but this moment – *here*,' said he.

'But what did he look like – what had he on – what did he wear – quick, quick,' urged his excited companion, ready to dart among the crowd and collar the delinquent on the spot.

'He touched your arm – he spoke to you – he pointed to me. God be merciful to me, there is no escape,' said Barton, in the low, subdued tones of despair.

Montague had already bustled away in all the flurry of mingled hope and rage; but though the singular aspect of the stranger who had accosted him was vividly impressed upon his recollection, he failed to discover among the crowd even the slightest resemblance to him.

After a fruitless search, in which he enlisted the services of several of the bystanders, who aided all the more zealously as they believed he had been robbed, he at length, out of breath and baffled, gave over the attempt.

'Ah, my friend, it won't do,' said Barton, with the faint voice and bewildered, ghastly look of one who had been stunned by some mortal shock; 'there is no use in contending; whatever it is, the dreadful association between me and it is now established – I shall never escape – never!'

'Nonsense, nonsense, my dear Barton; don't talk so,' said Montague, with something at once of irritation and dismay; 'you must not, I say; we'll jockey the scoundrel yet; never mind, I say – never mind.'

It was, however, but labour lost to endeavour henceforward to inspire Barton with one ray of hope; he became desponding.

This intangible and, as it seemed, utterly malign influence was fast destroying his energies of intellect, character and health. His first object was now to return to Ireland and there, as he believed and now almost hoped, speedily to die.

To Ireland accordingly he came, and one of the first faces he saw upon the shore was again that of his implacable and dreaded attendant. Barton seemed at last to have lost not only all enjoyment and every hope in existence, but all independence of will besides. He now submitted himself passively to the management of the friends most nearly interested in his welfare. With the apathy of entire despair, he implicitly assented to whatever measures they suggested and advised; and, as a last resource, it was determined to remove him to a house of Lady Rochdale's, in the neighbourhood of Clontarf, where, with the advice of his medical attendant, who persisted in his opinion that the whole train of consequences resulted merely from some nervous derangement, it was resolved that he was to confine himself strictly to the house, and make use only of those apartments which commanded a view of an enclosed yard, the gates of which were to be kept zealously locked.

Those precautions would certainly secure him against the casual appearance of any living form that his excited imagination might possibly confound with the spectre which, as it was contended, his fancy recognised in every figure that bore even a distant or general resemblance to the peculiarities with which his fancy had at first invested it.

A month or six weeks' absolute seclusion under these conditions, it was hoped, might, by interrupting the series of these terrible impressions, gradually dispel the predisposing apprehensions and the associations which had confirmed the supposed disease and rendered recovery hopeless.

Cheerful society and that of his friends was to be constantly supplied and, on the whole, very sanguine expectations were indulged in that under the treatment thus detailed the obstinate hypochondria of the patient might at length give way.

Accompanied, therefore, by Lady Rochdale, General Montague and his daughter – his own affianced bride – poor Barton – himself never daring to cherish a hope of his ultimate emancipation from the horrors under which his life was literally wasting away – took possession of the apartments whose situation protected him against the intrusions from which he shrank with such unutterable terror.

After a little time, a steady persistence in this system began to manifest its results in a very marked though gradual improvement alike in the health and spirits of the invalid. Not, indeed, that anything at all approaching complete recovery was yet discernible. On the contrary, to those who had not seen him since the commencement of his strange sufferings such an alteration would have been apparent as might well have shocked them.

The improvement, however, such as it was, was welcomed with gratitude and delight, especially by the young lady whom her attachment to him, as well as her now singularly painful position, consequent on his protracted illness, rendered an object scarcely one degree less to be commiserated than himself.

A week passed – a fortnight – a month – and yet there had been no recurrence of the hated visitation. The treatment had, so far forth, been followed by complete success. The chain of associations was broken. The constant pressure upon the overtasked spirits had been removed, and, under these comparatively favourable circumstances, the sense of social community with the world about him and something of human interest, if not of enjoyment, began to reanimate him.

It was about this time that Lady Rochdale who, like most old ladies of the day, was deep in family receipts and a great pretender to medical science, dispatched her own maid to the kitchen garden with a list of herbs to be carefully culled and brought back to her housekeeper for the purpose stated. The handmaiden, however, returned with her task scarce half completed and a good deal flurried and alarmed. Her mode of accounting for her precipitate retreat and evident agitation was odd, and, to the old lady, startling.

Softened

It appeared that she had repaired to the kitchen garden, pursuant to her mistress's directions, and had there begun to make the specified election among the rank and neglected herbs which crowded one corner of the enclosure, and while engaged in this pleasant labour, she carelessly sang a fragment of an old song, as she said, 'to keep herself company'. She was, however, interrupted by an ill-natured laugh; and, looking up, she saw through the old thorn hedge which surrounded the garden a singularly ill-looking little man, whose countenance wore the stamp of menace and malignity, standing close to her at the other side of the hawthorn screen.

She described herself as utterly unable to move or speak while he charged her with a message for Captain Barton; the substance of which she distinctly remembered to have been to the effect that he, Captain Barton, must come abroad as usual, and show himself to his friends, out of doors, or else prepare for a visit in his own chamber.

On concluding this brief message, the stranger had, with a threatening air, got down into the outer ditch, and seizing the hawthorn stems in his hands, seemed on the point of climbing through the fence, a feat which might have been accomplished without much difficulty.

Without, of course, awaiting this result, the girl – throwing down her treasures of thyme and rosemary – had turned and run, with the swiftness of terror, to the house. Lady Rochdale commanded her, on pain of instant dismissal, to observe an absolute silence respecting all that had passed of the incident which related to Captain Barton; and, at the same time, directed instant search to be made by her men in the garden and the fields adjacent. This measure, however, was as usual unsuccessful, and filled with undefinable misgivings, Lady Rochdale communicated the incident to her brother. The story, however, until long afterwards, went no further, and, of course, it was jealously guarded from Barton, who continued to amend, though slowly.

Barton now began to walk occasionally in the courtyard which I have mentioned and which, being enclosed by a high wall, commanded no view beyond its own extent. Here he, therefore, considered himself perfectly secure: and but for a careless violation of orders by one of the grooms, he might have enjoyed, at least for some time longer, his much prized immunity. Opening upon the public road, this yard was entered by a wooden gate, with a wicket in it, and was further defended by an iron gate upon the outside. Strict orders had been given to keep both carefully locked; but, spite of these, it happened that one day, as Barton was slowly pacing this narrow enclosure in his accustomed walk and, reaching the farther extremity, was turning to retrace his steps, he saw the boarded wicket ajar, and the face of his tormentor immovably looking at him through the iron bars. For a few seconds he stood riveted to the earth – breathless and bloodless – in the fascination of that dreaded gaze, and then fell helplessly insensible upon the pavement.

There he was found a few minutes afterwards, and conveyed to his room – the apartment which he was never afterwards to leave alive. Henceforward a marked and unaccountable change was observable in the tone of his mind. Captain Barton was now no longer the excited and despairing man he had been before; a strange alteration had passed upon him – an unearthly tranquillity reigned in his mind – it was the anticipated stillness of the grave.

'Montague, my friend, this struggle is nearly ended now,' he said, calmly, but with a look of fixed and fearful awe. 'I have, at last, some comfort from that world of spirits from which my punishment has come. I now know that my sufferings will soon be over.'

Montague pressed him to speak on.

'Yes,' said he, in a softened voice, 'my punishment is nearly ended. From sorrow, perhaps, I shall never, in time or eternity, escape; but my *agony* is almost over. Comfort has been revealed to me, and what remains of my allotted struggle I will bear with submission – even with hope.'

'I am glad to hear you speak so tranquilly, my dear Barton,' said Montague; 'peace and cheer of mind are all you need to make you what you were.'

'No, no – I never can be that,' said he mournfully. 'I am no longer fit for life. I am soon to die. I am to see him but once again, and then all is ended.'

'He said so, then?' suggested Montague.

'He? – No, no: good tidings could scarcely come through him; and these were good and welcome; and they came so solemnly and sweetly, with unutterable love and melancholy such as I could not – without saying more than is needful, or fitting, of other long past scenes and persons – fully explain to you.' As Barton said this he shed tears.

'Come, come,' said Montague, mistaking the source of his emotions, 'you must not give way. What is it, after all, but a pack of dreams and nonsense; or, at worst, the practices of a scheming rascal that enjoys his power of playing upon your nerves, and loves to exert it – a sneaking vagabond that owes you a grudge, and pays it off this way, not daring to try a more manly one.'

'A grudge, indeed, he owes me – you say rightly,' said Barton, with a sudden shudder; 'a grudge as you call it. Oh, my God! when the justice of heaven permits the Evil One to carry out a scheme of vengeance – when its execution is committed to the lost and terrible victim of sin, who owes his own ruin to the man, the very man, whom he is commissioned to pursue – then, indeed, the torments and terrors of hell are anticipated on earth. But heaven has dealt mercifully with me – hope has opened to me at last; and if death could come without the dreadful sight I am doomed to see, I would gladly close my eyes this moment upon the world. But though death is welcome, I shrink with an agony you cannot understand – an actual frenzy of terror – from the last encounter with that – that demon, who has drawn me thus to the verge of the chasm, and who is himself to plunge me down. I am to see him again – once more – but under circumstances unutterably more terrific than ever.'

As Barton thus spoke, he trembled so violently that Montague was really alarmed at the extremity of his sudden agitation, and hastened to lead him back to the topic which had before seemed to exert so tranquillising an effect upon his mind.

'It was not a dream,' he said, after a time; 'I was in a different state, I felt differently and strangely; and yet it was all as real, as clear and vivid as what I now see and hear – it was a reality.'

'And what *did* you see and hear?' urged his companion.

'When I wakened from the swoon I fell into on seeing *him*,' said Barton, continuing as if he had not heard the question, 'it was slowly, very slowly – I was lying by the margin of a broad lake, with misty hills all round, and a soft, melancholy, rose-coloured light illuminated it all. It was unusually sad and lonely, and yet more beautiful than any earthly scene. My head was leaning on the lap of a girl, and she was singing a song that told, I know not how – whether by words or harmonies – of all my life – all that is past, and all that is still to come; and with the song the old feelings that I thought had perished within me came back, and tears flowed from my eyes – partly for the song and its mysterious beauty, and partly for the unearthly sweetness of her voice; and yet I knew the voice – oh! how well; and I was spellbound as I listened and looked at the solitary scene, without stirring, almost without breathing – and, alas! alas! without turning my eyes towards the face that I knew was near me, so sweetly powerful was the enchantment that held me. And so, slowly, the song and scene grew fainter, and fainter, to my senses, till all was dark and still again. And then I awoke to this world, as you saw, comforted, for I knew that I was forgiven much.' Barton wept again long and bitterly.

From this time, as we have said, the prevailing tone of his mind was one of profound and tranquil melancholy. This, however, was not without its interruptions. He was thoroughly impressed with the conviction that he was to experience another and a final visitation, transcending in horror all he had before experienced. From this anticipated and unknown agony, he often shrank in such paroxysms of abject terror and distraction as filled the whole household with dismay and superstitious panic. Even those among them who affected to discredit the theory of a preternatural agency were often in their secret souls visited during the silence of night with qualms and apprehensions which they would not have readily confessed; and none of them attempted to dissuade Barton from the resolution on which he now systematically acted, of shutting himself up in his own apartment. The window-blinds of this room were kept jealously down; and his own man was seldom out of his presence, day or night, his bed being placed in the same chamber.

This man was an attached and respectable servant; and his duties, in addition to those ordinarily imposed upon valets, but which Barton's independent habits generally dispensed with, were to attend carefully to the simple precautions by means of which his master hoped to exclude the dreaded intrusion of the 'Watcher'. And, in addition to attending to those arrangements, which amounted merely to guarding against the possibility of his master's being, through any unscreened window or open door, exposed to the dreaded influence, the valet was never to suffer him to be alone – total solitude, even for a minute, had become to him now almost as intolerable as the idea of going abroad into the public ways; it was an instinctive anticipation of what was coming.

9

Requiescat

It is needless to say that, under these circumstances, no steps were taken toward the fulfilment of that engagement into which he had entered. There was quite disparity enough in point of years, and indeed of habits, between the young lady and Captain Barton to have precluded anything like a very vehement or romantic attachment on her part. Though grieved and anxious, therefore, she was very far from being heartbroken.

Miss Montague, however, devoted much of her time to a patient but fruitless attempt to cheer the unhappy invalid. She read to him and conversed with him; but it was apparent that whatever exertions he made, the endeavour to escape from the one ever-waking fear that preyed upon him was utterly and miserably unavailing.

Young ladies are much given to the cultivation of pets and among those who shared the favour of Miss Montague was a fine old owl, which the gardener, who caught him napping among the ivy of a ruined stable, had dutifully presented to that young lady.

The caprice which regulates such preferences was manifested in the extravagant favour with which this grim and ill-favoured bird was at once distinguished by his mistress; and, trifling as this whimsical circumstance may seem, I am forced to mention it, inasmuch as it is connected, oddly enough, with the concluding scene of the story.

Far from sharing in this liking for the new favourite, Barton regarded it from the first with an antipathy as violent as it was utterly unaccountable. Its very vicinity was unsupportable to him. He seemed to hate and dread it with a vehemence absolutely laughable, and which, to those who have never witnessed the exhibition of antipathies of this kind, would seem all but incredible.

With these few words of preliminary explanation, I shall proceed to state the particulars of the last scene in this strange series of incidents. It was almost two o'clock one winter's night, and Barton was, as usual at that hour, in his bed; the servant we have mentioned occupied a smaller bed in the same room, and a light was burning. The man was on a sudden aroused by his master, who said, 'I can't get it out of my head that that accursed bird has got out somehow and is lurking in some corner of the room. I have been dreaming about him. Get up, Smith, and look about; search for him. Such hateful dreams!'

The servant rose and examined the chamber, and while engaged in so doing, he heard the well-known sound, more like a long-drawn gasp than a hiss, with which these birds from their secret haunts affright the quiet of the night,

This ghostly indication of its proximity – for the sound proceeded from the passage upon which Barton's chamber-door opened – determined the search of the servant, who, opening the door, proceeded a step or two forward for the purpose of driving the bird away. He had, however, hardly entered the lobby, when the door behind him slowly swung to under the impulse, as it seemed, of some gentle current of air; but as immediately over the door there was a kind of window, intended in the daytime to aid in lighting the passage, through which at present the rays of the candle were issuing, the valet could see quite enough for his purpose.

As he advanced he heard his master – who, lying in a well-curtained bed, had not, as it seemed, perceived his exit from the room – call him by name, and direct him to place the candle on the table by his bed. The servant, who was now some way down the long passage and did not like to raise his voice for the purpose of replying lest he should startle the sleeping inmates of the house, began to walk hurriedly and softly back again, when, to his amazement, he heard a voice in the interior of the chamber answering calmly, and actually saw, through the window which overtopped the door, that the light was slowly shifting, as if being carried across the room in answer to his master's call. Palsied by a feeling akin to terror yet not unmingled with curiosity, he stood breathless and listening at the threshold, unable to summon resolution to push open the door and enter. Then came a rustling of the curtains, and a sound like that of one who in a low voice hushes a child to rest, in the midst of which he heard Barton say, in a tone of stifled horror, 'Oh, God – oh, my God!' and repeat the same exclamation several times. Then ensued a silence, which again was broken by the same strange soothing sound; and at last there burst forth, in one swelling peal, a yell of agony so appalling and hideous that, under some impulse of ungovernable horror, the man rushed to the door and with his whole strength strove to force it open. Whether it was that in his agitation he had himself but imperfectly turned the handle, or that the door was really secured upon the inside, he failed to effect an entrance; and as he tugged and pushed, yell after yell rang louder and wilder through the chamber, accompanied all the while by the same hushing sounds. Actually freezing with terror, and scarce knowing what he did, the man turned and ran down the passage, wringing his hands in the extremity of horror and irresolution. At the stair-head he was encountered by General Montague, scared and eager, and just as they met the fearful sounds ceased.

'What is it? Who – where is your master?' said Montague, with the incoherence of extreme agitation. 'Has anything – for God's sake is anything wrong?'

'Lord have mercy on us, it's all over,' said the man, staring wildly towards his master's chamber. 'He's dead, sir, I'm sure he's dead.'

Without waiting for enquiry or explanation, Montague, closely followed by the servant, hurried to the chamber door, turned the handle and pushed it open. As the door yielded to his pressure, the ill-omened bird of which the servant had been in search, uttering its spectral warning, started suddenly from the far side of the bed and, flying through the doorway close over their heads, and extinguishing in his passage the candle which Montague carried, crashed through the skylight that overlooked the lobby and sailed away into the darkness of the outer space.

'There it is, God bless us,' whispered the man after a breathless pause.

'Curse that bird,' muttered the general, startled by the suddenness of the apparition, and unable to conceal his discomposure.

'The candle is moved,' said the man, after another breathless pause, pointing to the candle that still burned in the room; 'see, they put it by the bed.'

'Draw the curtains, fellow, and don't stand gaping there,' whispered Montague, sternly.

The man hesitated.

'Hold this, then,' said Montague, and impatiently thrusting the candlestick into the servant's hand, he himself advanced to the bed-side and drew the curtains apart. The light of the candle, which was still burning at the bedside, fell upon a figure huddled together, half upright, at the head of the bed. It seemed as though it had slunk back as far as the solid panelling would allow, and the hands were still clutched in the bedclothes.

'*Barton, Barton!*' cried the general, with a strange mixture of awe and vehemence. He took the candle, and held it so that it shone full upon the face. The features were fixed, stern and white; the jaw was fallen; and the sightless eyes, still open, gazed vacantly forward towards the front of the bed. 'God Almighty! he's dead,' muttered the general, as he looked upon this fearful spectacle. They both continued to gaze upon it in silence for a minute or more. 'And cold, too,' whispered Montague, withdrawing his hand from that of the dead man.

'And see, see – may I never have life, sir,' added the man, after another pause, with a shudder, 'but there was something else on the bed with him. Look there – look there – see that, sir.'

As the man thus spoke he pointed to a deep indenture, as if caused by a heavy pressure, near the foot of the bed.

Montague was silent.

'Come, sir, come away, for God's sake,' whispered the man, drawing close up to him, and holding fast by his arm, while he glanced fearfully round; 'what good can be done here now – come away, for God's sake!'

At this moment they heard the steps of more than one approaching, and Montague, hastily desiring the servant to arrest their progress, endeavoured to loose the rigid grip with which the fingers of the dead man were clutched in the bedclothes, and drew, as well as he was able, the awful figure into a reclining posture; then closing the curtains carefully upon it, he hastened himself to meet those persons that were approaching.

It is needless to follow the personages so slightly connected with this narrative into the events of their after life; it is enough to say that no clue to the solution of these mysterious occurrences was ever after discovered; and so long an interval having now passed since the event which I have just described concluded this strange history, it is scarcely to be expected that time can throw any new light upon its dark and inexplicable outline. Until the secrets of the earth shall be no longer hidden, therefore, these transactions must remain shrouded in their original obscurity.

The only occurrence in Captain Barton's former life to which reference was ever made as having any possible connection with the sufferings with which his existence closed, and which he himself seemed to regard as working out a retribution for some grievous sin of his past life, was a circumstance which not for several years after his death was brought to light. The nature of this disclosure was painful to his relatives, and discreditable to his memory.

It appeared that some six years before Captain Barton's final return to Dublin, he had formed, in the town of Plymouth, a guilty attachment, the object of which was the daughter of one of the ship's crew under his command. The father had visited the frailty of his unhappy child with extreme harshness, and even brutality, and it was said that she had died heartbroken. Presuming upon Barton's implication in her guilt, this man had conducted himself towards him with marked insolence, and Barton repaid this – and, what he resented with still more exasperated bitterness, his treatment of the unfortunate girl – with a systematic exercise of those terrible and arbitrary severities which the regulations of the navy place at the command of those who are responsible for its discipline. The man had at length made his escape, while the vessel was in port at Naples, but died, as it was said, in a hospital in that town, of the wounds inflicted in one of his recent and sanguinary punishments.

Whether these circumstances in reality bear upon the occurrences of Barton's after life, it is, of course, impossible to say. It seems, however, more than probable that they were, at least in his own mind, closely associated with them. But whatever the truth may be as to the origin and motives of this mysterious persecution, there can be no doubt that, with respect to the agencies by which it was accomplished, absolute and impenetrable mystery is likely to prevail until the day of doom.

SHERIDAN LE FANU

Mr Justice Harbottle

PROLOGUE

On this case Dr Hesselius has inscribed nothing more than the words 'Harman's Report' and a simple reference to his own extraordinary essay on 'The Interior Sense and the Conditions of the Opening thereof'.

The reference is to Vol. I, Section 317, Note z. The note to which reference is thus made, simply says:

There are two accounts of the remarkable case of the Honourable Mr Justice Harbottle, one furnished to me by Mrs Trimmer, of Tunbridge Wells (June 1805); the other, at a much later date, by Anthony Harman Esq. I much prefer the former; in the first place, because it is minute and detailed, and written, it seems to me, with more caution and knowledge; and in the next, because the letters from Dr Hedstone, which are embodied in it, furnish matter of the highest value to a right apprehension of the nature of the case. It was one of the best declared cases of an opening of the interior sense which I have met with. It was affected, too, by the phenomenon which occurs so frequently as to indicate a law of these eccentric conditions; that is to say, it exhibited what I may term the contagious character of this sort of intrusion of the spirit-world upon the proper domain of matter. So soon as the spirit-action has established itself in the case of one patient, its developed energy begins to radiate, more or less effectually, upon others. The interior vision of the child was opened; as was, also, that of its mother, Mrs Pyneweck; and both the interior vision and hearing of the scullery-maid were opened on the same occasion. After-appearances are the result of the law explained in Vol. II, Sections 17 to 49. The common centre of association, simultaneously recalled, unites, or reunites, as the case may be, for a period measured, as we see in Section 37. The *maximum* will extend to days, the *minimum* is little more than a second. We see the operation of this principle perfectly displayed in certain cases of lunacy, of epilepsy, of catalepsy, and of mania of a peculiar and painful character, though unattended by incapacity of business.

The memorandum of the case of Judge Harbottle which was written by Mrs Trimmer of Tunbridge Wells and which Dr Hesselius thought the better of the two, I have been unable to discover among his papers. I found in his escritoire a note to the effect that he had lent the Report of Judge Harbottle's case, written by Mrs Trimmer, to Dr F. Heyne. To that learned and able gentleman accordingly I wrote, and received from him, in his reply, which was full of alarms and regrets, on account of the uncertain safety of that 'valuable manuscript', a line written long since by Dr Hesselius, which completely exonerated him, inasmuch as it acknowledged the safe return of the papers. The narrative of Mr Harman, is therefore, the only one available for this collection. The late Dr Hesselius, in another passage of the note that I have cited, says, 'As to the facts (non-medical) of the case, the narrative of Mr Harman exactly tallies with that furnished by Mrs Trimmer.' The strictly scientific view of the case would scarcely interest the popular reader; and, possibly, for the purposes of this selection, I should, even had I both papers to choose between, have preferred that of Mr Harman, which is given, in full, in the following pages.

The Judge's House

Thirty years ago, an elderly man, to whom I paid quarterly a small annuity charged on some property of mine, came on the quarter-day to receive it. He was a dry, sad, quiet man, who had known better days, and had always maintained an unexceptionable character. No better authority could be imagined for a ghost story.

He told me one, though with a manifest reluctance; he was drawn into the narration by his choosing to explain what I should not have remarked, that he had called two days earlier than that week after the strict day of payment which he had usually allowed to elapse. His reason was a sudden determination to change his lodgings, and the consequent necessity of paying his rent a little before it was due.

He lodged in a dark street in Westminster, in a spacious old house, very warm, being wainscoted from top to bottom and furnished with no undue abundance of windows, and those fitted with thick sashes and small panes.

This house was, as the bills upon the windows testified, offered to be sold or let. But no one seemed to care to look at it.

A thin matron, in rusty black silk, very taciturn, with large, steady, alarmed eyes that seemed to look in your face to read what you might have seen in the dark rooms and passages through which you had passed, was in charge of it, with a solitary 'maid-of-all-work' under her command. My poor friend had taken lodgings in this house, on account of their extraordinary cheapness. He had occupied them for nearly a year without the slightest disturbance, and was the only tenant, under rent, in the house. He had two rooms: a sitting-room and a bedroom with a closet opening from it, in which he kept his books and papers locked up. He had gone to his bed, having also locked the outer door. Unable to sleep, he had lighted a candle, and after having read for a time, had laid the book beside him. He heard the old clock at the stairhead strike one; and very shortly after, to his alarm, he saw the closet-door, which he thought he had locked, open stealthily, and a slight dark man, particularly sinister and somewhere about fifty, dressed in mourning of a very antique fashion (such a suit as we see in Hogarth) entered the room on tiptoe. He was followed by an elder man, stout and blotched with scurvy, whose features, fixed as a corpse's, were stamped with dreadful force with a character of sensuality and villainy.

This old man wore a flowered silk dressing-gown and ruffles, and he remarked a gold ring on his finger, and on his head a cap of velvet, such as, in the days of perukes, gentlemen wore in undress.

This direful old man carried in his ringed and ruffled hand a coil of rope; and these two figures crossed the floor diagonally, passing the foot of his bed, from the closet door at the farther end of the room, at the left, near the window, to the door opening upon the lobby, close to the bed's head, at his right.

He did not attempt to describe his sensations as these figures passed so near him. He merely said that so far from sleeping in that room again, no consideration the world could offer would induce him so much as to enter it again alone, even in the daylight. He found both doors, that of the closet and that of the room opening upon the lobby, in the morning as fast locked as he had left them before going to bed.

In answer to a question of mine, he said that neither appeared the least conscious of his presence. They did not seem to glide, but walked as living men do, but without any sound, and he felt a vibration on the floor as they crossed it. He so obviously suffered from speaking about the apparitions that I asked him no more questions.

There were in his description, however, certain coincidences so very singular as to induce me, by that very post, to write to a friend much my senior, then living in a remote part of England, for the information which I knew he could give me. He had himself more than once pointed out that old house to my attention, and told me, though very briefly, the strange story which I now asked him to give me in greater detail.

His answer satisfied me; and the following pages convey its substance.

Your letter [he wrote] tells me you desire some particulars about the closing years of the life of Mr Justice Harbottle, one of the judges of the Court of Common Pleas. You refer, of course, to the extraordinary occurrences that made that period of his life long after a theme for 'winter tales' and metaphysical speculation. I happen to know perhaps more than any other man living of those mysterious particulars.

The old family mansion, when I revisited London more than thirty years ago, I examined for the last time. During the years that have passed since then I hear that improvement, with its preliminary demolitions, has been doing wonders for the quarter of Westminster in which it stood. If I were quite certain that the house had been taken down, I should have no difficulty about naming the street in which it stood. As what I have to tell, however, is not likely to improve its letting value, and as I should not care to get into trouble, I prefer being silent on that particular point.

How old the house was, I can't tell. People said it was built by Roger Harbottle, a Turkey merchant, in the reign of King James I. I am not a good opinion upon such questions; but having been in it, though in its forlorn and deserted state, I can tell you in a general way what it was like. It was built of dark-red brick, and the door and windows were faced with stone that had turned yellow with time. It receded some feet from the line of the other houses in the street; and it had a florid and fanciful rail of iron about the broad steps that invited your ascent to the hall-door, in which were fixed, under a file of lamps among scrolls and twisted leaves, two immense 'extinguishers', like the conical caps of fairies, into which, in old times, the footmen used to thrust their flambeaux when their chairs or coaches had set down their great people, in the hall or at the steps, as the case might be. The hall is panelled up to the ceiling and has a large fireplace. Two or three stately old rooms open from it at each side. The windows of these are tall, with many small panes. Passing through the arch at the back of the hall, you come upon the wide and heavy well-staircase. There is a back staircase also. The mansion is large, and has not as much light, by any means, in proportion to its extent, as modern houses enjoy. When I saw it, it had long been untenanted and had the gloomy reputation beside of a haunted house. Cobwebs floated from the ceilings or spanned the corners of the cornices, and dust lay thick over everything. The windows were stained with the dust and rain of fifty years, and darkness had thus grown darker.

When I made it my first visit, it was in company with my father, when I was still a boy, in the year 1808. I was about twelve years old, and my imagination impressible, as it always is at that age. I looked about me with great awe. I was here in the very centre and scene of those occurrences which I had heard recounted at the fireside at home with so delightful a horror.

My father was an old bachelor of nearly sixty when he married. He had, when a child, seen Judge Harbottle on the bench in his robes and wig a dozen times at least before his death, which took place in 1748, and his appearance made a powerful and unpleasant impression, not only on his imagination, but upon his nerves.

The judge was at that time a man of some sixty-seven years. He had a great mulberry-coloured face, a big, carbuncled nose, fierce eyes and a grim and brutal mouth. My father, who was young at the time, thought it the most formidable face he had ever seen; for there were evidences of intellectual power in the formation and lines of the forehead. His voice was loud and harsh, and gave effect to the sarcasm which was his habitual weapon on the bench.

This old gentleman had the reputation of being about the wickedest man in England. Even on the bench he now and then showed his scorn of opinion. He had carried cases his own way, it was said, in spite of counsel, authorities and even of juries, by a sort of cajolery, violence and bamboozling that somehow confused and overpowered resistance. He had never actually committed himself; he was too cunning to do that. He had the character of being, however, a dangerous and unscrupulous judge; but his character did not trouble him. The associates he chose for his hours of relaxation cared as little as he did about it.

2

Mr Peters

One night during the session of 1746 this old judge went down in his chair to wait in one of the rooms of the House of Lords for the result of a division in which he and his order were interested.

This over, he was about to return to his house close by, in his chair; but the night had become so soft and fine that he changed his mind, sent it home empty, and with two footmen, each with a flambeau, set out on foot in preference. Gout had made him rather a slow pedestrian. It took him some time to get through the two or three streets he had to pass before reaching his house.

In one of those narrow streets of tall houses, perfectly silent at that hour, he overtook, slowly as he was walking, a very singular-looking old gentleman.

He had a bottle-green coat on, with a cape to it and large stone buttons, and a broad-leafed, low-crowned hat, from under which a big powdered wig escaped; he stooped very much, and supporting his bending knees with the aid of a crutch-handled cane, he shuffled and tottered along painfully.

'I ask your pardon, sir,' said this old man, in a very quavering voice as the burly judge came up with him, and he extended his hand feebly towards his arm.

Mr Justice Harbottle saw that the man was by no means poorly dressed, and his manner that of a gentleman. The judge stopped short, and said, in his harsh peremptory tones, 'Well, sir, how can I serve you?'

'Can you direct me to Judge Harbottle's house? I have some intelligence of the very last importance to communicate to him.'

'Can you tell it before witnesses?' asked the judge.

'By no means; it must reach *his* ear only,' quavered the old man earnestly.

'If that be so, sir, you have only to accompany me a few steps farther to reach my house and obtain a private audience; for I am Judge Harbottle.'

With this invitation the infirm gentleman in the white wig complied very readily; and in another minute the stranger stood in what was then termed the front parlour of the judge's house, tête-à-tête with that shrewd and dangerous functionary.

He had to sit down, being very much exhausted and unable for a little time to speak; and then he had a fit of coughing, and after that a fit of gasping; and thus two or three minutes passed, during which the judge dropped his roquelaure on an armchair, and threw his cocked-hat over that.

The venerable pedestrian in the white wig quickly recovered his voice. With closed doors they remained together for some time.

There were guests waiting in the drawing-rooms, and the sound of men's voices laughing, and then of a female voice singing to a harpsichord, were heard distinctly in the hall over the stairs; for old Judge Harbottle had arranged one of his dubious jollifications, such as might well make the hair of godly men's heads stand upright for that night.

This old gentleman in the powdered white wig that rested on his stooped shoulders must have had something to say that interested the judge very much, for he would not have parted on easy terms with the ten minutes and upwards which that conference filched from the sort of revelry in which he most delighted, and in which he was the roaring king, and in some sort the tyrant also, of his company.

The footman who showed the aged gentleman out observed that the judge's mulberry-coloured face, pimples and all, was bleached to a dingy yellow, and there was the abstraction of agitated thought in his manner as he bid the stranger good-night. The servant saw that the conversation had been of serious import, and that the judge was frightened.

Instead of stumping upstairs forthwith to his scandalous hilarities, his profane company and his great china bowl of punch – the identical bowl from which a bygone Bishop of London, good easy man, had baptised this judge's grandfather, but which now clinked round the rim with silver ladles and was hung with scrolls of lemon-peel – instead, I say, of stumping and clambering up the great staircase to the cavern of his Circean enchantment, he stood with his big nose flattened against the window pane, watching the progress of the feeble old man, who clung stiffly to the iron rail as he got down, step by step, to the pavement.

The hall-door had hardly closed when the old judge was in the hall bawling hasty orders, with such stimulating expletives as old colonels under excitement sometimes indulge in nowadays, with a stamp or two of his big foot, and a waving of his clenched fist in the air. He commanded the footman to overtake the old gentleman in the white wig, to offer him his protection on his way home, and in no case to show his face again without having ascertained where he lodged, and who he was, and all about him.

'By gad, sirrah! if you fail me in this, you doff my livery tonight!'

Forth bounced the stalwart footman, with his heavy cane under his arm; he skipped down the steps, and looked up and down the street after the singular figure, so easy to recognise. What were his adventures I shall not tell you just now.

The old man, in the conference to which he had been admitted in that stately panelled room, had just told the judge a very strange story. He might be himself a conspirator; he might possibly be crazed; or possibly his whole story was straight and true.

The aged gentleman in the bottle-green coat, on finding himself alone with Mr Justice Harbottle, had become agitated. He said, 'There is, perhaps you are not aware, my lord, a prisoner in Shrewsbury Gaol charged with having forged a bill of exchange for a hundred and twenty pounds, and his name is Lewis Pyneweck, a grocer of that town.'

'Is there?' says the judge, who knew well that there was.

'Yes, my lord,' says the old man.

'Then you had better say nothing to affect this case. If you do, by gad I'll commit you, for I'm to try it,' says the judge, with his terrible look and tone.

'I am not going to do anything of the kind, my lord; of him or his case I know nothing, and care nothing. But a fact has come to my knowledge which it behoves you well to consider.'

'And what may that fact be?' enquired the judge; 'I'm in haste, sir, and beg you will use dispatch.'

'It has come to my knowledge, my lord, that a secret tribunal is in process of formation, the object of which is to take cognisance of the conduct of the judges; and first, of *your* conduct, my lord: it is a wicked conspiracy.'

'Who are of it?' demanded the judge.

'I know not a single name as yet. I know but the fact, my lord; it is most certainly true.'

'I'll have you before the Privy Council, sir,' said the judge.

'That is what I most desire; but not for a day or two, my lord.'

'And why so?'

'I have not as yet a single name, as I told your lordship; but I expect to have a list of the most forward men in it, and some other papers connected with the plot, in two or three days.'

'You said one or two just now.'

'About that time, my lord.'

'Is this a Jacobite plot?'

'In the main I think it is, my lord.'

'Why, then, it is political. I have tried no state prisoners, nor am like to try any such. How, then, does it concern me?'

'From what I can gather, my lord, there are those in it who desire private revenges upon certain judges.'

'What do they call their cabal?'

'The High Court of Appeal, my lord.'

'Who are you, sir? What is your name?'

'Hugh Peters, my lord.'

'That should be a Whig name?'

'It is, my lord.'

'Where do you lodge, Mr Peters?'

'In Thames Street, my lord, over against the sign of the Three Kings.'

'Three Kings? Take care one be not too many for you, Mr Peters! How come you, an honest Whig, as you say, to be privy to a Jacobite plot? Answer me that.'

'My lord, a person in whom I take an interest has been seduced to take a part in it; and being frightened at the unexpected wickedness of their plans, he is resolved to become an informer for the crown.'

'He resolves like a wise man, sir. What does he say of the persons? Who are in the plot? Does he know them?'

'Only two, my lord; but he will be introduced to the club in a few days, and he will then have a list, and more exact information of their plans, and above all of their oaths, and their hours and places of meeting, with which he wishes to be acquainted before they can have any suspicions of his intentions. And being so informed, to whom, think you, my lord, had he best go then?'

'To the king's attorney-general straight. But you say this concerns me, sir, in particular? How about this prisoner, Lewis Pyneweck? Is he one of them?'

'I can't tell, my lord; but for some reason, it is thought your lord-ship will be well advised if you try him not. For if you do, it is feared 'twill shorten your days.'

'So far as I can learn, Mr Peters, this business smells pretty strong of blood and treason. The king's attorney-general will know how to deal with it. When shall I see you again, sir?'

'If you give me leave, my lord, either before your lordship's court sits, or after it rises, tomorrow. I should like to come and tell your lordship what has passed.'

'Do so, Mr Peters, at nine o'clock tomorrow morning. And see you play me no trick, sir, in this matter; if you do, by gad, sir, I'll lay you by the heels!'

'You need fear no trick from me, my lord; had I not wished to serve you, and acquit my own conscience, I never would have come all this way to talk with your lordship.'

'I'm willing to believe you, Mr Peters; I'm willing to believe you, sir.'

And upon this they parted.

'He has either painted his face, or he is consumedly sick,' thought the old judge.

The light had shone more effectually upon his features as he turned to leave the room with a low bow, and they looked, he fancied, unnaturally chalky.

'Damn him!' said the judge ungraciously, as he began to scale the stairs: 'he has half-spoiled my supper.'

But if he had, no one but the judge himself perceived it, and the evidence was all, as anyone might perceive, the other way.

3

Lewis Pyneweck

In the meantime the footman dispatched in pursuit of Mr Peters speedily overtook that feeble gentleman. The old man stopped when he heard the sound of pursuing steps, but any alarms that may have crossed his mind seemed to disappear on his recognising the livery. He very gratefully accepted the proffered assistance, and placed his tremulous arm within the servant's for support.

They had not gone far, however, when the old man stopped suddenly, saying, 'Dear me! as I live, I have dropped it. You heard it fall. My eyes, I fear, won't serve me, and I'm unable to stoop low enough; but if you will look, you shall have half the find. It is a guinea; I carried it in my glove.'

The street was silent and deserted. The footman had hardly

descended to what he termed his 'hunkers', and begun to search the pavement about the spot which the old man indicated, when Mr Peters, who seemed very much exhausted and breathed with difficulty, struck him a violent blow, from above, over the back of the head with a heavy instrument, and then another; and, leaving him bleeding and senseless in the gutter, ran like a lamplighter down a lane to the right and was gone.

When, an hour later, the watchman brought the man in livery home, still stupid and covered with blood, Judge Harbottle cursed his servant roundly, swore he was drunk, threatened him with an indictment for taking bribes to betray his master, and cheered him with a perspective of the broad street leading from the Old Bailey to Tyburn, the cart's tail and the hangman's lash.

Notwithstanding this demonstration, the judge was pleased. It was a disguised 'affidavit man', or footpad, no doubt, who had been employed to frighten him. The trick had fallen through.

A 'court of appeal', such as the false Hugh Peters had indicated, with assassination for its sanction, would be an uncomfortable institution for a 'hanging judge' like the Honourable Justice Harbottle. That sarcastic and ferocious administrator of the criminal code of England, at that time a rather pharisaical, bloody and heinous system of justice, had reasons of his own for choosing to try that very Lewis Pyneweck, on whose behalf this audacious trick was devised. Try him he would. No man living should take that morsel out of his mouth.

Of Lewis Pyneweck, of course, so far as the outer world could see, he knew nothing. He would try him after his fashion, without fear, favour or affection.

But did he not remember a certain thin man, dressed in mourning, in whose house in Shrewsbury the judge's lodgings used to be, until a scandal of his ill-treating his wife came suddenly to light? A grocer with a demure look, a soft step, and a lean face as dark as mahogany, with a nose sharp and long, standing ever so little awry, and a pair of dark steady brown eyes under thinly-traced black brows – a man whose thin lips wore always a faint unpleasant smile.

Had not that scoundrel an account to settle with the judge? had he not been troublesome lately? and was not his name Lewis Pyneweck, sometime grocer in Shrewsbury, and now prisoner in the gaol of that town?

The reader may take it, if he pleases, as a sign that Judge Harbottle was a good Christian that he suffered nothing ever from remorse. That was undoubtedly true. He had, nevertheless, done this grocer, forger, what you will, some five or six years before, a grievous wrong; but it was not that, but a possible scandal, and possible complications, that troubled the learned judge now.

Did he not, as a lawyer, know that to bring a man from his shop to the dock, the chances must be at least ninety-nine out of a hundred that he is guilty.

A weak man like his learned brother Withershins was not a judge to keep the high-roads safe and make crime tremble. Old Judge Harbottle was the man to make the evil-disposed quiver, and to refresh the world with showers of wicked blood, and thus save the innocent, to the refrain of the ancient law he loved to quote –

> Foolish pity
> Ruins a city.

In hanging that fellow he could not be wrong. The eye of a man accustomed to look upon the dock could not fail to read 'villain' written sharp and clear in his plotting face. Of course he would try him, and no one else should.

A saucy-looking woman, still handsome, in a mob-cap gay with blue ribbons, and a saque of flowered silk, with lace and rings on, much too fine for the judge's housekeeper, which nevertheless she was, peeped into his study next morning, and, seeing the judge alone, stepped in.

'Here's another letter from him, come by the post this morning. Can't you do nothing for him?' she said wheedlingly, with her arm over his neck, and her delicate finger and thumb fiddling with the lobe of his purple ear.

'I'll try,' said Judge Harbottle, not raising his eyes from the paper he was reading.

'I knew you'd do what I asked you,' she said.

The judge clapped his gouty claw over his heart and made her an ironical bow.

'What,' she asked, 'will you do?'

'Hang him,' said the judge with a chuckle.

'You don't mean to; no, you don't, my little man,' said she, surveying herself in a mirror on the wall.

'I'm damned but I think you're falling in love with your husband at last!' said Judge Harbottle.

'I'm blessed but I think you're growing jealous of him,' replied the lady with a laugh. 'But no; he was always a bad one to me; I've done with him long ago.'

'And he with you, by George! When he took your fortune, and your spoons, and your ear-rings, he had all he wanted of you. He drove you from his house; and when he discovered you had made yourself comfortable, and found a good situation, he'd have taken your guineas, and your silver, and your ear-rings over again, and then allowed you half a dozen years more to make a new harvest for his mill. You don't wish him good; if you say you do, you lie.'

She laughed a wicked, saucy laugh, and gave the terrible Rhada-manthus a playful tap on the chops. 'He wants me to send him money to fee a counsellor,' she said, while her eyes wandered over the pictures on the wall, and back again to the looking-glass; and certainly she did not look as if his jeopardy troubled her very much.

'Confound his impudence, the scoundrel!' thundered the old judge, throwing himself back in his chair, as he used to do *in furore* on the bench, and the lines of his mouth looked brutal, and his eyes ready to leap from their sockets. 'If you answer his letter from my house to please yourself, you'll write your next from somebody else's to please me. You understand, my pretty witch, I'll not be pestered. Come, no pouting; whimpering won't do. You don't care a brass farthing for the villain, body or soul. You came here but to make a row. You are one of Mother Carey's chickens; and where you come, the storm is up. Get you gone, baggage! *get you gone!*' he repeated, with a stamp; for a knock at the hall-door made her instantaneous disappearance indispensable.

I need hardly say that the venerable Hugh Peters did not appear again. The judge never mentioned him. But oddly enough, con-sidering how he laughed to scorn the weak invention which he had blown into dust at the very first puff, his white-wigged visitor and the conference in the dark front parlour was often in his memory.

His shrewd eye told him that allowing for a change of tints and such disguises as the playhouse affords every night, the features of this false old man, who had turned out too hard for his tall footman, were identical with those of Lewis Pyneweck.

Judge Harbottle made his registrar call upon the crown solicitor and tell him that there was a man in town who bore a wonderful resemblance to a prisoner in Shrewsbury Gaol named Lewis Pyneweck, and to make enquiry through the post forthwith whether anyone was personating Pyneweck in prison, and whether he had thus or otherwise made his escape.

The prisoner was safe, however, and there was no question as to his identity.

4

Interruption in Court

In due time Judge Harbottle went circuit; and in due time the judges were in Shrewsbury. News travelled slowly in those days, and newspapers, like the wagons and stage-coaches, took matters easily. Mrs Pyneweck, in the judge's house with a diminished household – the greater part of the judge's servants having gone with him, for he had given up riding circuit and travelled in his coach in state – kept house rather solitarily at home.

In spite of quarrels, in spite of mutual injuries – some of them, inflicted by herself, enormous – in spite of a married life of spiteful bickerings, a life in which there seemed no love or liking or forbearance, for years – now that Pyneweck stood in near danger of death, something like remorse came suddenly upon her. She knew that in Shrewsbury were being enacted the scenes which were to determine his fate. She knew she did not love him; but she could not have supposed, even a fortnight before, that the hour of suspense could have affected her so powerfully.

She knew the day on which the trial was expected to take place. She could not get it out of her head for a minute; she felt faint as it drew towards evening.

Two or three days passed; and then she knew that the trial must be over by this time. There were floods between London and Shrewsbury, and news was long delayed. She wished the floods would last for ever. It was dreadful waiting to hear; dreadful to know that the event was over, and that she could not hear till self-willed rivers subsided; dreadful to know that they must subside and the news come at last.

She had some vague trust in the judge's good-nature, and much in the resources of chance and accident. She had contrived to send the money he wanted. He would not be without legal advice and energetic and skilled support.

At last the news did come – a long arrear all in a gush: a letter from a female friend in Shrewsbury; a return of the sentences, sent up for the judge; and most important, because most easily got at, being told with great aplomb and brevity, the long-deferred intelligence of the Shrewsbury Assizes in the *Morning Advertiser*. Like an impatient reader of a novel, who reads the last page first, she read with dizzy eyes the list of the executions.

Two were respited, seven were hanged; and in that capital catalogue was this line: 'Lewis Pyneweck – forgery . . . ' She had to read it half a dozen times over before she was sure she understood it. Here was the paragraph:

Sentence of Death – 7

Executed accordingly, on Friday the 13th instant, to wit:

Thomas Primer, *alias* Duck – highway robbery;
Flora Guy – stealing to the value of 1s. 6d.;
Arthur Pounden – burglary;
Matilda Mummery – riot;
Lewis Pyneweck – forgery, bill of exchange . . .

And when she reached this, she read it over and over, feeling very cold and sick.

This buxom housekeeper was known in the house as Mrs Carwell – Carwell being her maiden name, which she had resumed. No one in the house except its master knew her history. Her introduction had been managed craftily. No one suspected that it had been concerted between her and the old reprobate in scarlet and ermine.

Flora Carwell ran up the stairs now, and snatched her little girl, hardly seven years of age, whom she met on the lobby, hurriedly up in her arms, and carried her into her bedroom, without well knowing what she was doing, and sat down, placing the child before her. She was not able to speak. She held the child before her, and looked in the little girl's wondering face, and burst into tears of horror.

She thought the judge could have saved him. I dare say he could.

For a time she was furious with him, and hugged and kissed her bewildered little girl, who returned her gaze with large round eyes.

That little girl had lost her father, and knew nothing of the matter. She had been always told that her father was dead long ago.

A woman, coarse, uneducated, vain and violent, does not reason, or even feel, very distinctly; but in these tears of consternation were mingling a self-upbraiding. She felt afraid of that little child.

But Mrs Carwell was a person who lived not upon sentiment, but upon beef and pudding; she consoled herself with punch; she did not trouble herself long even with resentments; she was a gross and material person, and could not mourn over the irrevocable for more than a limited number of hours, even if she would.

Judge Harbottle was soon in London again. Except the gout, this savage old epicurean never knew a day's sickness. He laughed, and coaxed, and bullied away the young woman's faint upbraidings, and in a little time Lewis Pyneweck troubled her no more; and the judge secretly chuckled over the perfectly fair removal of a bore, who might have grown little by little into something very like a tyrant.

It was the lot of the judge whose adventures I am now recounting to try criminal cases at the Old Bailey shortly after his return. He had commenced his charge to the jury in a case of forgery, and was, after his wont, thundering dead against the prisoner, with many a hard aggravation and cynical gibe, when suddenly all died away in silence and instead of looking at the jury the eloquent judge was gaping at some person in the body of the court.

Among the persons of small importance who stand and listen at the sides was one tall enough to show with a little prominence: a slight mean figure, dressed in seedy black, lean and dark of visage. He had just handed a letter to the crier, before he caught the judge's eye.

That judge descried, to his amazement, the features of Lewis Pyneweck. He had the usual faint thin-lipped smile; and with his blue chin raised in the air, and as it seemed quite unconscious of the distinguished notice he had attracted, he was stretching his low cravat with his crooked fingers, while he slowly turned his head from side to side – a process which enabled the judge to see distinctly a stripe of swollen blue round his neck, which indicated, he thought, the grip of the rope.

This man, with a few others, had got a footing on a step, from which he could better see the court. He now stepped down, and the judge lost sight of him.

His lordship signed energetically with his hand in the direction in which this man had vanished. He turned to the tipstaff. His first effort to speak ended in a gasp. He cleared his throat, and told the astounded official to arrest that man who had interrupted the court.

'He's but this moment gone down *there*. Bring him in custody before me, within ten minutes' time, or I'll strip your gown from your shoulders and fine the sheriff!' he thundered, while his eyes flashed round the court in search of the functionary.

Attorneys, counsellors, idle spectators, gazed in the direction in which Mr Justice Harbottle had shaken his gnarled old hand. They compared notes. Not one had seen anyone making a disturbance. They asked one another if the judge was losing his head.

Nothing came of the search. His lordship concluded his charge a great deal more tamely; and when the jury retired, he stared round the court with a wandering mind, and looked as if he would not have given sixpence to see the prisoner hanged.

5

Caleb Searcher

The judge had received the letter; had he known from whom it came, he would no doubt have read it instantaneously. As it was he simply read the direction:

To the Honourable
The Lord Justice
Elijah Harbottle,
One of His Majesty's Justices of
the Honourable Court of Common Pleas

It remained forgotten in his pocket till he reached home.

When he pulled out that and others from the capacious pocket of his coat, it had its turn, as he sat in his library in his thick silk dressing-gown; and then he found its contents to be a closely-written letter, in a clerk's hand, and an enclosure in 'secretary hand', as I believe the angular scrivinary of law-writings in those days was termed, engrossed on a bit of parchment about the size of this page. The letter said:

MR JUSTICE HARBOTTLE, MY LORD – I am ordered by the High Court of Appeal to acquaint your lordship, in order to your better preparing yourself for your trial, that a true bill hath been sent down, and the indictment lieth against your lordship for the murder of one Lewis Pyneweck of Shrewsbury, citizen, wrongfully executed for the forgery of a bill of exchange, on the 13th day of January last, by reason of the wilful perversion of the evidence, and the undue pressure put upon the jury, together with the illegal admission of evidence by your lordship, well knowing the same to be illegal, by all which the promoter of the prosecution of the said indictment, before the High Court of Appeal, hath lost his life.

And the trial of the said indictment, I am further ordered to acquaint your lordship, is fixed for the 10th day of February next ensuing, by the right honourable the Lord Chief Justice Twofold, of the court aforesaid, to wit, the High Court of Appeal, on which day it will most certainly take place. And I am further to acquaint your lordship, to prevent any surprise or miscarriage, that your case stands first for the said day, and that the said High Court of Appeal sits day and night, and never rises; and herewith, by order of the said court, I furnish your lordship with a copy (extract) of the record in this case, except of the indictment, whereof, not-withstanding, the substance and effect is supplied to your lordship in this notice. And further I am to inform you that in case the jury then to try your lordship should find you guilty, the right honourable the Lord Chief Justice will, in passing sentence of death upon you, fix the day of execution for the 10th day of March, being one calendar month from the day of your trial.

CALEB SEARCHER
Officer of the Crown Solicitor in the
Kingdom of Life and Death

The judge glanced through the parchment.

' 'Sblood! Do they think a man like me is to be bamboozled by their buffoonery?'

The judge's coarse features were wrung into one of his sneers; but he was pale. Possibly, after all, there was a conspiracy on foot. It was queer. Did they mean to pistol him in his carriage? or did they only aim at frightening him?

Judge Harbottle had more than enough of animal courage. He was not afraid of highwaymen, and he had fought more than his share of duels, being a foul-mouthed advocate while he held briefs at the bar. No one questioned his fighting qualities. But with respect to this particular case of Pyneweck, he lived in a house of glass. Was there not his pretty, dark-eyed, overdressed housekeeper, Mrs Flora Carwell? Very easy for people who knew Shrewsbury to identify Mrs Pyneweck, if once put upon the scent; and had he not stormed and worked hard in that case? Had he not made it hard sailing for the prisoner? Did he not know very well what the bar thought of it? It would be the worst scandal that ever blasted judge.

So much there was intimidating in the matter but nothing more. The judge was a little bit gloomy for a day or two after, and more testy with everyone than usual.

He locked up the papers; and about a week after he asked his house-keeper, one day, in the library: 'Had your husband never a brother?'

Mrs Carwell squalled on this sudden introduction of the funereal topic, and cried exemplary 'piggins full', as the judge used pleasantly to say. But he was in no mood for trifling now, and he said sternly: 'Come, madam! this wearies me. Do it another time; and give me an answer to my question.' So she did.

Pyneweck had no brother living. He once had one; but he died in Jamaica.

'How do you know he is dead?' asked the judge.

'Because he told me so.'

'Not the dead man.'

'Pyneweck told me so.'

'Is that all?' sneered the judge.

He pondered this matter; and time went on. The judge was growing a little morose, and enjoyed life less. The subject struck nearer to his thoughts than he fancied it could have done. But so it is with most undivulged vexations, and there was no one to whom he could tell this one.

It was now the ninth; and Mr Justice Harbottle was glad. He knew nothing would come of it. Still it bothered him; and tomorrow would see it well over.

[What of the paper I have cited? No one saw it during his life; no one, after his death. He spoke of it to Dr Hedstone; and what purported to be 'a copy', in the old judge's handwriting, was found. The original was nowhere. Was it a copy of an illusion, incident to brain disease? Such is my belief.]

6

Arrested

Judge Harbottle went this night to the play at Drury Lane. He was one of those old fellows who care nothing for late hours and occasional knocking about in pursuit of pleasure. He had appointed with two cronies of Lincoln's Inn to come home in his coach with him to sup after the play.

They were not in his box, but were to meet him near the entrance, and get into his carriage there; and Mr Justice Harbottle, who hated waiting, was looking a little impatiently from the window.

The judge yawned.

He told the footman to watch for Counsellor Thavies and Counsellor Beller, who were coming; and, with another yawn, he laid his cocked hat on his knees, closed his eyes, leaned back in his corner, wrapped his mantle closer about him, and began to think of pretty Mrs Abington.

And being a man who could sleep like a sailor, at a moment's notice, he was thinking of taking a nap. Those fellows had no business to keep a judge waiting.

He heard their voices now. Those rake-hell counsellors were laughing, and bantering, and sparring after their wont. The carriage swayed and jerked as one got in, and then again as the other followed. The door clapped, and the coach was now jogging and rumbling over the pavement. The judge was a little bit sulky. He did not care to sit up and open his eyes. Let them suppose he was asleep. He heard them laugh with more malice than good-humour, he thought, as they observed it. He would give them a damned hard knock or two when they got to his door, and till then he would counterfeit his nap.

The clocks were chiming twelve. Beller and Thavies were silent as tombstones. They were generally loquacious and merry rascals.

The judge suddenly felt himself roughly seized and thrust from his corner into the middle of the seat, and opening his eyes, instantly he found himself between his two companions.

Before he could blurt out the oath that was at his lips, he saw that they were two strangers – evil-looking fellows, each with a pistol in his hand, and dressed like Bow Street officers.

The judge clutched at the check-string. The coach pulled up. He stared about him. They were not among houses; but through the windows, under a broad moonlight, he saw a black moor stretching lifelessly from right to left, with rotting trees, pointing fantastic branches in the air, standing here and there in groups, as if they held up their arms and twigs like fingers, in horrible glee at the judge's coming.

A footman came to the window. He knew his long face and sunken eyes. He knew it was Dingly Chuff, fifteen years ago a footman in his service, whom he had turned off at a moment's notice, in a burst of jealousy, and indicted for a missing spoon. The man had died in prison of the jail-fever.

The judge drew back in utter amazement. His armed companions signed mutely; and they were again gliding over this unknown moor.

The bloated and gouty old man, in his horror considered the question of resistance. But his athletic days were long over. This moor was a desert. There was no help to be had. He was in the hands of strange servants, even if his recognition turned out to be a delusion, and they were under the command of his captors. There was nothing for it but submission, for the present.

Suddenly the coach was brought nearly to a standstill, so that the prisoner saw an ominous sight from the window.

It was a gigantic gallows beside the road; it stood three-sided, and from each of its three broad beams at top depended in chains some eight or ten bodies, from several of which the cere-clothes had dropped away, leaving the skeletons swinging lightly by their chains. A tall ladder reached to the summit of the structure, and on the peat beneath lay bones.

On top of the dark transverse beam facing the road, from which, as from the other two completing the triangle of death, dangled a row of these unfortunates in chains, a hangman, with a pipe in his mouth, much as we see him in the famous print of the 'Idle Apprentice', though here his perch was ever so much higher, was reclining at his ease and listlessly shying bones, from a little heap at his elbow, at the skeletons that hung round, bringing down now a rib or two, now a hand, now half a leg. A long-sighted man could have discerned that he was a dark fellow, lean; and from continually looking down on the earth from the elevation over which, in another sense, he always hung, his nose, his lips, his chin were pendulous and loose, and drawn down into a monstrous grotesque.

This fellow took his pipe from his mouth on seeing the coach, stood up, and cut some solemn capers high on his beam; he shook a new rope in the air, crying with a voice high and distant as the caw of a raven hovering over a gibbet, 'A rope for Judge Harbottle!'

The coach was now driving on at its old swift pace.

So high a gallows as that, the judge had never, even in his most hilarious moments, dreamed of. He thought he must be raving. He shook his ears and strained his eyelids; but if he was dreaming, he was unable to awake himself.

There was no good in threatening these scoundrels. A *brutum fulmen* might bring a real one on his head.

Any submission to get out of their hands; and then heaven and earth he would move to uncover and hunt them down.

Suddenly they drove round a corner of a vast white building, and under a *porte-cochère*.

7

Chief Justice Twofold

The judge found himself in a corridor lighted with dingy oil lamps, its walls of bare stone; it looked like a passage in a prison. His guards placed him in the hands of other people. Here and there he saw bony and gigantic soldiers passing to and fro, with muskets over their shoulders. They looked straight before them, grinding their teeth, in bleak fury, with no noise but the clank of their shoes. He saw these by glimpses, round corners, and at the ends of passages, but he did not actually pass them by.

And now, passing under a narrow doorway, he found himself in the dock, confronting a judge in his scarlet robes, in a large courthouse. There was nothing to elevate this Temple of Themis above its vulgar kind elsewhere. Dingy enough it looked, in spite of candles lighted in decent abundance. A case had just closed, and the last juror's back was seen escaping through the door in the wall of the jury-box. There were some dozen barristers, some fiddling with pen and ink, others buried in briefs, some beckoning, with the plumes of their pens, to their attorneys, of whom there was no lack; there were clerks to-ing and fro-ing, and the officers of the court, and the registrar, who was handing up a paper to the judge; and the tipstaff, who was presenting a note at the end of his wand to a king's counsel over the heads of the crowd between. If this was the High Court of Appeal, which never rose day or night, it might account for the pale and jaded aspect of everybody in it. An air of indescribable gloom hung upon the pallid features of all the people here; no one ever smiled; all looked more or less secretly suffering.

'The King against Elijah Harbottle!' shouted the officer.

'Is the appellant Lewis Pyneweck in court?' asked Chief Justice Twofold, in a voice of thunder that shook the woodwork of the court and boomed down the corridors.

Up stood Pyneweck from his place at the table.

'Arraign the prisoner!' roared the Chief Justice Twofold and Judge Harbottle felt the panels of the dock round him, and the floor, and the rails quiver with the vibrations of that tremendous voice.

The prisoner, *in limine*, objected to this pretended court as being a sham and non-existent in point of law; and then that, even if it were a court constituted by law (the judge was growing dazed), it had not and could not have any jurisdiction to try him for his conduct on the bench.

Whereupon the Chief Justice laughed suddenly, and everyone in court, turning round upon the prisoner, laughed also, till the laugh grew and roared all round like a deafening acclamation; he saw nothing but glittering eyes and teeth, a universal stare and grin; but though all the voices laughed, not a single face of all those that concentrated their gaze upon him looked like a laughing face. The mirth subsided as suddenly as it had begun.

The indictment was read. Judge Harbottle actually pleaded! He pleaded 'not guilty'. A jury was sworn. The trial proceeded. Judge Harbottle was bewildered. This could not be real. He must be either mad, or *going* mad, he thought.

One thing could not fail to strike even him. This Chief Justice Twofold, who was knocking him about at every turn with sneer and gibe, and roaring him down with his tremendous voice, was a dilated effigy of himself; an image of Mr Justice Harbottle, at least double his size, and with all his fierce colouring, and his ferocity of eye and visage, enhanced awfully.

Nothing the prisoner could argue, cite or state was permitted to retard for a moment the march of the case towards its catastrophe.

The Chief Justice seemed to feel his power over the jury, and to exult and riot in the display of it. He glared at them, he nodded to them; he seemed to have established an understanding with them. The lights were faint in that part of the court. The jurors were mere shadows, sitting in rows; the prisoner could see a dozen pair of white eyes shining, coldly, out of the darkness; and whenever the judge in his charge, which was contemptuously brief, nodded and grinned and gibed, the prisoner could see, in the obscurity, by the dip of all these rows of eyes together, that the jury nodded in acquiescence,

And now the charge was over, the huge Chief Justice leaned back panting and gloating on the prisoner. Everyone in the court turned about and gazed with steadfast hatred on the man in the dock. From the jury-box, where the twelve sworn brethren were whispering together, a sound in the general stillness like a prolonged 'hiss–s–s!' was heard; and then, in answer to the challenge of the officer, 'How say you, gentlemen of the jury, guilty or not guilty?' came in a melancholy voice the finding, 'Guilty.'

The place seemed to the eyes of the prisoner to grow gradually darker and darker, till he could discern nothing distinctly but the lumen of the eyes that were turned upon him from every bench and side and corner and gallery of the building. The prisoner doubtless thought that he had quite enough to say, and conclusively, why sentence of death should not be pronounced upon him; but the Lord Chief Justice puffed it contemptuously away, like so much smoke, and proceeded to pass sentence of death upon the prisoner, having named the tenth of the ensuing month for his execution.

Before he had recovered from the stun of this ominous farce, in obedience to the mandate, 'Remove the prisoner,' he was led from the dock. The lamps seemed all to have gone out, and there were stoves and charcoal-fires here and there that threw a faint crimson light on the walls of the corridors through which he passed. The stones that composed them looked now enormous, cracked and unhewn.

He came into a vaulted smithy, where two men, naked to the waist, with heads like bulls, round shoulders, and the arms of giants, were welding red-hot chains together with hammers that pelted like thunderbolts.

They looked on the prisoner with fierce red eyes, and rested on their hammers for a minute; then said the elder to his companion, 'Take out Elijah Harbottle's gyves;' and with a pincers he plucked the end which lay dazzling in the fire from the furnace.

'One end locks,' said he, taking the cool end of the iron in one hand, while with the grip of a vice he seized the leg of the judge and locked the ring round his ankle. 'The other,' he said with a grin, 'is welded.'

The iron band that was to form the ring for the other leg lay still red hot upon the stone floor, with brilliant sparks sporting up and down its surface.

His companion, in his gigantic hands, seized the old judge's other leg, and pressed his foot immovably to the stone floor; while his senior, in a twinkling, with a masterly application of pincers and hammer, sped the glowing bar round his ankle so tight that the skin and sinews smoked and bubbled, and old Judge Harbottle uttered a yell that seemed to chill the very stones and make the iron chains quiver on the wall.

Chains, vaults, smiths and smithy all vanished in a moment; but the pain continued. Mr Justice Harbottle was suffering torture all round the ankle on which the infernal smiths had just been operating.

His friends, Thavies and Beller, were startled by the judge's roar in the midst of their elegant trifling about a marriage-à-la-mode case which was going on. The judge was in panic as well as pain. The street lamps and the light of his own hall-door restored him.

'I'm very bad,' growled he between his set teeth; 'my foot's blazing. Who was he that hurt my foot? 'Tis the gout – 'tis the gout!' he said, awaking completely. 'How many hours have we been coming from the playhouse? 'S blood, what has happened on the way? I've slept half the night!'

There had been no hitch or delay, and they had driven home at a good pace.

The judge, however, was in gout; he was feverish too; and the attack, though very short, was sharp; and when, in about a fortnight, it subsided, his ferocious joviality did not return. He could not get this dream, as he chose to call it, out of his head.

8

Somebody Has Got into the House

People remarked that the judge was in the vapours. His doctor said he should go for a fortnight to Buxton.

Whenever the judge fell into a brown study, he was always conning over the terms of the sentence pronounced upon him in his vision – 'in one calendar month from the date of this day'; and then the usual form, 'and you shall be hanged by the neck till you are dead,' etc. 'That will be the 10th – I'm not much in the way of being hanged. I know what stuff dreams are, and I laugh at them; but this is continually in my thoughts, as if it forecast misfortune of some sort. I wish the day my dream gave me were passed and over. I wish I were well purged of my gout. I wish I were as I used to be. 'Tis nothing but vapours, nothing but a maggot.' The copy of the parchment and letter which had announced his trial with many a snort and sneer he would read over and over again, and the scenery and people of his dream would rise about him in places the most unlikely, and steal him in a moment from all that surrounded him into a world of shadows.

The judge had lost his iron energy and banter. He was growing taciturn and morose. The bar remarked the change, as well they might. His friends thought him ill. The doctor said he was troubled with hypochondria, and that his gout was still lurking in his system, and ordered him to that ancient haunt of crutches and chalk-stones, Buxton.

The judge's spirits were very low; he was frightened about himself; and he described to his housekeeper, having sent for her to his study to drink a dish of tea, his strange dream in his drive home from Drury Lane Playhouse. He was sinking into the state of nervous dejection in which men lose their faith in orthodox advice and in despair consult quacks, astrologers and nursery storytellers. Could such a dream mean that he was to have a fit, and so die on the 10th? She did not think so. On the contrary, it was certain some good luck must happen on that day.

The judge kindled; and for the first time for many days, he looked for a minute or two like himself, and he tapped her on the cheek with the hand that was not in flannel.

'Odsbud! odsheart! you dear rogue! I had forgot. There is young Tom – yellow Tom, my nephew, you know, lies sick at Harrogate; why shouldn't he go that day as well as another, and if he does, I get an estate by it? Why, lookee, I asked Dr Hedstone yesterday if I was like to take a fit any time, and he laughed, and swore I was the last man in town to go off that way.'

The judge sent most of his servants down to Buxton to make his lodgings and all things comfortable for him. He was to follow in a day or two.

It was now the 9th; and the next day well over, he might laugh at his visions and auguries.

On the evening of the 9th, Dr Hedstone's footman knocked at the judge's door. The doctor ran up the dusky stairs to the drawing-room. It was a March evening, near the hour of sunset, with an east wind whistling sharply through the chimney-stacks. A wood fire blazed cheerily on the hearth. And Judge Harbottle, in what was then called a brigadier-wig, with his red roquelaure on, helped the glowing effect of the darkened chamber, which looked red all over like a room on fire.

The judge had his feet on a stool, and his huge grim purple face confronted the fire and seemed to pant and swell as the blaze alternately spread upward and collapsed. He had fallen again among his blue devils, and was thinking of retiring from the bench, and of fifty other gloomy things.

But the doctor, who was an energetic son of Aesculapius, would listen to no croaking; he told the judge he was full of gout, and in his present condition no judge even of his own case, but promised him leave to pronounce on all those melancholy questions a fortnight later. In the meantime the judge must be very careful. He was over-charged with gout, and he must not provoke an attack, till the waters of Buxton should do that office for him, in their own salutary way.

The doctor did not think him perhaps quite so well as he pretended, for he told him he wanted rest, and would be better if he went forthwith to his bed.

Mr Gerningham, his valet, assisted him, and gave him his drops; and the judge told him to wait in his bedroom till he should go to sleep.

Three persons that night had specially odd stories to tell.

The housekeeper had got rid of the trouble of amusing her little girl at this anxious time by giving her leave to run about the sitting-rooms and look at the pictures and china, on the usual condition of touching nothing. It was not until the last gleam of sunset had for some time faded, and the twilight had so deepened that she could no longer discern the colours on the china figures on the chimney-piece or in the cabinets, that the child returned to the housekeeper's room to find her mother.

To her she related, after some prattle about the china, and the pictures, and the judge's two grand wigs in the dressing-room off the library, an adventure of an extraordinary kind.

In the hall was placed, as was customary in those times, the sedan-chair which the master of the house occasionally used, covered with stamped leather, and studded with gilt nails, and with its red-silk blinds down. In this case, the doors of this old-fashioned conveyance were locked, the windows up, and, as I said, the blinds down, but not so closely that the curious child could not peep underneath one of them and see into the interior.

A parting beam from the setting sun, admitted through the window of a back room, shot obliquely through the open door, and lighting on the chair, shone with a dull transparency through the crimson blind.

To her surprise, the child saw in the shadow a thin man, dressed in black, seated in it; he had sharp dark features; his nose, she fancied, a little awry, and his brown eyes were looking straight before him; his hand was on his thigh, and he stirred no more than the waxen figure she had seen at Southwark Fair.

A child is so often lectured for asking questions, and on the propriety of silence and the superior wisdom of its elders, that it accepts most things at last in good faith; and the little girl acquiesced respectfully in the occupation of the chair by this mahogany-faced person as being all right and proper.

It was not until she asked her mother who this man was, and observed her scared face as she questioned her more minutely upon the appearance of the stranger, that she began to understand that she had seen something unaccountable.

Mrs Carwell took the key of the chair from its nail over the foot-man's shelf, and led the child by the hand up to the hall, having a lighted candle in her other hand. She stopped at a distance from the chair and placed the candlestick in the child's hand.

'Peep in, Margery, again, and try if there's anything there,' she whispered; 'hold the candle near the blind so as to throw its light through the curtain.'

The child peeped, this time with a very solemn face, and intimated at once that he was gone.

'Look again, and be sure,' urged her mother.

The little girl was quite certain; and Mrs Carwell, with her mob-cap of lace and cherry-coloured ribbons, and her dark brown hair, not yet powdered, over a very pale face, unlocked the door, looked in, and beheld emptiness.

'All a mistake, child, you see.'

'*There!* ma'am! see there! He's gone round the corner,' said the child.

'Where?' said Mrs Carwell, stepping backwards a step.

'Into that room.'

'Tut, child, 'twas a shadow,' cried Mrs Carwell, angrily, because she was frightened. 'I moved the candle.' But she clutched one of the poles of the chair, which leant against the wall in the corner, and pounded the floor furiously with one end of it, being afraid to pass the open door the child had pointed to.

The cook and two kitchen-maids came running upstairs, not knowing what to make of this unwonted alarm.

They all searched the room; but it was still and empty, and no sign of anyone having been there.

Some people may suppose that the direction given to her thoughts by this odd little incident will account for a very strange illusion which Mrs Carwell herself experienced about two hours later.

9

The Judge Leaves His House

Mrs Flora Carwell was going up the great staircase with a posset for the judge in a china bowl on a little silver tray.

Across the top of the well-staircase there runs a massive oak rail; and, raising her eyes accidentally, she saw an extremely odd-looking stranger, slim and long, leaning carelessly over, with a pipe between his finger and thumb. Nose, lips and chin seemed all to droop downward into extraordinary length as he leant his odd peering face over the banister. In his other hand he held a coil of rope, one end of which escaped from under his elbow and hung over the rail.

Mrs Carwell, who had no suspicion at the moment that he was not a real person, and fancied that he was someone employed in cording the judge's luggage, called to know what he was doing there.

Instead of answering, he turned about and walked across the lobby, at about the same leisurely pace at which she was ascending, and entered a room, into which she followed him. It was an uncarpeted and unfurnished chamber. An open trunk lay upon the floor empty, and beside it the coil of rope; but except for herself there was no one in the room.

Mrs Carwell was very much frightened, and now concluded that the child must have seen the same ghost that had just appeared to her.

Perhaps, when she was able to think it over, it was a relief to believe so; for the face, figure and dress described by the child were awfully like Pyneweck; and this certainly was not he.

Very much scared and very hysterical, Mrs Carwell ran down to her room, afraid to look over her shoulder, and got some companions about her, and wept, and talked, and drank more than one cordial, and talked and wept again, and so on, until, in those early days, it was ten o'clock and time to go to bed.

A scullery-maid remained up finishing some of her scouring and 'scalding' for some time after the other servants – who, as I said, were few in number – that night had got to their beds. This was a low-browed, broad-faced, intrepid wench with black hair, who did not 'vally a ghost not a button', and treated the housekeeper's hysterics with measureless scorn.

The old house was quiet now. It was near twelve o'clock and no sounds were audible except the muffled wailing of the wintry winds, piping high among the roofs and chimneys, or rumbling at intervals, in under gusts, through the narrow channels of the street.

The spacious solitudes of the kitchen level were awfully dark, and this sceptical kitchen-wench was the only person now up and about in the house. She hummed tunes to herself for a time; and then stopped and listened; and then resumed her work again. At last, she was destined to be more terrified than even was the housekeeper.

There was a back kitchen in this house, and from this she heard, as if coming from below its foundations, a sound like heavy strokes that seemed to shake the earth beneath her feet. Sometimes a dozen in sequence, at regular intervals; sometimes fewer. She walked out softly into the passage, and was surprised to see a dusky glow issuing from this room, as if from a charcoal fire.

The room seemed thick with smoke

Looking in she very dimly beheld a monstrous figure, over a furnace, beating with a mighty hammer the rings and rivets of a chain.

The strokes, swift and heavy as they looked, sounded hollow and distant. The man stopped and pointed to something on the floor that, through the smoky haze, looked, she thought, like a dead body. She remarked no more; but the servants in the room close by, startled from their sleep by a hideous scream, found her in a swoon on the flags, close to the door from where she had just witnessed this ghastly vision.

Startled by the girl's incoherent asseverations that she had seen the judge's corpse on the floor, two servants, having first searched the lower part of the house, went rather frightened upstairs to enquire whether their master was well. They found him not in his bed but in his room. He had a table with candles burning at his bedside, and was getting on his clothes again; and he swore and cursed at them roundly in his old style, telling them that he had business and that he would discharge on the spot any scoundrel who should dare to disturb him again.

So the invalid was left to his quietude.

In the morning it was rumoured here and there in the street that the judge was dead. A servant was sent from the house three doors away, by Counsellor Traverse, to enquire at Judge Harbottle's hall-door.

The servant who opened it was pale and reserved, and would only say that the judge was ill. He had had a dangerous accident; Dr Hedstone had been with him at seven o'clock in the morning.

There were averted looks, short answers, pale and frowning faces, and all the usual signs that there was a secret that sat heavily upon their minds, the time for disclosing which had not yet come. That time would arrive when the coroner had been and the mortal scandal that had befallen the house could be no longer hidden. For that morning Mr Justice Harbottle had been found hanging by the neck from the banister at the top of the great staircase, and quite dead.

There was not the smallest sign of any struggle or resistance. There had not been heard a cry or any other noise in the slightest degree indicative of violence. There was medical evidence to show that, in his atrabilious state, it was quite on the cards that he might have made away with himself. The jury found accordingly that it was a case of suicide. But to those who were acquainted with the strange story which Judge Harbottle had related to at least two persons, the fact that the catastrophe occurred on the morning of March 10th seemed a startling coincidence.

A few days after, the pomp of a great funeral attended him to the grave; and so, in the language of Scripture, 'the rich man died, and was buried'.

SHERIDAN LE FANU

The Room in Le Dragon Volant

※

PROLOGUE

The curious case which I am about to place before you is referred to, very pointedly and more than once, in the extraordinary essay upon the drugs of the dark and middle ages from the pen of Dr Hesselius.

This essay he entitles '*Mortis Imago*', and he, therein, discusses the *Vinum Letiferum*, the *Beatifica*, the *Somnus Angelorum*, the *Hypnus Segarum*, the *Aqua Thessalliae*, and about twenty other infusions and distillations well known to the sages of eight hundred years ago; two of these are still, he alleges, known to the fraternity of thieves, and, among them, as police-office enquiries sometimes disclose to this day, in practical use.

The essay, '*Mortis Imago*', will occupy, as nearly as I can at present calculate, two volumes, the ninth and tenth, of the collected papers of Dr Martin Hesselius.

This essay, I may remark, in conclusion, is very curiously enriched by citations, in great abundance, from medieval verse and prose romance, some of the most valuable of which, strange to say, are Egyptian.

I have selected this particular statement from among many cases equally striking, but hardly, I think, so effective as mere narratives in this irregular form of publication; it is simply as a story that I present it.

On the Road

In the eventful year 1815, I was exactly three-and-twenty, and had just succeeded to a very large sum in consols and other securities. The first fall of Napoleon had thrown the continent open to English excursionists, anxious, let us suppose, to improve their minds by foreign travel; and I – the slight check of the 'hundred days' removed by the genius of Wellington on the field of Waterloo – was now added to the philosophic throng.

I was posting up to Paris from Brussels, following, I presume, the route that the allied army had pursued but a few weeks before – more carriages than you could believe were pursuing the same line. You could not look back or forward without seeing into far perspective the clouds of dust which marked the line of the long series of vehicles. We were perpetually passing relays of return-horses on their way, jaded and dusty, to the inns from which they had been taken. They were arduous times for those patient public servants. The whole world seemed posting up to Paris.

I ought to have noted it more particularly, but my head was so full of Paris and the future that I passed the intervening scenery with little patience and less attention; I think, however, that it was about four miles to the frontier side of a rather picturesque little town, the name of which, as of many more important places through which I posted in my hurried journey, I forget, and about two hours before sunset that we came up with a carriage in distress.

It was not quite an upset. But the two leaders were lying flat. The booted postilions had got down, and two servants, who seemed very much at sea in such matters, were by way of assisting them. A pretty little bonnet and head were popped out of the window of the carriage in distress. Its *tournure*, and that of the shoulders that also appeared for a moment, was captivating.

Resolving to play the part of a good Samaritan, I stopped my chaise, jumped out, and with my servant lent a very willing hand in the emergency. Alas! the lady with the pretty bonnet wore a very thick, black veil. I could see nothing but the pattern of the Brussels lace as she drew back.

A lean old gentleman, almost at the same time, stuck his head out of the window. An invalid he seemed, for although the day was hot, he wore a black muffler which came up to his ears and nose, quite covering the lower part of his face, an arrangement which he disturbed by pulling it down for a moment to pour forth a torrent of French thanks, uncovering his black wig as he gesticulated with grateful animation.

One of my very few accomplishments, besides boxing, which was cultivated by all Englishmen at that time, was French; and I replied, I hope and believe, grammatically. Many bows being exchanged the old gentleman's head went in again and the demure, pretty little bonnet once more appeared.

The lady must have heard me speak to my servant, for she framed her little speech in such pretty, broken English, and in a voice so sweet, that I more than ever cursed the black veil that baulked my romantic curiosity.

The arms that were emblazoned on the panel were peculiar; I remember especially one device – it was the figure of a stork, painted in carmine, upon what the heralds call a 'field or'. The bird was standing upon one leg, and in the other claw held a stone. This is, I believe, the emblem of vigilance. Its oddity struck me, and remained impressed upon my memory. There were supporters besides, but I forget what they were. The courtly manners of these people, the style of their servants, the elegance of their travelling carriage and the supporters to their arms satisfied me that they were noble.

The lady, you may be sure, was not the less interesting on that account. What a fascination a title exercises upon the imagination! I do not mean on that of snobs or moral flunkies. Superiority of rank is a powerful and genuine influence in love. The idea of superior refinement is associated with it. The careless notice of the squire tells more upon the heart of the pretty milkmaid than years of honest Dobbin's manly devotion, and so on and up. It is an unjust world!

But in this case there was something more. I was conscious of being good-looking. I really believe I was; and there could be no mistake about my being nearly six feet high. Why need this lady have thanked me? Had not her husband, for such I assumed him to be, thanked me quite enough and for both? I was instinctively aware that the lady was looking on me with no unwilling eyes; and, through her veil, I felt the power of her gaze.

She was now rolling away, with a train of dust behind her wheels in the golden sunlight, and a wise young gentleman followed her with ardent eyes, and sighed profoundly as the distance increased.

I told the positions on no account to pass the carriage, but to keep it steadily in view, and to pull up at whatever posting-house it should stop at. We were soon in the little town, and the carriage we followed drew up at the Belle Etoile, a comfortable old inn. They got out of the carriage and entered the house.

At a leisurely pace we followed. I got down, and mounted the steps listlessly, like a man quite apathetic and careless.

Audacious as I was, I did not care to enquire in what room I should find them. I peeped into the apartment to my right, and then into that on my left. My people were not there.

I ascended the stairs. A drawing-room door stood open. I entered with the most innocent air in the world. It was a spacious room, and, beside myself, contained but one living figure – a very pretty and ladylike one. There was the very bonnet with which I had fallen in love. The lady stood with her back towards me. I could not tell whether the envious veil was raised; she was reading a letter.

I stood for a minute in fixed attention, gazing upon her, in the vague hope that she might turn about and give me an opportunity of seeing her features. She did not; but with a step or two she placed herself before a little cabriole-table which stood against the wall and from which rose a tall mirror in a tarnished frame.

I might, indeed, have mistaken it for a picture, for it now reflected a half-length portrait of a singularly beautiful woman.

She was looking down upon a letter which she held in her slender fingers, and in which she seemed absorbed.

The face was oval, melancholy, sweet. It had in it, nevertheless, a faint and indefinably sensual quality also. Nothing could exceed the delicacy of its features, or the brilliancy of its tints. The eyes, indeed, were lowered, so that I could not see their colour; nothing but their long lashes, and delicate eyebrows. She continued reading. She must have been deeply interested; I never saw a living form so motionless – I gazed on a tinted statue.

Being at that time blessed with long and keen vision, I saw this beautiful face with perfect distinctness. I saw even the blue veins that traced their wanderings on the whiteness of her full throat.

I ought to have retreated as noiselessly as I came in, before my presence was detected. But I was too much interested to move from the spot for a few moments longer; and while they were passing, she raised her eyes. Those eyes were large, and of that hue which modern poets term 'violet'.

These splendid melancholy eyes were turned upon me from the glass with a haughty stare, and hastily the lady lowered her black veil and turned about.

I fancied that she hoped I had not seen her. I was watching every look and movement, the minutest, with an attention as intense as if an ordeal involving my life depended on them.

2

The Inn-yard of the Belle Etoile

The face was, indeed, one to fall in love with at first sight. Those sentiments that take such sudden possession of young men were now dominating my curiosity. My audacity faltered before her; and I felt that my presence in this room was probably an impertinence. This point she quickly settled, for the same very sweet voice I had heard before now said coldly, and this time in French, 'Monsieur cannot be aware that this apartment is not public.'

I bowed very low, faltered some apologies, and backed to the door.

I suppose I looked penitent and embarrassed – I certainly felt so – for the lady said, by way it seemed of softening matters, 'I am happy, however, to have an opportunity of again thanking monsieur for the assistance, so prompt and effectual, which he had the goodness to render us today.'

It was more the altered tone in which it was spoken, than the speech itself, that encouraged me. It was also true that she need not have recognised me; and if she had, she certainly was not obliged to thank me over again.

All this was indescribably flattering, and all the more so that it followed so quickly on her slight reproof.

The tone in which she spoke had become low and timid, and I observed that she turned her head quickly towards a second door of the room. I fancied that the gentleman in the black wig, a jealous husband, perhaps, might reappear through it. Almost at the same moment, a voice, at once reedy and nasal, was heard snarling some directions to a servant, and evidently approaching. It was the voice that had thanked me so profusely, from the carriage windows, about an hour before.

'Monsieur will have the goodness to retire,' said the lady, in a tone that resembled entreaty, at the same time gently waving her hand towards the door through which I had entered. Bowing again very low, I stepped back, and closed the door.

I ran down the stairs, very much elated. I saw the host of the Belle Etoile which, as I said, was the sign and designation of my inn.

I described the apartment I had just quitted, said I liked it, and asked whether I could have it. He was extremely troubled, but that apartment and the two adjoining rooms were engaged.

'By whom?'

'People of distinction.'

'But who are they? They must have names, or titles.'

'Undoubtedly, monsieur, but such a stream is rolling into Paris that we have ceased to enquire the names or titles of our guests – we designate them simply by the rooms they occupy.'

'What stay do they make?'

'Even that, monsieur, I cannot answer. It does not interest us. Our rooms, while this continues, can never be, for a moment, disengaged.'

'I should have liked those rooms so much! Is one of them a sleeping apartment?'

'Yes, sir, and monsieur will observe that people do not usually engage bedrooms, unless they mean to stay the night.'

'Well, I can, I suppose, have some rooms, any, I don't care in what part of the house?'

'Certainly, monsieur can have two apartments. They are the last at present disengaged.'

I took them instantly.

It was plain these people meant to make a stay here; at least they would not go till morning. I began to feel that I was all but engaged in an adventure.

I took possession of my rooms, and looked out of the window, which I found commanded the inn-yard. Many horses were being liberated from the traces, hot and weary, and others, fresh from the stables, being put to. A great many vehicles – some private carriages, others, like mine, of that public class which is equivalent to our old English post-chaise – were standing on the pavement, waiting their turn for relays. Fussy servants were to-ing and fro-ing, and idle ones lounging or laughing, and the scene, on the whole, was animated and amusing.

Among these objects I thought I recognised the travelling carriage and one of the servants of the 'persons of distinction' about whom I was, just then, so profoundly interested.

I therefore ran down the stairs, made my way to the back door; and so, behold me, in a moment, upon the uneven pavement, among all these sights and sounds which in such a place attend upon a period of extraordinary crush and traffic.

By this time the sun was near its setting, and threw its golden beams on the red-brick chimneys of the offices, and made the two barrels, that figured as pigeon-houses, on the tops of poles, look as if they were on fire. Everything in this light becomes picturesque; and things interest us which in the sober grey of morning are dull enough.

After a little search, I lighted upon the very carriage of which I was in quest. A servant was locking one of the doors, for it was made with the security of lock and key. I paused near, looking at the panel of the door.

'A very pretty device that red stork!' I observed, pointing to the shield on the door, 'and no doubt indicates a distinguished family?'

The servant looked at me for a moment as he placed the little key in his pocket, and said with a slightly sarcastic bow and smile, 'Monsieur is at liberty to conjecture.'

Nothing daunted, I forthwith administered that laxative which, on occasion, acts so happily upon the tongue – I mean a 'tip'.

The servant looked at the Napoleon in his hand, and then in my face, with a sincere expression of surprise.

'Monsieur is very generous!'

'Not worth mentioning – who are the lady and gentleman who came here, in this carriage, and whom, you may remember, I and my servant assisted today in an emergency, when their horses had come to the ground?'

'We call him the count, and the young lady we call the countess – but I know not, she may be his daughter.'

'Can you tell me where they live?'

'Upon my honour, monsieur, I am unable – I know not.'

'Not know where your master lives! Surely you know something about him?'

'Nothing worth relating, monsieur; in fact, I was hired in Brussels on the very day they started. Monsieur Picard, my fellow-servant, Monsieur the Comte's gentleman, he has been years in his service, and knows everything; but he never speaks except to communicate an order. From him I have learned nothing. We are going to Paris, however, and there I shall speedily pick up all about them. At present I am as ignorant of all that as monsieur himself.'

'And where is Monsieur Picard?'

'He has gone to the cutler's to get his razors set. But I do not think he will tell anything.'

This was a poor harvest for my golden sowing. The man, I think, spoke the truth, and would honestly have betrayed the secrets of the family if he had possessed any. I took my leave politely; and mounting the stairs, I found myself once more in my room.

Forthwith I summoned my servant. Though I had brought him with me from England, he was a native of France – a useful fellow, sharp, bustling and, of course, quite familiar with the ways and tricks of his countrymen.

'St Clair, shut the door; come here. I can't rest till I have made out something about those people of rank who have got the apartments under mine. Here are fifteen francs; make out the servants we assisted today; have them to a *petit souper*, and come back and tell me their entire history. I have, this moment, seen one of them who knows nothing, and has communicated it. The other, whose name I forget, is the unknown nobleman's valet, and knows everything. Him you must pump. It is, of course, the venerable peer, and not the young lady who accompanies him, that interests me – you understand? Begone! fly! and return with all the details I sigh for, and every circumstance that can possibly interest me.'

It was a commission which admirably suited the tastes and spirits of my worthy St Clair, to whom, you will have observed, I had accustomed myself to talk with the peculiar familiarity which the old French comedy establishes between master and valet.

I am sure he laughed at me in secret; but to my face no one could be more polite and deferential.

With several wise looks, nods and shrugs, he withdrew; and looking down from my window, I saw him, with incredible quickness, enter the yard where I soon lost sight of him among the carriages.

3

Death and Love Together Mated

When the day drags, when a man is solitary, and in a fever of impatience and suspense; when the minute hand of his watch travels as slowly as the hour hand used to do, and the hour hand has lost all appreciable motion; when he yawns, and beats the devil's tattoo, and flattens his handsome nose against the window, and whistles tunes he hates, and, in short, does not know what to do with himself, it is deeply to be regretted that he cannot make a solemn dinner of three courses more than once in a day. The laws of matter, to which we are slaves, deny us that resource.

But in the times I speak of, supper was still a substantial meal, and its hour was approaching. This was consolatory. Three-quarters of an hour, however, still interposed. How was I to dispose of that interval?

I had two or three idle books, it is true, as travelling-companions; but there are many moods in which one cannot read. My novel lay with my rug and walking-stick on the sofa, and I did not care if the heroine and the hero were both drowned together in the water barrel that I saw in the inn-yard under my window.

I took a turn or two up and down my room, and sighed, looking at myself in the glass, adjusted my great white 'choker', folded and tied after Brummel, the immortal 'Beau', put on a buff waistcoat and my blue swallow-tailed coat with gilt buttons; I deluged my pocket-handkerchief with eau-de-Cologne (we had not then the variety of bouquets with which the genius of perfumery has since blessed us); I arranged my hair, on which I piqued myself, and which I loved to groom in those days. That dark-brown *chevelure*, with its natural curl, is now represented by a few dozen perfectly white hairs, and its place – a smooth, bald, pink head – knows it no more. But let us forget these mortifications. It was then rich, thick and dark-brown. I was making a very careful toilet. I took my unexceptionable hat from its case, and placed it lightly on my wise head, as nearly as memory and practice enabled me to do so, at that very slight inclination which the immortal person I have mentioned was wont to give to his. A pair of light French gloves and a rather club-like knotted walking-stick, such as just then had come into vogue for a year or two again in England, in the phraseology of Sir Walter Scott's romances, 'completed my equipment'.

All this attention to effect, preparatory to a mere lounge in the yard or on the steps of the Belle Etoile, was a simple act of devotion to the wonderful eyes which I had that evening beheld for the first time, and never, never could forget. In plain terms, it was all done in the vague, very vague hope that those eyes might behold the unexceptionable get-up of a melancholy slave, and retain the image, not altogether without secret approbation.

As I completed my preparations the light failed me; the last level streak of sunlight disappeared, and a fading twilight only remained. I sighed in unison with the pensive hour, and threw open the window, intending to look out for a moment before going downstairs. I perceived instantly that the window underneath mine was also open, for I heard two voices in conversation, although I could not distinguish what they were saying.

The male voice was peculiar; it was, as I told you, reedy and nasal. I knew it, of course, instantly. The answering voice spoke in those sweet tones which I recognised only too easily. The dialogue was only for a minute; the repulsive male voice laughed, I fancied, with a kind of devilish satire, and retired from the window, so that I almost ceased to hear it.

The other voice remained nearer the window, but not so near as at first.

It was not an altercation; there was evidently nothing the least exciting in the colloquy. What would I not have given that it had been a quarrel – a violent one – and I the redresser of wrongs, and the defender of insulted beauty! Alas, so far as I could pronounce upon the character of the tones I heard, they might be as tranquil a pair as any in existence. In a moment more the lady began to sing an odd little chanson. I need not remind you how much farther the voice is heard singing than speaking. I could distinguish the words. The voice was of that exquisitely sweet kind which is called, I believe, a semi-contralto; it had something pathetic, and something, I fancied, a little mocking in its tones. I venture a clumsy, but adequate translation of the words:

> Death and Love, together mated,
>   Watch and wait in ambuscade;
> At early morn, or else belated,
>   They meet and mark the man or maid.
> Burning sigh, or breath that freezes,
>   Numbs or maddens man or maid;
> Death or Love the victim seizes,
>   Breathing from their ambuscade.

'Enough, madame!' said the old voice, with sudden severity. 'We do not desire, I believe, to amuse the grooms and hostlers in the yard with our music.'

The lady's voice laughed gaily.

'You desire to quarrel, madame?' And the old man, I presume, shut down the window. Down it went, at all events, with a rattle that might easily have broken the glass.

Of all thin partitions, glass is the most effectual excluder of sound. I heard no more, not even the subdued hum of the colloquy.

What a charming voice this countess had! How it melted, swelled and trembled! How it moved and even agitated me! What a pity that a hoarse old jackdaw should have power to crow down such a Philomel! 'Alas! what a life it is!' I moralised, wisely. 'That beautiful countess, with the patience of an angel and the beauty of a Venus and the accomplishments of all the Muses, a slave! She knows perfectly who occupies the apartments over hers; she heard me raise my window. One may conjecture pretty well for whom that music was intended – aye, old gentleman, and for whom you suspected it to be intended.'

In a very agreeable flutter I left my room, and descending the stairs, passed the count's door very much at my leisure. There was just a chance that the beautiful songstress might emerge. I dropped my stick on the lobby, near their door, and you may be sure it took me some little time to pick it up! Fortune, nevertheless, did not favour me. I could not stay on the lobby all night picking up my stick, so I went down to the hall.

I consulted the clock, and found that there remained but a quarter of an hour to the moment of supper.

Everyone was roughing it now, every inn in confusion; people might do at such a juncture what they never did before. Was it just possible that, for once, the count and countess would take their chairs at the table-d'hôte?

4

Monsieur Droqville

Full of this exciting hope, I sauntered out upon the steps of the Belle Etoile. It was now night, and a pleasant moonlight over everything. I had entered more into my romance since my arrival, and this poetic light heightened the sentiment. What a drama if she turned out to be the count's daughter, and in love with me! What a delightful *tragedy* if she turned out to be the count's wife!

In this luxurious mood, I was accosted by a tall and very elegantly made gentleman, who appeared to be about fifty. His air was courtly and graceful, and there was in his whole manner and appearance something so distinguished that it was impossible not to suspect him of being a person of rank.

He had been standing upon the steps, looking out, like me, upon the moonlight effects that transformed, as it were, the objects and buildings in the little street. He accosted me, as I say, with the politeness, at once easy and lofty, of a French nobleman of the old school. He asked me if I were not Mr Beckett? I assented; and he immediately introduced himself as the Marquis d'Harmonville (this information he gave me in a low tone), and asked leave to present me with a letter from Lord Rivers, who knew my father slightly, and had once done me, also, a trifling kindness.

This English peer, I may mention, stood very high in the political world, and was named as the most probable successor to the distinguished post of English minister at Paris.

I received it with a low bow, and read:

MY DEAR BECKETT – I beg to introduce my very dear friend, the Marquis d'Harmonville, who will explain to you the nature of the services it may be in your power to render him and us.

He went on to speak of the marquis as a man whose great wealth, whose intimate relations with the old families and whose legitimate influence with the court rendered him the fittest possible person for those friendly offices which, at the desire of his own sovereign and of our government, he had so obligingly undertaken.

It added a great deal to my perplexity, when I read, further –

By the by, Walton was here yesterday, and told me that your scat was likely to be attacked; something, he says, is unquestionably going on at Domwell. You know there is an awkwardness in my meddling ever so cautiously. But I advise, if it is not very officious, your making Haxton look after it, and report immediately. I fear it is serious. I ought to have mentioned that, for reasons that you will see when you have talked with him for five minutes, the marquis – with the concurrence of all our friends – drops his title, for a few weeks, and is at present plain Monsieur Droqville.

I am this moment going to town, and can say no more.

Yours faithfully,

RIVERS

I was utterly puzzled. I could scarcely boast of Lord Rivers' acquaintance. I knew no one named Haxton, and, except my hatter, no one called Walton; and this peer wrote as if we were intimate friends! I looked at the back of the letter, and the mystery was solved. To my consternation – for I was plain Richard Beckett – I read:

To George Stanhope Beckett Esq., MP

I looked with consternation in the face of the marquis.

'What apology can I offer to Monsieur the Mar – to Monsieur Droqville? It is true my name is Beckett – it is true I am known, though very slightly, to Lord Rivers; but the letter was not intended for me. My name is Richard Beckett – this is to Mr Stanhope Beckett, the member for Shillingsworth. What can I say, or do, in this unfortunate situation? I can only give you my honour as a gentleman that for me the letter, which I now return, shall remain as unviolated a secret as before I opened it. I am so shocked and grieved that such a mistake should have occurred!'

I dare say my honest vexation and good faith were pretty legibly written in my countenance; for the look of gloomy embarrassment which had for a moment settled on the face of the marquis brightened; he smiled, kindly, and extended his hand.

'I have not the least doubt that Monsieur Beckett will respect my little secret. As a mistake was destined to occur, I have reason to thank my good stars that it should have been with a gentleman of honour. Monsieur Beckett will permit me, I hope, to place his name among those of my friends?'

I thanked the marquis very much for his kind expressions.

He went on to say: 'If, monsieur, I can persuade you to visit me at Claironville in Normandy, where I hope to see on the 15th of August a great many friends whose acquaintance it might interest you to make, I shall be too happy.'

I thanked him, of course, very gratefully for his hospitality.

He continued: 'I cannot for the present see my friends, for reasons which you may surmise, at my house in Paris. But monsieur will be so good as to let me know the hotel he means to stay at in Paris; and he will find that, although the Marquis d'Harmonville is not in town, Monsieur Droqville will not lose sight of him.'

With many acknowledgements I gave him the information he desired.

'And in the meantime,' he continued, 'if you think of any way in which Monsieur Droqville can be of use to you, our communication shall not be interrupted, and I shall so manage matters that you can easily let me know.'

I was very much flattered. The marquis had, as we say, taken a fancy to me. Such likings at first sight often ripen into lasting friendships. To be sure it was just possible that the marquis might think it prudent to keep the involuntary depositary of a political secret, even so vague a one, in good humour.

Very graciously the marquis took his leave, going up the stairs of the Belle Etoile.

I remained upon the steps, for a minute lost in speculation upon this new theme of interest. But the wonderful eyes, the thrilling voice, the exquisite figure of the beautiful lady who had taken possession of my imagination, quickly reasserted their influence. I was again gazing at the sympathetic moon, and, descending the steps, I loitered along the pavements among strange objects, and houses that were antique and picturesque, in a dreamy state, thinking.

In a little while, I turned into the inn-yard again. There had come a lull. Instead of the noisy place it was an hour or two before, the yard was perfectly still and empty, except for the carriages that stood here and there. Perhaps there was a servants' table-d'hôte just then. I was rather pleased to find solitude; and undisturbed I found out my lady-love's carriage, in the moonlight. I mused, I walked round it; I was as utterly foolish and maudlin as very young men in my situation usually are. The blinds were down, the doors, I suppose, locked. The brilliant moonlight revealed everything, and cast sharp, black shadows of wheel, and bar, and spring, on the pavement. I stood before the escutcheon painted on the door, which I had examined in the daylight. I wondered how often her eyes had rested on the same object. I pondered in a charming dream. A harsh, loud voice, over my shoulder, said suddenly – 'A red stork – good! The stork is a bird of prey; it is vigilant, greedy, and catches gudgeons. Red, too! – blood red! Ha! ha! the symbol is appropriate.'

I had turned about, and beheld the palest face I ever saw. It was broad, ugly and malignant. The figure was that of a French officer, in undress, and was six feet high. Across the nose and eyebrow there was a deep scar, which made the repulsive face grimmer.

The officer elevated his chin and his eyebrows, with a scoffing chuckle, and said – 'I have shot a stork with a rifle bullet, when he thought himself safe in the clouds, for mere sport!' He shrugged, and laughed malignantly. 'See, monsieur; when a man like me – a man of energy, you understand, a man with all his wits about him, a man who has made the tour of Europe under canvas, and, *parbleu!* often without it – resolves to discover a secret, expose a crime, catch a thief, spit a robber on the point of his sword, it is odd if he does not succeed. Ha! ha! ha! Au revoir, monsieur!'

He turned with an angry whisk on his heel, and swaggered with long strides out of the gate.

5

Supper at the Belle Etoile

The French army were in a rather savage temper, just then. The English, especially, had but scant courtesy to expect at their hands. It was plain, however, that the cadaverous gentleman who had just apostrophised the heraldry of the count's carriage, with such mysterious acrimony, had not intended any of his malevolence for me. He was stung by some old recollection, and had marched off, seething with fury.

I had received one of those unacknowledged shocks which startle us when, fancying ourselves perfectly alone, we discover on a sudden that our antics have been watched by a spectator, almost at our elbow. In this case, the effect was enhanced by the extreme repulsiveness of the face, and, I may add, its proximity, for, as I think, it almost touched mine. The enigmatical harangue of this person, so full of hatred and implied denunciation, was still in my ears. Here at all events was new matter for the industrious fancy of a lover to work upon.

It was time now to go to the table-d'hôte. Who could tell what lights the gossip of the supper-table might throw upon the subject that interested me so powerfully!

I stepped into the room, my eyes searching the little assembly, about thirty people, for the persons who specially interested me.

It was not easy to induce people so hurried and overworked as those of the Belle Etoile just now to send meals up to one's private apartments in the midst of this unparalleled confusion; and, therefore, many people who did not like it, might find themselves reduced to the alternative of supping at the table-d'hôte or starving.

The count was not there, nor his beautiful companion; but the Marquis d'Harmonville, whom I hardly expected to see in so public a place, signed, with a significant smile, to a vacant chair beside himself. I secured it, and he seemed pleased, and almost immediately entered into conversation with me.

'This is probably your first visit to France?' he said.

I told him it was, and he said: 'You must not think me very curious and impertinent; but Paris is about the most dangerous capital a high-spirited and generous young gentleman could visit without a mentor. If you have not an experienced friend as a companion during your visit – ' He paused.

I told him I was not so provided, but that I had my wits about me; that I had seen a good deal of life in England, and that I fancied human nature was pretty much the same in all parts of the world. The marquis shook his head, smiling.

'You will find very marked differences, notwithstanding,' he said. 'Peculiarities of intellect and peculiarities of character, undoubtedly, do pervade different nations; and this results, among the criminal classes, in a style of villainy no less peculiar. In Paris, the class who live by their wits is three or four times as great as in London; and they live much better; some of them even splendidly. They are more ingenious than the London rogues; they have more animation, and invention, and the dramatic faculty, in which your countrymen are deficient, is everywhere. These invaluable attributes place them upon a totally different level. They can affect the manners and enjoy the luxuries of people of distinction. They live, many of them, by play.'

'So do many of our London rogues.'

'Yes, but in a totally different way. They are the *habitués* of certain gaming-tables, billiard-rooms and other places, including your races, where high play goes on; and by superior knowledge of chances, by masking their play, by means of confederates, by means of bribery and other artifices, varying with the subject of their imposture, they rob the unwary. But here it is more elaborately done, and with a really exquisite *finesse*. There are people whose manners, style, conversation, are unexceptionable, living in handsome houses in the best situations, with everything about them in the most refined taste, and exquisitely luxurious, who impose even upon the Parisian bourgeois, who believe them to be, in good faith, people of rank and fashion, because their habits are expensive and refined, and their houses are frequented by foreigners of distinction, and, to a degree, by foolish young French-men of rank. At all these houses play goes on. The ostensible host and hostess seldom join in it; they provide it simply to plunder their guests, by means of their accomplices, and thus wealthy strangers are inveigled and robbed.'

'But I have heard of a young Englishman, a son of Lord Rooksbury, who broke two Parisian gaming-tables only last year.'

'I see,' he said, laughing, 'you are come here to do likewise. I, myself, at about your age, undertook the same spirited enterprise. I raised no less a sum than five hundred thousand francs to begin with; I expected to carry all before me by the simple expedient of going on doubling my stakes. I had heard of it, and I fancied that the sharpers, who kept the table, knew nothing of the matter. I found, however, that they not only knew all about it, but had provided against the possibility of any such experiments; and I was pulled up before I had well begun by a rule which forbids the doubling of an original stake more than four times consecutively.'

'And is that rule in force still?' I enquired, chap-fallen.

He laughed and shrugged, 'Of course it is, my young friend. People who live by an art, always understand it better than an amateur. I see you had formed the same plan, and no doubt came provided.'

I confessed I had prepared for conquest upon a still grander scale. I had arrived with a purse of thirty thousand pounds sterling.

'Any acquaintance of my very dear friend Lord Rivers interests me; and, besides my regard for him, I am charmed with you; so you will pardon all my perhaps too officious questions and advice.'

I thanked him most earnestly for his valuable counsel, and begged that he would have the goodness to give me all the advice in his power.

'Then if you take my advice,' said he, 'you will leave your money in the bank where it lies. Never risk a Napoleon in a gaming house. The night I went to break the bank, I lost between seven and eight thousand pounds sterling of your English money; and for my next adventure, I had obtained an introduction to one of those elegant gaming-houses which affect to be the private mansions of persons of distinction, and was saved from ruin by a gentleman whom, ever since, I have regarded with increasing respect and friendship. It oddly happens he is in this house at this moment. I recognised his servant, and made him a visit in his apartments here, and found him the same brave, kind, honourable man I always knew him. But that he is living so entirely out of the world, now, I should have made a point of introducing you. Fifteen years ago he would have been the man of all others to consult. The gentleman I speak of is the Comte de St Alyre. He represents a very old family. He is the very soul of honour, and the most sensible man in the world, except in one particular.'

'And that particular?' I hesitated. I was now deeply interested.

'Is that he has married a charming creature, at least five-and-forty years younger than himself, and is, of course, although I believe absolutely without cause, horribly jealous.'

'And the lady?'

'The countess is, I believe, in every way worthy of so good a man,' he answered, a little drily.

'I think I heard her sing this evening.'

'Yes, I dare say; she is very accomplished.' After a few moments' silence he continued: 'I must not lose sight of you, for I should be sorry, when next you meet my friend Lord Rivers, that you had to tell him you had been pigeoned in Paris. A rich Englishman as you are, with so large a sum at his Paris bankers, young, gay, generous, a thousand ghouls and harpies will be contending who shall be the first to seize and devour you.'

At this moment I received something like a jerk from the elbow of the gentleman at my right. It was an accidental jog as he turned in his seat.

'On the honour of a soldier, there is no man's flesh in this company heals so fast as mine.'

The tone in which this was spoken was harsh and stentorian, and almost made me bounce. I looked round and recognised the officer whose large white face had half scared me in the inn-yard. Wiping his mouth furiously, and then with a gulp of Mâcon, he went on – 'No man's! It's not blood; it is ichor! it's miraculous! Set aside stature, thew, bone and muscle, set aside courage – and by all the angels of death, I'd fight a lion naked, and dash his teeth down his jaws with my fist, and flog him to death with his own tail! Set aside, I say, all those attributes, which I am allowed to possess, and I am worth six men in any campaign for that one quality of healing as I do – rip me up; punch me through, tear me to tatters with bombshells, and nature has me whole again while your tailor would fine-draw an old coat. *Parbleu!* gentlemen, if you saw me naked, you would laugh! Look at my hand, a sabre-cut across the palm, to the bone, to save my head, taken up with three stitches, and five days afterwards I was playing ball with an English general, a prisoner in Madrid, against

the wall of the convent of the Santa Maria de la Castita! At Arcola, by
the great devil himself that was an action. Every man there, gentlemen, swallowed as much smoke in five minutes as would smother
you all in this room! I received, at the same moment, two musket
balls in the thighs, a grape shot through the calf of my leg, a lance
through my left shoulder, a piece of shrapnel in the left deltoid,
a bayonet through the cartilage of my right ribs, a sabre-cut that
carried away a pound of flesh from my chest, and the better part of a
congreve rocket on my forehead. Pretty well, ha, ha! and all while
you'd say *bah!* and in eight days and a half I was making a forced
march, without shoes, and only one gaiter, the life and soul of my
company, and as sound as a roach!'

'Bravo! Bravissimo! Per Bacco! un gallant uomo!' exclaimed, in a
martial ecstasy, a fat little Italian, who manufactured toothpicks and
wicker cradles on the island of Notre Dame; 'your exploits should
resound through Europe and the history of those wars should be
written in your blood!'

'Never mind! a trifle!' exclaimed the soldier. 'At Ligny, the other
day, where we smashed the Prussians into ten hundred thousand
milliards of atoms, a bit of a shell cut me across the leg and opened an
artery. It was spouting as high as the chimney, and in half a minute I
had lost enough to fill a pitcher. I must have expired in another
minute if I had not whipped off my sash like a flash of lightning, tied
it round my leg above the wound, snatched a bayonet out of the back
of a dead Prussian and, passing it under, made a tourniquet of it with
a couple of twists and so stayed the haemorrhage and saved my life.
But, *sacré bleu!* gentlemen, I lost so much blood, I have been as pale as
the bottom of a plate ever since. No matter. A trifle. Blood well spent,
gentlemen.' He applied himself now to his bottle of *vin ordinaire*.

The marquis had closed his eyes, and looked resigned and disgusted
while all this was going on.

'Garçon,' said the officer, speaking in a low tone over the back of
his chair to the waiter; 'who came in that travelling carriage, dark
yellow and black, that stands in the middle of the yard, with arms and
supporters emblazoned on the door, and a red stork, as red as my
facings?'

The waiter could not say.

The eye of the eccentric officer, who had suddenly grown grim and serious, and seemed to have abandoned the general conversation to other people, lighted, as it were, accidentally, on me.

'Pardon me, monsieur,' he said. 'Did I not see you examining the panel of that carriage at the same time that I did so, this evening? Can you tell me who arrived in it?'

'I rather think the Count and Countess de St Alyre.'

'And are they here, in the Belle Etoile?' he asked.

'They have got apartments upstairs,' I answered.

He started up, and half pushed his chair from the table. He quickly sat down again, and I could hear him *sacré*-ing and muttering to himself, and grinning and scowling. I could not tell whether he was alarmed or furious.

I turned to say a word or two to the marquis, but he was gone. Several other people had dropped out also, and the supper party soon broke up.

Two or three substantial pieces of wood smouldered on the hearth, for the night had turned out chilly. I sat down by the fire in a great armchair of carved oak, with a marvellously high back, that looked as old as the days of Henry IV.

'Garçon,' said I, 'do you happen to know who that officer is?'

'That is Colonel Gaillarde, monsieur.'

'Has he been often here?'

'Once before, monsieur, for a week; it is a year since.'

'He is the palest man I ever saw.'

'That is true, monsieur; he has been often taken for a *revenant*.'

'Can you give me a bottle of really good Burgundy?'

'The best in France, monsieur.'

'Place it and a glass by my side, on this table, if you please. I may sit here for half an hour?'

'Certainly, monsieur.'

I was very comfortable, the wine excellent, and my thoughts glowing and serene. 'Beautiful countess! Beautiful countess! shall we ever be better acquainted.'

The Naked Sword

A man who has been posting all day long, and changing the air he breathes every half-hour, who is well pleased with himself, and has nothing on earth to trouble him, and who sits alone by a fire in a comfortable chair after having eaten a hearty supper, may be pardoned if he takes an accidental nap.

I had filled my fourth glass when I fell asleep. My head, I dare say, hung uncomfortably; and it is admitted, that a variety of French dishes is not the most favourable precursor to pleasant dreams.

I had a dream as I took mine ease in mine inn on this occasion. I fancied myself in a huge cathedral, without light except from four tapers that stood at the corners of a raised platform hung with black on which lay, draped also in black, what seemed to me the dead body of the Countess de St Alyre. The place seemed empty, it was cold, and I could see only (in the halo of the candles) a little way round.

The little I saw bore the character of Gothic gloom, and helped my fancy to shape and furnish the black void that yawned all round me. I heard a sound like the slow tread of two persons walking up the flagged aisle. A faint echo told of the vastness of the place. An awful sense of expectation was upon me, and I was horribly frightened when the body that lay on the catafalque said (without stirring), in a whisper that froze me, 'They come to place me in the grave alive; save me.'

I found that I could neither speak nor move. I was horribly frightened.

The two people who approached now emerged from the darkness. One, the Count de St Alyre, glided to the head of the figure and placed his long thin hands under it. The white-faced colonel, with the scar across his face, and a look of infernal triumph, placed his hands under her feet, and they began to raise her.

With an indescribable effort I broke the spell that bound me, and started to my feet with a gasp.

I was wide awake, but the broad, wicked face of Colonel Gaillarde was staring, white as death, at me, from the other side of the hearth. 'Where is she?' I shuddered.

'That depends on who she is, monsieur,' replied the colonel, curtly.

'Good heavens!' I gasped, looking about me.

The colonel, who was eyeing me sarcastically, had had his *demi-tasse* of *café noir*, and now drank his *tasse*, diffusing a pleasant perfume of brandy.

'I fell asleep and was dreaming,' I said, lest any strong language, founded on the role he played in my dream, should have escaped me. 'I did not know for some moments where I was.'

'You are the young gentleman who has the apartments over the Count and Countess de St Alyre?' he said, winking one eye closed in meditation and glaring at me with the other.

'I believe so – yes,' I answered.

'Well, younker, take care you have not worse dreams than that some night,' he said, enigmatically, and wagged his head with a chuckle. 'Worse dreams,' he repeated.

'What does Monsieur the Colonel mean?' I enquired.

'I am trying to find that out myself,' said the colonel; 'and I think I shall. When I get the first inch of the thread fast between my finger and thumb, it goes hard but I follow it up, bit by bit, little by little, tracing it this way and that, and up and down, and round about, until the whole clue is wound up on my thumb, and the end, and its secret, fast in my fingers. Ingenious! Crafty as five foxes! wide awake as a weazel! *Parbleu!* if I had descended to that occupation I should have made my fortune as a spy. Good wine here?' he glanced interrogatively at my bottle.

'Very good,' said I. 'Will Monsieur the Colonel try a glass?'

He took the largest he could find, and filled it, raised it with a bow, and drank it slowly. 'Ah! ah! Bah! That is not it,' he exclaimed, with some disgust, filling it again. 'You ought to have told me to order your Burgundy, and they would not have brought you that stuff.'

I got away from this man as soon as I civilly could, and, putting on my hat, I walked out with no other company than my sturdy walking-stick. I visited the inn-yard, and looked up to the windows of the countess's apartments. They were closed, however, and I had not even the insubstantial consolation of contemplating the light in which that beautiful lady was at that moment writing, or reading, or sitting and thinking of – anyone you please.

I bore this serious privation as well as I could, and took a little saunter through the town. I shan't bore you with moonlight effects, nor with the maunderings of a man who has fallen in love at first sight with a beautiful face. My ramble, it is enough to say, occupied about half an hour, and, returning by a slight *détour*, I found myself in a little square, with about two high-gabled houses on each side, and a rude stone statue, worn by centuries of rain, on a pedestal in the centre of the pavement. Looking at this statue was a slight and rather tall man, whom I instantly recognised as the Marquis d'Harmonville: he knew me almost as quickly. He walked a step towards me, shrugged and laughed: 'You are surprised to find Monsieur Droqville staring at that old stone figure by moonlight. Anything to pass the time. You, I see, suffer from *ennui* as I do. These little provincial towns! Heavens! what an effort it is to live in them! If I could regret having formed in early life a friendship that does me honour, I think its condemning me to a sojourn in such a place would make me do so. You go on towards Paris, I suppose, in the morning?'

'I have ordered horses.'

'As for me I await a letter, or an arrival, either would emancipate me; but I can't say how soon either event will happen.'

'Can I be of any use in this matter?' I began.

'None, monsieur, I thank you a thousand times. No, this is a piece in which every role is already cast. I am but an amateur, and induced, solely by friendship, to take a part.'

So he talked on, for a time, as we walked slowly towards the Belle Etoile, and then came a silence, which I broke by asking him if he knew anything of Colonel Gaillarde.

'Oh! yes, to be sure. He is a little mad; he has had some bad injuries of the head. He used to plague the people in the War Office to death. He has always some delusion. They contrived some employment for him – not regimental, of course – but in this last campaign Napoleon, who could spare nobody, placed him in command of a regiment. He was always a desperate fighter, and such men were more than ever needed.'

There is, or was, a second inn, in this town, called l'Ecu de France. At its door the marquis stopped, bade me a mysterious good-night, and disappeared.

As I walked slowly towards my inn, I met, in the shadow of a row of poplars, the *garçon* who had brought me my Burgundy a little time ago. I was thinking of Colonel Gaillarde, and I stopped the little waiter as he passed me.

'You said, I think, that Colonel Gaillarde was at the Belle Etoile for a week at one time.'

'Yes, monsieur.'

'Is he perfectly in his right mind?'

The waiter stared. 'Perfectly, monsieur.'

'Has he been suspected at any time of being out of his mind?'

'Never, monsieur; he is a little noisy, but a very shrewd man.'

'What is a fellow to think?' I muttered, as I walked on.

I was soon within sight of the lights of the Belle Etoile. A carriage, with four horses, stood in the moonlight at the door, and a furious altercation was going on in the hall, in which the yell of Colonel Gaillarde out-topped all other sounds.

Most young men like, at least, to witness a row. But, intuitively, I felt that this would interest me in a very special manner. I had only fifty yards to run before I found myself in the hall of the old inn. The principal actor in this strange drama was, indeed, the colonel, who stood facing the old Count de St Alyre, who, in his travelling costume, with his black muffler covering the lower part of his face, confronted him; he had evidently been intercepted in an endeavour to reach his carriage. A little in the rear of the count stood the countess, also in travelling costume, with her thick black veil down, and holding in her delicate fingers a white rose. You can't conceive a more diabolical effigy of hate and fury than the colonel; the knotted veins stood out on his forehead, his eyes were leaping from their sockets, he was grinding his teeth and froth was on his lips. His sword was drawn, in his hand, and he accompanied his yelling denunciations with stamps upon the floor and flourishes of his weapon in the air.

The host of the Belle Etoile was talking to the colonel in soothing terms utterly thrown away. Two waiters, pale with fear, stared uselessly from behind. The colonel screamed and thundered, and whirled his sword. 'I was not sure of your red birds of prey; I could not believe you would have the audacity to travel on high roads, and to stop at honest inns, and lie under the same roof with honest men. You! you! both – vampires, wolves, ghouls. Summon the gendarmes, I say. By St Peter and all the devils, if either of you tries to get out of that door I'll take your head off.'

For a moment I had stood aghast. Here was a situation! I walked up to the lady; she laid her hand wildly upon my arm. 'Oh! Monsieur,' she whispered, in great agitation, 'that dreadful madman! What are we to do? He won't let us pass; he will kill my husband.'

'Fear nothing, madame,' I answered with romantic devotion, stepping between the count and Gaillarde as he shrieked his invective. 'Hold your tongue, and clear the way, you ruffian, you bully, you coward!' I roared.

A faint cry escaped the lady, which more than repaid the risk I ran as the sword of the frantic soldier, after a moment's astonished pause, flashed in the air to cut me down.

7

The White Rose

I was too quick for Colonel Gaillarde. As he raised his sword, reckless of all consequences but my condign punishment, and quite resolved to cleave me to the teeth, I struck him across the side of his head with my heavy stick; and while he staggered back, I struck him another blow, nearly in the same place, that felled him to the floor, where he lay as if dead.

I did not care one of his own regimental buttons whether he was dead or not; I was, at that moment, carried away by such a tumult of delightful and diabolical emotions!

I broke his sword under my foot, and flung the pieces across the street. The old Count de St Alyre skipped nimbly without looking to the right or left, or thanking anybody, over the floor, out of the door, down the steps and into his carriage. Instantly I was at the side of the beautiful countess, thus left to shift for herself; I offered her my arm, which she took, and I led her to the carriage. She entered, and I shut the door. All this without a word.

I was about to ask if there were any commands with which she would honour me – my hand was laid upon the lower edge of the window, which was open.

The lady's hand was laid upon mine timidly and excitedly. Her lips almost touched my cheek as she whispered hurriedly, 'I may never see you more, and, oh! that I could forget you. Go – farewell – for God's sake, go!'

I pressed her hand for a moment. She withdrew it but tremblingly pressed into mine the rose which she had held in her fingers during the agitating scene she had just passed through.

All this took place while the count was commanding, entreating, cursing his servants, tipsy, and out of the way during the crisis, my conscience afterwards insinuated, by my clever contrivance. They now mounted to their places with the agility of alarm. The postilions' whips cracked, the horses scrambled into a trot, and away rolled the carriage, with its precious freightage, along the quaint main street, in the moonlight, towards Paris.

I stood on the pavement till it was quite lost to eye and ear in the distance.

With a deep sigh, I then turned, my white rose folded in my handkerchief – the little parting *gage*, the 'favour secret, sweet and precious', which no mortal eye but hers and mine had seen conveyed to me.

The care of the host of the Belle Etoile, and his assistants, had raised the wounded hero of a hundred fights partly against the wall, and propped him at each side with portmanteaus and pillows, and poured a glass of brandy, which was duly placed to his account, into his big mouth, where such a Godsend for the first time remained unswallowed.

A bald-headed little military surgeon of sixty, with spectacles, who had cut off eighty-seven legs and arms to his own share after the Battle of Eylau, having retired with his sword and his saw, his laurels and his sticking-plaster to this, his native town, was called in, and rather thought the gallant colonel's skull was fractured; at all events, there was concussion of the seat of thought, and quite enough work for his remarkable self-healing powers to occupy him for a fortnight.

I began to grow a little uneasy. A disagreeable surprise if my excursion, in which I was to break banks and hearts, and, as you see, heads, should end upon the gallows or the guillotine. I was not clear, in those times of political oscillation, which was the established apparatus.

The colonel was conveyed, snorting apoplectically to his room.

I saw my host in the apartment in which we had supped. Wherever you employ a force of any sort to carry a point of real importance, reject all nice calculations of economy. Better to be a thousand per cent over the mark, than the smallest fraction of a unit under it. I instinctively felt this.

I ordered a bottle of my landlord's very best wine; made him partake with me, in the proportion of two glasses to one; and then told him that he must not decline a trifling souvenir from a guest who had been so charmed with all he had seen of the renowned Belle Etoile. Thus saying, I placed five-and-thirty Napoleons in his hand. At touch of which his countenance, by no means encouraging before, grew sunny, his manners thawed, and it was plain, as he dropped the coins hastily into his pocket, that benevolent relations had been established between us.

I immediately placed the colonel's broken head upon the *tapis*. We both agreed that if I had not given him that rather smart tap of my walking-cane, he would have beheaded half the inmates of the Belle Etoile. There was not a waiter in the house who would not verify that statement on oath.

The reader may suppose that I had other motives, beside the desire to escape the tedious inquisition of the law, for desiring to recommence my journey to Paris with the least possible delay. Judge what was my horror then to learn that for love or money horses were nowhere to be had that night. The last pair in the town had been obtained from the Ecu de France by a gentleman who had dined and supped at the Belle Etoile and was obliged to proceed to Paris that night.

Who was the gentleman? Had he actually gone? Could he possibly be induced to wait till morning?

The gentleman was now upstairs getting his things together, and his name was Monsieur Droqville.

I ran upstairs. I found my servant St Clair in my room. At sight of him, for a moment, my thoughts were turned into a different channel.

'Well, St Clair, tell me this moment who the lady is?' I demanded.

'The lady is the daughter or wife, it matters not which, of the Count de St Alyre – the old gentleman who was so near being sliced like a cucumber tonight, I am informed, by the sword of the general whom monsieur, by a turn of fortune, has put to bed of an apoplexy.'

'Hold your tongue, fool! The man's beastly drunk – he's sulking – he could talk if he liked – who cares? Pack up my things. Which are Monsieur Droqville's apartments?'

He knew, of course; he always knew everything.

Half an hour later Monsieur Droqville and I were travelling towards Paris, in my carriage, and with his horses. I ventured to ask the Marquis d'Harmonville, in a little while, whether the lady who accompanied the count was certainly the countess. 'Has he not a daughter?'

'Yes; I believe a very beautiful and charming young lady. I cannot say – it may have been she, his daughter by an earlier marriage. I saw only the count himself today.'

The marquis was growing a little sleepy, and, in a little while, he actually fell asleep in his corner. I dozed and nodded; but the marquis slept like a top. He awoke at the next posting-house, where he had fortunately secured horses by sending on his man, he told me.

'You will excuse my being so dull a companion,' he said, 'but till tonight I have had but two hours' sleep in more than sixty hours. I shall have a cup of coffee here; I have had my nap. Permit me to recommend you to do likewise. Their coffee is really excellent.' He ordered two cups of *café noir*, and waited, with his head out of the window. 'We will keep the cups,' he said, as he received them from the waiter, 'and the tray. Thank you.'

There was a little delay as he paid for these things; and then he took in the little tray, and handed me a cup of coffee.

I declined the tray; so he placed it on his own knees, to act as a miniature table.

'I can't endure being waited for and hurried,' he said. 'I like to sip my coffee at leisure.'

I agreed. It really *was* the very perfection of coffee.

'I, like Monsieur le Marquis, have slept very little for the last two or three nights; and find it difficult to keep awake. This coffee will do wonders for me; it refreshes one so.'

Before we had half done, the carriage was again in motion.

For a time our coffee made us chatty, and our conversation was animated.

The marquis was extremely good-natured, as well as clever, and gave me a brilliant and amusing account of Parisian life, schemes and dangers, all put so as to furnish me with practical warnings of the most valuable kind.

In spite of the amusing and curious stories which the marquis related, with so much point and colour, I felt myself again becoming gradually drowsy and dreamy.

Perceiving this, no doubt, the marquis good-naturedly suffered our conversation to subside into silence. The window next him was open.

He threw his cup out of it and did the same kind office for mine, and finally the little tray flew after, and I heard it clank on the road; a valuable waif, no doubt, for some early wayfarer in wooden shoes.

I leaned back in my corner; I had my beloved *gage* – my white rose – close to my heart, folded now in white paper. It inspired all manner of romantic dreams. I began to grow more and more sleepy. But actual slumber did not come. I was still viewing, with my half-closed eyes, from my corner, diagonally, the interior of the carriage.

I wished for sleep; but the barrier between waking and sleeping seemed absolutely insurmountable; and, instead, I entered into a state of novel and indescribable indolence.

The marquis lifted his dispatch-box from the floor, placed it on his knees, unlocked it and took out what proved to be a lamp, which he hung by two hooks attached to it to the window opposite to him. He lighted it with a match, put on his spectacles, and taking out a bundle of letters, began to read them carefully.

We were making way very slowly. My impatience had hitherto employed four horses from stage to stage. We were, in this emergency, only too happy to have secured two. But the difference in pace was depressing.

I grew tired of the monotony of seeing the spectacled marquis reading, folding and docketing letter after letter. I wished to shut out the image which wearied me, but something prevented my being able to shut my eyes. I tried again and again; but, positively, I had lost the power of closing them.

I would have rubbed my eyes, but I could not stir my hand, my will no longer acted on my body – I found that I could not move one joint, or muscle, no more than I could, by an effort of my will, have turned the carriage about.

Up to this I had experienced no sense of horror. Whatever it was, simple nightmare was not the cause. I was awfully frightened. Was I in a fit?

It was horrible to see my good-natured companion pursue his occupation so serenely when he might have dissipated my horrors by a single shake.

I made a stupendous exertion to call out, but in vain; I repeated the effort again and again, with no result.

My companion now tied up his letters, and looked out of the

window, humming an air from an opera. He drew back his head, and said, turning to me – 'Yes, I see the lights; we shall be there in two or three minutes.'

He looked more closely at me, and with a kind smile, and a little shrug, he said, 'Poor child, how fatigued he must have been – how profoundly he sleeps; when the carriage stops he will waken.'

He then replaced his letters in the dispatch-box, locked it, put his spectacles in his pocket, and again looked out of the window.

We had entered a little town. I suppose it was past two o'clock by this time. The carriage drew up; I saw an inn-door open, and a light issuing from it.

'Here we are!' said my companion, turning gaily to me. But I did not awake. 'Yes, how tired he must have been!' he exclaimed, after he had waited for an answer.

My servant was at the carriage door, and opened it.

'Your master sleeps soundly, he is so fatigued! It would be cruel to disturb him. You and I will go in, while they change the horses, and take some refreshment, and choose something that Monsieur Beckett will like to take in the carriage; for when he awakes by and by, he will, I am sure, be hungry.'

He trimmed his lamp, poured in some oil; and taking care not to disturb me, with another kind smile, and another word of caution to my servant, he got out, and I heard him talking to St Clair, as they entered the inn-door, and I was left in my corner, in the carriage, in the same state.

8

A Three Minutes' Visit

I have suffered extreme and protracted bodily pain at different periods of my life, but anything like that misery, thank God, I never endured before or since. I earnestly hope it may not resemble any type of death to which we are liable. I was, indeed, a spirit in prison; and unspeakable was my dumb and unmoving agony.

The power of thought remained clear and active. Dull terror filled my mind. How would this end? Was it actual death?

You will understand that my faculty of observing was unimpaired. I could hear and see anything as distinctly as ever I did in my life. It was simply that my will had, as it were, lost its hold of my body.

I told you that the Marquis d'Harmonville had not extinguished his carriage lamp on going into this village inn. I was listening intently, longing for his return, which might result, by some lucky accident, in awaking me from my catalepsy.

Without any sound of steps approaching to announce an arrival, the carriage-door suddenly opened, and a total stranger got in silently and shut the door.

The lamp gave about as strong a light as a wax-candle, so I could see the intruder perfectly. He was a young man, with a dark grey loose surtout, made with a sort of hood, which was pulled over his head. I thought, as he moved, that I saw the gold band of a military undress cap under it; and I certainly saw the lace and buttons of a uniform on the cuffs of the coat that were visible under the wide sleeves of his outside wrapper.

This young man had thick moustaches, and an imperial, and I observed that he had a red scar running upward from his lip across his cheek.

He entered, shut the door softly, and sat down beside me. It was all done in a moment; leaning towards me, and shading his eyes with his gloved hand, he examined my face closely, for a few seconds.

This man had come as noiselessly as a ghost; and everything he did was accomplished with the rapidity and decision that indicated a well-defined and prearranged plan. His designs were evidently sinister. I thought he was going to rob, and, perhaps, murder me. I lay, nevertheless, like a corpse under his hands. He inserted his hand in my breast pocket, from which he took my precious white rose and all the letters it contained, among which was a paper of some consequence to me.

My letters he glanced at. They were plainly not what he wanted. My precious rose, too, he laid aside with them. It was evidently with the paper I have mentioned that he was concerned, for the moment he opened it, he began with a pencil, in a small pocket-book, to make rapid note of its contents.

This man seemed to glide through his work with the noiseless and cool celerity which argued, I thought, the training of the police department.

He rearranged the papers, possibly in the very order in which he had found them, replaced them in my breast-pocket, and was gone.

His visit, I think, did not quite last three minutes. Very soon after his disappearance, I heard the voice of the marquis once more. He got in, and I saw him look at me, and smile, half-envying me, I fancied, my sound repose. If he had but known all!

He resumed his reading and docketing by the light of the little lamp which had just subserved the purposes of a spy.

We were now out of the town, pursuing our journey at the same moderate pace. We had left the scene of my police visit, as I should have termed it, now two leagues behind us, when I suddenly felt a strange throbbing in one ear, and a sensation as if air passed through it into my throat. It seemed as if a bubble of air, formed deep in my ear, swelled and burst there. The indescribable tension of my brain seemed all at once to give way; there was an odd humming in my head, and a sort of vibration through every nerve of my body, such as I have experienced in a limb that has been, in popular phraseology, asleep. I uttered a cry and half rose from my seat, and then fell back trembling and with a sense of mortal faintness.

The marquis stared at me, took my hand, and earnestly asked if I was ill. I could answer only with a deep groan.

Gradually the process of restoration was completed; and I was able, though very faintly, to tell him how very ill I had been; and then to describe the violation of my letters during the time of his absence from the carriage.

'Good heaven!' he exclaimed, 'the miscreant did not get at my dispatch-box?'

I satisfied him, so far as I had observed, on that point. He placed the box on the seat beside him and opened and examined its contents very minutely.

'Yes, undisturbed; all safe, thank heaven!' he murmured. 'There are half a dozen letters here that I would not have some people read for a great deal.'

He now asked with a very kind anxiety all about the illness I complained of. When he had heard me, he said – 'A friend of mine once had an attack as like yours as possible. It was on board ship, and followed a state of high excitement. He was a brave man like you; and was called on to exert both his strength and his courage suddenly. An hour or two after, fatigue overpowered him, and he appeared to fall into a sound sleep. He really sank into a state which he afterwards described in such a way that I think it must have been precisely the same affection as yours.'

'I am happy to think that my attack was not unique. Did he ever experience a return of it?'

'I knew him for years after and never heard of any such thing. What strikes me is a parallel in the predisposing causes of each attack. Your unexpected and gallant hand-to-hand encounter, at such desperate odds, with an experienced swordsman like that insane colonel of dragoons, your fatigue, and, finally, your composing yourself, as my other friend did, to sleep.'

I was further reassured.

'I wish,' he resumed, 'one could make out who that *coquin* was who examined your letters. It is not worth turning back, however, because we should learn nothing. Those people always manage so adroitly. I am satisfied, however; that he must have been an agent of the police. A rogue of any other kind would have robbed you.'

I talked very little, being ill and exhausted, but the marquis talked on agreeably.

'We grow so intimate,' said he, at last, 'that I must remind you that I am not, for the present, the Marquis d'Harmonville, but only Monsieur Droqville; nevertheless, when we get to Paris, although I cannot see you often I may be of use. I shall ask you to name to me the hotel at which you mean to put up; because the marquis being, as you are aware, on his travels, the Hotel d'Harmonville is, for the present, tenanted only by two or three old servants, who must not even see Monsieur Droqville. That gentleman will, nevertheless, contrive to get you access to the box of Monsieur le Marquis, at the Opera, as well, possibly, as to other places more difficult; and so soon as the diplomatic office of the Marquis d'Harmonville is ended, and he is at liberty to declare himself, he will not excuse his friend, Monsieur Beckett, from fulfilling his promise to visit him this autumn at the Château d'Harmonville.'

You may be sure I thanked the marquis.

The nearer we got to Paris, the more I valued his protection. The countenance of a great man on the spot, just then, taking so kind an interest in the stranger whom he had, as it were, blundered upon, might make my visit ever so many degrees more delightful than I had anticipated.

Nothing could be more gracious than the manner and looks of the marquis; and, as I still thanked him, the carriage suddenly stopped in front of the place where a relay of horses awaited us, and where, as it turned out, we were to part.

9

Gossip and Counsel

My eventful journey was over, at last. I sat in my hotel window looking out upon brilliant Paris, which had, in a moment, recovered all its gaiety, and more than its accustomed bustle. Everyone has read of the kind of excitement that followed the catastrophe of Napoleon, and the second restoration of the Bourbons. I need not, therefore, even if, at this distance, I could, recall and describe my experiences and impressions of the peculiar aspect of Paris in those strange times. It was, to be sure, my first visit. But often as I have seen it since, I don't think I ever saw that delightful capital in a state so pleasurably excited and exciting.

I had been two days in Paris, and had seen all sorts of sights, and experienced none of that rudeness and insolence of which others complained from the exasperated officers of the defeated French army.

I must say this, also. My romance had taken complete possession of me; and the chance of seeing the object of my dream gave a secret and delightful interest to my rambles and drives in the streets and environs and my visits to the galleries and other sights of the metropolis.

I had neither seen nor heard of the count or countess, nor had the Marquis d'Harmonville made any sign. I had quite recovered from the strange indisposition under which I had suffered during my night journey.

It was now evening, and I was beginning to fear that my patrician acquaintance had quite forgotten me, when the waiter presented to me the card of 'Monsieur Droqville'; and, with no small elation and hurry, I desired him to show the gentleman up.

In came the Marquis d'Harmonville, kind and gracious as ever.

'I am a night-bird at present,' said he, as soon as we had exchanged the little speeches which are usual. 'I keep in the shade during the daytime, and even now I hardly ventured to come in a closed carriage. The friends for whom I have undertaken a rather critical service have so ordained it. They think all is lost if I am known to be in Paris. First, let me present you with these orders for my box. I am so vexed that I cannot command it oftener during the next fortnight; during my absence, I had directed my secretary to give it for any night to the first of my friends who might apply, and the result is that I find next to nothing left at my disposal.'

I thanked him very much.

'And now, a word, in my office of mentor. You have not come here, of course, without introductions?'

I produced half a dozen letters, the addresses of which he looked at.

'Don't mind these letters,' he said. 'I will introduce you. I will take you myself from house to house. One friend at your side is worth many letters. Make no intimacies, no acquaintances, until then. You young men like best to exhaust the public amusements of a great city, before embarrassing yourselves with the engagements of society. Go to all these. It will occupy you, day and night, for at least three weeks. When this is over, I shall be at liberty, and will myself introduce you to the brilliant but comparatively quiet routine of society. Place yourself in my hands; and in Paris remember, when once in society, you are always there.'

I thanked him very much, and promised to follow his counsels implicitly.

He seemed pleased, and said – 'I shall now tell you some of the places you ought to go to. Take your map, and write letters or numbers upon the points I will indicate, and we will make out a little list. All the places that I shall mention to you are worth seeing.'

In this methodical way, and with a great deal of amusing and scandalous anecdote, he furnished me with a catalogue and a guide, which, to a seeker of novelty and pleasure, was invaluable.

'In a fortnight, perhaps in a week,' he said, 'I shall be at leisure to be of real use to you. In the meantime, be on your guard. You must not play; you will be robbed if you do. Remember, you are surrounded here by plausible swindlers and villains of all kinds, who subsist by devouring strangers. Trust no one but those you know.'

I thanked him again, and promised to profit by his advice. But my heart was too full of the beautiful lady of the Belle Etoile to allow our interview to close without an effort to learn something about her. I therefore asked for the Count and Countess de St Alyre, whom I had had the good fortune to extricate from an extremely unpleasant row in the hall of the inn.

Alas, he had not seen them since. He did not know where they were staying. They had a fine old house only a few leagues from Paris; but he thought it probable that they would remain, for a few days at least, in the city, as preparations would, no doubt, be necessary, after so long an absence, for their reception at home.

'How long have they been away?'

'About eight months, I think.'

'They are poor, I think you said?'

'What you would consider poor. But, monsieur, the count has an income which affords them the comforts, and even the elegancies of life, living as they do in a very quiet and retired way in this cheap country.'

'Then they are very happy?'

'One would say they *ought* to be happy.'

'And what prevents it?'

'He is jealous.'

'But his wife – she gives him no cause?'

'I am afraid she does.'

'How, monsieur?'

'I always thought she was a little too – a *great deal* too –'

'Too *what*, monsieur?'

'Too handsome. But although she has remarkably fine eyes, exquisite features and the most delicate complexion in the world, I believe that she is a woman of probity. You have never seen her?'

'There was a lady, muffled up in a cloak, with a very thick veil on, the other night, in the hall of the Belle Etoile, when I broke that fellow's head who was bullying the old count. But her veil was so thick I could not see a feature through it.' My answer was diplomatic, you observe. 'She may have been the count's daughter. Do they quarrel?'

'Who, he and his wife?'

'Yes.'

'A little.'

'Oh! and what do they quarrel about?'

'It is a long story; about the lady's diamonds. They are valuable – they are worth, La Perelleuse says, about a million francs. The count wishes them sold and turned into revenue, which he offers to settle as she pleases. The countess, whose they are, resists, and for a reason which, I rather think, she can't disclose to him.'

'And pray what is that?' I asked, my curiosity a good deal piqued.

'She is thinking, I conjecture, how well she will look in them when she marries her second husband.'

'Oh? – yes, to be sure. But the Count de St Alyre is a good man?'

'Admirable, and extremely intelligent.'

'I should wish so much to be presented to the count: you tell me he's so – '

'So agreeably married. But they are living quite out of the world. He takes her now and then to the Opera, or to a public entertainment; but that is all.'

'And he must remember so much of the old *régime*, and so many of the scenes of the revolution!'

'Yes, the very man for a philosopher, like you. And he falls asleep after dinner; and his wife don't, But, seriously, he has retired from the gay and the great world and has grown apathetic; and so has his wife; and nothing seems to interest her now, not even – her husband!'

The marquis stood up to take his leave.

'Don't risk your money,' said he. 'You will soon have an opportunity of laying out some of it to great advantage. Several collections of really good pictures, belonging to persons who have mixed themselves up in this Bonapartist restoration, must come within a few weeks to the hammer. You can do wonders when these sales commence. There will be startling bargains! Reserve yourself for them. I shall let you know all about it. By the by,' he said, stopping short as he approached the door, 'I was so near forgetting. There is to be the very thing you would enjoy so much, because you see so little of it in England – I mean a *bal masqué*, conducted, it is said, with more than usual splendour. It takes place at Versailles – all the world will be there; there is such a rush for cards! But I think I may promise you one. Good-night!'

10

The Black Veil

Speaking the language fluently, and with unlimited money, there was nothing to prevent my enjoying all that was enjoyable in the French capital. You may easily suppose how two days were passed. At the end of that time, and at about the same hour, Monsieur Droqville called again.

Courtly, good-natured, gay as usual, he told me that the masquerade ball was fixed for the next day, and that he had applied for a card for me.

How awfully unlucky. I was so afraid I should not be able to go.

He stared at me for a moment with a suspicious and menacing look, which I did not understand, in silence, and then enquired rather sharply, 'And will Monsieur Beckett be good enough to say why not?'

I was a little surprised, but answered the simple truth: I had made an engagement for that evening with two or three English friends, and did not see how I could.

'Just so! You English, wherever you are, always look out for your English boors, your beer and "*bifstek*"; and when you come here, instead of trying to learn something of the people you visit and pretend to study, you are guzzling and swearing and smoking with one another, and no wiser or more polished at the end of your travels than if you had been all the time carousing in a booth at Greenwich.'

He laughed sarcastically, and looked as if he could have poisoned me.

'There it is,' said he, throwing the card on the table. 'Take it or leave it, just as you please. I suppose I shall have no thanks for my pains; but it is not usual when a man, such as I, takes trouble, asks a favour and secures a privilege for an acquaintance, for him to be treated so.'

This was astonishingly impertinent.

I was shocked, offended, penitent. I had possibly committed unwittingly a breach of good breeding, according to French ideas, which almost justified the brusque severity of the marquis's undignified rebuke.

In a confusion, therefore, of many feelings, I hastened to make my apologies, and to propitiate the chance friend who had showed me so much disinterested kindness.

I told him that I would, at any cost, break through the engagement in which I had unluckily entangled myself; that I had spoken with too little reflection, and that I certainly had not thanked him at all in proportion to his kindness, and to my real estimate of it.

'Pray say not a word more; my vexation was entirely on your account; and I expressed it, I am only too conscious, in terms a great deal too strong, which I am sure your good nature will pardon. Those who know me a little better are aware that I sometimes say a good deal more than I intend; and am always sorry when I do. Monsieur Beckett will forget that his old friend Monsieur Droqville has lost his temper in his cause, for a moment, and – we are as good friends as before.'

He smiled like the Monsieur Droqville of the Belle Etoile, and extended his hand, which I took very respectfully and cordially.

Our momentary quarrel had left us only better friends.

The marquis then told me I had better secure a bed in some hotel at Versailles as a rush would be made to take them; and advised my going down next morning for the purpose.

I ordered horses accordingly for eleven o'clock; and, after a little more conversation, the Marquis d'Harmonville bade me good-night, and ran down the stairs with his handkerchief to his mouth and nose and, as I saw from my window, jumped into his closed carriage again and drove away.

Next day I was at Versailles. As I approached the door of the Hôtel de France, it was plain that I was not a moment too soon, if, indeed, I were not already too late,

A crowd of carriages were drawn up about the entrance, so that I had no chance of approaching except by dismounting and pushing my way among the horses. The hall was full of servants and gentlemen screaming to the proprietor, who in a state of polite distraction, was assuring them, one and all, that there was not a room or a closet disengaged in his entire house.

I slipped out again, leaving the hall to those who were shouting, expostulating and wheedling, in the delusion that the host might, if he pleased, manage something for them. I jumped into my carriage and drove, at my horses' best pace, to the Hôtel du Reservoir. The blockade about this door was as complete as the other. The result was the same. It was very provoking, but what was to be done? My postilion had, a little officiously, while I was in the hall talking with the hotel authorities, got his horses bit by bit as other carriages moved away to the very steps of the inn door.

This arrangement was very convenient so far as getting in again was concerned. But, this accomplished, how were we to get out? There were carriages in front, and carriages behind, and no less than four rows of carriages, of all sorts, to the side of us.

I had at this time remarkably long and clear sight, and if I had been impatient before, guess what my feelings were when I saw an open carriage pass along the narrow strip of roadway left open at the other side, a barouche in which I was certain I recognised the veiled countess and her husband. This carriage had been brought to a walk by a cart which occupied the whole breadth of the narrow way, and was moving with the customary tardiness of such vehicles.

I should have done more wisely if I had jumped down on the *trottoir*, and run round the block of carriages in front of the barouche. But, unfortunately, I was more of a Murat than a Moltke, and preferred a direct charge upon my object to relying on *tactique*. I dashed across the back seat of a carriage which was next mine, I don't know how; tumbled through a sort of gig, in which an old gentleman and a dog were dozing; stepped with an incoherent apology over the side of an open carriage in which were four gentlemen engaged in a hot dispute; tripped at the far side in getting out, and fell flat across the backs of a pair of horses, who instantly began plunging and threw me head foremost in the dust.

To those who observed my reckless charge, without being in the secret of my object, I must have appeared demented. Fortunately, the interesting barouche had passed before the catastrophe, and covered as I was with dust, and my hat blocked, you may be sure I did not care to present myself before the object of my Quixotic devotion.

I stood for a while amid a storm of *sacré*-ing, tempered disagreeably with laughter; and in the midst of these, while endeavouring to beat the dust from my clothes with my handkerchief, I heard a voice with which I was acquainted call, 'Monsieur Beckett.'

I looked and saw the marquis peeping from a carriage-window. It was a welcome sight. In a moment I was at his carriage side.

'You may as well leave Versailles,' he said; 'you have learned, no doubt, that there is not a bed to hire in either of the hotels; and I can add that there is not a room to let in the whole town. But I have managed something for you that will answer just as well. Tell your servant to follow us, and get in here and sit beside me.'

Fortunately an opening in the closely-packed carriages had just occurred, and mine was approaching.

I directed the servant to follow us; and the marquis having said a word to his driver, we were immediately in motion.

'I will bring you to a comfortable place, the very existence of which is known to but few Parisians, where, knowing how things were here, I secured a room for you. It is only a mile away, and an old comfortable inn, called Le Dragon Volant. It was fortunate for you that my tiresome business called me to this place so early.'

I think we had driven about a mile and a half to the farther side of the palace when we found ourselves upon a narrow old road, with the woods of Versailles on one side, and much older trees, of a size seldom seen in France, on the other.

We pulled up before an antique and solid inn, built of Caen stone in a fashion richer and more florid than was ever usual in such houses, and which indicated that it was originally designed for the private mansion of some person of wealth, and probably, as the wall bore many carved shields and supporters, of distinction also. A kind of porch, less ancient than the rest, projected hospitably with a wide and florid arch, over which, cut in high relief in stone, and painted and gilded, was the sign of the inn. This was the Flying Dragon, with wings of brilliant red and gold, expanded, and its tail, pale green and gold, twisted and knotted into ever so many rings, and ending in a burnished point barbed like the dart of death.

'I shan't go in – but you will find it a comfortable place; at all events better than nothing. I would go in with you, but my incognito forbids. You will, I dare say, be all the better pleased to learn that the inn is haunted – I should have been, in my young days, I know. But don't allude to that awful fact in hearing of your host, for I believe it is a sore subject. Au revoir. If you want to enjoy yourself at the ball take my advice, and go in a domino. I think I shall look in; and certainly, if I do, in the same costume. How shall we recognise one another? Let me see, something held in the fingers – a flower won't do, so many people will have flowers. Suppose you get a red cross a couple of inches long – you're an Englishman – stitched or pinned on the breast of your domino, and I a white one? Yes, that will do very well; and whatever room you go into keep near the door till we meet. I shall look for you at all the doors I pass, and you, in the same way, look for me; and we *must* find each other soon. So that is understood. I can't enjoy a thing of that kind with any but a young person, a man of my age requires the contagion of young spirits and the companionship of someone who enjoys everything spontaneously. Farewell; we meet tonight.'

By this time I was standing on the road; I shut the carriage-door; bade him goodbye; and away he drove.

11

Le Dragon Volant

I took one look about me. The building was picturesque; the trees made it more so. The antique and sequestered character of the scene contrasted strangely with the glare and bustle of the Parisian life to which my eye and ear had become accustomed.

Then I examined the gorgeous old sign for a minute or two. Next I surveyed the exterior of the house more carefully. It was large and solid, and squared more with my ideas of an ancient English hostelry, such as the Canterbury Pilgrims might have put up at, than a French house of entertainment. Except, indeed, for a round turret that rose at the left flank of the house and terminated in the extinguisher-shaped roof that suggests a French château.

I entered and announced myself as Monsieur Beckett, for whom a room had been taken. I was received with all the consideration due to an English milord, with, of course, an unfathomable purse.

My host conducted me to my apartment. It was a large room, a little sombre, panelled with dark wainscoting, and furnished in a stately and sombre style, long out of date. There was a wide hearth, and a heavy mantelpiece, carved with shields, in which I might, had I been curious enough, have discovered a correspondence with the heraldry on the outer walls. There was something interesting, melancholy, and even depressing in all this. I went to the stone-shafted window, and looked out upon a small park, with a thick wood, forming the background of a château, which presented a cluster of such conical-topped turrets as I have just now mentioned.

The wood and château were melancholy objects. They showed signs of neglect, and almost of decay; and the gloom of fallen grandeur and a certain air of desertion hung oppressively over the scene.

I asked my host the name of the château.

'That, monsieur, is the Château de la Carque,' he answered.

'It is a pity it is so neglected,' I observed. 'I should say, perhaps, a pity that its proprietor is not more wealthy?'

'Perhaps so, monsieur.'

'*Perhaps?*' – I repeated, and looked at him. 'Then I suppose he is not very popular.'

'Neither one thing nor the other, monsieur,' he answered; 'I meant only that we could not tell what use he might make of riches.'

'And who is he?' I enquired.

'The Count de St Alyre.'

'Oh! The count! You are quite sure?' I asked, very eagerly.

It was now the innkeeper's turn to look at me.

'*Quite* sure, monsieur, the Count de St Alyre.'

'Do you see much of him in this part of the world?'

'Not a great deal, monsieur; he is often absent for a considerable time.'

'And is he poor?' I enquired.

'I pay rent to him for this house. It is not much; but I find he cannot wait long for it,' he replied, smiling satirically.

'From what I have heard, however, I should think he cannot be very poor?' I continued.

'They say, monsieur, he plays. I know not. He certainly is not rich. About seven months ago, a relation of his died in a distant place. His body was sent to the count's house here, and by him buried in Père Lachaise, as the poor gentleman had desired. The count was in profound affliction; although he got a handsome legacy, they say, by that death. But money never seems to do him good for any time.'

'He is old, I believe?'

'Old? We call him the "Wandering Jew", except, indeed, that he has not always the five sous in his pocket. Yet, monsieur, his courage does not fail him. He has taken a young and handsome wife.'

'And she?' I urged.

'Is the Countess de St Alyre.'

'Yes; but I fancy we may say something more? She has attributes?'

'Three, monsieur, three, at least, most amiable.'

'Ah! And what are they?'

'Youth, beauty, and – diamonds.'

I laughed. The sly old gentleman was compounding my curiosity.

'I see, my friend,' said I, 'you are reluctant – '

'To quarrel with the count,' he concluded. 'True. You see, monsieur, he could vex me in two or three ways, so could I him. But, on the whole, it is better each to mind his business, and to maintain peaceful relations; you understand.'

It was, therefore, no use pressing him further, at least for the present. Perhaps he had nothing to relate. Should I think differently, by and by, I could try the effect of a few Napoleons. Possibly he meant to extract them.

The host of Le Dragon Volant was an elderly man, thin, bronzed, intelligent, and with an air of decision, perfectly military. I learned afterwards that he had served under Napoleon in his early Italian campaigns.

'One question I think you may answer,' I said, 'without risking a quarrel. Is the count at home?'

'He has many homes, I conjecture,' said the host evasively. 'But – but I think I may say, monsieur, that he is, I believe, at present staying at the Château de la Carque.'

I looked out of the window, more interested than ever, across the undulating grounds to the château, with its gloomy background of foliage.

'I saw him today, in his carriage at Versailles,' I said.

'Very natural.'

'Then his carriage, and horses, and servants, are at the château?'

'The carriage he puts up here, monsieur, and the servants are hired for the occasion. There is but one who sleeps at the château. Such a life must be terrifying for Madame the Countess,' he replied.

'The old screw!' I thought. 'By this torture, he hopes to extract her diamonds. What a life! What fiends to contend with – jealousy and extortion!'

The knight, having made this speech to himself, cast his eyes once more upon the enchanter's castle, and heaved a gentle sigh – a sigh of longing, of resolution and of love.

What a fool I was! and yet, in the sight of angels, are we any wiser as we grow older? It seems to me only that our illusions change as we go on; but, still, we are madmen all the same.

'Well, St Clair,' said I, as my servant entered and began to arrange my things. 'You have got a bed?'

'In the cock-loft, monsieur, among the spiders, and, *par ma foi!* the cats and the owls. But we agree very well. *Vive la bagatelle!*'

'I had no idea it was so full.'

'Chiefly the servants, monsieur, of those persons who were fortunate enough to get apartments at Versailles.'

'And what do you think of Le Dragon Volant?'

'Le Dragon Volant, Monsieur? the old fiery dragon? The devil himself, if all is true! On the faith of a Christian, monsieur, they say that diabolical miracles have taken place in this house.'

'What do you mean? *Revenants*?'

'Not at all, sir; I wish it was no worse. *Revenants*? No! People who have never returned – who vanished, before the eyes of half a dozen men all looking at them.'

'What do you mean, St Clair? Let us hear the story, or miracle, or whatever it is.'

'It is only this, monsieur, that an ex-master-of-the-horse of the late king who lost his head – monsieur will have the goodness to recollect, in the revolution – being permitted by the emperor to return to France, lived here in this hotel, for a month, and at the end of that time vanished, visibly, as I told you, before the faces of half a dozen credible witnesses! The other was a Russian nobleman, six feet high and upwards, who, standing in the centre of the room downstairs, describing to seven gentlemen of unquestionable veracity the last moments of Peter the Great, and having a glass of *eau de vie* in his left hand and his *tasse de café*, nearly finished, in his right, in like manner vanished. His boots were found on the floor where he had been standing; and the gentleman at his right found, to his astonishment, his cup of coffee in his fingers, and the gentleman at his left, his glass of *eau de vie* –'

'Which he swallowed in his confusion,' I suggested.

'Which was preserved for three years among the curious articles of this house, and was broken by the *curé* while conversing with Mademoiselle Fidone in the housekeeper's room; but of the Russian nobleman himself, nothing more was ever seen or heard. *Parbleu!* when *we* go out of Le Dragon Volant, I hope it may be by the door. I heard all this, monsieur, from the postilion who drove us.'

'Then it *must* be true!' said I, jocularly: but I was beginning to feel the gloom of the view, and of the chamber in which I stood; there had stolen over me, I know not how, a presentiment of evil; and my joke was with an effort, and my spirit flagged.

12

The Magician

No more brilliant spectacle than this masked ball could be imagined. Among other *salons* and galleries thrown open was the enormous perspective of the Grande Galerie des Glaces, lighted up for the occasion with no less than four thousand wax candles, reflected and repeated by all the mirrors, so that the effect was almost dazzling. The grand suite of salons was thronged with masquers in every conceivable costume. There was not a single room deserted. Every place was animated with music, voices, brilliant colours, flashing jewels, the hilarity of extemporised comedy, and all the spirited incidents of a cleverly sustained masquerade. I had never seen before anything in the least comparable to this magnificent fête. I moved along, indolently, in my domino and mask, loitering, now and then, to enjoy a clever dialogue, a farcical song or an amusing monologue, but, at the same time, keeping my eyes about me, lest my friend in the black domino, with the little white cross on his breast, should pass me by.

I had delayed and looked about me, specially at every door I passed, as the marquis and I had agreed; but he had not yet appeared.

While I was thus employed in the very luxury of lazy amusement, I saw a gilded sedan chair, or, rather, a Chinese palanquin, exhibiting the fantastic exuberance of 'celestial' decoration, borne forward on gilded poles by four richly dressed Chinese; one with a wand in his hand marched in front, and another behind; and a slight and solemn man, with a long black beard and a tall fez, such as a dervish is represented as wearing, walked close to its side. A strangely-embroidered robe fell over his shoulders, covered with hieroglyphic symbols; the embroidery was in black and gold upon a variegated ground of brilliant colours. The robe was bound about his waist with a broad belt of gold, with cabbalistic devices traced on it in dark red and black; red stockings, and shoes embroidered with gold, and pointed and curved upward at the toes, in Oriental fashion, appeared below the skirt of the robe. The man's face was dark, fixed and solemn, his eyebrows black and enormously heavy, and he carried a singular-looking book under one arm, a wand of polished black wood in his other hand and walked with his chin sunk on his breast and his eyes fixed upon the floor. The man in front waved his wand right and left to clear the way for the advancing palanquin, the curtains of which were closed; and there was something so singular, strange and solemn about the whole thing that I felt at once interested.

I was very well pleased when I saw the bearers set down their burden within a few yards of the spot on which I stood.

The bearers and the men with the gilded wands forthwith clapped their hands, and in silence danced round the palanquin a curious and half-frantic dance, which was yet, as to figures and postures, perfectly methodical. This was soon accompanied by a clapping of hands and a ha-ha-ing, rhythmically delivered.

While the dance was going on a hand was lightly laid on my arm, and, looking round, I saw that a black domino with a white cross stood beside me.

'I am so glad I have found you,' said the marquis; 'and at this moment. This is the best group in the rooms. You must speak to the wizard. About an hour ago I lighted upon them, in another salon, and consulted the oracle by putting questions. I never was more amazed. Although his answers were a little disguised it was soon perfectly plain that he knew every detail about the business, which no one on earth had heard of but myself and two or three other men, about the most cautious persons in France. I shall never forget that shock. I saw other people who consulted him, evidently as much surprised, and more frightened than I. I came with the Count de St Alyre and the countess.'

He nodded toward a thin figure, also in a domino. It was the count.

'Come,' he said to me, 'I'll introduce you.'

I followed, you may suppose, readily enough.

The marquis presented me, with a very prettily-turned allusion to my fortunate intervention in his favour at the Belle Etoile; and the count overwhelmed me with polite speeches, and ended by saying what pleased me better still: 'The countess is near us, in the next salon but one, chatting with her old friend the Duchesse d'Argensaque; I shall go for her in a few minutes; and when I bring her here, she shall make your acquaintance; and thank you, also, for your assistance, rendered with so much courage when we were so very disagreeably interrupted.'

'You must, positively, speak with the magician,' said the marquis to the Count de St Alyre, 'you will be so much amused. I did so; and, I assure you, I could not have anticipated such answers! I don't know what to believe.'

'Really! Then, by all means, let us try,' he replied.

We three approached, together, the side of the palanquin at which the black-bearded magician stood.

A young man, in a Spanish dress, who, with a friend at his side, had just conferred with the conjuror, was saying, as he passed us by: 'Ingenious mystification! Who is that in the palanquin? He seems to know everybody!'

The count, in his mask and domino, moved along stiffly with us towards the palanquin. A clear circle was maintained by the Chinese attendants, and the spectators crowded round in a ring. One of these men – he who with a gilded wand had preceded the procession – advanced, extending his empty hand, palm upward.

'Money?' enquired the count.

'Gold,' replied the usher.

The count placed a piece of money in his hand; and I and the marquis were each called on in turn to do likewise as we entered the circle. We paid accordingly.

The conjuror stood beside the palanquin, its silk curtain in his hand; his chin sunk, with its long, jet-black beard, on his chest; the outer hand grasping the black wand, on which he leaned; his eyes were lowered, as before, to the ground; his face looked absolutely lifeless. Indeed, I never saw face or figure so moveless, except in death.

The first question the count put was – 'Am I married, or unmarried?'

The conjuror drew back the curtain quickly, placed his ear towards a richly dressed Chinese who sat in the litter, withdrew his head and closed the curtain again; then he answered – 'Yes.'

The same preliminary was observed each time, so that the man with the black wand presented himself, not as a prophet, but as a medium; and answered, as it seemed, in the words of a greater than himself.

Two or three questions followed, the answers to which seemed to amuse the marquis very much; but the point of which I could not see, for I knew next to nothing of the count's peculiarities and adventures.

'Does my wife love me?' asked he, playfully.

'As well as you deserve.'

'Whom do I love best in the world?'

'Self.'

'Oh! That I fancy is pretty much the case with everyone. But, putting myself out of the question, do I love anything on earth better than my wife?'

'Her diamonds.'

'Oh!' said the count.

The marquis, I could see, laughed.

'Is it true,' said the count, changing the conversation peremptorily, 'that there has been a battle in Naples?'

'No; in France.'

'Indeed,' said the count, satirically, with a glance round. 'And may I enquire between what powers, and on what particular quarrel?'

'Between the Count and Countess de St Alyre, and about a document they subscribed on the 25th July 1811.'

The marquis afterwards told me that this was the date of their marriage settlement.

The count stood stock-still for a minute or so; and one could fancy that they saw his face flushing through his mask.

Nobody, but we two, knew that the enquirer was the Count de St Alyre.

I thought he was puzzled to find a subject for his next question, and perhaps repented having entangled himself in such a colloquy. If so, he was relieved; for the marquis, touching his arm, whispered, 'Look to your right, and see who is coming.'

I looked in the direction indicated by the marquis, and I saw a gaunt figure stalking towards us. It wore no mask. The face was broad, scarred and white. In a word, it was the ugly face of Colonel Gaillarde,

who, in the costume of a corporal of the Imperial Guard, had his left
arm so adjusted as to look like a stump, leaving the lower part of the
coat-sleeve empty and pinned up to the breast. There were strips of
very real sticking-plaster across his eyebrow and temple, where my
stick had left its mark, to score, hereafter, among the more honourable
scars of war.

13

The Oracle Tells Me Wonders

I forgot for a moment how impervious my mask and domino were
to the hard stare of the old campaigner and was preparing for an
animated scuffle. It was only for a moment, of course; but the count
cautiously drew a little back as the Gasconading corporal, in blue
uniform, white vest and white gaiters – for my friend Gaillarde was as
loud and swaggering in his assumed character as in his real one of a
colonel of dragoons – drew near. He had already twice all but got
himself turned out of doors for vaunting the exploits of Napoleon le
Grand in terrific mock-heroics, and had very nearly come to hand-
grips with a Prussian hussar. In fact, he would have been involved in
several sanguinary rows already had not his discretion reminded him
that the object of his coming there at all, namely, to arrange a meeting
with an affluent widow, on whom he believed he had made a tender
impression, would not have been promoted by his premature removal
from the festive scene, of which he was an ornament, in charge of a
couple of gendarmes.

'Money! Gold! Bah! What money can a wounded soldier like your
humble servant have amassed with but his sword-hand left, which,
being necessarily occupied, places not a finger at his command with
which to scrape together the spoils of a routed enemy?'

'No gold from him,' said the magician. 'His scars frank him.'

'Bravo, Monsieur le Prophète! Bravissimo! Here I am. Shall I begin,
mon sorcier, without further loss of time, to question you?'

Without waiting for an answer, he commenced, in stentorian tones.

After half a dozen questions and answers, he asked – 'Whom do I
pursue at present?'

'Two persons.'

'Ha! Two? Well, who are they?'

'An Englishman, whom, if you catch, he will kill you; and a French widow, whom, if you find, she will spit in your face.'

'Monsieur le Magicien calls a spade a spade, and knows that his cloth protects him. No matter! Why do I pursue them?'

'The widow has inflicted a wound on your heart, and the Englishman a wound on your head. They are each separately too strong for you; take care your pursuit does not unite them.'

'Bah! How could that be?'

'The Englishman protects ladies. He has got that fact into your head. The widow, if she sees him, will marry him. It takes some time, she will reflect, to become a colonel, and the Englishman is unquestionably young.'

'I will cut his cock's-comb for him,' he ejaculated with an oath and a grin; and in a softer tone he asked, 'Where is she?'

'Near enough to be offended if you fail.'

'So she ought, by my faith. You are right, Monsieur le Prophète! A hundred thousand thanks! Farewell!' And staring about him, and stretching his lank neck as high as he could, he strode away with his scars and white waistcoat and gaiters, and his bearskin shako.

I had been trying to see the person who sat in the palanquin. I had only once an opportunity of a tolerably steady peep. What I saw was singular. The oracle was dressed, as I have said, very richly, in the Chinese fashion. He was a figure altogether on a larger scale than the interpreter who stood outside. The features seemed to me large and heavy, and the head was carried with a downward inclination; the eyes were closed, and the chin rested on the breast of his embroidered pelisse. The face seemed fixed, and the very image of apathy. Its character and pose seemed an exaggerated repetition of the immobility of the figure who communicated with the noisy outer world. This face looked blood-red; but that was caused, I concluded, by the light entering through the red silk curtains. All this struck me almost at a glance; I had not many seconds in which to make my observation. The ground was now clear, and the marquis said, 'Go forward, my friend.'

I did so. When I reached the magician, as we called the man with the black wand, I glanced over my shoulder to see whether the count was near.

No, he was some yards behind; and he and the marquis, whose curiosity seemed to be by this time satisfied, were now conversing generally upon some subject of course quite different.

I was relieved, for the sage seemed to blurt out secrets in an unexpected way; and some of mine might not have amused the count.

I thought for a moment. I wished to test the prophet. A Church of England man was a *rara avis* in Paris.

'What is my religion?' I asked.

'A beautiful heresy,' answered the oracle instantly.

'A heresy? – and pray how is it named?'

'Love.'

'Oh! Then I suppose I am a polytheist, and love a great many?'

'One.'

'But, seriously,' I asked, intending to turn the course of our colloquy a little out of an embarrassing channel, 'have I ever learned any words of devotion by heart?'

'Yes.'

'Can you repeat them?'

'Approach.'

I did, and lowered my ear.

The man with the black wand closed the curtains, and whispered, slowly and distinctly, these words which, I need scarcely tell you, I instantly recognised: '*I may never see you more; and, oh! that I could forget you! go – farewell – for God's sake, go!*'

I started as I heard them. They were, you know, the last words whispered to me by the countess.

Good heavens! How miraculous! Words heard most assuredly by no ear on earth but my own and the lady's who uttered them, till now!

I looked at the impassive face of the spokesman with the wand. There was no trace of meaning, or even of a consciousness that the words he had uttered could possible interest me.

'What do I most long for?' I asked, scarcely knowing what I said.

'Paradise.'

'And what prevents my reaching it?'

'A black veil.'

Stronger and stronger! The answers seemed to me to indicate the minutest acquaintance with every detail of my little romance, of which not even the marquis knew anything! And I, the questioner, masked and robed so that my own brother could not have known me!

'You said I loved someone. Am I loved in return?' I asked.

'Try.'

I was speaking lower than before, and stood near the dark man with the beard, to prevent the necessity of his speaking in a loud key.

'Does anyone love me?' I repeated.

'Secretly,' was the answer.

'Much or little?' I enquired.

'Too well.'

'How long will that love last?'

'Till the rose casts its leaves.'

'The rose – another allusion!'

'Then – darkness!' I sighed. 'But till then I live in light.'

'The light of violet eyes.'

Love, if not a religion, as the oracle had just pronounced it, is at least a superstition. How it exalts the imagination! How it enervates the reason! How credulous it makes us!

All this which, in the case of another, I should have laughed at, most powerfully affected me in my own. It inflamed my ardour, and half crazed my brain, and even influenced my conduct.

The spokesman of this wonderful trick – if trick it were – now waved me backward with his wand, and I withdrew, my eyes still fixed upon the group, by this time encircled with an aura of mystery in my fancy; backing towards the ring of spectators, I saw him raise his hand suddenly, with a gesture of command, as a signal to the usher who carried the golden wand in front.

The usher struck his wand on the ground, and, in a shrill voice, proclaimed: 'The great Confu is silent for an hour.'

Instantly the bearers pulled down a sort of blind of bamboo, which descended with a sharp clatter, and secured it at the bottom; and then the man in the tall fez, with the black beard and wand, began a sort of dervish dance. In this the men with the gold wands joined, and finally, in an outer ring, the bearers, the palanquin being the centre of the circles described by these solemn dancers, whose pace, little by little, quickened, whose gestures grew sudden, strange, frantic, as the motion became swifter and swifter, until at length the whirl became so rapid that the dancers seemed to fly by with the speed of a mill-wheel, and amid a general clapping of hands, and universal wonder, these strange performers mingled with the crowd, and the exhibition, for the time at least, ended.

The Marquis d'Harmonville was standing not far away, looking on the ground, as one could judge by his attitude and musing. I approached, and he said: 'The count has just gone away to look for his wife. It is a pity she was not here to consult the prophet; it would have been amusing, I dare say, to see how the count bore it. Suppose we follow him. I have asked him to introduce you.'

With a beating heart, I accompanied the Marquis d'Harmonville.

14

Mademoiselle de la Vallière

We wandered through the *salons*, the marquis and I. It was no easy matter to find a friend in rooms so crowded.

'Stay here,' said the Marquis, 'I have thought of a way of finding him. Besides, his jealousy may have warned him that there is no particular advantage to be gained by presenting you to his wife. I had better go and reason with him as you seem to wish an introduction so very much.'

This occurred in the room that is now called the Salon d'Apollon. The paintings remain in my memory, and my adventure of that evening was destined to occur there.

I sat down upon a sofa and looked about me. Three or four persons beside myself were seated on this roomy piece of gilded furniture. They were chatting all very gaily; all – except the person who sat next me, and she was a lady. Hardly two feet interposed between us. The lady sat apparently in a reverie. Nothing could be more graceful. She wore the costume perpetuated in Collignan's full-length portrait of Mademoiselle de la Vallière. It is, as you know, not only rich, but elegant. Her hair was powdered, but one could perceive that it was naturally a dark brown. One pretty little foot appeared, and could anything be more exquisite than her hand?

It was extremely provoking that this lady wore her mask, and did not, as many did, hold it for a time in her hand.

I was convinced that she was pretty. Availing myself of the privilege of a masquerade, a microcosm in which it is impossible, except by voice and allusion, to distinguish friend from foe, I spoke. 'It is not easy, mademoiselle, to deceive me,' I began.

'So much the better for monsieur,' answered the masquer, quietly.

'I mean,' I said, determined to tell my fib, 'that beauty is a gift more difficult to conceal than mademoiselle supposes.'

'Yet monsieur has succeeded very well,' she said in the same sweet and careless tones.

'I see the costume of this, the beautiful Mademoiselle de la Vallière, upon a form that surpasses her own; I raise my eyes, and I behold a mask, and yet I recognise the lady; beauty is like that precious stone in *The Arabian Nights*, which emits, no matter how concealed, a light that betrays it.'

'I know the story,' said the young lady. 'The light betrayed it, not in the sun, but in darkness. Is there so little light in these rooms, monsieur, that a poor glowworm can show so brightly. I thought we were in a luminous atmosphere, wherever a certain countess moved?'

Here was an awkward speech! How was I to answer? This lady might be, as they say some ladies are, a lover of mischief, or an intimate of the Countess de St Alyre. Cautiously, therefore, I enquired, 'What countess?'

'If you know me, you must know that she is my dearest friend. Is she not beautiful?'

'How can I answer, there are so many countesses.'

'Everyone who knows me, knows who my best beloved friend is. You don't know me.'

'That is cruel. I can scarcely believe I am mistaken.'

'With whom were you walking, just now?' she asked.

'A gentleman, a friend,' I answered,

'I saw him, of course; a friend; but I think I know him, and should like to be certain. Is he not a certain marquis?'

Here was another question that was extremely awkward.

'There are so many people here, and one may walk at one time with one, and at another with a different one, that – '

'That an unscrupulous person has no difficulty in evading a simple question like mine. Know then, once for all, that nothing disgusts a person of spirit so much as suspicion. You, monsieur, are a gentleman of discretion. I shall respect you accordingly.'

'Mademoiselle would despise me, were I to violate a confidence.'

'But you don't deceive me. You imitate your friend's diplomacy. I hate diplomacy. It means fraud and cowardice. Don't you think I know him. The gentleman with the cross of white ribbon on his breast. I know the Marquis d'Harmonville perfectly. You see to what good purpose your ingenuity has been expended.'

'To that conjecture I can answer neither yes nor no.'

'You need not. But what was your motive in mortifying a lady?'

'It is the last thing on earth I should do.'

'You affected to know me, and you don't; through caprice, or listlessness, or curiosity, you wished to converse, not with a lady, but with a costume. You admired, and you pretend to mistake me for another. But who is quite perfect? Is truth any longer to be found on earth?'

'Mademoiselle has formed a mistaken opinion of me.'

'And you also of me; you find me less foolish than you supposed. I know perfectly whom you intend amusing with compliments and melancholy declamation, and whom, with that amiable purpose, you have been seeking.'

'Tell me whom you mean,' I entreated.

'Upon one condition.'

'What is that?'

'That you will confess if I name the lady.'

'You describe my object unfairly,' I objected. 'I can't admit that I proposed speaking to any lady in the tone you describe.'

'Well, I shan't insist on that; only if I name the lady, you will promise to admit that I am right.'

'*Must* I promise?'

'Certainly not, there is no compulsion; but your promise is the only condition on which I will speak to you again.'

I hesitated for a moment; but how could she possibly tell? The countess would scarcely have admitted this little romance to anyone; and the masquer in the La Vallière costume could not possibly know who the masked domino beside her was. 'I consent,' I said, 'I promise.'

'You must promise on the honour of a gentleman.'

'Well, I do; on the honour of a gentleman.'

'Then this lady is the Countess de St Alyre.'

I was unspeakably surprised; I was disconcerted; but I remembered my promise, and said, 'The Countess de St Alyre *is*, unquestionably, the lady to whom I hoped for an introduction tonight; but I beg to assure you also, on the honour of a gentleman, that she has not the faintest imaginable suspicion that I was seeking such an honour, nor, in all probability, does she remember that such a person as I exists. I had the honour to render her and the count a trifling service, too trifling, I fear, to have earned more than an hour's recollection.'

'The world is not so ungrateful as you suppose; or if it be, there are, nevertheless, a few hearts that redeem it. I can answer for the Countess de St Alyre, she never forgets a kindness. She does not show all she feels; for she is unhappy, and cannot.'

'Unhappy! I feared, indeed, that might be. But for all the rest that you are good enough to suppose, it is but a flattering dream.'

'I told you that I am the countess's friend, and being so I must know something of her character; also, there are confidences between us, and I may know more than you think of those trifling services of which you suppose the recollection is so transitory.'

I was becoming more and more interested. I was as wicked as other young men, and the heinousness of such a pursuit was as nothing now that self-love and all the passions that mingle in such a romance were roused. The image of the beautiful countess had now again quite superseded the pretty counterpart of La Vallière, who was before me. I would have given a great deal to hear, in solemn earnest, that she did remember the champion who, for her sake, had thrown himself before the sabre of an enraged dragoon, with only a cudgel in his hand, and conquered.

'You say the countess is unhappy,' said I. 'What causes her unhappiness?'

'Many things. Her husband is old, jealous and tyrannical. Is not that enough? Even when relieved from his society, she is lonely.'

'But you are her friend?' I suggested.

'And you think one friend enough?' she answered; 'she has one alone, to whom she can open her heart.'

'Is there room for another friend?'

'Try.'

'How can I find a way?'

'She will aid you.'

'How?'

She answered by a question. 'Have you secured rooms in either of the hotels of Versailles?'

'No, I could not. I am lodged in Le Dragon Volant, which stands at the verge of the grounds of the Château de la Carque.'

'That is better still. I need not ask if you have courage for an adventure. I need not ask if you are a man of honour. A lady may trust herself to you, and fear nothing. There are few men to whom the interview, such as I shall arrange, could be granted with safety. You shall meet her at two o'clock this morning in the park of the Château de la Carque. What room do you occupy in Le Dragon Volant?'

I was amazed at the audacity and decision of this girl. Was she, as we say in England, hoaxing me?

'I can describe that accurately,' said I. 'As I look from the rear of the house in which my apartment is, I am at the extreme right, next the angle; and one pair of stairs up from the hall.'

'Very well; you must have observed, if you looked into the park, two or three clumps of chestnut and lime trees, growing so close together as to form a small grove. You must return to your hotel, change your dress and, preserving a scrupulous secrecy as to why or where you go, leave Le Dragon Volant and climb the park wall unseen; you will easily recognise the grove I have mentioned; there you will meet the countess, who will grant you an audience of a few minutes, who will expect the most scrupulous reserve on your part, and who will explain to you, in a few words, a great deal which I could not so well tell you here.'

I cannot describe the feeling with which I heard these words. I was astounded. Doubt succeeded. I could not believe these agitating words.

'Mademoiselle will believe that if I only dared assure myself that so great a happiness and honour were really intended for me my gratitude would be as lasting as my life. But how dare I believe that mademoiselle does not speak rather from her own sympathy or goodness than from a certainty that the Countess de St Alyre would concede so great an honour?'

'Monsieur believes either that I am not, as I pretend to be, in the secret which he hitherto supposed to be shared by no one but the countess and himself, or else that I am cruelly mystifying him. That I am in her confidence, I swear by all that is dear in a whispered farewell. By the last companion of this flower!' and she took for a moment in her fingers the nodding head of a white rosebud that was nestled in her bouquet. 'By my own good star, and hers – or shall I call it our "*belle étoile*"? Have I said enough?'

'Enough?' I repeated; 'more than enough – a thousand thanks.'

'And being thus in her confidence, I am clearly her friend; and being a friend would it be friendly to use her dear name so; and all for sake of practising a vulgar trick upon you – a stranger?'

'Mademoiselle will forgive me. Remember how very precious is the hope of seeing and speaking to the countess. Is it wonderful, then, that I should falter in my belief? You have convinced me, however, and will forgive my hesitation.'

'You will be at the place I have described, then, at two o'clock?'

'Assuredly,' I answered.

'And monsieur, I know, will not fail through fear. No, he need not assure me; his courage is already proved.'

'No danger, in such a case, will be unwelcome to me.'

'Had you not better go now, monsieur, and rejoin your friend.'

'I promised to wait here for my friend's return. The Count de St Alyre said that he intended to introduce me to the countess.'

'And monsieur is so simple as to believe him?'

'Why should I not?'

'Because he is jealous and cunning. You will see. He will never introduce you to his wife. He will come here and say he cannot find her, and promise another time.'

'I think I see him approaching, with my friend. No – there is no lady with him.'

'I told you so. You will wait a long time for that happiness if it is never to reach you except through his hands. In the meantime, you had better not let him see you so near me. He will suspect that we have been talking of his wife; and that will whet his jealousy and his vigilance.'

I thanked my unknown friend in the mask, and withdrawing a few steps, came by a little *circumbendibus* upon the flank of the count.

I smiled under my mask as he assured me that the Duchess de la Roquème had changed her place and taken the countess with her; but he hoped, at some very early time, to have an opportunity of enabling her to make my acquaintance.

I avoided the Marquis d'Harmonville, who was following the count.

I was afraid he might propose accompanying me home, and had no wish to be forced to make an explanation.

I lost myself quickly, therefore, in the crowd, and moved, as rapidly as it would allow me, toward the Galerie des Glaces, which lay in the direction opposite to that in which I saw the count and my friend the marquis moving.

15

Strange Story of Le Dragon Volant

These fêtes were earlier in those days, and in France, than our modern balls are in London. I consulted my watch. It was a little past twelve.

It was a still and sultry night; the magnificent suite of rooms, vast as some of them were, could not be kept at a temperature less than oppressive, especially to people with masks on. In some places the crowd was inconvenient, and the profusion of lights added to the heat. I removed my mask, therefore, as I saw some other people do, who were as careless of mystery as I. I had hardly done so, and begun to breathe more comfortably, when I heard a friendly English voice call me by my name. It was Tom Whistlewick, of the 8th Dragoons. He had unmasked, with a very flushed face, as I did. He was one of those Waterloo heroes, new from the mint of glory, whom, as a body, all the world, except France, revered; and the only thing I knew against him was a habit of allaying his thirst, which was excessive, at balls, fêtes, musical parties and all gatherings where it was to be had, with champagne; and, as he introduced me to his friend, Monsieur Carmaignac, I observed that he spoke a little thick. Monsieur Carmaignac was little, lean and as straight as a ramrod. He was bald, took snuff and wore spectacles; and, as I soon learned, held an official position.

Tom was facetious, sly, and rather difficult to understand in his present pleasant mood. He was elevating his eyebrows and screwing his lips oddly, and fanning himself vaguely with his mask.

After some agreeable conversation, I was glad to observe that he preferred silence, and was satisfied with the role of listener, as I and Monsieur Carmaignac chatted; and he seated himself, with extraordinary caution and indecision, upon a bench beside us, and seemed very soon to find a difficulty in keeping his eyes open.

'I heard you mention,' said the French gentleman, 'that you had engaged an apartment at Le Dragon Volant, about half a league from this. When I was in a different police department, about four years ago, two very strange cases were connected with that house. One was of a wealthy *émigré*, permitted to return to France, by the Em – by Napoleon. He vanished. The other – equally strange – was the case of a Russian of rank and wealth. He disappeared just as mysteriously.'

'My servant,' I said, 'gave me a confused account of some occurrences, and, as well as I recollect he described the same persons – I mean a returned French nobleman and a Russian gentleman. But he made the whole story so marvellous – I mean in the supernatural sense – that, I confess, I did not believe a word of it.'

'No, there was nothing supernatural; but a great deal inexplicable,' said the French gentleman. 'Of course, there may be theories; but the thing was never explained, nor, so far as I know, was a ray of light ever thrown upon it.'

'Pray let me hear the story,' I said. 'I think I have a claim, as it affects my quarters. You don't suspect the people of the house?'

'Oh! it has changed hands since then. But there seemed to be a fatality about a particular room.'

'Could you describe that room?'

'Certainly. It is a spacious, panelled bedroom, up one pair of stairs, in the back of the house, and at the extreme right, as you look from its windows.'

'Ho! Really? Why, then, I have got the very room!' I said, beginning to be more interested – perhaps the least bit in the world disagreeably. 'Did the people die, or were they actually spirited away?'

'No, they did not die – they disappeared very oddly. I'll tell you the particulars – I happen to know them exactly, because I made an official visit, on the first occasion, to the house, to collect evidence; and although I did not go down there upon the second, the papers came before me, and I dictated the official letter dispatched to the relations of the people who had disappeared; they had applied to the government to investigate the affair. We had letters from the same relations more than two years later, from which we learned that the missing men had never turned up.'

He took a pinch of snuff, and looked steadily at me.

'Never! I shall relate all that happened, so far as we could discover. The French noble, who was the Chevalier Château Blassemare, unlike most *émigrés* had taken the matter in time, sold a large portion of his property before the revolution had proceeded so far as to render that next to impossible, and retired with a large sum. He brought with him about half a million francs, the greater part of which he invested in French funds; a much larger sum remained in Austrian land and securities. You will observe then that this gentleman was rich, and there was no allegation of his having lost money, or being, in any way, embarrassed. You see?'

I assented.

'This gentleman's habits were not expensive in proportion to his means. He had suitable lodgings in Paris; and for a time, society, the theatres and other reasonable amusements engrossed him. He did not play. He was a middle-aged man, affecting youth, with the vanities which are usual in such persons; but, for the rest, he was a gentle and polite person, who disturbed nobody – a person, you see, not likely to provoke an enmity.'

'Certainly not,' I agreed.

'Early in the summer of 1811, he got an order permitting him to copy a picture in one of these *salons*, and came down here, to Versailles, for the purpose. His work was getting on slowly. After a time he left his hotel, here, and went, by way of change, to Le Dragon Volant; there he took, by special choice, the bedroom which has fallen to you by chance. From this time, it appeared, he painted little; and seldom visited his apartments in Paris. One night he saw the host of Le Dragon Volant, and told him that he was going into Paris, to remain for a day or two, on very particular business; that his servant would accompany him, but that he would retain his apartments at Le Dragon Volant, and return in a few days. He left some clothes there, but packed a portmanteau, took his dressing case, and the rest, and, with his servant behind his carriage, drove into Paris. You observe all this, monsieur?'

'Most attentively,' I answered.

'Well, monsieur, as soon as they were approaching his lodgings, he stopped the carriage on a sudden, told his servant that he had changed his mind; that he would sleep elsewhere that night, that he had very particular business in the north of France, not far from Rouen, that he would set out before daylight on his journey, and return in a fortnight. He called a *fiacre*, took in his hand a leather bag which, the servant said, was just large enough to hold a few shirts and a coat, but that it was enormously heavy, as he could testify, for he held it in his hand, while his master took out his purse to count thirty-six Napoleons, for which the servant was to account when he should return. He then sent him on, in the carriage; and he, with the bag I have mentioned, got into the *fiacre*. Up to that, you see, the narrative is quite clear.'

'Perfectly,' I agreed.

'Now comes the mystery,' said Monsieur Carmaignac. 'After that, the Count Château Blassemare was never more seen, so far as we can make out, by acquaintance or friend. We learned that the day before the count's stockbroker had, by his direction, sold all his stock in the French funds, and handed him the cash it realised. The reason he gave him for this measure tallied with what he said to his servant He told him that he was going to the north of France to settle some claims, and did not know exactly how much might be required. The bag, which had puzzled the servant by its weight, contained, no doubt, a large sum in gold. Will Monsieur try my snuff?'

He politely tendered his open snuff-box, of which I partook, experimentally.

'A reward was offered,' he continued, 'when the enquiry was instituted, for any information tending to throw a light upon the mystery which might be afforded by the driver of the *fiacre*, "employed on the night of" (so and so), "at about the hour of half-past ten, by a gentleman with a black-leather travelling-bag in his hand, who descended from a private carriage, and gave his servant some money, which he counted twice over". About a hundred and fifty drivers applied, but not one of them was the right man. We did, however, elicit a curious and unexpected piece of evidence in quite another quarter. What a racket that plaguey harlequin makes with his sword!'

'Intolerable!' I chimed in.

The harlequin was soon gone, and he resumed,

'The evidence I speak of came from a boy, about twelve years old, who knew the appearance of the count perfectly, having been often employed by him as a messenger. He stated that about half-past twelve o'clock on the same night – upon which you are to observe, there was a brilliant moon – he was sent (his mother having been suddenly taken ill) for the sage *femme* who lived within a stone's throw of Le Dragon Volant. His father's house, from which he started, was a mile away, or more, from that inn, in order to reach which he had to pass round the park of the Château de la Carque, at the site most remote from the point to which he was going. It passes the old churchyard of St Aubin, which is separated from the road only by a very low fence, and two or three enormous old trees. The boy was a little nervous as he approached this ancient cemetery; and, under the bright moonlight, he saw a man whom he distinctly recognised as the count, whom they designated by a sobriquet which means "the man of smiles". He was looking rueful enough now, and was seated on the side of a tombstone on which he had laid a pistol, while he was ramming home the charge of another.

'The boy got cautiously by, on tiptoe, with his eyes all the time on the Count Château Blassemare, or the man he mistook for him: his dress was not what he usually wore, but the witness swore that he could not be mistaken as to his identity. He said his face looked grave and stern; but though he did not smile, it was the same face he knew so well. Nothing would make him swerve from that. If that were he, it was the last time he was seen. He has never been heard of since. Nothing could be heard of him in the neighbourhood of Rouen. There has been no evidence of his death; and there is no sign that he is living.'

'That certainly is a most singular case,' I replied, and was about to ask a question or two, when Tom Whistlewick who, without my observing it, had been taking a ramble, returned, a great deal more awake and a great deal less tipsy.

'I say, Carmaignac, it is getting late, and I must go; I really must, for the reason I told you – and, Beckett, we must soon meet again.'

'I regret very much, monsieur, my not being able at present to relate to you the other case, that of another tenant of the very same room – a case more mysterious and sinister than the last – and which occurred in the autumn of the same year.'

'Will you both do a very good-natured thing, and come and dine with me at Le Dragon Volant tomorrow?'

So, as we pursued our way along the Galerie des Glaces, I extracted their promise.

'By Jove!' said Whistlewick, when this was done; 'look at that pagoda, or sedan chair, or whatever it is, just where those fellows set it down, and not one of them near it! I can't imagine how they tell fortunes so devilish well. Jack Nuffles – I met him here tonight – says they are gypsies. Where are they, I wonder? I'll go over and have a peep at the prophet.'

I saw him plucking at the blinds, which were constructed something on the principle of Venetian blinds; the red curtains were inside; but they did not yield, and he could only peep under one that did not come quite down.

When he rejoined us, he related: 'I could scarcely see the old fellow, it's so dark. He is covered with gold and red, and has an embroidered hat on like a mandarin's; he's fast asleep; and, by Jove, he smells like a polecat! It's worth going over only to have it to say. Fiew! pooh! oh! It *is* a perfume. Faugh!'

Not caring to accept this tempting invitation, we got along slowly toward the door. I bade them good-night, reminding them of their promise. And so I found my way at last to my carriage, and was soon rolling slowly towards Le Dragon Volant, on the loneliest of roads, under old trees, and in the soft moonlight.

What a number of things had happened within the last two hours! what a variety of strange and vivid pictures were crowded together in that brief space! What an adventure was before me!

The silent, moonlighted, solitary road, how it contrasted with the many-eddied whirl of pleasure from whose roar and music, lights, diamonds and colours, I had just extricated myself!

The sight of lonely nature at such an hour acts like a sudden sedative. The madness and guilt of my pursuit struck me with a momentary compunction and horror. I wished I had never entered the labyrinth which was leading me, I knew not whither. It was too late to think of that now; but the bitter was already stealing into my cup; and vague anticipations lay, for a few minutes, heavy on my heart. It would not have taken much to make me disclose my unmanly state of mind to my lively friend, Alfred Ogle, nor even to the milder ridicule of the agreeable Tom Whistlewick.

16

The Park of the Château de la Carque

There was no danger of Le Dragon Volant's closing its doors on that occasion till three or four in the morning. There were quartered there many servants of great people, whose masters would not leave the ball till the last moment and who could not return to their corners in Le Dragon Volant till their last services had been rendered.

I knew, therefore, I should have ample time for my mysterious excursion without exciting curiosity by being shut out.

And now we pulled up under the canopy of boughs before the sign of Le Dragon Volant and the light that shone from its hall-door.

I dismissed my carriage, ran up the broad staircase, mask in hand, with my domino fluttering about me, and entered the large bedroom. The black wainscoting and stately furniture, with the dark curtains of the very tall bed, made the night there more sombre.

An oblique patch of moonlight was thrown upon the floor from the window to which I hastened. I looked out upon the landscape slumbering in those silvery beams. There stood the outline of the Château de la Carque, its chimneys and many turrets with their extinguisher-shaped roofs black against the soft grey sky. There, also, more in the foreground, about midway between the window where I stood and the château but a little to the left, I traced the tufted masses of the grove which the lady in the mask had appointed as the trysting-place where I and the beautiful countess were to meet that night.

I took 'the bearings' of this gloomy bit of wood, whose foliage glimmered softly at top in the light of the moon.

You may guess with what a strange interest and swelling of the heart I gazed on the unknown scene of my coming adventure.

But time was flying, and the hour already near. I threw my robe upon a sofa and groped out a pair of boots, which I substituted for those thin heel-less shoes, in those days called 'pumps', without which a gentleman could not attend an evening party. I put on my hat, and lastly I took a pair of loaded pistols, which I had been advised were satisfactory companions in the then unsettled state of French society; swarms of disbanded soldiers, some of them alleged to be desperate characters, being everywhere to be met with. These preparations made, I confess I took a looking-glass to the window to see how I looked in the moonlight; and being satisfied, I replaced it, and ran downstairs.

In the hall I called for my servant.

'St Clair,' said I, 'I mean to take a little moonlight ramble, only ten minutes or so. You must not go to bed until I return. If the night is very beautiful, I may possibly extend my ramble a little.'

So down the steps I lounged, looking first over my right and then over my left shoulder, like a man uncertain which direction to take, and I sauntered up the road, gazing now at the moon and now at the thin white clouds in the opposite direction, whistling, all the time, an air which I had picked up at one of the theatres.

When I had got a couple of hundred yards away from Le Dragon Volant, my minstrelsy totally ceased; and I turned about and glanced sharply down the road, that looked as white as hoar-frost under the moon, and saw the gable of the old inn, and a window, partly concealed by the foliage, with a dusky light shining from it.

No sound of footstep was stirring; no sign of human figure in sight. I consulted my watch, which the light was sufficiently strong to enable me to do. It now wanted but eight minutes of the appointed hour. A thick mantle of ivy at this point covered the wall and rose in a clustering head at the top. It afforded me facilities for scaling the wall, and a partial screen for my operations, if any eye should chance to be looking that way. And now it was done. I was in the park of the Château de la Carque, as nefarious a poacher as ever trespassed on the grounds of unsuspicious lord!

Before me rose the appointed grove, which looked as black as a clump of gigantic hearse plumes. It seemed to tower higher and higher at every step and cast a broader and blacker shadow towards my feet. On I marched, and was glad when I plunged into the shadow, which concealed me. Now I was among the grand old lime and chestnut trees – my heart beat fast with expectation.

This grove opened, a little, near the middle; and in the space thus cleared, there stood, with a surrounding flight of steps, a small Greek temple or shrine, with a statue in the centre. It was built of white marble with fluted Corinthian columns, and the crevices were tufted with grass; moss had shown itself on pedestal and cornice, and signs of long neglect and decay were apparent in its discoloured and weather-worn marble. A few feet in front of the steps a fountain, fed from the great ponds at the other side of the château, was making a constant tinkle and plashing in a wide marble basin, and the jet of water glimmered like a shower of diamonds in the broken moonlight. The very neglect and half-ruinous state of all this made it only the prettier, as well as sadder. I was too intently watching for the arrival of the lady, in the direction of the château, to study these things; but the half-noted effect of them was romantic, and suggested somehow the grotto and the fountain and the apparition of Egeria.

As I watched a voice spoke to me, a little behind my left shoulder. I turned, almost with a start, and the masquer in the costume of Mademoiselle de la Vallière stood there.

'The countess will be here presently,' she said. The lady stood upon the open space, and the moonlight fell unbroken upon her. Nothing could be more becoming; her figure looked more graceful and elegant than ever. 'In the meantime I shall tell you some peculiarities of her situation. She is unhappy; miserable in an ill-assorted marriage, with a jealous tyrant who now would constrain her to sell her diamonds, which are – '

'Worth thirty thousand pounds sterling. I heard all that from a friend. Can I aid the countess in her unequal struggle? Say but how, and the greater the danger or the sacrifice, the happier will it make me. Can I aid her?'

'If you despise a danger – which, yet, is not a danger; if you despise, as she does, the tyrannical canons of the world; and, if you are chivalrous enough to devote yourself to a lady's cause, with no reward but her poor gratitude; if you can do these things you can aid her, and earn a foremost place, not in her gratitude only, but in her friendship.'

At those words the lady in the mask turned away and seemed to weep.

I vowed myself the willing slave of the countess. 'But,' I added, 'you told me she would soon be here.'

'That is, if nothing unforeseen should happen; but with the eye of the Count de St Alyre in the house, and open, it is seldom safe to stir.'

'Does she wish to see me?' I asked, with a tender hesitation.

'First, say have you really thought of her, more than once, since the adventure of the Belle Etoile?'

'She never leaves my thoughts; day and night her beautiful eyes haunt me; her sweet voice is always in my ear.'

'Mine is said to resemble hers,' said the masquer.

'So it does,' I answered. 'But it is only a resemblance.'

'Oh! then mine is better?'

'Pardon me, mademoiselle, I did not say that. Yours is a sweet voice, but I fancy a little higher.'

'A little shriller, you would say,' answered the de la Vallière, I fancied a good deal vexed.

'No, not shriller: your voice is not shrill, it is beautifully sweet; but not so pathetically sweet as hers.'

'That is prejudice, monsieur; it is not true.'

I bowed; I could not contradict a lady.

'I see, monsieur, you laugh at me; you think me vain, because I claim in some points to be equal to the Countess de St Alyre. I challenge you to say my hand, at least, is less beautiful than hers.' As she thus spoke, she drew her glove off and extended her hand, back upward, in the moonlight.

The lady seemed really nettled. It was undignified and irritating; for in this uninteresting competition the precious moments were flying, and my interview leading apparently to nothing.

'You will admit, then, that my hand is as beautiful as hers?'

'I cannot admit it, mademoiselle,' said I, with the honesty of irritation. 'I will not enter into comparisons, but the Countess de St Alyre is, in all respects, the most beautiful lady I ever beheld.'

The masquer laughed coldly, and then, more and more softly, said, with a sigh, 'I will prove all I say.' And as she spoke she removed the mask and the Countess de St Alyre, smiling, confused, bashful, more beautiful than ever, stood before me!

'Good heavens!' I exclaimed. 'How monstrously stupid I have been. And it was to Madame la Comtesse that I spoke for so long in the *salon*!' I gazed on her in silence. And with a low sweet laugh of good nature she extended her hand. I took it, and carried it to my lips.

'No, you must not do that,' she said, quietly, 'we are not old enough friends yet. I find, although you were mistaken, that you do remember the Countess of the Belle Etoile, and that you are a champion true and fearless. Had you yielded to the claims just now pressed upon you by the rivalry of Mademoiselle de la Vallière, in her mask, the Countess de St Alyre should never have trusted or seen you more. I now am sure that you are true, as well as brave. You now know that I have not forgotten you; and, also, that if you would risk your life for me, I, too, would brave some danger, rather than lose my friend for ever. I have but a few moments more. Will you come here again tomorrow night, at a quarter past eleven? I will be here at that moment; you must exercise the most scrupulous care to prevent suspicion that you have come here, monsieur. *You owe that to me.*'

She spoke these last words with the most solemn entreaty.

I vowed again and again that I would die rather than permit the least rashness to endanger the secret which made all the interest and value of my life.

She was looking, I thought, more and more beautiful every moment. My enthusiasm expanded in proportion.

'You must come tomorrow night by a different route,' she said; 'and if you come again, we can change it once more. At the other side of the château there is a little churchyard with a ruined chapel. The neighbours are afraid to pass it by night. The road is deserted there, and a stile opens a way into these grounds. Cross it and you can find a covert of thickets to within fifty steps of this spot.'

I promised, of course, to observe her instructions implicitly.

'I have lived for more than a year in an agony of irresolution. I have decided at last. I have lived a melancholy life; a lonelier life than is passed in the cloister. I have had no one to confide in; no one to advise me; no one to save me from the horrors of my existence. I have found a brave and prompt friend at last. Shall I ever forget the heroic tableau of the hall of the Belle Etoile? Have you – have you really kept the rose I gave you, as we parted? Yes – you swear it. You need not; I trust you. Richard, how often have I in solitude repeated your name, learned from my servant. Richard, my hero! Oh! Richard! Oh, my king! I love you!'

I would have folded her to my heart – thrown myself at her feet. But this beautiful and – shall I say it – inconsistent woman constrained me.

'No, we must not waste our moments in extravagances. Understand my case. There is no such thing as indifference in the married state. Not to love one's husband,' she continued, 'is to hate him. The count, ridiculous in all else, is formidable in his jealousy. In mercy, then, to me, observe caution. Affect to all you speak to the most complete ignorance of all the people in the Château de la Carque; and, if anyone in your presence mentions the Count or Countess de St Alyre, be sure you say you never saw either. I shall have more to say to you tomorrow night. I have reasons that I cannot now explain for all I do and all I postpone. Farewell. Go! Leave me.'

She waved me back, peremptorily. I echoed her 'farewell', and obeyed.

This interview had not lasted, I think, more than ten minutes. I scaled the park wall again, and reached Le Dragon Volant before its doors were closed.

I lay awake in my bed, in a fever of elation. I saw, till the dawn broke and chased the vision, the beautiful Countess de St Alyre, always in the dark, before me.

17

The Tenant of the Palanquin

The marquis called on me next day. My late breakfast was still upon the table.

He had come, he said, to ask a favour. An accident had happened to his carriage in the crowd on leaving the ball, and he begged, if I were going into Paris, a seat in mine. I was going in, and was extremely glad of his company. He came with me to my hotel; we went up to my rooms. I was surprised to see a man seated in an easy chair, with his back towards us, reading a newspaper. He rose. It was the Count de St Alyre, his gold spectacles on his nose; his black wig, in oily curls, lying close to his narrow head and looking like carved ebony over a repulsive visage of boxwood. His black muffler had been pulled down. His right arm was in a sling. I don't know whether there was anything unusual in his countenance that day or whether it was but the effect of prejudice arising from all I had heard in my mysterious interview in his park, but I thought his countenance was more strikingly forbidding than I had seen it before.

I was not callous enough in the ways of sin to meet this man, injured at least in intent, thus suddenly without a momentary disturbance.

He smiled.

'I called, Monsieur Beckett, in the hope of finding you here,' he croaked, 'and I meditated, I fear, taking a great liberty, but my friend the Marquis d'Harmonville, on whom I have perhaps some claim, will perhaps give me the assistance I require so much.'

'With great pleasure,' said the marquis, 'but not till after six o'clock. I must go this moment to a meeting of three or four people, whom I cannot disappoint, and I know, perfectly, we cannot break up earlier.'

'What am I to do?' exclaimed the count, 'an hour would have done it all. Was ever *contretemps* so unlucky?'

'I'll give you an hour, with pleasure,' said I.

'How very good of you, monsieur, I hardly dare to hope it. The business, for so gay and charming a man as Monsieur Beckett, is a little *funeste*. Pray read this note which reached me this morning.'

It certainly was not cheerful. It was a note stating that the body of the count's cousin, Monsieur de St Amand, who had died at his house, the Château Clery, had been, in accordance with his written directions, sent for burial at Père Lachaise, and, with the permission of the Count de St Alyre, would reach his house (the Château de la Carque) at about ten o'clock on the night following, to be conveyed thence in a hearse, with any member of the family who might wish to attend the obsequies.

'I did not see the poor gentleman twice in my life,' said the count, 'but this office, as he has no other kinsman, disagreeable as it is, I could scarcely decline, and so I want to attend at the cemetery to have the book signed, and the order entered. But here is another misery. By ill luck, I have sprained my thumb, and can't sign my name for a week to come. However, one name answers as well as another. Yours as well as mine. And as you are so good as to come with me, all will go right.'

Away we drove. The count gave me a memorandum of the Christian and surnames of the deceased, his age, the complaint he died of, and the usual particulars; also a note of the exact position in which a grave, the dimensions of which were described, of the ordinary simple kind, was to be dug, between two vaults belonging to the family of St Amand. The funeral, it was stated, would arrive at half-past one o'clock a.m. (the next night but one); and he handed me the money, with extra fees for a burial by night. It was a good deal; and I asked him, as he entrusted the whole affair to me, in whose name I should take the receipt.

'Not in mine, my good friend. They wanted me to become an executor, which I, yesterday, wrote to decline; and I am informed that if the receipt were in my name it would constitute me an executor in the eye of the law, and fix me in that position. Take it, pray, if you have no objection, in your own name.'

This, accordingly, I did.

You will see, by and by, why I am obliged to mention all these particulars.

The count, meanwhile, was leaning back in the carriage, with his black silk muffler up to his nose, and his hat shading his eyes, while he dozed in his corner; in which state I found him on my return.

Paris had lost its charm for me. I hurried through the little business I had to do, longing once more for my quiet room in Le Dragon Volant, the melancholy woods of the Château de la Carque and the tumultuous and thrilling influence of proximity to the object of my wild but wicked romance.

I was delayed some time by my stockbroker. I had a very large sum, as I told you, at my banker's, uninvested. I cared very little for a few days' interest – very little for the entire sum, compared with the image that occupied my thoughts and beckoned me with a white arm through the dark towards the spreading lime trees and chestnuts of the Château de la Carque. But I had fixed this day to meet him, and was relieved when he told me that I had better let it lie in my banker's hands for a few days longer as the funds would certainly fall immediately. This accident, too, was not without its immediate bearing on my subsequent adventures.

When I reached Le Dragon Volant, I found in my sitting-room, a good deal to my chagrin, my two guests, whom I had quite forgotten. I inwardly cursed my own stupidity for having embarrassed myself with their agreeable society. It could not be helped now, however, and a word to the waiters put all things in train for dinner.

Tom Whistlewick was in great force; and he commenced almost immediately with a very odd story.

He told me that not only Versailles, but all Paris, was in a ferment, in consequence of a revolting, and all but sacrilegious, practical joke, played off on the night before.

The pagoda, as he persisted in calling the palanquin, had been left standing on the spot where we last saw it. Neither conjuror, nor usher, nor bearers had ever returned. When the ball closed, and the company at length retired, the servants who attended to put out the lights and secure the doors found it still there.

It was determined, however, to let it stand where it was until next morning, by which time, it was conjectured, its owners would send messengers to remove it.

None arrived. The servants were then ordered to take it away; and its extraordinary weight, for the first time, reminded them of its forgotten human occupant. Its door was forced; and judge what was their disgust when they discovered not a living man but a corpse! Three or four days must have passed since the death of the burly man in the Chinese tunic and painted cap. Some people thought it was a trick designed to insult the allies, in whose honour the ball was got up. Others were of opinion that it was nothing worse than a daring and cynical jocularity which, shocking as it was, might yet be forgiven as arising from the high spirits and irrepressible buffoonery of youth. Others, again, fewer in number, and mystically given, insisted that the corpse was *bona fide* necessary to the exhibition, and that the disclosures and allusions which had astonished so many people were distinctly due to necromancy.

'The matter, however, is now in the hands of the police,' observed Monsieur Carmaignac, 'and we are not the force we were two or three months ago if the offenders against propriety and public feeling are not traced and convicted, unless, indeed, they have been a great deal more cunning than such fools generally are.'

I was thinking within myself how utterly inexplicable was my colloquy with the conjuror, so cavalierly dismissed by Monsieur Carmaignac as a 'fool'; and the more I thought the more marvellous it seemed.

'It certainly was an original joke, though not a very clear one,' said Whistlewick.

'Not even original,' said Carmaignac. 'Very nearly the same thing was done, a hundred years ago or more, at a state ball in Paris; and the rascals who played the trick were never found out.'

In this Monsieur Carmaignac, as I afterwards discovered, spoke truly; for, among my books of French anecdote and memoir, the very incident is marked, by my own hand.

While we were thus talking, the waiter told us that dinner was served; and we withdrew accordingly; my guests more than making amends for my comparative taciturnity.

18

The Churchyard

Our dinner was really good, so were the wines; better, perhaps, at this out-of-the-way inn than at some of the more pretentious hotels in Paris. The moral effect of a really good dinner is immense – we all felt it. The serenity and good nature that follow are more solid and comfortable than the tumultuous benevolences of Bacchus.

My friends were happy, therefore, and very chatty; which latter relieved me of the trouble of talking, and prompted them to entertain me and one another incessantly with agreeable stories and conversation, of which, until suddenly a subject emerged which interested me powerfully, I confess, so much were my thoughts engaged elsewhere, I heard next to nothing.

'Yes,' said Carmaignac, continuing a conversation which had escaped me, 'there was another case, beside that Russian nobleman, odder still. I remembered it this morning, but cannot recall the name. He was a tenant of the very same room. By the by, monsieur, might it not be as well,' he added, turning to me, with a laugh, half joke whole earnest, as they say, 'if you were to get into another apartment now that the house is no longer crowded? that is, if you mean to make any stay here.'

'A thousand thanks, no. I'm thinking of changing my hotel; and I can run into town so easily at night; and though I stay here, for this night, at least, I don't expect to vanish like those others. But you say there is another adventure, of the same kind, connected with the same room. Do let us hear it. But take some wine first.'

The story he told was curious.

'It happened,' said Carmaignac, 'as well as I recollect, before either of the other cases. A French gentleman – I wish I could remember his name – the son of a merchant, came to this inn (Le Dragon Volant), and was put by the landlord into the same room of which we have been speaking. Your apartment, monsieur. He was by no means young – past forty – and very far from good-looking. The people here said that he was the ugliest man, and the most good-natured, that ever lived. He played on the fiddle, sang and wrote poetry. His habits were odd and desultory. He would sometimes sit all day in his room writing, singing and fiddling, and go out at night for a walk. An eccentric man! He was by no means a millionaire, but he had a *modicum bonum*, you understand – a trifle more than half a million francs. He consulted his stockbroker about investing this money in foreign stocks, and drew the entire sum from his banker. You now have the situation of affairs when the catastrophe occurred.'

'Pray fill your glass,' I said.

'Dutch courage, monsieur, to face the catastrophe!' said Whistlewick, filling his own.

'Now, that was the last that ever was heard of his money,' resumed Carmaignac. 'You shall hear about events. The night after this financial operation, he was seized with a poetic frenzy: he sent for the then landlord of this house, and told him that he had long meditated an epic, and meant to commence that night, and that he was on no account to be disturbed until nine o'clock in the morning. He had two pairs of wax candles, a little cold supper on a side table, his desk open, paper enough upon it to contain the entire *Henriade*, and a proportionate store of pens and ink.

'Seated at this desk he was seen by the waiter who brought him a cup of coffee at nine o'clock, at which time the intruder said he was writing fast enough to set fire to the paper – that was his phrase; he did not look up, he appeared too much engrossed. But when the waiter came back, half an hour afterwards, the door was locked; and the poet, from within, answered that he must not be disturbed.

'Away went the *garçon*. Next morning at nine o'clock he knocked at the door, and receiving no answer, looked through the keyhole; the lights were still burning, the window-shutters were closed as he had left them; he renewed his knocking, knocked louder, no answer came. He reported this continued and alarming silence to the innkeeper, who, finding that his guest had not left his key in the lock, succeeded in finding another that opened it. The candles were just giving up the ghost in their sockets, but there was light enough to ascertain that the tenant of the room was gone! The bed had not been disturbed; the window-shutter was barred. He must have let himself out, and locking the door on the outside, put the key in his pocket, and so made his way out of the house. Here, however, was another difficulty: Le Dragon Volant shut its doors and made all fast at twelve o'clock; after that hour no one could leave the house, except by obtaining the key and letting himself out, and of necessity leaving the door unsecured, unless he had the collusion and aid of some person in the house.

'Now it happened that some time after the doors were secured, at half-past twelve, a servant who had not been apprised of his order to be left undisturbed, seeing a light shine through the keyhole, knocked at the door to enquire whether the poet wanted anything. He was very little obliged to his disturber, and dismissed him with a renewed charge that he was not to be interrupted again during the night. This incident established the fact that he was in the house after the doors had been locked and barred. The innkeeper himself kept the keys, and swore that he found them hung on the wall above his head over his bed, in their usual place, in the morning; and that nobody could have taken them away without awakening him. That was all we could discover. The Count de St Alyre, to whom this house belongs, was very active and very much chagrined. But nothing was discovered.'

'And nothing heard since of the epic poet?' I asked.

'Nothing – not the slightest clue – he never turned up again. I suppose he is dead; if he is not, he must have got into some devilish bad scrape, of which we have heard nothing, that compelled him to abscond with all the secrecy and expedition in his power. All that we know for certain is that, having occupied the room in which you sleep, he vanished, nobody ever knew how, and never was heard of since.'

'You have now mentioned three cases,' I said, 'and all from the same room.'

'Three. Yes, all equally unintelligible. When men are murdered, the great and immediate difficulty the assassins encounter is how to conceal the body. It is very hard to believe that three persons should have been consecutively murdered, in the same room, and their bodies so effectually disposed of that no trace of them was ever discovered.'

From this we passed to other topics, and the grave Monsieur Carmaignac amused us with a perfectly prodigious collection of scandalous anecdotes, which his opportunities in the police department had enabled him to accumulate.

My guests happily had engagements in Paris, and left me about ten.

I went up to my room, and looked out upon the grounds of the Château de la Carque. The moonlight was broken by clouds, and the view of the park in this desultory light acquired a melancholy and fantastic character.

The strange anecdotes, recounted of the room in which I stood by Monsieur Carmaignac, returned vaguely upon my mind, drowning in sudden shadows the gaiety of the more frivolous stories with which he had followed them. I looked round me on the room that lay in ominous gloom with an almost disagreeable sensation. I took my pistols now with an undefined apprehension that they might be really needed before my return tonight. This feeling, be it understood, in no wise chilled my ardour. Never had my enthusiasm mounted higher. My adventure absorbed and carried me away; but it added a strange and stern excitement to the expedition.

I loitered for a time in my room. I had ascertained the exact point at which the little churchyard lay. It was about a mile away. I did not wish to reach it earlier than necessary.

I stole quietly out, and sauntered along the road to my left, and thence entered a narrower track, still to my left, which, skirting the park wall, and describing a circuitous route all the way, under grand old trees, passes the ancient cemetery. That cemetery is embowered in trees, and occupies little more than half an acre of ground to the left of the road interposing between it and the park of the Château de la Carque.

Here, at this haunted spot, I paused and listened. The place was utterly silent. A thick cloud had darkened the moon, so that I could distinguish little more than the outlines of near objects, and that vaguely enough; and sometimes, as it were floating in black fog, the white surface of a tombstone emerged.

Among the forms that met my eye against the iron-grey of the horizon were some of those shrubs or trees that grow like our junipers, some six feet high, in form like a miniature poplar, with the darker foliage of the yew. I do not know the name of the plant, but I have often seen it in such funereal places.

Knowing that I was a little too early, I sat down upon the edge of a tombstone to wait, as, for aught I knew, the beautiful countess might have wise reasons for not caring that I should enter the grounds of the château earlier than she had appointed. In the listless state induced by waiting, I sat there, with my eyes on the object straight before me, which chanced to be the faint black outline of a tree such as I have described. It was right before me, about half a dozen steps away.

The moon now began to escape from under the skirt of the cloud that had hid her face for so long; and, as the light gradually improved, the tree on which I had been lazily staring began to take a new shape. It was no longer a tree, but a man standing motionless. Brighter and brighter grew the moonlight, clearer and clearer the image became, and at last stood out perfectly distinctly. It was Colonel Gaillarde.

Luckily, he was not looking towards me. I could only see him in profile; but there was no mistaking the white moustache, the *farouche* visage, and the gaunt six-foot stature. There he was, his shoulder towards me, listening and watching, plainly, for some signal or person expected, straight in front of him.

If he were by chance to turn his eyes in my direction, I knew that I must reckon upon an instantaneous renewal of the combat only commenced in the hall of the Belle Etoile. In any case, could malignant fortune have posted, at this place and hour, a more dangerous watcher? What ecstasy to him, by a single discovery, to hit me so hard, and blast the Countess de St Alyre, whom he seemed to hate.

He raised his arm; he whistled softly; I heard an answering whistle as low; and, to my relief, the colonel advanced in the direction of this sound, widening the distance between us at every step; and immediately I heard talking, but in a low and cautious key.

I recognised, I thought, even so, the peculiar voice of Gaillarde.

I stole softly forward in the direction in which those sounds were audible. In doing so, I had, of course, to use the extremest caution.

I thought I saw a hat above a jagged piece of ruined wall, and then a second – yes, I saw two hats conversing; the voices came from under them. They moved off, not in the direction of the park, but of the road, and I lay along the grass, peeping over a grave, as a skirmisher might, observing the enemy. One after the other, the figures emerged full into view as they mounted the stile at the roadside. The colonel, who was last, stood on the wall for awhile, looking about him, and then jumped down on the road. I heard their steps and talk as they moved away together, with their backs towards me, in the direction which led them farther and farther from Le Dragon Volant.

I waited until these sounds were quite lost in distance before I entered the park. I followed the instructions I had received from the Countess de St Alyre and made my way among brushwood and thickets to the point nearest the ruinous temple, and then crossed the short intervening space of open ground rapidly.

I was now once more under the gigantic boughs of the old lime and chestnut trees; softly, and with a heart throbbing fast, I approached the little structure.

The moon was now shining steadily, pouring down its radiance on the soft foliage, and here and there mottling the verdure under my feet.

I reached the steps; I was among its worn marble shafts. She was not there, nor in the inner sanctuary, the arched windows of which were screened almost entirely by masses of ivy. The lady had not yet arrived.

19

The Key

I stood now upon the steps, watching and listening. In a minute or two I heard the crackle of withered sticks trod upon, and, looking in the direction, I saw a figure approaching among the trees, wrapped in a mantle.

I advanced eagerly. It was the countess. She did not speak, but gave me her hand, and I led her to the scene of our last interview. She repressed the ardour of my impassioned greeting with a gentle but peremptory firmness. She removed her hood, shook back her beautiful hair, and, gazing on me with sad and glowing eyes, sighed deeply. Some awful thought seemed to weigh upon her.

'Richard, I must speak plainly. The crisis of my life has come. I am sure you would defend me. I think you pity me; perhaps you even love me.'

At these words I became eloquent, as young madmen in my plight do. She silenced me, however with the same melancholy firmness.

'Listen, dear friend, and then say whether you can aid me. How madly I am trusting you; and yet my heart tells me how wisely! To meet you here as I do – what insanity it seems! How poorly you must think of me! But when you know all, you will judge me fairly. Without your aid I cannot accomplish my purpose. That purpose unaccomplished, I must die. I am chained to a man whom I despise – whom I abhor. I have resolved to fly. I have jewels, principally diamonds, for which I am offered thirty thousand pounds of your English money. They are my separate property by my marriage settlement; I will take them with me. You are a judge, no doubt, of jewels. I was counting mine when the hour came, and brought this in my hand to show you. Look.'

'It is magnificent!' I exclaimed, as a collar of diamonds twinkled and flashed in the moonlight, suspended from her pretty fingers. I thought, even at that tragic moment, that she prolonged the show, with a feminine delight in these brilliant toys.

'Yes,' she said, 'I shall part with them all. I will turn them into money, and break, for ever, the unnatural and wicked bonds that tied me, in the name of a sacrament, to a tyrant. A man young, handsome, generous, brave as you, can hardly be rich. Richard, you say you love me; you shall share all this with me. We will fly together to Switzerland; we will evade pursuit; my powerful friends will intervene and arrange a separation, and I shall, at length, be happy and reward my hero.'

You may suppose the style, florid and vehement, in which I poured forth my gratitude, vowed the devotion of my life, and placed myself absolutely at her disposal.

'Tomorrow night,' she said, 'my husband will attend the remains of his cousin, Monsieur de St Amand, to Père Lachaise. The hearse, he says, will leave this at half-past nine. You must be here, where we stand, at nine o'clock.'

I promised punctual obedience.

'I will not meet you here; but you see a red light in the window of the tower at that angle of the château?'

I assented.

'I placed it there that tomorrow night, when it comes, you may recognise it. So soon as that rose-coloured light appears at that window, it will be a signal to you that the funeral has left the château, and that you may approach safely. Come, then, to that window; I will open it and admit you. Five minutes after, a travelling-carriage, with four horses, shall stand ready in the *porte-cochère*. I will place my diamonds in your hands; and so soon as we enter the carriage, our flight commences. We shall have at least five hours' start; and with energy, stratagem and resource, I fear nothing. Are you ready to undertake all this for my sake?'

Again I vowed myself her slave.

'My only difficulty,' she said, 'is how we shall quickly enough convert my diamonds into money; I dare not remove them while my husband is in the house.'

Here was the opportunity I wished for. I now told her that I had in my banker's hands no less a sum than thirty thousand pounds, with which, in the shape of gold and notes, I should come furnished, and thus the risk and loss of disposing of her diamonds in too much haste would be avoided.

'Good heaven!' she exclaimed, with a kind of disappointment. 'You are rich, then? and I have lost the felicity of making my generous friend more happy. Be it so, since so it must be. Let us contribute, each, in equal shares, to our common fund. Bring you, your money; I, my jewels. There is a happiness to me even in mingling my resources with yours.'

On this there followed a romantic colloquy, all poetry and passion, such as I should in vain endeavour to reproduce.

Then came a very special instruction.

'I have come provided, too, with a key, the use of which I must explain.'

It was a double key – a long, slender stem, with a key at each end – one about the size which opens an ordinary room door; the other, as small, almost, as the key of a dressing-case.

'You cannot employ too much caution tomorrow night. An interruption would murder all my hopes. I have learned that you occupy the haunted room in Le Dragon Volant. It is the very room I would have wished you in. I will tell you why – there is a story of a man who, having shut himself up in that room one night, disappeared before morning. The truth is, he wanted, I believe, to escape from creditors; and the host of Le Dragon Volant, at that time, being a rogue, aided him in absconding. My husband investigated the matter, and discovered how his escape was made. It was by means of this key. Here is a memorandum and a plan describing how it is to be applied. I have taken it from the count's escritoire. And now, once more I must leave to your ingenuity how to mystify the people at Le Dragon Volant. Be sure you try the keys first, to see that the locks turn freely. I will have my jewels ready. You, whatever we divide, had better bring your money, because it may be many months before you can revisit Paris, or disclose our place of residence to anyone; and our passports – arrange all that, in what names and whither you please. And now, dear Richard' (she leaned her arm fondly on my shoulder, and looked with ineffable passion in my eyes, with her other hand clasped in mine), 'my very life is in your hands; I have staked all on your fidelity.'

As she spoke the last word, she, on a sudden, grew deadly pale, and gasped, 'Good God! who is here?'

At the same moment she receded through the door in the marble screen, close to which she stood, and behind which was a small roofless chamber, as small as the shrine, the window of which was darkened by a clustering mass of ivy so dense that hardly a gleam of light came through the leaves.

I stood upon the threshold which she had just crossed, looking in the direction in which she had thrown that one terrified glance. No wonder she was frightened. Quite close upon us, not twenty yards away, and approaching at a quick step, very distinctly lighted by the moon, Colonel Gaillarde and his companion were coming. The shadow of the cornice and a piece of wall were upon me. Unconscious of this, I was expecting the moment when, with one of his frantic yells, he should spring forward to assail me.

I made a step backwards, drew one of my pistols from my pocket and cocked it. It was obvious he had not seen me.

I stood, with my finger on the trigger, determined to shoot him dead if he should attempt to enter the place where the countess was. It would, no doubt, have been a murder; but, in my mind, I had no question or qualm about it. When once we engage in secret and guilty practices we are nearer other and greater crimes than we at all suspect.

There's the statue,' said the colonel, in his brief discordant tones. 'That's the figure.'

'Alluded to in the stanzas?' enquired his companion.

'The very thing. We shall see more next time. Forward, monsieur; let us march.'

And, much to my relief, the gallant colonel turned on his heel, and marched through the trees, with his back towards the château, striding over the grass, as I quickly saw, to the park wall, which they crossed not far from the gables of Le Dragon Volant.

I found the countess trembling in no affected, but a very real terror. She would not hear of my accompanying her towards the château. But I told her that I would prevent the return of the mad colonel; and upon that point, at least, she need fear nothing. She quickly recovered, again bade me a fond and lingering good-night, and left me, gazing after her, with the key in my hand, and such a phantasmagoria floating in my brain as amounted very nearly to madness.

There was I, ready to brave all dangers, all right and reason, plunge into murder itself, on the first summons, and entangle myself in consequences inextricable and horrible (what cared I?) for a woman of whom I knew nothing but that she was beautiful and reckless!

I have often thanked heaven for its mercy in conducting me through the labyrinths in which I had all but lost myself.

20

A High-Cauld-Cap

I was now upon the road, within two or three hundred yards of Le Dragon Volant. I had undertaken an adventure with a vengeance! And by way of prelude, there not improbably awaited me, at my inn, another encounter, perhaps this time not so lucky, with the grotesque sabreur.

I was glad I had my pistols. I certainly was bound by no law to allow a ruffian to cut me down, unresisting.

Stooping boughs from the old park, gigantic poplars on the other side, and the moonlight over all, made the narrow road to the inn-door picturesque.

I could not think very clearly just now; events were succeeding one another so rapidly, and I, involved in the action of a drama so extravagant and guilty, hardly knew myself or believed my own story as I slowly paced towards the still open door of the inn.

No sign of the colonel, visible or audible, was there. In the hall I enquired. No gentleman had arrived at the inn for the last half-hour. I looked into the public room. It was deserted. The clock struck twelve, and I heard the servant barring the great door. I took my candle. The lights in this rural hostelry were by this time out, and the house had the air of one that had settled to slumber for many hours. The cold moonlight streamed in at the window on the landing as I ascended the broad staircase; and I paused for a moment to look over the wooded grounds to the turreted château, to me so full of interest. I bethought me, however, that prying eyes might read a meaning in this midnight gazing, and possibly the count himself might, in his jealous mood, surmise a signal in this unwonted light in the stair-window of Le Dragon Volant.

On opening my room door, with a little start I met an extremely old woman with the longest face I ever saw; she had what used to be termed a high-cauld-cap on, the white border of which contrasted with her brown and yellow skin and made her wrinkled face more ugly. She raised her curved shoulders, and looked up in my face, with eyes unnaturally black and bright.

'I have lighted a little wood, monsieur, because the night is chill.'

I thanked her, but she did not go. She stood with her candle in her tremulous fingers.

'Excuse an old woman, monsieur,' she said; 'but what on earth can a young English milord, with all Paris at his feet, find to amuse him in Le Dragon Volant?'

Had I been at the age of fairy tales, and in daily intercourse with the delightful Countess d'Aulnois, I should have seen in this withered apparition the *genius loci*, the malignant fairy, at the stamp of whose foot the ill-fated tenants of this very room had, from time to time, vanished. I was past that, however; but the old woman's dark eyes were fixed on mine with a steady meaning that plainly told me that my secret was known. I was embarrassed and alarmed; I never thought of asking her what business that was of hers.

'These old eyes saw you in the park of the château tonight.'

'*I!*' I began, with all the scornful surprise I could affect.

'It avails nothing, monsieur; I know why you stay here; and I tell you to begone. Leave this house tomorrow morning, and never come again.'

She lifted her disengaged hand, as she looked at me with intense horror in her eyes.

'There is nothing on earth – I don't know what you mean,' I answered; 'and why should you care about me?'

'I don't care about you, monsieur – I care about the honour of an ancient family, whom I served in their happier days, when to be noble was to be honoured. But my words are thrown away, monsieur; you are insolent. I will keep my secret, and you, yours; that is all. You will soon find it hard enough to divulge it.'

The old woman went slowly from the room and shut the door, before I had made up my mind to say anything. I was standing where she had left me, nearly five minutes later. The jealousy of Monsieur the Count, I assumed, appears to this old creature about the most terrible thing in creation. Whatever contempt I might entertain for the dangers which this old lady so darkly intimated, it was by no means pleasant, you may suppose, that a secret so dangerous should be so much as suspected by a stranger, and that stranger a partisan of the Count de St Alyre.

Ought I not, at all risks, to apprise the countess, who had trusted me so generously, or, as she said herself, so madly, of the fact that our secret was, at least, suspected by another? But was there not greater danger in attempting to communicate? What did the beldame mean by saying, 'Keep your secret, and I'll keep mine?'

I had a thousand distracting questions before me. My progress seemed like a journey through the Spessart, where at every step some new goblin or monster starts from the ground or steps from behind a tree.

Peremptorily I dismissed these harassing and frightful doubts. I secured my door, sat myself down at my table, and with a candle at each side, placed before me the piece of vellum which contained the drawings and notes on which I was to rely for full instructions as to how to use the key.

When I had studied this for a while, I made my investigation. The angle of the room at the right side of the window was cut off by an oblique turn in the wainscot. I examined this carefully, and, on pressure, a small bit of the frame of the woodwork slid aside, and disclosed a keyhole. On my removing my finger, it shot back to its place again, with a spring. So far I had interpreted my instructions successfully. A similar search, next the door, and directly under this, was rewarded by a like discovery. The small end of the key fitted this, as it had the upper keyhole; and now, with two or three hard jerks at the key, a door in the panel opened, showing a strip of the bare wall, and a narrow, arched doorway, piercing the thickness of the wall, within which I saw a screw staircase of stone.

Candle in hand, I stepped in. I do not know whether the quality of air, long undisturbed, is peculiar; to me it has always seemed so, and the damp smell of the old masonry hung in this atmosphere. My candle faintly lighted the bare stone wall that enclosed the stair, the foot of which I could not see. Down I went, and a few turns brought me to the stone floor. Here was another door, of the simple old oak kind, deep sunk in the thickness of the wall. The large end of the key fitted this. The lock was stiff; I set the candle down upon the stair, and applied both hands; it turned with difficulty, and as it revolved, uttered a shriek that alarmed me for my secret.

For some minutes I did not move. In a little time, however, I took courage and opened the door. The night-air floating in, puffed out the candle. There was a thicket of holly and underwood, as dense as a jungle, close about the door. I should have been in pitch-darkness were it not that through the topmost leaves there twinkled, here and there, a glimmer of moonshine.

Softly, lest anyone should have opened his window at the sound of the rusty bolt, I struggled through this till I gained a view of the open grounds. Here I found that the brushwood spread a good way up the park, uniting with the wood that approached the little temple I have described.

A general could not have chosen a more effectually covered approach from Le Dragon Volant to the trysting-place where hitherto I had conferred with the idol of my lawless adoration.

Looking back upon the old inn, I discovered that the stair I had descended was enclosed in one of those slender turrets that decorate such buildings. It was placed at that angle which corresponded with the part of the panelling of my room indicated in the plan I had been studying.

Thoroughly satisfied with my experiment, I made my way back to the door, with some little difficulty remounted to my room, locked my secret door again, kissed the mysterious key that her hand had pressed that night and placed it under my pillow, upon which, very soon after, my giddy head was laid, not, for some time, to sleep soundly.

I See Three Men in a Mirror

I awoke very early next morning, and was too excited to sleep again. As soon as I could, without exciting remark, I saw my host. I told him that I was going into town that night, and thence to Rouen, where I had to see some people on business, and requested him to mention my being there to any friend who might call. That I expected to be back in about a week, and that in the meantime my servant, St Clair, would keep the key of my room, and look after my things.

Having prepared this mystification for my landlord, I drove into Paris, and there transacted the financial part of the affair. The problem was to reduce my balance, nearly thirty thousand pounds, to a shape in which it would be not only easily portable, but available, wherever I might go, without involving correspondence or any other incident which would disclose my place of residence for the time being. All these points were as nearly provided for as they could be. I need not trouble you about my arrangements for passports. It is enough to say that the point I selected for our flight was, in the spirit of romance, one of the most beautiful and sequestered nooks in Switzerland.

Luggage, I should start with none. The first considerable town we reached next morning would supply an extemporised wardrobe. It was now two o'clock; only two! How on earth was I to dispose of the remainder of the day?

I had not yet seen the cathedral of Notre Dame and thither I drove. I spent an hour or more there and then visited the Conciergerie, the Palais de Justice and the beautiful Sainte Chapelle. Still there remained some time to get rid of, and I strolled into the narrow streets adjoining the cathedral. I recollect seeing, in one of them, an old house with a mural inscription stating that it had been the residence of Canon Fulbert, the uncle of Abelard's Eloise. I don't know whether these curious old streets, in which I observed fragments of ancient Gothic churches fitted up as warehouses, are still extant. I lighted, among other dingy and eccentric shops, upon one that seemed that of a broker of all sorts of old decorations, armour, china, furniture. I entered the shop; it was dark, dusty and low. The proprietor was busy scouring a piece of inlaid armour, and allowed me to poke about his shop, and examine the curious things accumulated there, just as I pleased. Gradually I made my way to the farther end of it, where there was but one window with many panes, each with a bull's-eye in it, and in the dirtiest possible state. When I reached this window, I turned about, and in a recess, standing at right angles with the side wall of the shop, was a large mirror in an old-fashioned dingy frame. Reflected in this I saw what in old houses I have heard termed an 'alcove', in which, among lumber, and various dusty articles hanging on the wall, there stood a table, at which three persons were seated, as it seemed to me, in earnest conversation. Two of these persons I instantly recognised; one was Colonel Gaillarde, the other was the Marquis d'Harmonville. The third, who was fiddling with a pen, was a lean, pale man, pitted with the smallpox, with lank black hair, and about as mean-looking a person as I had ever seen in my life. The marquis looked up, and his glance was instantaneously followed by his two companions. For a moment I hesitated what to do. But it was plain that I was not recognised, as indeed I could hardly have been, the light from the window being behind me and the portion of the shop immediately before me being very dark indeed.

Perceiving this, I had the presence of mind to affect being entirely engrossed by the objects before me, and strolled slowly down the shop again. I paused for a moment to hear whether I was followed and was relieved when I heard no step. You may be sure I did not waste more time in that shop, where I had just made a discovery so curious and so unexpected.

It was no business of mine to enquire what brought Colonel Gaillarde and the marquis together in so shabby and even dirty a place, or who the mean person biting the feather end of his pen might be. Such employments as the marquis had accepted sometimes make strange bedfellows.

I was glad to get away, and just as the sun set, I reached the steps of Le Dragon Volant and dismissed the vehicle in which I had arrived, carrying in my hand a strong box, of marvellously small dimensions considering all it contained, strapped in a leather cover, which disguised its real character.

When I got to my room, I summoned St Clair. I told him nearly the same story I had already told my host. I gave him fifty pounds, with orders to expend whatever was necessary on himself and in payment for my rooms till my return. I then ate a slight and hasty dinner. My eyes were often upon the solemn old clock over the chimney-piece, which was my sole accomplice in keeping tryst in this iniquitous venture. The sky favoured my design, and darkened all things with a sea of clouds.

The innkeeper met me in the hall, to ask whether I should want a vehicle to Paris? I was prepared for this question, and instantly answered that I meant to walk to Versailles, and take a carriage there. I called St Clair.

'Go,' said I, 'and drink a bottle of wine with your friends. I shall call you if I should want anything; in the meantime, here is the key of my room; I shall be writing some notes, so don't allow anyone to disturb me for at least half an hour. At the end of that time you will probably find that I have left for Versailles; should you not find me in the room, you may take that for granted; thereupon take charge of everything, and lock the door, you understand?'

St Clair took his leave, wishing me all happiness and no doubt promising himself some little amusement with my money. With my candle in my hand, I hastened upstairs. It wanted now but five minutes to the appointed time. I do not think there is anything of the coward in my nature; but I confess, as the crisis approached, I felt something of the suspense and awe of a soldier going into action. Would I have receded? Not for all this earth could offer.

I bolted my door, put on my greatcoat and placed my pistols one in each pocket. I now applied my key to the secret locks, drew the wainscot door a little open, took my strong box under my arm, extinguished my candle, unbolted my door, listened at it for a few moments to be sure that no one was approaching, and then crossed the floor of my room swiftly, entered the secret door and closed the spring lock after me. I was upon the screw-stair in total darkness, the key in my fingers. Thus far the undertaking was successful.

Rapture

Down the screw-stair I went in utter darkness; and having reached the stone floor, I discerned the door and groped out the keyhole. With more caution and less noise than upon the night before, I opened the door, and stepped out into the thick brushwood. It was almost as dark in this jungle.

Having secured the door, I slowly pushed my way through the bushes, which soon became less dense. Then, with more ease, but still under thick cover, I pursued in the track of the wood, keeping near its edge.

At length, in the darkened air, about fifty yards away, the shafts of the marble temple rose like phantoms before me, seen through the trunks of the old trees. Everything favoured my enterprise. I had effectually mystified my servant and the people of Le Dragon Volant, and so dark was the night that even had I alarmed the suspicions of all the tenants of the inn, I might safely defy their united curiosity, though posted at every window of the house.

Through the trunks, over the roots of the old trees, I reached the appointed place of observation. I laid my treasure, in its leathern case, in the embrasure, and leaning my arms upon it, looked steadily in the direction of the château. The outline of the building was scarcely discernible, blending dimly, as it did, with the sky. No light in any window was visible. I was plainly to wait; but for how long?

Leaning on my box of treasure, gazing toward the massive shadow that represented the château, in the midst of my ardent and elated longings, there came upon me an odd thought – which you will think might well have struck me long before. It came on a sudden, and as it came the darkness deepened, and a chill stole into the air around me. Suppose I were to disappear finally, like those other men whose stories I had listened to! Had I not been at all the pains that mortal could to obliterate every trace of my real proceedings, and to mislead everyone to whom I spoke as to the direction in which I had gone?

This icy, snakelike thought stole through my mind, and was gone.

Did I not rejoice in the full-blooded season of youth, conscious strength, rashness, passion, pursuit, the adventure! Here were a pair of double-barrelled pistols, four lives in my hands? What could possibly happen? The count – except for the sake of my Dulcinea, what was it to me whether the old coward whom I had seen in an ague of terror before the brawling colonel interposed or not? I was assuming the worst that could happen. But with an ally so clever and courageous as my beautiful countess, could any such misadventure befall? Bah! I laughed at all such fancies.

As I thus communed with myself, the signal light sprang up. The rose-coloured light, *couleur de rose*, emblem of sanguine hope and the dawn of a happy day.

Clear, soft and steady glowed the light from the window. The stone shafts showed black against it. Murmuring words of passionate love as I gazed upon the signal, I grasped my strong box under my arm and with rapid strides approached the Château de la Carque. No sign of light or life, no human voice, no tread of foot, no bark of dog indicated a chance of interruption. A blind was down; and as I came close to the tall window, I found that half a dozen steps led up to it, and that a large lattice, answering for a door, lay open.

A shadow from within fell upon the blind; it was drawn aside, and as I ascended the steps, a soft voice murmured – 'Richard, dearest Richard, come, oh, come! how I have longed for this moment!'

Never did she look so beautiful. My love rose to passionate enthusiasm. I only wished there were some real danger in the adventure worthy of such a creature. When the first tumultuous greeting was over, she made me sit beside her on a sofa. There we talked for a minute or two. She told me that the count had gone and was by that time more than a mile on his way, with the funeral, to Père Lachaise. Here were her diamonds. She exhibited, hastily, an open casket containing a profusion of the largest brilliants.

'What is this?' she asked.

'A box containing money to the amount of thirty thousand pounds,' I answered.

'What! all that money?' she exclaimed.

'Every sou.'

'Was it not unnecessary to bring so much, seeing all these,' she said, touching her diamonds. 'It would have been kind of you to allow me to provide for us both, for a time at least. It would have made me happier even than I am.'

'Dearest, generous angel!' Such was my extravagant declamation. 'You forget that it may be necessary, for a long time, to observe silence as to where we are, and impossible to communicate safely with anyone.'

'You have then here this great sum – are you certain; have you counted it?'

'Yes, certainly; I received it today,' I answered, perhaps showing a little surprise in my face. 'I counted it, of course, on drawing it from my bankers.'

'It makes me feel a little nervous, travelling with so much money; but these jewels make as great a danger; *that* can add but little to it. Place them side by side; you shall take off your greatcoat when we are ready to go, and with it manage to conceal these boxes. I should not like the drivers to suspect that we were conveying such a treasure. I must ask you now to close the curtains of that window, and bar the shutters.'

I had hardly done this when a knock was heard at the room door.

'I know who this is,' she said, in a whisper to me. I saw that she was not alarmed. She went softly to the door, and a whispered conversation for a minute followed.

'My trusty maid, who is coming with us. She says we cannot safely go sooner than ten minutes. She is bringing some coffee to the next room.'

She opened the door and looked in.

'I must tell her not to take too much luggage. She is so odd! Don't follow – stay where you are – it is better that she should not see you.'

She left the room with a gesture of caution.

A change had come over the manner of this beautiful woman. For the last few minutes a shadow had been stealing over her, an air of abstraction, a look bordering on suspicion. Why was she pale? Why had there come that dark look in her eyes? Why had her very voice become changed? Had anything gone suddenly wrong? Did some danger threaten?

This doubt, however, speedily quieted itself. If there had been anything of the kind, she would, of course, have told me. It was only natural that, as the crisis approached, she should become more and more nervous. She did not return quite so soon as I had expected. To a man in my situation absolute quietude is next to impossible. I moved restlessly about the room. It was a small one. There was a door at the other end. I opened it, rashly enough. I listened, it was perfectly silent. I was in an excited, eager state with every faculty focused on what lay ahead and, in so far, detached from the immediate present. I can't account, in any other way, for my having done so many foolish things that night, for I was, naturally, by no means deficient in cunning. About the most stupid of those was that instead of immediately closing that door, which I never ought to have opened, I actually took a candle and walked into the room.

There I made, quite unexpectedly, a rather startling discovery.

23

A Cup of Coffee

The room was carpetless. On the floor were a quantity of shavings and some score of bricks. Beyond these, on a narrow table, lay an object, which I could hardly believe I saw aright.

I approached and drew from it a sheet which had very slightly disguised its shape. There was no mistake about it. It was a coffin; and on the lid was a plate, with the inscription in French:

PIERRE DE LA ROCHE ST AMAND

AGÉ DE XXIII ANS

I drew back with a double shock. So, then, the funeral after all had not yet left! Here lay the body. I had been deceived. This, no doubt, accounted for the embarrassment so manifest in the countess's manner. She would have done more wisely had she told me the true state of the case.

I drew back from this melancholy room, and closed the door. Her distrust of me was the worst rashness she could have committed. There is nothing more dangerous than misapplied caution. In entire ignorance of the fact I had entered the room, and there I might have lighted upon some of the very persons it was our special anxiety that I should avoid.

These reflections were interrupted, almost as soon as begun, by the return of the Countess de St Alyre. I saw at a glance that she detected in my face some evidence of what had happened, for she threw a hasty look towards the door.

'Have you seen anything – anything to disturb you, dear Richard? Have you been out of this room?'

I answered promptly, 'Yes,' and told her frankly what had happened.

'Well, I did not like to make you more uneasy than necessary. Besides, it is disgusting and horrible. The body is there; but the count had departed a quarter of an hour before I lighted the coloured lamp and prepared to receive you. The body did not arrive till eight or ten minutes after he had set out. He was afraid lest the people at Père Lachaise should suppose that the funeral was postponed. He knew that the remains of poor Pierre would certainly reach here tonight, although an unexpected delay had occurred; and there are reasons why he wishes the funeral completed before tomorrow. The hearse with the body must leave here in ten minutes. So soon as it is gone, we shall be free to set out upon our wild and happy journey. The horses are to the carriage in the *porte-cochère*. As for this *funeste* horror' (she shuddered very prettily), 'let us think of it no more.'

She bolted the door of communication, and when she turned, it was with such a pretty penitence in her face and attitude that I was ready to throw myself at her feet.

'It is the last time,' she said, in a sweet sad little pleading, 'I shall ever practise a deception on my brave and beautiful Richard – my hero! Am I forgiven?'

There was another scene of passionate effusion, and lovers' raptures and declamations, but only murmured, lest the ears of listeners should be busy.

At length, on a sudden, she raised her hand as if to prevent my stirring, her eyes fixed on me and her ear towards the door of the room in which the coffin was placed, and remained breathless in that attitude for a few moments. Then, with a little nod towards me, she moved on tiptoe to the door and listened, extending her hand backward as if to warn me against advancing; and, after a little time, she returned, still on tiptoe, and whispered to me, 'They are removing the coffin – come with me.'

I accompanied her into the room from which her maid, as she

told me, had spoken to her. Coffee and some old china cups, which appeared to me quite beautiful, stood on a silver tray; and some liqueur glasses, with a flask, which turned out to be noyeau, on a salver beside it.

'I shall attend you. I'm to be your servant here; I am to have my own way; I shall not think myself forgiven by my darling if he refuses to indulge me in anything.'

She filled a cup with coffee and handed it to me with her left hand; her right arm she fondly passed over my shoulder, and with her fingers through my curls caressingly, she whispered, 'Take this, I shall take some just now.'

It was excellent; and when I had done she handed me the liqueur, which I also drank.

'Come back, dearest, to the next room,' she said. 'By this time those terrible people must have gone away, and we shall be safer there, for the present, than here.'

'You shall direct, and I obey; you shall command me, not only now, but always, and in all things, my beautiful queen!' I murmured.

My heroics were unconsciously, I dare say, founded upon my ideal of the French school of lovemaking. I am, even now, ashamed as I recall the bombast to which I treated the Countess de St Alyre.

'There, you shall have another miniature glass – a fairy glass – of noyeau,' she said gaily. In this volatile creature, the funereal gloom of the moment before, and the suspense of an adventure on which all her future was staked, disappeared in a moment. She ran and returned with another tiny glass, which, with an eloquent or tender little speech, I placed to my lips and sipped.

I kissed her hand, I kissed her lips, I gazed in her beautiful eyes and kissed her again unresisting.

'You call me Richard, by what name am I to call my beautiful divinity?' I asked.

'You must call me Eugénie, it is my name. Let us be quite real; that is, if you love as entirely as I do.'

'Eugénie!' I exclaimed, and broke into a new rapture upon the name. It ended by my telling her how impatient I was to set out upon our journey; and, as I spoke, suddenly an odd sensation overcame me. It was not in the slightest degree like faintness. I can find no phrase to describe it except as a sudden constraint of the brain; it was as if the membrane in which it lies, if there be such a thing, contracted, and became inflexible.

'Dear Richard! what is the matter?' she exclaimed, with terror in her looks. 'Good heavens! are you ill? I conjure you, sit down; sit in this chair.' She almost forced me into one; I was in no condition to offer the least resistance. I recognised but too truly the sensations that supervened. I was lying back in the chair without the power, by this time, of uttering a syllable, of closing my eyelids, of moving my eyes, of stirring a muscle. I had in a few seconds glided into precisely the state in which I had passed so many appalling hours when approaching Paris in my night-drive with the Marquis d'Harmonville.

Great and loud was the lady's agony. She seemed to have lost all sense of fear. She called me by my name, shook me by the shoulder, raised my arm and let it fall, all the time imploring of me, in distracting sentences, to make the slightest sign of life, and vowing that if I did not, she would make away with herself.

These ejaculations, after a minute or two, suddenly subsided. The lady was perfectly silent and cool. In a very businesslike way she took a candle and stood before me, pale indeed, very pale, but with an expression only of intense scrutiny with a dash of horror in it. She moved the candle before my eyes slowly, evidently watching the effect. She then set it down, and rang a handbell two or three times sharply. She placed the two cases (I mean hers containing the jewels, and my strong box) side by side on the table; and I saw her carefully lock the door that gave access to the room in which I had just now sipped my coffee.

24

Hope

She had scarcely set down my heavy box, which she seemed to have considerable difficulty in raising on the table, when the door of the room in which I had seen the coffin opened, and a sinister and unexpected apparition entered.

It was the Count de St Alyre, who had been, as I have told you, reported to me to be, for some considerable time, on his way to Père

Lachaise. He stood before me for a moment, with the frame of the doorway and a background of darkness enclosing him, like a portrait. His slight, mean figure was draped in the deepest mourning. He had in his hand a pair of black gloves and his hat with crape round it.

When he was not speaking his face showed signs of agitation; his mouth was puckering and working. He looked damnably wicked and frightened.

'Well, my dear Eugénie? Well, child – eh? Well, it all goes admirably?'

'Yes,' she answered, in a low, hard tone. 'But you and Planard should not have left that door open.'

This she said sternly. 'He went in there and looked about wherever he liked; it was fortunate he did not move aside the lid of the coffin.'

'Planard should have seen to that,' said the count, sharply. '*Ma foi!* I can't be everywhere!' He advanced half a dozen short quick steps into the room toward me, and placed his glasses to his eyes.

'Monsieur Beckett,' he cried sharply, two or three times, 'Hi! don't you know me?'

He approached and peered more closely in my face; raised my hand and shook it, calling me again, then let it drop, and said – 'It has set in admirably, my pretty *mignonne*. When did it commence?'

The countess came and stood beside him, and looked at me steadily for some seconds.

You can't conceive the effect of the silent gaze of those two pairs of evil eyes.

The lady glanced to where, I recollected, the mantelpiece stood, and upon it a clock, the regular click of which I sharply heard.

'Four – five – six minutes and a half,' she said slowly, in a cold hard way.

'Brava! Bravissima! my beautiful queen! my little Venus! my Joan of Arc! my heroine! my paragon of women!'

He was gloating on me with an odious curiosity, smiling, as he groped backwards with his thin brown fingers to find the lady's hand; but she, not (I dare say) caring for his caresses, drew back a little.

'Come, *ma chère*, let us count his things. What is it? Pocket-book? Or – or – what?'

'It is that!' said the lady, pointing with a look of disgust to the box, which lay in its leather case on the table.

'Oh! Let us see – let us count – let us see,' he said, as he was unbuckling the straps with his tremulous fingers. 'We must count all – we must see to it. I have pencil and pocket-book – but – where's the key? See this cursed lock! My faith! What is it? Where's the key?' He was standing before the countess, shuffling his feet, with his hands extended and all his fingers quivering.

'I have not got it; how could I? It is in his pocket, of course,' said the lady.

In another instant the fingers of the old miscreant were in my pockets; he plucked out everything they contained, and some keys among the rest.

I lay in precisely the state in which I had been during my drive with the marquis to Paris. This wretch I knew was about to rob me. The whole drama, and the countess's role in it, I could not yet comprehend. I could not be sure – so much more presence of mind and histrionic resource have women than fall to the lot of our clumsy sex – whether the return of the count was not, in truth, a surprise to her; and this scrutiny of the contents of my strong box, an extempore undertaking of the count's. But it was clearing more and more every moment: and I was destined, very soon, to comprehend minutely my appalling situation.

I had not the power of turning my eyes this way or that the smallest fraction of a hair's breadth. But let anyone, placed as I was at the end of a room, ascertain for himself by experiment how wide is the field of sight, without the slightest alteration in the line of vision, he will find that it takes in the entire breadth of a large room, and that up to a very short distance before him; and imperfectly, by a refraction, I believe, in the eye itself, to a point very near indeed. Next to nothing that passed in the room, therefore, was hidden from me.

The old man had, by this time, found the key. The leather case was open. The box cramped round with iron was next unlocked. He turned out its contents upon the table.

'*Rouleaux* of a hundred Napoleons each. One, two, three. Yes, quick. Write down a thousand Napoleons. One, two; yes, right. Another thousand, *write*!' And so on and on still he rapidly counted. Then came the notes.

'Ten thousand francs. *Write*. Ten thousand francs again: is it

would have been better. They should have been smaller. These are
horribly embarrassing. Bolt that door again; Planard would become
unreasonable if he knew the amount. Why did you not tell him to get
it in smaller notes? No matter now – go on – it can't be helped –
write – another ten thousand francs – another – another.' And so on,
till my treasure was counted out, before my face, while I saw and
heard all that passed with the sharpest distinctness, and my mental
perceptions were horribly vivid. But in all other respects I was dead.

He had replaced in the box every note and *rouleau* as he counted it,
and now having ascertained the sum total, he locked it, replaced it, very
methodically, in its cover, opened a buffet in the wainscoting, and,
having placed the countess's jewel-case and my strong box in it, he
locked it; and immediately on completing these arrangements he began
to complain with fresh acrimony and maledictions of Planard's delay.

He unbolted the door, looked in the dark room beyond, and listened.
He closed the door again and returned. The old man was in a fever of
suspense.

'I have kept ten thousand francs for Planard,' said the count,
touching his waistcoat pocket.

'Will that satisfy him?' asked the lady.

'Why – curse him!' screamed the count. 'Has he no conscience? I'll
swear to him it's half the entire thing.'

He and the lady again came and looked at me anxiously for a while,
in silence; and then the old count began to grumble again about
Planard, and to compare his watch with the clock. The lady seemed
less impatient; she sat no longer looking at me, but across the room, so
that her profile was towards me – and strangely changed, dark and
witchlike it looked. My last hope died as I beheld that jaded face from
which the mask had dropped. I was certain that they intended to
crown their robbery by murder. Why did they not dispatch me at
once? What object could there be in postponing the catastrophe which
would expedite their own safety. I cannot recall, even to myself,
adequately the horrors unutterable that I underwent. You must
suppose a real nightmare – I mean a nightmare in which the objects
and the danger are real, and the spell of corporal death appears to
be protractable at the pleasure of the persons who preside at your
unearthly torments. I could have no doubt as to the cause of the state
in which I was.

In this agony, to which I could not give the slightest expression, I saw the door of the room where the coffin had been open slowly, and the Marquis d'Harmonville entered the room.

25

Despair

A moment's hope, hope violent and fluctuating, hope that was nearly torture, and then came a dialogue and with it the terrors of despair.

'Thank heaven, Planard, you have come at last,' said the count, taking him with both hands by the arm and clinging to it and drawing him towards me. 'See, look at him. It has all gone sweetly, sweetly, sweetly up to this. Shall I hold the candle for you?'

My friend d'Harmonville, Planard, whoever he was, came to me, pulling off his gloves, which he popped into his pocket.

'The candle, a little this way,' he said, and stooping over me he looked earnestly in my face. He touched my forehead, drew his hand across it, and then looked in my eyes for a time.

'Well, doctor, what do you think?' whispered the count.

'How much did you give him?' said the marquis, thus suddenly stunted down to a doctor.

'Seventy drops,' said the lady.

'In the hot coffee?'

'Yes; sixty in a hot cup of coffee and ten in the liqueur.'

Her voice, low and hard, seemed to me to tremble a little. It takes a long course of guilt to subjugate nature completely, and prevent those exterior signs of agitation that outlive all good.

The doctor, however, was treating me as coolly as he might a subject which he was about to place on the dissecting-table for a lecture.

He looked into my eyes again for a while, took my wrist and applied his fingers to the pulse.

'That action suspended,' he said to himself.

Then again he placed something that, for the moment I saw it, looked like a piece of gold-beater's leaf to my lips, holding his head so far that his own breathing could not affect it.

'Yes,' he said in soliloquy, very low.

Then he plucked my shirt-breast open and applied the stethoscope, shifted it from point to point, listened with his ear to its end, as if for a very far-off sound, raised his head, and said, in like manner, softly to himself, 'All appreciable action of the lungs has subsided.'

Then turning from the sound, as I conjectured, he said: 'Seventy drops, allowing ten for waste, ought to hold him fast for six hours and a half – that is ample. The experiment I tried in the carriage was only thirty drops, and showed a highly sensitive brain. It would not do to kill him, you know. You are certain you did not exceed seventy?'

'Perfectly,' said the lady.

'If he were to die the evaporation would be arrested, and foreign matter, some of it poisonous, would be found in the stomach, don't you see? If you are doubtful, it would be well to use the stomach-pump.'

'Dearest Eugénie, be frank, be frank, do be frank,' urged the count.

'I am *not* doubtful, I am *certain*,' she answered.

'How long ago, exactly? I told you to observe the time.'

'I did; the minute-hand was exactly there, under the point of that cupid's foot.'

'It will last, then, probably for seven hours. He will recover then; the evaporation will be complete, and not one particle of the fluid will remain in the stomach.'

It was reassuring, at all events, to hear that there was no intention to murder me. No one who has not tried it knows the terror of the approach of death, when the mind is clear, the instincts of life unimpaired, and no excitement to disturb the appreciation of that entirely new horror.

The nature and purpose of this tenderness was very, very peculiar, and as yet I had not a suspicion of it.

'You leave France, I suppose?' said the ex-marquis.

'Yes, certainly, tomorrow,' answered the count.

'And where do you mean to go?'

'That I have not yet settled,' he answered quickly.

'You won't tell a friend, eh?'

'I can't till I know. This has turned out an unprofitable affair.'

'We shall settle that by and by.'

'It is time we should get him lying down, eh,' said the count, indicating me with one finger.

'Yes, we must proceed rapidly now. Are his nightshirt and night–cap – you understand – here?'

'All ready,' said the count.

'Now, madame,' said the doctor, turning to the lady, and making her, in spite of the emergency, a bow, 'it is time you should retire.'

The lady passed into the room in which I had taken my cup of treacherous coffee, and I saw her no more.

The count took a candle, and passed through the door at the farther end of the room, returning with a roll of linen in his hand. He bolted first one door then the other.

They now, in silence, proceeded to undress me rapidly. They were not many minutes in accomplishing this.

What the doctor had termed my nightshirt, a long garment which reached below my feet, was now on, and a cap that resembled a female nightcap more than anything I had ever seen upon a male head was fitted upon mine and tied under my chin.

And now, I thought, I shall be laid in a bed to recover how I can, and, in the meantime, the conspirators will have escaped with their booty and pursuit be in vain.

This was my best hope at the time; but it was soon clear that their plans were very different.

The count and Planard now went together into the room that lay straight before me. I heard them talking low, and a sound of shuffling feet; then a long rumble; it suddenly stopped; it recommenced; it continued; side by side they came in at the door, their backs toward me. They were dragging something along the floor that made a continued boom and rumble, but they were interposed between me and it, so that I could not see it until they had dragged it almost beside me; and then, merciful heaven! I saw it plainly enough. It was the coffin I had seen in the next room. It now lay flat on the floor, its edge against the chair in which I sat. Planard removed the lid. The coffin was empty.

26

Catastrophe

'Those seem to be good horses, and we change on the way,' said Planard. 'You give the men a Napoleon or two; we must do it within three hours and a quarter. Now, come; I'll lift him upright so as to place his feet in their proper berth, and you must keep them together, and draw the white shirt well down over them.'

In another moment I was placed, as he described, sustained in Planard's arms, standing at the foot of the coffin, and so lowered backwards, gradually, till I lay my length in it. Then the man, whom the count called Planard, stretched my arms by my sides, and carefully arranged the frills at my breast, and the folds of the shroud, and after that, taking his stand at the foot of the coffin, made a survey which seemed to satisfy him.

The count, who was very methodical, took my clothes which had just been removed, folded them rapidly together and locked them up, as I afterwards heard, in one of the three presses which opened by doors in the panel.

I now understood their frightful plan. This coffin had been prepared for *me*; the funeral of St Amand was a sham to mislead enquiry; I had myself given the order at Père Lachaise, signed it, and paid the fees for the interment of the fictitious Pierre de St Amand, whose place I was to take, to lie in his coffin with his name on the plate above my breast, and with a ton of clay packed down upon me; to waken from this catalepsy, after I had been for hours in the grave, there to perish by a death the most horrible that imagination can conceive.

If, hereafter, by any caprice of curiosity or suspicion, the coffin should be exhumed and the body it enclosed examined, no chemistry could detect a trace of poison, nor the most cautious examination the slightest mark of violence.

I had myself been at the utmost pains to mystify enquiry, should my disappearance excite surmises, and had even written to my few correspondents in England to tell them that they were not to look for a letter from me for three weeks at least.

In the moment of my guilty elation death had caught me, and there was no escape. I tried to pray to God in my unearthly panic, but only thoughts of terror, judgment and eternal anguish crossed the distraction of my immediate doom.

I must not try to recall what is indeed indescribable – the multiform horrors of my own thoughts. I will relate, simply, what befell, every detail of which remains sharp in my memory as if cut in steel.

'The undertaker's men are in the hall,' said the count.

'They must not come till this is fixed,' answered Planard. 'Be good enough to take hold of the lower part while I take this end.' I was not left long to conjecture what was coming, for in a few seconds more something slid across, a few inches above my face, and entirely excluded the light, and muffled sound so that nothing that was not very distinct reached my ears henceforward; but very distinctly came the working of a turnscrew, and the crunching home of screws in succession. Than these vulgar sounds no doom spoken in thunder could have been more tremendous.

The rest I must relate, not as it then reached my ears, which was too imperfectly and interruptedly to supply a connected narrative, but as it was afterwards told me by other people.

The coffin-lid being screwed down, the two gentlemen arranged the room and adjusted the coffin so that it lay perfectly straight along the boards, the count being specially anxious that there should be no appearance of hurry or disorder in the room, which might have excited remark and conjecture.

When this was done, Dr Planard said he would go to the hall to summon the men who were to carry the coffin out and place it in the hearse. The count pulled on his black gloves, and held his white handkerchief in his hand, a very impressive chief-mourner. He stood a little behind the head of the coffin, awaiting the arrival of the persons who accompanied Planard, and whose fast steps he soon heard approaching.

Planard came first. He entered the room through the apartment in which the coffin had been originally placed. His manner was changed; there was something of a swagger in it.

'Monsieur le Comte,' he said, as he strode through the door, followed by half a dozen persons. 'I am sorry to have to announce a most unseasonable interruption. Here is Monsieur Carmaignac, a gentleman holding an office in the police department, who has information to the effect that large quantities of smuggled English and other goods have been distributed in this neighbourhood and that a portion of them is concealed in your house. I have ventured to assure him, of my own knowledge, that nothing can be more false than that information, and that you would be only too happy to throw open for his inspection, at a moment's notice, every room, closet and cupboard in your house.'

'Most assuredly,' exclaimed the count, with a stout voice, but a very white face. 'Thank you, my good friend, for having anticipated me. I will place my house and keys at his disposal, for the purpose of his scrutiny, so soon as he is good enough to inform me of what specific contraband goods he comes in search.'

'The Count de St Alyre will pardon me,' answered Carmaignac, a little drily. 'I am forbidden by my instructions to make that disclosure; and that I am instructed to make a general search, this warrant will satisfy Monsieur le Comte.'

'Monsieur Carmaignac, may I hope,' interposed Planard, 'that you will permit the Count de St Alyre to attend the funeral of his kinsman, who lies here, as you see' (he pointed to the plate upon the coffin), 'and to convey whom to Père Lachaise, a hearse waits at this moment at the door?'

'That, I regret to say, I cannot permit. My instructions are precise; but the delay, I trust, will be but trifling. Monsieur le Comte will not suppose for a moment that I suspect him; but we have a duty to perform, and I must act as if I did. When I am ordered to search, I search; things are sometimes hid in such bizarre places. I can't say, for instance, what that coffin may contain.'

'The body of my kinsman, Monsieur Pierre de St Amand,' answered the count, loftily.

'Oh! then you've seen him?'

'Seen him? Often, too often!' The count was evidently a good deal moved.

'I mean the body?'

The count stole a quick glance at Planard.

'N–no, monsieur – that is, I mean only for a moment.' Another quick glance at Planard.

'But quite long enough, I fancy, to recognise him?' insinuated that gentleman.

'Of course – of course; instantly – perfectly. What! Pierre de St Amand? Not know him at a glance? No, no, poor fellow, I know him too well for that.'

'The things I am in search of,' said Monsieur Carmaignac, 'would fit in a narrow compass – servants are so ingenious sometimes. Let us raise the lid.'

'Pardon me, monsieur,' said the count, peremptorily, advancing to the side of the coffin, and extending his arm across it, 'I cannot permit that indignity – that desecration.'

'There shall be none, sir – simply the raising of the lid; you shall remain in the room. If it should prove as we all hope, you shall have the pleasure of one final look, really the last, upon your beloved kinsman.'

'But, sir, I can't.'

'But, monsieur, I must.'

'But, besides, the thing, the turnscrew, broke when the last screw was turned; and I give you my sacred honour there is nothing but the body in this coffin.'

'Of course, Monsieur le Comte believes all that; but he does not know so well as I the legerdemain in use among servants who are accustomed to smuggling. Here, Philippe, you must take off the lid of that coffin.'

The count protested; but Philippe – a man with a bald head, and a smirched face, looking like a working blacksmith – placed on the floor a leather bag of tools, from which, having looked at the coffin and picked with his nail at the screw-heads, he selected a turnscrew; after a few deft twirls at each of the screws, they stood up like little rows of mushrooms, and the lid was raised. I saw the light, of which I thought I had seen my last, once more; but the axis of vision remained fixed. As I was reduced to the cataleptic state in a position nearly perpendicular, I continued looking straight before me, and thus my gaze was now fixed upon the ceiling. I saw the face of Carmaignac leaning over me with a curious frown. It seemed to me that there was no recognition in his eyes. Oh, heaven! that I could have uttered were it but one cry! I saw the dark, mean mask of the little count staring down at me from the other side; the face of the pseudo-marquis also peering at me, but not so full in the line of vision; there were other faces also.

'I see, I see,' said Carmaignac, withdrawing. 'Nothing of the kind there.'

'You will be good enough to direct your man to readjust the lid of the coffin, and to fix the screws,' said the count, taking courage; 'and – and – really the funeral must proceed. It is not fair to the people who have but moderate fees for night-work, to keep them hour after hour beyond the time.'

'Count de St Alyre, you shall go in a very few minutes. I will direct, just now, all about the coffin.'

The count looked toward the door, and there saw a gendarme; and two or three more grave and stalwart specimens of the same force were also in the room. The count was very uncomfortably excited; it was growing insupportable.

'As this gentleman makes a difficulty about my attending the obsequies of my kinsman, I will ask you, Planard, to accompany the funeral in my stead.'

'In a few minutes,' answered the incorrigible Carmaignac. 'I must first trouble you for the key that opens that press.'

He pointed directly at the press in which my clothes had just been locked up.

'I – I have no objection,' said the count – 'none, of course; only they have not been used for an age. I'll direct someone to look for the key.'

'If you have not got it about you, it is quite unnecessary. Philippe, try your skeleton-keys with that press. I want it opened. Whose clothes are these?' enquired Carmaignac, when, the press having been opened, he took out the suit that had been placed there scarcely two minutes since.

'I can't say,' answered the count. 'I know nothing of the contents of that press. A roguish servant, named Lablais, whom I dismissed about a year ago, had the key. I have not seen it open for ten years or more. The clothes are probably his.'

'Here are visiting cards, see, and here a marked pocket-handker–chief – "R. B." upon it. He must have stolen them from a person named Beckett – R. Beckett. "Mr Beckett, Berkeley Square", the card says; and, my faith! here's a watch and a bunch of seals; one of them with the initials "R. B" upon it. That servant, Lablais, must have been a consummate rogue!'

'So he was; you are right, sir.'

'It strikes me that he possibly stole these clothes,' continued Carmaignac, 'from the man in the coffin, who, in that case, would be

Monsieur Beckett, and not Monsieur de St Amand. For, wonderful to relate, monsieur, the watch is still going! That man in the coffin, I believe is not dead, but simply drugged. And for having robbed and intended to murder him, I arrest you, Nicolas de la Marque, Count de St Alyre.'

In another moment the old villain was a prisoner. I heard his discordant voice break quaveringly into sudden vehemence and volubility, now croaking, now shrieking, as he oscillated between protests, threats and impious appeals to the God who will 'judge the secrets of men'! And thus lying and raving, he was removed from the room, and placed in the same coach with his beautiful and abandoned accomplice, already arrested; and, with two gendarmes sitting beside them, they were immediately driving at a rapid pace towards the Conciergerie.

There were now added to the general chorus two voices, very different in quality; one was that of the Gasconading Colonel Gaillarde, who had with difficulty been kept in the background up to this; the other was that of my jolly friend Whistlewick, who had come to identify me.

I shall tell you, just now, how this project against my property and life, so ingenious and monstrous, was exploded. I must first say a word about myself. I was placed in a hot bath, under the direction of Planard, as consummate a villain as any of the gang, but now thoroughly in the interests of the prosecution. Thence I was laid in a warm bed, the window of the room being open. These simple measures restored me in about three hours; I should otherwise, probably, have continued under the spell for nearly seven.

The practices of these nefarious conspirators had been carried on with consummate skill and secrecy. Their dupes were led, as I was, to be themselves auxiliary to the mystery which made their own destruction both safe and certain.

A search was, of course, instituted. Graves were opened in Père Lachaise. The bodies exhumed had lain there too long, and were too much decomposed to be recognised. One only was identified. The notice for the burial, in this particular case, had been signed, the order given and the fees paid by Gabriel Gaillarde, who was known to the official clerk who had to transact with him this little funereal business. The very trick that had been arranged for me, had been successfully practised in his case. The person for whom the grave had been ordered was purely fictitious; and Gabriel Gaillarde himself filled the coffin, on the cover of which that false name was inscribed as well as upon a tombstone over the grave. Possibly, the same honour, under my pseudonym, may have been intended for me.

The identification was curious. This Gabriel Gaillarde had had a bad fall from a runaway horse, about five years before his mysterious disappearance. He had lost an eye and some teeth, in this accident, besides sustaining a fracture of the right leg, immediately above the ankle. He had kept the injuries to his face as profound a secret as he could. The result was that the glass eye which had done duty for the one he had lost remained in the socket, slightly displaced, of course, but recognisable by the 'artist' who had supplied it.

More pointedly recognisable were the teeth, peculiar in workmanship, which one of the ablest dentists in Paris had himself adapted to the chasms, the cast of which, owing to peculiarities in the accident, he happened to have preserved. This cast precisely fitted the gold plate found in the mouth of the skull. The mark, also, above the ankle, in the bone, where it had reunited, corresponded exactly with the place where the fracture had knit in the limb of Gabriel Gaillarde.

The colonel, his younger brother, had been furious about the disappearance of Gabriel, and still more so about that of his money, which he had long regarded as his proper keepsake whenever death should remove his brother from the vexations of living. He had suspected for a long time, for certain adroitly discovered reasons, that the Count de St Alyre and the beautiful lady, his companion, countess, or whatever else she was, had pigeoned him. To this suspicion were added some others of a still darker kind – but in their first shape, rather the exaggerated reflections of his fury, ready to believe anything, than well-defined conjectures.

At length an accident had placed the colonel very nearly upon the right scent; a chance, possibly lucky for himself, had apprised the scoundrel Planard that the conspirators – himself among the number – were in danger. The result was that he made terms for himself, became an informer, and concerted with the police this visit made to the Château de la Carque at the critical moment, when every measure had been completed that was necessary to construct a perfect case against his guilty accomplices.

I need not describe the minute industry or forethought with which the police agents collected all the details necessary to support the case. They had brought an able physician, who, even had Planard failed, would have supplied the necessary medical evidence.

My trip to Paris, you will believe, had not turned out quite so agreeably as I had anticipated. I was the principal witness for the prosecution in this *cause célèbre*, with all the *agrément* that attends that enviable position. Having had an escape, as my friend Whistlewick said, 'within a squeak' of my life, I innocently fancied that I should have been an object of considerable interest to Parisian society; but, a good deal to my mortification, I discovered that I was the object of a good-natured but contemptuous merriment. I was a *balourd*, a *benêt*, *un âne*, and figured even in caricatures. I became a sort of public character, a figure of fun, 'unto which I was not born' and from which I fled as soon as I conveniently could, without even paying my friend, the Marquis d'Harmonville, a visit at his hospitable château.

The marquis escaped scot-free. His accomplice, the count, was executed. The fair Eugénie, under extenuating circumstances – consisting, so far as I could discover, of her good looks – got off with six years' imprisonment.

Colonel Gaillarde recovered some of his brother's money, out of the not very affluent estate of the count and *soi-disant* countess. This, and the execution of the count, put him in high good humour. So far from insisting on a hostile meeting, he shook me very graciously by the hand and told me that he looked upon the wound to his head, inflicted by the knob of my stick, as having been received in an honourable though irregular duel, in which he had no disadvantage or unfairness to complain of.

I think I have only two additional details to mention. The bricks discovered in the room with the coffin had been packed in it, in straw, to supply the weight of a dead body and to prevent the suspicions and contradictions that might have been excited by the arrival of an empty coffin at the château.

Secondly, the countess's magnificent brilliants were examined by a lapidary and pronounced to be worth about five pounds to a tragedy queen who happened to be in want of a suite of paste.

The countess had figured some years before as one of the cleverest actresses on the minor stage of Paris, where she had been picked up by the count and used as his principal accomplice.

She it was who, admirably disguised, had rifled my papers in the carriage on my memorable night-journey to Paris. She also had figured as the interpreting magician of the palanquin at the ball at Versailles. So far as I was affected by that elaborate mystification it was intended to reanimate my interest, which, they feared, might flag, in the beautiful countess. It had its design and action upon other intended victims also; but of them there is, at present, no need to speak. The introduction of a real corpse – procured from a person who supplied the Parisian anatomists – involved no real danger, while it heightened the mystery and kept the prophet alive in the gossip of the town and in the thoughts of the noodles with whom he had conferred.

I divided the remainder of the summer and autumn between Switzerland and Italy.

As the well-worn phrase goes, I was a sadder if not a wiser man. A great deal of the horrible impression left upon my mind was due, of course, to the mere action of nerves and brain. But serious feelings of another and deeper kind remained. My after life was ultimately formed by the shock I had then received. Those impressions led me – but not till after many years – to happier though not less serious thoughts; and I have deep reason to be thankful to the all-merciful Ruler of Events, for an early and terrible lesson in the ways of sin.

SHERIDAN LE FANU

Carmilla

❧❧❧

PROLOGUE

Upon a paper attached to the narrative which follows, Dr Hesselius has written a rather elaborate note, which he accompanies with a reference to his essay on the strange subject which the manuscript illuminates.

This mysterious subject he treats, in that essay, with his usual learning and acumen, and with remarkable directness and condensation. It will form but one volume of the series of that extraordinary man's collected papers.

As I publish the case in this volume simply to interest the 'laity', I shall forestall the intelligent lady who relates it in nothing; and, after due consideration, I have determined, therefore, to abstain from presenting any *précis* of the learned doctor's reasoning, or extract from his statement on a subject which he describes as 'involving, not improbably, some of the profoundest arcana of our dual existence and its intermediates'.

I was anxious, on discovering this paper, to reopen the correspondence commenced by Dr Hesselius, so many years before, with a person so clever and careful as his informant seems to have been. Much to my regret, however, I found that she had died in the interval. She probably could have added little to the narrative which she communicates in the following pages with, so far as I can pronounce, such a conscientious particularity.

An Early Fright

In Styria, we, though by no means magnificent people, inhabit a castle, or *schloss*. A small income, in that part of the world, goes a great way. Eight or nine hundred a year does wonders. Scantily enough would it answer among wealthy people at home. My father is English, and I bear an English name, although I never saw England. But here, in this lonely and primitive place, where everything is so marvellously cheap, I really don't see how ever so much more money would at all materially add to our comforts, or even luxuries.

My father was in the Austrian service, and retired upon a pension and his patrimony; he purchased this feudal residence, and the small estate on which it stands, at a bargain price.

Nothing can be more picturesque or solitary. It stands on a slight eminence in a forest. The road, very old and narrow, passes in front of its drawbridge, never raised in my time, and its moat, stocked with perch and sailed over by many swans, with floating on its surface white fleets of water-lilies.

Over all this the *schloss* shows its many-windowed front, its towers and its Gothic chapel.

The forest opens in an irregular and very picturesque glade before its gate, and at the right a steep Gothic bridge carries the road over a stream that winds in deep shadow through the wood.

I have said that this is a very lonely place. Judge whether I say truth. Looking from the hall-door towards the road, the forest in which our castle stands extends fifteen miles to the right and twelve to the left. The nearest inhabited village is about seven of your English miles to the left. The nearest inhabited *schloss* of any historic associations is that of old General Spielsdorf, nearly twenty miles away to the right.

I have said 'the nearest *inhabited* village', because there is, only three miles westward, that is to say in the direction of General Spielsdorf's *schloss*, a ruined village; it has a quaint little church, now roofless, in the aisle of which are the mouldering tombs of the proud family of

Karnstein, now extinct, who once owned the equally desolate château which, in the thick of the forest, overlooks the silent ruins of the town.

Respecting the cause of the desertion of this striking and melancholy spot, there is a legend which I shall relate to you another time.

I must tell you now how very small in number is the usual party of inhabitants of our castle. I don't include servants, or those dependants who occupy rooms in the buildings attached to the *schloss*. Listen, and wonder! My father, who is the kindest man on earth, but growing old, and I, then only nineteen, constituted the family at the *schloss* at the date of my story. Eight years have passed since then. My mother, a Styrian lady, died in my infancy, but I had a good-natured governess, who had been with me from, I might almost say, my infancy. I could not remember the time when her fat, benignant face was not a familiar picture in my memory. This was Madame Perrodon, a native of Berne, whose care and good nature in part supplied to me the loss of my mother, whom I do not even remember, so early did I lose her. She made a third at our little dinner party. There was a fourth, Mademoiselle de Lafontaine, a lady such as you term, I believe, a 'finishing governess'. She spoke French and German, Madame Perrodon French and broken English, to which my father and I added English, which, partly to prevent its becoming a lost language among us, and partly from patriotic motives, we spoke every day. The consequence was a Babel, at which strangers used to laugh, and which I shall make no attempt to reproduce in this narrative. And there were two or three young lady friends besides, pretty nearly of my own age, who were occasional visitors, for longer or shorter terms; and these visits I sometimes returned.

These were our regular social resources; but of course there were chance visits from 'neighbours' of only five or six leagues' distance. My life was, notwithstanding, rather a solitary one, I can assure you.

My *gouvernantes* had just so much control over me as you might conjecture such sage persons would have in the case of a rather spoiled girl whose only parent allowed her pretty nearly her own way in everything.

The first occurrence in my existence which produced a terrible impression upon my mind – one which, indeed, has never been effaced – was one of the very earliest incidents of my life which I can recollect. Some people will think it so trifling that it should not be recorded here. You will see, however, by and by, why I mention it. The nursery, as it was called, though I had it all to myself, was a large room in the upper story of the castle, with a steep oak roof. I can't have been more than six years old, when one night I awoke, and looking round the room from my bed, failed to see the nurserymaid. Neither was my nurse there; and I thought myself alone. I was not frightened, for I was one of those happy children who are studiously kept in ignorance of ghost stories, of fairy tales, and of all such lore as makes us cover up our heads when the door creaks suddenly, or the flicker of an expiring candle makes the shadow of a bedpost dance upon the wall, nearer to our faces. I was vexed and insulted at finding myself, as I conceived, neglected, and I began to whimper, preparatory to a hearty bout of roaring; when, to my surprise, I saw a solemn but very pretty face looking at me from the side of the bed. It was that of a young lady who was kneeling, with her hands under the coverlet. I looked at her with a kind of pleased wonder, and ceased whimpering. She caressed me with her hands, and lay down beside me on the bed, and drew me towards her, smiling; I felt immediately delightfully soothed, and fell asleep again. I was wakened by a sensation as if two needles ran into my breast, just below my throat, very deep at the same moment, and I cried loudly. The lady started back, with her eyes fixed on me, and then slipped down upon the floor, and, as I thought, hid herself under the bed.

I was now for the first time frightened, and I yelled with all my might and main. Nurse, nurserymaid, housekeeper, all came running in, and hearing my story, they made light of it, soothing me all they could meanwhile. But, child as I was, I could perceive that their faces were pale with an unwonted look of anxiety, and I saw them look under the bed and about the room, and peep under tables and pluck open cupboards; and the housekeeper whispered to the nurse: 'Lay your hand along that hollow in the bed; someone did lie there, so sure as you did not; the place is still warm.'

I remember the nurserymaid petting me, and all three examining my chest, where I told them I felt the puncture, and pronouncing that there was no sign visible that any such thing had happened to me.

The housekeeper and the two other servants who were in charge of the nursery, remained sitting up all night; and from that time a servant always sat up in the nursery until I was about fourteen.

I was very nervous for a long time after this. A doctor was called in, he was pallid and elderly. How well I remember his long saturnine face, slightly pitted with smallpox, and his chestnut wig. For a good while, every second day, he came and gave me medicine, which of course I hated.

The morning after I saw this apparition I was in a state of terror, and could not bear to be left alone, daylight though it was, for a moment.

I remember my father coming up and standing at the bedside, and talking cheerfully, and asking the nurse a number of questions, and laughing very heartily at one of the answers; and patting me on the shoulder, and kissing me, and telling me not to be frightened, that it was nothing but a dream and could not hurt me.

But I was not comforted, for I knew the visit of the strange woman was *not* a dream; and I was *awfully* frightened.

I was a little consoled by the nurserymaid's assuring me that it was she who had come and looked at me, and lain down beside me in the bed, and that I must have been half-dreaming not to have known her face. But this, though supported by the nurse, did not quite satisfy me.

I remember, in the course of that day, a venerable old man, in a black cassock, coming into the room with the nurse and housekeeper, and talking a little to them, and very kindly to me; his face was very sweet and gentle, and he told me they were going to pray, and joined my hands together, and desired me to say, softly, while they were praying, 'Lord, hear all good prayers for us, for Jesus' sake.' I think these were the very words, for I often repeated them to myself, and my nurse used for years to make me say them in my prayers.

I remember so well the thoughtful sweet face of that white-haired old man, in his black cassock, as he stood in that rude, lofty, brown room, with the clumsy furniture of a fashion three hundred years old, about him, and the scanty light entering its shadowy atmosphere through the small lattice. He kneeled, and the three women with him, and he prayed aloud with an earnest quavering voice for, what appeared to me, a long time. I forget all my life preceding that event, and for some time after it is all obscure also; but the scenes I have just described stand out vivid as the isolated pictures of the phantasmagoria surrounded by darkness.

2

A Guest

I am now going to tell you something so strange that it will require all your faith in my veracity to believe my story. It is not only the truth, nevertheless, but truth of which I have been an eyewitness.

It was a sweet summer evening, and my father asked me, as he sometimes did, to take a little ramble with him along that beautiful forest vista which I have mentioned as lying in front of the *schloss*.

'General Spielsdorf cannot come to us so soon as I had hoped,' said my father, as we pursued our walk.

He was to have paid us a visit of some weeks, and we had expected his arrival next day. He was to have brought with him a young lady, his niece and ward, Mademoiselle Rheinfeldt, whom I had never seen, but whom I had heard described as a very charming girl, and in whose society I had promised myself many happy days. I was more disappointed than a young lady living in a town or a bustling neighbourhood can possibly imagine. This visit, and the new acquaintance it promised, had furnished my daydreams for many weeks.

'And how soon does he come?' I asked.

'Not till autumn. Not for two months, I dare say,' he answered. 'And I am very glad now, dear, that you never knew Mademoiselle Rheinfeldt.'

'And why?' I asked, both mortified and curious.

'Because the poor young lady is dead,' he replied. 'I quite forgot I had not told you, but you were not in the room when I received the general's letter this evening.'

I was very much shocked. General Spielsdorf had mentioned in his first letter, six or seven weeks before, that she was not so well as he would wish her, but there was nothing to suggest the remotest suspicion of danger.

'Here is the general's letter,' he said, handing it to me. 'I am afraid he is in great affliction; the letter appears to me to have been written very nearly in distraction.'

We sat down on a rude bench, under a group of magnificent lime trees. The sun was setting with all its melancholy splendour behind the sylvan horizon, and the stream that flows beside our home, and passes under the steep old bridge I have mentioned, wound through many a group of noble trees, almost at our feet, reflecting in its current the fading crimson of the sky. General Spieldorf's letter was so extraordinary, so vehement, and in some places so self-contradictory, that I read it twice over – the second time aloud to my father – and was still unable to account for it, except by supposing that grief had unsettled his mind. He wrote:

> I have lost my darling daughter, for as such I loved her. During the last days of dear Bertha's illness I was not able to write to you. Before then I had no idea of her danger. I have lost her, and now learn *all*, too late. She died in the peace of innocence, and in the glorious hope of a blessed futurity. The fiend who betrayed our infatuated hospitality has done it all. I thought I was receiving into my house innocence, gaiety, a charming companion for my lost Bertha. Heavens! what a fool have I been! I thank God my child died without a suspicion of the cause of her sufferings. She is gone without so much as conjecturing the nature of her illness, and the accursed passion of the agent of all this misery. I devote my remaining days to tracking and extinguishing a monster. I am told I may hope to accomplish my righteous and merciful purpose. At present there is scarcely a gleam of light to guide me. I curse my conceited incredulity, my despicable affectation of superiority, my blindness, my obstinacy – all – too late. I cannot write or talk collectedly now. I am distracted. So soon as I shall have a little recovered, I mean to devote myself for a time to enquiry, which may possibly lead me as far as Vienna. Sometime in the autumn, two months hence, or earlier if I live, I will see you – that is, if you permit me; I will then tell you all that I scarce dare put upon paper now. Farewell. Pray for me, dear friend.

In these terms ended this strange letter. Though I had never seen Bertha Rheinfeldt, my eyes filled with tears at the sudden intelligence; I was startled, as well as profoundly disappointed.

The sun had now set, and it was twilight by the time I had returned the general's letter to my father. It was a soft clear evening, and we loitered, speculating upon the possible meanings of the violent and incoherent sentences which I had just been reading. We had nearly a mile to walk before reaching the road that passes the *schloss* in front, and by that time the moon was shining brilliantly. At the drawbridge we met Madame Perrodon and Mademoiselle de Lafontaine, who had come out, without their bonnets, to enjoy the exquisite moonlight.

We heard their voices gabbling in animated dialogue as we approached. We joined them at the drawbridge, and turned about to admire with them the beautiful scene.

The glade through which we had just walked lay before us. At our left the narrow road wound away under clumps of lordly trees and was lost to sight amid the thickening forest. At the right the same road crosses the steep and picturesque bridge, near which stands a ruined tower, which once guarded that pass; and beyond the bridge an abrupt eminence rises, covered with trees and showing in the shadow some grey ivy-clustered rocks.

Over the sward and low ground, a thin film of mist was stealing, like smoke, marking the distances with a transparent veil; and here and there we could see the river faintly flashing in the moonlight. No softer, sweeter scene could be imagined. The news I had just heard made it melancholy; but nothing could disturb its character of pro-found serenity, and the enchanted glory and vagueness of the prospect.

My father, who enjoyed the picturesque, and I, stood looking in silence over the expanse beneath us. The two good governesses, standing a little way behind us, discoursed upon the scene, and were eloquent upon the moon.

Madame Perrodon was fat, middle-aged and romantic, and talked and sighed poetically. Mademoiselle de Lafontaine – in right of her father, who was a German and assumed to be psychological, meta-physical and something of a mystic – now declared that when the moon shone with a light so intense it was well known that it indicated a special spiritual activity. The effect of the full moon in such a state of brilliancy was manifold. It acted on dreams, it acted on lunacy, it acted on nervous people; it had marvellous physical influences connected with life. Mademoiselle related that her cousin, who was mate of a merchant ship, having taken a nap on deck on such a night, lying on his back, with his face full in the light of the moon, had wakened, after a dream of an old woman clawing him by the cheek, with his features horribly drawn to one side; and his countenance had never quite recovered its equilibrium.

'The moon, this night,' she said, 'is full of odylic and magnetic influence – and see, when you look behind you at the front of the *schloss*, how all its windows flash and twinkle with that silvery splendour, as if unseen hands had lighted up the rooms to receive fairy guests.'

There are indolent states of the spirits in which, indisposed to talk ourselves, the talk of others is pleasant to our listless ears; and I gazed on, pleased with the tinkle of the ladies' conversation.

'I have got into one of my moping moods tonight,' said my father, after a silence; then quoting Shakespeare, whom, by way of keeping up our English, he used to read aloud, he said:

> 'In truth I know not why I am so sad:
> It wearies me; you say it wearies you;
> But how I got it – came by it . . .

I forget the rest. But I feel as if some great misfortune were hanging over us. I suppose the poor general's afflicted letter has had something to do with it.'

At this moment the unwonted sound of carriage wheels and many hoofs upon the road, arrested our attention.

They seemed to be approaching from the high ground overlooking the bridge, and very soon the equipage emerged from that point. Two horsemen first crossed the bridge, then came a carriage drawn by four horses, and two men rode behind.

It seemed to be the travelling carriage of a person of rank; and we were all immediately absorbed in watching that very unusual spectacle. It became, in a few moments, greatly more interesting, for just as the carriage had passed the summit of the steep bridge, one of the leaders, taking fright, communicated his panic to the rest, and, after a plunge or two, the whole team broke into a wild gallop together, and dashing between the horsemen who rode in front, came thundering along the road towards us with the speed of a hurricane.

The excitement of the scene was made more painful by the clear, long-drawn screams of a female voice from the carriage window.

We all advanced in curiosity and horror; my father in silence, the rest with various ejaculations of terror.

Our suspense did not last long. Just before you reach the castle drawbridge, on the route they were coming, there stands by the roadside a magnificent lime tree; on the other stands an ancient stone cross, at sight of which the horses, now going at a pace that was perfectly frightful, swerved so as to bring the wheel over the projecting roots of the tree.

I knew what was coming. I covered my eyes, unable to see it out, and turned my head away; at the same moment I heard a cry from my lady-friends, who had gone on a little.

Curiosity opened my eyes, and I saw a scene of utter confusion. Two of the horses were on the ground, the carriage lay upon its side, with two wheels in the air; the men were busy removing the traces, and a lady, with a commanding air and figure had got out, and stood with clasped hands, raising the handkerchief that was in them every now and then to her eyes. Through the carriage door was now lifted a young lady, who appeared to be lifeless. My dear old father was already beside the elder lady, with his hat in his hand, evidently tendering his aid and the resources of his *schloss*. The lady did not appear to hear him, or to have eyes for anything but the slender girl who was being placed against the slope of the bank.

I approached; the young lady was apparently stunned, but she was certainly not dead. My father, who piqued himself on being something of a physician, had just had his fingers to her wrist and assured the lady, who declared herself her mother, that her pulse, though faint and irregular, was undoubtedly still distinguishable. The lady clasped her hands and looked upward, as if in a momentary transport of gratitude; but immediately she broke out again in that theatrical way which is, I believe, natural to some people.

She was what is called a fine-looking woman for her time of life, and must have been handsome; she was tall, but not thin, and dressed in black velvet, and looked rather pale, but with a proud and commanding countenance, though now agitated strangely.

'Was ever being so born to calamity?' I heard her say, with clasped hands, as I came up. 'Here am I, on a journey of life and death, in prosecuting which to lose an hour is possibly to lose all. My child will not have recovered sufficiently to resume her route for who can say how long. I must leave her; I cannot, dare not, delay. How far on, sir, can you tell, is the nearest village? I must leave her there; and shall not see my darling or even hear of her till my return, three months hence.'

I plucked my father by the coat, and whispered earnestly in his ear, 'Oh! papa, pray ask her to let her stay with us – it would be so delightful. Do, pray.'

'If madame will entrust her child to the care of my daughter and of her good *gouvernante*, Madame Perrodon, and permit her to remain as our guest, under my charge, until her return, it will confer a distinction and an obligation upon us, and we shall treat her with all the care and devotion which so sacred a trust deserves.'

'I cannot do that, sir, it would be to task your kindness and chivalry too cruelly,' said the lady, distractedly.

'It would, on the contrary, be to confer on us a very great kindness at the moment when we most need it. My daughter has just been disappointed, by a cruel misfortune, in a visit from which she had long anticipated a great deal of happiness. If you confide this young lady to our care it will be her best consolation. The nearest village on your route is distant, and affords no such inn as you could think of placing your daughter at; you cannot allow her to continue her journey for any considerable distance without danger. If, as you say, you cannot suspend your journey, you must part with her tonight, and nowhere could you do so with more honest assurances of care and tenderness than here.'

There was something in this lady's air and appearance so distinguished, and even imposing, and in her manner so engaging, as to impress one, quite apart from the dignity of her equipage, with a conviction that she was a person of consequence.

By this time the carriage was replaced in its upright position, and the horses, quite tractable, in the traces again.

The lady threw on her daughter a glance which I fancied was not quite so affectionate as one might have anticipated from the beginning of the scene; then she beckoned slightly to my father, and withdrew two or three steps with him out of hearing; and talked to him with a fixed and stern countenance, not at all like that with which she had hitherto spoken.

I was filled with wonder that my father did not seem to perceive the change, and also unspeakably curious to learn what it could be that she was speaking of, almost in his ear, with so much earnestness and rapidity.

Two or three minutes at most, I think, she remained thus employed, then she turned, and a few steps brought her to where her daughter lay, supported by Madame Perrodon. She kneeled beside her for a moment and whispered, as Madame supposed, a little benediction in her ear; then hastily kissing her, she stepped into her carriage, the door was closed, the footmen in stately liveries jumped up behind, the outriders spurred on, the postilions cracked their whips, the horses plunged and broke suddenly into a furious canter that threatened soon again to become a gallop, and the carriage whirled away, followed at the same rapid pace by the two horsemen in the rear.

3

We Compare Notes

We followed the *cortège* with our eyes until it was swiftly lost to sight in the misty wood, and the very sound of the hoofs and wheels died away in the silent night air.

Nothing remained to assure us that the adventure had not been an illusion except the young lady, who just at that moment opened her eyes. I could not see, for her face was turned from me, but she raised her head, evidently looking about her, and I heard a very sweet voice ask complainingly, 'Where is mamma?'

Our good Madame Perrodon answered tenderly, and added some comfortable assurances.

I then heard her ask: 'Where am I? What is this place?' and after that she said, 'I don't see the carriage; and Matska, where is she?'

Madame answered all her questions in so far as she understood them; and gradually the young lady remembered how the misadventure came about, and was glad to hear that no one in, or in attendance on, the carriage was hurt; and on learning that her mamma had left her here, till her return in about three months, she wept.

I was going to add my consolations to those of Madame Perrodon when Mademoiselle de Lafontaine placed her hand upon my arm, saying: 'Don't approach, one at a time is as much as she can at present converse with; a very little excitement would possibly overpower her now.'

As soon as she is comfortably in bed, I thought, I will run up to her room and see her.

My father in the meantime had sent a servant on horseback for the physician, who lived about two leagues away; and a bedroom was being prepared for the young lady's reception.

The stranger now rose, and leaning on Madame's arm, walked slowly over the drawbridge and into the castle gate.

In the hall, servants waited to receive her, and she was conducted forthwith to her room.

The room we usually sat in as our drawing-room is long, having four windows that look over the moat and drawbridge upon the forest scene I have just described. It is furnished in old carved oak, with large carved cabinets, and the chairs are cushioned with crimson Utrecht velvet. The walls are covered with tapestries surrounded with great gold frames, the figures being as large as life, in ancient and zvery curious costume, and the subjects represented are hunting and hawking, and are generally festive. It is not too stately to be extremely comfortable; and here we had our tea, for with his usual patriotic leanings, my father insisted that the national beverage should make its appearance regularly with our coffee and chocolate.

We sat here this night, and with candles lighted, were talking over the adventure of the evening.

Madame Perrodon and Mademoiselle de Lafontaine were both of our party. The young stranger had hardly lain down in her bed when she sank into a deep sleep, so the ladies had left her in the care of a servant.

'How do you like our guest?' I asked, as soon as Madame entered. 'Tell me all about her?'

'I like her extremely,' answered Madame; 'she is, I almost think, the prettiest creature I ever saw; about your age, and so gentle and nice.'

'She is absolutely beautiful,' threw in Mademoiselle, who had peeped for a moment into the stranger's room.

'And such a sweet voice!' added Madame Perrodon.

'Did you remark a woman in the carriage, after it was set up again, who did not get out,' enquired Mademoiselle, 'but only looked from the window?'

No, we had not seen her.

Then she described a hideous black woman, with a sort of coloured turban on her head, who was gazing all the time from the carriage window, nodding and grinning derisively towards the ladies, with gleaming eyes and large white eyeballs, and her teeth set as if in fury.

'Did you remark what an ill-looking pack of men the servants were?' asked Madame.

'Yes,' said my father, who had just come in, 'ugly, hangdog-looking fellows, as ever I beheld in my life. I hope they mayn't rob the poor lady in the forest. They are clever rogues, however; they got everything to rights in a minute.'

'I dare say they are worn out with too long travelling,' said Madame. 'Besides looking wicked, their faces were so strangely lean, and dark, and sullen. I am very curious, I own; but I dare say the young lady will tell us all about it tomorrow, if she is sufficiently recovered.'

'I don't think she will,' said my father, with a mysterious smile, and a little nod of his head, as if he knew more about it than he cared to tell us.

This made me all the more inquisitive as to what had passed between him and the lady in the black velvet in the brief but earnest interview that had immediately preceded her departure.

We were scarcely alone, when I entreated him to tell me. He did not need much pressing.

'There is no particular reason why I should not tell you. She expressed a reluctance to trouble us with the care of her daughter, saying she was in delicate health, and nervous, but not subject to any kind of seizure – she volunteered that – nor to any illusion; being, in fact, perfectly sane.'

'How very odd to say all that!' I interpolated. 'It was so unnecessary.'

'At all events it *was* said,' he laughed, 'and as you wish to know all that passed, which was indeed very little, I tell you. She then said, "I am making a long journey of *vital* importance" – she emphasised the word – "rapid and secret; I shall return for my child in three months; in the meantime, she will be silent as to who we are, whence we come, and whither we are travelling." That is all she said. She spoke very pure French. When she said the word "secret", she paused for a few seconds, looking sternly, her eyes fixed on mine. I fancy she makes a great point of that. You saw how quickly she was gone. I hope I have not done a very foolish thing in taking charge of the young lady.'

For my part, I was delighted. I was longing to see and talk to her;

and only waiting till the doctor should give me leave. You, who live in towns, can have no idea how great an event the introduction of a new friend is in such a solitude as surrounded us.

The doctor did not arrive till nearly one o'clock; but I could no more have gone to my bed and slept than I could have overtaken, on foot, the carriage in which the princess in black velvet had driven away.

When the physician came down to the drawing-room, it was to report very favourably upon his patient. She was now sitting up, her pulse quite regular, apparently perfectly well. She had sustained no injury, and the little shock to her nerves had passed away quite harmlessly. There could be no harm certainly in my seeing her, if we both wished it; and, with this permission, I sent, forthwith, to know whether she would allow me to visit her for a few minutes in her room.

The servant returned immediately to say that she desired nothing more.

You may be sure I was not long in availing myself of this permission.

Our visitor lay in one of the handsomest rooms in the *schloss*. It was perhaps a little stately. There was a sombre piece of tapestry opposite the foot of the bed, representing Cleopatra with the asp to her bosom; and other solemn classic scenes were displayed, a little faded, upon the other walls. But there was gold carving and rich and varied colour enough in the other decorations of the room to more than redeem the gloom of the old tapestries.

There were candles at the bedside. She was sitting up; her slender pretty figure enveloped in the soft silk dressing-gown, embroidered with flowers, and lined with thick quilted silk, which her mother had thrown over her feet as she lay upon the ground.

What was it that, as I reached the bedside and had just begun my little greeting, struck me dumb in a moment, and made me recoil a step or two from before her? I will tell you. I saw the very face which had visited me in my childhood at night, which had remained fixed in my memory and on which I had for so many years often ruminated with horror, when no one suspected of what I was thinking.

It was pretty, even beautiful; and when I first beheld it, wore the same melancholy expression.

But this almost instantly lighted into a strange fixed smile of recognition.

There was a silence of fully a minute, and then at length she spoke; I could not.

'How wonderful!' she exclaimed. 'Twelve years ago, I saw your face in a dream, and it has haunted me ever since.'

'Wonderful indeed!' I repeated, overcoming with an effort the horror that had for a time suspended my utterances. 'Twelve years ago, in vision or reality, *I* certainly saw you. I could not forget your face. It has remained before my eyes ever since.'

Her smile had softened. Whatever I had fancied strange in it, was gone, and it and her dimpling cheeks were now delightfully pretty and intelligent.

I felt reassured and continued more in the vein which hospitality indicated to bid her welcome, and to tell her how much pleasure her accidental arrival had given us all, and especially what a happiness it was to me.

I took her hand as I spoke. I was a little shy, as lonely people are, but the situation made me eloquent, and even bold. She pressed my hand, she laid hers upon it, and her eyes glowed, as, looking hastily into mine, she smiled again and blushed.

She answered my welcome very prettily. I sat down beside her, still wondering; and she said: 'I must tell you my vision about you; it is so very strange that you and I should have had, each of the other, so vivid a dream that each should have seen, I you and you me, looking as we do now, when of course we both were mere children. I was a child, about six years old, and I awoke from a confused and troubled dream, and found myself in a room, unlike my nursery, wainscoted clumsily in some dark wood, and with cupboards and bedsteads, and chairs and benches placed about it. The beds were, I thought, all empty, and the room itself without anyone but myself in it; and I, after looking about me for some time, and admiring especially an iron candlestick, with two branches, which I should certainly know again, crept under one of the beds to reach the window; but as I got from under the bed, I heard someone crying; and looking up, while I was still upon my knees, I saw you – most assuredly you – as I see you now; a beautiful young lady, with golden hair and large blue eyes, and lips – your lips – you, as you are here. Your looks won me; I climbed on the bed and put my arms about you, and I think we both fell asleep. I was aroused by a scream; you were sitting up screaming. I was frightened, and slipped down upon the ground, and, it seemed to me, lost consciousness for a moment; and when I came to myself, I was again in my nursery at home. Your face I have never forgotten since. I could not be misled by mere resemblance. You are the lady whom I then saw.'

It was now my turn to relate my corresponding vision, which I did, to the undisguised wonder of my new acquaintance.

'I don't know which should be most afraid of the other,' she said, again smiling. 'If you were less pretty I think I should be very much afraid of you, but being as you are, and you and I both so young, I feel only that I made your acquaintance twelve years ago, and have already a right to your intimacy; at all events, it does seem as if we were destined, from our earliest childhood, to be friends. I wonder whether you feel as strangely drawn towards me as I do to you; I have never had a friend – shall I find one now?' She sighed, and her fine dark eyes gazed passionately on me.

Now the truth is, I felt rather unaccountably towards the beautiful stranger. I did feel, as she said, 'drawn towards her', but there was also something of repulsion. In this ambiguous feeling, however, the sense of attraction immensely prevailed She interested and won me; she was so beautiful and so indescribably engaging.

I perceived now something of languor and exhaustion stealing over her, and hastened to bid her good-night.

'The doctor thinks,' I added, 'that you ought to have a maid to sit up with you tonight; one of ours is waiting, and you will find her a very useful and quiet creature.'

'How kind of you, but I could not sleep – I never could – with an attendant in the room. I shan't require any assistance but – shall I confess my weakness – I am haunted with a terror of robbers. Our house was robbed once, and two servants murdered, so I always lock my door. It has become a habit – and you look so kind I know you will forgive me. I see there is a key in the lock.'

She held me close in her pretty arms for a moment and whispered in my ear, 'Good-night, darling, it is very hard to part with you, but good-night; tomorrow, but not early, I shall see you again.'

She sank back on the pillow with a sigh, and her fine eyes followed me with a fond and melancholy gaze, and she murmured again, 'Good-night, dear friend.'

Young people like, and even love, on impulse. I was flattered by the evident, though as yet undeserved, fondness she showed me. I liked the confidence with which she at once received me. She was determined that we should be very dear friends.

Next day came and we met again. I was delighted with my companion; that is to say, in many respects.

Her looks lost nothing in daylight – she was certainly the most beautiful creature I had ever seen, and the unpleasant remembrance of the face presented in my early dream had lost the effect of the first unexpected recognition.

She confessed that she had experienced a similar shock on seeing me, and precisely the same faint antipathy that had mingled with my admiration of her. We now laughed together over our momentary horrors.

4

Her Habits – A Saunter

I told you that I was charmed with her in most particulars. There were some that did not please me so well.

She was above the middle height of women. I shall begin by describing her. She was slender, and wonderfully graceful. Except that her movements were languid – very languid – and yet there was nothing in her appearance to indicate an invalid. Her complexion was rich and brilliant; her features were small and beautifully formed; her eyes large, dark and lustrous; her hair was quite wonderful, I never saw hair so magnificently thick and long when it was down about her shoulders; I have often placed my hands under it, and laughed with wonder at its weight. It was exquisitely fine and soft, and in colour a rich, very dark brown, with something of gold. I loved to let it down, tumbling with its own weight, as, in her room, she lay back in her chair talking in her sweet low voice; I used to fold and braid it, and spread it out and play with it. Heavens! If I had but known all!

I said there were particulars which did not please me. I have told you that her confidence won me the first night I saw her; but I found that she exercised with respect to herself, her mother, her history, everything in fact connected with her life, plans, and people, an ever-wakeful reserve. I dare say I was unreasonable, perhaps I was wrong; I dare say I ought to have respected the solemn injunction laid upon my father by the stately lady in black velvet. But curiosity is a restless and unscrupulous passion, and no one girl can endure, with patience, that her's should be baffled by another. What harm could it do anyone to tell me what I so ardently desired to know? Had she no trust in my good sense or honour? Why would she not believe me when I assured her, so solemnly, that I would not divulge one syllable of what she told me to any mortal breathing.

There was a coldness, it seemed to me, beyond her years, in her smiling, melancholy, persistent refusal to afford me the least ray of light.

I cannot say we quarrelled upon this point, for she would not quarrel upon any. It was, of course, very unfair of me to press her, very ill-bred, but I really could not help it; though I might just as well have let it alone.

What she did tell me amounted, in my unconscionable estimation, to nothing.

It was all summed up in three very vague disclosures: first – her name was Carmilla; second – her family was very ancient and noble; third – her home lay in the direction of the west.

She would not tell me the name of her family, nor their armorial bearings, nor the name of their estate, nor even that of the country they lived in.

You are not to suppose that I worried her incessantly on these subjects. I watched for an opportunity and rather insinuated than urged my enquiries. Once or twice, indeed, I did attack her more directly. But no matter what my tactics, utter failure was invariably the result. Reproaches and caresses were all lost upon her. But I must add this, that her evasion was conducted with so pretty a melancholy and deprecation, with so many, and even passionate, declarations of her liking for me and trust in my honour, and with so many promises that I should at last know all, that I could not find it in my heart long to be offended with her.

She used to place her pretty arms about my neck, draw me to her, and laying her cheek to mine, murmur with her lips near my ear, 'Dearest, your little heart is wounded; think me not cruel because I

obey the irresistible law of my strength and weakness; if your dear
heart is wounded, my wild heart bleeds with yours. In the rapture of
my enormous humiliation I live in your warm life, and you shall die –
die, sweetly die – into mine. I cannot help it; as I draw near to you,
you, in your turn, will draw near to others, and learn the rapture of
that cruelty, which yet is love; so, for a while, seek to know no more of
me and mine, but trust me with all your loving spirit.'

And when she had spoken such a rhapsody, she would press me
more closely in her trembling embrace, and her lips in soft kisses
gently glow upon my cheek.

Her agitations and her language were unintelligible to me.

From these foolish embraces, which were not of very frequent
occurrence, I must allow, I used to wish to extricate myself; but my
energies seemed to fail me. Her murmured words sounded like a
lullaby in my ear, and soothed my resistance into a trance, from which
I only seemed to recover myself when she withdrew her arms.

In these mysterious moods I did not like her. I experienced a
strange tumultuous excitement that was pleasurable but was ever and
anon mingled with a vague sense of fear and disgust. I had no distinct
thoughts about her while such scenes lasted, but I was conscious of a
love growing into adoration, and also of abhorrence. This I know is
paradox, but I can make no other attempt to explain the feeling.

I now write, after an interval of more than ten years, with a trembling
hand, with a confused and horrible recollection of certain occurrences
and situations in the ordeal through which I was unconsciously passing;
though with a vivid and very sharp remembrance of the main current of
my story. But, I suspect in all lives there are certain emotional scenes,
those in which our passions have been most wildly and terribly roused,
that are of all others the most vaguely and dimly remembered.

Sometimes, after an hour of apathy, my strange and beautiful
companion would take my hand and hold it with a fond pressure,
renewed again and again; blushing softly, she would gaze in my face
with languid and burning eyes, breathing so fast that her dress rose
and fell with the tumultuous respiration. It was like the ardour of a
lover; it embarrassed me; it was hateful and yet overpowering; and
with gloating eyes she drew me to her, and her hot lips travelled along
my cheek in kisses; and she would whisper, almost in sobs, 'You are
mine, you shall be mine, and you and I are one for ever.' Then she

would throw herself back in her chair, with her small hands over her eyes, leaving me trembling.

'Are we related,' I used to ask; 'what can you mean by all this? I remind you perhaps of someone whom you love; but you must not, I hate it; I don't know you – I don't know myself when you look so and talk so.'

She used to sigh at my vehemence , then turn away and drop my hand.

Respecting these very extraordinary manifestations I strove in vain to form any satisfactory theory – I could not refer them to affectation or trick. It was unmistakably the momentary breaking out of suppressed instinct and emotion. Was she, notwithstanding her mother's volunteered denial, subject to brief visitations of insanity; or was there here a disguise and a romance? I had read in old story books of such things. What if a boyish lover had found his way into the house, and sought to prosecute his suit in masquerade, with the assistance of a clever old adventuress. But there were many things against this hypothesis, highly interesting as it was to my vanity.

I could boast of no little attentions such as masculine gallantry delights to offer. Between these passionate moments there were long intervals of commonplace intercourse, of gaiety, of brooding melancholy, during which, except that I detected her eyes, so full of melancholy fire, following me at times, I might have been as nothing to her. Except in these brief periods of mysterious excitement her ways were girlish; and there was always a languor about her, quite incompatible with a masculine system in a state of health.

In some respects her habits were odd. Perhaps not so singular in the opinion of a town lady, like you, as they appeared to us rustic people. She used to come down very late, generally not till one o'clock, she would then take a cup of chocolate, but eat nothing; we then went out for a walk, which was a mere saunter, and she seemed, almost immediately, exhausted, and either returned to the *schloss* or sat on one of the benches that were placed, here and there, among the trees. This was a bodily languor in which her mind did not sympathise. She was always an animated talker, and very intelligent.

She sometimes alluded for a moment to her own home, or mentioned an adventure or situation, or an early recollection, which indicated a people of strange manners and described customs of which we knew nothing. I gathered from these chance hints that her native country was much more remote than I had at first fancied.

As we sat thus one afternoon under the trees a funeral passed us by. It was that of a pretty young girl, whom I had often seen, the daughter of one of the rangers of the forest. The poor man was walking behind the coffin of his darling; she was his only child, and he looked quite heartbroken. Peasants walking two-and-two came behind; they were singing a funeral hymn.

I rose to mark my respect as they passed, and joined in the hymn they were very sweetly singing.

My companion shook me a little roughly, and I turned surprised.

She said brusquely, 'Don't you perceive how discordant that is?'

'I think it very sweet, on the contrary,' I answered, vexed at the interruption, and very uncomfortable, lest the people who composed the little procession should observe and resent what was passing.

I resumed, therefore, instantly, and was again interrupted. 'You pierce my ears,' said Carmilla, almost angrily, and stopping her ears with her tiny fingers. 'Besides, how can you tell that your religion and mine are the same; your forms wound me, and I hate funerals. What a fuss! Why, you must die – *everyone* must die; and all are happier when they do. Come home.'

'My father has gone on with the clergyman to the churchyard. I thought you knew she was to be buried today.'

'*She?* I don't trouble my head about peasants. I don't know who she is,' answered Carmilla, with a flash from her fine eyes.

'She is the poor girl who fancied she saw a ghost a fortnight ago, and has been dying ever since, till yesterday, when she expired.'

'Tell me nothing about ghosts, I shan't sleep tonight if you do.'

'I hope there is no plague or fever coming; all this looks very like it,' I continued. 'The swineherd's young wife died only a week ago, and she thought something seized her by the throat as she lay in her bed and nearly strangled her. Papa says such horrible fancies do accompany some forms of fever. She was quite well the day before. She sank afterwards, and died before a week.'

'Well, her funeral is over, I hope, and her hymn sung; and our ears shan't be tortured with that discord and jargon. It has made me nervous. Sit down here, beside me; sit close; hold my hand; press it hard – hard – harder.'

We had moved a little back, and had come to another seat.

She sat down. Her face underwent a change that alarmed and even terrified me for a moment. It darkened, and became horribly livid; her teeth and hands were clenched, and she frowned and compressed her lips, while she stared down upon the ground at her feet, and trembled all over with a continued shudder as irrepressible as ague. All her energies seemed strained to suppress a fit, with which she was then breathlessly tugging; and at length a low convulsive cry of suffering broke from her, and gradually the hysteria subsided. 'There! That comes of strangling people with hymns!' she said at last. 'Hold me, hold me still. It is passing away.'

And so gradually it did; and perhaps to dissipate the sombre impression which the spectacle had left upon me, she became unusually animated and chatty; and so we got home.

This was the first time I had seen her exhibit any definable symptoms of that delicacy of health which her mother had spoken of. It was the first time, also, I had seen her exhibit anything like temper.

Both passed away like a summer cloud; and never but once afterwards did I witness on her part a momentary sign of anger. I will tell you how it happened.

She and I were looking out of one of the long drawing-room windows, when there entered the courtyard, over the drawbridge, a figure of a wanderer whom I knew very well. He used to visit the *schloss* generally twice a year.

It was the figure of a hunchback, with the sharp lean features that generally accompany deformity. He wore a pointed black beard, and he was smiling from ear to ear, showing his white fangs. He was dressed in buff, black and scarlet, and crossed with more straps and belts than I could count from which hung all manner of things. Behind, he carried a magic-lantern, and two boxes, which I well knew, in one of which was a salamander, and in the other a mandrake. These monsters used to make my father laugh. They were compounded of parts of monkeys, parrots, squirrels, fish and hedgehogs, dried and stitched together with great neatness and startling effect. He had a fiddle, a box of conjuring apparatus, a pair of foils and masks attached to his belt, several other mysterious cases dangling about him, and a black staff with copper ferrules in his hand. His companion was a rough spare dog that followed at his heels, but stopped short

suspiciously at the drawbridge, and in a little while began to howl
dismally.

In the meantime, the mountebank, standing in the midst of the
courtyard, raised his grotesque hat and made us a very ceremonious
bow, paying his compliments very volubly in execrable French, and
German not much better. Then, disengaging his fiddle, he began to
scrape a lively air, to which he sang with a merry discord, dancing with
ludicrous airs and activity that made me laugh, in spite of the dog's
howling.

Then he advanced to the window with many smiles and salutations
and, his hat in his left hand, his fiddle under his arm and with a fluency
that never took breath, he gabbled a long advertisement of all his
accomplishments, and the resources of the various arts which he placed
at our service, and the curiosities and entertainments which it was in
his power, at our bidding, to display.

'Will your ladyships be pleased to buy an amulet against the vampire
which is going like the wolf, I hear, through these woods,' he said,
dropping his hat on the pavement. 'They are dying of it right and left,
and here is a charm that never fails; only pin it to the pillow, and you
may laugh in his face.'

These charms consisted of oblong slips of vellum with cabbalistic
ciphers and diagrams upon them.

Carmilla instantly purchased one, and so did I.

He was looking up, and we were smiling down upon him, amused;
at least, I can answer for myself. His piercing black eye, as he looked
up in our faces, seemed to detect something that fixed for a moment
his curiosity.

In an instant he unrolled a leather case, full of all manner of odd
little steel instruments.

'See here, my lady,' he said, displaying it, and addressing me, 'I
profess, among other things less useful, the art of dentistry. Plague
take the dog!' he interpolated. 'Silence, beast! He howls so that your
ladyships can scarcely hear a word. Your noble friend, the young lady
at your right, has the sharpest tooth – long, thin, pointed, like an awl,
like a needle; ha, ha! With my sharp and long sight, as I look up, I have
seen it distinctly; now if it happens to hurt the young lady, and I think
it must, here am I, here are my file, my punch, my nippers; I will make
it round and blunt, if her ladyship pleases; no longer the tooth of a

fish, but of a beautiful young lady as she is. Hey? Is the young lady displeased? Have I been too bold? Have I offended her?'

The young lady, indeed, looked very angry as she drew back from the window.

'How dares that mountebank insult us so? Where is your father? I shall demand redress from him. My father would have had the wretch tied up to the pump, and flogged with a cart-whip, and burnt to the bones with the castle brand!'

She retired from the window a step or two, and sat down, and had hardly lost sight of the offender, when her wrath subsided as suddenly as it had risen, and she gradually recovered her usual tone, and seemed to forget the little hunchback and his follies.

My father was out of spirits that evening. On coming in he told us that there had been another case very similar to the two fatal ones which had lately occurred. The sister of a young peasant on his estate, only a mile away, was very ill, had been, as she described it, attacked very nearly in the same way, and was now slowly but steadily sinking.

'All this,' said my father, 'is strictly referable to natural causes. These poor people infect one another with their superstitions, and so repeat in imagination the images of terror that have infested their neighbours.'

'But that very circumstance frightens one horribly,' said Carmilla.

'How so?' enquired my father.

'I am so afraid of fancying I see such things; I think it would be as bad as reality.'

'We are in God's hands; nothing can happen without his permission, and all will end well for those who love Him. He is our faithful creator; He has made us all, and will take care of us.'

'Creator? *Nature!*' said the young lady in answer to my gentle father. 'All this disease that invades the country is natural. Nature. All things proceed from Nature – don't they? All things in the heaven, in the earth, and under the earth, act and live as Nature ordains? I think so.'

'The doctor said he would come here today,' said my father, after a silence. 'I want to know what he thinks about it, and what he thinks we had better do.'

'Doctors never did me any good,' said Carmilla.

'Then you have been ill?' I asked.

'More ill than ever you were,' she answered.

'Long ago?'

'Yes, a long time. I suffered from this very illness; but I forget all but my pain and weakness, and they were not so bad as are suffered in other diseases.'

'You were very young then?'

'I dare say; let us talk no more of it. You would not wound a friend?' She looked languidly in my eyes, and passed her arm round my waist lovingly, and led me out of the room. My father was busy over some papers near the window.

'Why does your papa like to frighten us?' said the pretty girl, with a sigh and a little shudder.

'He doesn't, dear Carmilla, it is the very furthest thing from his mind.'

'Are you afraid, dearest?'

'I should be very much if I fancied there was any real danger of my being attacked as those poor people were.'

'You are afraid to die?'

'Yes, everyone is.'

'But to die as lovers may – to die together, so that they may live together. Girls are caterpillars while they live in the world, to be finally butterflies when the summer comes; but in the meantime they are grubs and larvae, don't you see – each with their peculiar propensities, necessities and structure. So says Monsieur Buffon, in his big book, in the next room.'

Later in the day the doctor came, and was closeted with papa for some time. He was a skilful man, of sixty and upwards, he wore powder, and shaved his pale face as smooth as a pumpkin. He and papa emerged from the room together, and I heard papa laugh, and say as they came out: 'Well, I do wonder at a wise man like you. What do you say to hippogriffs and dragons?'

The doctor was smiling, and made answer, shaking his head, 'Nevertheless, life and death are mysterious states, and we know little of the resources of either.'

And so they walked on, and I heard no more. I did not then know what the doctor had been broaching, but I think I guess it now.

A Wonderful Likeness

That evening there arrived from Gratz the grave, dark-faced son of the picture-cleaner, with a horse and cart laden with two large packing-cases, having many pictures in each. It was a journey of ten leagues, and whenever a messenger arrived at the *schloss* from our little capital of Gratz, we used to crowd about him in the hall, to hear the news.

This arrival created in our secluded quarters quite a sensation. The cases remained in the hall, and the messenger was taken charge of by the servants till he had eaten his supper. Then with assistants, and armed with hammer, ripping chisel and turnscrew, he met us in the hall, where we had assembled to witness the unpacking of the cases.

Carmilla sat looking listlessly on, while one after the other the old pictures, nearly all portraits, which had undergone the process of renovation, were brought to light. My mother was of an old Hungarian family, and most of these pictures, which were about to be restored to their places, had come to us through her.

My father had a list in his hand, from which he read as the artist rummaged out the corresponding numbers. I don't know that the pictures were very good, but they were undoubtedly very old, and some of them very curious also. They had, for the most part, the merit of being now seen by me, I may say, for the first time; for the smoke and dust of time had all but obliterated them.

'There is a picture that I have not seen yet,' said my father. 'In one corner, at the top of it, is the name, as well as I could read, "Marcia Karnstein", and the date "1698"; and I am curious to see how it has turned out.'

I remembered it; it was a small picture, about a foot and a half high, and nearly square, without a frame; but it was so blackened by age that I had not been able to make it out.

The artist now produced it, with evident pride. It was quite beautiful; it was startling; it seemed to live. It was the effigy of Carmilla!

'Carmilla, dear, here is an absolute miracle. Here you are, living, smiling, ready to speak, in this picture. Isn't it beautiful, papa? And see, even the little mole on her throat.'

My father laughed, and said, 'Certainly it is a wonderful likeness,' but he looked away, and to my surprise seemed but little struck by it, and went on talking to the picture-cleaner, who was also something of an artist, and discoursed with intelligence about the other works which his art had just brought into light and colour, while *I* was more and more lost in wonder the more I looked at the picture.

'Will you let me hang this picture in my room, papa?' I asked.

'Certainly, dear,' said he, smiling, 'I'm very glad you think it so like. It must be prettier even than I thought it, if it is.'

The young lady did not acknowledge this pretty speech, did not seem to hear it. She was leaning back in her seat, her fine eyes under their long lashes gazing on me in contemplation, and she smiled in a kind of rapture.

'And now you can read quite plainly the name that is written in the corner. It is not Marcia; it looks as if it was done in gold. The name is Mircalla, Countess Karnstein, and this is a little coronet over it, and underneath A.D.1698. I am descended from the Karnsteins; that is, mamma was.'

'Ah!' said the lady, languidly, 'so am I, I think, a very long descent, very ancient. Are there any Karnsteins living now?'

'None who bear the name, I believe. The family were ruined, it seems, in some civil wars long ago, but the ruins of the castle are only about three miles away.'

'How interesting!' she said, languidly. 'But see what beautiful moonlight!' She glanced through the hall-door, which stood a little open. 'Suppose we take a little ramble round the court, and look down at the road and river.'

'It is so like the night you came to us,' I said.

She sighed, smiling.

She rose, and each with her arm about the other's waist, we walked out upon the pavement.

In silence, slowly we walked down to the drawbridge, where the beautiful landscape opened before us.

'And so you were thinking of the night I came here?' she almost whispered. 'Are you glad I came?'

'Delighted, dear Carmilla,' I answered.

'And you ask for the picture you think like me, to hang in your room,' she murmured with a sigh, as she drew her arm closer about my waist, and let her pretty head sink upon my shoulder.

'How romantic you are, Carmilla,' I said. 'Whenever you tell me your story, it will be made up chiefly of some one great romance.'

She kissed me silently.

'I am sure, Carmilla, you have been in love; that there is, at this moment, an affair of the heart going on.'

'I have been in love with no one, and never shall,' she whispered, 'unless it should be with you.'

How beautiful she looked in the moonlight!

Shy and strange was the look with which she quickly hid her face in my neck and hair, with tumultuous sighs, that seemed almost to sob, and pressed in mine a hand that trembled.

Her soft cheek was glowing against mine. 'Darling, darling,' she murmured, 'I live in you; and you would die for me, I love you so.'

I started from her.

She was gazing on me with eyes from which all fire, all meaning had flown, and a face colourless and apathetic.

'Is there a chill in the air, dear?' she said drowsily. 'I almost shiver; have I been dreaming? Let us come in. Come, come; come in.'

'You look ill, Carmilla; a little faint. You certainly must take some wine,' I said.

'Yes, I will. I'm better now. I shall be quite well in a few minutes. Yes, do give me a little wine,' answered Carmilla, as we approached the door. 'Let us look again for a moment; it is the last time, perhaps, I shall see the moonlight with you.'

'How do you feel now, dear Carmilla? Are you really better?' I asked.

I was beginning to take alarm, lest she were becoming a victim of the strange epidemic that they said had invaded the country about us.

'Papa would be grieved beyond measure,' I added, 'if he thought you were ever so little ill without immediately letting us know. We have a very skilful doctor near here, the physician who was with papa today.'

'I'm sure he is. I know how kind you all are; but, dear child, I am quite well again. There is nothing ever wrong with me, but a little weakness. People say I am languid; I am incapable of exertion; I can scarcely walk as far as a child of three years old; and every now and then the little strength I have falters, and I become as you have just seen me. But after all I am very easily set up again; in a moment I am perfectly myself. See how I have recovered.'

So, indeed, she had; and she and I talked a great deal, and very animated she was; and the remainder of that evening passed without any recurrence of what I called her infatuations. I mean her crazy talk and looks, which embarrassed, and even frightened me.

But there occurred that night an event which gave my thoughts quite a new turn, and seemed to startle even Carmilla's languid nature into momentary energy.

6

A Very Strange Agony

When we got into the drawing-room, and had sat down to our coffee and chocolate, although Carmilla did not take any she seemed quite herself again, and Madame and Mademoiselle de Lafontaine joined us, and made a little card party, in the course of which papa came in for what he called his 'dish of tea'.

When the game was over he sat down beside Carmilla on the sofa, and asked her, a little anxiously, whether she had heard from her mother since her arrival.

She answered, 'No.'

He then asked her whether she knew where a letter would reach her at present.

'I cannot tell,' she answered, ambiguously, 'but I have been thinking of leaving you; you have been already too hospitable and too kind to me. I have given you an infinity of trouble, and I should wish to take a carriage tomorrow, and post in pursuit of her; I know where I shall ultimately find her, although I dare not yet tell you.'

'But you must not dream of any such thing,' exclaimed my father, to my great relief. 'We can't afford to lose you so, and I won't consent to your leaving us except under the care of your mother, who was so good as to consent to your remaining with us till she should herself return. I should be quite happy if I knew that you heard from her; but this evening the accounts of the progress of the mysterious disease that has invaded our neighbourhood grow even more alarming; and, my beautiful guest, I do feel the responsibility, unaided by advice from your mother, very much. But I shall do my best; and one thing is certain, that you must not think of leaving us without her distinct direction to that effect. We should suffer too much in parting from you to consent to it easily.'

'Thank you, sir, a thousand times for your hospitality,' she answered, smiling bashfully. 'You have all been too kind to me; I have seldom been so happy in all my life before as in your beautiful château, under your care, and in the society of your dear daughter.'

So he gallantly, in his old-fashioned way, kissed her hand, smiling, and pleased at her little speech.

I accompanied Carmilla as usual to her room, and sat and chatted with her while she was preparing for bed.

'Do you think,' I said, at length, 'that you will ever confide fully in me?'

She turned round smiling, but made no answer – only continued to smile on me.

'You won't answer that?' I said. 'You can't answer pleasantly; I ought not to have asked you.'

'You were quite right to ask me that, or anything. You do not know how dear you are to me, or you could not think any confidence too great to look for. But I am under vows, no nun half so awfully, and I dare not tell my story yet, even to you. The time is very near when you shall know everything. You will think me cruel, very selfish, but love is always selfish; the more ardent, the more selfish. How jealous I am you cannot know. You must come with me, loving me, to death; or else hate me, and still come with me, hating me through death and after. There is no such word as indifference in my apathetic nature.'

'Now, Carmilla, you are going to talk your wild nonsense again,' I said hastily.

'Not I, silly little fool as I am, and full of whims and fancies; for your sake I'll talk like a sage. Were you ever at a ball?'

'No; how you do run on. What is it like? How charming it must be.'

'I almost forget, it is years ago.'

I laughed.

'You are not so old. Your first ball can hardly be forgotten yet.'

'I remember everything about it – with an effort. I see it all, as divers see what is going on above them, through a medium, dense, rippling, but transparent. There occurred that night what has confused the picture, and made its colours faint. I was all but assassinated in my bed, wounded *here*,' she touched her breast, 'and never was the same since.'

'Were you near dying?'

'Yes, very – a cruel love – strange love, that would have taken my life. Love will have its sacrifices. No sacrifice without blood. Let us go to sleep now; I feel so lazy. How can I get up just now and lock my door?'

She was lying with her tiny hands buried in her rich wavy hair, under her cheek, her little head upon the pillow, and her glittering eyes followed me wherever I moved, with a kind of shy smile that I could not decipher.

I bid her good-night, and crept from the room with an uncomfortable sensation.

I often wondered whether our pretty guest ever said her prayers. I certainly had never seen her upon her knees. In the morning she never came down until long after our family prayers were over, and at night she never left the drawing-room to attend our brief evening prayers in the hall.

If it had not been that it had casually come out in one of our careless talks that she had been baptised, I should have doubted her being a Christian. Religion was a subject on which I had never heard her speak a word. If I had known the world better, this particular neglect or antipathy would not have so much surprised me.

The precautions of nervous people are infectious, and persons of a like temperament are pretty sure, after a time, to imitate them. I had adopted Carmilla's habit of locking her bedroom door, having taken into my head all her whimsical alarms about midnight invaders and prowling assassins. I had also adopted her precaution of making a brief search through her room, to satisfy herself that no lurking assassin or robber was 'ensconced'.

These wise measures taken, I got into my bed and fell asleep. A light was burning in my room. This was an old habit, of very early date, which nothing could have tempted me to dispense with.

Thus fortified I might take my rest in peace. But dreams come through stone walls, light up dark rooms or darken light ones, and their persons make their exits and their entrances as they please and laugh at locksmiths.

I had a dream that night that was the beginning of a very strange agony.

I cannot call it a nightmare, for I was quite conscious of being asleep. But I was equally conscious of being in my room, and lying in bed, precisely as I actually was. I saw, or fancied I saw, the room and its furniture just as I had seen it last, except that it was very dark, and I saw something moving round the foot of the bed, which at first I could not accurately distinguish. But I soon saw that it was a sooty-black animal that resembled a monstrous cat. It appeared to me about four or five feet long, for it measured fully the length of the hearth-rug as it passed over it; and it continued to-ing and fro-ing with the lithe sinister restlessness of a beast in a cage. I could not cry out, although, as you may suppose, I was terrified. Its pace was growing faster, and the room rapidly darker and darker, and at length so dark that I could no longer see anything of it but its eyes. I felt it spring lightly on the bed. The two broad eyes approached my face, and suddenly I felt a stinging pain as if two large needles darted, an inch or two apart, deep into my breast a little below my throat. I waked with a scream. The room was lighted by the candle that burnt there all through the night, and I saw a female figure standing at the foot of the bed, a little at the right side. It was in a dark loose dress, and its hair was down and covered its shoulders. A block of stone could not have been more still. There was not the slightest stir of respiration. As I stared at it, the figure appeared to have changed its place, and was now nearer the door; then, close to it; then the door opened, and it passed out.

I was now relieved, and able to breathe and move. My first thought was that Carmilla had been playing a trick on me, and that I had forgotten to secure my door. I hastened to it, and found it locked as usual on the inside. I was afraid to open it – I was horrified. I sprang into my bed and covered my head up in the bedclothes, and lay there more dead than alive till morning.

Descending

It would be vain my attempting to tell you the horror with which, even now, I recall the occurrence of that night. It was no such transitory terror as a dream leaves behind it. It seemed to deepen by time, and communicated itself to the room and the very furniture that had encompassed the apparition.

I could not bear next day to be alone for a moment. I should have told papa, but for two opposite reasons. At one time I thought he would laugh at my story, and I could not bear its being treated as a jest; and at another, I thought he might fancy that I had been attacked by the mysterious complaint which had invaded our neighbourhood. I had myself no misgivings of the kind, and as he had been rather an invalid for some time, I was afraid of alarming him.

I was comfortable enough with my good-natured companions, Madame Perrodon and the vivacious Mademoiselle Lafontaine. They both perceived that I was out of spirits and nervous, and at length I told them what lay so heavy at my heart.

Mademoiselle laughed, but I fancied that Madame Perrodon looked anxious.

'By the by,' said Mademoiselle, laughing, 'the long lime tree walk, below Carmilla's bedroom window, is haunted!'

'Nonsense!' exclaimed Madame, who probably, thought the theme rather inopportune, 'and who tells that story, my dear?'

'Martin says that he came up twice, when the old yard-gate was being repaired, before sunrise, and twice saw the same female figure walking down the lime tree avenue.'

'So he well might, as long as there are cows to milk in the river fields,' said Madame.

'I dare say; but Martin chooses to be frightened, and never did I see fool more frightened.'

'You must not say a word about it to Carmilla, because she can see down that walk from her room window,' I interposed, 'and she is, if possible, a greater coward than I.'

Carmilla came down rather later than usual that day.

'I was so frightened last night,' she said, as soon as we were together, 'and I am sure I should have seen something dreadful if it had not been for that charm I bought from the poor little hunchback whom I called such hard names. I had a dream of something black coming round my bed, and I awoke in a perfect horror, and I really thought, for some seconds, I saw a dark figure near the chimney-piece, but I felt under my pillow for my charm, and the moment my fingers touched it, the figure disappeared, and I felt quite certain, if I hadn't had it by me, that something frightful would have made its appearance, and perhaps throttled me, as it did those poor people we heard of.'

'Well, listen to me,' I began, and recounted my adventure, at the recital of which she appeared horrified.

'And had you your charm near you?' she asked, earnestly.

'No, I had dropped it into a china vase in the drawing-room, but I shall certainly take it with me tonight, as you have so much faith in it.'

At this distance of time I cannot tell you, or even understand, how I overcame my horror so effectually as to lie alone in my room that night. I remember distinctly that I pinned the charm to my pillow. I fell asleep almost immediately, and slept even more soundly than usual all night.

Next night I passed as well. My sleep was delightfully deep and dreamless. But I wakened with a sense of lassitude and melancholy, which, however, did not exceed a degree that was almost luxurious.

'Well, I told you so,' said Carmilla, when I described my quiet sleep. 'I had such delightful sleep myself last night; I pinned the charm to the breast of my nightdress. It was too far away the night before. I am quite sure it was all fancy, except the dreams. I used to think that evil spirits made dreams, but our doctor told me it is no such thing. Only a fever passing by, or some other malady, as they often do, he said, knocks at the door, and not being able to get in, passes on, with that alarm.'

'And what do you think the charm is?' said I.

'It has been fumigated or immersed in some drug, and is an antidote against the malaria,' she answered.

'Then it acts only on the body?'

'Certainly; you don't suppose that evil spirits are frightened by bits of ribbon, or the perfumes of a druggist's shop? No, these complaints, wandering in the air, begin by trying the nerves, and so infect the brain; but before they can seize upon you, the antidote repels them. That I am sure is what the charm has done for us. It is nothing magical, it is simply natural.'

I should have been happier if I could quite have agreed with Carmilla, but I did my best, and the impression was a little losing its force.

For some nights I slept profoundly; but still every morning I felt the same lassitude, and a languor weighed upon me all day. I felt myself a changed girl. A strange melancholy was stealing over me, a melancholy that I would not have interrupted. Dim thoughts of death began to open, and an idea that I was slowly sinking took gentle, and, somehow, not unwelcome possession of me. If it was sad, the tone of mind which this induced was also sweet. Whatever it might be, my soul acquiesced in it.

I would not admit that I was ill, I would not consent to tell my papa, or to have the doctor sent for.

Carmilla became more devoted to me than ever, and her strange paroxysms of languid adoration more frequent. She used to gloat on me with increasing ardour the more my strength and spirits waned. This always shocked me like a momentary glare of insanity.

Without knowing it, I was now in a pretty advanced stage of the strangest illness under which mortal ever suffered. There was an unaccountable fascination in its earlier symptoms that more than reconciled me to the incapacitating effect of that stage of the malady. This fascination increased for a time, until it reached a certain point when gradually a sense of the horrible mingled itself with it, deepening, as you shall hear, until it discoloured and perverted the whole state of my life.

The first change I experienced was rather agreeable. It was very near the turning point from which began the descent of Avernus.

Certain vague and strange sensations visited me in my sleep. The prevailing one was of that pleasant, peculiar cold thrill which we feel in bathing, when we move against the current of a river. This was soon accompanied by dreams that seemed interminable, and were so vague that I could never recollect their scenery and persons or any one connected portion of their action. But they left an awful impression, and a sense of exhaustion, as if I had passed through a long period of great mental exertion and danger. After all these dreams there remained on waking a remembrance of having been in a place very nearly dark, and of having spoken to people whom I could not see; and especially of one clear voice, of a female's, very deep, that spoke as if at a distance, slowly, and producing always the same sensation of indescribable solemnity and fear. Sometimes there came a sensation as if a hand was drawn softly along my cheek and neck. Sometimes it was as if warm lips kissed me, and longer and more lovingly as they reached my throat, but there the caress fixed itself. My heart beat faster, my breathing rose and fell rapidly and full drawn; a sobbing, that rose into a sense of strangulation, supervened, and turned into a dreadful convulsion, in which my senses left me, and I became unconscious.

It was now three weeks since the commencement of this un-accountable state. My sufferings had, during the last week, told upon my appearance. I had grown pale, my eyes were dilated and darkened underneath, and the languor which I had long felt began to display itself in my countenance.

My father asked me often whether I was ill; but, with an obstinacy which now seems to me unaccountable, I persisted in assuring him that I was quite well.

In a sense this was true. I had no pain, I could complain of no bodily derangement. My complaint seemed to be one of the imagination, or the nerves, and, horrible as my sufferings were, I kept them, with a morbid reserve, very nearly to myself.

It could not be that terrible complaint which the peasants attribute to a vampire, for I had now been suffering for three weeks, and they were seldom ill for much more than three days when death put an end to their miseries.

Carmilla complained of dreams and feverish sensations, but by no means of so alarming a kind as mine. I say that mine were extremely alarming. Had I been capable of comprehending my condition, I would have invoked aid and advice on my knees. The narcotic of an unsuspected influence was acting upon me, and my perceptions were benumbed.

I am going to tell you now of a dream that led immediately to an odd discovery.

One night, instead of the voice I was accustomed to hear in the dark, I heard one, sweet and tender, and at the same time terrible, which said, 'Your mother warns you to beware of the assassin.' At the same time a light unexpectedly sprang up, and I saw Carmilla, standing near the foot of my bed in her white nightdress, bathed, from her chin to her feet, in one great stain of blood.

I wakened with a shriek, possessed with the one idea that Carmilla was being murdered. I remember springing from my bed, and my next recollection is that of standing on the landing, crying for help.

Madame and Mademoiselle came scurrying out of their rooms in alarm; a lamp burned always on the landing, and seeing me, they soon learned the cause of my terror.

I insisted on our knocking at Carmilla's door. Our knocking was unanswered. It soon became a pounding and an uproar. We shrieked her name, but all was vain. We all grew frightened, for the door was locked. We hurried back, in panic, to my room. There we rang the bell long and furiously. If my father's room had been at that side of the house, we would have called him up at once to our aid. But, alas! he was quite out of hearing, and to reach him involved an excursion for which we none of us had courage.

Servants, however, soon came running up the stairs; I had got on my dressing-gown and slippers meanwhile, and my companions were already similarly furnished. Recognising the voices of the servants on the landing, we sallied out together; and having renewed, as fruitlessly, our summons at Carmilla's door, I ordered the men to force the lock. They did so, and we stood, holding our lights aloft, in the doorway, and so stared into the room.

We called her by name; but there was still no reply. We looked round the room. Everything was undisturbed. It was exactly in the state in which I had left it on bidding her good-night. But Carmilla was gone.

Search

At sight of the room, perfectly undisturbed except for our violent entrance, we began to cool a little, and soon recovered our senses sufficiently to dismiss the men. It had struck Mademoiselle that possibly Carmilla had been wakened by the uproar at her door, and in her first panic had jumped from her bed and hidden herself in a press, or behind a curtain, from which she could not, of course, emerge until the major-domo and his myrmidons had withdrawn. We now recommenced our search, and began to call her by name again.

It was all to no purpose. Our perplexity and agitation increased. We examined the windows, but they were secured. I implored of Carmilla, if she had concealed herself, to play this cruel trick no longer – to come out, and to end our anxieties. It was all useless. I was by this time convinced that she was not in the room, nor in the dressing-room, the door of which was still locked on this side. She could not have passed through it. I was utterly puzzled. Had Carmilla discovered one of those secret passages which the old housekeeper said were known to exist in the *schloss*, although the tradition of their exact situation had been lost. A little time would, no doubt, explain all – utterly perplexed as, for the present, we were.

It was past four o'clock, and I preferred passing the remaining hours of darkness in Madame's room. Daylight brought no solution of the difficulty.

The whole household, with my father at its head, was in a state of agitation next morning. Every part of the château was searched. The grounds were explored. Not a trace of the missing lady could be discovered. The stream was about to be dragged; my father was in distraction; what a tale to have to tell the poor girl's mother on her return. I, too, was almost beside myself, though my grief was quite of a different kind.

The morning was passed in alarm and excitement. It was now one o'clock, and still no tidings. I ran up to Carmilla's room, and found her standing at her dressing-table. I was astounded. I could not believe my eyes. She beckoned me to her with her pretty finger, in silence. Her face expressed extreme fear.

I ran to her in an ecstasy of joy; I kissed and embraced her again and again. I ran to the bell and rang it vehemently, to bring others to the spot, who might at once relieve my father's anxiety.

'Dear Carmilla, what has become of you all this time? We have been in agonies of anxiety about you,' I exclaimed. 'Where have you been? How did you come back?'

'Last night was a night of wonders,' she said.

'For mercy's sake, explain all you can.'

'It was past two last night,' she said, 'when I went to sleep as usual in my bed with my doors locked, that of the dressing-room and that opening upon the gallery. My sleep was uninterrupted, and, so far as I know, dreamless; but I awoke just now on the sofa in the dressing-room there, and I found the door between the rooms open, and the other door forced. How could all this have happened without my being wakened? It must have been accompanied with a great deal of noise, and I am particularly easily wakened; and how could I have been carried out of my bed without my sleep having been interrupted, I whom the slightest stir startles?'

By this time, Madame, Mademoiselle, my father, and a number of the servants were in the room. Carmilla was, of course, overwhelmed with enquiries, congratulations and welcomes. She had but one story to tell, and seemed the least able of all the party to suggest any way of accounting for what had happened.

My father took a turn up and down the room, thinking. I saw Carmilla's eye follow him for a moment with a sly, dark glance.

When my father had sent the servants away, Mademoiselle having gone in search of a little bottle of valerian and sal-volatile, and there being no one now in the room with Carmilla except my father, Madame and myself, he came to her thoughtfully, took her hand very kindly, led her to the sofa and sat down beside her.

'Will you forgive me, my dear, if I risk a conjecture, and ask a question?'

'Who can have a better right?' she said. 'Ask what you please, and I will tell you everything. But my story is simply one of bewilderment and darkness. I know absolutely nothing. Put any question you please. But you know, of course, the limitations mamma has placed me under.'

'Perfectly, my dear child. I need not approach the topics on which she desires our silence. Now, the marvel of last night consists in your having been removed from your bed and your room without being wakened, and this removal having occurred apparently while the windows were still secured, and the two doors locked upon the inside. I will tell you my theory, and first ask you a question.'

Carmilla was leaning on her hand dejectedly; Madame and I were listening breathlessly.

'Now, my question is this. Have you ever been suspected of walking in your sleep?'

'Never since I was very young indeed.'

'But you did walk in your sleep when you were young?'

'Yes; I know I did. I have been told so often by my old nurse.'

My father smiled and nodded.

'Well, what has happened is this. You got up in your sleep, unlocked the door, not leaving the key, as usual, in the lock, but taking it out and locking it on the outside; you again took the key out, and carried it away with you to some one of the five-and-twenty rooms on this floor, or perhaps upstairs or downstairs. There are so many rooms and closets, so much heavy furniture, and such accumulations of lumber, that it would require a week to search this old house thoroughly. Do you see, now, what I mean?'

'I do, but not all,' she answered.

'And how, papa, do you account for her finding herself on the sofa in the dressing-room, which we had searched so carefully?'

'She came there after you had searched it, still in her sleep, and at last awoke spontaneously, and was as much surprised to find herself where she was as anyone else. I wish all mysteries were as easily and innocently explained as yours, Carmilla,' he said, laughing. 'And so we may congratulate ourselves on the certainty that the most natural explanation of the occurrence is one that involves no drugging, no tampering with locks, no burglars, or poisoners, or witches – nothing that need alarm Carmilla, or anyone else, for our safety.'

Carmilla was looking charmingly. Nothing could be more beautiful than her tints. Her beauty was, I think, enhanced by that graceful languor that was peculiar to her. I think my father was silently contrasting her looks with mine, for he said: 'I wish my poor Laura was looking more like herself;' and he sighed.

So our alarms were happily ended, and Carmilla restored to her friends.

9

The Doctor

As Carmilla would not hear of an attendant sleeping in her room, my father arranged that a servant should sleep outside her door, so that she could not attempt to make another such excursion without being arrested at her own door.

That night passed quietly; and next morning early, the doctor, whom my father had sent for without telling me a word about it, arrived to see me.

Madame accompanied me to the library; and there the grave little doctor, with white hair and spectacles, whom I mentioned before, was waiting to receive me.

I told him my story, and as I proceeded he grew graver and graver.

We were standing, he and I, in the recess of one of the windows, facing one another. When my statement was over, he leaned with his shoulders against the wall and with his eyes fixed on me earnestly, with an interest in which was a dash of horror.

After a minute's reflection, he asked Madame if he could see my father.

He was sent for accordingly, and as he entered, smiling, he said: 'I dare say, doctor, you are going to tell me that I am an old fool for having brought you here; I hope I am.'

But his smile faded into shadow as the doctor, with a very grave face, beckoned him to him.

He and the doctor talked for some time in the same recess where I had just conferred with the physician. It seemed an earnest and argumentative conversation. The room is very large, and I and Madame stood together, burning with curiosity, at the farther end. Not a word could we hear, however, for they spoke in a very low tone, and the deep recess of the window quite concealed the doctor from view, and very nearly my father, whose foot, arm and shoulder only could we see; and the voices were, I suppose, all the less audible for the sort of closet which the thick wall and window formed.

After a time my father's face looked into the room; it was pale, thoughtful and, I fancied, agitated.

'Laura dear, come here for a moment. Madame, we shan't trouble you, the doctor says, at present.'

Accordingly I approached, for the first time a little alarmed; for, although I felt very weak, I did not feel ill; and strength, one always fancies, is a thing that may be picked up when we please.

My father held out his hand to me as I drew near, but he was looking at the doctor, and he said: 'It certainly *is* very odd; I don't understand it quite. Laura, come here, dear; now attend to Dr Spielsberg, and recollect yourself.'

'You mentioned a sensation like that of two needles piercing the skin, somewhere about your neck, on the night when you experienced your first horrible dream. Is there still any soreness?'

'None at all,' I answered.

'Can you indicate with your finger about the point at which you think this occurred?'

'Very little below my throat – *here*,' I answered. I wore a morning dress, which covered the place I pointed to.

'Now you can satisfy yourself,' said the doctor. 'You won't mind your papa's lowering your dress a very little. It is necessary, to detect a symptom of the complaint under which you have been suffering.'

I acquiesced. It was only an inch or two below the edge of my collar.

'God bless me! – so it is,' exclaimed my father, growing pale.

'You see it now with your own eyes,' said the doctor, with a gloomy triumph.

'What is it?' I exclaimed, beginning to be frightened.

'Nothing, my dear young lady, but a small blue spot, about the size of the tip of your little finger; and now,' he continued, turning to papa, 'the question is what is best to be done?'

'Is there any danger?' I urged, in great trepidation.

'I trust not, my dear,' answered the doctor. 'I don't see why you should not recover. I don't see why you should not begin *immediately* to get better. That is the point at which the sense of strangulation begins?'

'Yes,' I answered.

'And – recollect as well as you can – the same point was a kind of centre of that thrill which you described just now, like the current of a cold stream running against you?'

'It may have been; I think it was.'

'Ay, you see?' he added, turning to my father. 'Shall I say a word to Madame?'

'Certainly,' said my father.

He called Madame to him, and said: 'I find my young friend here far from well. It won't be of any great consequence, I hope; but it will be necessary that some steps be taken, which I will explain by and by; but in the meantime, Madame, you will be so good as not to let Miss Laura be left alone for one moment. That is the only direction I need give for the present. It is indispensable.'

'We may rely upon your kindness, Madame, I know,' added my father.

Madame satisfied him eagerly.

'And you, dear Laura, I know you will observe the doctor's direction.'

My father turned back to the doctor. 'I shall have to ask your opinion upon another patient, whose symptoms slightly resemble those of my daughter; they are very much milder in degree, but I believe quite of the same sort. She is a young lady – our guest; but as you say you will be passing this way again this evening, you can't do better than take your supper here, and you can see her then. She does not come down till the afternoon.'

'I thank you,' said the doctor. 'I shall be with you, then, at about seven this evening.'

They repeated their directions to me and to Madame, and with this parting charge my father left us, and walked out with the doctor; and I saw them pacing together up and down between the road and the moat, on the grassy platform in front of the castle, evidently absorbed in earnest conversation.

The doctor did not return. I saw him mount his horse there, take his leave and ride away eastward through the forest. Nearly at the same time I saw the man arrive from Dranfeld with the letters, and dismount and hand the bag to my father.

In the meantime, Madame and I were both busy, lost in conjecture as to the reasons for the singular and earnest direction which the doctor and my father had concurred in imposing. Madame, as she afterwards told me, was afraid the doctor apprehended a sudden seizure, and that, without prompt assistance, I might either lose my life in a fit, or at least be seriously hurt.

This interpretation did not strike me; and I fancied, perhaps luckily for my nerves, that the arrangement was prescribed simply to secure a companion who would prevent my taking too much exercise, or eating unripe fruit, or doing any of the fifty foolish things to which young people are supposed to be prone.

About half an hour later my father came in – he had a letter in his hand – and said: 'This letter has been delayed; it is from General Spielsdorf. He might have been here yesterday, he may not come till tomorrow, or he may be here today.'

He put the open letter into my hand; but he did not look as pleased as he usually did when a guest, especially one so much loved as the general, was coming. On the contrary, he looked as if he wished him at the bottom of the Red Sea. There was plainly something on his mind which he did not choose to divulge.

'Papa, darling, will you tell me this?' said I, suddenly laying my hand on his arm, and looking, I am sure, imploringly in his face.

'Perhaps,' he answered, smoothing my hair caressingly over my eyes.

'Does the doctor think me very ill?'

'No, dear; he thinks, if right steps are taken, you will be quite well again, at least on the high road to a complete recovery, in a day or two,' he answered, a little drily. 'I wish our good friend the general had chosen any other time; that is, I wish you had been perfectly well to receive him.'

'But do tell me, papa,' I insisted, 'what does he think is the matter with me?'

'Nothing; you must not plague me with questions,' he answered, with more irritation than I ever remember him to have displayed before; and seeing that I looked wounded, I suppose, he kissed me, and added, 'You shall know all about it in a day or two; that is, all that I know. In the meantime, you are not to trouble your head about it.'

He turned and left the room, but came back before I had done wondering and puzzling over the oddity of all this; it was merely to say that he was going to Karnstein, and had ordered the carriage to be ready at twelve, and that I and Madame should accompany him; he was going to see the priest who lived near those picturesque grounds, upon business, and as Carmilla had never seen them, she could follow, when she came down, with Mademoiselle, who would bring materials for what you call a picnic, which might be laid for us in the ruined castle.

At twelve o'clock, accordingly, I was ready, and not long after, my father, Madame and I set out upon our projected drive. Passing the drawbridge, we turned to the right and followed the road over the steep Gothic bridge, westward, to reach the deserted village and ruined castle of Karnstein.

No sylvan drive can be fancied prettier. The ground breaks into gentle hills and hollows, all clothed with beautiful woods, totally destitute of the comparative formality which artificial planting and early culture and pruning impart.

The irregularities of the ground often lead the road out of its course, and cause it to wind beautifully round the sides of broken hollows and the steeper sides of the hills, among varieties of ground almost inexhaustible.

Turning one of these points, we suddenly encountered our old friend the general riding towards us, attended by a mounted servant. His portmanteaus were following in a hired wagon, such as we term a cart.

The general dismounted as we pulled up, and, after the usual greetings, was easily persuaded to accept the vacant seat in the carriage and send his horse on with his servant to the *schloss*.

10

Bereaved

It was about ten months since we had last seen him; but that time had sufficed to make an alteration of years in his appearance. He had grown thinner; something of gloom and anxiety had taken the place of that cordial serenity which used to characterise his features. His dark blue eyes, always penetrating, now gleamed with a sterner light from under his shaggy grey eyebrows. It was not such a change as grief alone usually induces, and angrier passions seemed to have had their share in bringing it about.

We had not long resumed our drive, when the general began to talk, with his usual soldierly directness, of the bereavement, as he termed it, which he had sustained in the death of his beloved niece and ward; and he then broke out in a tone of intense bitterness and fury, inveighing against the 'hellish arts' to which she had fallen a victim, and expressing, with more exasperation than piety, his wonder that heaven should tolerate so monstrous an indulgence of the lusts and malignity of hell.

My father, who saw at once that something very extraordinary had befallen, asked him, if it would not be too painful for him, to detail the circumstances which he thought justified the strong terms in which he expressed himself.

'I should tell you all with pleasure,' said the general, 'but you would not believe me.'

'Why should I not?' asked my father.

'Because,' he answered testily, 'you believe in nothing but what consists with your own prejudices and illusions. I remember when I was like you, but I have learned better.'

'Try me,' said my father; 'I am not such a dogmatist as you suppose. Besides which, I very well know that you generally require proof for what you believe, and am, therefore, very strongly predisposed to respect your conclusions.'

'You are right in supposing that I have not been led lightly into a belief in the marvellous – for what I have experienced is marvellous – and I have been forced by extraordinary evidence to credit that which ran counter, diametrically, to all my theories. I have been made the dupe of a preternatural conspiracy.'

Notwithstanding his professions of confidence in the general's penetration, I saw my father, at this point, glance at the general with, as I thought, a marked suspicion of his sanity.

The general did not see it, luckily. He was looking gloomily and curiously into the glades and vistas of the woods that were opening before us.

'You are going to the ruins of Karnstein?' he said. 'Yes, it is a lucky coincidence; do you know I was going to ask you to bring me there to inspect them. I have a special object in exploring them. There is a ruined chapel, ain't there, and a great many tombs of that extinct family?'

'So there are – highly interesting,' said my father. 'I hope you are thinking of claiming the title and estates?'

My father said this gaily, but the general did not recollect the laugh, or even the smile, which courtesy exacts for a friend's joke; on the contrary, he looked grave and even fierce, ruminating on a matter that stirred his anger and horror.

'Something very different,' he said, gruffly. 'I mean to unearth some of those fine people. I hope, by God's blessing, to accomplish a pious sacrilege here, which will relieve our earth of certain monsters, and enable honest people to sleep in their beds without being assailed by murderers. I have strange things to tell you, my dear friend, such as I myself would have counted as incredible a few months since.'

My father looked at him again, but this time not with a glance of suspicion – with an eye, rather, of keen intelligence and alarm. 'The house of Karnstein,' he said, 'has been long extinct: a hundred years at least. My dear wife was maternally descended from the Karnsteins. But the name and title have long ceased to exist. The castle is a ruin; the very village is deserted; it is fifty years since the smoke of a chimney was seen there; not a roof left.'

'Quite true. I have heard a great deal about that since I last saw you; a great deal that will astonish you. But I had better relate everything in the order in which it occurred,' said the general. 'You saw my dear ward – my child, I may call her. No creature could have been more beautiful, and only three months ago none more blooming.'

'Yes, poor thing! when I saw her last she certainly was quite lovely,' said my father. 'I was grieved and shocked more than I can tell you, my dear friend; I knew what a blow it was to you.'

He took the general's hand, and they exchanged a kind pressure. Tears gathered in the old soldier's eyes. He did not seek to conceal them. He said: 'We have been very old friends; I knew you would feel for me, childless as I am. She had become an object of very dear interest to me, and repaid my care by an affection that cheered my home and made my life happy. That is all gone. The years that remain to me on earth may not be very long; but by God's mercy I hope to accomplish a service to mankind before I die, and to subserve the vengeance of heaven upon the fiends who have murdered my poor child in the spring of her hopes and beauty!'

'You said, just now, that you intended relating everything as it occurred,' said my father. 'Pray do; I assure you that it is not mere curiosity that prompts me.'

By this time we had reached the point at which the Drunstall road, by which the general had come, diverges from the road which we were travelling to Karnstein.

'How far is it to the ruins?' enquired the general, looking anxiously forward.

'About half a league,' answered my father. 'Pray let us hear the story you were so good as to promise.'

11

The Story

'With all my heart,' said the general, with an effort; and after a short pause in which to arrange his subject, he commenced one of the strangest narratives I ever heard.

'My dear child was looking forward with great pleasure to the visit you had been so good as to arrange for her to your charming daughter.' Here he made me a gallant but melancholy bow. 'In the meantime we had an invitation to my old friend the Count Carlsfeld, whose *schloss* is about six leagues to the other side of Karnstein. It was to attend the series of fêtes which, you remember, were given by him in honour of his illustrious visitor, the Grand Duke Charles.'

'Yes; and very splendid, I believe, they were,' said my father.

'Princely! But then his hospitalities are quite regal. He has Aladdin's lamp. The night from which my sorrow dates was devoted to a magnificent masquerade. The grounds were thrown open, the trees hung with coloured lamps. There was such a display of fireworks as Paris itself had never witnessed. And such music – music, you know, is my weakness – such ravishing music! The finest instrumental band, perhaps, in the world, and the finest singers who could be collected from all the great operas in Europe. As you wandered through these fantastically illuminated grounds, the moon-lighted château throwing a rosy light from its long rows of windows, you would suddenly hear these ravishing voices stealing from the silence of some grove, or rising from boats upon the lake. I felt myself, as I looked and listened, carried back into the romance and poetry of my early youth.

'When the fireworks were ended and the ball beginning, we

returned to the noble suite of rooms that were thrown open to the dancers. A masked ball, you know, is a beautiful sight; but so brilliant a spectacle of the kind I never saw before.

'It was a very aristocratic assembly. I was myself almost the only "nobody" present.

'My dear child was looking quite beautiful. She wore no mask. Her excitement and delight added an unspeakable charm to her features, always lovely. I remarked a young lady, dressed magnificently, but wearing a mask, who appeared to me to be observing my ward with extraordinary interest. I had seen her, earlier in the evening, in the great hall, and again, for a few minutes, walking near us on the terrace under the castle windows, similarly employed. A lady, also masked, richly and gravely dressed, and with a stately air, like a person of rank, accompanied her as a chaperon. Had the young lady not worn a mask, I could, of course, have been much more certain upon the question as to whether she was really watching my poor darling. I am now well assured that she was.

'We were now in one of the *salons*. My poor dear child had been dancing, and was resting a little in one of the chairs near the door; I was standing near. The two ladies I have mentioned had approached, and the younger took the chair next my ward; her companion stood beside me, and for a little time addressed herself, in a low tone, to her charge.

'Availing herself of the privilege of her mask, she turned to me, and in the tone of an old friend, and calling me by my name, opened a conversation with me which piqued my curiosity a good deal. She referred to many scenes where she had met me – at court, and at distinguished houses. She alluded to little incidents which I had long ceased to think of, but which, I found, had only lain in abeyance in my memory, for they instantly started into life at her touch.

'I became more and more curious to ascertain who she was, every moment. She parried my attempts to discover very adroitly and pleasantly. The knowledge she showed of many passages in my life seemed to me all but unaccountable; and she appeared to take a not unnatural pleasure in foiling my curiosity, and in seeing me flounder, in my eager perplexity, from one conjecture to another.

'In the meantime, the young lady, whom her mother called by the odd name of Millarca, when she once or twice addressed her, had, with the same ease and grace, got into conversation with my ward.

'She introduced herself by saying that her mother was a very old acquaintance of mine. She spoke of the agreeable audacity which a mask rendered practicable; she talked like a friend; she admired her dress, and insinuated very prettily her admiration of her beauty. She amused her with laughing criticisms upon the people who crowded the ballroom, and laughed at my poor child's fun. She was very witty and lively when she pleased, and after a time they had grown very good friends, and the young stranger lowered her mask, displaying a remarkably beautiful face. I had never seen it before, neither had my dear child. But though it was new to us, the features were so engaging, as well as lovely, that it was impossible not to feel the attraction powerfully. My poor girl did so. I never saw anyone more taken with another at first sight – unless, indeed, it was the stranger herself, who seemed quite to have lost her heart to my ward.

'In the meantime, availing myself of the licence of a masquerade, I put not a few questions to the elder lady.

' "You have puzzled me utterly," I said, laughing. "Is that not enough? won't you, now, consent to stand on equal terms, and do me the kindness to remove your mask?"

' "Can any request be more unreasonable?" she replied. "Ask a lady to yield an advantage! Beside, how do you know you would recognise me? Years make changes."

' "As you see," I said, with a bow, and, I suppose, a rather melancholy little laugh.

' "As philosophers tell us," she said; "so how do you know that a sight of my face would help you?"

' "I would take a chance on that," I answered. "It is vain trying to make yourself out an old woman; your figure betrays you."

' "Years, nevertheless, have passed since I saw you – rather since you saw me, for that is what I am considering. Millarca, there, is my daughter; I cannot then be young, even in the opinion of people whom time has taught to be indulgent, and I may not like to be compared with what you remember me as. You have no mask to remove. You can offer me nothing in exchange."

' "My petition is to your pity, to remove it."

' "And mine to yours, to let it stay where it is," she replied.

' "Well, then, at least you will tell me whether you are French or German; you speak both languages so perfectly."

' "I don't think I shall tell you that, general; you intend a surprise, and are meditating the particular point of attack."

' "At all events, you won't deny this," I said, "that being honoured by your permission to converse, I ought to know how to address you. Shall I say Madame la Comtesse?"

'She laughed, and she would, no doubt, have met me with another evasion – if, indeed, I can treat any occurrence, in an interview every circumstance of which was prearranged, as I now believe, with the profoundest cunning, as liable to be modified by accident.

' "As to that," she began; but she was interrupted, almost as she opened her lips, by a gentleman, dressed in black, who looked particularly elegant and distinguished, with this drawback, that his face was the most deadly pale I ever saw, except in death. He was in no masquerade but in the plain evening dress of a gentleman; and he said, without a smile, but with a courtly and unusually low bow: "Will Madame la Comtesse permit me to say a very few words which may interest her?"

'The lady turned quickly to him, and touched her lip in token of silence; she then said to me, "Keep my place for me, general; I shall return when I have said a few words."

'And with this injunction, playfully given, she walked a little aside with the gentleman in black, and talked for some minutes, apparently very earnestly. They then walked away slowly together in the crowd, and I lost them for some minutes.

'I spent the interval in cudgelling my brains for conjecture as to the identity of the lady who seemed to remember me so kindly, and I was thinking of turning about and joining in the conversation between my pretty ward and the countess's daughter, and trying whether, by the time she returned, I might not have a surprise in store for her, by having her name, title, château and estates at my fingers' ends. But at this moment she returned, accompanied by the pale man in black, who said: "I shall return and inform Madame la Comtesse when her carriage is at the door."

'He withdrew with a bow.'

12

A Petition

' "Then we are to lose Madame la Comtesse, but I hope only for a few hours," I said, with a low bow.

' "It may be that only, or it may be a few weeks. It was very unlucky his speaking to me just now as he did. Do you now know me?"

'I assured her I did not.

' "You shall know me," she said, "but not at present. We are older and better friends than, perhaps, you suspect. I cannot yet declare myself. I shall in three weeks pass your beautiful *schloss* about which I have been making enquiries. I shall then look in upon you for an hour or two, and renew a friendship which I never think of without a thousand pleasant recollections. This moment a piece of news has reached me like a thunderbolt. I must set out now, and travel by a devious route, nearly a hundred miles, with all the dispatch I can possibly make. My perplexities multiply. I am only deterred by the compulsory reserve I practise as to my name from making a very singular request of you. My poor child has not quite recovered her strength. Her horse fell with her, at a hunt which she had ridden out to witness; her nerves have not yet recovered the shock, and our physician says that she must on no account exert herself for some time to come. We came here, in consequence, by very easy stages – hardly six leagues a day. I must now travel day and night, on a mission of life and death – a mission the critical and momentous nature of which I shall be able to explain to you when we meet, as I hope we shall, in a few weeks, without the necessity of any concealment."

'She went on to make her petition, and it was in the tone of a person from whom such a request amounted to conferring rather than seeking a favour. This was only in manner, and, as it seemed, quite unconsciously. Than the terms in which it was expressed, nothing could have been more deprecatory. It was simply that I would consent to take charge of her daughter during her absence.

'This was, all things considered, a strange, not to say an audacious, request. She in some sort disarmed me by stating and admitting everything that could be urged against it, and throwing herself entirely upon my chivalry. At the same moment, by a fatality that seems to have predetermined all that happened, my poor child came to my side, and, in an undertone, besought me to invite her new friend, Millarca, to pay us a visit. She had just been sounding her, and thought, if her mamma would allow her, she would like it extremely.

'At another time I should have told her to wait a little, until at least we knew who they were. But I had not a moment to think in. The two ladies assailed me together, and I must confess the refined and beautiful face of the young lady, about which there was something extremely engaging, as well as the elegance and fire of high birth, determined me; and quite overpowered, I submitted, and undertook, too easily, the care of the young lady, whom her mother called Millarca.

'The countess beckoned to her daughter, who listened with grave attention while she told her, in general terms, how suddenly and peremptorily she had been summoned, and also of the arrangement she had made for her under my care, adding that I was one of her earliest and most valued friends.

'I made, of course, such speeches as the case seemed to call for, and found myself, on reflection, in a position which I did not half like.

'The gentleman in black returned, and very ceremoniously conducted the lady from the room.

'The demeanour of this gentleman was such as to impress me with the conviction that the countess was a lady of very much more importance than her modest title alone might have led me to assume.

'Her last charge to me was that no attempt was to be made to learn more about her than I might have already guessed until her return. Our distinguished host, whose guest she was, knew her reasons.

' "But here," she said, "neither I nor my daughter could safely remain for more than a day. I removed my mask imprudently for a moment, about an hour ago, and, too late, I fancied you saw me. So I resolved to seek an opportunity of talking a little to you. Had I found that you *had* seen me, I should have thrown myself on your high sense of honour to keep my secret for some weeks. As it is, I am satisfied that you did not see me; but if you now *suspect*, or, on reflection, should *suspect*, who I am, I commit myself, in like manner, entirely to your honour. My daughter will observe the same secrecy, and I well know that you will, from time to time, remind her, lest she should thoughtlessly disclose it."

'She whispered a few words to her daughter, kissed her hurriedly twice, and went away, accompanied by the pale gentleman in black, and disappeared in the crowd.

' "In the next room," said Millarca, "there is a window that looks upon the hall-door. I should like to see the last of mamma, and to kiss my hand to her."

'We assented, of course, and accompanied her to the window. We looked out and saw a handsome old-fashioned carriage, with a troop of couriers and footmen. We saw the slim figure of the pale gentleman in black, as he held a thick velvet cloak and placed it about her shoulders and threw the hood over her head. She nodded to him, and just touched his hand with hers. He bowed low repeatedly as the door closed, and the carriage began to move.

' "She is gone," said Millarca, with a sigh.

' "She is gone," I repeated to myself, for the first time – in the hurried moments that had elapsed since my consent – reflecting upon the folly of my act.

' "She did not look up," said the young lady, plaintively.

' "The countess had taken off her mask, perhaps, and did not care to show her face," I said; "and she could not know that you were in the window."

'She sighed and looked in my face. She was so beautiful that I relented. I was sorry I had for a moment repented of my hospitality, and I determined to make her amends for the unavowed churlishness of my reception.

'The young lady, replacing her mask, joined my ward in persuading me to return to the grounds, where the concert was soon to be renewed. We did so, and walked up and down the terrace that lies under the castle windows. Millarca became very intimate with us, and amused us with lively descriptions and stories of most of the great people whom we saw upon the terrace. I liked her more and more every minute. Her gossip, without being ill-natured, was extremely diverting to me, who had been so long out of the great world. I thought what life she would give to our sometimes lonely evenings at home.

'This ball was not over until the morning sun had almost reached the horizon. It pleased the Grand Duke Charles to dance till then, so loyal people could not go away, or think of bed.

'We had just got through a crowded saloon, when my ward asked me what had become of Millarca. I thought she had been by her side, and she fancied she was by mine. The fact was, we had lost her.

'All my efforts to find her were vain. I feared that she had mistaken, in the confusion of a momentary separation from us, other people for her new friends, and had, possibly, pursued and lost them in the extensive grounds which were thrown open to us.

'Now, in its full force, I recognised a new folly in my having undertaken the charge of a young lady without so much as knowing her name; and fettered as I was by promises, of the reasons for imposing which I knew nothing, I could not even point my enquiries by saying that the missing young lady was the daughter of the countess who had taken her departure a few hours before.

'Morning broke. It was clear daylight before I gave up my search. It was not till near two o'clock next day that we heard anything of my missing charge.

'At about that time a servant knocked at my niece's door, to say that he had been earnestly requested by a young lady, who appeared to be in great distress, to make out where she could find the General Baron Spielsdorf and the young lady, his daughter, in whose charge she had been left by her mother.

'There could be no doubt, notwithstanding the slight inaccuracy, that our young friend had turned up; and so she had. Would to heaven we had lost her!

'She told my poor child a story to account for her having failed to recover us for so long. Very late, she said, she had got into the housekeeper's bedroom in despair of finding us, and had then fallen into a deep sleep which, long as it was, had hardly sufficed to recruit her strength after the fatigues of the ball.

'That day Millarca came home with us. I was only too happy, after all, to have secured so charming a companion for my dear girl.'

13

The Woodman

'There soon, however, appeared some drawbacks. In the first place, Millarca complained of extreme languor – the weakness that remained after her late illness – and she never emerged from her room till the afternoon was pretty far advanced. In the next place, it was accidentally discovered, although she always locked her door on the inside, and never disturbed the key from its place till she admitted the maid to assist at her toilet, that she was undoubtedly sometimes absent from her room in the very early morning, and at various times later in the day, before she wished it to be understood that she was stirring. She was repeatedly seen from the windows of the *schloss*, in the first faint grey of the morning, walking through the trees in an easterly direction, and looking like a person in a trance. This convinced me that she walked in her sleep. But this hypothesis did not solve the puzzle. How did she pass out from her room, leaving the door locked on the inside. How did she escape from the house without unbarring door or window?

'In the midst of my perplexities, an anxiety of a far more urgent kind presented itself.

'My dear child began to lose her looks and health, and that in a manner so mysterious, and even horrible, that I became thoroughly frightened.

'She was at first visited by appalling dreams; then, as she fancied, by a spectre, sometimes resembling Millarca, sometimes in the shape of a beast, indistinctly seen, walking round the foot of her bed, from side to side. Lastly came sensations. One, not unpleasant, but very peculiar, she said, resembled the flow of an icy stream against her breast. At a later time, she felt something like a pair of large needles pierce her, a little below the throat, with a very sharp pain. A few nights after, followed a gradual and convulsive sense of strangulation; then came unconsciousness.'

I could hear distinctly every word the kind old general was saying, because by this time we were driving upon the short grass that spreads on either side of the road as you approach the roofless village which had not shown the smoke of a chimney for more than half a century.

You may guess how strangely I felt as I heard my own symptoms so exactly described in those which had been experienced by the poor girl who, but for the catastrophe which followed, would have been at that moment a visitor at my father's château. You may suppose, also, how I felt as I heard him detail habits and mysterious peculiarities which were, in fact, those of our beautiful guest, Carmilla!

A vista opened in the forest; we were on a sudden under the chimneys and gables of the ruined village, and the towers and battlements of the dismantled castle, round which gigantic trees are grouped, overhung us from a slight eminence.

In a frightened dream I got down from the carriage, and in silence, for we had each abundant matter for thinking; we soon mounted the ascent, and were among the spacious chambers, winding stairs and dark corridors of the castle.

'And this was once the palatial residence of the Karnsteins!' said the old general at length, as from a great window he looked out across the village, and saw the wide, undulating expanse of forest. 'It was a bad family, and here its blood-stained annals were written,' he continued. 'It is hard that they should, after death, continue to plague the human race with their atrocious lusts. That is the chapel of the Karnsteins, down there.'

He pointed down to the grey walls of the Gothic building, partly visible through the foliage, a little way down the steep. 'And I hear the axe of a wood-man,' he added, 'busy among the trees that surround it; he possibly may give us the information of which I am in search, and point out the grave of Mircalla, Countess of Karnstein. These rustics preserve the local traditions of great families, whose stories die out among the rich and titled so soon as the families themselves become extinct.'

'We have a portrait, at home, of Mircalla, the Countess Karnstein; should you like to see it?' asked my father.

'Time enough, dear friend,' replied the general. 'I believe that I have seen the original; and one motive which has led me to you earlier than I at first intended was to explore the chapel which we are now approaching.'

'What! seen the Countess Mircalla,' exclaimed my father; 'why, she has been dead more than a century!'

'Not so dead as you fancy, I am told,' answered the general.

'I confess, general, you puzzle me utterly,' replied my father, looking at him, I fancied, for a moment with a return of the suspicion I detected before. But although there was anger and detestation, at times, in the old general's manner, there was nothing flighty.

'There remains,' he said, as we passed under the heavy arch of the Gothic church – for its dimensions would have justified its being so styled – 'but one object which can interest me during the few years that remain to me on earth, and that is to wreak on her the vengeance which, I thank God, may still be accomplished by a mortal arm.'

'What vengeance can you mean?' asked my father, in increasing amazement.

'I mean, to decapitate the monster,' he answered, with a fierce flush and a stamp that echoed mournfully through the hollow ruin, and his clenched hand was at the same moment raised, as if it grasped the handle of an axe, while he shook it ferociously in the air.

'What!' exclaimed my father, more than ever bewildered.

'To strike her head off.'

'Cut her head off!'

'Aye, with a hatchet, with a spade, or with anything that can cleave through her murderous throat. You shall hear,' he answered, trembling with rage. And hurrying forward he said: 'That beam will answer for a seat; your dear child is fatigued; let her be seated, and I will, in a few sentences, close my dreadful story.'

The squared block of wood, which lay on the grass-grown pavement of the chapel, formed a bench on which I was very glad to seat myself, and in the meantime the general called to the woodman, who had been removing some boughs which leaned upon the old walls, and axe in hand the hardy old fellow stood before us.

He could not tell us anything of these monuments; but there was an old man, he said, a ranger of this forest, at present sojourning in the house of the priest, about two miles away, who could point out every monument of the old Karnstein family; and, for a trifle, he undertook to bring him back with him, if we would lend him one of our horses, in little more than half an hour.

'Have you been long employed about this forest?' asked my father of the old man.

'I have been a woodman here,' he answered in his *patois*, 'under the forester, all my days; so was my father before me, and so on, as many generations as I can count up. I could show you the very house in the village here in which my ancestors lived.'

'How came the village to be deserted?' asked the general.

'It was troubled by *revenants*, sir; several were tracked to their graves and there detected by the usual tests and extinguished in the usual way, by decapitation, by the stake and by burning; but not until many of the villagers had been killed.

'But after all these proceedings according to law,' he continued – 'so many graves opened, and so many vampires deprived of their horrible animation – the village was not relieved. But a Moravian nobleman, who happened to be travelling this way, heard how matters were, and being skilled – as many people are in his country – in such affairs, he offered to deliver the village from its tormentor. There being a bright moon that night, he ascended, shortly after sunset, the tower of the chapel here, from whence he could distinctly see the churchyard beneath him; you can see it from that window. From this point he watched until he saw the vampire come out of his grave and place near it the linen clothes in which he had been folded and glide away towards the village to plague its inhabitants.

'The stranger, having seen all this, came down from the steeple, took the linen wrappings of the vampire, and carried them up to the top of the tower, which he again mounted. When the vampire returned from his prowlings and missed his clothes, he cried furiously to the Moravian, whom he saw at the summit of the tower, and who, in reply, beckoned him to ascend and take them. Whereupon the vampire, accepting his invitation, began to climb the steeple; but as soon as he had reached the battlements, the Moravian, with a stroke of his sword, clove his skull in twain, and hurled him down to the churchyard. Then, descending by the winding stairs, he followed and cut the vampire's head off, and next day delivered head and body to the villagers, who duly impaled and burnt them.

'This Moravian nobleman had authority from the senior member of the family to remove the tomb of Mircalla, Countess Karnstein, which he did effectually, so that in a little while its site was quite forgotten.'

'Can you point out where it stood?' asked the general, eagerly.

The forester shook his head and smiled. 'Not a soul living could tell you that now,' he said; 'besides, they say her body was removed; but no one is sure of that either.'

Having thus spoken, as time pressed, he dropped his axe and departed, leaving us to hear the remainder of the general's strange story.

14

The Meeting

'My beloved child,' he resumed, 'was now growing rapidly worse. The physician who attended her had failed to produce the slightest impression upon her disease, for such I then supposed it to be. He saw my alarm, and suggested a consultation. I called in an abler physician, from Gratz. Several days elapsed before he arrived. He was a good and pious, as well as a learned, man. Having seen my poor ward together, they withdrew to my library to confer and discuss. I, from the adjoining room, where I awaited their summons, heard these two gentlemen's voices raised in something sharper than a strictly philosophical discussion. I knocked at the door and entered. I found the old physician from Gratz maintaining his theory. His rival was combating it with undisguised ridicule, accompanied with bursts of laughter. This unseemly manifestation subsided and the altercation ended on my entrance.

' "Sir," said my first physician, "my learned brother seems to think that you want a conjuror, and not a doctor."

' "Pardon me," said the old physician from Gratz, looking displeased, "I shall state my own view of the case in my own way another time. I grieve, Monsieur le General, that by my skill and science I can be of no use. Before I go I shall do myself the honour to suggest something to you."

'He seemed thoughtful, and sat down at a table and began to write. Profoundly disappointed, I made my bow, and as I turned to go, the other doctor pointed over his shoulder to his companion who was writing, and then, with a shrug, significantly touched his forehead.

'This consultation, then, left me precisely where I was. I walked out into the grounds, all but distracted. The doctor from Gratz, in ten or fifteen minutes, overtook me. He apologised for having followed me, but said that he could not conscientiously take his leave without a few words more. He told me that he could not be mistaken; no natural disease exhibited the same symptoms; and that death was already very near. There remained, however, a day, or possibly two, of life. If the fatal seizure were at once arrested, with great care and skill her strength might possibly return. But all hung now upon the confines of the irrevocable. One more assault might extinguish the last spark of vitality which was, every moment, ready to die.

' "And what is the nature of the seizure you speak of?" I entreated.

' "I have stated all fully in this note, which I place in your hands, upon the distinct condition that you send for the nearest clergyman, and open my letter in his presence, and on no account read it till he is with you; you would despise it else, and it is a matter of life and death. Should the priest fail you, then, indeed, you may read it."

'He asked me, before taking his leave finally, whether I would wish to see a man curiously learned upon the very subject, which, after I had read his letter, would probably interest me above all others, and he urged me earnestly to invite him to visit him there; and so took his leave.

'The ecclesiastic was absent, and I read the letter by myself. At another time, or in another case, it might have excited my ridicule. But into what quackeries will not people rush for a last chance, where all accustomed means have failed, and the life of a beloved object is at stake?

'Nothing, you will say, could be more absurd than the learned man's letter. It was monstrous enough to have consigned him to a madhouse. He said that the patient was suffering from the visits of a vampire! The punctures which she described as having occurred near the throat, were, he insisted, the insertion of those two long, thin and sharp teeth which, it is well known, are peculiar to vampires; and there could be no doubt, he added, as to the well-defined presence of the small livid mark which all concurred in describing as that induced by the demon's lips; and every symptom described by the sufferer was in exact conformity with those recorded in every case of a similar visitation.

'Being myself wholly sceptical as to the existence of any such portent as the vampire, the supernatural theory of the good doctor furnished, in my opinion, but another instance of learning and intelligence oddly associated with some one hallucination. I was so miserable, however, that, rather than try nothing, I acted upon the instructions in the letter.

'I concealed myself in the dark dressing-room that opened upon the poor patient's room, in which a candle was burning, and watched there till she was fast asleep. I stood at the door, peeping through the small crevice, my sword laid on the table beside me, as my directions prescribed, until, a little after one, I saw a large black object, very ill-defined, crawl, as it seemed to me, over the foot of the bed, and swiftly spread itself up to the poor girl's throat, where it swelled, in a moment, into a great, palpitating mass.

'For a few moments I had stood petrified. I now sprang forward, with my sword in my hand. The black creature suddenly contracted towards the foot of the bed, glided over it, and, standing on the floor about a yard from the bed, with a glare of skulking ferocity and horror fixed on me, I saw Millarca. Speculating I know not what, I struck at her instantly with my sword, but then saw her standing near the door, unscathed. Horrified, I pursued, and struck again. She was gone, and my sword flew to shivers against the door.

'I can't describe to you all that passed on that horrible night. The whole house was up and stirring. The spectre Millarca was gone. But her victim was sinking fast, and before the morning dawned, she died.'

The old general was agitated. We did not speak to him. My father walked to some little distance, and began reading the inscriptions on the tombstones; and thus occupied, he strolled into the door of a side chapel to prosecute his researches. The general leaned against the wall, dried his eyes, and sighed heavily. I was relieved on hearing the voices of Carmilla and Madame, who were at that moment approaching. The voices died away.

In this solitude, having just listened to so strange a story, connected, as it was, with the great and titled dead whose monuments were mouldering among the dust and ivy round us, and every incident of which bore so awfully upon my own mysterious case – in this haunted spot, darkened by the towering foliage that rose on every side, dense and high above its noiseless walls – a horror began to steal over me, and my heart sank as I thought that my friends were, after all, not about to enter and disturb this triste and ominous scene.

The old general's eyes were fixed on the ground as he leaned with his hand upon the pedestal of a shattered monument.

Under a narrow, arched doorway, surmounted by one of those demoniacal grotesques in which the cynical and ghastly fancy of old Gothic carving delights, I saw very gladly the beautiful face and figure of Carmilla enter the shadowy chapel.

I was just about to rise and speak, having nodded, smiling, in answer to her peculiarly engaging smile, when, with a cry, the old man by my side caught up the woodman's hatchet and started forward. On seeing him, a brutalised change came over her features. It was an instantaneous and horrible transformation, as she made a crouching step backwards. Before I could utter a scream, he struck at her with all his force, but she dived under his blow and, unscathed, caught him in her tiny grasp by the wrist. He struggled for a moment to release his arm, but his hand opened, the axe fell to the ground, and the girl was gone.

He staggered against the wall. His grey hair stood upon his head, and a moisture shone over his face, as if he were at the point of death.

The frightful scene had passed in a moment. The first thing I recollect after, is Madame standing before me and impatiently repeating, again and again, the question, 'Where is Mademoiselle Carmilla?'

I answered at length, 'I don't know – I can't tell – she went there,' and I pointed to the door through which Madame had just entered; 'only a minute or two since.'

'But I have been standing there, in the passage, ever since Mademoiselle Carmilla entered; and she did not return.'

She then began to call, 'Carmilla,' through every door and passage and from the windows, but no answer came.

'She called herself Carmilla?' asked the general, still agitated.

'Carmilla, yes,' I answered.

'Aye,' he said; 'that is Millarca. That is the same person who long ago was called Mircalla, Countess Karnstein. Depart from this accursed ground, my poor child, as quickly as you can. Drive to the clergyman's house, and stay there till we come. Begone! May you never behold Carmilla more; you will not find her here.'

15

Ordeal and Execution

As he spoke, one of the strangest-looking men I ever beheld entered the chapel at the door through which Carmilla had made her entrance and her exit. He was tall, narrow-chested, stooping, with high shoulders, and dressed in black. His face was brown and dried into deep furrows; he wore an oddly-shaped hat with a broad brim. His hair, long and grizzled, hung on his shoulders. He wore a pair of gold spectacles, and walked slowly, with an odd shambling gait, and his face, sometimes turned up to the sky and sometimes bowed down towards the ground, seemed to wear a perpetual smile; his long thin arms were swinging, and his lank hands, in old black gloves ever so much too wide for them, waved and gesticulated in utter abstraction.

'The very man!' exclaimed the general, advancing with manifest delight. 'My dear baron, how happy I am to see you, I had no hope of meeting you so soon.' He signed to my father, who had by this time returned, and leading the fantastic old gentleman, whom he called the baron, to meet him, he introduced him formally, and they at once entered into earnest conversation. The stranger took a roll of paper from his pocket, and spread it on the worn surface of a tomb that stood by. He had a pencil-case in his fingers with which he traced imaginary lines from point to point on the paper, which, from their often glancing from it together at certain points of the building, I concluded to be a plan of the chapel. He accompanied what I may term his lecture with occasional readings from a dirty little book, whose yellow leaves were closely written over.

They sauntered together down the side aisle, opposite to the spot where I was standing, conversing as they went; then they began measuring distances by paces, and finally they all stood together facing a piece of the side-wall, which they began to examine with great minuteness, pulling off the ivy that clung over it and rapping the plaster with the ends of their sticks, scraping here and knocking there. At length they ascertained the existence of a broad marble tablet, with letters carved in relief upon it.

With the assistance of the woodman, who had reappeared, a monumental inscription and carved escutcheon were disclosed. They proved to be those of the long-lost monument of Mircalla, Countess Karnstein.

The old general, though not I fear given to the praying mode, raised his hands and eyes to heaven in mute thanksgiving for some moments.

'Tomorrow,' I heard him say, 'the commissioner will be here, and the inquisition will be held according to law.'

Then turning to the old man with the gold spectacles, whom I have described, he shook him warmly by both hands and said: 'Baron, how can I thank you? How can we all thank you? You will have delivered this region from a plague that has scourged its inhabitants for more than a century. The horrible enemy, thank God, is at last tracked.'

My father led the stranger aside, and the general followed. I knew that he had led them out of hearing so that he might relate my case, and I saw them glance often quickly at me as the discussion proceeded.

My father came to me, kissed me again and again, and leading me from the chapel, said: 'It is time to return, but before we go home, we must add to our party the good priest, who lives but a little way from here, and persuade him to accompany us to the *schloss*.'

In this quest we were successful: and I was glad, being unspeakably fatigued when we reached home. But my satisfaction was changed to dismay on discovering that there were no tidings of Carmilla. Of the scene that had occurred in the ruined chapel, no explanation was offered to me, and it was clear that it was a secret which my father for the present determined to keep from me.

The sinister absence of Carmilla made the remembrance of the scene more horrible to me. The arrangements for that night were singular. Two servants and Madame were to sit up in my room that night; and the ecclesiastic with my father kept watch in the adjoining dressing-room.

The priest had performed certain solemn rites that night, the purport of which I did not understand any more than I comprehended the reason of this extraordinary precaution taken for my safety during sleep.

I saw all clearly a few days later.

The disappearance of Carmilla was followed by the discontinuance of my nightly sufferings.

You have heard, no doubt, of the appalling superstition that prevails in Upper and Lower Styria, in Moravia, Silesia, in Turkish Servia, in Poland, even in Russia; the superstition, so we must call it, of the vampire.

If human testimony – taken with every care and solemnity, judicially, before commissions innumerable, each consisting of many members, all chosen for integrity and intelligence, and constituting reports more voluminous perhaps than exist upon any one other class of cases – is worth anything, it is difficult to deny or even to doubt the existence of such a phenomenon as the vampire.

For my part, I have heard no theory by which to explain what I myself have witnessed and experienced other than that supplied by the ancient and well-attested belief of the country.

The next day the formal proceedings took place in the chapel of Karnstein. The grave of the Countess Mircalla was opened; and the general and my father recognised each his perfidious and beautiful guest in the face now disclosed to view. The features, though a hundred and fifty years had passed since her funeral, were tinted with the warmth of life. Her eyes were open; no cadaverous smell exhaled from the coffin. The two medical men, one officially present, the other there on behalf of the promoter of the enquiry, attested to the marvellous fact that there was a faint but appreciable respiration and a corresponding action of the heart. The limbs were perfectly flexible, the flesh elastic; and the leaden coffin floated with blood, in which, to a depth of seven inches, the body lay immersed. Here, then, were all the admitted signs and proofs of vampirism. The body, therefore, in accordance with the ancient practice, was raised, and a sharp stake driven through the heart of the vampire, who uttered a piercing shriek at the moment, in all respects such as might escape from a living person in the last agony. Then the head was struck off, and a torrent of blood flowed from the severed neck. The body and head were next placed on a pile of wood, and reduced to ashes, which were thrown upon the river and borne away, and that territory has never since been plagued by the visits of a vampire.

My father has a copy of the report of the Imperial Commission, with the signatures of all who were present at these proceedings attached in verification of the statement. It is from this official paper that I have summarised my account of this last shocking scene.

16

Conclusion

I write all this you suppose with composure. But far from it; I cannot think of it without agitation. Nothing but your earnest desire, so repeatedly expressed, could have induced me to sit down to a task that has unstrung my nerves for months to come, and reinduced a shadow of the unspeakable horror which years after my deliverance continued to make my days and nights dreadful, and solitude insupportably terrific.

Let me add a word or two about that quaint Baron Vordenburg, to whose curious lore we were indebted for the discovery of the Countess Mircalla's grave.

He had taken up his abode in Gratz, where, living upon a mere pittance, which was all that remained to him of the once princely estates of his family in Upper Styria, he devoted himself to the minute and laborious investigation of the marvellously authenticated tradition of vampirism. He had at his fingers' ends all the great and little works upon the subject: *Magia Posthuma*, *Phlegon de Mirabilibus*, *Augustinus de Cura pro Mortuis*, *Philosophicae et Christianae Cogitationes de Vampiris* by John Christofer Herenberg and a thousand others, among which I remember only a few of those which he lent to my father. He had a voluminous digest of all the judicial cases, from which he had extracted a system of principles that appear to govern – some always, and others occasionally only – the condition of the vampire. I may mention, in passing, that the deadly pallor attributed to that sort of *revenant* is a mere melodramatic fiction. They present, in the grave, and when they show themselves in human society, the appearance of healthy life. When disclosed to light in their coffins, they exhibit all the symptoms that are enumerated as those which proved the vampire-life of the long-dead Countess Karnstein.

How they escape from their graves and return to them for certain hours every day, without displacing the clay or leaving any trace of disturbance in the state of the coffin or the cerements, has always been admitted to be utterly inexplicable. The amphibious existence of the vampire is sustained by daily renewed slumber in the grave. Its horrible lust for living blood supplies the vigour of its waking existence. The vampire is prone to be fascinated with an engrossing vehemence, resembling the passion of love, by particular persons. In pursuit of these it will exercise inexhaustible patience and stratagem, for access to a particular object may be obstructed in a hundred ways. It will never desist until it has satiated its passion, and drained the very life of its coveted victim. But it will, in these cases, husband and protract its murderous enjoyment with the refinement of an epicure, and heighten it by the gradual approaches of an artful courtship. In these cases it seems to yearn for something like sympathy and consent. In ordinary cases it goes direct to its object, overpowers with violence, and strangles and exhausts often at a single feast.

The vampire is apparently subject, in certain situations, to special conditions. In the particular instance of which I have given you an account, Mircalla seemed to be limited to a name which, if not her real one, should at least reproduce, without the omission or addition of a single letter, those, as we say, anagrammatically, which compose it. Carmilla did this; so did Millarca.

My father related to the Baron Vordenburg, who remained with us for two or three weeks after the expulsion of Carmilla, the story about the Moravian nobleman and the vampire at Karnstein churchyard, and then he asked the baron how he had discovered the exact position of the long-concealed tomb of the Countess Millarca? The baron's grotesque features puckered up into a mysterious smile; he looked down, still smiling on his worn spectacle-case and fumbled with it. Then looking up, he said: 'I have many journals, and other papers, written by that remarkable man; the most curious among them is one treating of the visit of which you speak to Karnstein. The tradition, of course, discolours and distorts a little. He might have been termed a Moravian nobleman, for he had changed his abode to that territory, and was, beside, a noble. But he was, in truth, a native of Upper Styria. It is enough to say that in very early youth he had been a passionate and favoured lover of the beautiful Mircalla, Countess Karnstein. Her early death plunged him into inconsolable grief. It is the nature of vampires to increase and multiply, according, that is, to an ascertained and ghostly law.

'Assume, at starting, a territory perfectly free from that pest. How does it begin, and how does it multiply itself? I will tell you. A person, more or less wicked, puts an end to himself. A suicide, under certain circumstances, becomes a vampire. That spectre visits living people in their slumbers; they die, and almost invariably, in the grave, develop into vampires. This happened in the case of the beautiful Mircalla, who was haunted by one of those demons. My ancestor, Vordenburg, whose title I still bear, soon discovered this, and in the course of the studies to which he devoted himself, learned a great deal more.

'Among other things, he concluded that suspicion of vampirism would probably fall, sooner or later, upon the dead countess, who in life had been his idol. He conceived a horror, be she what she might, of her remains being profaned by the outrage of a posthumous execution. He has left a curious paper to prove that the vampire, on its expulsion from its amphibious existence, is projected into a far more horrible life; and he resolved to save his once beloved Mircalla from this.

'He adopted the stratagem of a journey here, a pretended removal of her remains, and a real obliteration of her monument. When age had stolen upon him, and from the vale of years he looked back on the scenes he was leaving, he considered, in a different spirit, what he had done, and a horror took possession of him. He made the tracings and notes which have guided me to the very spot, and drew up a confession of the deception that he had practised. If he had intended any further action in this matter, death prevented him; and the hand of a remote descendant has, too late for many, directed the pursuit to the lair of the beast.'

We talked a little more, and among other things he said was this: 'One sign of the vampire is the power of the hand. The slender hand of Carmilla closed like a vice of steel on the general's wrist when he raised the hatchet to strike. But its power is not confined to its grasp; it leaves a numbness in the limb it seizes, which is slowly, if ever, recovered from.'

The following spring my father took me on a tour through Italy. We remained away for more than a year. It was long before the terror of recent events subsided; and to this hour the image of Carmilla returns to memory with ambiguous alternations – sometimes the playful, languid, beautiful girl; sometimes the writhing fiend I saw in the ruined church; and often I have started from a reverie, fancying I heard the light step of Carmilla at the drawing-room door.

SHERIDAN LE FANU

Madam Crowl's Ghost

I'm an old woman now; and I was but thirteen my last birthday, the night I came to Applewale House. My aunt was the housekeeper there, and a sort o' one-horse carriage was down at Lexhoe to take me and my box up to Applewale.

I was a bit frightened by the time I got to Lexhoe, and when I saw the carriage and horse, I wished myself back again with my mother at Hazelden. I was crying when I got into the 'shay' – that's what we used to call it and old John Mulbery that drove it, and was a good-natured fellow, bought me a handful of apples at the Golden Lion, to cheer me up a bit; and he told me that there was a currant-cake, and tea, and pork-chops, waiting for me, all hot, in my aunt's room at the great house. It was a fine moonlight night and I eat the apples, lookin' out o' the shay winda.

It is a shame for gentlemen to frighten a poor foolish child like I was. I sometimes think it might be tricks. There was two on 'em on the tap o' the coach beside me. And they began to question me after nightfall, when the moon rose, where I was going to. Well, I told them it was to wait on Dame Arabella Crowl, of Applewale House, near by Lexhoe.

'Ho, then,' says one of them, 'you'll not be long there!'

And I looked at him as much as to say, 'Why not?' for I had spoke out when I told them where I was goin', as if 'twas something clever I had to say.

'Because,' says he – 'and don't you for your life tell no one, only watch her and see – she's possessed by the devil, and more an half a ghost. Have you got a Bible?'

'Yes, sir,' says I. For my mother put my little Bible in my box, and I knew it was there and by the same token, though the print's too small for my old eyes, I have it in my press to this hour.

As I looked up at him, saying 'Yes, sir,' I thought I saw him winkin' at his friend; but I could not be sure.

'Well,' says he, 'be sure you put it under your bolster every night, it will keep the old girl's claws aff ye.'

And I got such a fright when he said that, you wouldn't fancy! And I'd a liked to ask him a lot about the old lady, but I was too shy, and he and his friend began talkin' together about their own consarns, and dowly enough I got down, as I told ye, at Lexhoe. My heart sank as I drove into the dark avenue. The trees stands very thick and big, as old as the old house almost, and four people, with their arms out and fingertips touchin', barely girds round some of them.

Well, my neck was stretched out o' the winda, looking for the first view o' the great house; and, all at once we pulled up in front of it.

A great white-and-black house it is, wi' great black beams across and right up it, and gables lookin' out, as white as a sheet, to the moon, and the shadows o' the trees, two or three up and down upon the front, you could count the leaves on them, and all the little diamond-shaped winda-panes, glimmering on the great hall winda, and great shutters, in the old fashion, hinged on the wall outside, boulted across all the rest o' the windas in front, for there was but three or four servants, and the old lady in the house, and most o' t'rooms was locked up.

My heart was in my mouth when I sid the journey was over, and this, the great house afore me, and I sa near my aunt that I never sid till noo, and Dame Crowl, that I was come to wait upon, and was afeard on already.

My aunt kissed me in the hall, and brought me to her room. She was tall and thin, wi' a pale face and black eyes, and long thin hands wi' black mittins on. She was past fifty, and her word was short; but her word was law. I hev no complaints to make of her; but she was a hard woman, and I think she would hev bin kinder to me if I had bin her sister's child in place of her brother's. But all that's o' no consequence noo.

The squire – his name was Mr Chevenix Crowl, he was Dame Crowl's grandson – came down there, by way of seeing that the old lady was well treated, about twice or thrice in the year. I sid him but twice all the time I was at Applewale House.

I can't say but she was well taken care of, notwithstandin', but that was because my aunt and Meg Wyvern, that was her maid, had a conscience, and did their duty by her.

Mrs Wyvern – Meg Wyvern my aunt called her to herself, and Mrs Wyvern to me – was a fat, jolly lass of fifty, a good height and a good breadth, always good-humoured, and walked slow. She had fine wages, but she was a bit stingy, and kept all her fine clothes under lock and key, and wore, mostly, a twilled chocolate cotton, wi' red, and yellow, and green sprigs and balls on it, and it lasted wonderful.

She never gave me nout, not the vally o' a brass thimble, all the time I was there; but she was good-humoured, and always laughin', and she talked no end o' proas over her tea; and, seeing me sa sackless and dowly, she roused me up wi' her laughin' and stories; and I think I liked her better than my aunt – children is so taken wi' a bit o' fun or a story – though my aunt was very good to me, but a hard woman about some things, and silent always.

My aunt took me into her bedchamber, that I might rest myself a bit while she was settin' the tea in her room. But first she patted me on the shouther, and said I was a tall lass o' my years, and had spired up well, and asked me if I could do plain work and stitchin'; and she looked in my face, and said I was like my father, her brother, that was dead and gone, and she hoped I was a better Christian, and wad na du a' that lids.

It was a hard sayin' the first time I set my foot in her room, I thought.

When I went into the next room, the housekeeper's room – very comfortable, yak (oak) all round – there was a fine fire blazin' away, wi' coal, and peat, and wood, all in a low together, and tea on the table, and hot cake, and smokin' meat; and there was Mrs Wyvern, fat, jolly, and talkin' away, more in an hour than my aunt would in a year.

While I was still at my tea my aunt went upstairs to see Madam Crowl.

'She's agone up to see that old Judith Squailes is awake,' says Mrs Wyvern. 'Judith sits with Madam Crowl when me and Mrs Shutters' – that was my aunt's name – 'is away. She's a troublesome old lady. Ye'll hev to be sharp wi' her, or she'll be into the fire, or out o' t' winda. She goes on wires, she does, old though she be.'

'How old, ma'am?' says I.

'Ninety-three her last birthday, and that's eight months gone,' says she; and she laughed. 'And don't be askin' questions about her before your aunt – mind, I tell ye; just take her as you find her, and that's all.'

'And what's to be my business about her, please ma'am?' says I.

'About the old lady? Well,' says she, 'your aunt, Mrs Shutters, will tell you that; but I suppose you'll hev to sit in the room with your work, and see she's at no mischief, and let her amuse herself with her things on the table, and get her her food or drink as she calls for it, and keep her out o' mischief, and ring the bell hard if she's troublesome.'

'Is she deaf, ma'am?'

'No, nor blind,' says she; 'as sharp as a needle, but she's gone quite aupy, and can't remember nout rightly; and Jack the Giant Killer, or Goody Twoshoes will please her as well as the King's court, or the affairs of the nation.'

'And what did the little girl go away for, ma'am, that went on Friday last? My aunt wrote to my mother she was to go.'

'Yes; she's gone.'

'What for?' says I again.

'She didn't answer Mrs Shutters, I do suppose,' says she. 'I don't know. Don't be talkin'; your aunt can't abide a talkin' child.'

'And please, ma'am, is the old lady well in health?' says I.

'It ain't no harm to ask that,' says she. 'She's torflin' a bit lately, but better this week past, and I dare say she'll last out her hundred years yet. Hish! Here's your aunt coming down the passage.'

In comes my aunt, and begins talkin' to Mrs Wyvern, and I, beginnin' to feel more comfortable and at home like, was walkin' about the room lookin' at this thing and at that. There was pretty old china things on the cupboard, and pictures again the wall; and there was a door open in the wainscot, and I sees a queer old leathern jacket, wi' straps and buckles to it, and sleeves as long as the bedpost, hangin' up inside.

'What's that you're at, child?' says my aunt, sharp enough, turning about when I thought she least minded. 'What's that in your hand?'

'This, ma'am?' says I, turning about with the leathern jacket. 'I don't know what it is, ma'am.'

Pale as she was, the red came up in her cheeks, and her eyes flashed wi' anger, and I think only she had half a dozen steps to take, between her and me, she'd a gov me a sizzup. But she did give me a shake by the shouther, and she plucked the thing out o' my hand, and says she,

'While ever you stay here, don't ye meddle wi' nout that don't belong to ye,' and she hung it up on the pin that was there, and shut the door wi' a bang and locked it fast.

Mrs Wyvern was liftin' up her hands and laughin' all this time, quietly in her chair, rolling herself a bit in it, as she used when she was kinkin'.

The tears was in my eyes, and she winked at my aunt, and says she, dryin' her own eyes that was wet wi' the laughin', 'Tut, the child meant no harm – come here to me, child. It's only a pair o' crutches for lame ducks, and ask us no questions mind, and we'll tell ye no lies; and come here and sit down, and drink a mug o' beer before ye go to your bed.'

My room, mind ye, was upstairs, next to the old lady's, and Mrs Wyvern's bed was near hers in her room and I was to be ready at call, if need should be.

The old lady was in one of her tantrums that night and part of the day before. She used to take fits o' the sulks. Sometimes she would not let them dress her, and other times she would not let them take her clothes off. She was a great beauty, they said, in her day. But there was no one about Applewale that remembered her in her prime. And she was dreadful fond o' dress, and had thick silks, and stiff satins, and velvets, and laces, and all sorts, enough to set up seven shops at the least. All her dresses was old fashioned and queer, but worth a fortune.

Well, I went to my bed. I lay for a while awake; for a' things was new to me; and I think the tea was in my nerves, too, for I wasn't used to it, except now and then on a holiday, or the like. And I heard Mrs Wyvern talkin', and I listened with my hand to my ear; but I could not hear Mrs Crowl, and I don't think she said a word.

There was great care took of her. The people at Applewale knew that when she died they would everyone get the sack; and their situations was well paid and easy.

The doctor come twice a week to see the old lady, and you may be sure they all did as he bid them. One thing was the same every time; they were never to cross or frump her in any way, but to humour and please her in everything.

So she lay in her clothes all that night, and next day, not a word she said, and I was at my needlework all that day, in my own room, except when I went down to my dinner.

I would a liked to see the old lady, and even to hear her speak. But she might as well a'bin in Lunnon a' the time for me.

When I had my dinner my aunt sent me out for a walk for an hour. I was glad when I came back, the trees was so big, and the place so dark and lonesome, and 'twas a cloudy day, and I cried a deal, thinkin' of home, while I was walkin' alone there. That evening, the candles bein' alight, I was sittin' in my room, and the door was open into Madam Crowl's chamber, where my aunt was. It was, then, for the first time I heard what I suppose was the old lady talking.

It was a queer noise like, I couldn't well say which, a bird, or a beast, only it had a bleatin' sound in it, and was very small.

I pricked my ears to hear all I could. But I could not make out one word she said. And my aunt answered: 'The evil one can't hurt no one, ma'am, bout the Lord permits.'

Then the same queer voice from the bed says something more that I couldn't make head nor tail on.

And my aunt med answer again: 'Let them pull faces, ma'am, and say what they will; if the Lord be for us, who can be against us?'

I kept listenin' with my ear turned to the door, holdin' my breath, but not another word or sound came in from the room. In about twenty minutes, as I was sittin' by the table, lookin' at the pictures in the old Aesop's Fables, I was aware o' something moving at the door, and lookin' up I sid my aunt's face lookin' in at the door, and her hand raised.

'Hish!' says she, very soft, and comes over to me on tiptoe, and she says in a whisper: 'Thank God, she's asleep at last, and don't ye make no noise till I come back, for I'm going' down to take my cup o' tea, and I'll be back i' noo – me and Mrs Wyvern, and she'll be sleepin' in the room, and you can run down when we come up, and Judith will gie ye yaur supper in my room.'

And with that away she goes.

I kep' looking at the picture-book, as before, listenin' every noo and then, but there was no sound, not a breath, that I could hear; an' I began whisperin' to the pictures and talkin' to myself to keep my heart up, for I was growin' feared in that big room.

And at last up I got, and began walkin' about the room, lookin' at this and peepin' at that, to amuse my mind, ye'll understand. And at last what sud I do but peeps into Madame Crowl's bedchamber.

A grand chamber it was, wi' a great four-poster, wi' flowered silk curtains as tall as the ceilin', and foldin' down on the floor, and drawn close all round. There was a lookin'-glass, the biggest I ever sid before, and the room was a blaze o' light. I counted twenty-two wax-candles, all alight. Such was her fancy, and no one dared say her nay.

I listened at the door, and gaped and wondered all round. When I heard there was not a breath, and did not see so much as a stir in the curtains, I took heart, and I walked into the room on tiptoe and looked round again. Then I takes a keek at myself in the big glass; and at last it came in my head, 'Why couldn't I ha' a keek at the old lady herself in the bed?'

Ye'd think me a fule if ye knew half how I longed to see Dame Crowl, and I thought to myself if I didn't peep now I might wait many a day before I got so gude a chance again.

Well, my dear, I came to the side o' the bed, the curtains bein' close, and my heart a'most failed me. But I took courage, and I slips my finger in between the thick curtains, and then my hand. So I waits a bit, but all was still as death. So, softly, softly I draws the curtain, and there, sure enough, I sid before me, stretched out like the painted lady on the tomb-stean in Lexhoe Church, the famous Dame Crowl, of Applewale House. There she was, dressed out. You never sid the like in they days. Satin and silk, and scarlet and green, and gold and pint lace; by Jen! 'twas a sight! A big powdered wig, half as high as herself, was a-top o' her head, and, wow! – was ever such wrinkles? – and her old baggy throat all powdered white, and her cheeks rouged, and mouse-skin eyebrows, that Mrs Wyvern used to stick on, and there she lay grand and stark, wi' a pair o' clocked silk hose on, and heels to her shoon as tall as nine-pins. Lawk! But her nose was crooked and thin, and half the whites o' her eyes was open. She used to stand, dressed as she was, gigglin' and dribblin' before the lookin'-glass, wi' a fan in her hand, and a big nosegay in her bodice. Her wrinkled little hands was stretched down by her sides, and such long nails, all cut into points, I never sid in my days. Could it ever a bin the fashion for grit fowk to wear their fingernails so?

Well, I think ye'd a-bin frightened yourself if ye'd a sid such a sight. I couldn't let go the curtain, nor move an inch, not take my eyes off her; my very heart stood still. And in an instant she opens her eyes, and up she sits, and spins herself round, and down wi' her, wi' a clack on her two tall heels on the floor, facin' me, ogglin' in my face wi' her two great glassy eyes, and a wicked simper wi' her old wrinkled lips, and lang fause teeth.

Well, a corpse is a natural thing; but this was the dreadfullest sight I ever sid. She had her fingers straight out pointin' at me, and her back was crooked, round again wi' age. Says she: 'Ye little limb! what for did ye say I killed the boy? I'll tickle ye till ye're stiff!'

If I'd a thought an instant, I'd a turned about and run. But I couldn't take my eyes off her, and I backed from her as soon as I could; and she came clatterin' after, like a thing on wires, with her fingers pointing to my throat, and she makin' all the time a sound with her tongue like zizz-zizz-zizz.

I kept backin' and backin' as quick as I could, and her fingers was only a few inches away from my throat, and I felt I'd lose my wits if she touched me.

I went back this way, right into the corner, and I gev a yellock, ye'd think saul and body was partin', and that minute my aunt, from the door, calls out wi' a blare, and the old lady turns round on her, and I turns about, and ran through my room, and down the back stairs, as hard as my legs could carry me.

I cried hearty, I can tell you, when I got down to the housekeeper's room. Mrs Wyvern laughed a deal when I told her what happened. But she changed her key when she heard the old lady's words.

'Say them again,' says she.

So I told her.

'Ye little limb! What for did ye say I killed the boy? I'll tickle ye till ye're stiff.'

'And did ye say she killed a boy?' says she.

'Not I, ma'am,' says I.

Judith was always up with me, after that, when the two elder women was away from her. I would a jumped out at winda, rather than stay alone in the same room wi' her.

It was about a week after, as well as I can remember, Mrs Wyvern, one day when me and her was alone, told me a thing about Madam Crowl that I did not know before.

She being young, and a great beauty, full seventy years before, had married Squire Crowl of Applewale. But he was a widower, and had a son about nine year old.

There never was tale or tidings of this boy after one mornin'. No one could say where he went to. He was allowed too much liberty, and used to be off in the morning, one day, to the keeper's cottage, and breakfast wi' him, and away to the warren, and not home, mayhap, till evening, and another time down to the lake, and bathe there, and spend the day fishin' there, or paddlin' about in the boat. Well, no one could say what was gone wi' him; only this, that his hat was found by the lake, under a haathorn that grows thar to this day, and 'twas thought he was drowned bathin'. And the squire's son, by his second marriage, by this Madam Crowl that lived sa dreadful lang, came in for the estates. It was his son, the old lady's grandson, Squire Chevenix Crowl, that owned the estates at the time I came to Applewale.

There was a deal o' talk lang before my aunt's time about it; and 'twas said the stepmother knew more than she was like to let out. And she managed her husband, the old squire, wi' her whiteheft and flatteries. And as the boy was never seen more, in course of time the thing died out of fowks' minds.

I'm going' to tell ye noo about what I sid wi' my own een.

I was not there six months, and it was winter time, when the old lady took her last sickness.

The doctor was afeard she might a took a fit o' madness, as she did, fifteen years before, and was buckled up, many a time, in a strait-waistcoat, which was the very leathern jerkin' I sid in the closet, off my aunt's room.

Well, she didn't. She pined, and windered, and went off, torflin', torflin', quiet enough, till a day or two before her flittin', and then she took to rabblin', and sometimes skirlin' in the bed, ye'd think a robber had a knife to her throat, and she used to work out o' the bed, and not being strong enough, then, to walk or stand, she'd fall on the flure, wi' her old wizened hands stretched before her face, and skirlin' still for mercy.

Ye may guess I didn't go into the room, and I used to be shiverin' in my bed wi' fear, at her skirlin' and scrafflin' on the flure, and blarin' out words that id make your skin turn blue.

My aunt, and Mrs Wyvern, and Judith Squailes, and a woman from Lexhoe, was always about her. At last she took fits, and they wore her out.

T' sir (parson) was there, and prayed for her; but she was past

praying with. I suppose it was right, but none could think there was
much good in it, and sa at lang last she made her flittin', and a' was
over, and old Dame Crowl was shrouded and coffined and Squire
Chevenix was wrote for. But he was away in France, and the delay was
sa lang, that t' sir and doctor both agreed it would not du to keep her
langer out o' her place, and no one cared but just them two, and my
aunt and the rest o' us, from Applewale, to go to the buryin'. So the
old lady of Applewale was laid in the vault under Lexhoe Church; and
we lived up at the great house till such time as the squire should come
to tell his will about us, and pay off such as he chose to discharge.

I was put into another room, two doors away from what was Dame
Crowl's chamber, after her death, and this thing happened the night
before Squire Chevenix came to Applewale.

The room I was in now was a large square chamber, covered wi' yak
panels, but unfurnished except for my bed, which had no curtains to
it, and a chair and a table, so, that looked nothing at all in such a big
room. And the big looking-glass, that the old lady used to keek into
and admire herself from head to heel, now that there was na mair o'
that wark, was put out of the way, and stood against the wall in my
room, for there was shiftin' o' many things in her chambers ye may
suppose, when she came to be coffined.

The news had come that day that the squire was to be down next
morning at Applewale; and not sorry was I, for I thought I was sure to
be sent home again to my mother. And right glad was I, and I was
thinkin' of a' at hame, and my sister, Janet, and the kitten and the
pymag, and Trimmer the tike, and all the rest, and I got sa fidgetty, I
couldn't sleep, and the clock struck twelve, and me wide awake, and
the room as dark as pick. My back was turned to the door, and my eyes
toward the wall opposite.

Well, it could na be a full quarter past twelve, when I sees a lightin'
on the wall before me, as if something took fire behind, and the shadas
o' the bed, and the chair, and my gown, that was hangin' from the
wall, was dancin' up and down, on the ceilin' beams and the yak
panels; and I turns my head ower my shouther quick, thinkin' something must a gone a' fire.

And what sud I see, by Jen! but the likeness o' the old beldame,
bedizened out in her satins and velvets, on her dead body, simperin',
wi' her eyes as wide as saucers, and her face like the fiend himself.

'Twas a red light that rose about her in a fuffin low, as if her dress round her feet was blazin'. She was drivin' on right for me, wi' her old shrivelled hands crooked as if she was goin' to claw me. I could not stir, but she passed me straight by, wi' a blast o' cald air, and I sid her, at the wall, in the alcove as my aunt used to call it, which was a recess where the state bed used to stand in old times, wi' a door open wide, and her hands gropin' in at somethin' was there. I never sid that door before. And she turned round to me, like a thing on a pivot, flyrin' (grinning), and all at once the room was dark, and I standin' at the far side o' the bed; I don't know how I got there, and I found my tongue at last, and if I did na blare a yellock, rennin' down the gallery and almost pulled Mrs Wyvern's door, off t'hooks, and frightened her half out o' her wits.

Ye may guess I did na sleep that night; and wi' the first light, down wi' me to my aunt, as fast as my two legs cud carry me.

Well, my aunt did na frump or flite me, as I thought she would, but she held me by the hand, and looked hard in my face all the time. And she telt me not to be feared; and says she: 'Hed the appearance a key in its hand?'

'Yes,' says I, bringin' it to mind, 'a big key in a queer brass handle.'

'Stop a bit,' says she, lettin' go ma hand, and openin' the cupboard-door. 'Was it like this?' says she, takin' one out in her fingers and showing it to me, with a dark look in my face.

'That was it,' says I, quick enough.

'Are ye sure?' she says, turnin' it round.

'Sart,' says I, and I felt like I was gain' to faint when I sid it.

'Well, that will do, child,' says she, saftly thinkin', and she locked it up again.

'The squire himself will be here today, before twelve o'clock, and ye must tell him all about it,' says she, thinkin', 'and I suppose I'll be leavin' soon, and so the best thing for the present is, that ye should go home this afternoon, and I'll look out another place for you when I can.'

Fain was I, ye may guess, at that word.

My aunt packed up my things for me, and the three pounds that was due to me, to bring home, and Squire Crowl himself came down to Applewale that day, a handsome man, about thirty years old. It was the second time I sid him. But this was the first time he spoke to me.

My aunt talked wi' him in the housekeeper's room, and I don't know what they said. I was a bit feared on the squire, he bein' a great gentleman down in Lexhoe, and I darn't go near till I was called. And says he, smilin': 'What's a' this ye a sen, child? it mun be a dream, for ye know there's na sic a thing as a bo or a freet in a' the world. But whatever it was, ma little maid, sit ye down and tell us all about it from first to last.'

Well, so soon as I med an end, he thought a bit, and says he to my aunt: 'I mind the place well. In old Sir Oliver's time lame Wyndel told me there was a door in that recess, to the left, where the lassie dreamed she saw my grandmother open it. He was past eighty when he telt me that, and I but a boy. It's twenty year sen. The plate and jewels used to be kept there, long ago, before the iron closet was made in the arras chamber, and he told me the key had a brass handle, and this ye say was found in the bottom o' the kist where she kept her old fans. Now, would not it be a queer thing if we found some spoons or diamonds forgot there? Ye mun come up wi' us, lassie, and point to the very spot.'

Loth was I, and my heart in my mouth, and fast I held by my aunt's hand as I stepped into that awsome room, and showed them both how she came and passed me by, and the spot where she stood, and where the door seemed to open.

There was an old empty press against the wall then, and shoving it aside, sure enough there was the tracing of a door in the wainscot, and a keyhole stopped with wood, and planed across as smooth as the rest, and the joining of the door all stopped wi' putty the colour o' yak, and, but for the hinges that showed a bit when the press was shoved aside, ye would not consayt there was a door there at all.

'Ha!' says he, wi' a queer smile, 'this looks like it.'

It took some minutes wi' a small chisel and hammer to pick the bit o' wood out o' the keyhole. The key fitted, sure enough, and, wi' a strang twist and a lang skreeak, the boult went back and he pulled the door open.

There was another door inside, stranger than the first, but the lacks was gone, and it opened easy. Inside was a narrow floor and walls and vault o' brick; we could not see what was in it, for 'twas dark as pick.

When my aunt had lighted the candle the squire held it up and stepped in.

My aunt stood on tiptoe tryin' to look over his shouther, and I did na see nout.

'Ha! ha!' says the squire, steppin' backward. 'What's that? Gi'ma the poker – quick!' says he to my aunt. And as she went to the hearth I peeps beside his arm, and I sid squat down in the far corner a monkey or a flayin' on the chest, or else the maist shrivelled up, wizzened old wife that ever was sen on yearth.

'By Jen!' says my aunt, as, puttin' the poker in his hand, she keeked by his shouther, and sid the ill-favoured thing, 'hae a care sir, what ye're doin'. Back wi' ye, and shut to the door!'

But in place o' that he steps in saftly, wi' the poker pointed like a sword, and he gies it a poke, and down it a' tumbles together, head and a', in a heap o' bayans and dust, little meyar an' a hatful.

'Twas the bayans o' a child; a' the rest went to dust at a touch. They said nout for a while, but he turns round the skull as it lay on the floor.

Young as I was I consayted I knew well enough what they was thinkin' on.

'A dead cat!' says he, pushin' back and blowin' out the can'le, and shuttin' to the door. 'We'll come back, you and me, Mrs Shutters, and look on the shelves by and by. I've other matters first to speak to ye about; and this little girl's going' hame, ye say. She has her wages, and I mun mak' her a present,' says he, pattin' my shoulder wi' his hand.

And he did gimma a goud pound, and I went aff to Lexhoe about an hour after, and sa hame by the stagecoach, and fain was I to be at hame again; and I never sa old Dame Crowl o' Applewale, God be thanked, either in appearance or in dream, at-efter. But when I was grown to be a woman my aunt spent a day and night wi' me at Littleham, and she telt me there was na doubt it was the poor little boy that was missing sa lang sen that was shut up to die thar in the dark by that wicked beldame, whar his skirls, or his prayers, or his thumpin' cud na be heard, and his hat was left by the water's edge, whoever did it, to mak' belief he was drowned. The clothes, at the first touch, a' ran into a snuff o' dust in the cell whar the bayans was found. But there was a handful o' jet buttons, and a knife with a green handle, together wi' a couple o' pennies the poor little fella had in his pocket, I suppose, when he was decoyed in thar, and sid his last o' the light. And there was, amang the squire's papers, a copy o' the notice that was prented after he was lost, when the old squire thought he might 'a run away, or bin took by gypsies, and it said he had a green-hefted knife wi' him, and that his buttons were o' cut jet. Sa that is a' I hev to say consarnin' old Dame Crowl, o' Applewale House.

SHERIDAN LE FANU

Squire Toby's Will

A Ghost Story

Many persons accustomed to travel the old York and London road, in the days of stage-coaches, will remember passing, in the afternoon, say, of an autumn day, in their journey to the capital, about three miles south of the town of Applebury, and a mile and a half before you reach the Old Angel Inn, a large black-and-white house, as those old fashioned cage-work habitations are termed, dilapidated and weather-stained, with broad lattice windows glimmering all over in the evening sun with little diamond panes, and thrown into relief by a dense background of ancient elms. A wide avenue, now overgrown like a churchyard with grass and weeds, and flanked by double rows of the same dark trees, old and gigantic, with here and there a gap in their solemn files, and sometimes a fallen tree lying across on the avenue, leads up to the hall-door.

Looking up its sombre and lifeless avenue from the top of the London coach, as I have often done, you are struck with so many signs of desertion and decay, the tufted grass sprouting in the chinks of the steps and window-stones, the smokeless chimneys over which the jackdaws are wheeling, the absence of human life and all its evidence, that you conclude at once that the place is uninhabited and abandoned to decay. The name of this ancient house is Gylingden Hall. Tall hedges and old timber quickly shroud the old place from view, and about a quarter of a mile further on you pass, embowered in melancholy trees, a small and ruinous Saxon chapel, which, time out of mind, has been the burying-place of the family of Marston, and partakes of the neglect and desolation which brood over their ancient dwelling-place.

The grand melancholy of the secluded valley of Gylingden, lonely as an enchanted forest, in which the crows returning to their roosts among the trees, and the straggling deer who peep from beneath their branches, seem to hold a wild and undisturbed dominion, heightens the forlorn aspect of Gylingden Hall.

Of late years repairs have been neglected, and here and there the roof is stripped, and 'the stitch in time' has been wanting. At the side of the house exposed to the gales that sweep through the valley like a torrent through its channel, there is not a perfect window left, and the shutters but imperfectly exclude the rain. The ceilings and walls are mildewed and green with damp stains. Here and there, where the drip falls from the ceiling, the floors are rotting. On stormy nights, as the guard described, you can hear the doors clapping in the old house, as far away as old Gryston bridge, and the howl and sobbing of the wind through its empty galleries.

About seventy years ago died the old Squire, Toby Marston, famous in that part of the world for his hounds, his hospitality, and his vices. He had done kind things, and he had fought duels: he had given away money and he had horse-whipped people. He carried with him some blessings and a good many curses, and left behind him an amount of debts and charges upon the estates which appalled his two sons, who had no taste for business or accounts, and had never suspected, till that wicked, open-handed, and swearing old gentleman died, how very nearly he had run the estates into insolvency.

They met at Gylingden Hall. They had the will before them, and lawyers to interpret, and information without stint, as to the encumbrances with which the deceased had saddled them. The will was so framed as to set the two brothers instantly at deadly feud.

These brothers differed in some points; but in one material characteristic they resembled one another, and also their departed father. They never went into a quarrel by halves, and once in, they did not stick at trifles.

The elder, Scroope Marston, the more dangerous man of the two, had never been a favourite of the old Squire. He had no taste for the sports of the field and the pleasures of a rustic life. He was no athlete, and he certainly was not handsome. All this the Squire resented. The young man, who had no respect for him, and outgrew his fear of his violence as he came to manhood, retorted. This aversion, therefore, in the ill-conditioned old man grew into positive hatred. He used to wish that d—d pippin-squeezing, humpbacked rascal Scroope, out of the way of better men – meaning his younger son Charles; and in his cups would talk in a way which even the old and young fellows who followed his hounds, and drank his port, and could stand a reasonable amount of brutality, did not like.

Scroope Marston was slightly deformed, and he had the lean sallow face, piercing black eyes, and black lank hair, which sometimes accompany deformity.

'I'm no feyther o' that hog-backed creature. I'm no sire of hisn, d—n him! I'd as soon call that tongs son o' mine,' the old man used to bawl, in allusion to his son's long, lank limbs: 'Charlie's a man, but that's a jack-an-ape. He has no good-nature; there's nothing handy, nor manly, nor no one turn of a Marston in him.'

And when he was pretty drunk, the old Squire used to swear he should never 'sit at the head o' that board; nor frighten away folk from Gylingden Hall wi' his d—d hatchet-face – the black loon!'

Handsome Charlie was the man for his money. He knew what a horse was, and could sit to his bottle; and the lasses were all clean *wad* about him. He was a Marston every inch of his six foot two.

Handsome Charlie and he, however, had also had a row or two. The old Squire was free with his horsewhip as with his tongue, and on occasion when neither weapon was quite practicable, had been known to give a fellow 'a tap o' his knuckles.' Handsome Charlie, however, thought there was a period at which personal chastisement should cease; and one night, when the port was flowing, there was some allusion to Marion Hayward, the miller's daughter, which for some reason the old gentleman did not like. Being 'in liquor,' and having clearer ideas about pugilism than self-government, he struck out, to the surprise of all present, at Handsome Charlie. The youth threw back his head scientifically, and nothing followed but the crash of a decanter on the floor. But the old Squire's blood was up, and he bounced from his chair. Up jumped Handsome Charlie, resolved to stand no nonsense. Drunken Squire Lilbourne, intending to mediate, fell flat on the floor, and cut his ear among the glasses. Handsome Charlie caught the thump which the old Squire discharged at him upon his open hand, and catching him by the cravat, swung him with his back to the wall. They said the old man never looked so purple, nor his eyes so goggle before; and then Handsome Charlie pinioned him tight to the wall by both arms.

'Well, I say – come, don't you talk no more nonsense o' that sort, and I won't lick you,' croaked the old Squire. 'You stopped that un clever, you did. Didn't he? Come, Charlie, man, gie us your hand, I say, and sit down again, lad.'

And so the battle ended; and I believe it was the last time the Squire raised his hand to Handsome Charlie.

But those days were over. Old Toby Marston lay cold and quiet enough now, under the drip of the mighty ash tree within the Saxon ruin where so many of the old Marston race returned to dust, and were forgotten. The weather-stained top-boots and leather-breeches, the three-cornered cocked hat to which old gentlemen of that day still clung, and the well-known red waistcoat that reached below his hips, and the fierce pug face of the old Squire, were now but a picture of memory. And the brothers between whom he had planted an irreconcilable quarrel, were now in their new mourning suits, with the gloss still on, debating furiously across the table in the great oak parlour, which had so often resounded to the banter and coarse songs, the oaths and laughter of the congenial neighbours whom the old Squire of Gylingden Hall loved to assemble there.

These young gentlemen, who had grown up in Gylingden Hall, were not accustomed to bridle their tongues, nor, if need be, to hesitate about a blow. Neither had been at the old man's funeral. His death had been sudden. Having been helped to his bed in that hilarious and quarrelsome state which was induced by port and punch, he was found dead in the morning – his head hanging over the side of the bed, and his face very black and swollen.

Now the Squire's will despoiled his eldest son of Gylingden, which had descended to the heir time out of mind. Scroope Marston was furious. His deep stern voice was heard inveighing against his dead father and living brother, and the heavy thumps on the table with which he enforced his stormy recriminations resounded through the large chamber. Then broke in Charles's rougher voice, and then came a quick alternation of short sentences, and then both voices together in growing loudness and anger, and at last, swelling the tumult, the expostulations of pacific and frightened lawyers, and at last a sudden break up of the conference. Scroope broke out of the room, his pale furious face showing whiter against his long black hair, his dark fierce eyes blazing, his hands clenched, and looking more ungainly and deformed than ever in the convulsions of his fury.

Very violent words must have passed between them; for Charlie, though he was the winning man, was almost as angry as Scroope. The elder brother was for holding possession of the house, and putting his rival to legal process to oust him. But his legal advisers were clearly against it. So, with a heart boiling over with gall, up he went to London, and found the firm who had managed his father's business fair and communicative enough. They looked into the settlements, and found that Gylingden was excepted. It was very odd, but so it was, specially excepted; so that the right of the old Squire to deal with it by his will could not be questioned.

Notwithstanding all this, Scroope, breathing vengeance and aggression, and quite willing to wreck himself provided he could run his brother down, assailed Handsome Charlie, and battered old Squire Toby's will in the Prerogative Court and also at common law, and the feud between the brothers was knit, and every month their exasperation was heightened.

Scroope was beaten, and defeat did not soften him. Charles might have forgiven hard words; but he had been himself worsted during the long campaign in some of those skirmishes, special motions, and so forth, that constitute the episodes of a legal epic like that in which the Marston brothers figured as opposing combatants; and the blight of law-costs had touched him, too, with the usual effect upon the temper of a man of embarrassed means.

Years flew, and brought no healing on their wings. On the contrary, the deep corrosion of this hatred bit deeper by time. Neither brother married. But an accident of a different kind befell the younger, Charles Marston, which abridged his enjoyments very materially.

This was a bad fall from his hunter. There were severe fractures, and there was concussion of the brain. For some time it was thought that he could not recover. He disappointed these evil auguries, however. He did recover, but changed in two essential particulars. He had received an injury in his hip, which doomed him never more to sit in the saddle. And the rollicking animal spirits which hitherto had never failed him, had now taken flight for ever.

He had been for five days in a state of coma – absolute insensibility –

and when he recovered consciousness he was haunted by an indescribable anxiety.

Tom Cooper, who had been butler in the palmy days of Gyling–den Hall, under old Squire Toby, still maintained his post with old-fashioned fidelity, in these days of faded splendour and frugal housekeeping. Twenty years had passed since the death of his old master. He had grown lean, and stooped, and his face, dark with the peculiar brown of age, furrowed and gnarled, and his temper, except with his master, had waxed surly.

His master had visited Bath and Buxton, and came back, as he went, lame, and halting gloomily about with the aid of a stick. When the hunter was sold, the last tradition of the old life at Gylingden dis-appeared. The young Squire, as he was still called, excluded by his mischance from the hunting field, dropped into a solitary way of life, and halted slowly and solitarily about the old place, seldom raising his eyes, and with an appearance of indescribable gloom.

Old Cooper could talk freely on occasion with his master; and one day he said, as he handed him his hat and stick in the hall: 'You should rouse yourself up a bit, Master Charles!'

'It's past rousing with me, old Cooper.'

'It's just this, I'm thinking: there's something on your mind, and you won't tell no one. There's no good keeping it on your stomach. You'll be a deal lighter if you tell it. Come, now, what is it, Master Charlie?'

The Squire looked with his round grey eyes straight into Cooper's eyes. He felt that there was a sort of spell broken. It was like the old rule of the ghost who can't speak till it is spoken to. He looked earnestly into old Cooper's face for some seconds, and sighed deeply.

'It ain't the first good guess you've made in your day, old Cooper, and I'm glad you've spoke. It's bin on my mind, sure enough, ever since I had that fall. Come in here after me, and shut the door.'

The Squire pushed open the door of the oak parlour, and looked round on the pictures abstractedly. He had not been there for some time, and, seating himself on the table, he looked again for a while in Cooper's face before he spoke.

'It's not a great deal, Cooper, but it troubles me, and I would not tell it to the parson nor the doctor; for, God knows what they'd say, though there's nothing to signify in it. But you were always true to the family, and I don't mind if I tell you.'

' 'Tis as safe with Cooper, Master Charles, as if 'twas locked in a chest, and sunk in a well.'

'It's only this,' said Charles Marston, looking down on the end of his stick, with which he was tracing lines and circles, 'all the time I was lying like dead, as you thought, after that fall, I was with the old master.' He raised his eyes to Cooper's again as he spoke, and with an awful oath he repeated – 'I was with him, Cooper!'

'He was a good man, sir, in his way,' repeated old Cooper, returning his gaze with awe. 'He was a good master to me, and a good father to you, and I hope he's happy. May God rest him!'

'Well,' said Squire Charles, 'it's only this: the whole of that time I was with him, or he was with me – I don't know which. The upshot is, we were together, and I thought I'd never get out of his hands again, and all the time he was bullying me about some one thing; and if it was to save my life, Tom Cooper, by – from the time I waked I never could call to mind what it was; and I think I'd give that hand to know; and if you can think of anything it might be – for God's sake! don't be afraid, Tom Cooper, but speak it out, for he threatened me hard, and it was surely him.'

Here ensued a silence.

'And what did you think it might be yourself, Master Charles?' said Cooper.

'I han't thought of aught that's likely. I'll never hit on't – *never*. I thought it might happen he knew something about that d—d humpbacked villain, Scroope, that swore before Lawyer Gingham I made away with a paper of settlements – me and father; and, as I hope to be saved, Tom Cooper, there never was a bigger lie! I'd a had the law of him for them identical words, and cast him for more than he's worth; only Lawyer Gingham never goes into nothing for me since money grew scarce in Gylingden; and I can't change my lawyer, I owe him such a hatful of money. But he did, he swore he'd hang me yet for it. He said it in them identical words – he'd never rest till he *hanged* me for it, and I think it was, like enough, something about *that*, the old master was troubled; but it's enough to drive a man mad. I *can't* bring it to mind – I can't remember a word he said, only he threatened awful, and looked – Lord a mercy on us! – frightful bad.'

'There's no need he should. May the Lord a-mercy on him!' said the old butler.

'No, of course; and you're not to tell a soul, Cooper – not a living soul, mind, that I said he looked bad, nor nothing about it.'

'God forbid!' said old Cooper, shaking his head. 'But I was thinking, sir, it might ha' been about the slight that's bin so long put on him by having no stone over him, and never a scratch o' a chisel to say who he is.'

'Ay! Well, I didn't think o' that. Put on your hat, old Cooper, and come down wi' me; for I'll look after that, at any rate.'

There is a bye-path leading by a turnstile to the park, and thence to the picturesque old burying-place, which lies in a nook by the road-side, embowered in ancient trees. It was a fine autumnal sunset, and melancholy lights and long shadows spread their peculiar effects over the landscape as 'Handsome Charlie' and the old butler made their way slowly toward the place where Handsome Charlie was himself to lie at last.

'Which of the dogs made that howling all last night?' asked the Squire, when they had got on a little way.

' 'Twas a strange dog, Master Charlie, in front of the house; ours was all in the yard – a white dog wi' a black head, he looked to be, and he was smelling round them mounting-steps the old master, God be wi' him! set up the time his knee was bad. When the tyke got up a' top of them, howlin' up at the windows, I'd a liked to shy something at him.'

'Hullo! Is that like him?' said the Squire, stopping short, and pointing with his stick at a dirty-white dog with a large black head, which was scampering round them in a wide circle, half crouching with that air of uncertainty and deprecation which dogs so well know how to assume.

He whistled the dog up. He was a large, half-starved bulldog.

'That fellow has made a long journey – thin as a whipping-post, and stained all over, and his claws worn to the stumps,' said the Squire, musingly. 'He isn't a bad dog, Cooper. My poor father liked a good bulldog, and knew a cur from a good 'un.'

The dog was looking up into the Squire's face with the peculiar grim visage of his kind, and the Squire was thinking irreverently how strong a likeness it presented to the character of his father's fierce pug features when he was clutching his horsewhip and swearing at a keeper.

'If I did right I'd shoot him. He'll worry the cattle, and kill our dogs,' said the Squire. 'Hey, Cooper? I'll tell the keeper to look after him. That fellow could pull down a sheep, and he shan't live on my mutton.'

But the dog was not to be shaken off. He looked wistfully after the Squire, and after they had got a little way on, he followed timidly.

It was vain trying to drive him off. The dog ran round them in wide circles, like the infernal dog in 'Faust'; only he left no track of thin flame behind him. These manoeuvres were executed with a sort of beseeching air, which flattered and touched the object of this odd preference. So he called him up again, patted him, and then and there in a manner adopted him.

The dog now followed their steps dutifully, as if he had belonged to Handsome Charlie all his days. Cooper unlocked the little iron door, and the dog walked in close behind their heels, and followed them as they visited the roofless chapel.

The Marstons were lying under the floor of this little building in rows. There is not a vault. Each has his distinct grave enclosed in a lining of masonry. Each is surmounted by a stone kist, on the upper flag of which is enclosed his epitaph, except that of poor old Squire Toby. Over him was nothing but the grass and the line of masonry which indicate the site of the kist, whenever his family should afford him one like the rest.

'Well, it does look shabby. It's the elder brother's business; but if he won't, I'll see to it myself, and I'll take care, old boy, to cut sharp and deep in it, that the elder son having refused to lend a hand the stone was put there by the younger.'

They strolled round this little burial-ground. The sun was now below the horizon, and the red metallic glow from the clouds, still illuminated by the departed sun, mingled luridly with the twilight. When Charlie peeped again into the little chapel, he saw the ugly dog stretched upon Squire Toby's grave, looking at least twice his natural length, and performing such antics as made the young Squire stare. If you have ever seen a cat stretched on the floor, with a bunch of Valerian, straining, writhing, rubbing its jaws in long-drawn caresses, and in the absorption of a sensual ecstasy, you have seen a phenomenon resembling that which Handsome Charlie witnessed on looking in.

The head of the brute looked so large, its body so long and thin, and its joints so ungainly and dislocated, that the Squire, with old Cooper beside him, looked on with a feeling of disgust and astonishment, which, in a moment or two more, brought the Squire's stick down upon him with a couple of heavy thumps. The beast awakened from his ecstasy, sprang to the head of the grave, and there on a sudden, thick and bandy as before, confronted the Squire, who stood at its foot, with a terrible grin, and eyes that glared with the peculiar green of canine fury.

The next moment the dog was crouching abjectly at the Squire's feet.

'Well, he's a rum 'un!' said old Cooper, looking hard at him.

'I like him,' said the Squire.

'I don't,' said Cooper.

'But he shan't come in here again,' said the Squire.

'I shouldn't wonder if he was a witch,' said old Cooper, who remembered more tales of witchcraft than are now current in that part of the world.

'He's a good dog,' said the Squire, dreamily. 'I remember the time I'd a given a handful for him – but I'll never be good for nothing again. Come along.'

And he stooped down and patted him. So up jumped the dog and looked up in his face, as if watching for some sign, ever so slight, which he might obey.

Cooper did not like a bone in that dog's skin. He could not imagine what his master saw to admire in him. He kept him all night in the gunroom, and the dog accompanied him in his halting rambles about the place. The fonder his master grew of him, the less did Cooper and the other servants like him.

'He hasn't a point of a good dog about him,' Cooper would growl. 'I think Master Charlie be blind. And old Captain (an old red parrot, who sat chained to a perch in the oak parlour, and conversed with himself, and nibbled at his claws and bit his perch all day), – old Captain, the only living thing, except one or two of us, and the Squire himself, that remembers the old master, the minute he saw the dog, screeched as if he was struck, shakin' his feathers out quite wild, and drops down, poor old soul, a-hangin' by his foot, in a fit.'

But there is no accounting for fancies, and the Squire was one of those dogged persons who persist more obstinately in their whims the more they are opposed. But Charles Marston's health suffered by his lameness. The transition from habitual and violent exercise to such a life as his privation now consigned him to, was never made without a risk to health; and a host of dyspeptic annoyances, the existence of which he had never dreamed of before, now beset him in sad earnest. Among these was the now not unfrequent troubling of his sleep with dreams and nightmares. In these his canine favourite invariably had a part and was generally a central, and sometimes a solitary figure. In these visions the dog seemed to stretch himself up the side of the Squire's bed, and in dilated proportions to sit at his feet, with a horrible likeness to the pug features of old Squire Toby, with his tricks of wagging his head and throwing up his chin; and then he would talk to him about Scroope, and tell him 'all wasn't straight', and that he 'must make it up wi' Scroope', that he, the old Squire, had 'served him an ill turn', that 'time was nigh up', and that 'fair was fair', and he was 'troubled where he was, about Scroope'.

Then in his dream this semi-human brute would approach his face to his, crawling and crouching up his body, heavy as lead, till the face of the beast was laid on his, with the same odious caresses and stretchings and writhings which he had seen over the old Squire's grave. Then Charlie would wake up with a gasp and a howl, and start upright in the bed, bathed in a cold moisture, and fancy he saw something white sliding off the foot of the bed. Sometimes he thought it might be the curtain with white lining that slipped down, or the coverlet disturbed by his uneasy turnings; but he always fancied, at such moments, that he saw something white sliding hastily off the bed; and always when he had been visited by such dreams the dog next morning was more than usually caressing and servile, as if to obliterate, by a more than ordinary welcome, the sentiment of disgust which the horror of the night had left behind it.

The doctor half satisfied the Squire that there was nothing in these dreams, which, in one shape or another, invariably attended forms of indigestion such as he was suffering from.

For a while, as if to corroborate this theory, the dog ceased altogether to figure in them. But at last there came a vision in which, more unpleasantly than before, he did resume his old place.

In his nightmare the room seemed all but dark; he heard what he knew to be the dog walking from the door round his bed slowly, to the side from which he always had come upon it. A portion of the room was uncarpeted, and he said he distinctly heard the peculiar tread of a dog, in which the faint clatter of the claws is audible. It was a light stealthy step, but at every tread the whole room shook heavily; he felt something place itself at the foot of his bed, and saw a pair of green eyes staring at him in the dark, from which he could not remove his own. Then he heard, as he thought, the old Squire Toby say – 'The eleventh hour be passed, Charlie, and ye've done nothing – you and I 'a done Scroope a wrong!' and then came a good deal more, and then – 'The time's nigh up, it's going to strike.' And with a long low growl, the thing began to creep up upon his feet; the growl continued, and he saw the reflection of the up-turned green eyes upon the bedclothes, as it began slowly to stretch itself up his body towards his face. With a loud scream, he waked. The light, which of late the Squire was accustomed to have in his bedroom, had accidentally gone out. He was afraid to get up, or even to look about the room for some time; so sure did he feel of seeing the green eyes in the dark fixed on him from some corner. He had hardly recovered from the first agony which nightmare leaves behind it, and was beginning to collect his thoughts, when he heard the clock strike twelve. And he bethought him of the words 'the eleventh hour be passed – time's nigh up – it's going to strike!' and he almost feared that he would hear the voice reopening the subject.

Next morning the Squire came down looking ill.

'Do you know a room, old Cooper,' said he, 'they used to call King Herod's Chamber?'

'Ay, sir; the story of King Herod was on the walls o't when I was a boy.'

'There's a closet off it – is there?'

'I can't be sure o' that; but 'tisn't worth your looking at, now; the hangings was rotten, and took off the walls, before you was born; and there's nou't there but some old broken things and lumber. I seed them put there myself by poor Twinks; he was blind of an eye, and footman afterwards. You'll remember Twinks? He died here, about the time o' the great snow. There was a deal o' work to bury him, poor fellow!'

'Get the key, old Cooper; I'll look at the room,' said the Squire.

'And what the devil can you want to look at it for?' said Cooper, with the old-world privilege of a rustic butler.

'And what the devil's that to you? But I don't mind if I tell you. I don't want that dog in the gunroom, and I'll put him somewhere else; and I don't care if I put him there.'

'A bulldog in a bedroom! Oons, sir! the folks 'ill say you're clean mad!'

'Well, let them; get you the key, and let us look at the room.'

'You'd shoot him if you did right, Master Charlie. You never heard what a noise he kept up all last night in the gunroom, walking to and fro growling like a tiger in a show; and, say what you like, the dog's not worth his feed; he hasn't a point of a dog; he's a bad dog.'

'I know a dog better than you – and he's a good dog!' said the Squire, testily.

'If you was a judge of a dog you'd hang that 'un,' said Cooper.

'I'm not a-going to hang him, so there's an end. Go you, and get the key; and don't be talking, mind, when you go down. I may change my mind.'

Now this freak of visiting King Herod's room had, in truth, a totally different object from that pretended by the Squire. The voice in his nightmare had uttered a particular direction, which haunted him, and would give him no peace until he had tested it. So far from liking that dog today, he was beginning to regard it with a horrible suspicion; and if old Cooper had not stirred his obstinate temper by seeming to dictate, I dare say he would have got rid of that inmate effectually before evening.

Up to the third storey, long disused, he and old Cooper mounted. At the end of a dusty gallery, the room lay. The old tapestry, from which the spacious chamber had taken its name, had long given place to modern paper, and this was mildewed, and in some places hanging from the walls. A thick mantle of dust lay over the floor. Some broken chairs and boards, thick with dust, lay, along with other lumber, piled together at one end of the room.

They entered the closet, which was quite empty. The Squire looked round, and you could hardly have said whether he was relieved or disappointed.

'No furniture here,' said the Squire, and looked through the dusty window. 'Did you say anything to me lately – I don't mean this morning – about this room, or the closet – or anything – I forget – '

'Lor' bless you! Not I. I han't been thinkin' o' this room this forty year.'

'Is there any sort of old furniture called a *buffet* – do you remember?' asked the Squire.

'A buffet? why, yes – to be sure – there was a buffet, sure enough, in this closet, now you bring it to my mind,' said Cooper. 'But it's papered over.'

'And what is it?'

'A little cupboard in the wall,' answered the old man.

'Ho – I see – and there's such a thing here, is there, under the paper? Show me whereabouts it was.'

'Well – I think it was somewhere about here,' answered he, rapping his knuckles along the wall opposite the window. 'Ay, there it is,' he added, as the hollow sound of a wooden door was returned to his knock.

The Squire pulled the loose paper from the wall, and disclosed the doors of a small press, about two feet square, fixed in the wall.

'The very thing for my buckles and pistols, and the rest of my gimcracks,' said the Squire. 'Come away, we'll leave the dog where he is. Have you the key of that little press?'

No, he had not. The old master had emptied and locked it up, and desired that it should be papered over, and that was the history of it.

Down came the Squire, and took a strong turn-screw from his gun-case; and quietly he reascended to King Herod's room, and, with little trouble, forced the door of the small press in the closet wall. There were in it some letters and cancelled leases, and also a parchment deed which he took to the window and read with much agitation. It was a supplemental deed executed about a fortnight after the others, and previously to his father's marriage, placing Gylingden under strict settlement to the elder son, in what is called 'tail male'. Handsome Charlie, in his fraternal litigation, had acquired a smattering of technical knowledge, and he perfectly well knew that the effect of this would be not only to transfer the house and lands to his brother Scroope, but to leave him at the mercy of that exasperated brother, who might recover from him personally every guinea he had ever received by way of rent, from the date of his father's death.

It was a dismal, clouded day, with something threatening in its aspect, and the darkness, where he stood, was made deeper by the top of one of the huge old trees over-hanging the window.

In a state of awful confusion he attempted to think over his position. He placed the deed in his pocket, and nearly made up his mind to destroy it. A short time ago he would not have hesitated for a moment under such circumstances; but now his health and his nerves were shattered, and he was under a supernatural alarm which the strange discovery of this deed had powerfully confirmed.

In this state of profound agitation he heard a sniffing at the closet-door, and then an impatient scratch and a long low growl. He screwed his courage up, and, not knowing what to expect, threw the door open and saw the dog, not in his dream-shape, but wriggling with joy, and crouching and fawning with eager submission; and then wandering about the closet, the brute growled awfully into the corners of it, and seemed in an unappeasable agitation.

Then the dog returned and fawned and crouched again at his feet.

After the first moment was over, the sensations of abhorrence and fear began to subside, and he almost reproached himself for requiting the affection of this poor friendless brute with the antipathy which he had really done nothing to earn.

The dog pattered after him down the stairs. Oddly enough, the sight of this animal, after the first revulsion, reassured him; it was, in his eyes, so attached, so good-natured, and palpably so mere a dog.

By the hour of evening the Squire had resolved on a middle course; he would not inform his brother of his discovery, nor yet would he destroy the deed. He would never marry. He was past that time. He would leave a letter, explaining the discovery of the deed, addressed to the only surviving trustee – who had probably forgotten everything about it – and having seen out his own tenure, he would provide that all should be set right after his death. Was not that fair? at all events it quite satisfied what he called his conscience, and he thought it a devilish good compromise for his brother; and he went out, towards sunset, to take his usual walk.

Returning in the darkening twilight, the dog, as usual attending him, began to grow frisky and wild, at first scampering round him in great circles, as before, nearly at the top of his speed, his great head between his paws as he raced. Gradually more excited grew the pace and narrower his circuit, louder and fiercer his continuous growl, and the Squire stopped and grasped his stick hard, for the lurid eyes and grin of the brute threatened an attack. Turning round and round as the excited brute encircled him, and striking vainly at him with his stick, he grew at last so tired that he almost despaired of keeping him longer at bay; when on a sudden the dog stopped short and crawled up to his feet wriggling and crouching submissively.

Nothing could be more apologetic and abject; and when the Squire dealt him two heavy thumps with his stick, the dog whimpered only, and writhed and licked his feet. The Squire sat down on a prostrate tree; and his dumb companion, recovering his wonted spirits immediately, began to sniff and nuzzle among the roots. The Squire felt in his breast-pocket for the deed – it was safe; and again he pondered, in this loneliest of spots, on the question whether he should preserve it for restoration after his death to his brother, or destroy it forthwith. He began rather to lean toward the latter solution, when the long low growl of the dog not far off startled him.

He was sitting in a melancholy grove of old trees, that slants gently westward. Exactly the same odd effect of light I have before described – a faint red glow reflected downward from the upper sky, after the sun had set, now gave to the growing darkness a lurid uncertainty. This grove, which lies in a gentle hollow, owing to its circumscribed horizon on all but one side, has a peculiar character of loneliness.

He got up and peeped over a sort of barrier, accidentally formed of the trunks of felled trees laid one over the other, and saw the dog straining up the other side of it, and hideously stretched out, his ugly head looking in consequence twice the natural size. His dream was coming over him again. And now between the trunks the brute's ungainly head was thrust, and the long neck came straining through, and the body, twining after it like a huge white lizard; and as it came striving and twisting through, it growled and glared as if it would devour him.

As swiftly as his lameness would allow, the Squire hurried from this solitary spot towards the house. What thoughts exactly passed through his mind as he did so, I am sure he could not have told. But when the dog came up with him it seemed appeased, and even in high good-humoured, and no longer resembled the brute that haunted his dreams.

That night, near ten o'clock, the Squire, a good deal agitated, sent for the keeper, and told him that he believed the dog was mad, and that he must shoot him. He might shoot the dog in the gunroom, where he was – a grain of shot or two in the wainscot did not matter, and the dog must not have a chance of getting out.

The Squire gave the gamekeeper his double-barrelled gun, loaded with heavy shot. He did not go with him beyond the hall. He placed his hand on the keeper's arm; the keeper said his hand trembled, and that he looked 'as white as curds'.

'Listen a bit!' said the Squire under his breath.

They heard the dog in a state of high excitement in the room – growling ominously, jumping on the window-stool and down again, and running round the room.

'You'll need to be sharp, mind – don't give him a chance – slip in edgeways, d'ye see? and give him both barrels!'

'Not the first mad dog I've knocked over, sir,' said the man, looking very serious as he cocked the gun.

As the keeper opened the door, the dog had sprung into the empty grate. He said he 'never see sich a stark, staring devil.' The beast made a twist round, as if, he thought, to jump up the chimney – 'but that wasn't to be done at no price,' – and he made a yell – not like a dog – like a man caught in a mill-crank, and before he could spring at the keeper, he fired one barrel into him. The dog leaped towards him, and rolled over, receiving the second barrel in his head, as he lay snorting at the keeper's feet!

'I never seed the like; I never heard a screech like that!' said the keeper, recoiling. 'It makes a fellow feel queer.'

'Quite dead?' asked the Squire.

'Not a stir in him, sir,' said the man, pulling him along the floor by the neck.

'Throw him outside the hall-door now,' said the Squire; 'and mind you pitch him outside the gate tonight – old Cooper says he's a witch,' and the pale Squire smiled, 'so he shan't lie in Gylingden.'

Never was man more relieved than the Squire, and he slept better for a week after this than he had done for many weeks before.

It behoves us all to act promptly on our good resolutions. There is a determined gravitation towards evil, which, if left to itself, will bear down first intentions. If at one moment of superstitious fear, the Squire had made up his mind to a great sacrifice, and resolved in the matter of that deed so strangely recovered, to act honestly by his brother, that resolution very soon gave place to the compromise with fraud, which so conveniently postponed the restitution to the period when further enjoyment on his part was impossible. Then came more tidings of Scroope's violent and minatory language, with always the same burthen – that he would leave no stone unturned to show that there had existed a deed which Charles had either secreted or destroyed, and that he would never rest till he had hanged him.

This of course was wild talk. At first it had only enraged him; but, with his recent guilty knowledge and suppression, had come fear. His danger was the existence of the deed, and little by little he brought himself to a resolution to destroy it. There were many falterings and recoils before he could bring himself to commit this crime. At length, however, he did it, and got rid of the custody of that which at any time might become the instrument of disgrace and ruin. There was relief in this, but also the new and terrible sense of actual guilt.

He had got pretty well rid of his supernatural qualms. It was a different kind of trouble that agitated him now.

But this night, he imagined, he was awakened by a violent shaking of his bed. He could see, in the very imperfect light, two figures at the foot of it, holding each a bedpost. One of these he half fancied was his brother Scroope, but the other was the old Squire – of that he was sure – and he fancied that they had shaken him up from his sleep. Squire Toby was talking as Charlie wakened, and he heard him say: 'Put out of our own house by you! It won't hold for long. We'll come in together, friendly, and stay. Forewarned, wi' yer eyes open, ye did it; and now Scroope'll hang you! We'll hang you together! Look at me, you devil's limb.'

And the old Squire tremblingly stretched his face, torn with shot and bloody, and growing every moment more and more into the likeness of the dog, and began to stretch himself out and climb the bed over the foot-board; and he saw the figure at the other side, little more than a black shadow, begin also to scale the bed; and there was instantly a dreadful confusion and uproar in the room, and such a gabbling and laughing; he could not catch the words; but, with a scream, he woke, and found himself standing on the floor. The phantoms and the clamour were gone, but a crash and ringing of fragments was in his ears. The great china bowl, from which for generations the Marstons of Gylingden had been baptised, had fallen from the mantelpiece, and was smashed on the hearthstone.

'I've bin dreamin' all night about Mr Scroope, and I wouldn't wonder, old Cooper, if he was dead,' said the Squire, when he came down in the morning.

'God forbid! I was adreamed about him, too, sir: I dreamed he was dammin' and sinkin' about a hole was burnt in his coat, and the old master, God be wi' him! said – quite plain – I'd 'a swore 'twas himself – "Cooper, get up, ye d—d land-loupin' thief, and lend a hand to hang him – for he's a daft cur, and no dog o' mine." 'Twas the dog shot over night, I do suppose, as was runnin' in my old head. I thought old master gied me a punch wi' his knuckles, and says I, wakenin' up, "At yer service, sir"; and for a while I couldn't get it out o' my head, master was in the room still.'

Letters from town soon convinced the Squire that his brother Scroope, so far from being dead, was particularly active; and Charlie's attorney wrote to say, in serious alarm, that he had heard, accidentally, that he intended setting up a case, of a supplementary deed of settlement, of which he had secondary evidence, which would give him Gylingden. And at this menace Handsome Charlie snapped his fingers, and wrote courageously to his attorney; abiding what might follow with, however, a secret foreboding.

Scroope threatened loudly now, and swore after his bitter fashion, and reiterated his old promise of hanging that cheat at last. In the midst of these menaces and preparations, however, a sudden peace proclaimed itself: Scroope died, without time even to make provisions for a posthumous attack upon his brother. It was one of those cases of disease of the heart in which death is as sudden as by a bullet.

Charlie's exultation was undisguised. It was shocking. Not, of course, altogether malignant. For there was the expansion consequent on the removal of a secret fear. There was also the comic piece of luck, that only the day before Scroope had destroyed his old will, which left to a stranger every farthing he possessed, intending in a day or two to execute another to the same person, charged with the express condition of prosecuting the suit against Charlie.

The result was, that all his possessions went unconditionally to his brother Charles as his heir. Here were grounds for abundance of savage elation. But there was also the deep-seated hatred of half a life of mutual and persistent aggression and revilings; and Handsome Charlie was capable of nursing a grudge, and enjoying a revenge with his whole heart.

He would gladly have prevented his brother's being buried in the old Gylingden chapel, where he wished to lie; but his lawyers doubted his power, and he was not quite proof against the scandal which would attend his turning back the funeral, which would, he knew, be attended by some of the country gentry and others, with an hereditary regard for the Marstons.

But he warned his servants that not one of them were to attend it; promising, with oaths and curses not to be disregarded, that any one of them who did so, should find the door shut in his face on his return.

I don't think, with the exception of old Cooper, that the servants cared for this prohibition, except as it baulked a curiosity always strong in the solitude of the country. Cooper was very much vexed that the eldest son of the old Squire should be buried in the old family chapel, and no sign of decent respect from Gylingden Hall. He asked his master, whether he would not, at least, have some wine and refreshments in the oak parlour, in case any of the country gentlemen who paid this respect to the old family should come up to the house? But the Squire only swore at him, told him to mind his own business, and ordered him to say, if such a thing happened, that he was out, and no preparations made, and, in fact, to send them away as they came. Cooper expostulated stoutly, and the Squire grew angrier; and after a tempestuous scene, took his hat and stick and walked out, just as the funeral descending the valley from the direction of the Old Angel Inn came in sight.

Old Cooper prowled about disconsolately, and counted the carriages as well as he could from the gate. When the funeral was over, and they began to drive away, he returned to the hall, the door of which lay open, and as usual deserted. Before he reached it quite, a mourning coach drove up, and two gentlemen in black cloaks, and with crapes to their hats, got out, and without looking to the right or the left, went up the steps into the house. Cooper followed them slowly. The carriage had, he supposed, gone round to the yard, for, when he reached the door, it was no longer there.

So he followed the two mourners into the house. In the hall he found a fellow-servant, who said he had seen two gentlemen, in black cloaks, pass through the hall, and go up the stairs without removing their hats, or asking leave of anyone. This was very odd, old Cooper thought, and a great liberty; so upstairs he went to make them out.

But he could not find them then, nor ever. And from that hour the house was troubled.

In a little time there was not one of the servants who had not something to tell. Steps and voices followed them sometimes in the passages, and tittering whispers, always minatory, scared them at corners of the galleries, or from dark recesses; so that they would return panic-stricken to be rebuked by thin Mrs Beckett, who looked on such stories as worse than idle. But Mrs Beckett herself, a short time after, took a very different view of the matter.

She had herself begun to hear these voices, and with this formidable aggravation, that they came always when she was at her prayers, which she had been punctual in saying all her life, and utterly interrupted them. She was scared at such moments by dropping words and sentences, which grew, as she persisted, into threats and blasphemies.

These voices were not always in the room. They called, as she fancied, through the walls, very thick in that old house, from the neighbouring apartments, sometimes on one side, sometimes on the other; sometimes they seemed to holloa from distant lobbies, and came muffled, but threateningly, through the long panelled passages. As they approached they grew furious, as if several voices were speaking together. Whenever, as I said, this worthy woman applied herself to her devotions, these horrible sentences came hurrying towards the door, and, in panic, she would start from her knees, and all then would subside except the thumping of her heart against her stays, and the dreadful tremors of her nerves.

What these voices said, Mrs Beckett never could quite remember one minute after they had ceased speaking; one sentence chased another away; gibe and menace and impious denunciation, each hideously articulate, were lost as soon as heard. And this added to the effect of these terrifying mockeries and invectives, that she could not, by any effort, retain their exact import, although their horrible character remained vividly present to her mind.

For a long time the Squire seemed to be the only person in the house absolutely unconscious of these annoyances. Mrs Beckett had twice made up her mind within the week to leave. A prudent woman, however, who has been comfortable for more than twenty years in a place, thinks oftener than twice before she leaves it. She and old Cooper were the only servants in the house who remembered the good old housekeeping in Squire Toby's day. The others were few, and such as could hardly be accounted regular servants. Meg Dobbs, who acted as housemaid, would not sleep in the house, but walked home, in trepidation, to her father's, at the gatehouse, under the escort of her little brother, every night. Old Mrs Beckett, who was high and mighty with the makeshift servants of fallen Gylingden, let herself down all at once, and made Mrs Kymes and the kitchen-maid move their beds into her large and faded room, and there, very frankly, shared her nightly terrors with them.

Old Cooper was testy and captious about these stories. He was already uncomfortable enough by reason of the entrance of the two muffled figures into the house, about which there could be no mistake. His own eyes had seen them. He refused to credit the stories of the women, and affected to think that the two mourners might have left the house and driven away, on finding no one to receive them.

Old Cooper was summoned at night to the oak parlour, where the Squire was smoking.

'I say, Cooper,' said the Squire, looking pale and angry, 'what for ha' you been frightenin' they crazy women wi' your plaguy stories? d—n me, if you see ghosts here it's no place for you, and it's time you should pack. I won't be left without servants. Here has been old Beckett, wi' the cook and the kitchen-maid, as white as pipeclay, all in a row, to tell me I must have a parson to sleep among them, and preach down the devil! Upon my soul, you're a wise old body, filling their heads wi' maggots! and Meg goes down to the lodge every night, afeared to lie in the house – all your doing, wi' your old wives' stories, – ye withered old Tom o' Bedlam!'

'I'm not to blame, Master Charles. 'Tisn't along o' no stories o' mine, for I'm never done tellin' 'em it's all vanity and vapours. Mrs Beckett 'ill tell you that, and there's been many a wry word betwixt us on the head o't. Whate'er I may *think*,' said old Cooper, significantly, and looking askance, with the sternness of fear in the Squire's face.

The Squire averted his eyes, and muttered angrily to himself, and turned away to knock the ashes out of his pipe on the hob, and then turning suddenly round upon Cooper again, he spoke, with a pale face, but not quite so angrily as before.

'I know you're no fool, old Cooper, when you like. Suppose there was such a thing as a ghost here, don't you see, it ain't to them snipe-headed women it 'id go to tell its story. What ails you, man, that you should think aught about it, but just what *I* think? You had a good headpiece o' yer own once, Cooper, don't be you clappin' a goosecap over it, as my poor father used to say; d— it, old boy, you mustn't let 'em be fools, settin' one another wild wi' their blether, and makin' the folk talk what they shouldn't, about Gylingden and the family. I don't think ye'd like that, old Cooper, I'm sure ye wouldn't. The women has gone out o' the kitchen, make up a bit o' fire, and get your pipe. I'll go to you, when I finish this one, and we'll smoke a bit together, and a glass o' brandy and water.'

Down went the old butler, not altogether unused to such con-descensions in that disorderly and lonely household; and let not those who can choose their company, be too hard on the Squire who couldn't.

When he had got things tidy, as he said, he sat down in that big old kitchen, with his feet on the fender, the kitchen candle burning in a great brass candlestick, which stood on the deal table at his elbow, with the brandy bottle and tumblers beside it, and Cooper's pipe also in readiness. And these preparations completed, the old butler, who had remembered other generations and better times, fell into rumination, and so, gradually, into a deep sleep.

Old Cooper was half awakened by someone laughing low, near his head. He was dreaming of old times in the Hall, and fancied one of 'the young gentlemen' going to play him a trick, and he mumbled something in his sleep, from which he was awakened by a stern deep voice, saying, 'You wern't at the funeral; I might take your life, I'll take your ear.' At the same moment, the side of his head received a violent push, and he started to his feet.

The fire had gone down, and he was chilled. The candle was expiring in the socket, and threw on the white wall long shadows, that danced up and down from the ceiling to the ground, and their black outlines he fancied resembled the two men in cloaks, whom he remembered with a profound horror.

He took the candle, with all the haste he could, getting along the passage, on whose walls the same dance of black shadows was continued, very anxious to reach his room before the light should go out. He was startled half out of his wits by the sudden clang of his master's bell, close over his head, ringing furiously.

'Ha, ha! There it goes – yes, sure enough,' said Cooper, reassuring himself with the sound of his own voice, as he hastened on, hearing more and more distinct every moment the same furious ringing. 'He's fell asleep, like me; that's it, and his lights is out, I lay you fifty – '

When he turned the handle of the door of the oak parlour, the Squire wildly called, 'Who's *there*?' in the tone of a man who expects a robber.

'It's me, old Cooper, all right, Master Charlie, you didn't come to the kitchen after all, sir.'

'I'm very bad, Cooper; I don't know how I've been. Did you meet anything?' asked the Squire.

'No,' said Cooper.

They stared on one another.

'Come here – stay here! Don't you leave me! Look round the room, and say is all right; and gie us your hand, old Cooper, for I must hold it.' The Squire's was damp and cold, and trembled very much. It was not very far from daybreak now.

After a time he spoke again: 'I 'a done many a thing I shouldn't; I'm not fit to go, and wi' God's blessin' I'll look to it – why shouldn't I? I'm as lame as old Billy – I'll never be able to do any good no more, and I'll give over drinking, and marry, as I ought to 'a done long ago – none o' yer fine ladies, but a good homely wench; there's Farmer Crump's youngest daughter, a good lass, and discreet. What for shouldn't I take her? She'd take care o' me, and wouldn't bring a head full o' romances here, and mantua-makers' trumpery, and I'll talk with the parson, and I'll do what's fair wi' everyone; and mind, I said I'm sorry for many a thing I 'a done.'

A wild cold dawn had by this time broken. The Squire, Cooper said, looked 'awful bad,' as he got his hat and stick, and sallied out for a walk, instead of going to his bed, as Cooper besought him, looking so wild and distracted, that it was plain his object was simply to escape from the house. It was twelve o'clock when the Squire walked into the kitchen, where he was sure of finding some of the servants, looking as if ten years had passed over him since yesterday. He pulled a stool by the fire, without speaking a word, and sat down. Cooper had sent to Applebury for the doctor, who had just arrived, but the Squire would not go to him. 'If he wants to see me, he may come here,' he muttered as often as Cooper urged him. So the doctor did come, charily enough, and found the Squire very much worse than he had expected.

The Squire resisted the order to get to his bed. But the doctor insisted under a threat of death, at which his patient quailed.

'Well, I'll do what you say – only this – you must let old Cooper and Dick Keeper stay wi' me. I mustn't be left alone, and they must keep awake o' nights; and stay a while, do *you*. When I get round a bit, I'll go and live in a town. It's dull livin' here, now that I can't do nou't, as I used, and I'll live a better life, mind ye; ye heard me say that, and I don't care who laughs, and I'll talk wi' the parson. I like 'em to laugh, hang 'em, it's a sign I'm doin' right, at last.'

The doctor sent a couple of nurses from the County Hospital, not choosing to trust his patient to the management he had selected, and he went down himself to Gylingden to meet them in the evening. Old Cooper was ordered to occupy the dressing-room, and sit up at night, which satisfied the Squire, who was in a strangely excited state, very low, and threatened, the doctor said, with fever.

The clergyman came, an old, gentle, 'book-learned' man, and talked and prayed with him late that evening. After he had gone the Squire called the nurses to his bedside, and said: 'There's a fellow sometimes comes; you'll never mind him. He looks in at the door and beckons, – a thin, humpbacked chap in mourning, wi' black gloves on; ye'll know him by his lean face, as brown as the wainscot: don't ye mind his smilin'. You don't go out to him, nor ask him in; he won't say nout; and if he grows anger'd and looks awry at ye, don't ye be afeared, for he can't hurt ye, and he'll grow tired waitin', and go away; and for God's sake mind ye don't ask him in, nor go out after him!'

The nurses put their heads together when this was over, and held afterwards a whispering conference with old Cooper. 'Law bless ye! – no, there's no madman in the house,' he protested; 'not a soul but what ye saw, – it's just a trifle o' the fever in his head – no more.'

The Squire grew worse as the night wore on. He was heavy and delirious, talking of all sorts of things – of wine, and dogs, and lawyers; and then he began to talk, as it were, to his brother Scroope. As he did so, Mrs Oliver, the nurse, who was sitting up alone with him, heard, as she thought, a hand softly laid on the door handle outside, and a stealthy attempt to turn it. 'Lord bless us! who's there?' she cried, and her heart jumped into her mouth, as she thought of the humpbacked man in black, who was to put in his head smiling and beckoning – 'Mr Cooper! sir! are you there?' she cried. 'Come here, Mr Cooper, please – do, sir, quick!'

Old Cooper, called up from his doze by the fire, stumbled in from the dressing-room, and Mrs Oliver seized him tightly as he emerged.

'The man with the hump has been atryin' the door, Mr Cooper, as sure as I am here.' The Squire was moaning and mumbling in his fever, understanding nothing, as she spoke. 'No, no! Mrs Oliver, ma'am, it's impossible, for there's no sich man in the house: what is Master Charlie sayin'?'

'He's saying *Scroope* every minute, whatever he means by that, and – and – hisht! – listen – there's the handle again,' and, with a loud scream, she added – 'Look at his head and neck in at the door!' and in her tremor she strained old Cooper in an agonising embrace.

The candle was flaring, and there was a wavering shadow at the door that looked like the head of a man with a long neck, and a longish sharp nose, peeping in and drawing back.

'Don't be a d—n fool, ma'am!' cried Cooper, very white, and shaking her with all his might. 'It's only the candle, I tell you – nothing in life but that. Don't you see?' and he raised the light; 'and I'm sure there was no one at the door, and I'll try, if you let me go.'

The other nurse was asleep on a sofa, and Mrs Oliver called her up in a panic, for company, as old Cooper opened the door. There was no one near it, but at the angle of the gallery was a shadow resembling that which he had seen in the room. He raised the candle a little, and it seemed to beckon with a long hand as the head drew back. 'Shadow from the candle!' exclaimed Cooper aloud, resolved not to yield to Mrs Oliver's panic; and, candle in hand, he walked to the corner. There was nothing. He could not forbear peeping down the long gallery from this point, and as he moved the light, he saw precisely the same sort of shadow, a little further down, and as he advanced the same withdrawal, and beckon. 'Gammon!' said he; 'it is nout but the candle.' And on he went, growing half angry and half frightened at the persistency with which this ugly shadow – a literal shadow he was sure it was – presented itself. As he drew near the point where it now appeared, it seemed to collect itself, and nearly dissolve in the central panel of an old carved cabinet which he was now approaching.

In the centre panel of this is a sort of boss carved into a wolf's head. The light fell oddly upon this, and the fugitive shadow seemed to be breaking up, and rearranging itself as oddly. The eyeball gleamed with a point of reflected light, which glittered also upon the grinning mouth, and he saw the long, sharp nose of Scroope Marston, and his fierce eye looking at him, he thought, with a steadfast meaning.

Old Cooper stood gazing upon this sight, unable to move, till he saw the face, and the figure that belonged to it, begin gradually to emerge from the wood. At the same time he heard voices approaching rapidly up a side gallery, and Cooper, with a loud 'Lord a-mercy on us!' turned and ran back again, pursued by a sound that seemed to shake the old house like a mighty gust of wind.

Into his master's room burst old Cooper, half wild with fear, and clapped the door and turned the key in a twinkling, looking as if he had been pursued by murderers.

'Did you hear it?' whispered Cooper, now standing near the dressing-room door. They all listened, but not a sound from without disturbed the utter stillness of night. 'God bless us! I doubt it's my old head that's gone crazy!' exclaimed Cooper.

He would tell them nothing but that he was himself 'an old fool,' to be frightened by their talk, and that 'the rattle of a window, or the dropping o' a pin' was enough to scare him now; and so he helped himself through that night with brandy, and sat up talking by his master's fire.

The Squire recovered slowly from his brain fever, but not perfectly. A very little thing, the doctor said, would suffice to upset him. He was not yet sufficiently strong to remove for change of scene and air, which were necessary for his complete restoration.

Cooper slept in the dressing-room, and was now his only nightly attendant. The ways of the invalid were odd: he liked, half sitting up in his bed, to smoke his churchwarden o' nights, and made old Cooper smoke, for company, at the fireside. As the Squire and his humble friend indulged in it, smoking is a taciturn pleasure, and it was not until the Master of Gylingden had finished his third pipe that he essayed conversation, and when he did, the subject was not such as Cooper would have chosen.

'I say, old Cooper, look in my face, and don't be afeared to speak out,' said the Squire, looking at him with a steady, cunning smile; 'you know all this time, as well as I do, who's in the house. You needn't deny – hey? – Scroope and my father?'

'Don't you be talking like that, Charlie,' said old Cooper, rather sternly and frightened, after a long silence; still looking in his face, which did not change.

'What's the good o' shammin', Cooper? Scroope's took the hearin' o' yer right ear – you know he did. He's looking angry. He's nigh took my life wi' this fever. But he's not done wi' me yet, and he looks awful wicked. Ye saw him – ye know ye did.'

Cooper was awfully frightened, and the odd smile on the Squire's lips frightened him still more. He dropped his pipe, and stood gazing in silence at his master, and feeling as if he were in a dream.

'If ye think so, ye should not be smiling like that,' said Cooper, grimly.

'I'm tired, Cooper, and it's as well to smile as t'other thing; so I'll even smile while I can. You know what they mean to do wi' me. That's all I wanted to say. Now, lad, go on wi' yer pipe – I'm going' asleep.'

So the Squire turned over in his bed, and lay down serenely, with his head on the pillow. Old Cooper looked at him, and glanced at the door, and then half filled his tumbler with brandy, and drank it off, and felt better, and got to his bed in the dressing-room.

In the dead of night he was suddenly awakened by the Squire, who was standing, in his dressing-gown and slippers, by his bed.

'I've brought you a bit o' a present. I got the rents o' Hazelden yesterday, and ye'll keep that for yourself – it's a fifty – and give t' other to Nelly Carwell, tomorrow; I'll sleep the sounder; and I saw Scroope since; he's not such a bad 'un after all, old fellow! He's got a crape over his face – for I told him I couldn't bear it; and I'd do many a thing for him now. I never could stand shillyshally. Good-night, old Cooper!'

And the Squire laid his trembling hand kindly on the old man's shoulder, and returned to his own room. 'I don't half like how he is. Doctor don't come half often enough. I don't like that queer smile o' his, and his hand was as cold as death. I hope in God his brain's not a-turnin'!'

With these reflections, he turned to the pleasanter subject of his present, and at last fell asleep.

In the morning, when he went into the Squire's room, the Squire had left his bed. 'Never mind; he'll come back, like a bad shillin',' thought old Cooper, preparing the room as usual. But he did not return. Then began an uneasiness, succeeded by a panic, when it began to be plain that the Squire was not in the house. What had become of him? None of his clothes, but his dressing-down and slippers, were missing. Had he left the house, in his present sickly state, in that garb? and, if so, could he be in his right senses; and was there a chance of his surviving a cold, damp night, so passed, in the open air?

Tom Edwards was up to the house, and told them, that, walking a mile or so that morning, at four o'clock – there being no moon – along with Farmer Nokes, who was driving his cart to market, in the dark, three men walked, in front of the horse, not twenty yards before them, all the way from near Gylingden Lodge to the burial-ground, the gate of which was opened for them from within, and the three men entered, and the gate was shut. Tom Edwards thought they were gone in to make preparation for a funeral of some member of the Marston family. But the occurrence seemed to Cooper, who knew there was no such thing, horribly ominous.

He now commenced a careful search, and at last bethought him of the lonely upper storey, and King Herod's chamber. He saw nothing changed there, but the closet door was shut, and, dark as was the morning, something, like a large white knot sticking out over the door, caught his eye.

The door resisted his efforts to open it for a time; some great weight forced it down against the floor; at length, however, it did yield a little, and a heavy crash, shaking the whole floor, and sending an echo flying through all the silent corridors, with a sound like receding laughter, half stunned him.

When he pushed open the door, his master was lying dead upon the floor. His cravat was drawn halter-wise tight round his throat, and had done its work well. The body was cold, and had been long dead.

In due course the coroner held his inquest, and the jury pronounced, 'that the deceased, Charles Marston, had died by his own hand, in a state of temporary insanity.' But old Cooper had his own opinion about the Squire's death, though his lips were sealed, and he never spoke about it. He went and lived for the residue of his days in York, where there are still people who remember him, a taciturn and surly old man, who attended church regularly, and also drank a little, and was known to have saved some money.

SHERIDAN LE FANU

Dickon the Devil

About thirty years ago I was selected by two rich old maids to visit a property in that part of Lancashire which lies near the famous forest of Pendle, with which Mr Ainsworth's 'Lancashire Witches' has made us so pleasantly familiar. My business was to make partition of a small property, including a house and demesne, to which they had a long time before succeeded as co-heiresses.

The last forty miles of my journey I was obliged to post, chiefly by crossroads, little known, and less frequented, and presenting scenery often extremely interesting and pretty. The picturesqueness of the landscape was enhanced by the season, the beginning of September, at which I was travelling.

I had never been in this part of the world before; I am told it is now a great deal less wild, and, consequently, less beautiful.

At the inn where I had stopped for a relay of horses and some dinner – for it was then past five o'clock – I found the host, a hale old fellow of five-and-sixty, as he told me, a man of easy and garrulous benevolence, willing to accommodate his guests with any amount of talk, which the slightest tap sufficed to set flowing, on any subject you pleased.

I was curious to learn something about Barwyke, which was the name of the demesne and house I was going to. As there was no inn within some miles of it, I had written to the steward to put me up there, the best way he could, for a night.

The host of the 'Three Nuns', which was the sign under which he entertained wayfarers, had not a great deal to tell. It was twenty years, or more, since old Squire Bowes died, and no one had lived in the Hall ever since, except the gardener and his wife.

'Tom Wyndsour will be as old a man as myself; but he's a bit taller, and not so much in flesh, quite,' said the fat innkeeper.

'But there were stories about the house,' I repeated, 'that they said, prevented tenants from coming into it?'

'Old wives' tales; many years ago, that will be, sir; I forget 'em; I forget 'em all. Oh yes, there always will be, when a house is left so; foolish folk will always be talkin'; but I hadn't heard a word about it this twenty year.'

It was vain trying to pump him; the old landlord of the 'Three Nuns,' for some reason, did not choose to tell tales of Barwyke Hall, if he really did, as I suspected, remember them.

I paid my reckoning, and resumed my journey, well pleased with the good cheer of that old-world inn, but a little disappointed.

We had been driving for more than an hour, when we began to cross a wild common; and I knew that, this passed, a quarter of an hour would bring me to the door of Barwyke Hall.

The peat and furze were pretty soon left behind; we were again in the wooded scenery that I enjoyed so much, so entirely natural and pretty, and so little disturbed by traffic of any kind. I was looking from the chaise-window, and soon detected the object of which, for some time, my eye had been in search. Barwyke Hall was a large, quaint house, of that cage-work fashion known as 'black and white,' in which the bars and angles of an oak framework contrast, black as ebony, with the white plaster that overspreads the masonry built into its interstices. This steep-roofed Elizabethan house stood in the midst of park-like grounds of no great extent, but rendered imposing by the noble stature of the old trees that now cast their lengthening shadows eastward over the sward, from the declining sun.

The park-wall was grey with age, and in many places laden with ivy. In deep grey shadow, that contrasted with the dim fires of evening reflected on the foliage above it, in a gentle hollow, stretched a lake that looked cold and black, and seemed, as it were, to skulk from observation with a guilty knowledge.

I had forgot that there was a lake at Barwyke; but the moment this caught my eye, like the cold polish of a snake in the shadow, my instinct seemed to recognise something dangerous, and I knew that the lake was connected, I could not remember how, with the story I had heard of this place in my boyhood.

I drove up a grass-grown avenue, under the boughs of these noble trees, whose foliage, dyed in autumnal red and yellow, returned the beams of the western sun gorgeously.

We drew up at the door. I got out, and had a good look at the front of the house; it was a large and melancholy mansion, with signs of long neglect upon it; great wooden shutters, in the old fashion, were barred, outside, across the windows; grass, and even nettles, were growing thick on the courtyard, and a thin moss streaked the timber beams; the plaster was discoloured by time and weather, and bore great russet and yellow stains. The gloom was increased by several grand old trees that crowded close about the house.

I mounted the steps, and looked round; the dark lake lay near me now, a little to the left. It was not large; it may have covered some ten or twelve acres; but it added to the melancholy of the scene. Near the centre of it was a small island, with two old ash trees, leaning toward each other, their pensive images reflected in the stirless water. The only cheery influence in this scene of antiquity, solitude, and neglect was that the house and landscape were warmed with the ruddy western beams. I knocked, and my summons resounded hollow and ungenial in my ear; and the bell, from far away, returned a deep-mouthed and surly ring, as if it resented being roused from a score years' slumber.

A light-limbed, jolly-looking old fellow, in a barracan jacket and gaiters, with a smile of welcome, and a very sharp, red nose, that seemed to promise good cheer, opened the door with a promptitude that indicated a hospitable expectation of my arrival.

There was but little light in the hall, and that little lost itself in darkness in the background. It was very spacious and lofty, with a gallery running round it, which, when the door was open, was visible at two or three points. Almost in the dark my new acquaintance led me across this wide hall into the room destined for my reception. It was spacious, and wainscoted up to the ceiling. The furniture of this capacious chamber was old fashioned and clumsy. There were curtains still to the windows, and a piece of Turkey carpet lay upon the floor; those windows were two in number, looking out, through the trunks of the trees close to the house, upon the lake. It needed all the fire, and all the pleasant associations of my entertainer's red nose, to light up this melancholy chamber. A door at its farther end admitted to the room that was prepared for my sleeping apartment. It was wainscoted, like the other. It had a four-post bed, with heavy tapestry curtains, and in other respects was furnished in the same old-world and ponderous style as the other room. Its window, like those of that apartment, looked out upon the lake.

Sombre and sad as these rooms were, they were yet scrupulously clean. I had nothing to complain of; but the effect was rather dispiriting. Having given some directions about supper – a pleasant incident to look forward to – and made a rapid toilet, I called on my friend with the gaiters and red nose (Tom Wyndsour) whose occupation was that of a 'bailiff', or under-steward, of the property, to accompany me, as we had still an hour or so of sun and twilight, in a walk over the grounds.

It was a sweet autumn evening, and my guide, a hardy old fellow, strode at a pace that tasked me to keep up with.

Among clumps of trees at the northern boundary of the demesne we lighted upon the little antique parish church. I was looking down upon it, from an eminence, and the park-wall interposed; but a little way down was a stile affording access to the road, and by this we approached the iron gate of the churchyard. I saw the church door open; the sexton was replacing his pick, shovel and spade, with which he had just been digging a grave in the churchyard, in their little repository under the stone stair of the tower. He was a polite, shrewd little hunchback, who was very happy to show me over the church. Among the monuments was one that interested me; it was erected to commemorate the very Squire Bowes from whom my two old maids had inherited the house and estate of Barwyke. It spoke of him in terms of grandiloquent eulogy, and informed the Christian reader that he had died, in the bosom of the Church of England, at the age of seventy-one.

I read this inscription by the parting beams of the setting sun, which disappeared behind the horizon just as we passed out from under the porch.

'Twenty years since the Squire died,' said I, reflecting as I loitered still in the churchyard.

'Ay, sir; 'twill be twenty year the ninth o' last month.'

'And a very good old gentleman?'

'Good-natured enough, and an easy gentleman he was, sir; I don't think while he lived he ever hurt a fly,' acquiesced Tom Wyndsour. 'It ain't always easy sayin' what's in 'em though, and what they may take or turn to afterwards; and some o' them sort, I think, goes mad.'

'You don't think he was out of his mind?' I asked.

'He? La! no; not he, sir; a bit lazy, mayhap, like other old fellows; but a knew devilish well what he was about.'

Tom Wyndsour's account was a little enigmatical; but, like old Squire Bowes, I was 'a bit lazy' that evening, and asked no more questions about him.

We got over the stile upon the narrow road that skirts the church-yard. It is overhung by elms more than a hundred years old, and in the twilight, which now prevailed, was growing very dark. As side by side we walked along this road, hemmed in by two loose stonelike walls, something running towards us in a zig-zag line passed us at a wild pace, with a sound like a frightened laugh or a shudder, and I saw, as it passed, that it was a human figure. I may confess now, that I was a little startled. The dress of this figure was, in part, white: I know I mistook it at first for a white horse coming down the road at a gallop. Tom Wyndsour turned about and looked after the retreating figure.

'He'll be on his travels tonight,' he said, in a low tone. 'Easy served with a bed, *that* lad be; six foot o' dry peat or heath, or a nook in a dry ditch. That lad hasn't slept once in a house this twenty year, and never will while grass grows.'

'Is he mad?' I asked.

'Something that way, sir; he's an idiot, an awpy; we call him "Dickon the devil," because the devil's almost the only word that's ever in his mouth.'

It struck me that this idiot was in some way connected with the story of old Squire Bowes.

'Queer things are told of him, I dare say?' I suggested.

'More or less, sir; more or less. Queer stories, some.'

'Twenty years since he slept in a house? That's about the time the Squire died,' I continued.

'So it will be, sir; and not very long after.'

'You must tell me all about that, Tom, tonight, when I can hear it comfortably, after supper.'

Tom did not seem to like my invitation; and looking straight before him as we trudged on, he said,

'You see, sir, the house has been quiet, and nout's been troubling folk inside the walls or out, all round the woods of Barwyke, this ten year, or more; and my old woman, down there, is clear against talking about such matters, and thinks it best – and so do I – to let sleepin' dogs be.'

He dropped his voice towards the close of the sentence, and nodded significantly.

We soon reached a point where he unlocked a wicket in the park wall, by which we entered the grounds of Barwyke once more.

The twilight deepening over the landscape, the huge and solemn trees, and the distant outline of the haunted house, exercised a sombre influence on me, which, together with the fatigue of a day of travel, and the brisk walk we had had, disinclined me to interrupt the silence in which my companion now indulged.

A certain air of comparative comfort, on our arrival, in great measure dissipated the gloom that was stealing over me. Although it was by no means a cold night, I was very glad to see some wood blazing in the grate; and a pair of candles aiding the light of the fire, made the room look cheerful. A small table, with a very white cloth, and preparations for supper, was also a very agreeable object.

I should have liked very well, under these influences, to have listened to Tom Wyndsour's story; but after supper I grew too sleepy to attempt to lead him to the subject; and after yawning for a time, I found there was no use in contending against my drowsiness, so I betook myself to my bedroom, and by ten o'clock was fast asleep.

What interruption I experienced that night I shall tell you presently. It was not much, but it was very odd.

By next night I had completed my work at Barwyke. From early morning till then I was so incessantly occupied and hard-worked, that I had no time to think over the singular occurrence to which I have just referred. Behold me, however, at length once more seated at my little supper-table, having ended a comfortable meal. It had been a sultry day, and I had thrown one of the large windows up as high as it would go. I was sitting near it, with my brandy and water at my elbow, looking out into the dark. There was no moon, and the trees that are grouped about the house make the darkness round it supernaturally profound on such nights.

'Tom,' said I, so soon as the jug of hot punch I had supplied him with began to exercise its genial and communicative influence; 'you must tell me who beside your wife and you and myself slept in the house last night.'

Tom, sitting near the door, set down his tumbler, and looked at me askance, while you might count seven, without speaking a word.

'Who else slept in the house?' he repeated, very deliberately. 'Not a living soul, sir'; and he looked hard at me, still evidently expecting something more.

'That *is* very odd,' I said returning his stare, and feeling really a little odd. 'You are sure *you* were not in my room last night?'

'Not till I came to call you, sir, this morning; *I* can make oath of that.'

'Well,' said I, 'there was someone there, *I* can make oath of that. I was so tired I could not make up my mind to get up; but I was waked by a sound that I thought was someone flinging down the two tin boxes in which my papers were locked up violently on the floor. I heard a slow step on the ground, and there was light in the room, although I remembered having put out my candle. I thought it must have been you, who had come in for my clothes, and upset the boxes by accident. Whoever it was, he went out and the light with him. I was about to settle again, when, the curtain being a little open at the foot of the bed, I saw a light on the wall opposite; such as a candle from outside would cast if the door were very cautiously opening. I started up in the bed, drew the side curtain, and saw that the door *was* opening, and admitting light from outside. It is close, you know, to the head of the bed. A hand was holding on the edge of the door and pushing it open; not a bit like yours; a very singular hand. Let me look at yours.'

He extended it for my inspection.

'Oh no; there's nothing wrong with your hand. This was differently shaped; fatter; and the middle finger was stunted, and shorter than the rest, looking as if it had once been broken, and the nail was crooked like a claw. I called out "Who's there?" and the light and the hand were withdrawn, and I saw and heard no more of my visitor.'

'So sure as you're a living man, that was him!' exclaimed Tom Wyndsour, his very nose growing pale, and his eyes almost starting out of his head.

'Who?' I asked.

'Old Squire Bowes; 'twas *his* hand you saw; the Lord a' mercy on us!' answered Tom. 'The broken finger, and the nail bent like a hoop. Well for you, sir, he didn't come back when you called, that time. You came here about them Miss Dymock's business, and he never meant they should have a foot o' ground in Barwyke; and he was making a will to give it away quite different, when death took him short. He never was uncivil to no one; but he couldn't abide them ladies. My mind misgave me when I heard 'twas about their business you were coming; and now you see how it is; he'll be at his old tricks again!'

With some pressure and a little more punch, I induced Tom Wyndsour to explain his mysterious allusions by recounting the occurrences which followed the old Squire's death.

'Squire Bowes of Barwyke died without making a will, as you know,' said Tom. 'And all the folk round were sorry; that is to say, sir, as sorry as folk will be for an old man that has seen a long tale of years, and has no right to grumble that death has knocked an hour too soon at his door. The Squire was well liked; he was never in a passion, or said a hard word; and he would not hurt a fly; and that made what happened after his decease the more surprising.

'The first thing these ladies did, when they got the property was to buy stock for the park.

'It was not wise, in any case, to graze the land on their own account. But they little knew all they had to contend with.

'Before long something went wrong with the cattle first one, and then another, took sick and died, and so on, till the loss began to grow heavy. Then, queer stories, little by little, began to be told. It was said, first by one, then by another, that Squire Bowes was seen, about evening time, walking, just as he used to do when he was alive, among the old trees, leaning on his stick; and sometimes when he came up with the cattle, he would stop and lay his hand kindly like on the back of one of them; and that one was sure to fall sick next day, and die soon after.

'No one ever met him in the park, or in the woods, or ever saw him, except a good distance off. But they knew his gait and his figure well, and the clothes he used to wear; and they could tell the beast he laid his hand on by its colour – white, dun, or black; and that beast was sure to sicken and die. The neighbours grew shy of taking the path over the park; and no one liked to walk in the woods, or come inside the bounds of Barwyke: and the cattle went on sickening and dying as before.

'At that time there was one Thomas Pyke; he had been a groom to the old Squire; and he was in care of the place, and was the only one that used to sleep in the house.

'Tom was vexed, hearing these stories; which he did not believe the half on 'em; and more especial as he could not get man or boy to herd the cattle; all being afeared. So he wrote to Matlock in Derbyshire, for his brother, Richard Pyke, a clever lad, and one that knew nout o' the story of the old Squire walking.

'Dick came; and the cattle was better; folk said they could still see the old Squire, sometimes, walking, as before, in openings of the wood, with his stick in his hand; but he was shy of coming nigh the cattle, whatever his reason might be, since Dickon Pyke came; and he used to stand a long bit off, looking at them, with no more stir in him than a trunk o' one of the old trees, for an hour at a time, till the shape melted away, little by little, like the smoke of a fire that burns out.

'Tom Pyke and his brother Dickon, being the only living souls in the house, lay in the big bed in the servants' room, the house being fast barred and locked, one night in November.

'Tom was lying next the wall, and he told me, as wide awake as ever he was at noonday. His brother Dickon lay outside, and was sound asleep.

'Well, as Tom lay thinking, with his eyes turned toward the door, it opens slowly, and who should come in but old Squire Bowes, his face lookin' as dead as he was in his coffin.

'Tom's very breath left his body; he could not take his eyes off him; and he felt the hair rising up on his head.

'The Squire came to the side of the bed, and put his arms under Dickon, and lifted the boy – in a dead sleep all the time – and carried him out so, at the door.

'Such was the appearance, to Tom Pyke's eyes, and he was ready to swear to it, anywhere.

'When this happened, the light, wherever it came from, all on a sudden went out, and Tom could not see his own hand before him.

'More dead than alive, he lay till daylight.

'Sure enough his brother Dickon was gone. No sign of him could he discover about the house, and with some trouble he got a couple of the neighbours to help him to search the woods and grounds. Not a sign of him anywhere.

'At last one of them thought of the island in the lake; the little boat was moored to the old post at the water's edge In they got, though with small hope of finding him there. Find him, nevertheless, they did, sitting under the big ash tree, quite out of his wits; and to all their questions he answered nothing but one cry – 'Bowes, the devil! See him; see him; Bowes, the devil!' An idiot they found him; and so he will be till God sets all things right. No one could ever get him to sleep under roof tree more. He wanders from house to house while daylight lasts; and no one cares to lock the harmless creature in the workhouse. And folk would rather not meet him after nightfall, for they think where he is there may be worse things near.'

A silence followed Tom's story. He and I were alone in that large room; I was sitting near the open window, looking into the dark night air. I fancied I saw something white move across it; and I heard a sound like low talking that swelled into a discordant shriek – 'Hoo-oo-oo! Bowes, the devil! Over your shoulder. Hoo-oo-oo! ha! ha! ha!' I started up, and saw, by the light of the candle with which Tom strode to the window, the wild eyes and blighted face of the idiot, as, with a sudden change of mood, he drew off, whispering and tittering to himself, and holding up his long fingers, and looking at the tips like a 'hand of glory.'

Tom pulled down the window. The story and its epilogue were over. I confess I was rather glad when I heard the sound of the horses' hoofs on the courtyard, a few minutes later; and still gladder when, having bidden Tom a kind farewell, I had left the neglected house of Barwyke a mile behind me.

SHERIDAN LE FANU

The Child that Went with the Fairies

✦

Eastward of the old city of Limerick, about ten Irish miles under the range of mountains known as the Slieveelim hills, famous as having afforded Sarsfield a shelter among their rocks and hollows, when he crossed them in his gallant descent upon the cannon and ammunition of King William, on its way to the beleaguering army, there runs a very old and narrow road. It connects the Limerick road to Tipperary with the old road from Limerick to Dublin, and runs by bog and pasture, hill and hollow, straw-thatched village, and roofless castle, not far from twenty miles.

Skirting the heathy mountains of which I have spoken, at one part it becomes singularly lonely. For more than three Irish miles it traverses a deserted country. A wide, black bog, level as a lake, skirted with copse, spreads at the left, as you journey northward, and the long and irregular line of mountain rises at the right, clothed in heath, broken with lines of grey rock that resemble the bold and irregular outlines of fortifications, and riven with many a gully, expanding here and there into rocky and wooded glens, which open as they approach the road.

A scanty pasturage, on which browsed a few scattered sheep or kine, skirts this solitary road for some miles, and under shelter of a hillock, and of two or three great ash trees, stood, not many years ago, the little thatched cabin of a widow named Mary Ryan.

Poor was this widow in a land of poverty. The thatch had acquired the grey tint and sunken outlines, that show how the alternations of rain and sun have told upon that perishable shelter.

But whatever other dangers threatened, there was one well provided against by the care of other times. Round the cabin stood half a dozen mountain ashes, as the rowans, inimical to witches, are there called.

On the worn planks of the door were nailed two horseshoes, and over the lintel and spreading along the thatch, grew, luxuriant, patches of that ancient cure for many maladies, and prophylactic against the machinations of the evil one, the house-leek. Descending into the doorway, in the *chiaroscuro* of the interior, when your eye grew sufficiently accustomed to that dim light, you might discover, hanging at the head of the widow's wooden-roofed bed, her beads and a phial of holy water.

Here certainly were defences and bulwarks against the intrusion of that unearthly and evil power, of whose vicinity this solitary family were constantly reminded by the outline of Lisnavoura, that lonely hill-haunt of the 'good people', as the fairies are called euphemistically, whose strangely domelike summit rose not half a mile away, looking like an outwork of the long line of mountain that sweeps by it.

It was at the fall of the leaf, and an autumnal sunset threw the lengthening shadow of haunted Lisnavoura, close in front of the solitary little cabin, over the undulating slopes and sides of Slieveelim. The birds were singing among the branches in the thinning leaves of the melancholy ash trees that grew at the roadside in front of the door. The widow's three younger children were playing on the road, and their voices mingled with the evening song of the birds. Their elder sister, Nell, was 'within in the house', as their phrase is, seeing after the boiling of the potatoes for supper.

Their mother had gone down to the bog, to carry up a hamper of turf on her back. It is, or was at least, a charitable custom – and if not disused, long may it continue – for the wealthier people when cutting their turf and stacking it in the bog, to make a smaller stack for the behoof of the poor, who were welcome to take from it so long as it lasted, and thus the potato pot was kept boiling, and the hearth warm that would have been cold enough but for that good-natured bounty, through wintry months.

Moll Ryan trudged up the steep 'bohereen' whose banks were overgrown with thorn and brambles, and stooping under her burden, re-entered her door, where her dark-haired daughter Nell met her with a welcome, and relieved her of her hamper.

Moll Ryan looked round with a sigh of relief, and drying her forehead, uttered the Munster ejaculation: 'Eiah, wisha! It's tired I am with it, God bless it. And where's the craythurs, Nell?'

'Playin' out on the road, mother; didn't ye see them and you comin' up?'

'No; there was no one before me on the road,' she said, uneasily; 'not a soul, Nell; and why didn't ye keep an eye on them?'

'Well, they're in the haggard, playin' there, or round by the back o' the house. Will I call them in?'

'Do so, good girl, in the name o' God. The hens is comin' home, see, and the sun was just down over Knockdoulah, an' I comin' up.'

So out ran tall, dark-haired Nell, and standing on the road, looked up and down it; but not a sign of her two little brothers, Con and Bill, or her little sister, Peg, could she see. She called them; but no answer came from the little haggard, fenced with straggling bushes. She listened, but the sound of their voices was missing. Over the stile, and behind the house she ran – but there all was silent and deserted.

She looked down toward the bog, as far as she could see; but they did not appear. Again she listened – but in vain. At first she had felt angry, but now a different feeling overcame her, and she grew pale. With an undefined boding she looked toward the heathy boss of Lisnavoura, now darkening into the deepest purple against the flaming sky of sunset.

Again she listened with a sinking heart, and heard nothing but the farewell twitter and whistle of the birds in the bushes around. How many stories had she listened to by the winter hearth, of children stolen by the fairies, at nightfall, in lonely places! With this fear she knew her mother was haunted.

No one in the country round gathered her little flock about her so early as this frightened widow, and no door 'in the seven parishes' was barred so early.

Sufficiently fearful, as all young people in that part of the world are of such dreaded and subtle agents, Nell was even more than usually afraid of them, for her terrors were infected and redoubled by her mother's. She was looking towards Lisnavoura in a trance of fear, and crossed herself again and again, and whispered prayer after prayer. She was interrupted by her mother's voice on the road calling her loudly. She answered, and ran round to the front of the cabin, where she found her standing.

'And where in the world's the craythurs – did ye see sight o' them anywhere?' cried Mrs Ryan, as the girl came over the stile.

'Arrah! mother, 'tis only what they're run down the road a bit. We'll see them this minute coming back. It's like goats they are, climbin' here and runnin' there; an' if I had them here, in my hand, maybe I wouldn't give them a hiding all round.'

'May the Lord forgive you, Nell! the childhers gone. They're took, and not a soul near us, and Father Tom three miles away! And what'll I do, or who's to help us this night? Oh, wirristhru, wirristhru! The craythurs is gone!'

'Whisht, mother, be aisy: don't ye see them comin' up.'

And then she shouted in menacing accents, waving her arm, and beckoning the children, who were seen approaching on the road, which some little way off made a slight dip, which had concealed them. They were approaching from the westward, and from the direction of the dreaded hill of Lisnavoura.

But there were only two of the children, and one of them, the little girl, was crying. Their mother and sister hurried forward to meet them, more alarmed than ever.

'Where is Billy – where is he?' cried the mother, nearly breathless, so soon as she was within hearing.

'He's gone – they took him away; but they said he'll come back again,' answered little Con, with the dark brown hair.

'He's gone away with the grand ladies,' blubbered the little girl.

'What ladies – where? Oh, Leum, asthora! My darlin', are you gone away at last? Where is he? Who took him? What ladies are you talkin' about? What way did he go?' she cried in distraction.

'I couldn't see where he went, mother; 'twas like as if he was going to Lisnavoura.'

With a wild exclamation the distracted woman ran on towards the hill alone, clapping her hands, and crying aloud the name of her lost child.

Scared and horrified, Nell, not daring to follow, gazed after her, and burst into tears; and the other children raised high their lamentations in shrill rivalry.

Twilight was deepening. It was long past the time when they were usually barred securely within their habitation. Nell led the younger children into the cabin, and made them sit down by the turf fire, while she stood in the open door, watching in great fear for the return of her mother.

After a long while they did see their mother return. She came in and sat down by the fire, and cried as if her heart would break.

'Will I bar the doore, mother?' asked Nell.

'Ay, do – didn't I lose enough, this night, without lavin' the doore open, for more o' yez to go; but first take an' sprinkle a dust o' the holy waters over ye, acuishla, and bring it here till I throw a taste iv it over myself and the craythurs; an' I wondher, Nell, you'd forget to do the like yourself, lettin' the craythurs out so near nightfall. Come here and sit on my knees, asthora, come to me, mavourneen, and hould me fast, in the name o' God, and I'll hould you fast that none can take yez from me, and tell me all about it, and what it was – the Lord between us and harm – an' how it happened, and who was in it.'

And the door being barred, the two children, sometimes speaking together, often interrupting one another, often interrupted by their mother, managed to tell this strange story, which I had better relate connectedly and in my own language.

The Widow Ryan's three children were playing, as I have said, upon the narrow old road in front of her door. Little Bill or Leum, about five years old, with golden hair and large blue eyes, was a very pretty boy, with all the clear tints of healthy childhood, and that gaze of earnest simplicity which belongs not to town children of the same age. His little sister Peg, about a year elder, and his brother Con, a little more than a year elder than she, made up the little group.

Under the great old ash trees, whose last leaves were falling at their feet, in the light of an October sunset, they were playing with the hilarity and eagerness of rustic children, clamouring together, and their faces were turned toward the west and storeyed hill of Lisnavoura.

Suddenly a startling voice with a screech called to them from behind, ordering them to get out of the way, and turning, they saw a sight, such as they never beheld before. It was a carriage drawn by four horses that were pawing and snorting, in impatience, as if just pulled up. The children were almost under their feet, and scrambled to the side of the road next their own door.

This carriage and all its appointments were old fashioned and gorgeous, and presented to the children, who had never seen anything finer than a turf car, and once, an old chaise that passed that way from Killaloe, a spectacle perfectly dazzling.

Here was antique splendour. The harness and trappings were scarlet, and blazing with gold. The horses were huge, and snow white, with great manes, that as they tossed and shook them in the air, seemed to stream and float sometimes longer and sometimes shorter, like so much smoke – their tails were long, and tied up in bows of broad scarlet and gold ribbon. The coach itself was glowing with colours, gilded and emblazoned. There were footmen in gay liveries, and three-cocked hats, like the coachman's; but he had a great wig, like a judge's, and their hair was frizzed out and powdered, and a long thick 'pigtail,' with a bow to it, hung down the back of each.

All these servants were diminutive, and ludicrously out of proportion with the enormous horses of the equipage, and had sharp, sallow features, and small, restless fiery eyes, and faces of cunning and malice that chilled the children. The little coachman was scowling and showing his white fangs under his cocked hat, and his little blazing beads of eyes were quivering with fury in their sockets as he whirled his whip round and round over their heads, till the lash of it looked like a streak of fire in the evening sun, and sounded like the cry of a legion of 'fillapoueeks' in the air.

'Stop the princess on the highway!' cried the coachman, in a piercing treble.

'Stop the princess on the highway!' piped each footman in turn, scowling over his shoulder down on the children, and grinding his keen teeth.

The children were so frightened they could only gape and turn white in their panic. But a very sweet voice from the open window of the carriage reassured them, and arrested the attack of the lackeys.

A beautiful and 'very grand-looking' lady was smiling from it on them, and they all felt pleased in the strange light of that smile.

'The boy with the golden hair, I think,' said the lady, bending her large and wonderfully clear eyes on little Leum.

The upper sides of the carriage were chiefly of glass, so that the children could see another woman inside, whom they did not like so well.

This was a black woman, with a wonderfully long neck, hung round with many strings of large variously-coloured beads, and on her head was a sort of turban of silk striped with all the colours of the rainbow, and fixed in it was a golden star.

This black woman had a face as thin almost as a death's-head, with high cheekbones, and great goggle eyes, the whites of which, as well as her wide range of teeth, showed in brilliant contrast with her skin, as she looked over the beautiful lady's shoulder, and whispered something in her ear.

'Yes; the boy with the golden hair, I think,' repeated the lady.

And her voice sounded sweet as a silver bell in the children's ears, and her smile beguiled them like the light of an enchanted lamp, as she leaned from the window with a look of ineffable fondness on the golden-haired boy, with the large blue eyes; insomuch that little Billy, looking up, smiled in return with a wondering fondness, and when she stooped down, and stretched her jewelled arms towards him, he stretched his little hands up, and how they touched the other children did not know; but, saying, 'Come and give me a kiss, my darling,' she raised him, and he seemed to ascend in her small fingers as lightly as a feather, and she held him in her lap and covered him with kisses.

Nothing daunted, the other children would have been only too happy to change places with their favoured little brother. There was only one thing that was unpleasant, and a little frightened them, and that was the black woman, who stood and stretched forward, in the carriage as before. She gathered a rich silk and gold handkerchief that was in her fingers up to her lips, and seemed to thrust ever so much of it, fold after fold, into her capacious mouth, as they thought to smother her laughter, with which she seemed convulsed, for she was shaking and quivering, as it seemed, with suppressed merriment; but her eyes, which remained uncovered, looked angrier than they had ever seen eyes look before.

But the lady was so beautiful they looked on her instead, and she continued to caress and kiss the little boy on her knee; and smiling at the other children she held up a large russet apple in her fingers, and the carriage began to move slowly on, and with a nod inviting them to take the fruit, she dropped it on the road from the window; it rolled some way beside the wheels, they following, and then she dropped another, and then another, and so on. And the same thing happened to all; for just as either of the children who ran beside had caught the rolling apple, somehow it slipped into a hole or ran into a ditch, and looking up they saw the lady drop another from the window, and so the chase was taken up and continued till they got, hardly knowing how far they had gone, to the old cross-road that leads to Owney.

It seemed that there the horses' hoofs and carriage-wheels rolled up a wonderful dust, which being caught in one of those eddies that whirl the dust up into a column, on the calmest day, enveloped the children for a moment, and passed whirling on towards Lisnavoura, the carriage, as they fancied, driving in the centre of it; but suddenly it subsided, the straws and leaves floated to the ground, the dust dissipated itself, but the white horses and the lackeys, the gilded carriage, the lady and their little golden-haired brother were gone.

At the same moment suddenly the upper rim of the clear setting sun disappeared behind the hill of Knockdoula, and it was twilight. Each child felt the transition like a shock – and the sight of the rounded summit of Lisnavoura, now closely overhanging them, struck them with a new fear.

They screamed their brother's name after him, but their cries were lost in the vacant air. At the same time they thought they heard a hollow voice say, close to them, 'Go home.'

Looking round and seeing no one, they were scared, and hand in hand – the little girl crying wildly, and the boy white as ashes, from fear, they trotted homeward, at their best speed, to tell, as we have seen, their strange story.

Molly Ryan never more saw her darling. But something of the lost little boy was seen by his former playmates.

Sometimes when their mother was away earning a trifle at hay-making, and Nelly washing the potatoes for their dinner, or 'beatling' clothes in the little stream that flows in the hollow close by, they saw the pretty face of little Billy peeping in archly at the door, and smiling silently at them, and as they ran to embrace him, with cries of delight, he drew back, still smiling archly, and when they got out into the open day, he was gone, and they could see no trace of him anywhere.

This happened often, with slight variations in the circumstances of the visit. Sometimes he would peep for a longer time, sometimes for a shorter time, sometimes his little hand would come in, and, with bended finger, beckon them to follow; but always he was smiling with the same arch look and wary silence – and always he was gone when they reached the door. Gradually these visits grew less and less frequent, and in about eight months they ceased altogether, and little Billy, irretrievably lost, took rank in their memories with the dead.

One wintry morning, nearly a year and a half after his disappearance, their mother having set out for Limerick soon after cockcrow, to sell some fowls at the market, the little girl, lying by the side of her elder sister, who was fast asleep, just at the grey of the morning heard the latch lifted softly, and saw little Billy enter and close the door gently after him. There was light enough to see that he was barefoot and ragged, and looked pale and famished. He went straight to the fire, and cowered over the turf embers, and rubbed his hands slowly, and seemed to shiver as he gathered the smouldering turf together.

The little girl clutched her sister in terror and whispered, 'Waken, Nelly, waken; here's Billy come back!'

Nelly slept soundly on, but the little boy, whose hands were extended close over the coals, turned and looked toward the bed, it seemed to her, in fear, and she saw the glare of the embers reflected on his thin cheek as he turned toward her. He rose and went, on tiptoe, quickly to the door, in silence, and let himself out as softly as he had come in.

After that, the little boy was never seen any more by any one of his kindred.

'Fairy doctors', as the dealers in the preternatural, who in such cases were called in, are termed, did all that in them lay – but in vain. Father Tom came down, and tried what holier rites could do, but equally without result. So little Billy was dead to mother, brother, and sisters; but no grave received him. Others whom affection cherished, lay in holy ground, in the old churchyard of Abington, with headstone to mark the spot over which the survivor might kneel and say a kind prayer for the peace of the departed soul. But there was no landmark to show where little Billy was hidden from their loving eyes, unless it was in the old hill of Lisnavoura, that cast its long shadow at sunset before the cabin-door; or that, white and filmy in the moonlight, in later years, would occupy his brother's gaze as he returned from fair or market, and draw from him a sigh and a prayer for the little brother he had lost so long ago, and was never to see again.

SHERIDAN LE FANU

The White Cat of Drumgunniol

There is a famous story of a white cat, with which we all become acquainted in the nursery. I am going to tell a story of a white cat very different from the amiable and enchanted princess who took that disguise for a season. The white cat of which I speak was a more sinister animal.

The traveller from Limerick toward Dublin, after passing the hills of Killaloe upon the left, as Keeper Mountain rises high in view, finds himself gradually hemmed in, up the right, by a range of lower hills. An undulating plain that dips gradually to a lower level than that of the road interposes, and some scattered hedgerows relieve its somewhat wild and melancholy character.

One of the few human habitations that send up their films of turf-smoke from that lonely plain, is the loosely-thatched, earth-built dwelling of a 'strong farmer,' as the more prosperous of the tenant-farming classes are termed in Munster. It stands in a clump of trees near the edge of a wandering stream, about halfway between the mountains and the Dublin road, and had been for generations tenanted by people named Donovan.

In a distant place, desirous of studying some Irish records which had fallen into my hands, and enquiring for a teacher capable of instructing me in the Irish language, a Mr Donovan, dreamy, harmless, and learned, was recommended to me for the purpose.

I found that he had been educated as a Sizar in Trinity College, Dublin. He now supported himself by teaching, and the special direction of my studies, I suppose, flattered his national partialities, for he unbosomed himself of much of his long-reserved thoughts, and recollections about his country and his early days. It was he who told me this story, and I mean to repeat it, as nearly as I can, in his own words.

I have myself seen the old farmhouse, with its orchard of huge moss-grown apple trees. I have looked round on the peculiar landscape; the roofless, ivy-covered tower, that two hundred years before had afforded a refuge from raid and rapparee, and which still occupies its old place in the angle of the haggard; the bush-grown 'liss', that scarcely a hundred and fifty steps away records the labours of a bygone race; the dark and towering outline of old Keeper in the background; and the lonely range of furze and heath-clad hills that form a nearer barrier, with many a line of grey rock and clump of dwarf oak or birch. The pervading sense of loneliness made it a scene not unsuited for a wild and unearthly story. And I could quite fancy how, seen in the grey of a wintry morning, shrouded far and wide in snow, or in the melancholy glory of an autumnal sunset, or in the chill splendour of a moonlight night, it might have helped to tone a dreamy mind like honest Dan Donovan's to superstition and a proneness to the illusions of fancy. It is certain, however, that I never anywhere met with a more simple-minded creature, or one on whose good faith I could more entirely rely.

When I was a boy, said he, living at home at Drumgunniol, I used to take my Goldsmith's *Roman History* in my hand and go down to my favourite seat, the flat stone, sheltered by a hawthorn tree beside the little lough, a large and deep pool, such as I have heard called a tarn in England. It lay in the gentle hollow of a field that is overhung toward the north by the old orchard, and being a deserted place was favourable to my studious quietude.

One day reading here, as usual, I wearied at last, and began to look about me, thinking of the heroic scenes I had just been reading of. I was as wide awake as I am at this moment, and I saw a woman appear at the corner of the orchard and walk down the slope. She wore a long, light grey dress, so long that it seemed to sweep the grass behind her, and so singular was her appearance in a part of the world where female attire is so inflexibly fixed by custom, that I could not take my eyes off her. Her course lay diagonally from corner to corner of the field, which was a large one, and she pursued it without swerving.

When she came near I could see that her feet were bare, and that she seemed to be looking steadfastly upon some remote object for guidance. Her route would have crossed me – had the tarn not interposed – about ten or twelve yards below the point at which I was sitting. But instead of arresting her course at the margin of the lough, as I had expected, she went on without seeming conscious of its existence, and I saw her, as plainly as I see you, sir, walk across the surface of the water, and pass, without seeming to see me, at about the distance I had calculated.

I was ready to faint from sheer terror. I was only thirteen years old then, and I remember every particular as if it had happened this hour.

The figure passed through the gap at the far corner of the field, and there I lost sight of it. I had hardly strength to walk home, and was so nervous, and ultimately so ill, that for three weeks I was confined to the house, and could not bear to be alone for a moment. I never entered that field again, such was the horror with which from that moment every object in it was clothed. Even at this distance of time I should not like to pass through it.

This apparition I connected with a mysterious event; and, also, with a singular liability, that has for nearly eight years distinguished, or rather afflicted, our family. It is no fancy. Everybody in that part of the country knows all about it. Everybody connected what I had seen with it.

I will tell it all to you as well as I can.

When I was about fourteen years old – that is about a year after the sight I had seen in the lough field – we were one night expecting my father home from the fair of Killaloe. My mother sat up to welcome him home, and I with her, for I liked nothing better than such a vigil. My brothers and sisters, and the farm servants, except the men who were driving home the cattle from the fair, were asleep in their beds. My mother and I were sitting in the chimney corner chatting together, and watching my father's supper, which was kept hot over the fire. We knew that he would return before the men who were driving home the cattle, for he was riding, and told us that he would only wait to see them fairly on the road, and then push homeward.

At length we heard his voice and the knocking of his loaded whip at the door, and my mother let him in. I don't think I ever saw my father drunk, which is more than most men of my age, from the same part of the country, could say of theirs. But he could drink his glass of whisky as well as another, and he usually came home from fair or market a little merry and mellow, and with a jolly flush in his cheeks.

Tonight he looked sunken, pale and sad. He entered with the saddle and bridle in his hand, and he dropped them against the wall, near the door, and put his arms round his wife's neck, and kissed her kindly.

'Welcome home, Meehal,' said she, kissing him heartily.

'God bless you, mavourneen,' he answered.

And hugging her again, he turned to me, who was plucking him by the hand, jealous of his notice. I was little, and light of my age, and he lifted me up in his arms and kissed me, and my arms being about his neck, he said to my mother: 'Draw the bolt, acuishla.'

She did so, and setting me down very dejectedly, he walked to the fire and sat down on a stool, and stretched his feet toward the glowing turf, leaning with his hands on his knees.

'Rouse up, Mick, darlin',' said my mother, who was growing anxious, 'and tell me how did the cattle sell, and did everything go lucky at the fair, or is there anything wrong with the landlord, or what in the world is it that ails you, Mick, jewel?'

'Nothin', Molly. The cows sould well, thank God, and there's nothin' fell out between me an' the landlord, an' everything's the same way. There's no fault to find anywhere.'

'Well, then, Mickey, since so it is, turn round to your hot supper, and ate it, and tell us is there anything new.'

'I got my supper, Molly, on the way, and I can't ate a bit,' he answered.

'Got your supper on the way, an' you knowin' 'twas waiting for you at home, an' your wife sittin' up an' all!' cried my mother, reproachfully.

'You're takin' a wrong meanin' out of what I say,' said my father. 'There's something happened that leaves me that I can't ate a mouthful, and I'll not be dark with you, Molly, for, maybe, it ain't very long I have to be here, an' I'll tell you what it was. It's what I've seen, the white cat.'

'The Lord between us and harm!' exclaimed my mother, in a moment as pale and as chap-fallen as my father; and then, trying to rally, with a laugh, she said: 'Ha! 'tis only funnin' me you are. Sure a white rabbit was snared a Sunday last, in Grady's wood; an' Teigue seen a big white rat in the haggard yesterday.'

' 'Twas neither rat nor rabbit was in it. Don't ye think but I'd know a rat or a rabbit from a big white cat, with green eyes as big as halfpennies, and its back riz up like a bridge, trottin' on and across me, and ready, if I dar' stop, to rub its sides against my shins, and maybe to make a jump and seize my throat, if that it's a cat, at all, an' not something worse?'

As he ended his description in a low tone, looking straight at the fire, my father drew his big hand across his forehead once or twice, his face being damp and shining with the moisture of fear, and he sighed, or rather groaned, heavily.

My mother had relapsed into panic, and was praying again in her fear. I, too, was terribly frightened, and on the point of crying, for I knew all about the white cat.

Clapping my father on the shoulder, by way of encouragement, my mother leaned over him, kissing him, and at last began to cry. He was wringing her hands in his, and seemed in great trouble.

'There was nothin' came into the house with me?' he asked, in a very low tone, turning to me.

'There was nothin', father,' I said, 'but the saddle and bridle that was in your hand.'

'Nothin' white kem in at the doore wid me,' he repeated.

'Nothin' at all,' I answered.

'So best,' said my father, and making the sign of the cross, he began mumbling to himself, and I knew he was saying his prayers.

Waiting for a while, to give him time for this exercise, my mother asked him where he first saw it.

'When I was riding up the bohereen,' – the Irish term meaning a little road, such as leads up to a farmhouse – 'I bethought myself that the men was on the road with the cattle, and no one to look to the horse barrin' myself, so I thought I might as well leave him in the crooked field below, an' I tuck him there, he bein' cool, and not a hair turned, for I rode him aisy all the way. It was when I turned, after lettin' him go – the saddle and bridle bein' in my hand – that I saw it, pushin' out o' the long grass at the side o' the path, an' it walked across it, in front of me, an' then back again, before me, the same way, an' sometimes at one side, an' then at the other, lookin' at me wid them shinin' eyes; and I consayted I heard it growlin' as it kep' beside me – as close as ever you see – till I kem up to the doore, here, an' knocked an' called, as ye heerd me.'

Now, what was it, in so simple an incident, that agitated my father, my mother, myself, and finally, every member of this rustic household, with a terrible foreboding? It was this that we, one and all, believed that my father had received, in thus encountering the white cat, a warning of his approaching death.

The omen had never failed hitherto. It did not fail now. In a week after my father took the fever that was going, and before a month he was dead.

My honest friend, Dan Donovan, paused here; I could perceive that he was praying, for his lips were busy, and I concluded that it was for the repose of that departed soul.

In a little while he resumed.

It is eighty years now since that omen first attached to my family. Eighty years? Ay, is it. Ninety is nearer the mark. And I have spoken to many old people, in those earlier times, who had a distinct recollection of everything connected with it.

It happened in this way.

My grand-uncle, Connor Donovan, had the old farm of Drumgunniol in his day. He was richer than ever my father was, or my father's father either, for he took a short lease of Balraghan, and made money of it. But money won't soften a hard heart, and I'm afraid my grand-uncle was a cruel man – a profligate man he was, surely, and that is mostly a cruel man at heart. He drank his share, too, and cursed and swore, when he was vexed, more than was good for his soul, I'm afraid.

At that time there was a beautiful girl of the Colemans, up in the mountains, not far from Capper Cullen. I'm told that there are no Colemans there now at all, and that family has passed away. The famine years made great changes.

Ellen Coleman was her name. The Colemans were not rich. But, being such a beauty, she might have made a good match. Worse than she did for herself, poor thing, she could not.

Con Donovan – my grand-uncle, God forgive him! – sometimes in his rambles saw her at fairs or patterns, and he fell in love with her, as who might not?

He used her ill. He promised her marriage, and persuaded her to come away with him; and, after all, he broke his word. It was just the old story. He tired of her, and he wanted to push himself in the world; and he married a girl of the Collopys, that had a great fortune – twenty-four cows, seventy sheep, and a hundred and twenty goats.

He married this Mary Collopy, and grew richer than before; and Ellen Coleman died broken-hearted. But that did not trouble the strong farmer much.

He would have liked to have children, but he had none, and this was the only cross he had to bear, for everything else went much as he wished.

One night he was returning from the fair of Nenagh. A shallow stream at that time crossed the road – they have thrown a bridge over it, I am told, some time since – and its channel was often dry in summer weather. When it was so, as it passes close by the old farmhouse of Drumgunniol, without a great deal of winding, it makes a sort of road, which people then used as a short cut to reach the house by. Into this dry channel, as there was plenty of light from the moon, my grand-uncle turned his horse, and when he had reached the two ash trees at the meering of the farm he turned his horse short into the river-field, intending to ride through the gap at the other end, under the oak tree, and so he would have been within a few hundred yards of his door.

As he approached the 'gap' he saw, or thought he saw, with a slow motion, gliding along the ground toward the same point, and now and then with a soft bound, a white object, which he described as being no bigger than his hat, but what it was he could not see, as it moved along the hedge and disappeared at the point to which he was himself tending.

When he reached the gap the horse stopped short. He urged and coaxed it in vain. He got down to lead it through, but it recoiled, snorted, and fell into a wild trembling fit. He mounted it again. But its terror continued, and it obstinately resisted his caresses and his whip. It was bright moonlight, and my grand-uncle was chafed by the horse's resistance, and, seeing nothing to account for it, and being so near home, what little patience he possessed forsook him, and, plying his whip and spur in earnest, he broke into oaths and curses.

All on a sudden the horse sprang through, and Con Donovan, as he passed under the broad branch of the oak, saw clearly a woman standing on the bank beside him, her arm extended, with the hand of which, as he flew by, she struck him a blow upon the shoulders. It threw him forward upon the neck of the horse, which, in wild terror, reached the door at a gallop, and stood there quivering and steaming all over.

Less alive than dead, my grand-uncle got in. He told his story, at least, so much as he chose. His wife did not quite know what to think. But that something very bad had happened she could not doubt. He was very faint and ill, and begged that the priest should be sent for forthwith. When they were getting him to his bed they saw distinctly the marks of five fingerpoints on the flesh of his shoulder, where the spectral blow had fallen. These singular marks – which they said resembled in tint the hue of a body struck by lightning – remained imprinted on his flesh, and were buried with him.

When he had recovered sufficiently to talk with the people about him – speaking, like a man at his last hour, from a burdened heart, and troubled conscience – he repeated his story, but said he did not see, or, at all events, know, the face of the figure that stood in the gap. No one believed him. He told more about it to the priest than to others. He certainly had a secret to tell. He might as well have divulged it frankly, for the neighbours all knew well enough that it was the face of dead Ellen Coleman that he had seen.

From that moment my grand-uncle never raised his head. He was a scared, silent, broken-spirited man. It was early summer then, and at the fall of the leaf in the same year he died.

Of course there was a wake, such as beseemed a strong farmer so rich as he. For some reason the arrangements of this ceremonial were a little different from the usual routine.

The usual practice is to place the body in the great room, or kitchen, as it is called, of the house. In this particular case there was, as I told you, for some reason, an unusual arrangement. The body was placed in a small room that opened upon the greater one. The door of this, during the wake, stood open. There were candles about the bed, and pipes and tobacco on the table, and stools for such guests as chose to enter, the door standing open for their reception.

The body, having been laid out, was left alone, in this smaller room, during the preparations for the wake. After nightfall one of the women, approaching the bed to get a chair which she had left near it, rushed from the room with a scream, and, having recovered her speech at the further end of the 'kitchen', and surrounded by a gaping audience, she said, at last: 'May I never sin, if his face bain't riz up again the back o' the bed, and he starin' down to the doore, wid eyes as big as pewter plates, that id be shinin' in the moon!'

'Arra, woman! Is it cracked you are?' said one of the farm boys as they are termed, being men of any age you please.

'Agh, Molly, don't be talkin', woman! 'Tis what ye consayted it, going' into the dark room, out o' the light. Why didn't ye take a candle in your fingers, ye aumadhaun?' said one of her female companions.

'Candle, or no candle; I seen it,' insisted Molly.

'An' what's more, I could a'most tak' my oath I seen his arum, too, stretchin' out o' the bed along the flure, three times as long as it should be, to take hould o' me be the fut.'

'Nansinse! ye fool, what id he want o' yer fut?' exclaimed one scornfully.

'Gi' me the candle, some o' yez – in the name o' God,' said old Sal Doolan, that was straight and lean, and a woman that could pray like a priest almost.

'Give her a candle!' agreed all.

But whatever they might say, there wasn't one among them that did not look pale and stern enough as they followed Mrs Doolan, who was praying as fast as her lips could patter, and leading the van with a tallow candle, held like a taper, in her fingers.

The door was half open, as the panic-stricken girl had left it; and holding the candle on high the better to examine the room, she made a step or so into it.

If my grand-uncle's hand had been stretched along the floor, in the unnatural way described, he had drawn it back again under the sheet that covered him. And tall Mrs Doolan was in no danger of tripping over his arm as she entered. But she had not gone more than a step or two with her candle aloft, when, with a drowning face, she suddenly stopped short, staring at the bed which was now fully in view.

'Lord, bless us, Mrs Doolan, ma'am, come back,' said the woman next her, who had fast hold of her dress, or her "coat", as they call it, and drawing her backwards with a frightened pluck, while a general recoil among her followers betokened the alarm which her hesitation had inspired.

'Whisht, will yez?' said the leader, peremptorily, 'I can't hear my own ears wid the noise ye're makin', an' which iv yez let the cat in here, an' whose cat is it?' she asked, peering suspiciously at a white cat that was sitting on the breast of the corpse.

'Put it away, will yez?' she resumed, with horror at the

profanation. 'Many a corpse as I stretched and crossed in the bed, the likes o' that I never seen yet. The man o' the house, wid a brute baste like that mounted on him, like a phooka, Lord forgi' me for namin' the like in this room. Dhrive it away, some o' yez! out o' that, this minute, I tell ye.'

Each repeated the order, but no one seemed inclined to execute it. They were crossing themselves, and whispering their conjectures and misgivings as to the nature of the beast, which was no cat of that house, nor one that they had ever seen before. On a sudden, the white cat placed itself on the pillow over the head of the body, and having from that place glared for a time at them over the features of the corpse, it crept softly along the body towards them, growling low and fiercely as it drew near.

Out of the room they bounced, in dreadful confusion, shutting the door fast after them, and not for a good while did the hardiest venture to peep in again.

The white cat was sitting in its old place, on the dead man's breast, but this time it crept quietly down the side of the bed, and disappeared under it, the sheet which was spread like a coverlet, and hung down nearly to the floor, concealing it from view.

Praying, crossing themselves, and not forgetting a sprinkling of holy water, they peeped, and finally searched, poking spades, 'wattles,' pitchforks and such implements under the bed. But the cat was not to be found, and they concluded that it had made its escape among their feet as they stood near the threshold. So they secured the door carefully, with hasp and padlock.

But when the door was opened next morning they found the white cat sitting, as if it had never been disturbed, upon the breast of the dead man.

Again occurred very nearly the same scene with a like result, only that some said they saw the cat afterwards lurking under a big box in a corner of the outer-room where my grand-uncle kept his leases and papers, and his prayer-book and beads.

Mrs Doolan heard it growling at her heels wherever she went; and although she could not see it, she could hear it spring on the back of her chair when she sat down, and growl in her ear, so that she would bounce up with a scream and a prayer, fancying that it was on the point of taking her by the throat.

And the priest's boy, looking round the corner, under the branches of the old orchard, saw a white cat sitting under the little window of the room where my grand-uncle was laid out and looking up at the four small panes of glass as a cat will watch a bird.

The end of it was that the cat was found on the corpse again, when the room was visited, and do what they might, whenever the body was left alone, the cat was found again in the same ill-omened contiguity with the dead man. And this continued, to the scandal and fear of the neighbourhood, until the door was opened finally for the wake.

My grand-uncle being dead, and, with all due solemnities, buried, I have done with him. But not quite yet with the white cat. No banshee ever yet was more inalienably attached to a family than this ominous apparition is to mine. But there is this difference. The banshee seems to be animated with an affectionate sympathy with the bereaved family to whom it is hereditarily attached whereas this thing has about it a suspicion of malice. It is the messenger simply of death. And its taking the shape of a cat – the coldest, and they say, the most vindictive of brutes – is indicative of the spirit of its visit.

When my grandfather's death was near, although he seemed quite well at the time, it appeared not exactly, but very nearly in the same way in which I told you it showed itself to my father.

The day before my Uncle Teigue was killed by the bursting of his gun, it appeared to him in the evening, at twilight, by the lough, in the field where I saw the woman who walked across the water, as I told you. My uncle was washing the barrel of his gun in the lough. The grass is short there, and there is no cover near it. He did not know how it approached; but the first he saw of it, the white cat was walking close round his feet, in the twilight, with an angry twist of its tail, and a green glare in its eyes, and do what he would, it continued walking round and round him, in larger or smaller circles, till he reached the orchard, and there he lost it.

My poor Aunt Peg – she married one of the O'Brians, near Oolah – came to Drumgunniol to go to the funeral of a cousin who died about a mile away. She died herself, poor woman, only a month after.

Coming from the wake, at two or three o'clock in the morning, as she got over the style into the farm of Drumgunniol, she saw the white cat at her side, and it kept close beside her, she ready to faint all the time, till she reached the door of the house, where it made a spring up into the white-thorn tree that grows close by, and so it parted from her. And my little brother Jim saw it also, just three weeks before he died. Every member of our family who dies, or takes his death-sickness, at Drumgunniol, is sure to see the white cat, and no one of us who sees it need hope for long life after.

SHERIDAN LE FANU

An Account of Some Strange
Disturbances in Aungier Street

※⁂※

It is not worth telling, this story of mine – at least, not worth writing. Told, indeed, as I have sometimes been called upon to tell it, to a circle of intelligent and eager faces, lighted up by a good after-dinner fire on a winter's evening, with a cold wind rising and wailing outside, and all snug and cosy within, it has gone off – though I say it, who should not – indifferent well. But it is a venture to do as you would have me. Pen, ink, and paper are cold vehicles for the marvellous, and a 'reader' decidedly a more critical animal than a 'listener.' If, however, you can induce your friends to read it after nightfall, and when the fireside talk has run for a while on thrilling tales of shapeless terror; in short, if you will secure me the *mollia tempora fandi*, I will go to my work, and say my say, with better heart. Well, then, these conditions presupposed, I shall waste no more words, but tell you simply how it all happened.

My cousin (Tom Ludlow) and I studied medicine together. I think he would have succeeded, had he stuck to the profession; but he preferred the Church, poor fellow, and died early, a sacrifice to contagion, contracted in the noble discharge of his duties. For my present purpose, I say enough of his character when I mention that he was of a sedate but frank and cheerful nature; very exact in his observance of truth, and not by any means like myself – of an excitable or nervous temperament.

My Uncle Ludlow – Tom's father – while we were attending lectures, purchased three or four old houses in Aungier Street, one of which was unoccupied. *He* resided in the country, and Tom proposed that we should take up our abode in the untenanted house, so long as it should continue unlet; a move which would accomplish the double end of settling us nearer alike to our lecture-rooms and to our amusements, and of relieving us from the weekly charge of rent for our lodgings.

Our furniture was very scant – our whole equipage remarkably modest and primitive; and, in short, our arrangements pretty nearly as simple as those of a bivouac. Our new plan was, therefore, executed almost as soon as conceived. The front drawing-room was our sitting-room. I had the bedroom over it, and Tom the back bedroom on the same floor, which nothing could have induced me to occupy.

The house, to begin with, was a very old one. It had been, I believe, newly fronted about fifty years before; but with this exception, it had nothing modern about it. The agent who bought it and looked into the titles for my uncle, told me that it was sold, along with much other forfeited property, at Chichester House, I think, in 1702; and had belonged to Sir Thomas Hacket, who was Lord Mayor of Dublin in James II's time. How old it was *then*, I can't say; but, at all events, it had seen years and changes enough to have contracted all that mysterious and saddened air, at once exciting and depressing, which belongs to most old mansions.

There had been very little done in the way of modernising details; and, perhaps, it was better so; for there was something queer and bygone in the very walls and ceilings – in the shape of doors and windows – in the odd diagonal site of the chimney-pieces – in the beams and ponderous cornices – not to mention the singular solidity of all the woodwork, from the bannisters to the window-frames, which hopelessly defied disguise, and would have emphatically proclaimed their antiquity through any conceivable amount of modern finery and varnish.

An effort had, indeed, been made, to the extent of papering the drawing-rooms; but somehow, the paper looked raw and out of keeping; and the old woman, who kept a little dirt-pie of a shop in the lane, and whose daughter – a girl of two and fifty – was our solitary handmaid, coming in at sunrise, and chastely receding again as soon as she had made all ready for tea in our state apartment; – this woman, I say, remembered it, when old Judge Horrocks (who, having earned the reputation of a particularly 'hanging judge,' ended by hanging himself, as the coroner's jury found, under an impulse of 'temporary insanity,' with a child's skipping-rope, over the massive old bannisters) resided there, entertaining good company, with fine venison and rare old port. In those halcyon days, the drawing-rooms were hung with gilded leather, and, I dare say, cut a good figure, for they were really spacious rooms.

The bedrooms were wainscoted, but the front one was not gloomy; and in it the cosiness of antiquity quite overcame its sombre associations. But the back bedroom, with its two queerly-placed melancholy windows, staring vacantly at the foot of the bed, and with the shadowy recess to be found in most old houses in Dublin, like a large ghostly closet, which, from congeniality of temperament, had amalgamated with the bedchamber, and dissolved the partition. At night-time, this 'alcove' – as our 'maid' was wont to call it – had, in my eyes, a specially sinister and suggestive character. Tom's distant and solitary candle glimmered vainly into its darkness. *There* it was always overlooking him – always itself impenetrable. But this was only part of the effect. The whole room was, I can't tell how, repulsive to me. There was, I suppose, in its proportions and features, a latent discord – a certain mysterious and indescribable relation, which jarred indistinctly upon some secret sense of the fitting and the safe, and raised indefinable suspicions and apprehensions of the imagination. On the whole, as I began by saying, nothing could have induced me to pass a night alone in it.

I had never pretended to conceal from poor Tom my superstitious weakness; and he, on the other hand, most unaffectedly ridiculed my tremors. The sceptic was, however, destined to receive a lesson, as you shall hear.

We had not been very long in occupation of our respective dormitories, when I began to complain of uneasy nights and disturbed sleep. I was, I suppose, the more impatient under this annoyance, as I was usually a sound sleeper, and by no means prone to nightmares. It was now, however, my destiny, instead of enjoying my customary repose, every night to 'sup full of horrors'. After a preliminary course of disagreeable and frightful dreams, my troubles took a definite form, and the same vision, without an appreciable variation in a single detail, visited me at least (on an average) every second night in the week.

Now, this dream, nightmare, or infernal illusion – which you please – of which I was the miserable sport, was on this wise – I saw, or thought I saw, with the most abominable distinctness, although at the time in profound darkness, every article of furniture and accidental arrangement of the chamber in which I lay. This, as you know, is incidental to ordinary nightmare. Well, while in this clair-voyant condition, which seemed but the lighting up of the theatre in which was to be exhibited the monotonous tableau of horror, which made my nights insupportable, my attention invariably became, I know not why, fixed upon the windows opposite the foot of my bed; and, uniformly with the same effect, a sense of dreadful anticipation always took slow but sure possession of me. I became somehow conscious of a sort of horrid but undefined preparation going forward in some unknown quarter, and by some unknown agency, for my torment; and, after an interval, which always seemed to me of the same length, a picture suddenly flew up to the window, where it remained fixed, as if by an electrical attraction, and my discipline of horror then commenced, to last perhaps for hours. The picture thus mysteriously glued to the window-panes, was the portrait of an old man, in a crimson flowered silk dressing-gown, the folds of which I could now describe, with a countenance embodying a strange mixture of intellect, sensuality, and power, but withal sinister and full of malignant omen. His nose was hooked, like the beak of a vulture; his eyes large, grey, and prominent, and lighted up with a more than mortal cruelty and coldness. These features were surmounted by a crimson velvet cap, the hair that peeped from under which was white with age, while the eyebrows retained their original blackness. Well I remember every line, hue, and shadow of that stony countenance, and well I may! The gaze of this hellish visage was fixed upon me, and mine returned it with the inexplicable fascination of nightmare, for what appeared to me to be hours of agony. At last – 'The cock he crew, away then flew', the fiend who had enslaved me through the awful watches of the night; and, harassed and nervous, I rose to the duties of the day.

I had – I can't say exactly why, but it may have been from the exquisite anguish and profound impressions of unearthly horror, with which this strange phantasmagoria was associated – an insurmountable antipathy to describing the exact nature of my nightly troubles to my friend and comrade. Generally, however, I told him that I was haunted by abominable dreams; and, true to the imputed materialism of medicine, we put our heads together to dispel my horrors, not by exorcism, but by a tonic.

I will do this tonic justice, and frankly admit that the accursed portrait began to intermit its visits under its influence. What of that? Was this singular apparition – as full of character as of terror – therefore the creature of my fancy, or the invention of my poor stomach? Was it, in short, *subjective* (to borrow the technical slang of the day) and not the palpable aggression and intrusion of an external agent? That, good friend, as we will both admit, by no means follows. The evil spirit, who enthralled my senses in the shape of that portrait, may have been just as near me, just as energetic, just as malignant, though I saw him not. What means the whole moral code of revealed religion regarding the due keeping of our own bodies, soberness, temperance, etc.? here is an obvious connection between the material and the invisible; the healthy tone of the system, and its unimpaired energy, may, for aught we can tell, guard us against influences which would otherwise render life itself terrific. The mesmerist and the electro-biologist will fail upon an average with nine patients out of ten – so may the evil spirit. Special conditions of the corporeal system are indispensable to the production of certain spiritual phenomena. The operation succeeds sometimes – sometimes fails – that is all.

I found afterwards that my would-be sceptical companion had his troubles too. But of these I knew nothing yet. One night, for a wonder, I was sleeping soundly, when I was roused by a step on the lobby outside my room, followed by the loud clang of what turned out to be a large brass candlestick, flung with all his force by poor Tom Ludlow over the banisters, and rattling with a rebound down the second flight of stairs; and almost concurrently with this, Tom burst open my door, and bounced into my room backwards, in a state of extraordinary agitation.

I had jumped out of bed and clutched him by the arm before I had any distinct idea of my own whereabouts. There we were – in our shirts – standing before the open door – staring through the great old banister opposite, at the lobby window, through which the sickly light of a clouded moon was gleaming.

'What's the matter, Tom? What's the matter with you? What the devil's the matter with you, Tom?' I demanded shaking him with nervous impatience.

He took a long breath before he answered me, and then it was not very coherently.

'It's nothing, nothing at all – did I speak? – what did I say? – where's the candle, Richard? It's dark; I – I had a candle!'

'Yes, dark enough,' I said; 'but what's the matter? – what is it? – why don't you speak, Tom? – have you lost your wits? – what is the matter?'

'The matter? – oh, it is all over. It must have been a dream – nothing at all but a dream – don't you think so? It could not be anything more than a dream.'

'Of *course*,' said I, feeling uncommonly nervous, 'it *was* a dream.'

'I thought,' he said, 'there was a man in my room, and – and I jumped out of bed; and – and – where's the candle?'

'In your room, most likely,' I said, 'shall I go and bring it?'

'No; stay here – don't go; it's no matter – don't, I tell you; it was all a dream. Bolt the door, Dick; I'll stay here with you – I feel nervous. So, Dick, like a good fellow, light your candle and open the window – I am in a *shocking state*.'

I did as he asked me, and robing himself like Granuaile in one of my blankets, he seated himself close beside my bed.

Everybody knows how contagious is fear of all sorts, but more especially that particular kind of fear under which poor Tom was at that moment labouring. I would not have heard, nor I believe would he have recapitulated, just at that moment, for half the world, the details of the hideous vision which had so unmanned him.

'Don't mind telling me anything about your nonsensical dream, Tom,' said I, affecting contempt, really in a panic; 'let us talk about something else; but it is quite plain that this dirty old house disagrees with us both, and hang me if I stay here any longer, to be pestered with indigestion and – and – bad nights, so we may as well look out for lodgings – don't you think so? – at once.'

Tom agreed, and, after an interval, said – 'I have been thinking, Richard, that it is a long time since I saw my father, and I have made up my mind to go down tomorrow and return in a day or two, and you can take rooms for us in the meantime.'

I fancied that this resolution, obviously the result of the vision which had so profoundly scared him, would probably vanish next morning with the damps and shadows of night. But I was mistaken. Off went Tom at peep of day to the country, having agreed that so soon as I had secured suitable lodgings, I was to recall him by letter from his visit to my Uncle Ludlow.

Now, anxious as I was to change my quarters, it so happened, owing to a series of petty procrastinations and accidents, that nearly a week elapsed before my bargain was made and my letter of recall on the wing to Tom; and, in the meantime, a trifling adventure or two had occurred to your humble servant, which, absurd as they now appear, diminished by distance, did certainly at the time serve to whet my appetite for change considerably.

A night or two after the departure of my comrade, I was sitting by my bedroom fire, the door locked, and the ingredients of a tumbler of hot whisky-punch upon the crazy spider-table; for, as the best mode of keeping the

> Black spirits and white,
> Blue spirits and grey,

with which I was environed, at bay, I had adopted the practice recommended by the wisdom of my ancestors, and 'kept my spirits up by pouring spirits down.' I had thrown aside my volume of Anatomy, and was treating myself by way of a tonic, preparatory to my punch and bed, to half a dozen pages of the *Spectator*, when I heard a step on the flight of stairs descending from the attics. It was two o'clock, and the streets were as silent as a churchyard – the sounds were, therefore, perfectly distinct. There was a slow, heavy tread, characterised by the emphasis and deliberation of age, descending by the narrow staircase from above; and, what made the sound more singular, it was plain that the feet which produced it were perfectly bare, measuring the descent with something between a pound and a flop, very ugly to hear.

I knew quite well that my attendant had gone away many hours before, and that nobody but myself had any business in the house. It was quite plain also that the person who was coming downstairs had no intention whatever of concealing his movements; but, on the contrary, appeared disposed to make even more noise, and proceed more deliberately, than was at all necessary. When the step reached the foot of the stairs outside my room, it seemed to stop; and I expected every moment to see my door open spontaneously, and give admission to the original of my detested portrait. I was, however, relieved in a few seconds by hearing the descent renewed, just in the same manner, upon the staircase leading down to the drawing-rooms, and thence, after another pause, down the next flight, and so on to the hall, whence I heard no more.

Now, by the time the sound had ceased, I was wound up, as they say, to a very unpleasant pitch of excitement. I listened, but there was not a stir. I screwed up my courage to a decisive experiment – opened my door, and in a stentorian voice bawled over the banisters, 'Who's there?' There was no answer but the ringing of my own voice through the empty old house, – no renewal of the movement; nothing, in short, to give my unpleasant sensations a definite direction. There is, I think, something most disagreeably disenchanting in the sound of one's own voice under such circumstances, exerted in solitude, and in vain. It redoubled my sense of isolation and my misgivings increased on perceiving that the door, which I certainly thought I had left open, was closed behind me; in a vague alarm, lest my retreat should be cut off, I got again into my room as quickly as I could, where I remained in a state of imaginary blockade, and very uncomfortable indeed, till morning.

Next night brought no return of my barefooted fellow-lodger; but the night following, being in my bed, and in the dark – somewhere, I suppose, about the same hour as before, I distinctly heard the old fellow again descending from the garrets.

This time I had had my punch, and the *morale* of the garrison was consequently excellent. I jumped out of bed, clutched the poker as I passed the expiring fire, and in a moment was upon the lobby. The sound had ceased by this time – the dark and chill were discouraging; and, guess my horror, when I saw, or thought I saw, a black monster, whether in the shape of a man or a bear I could not say, standing, with its back to the wall, on the lobby, facing me, with a pair of great greenish eyes shining dimly out. Now, I must be frank, and confess that the cupboard which displayed our plates and cups stood just there, though at the moment I did not recollect it. At the same time I must honestly say, that making every allowance for an excited imagination, I never could satisfy myself that I was made the dupe of my own fancy in this matter; for this apparition, after one or two shiftings of shape, as if in the act of incipient transformation, began, as it seemed on second thoughts, to advance upon me in its original form. From an instinct of terror rather than of courage, I hurled the poker, with all my force, at its head; and to the music of a horrid crash made my way into my room, and double-locked the door. Then, in a minute more, I heard the horrid bare feet walk down the stairs, till the sound ceased in the hall, as on the former occasion.

If the apparition of the night before was an ocular delusion of my fancy sporting with the dark outlines of our cupboard, and if its horrid eyes were nothing but a pair of inverted teacups, I had, at all events, the satisfaction of having launched the poker with admirable effect, and in true 'fancy' phrase, 'knocked its two daylights into one', as the commingled fragments of my tea-service testified. I did my best to gather comfort and courage from these evidences; but it would not do. And then what could I say of those horrid bare feet, and the regular tramp, tramp, tramp, which measured the distance of the entire stair-case through the solitude of my haunted dwelling, and at an hour when no good influence was stirring? Confound it! – the whole affair was abominable. I was out of spirits, and dreaded the approach of night.

It came, ushered ominously in with a thunderstorm and dull torrents of depressing rain. Earlier than usual the streets grew silent; and by twelve o'clock nothing but the comfortless pattering of the rain was to be heard.

I made myself as snug as I could. I lighted *two* candles instead of one. I forswore bed, and held myself in readiness for a sally, candle in hand; for, *coute qui coute*, I was resolved to *see* the being, if visible at all, who troubled the nightly stillness of my mansion. I was fidgetty and nervous and, tried in vain to interest myself with my books. I walked up and down my room, whistling in turn martial and hilarious music, and listening ever and anon for the dreaded noise. I sate down and stared at the square label on the solemn and reserved-looking black bottle, until 'Flanagan & Co.'s Best Old Malt Whisky' grew into a sort of subdued accompaniment to all the fantastic and horrible speculations which chased one another through my brain.

Silence, meanwhile, grew more silent, and darkness darker. I listened in vain for the rumble of a vehicle, or the dull clamour of a distant row. There was nothing but the sound of a rising wind, which had succeeded the thunderstorm that had travelled over the Dublin mountains quite out of hearing. In the middle of this great city I began to feel myself alone with nature, and Heaven knows what beside. My courage was ebbing. Punch, however, which makes beasts of so many, made a man of me again – just in time to hear with tolerable nerve and firmness the lumpy, flabby, naked feet deliberately descending the stairs again.

I took a candle, not without a tremor. As I crossed the floor I tried to extemporise a prayer, but stopped short to listen, and never finished it. The steps continued. I confess I hesitated for some seconds at the door before I took heart of grace and opened it. When I peeped out the lobby was perfectly empty – there was no monster standing on the staircase; and as the detested sound ceased, I was reassured enough to venture forward nearly to the banisters. Horror of horrors! within a stair or two beneath the spot where I stood the unearthly tread smote the floor. My eye caught something in motion; it was about the size of Goliah's foot – it was grey, heavy, and flapped with a dead weight from one step to another. As I am alive, it was the most monstrous grey rat I ever beheld or imagined.

Shakespeare says – 'Some men there are cannot abide a gaping pig, and some that are mad if they behold a cat.' I went well-nigh out of my wits when I beheld this *rat*; for, laugh at me as you may, it fixed upon me, I thought, a perfectly human expression of malice; and, as it shuffled about and looked up into my face almost from between my feet, I saw, I could swear it – I felt it then, and know it now, the infernal gaze and the accursed countenance of my old friend in the portrait, transfused into the visage of the bloated vermin before me.

I bounced into my room again with a feeling of loathing and horror I cannot describe, and locked and bolted my door as if a lion had been at the other side. D—n him or *it*; curse the portrait and its original! I felt in my soul that the rat – yes, the *rat*, the rat I had just seen, was that evil being in masquerade, and rambling through the house upon some infernal night lark.

Next morning I was early trudging through the miry streets; and, among other transactions, posted a peremptory note recalling Tom. On my return, however, I found a note from my absent 'chum,' announcing his intended return next day. I was doubly rejoiced at this, because I had succeeded in getting rooms; and because the change of scene and return of my comrade were rendered specially pleasant by the last night's half ridiculous half horrible adventure.

I slept extemporaneously in my new quarters in Digges' Street that night, and next morning returned for breakfast to the haunted mansion, where I was certain Tom would call immediately on his arrival.

I was quite right – he came; and almost his first question referred to the primary object of our change of residence.

'Thank God,' he said with genuine fervour, on hearing that all was arranged. 'On *your* account I am delighted. As to myself, I assure you that no earthly consideration could have induced me ever again to pass a night in this disastrous old house.'

'Confound the house!' I ejaculated, with a genuine mixture of fear and detestation, 'we have not had a pleasant hour since we came to live here'; and so I went on, and related incidentally my adventure with the plethoric old rat.

'Well, if that were *all*,' said my cousin, affecting to make light of the matter, 'I don't think I should have minded it very much.'

'Ay, but its eye – its countenance, my dear Tom,' – urged I; 'if you had seen that, *you* would have felt it might be *anything* but what it seemed.'

'I inclined to think the best conjurer in such a case would be an able-bodied cat,' he said, with a provoking chuckle.

'But let us hear your own adventure,' I said tartly.

At this challenge he looked uneasily round him. I had poked up a very unpleasant recollection.

'You shall hear it, Dick; I'll tell it to you,' he said. 'Begad, sir, I should feel quite queer, though, telling it *here*, though we are too strong a body for ghosts to meddle with just now.'

Though he spoke this like a joke, I think it was serious calculation. Our Hebe was in a corner of the room, packing our cracked delft tea and dinner-services in a basket. She soon suspended operations, and with mouth and eyes wide open became an absorbed listener. Tom's experiences were told nearly in these words: 'I saw it three times, Dick – three distinct times; and I am perfectly certain it meant me some infernal harm. I was, I say, in danger – in *extreme* danger; for, if nothing else had happened, my reason would most certainly have failed me, unless I had escaped so soon. Thank God. I *did* escape.

'The first night of this hateful disturbance, I was lying in the attitude of sleep, in that lumbering old bed. I hate to think of it. I was really wide awake, though I had put out my candle, and was lying as quietly as if I had been asleep; and although accidentally restless, my thoughts were running in a cheerful and agreeable channel.

'I think it must have been two o'clock at least when I thought I heard a sound in that – that odious dark recess at the far end of the bedroom. It was as if someone was drawing a piece of cord slowly along the floor, lifting it up, and dropping it softly down again in coils. I sate up once or twice in my bed, but could see nothing, so I concluded it must be mice in the wainscot. I felt no emotion graver than curiosity, and after a few minutes ceased to observe it.

'While lying in this state, strange to say; without at first a suspicion of anything supernatural, on a sudden I saw an old man, rather stout and square, in a sort of roan-red dressing-gown, and with a black cap on his head, moving stiffly and slowly in a diagonal direction, from the recess, across the floor of the bedroom, passing my bed at the foot, and entering the lumber-closet at the left. He had something under his arm; his head hung a little at one side; and, merciful God! when I saw his face.'

Tom stopped for a while, and then said: 'That awful countenance, which living or dying I never can forget, disclosed what he was. Without turning to the right or left, he passed beside me, and entered the closet by the bed's head.

'While this fearful and indescribable type of death and guilt was passing, I felt that I had no more power to speak or stir than if I had been myself a corpse. For hours after it had disappeared, I was too terrified and weak to move. As soon as daylight came, I took courage, and examined the room, and especially the course which the frightful intruder had seemed to take, but there was not a vestige to indicate anybody's having passed there; no sign of any disturbing agency visible among the lumber that strewed the floor of the closet.

'I now began to recover a little. I was fagged and exhausted, and at last, overpowered by a feverish sleep. I came down late; and finding you out of spirits, on account of your dreams about the portrait, whose *original* I am now certain disclosed himself to me, I did not care to talk about the infernal vision. In fact, I was trying to persuade myself that the whole thing was an illusion, and I did not like to revive in their intensity the hated impressions of the past night – or, to risk the constancy of my scepticism, by recounting the tale of my sufferings.

'It required some nerve, I can tell you, to go to my haunted chamber next night, and lie down quietly in the same bed,' continued Tom. 'I did so with a degree of trepidation, which, I am not ashamed to say, a very little matter would have sufficed to stimulate to downright panic. This night, however, passed off quietly enough, as also the next; and so too did two or three more. I grew more confident, and began to fancy that I believed in the theories of spectral illusions, with which I had at first vainly tried to impose upon my convictions.

'The apparition had been, indeed, altogether anomalous. It had crossed the room without any recognition of my presence: I had not disturbed *it*, and *it* had no mission to *me*. What, then, was the imaginable use of its crossing the room in a visible shape at all? Of course it might have *been* in the closet instead of *going* there, as easily as it introduced itself into the recess without entering the chamber in a shape discernible by the senses. Besides, how the deuce *had* I seen it? It was a dark night; I had no candle; there was no fire; and yet I saw it as distinctly, in colouring and outline, as ever I beheld human form! A cataleptic dream would explain it all; and I was determined that a dream it should be.

'One of the most remarkable phenomena connected with the practice of mendacity is the vast number of deliberate lies we tell ourselves, whom, of all persons, we can least expect to deceive. In all this, I need hardly tell you, Dick, I was simply lying to myself, and did not believe one word of the wretched humbug. Yet I went on, as men will do, like persevering charlatans and impostors, who tire people into credulity by the mere force of reiteration; so I hoped to win myself over at last to a comfortable scepticism about the ghost.

'He had not appeared a second time – that certainly was a comfort; and what, after all, did I care for him, and his queer old toggery and strange looks? Not a fig! I was nothing the worse for having seen him, and a good story the better. So I tumbled into bed, put out my candle, and, cheered by a loud drunken quarrel in the back lane, went fast asleep.

'From this deep slumber I awoke with a start. I knew I had had a horrible dream; but what it was I could not remember. My heart was thumping furiously; I felt bewildered and feverish; I sate up in the bed and looked about the room. A broad flood of moonlight came in through the curtainless window; everything was as I had last seen it;

and though the domestic squabble in the back lane was, unhappily for
me, allayed, I yet could hear a pleasant fellow singing, on his way
home, the then popular comic ditty called, "Murphy Delany". Taking
advantage of this diversion I lay down again, with my face towards the
fireplace, and closing my eyes, did my best to think of nothing else but
the song, which was every moment growing fainter in the distance:

> 'Twas Murphy Delany, so funny and frisky,
>   Stepped into a shebeen shop to get his skin full;
> He reeled out again pretty well lined with whiskey,
>   As fresh as a shamrock, as blind as a bull.

'The singer, whose condition I dare say resembled that of his hero,
was soon too far off to regale my ears any more; and as his music
died away, I myself sank into a doze, neither sound nor refreshing.
Somehow the song had got into my head, and I went meandering on
through the adventures of my respectable fellow-countryman, who,
on emerging from the "shebeen shop," fell into a river, from which he
was fished up to be "sat upon" by a coroner's jury, who having learned
from a "horse-doctor" that he was "dead as a doornail, so there was an
end," returned their verdict accordingly, just as he returned to his
senses, when an angry altercation and a pitched battle between the
body and the coroner winds up the lay with due spirit and pleasantry.

'Through this ballad I continued with a weary monotony to
plod, down to the very last line, and then *da capo*, and so on, in my
uncomfortable half sleep, for how long, I can't conjecture. I found
myself at last, however, muttering, "*dead* as a doornail, so there was an
end"; and something like another voice within me, seemed to say, very
faintly, but sharply, "dead! dead! *dead!* and may the Lord have mercy
on your soul!" and instantaneously I was wide awake, and staring right
before me from the pillow.

'Now – will you believe it, Dick? – I saw the same accursed figure
standing full front, and gazing at me with its stony and fiendish
countenance, not two yards from the bedside.'

Tom stopped here, and wiped the perspiration from his face. I felt
very queer. The girl was as pale as Tom; and, assembled as we were in
the very scene of these adventures, we were all, I dare say, equally
grateful for the clear daylight and the resuming bustle out of doors.

'For about three seconds only I saw it plainly; then it grew indistinct; but, for a long time, there was something like a column of dark vapour where it had been standing, between me and the wall; and I felt sure that he was still there. After a good while, this appearance went too. I took my clothes downstairs to the hall, and dressed there, with the door half open; then went out into the street, and walked about the town till morning when I came back, in a miserable state of nervousness and exhaustion. I was such a fool, Dick, as to be ashamed to tell you how I came to be so upset. I thought you would laugh at me; especially as I had always talked philosophy, and treated your ghosts with contempt. I concluded you would give me no quarter; and so kept my tale of horror to myself.

'Now, Dick, you will hardly believe me, when I assure you, that for many nights after this last experience, I did not go to my room at all. I used to sit up for a while in the drawing-room after you had gone up to your bed; and then steal down softly to the hall-door, let myself out, and sit in the "Robin Hood" tavern until the last guest went off; and then I got through the night like a sentry, pacing the streets till morning.

'For more than a week I never slept in bed. I sometimes had a snooze on a form in the "Robin Hood", and sometimes a nap in a chair during the day; but regular sleep I had absolutely none.

'I was quite resolved that we should get into another house; but I could not bring myself to tell you the reason, and I somehow put it off from day to day, although my life was, during every hour of this procrastination, rendered as miserable as that of a felon with the constables on his track. I was growing absolutely ill from this wretched mode of life.

'One afternoon I determined to enjoy an hour's sleep upon your bed. I hated mine; so that I had never, except in a stealthy visit every day to unmake it, lest Martha should discover the secret of my nightly absence, entered the ill-omened chamber.

'As ill-luck would have it, you had locked your bedroom, and taken away the key. I went into my own to unsettle the bedclothes, as usual, and give the bed the appearance of having been slept in. Now, a variety of circumstances concurred to bring about the dreadful scene through which I was that night to pass. In the first place, I was literally overpowered with fatigue, and longing for sleep; in the next place, the effect of this extreme exhaustion upon my nerves resembled that of a narcotic, and rendered me less susceptible than, perhaps I should in any other condition have been, of the exciting fears which had become habitual to me. Then again, a little bit of the window was open, a pleasant freshness pervaded the room, and, to crown all, the cheerful sun of day was making the room quite pleasant. What was to prevent my enjoying an hour's nap *here*? The whole air was resonant with the cheerful hum of life, and the broad matter-of-fact light of day filled every corner of the room.

'I yielded – stifling my qualms – to the almost overpowering tempt-ation; and merely throwing off my coat, and loosening my cravat, I lay down, limiting myself to *half* an hour's doze in the unwonted enjoyment of a feather bed, a coverlet, and a bolster.

'It was horribly insidious; and the demon, no doubt, marked my infatuated preparations. Dolt that I was, I fancied, with mind and body worn out for want of sleep, and an arrear of a full week's rest to my credit, that such measure as *half* an hour's sleep, in such a situation, was possible. My sleep was deathlike, long, and dreamless.

'Without a start or fearful sensation of any kind, I waked gently, but completely. It was, as you have good reason to remember, long past midnight – I believe, about two o'clock. When sleep has been deep and long enough to satisfy nature thoroughly, one often wakens in this way, suddenly, tranquilly, and completely.

'There was a figure seated in that lumbering, old sofa-chair, near the fireplace. Its back was rather towards me, but I could not be mistaken; it turned slowly round, and, merciful heavens! there was the stony face, with its infernal lineaments of malignity and despair, gloating on me. There was now no doubt as to its consciousness of my presence, and the hellish malice with which it was animated, for it arose, and drew close to the bedside. There was a rope about its neck, and the other end, coiled up, it held stiffly in its hand.

'My good angel nerved me for this horrible crisis. I remained for some seconds transfixed by the gaze of this tremendous phantom. He came close to the bed, and appeared on the point of mounting upon it. The next instant I was upon the floor at the far side, and in a moment more was, I don't know how, upon the lobby.

'But the spell was not yet broken; the valley of the shadow of death was not yet traversed. The abhorred phantom was before me there; it was standing near the banisters, stooping a little, and with one end of the rope round its own neck, was poising a noose at the other, as if to throw over mine; and while engaged in this baleful pantomime, it wore a smile so sensual, so unspeakably dreadful, that my senses were nearly overpowered. I saw and remember nothing more, until I found myself in your room.

'I had a wonderful escape, Dick – there is no disputing *that* – an escape for which, while I live, I shall bless the mercy of heaven. No one can conceive or imagine what it is for flesh and blood to stand in the presence of such a thing, but one who has had the terrific experience. Dick, Dick, a shadow has passed over me – a chill has crossed my blood and marrow, and I will never be the same again – never, Dick – never!'

Our handmaid, a mature girl of two-and-fifty, as I have said, stayed her hand, as Tom's story proceeded, and by little and little drew near to us, with open mouth, and her brows contracted over her little, beady black eyes, till stealing a glance over her shoulder now and then, she established herself close behind us. During the relation, she had made various earnest comments, in an undertone; but these and her ejaculations, for the sake of brevity and simplicity, I have omitted in my narration.

'It's often I heard tell of it,' she now said, 'but I never believed it rightly till now – though, indeed, why should not I? Does not my mother, down there in the lane, know quare stories, God bless us, beyant telling about it? But you ought not to have slept in the back bedroom. She was loath to let me be going in and out of that room even in the day time, let alone for any Christian to spend the night in it; for sure she says it was his own bedroom.'

'*Whose* own bedroom?' we asked, in a breath.

'Why, *his* – the ould Judge's – Judge Horrock's, to be sure, God rest his sowl'; and she looked fearfully round.

'Amen!' I muttered. 'But did he die there?'

'Die there! No, not quite *there*,' she said. 'Shure, was not it over the bannisters he hung himself, the ould sinner, God be merciful to us all? and was not it in the alcove they found the handles of the skipping-rope cut off, and the knife where he was settling the cord, God bless us, to hang himself with? It was his housekeeper's daughter owned the rope, my mother often told me, and the child never throve after, and used to be starting up out of her sleep, and screeching in the night

time, wid dhrames and frights that cum an her; and they said how it
was the speerit of the ould Judge that was tormentin' her; and she used
to be roaring and yelling out to hould back the big ould fellow with
the crooked neck; and then she'd screech "Oh, the master! the master!
he's stampin' at me, and beckoning to me! Mother, darling, don't let
me go!" And so the poor crathure died at last, and the docthers said it
was wather on the brain, for it was all they could say.'

'How long ago was all this?' I asked.

'Oh, then, how would I know?' she answered. 'But it must be a
wondherful long time ago, for the housekeeper was an ould woman,
with a pipe in her mouth, and not a tooth left, and better nor eighty
years ould when my mother was first married; and they said she was a
rale buxom, fine-dressed woman when the ould Judge come to his
end; an', indeed, my mother's not far from eighty years ould herself
this day; and what made it worse for the unnatural ould villain, God
rest his soul, to frighten the little girl out of the world the way he did,
was what was mostly thought and believed by everyone. My mother
says how the poor little crathure was his own child; for he was by all
accounts an ould villain every way, an' the hangin'est judge that ever
was known in Ireland's ground.'

'From what you said about the danger of sleeping in that bedroom,'
said I, 'I suppose there were stories about the ghost having appeared
there to others.'

'Well, there *was* things said – quare things, surely,' she answered, as
it seemed, with some reluctance. 'And why would not there? Sure was
it not up in that same room he slept for more than twenty years? and
was it not in the *alcove* he got the rope ready that done his own
business at last, the way he done many a betther man's in his lifetime?
– and was not the body lying in the same bed after death, and put in
the coffin there, too, and carried out to his grave from it in Pether's
churchyard, after the coroner was done? But there was quare stories –
my mother has them all – about how one Nicholas Spaight got into
trouble on the head of it.'

'And what did they say of this Nicholas Spaight?' I asked.

'Oh, for that matther, it's soon told,' she answered.

And she certainly did relate a very strange story, which so piqued
my curiosity, that I took occasion to visit the ancient lady, her mother,
from whom I learned many very curious particulars. Indeed, I am

tempted to tell the tale, but my fingers are weary, and I must defer it. But if you wish to hear it another time, I shall do my best.

When we had heard the strange tale I have *not* told you, we put one or two further questions to her about the alleged spectral visitations, to which the house had, ever since the death of the wicked old Judge, been subjected.

'No one ever had luck in it,' she told us. 'There was always cross accidents, sudden deaths, and short times in it. The first that tuck it was a family – I forget their name – but at any rate there was two young ladies and their papa. He was about sixty, and a stout healthy gentleman as you'd wish to see at that age. Well, he slept in that unlucky back bedroom; and, God between us an' harm! sure enough he was found dead one morning, half out of the bed, with his head as black as a sloe, and swelled like a puddin', hanging down near the floor. It was a fit, they said. He was as dead as a mackerel, and so *he* could not say what it was; but the ould people was all sure that it was nothing at all but the ould Judge, God bless us! that frightened him out of his senses and his life together.

'Some time after there was a rich old maiden lady took the house. I don't know which room *she* slept in, but she lived alone; and at any rate, one morning, the servants going down early to their work, found her sitting on the passage-stairs, shivering and talkin' to herself, quite mad; and never a word more could any of *them* or her friends get from her ever afterwards but, "Don't ask me to go, for I promised to wait for him." They never made out from her who it was she meant by *him*, but of course those that knew all about the ould house were at no loss for the meaning of all that happened to her.

'Then afterwards, when the house was let out in lodgings, there was Micky Byrne that took the same room, with his wife and three little children; and sure I heard Mrs Byrne myself telling how the children used to be lifted up in the bed at night, she could not see by what mains; and how they were starting and screeching every hour, just all as one as the housekeeper's little girl that died, till at last one night poor Micky had a dhrop in him, the way he used now and again; and what do you think in the middle of the night he thought he heard a noise on the stairs, and being in liquor, nothing less id do him but out he must go himself to see what was wrong. Well, after that, all she ever heard of him was himself sayin', "Oh, God!" and a tumble that shook the very house; and there, sure enough, he was lying on the lower stairs, under the lobby, with his neck smashed double undher him, where he was flung over the banisters.'

Then the hándmaiden added: 'I'll go down to the lane, and send up Joe Gavvey to pack up the rest of the taythings, and bring all the things across to your new lodgings.'

And so we all sallied out together, each of us breathing more freely, I have no doubt, as we crossed that ill-omened threshold for the last time.

Now, I may add thus much, in compliance with the immemorial usage of the realm of fiction, which sees the hero not only through his adventures, but fairly out of the world. You must have perceived that what the flesh, blood, and bone hero of romance proper is to the regular compounder of fiction, this old house of brick, wood, and mortar is to the humble recorder of this true tale. I, therefore, relate, as in duty bound, the catastrophe which ultimately befell it, which was simply this – that about two years subsequently to my story it was taken by a quack doctor, who called himself Baron Duhlstoerf, and filled the parlour windows with bottles of indescribable horrors preserved in brandy, and the newspapers with the usual grandiloquent and mendacious advertisements. This gentleman among his virtues did not reckon sobriety, and one night, being overcome with much wine, he set fire to his bed curtains, partially burned himself, and totally consumed the house. It was afterwards rebuilt, and for a time an undertaker established himself in the premises.

I have now told you my own and Tom's adventures, together with some valuable collateral particulars; and having acquitted myself of my engagement, I wish you a very good night, and pleasant dreams.

SHERIDAN LE FANU

Ghost Stories of Chapelizod

჻

Take my word for it, there is no such thing as an ancient village, especially if it has seen better days, unillustrated by its legends of terror. You might as well expect to find a decayed cheese without mites, or an old house without rats, as an antique and dilapidated town without an authentic population of goblins. Now, although this class of inhabitants are in nowise amenable to the police authorities, yet, as their demeanour directly affects the comforts of her Majesty's subjects, I cannot but regard it as a grave omission that the public have hitherto been left without any statistical returns of their numbers, activity, etc., etc. And I am persuaded that a Commission to enquire into and report upon the numerical strength, habits, haunts, etc., etc., of supernatural agents resident in Ireland, would be a great deal more innocent and entertaining than half the Commissions for which the country pays, and at least as instructive. This I say, more from a sense of duty, and to deliver my mind of a grave truth, than with any hope of seeing the suggestion adopted. But, I am sure, my readers will deplore with me that the comprehensive powers of belief, and apparently illimitable leisure, possessed by parliamentary commissions of enquiry, should never have been applied to the subject I have named, and that the collection of that species of information should be confided to the gratuitous and desultory labours of individuals, who, like myself, have other occupations to attend to. This, however, by the way.

Among the village outposts of Dublin, Chapelizod once held a considerable, if not a foremost rank. Without mentioning its connection with the history of the great Kilmainham Preceptory of the Knights of St John, it will be enough to remind the reader of its ancient and celebrated Castle, not one vestige of which now remains, and of the fact that it was for, we believe, some centuries, the summer residence of the Viceroys of Ireland. The circumstance of its being up, we believe, to the period at which that corps was disbanded, the headquarters of the Royal Irish Artillery, gave it also a consequence of an humbler, but not less substantial kind. With these advantages in its favour, it is not wonderful that the town exhibited at one time an air of substantial and semi-aristocratic prosperity unknown to Irish villages in modern times.

A broad street, with a well-paved footpath, and houses as lofty as were at that time to be found in the fashionable streets of Dublin; a goodly stone-fronted barrack; an ancient church, vaulted beneath, and with a tower clothed from its summit to its base with the richest ivy; an humble Roman Catholic chapel; a steep bridge spanning the Liffey, and a great old mill at the near end of it, were the principal features of the town. These, or at least most of them, remain still, but the greater part in a very changed and forlorn condition. Some of them indeed are superseded, though not obliterated by modern erections, such as the bridge, the chapel, and the church in part; the rest forsaken by the order who originally raised them, and delivered up to poverty, and in some cases to absolute decay.

The village lies in the lap of the rich and wooded valley of the Liffey, and is overlooked by the high grounds of the beautiful Phoenix Park on the one side, and by the ridge of the Palmerstown hills on the other. Its situation, therefore, is eminently picturesque; and factory-fronts and chimneys notwithstanding, it has, I think, even in its decay, a sort of melancholy picturesqueness of its own. Be that as it may, I mean to relate two or three stories of that sort which may be read with very good effect by a blazing fire on a shrewd winter's night, and are all directly connected with the altered and somewhat melancholy little town I have named. The first I shall relate concerns

THE VILLAGE BULLY

About thirty years ago there lived in the town of Chapelizod an ill-conditioned fellow of herculean strength, well known throughout the neighbourhood by the title of Bully Larkin. In addition to this remarkable physical superiority, this fellow had acquired a degree of skill as a pugilist which alone would have made him formidable. As it was, he was the autocrat of the village, and carried not the sceptre in vain. Conscious of his superiority, and perfectly secure of impunity, he lorded it over his fellows in a spirit of cowardly and brutal insolence, which made him hated even more profoundly than he was feared.

Upon more than one occasion he had deliberately forced quarrels upon men whom he had singled out for the exhibition of his savage prowess; and in every encounter his over-matched antagonist had received an amount of 'punishment' which edified and appalled the spectators, and in some instances left ineffaceable scars and lasting injuries after it.

Bully Larkin's pluck had never been fairly tried. For, owing to his prodigious superiority in weight, strength, and skill, his victories had always been certain and easy; and in proportion to the facility with which he uniformly smashed an antagonist, his pugnacity and insolence were inflamed. He thus became an odious nuisance in the neighbourhood, and the terror of every mother who had a son, and of every wife who had a husband who possessed a spirit to resent insult, or the smallest confidence in his own pugilistic capabilities.

Now it happened that there was a young fellow named Ned Moran better known by the soubriquet of 'Long Ned', from his slender, lathy proportions at that time living in the town. He was, in truth, a mere lad, nineteen years of age, and fully twelve years younger than the stalwart bully. This, however, as the reader will see secured for him no exemption from the dastardly provocations of the ill-conditioned pugilist. Long Ned, in an evil hour, had thrown eyes of affection upon a certain buxom damsel, who, notwithstanding Bully Larkin's amorous rivalry, inclined to reciprocate them.

I need not say how easily the spark of jealousy, once kindled, is blown into a flame, and how naturally, in a coarse and ungoverned nature, it explodes in acts of violence and outrage.

'The bully' watched his opportunity, and contrived to provoke Ned Moran, while drinking in a public-house with a party of friends, into an altercation, in the course of which he failed not to put such insults upon his rival as manhood could not tolerate. Long Ned, though a simple, good-natured sort of fellow, was by no means deficient in spirit, and retorted in a tone of defiance which edified the more timid, and gave his opponent the opportunity he secretly coveted.

Bully Larkin challenged the heroic youth, whose pretty face he had privately consigned to the mangling and bloody discipline he was himself so capable of administering. The quarrel, which he had himself contrived to get up, to a certain degree covered the ill blood and malignant premeditation which inspired his proceedings, and Long Ned, being full of generous ire and whiskey punch, accepted the gauge of battle on the instant. The whole party, accompanied by a mob of idle men and boys, and in short by all who could snatch a moment from the calls of business, proceeded in slow procession through the old gate into the Phoenix Park, and mounting the hill overlooking the town, selected near its summit a level spot on which to decide the quarrel.

The combatants stripped, and a child might have seen in the contrast presented by the slight, lank form and limbs of the lad, and the muscular and massive build of his veteran antagonist, how desperate was the chance of poor Ned Moran.

'Seconds' and 'bottle-holders' – selected of course for their love of the game – were appointed, and 'the fight' commenced.

I will not shock my readers with a description of the cool-blooded butchery that followed. The result of the combat was what anybody might have predicted. At the eleventh round, poor Ned refused to 'give in'; the brawny pugilist, unhurt, in good wind, and pale with concentrated and as yet unslaked revenge, had the gratification of seeing his opponent seated upon his second's knee, unable to hold up his head, his left arm disabled; his face a bloody, swollen, and shapeless mass; his breast scarred and bloody, and his whole body panting and quivering with rage and exhaustion.

'Give in Ned, my boy,' cried more than one of the bystanders.

'Never, never,' shrieked he, with a voice hoarse and choking.

Time being 'up,' his second placed him on his feet again. Blinded with his own blood, panting and staggering, he presented but a helpless mark for the blows of his stalwart opponent. It was plain that a touch would have been sufficient to throw him to the earth. But Larkin had no notion of letting him off so easily. He closed with him without striking a blow (the effect of which, prematurely dealt, would have been to bring him at once to the ground, and so put an end to the combat), and getting his battered and almost senseless head under his arm, fast in that peculiar 'fix' known to the fancy pleasantly by the name of 'chancery,' he held him firmly, while with monotonous and brutal strokes he beat his fist, as it seemed, almost into his face. A cry of 'shame' broke from the crowd, for it was plain that the beaten man was now insensible, and supported only by the herculean arm of the bully. The round and the fight ended by his hurling him upon the ground, falling upon him at the same time with his knee upon his chest.

The bully rose, wiping the perspiration from his white face with his blood-stained hands, but Ned lay stretched and motionless upon the grass. It was impossible to get him upon his legs for another round. So he was carried down, just as he was, to the pond which then lay close to the old Park gate, and his head and body were washed beside it. Contrary to the belief of all he was not dead. He was carried home, and after some months to a certain extent recovered. But he never held up his head again, and before the year was over he had died of consumption. Nobody could doubt how the disease had been induced, but there was no actual proof to connect the cause and effect, and the ruffian Larkin escaped the vengeance of the law. A strange retribution, however, awaited him.

After the death of Long Ned, he became less quarrelsome than before, but more sullen and reserved. Some said 'he took it to heart', and others, that his conscience was not at ease about it. Be this as it may, however, his health did not suffer by reason of his presumed agitations, nor was his worldly prosperity marred by the blasting curses with which poor Moran's enraged mother pursued him; on the contrary, he had rather risen in the world, and obtained regular and well-remunerated employment from the Chief Secretary's gardener, at the other side of the Park. He still lived in Chapelizod, whither, on the close of his day's work, he used to return across the Fifteen Acres.

It was about three years after the catastrophe we have mentioned, and late in the autumn, when, one night, contrary to his habit, he did not appear at the house where he lodged, neither had he been seen anywhere, during the evening, in the village. His hours of return had been so very regular, that his absence excited considerable surprise, though, of course, no actual alarm; and, at the usual hour, the house was closed for the night, and the absent lodger consigned to the mercy of the elements, and the care of his presiding star. Early in the morning, however, he was found lying in a state of utter helplessness upon the slope immediately overlooking the Chapelizod gate. He had been smitten with a paralytic stroke: his right side was dead; and it was many weeks before he had recovered his speech sufficiently to make himself at all understood.

He then made the following relation: He had been detained, it appeared, later than usual, and darkness had closed before he commenced his homeward walk across the Park. It was a moonlit night, but masses of ragged clouds were slowly drifting across the heavens. He had not encountered a human figure, and no sounds but the softened rush of the wind sweeping through bushes and hollows met his ear. These wild and monotonous sounds, and the utter solitude which surrounded him, did not however, excite any of those uneasy sensations which are ascribed to superstition, although he said he did feel depressed, or, in his own phraseology, 'lonesome.' Just as he crossed the brow of the hill which shelters the town of Chapelizod, the moon shone out for some moments with unclouded lustre, and his eye, which happened to wander by the shadowy enclosures which lay at the foot of the slope, was arrested by the sight of a human figure climbing, with all the haste of one pursued, over the churchyard wall, and running up the steep ascent directly towards him. Stories of 'resurrectionists' crossed his recollection, as he observed this sus-picious-looking figure. But he began, momentarily, to be aware with a sort of fearful instinct which he could not explain, that the running figure was directing his steps, with a sinister purpose, towards himself.

The form was that of a man with a loose coat about him, which, as he ran, he disengaged, and as well as Larkin could see, for the moon was again wading in clouds, threw from him. The figure thus advanced until within some two score yards of him, it arrested its speed, and approached with a loose, swaggering gait. The moon again shone out bright and clear, and, gracious God! what was the spectacle before him? He saw as distinctly as if he had been presented there in the flesh, Ned Moran, himself, stripped naked from the waist upward, as if for pugilistic combat, and drawing towards him in silence. Larkin would have shouted, prayed, cursed, fled across the Park, but he was absolutely powerless; the apparition stopped within a few steps, and leered on him with a ghastly mimicry of the defiant stare with which pugilists strive to cow one another before combat. For a time, which he could not so much as conjecture, he was held in the fascination of that unearthly gaze, and at last the thing, whatever it was, on a sudden swaggered close up to him with extended palms. With an impulse of horror, Larkin put out his hand to keep the figure off, and their palms touched – at least, so he believed – for a thrill of unspeakable agony, running through his arm, pervaded his entire frame, and he fell senseless to the earth.

Though Larkin lived for many years after, his punishment was terrible. He was incurably maimed; and being unable to work, he was forced, for existence, to beg alms of those who had once feared and flattered him. He suffered, too, increasingly, under his own horrible interpretation of the preternatural encounter which was the beginning of all his miseries. It was vain to endeavour to shake his faith in the reality of the apparition, and equally vain, as some compassionately did, to try to persuade him that the greeting with which his vision closed was intended, while inflicting a temporary trial, to signify a compensating reconciliation.

'No, no,' he used to say, 'all won't do. I know the meaning of it well enough; it is a challenge to meet him in the other world – in Hell, where I am going – that's what it means, and nothing else.'

And so, miserable and refusing comfort, he lived on for some years, and then died, and was buried in the same narrow churchyard which contains the remains of his victim.

I need hardly say, how absolute was the faith of the honest inhabitants, at the time when I heard the story, in the reality of the preternatural summons which, through the portals of terror, sickness, and misery, had summoned Bully Larkin to his long, last home, and that, too, upon the very ground on which he had signalised the guiltiest triumph of his violent and vindictive career.

I recollect another story of the preternatural sort, which made no small sensation, some five-and-thirty years ago, among the good gossips of the town; and, with your leave, courteous reader, I shall relate it.

THE SEXTON'S ADVENTURE

Those who remember Chapelizod a quarter of a century ago, or more, may possibly recollect the parish sexton. Bob Martin was held much in awe by truant boys who sauntered into the churchyard on Sundays, to read the tombstones, or play leap frog over them, or climb the ivy in search of bats or sparrows' nests, or peep into the mysterious aperture under the eastern window, which opened a dim perspective of descending steps losing themselves among profounder darkness, where lidless coffins gaped horribly among tattered velvet, bones, and dust, which time and mortality had strewn there. Of such horribly curious, and otherwise enterprising juveniles, Bob was, of course, the special scourge and terror. But terrible as was the official aspect of the sexton, and repugnant as his lank form, clothed in rusty, sable vesture, his small, frosty visage, suspicious grey eyes, and rusty, brown scratch-wig, might appear to all notions of genial frailty; it was yet true, that Bob Martin's severe morality sometimes nodded, and that Bacchus did not always solicit him in vain.

Bob had a curious mind, a memory well stored with 'merry tales', and tales of terror. His profession familiarised him with graves and goblins, and his tastes with weddings, wassail, and sly frolics of all sorts. And as his personal recollections ran back nearly three score years into the perspective of the village history, his fund of local anecdote was copious, accurate, and edifying.

As his ecclesiastical revenues were by no means considerable, he was not unfrequently obliged, for the indulgence of his tastes, to arts which were, at the best, undignified.

He frequently invited himself when his entertainers had forgotten to do so; he dropped in accidentally upon small drinking parties of his acquaintance in public-houses, and entertained them with stories, queer or terrible, from his inexhaustible reservoir, never scrupling to accept an acknowledgment in the shape of hot whiskey-punch, or whatever else was going.

There was at that time a certain atrabilious publican, called Philip Slaney, established in a shop nearly opposite the old turnpike. This man was not, when left to himself, immoderately given to drinking; but being naturally of a saturnine complexion, and his spirits constantly requiring a fillip, he acquired a prodigious liking for Bob Martin's company. The sexton's society, in fact, gradually became the solace of his existence, and he seemed to lose his constitutional melancholy in the fascination of his sly jokes and marvellous stories.

This intimacy did not redound to the prosperity or reputation of the convivial allies. Bob Martin drank a good deal more punch than was good for his health, or consistent with the character of an ecclesiastical functionary. Philip Slaney, too, was drawn into similar indulgences, for it was hard to resist the genial seductions of his gifted companion; and as he was obliged to pay for both, his purse was believed to have suffered even more than his head and liver.

Be this as it may, Bob Martin had the credit of having made a drunkard of 'black Phil Slaney' – for by this cognomen was he distinguished; and Phil Slaney had also the reputation of having made the sexton, if possible, a 'bigger bliggard' than ever. Under these circumstances, the accounts of the concern opposite the turnpike became somewhat entangled; and it came to pass one drowsy summer morning, the weather being at once sultry and cloudy, that Phil Slaney went into a small back parlour, where he kept his books, and which commanded, through its dirty window-panes, a full view of a dead wall, and having bolted the door, he took a loaded pistol, and clapping the muzzle in his mouth, blew the upper part of his skull through the ceiling.

This horrid catastrophe shocked Bob Martin extremely; and partly on this account, and partly because having been, on several late occasions, found at night in a state of abstraction, bordering on insensibility, upon the high road, he had been threatened with dismissal; and, as some said, partly also because of the difficulty of finding anybody to 'treat' him as poor Phil Slaney used to do, he for a time forswore alcohol in all its combinations, and became an eminent example of temperance and sobriety.

Bob observed his good resolutions, greatly to the comfort of his wife, and the edification of the neighbourhood, with tolerable punctuality. He was seldom tipsy, and never drunk, and was greeted by the better part of society with all the honours of the prodigal son.

Now it happened, about a year after the grisly event we have mentioned, that the curate having received, by the post, due notice of a funeral to be consummated in the churchyard of Chapelizod, with certain instructions respecting the site of the grave, despatched a summons for Bob Martin, with a view to communicate to that functionary these official details.

It was a lowering autumn night: piles of lurid thunderclouds, slowly rising from the earth, had loaded the sky with a solemn and boding canopy of storm. The growl of the distant thunder was heard afar off upon the dull, still air, and all nature seemed, as it were, hushed and cowering under the oppressive influence of the approaching tempest.

It was past nine o'clock when Bob, putting on his official coat of seedy black, prepared to attend his professional superior.

'Bobby, darlin',' said his wife, before she delivered the hat she held in her hand to his keeping, 'sure you won't, Bobby, darlin' – you won't – you know what.'

'I *don't* know what,' he retorted, smartly, grasping at his hat.

'You won't be throwing up the little finger, Bobby, acushla?' she said, evading his grasp. .

'Arrah, why would I, woman? there, give me my hat, will you?'

'But won't you promise me, Bobby darlin' – won't you, alanna?'

'Ay, ay, to be sure I will – why not? – there, give me my hat, and let me go.'

'Ay, but you're not promisin', Bobby, mavourneen; you're not promisin' all the time.'

'Well, divil carry me if I drink a drop till I come back again,' said the sexton, angrily; 'will that do you? And *now* will you give me my hat?'

'Here it is, darlin',' she said, 'and God send you safe back.'

And with this parting blessing she closed the door upon his retreating figure, for it was now quite dark, and resumed her knitting till his return, very much relieved; for she thought he had of late been oftener tipsy than was consistent with his thorough reformation, and feared the allurements of the half-dozen 'publics' which he had at that time to pass on his way to the other end of the town.

They were still open, and exhaled a delicious reek of whiskey, as Bob glided wistfully by them; but he stuck his hands in his pockets and looked the other way, whistling resolutely, and filling his mind with the image of the curate and anticipations of his coming fee. Thus he steered his morality safely through these rocks of offence, and reached the curate's lodging in safety.

He had, however, an unexpected sick call to attend, and was not at home, so that Bob Martin had to sit in the hall and amuse himself with the devil's tattoo until his return. This, unfortunately, was very long delayed, and it must have been fully twelve o'clock when Bob Martin set out upon his homeward way. By this time the storm had gathered to a pitchy darkness, the bellowing thunder was heard among the rocks and hollows of the Dublin mountains, and the pale, blue lightning shone upon the staring fronts of the houses.

By this time, too, every door was closed; but as Bob trudged home-ward, his eye mechanically sought the public-house which had once belonged to Phil Slaney. A faint light was making its way through the shutters and the glass panes over the doorway, which made a sort of dull, foggy halo about the front of the house.

As Bob's eyes had become accustomed to the obscurity by this time, the light in question was quite sufficient to enable him to see a man in a sort of loose riding-coat seated upon a bench which, at that time, was fixed under the window of the house. He wore his hat very much over his eyes, and was smoking a long pipe. The outline of a glass and a quart bottle were also dimly traceable beside him; and a large horse saddled, but faintly discernible, was patiently awaiting his master's leisure.

There was something odd, no doubt, in the appearance of a traveller refreshing himself at such an hour in the open street; but the sexton accounted for it easily by supposing that, on the closing of the house for the night, he had taken what remained of his refection to the place where he was now discussing it alfresco.

At another time Bob might have saluted the stranger as he passed with a friendly 'good-night'; but, somehow, he was out of humour and in no genial mood, and was about passing without any courtesy of the sort, when the stranger, without taking the pipe from his mouth, raised the bottle, and with it beckoned him familiarly, while, with a sort of lurch of the head and shoulders, and at the same time shifting his seat to the end of the bench, he pantomimically invited him to share his seat and his cheer. There was a divine fragrance of whiskey about the spot, and Bob half relented; but he remembered his promise just as he began to waver, and said: 'No, I thank you, sir, I can't stop tonight.'

The stranger beckoned with vehement welcome, and pointed to the vacant space on the seat beside him.

'I thank you for your polite offer,' said Bob, 'but it's what I'm too late as it is, and haven't time to spare, so I wish you a good night.'

The traveller jingled the glass against the neck of the bottle, as if to intimate that he might at least swallow a dram without losing time. Bob was mentally quite of the same opinion; but, though his mouth watered, he remembered his promise, and shaking his head with incorruptible resolution, walked on.

The stranger, pipe in mouth, rose from his bench, the bottle in one hand, and the glass in the other, and followed at the Sexton's heels, his dusky horse keeping close in his wake.

There was something suspicious and unaccountable in this importunity.

Bob quickened his pace, but the stranger followed close. The sexton began to feel queer, and turned about. His pursuer was behind, and still inviting him with impatient gestures to taste his liquor.

'I told you before,' said Bob, who was both angry and frightened, 'that I would not taste it, and that's enough. I don't want to have anything to say to you or your bottle; and in God's name,' he added, more vehemently, observing that he was approaching still closer, 'fall back and don't be tormenting me this way.'

These words, as it seemed, incensed the stranger, for he shook the bottle with violent menace at Bob Martin; but, notwithstanding this gesture of defiance, he suffered the distance between them to increase. Bob, however, beheld him dogging him still in the distance, for his pipe shed a wonderful red glow, which duskily illuminated his entire figure like the lurid atmosphere of a meteor.

'I wish the devil had his own, my boy,' muttered the excited sexton, 'and I know well enough where you'd be.'

The next time he looked over his shoulder, to his dismay he observed the importunate stranger as close as ever upon his track.

'Confound you,' cried the man of skulls and shovels, almost beside himself with rage and horror, 'what is it you want of me?'

The stranger appeared more confident, and kept wagging his head and extending both glass and bottle toward him as he drew near, and Bob Martin heard the horse snorting as it followed in the dark.

'Keep it to yourself, whatever it is, for there is neither grace nor luck about you,' cried Bob Martin, freezing with terror; 'leave me alone, will you.'

And he fumbled in vain among the seething confusion of his ideas for a prayer or an exorcism. He quickened his pace almost to a run; he was now close to his own door, under the impending bank by the river side.

'Let me in, let me in, for God's sake; Molly, open the door,' he cried, as he ran to the threshold, and leant his back against the plank. His pursuer confronted him upon the road; the pipe was no longer in his mouth, but the dusky red glow still lingered round him. He uttered some inarticulate cavernous sounds, which were wolfish and indescribable, while he seemed employed in pouring out a glass from the bottle.

The sexton kicked with all his force against the door, and cried at the same time with a despairing voice.

'In the name of God Almighty, once for all, leave me alone.'

His pursuer furiously flung the contents of the bottle at Bob Martin; but instead of fluid it issued out in a stream of flame, which expanded and whirled round them, and for a moment they were both enveloped in a faint blaze; at the same instant a sudden gust whisked off the stranger's hat, and the sexton beheld that his skull was roofless. For an instant he beheld the gaping aperture, black and shattered, and then he fell senseless into his own doorway, which his affrighted wife had just unbarred.

I need hardly give my reader the key to this most intelligible and authentic narrative. The traveller was acknowledged by all to have been the spectre of the suicide, called up by the Evil One to tempt the convivial sexton into a violation of his promise, sealed, as it was, by an imprecation. Had he succeeded, no doubt the dusky steed, which Bob had seen saddled in attendance, was destined to have carried back a double burden to the place from whence he came.

As an attestation of the reality of this visitation, the old thorn tree which overhung the doorway was found in the morning to have been blasted with the infernal fires which had issued from the bottle, just as if a thunderbolt had scorched it.

The moral of the above tale is upon the surface, apparent, and, so to speak, *self-acting* – a circumstance which happily obviates the necessity of our discussing it together. Taking our leave, therefore, of honest Bob Martin, who now sleeps soundly in the same solemn dormitory where, in his day, he made so many beds for others, I come to a legend of the Royal Irish Artillery, whose headquarters were for so long a time in the town of Chapelizod. I don't mean to say that I cannot tell a great many more stories, equally authentic and marvellous, touching this old town; but as I may possibly have to perform a like office for other localities, and as Anthony Poplar is known, like Atropos, to carry a shears, wherewith to snip across all 'yarns' which exceed reasonable bounds, I consider it, on the whole, safer to despatch the traditions of Chapelizod with one tale more.

Let me, however, first give it a name; for an author can no more despatch a tale without a title, than an apothecary can deliver his physic without a label. We shall, therefore, call it –

THE SPECTRE LOVERS

There lived some fifteen years since in a small and ruinous house, little better than a hovel, an old woman who was reported to have considerably exceeded her eightieth year, and who rejoiced in the name of Alice, or popularly, Ally Moran. Her society was not much courted, for she was neither rich, nor, as the reader may suppose, beautiful. In addition to a lean cur and a cat she had one human companion, her grandson, Peter Brien, whom, with laudable good nature, she had supported from the period of his orphanage down to that of my story, which finds him in his twentieth year. Peter was a good-natured slob of a fellow, much more addicted to wrestling, dancing, and lovemaking, than to hard work, and fonder of whiskey punch than good advice. His grandmother had a high opinion of his accomplishments, which indeed was but natural, and also of his genius, for Peter had of late years begun to apply his mind to politics; and as it was plain that he had a mortal hatred of honest labour, his grandmother predicted, like a true fortune-teller, that he was born to marry an heiress, and Peter himself (who had no mind to forego his freedom even on such terms) that he was destined to find a pot of gold. Upon one point both agreed, that being unfitted by the peculiar bias of his genius for work, he was to acquire the immense fortune to which his merits entitled him by means of a pure run of good luck. This solution of Peter's future had the double effect of reconciling both himself and his grandmother to his idle courses, and also of maintaining that even flow of hilarious spirits which made him everywhere welcome, and which was in truth the natural result of his consciousness of approaching affluence.

It happened one night that Peter had enjoyed himself to a very late hour with two or three choice spirits near Palmerstown. They had talked politics and love, sung songs, and told stories, and, above all, had swallowed, in the chastened disguise of punch, at least a pint of good whiskey, every man.

It was considerably past one o'clock when Peter bid his companions goodbye, with a sigh and a hiccough, and lighting his pipe set forth on his solitary homeward way.

The bridge of Chapelizod was pretty nearly the midway point of his night march, and from one cause or another his progress was rather slow, and it was past two o'clock by the time he found himself leaning over its old battlements, and looking up the river, over whose winding current and wooded banks the soft moonlight was falling.

The cold breeze that blew lightly down the stream was grateful to him. It cooled his throbbing head, and he drank it in at his hot lips. The scene, too, had, without his being well sensible of it, a secret fascination. The village was sunk in the profoundest slumber, not a mortal stirring, not a sound afloat, a soft haze covered it all, and the fairy moonlight hovered over the entire landscape.

In a state between rumination and rapture, Peter continued to lean over the battlements of the old bridge, and as he did so he saw, or fancied he saw, emerging one after another along the river bank in the little gardens and enclosures in the rear of the street of Chapelizod, the queerest little white-washed huts and cabins he had ever seen there before. They had not been there that evening when he passed the bridge on the way to his merry tryst. But the most remarkable thing about it was the odd way in which these quaint little cabins showed themselves. First he saw one or two of them just with the corner of his eye, and when he looked full at them, strange to say, they faded away and disappeared. Then another and another came in view, but all in the same coy way, just appearing and gone again before he could well fix his gaze upon them; in a little while, however, they began to bear a fuller gaze, and he found, as it seemed to himself, that he was able by an effort of attention to fix the vision for a longer and a longer time, and when they waxed faint and nearly vanished, he had the power of recalling them into light and substance, until at last their vacillating indistinctness became less and less, and they assumed a permanent place in the moonlit landscape.

'Be the hokey,' said Peter, lost in amazement, and dropping his pipe into the river unconsciously, 'them is the quarist bits iv mud cabins I ever seen, growing up like musharoons in the dew of an evening, and poppin' up here and down again there, and up again in another place, like so many white rabbits in a warren; and there they stand at last as firm and fast as if they were there from the Deluge; bedad it's enough to make a man a'most believe in the fairies.'

This latter was a large concession from Peter, who was a bit of a free-thinker, and spoke contemptuously in his ordinary conversation of that class of agencies.

Having treated himself to a long last stare at these mysterious fabrics, Peter prepared to pursue his homeward way; having crossed the bridge and passed the mill, he arrived at the corner of the main street of the little town, and casting a careless look up the Dublin road, his eye was arrested by a most unexpected spectacle.

This was no other than a column of foot-soldiers, marching with perfect regularity towards the village, and headed by an officer on horseback. They were at the far side of the turnpike, which was closed; but much to his perplexity he perceived that they marched on through it without appearing to sustain the least check from that barrier.

On they came at a slow march; and what was most singular in the matter was, that they were drawing several cannons along with them; some held ropes, others spoked the wheels, and others again marched in front of the guns and behind them, with muskets shouldered, giving a stately character of parade and regularity to this, as it seemed to Peter, most unmilitary procedure.

It was owing either to some temporary defect in Peter's vision, or to some illusion attendant upon mist and moonlight, or perhaps to some other cause, that the whole procession had a certain waving and vapoury character which perplexed and tasked his eyes not a little. It was like the pictured pageant of a phantasmagoria reflected upon smoke. It was as if every breath disturbed it; sometimes it was blurred, sometimes obliterated; now here, now there. Sometimes, while the upper part was quite distinct, the legs of the column would nearly fade away or vanish outright, and then again they would come out into clear relief, marching on with measured tread, while the cocked hats and shoulders grew, as it were, transparent, and all but disappeared.

Notwithstanding these strange optical fluctuations, however, the column continued steadily to advance. Peter crossed the street from the corner near the old bridge, running on tiptoe, and with his body stooped to avoid observation, and took up a position upon the raised footpath in the shadow of the houses, where, as the soldiers kept the middle of the road, he calculated that he might, himself undetected, see them distinctly enough as they passed.

'What the div—, what on airth,' he muttered, checking the irreligious ejaculation with which he was about to start, for certain queer misgivings were hovering about his heart, notwithstanding the factitious courage of the whiskey bottle. 'What on airth is the manin' of all this? is it the French that's landed at last to give us a hand and help us in airnest to this blessed repale? If it is not them, I simply ask who the div—, I mane who on airth are they, for such sogers as them I never seen before in my born days?'

By this time the foremost of them were quite near, and truth to say they were the queerest soldiers he had ever seen in the course of his life. They wore long gaiters and leather breeches, three-cornered hats, bound with silver lace, long blue coats, with scarlet facings and linings, which latter were shewn by a fastening which held together the two opposite corners of the skirt behind; and in front the breasts were in like manner connected at a single point, where and below which they sloped back, disclosing a long-flapped waistcoat of snowy whiteness; they had very large, long cross-belts, and wore enormous pouches of white leather hung extraordinarily low, and on each of which a little silver star was glittering. But what struck him as most grotesque and outlandish in their costume was their extraordinary display of shirt-frill in front, and of ruffle about their wrists, and the strange manner in which their hair was frizzled out and powdered under their hats, and clubbed up into great rolls behind. But one of the party was mounted. He rode a tall white horse, with high action and arching neck; he had a snow-white feather in his three-cornered hat, and his coat was shimmering all over with a profusion of silver lace. From these circumstances Peter concluded that he must be the commander of the detachment, and examined him as he passed attentively. He was a slight, tall man, whose legs did not half fill his leather breeches, and he appeared to be at the wrong side of sixty. He had a shrunken, weather-beaten, mulberry-coloured face, carried a large black patch over one eye, and turned neither to the right nor to the left, but rode on at the head of his men, with a grim, military inflexibility.

The countenances of these soldiers, officers as well as men, seemed all full of trouble, and, so to speak, scared and wild. He watched in vain for a single contented or comely face. They had, one and all, a melancholy and hang-dog look; and as they passed by, Peter fancied that the air grew cold and thrilling.

He had seated himself upon a stone bench, from which, staring with all his might, he gazed upon the grotesque and noiseless procession as it filed by him. Noiseless it was; he could neither hear the jingle of accoutrements, the tread of feet, nor the rumble of the wheels; and when the old colonel turned his horse a little, and made as though he were giving the word of command, and a trumpeter, with a swollen blue nose and white feather fringe round his hat, who was walking beside him, turned about and put his bugle to his lips, still Peter heard nothing, although it was plain the sound had reached the soldiers, for they instantly changed their front to three abreast.

'Botheration!' muttered Peter, 'is it deaf I'm growing?'

But that could not be, for he heard the sighing of the breeze and the rush of the neighbouring Liffey plain enough.

'Well,' said he, in the same cautious key, 'by the piper, this bangs Banagher fairly! It's either the Frinch army that's in it, come to take the town iv Chapelizod by surprise, an' makin' no noise for feard iv wakenin' the inhabitants; or else it's – it's – what it's – somethin' else. But, tundher-an-ouns, what's gone wid Fitzpatrick's shop across the way?'

The brown, dingy stone building at the opposite side of the street looked newer and cleaner than he had been used to see it; the front door of it stood open, and a sentry, in the same grotesque uniform, with shouldered musket, was pacing noiselessly to and fro before it. At the angle of this building, in like manner, a wide gate (of which Peter had no recollection whatever) stood open, before which, also, a similar sentry was gliding, and into this gateway the whole column gradually passed, and Peter finally lost sight of it.

'I'm not asleep; I'm not dhramin',' said he, rubbing his eyes, and stamping slightly on the pavement, to assure himself that he was wide awake. 'It is a quare business, whatever it is; an' it's not alone that, but everything about the town looks strange to me. There's Tresham's house new painted, bedad, an' them flowers in the windies! An' Delany's house, too, that had not a whole pane of glass in it this morning, and scarce a slate on the roof of it! It is not possible it's what it's dhrunk I am. Sure there's the big tree, and not a leaf of it changed since I passed, and the stars overhead, all right. I don't think it is in my eyes it is.'

And so looking about him, and every moment finding or fancying new food for wonder, he walked along the pavement, intending, without further delay, to make his way home.

But his adventures for the night were not concluded. He had nearly reached the angle of the short lane that leads up to the church, when for the first time he perceived that an officer, in the uniform he had just seen, was walking before, only a few yards in advance of him.

The officer was walking along at an easy, swinging gait, and carried his sword under his arm, and was looking down on the pavement with an air of reverie.

In the very fact that he seemed unconscious of Peter's presence, and disposed to keep his reflections to himself, there was something reassuring. Besides, the reader must please to remember that our hero had a *quantum sufficit* of good punch before his adventure commenced, and was thus fortified against those qualms and terrors under which, in a more reasonable state of mind, he might not impossibly have sunk.

The idea of the French invasion revived in full power in Peter's fuddled imagination, as he pursued the nonchalant swagger of the officer.

'Be the powers iv Moll Kelly, I'll ax him what it is,' said Peter, with a sudden accession of rashness. 'He may tell me or not, as he plases, but he can't be offinded, anyhow.'

With this reflection having inspired himself, Peter cleared his voice and began: 'Captain!' said he, 'I ax your pardon, captain, an' maybe you'd be so condescindin' to my ignorance as to tell me, if it's plasin' to yer honour, whether your honour is not a Frinchman, if it's plasin' to you.'

This he asked, not thinking that, had it been as he suspected, not one word of his question in all probability would have been intelligible to the person he addressed. He was, however, understood, for the officer answered him in English, at the same time slackening his pace and moving a little to the side of the pathway, as if to invite his interrogator to take his place beside him.

'No; I am an Irishman,' he answered.

'I humbly thank your honour,' said Peter, drawing nearer – for the affability and the nativity of the officer encouraged him – 'but maybe your honour is in the *sarvice* of the King of France?'

'I serve the same King as you do,' he answered, with a sorrowful significance which Peter did not comprehend at the time; and, interrogating in turn, he asked, 'But what calls you forth at this hour of the day?'

'The *day*, your honour! – the night, you mane.'

'It was always our way to turn night into day, and we keep to it still,' remarked the soldier. 'But, no matter, come up here to my house; I have a job for you, if you wish to earn some money easily. I live here.'

As he said this, he beckoned authoritatively to Peter, who followed almost mechanically at his heels, and they turned up a little lane near the old Roman Catholic chapel, at the end of which stood, in Peter's time, the ruins of a tall, stone-built house.

Like everything else in the town, it had suffered a metamorphosis. The stained and ragged walls were now erect, perfect, and covered with pebble-dash; windowpanes glittered coldly in every window; the green hall-door had a bright brass knocker on it. Peter did not know whether to believe his previous or his present impressions; seeing is believing, and Peter could not dispute the reality of the scene. All the records of his memory seemed but the images of a tipsy dream. In a trance of astonishment and perplexity, therefore, he submitted himself to the chances of his adventure.

The door opened, the officer beckoned with a melancholy air of authority to Peter, and entered. Our hero followed him into a sort of hall, which was very dark, but he was guided by the steps of the soldier, and, in silence, they ascended the stairs. The moonlight, which shone in at the lobbies, showed an old, dark wainscoting, and a heavy, oak banister. They passed by closed doors at different landing-places, but all was dark and silent as, indeed, became that late hour of the night.

Now they ascended to the topmost floor. The captain paused for a minute at the nearest door, and, with a heavy groan, pushing it open, entered the room. Peter remained at the threshold. A slight female form in a sort of loose, white robe, and with a great deal of dark hair hanging loosely about her, was standing in the middle of the floor, with her back towards them.

The soldier stopped short before he reached her, and said, in a voice of great anguish, 'Still the same, sweet bird – sweet bird! still the same.' Whereupon, she turned suddenly, and threw her arms about the neck of the officer, with a gesture of fondness and despair, and her frame was agitated as if by a burst of sobs. He held her close to his breast in silence; and honest Peter felt a strange terror creep over him, as he witnessed these mysterious sorrows and endearments.

'Tonight, tonight – and then ten years more – ten long years another ten years.'

The officer and the lady seemed to speak these words together; her voice mingled with his in a musical and fearful wail, like a distant summer wind, in the dead hour of night, wandering through ruins. Then he heard the officer say, alone, in a voice of anguish: 'Upon me be it all, for ever, sweet birdie, upon me.'

And again they seemed to mourn together in the same soft and desolate wail, like sounds of grief heard from a great distance.

Peter was thrilled with horror, but he was also under a strange fascination; and an intense and dreadful curiosity held him fast.

The moon was shining obliquely into the room, and through the window Peter saw the familiar slopes of the Park, sleeping mistily under its shimmer. He could also see the furniture of the room with tolerable distinctness – the old balloon-backed chairs, a four-post bed in a sort of recess, and a rack against the wall, from which hung some military clothes and accoutrements; and the sight of all these homely objects reassured him somewhat, and he could not help feeling unspeakably curious to see the face of the girl whose long hair was streaming over the officer's epaulet.

Peter, accordingly, coughed, at first slightly, and afterward more loudly, to recall her from her reverie of grief; and, apparently, he succeeded; for she turned round, as did her companion, and both, standing hand in hand, gazed upon him fixedly. He thought he had never seen such large, strange eyes in all his life; and their gaze seemed to chill the very air around him, and arrest the pulses of his heart. An eternity of misery and remorse was in the shadowy faces that looked upon him.

If Peter had taken less whisky by a single thimbleful, it is probable that he would have lost heart altogether before these figures, which seemed every moment to assume a more marked and fearful, though hardly definable, contrast to ordinary human shapes.

'What is it you want with me?' he stammered.

'To bring my lost treasure to the churchyard,' replied the lady, in a silvery voice of more than mortal desolation.

The word 'treasure' revived the resolution of Peter, although a cold sweat was covering him, and his hair was bristling with horror; he believed, however, that he was on the brink of fortune, if he could but command nerve to brave the interview to its close.

'And where,' he gasped, 'is it hid – where will I find it?'

They both pointed to the sill of the window, through which the moon was shining at the far end of the room, and the soldier said: 'Under that stone.'

Peter drew a long breath, and wiped the cold dew from his face, preparatory to passing to the window, where he expected to secure the reward of his protracted terrors. But looking steadfastly at the window, he saw the faint image of a new-born child sitting upon the sill in the moonlight, with its little arms stretched toward him, and a smile so heavenly as he never beheld before.

At sight of this, strange to say, his heart entirely failed him, he looked on the figures that stood near, and beheld them gazing on the infantine form with a smile so guilty and distorted, that he felt as if he were entering alive among the scenery of hell, and shuddering, he cried in an irrepressible agony of horror: 'I'll have nothing to say with you, and nothing to do with you; I don't know what yez are or what yez want iv me, but let me go this minute, everyone of yez, in the name of God.'

With these words there came a strange rumbling and sighing about Peter's ears; he lost sight of everything, and felt that peculiar and not unpleasant sensation of falling softly, that sometimes supervenes in sleep, ending in a dull shock. After that he had neither dream nor consciousness till he wakened, chill and stiff, stretched between two piles of old rubbish, among the black and roofless walls of the ruined house.

We need hardly mention that the village had put on its wonted air of neglect and decay, or that Peter looked around him in vain for traces of those novelties which had so puzzled and distracted him upon the previous night.

'Ay, ay,' said his grandmother, removing her pipe, as he ended his description of the view from the bridge, 'sure enough I remember myself, when I was a slip of a girl, these little white cabins among the gardens by the river side. The artillery sogers that was married, or had not room in the barracks, used to be in them, but they're all gone long ago.'

'The Lord be merciful to us!' she resumed, when he had described the military procession, 'it's often I seen the regiment marchin' into the town, jist as you saw it last night, acushla. Oh, voch, but it makes my heart sore to think iv them days; they were pleasant times, sure enough; but is not it terrible, avick, to think its what it was the ghost of the rigiment you seen? The Lord betune us an' harm, for it was nothing else, as sure as I'm sittin' here.'

When he mentioned the peculiar physiognomy and figure of the old officer who rode at the head of the regiment: '*That*,' said the old crone, dogmatically, 'was ould Colonel Grimshaw, the Lord presarve us! he's buried in the churchyard iv Chapelizod, and well I remember him, when I was a young thing, an' a cross ould floggin' fellow he was wid the men, an' a devil's boy among the girls – rest his soul!'

'Amen!' said Peter; 'it's often I read his tombstone myself; but he's a long time dead.'

'Sure, I tell you he died when I was no more nor a slip iv a girl – the Lord betune us and harm!'

'I'm afeard it is what I'm not long for this world myself, afther seeing such a sight as that,' said Peter, fearfully.

'Nonsinse, avourneen,' retorted his grandmother, indignantly, though she had herself misgivings on the subject; 'sure there was Phil Doolan, the ferryman, that seen black Ann Scanlan in his own boat, and what harm ever kem of it?'

Peter proceeded with his narrative, but when he came to the description of the house, in which his adventure had had so sinister a conclusion, the old woman was at fault.

'I know the house and the ould walls well, an' I can remember the time there was a roof on it, and the doors an' windows in it, but it had a bad name about being haunted, but by who, or for what, I forget intirely.'

'Did you ever hear was there goold or silver there?' he enquired.

'No, no, avick, don't be thinking about the likes; take a fool's advice, and never go next or near them ugly black walls again the longest day you have to live; an' I'd take my davy, it's what it's the same word the priest himself I'd be afther sayin' to you if you wor to ax his raverence consarnin' it, for it's plain to be seen it was nothing good you seen there, and there's neither luck nor grace about it.'

Peter's adventure made no little noise in the neighbourhood, as the reader may well suppose; and a few evenings after it, being on an errand to old Major Vandeleur, who lived in a snug old fashioned house, close by the river, under a perfect bower of ancient trees, he was called on to relate the story in the parlour.

The Major was, as I have said, an old man; he was small, lean, and upright, with a mahogany complexion, and a wooden inflexibility of face; he was a man, besides, of few words, and if *he* was old, it follows plainly that his mother was older still. Nobody could guess or tell *how* old, but it was admitted that her own generation had long passed away, and that she had not a competitor left. She had French blood in her veins, and although she did not retain her charms quite so well as Ninon de l'Enclos, she was in full possession of all her mental activity, and talked quite enough for herself and the Major.

'So, Peter,' she said, 'you have seen the dear, old Royal Irish again in the streets of Chapelizod. Make him a tumbler of punch, Frank; and Peter, sit down, and while you take it let us have the story.'

Peter accordingly, seated near the door, with a tumbler of the nectarian stimulant steaming beside him, proceeded with marvellous courage, considering they had no light but the uncertain glare of the fire, to relate with minute particularity his awful adventure. The old lady listened at first with a smile of good-natured incredulity; her cross examination touching the drinking-bout at Palmerstown had been teazing, but as the narrative proceeded she became attentive, and at length absorbed, and once or twice she uttered ejaculations of pity or awe. When it was over, the old lady looked with a somewhat sad and stern abstraction on the table, patting her cat assiduously meanwhile, and then suddenly looking upon her son, the Major, she said; 'Frank, as sure as I live he has seen the wicked Captain Devereux.'

The Major uttered an inarticulate expression of wonder.

'The house was precisely that he has described. I have told you the story often, as I heard it from your dear grandmother, about the poor young lady he ruined, and the dreadful suspicion about the little baby. *She*, poor thing, died in that house heart-broken, and you know he was shot shortly after in a duel.'

This was the only light that Peter ever received respecting his adventure. It was supposed, however, that he still clung to the hope that treasure of some sort was hidden about the old house, for he was often seen lurking about its walls, and at last his fate overtook him, poor fellow, in the pursuit; for climbing near the summit one day, his holding gave way, and he fell upon the hard uneven ground, fracturing a leg and a rib, and after a short interval died, and he, like the other heroes of these true tales, lies buried in the little churchyard of Chapelizod.

SHERIDAN LE FANU

Wicked Captain Walshawe of Wauling

❧

CHAPTER ONE

Peg O'Neill Pays the Captain's Debts

A very odd thing happened to my uncle, Mr Watson, of Haddlestone;
and to enable you to understand it, I must begin at the beginning.

In the year 1822, Mr James Walshawe, more commonly known as
Captain Walshawe, died at the age of eighty-one years. The Captain in
his early days, and so long as health and strength permitted, was a
scamp of the active, intriguing sort; and spent his days and nights in
sowing his wild oats, of which he seemed to have an inexhaustible stock.
The harvest of this tillage was plentifully interspersed with thorns,
nettles, and thistles, which stung the husbandman unpleasantly, and did
not enrich him.

Captain Walshawe was very well known in the neighbourhood of
Wauling, and very generally avoided there. A 'captain' by courtesy, for
he had never reached that rank in the army list. He had quitted the
service in 1766, at the age of twenty-five; immediately previous to
which period his debts had grown so troublesome, that he was induced
to extricate himself by running away with and marrying an heiress.

Though not so wealthy quite as he had imagined, she proved a very
comfortable investment for what remained of his shattered affections;
and he lived and enjoyed himself very much in his old way, upon her
income, getting into no end of scrapes and scandals, and a good deal
of debt and money trouble.

When he married his wife, he was quartered in Ireland, at Clonmel,
where was a nunnery, in which, as pensioner resided Miss O'Neill, or

as she was called in the country, Peg O'Neill – the heiress of whom I have spoken.

Her situation was the only ingredient of romance in the affair, for the young lady was decidedly plain, though good-humoured looking, with that style of features which is termed *potato*; and in figure she was a little too plump, and rather short. But she was impressible; and the handsome young English Lieutenant was too much for her monastic tendencies, and she eloped.

In England there are traditions of Irish fortune-hunters, and in Ireland of English. The fact is, it was the vagrant class of each country that chiefly visited the other in old times; and a handsome vagabond, whether at home or abroad, I suppose, made the most of his face, which was also his fortune.

At all events, he carried off the fair one from the sanctuary; and for some sufficient reason, I suppose, they took up their abode at Wauling, in Lancashire.

Here the gallant captain amused himself after his fashion, sometimes running up, of course on business, to London. I believe few wives have ever cried more in a given time than did that poor, dumpy, potato-faced heiress, who got over the nunnery garden wall, and jumped into the handsome Captain's arms, for love.

He spent her income, frightened her out of her wits with oaths and threats, and broke her heart.

Latterly she shut herself up pretty nearly altogether in her room. She had an old, rather grim, Irish servant-woman in attendance upon her. This domestic was tall, lean, and religious, and the Captain knew instinctively she hated him; and he hated her in return, and often threatened to put her out of the house, and sometimes even to kick her out of the window. And whenever a wet day confined him to the house, or the stable, and he grew tired of smoking, he would begin to swear and curse at her for a *diddled* old mischief-maker, that could never be easy, and was always troubling the house with her cursed stories, and so forth.

But years passed away and old Molly Doyle remained still in her original position. Perhaps he thought that there must be somebody there, and that he was not, after all, very likely to change for the better.

CHAPTER TWO

The Blessed Candle

He tolerated another intrusion, too, and thought himself a paragon of patience and easy good-nature for so doing. A Roman Catholic clergyman, in a long black frock, with a low standing collar, and a little white muslin fillet round his neck – tall, sallow, with blue chin, and dark steady eyes – used to glide up and down the stairs, and through the passages; and the Captain sometimes met him in one place and sometimes in another. But by a caprice incident to such tempers he treated this cleric exceptionally, and even with a surly sort of courtesy, though he grumbled about his visits behind his back.

I do not know that he had a great deal of moral courage, and the ecclesiastic looked severe and self-possessed; and somehow he thought he had no good opinion of him, and if a natural occasion were offered, might say extremely unpleasant things, and hard to be answered.

Well the time came at last, when poor Peg O'Neill – in an evil hour Mrs James Walshawe – must cry, and quake, and pray her last. The doctor came from Penlynden, and was just as vague as usual, but more gloomy, and for about a week came and went oftener. The cleric in the long black frock was also daily there. And at last came that last sacrament in the gates of death, when the sinner is traversing those dread steps that never can be retraced; when the face is turned for ever from life, and we see a receding shape, and hear a voice already irrevocably in the land of spirits.

So the poor lady died; and some people said the Captain 'felt it very much'. I don't think he did. But he was not very well just then, and looked the part of mourner and penitent to admiration – being seedy and sick. He drank a great deal of brandy and water that night, and called in Farmer Dobbs, for want of better company, to drink with him; and told him all his grievances, and how happy he and 'the poor lady upstairs' might have been, had it not been for liars, and pick-thanks, and tale-bearers, and the like, who came between them – meaning Molly Doyle – whom, as he waxed eloquent over his liquor, he came at last to curse and rail at by name, with more than his accustomed freedom. And he described his own natural character and amiability in such moving terms, that he wept maudlin tears of sensibility over his theme; and when Dobbs was gone, drank some more grog, and took to railing and cursing again by himself; and then mounted the stairs unsteadily, to see 'what the devil Doyle and the other old witches were about in poor Peg's room.'

When he pushed open the door, he found some half-dozen crones, chiefly Irish, from the neighbouring town of Hackleton, sitting over tea and snuff, etc., with candles lighted round the corpse, which was arrayed in a strangely cut robe of brown serge. She had secretly belonged to some order – I think the Carmelite, but I am not certain – and wore the habit in her coffin.

'What the d— are you doing with my wife?' cried the Captain, rather thickly. 'How dare you dress her up in this trumpery, you – you cheating old witch; and what's that candle doing in her hand?'

I think he was a little startled, for the spectacle was grisly enough. The dead lady was arrayed in this strange brown robe, and in her rigid fingers, as in a socket, with the large wooden beads and cross wound round it, burned a wax candle, shedding its white light over the sharp features of the corpse. Moll Doyle was not to be put down by the Captain, whom she hated, and accordingly, in her phrase, 'he got as good as he gave.' And the Captain's wrath waxed fiercer, and he chucked the wax taper from the dead hand, and was on the point of flinging it at the old serving-woman's head.

'The holy candle, you sinner!' cried she.

'I've a mind to make you eat it, you beast,' cried the Captain.

But I think he had not known before what it was, for he subsided a little sulkily, and he stuffed his hand with the candle (quite extinct by this time) into his pocket, and said he: 'You know devilish well you had no business going on with y–y–your d—n *witchcraft* about my poor wife, without my leave – you do – and you'll please to take off that d—n brown pinafore, and get her decently into her coffin, and I'll pitch your devil's waxlight into the sink.'

And the Captain stalked out of the room.

'An' now her poor sowl's in prison, you wretch, be the mains o' ye; an' may yer own be shut into the wick o' that same candle, till it's burned out, ye savage.'

'I'd have you ducked for a witch, for twopence,' roared the Captain up the staircase, with his hand on the banisters, standing on the lobby. But the door of the chamber of death clapped angrily, and he went down to the parlour, where he examined the holy candle for a while, with a tipsy gravity, and then with something of that reverential feeling for the symbolic, which is not uncommon in rakes and scamps, he thoughtfully locked it up in a press, where were accumulated all sorts of obsolete rubbish – soiled packs of cards, disused tobacco-pipes, broken powder-flasks, his military sword, and a dusky bundle of the 'Flash Songster,' and other questionable literature.

He did not trouble the dead lady's room any more. Being a volatile man it is probable that more cheerful plans and occupations began to entertain his fancy.

CHAPTER THREE

My Uncle Watson Visits Wauling

So the poor lady was buried decently, and Captain Walshawe reigned alone for many years at Wauling. He was too shrewd and too experienced by this time to run violently down the steep hill that leads to ruin. So there was a method in his madness; and after a widowed career of more than forty years, he, too, died at last with some guineas in his purse.

Forty years and upwards is a great *edax rerum*, and a wonderful chemical power. It acted forcibly upon the gay Captain Walshawe. Gout supervened, and was no more conducive to temper than to enjoyment, and made his elegant hands lumpy at all the small joints, and turned them slowly into crippled claws. He grew stout when his exercise was interfered with, and ultimately almost corpulent. He suffered from what Mr Holloway calls 'bad legs', and was wheeled about in a great leathern-backed chair, and his infirmities went on accumulating with his years.

I am sorry to say, I never heard that he repented, or turned his thoughts seriously to the future. On the contrary, his talk grew fouler, and his fun ran upon his favourite sins, and his temper waxed more truculent. But he did not sink into dotage. Considering his bodily infirmities, his energies and his malignities, which were many and

active, were marvellously little abated by time. So he went on to the
close. When his temper was stirred, he cursed and swore in a way that
made decent people tremble. It was a word and a blow with him; the
latter, luckily, not very sure now. But he would seize his crutch and
make a swoop or a pound at the offender, or shy his medicine-bottle,
or his tumbler, at his head.

It was a peculiarity of Captain Walshawe, that he, by this time,
hated nearly everybody. My Uncle, Mr Watson, of Haddlestone, was
cousin to the Captain, and his heir-at-law. But my uncle had lent him
money on mortgage of his estates, and there had been a treaty to sell,
and terms and a price were agreed upon, in 'articles' which the lawyers
said were still in force.

I think the ill-conditioned Captain bore him a grudge for being
richer than he, and would have liked to do him an ill turn. But it did
not lie in his way; at least while he was living.

My Uncle Watson was a Methodist, and what they call a 'class-
leader'; and, on the whole, a very good man. He was now near fifty –
grave, as beseemed his profession – somewhat dry – and a little severe,
perhaps – but a just man.

A letter from the Penlynden doctor reached him at Haddlestone,
announcing the death of the wicked old Captain; and suggesting his
attendance at the funeral, and the expediency of his being on the spot
to look after things at Wauling. The reasonableness of this striking
my good Uncle, he made his journey to the old house in Lancashire
incontinently, and reached it in time for the funeral.

My Uncle, whose traditions of the Captain were derived from his
mother, who remembered him in his slim, handsome youth – in
shorts, cocked-hat and lace, was amazed at the bulk of the coffin
which contained his mortal remains; but the lid being already screwed
down, he did not see the face of the bloated old sinner.

CHAPTER FOUR

In the Parlour

What I relate, I had from the lips of my uncle, who was a truthful man, and not prone to fancies.

The day turning out awfully rainy and tempestuous, he persuaded the doctor and the attorney to remain for the night at Wauling.

There was no will – the attorney was sure of that; for the Captain's enmities were perpetually shifting, and he could never quite make up his mind, as to how best to give effect to a malignity whose direction was being constantly modified. He had had instructions for drawing a will a dozen times over. But the process had always been arrested by the intending testator.

Search being made, no will was found. The papers, indeed were all right, with one important exception: the leases were nowhere to be seen. There were special circumstances connected with several of the principal tenancies on the estate – unnecessary here to detail – which rendered the loss of these documents one of very serious moment, and even of very obvious danger.

My uncle, therefore, searched strenuously. The attorney was at his elbow, and the doctor helped with a suggestion now and then. The old serving-man seemed an honest deaf creature, and really knew nothing.

My Uncle Watson was very much perturbed. He fancied – but this possibly was only fancy – that he had detected for a moment a queer look in the attorney's face; and from that instant it became fixed in his mind that he knew all about the leases. Mr Watson expounded that evening in the parlour to the doctor, the attorney, and the deaf servant. Ananias and Sapphira figured in the foreground; and the awful nature of fraud and theft, or tampering in anywise with the plain rule of honesty in matters pertaining to estates, etc., were pointedly dwelt upon; and then came a long and strenuous prayer, in which he entreated with fervour and aplomb that the hard heart of the sinner who had abstracted the leases might be softened or broken in such a way as to lead to their restitution; or that, if he continued reserved and contumacious, it might at least be the will of Heaven to bring him to public justice and the documents to light. The fact is, that he was praying all this time at the attorney.

When these religious exercises were over, the visitors retired to their rooms, and my Uncle Watson wrote two or three pressing letters by the fire. When his task was done, it had grown late; the candles were flaring in their sockets, and all in bed, and, I suppose, asleep, but he.

The fire was nearly out, he chilly, and the flame of the candles throbbing strangely in their sockets shed alternate glare and shadow round the old wainscoted room and its quaint furniture. Outside were the wild thunder and piping of the storm; and the rattling of distant windows sounded through the passages, and down the stairs, like angry people astir in the house.

My Uncle Watson belonged to a sect who by no means reject the supernatural, and whose founder, on the contrary, has sanctioned ghosts in the most emphatic way. He was glad therefore to remember, that in prosecuting his search that day, he had seen some six inches of wax candle in the press in the parlour; for he had no fancy to be overtaken by darkness in his present situation. He had no time to lose; and taking the bunch of keys – of which he was now master – he soon fitted the lock, and secured the candle – a treasure in his circumstances; and lighting it, he stuffed it into the socket of one of the expiring candles, and extinguishing the other, he looked round the room in the steady light reassured. At the same moment, an unusually violent gust of the storm blew a handful of gravel against the parlour window, with a sharp rattle that startled him in the midst of the roar and hubbub; and the flame of the candle itself was agitated by the air.

CHAPTER FIVE

The Bed Chamber

My Uncle walked up to bed guarding his candle with his hand, for the lobby windows were rattling furiously, and he disliked the idea of being left in the dark more than ever.

His bedroom was comfortable, though old fashioned. He shut and bolted the door. There was a tall looking-glass opposite the foot of his four-poster, on the dressing-table between the windows. He tried to make the curtains meet, but they would not draw; and like many a gentleman in a like perplexity, he did not possess a pin, nor was there one in the huge pincushion beneath the glass.

He turned the face of the mirror away therefore, so that its back was presented to the bed, pulled the curtains together, and placed a chair against them, to prevent their falling open again. There was a good fire, and a reinforcement of round coal and wood inside the fender. So he piled it up to ensure a cheerful blaze through the night, and placing a little black mahogany table, with the legs of a Satyr, beside the bed, and his candle upon it, he got between the sheets, and laid his red night-capped head upon his pillow, and disposed himself to sleep.

The first thing that made him uncomfortable was a sound at the foot of his bed, quite distinct in a momentary lull of the storm. It was only the gentle rustle and rush of the curtains, which fell open again; and as his eyes opened, he saw them resuming their perpendicular dependence, and sat up in his bed almost expecting to see something uncanny in the aperture.

There was nothing, however, but the dressing-table, and other dark furniture, and the window-curtains faintly undulating in the violence of the storm. He did not care to get up, therefore – the fire being bright and cheery – to replace the curtains by a chair, in the position in which he had left them, anticipating possibly a new recurrence of the relapse which had startled him from his incipient doze.

So he got to sleep in a little while again, but he was disturbed by a sound, as he fancied, at the table on which stood the candle. He could not say what it was, only that he wakened with a start, and lying so in some amaze, he did distinctly hear a sound which startled him a good deal, though there was nothing necessarily supernatural in it. He described it as resembling what would occur if you fancied a thinnish table-leaf, with a convex warp in it, depressed the reverse way, and suddenly with a spring recovering its natural convexity. It was a loud, sudden thump, which made the heavy candlestick jump, and there was an end, except that my uncle did not get again into a doze for ten minutes at least.

The next time he awoke, it was in that odd, serene way that some-times occurs. We open our eyes, we know not why, quite placidly, and are on the instant wide awake. He had had a nap of some duration this time, for his candle-flame was fluttering and flaring, *in articulo*, in the silver socket. But the fire was still bright and cheery; so he popped the extinguisher on the socket, and almost at the same time there came a tap at his door, and a sort of crescendo 'hush–sh–sh!' Once more my Uncle was sitting up, scared and perturbed, in his bed. He recollected, however, that he had bolted his door; and such inveterate materialists are we in the midst of our spiritualism, that this reassured him, and he breathed a deep sigh, and began to grow tranquil. But after a rest of a minute or two, there came a louder and sharper knock at his door; so that instinctively he called out, 'Who's there?' in a loud, stern key. There was no sort of response, however. The nervous effect of the start subsided; and I think my uncle must have remembered how constantly, especially on a stormy night, these creaks or cracks which simulate all manner of goblin noises, make themselves naturally audible.

CHAPTER SIX

The Extinguisher is Lifted

After a while, then, he lay down with his back turned toward that side of the bed at which was the door, and his face toward the table on which stood the massive old candlestick, capped with its extinguisher, and in that position he closed his eyes. But sleep would not revisit them. All kinds of queer fancies began to trouble him – some of them I remember.

He felt the point of a finger, he averred, pressed most distinctly on the tip of his great toe, as if a living hand were between his sheets, and making a sort of signal of attention or silence. Then again he felt something as large as a rat make a sudden bounce in the middle of his bolster, just under his head. Then a voice said 'Oh!' very gently, close at the back of his head. All these things he felt certain of, and yet investigation led to nothing. He felt odd little cramps stealing now and then about him; and then, on a sudden, the middle finger of his right hand was plucked backwards, with a light playful jerk that frightened him awfully.

Meanwhile the storm kept singing, and howling, and ha–ha–hooing hoarsely among the limbs of the old trees and the chimney-pots; and my Uncle Watson, although he prayed and meditated as was his wont when he lay awake, felt his heart throb excitedly, and sometimes thought he was beset with evil spirits, and at others that he was in the early stage of a fever.

He resolutely kept his eyes closed, however, and, like St Paul's shipwrecked companions, wished for the day. At last another little doze seems to have stolen upon his senses, for he awoke quietly and completely as before – opening his eyes all at once, and seeing everything as if he had not slept for a moment.

The fire was still blazing redly – nothing uncertain in the light – the massive silver candlestick, topped with its tall extinguisher, stood on the centre of the black mahogany table as before; and, looking by what seemed a sort of accident to the apex of this, he beheld something which made him quite misdoubt the evidence of his eyes.

He saw the extinguisher lifted by a tiny hand, from beneath, and a small human face, no bigger than a thumbnail, with nicely proportioned features peep from beneath it. In this Lilliputian countenance was such a ghastly consternation as horrified my Uncle unspeakably. Out came a little foot then and there, and a pair of wee legs, in short silk stockings and buckled shoes, then the rest of the figure; and, with the arms holding about the socket, the little legs stretched and stretched, hanging about the stem of the candlestick till the feet reached the base, and so down the Satyr-like leg of the table, till they reached the floor, extending elastically, and strangely enlarging in all proportions as they approached the ground, where the feet and buckles were those of a well-shaped, full grown man, and the figure tapering upward until it dwindled to its original fairy dimensions at the top, like an object seen in some strangely curved mirror.

Standing upon the floor he expanded, my amazed uncle could not tell how, into his proper proportions; and stood pretty nearly in profile at the bedside, a handsome and elegantly shaped young man, in a bygone military costume, with a small laced, three-cocked hat and plume on his head, but looking like a man going to be hanged – in unspeakable despair.

He stepped lightly to the hearth, and turned for a few seconds very dejectedly with his back toward the bed and the mantelpiece, and he saw the hilt of his rapier glittering in the firelight; and then walking across the room he placed himself at the dressing-table, visible through the divided curtains at the foot of the bed. The fire was blazing still so brightly that my uncle saw him as distinctly as if half a dozen candles were burning.

CHAPTER SEVEN

The Visitation Culminates

The looking-glass was an old fashioned piece of furniture and had a drawer beneath it. My Uncle had searched it carefully for the papers in the daytime; but the silent figure pulled the drawer quite out, pressed a spring at the side, disclosing a false receptacle behind it, and from this he drew a parcel of papers tied together with pink tape.

All this time my Uncle was staring at him in a horrified state, neither winking nor breathing, and the apparition had not once given the smallest intimation of consciousness that a living person was in the same room. But now, for the first time, it turned its livid stare full upon my Uncle with a hateful smile of significance, lifting up the little parcel of papers between his slender finger and thumb. Then he made a long, cunning wink at him, and seemed to blow out one of his cheeks in a burlesque grimace, which, but for the horrific circumstances, would have been ludicrous. My Uncle could not tell whether this was really an intentional distortion or only one of those horrid ripples and deflections which were constantly disturbing the proportions of the figure, as if it were seen through some unequal and perverting medium.

The figure now approached the bed, seeming to grow exhausted and malignant as it did so. My Uncle's terror nearly culminated at this point, for he believed it was drawing near him with an evil purpose. But it was not so; for the soldier, over whom twenty years seemed to have passed in his brief transit to the dressing-table and back again, threw himself into a great high-backed armchair of stuffed leather at the far side of the fire, and placed his heels on the fender. His feet and legs seemed indistinctly to swell, and swathings showed themselves round them, and they grew into something enormous, and the upper figure swayed and shaped itself into corresponding proportions, a great mass of corpulence, with a cadaverous and malignant face, and the furrows of a great old age, and colourless glassy eyes; and with these changes, which came indefinitely but rapidly as those of a sunset cloud, the fine regimentals faded away, and a loose, gray, woollen drapery, somehow, was there in its stead; and all seemed to be stained and rotten, for swarms of worms seemed creeping in and out, while the figure grew paler and paler, till my Uncle, who liked his pipe, and employed the simile naturally, said the whole effigy grew to the colour of tobacco ashes, and the clusters of worms into little wriggling knots of sparks such as we see running over the residuum of a burnt sheet of paper. And so with the strong draught caused by the fire, and the current of air from the window, which was rattling in the storm, the feet seemed to be drawn into the fireplace, and the whole figure, light as ashes, floated away with them, and disappeared with a whisk up the capacious old chimney.

It seemed to my Uncle that the fire suddenly darkened and the air grew icy cold, and there came an awful roar and riot of tempest, which shook the old house from top to base, and sounded like the yelling of a bloodthirsty mob on receiving a new and long-expected victim.

Good Uncle Watson used to say, 'I have been in many situations of fear and danger in the course of my life, but never did I pray with so much agony before or since; for then, as now, it was clear beyond a cavil that I had actually beheld the phantom of an evil spirit.'

CONCLUSION

Now there are two curious circumstances to be observed in this relation of my Uncle's, who was, as I have said, a perfectly veracious man.

First – The wax candle which he took from the press in the parlour and burnt at his bedside on that horrible night was unquestionably, according to the testimony of the old deaf servant, who had been fifty years at Wauling, that identical piece of 'holy candle' which had stood in the fingers of the poor lady's corpse, and concerning which the old Irish crone, long since dead, had delivered the curious curse I have mentioned against the Captain.

Secondly – Behind the drawer under the looking-glass, he did actually discover a second but secret drawer, in which were concealed the identical papers which he had suspected the attorney of having made away with. There were circumstances, too, afterwards disclosed, which convinced my Uncle that the old man had deposited them there preparatory to burning them, which he had nearly made up his mind to do.

Now, a very remarkable ingredient in this tale of my Uncle Watson was this, that so far as my father, who had never seen Captain Walshawe in the course of his life, could gather, the phantom had exhibited a horrible and grotesque, but unmistakeable resemblance to that defunct scamp in the various stages of his long life.

Wauling was sold in the year 1837, and the old house shortly after pulled down, and a new one built nearer to the river. I often wonder whether it was rumoured to be haunted, and, if so, what stories were current about it. It was a commodious and stanch old house, and withal rather handsome; and its demolition was certainly suspicious.

SHERIDAN LE FANU

Sir Dominick's Bargain

A Legend of Dunoran

❧❦❧

In the early autumn of the year 1838, business called me to the south of Ireland. The weather was delightful, the scenery and people were new to me, and sending my luggage on by the mail-coach route in charge of a servant, I hired a serviceable nag at a posting-house, and, full of the curiosity of an explorer, I commenced a leisurely journey of five-and-twenty miles on horseback, by sequestered crossroads, to my place of destination. By bog and hill, by plain and ruined castle, and many a winding stream, my picturesque road led me.

I had started late, and having made little more than half my journey, I was thinking of making a short halt at the next convenient place, and letting my horse have a rest and a feed, and making some provision also for the comforts of his rider.

It was about four o'clock when the road, ascending a gradual steep, found a passage through a rocky gorge between the abrupt termination of a range of mountain to my left and a rocky hill, that rose dark and sudden at my right. Below me lay a little thatched village, under a long line of gigantic beech trees, through the boughs of which the lowly chimneys sent up their thin turf-smoke. To my left, stretched away for miles, ascending the mountain range I have mentioned, a wild park, through whose sward and ferns the rock broke, time-worn and lichen-stained. This park was studded with straggling wood, which thickened to something like a forest, behind and beyond the little village I was approaching, clothing the irregular ascent of the hillsides with beautiful, and in some places discoloured foliage.

As you descend, the road winds slightly, with the grey park-wall, built of loose stone, and mantled here and there with ivy, at its left, and crosses a shallow ford; and as I approached the village, through breaks in the woodlands, I caught glimpses of the long front of an old ruined house, placed among the trees, about halfway up the picturesque mountainside.

The solitude and melancholy of this ruin piqued my curiosity, and when I had reached the rude thatched public-house, with the sign of St Columbkill, with robes, mitre, and crozier displayed over its lintel, having seen to my horse and made a good meal myself on a rasher and eggs, I began to think again of the wooded park and the ruinous house, and resolved on a ramble of half an hour among its sylvan solitudes.

The name of the place, I found, was Dunoran; and beside the gate a stile admitted to the grounds, through which, with a pensive enjoyment, I began to saunter towards the dilapidated mansion.

A long grass-grown road, with many turns and windings, led up to the old house, under the shadow of the wood.

The road, as it approached the house skirted the edge of a precipitous glen, clothed with hazel, dwarf-oak, and thorn, and the silent house stood with its wide-open hall-door facing this dark ravine, the further edge of which was crowned with towering forest; and great trees stood about the house and its deserted courtyard and stables.

I walked in and looked about me, through passages overgrown with nettles and weeds; from room to room with ceilings rotted, and here and there a great beam dark and worn, with tendrils of ivy trailing over it. The tall walls with rotten plaster were stained and mouldy, and in some rooms the remains of decayed wainscoting crazily swung to and fro. The almost sashless windows were darkened also with ivy, and about the tall chimneys the jackdaws were wheeling, while from the huge trees that overhung the glen in sombre masses at the other side, the rooks kept up a ceaseless cawing.

As I walked through these melancholy passages – peeping only into some of the rooms, for the flooring was quite gone in the middle, and bowed down toward the centre, and the house was very nearly unroofed, a state of things which made the exploration a little critical – I began to wonder why so grand a house, in the midst of scenery so picturesque, had been permitted to go to decay; I dreamed of the hospitalities of which it had long ago been the rallying place, and I thought what a scene of Redgauntlet revelries it might disclose at midnight.

The great staircase was of oak, which had stood the weather wonderfully, and I sat down upon its steps, musing vaguely on the transitoriness of all things under the sun.

Except for the hoarse and distant clamour of the rooks, hardly audible where I sat, no sound broke the profound stillness of the spot. Such a sense of solitude I have seldom experienced before. The air was stirless, there was not even the rustle of a withered leaf along the passage. It was oppressive. The tall trees that stood close about the building darkened it, and added something of awe to the melancholy of the scene.

In this mood I heard, with an unpleasant surprise, close to me, a voice that was drawling, and, I fancied, sneering, repeat the words: 'Food for worms, dead and rotten; God over all.'

There was a small window in the wall, here very thick, which had been built up, and in the dark recess of this, deep in the shadow, I now saw a sharp-featured man, sitting with his feet dangling. His keen eyes were fixed on me, and he was smiling cynically, and before I had well recovered my surprise, he repeated the distich:

> 'If death was a thing that money could buy,
> The rich they would live, and the poor they would die.'

'It was a grand house in its day, sir,' he continued, 'Dunoran House, and the Sarsfields. Sir Dominick Sarsfield was the last of the old stock. He lost his life not six foot away from where you are sitting.'

As he thus spoke he let himself down, with a little jump, on to the ground.

He was a dark-faced, sharp-featured, little hunchback, and had a walking-stick in his hand, with the end of which he pointed to a rusty stain in the plaster of the wall.

'Do you mind that mark, sir?' he asked.

'Yes,' I said, standing up, and looking at it, with a curious anticipation of something worth hearing.

'That's about seven or eight feet from the ground, sir, and you'll not guess what it is.'

'I dare say not,' said I, 'unless it is a stain from the weather.'

' 'Tis nothing so lucky, sir,' he answered, with the same cynical smile and a wag of his head, still pointing at the mark with his stick.

'That's a splash of brains and blood. It's there this hundred years; and it will never leave it while the wall stands.'

'He was murdered, then?'

'Worse than that, sir,' he answered.

'He killed himself, perhaps?'

'Worse than that, itself, this cross between us and harm! I'm oulder than I look, sir; you wouldn't guess my years.'

He became silent, and looked at me, evidently inviting a guess.

'Well, I should guess you to be about five-and-fifty.'

He laughed, and took a pinch of snuff, and said: 'I'm that, your honour, and something to the back of it. I was seventy last Candlemas. You would not a' thought that, to look at me.'

'Upon my word I should not; I can hardly believe it even now. Still, you don't remember Sir Dominick Sarsfield's death?' I said, glancing up at the ominous stain on the wall.

'No, sir, that was a long while before I was born. But my grand-father was butler here long ago, and many a time I heard tell how Sir Dominick came by his death. There was no masther in the great house ever sinst that happened. But there was two sarvants in care of it, and my aunt was one o' them; and she kep' me here wid her till I was nine year old, and she was lavin' the place to go to Dublin; and from that time it was let to go down. The wind sthript the roof, and the rain rotted the timber, and little by little, in sixty years' time, it kem to what you see. But I have a likin' for it still, for the sake of ould times; and I never come this way but I take a look in. I don't think it's many more times I'll be turnin' to see the ould place, for I'll be undher the sod myself before long.'

'You'll outlive younger people,' I said.

And, quitting that trite subject, I ran on: 'I don't wonder that you like this old place; it is a beautiful spot, such noble trees.'

'I wish ye seen the glin when the nuts is ripe; they're the sweetest nuts in all Ireland, I think,' he rejoined, with a practical sense of the picturesque. 'You'd fill your pockets while you'd be lookin' about you.'

'These are very fine old woods,' I remarked. 'I have not seen any in Ireland I thought so beautiful.'

'Eiah! your honour, the woods about here is nothing to what they wor. Al the mountains along here was wood when my father was a gossoon, and Murroa Wood was the grandest of them all. All oak mostly, and all cut down as bare as the road. Not one left here that's fit to compare with them. Which way did your honour come hither – from Limerick?'

'No. Killaloe.'

'Well, then, you passed the ground where Murroa Wood was in former times. You kem undher Lisnavourra, the steep knob of a hill about a mile above the village here. 'Twas near that Murroa Wood was, and 'twas there Sir Dominick Sarsfield first met the devil, the Lord between us and harm, and a bad meeting it was for him and his.'

I had become interested in the adventure which had occurred in the very scenery which had so greatly attracted me, and my new acquaintance, the little hunchback, was easily entreated to tell me the story, and spoke thus, so soon as we had each resumed his seat: 'It was a fine estate when Sir Dominick came into it; and grand doings there was entirely, feasting and fiddling, free quarters for all the pipers in the counthry round, and a welcome for everyone that liked to come. There was wine, by the hogshead, for the quality; and potteen enough to set a town a-fire, and beer and cidher enough to float a navy, for the boys and girls, and the likes o' me. It was kep' up the best part of a month, till the weather broke, and the rain spoilt the sod for the moneen jigs, and the fair of Allybally Killudeen comin' on they wor obliged to give over their diversion, and attind to the pigs.

But Sir Dominick was only beginnin' when they wor lavin' off. There was no way of gettin' rid of his money and estates he did not try – what with drinkin', dicin', racin', cards, and all soarts, it was not many years before the estates wor in debt, and Sir Dominick a distressed man. He showed a bold front to the world as long as he could; and then he sould off his dogs, and most of his horses, and gev out he was going to thravel in France, and the like; and so off with him for awhile; and no one in these parts heard tale or tidings of him for two or three years. Till at last quite unexpected, one night there comes a rapping at the big kitchen window. It was past ten o'clock, and old Connor Hanlon, the butler, my grandfather, was sittin' by the fire alone, warming his shins over it. There was keen east wind blowing along the mountains that night, and whistling cowld enough, through the tops of the trees, and soundin' lonesome through the long chimneys.

(And the storyteller glanced up at the nearest stack visible from his seat.)

So he wasn't quite sure of the knockin' at the window, and up he gets, and sees his master's face.

My grandfather was glad to see him safe, for it was a long time since there was any news of him; but he was sorry, too, for it was a changed place and only himself and old Juggy Broadrick in charge of the house, and a man in the stables, and it was a poor thing to see him comin' back to his own like that.

He shook Con by the hand, and says he: 'I came here to say a word to you. I left my horse with Dick in the stable; I may want him again before morning, or I may never want him.'

And with that he turns into the big kitchen, and draws a stool, and sits down to take an air of the fire.

'Sit down, Connor, opposite me, and listen to what I tell you, and don't be afeard to say what you think.'

He spoke all the time lookin' into the fire, with his hands stretched over it, and a tired man he looked.

'An' why should I be afeard, Masther Dominick?' says my grandfather. 'Yourself was a good masther to me, and so was your father, rest his soul, before you, and I'll say the truth, and dar' the devil, and more than that for any Sarsfield of Dunoran, much less yourself, and a good right I'd have.'

'It's all over with me, Con,' says Sir Dominick.

'Heaven forbid!' says my grandfather.

' 'Tis past praying for,' says Sir Dominick. 'The last guinea's gone; the ould place will follow it. It must be sold, and I'm come here, I don't know why, like a ghost to have a last look round me, and go off in the dark again.'

And with that he told him to be sure, in case he should hear of his death, to give the oak box, in the closet off his room, to his cousin, Pat Sarsfield, in Dublin, and the sword and pistols his grandfather carried in Aughrim, and two or three trifling things of the kind.

And says he, 'Con, they say if the divil gives you money overnight, you'll find nothing but a bagful of pebbles, and chips, and nutshells, in the morning. If I thought he played fair, I'm in the humour to make a bargain with him tonight.'

'Lord forbid!' says my grandfather, standing up, with a start and crossing himself.

'They say the country's full of men, listin' sogers for the King o'

France. If I light on one o' them, I'll not refuse his offer. How contrary things goes! How long is it since me an Captain Waller fought the jewel at New Castle?'

'Six years, Masther Dominick, and ye broke his thigh with the bullet the first shot.'

'I did, Con,' says he, 'and I wish, instead, he had shot me through the heart. Have you any whisky?'

My grandfather took it out of the buffet, and the master pours out some into a bowl, and drank it off.

'I'll go out and have a look at my horse,' says he, standing up. There was sort of a stare in his eyes, as he pulled his riding-cloak about him, as if there was something bad in his thoughts.

'Sure, I won't be a minute running out myself to the stable, and looking after the horse for you myself,' says my grandfather.

'I'm not goin' to the stable,' says Sir Dominick; 'I may as well tell you, for I see you found it out already – I'm goin' across the deer-park; if I come back you'll see me in an hour's time. But, anyhow, you'd better not follow me, for if you do I'll shoot you, and that 'id be a bad ending to our friendship.'

And with that he walks down this passage here, and turns the key in the side door at that end of it, and out wid him on the sod into the moonlight and the cowld wind; and my grandfather seen him walkin' hard towards the park-wall, and then he comes in and closes the door with a heavy heart.

Sir Dominick stopped to think when he got to the middle of the deer-park, for he had not made up his mind, when he left the house, and the whisky did not clear his head, only it gev him courage.

He did not feel the cowld wind now, nor fear death, nor think much of anything but the shame and fall of the old family.

And he made up his mind, if no better thought came to him between that and there, so soon as he came to Murroa Wood, he'd hang himself from one of the oak branches with his cravat.

It was a bright moonlight night, there was just a bit of a cloud driving across the moon now and then, but, only for that, as light a'most as day.

Down he goes, right for the wood of Murroa. It seemed to him every step he took was as long as three, and it was no time till he was among the big oak trees with their roots spreading from one to another, and their branches stretching overhead like the timbers of a naked roof, and the moon shining down through them, and casting their shadows thick and twist abroad on the ground as black as my shoe.

He was sobering a bit by this time, and he slacked his pace, and he thought 'twould be better to list in the French king's army, and thry what that might do for him, for he knew a man might take his own life any time, but it would puzzle him to take it back again when he liked.

Just as he made up his mind not to make away with himself, what should he hear but a step clinkin' along the dry ground under the trees, and soon he sees a grand gentleman right before him comin' up to meet him.

He was a handsome young man like himself, and he wore a cocked-hat with gold-lace round it, such as officers wears on their coats, and he had on a dress the same as French officers wore in them times.

He stopped opposite Sir Dominick, and he cum to a standstill also.

The two gentlemen took off their hats to one another, and says the stranger: 'I am recruiting, sir,' says he, 'for my sovereign, and you'll find my money won't turn into pebbles, chips, and nutshells, by tomorrow.'

At the same time he pulls out a big purse full of gold.

The minute he set eyes on that gentleman, Sir Dominick had his own opinion of him; and at those words he felt the very hair standing up on his head.

'Don't be afraid,' says he, 'the money won't burn you. If it proves honest gold, and if it prospers with you, I'm willing to make a bargain. This is the last day of February,' says he; 'I'll serve you seven years, and at the end of that time you shall serve me, and I'll come for you when the seven years is over, when the clock turns the minute between February and March; and the first of March ye'll come away with me, or never. You'll not find me a bad master, any more than a bad servant. I love my own; and I command all the pleasures and the glory of the world. The bargain dates from this day, and the lease is out at midnight on the last day I told you; and in the year' – he told him the year, it was easy reckoned, but I forget it – 'and if you'd rather wait,' he says, 'for eight months and twenty eight days, before you sign the writin', you may, if you meet me here. But I can't do a great deal for you in the mean time; and if you don't sign then, all you get from me, up to that time, will vanish away, and you'll be just as you are tonight, and ready to hang yourself on the first tree you meet.'

Well, the end of it was, Sir Dominick chose to wait, and he came back to the house with a big bag full of money, as round as your hat a'most.

My grandfather was glad enough, you may be sure, to see the master safe and sound again so soon. Into the kitchen he bangs again, and swings the bag o' money on the table; and he stands up straight, and heaves up his shoulders like a man that has just got shut of a load; and he looks at the bag, and my grandfather looks at him, and from him to it, and back again. Sir Dominick looked as white as a sheet, and says he: 'I don't know, Con, what's in it; it's the heaviest load I ever carried.'

He seemed shy of openin' the bag; and he made my grandfather heap up a roaring fire of turf and wood, and then, at last, he opens it, and, sure enough, 'twas stuffed full o' golden guineas, bright and new, as if they were only that minute out o' the Mint.

Sir Dominick made my grandfather sit at his elbow while he counted every guinea in the bag.

When he was done countin,' and it wasn't far from daylight when that time came, Sir Dominick made my grandfather swear not to tell a word about it. And a close secret it was for many a day after.

When the eight months and twenty-eight days were pretty near spent and ended, Sir Dominick returned to the house here with a troubled mind, in doubt what was best to be done, and no one alive but my grandfather knew anything about the matter, and he not half what had happened.

As the day drew near, towards the end of October, Sir Dominick grew only more and more troubled in mind.

One time he made up his mind to have no more to say to such things, nor to speak again with the like of them he met with in the wood of Murroa. Then, again, his heart failed him when he thought of his debts, and he not knowing where to turn. Then, only a week before the day, everything began to go wrong with him. One man wrote from London to say that Sir Dominick paid three thousand pounds to the wrong man, and must pay it over again; another demanded a debt he never heard of before; and another, in Dublin, denied the payment of a thundherin' big bill, and Sir Dominick could nowhere find the receipt, and so on, wid fifty other things as bad.

Well, by the time the night of the 28th of October came round, he was a'most ready to lose his senses with all the demands that was risin' up again him on all sides, and nothing to meet them but the help of the one dhreadful friend he had to depind on at night in the oak-wood down there below.

So there was nothing for it but to go through with the business that was begun already, and about the same hour as he went last, he takes off the little crucifix he wore round his neck, for he was a Catholic, and his gospel, and his bit o' the thrue cross that he had in a locket, for since he took the money from the Evil One he was growin' frightful in himself, and got all he could to guard him from the power of the devil. But tonight, for his life, he daren't take them with him. So he gives them into my grandfather's hands without a word, only he looked as white as a sheet o' paper; and he takes his hat and sword, and telling my grandfather to watch for him, away he goes, to try what would come of it.

It was a fine still night, and the moon – not so bright, though, now as the first time – was shinin' over heath and rock, and down on the lonesome oak-wood below him.

His heart beat thick as he drew near it. There was not a sound, not even the distant bark of a dog from the village behind him. There was not a lonesomer spot in the country round, and if it wasn't for his debts and losses that was drivin' him on half mad, in spite of his fears for his soul and his hopes of paradise, and all his good angel was whisperin' in his ear, he would a' turned back, and sent for his clargy, and made his confession and his penance, and changed his ways, and led a good life, for he was frightened enough to have done a great dale.

Softer and slower he stepped as he got, once more, in undher the big branches of the oak-threes; and when he got in a bit, near where he met with the bad spirit before, he stopped and looked round him, and felt himself, every bit, turning as cowld as a dead man, and you may be sure he did not feel much betther when he seen the same man steppin' from behind the big tree that was touchin' his elbow a'most.

'You found the money good,' says he, 'but it was not enough. No matter, you shall have enough and to spare. I'll see after your luck, and I'll give you a hint whenever it can serve you; and any time you want to see me you have only to come down here, and call my face to mind, and wish me present. You shan't owe a shilling by the end of the year, and you shall never miss the right card, the best throw, and the winning horse. Are you willing?'

The young gentleman's voice almost stuck in his throat, and his hair was rising on his head, but he did get out a word or two to signify that he consented; and with that the Evil One handed him a needle, and bid him give him three drops of blood from his arm; and he took them in the cup of an acorn, and gave him a pen, and bid him write some words that he repeated, and that Sir Dominick did not understand, on two thin slips of parchment. He took one himself and the other he sunk in Sir Dominick's arm at the place where he drew the blood, and he closed the flesh over it. And that's as true as you're sittin' there!

Well, Sir Dominick went home. He was a frightened man, and well he might be. But in a little time he began to grow aisier in his mind. Anyhow, he got out of debt very quick, and money came tumbling in to make him richer, and everything he took in hand prospered, and he never made a wager, or played a game, but he won; and for all that, there was not a poor man on the estate that was not happier than Sir Dominick.

So he took again to his old ways; for, when the money came back, all came back, and there were hounds and horses, and wine galore, and no end of company, and grand doin's, and divarsion, up here at the great house. And some said Sir Dominick was thinkin' of gettin' married; and more said he wasn't. But, anyhow, there was somethin' troublin' him more than common, and so one night, unknownst to all, away he goes to the lonesome oak-wood. It was something, maybe, my grandfather thought was troublin' him about a beautiful young lady he was jealous of, and mad in love with her. But that was only guess.

Well, when Sir Dominick got into the wood this time, he grew more in dread than ever; and he was on the point of turnin' and lavin' the place, when who should he see, close beside him, but my gentleman, seated on a big stone undher one of the trees. In place of looking the fine young gentleman in goold lace and grand clothes he appeared before, he was now in rags, he looked twice the size he had been, and his face smutted with soot, and he had a murtherin' big steel hammer, as heavy as a half-hundred, with a handle a yard long, across his knees. It was so dark under the tree, he did not see him quite clear for some time.

He stood up, and he looked awful tall entirely. And what passed between them in that discourse my grandfather never heered. But Sir

Dominick was as black as night afterwards, and hadn't a laugh for anything nor a word a'most for anyone, and he only grew worse and worse, and darker and darker. And now this thing, whatever it was, used to come to him of its own accord, whether he wanted it or no; sometimes in one shape, and sometimes in another, in lonesome places, and sometimes at his side by night when he'd be ridin' home alone, until at last he lost heart altogether and sent for the priest.

The priest was with him a long time, and when he heered the whole story, he rode off all the way for the bishop, and the bishop came here to the great house next day, and he gev Sir Dominick a good advice. He toult him he must give over dicin', and swearin,' and drinkin', and all bad company, and live a vartuous steady life until the seven years bargain was out, and if the divil didn't come for him the minute afther the stroke of twelve the first morning of the month of March, he was safe out of the bargain. There was not more than eight or ten months to run now before the seven years wor out, and he lived all the time according to the bishop's advice, as strict as if he was 'in retreat.'

Well, you may guess he felt quare enough when the mornin' of the 28th of February came.

The priest came up by appointment, and Sir Dominick and his raverence wor together in the room you see there, and kep' up their prayers together till the clock struck twelve, and a good hour after, and not a sign of a disturbance, nor nothing came near them, and the priest slep' that night in the house in the room next Sir Dominick's, and all went over as comfortable as could be, and they shook hands and kissed like two comrades after winning a battle.

So, now, Sir Dominick thought he might as well have a pleasant evening, after all his fastin' and praying; and he sent round to half a dozen of the neighbouring gentlemen to come and dine with him, and his raverence stayed and dined also, and a roarin' bowl o' punch they had, and no end o' wine, and the swearin' and dice, and cards and guineas changing hands, and songs and stories, that wouldn't do anyone good to hear, and the priest slipped away, when he seen the turn things was takin', and it was not far from the stroke of twelve when Sir Dominick, sitting at the head of his table, swears, 'this is the best first of March I ever sat down with my friends.'

'It ain't the first o' March,' says Mr Hiffernan of Ballyvoreen. He was a scholard, and always kep' an almanack.

'What is it, then?' says Sir Dominick, startin' up, and dhroppin' the ladle into the bowl, and starin' at him as if he had two heads.

' 'Tis the twenty-ninth of February, leap year,' says he. And just as they were talkin', the clock strikes twelve; and my grandfather, who was half asleep in a chair by the fire in the hall, openin' his eyes, sees a short square fellow with a cloak on, and long black hair bushin' out from under his hat, standin' just there where you see the bit o' light shinin' again' the wall.

(My hunchbacked friend pointed with his stick to a little patch of red sunset light that relieved the deepening shadow of the passage.)

'Tell your master,' says he, in an awful voice, like the growl of a baist, 'that I'm here by appointment, and expect him downstairs this minute.'

Up goes my grandfather, by these very steps you are sittin' on.

'Tell him I can't come down yet,' says Sir Dominick, and he turns to the company in the room, and says he with a cold sweat shinin' on his face, 'for God's sake, gentlemen, will any of you jump from the window and bring the priest here?' One looked at another and no one knew what to make of it, and in the mean time, up comes my grandfather again, and says he, tremblin', 'He says, sir, unless you go down to him, he'll come up to you.'

'I don't understand this, gentlemen, I'll see what it means,' says Sir Dominick, trying to put a face on it, and walkin' out o' the room like a man through the press-room, with the hangman waitin' for him outside. Down the stairs he comes, and two or three of the gentlemen peeping over the banisters, to see. My grandfather was walking six or eight steps behind him, and he seen the stranger take a stride out to meet Sir Dominick, and catch him up in his arms, and whirl his head against the wall, and wi' that the hall-doore flies open, and out goes the candles, and the turf and wood-ashes flyin' with the wind out o' the hall-fire, ran in a drift o' sparks along the floore by his feet.

Down runs the gintlemen. Bang goes the hall-doore. Some comes runnin' up, and more runnin' down, with lights. It was all over with Sir Dominick. They lifted up the corpse, and put its shoulders again' the wall; but there was not a gasp left in him. He was cowld and stiffenin' already.

Pat Donovan was comin' up to the great house late that night and after he passed the little brook, that the carriage track up to the house crosses, and about fifty steps to this side of it, his dog, that was by his side, makes a sudden wheel, and springs over the wall, and sets up a yowlin' inside you'd hear a mile away; and that minute two men passed him by in silence, goin' down from the house, one of them short and square, and the other like Sir Dominick in shape, but there was little light under the trees where he was, and they looked only like shadows; and as they passed him by he could not hear the sound of their feet and he drew back to the wall frightened; and when he got up to the great house, he found all in confusion, and the master's body, with the head smashed to pieces, lying just on *that spot*.

The narrator stood up and indicated with the point of his stick the exact site of the body, and, as I looked, the shadow deepened, the red stain of sunlight vanished from the wall, and the sun had gone down behind the distant hill of New Castle, leaving the haunted scene in the deep grey of darkening twilight.

So I and the storyteller parted, not without good wishes on both sides, and a little 'tip,' which seemed not unwelcome, from me.

It was dusk and the moon up by the time I reached the village, remounted my nag, and looked my last on the scene of the terrible legend of Dunoran.

SHERIDAN LE FANU

Ultor de Lacy
A Legend of Cappercullen

❧

CHAPTER ONE

The Jacobite Legacy

In my youth I heard a great many Irish family traditions, more or less of a supernatural character, some of them very peculiar, and all, to a child at least, highly interesting. One of these I will now relate, though the translation to cold type from oral narrative, with all the aids of animated human voice and countenance, and the appropriate *mise en scéne* of the old fashioned parlour fireside and its listening circle of excited faces, and, outside, the wintry blast and the moan of leafless boughs, with the occasional rattle of the clumsy old window-frame behind shutter and curtain, as the blast swept by, is at best a trying one.

About midway up the romantic glen of Cappercullen, near the point where the counties of Limerick, Clare, and Tipperary converge, upon the then sequestered and forest-bound range of the Slieve-Felim hills, there stood, in the reigns of the two earliest Georges, the picturesque and massive remains of one of the finest of the Anglo-Irish castles of Munster – perhaps of Ireland.

It crowned the precipitous edge of the wooded glen, itself half buried among the wild forest that covered that long and solitary range. There was no human habitation within a circle of many miles, except the half-dozen hovels and the small thatched chapel composing the little village of Murroa, which lay at the foot of the glen among the straggling skirts of the noble forest.

Its remoteness and difficulty of access saved it from demolition. It was worth nobody's while to pull down and remove the ponderous and clumsy oak, much less the masonry or flagged roofing of the pile. Whatever would pay the cost of removal had been long since carried away. The rest was abandoned to time – the destroyer.

The hereditary owners of this noble building and of a wide territory in the contiguous counties I have named, were English – the de Lacys – long naturalised in Ireland. They had acquired at least this portion of their estate in the reign of Henry VIII, and held it, with some vicissitudes, down to the establishment of the revolution in Ireland, when they suffered attainder, and, like other great families of that period, underwent a final eclipse.

The de Lacy of that day retired to France, and held a brief command in the Irish Brigade, interrupted by sickness. He retired, became a poor hanger-on of the Court of St Germains, and died early in the eighteenth century – as well as I remember, 1705 – leaving an only son, hardly twelve years old, called by the strange but significant name of Ultor.

At this point commences the marvellous ingredient of my tale.

When his father was dying, he had him to his bedside, with no one by except his confessor; and having told him, first, that on reaching the age of twenty-one, he was to lay claim to a certain small estate in the county of Clare, in Ireland, in right of his mother the title-deeds of which he gave him – and next, having enjoined him not to marry before the age of thirty, on the ground that earlier marriages destroyed the spirit and the power of enterprise, and would incapacitate him from the accomplishment of his destiny – the restoration of his family – he then went on to open to the child a matter which so terrified him that he cried lamentably, trembling all over, clinging to the priest's gown with one hand and to his father's cold wrist with the other, and imploring him, with screams of horror, to desist from his communication.

But the priest, impressed, no doubt, himself, with its necessity, compelled him to listen. And then his father showed him a small picture, from which also the child turned with shrieks, until similarly constrained to look. They did not let him go until he had carefully conned the features, and was able to tell them, from memory, the colour of the eyes and hair, and the fashion and hues of the dress. Then his father gave him a black box containing this portrait, which was a full-length miniature, about nine inches long, painted very finely in oils, as smooth as enamel, and folded above it a sheet of paper, written over in a careful and very legible hand.

The deeds and this black box constituted the most important legacy bequeathed to his only child by the ruined Jacobite, and he deposited them in the hands of the priest, in trust, till his boy, Ultor, should have attained to an age to understand their value, and to keep them securely.

When this scene was ended, the dying exile's mind, I suppose, was relieved, for he spoke cheerily, and said he believed he would recover; and they soothed the crying child, and his father kissed him, and gave him a little silver coin to buy fruit with; and so they sent him off with another boy for a walk, and when he came back his father was dead.

He remained in France under the care of this ecclesiastic until he had attained the age of twenty-one, when he repaired to Ireland, and his title being unaffected by his father's attainder, he easily made good his claim to the small estate in the county of Clare.

There he settled, making a dismal and solitary tour now and then of the vast territories which had once been his father's, and nursing those gloomy and impatient thoughts which befitted the enterprises to which he was devoted.

Occasionally he visited Paris, that common centre of English, Irish, and Scottish disaffection; and there, when a little past thirty, he married the daughter of another ruined Irish house. His bride returned with him to the melancholy seclusion of their Munster residence, where she bore him in succession two daughters – Alice, the elder, dark-eyed and dark-haired, grave and sensible – Una, four years younger, with large blue eyes and long and beautiful golden hair.

Their poor mother was, I believe, naturally a light-hearted, sociable, high-spirited little creature; and her gay and childish nature pined in the isolation and gloom of her lot. At all events she died young, and the children were left to the sole care of their melancholy and embittered father. In process of time the girls grew up, tradition says, beautiful. The elder was designed for a convent, the younger her father hoped to mate as nobly as her high blood and splendid beauty seemed to promise, if only the great game on which he had resolved to stake all succeeded.

CHAPTER TWO

The Fairies in the Castle

The Rebellion of '45 came, and Ultor de Lacy was one of the few Irishmen implicated treasonably in that daring and romantic insurrection. Of course there were warrants out against him, but he was not to be found. The young ladies, indeed, remained as heretofore in their father's lonely house in Clare; but whether he had crossed the water or was still in Ireland was for some time unknown, even to them. In due course he was attainted, and his little estate forfeited. It was a miserable catastrophe – a tremendous and beggarly waking up from a life-long dream of returning principality.

In due course the officers of the crown came down to take possession, and it behoved the young ladies to flit. Happily for them the ecclesiastic I have mentioned was not quite so confident as their father, of his winning back the magnificent patrimony of his ancestors; and by his advice the daughters had been secured twenty pounds a year each, under the marriage settlement of their parents, which was all that stood between this proud house and literal destitution.

Late one evening, as some little boys from the village were returning from a ramble through the dark and devious glen of Cappercullen, with their pockets laden with nuts and 'frahans', to their amazement and even terror they saw a light streaming redly from the narrow window of one of the towers overhanging the precipice among the ivy and the lofty branches, across the glen, already dim in the shadows of the deepening night.

'Look – look – look – 'tis the Phooka's tower!' was the general cry, in the vernacular Irish, and a universal scamper commenced.

The bed of the glen, strewn with great fragments of rock, among which rose the tall stems of ancient trees, and overgrown with a tangled copse, was at the best no favourable ground for a run. Now it was dark; and, terrible work breaking through brambles and hazels, and tumbling over rocks. Little Shaeen Mull Ryan, the last of the panic rout, screaming to his mates to wait for him – saw a whitish figure emerge from the thicket at the base of the stone flight of steps

that descended the side of the glen, close by the castle-wall, intercepting his flight, and a discordant male voice shrieked: 'I have you!'

At the same time the boy, with a cry of terror, tripped and tumbled;
and felt himself roughly caught by the arm, and hauled to his feet with
a shake.

A wild yell from the child, and a volley of terror and entreaty
followed.

'Who is it, Larry; what's the matter?' cried a voice, high in air, from
the turret window. The words floated down through the trees, clear
and sweet as the low notes of a flute.

'Only a child, my lady; a boy.'

'Is he hurt?'

'Are you hurted?' demanded the whitish man, who held him fast,
and repeated the question in Irish; but the child only kept blubbering
and crying for mercy, with his hands clasped, and trying to drop on his
knees.

Larry's strong old hand held him up. He *was* hurt, and bleeding
from over his eye.

'Just a trifle hurted, my lady!'

'Bring him up here.'

Shaeen Mull Ryan gave himself over. He was among 'the good
people,' who he knew would keep him prisoner for ever and a day.
There was no good in resisting. He grew bewildered, and yielded
himself passively to his fate, and emerged from the glen on the platform above; his captor's knotted old hand still on his arm, and looked
round on the tall mysterious trees, and the gray front of the castle,
revealed in the imperfect moonlight, as upon the scenery of a dream.

The old man who, with thin wiry legs, walked by his side, in a
dingy white coat, and blue facings, and great pewter buttons, with his
silver gray hair escaping from under his battered three-cocked hat;
and his shrewd puckered resolute face, in which the boy could read
no promise of sympathy, showing so white and phantom-like in the
moonlight, was, as he thought, the incarnate ideal of a fairy.

This figure led him in silence under the great arched gateway, and
across the grass-grown court, to the door in the far angle of the
building; and so, in the dark, round and round, up a stone screw stair,
and with a short turn into a large room, with a fire of turf and wood,
burning on its long unused hearth, over which hung a pot, and

about it an old woman with a great wooden spoon was busy. An iron candlestick supported their solitary candle; and about the floor of the room, as well as on the table and chairs, lay a litter of all sorts of things; piles of old faded hangings, boxes, trunks, clothes, pewter-plates, and cups; and I know not what more.

But what instantly engaged the fearful gaze of the boy were the figures of two ladies; red drugget cloaks they had on, like the peasant girls of Munster and Connaught, and the rest of their dress was pretty much in keeping. But they had the grand air, the refined expression and beauty, and above all, the serene air of command that belong to people of a higher rank.

The elder, with black hair and full brown eyes sat writing at the deal table on which the candle stood, and raised her dark gaze to the boy as he came in. The other, with her hood thrown back, beautiful and *riant*, with a flood of wavy golden hair, and great blue eyes, and with something kind, and arch, and strange in her countenance, struck him as the most wonderful beauty he could have imagined.

They questioned the man in a language strange to the child. It was not English, for he had a smattering of that, and the man's story seemed to amuse them. The two young ladies exchanged a glance, and smiled mysteriously. He was more convinced than ever that he was among the good people. The younger stepped gaily forward and said: 'Do you know who *I* am, my little man? Well, I'm the fairy Una, and this is my palace; and that fairy you see there (pointing to the dark lady, who was looking out something in a box), is my sister and family physician, the Lady Graveairs; and these (glancing at the old man and woman), are some of my courtiers; and I'm considering now what I shall do with you, whether I shall send *you* tonight to Lough Guir, riding on a rush, to make my compliments to the Earl of Desmond in his enchanted castle; or, straight to your bed, two thousand miles under ground, among the gnomes; or to prison in that little corner of the moon you see through the window – with the man-in-the-moon for your gaoler, for thrice three hundred years and a day! There, don't cry. You only see how serious a thing it is for you, little boys, to come so near my castle. Now, for this once, I'll let you go. But, hence-forward, any boys I, or my people, may find within half a mile round my castle, shall belong to me for life, and never behold their home or their people more.'

And she sang a little air and chased mystically half a dozen steps before him, holding out her cloak with her pretty fingers, and courtesying very low, to his indescribable alarm.

Then, with a little laugh, she said: 'My little man, we must mend your head.'

And so they washed his scratch, and the elder one applied a plaister to it. And she of the great blue eyes took out of her pocket a little French box of *bon-bons* and emptied it into his hand, and she said: 'You need not be afraid to eat these – they are very good – and I'll send my fairy, Blanc-et-bleu, to set you free. Take him (she addressed Larry), and let him go, with a solemn charge.'

The elder, with a grave and affectionate smile, said, looking on the fairy: 'Brave, dear, wild Una! nothing can ever quell your gaiety of heart.'

And Una kissed her merrily on the cheek.

So the oak door of the room again opened, and Shaeen, with his conductor, descended the stair. He walked with the scared boy in grim silence near halfway down the wild hillside toward Murroa, and then he stopped, and said in Irish: 'You never saw the fairies before, my fine fellow, and 'tisn't often those who once set eyes on us return to tell it. Whoever comes nearer, night or day, than this stone,' and he tapped it with the end of his cane, 'will never see his home again, for we'll keep him till the day of judgment; good-night, little gossoon – and away with you.'

So these young ladies, Alice and Una, with two old servants, by their father's direction, had taken up their abode in a portion of that side of the old castle which overhung the glen; and with the furniture and hangings they had removed from their late residence, and with the aid of glass in the casements and some other indispensable repairs, and a thorough airing, they made the rooms they had selected just habitable, as a rude and temporary shelter.

CHAPTER THREE

The Priest's Adventure in the Glen

At first, of course, they saw or heard little of their father. In general, however, they knew that his plan was to procure some employment in France, and to remove them there. Their present strange abode was only an adventure and an episode, and they believed that any day they might receive instructions to commence their journey.

After a little while the pursuit relaxed. The government, I believe, did not care, provided he did not obtrude himself, what became of him, or where he concealed himself. At all events, the local authorities showed no disposition to hunt him down. The young ladies' charges on the little forfeited property were paid without any dispute, and no vexatious enquiries were raised as to what had become of the furniture and other personal property which had been carried away from the forfeited house.

The haunted reputation of the castle – for in those days, in matters of the marvellous, the oldest were children – secured the little family in the seclusion they coveted. Once, or sometimes twice a week, old Laurence, with a shaggy little pony, made a secret expedition to the city of Limerick, starting before dawn, and returning under the cover of the night, with his purchases. There was beside an occasional sly moonlit visit from the old parish priest, and a midnight mass in the old castle for the little outlawed congregation.

As the alarm and enquiry subsided, their father made them, now and then, a brief and stealthy visit. At first these were but of a night's duration, and with great precaution; but gradually they were extended and less guarded. Still he was, as the phrase is in Munster, 'on his keeping.' He had firearms always by his bed, and had arranged places of concealment in the castle in the event of a surprise. But no attempt nor any disposition to molest him appearing, he grew more at ease, if not more cheerful.

It came, at last, that he would sometimes stay so long as two whole months at a time, and then depart as suddenly and mysteriously as he came. I suppose he had always some promising plot on hand, and his head full of ingenious treason, and lived on the sickly and exciting dietary of hope deferred.

Was there a poetical justice in this, that the little *ménage* thus secretly established, in the solitary and timeworn pile, should have themselves experienced, but from causes not so easily explicable, those very supernatural perturbations which they had themselves essayed to inspire?

The interruption of the old priest's secret visits was the earliest consequence of the mysterious interference which now began to display itself. One night, having left his cob in care of his old sacristan in the little village, he trudged on foot along the winding pathway, among the gray rocks and ferns that threaded the glen, intending a ghostly visit to the fair recluses of the castle, and he lost his way in this strange fashion.

There was moonlight, indeed, but it was little more than quarter-moon, and a long train of funereal clouds were sailing slowly across the sky – so that, faint and wan as it was, the light seldom shone full out, and was often hidden for a minute or two altogether. When he reached the point in the glen where the castle-stairs were wont to be, he could see nothing of them, and above, no trace of the castle-towers. So, puzzled somewhat, he pursued his way up the ravine, wondering how his walk had become so unusually protracted and fatiguing.

At last, sure enough, he saw the castle as plain as could be, and a lonely streak of candle-light issuing from the tower, just as usual, when his visit was expected. But he could not find the stair; and had to clamber among the rocks and copse-wood the best way he could. But when he emerged at top, there was nothing but the bare heath. Then the clouds stole over the moon again, and he moved along with hesitation and difficulty, and once more he saw the outline of the castle against the sky, quite sharp and clear. But this time it proved to be a great battlemented mass of cloud on the horizon. In a few minutes more he was quite close, all of a sudden, to the great front, rising gray and dim in the feeble light, and not till he could have struck it with his good oak 'wattle' did he discover it to be only one of those wild, gray frontages of living rock that rise here and there in picturesque tiers along the slopes of those solitary mountains. And so, till dawn, pursuing this mirage of the castle, through pools and among ravines, he wore out a night of miserable misadventure and fatigue.

Another night, riding up the glen, so far as the level way at bottom would allow, and intending to make his nag fast at his customary tree, he hears on a sudden a horrid shriek at top of the steep rocks above his head, and something – a gigantic human form, it seemed – came tumbling and bounding headlong down through the rocks, and fell with a fearful impetus just before his horse's hoofs and there lay like a huge palpitating carcass. The horse was scared, as, indeed, was his rider, too, and more so when this apparently lifeless thing sprang up to his legs, and throwing his arms apart to bar their further progress, advanced his white and gigantic face towards them. Then the horse started about, with a snort of terror, nearly unseating the priest, and broke away into a furious and uncontrollable gallop.

I need not recount all the strange and various misadventures which the honest priest sustained in his endeavours to visit the castle, and its isolated tenants. They were enough to wear out his resolution, and frighten him into submission. And so at last these spiritual visits quite ceased; and fearing to awaken enquiry and suspicion, he thought it only prudent to abstain from attempting them in the daytime.

So the young ladies of the castle were more alone than ever. Their father, whose visits were frequently of long duration, had of late ceased altogether to speak of their contemplated departure for France, grew angry at any allusion to it, and they feared, had abandoned the plan altogether.

CHAPTER FOUR

The Light in the Bell Tower

Shortly after the discontinuance of the priest's visits, old Laurence, one night, to his surprise, saw light issuing from a window in the Bell Tower. It was at first only a tremulous red ray, visible only for a few minutes, which seemed to pass from the room, through whose window it escaped upon the courtyard of the castle, and so to lose itself. This tower and casement were in the angle of the building, exactly confronting that in which the little outlawed family had taken up their quarters.

The whole family were troubled at the appearance of this dull red ray from the chamber in the Bell Tower. Nobody knew what to make of it. But Laurence, who had campaigned in Italy with his old master, the young ladies' grandfather – 'the heavens be his bed this night!' – was resolved to see it out, and took his great horse-pistols with him, and ascended to the corridor leading to the tower. But his search was vain.

This light left a sense of great uneasiness among the inmates, and most certainly it was not pleasant to suspect the establishment of an independent and possibly dangerous lodger or even colony, within the walls of the same old building.

The light very soon appeared again, steadier and somewhat brighter, in the same chamber. Again old Laurence buckled on his armour, swearing ominously to himself, and this time bent in earnest upon conflict. The young ladies watched in thrilling suspense from the great window in *their* stronghold, looking diagonally across the court. But as Laurence, who had entered the massive range of buildings opposite, might be supposed to be approaching the chamber from which this ill-omened glare proceeded, it steadily waned, finally disappearing altogether, just a few seconds before his voice was heard shouting from the arched window to know which way the light had gone.

This lighting up of the great chamber of the Bell Tower grew at last to be of frequent and almost continual recurrence. It was, there, long ago, in times of trouble and danger, that the de Lacys of those evil days used to sit in feudal judgment upon captive adversaries, and, as tradition alleged, often gave them no more time for shrift and prayer, than it needed to mount to the battlement of the turret overhead, from which they were forthwith hung by the necks, for a caveat and admonition to all evil disposed persons viewing the same from the country beneath.

Old Laurence observed these mysterious glimmerings with an evil and an anxious eye, and many and various were the stratagems he tried, but in vain, to surprise the audacious intruders. It is, however, I believe, a fact that no phenomenon, no matter how startling at first, if prosecuted with tolerable regularity, and unattended with any new circumstances of terror, will very long continue to excite alarm or even wonder.

So the family came to acquiesce in this mysterious light. No harm accompanied it. Old Laurence, as he smoked his lonely pipe in the grass-grown courtyard, would cast a disturbed glance at it, as it softly glowed out through the darking aperture, and mutter a prayer or an oath. But he had given over the chase as a hopeless business. And Peggy Sullivan, the old dame of all work, when, by chance, for she never willingly looked toward the haunted quarter, she caught the faint reflection of its dull effulgence with the corner of her eye, would sign herself with the cross or fumble at her beads, and deeper furrows would gather in her forehead, and her face grow ashen and perturbed. And this was not mended by the levity with which the young ladies, with whom the spectre had lost his influence, familiarity, as usual, breeding contempt, had come to talk, and even to jest, about it.

CHAPTER FIVE

The Man with the Claret-mark

But as the former excitement flagged, old Peggy Sullivan produced a new one; for she solemnly avowed that she had seen a thin-faced man, with an ugly red mark all over the side of his cheek, looking out of the same window, just at sunset, before the young ladies returned from their evening walk.

This sounded in their ears like an old woman's dream, but still it was an excitement, jocular in the morning, and just, perhaps, a little fearful as night overspread the vast and desolate building, but still, not wholly unpleasant. This little flicker of credulity suddenly, however, blazed up into the full light of conviction.

Old Laurence, who was not given to dreaming, and had a cool, hard head, and an eye like a hawk, saw the same figure, just about the same hour, when the last level gleam of sunset was tinting the summits of the towers and the tops of the tall trees that surrounded them.

He had just entered the court from the great gate, when he heard all at once the hard peculiar twitter of alarm which sparrows make when a cat or a hawk invades their safety, rising all round from the thick ivy that overclimbed the wall on his left, and raising his eyes listlessly, he saw, with a sort of shock, a thin, ungainly man, standing with his legs crossed in the recess of the window from which the light was wont to issue, leaning with his elbows on the stone mullion, and looking down with a sort of sickly sneer, his hollow yellow cheeks being deeply stained on one side with what is called a 'claret mark.'

'I have you at last, you villain!' cried Larry, in a strange rage and panic: 'drop down out of that on the grass here, and give yourself up, or I'll shoot you.'

The threat was backed with an oath, and he drew from his coat pocket the long holster pistol he was wont to carry, and covered his man cleverly.

'I give you while I count ten – one-two-three-four. If you draw back, I'll fire, mind; five-six – you'd better be lively – seven-eight-nine – one chance more; will you come down? Then take it – ten!'

Bang went the pistol. The sinister stranger was hardly fifteen feet removed from him, and Larry was a dead shot. But this time he made a scandalous miss, for the shot knocked a little white dust from the stone wall a full yard at one side; and the fellow never shifted his negligent posture or qualified his sardonic smile during the procedure.

Larry was mortified and angry.

'You'll not get off this time, my tulip!' he said with a grin, exchanging the smoking weapon for the loaded pistol in reserve.

'What are you pistolling, Larry?' said a familiar voice close by his elbow, and he saw his master, accompanied by a handsome young man in a cloak.

'That villain, your honour, in the window, there.'

'Why there's nobody there, Larry,' said de Lacy, with a laugh, though that was no common indulgence with him.

As Larry gazed, the figure somehow dissolved and broke up without receding. A hanging tuft of yellow and red ivy nodded queerly in place of the face, some broken and discoloured masonry in perspective took up the outline and colouring of the arms and figure, and two imperfect red and yellow lichen streaks carried on the curved tracing of the long spindle shanks. Larry blessed himself, and drew his hand across his damp forehead, over his bewildered eyes, and could not speak for a minute. It was all some devilish trick; he could take his oath he saw every feature in the fellow's face, the lace and buttons of his cloak and doublet, and even his long finger nails and thin yellow fingers that overhung the cross-shaft of the window, where there was now nothing but a rusty stain left.

The young gentleman who had arrived with de Lacy, staid that night and shared with great apparent relish the homely fare of the family. He was a gay and gallant Frenchman, and the beauty of the younger lady, and her pleasantry and spirit, seemed to make his hours pass but too swiftly, and the moment of parting sad.

When he had departed early in the morning, Ultor de Lacy had a long talk with his elder daughter, while the younger was busy with her early dairy task, for among their retainers this *proles generosa* reckoned a 'kind' little Kerry cow.

He told her that he had visited France since he had been last at Cappercullen, and how good and gracious their sovereign had been, and how he had arranged a noble alliance for her sister Una. The young gentleman was of high blood, and though not rich, had, nevertheless, his acres and his *nom de terre*, besides a captain's rank in the army. He was, in short, the very gentleman with whom they had parted only that morning. On what special business he was now in Ireland there was no necessity that he should speak; but being here he had brought him hither to present him to his daughter, and found that the impression she had made was quite what was desirable.

'You, you know, dear Alice, are promised to a conventual life. Had it been otherwise – '

He hesitated for a moment.

'You are right, dear father,' she said, kissing his hand, 'I *am* so promised, and no earthly tie or allurement has power to draw me from that holy engagement.'

'Well,' he said, returning her caress, 'I do not mean to urge you upon that point. It must not, however, be until Una's marriage has taken place. That cannot be, for many good reasons, sooner than this time twelve months; we shall then exchange this strange and barbarous abode for Paris, where are many eligible convents, in which are entertained as sisters some of the noblest ladies of France; and there, too, in Una's marriage will be continued, though not the name, at all events the blood, the lineage, and the title which, so sure as justice ultimately governs the course of human events, will be again established, powerful and honoured in this country, the scene of their ancient glory and transitory misfortunes. Meanwhile, we must not mention this engagement to Una. Here she runs no risk of being sought or won; but the mere knowledge that her hand was absolutely pledged, might excite a capricious opposition and repining such as neither I nor you would like to see; therefore be secret.'

The same evening he took Alice with him for a ramble round the castle wall, while they talked of grave matters, and he as usual allowed her a dim and doubtful view of some of those cloud-built castles in which he habitually dwelt, and among which his jaded hopes revived.

They were walking upon a pleasant short sward of darkest green, on one side overhung by the gray castle walls, and on the other by the forest trees that here and there closely approached it, when precisely as they turned the angle of the Bell Tower, they were encountered by a person walking directly towards them. The sight of a stranger, with the exception of the one visitor introduced by her father, was in this place so absolutely unprecedented, that Alice was amazed and affrighted to such a degree that for a moment she stood stock-still.

But there was more in this apparition to excite unpleasant emotions, than the mere circumstance of its unexpectedness. The figure was very strange, being that of a tall, lean, ungainly man, dressed in a dingy suit, somewhat of a Spanish fashion, with a brown laced cloak, and faded red stockings. He had long lank legs, long arms, hands, and fingers, and a very long sickly face, with a drooping nose, and a sly, sarcastic leer, and a great purplish stain over-spreading more than half of one cheek.

As he strode past, he touched his cap with his thin, discoloured fingers, and an ugly side glance, and disappeared round the corner. The eyes of father and daughter followed him in silence.

Ultor de Lacy seemed first absolutely terror-stricken, and then suddenly inflamed with ungovernable fury. He dropped his cane on the ground, drew his rapier, and, without wasting a thought on his daughter, pursued.

He just had a glimpse of the retreating figure as it disappeared round the far angle. The plume, and the lank hair, the point of the rapier-scabbard, the flutter of the skirt of the cloak, and one red stocking and heel; and this was the last he saw of him.

When Alice reached his side, his drawn sword still in his hand, he was in a state of abject agitation.

'Thank Heaven, he's gone!' she exclaimed.

'He's gone,' echoed Ultor, with a strange glare.

'And you are safe,' she added, clasping his hand.

He sighed a great sigh.

'And you don't think he's coming back?'

'He! – who?'

'The stranger who passed us but now. Do you know him, father?'

'Yes – and – no, child – I know him not – and yet I know him too well. Would to heaven we could leave this accursed haunt tonight. Cursed be the stupid malice that first provoked this horrible feud, which no sacrifice and misery can appease, and no exorcism can quell or even suspend. The wretch has come from afar with a sure instinct to devour my last hope – to dog us into our last retreat – and to blast with his triumph the very dust and ruins of our house. What ails that stupid priest that he has given over his visits? Are *my* children to be left without mass or confession – the sacraments which *guard* as well as save – because he once loses his way in a mist, or mistakes a streak of foam in the brook for a dead man's face? D—n him!'

'See, Alice, if he won't come,' he resumed, 'you must only *write* your confession to him in full – you and Una. Laurence is trusty, and will carry it – and we'll get the bishop's – or, if need be, the Pope's leave for him to give you absolution. I'll move heaven and earth, but you *shall* have the sacraments, poor children! – and see him. I've been a wild fellow in my youth, and never pretended to sanctity; but I know there's but one safe way – and – and – keep you each a bit of this – (he opened a small silver box) – about you while you stay here – fold and sew it up reverently in a bit of the old psaltery parchment and wear it next your hearts – 'tis a fragment of the consecrated wafer – and will help, with the saints' protection, to guard you from harm – and be strict in fasts, and constant in prayer – *I* can do nothing – nor devise any help. The curse has fallen, indeed, on me and mine.'

And Alice, saw, in silence, the tears of despair roll down his pale and agitated face.

This adventure was also a secret, and Una was to hear nothing of it.

CHAPTER SIX

Voices

Now Una, nobody knew why, began to lose spirit, and to grow pale. Her fun and frolic were quite gone! Even her songs ceased. She was silent with her sister, and loved solitude better. She said she was well, and quite happy, and could in no wise be got to account for the lamentable change that had stolen over her. She had grown odd too, and obstinate in trifles; and strangely reserved and cold.

Alice was very unhappy in consequence. What was the cause of this estrangement – had she offended her, and how? But Una had never before borne resentment for an hour. What could have altered her entire nature so? Could it be the shadow and chill of coming insanity?

Once or twice, when her sister urged her with tears and entreaties to disclose the secret of her changed spirits and demeanour, she seemed to listen with a sort of silent wonder and suspicion, and then she looked for a moment full upon her, and seemed on the very point of revealing all. But the earnest dilated gaze stole downward to the floor, and subsided into an odd wily smile, and she began to whisper to herself, and the smile and the whisper were both a mystery to Alice.

She and Alice slept in the same bedroom – a chamber in a projecting tower – which on their arrival, when poor Una was so merry, they had hung round with old tapestry, and decorated fantastically according to their skill and frolic. One night, as they went to bed, Una said, as if speaking to herself: ' 'Tis my last night in this room – I shall sleep no more with Alice.'

'And what has poor Alice done, Una, to deserve your strange unkindness?'

Una looked on her curiously, and half frightened, and then the odd smile stole over her face like a gleam of moonlight.

'My poor Alice, what have you to do with it?' she whispered.

'And why do you talk of sleeping no more with me?' said Alice.

'Why? Alice dear – no why – no reason – only a knowledge that it must be so, or Una will die.'

'Die, Una darling! – what can you mean?'

'Yes, sweet Alice, die, indeed. We must all die sometime, you know, or – or undergo a change; and my time is near – *very* near – unless I sleep apart from you.'

'Indeed, Una, sweetheart, I think you *are* ill, but not near death.'

'Una knows what you think, wise Alice – but she's not mad – on the contrary, she's wiser than other folks.'

'She's sadder and stranger too,' said Alice, tenderly.

'Knowledge is sorrow,' answered Una, and she looked across the room through her golden hair which she was combing – and through the window, beyond which lay the tops of the great trees, and the still foliage of the glen in the misty moonlight.

' 'Tis enough, Alice dear; it must be so. The bed must move hence, or Una's bed will be low enough ere long. See, it shan't be far though, only into that small room.'

She pointed to an inner room or closet opening from that in which they lay. The walls of the building were hugely thick, and there were double doors of oak between the chambers, and Alice thought, with a sigh, how completely separated they were going to be.

However she offered no opposition. The change was made, and the girls for the first time since childhood lay in separate chambers. A few nights afterwards Alice, awoke late in the night from a dreadful dream, in which the sinister figure which she and her father had encountered in their ramble round the castle walls, bore a principal part.

When she awoke there were still in her ears the sounds which had mingled in her dream. They were the notes of a deep, ringing, bass voice rising from the glen beneath the castle walls – something between humming and singing – listlessly unequal and intermittent, like the melody of a man whiling away the hours over his work. While she was wondering at this unwonted minstrelsy, there came a silence, and – could she believe her ears? – it certainly was Una's clear low contralto – softly singing a bar or two from the window. Then once more silence – and then again the strange manly voice, faintly chaunting from the leafy abyss.

With a strange wild feeling of suspicion and terror, Alice glided to the window. The moon who sees so many things, and keeps all secrets, with her cold impenetrable smile, was high in the sky. But Alice saw the red flicker of a candle from Una's window, and, she thought, the shadow of her head against the deep side wall of its recess. Then this was gone, and there were no more sights or sounds that night.

As they sate at breakfast, the small birds were singing merrily from among the sun-tipped foliage.

'I love this music,' said Alice, unusually pale and sad; 'it comes with the pleasant light of morning. I remember, Una, when *you* used to sing, like those gay birds, in the fresh beams of the morning; that was in the old time, when Una kept no secret from poor Alice.'

'And Una knows what her sage Alice means; but there are other birds, silent all day long, and, they say, the sweetest too, that love to sing by *night* alone.'

So things went on – the elder girl pained and melancholy – the younger silent, changed, and unaccountable.

A little while after this, very late one night, on awaking, Alice heard a conversation being carried on in her sister's room. There seemed to be no disguise about it. She could not distinguish the words, indeed, the walls being some six feet thick, and two great oak doors intercepting. But Una's clear voice, and the deep bell-like tones of the unknown, made up the dialogue.

Alice sprung from her bed, threw her clothes about her, and tried to enter her sister's room; but the inner door was bolted. The voices ceased to speak as she knocked, and Una opened it, and stood before her in her nightdress, candle in hand.

'Una – Una, darling, as you hope for peace, tell me who is here?' cried frightened Alice, with her trembling arms about her neck.

Una drew back, with her large, innocent blue eyes fixed full upon her.

'Come in, Alice,' she said, coldly.

And in came Alice, with a fearful glance around. There was no hiding place there; a chair, a table, a little bedstead, and two or three pegs in the wall to hang clothes on; a narrow window, with two iron bars across; no hearth or chimney – nothing but bare walls.

Alice looked round in amazement, and her eyes glanced with painful enquiry into those of her sister's. Una smiled one of her peculiar sidelong smiles, and said: 'Strange dreams! I've been dreaming – so has Alice. She hears and sees Una's dreams, and wonders – and well she may.'

And she kissed her sister's cheek with a cold kiss and lay down in her little bed, her slender hand under her head, and spoke no more.

Alice, not knowing what to think, went back to hers.

About this time Ultor de Lacy returned. He heard his elder daughter's strange narrative with marked uneasiness, and his agitation seemed to grow rather than subside. He enjoined her, however, not to mention it to the old servant, nor in presence of anybody she might chance to see, but only to him and to the priest, if he could be persuaded to resume his duty and return. The trial, however, such as it was, could not endure very long; matters had turned out favourably. The union of his younger daughter might be accomplished within a few months, and in eight or nine weeks they should be on their way to Paris.

A night or two after her father's arrival, Alice, in the dead of the night, heard the well-known strange deep voice speaking softly, as it seemed, close to her own window on the outside; and Una's voice, clear and tender, spoke in answer. She hurried to her own casement, and pushed it open, kneeling in the deep embrasure, and looking with a stealthy and affrighted gaze towards her sister's window. As she crossed the floor the voices subsided, and she saw a light withdrawn from within. The moonbeams slanted bright and clear on the whole side of the castle overlooking the glen, and she plainly beheld the shadow of a man projected on the wall as on a screen.

This black shadow recalled with a horrid thrill the outline and fashion of the figure in the Spanish dress. There were the cap and mantle, the rapier, the long thin limbs and sinister angularity. It was so thrown obliquely that the hands reached to the windowsill, and the feet stretched and stretched, longer and longer as she looked, toward the ground, and disappeared in the general darkness; and the rest, with a sudden flicker, shot downwards, as shadows will on the sudden movement of a light, and was lost in one gigantic leap down the castle wall.

'I do not know whether I dream or wake when I hear and see these sights; but I will ask my father to sit up with me, and we *two* surely cannot be mistaken. May the holy saints keep and guard us!' And in her terror she buried her head under the bedclothes, and whispered her prayers for an hour.

CHAPTER SEVEN

Una's Love

'I have been with Father Denis,' said de Lacy, next day, 'and he will come tomorrow; and, thank Heaven! you may both make your confession and hear mass, and my mind will be at rest; and you'll find poor Una happier and more like herself.'

But 'tween cup and lip there's many a slip. The priest was not destined to hear poor Una's shrift. When she bid her sister good-night she looked on her with her large, cold, wild eyes, till something of her old human affections seemed to gather there, and they slowly filled with tears, which dropped one after the other on her homely dress as she gazed in her sister's face.

Alice, delighted, sprang up, and clasped her arms about her neck. 'My own darling treasure, 'tis all over; you love your poor Alice again, and will be happier than ever.'

But while she held her in her embrace Una's eyes were turned towards the window, and her lips apart, and Alice felt instinctively that her thoughts were already far away.

'Hark! – listen! – hush!' and Una, with her delighted gaze fixed, as if she saw far away beyond the castle wall, the trees, the glen, and the night's dark curtain, held her hand raised near her ear, and waved her head slightly in time, as it seemed, to music that reached not Alice's ear, and smiled her strange pleased smile, and then the smile slowly faded away, leaving that sly suspicious light behind it which somehow scared her sister with an uncertain sense of danger; and she sang in tones so sweet and low that it seemed but a reverie of a song, recalling, as Alice fancied, the strain to which she had just listened in that strange ecstasy, the plaintive and beautiful Irish ballad, 'Shule, shule, shule, aroon,' the midnight summons of the outlawed Irish soldier to his darling to follow him.

Alice had slept little the night before. She was now overpowered with fatigue; and leaving her candle burning by her bedside, she fell into a deep sleep. From this she awoke suddenly, and completely, as will sometimes happen without any apparent cause, and she saw

Una come into the room. She had a little purse of embroidery – her own work – in her hand; and she stole lightly to the bedside, with her peculiar oblique smile, and evidently thinking that her sister was asleep.

Alice was thrilled with a strange terror, and did not speak or move; and her sister, slipped her hand softly under her bolster, and withdrew it. Then Una stood for a while by the hearth, and stretched her hand up to the mantelpiece, from which she took a little bit of chalk, and Alice thought she saw her place it in the fingers of a long yellow hand that was stealthily introduced from her own chamber door to receive it; and Una paused in the dark recess of the door, and smiled over her shoulder toward her sister, and then glided into her room, closing the doors.

Almost freezing with terror, Alice rose and glided after her, and stood in her chamber, screaming: 'Una, Una, in heaven's name what troubles you?'

But Una seemed to have been sound asleep in her bed, and raised herself with a start, and looking upon her with a peevish surprise, said: 'What does Alice seek here?'

'You were in my room, Una, dear; you seem disturbed and troubled.'

'Dreams, Alice. My dreams crossing your brain; only dreams – dreams. Get you to bed, and sleep.'

And to bed she went, but *not* to sleep. She lay awake more than an hour; and then Una emerged once more from her room. This time she was fully dressed, and had her cloak and thick shoes on, as their rattle on the floor plainly discovered. She had a little bundle tied up in a handkerchief in her hand, and her hood was drawn about her head; and thus equipped, as it seemed, for a journey, she came and stood at the foot of Alice's bed, and stared on her with a look so soulless and terrible that her senses almost forsook her. Then she turned and went back into her own chamber.

She may have returned; but Alice thought not – at least she did not see her. But she lay in great excitement and perturbation; and was terrified, about an hour later, by a knock at her chamber door – not that opening into Una's room, but upon the little passage from the stone screw staircase. She sprang from her bed; but the door was secured on the inside, and she felt relieved. The knock was repeated, and she heard someone laughing softly on the outside.

The morning came at last; that dreadful night was over. But Una! Where was Una?

Alice never saw her more. On the head of her empty bed were traced in chalk the words – Ultor de Lacy, Ultor O'Donnell. And Alice found beneath her own pillow the little purse of embroidery she had seen in Una's hand. It was her little parting token, and bore the simple legend – 'Una's love!'

De Lacy's rage and horror were boundless. He charged the priest, in frantic language, with having exposed his child, by his cowardice and neglect, to the machinations of the Fiend, and raved and blasphemed like a man demented.

It is said that he procured a solemn exorcism to be performed, in the hope of disenthralling and recovering his daughter. Several times, it is alleged, she was seen by the old servants. Once on a sweet summer morning, in the window of the tower, she was perceived combing her beautiful golden tresses, and holding a little mirror in her hand; and first, when she saw herself discovered, she looked affrighted, and then smiled, her slanting, cunning smile. Sometimes, too, in the glen, by moonlight, it was said belated villagers had met her, always startled first, and then smiling, generally singing snatches of old Irish ballads, that seemed to bear a sort of dim resemblance to her melancholy fate. The apparition has long ceased. But it is said that now and again, perhaps once in two or three years late on a summer night, you may hear – but faint and far away in the recesses of the glen – the sweet, sad notes of Una's voice, singing those plaintive melodies. This, too, of course, in time will cease, and all be forgotten.

CHAPTER EIGHT

Sister Agnes and the Portrait

When Ultor de Lacy died, his daughter Alice found among his effects a small box, containing a portrait such as I have described. When she looked on it, she recoiled in horror. There, in the plenitude of its sinister peculiarities, was faithfully portrayed the phantom which lived with a vivid and horrible accuracy in her remembrance. Folded in the same box was a brief narrative, stating that, 'A.D. 1601, in the month of

December, Walter de Lacy, of Cappercullen, made many prisoners at the ford of Ownhey, or Abington, of Irish and Spanish soldiers, flying from the great overthrow of the rebel powers at Kinsale, and among the number one Roderic O'Donnell, an arch traitor, and near kinsman to that other O'Donnell who led the rebels; who, claiming kindred through his mother to de Lacy, sued for his life with instant and miserable entreaty, and offered great ransom, but was by de Lacy, through great zeal for the queen, as some thought, cruelly put to death. When he went to the tower-top, where was the gallows, finding himself in extremity, and no hope of mercy, he swore that though he could work them no evil before his death, yet that he would devote himself thereafter to blast the greatness of the de Lacys, and never leave them till his work was done. He hath been seen often since, and always for that family perniciously, insomuch that it hath been the custom to show to young children of that lineage the picture of the said O'Donnell, in little, taken among his few valuables, to prevent their being misled by him unawares, so that he should not have his will, who by devilish wiles and hell-born cunning, hath steadfastly sought the ruin of that ancient house, and especially to leave that *stemma generosum* destitute of issue for the transmission of their pure blood and worshipful name.'

Old Miss Croker, of Ross House, who was near seventy in the year 1821, when she related this story to me, had seen and conversed with Alice de Lacy, a professed nun, under the name of Sister Agnes, in a religious house in King Street, in Dublin, founded by the famous Duchess of Tyrconnell, and had the narrative from her own lips. I thought the tale worth preserving, and have no more to say.

SHERIDAN LE FANU

The Vision of Tom Chuff

At the edge of melancholy Catstean Moor, in the north of England, with half a dozen ancient poplar trees with rugged and hoary stems around, one smashed across the middle by a flash of lightning thirty summers before, and all by their great height dwarfing the abode near which they stand, there squats a rude stone house, with a thick chimney, a kitchen and bedroom on the ground floor, and a loft, accessible by a ladder, under the shingle roof, divided into two rooms.

Its owner was a man of ill repute. Tom Chuff was his name. A shock-headed, broad-shouldered, powerful man, though somewhat short, with lowering brows and a sullen eye. He was a poacher, and hardly made an ostensible pretence of earning his bread by any honest industry. He was a drunkard. He beat his wife, and led his children a life of terror and lamentation, when he was at home. It was a blessing to his frightened little family when he absented himself, as he some-times did, for a week or more together.

On the night I speak of he knocked at the door with his cudgel at about eight o'clock. It was winter, and the night was very dark. Had the summons been that of a bogie from the moor, the inmates of this small house could hardly have heard it with greater terror.

His wife unbarred the door in fear and haste. Her hunchbacked sister stood by the hearth, staring toward the threshold. The children cowered behind.

Tom Chuff entered with his cudgel in his hand, without speaking, and threw himself into a chair opposite the fire. He had been away two or three days. He looked haggard, and his eyes were bloodshot. They knew he had been drinking.

Tom raked and knocked the peat fire with his stick, and thrust his feet close to it. He signed towards the little dresser, and nodded to his wife, and she knew he wanted a cup, which in silence she gave him. He pulled a bottle of gin from his coat-pocket, and nearly filling the teacup, drank off the dram at a few gulps.

He usually refreshed himself with two or three drams of this kind before beating the inmates of his house. His three little children, cowering in a corner, eyed him from under a table, as Jack did the ogre in the nursery tale. His wife, Nell, standing behind a chair, which she was ready to snatch up to meet the blow of the cudgel, which might be levelled at her at any moment, never took her eyes off him; and hunchbacked Mary showed the whites of a large pair of eyes, similarly employed, as she stood against the oaken press, her dark face hardly distinguishable in the distance from the brown panel behind it.

Tom Chuff was at his third dram, and had not yet spoken a word since his entrance, and the suspense was growing dreadful, when, on a sudden, he leaned back in his rude seat, the cudgel slipped from his hand, a change and a deathlike pallor came over his face.

For a while they all stared on; such was their fear of him, they dared not speak or move, lest it should prove to have been but a doze, and Tom should wake up and proceed forthwith to gratify his temper and exercise his cudgel.

In a very little time, however, things began to look so odd, that they ventured, his wife and Mary, to exchange glances full of doubt and wonder. He hung so much over the side of the chair, that if it had not been one of cyclopean clumsiness and weight, he would have borne it to the floor. A leaden tint was darkening the pallor of his face. They were becoming alarmed, and finally braving everything his wife timidly said, 'Tom!' and then more sharply repeated it, and finally cried the appellative loudly, and again and again, with the terrified accompaniment, 'He's dying – he's dying!' her voice rising to a scream, as she found that neither it nor her plucks and shakings of him by the shoulder had the slightest effect in recalling him from his torpor.

And now from sheer terror of a new kind the children added their shrilly piping to the talk and cries of their seniors; and if anything could have called Tom up from his lethargy, it might have been the piercing chorus that made the rude chamber of the poacher's habitation ring again. But Tom continued unmoved, deaf, and stirless.

His wife sent Mary down to the village, hardly a quarter of a mile away, to implore of the doctor, for whose family she did duty as laundress, to come down and look at her husband, who seemed to be dying.

The doctor, who was a good-natured fellow, arrived. With his hat still on, he looked at Tom, examined him, and when he found that the emetic he had brought with him, on conjecture from Mary's description, did not act, and that his lancet brought no blood, and that he felt a pulseless wrist, he shook his head, and inwardly thought: 'What the plague is the woman crying for? Could she have desired a greater blessing for her children and herself than the very thing that has happened?'

Tom, in fact, seemed quite gone. At his lips no breath was perceptible. The doctor could discover no pulse. His hands and feet were cold, and the chill was stealing up into his body.

The doctor, after a stay of twenty minutes, had buttoned up his greatcoat again and pulled down his hat, and told Mrs Chuff that there was no use in his remaining any longer, when, all of a sudden, a little rill of blood began to trickle from the lancet-cut in Tom Chuff's temple.

'That's very odd,' said the doctor. 'Let us wait a little.'

I must describe now the sensations which Tom Chuff had experienced.

With his elbows on his knees, and his chin upon his hands, he was staring into the embers, with his gin beside him, when suddenly a swimming came in his head, he lost sight of the fire, and a sound like one stroke of a loud church bell smote his brain.

Then he heard a confused humming, and the leaden weight of his head held him backward as he sank in his chair, and consciousness quite forsook him.

When he came to himself he felt chilled, and was leaning against a huge leafless tree. The night was moonless, and when he looked up he thought he had never seen stars so large and bright, or sky so black. The stars, too, seemed to blink down with longer intervals of darkness, and fiercer and more dazzling emergence, and something, he vaguely thought, of the character of silent menace and fury.

He had a confused recollection of having come there, or rather of having been carried along, as if on men's shoulders, with a sort of rushing motion. But it was utterly indistinct; the imperfect recollection simply of a sensation. He had seen or heard nothing on his way.

He looked round. There was not a sign of a living creature near. And he began with a sense of awe to recognise the place.

The tree against which he had been leaning was one of the noble old beeches that surround at irregular intervals the churchyard of Shackleton, which spreads its green and wavy lap on the edge of the Moor of Catstean, at the opposite side of which stands the rude cottage in which he had just lost consciousness. It was six miles or more across the moor to his habitation, and the black expanse lay before him, disappearing dismally in the darkness. So that, looking straight before him, sky and land blended together in an undistinguishable and awful blank.

There was a silence quite unnatural over the place. The distant murmur of the brook, which he knew so well, was dead; not a whisper in the leaves above him; the air, earth, everything about and above was indescribably still; and he experienced that quaking of the heart that seems to portend the approach of something awful. He would have set out upon his return across the moor, had he not an undefined presentiment that he was waylaid by something he dared not pass.

The old grey church and tower of Shackleton stood like a shadow in the rear. His eye had grown accustomed to the obscurity, and he could just trace its outline. There were no comforting associations in his mind connected with it; nothing but menace and misgiving. His early training in his lawless calling was connected with this very spot. Here his father used to meet two other poachers, and bring his son, then but a boy, with him.

Under the church porch, towards morning, they used to divide the game they had taken, and take account of the sales they had made on the previous day, and make partition of the money, and drink their gin. It was here he had taken his early lessons in drinking, cursing and lawlessness. His father's grave was hardly eight steps from the spot where he stood. In his present state of awful dejection, no scene on earth could have so helped to heighten his fear.

There was one object close by which added to his gloom. About a yard away, in rear of the tree, behind himself, and extending to his left, was an open grave, the mould and rubbish piled on the other side. At the head of this grave stood the beech tree; its columnar stem rose like a huge monumental pillar. He knew every line and crease on its smooth surface. The initial letters of his own name, cut in its bark long ago, had spread out and wrinkled like the grotesque capitals of a fanciful engraver, and now with a sinister significance overlooked the open grave, as if answering his mental question, 'Who for is t' grave cut?'

He felt still a little stunned, and there was a faint tremor in his joints that disinclined him to exert himself; and, further, he had a vague apprehension that take what direction he might, there was danger around him worse than that of staying where he was.

On a sudden the stars began to blink more fiercely, a faint wild light overspread for a minute the bleak landscape, and he saw approaching from the moor a figure at a kind of swinging trot, with now and then a zig-zag hop or two, such as men accustomed to cross such places make, to avoid the patches of slob or quag that meet them here and there. This figure resembled his father's, and like him, whistled through his finger by way of signal as he approached; but the whistle sounded not now shrilly and sharp, as in old times, but immensely far away, and seemed to sing strangely through Tom's head. From habit or from fear, in answer to the signal, Tom whistled as he used to do five-and-twenty years ago and more, although he was already chilled with an unearthly fear.

Like his father, too, the figure held up the bag that was in his left hand as he drew near, when it was his custom to call out to him what was in it. It did not reassure the watcher, you may be certain, when a shout unnaturally faint reached him, as the phantom dangled the bag in the air, and he heard with a faint distinctness the words, 'Tom Chuff's soul!'

Scarcely fifty yards away from the low churchyard fence at which Tom was standing, there was a wider chasm in the peat, which there threw up a growth of reeds and bulrushes, among which, as the old poacher used to do on a sudden alarm, the approaching figure suddenly cast itself down.

From the same patch of tall reeds and rushes emerged instantaneously what he at first mistook for the same figure creeping on all-fours, but what he soon perceived to be an enormous black dog with a rough coat like a bear's, which at first sniffed about, and then started towards him in what seemed to be a sportive amble, bouncing this way and that, but as it drew near it displayed a pair of fearful eyes that glowed like live coals, and emitted from the monstrous expanse of its jaws a terrifying growl.

This beast seemed on the point of seizing him, and Tom recoiled in panic and fell into the open grave behind him. The edge which he caught as he tumbled gave way, and down he went, expecting almost at the same instant to reach the bottom. But never was such a fall! Bottomless seemed the abyss! Down, down, down, with immeasurable and still increasing speed, through utter darkness, with hair streaming straight upward, breathless, he shot with a rush of air against him, the force of which whirled up his very arms, second after second, minute after minute, through the chasm downward he flew, the icy perspiration of horror covering his body, and suddenly, as he expected to be dashed into annihilation, his descent was in an instant arrested with a tremendous shock, which, however, did not deprive him of consciousness even for a moment.

He looked about him. The place resembled a smoke-stained cavern or catacomb, the roof of which, except for a ribbed arch here and there faintly visible, was lost in darkness. From several rude passages, like the galleries of a gigantic mine, which opened from this centre chamber, was very dimly emitted a dull glow as of charcoal, which was the only light by which he could imperfectly discern the objects immediately about him.

What seemed like a projecting piece of the rock, at the corner of one of these murky entrances, moved on a sudden, and proved to be a human figure, that beckoned to him. He approached, and saw his father. He could barely recognise him, he was so monstrously altered.

'I've been looking for you, Tom. Welcome home, lad; come along to your place.'

Tom's heart sank as he heard these words, which were spoken in a hollow and, he thought, derisive voice that made him tremble. But he could not help accompanying the wicked spirit, who led him into a place, in passing which he heard, as it were from within the rock, dreadful cries and appeals for mercy.

'What is this?' said he.

'Never mind.'

'Who are they?'

'New-comers, like yourself, lad,' answered his father apathetically. 'They give over that work in time, finding it is no use.'

'What shall I do?' said Tom, in an agony.

'It's all one.'

'But what shall I do?' reiterated Tom, quivering in every joint and nerve.

'Grin and bear it, I suppose.'

'For God's sake, if ever you cared for me, as I am your own child, let me out of this!'

'There's no way out.'

'If there's a way in there's a way out, and for Heaven's sake let me out of this.'

But the dreadful figure made no further answer, and glided backwards by his shoulder to the rear; and others appeared in view, each with a faint red halo round it, staring on him with frightful eyes, images, all in hideous variety, of eternal fury or derision. He was growing mad, it seemed, under the stare of so many eyes, increasing in number and drawing closer every moment, and at the same time myriads and myriads of voices were calling him by his name, some far away, some near, some from one point, some from another, some from behind, close to his ears. These cries were increased in rapidity and multitude, and mingled with laughter, with flitting blasphemies, with broken insults and mockeries, succeeded and obliterated by others, before he could half catch their meaning.

All this time, in proportion to the rapidity and urgency of these dreadful sights and sounds, the epilepsy of terror was creeping up to his brain, and with a long and dreadful scream he lost consciousness.

When he recovered his senses, he found himself in a small stone chamber, vaulted above, and with a ponderous door. A single point of light in the wall, with a strange brilliancy illuminated this cell.

Seated opposite to him was a venerable man with a snowy beard of immense length; an image of awful purity and severity. He was dressed in a coarse robe, with three large keys suspended from his girdle. He might have filled one's idea of an ancient porter of a city gate; such spiritual cities, I should say, as John Bunyan loved to describe.

This old man's eyes were brilliant and awful, and fixed on him as they were, Tom Chuff felt himself helplessly in his power. At length he spoke: 'The command is given to let you forth for one trial more. But if you are found again drinking with the drunken, and beating your fellow-servants, you shall return through the door by which you came, and go out no more.'

With these words the old man took him by the wrist and led him through the first door, and then unlocking one that stood in the cavern outside, he struck Tom Chuff sharply on the shoulder, and the door shut behind him with a sound that boomed peal after peal of thunder near and far away, and all round and above, till it rolled off gradually into silence. It was totally dark, but there was a fanning of fresh cool air that overpowered him. He felt that he was in the upper world again.

In a few minutes he began to hear voices which he knew, and first a faint point of light appeared before his eyes, and gradually he saw the flame of the candle, and, after that, the familiar faces of his wife and children, and he heard them faintly when they spoke to him, although he was as yet unable to answer.

He also saw the doctor, like an isolated figure in the dark, and heard him say: 'There, now, you have him back. He'll do, I think.'

His first words, when he could speak and saw clearly all about him, and felt the blood on his neck and shirt, were: 'Wife, forgie me. I'm a changed man. Send for 't sir.'

Which last phrase means, 'Send for the clergyman.'

When the vicar came and entered the little bedroom where the scared poacher, whose soul had died within him, was lying, still sick and weak, in his bed, and with a spirit that was prostrate with terror, Tom Chuff feebly beckoned the rest from the room, and, the door being closed, the good parson heard the strange confession, and with equal amazement the man's earnest and agitated vows of amendment, and his helpless appeals to him for support and counsel.

These, of course, were kindly met; and the visits of the rector, for some time, were frequent.

One day, when he took Tom Chuff's hand on bidding him goodbye, the sick man held it still, and said: 'Ye'r vicar o' Shackleton, sir, and if I sud dee, ye'll promise me a'e thing, as I a promised ye a many. I a said I'll never gie wife, nor barn, nor folk o' no sort, skelp nor sizzup more, and ye'll know o' me no more among the sipers. Nor never will Tom draw trigger, nor set a snare again, but in an honest way, and after that ye'll no make it a bootless bene for me, but bein', as I say, vicar o' Shackleton, and able to do as ye list, ye'll no let them bury me within twenty good yerd-wands measure o' the a'd beech trees that's round the churchyard of Shackleton.'

'I see; you would have your grave, when your time really comes, a good way from the place where lay the grave you dreamed of.'

'That's jest it. I'd lie at the bottom o' a marl-pit liefer! And I'd be laid in anither churchyard just to be shut o' my fear o' that, but that a' my kinsfolk is buried beyond in Shackleton, and ye'll gie me yer promise, and no break yer word.'

'I do promise, certainly. I'm not likely to outlive you; but, if I should, and still be vicar of Shackleton, you shall be buried somewhere as near the middle of the churchyard as we can find space.'

'That'll do.'

And so content they parted.

The effect of the vision upon Tom Chuff was powerful, and promised to be lasting. With a sore effort he exchanged his life of desultory adventure and comparative idleness for one of regular industry. He gave up drinking; he was as kind as an originally surly nature would allow to his wife and family; he went to church; in fine weather they crossed the moor to Shackleton Church; the vicar said he came there to look at the scenery of his vision, and to fortify his good resolutions by the reminder.

Impressions upon the imagination, however, are but transitory, and a bad man acting under fear is not a free agent; his real character does not appear. But as the images of the imagination fade, and the action of fear abates, the essential qualities of the man reassert themselves.

So, after a time, Tom Chuff began to grow weary of his new life; he grew lazy, and people began to say that he was catching hares, and pursuing his old contraband way of life, under the rose.

He came home one hard night, with signs of the bottle in his thick speech and violent temper. Next day he was sorry, or frightened, at all events repentant, and for a week or more something of the old horror returned, and he was once more on his good behaviour. But in a little time came a relapse, and another repentance, and then a relapse again, and gradually the return of old habits and the flooding in of all his old way of life, with more violence and gloom, in proportion as the man was alarmed and exasperated by the remembrance of his despised, but terrible, warning.

With the old life returned the misery of the cottage. The smiles, which had begun to appear with the unwonted sunshine, were seen no more. Instead, returned to his poor wife's face the old pale and heartbroken look. The cottage lost its neat and cheerful air, and the melancholy of neglect was visible. Sometimes at night were overheard, by a chance passer-by, cries and sobs from that ill-omened dwelling. Tom Chuff was now often drunk, and not very often at home, except when he came in to sweep away his poor wife's earnings.

Tom had long lost sight of the honest old parson. There was shame mixed with his degradation. He had grace enough left when he saw the thin figure of 't' sir' walking along the road to turn out of his way and avoid meeting him. The clergyman shook his head, and some-times groaned, when his name was mentioned. His horror and regret were more for the poor wife than for the relapsed sinner, for her case was pitiable indeed.

Her brother, Jack Everton, coming over from Hexley, having heard stories of all this, determined to beat Tom, for his ill-treatment of his sister, within an inch of his life. Luckily, perhaps, for all concerned, Tom happened to be away upon one of his long excursions, and poor Nell besought her brother, in extremity of terror, not to interpose between them. So he took his leave and went home muttering and sulky.

Now it happened a few months later that Nelly Chuff fell sick. She had been ailing, as heartbroken people do, for a good while. But now the end had come.

There was a coroner's inquest when she died, for the doctor had doubts as to whether a blow had not, at least, hastened her death. Nothing certain, however, came of the enquiry. Tom Chuff had left his home more than two days before his wife's death. He was absent upon his lawless business still when the coroner had held his quest.

Jack Everton came over from Hexley to attend the dismal obsequies of his sister. He was more incensed than ever with the wicked husband, who, one way or other, had hastened Nelly's death. The inquest had closed early in the day. The husband had not appeared.

An occasional companion – perhaps I ought to say accomplice – of Chuff's happened to turn up. He had left him on the borders of Westmoreland, and said he would probably be home next day. But Everton affected not to believe it. Perhaps it was to Tom Chuff, he suggested, a secret satisfaction to crown the history of his bad married life with the scandal of his absence from the funeral of his neglected and abused wife.

Everton had taken on himself the direction of the melancholy preparations. He had ordered a grave to be opened for his sister beside her mother's, in Shackleton churchyard, at the other side of the moor. For the purpose, as I have said, of marking the callous neglect of her husband, he determined that the funeral should take place that night. His brother Dick had accompanied him, and they and his sister, with Mary and the children, and a couple of the neighbours, formed the humble cortège.

Jack Everton said he would wait behind, on the chance of Tom Chuff coming in time, that he might tell him what had happened, and make him cross the moor with him to meet the funeral. His real object, I think, was to inflict upon the villain the drubbing he had so long wished to give him. Anyhow, he was resolved, by crossing the moor, to reach the churchyard in time to anticipate the arrival of the funeral, and to have a few words with the vicar, clerk, and sexton, all old friends of his, for the parish of Shackleton was the place of his birth and early recollections.

But Tom Chuff did not appear at his house that night. In surly mood, and without a shilling in his pocket, he was making his way homeward. His bottle of gin, his last investment, half emptied, with its neck protruding, as usual on such returns, was in his coat-pocket.

His way home lay across the moor of Catstean, and the point at which he best knew the passage was from the churchyard of Shackleton. He vaulted the low wall that forms its boundary, and strode across the graves, and over many a flat, half-buried tombstone, toward the side of the churchyard next Catstean Moor.

The old church of Shackleton and its tower rose, close at his right, like a black shadow against the sky. It was a moonless night, but clear. By this time he had reached the low boundary wall, at the other side, that overlooks the wide expanse of Catstean Moor. He stood by one of the huge old beech trees, and leaned his back to its smooth trunk. Had he ever seen the sky look so black, and the stars shine out and blink so vividly? There was a deathlike silence over the scene, like the hush that precedes thunder in sultry weather. The expanse before him was lost in utter blackness. A strange quaking unnerved his heart. It was the sky and scenery of his vision! The same horror and misgiving. The same invincible fear of venturing from the spot where he stood. He would have prayed if he dared. His sinking heart demanded a restorative of some sort, and he grasped the bottle in his coat-pocket.

Turning to his left, as he did so, he saw the piled-up mould of an open grave that gaped with its head close to the base of the great tree against which he was leaning.

He stood aghast. His dream was returning and slowly enveloping him. Everything he saw was weaving itself into the texture of his vision. The chill of horror stole over him.

A faint whistle came shrill and clear over the moor, and he saw a figure approaching at a swinging trot, with a zig-zag course, hopping now here and now there, as men do over a surface where one has need to choose their steps. Through the jungle of reeds and bulrushes in the foreground this figure advanced; and with the same unaccountable impulse that had coerced him in his dream, he answered the whistle of the advancing figure.

On that signal it directed its course straight toward him. It mounted the low wall, and, standing there, looked into the graveyard.

'Who med answer?' challenged the new-comer from his post of observation.

'Me,' answered Tom.

'Who are you?' repeated the man upon the wall.

'Tom Chuff; and who's this grave cut for?' He answered in a savage tone, to cover the secret shudder of his panic.

'I'll tell you that, ye villain!' answered the stranger, descending from the wall, 'I a' looked for you far and near, and waited long, and now you're found at last.'

Not knowing what to make of the figure that advanced upon him, Tom Chuff recoiled, stumbled, and fell backward into the open grave. He caught at the sides as he fell, but without retarding his fall.

An hour after, when lights came with the coffin, the corpse of Tom Chuff was found at the bottom of the grave. He had fallen direct upon his head, and his neck was broken. His death must have been simultaneous with his fall. Thus far his dream was accomplished.

It was his brother-in-law who had crossed the moor and approached the churchyard of Shackleton, exactly in the line which the image of his father had seemed to take in his strange vision. Fortunately for Jack Everton, the sexton and clerk of Shackleton church were, unseen by him, crossing the churchyard toward the grave of Nelly Chuff, just as Tom the poacher stumbled and fell. Suspicion of direct violence would otherwise have inevitably attached to the exasperated brother. As it was, the catastrophe was followed by no legal consequences.

The good vicar kept his word, and the grave of Tom Chuff is still pointed out by the old inhabitants of Shackleton pretty nearly in the centre of the churchyard. This conscientious compliance with the entreaty of the panic-stricken man as to the place of his sepulture gave a horrible and mocking emphasis to the strange combination by which fate had defeated his precaution, and fixed the place of his death.

The story was for many a year, and we believe still is, told round many a cottage hearth, and though it appeals to what many would term superstition, it yet sounded, in the ears of a rude and simple audience, a thrilling, and, let us hope, not altogether fruitless homily.

SHERIDAN LE FANU

Stories of Lough Guir

❧❀❧

When the present writer was a boy of twelve or thirteen, he first made
the acquaintance of Miss Anne Baily, of Lough Guir, in the county of
Limerick. She and her sister were the last representatives at that place,
of an extremely good old name in the county. They were both what is
termed 'old maids,' and at that time past sixty. But never were old
ladies more hospitable, lively, and kind, especially to young people.
They were both remarkably agreeable and clever. Like all old county
ladies of their time, they were great genealogists, and could recount
the origin, generations, and intermarriages, of every county family of
note.

These ladies were visited at their house at Lough Guir by Mr
Crofton Croker; and are, I think, mentioned, by name, in the second
series of his fairy legends; the series in which (probably communicated
by Miss Anne Baily), he recounts some of the picturesque traditions of
those beautiful lakes – lakes, I should no longer say, for the smaller
and prettier has since been drained, and gave up from its depths some
long lost and very interesting relics.

In their drawing-room stood a curious relic of another sort: old
enough, too, though belonging to a much more modern period. It
was the ancient stirrup cup of the hospitable house of Lough Guir.
Crofton Croker has preserved a sketch of this curious glass. I have
often had it in my hand. It had a short stem; and the cup part, having
the bottom rounded, rose cylindrically, and, being of a capacity to
contain a whole bottle of claret, and almost as narrow as an old
fashioned ale glass, was tall to a degree that filled me with wonder. As
it obliged the rider to extend his arm as he raised the glass, it must
have tried a tipsy man, sitting in the saddle, pretty severely. The

wonder was that the marvellous tall glass had come down to our times without a crack.

There was another glass worthy of remark in the same drawing-room. It was gigantic, and shaped conically, like one of those old fashioned jelly glasses which used to be seen upon the shelves of confectioners. It was engraved round the rim with the words, 'The glorious, pious, and immortal memory'; and on grand occasions, was filled to the brim, and after the manner of a loving cup, made the circuit of the Whig guests, who owed all to the hero whose memory its legend invoked.

It was now but the transparent phantom of those solemn con-vivialities of a generation, who lived, as it were, within hearing of the cannon and shoutings of those stirring times. When I saw it, this glass had long retired from politics and carousals, and stood peacefully on a little table in the drawing-room, where ladies' hands replenished it with fair water, and crowned it daily with flowers from the garden.

Miss Anne Baily's conversation ran oftener than her sister's upon the legendary and supernatural; she told her stories with the sympathy, the colour, and the mysterious air which contribute so powerfully to effect, and never wearied of answering questions about the old castle, and amusing her young audience with fascinating little glimpses of old adventure and bygone days. My memory retains the picture of my early friend very distinctly. A slim straight figure, above the middle height; a general likeness to the full-length portrait of that delightful Countess D'Aulnois, to whom we all owe our earliest and most brilliant glimpses of fairyland; something of her gravely-pleasant countenance, plain, but refined and ladylike, with that kindly mystery in her sidelong glance and uplifted finger, which indicated the approaching climax of a tale of wonder.

Lough Guir is a kind of centre of the operations of the Munster fairies. When a child is stolen by the 'good people,' Lough Guir is conjectured to be the place of its unearthly transmutation from the human to the fairy state. And beneath its waters lie enchanted, the grand old castle of the Desmonds, the great earl himself, his beautiful young countess, and all the retinue that surrounded him in the years of his splendour, and at the moment of his catastrophe.

Here, too, are historic associations. The huge square tower that rises at one side of the stable-yard close to the old house, to a height that amazed my young eyes, though robbed of its battlements and one story, was a stronghold of the last rebellious Earl of Desmond, and is specially mentioned in that delightful old folio, the *Hibernia Pacata*, as having, with its Irish garrison on the battlements, defied the army of the lord deputy, then marching by upon the summits of the overhanging hills. The house, built under shelter of this stronghold of the once proud and turbulent Desmonds, is old, but snug, with a multitude of small low rooms, such as I have seen in houses of the same age in Shropshire and the neighbouring English counties.

The hills that overhang the lakes appeared to me, in my young days (and I have not seen them since), to be clothed with a short soft verdure, of a hue so dark and vivid as I had never seen before.

In one of the lakes is a small island, rocky and wooded, which is believed by the peasantry to represent the top of the highest tower of the castle which sank, under a spell, to the bottom. In certain states of the atmosphere, I have heard educated people say, when in a boat you have reached a certain distance, the island appears to rise some feet from the water, its rocks assume the appearance of masonry, and the whole circuit presents very much the effect of the battlements of a castle rising above the surface of the lake.

This was Miss Anne Baily's story of the submersion of this lost castle:

THE MAGICIAN EARL

It is well known that the great Earl of Desmond, though history pretends to dispose of him differently, lives to this hour enchanted in his castle, with all his household, at the bottom of the lake.

There was not, in his day, in all the world, so accomplished a magician as he. His fairest castle stood upon an island in the lake, and to this he brought his young and beautiful bride, whom he loved but too well; for she prevailed upon his folly to risk all to gratify her imperious caprice.

They had not been long in this beautiful castle, when she one day presented herself in the chamber in which her husband studied his forbidden art, and there implored him to exhibit before her some of the wonders of his evil science. He resisted long; but her entreaties, tears, and wheedlings were at length too much for him and he consented.

But before beginning those astonishing transformations with which he was about to amaze her, he explained to her the awful conditions and dangers of the experiment.

Alone in this vast apartment, the walls of which were lapped, far below, by the lake whose dark waters lay waiting to swallow them, she must witness a certain series of frightful phenomena, which once commenced, he could neither abridge nor mitigate; and if throughout their ghastly succession she spoke one word, or uttered one exclamation, the castle and all that it contained would in one instant subside to the bottom of the lake, there to remain, under the servitude of a strong spell, for ages.

The dauntless curiosity of the lady having prevailed, and the oaken door of the study being locked and barred, the fatal experiments commenced.

Muttering a spell, as he stood before her, feathers sprouted thickly over him, his face became contracted and hooked, a cadaverous smell filled the air, and, with heavy winnowing wings, a gigantic vulture rose in his stead, and swept round and round the room, as if on the point of pouncing upon her.

The lady commanded herself through this trial, and instantly another began.

The bird alighted near the door, and in less than a minute changed, she saw not how, into a horribly deformed and dwarfish hag: who, with yellow skin hanging about her face and enormous eyes, swung herself on crutches toward the lady, her mouth foaming with fury, and her grimaces and contortions becoming more and more hideous every moment, till she rolled with a yell on the floor, in a horrible convulsion, at the lady's feet, and then changed into a huge serpent, with crest erect, and quivering tongue. Suddenly, as it seemed on the point of darting at her, she saw her husband in its stead, standing pale before her, and, with his finger on his lip, enforcing the continued necessity of silence. He then placed himself at his length on the floor, and began to stretch himself out and out, longer and longer, until his head nearly reached to one end of the vast room, and his feet to the other.

This horror overcame her. The ill-starred lady uttered a wild scream, whereupon the castle and all that was within it, sank in a moment to the bottom of the lake.

But, once in every seven years, by night, the Earl of Desmond and his retinue emerge, and cross the lake, in shadowy cavalcade. His white horse is shod with silver. On that one night, the earl may ride till daybreak, and it behoves him to make good use of his time; for, until the silver shoes of his steed be worn through, the spell that holds him and his beneath the lake, will retain its power.

When I (Miss Anne Baily) was a child, there was still living a man named Teigue O'Neill, who had a strange story to tell.

He was a smith, and his forge stood on the brow of the hill, over-looking the lake, on a lonely part of the road to Cahir Conlish. One bright moonlight night, he was working very late, and quite alone. The clink of his hammer, and the wavering glow reflected through the open door on the bushes at the other side of the narrow road, were the only tokens that told of life and vigil for miles around.

In one of the pauses of his work, he heard the ring of many hoofs ascending the steep road that passed his forge, and, standing in his doorway, he was just in time to see a gentleman, on a white horse, who was dressed in a fashion the like of which the smith had never seen before. This man was accompanied and followed by a mounted retinue, as strangely dressed as he.

They seemed, by the clang and clatter that announced their approach, to be riding up the hill at a hard hurry-scurry gallop; but the pace abated as they drew near, and the rider of the white horse who, from his grave and lordly air, he assumed to be a man of rank, and accustomed to command, drew bridle and came to a halt before the smith's door.

He did not speak, and all his train were silent, but he beckoned to the smith, and pointed down to one of his horse's hoofs.

Teigue stooped and raised it, and held it just long enough to see that it was shod with a silver shoe; which, in one place, he said, was worn as thin as a shilling. Instantaneously, his situation was made apparent to him by this sign, and he recoiled with a terrified prayer. The lordly rider, with a look of pain and fury, struck at him suddenly, with something that whistled in the air like a whip; and an icy streak seemed to traverse his body as if he had been cut through with a leaf of steel. But he was without scathe or scar, as he afterwards found. At the same moment he saw the whole cavalcade break into a gallop and disappear down the hill, with a momentary hurtling in the air, like the flight of a volley of cannon shot.

Here had been the earl himself. He had tried one of his accustomed stratagems to lead the smith to speak to him. For it is well known that either for the purpose of abridging or of mitigating his period of enchantment, he seeks to lead people to accost him. But what, in the event of his succeeding, would befall the person whom he had thus ensnared, no one knows.

MOLL RIAL'S ADVENTURE

When Miss Anne Baily was a child, Moll Rial was an old woman. She had lived all her days with the Bailys of Lough Guir; in and about whose house, as was the Irish custom of those days, were a troop of bare-footed country girls, scullery maids, or laundresses, or employed about the poultry yard, or running of errands.

Among these was Moll Rial, then a stout good-humoured lass, with little to think of, and nothing to fret about. She was once washing clothes by the process known universally in Munster as beetling. The washer stands up to her ankles in water, in which she has immersed the clothes, which she lays in that state on a great flat stone, and smacks with lusty strokes of an instrument which bears a rude resemblance to a cricket bat, only shorter, broader, and light enough to be wielded freely with one hand. Thus, they smack the dripping clothes, turning them over and over, sousing them in the water, and replacing them on the same stone, to undergo a repetition of the process, until they are thoroughly washed.

Moll Rial was plying her 'beetle' at the margin of the lake, close under the old house and castle. It was between eight and nine o'clock on a fine summer morning, everything looked bright and beautiful. Though quite alone, and though she could not see even the windows of the house (hidden from her view by the irregular ascent and some interposing bushes), her loneliness was not depressing.

Standing up from her work, she saw a gentleman walking slowly down the slope toward her. He was a 'grand-looking' gentleman, arrayed in a flowered silk dressing-gown, with a cap of velvet on his head; and as he stepped toward her, in his slippered feet, he showed a very handsome leg. He was smiling graciously as he approached, and drawing a ring from his finger with an air of gracious meaning, which seemed to imply that he wished to make her a present, he raised it in his fingers with a pleased look, and placed it on the flat stones beside the clothes she had been beetling so industriously.

He drew back a little, and continued to look at her with an encouraging smile, which seemed to say: 'You have earned your reward; you must not be afraid to take it.'

The girl fancied that this was some gentleman who had arrived, as often happened in those hospitable and haphazard times, late and unexpectedly the night before, and who was now taking a little indolent ramble before breakfast.

Moll Rial was a little shy, and more so at having been discovered by so grand a gentleman with her petticoats gathered a little high about her bare shins. She looked down, therefore, upon the water at her feet, and then she saw a ripple of blood, and then another, ring after ring, coming and going to and from her feet. She cried out the sacred name in horror, and, lifting her eyes, the courtly gentleman was gone, but the blood-rings about her feet spread with the speed of light over the surface of the lake, which for a moment glowed like one vast estuary of blood.

Here was the earl once again, and Moll Rial declared that if it had not been for that frightful transformation of the water she would have spoken to him next minute, and would thus have passed under a spell, perhaps as direful as his own.

THE BANSHEE

So old a Munster family as the Bailys, of Lough Guir, could not fail to have their attendant banshee. Everyone attached to the family knew this well, and could cite evidences of that unearthly distinction. I heard Miss Baily relate the only experience she had personally had of that wild spiritual sympathy.

She said that, being then young, she and Miss Susan undertook a long attendance upon the sick bed of their sister, Miss Kitty, whom I have heard remembered among her contemporaries as the merriest and most entertaining of human beings. This light-hearted young lady was dying of consumption. The sad duties of such attendance being divided among many sisters, as there then were, the night watches devolved upon the two ladies I have named: I think, as being the eldest.

It is not improbable that these long and melancholy vigils, lowering the spirits and exciting the nervous system, prepared them for illusions. At all events, one night at dead of night, Miss Baily and her sister, sitting in the dying lady's room, heard such sweet and melancholy music as they had never heard before. It seemed to them like distant cathedral music. The room of the dying girl had its windows toward the yard, and the old castle stood near, and full in sight. The music was not in the house but seemed to come from the yard, or beyond it. Miss Anne Baily took a candle, and went down the back stairs. She opened the back door, and, standing there heard the same faint but solemn harmony, and could not tell whether it most resembled the distant music of instruments, or a choir of voices. It seemed to come through the windows of the old castle, high in the air. But when she approached the tower, the music, she thought, came from above the house, at the other side of the yard; and thus perplexed, and at last frightened, she returned.

This aerial music both she and her sister, Miss Susan Baily, avowed that they distinctly heard, and for a long time. Of the fact she was clear, and she spoke of it with great awe.

THE GOVERNESS'S DREAM

This lady, one morning, with a grave countenance that indicated something weighty upon her mind, told her pupils that she had, on the night before, had a very remarkable dream.

The first room you enter in the old castle, having reached the foot of the spiral stone stair, is a large hall, dim and lofty, having only a small window or two, set high in deep recesses in the wall. When I saw the castle many years ago, a portion of this capacious chamber was used as a store for the turf laid in to last the year.

Her dream placed her, alone, in this room, and there entered a grave-looking man, having something very remarkable in his countenance: which impressed her, as a fine portrait sometimes will, with a haunting sense of character and individuality.

In his hand this man carried a wand, about the length of an ordinary walking cane. He told her to observe and remember its length, and to mark well the measurements he was about to make, the result of which she was to communicate to Mrs Baily of Lough Guir.

From a certain point in the wall, with this wand, he measured along the floor, at right angles with the wall, a certain number of its lengths, which he counted aloud; and then, in the same way, from the adjoining wall he measured a certain number of its lengths, which he also counted distinctly. He then told her that at the point where these two lines met, at a depth of a certain number of feet which he also told her, treasure lay buried. And so the dream broke up, and her remarkable visitant vanished.

She took the girls with her to the old castle, where, having cut a switch to the length represented to her in her dream, she measured the distances, and ascertained, as she supposed, the point on the floor beneath which the treasure lay. The same day she related her dream to Mr Baily. But he treated it laughingly, and took no step in consequence.

Some time after this, she again saw, in a dream, the same remarkable-looking man, who repeated his message, and appeared displeased. But the dream was treated by Mr Baily as before.

The same dream occurred again, and the children became so clamorous to have the castle floor explored, with pick and shovel, at the point indicated by the thrice-seen messenger, that at length Mr Baily consented, and the floor was opened, and a trench was sunk at the spot which the governess had pointed out.

Miss Anne Baily, and nearly all the members of the family, her father included, were present at this operation. As the workmen approached the depth described in the vision, the interest and suspense of all increased; and when the iron implements met the solid resistance of a broad flagstone, which returned a cavernous sound to the stroke, the excitement of all present rose to its acme.

With some difficulty the flag was raised, and a chamber of stone work, large enough to receive a moderately-sized crock or pit, was disclosed. Alas! it was empty. But in the earth at the bottom of it, Miss Baily said, she herself saw, as every other bystander plainly did, the circular impression of a vessel: which had stood there, as the mark seemed to indicate, for a very long time.

Both the Miss Bailys were strong in their belief here-afterwards, that the treasure which they were convinced had actually been deposited there, had been removed by some more trusting and active listener than their father had proved.

This same governess remained with them to the time of her death, which occurred some years later, under the following circumstances as extraordinary as her dream.

The good governess had a particular liking for the old castle, and when lessons were over, would take her book or her work into a large room in the ancient building, called the Earl's Hall. Here she caused a table and chair to be placed for her use, and in the chiaroscuro would so sit at her favourite occupations, with just a little ray of subdued light, admitted through one of the glassless windows above her, and falling upon her table.

The Earl's Hall is entered by a narrow-arched door, opening close to the winding stair. It is a very large and gloomy room, pretty nearly square, with a lofty vaulted ceiling, and a stone floor. Being situated high in the castle, the walls of which are immensely thick, and the windows very small and few, the silence that reigns here is like that of a subterranean cavern. You hear nothing in this solitude, except perhaps twice in a day, the twitter of a swallow in one of the small windows high in the wall.

This good lady having one day retired to her accustomed solitude, was missed from the house at her wonted hour of return. This in a country house, such as Irish houses were in those days, excited little surprise, and no harm. But when the dinner hour came, which was then, in country houses, five o'clock, and the governess had not appeared, some of her young friends, it being not yet winter, and sufficient light remaining to guide them through the gloom of the dim ascent and passages, mounted the old stone stair to the level of the Earl's Hall, gaily calling to her as they approached.

There was no answer. On the stone floor, outside the door of the Earl's Hall, to their horror, they found her lying insensible. By the usual means she was restored to consciousness; but she continued very ill, and was conveyed to the house, where she took to her bed.

It was there and then that she related what had occurred to her. She had placed herself, as usual, at her little work table, and had been either working or reading – I forget which – for some time, and felt in her usual health and serene spirits. Raising her eyes, and looking towards the door, she saw a horrible-looking little man enter. He was dressed in red, was very short, had a singularly dark face, and a most atrocious countenance. Having walked some steps into the room, with his eyes fixed on her, he stopped, and beckoning to her to follow, moved back toward the door. About halfway, again he stopped once more and turned. She was so terrified that she sat staring at the apparition without moving or speaking. Seeing that she had not obeyed him, his face became more frightful and menacing, and as it underwent this change, he raised his hand and stamped on the floor. Gesture, look, and all, expressed diabolical fury. Through sheer extremity of terror she did rise, and, as he turned again, followed him a step or two in the direction of the door. He again stopped, and with the same mute menace, compelled her again to follow him.

She reached the narrow stone doorway of the Earl's Hall, through which he had passed; from the threshold she saw him standing a little way off, with his eyes still fixed on her. Again he signed to her, and began to move along the short passage that leads to the winding stair. But instead of following him further, she fell on the floor in a fit.

The poor lady was thoroughly persuaded that she was not long to survive this vision, and her foreboding proved true. From her bed she never rose. Fever and delirium supervened in a few days and she died. Of course it is possible that fever, already approaching, had touched her brain when she was visited by the phantom, and that it had no external existence.

MICHAEL BANIM

The Rival Dreamers

ॐ

Mr Washington Irving has already given to the public a version of an American legend, which, in a principal feature, bears some likeness to the following transcript of a popular Irish one. It may, however, be interesting to show this very coincidence between the descendants of a Dutch transatlantic colony and the native peasantry of Ireland, in the superstitious annals of both. Our tale, moreover, will be found original in all its circumstances, that alluded to only excepted.

Shamus Dempsey returned a silent, plodding, sorrowful man, though a young one, to his poor home, after seeing laid in the grave his aged decrepit father. The last rays of the setting sun were glorious, shooting through the folds of their pavilion of scarlet clouds; the last song of the thrush, chanted from the bough nearest to his nest, was gladdening; the abundant though but half-matured crops around breathed of hope for the future. But Shamus's bosom was covered with the darkness that inward sunshine alone can illumine. The chord that should respond to song and melody had snapped in it; for him the softly undulating fields of light-green wheat, or the silken surfaced patches of barley, made a promise in vain. He was poor, penniless, friendless, and yet groaning under responsibilities; worn out by past and present suffering, and without a consoling prospect. His father's corpse had been just buried by a subscription among his neighbours, collected in an old glove, a penny or a halfpenny from each, by the most active of the humble community to whom his sad state was a subject of pity. In the wretched shed which he called 'home', a young wife lay on a truss of straw, listening to the hungry cries of two little children, and awaiting her hour to become the weeping mother of a third. And the recollection that but for an act of domestic treachery experienced by his father and himself, both would have been comfortable and respectable in the world, aggravated the bitterness of the feeling in which Shamus contemplated this lot. He could himself faintly call to mind a time of early childhood, when he lived with his parents in a roomy house, eating and sleeping and dressing well, and surrounded by servants and workmen; he further remembered that a day of great affliction came, upon which strange and rude persons forced their way into the house; and, for some cause his infant observation did not reach, father, servants, and workmen (his mother had just died), were all turned out upon the road, and doomed to seek the shelter of a mean roof. But his father's discourse, since he gained the years of manhood, supplied Shamus with an explanation of all these circumstances, as follows.

Old Dempsey had been the youngest son of a large farmer, who divided his lands between two elder children, and destined Shamus's father to the Church, sending him abroad for education, and, during its course, supplying him with liberal allowances. Upon the eve of ordination, the young student returned home to visit his friends; was much noticed by neighbouring small gentry of each religion; at the house of one of the opposite persuasion from his, met a sister of the proprietor, who had a fortune in her own right; abandoned his clerical views for her smiles; eloped with her; married her privately; incurred thereby the irremovable hostility of his own family; but, after a short time, was received, along with his wife, by his generous brother-in-law, under whose guidance both became reputably settled in the house to which Shamus's early recollections pointed, and where, till he was about six years old, he passed indeed a happy childhood.

But, a little previous to this time, his mother's good brother died unmarried, and was succeeded by another of her brothers, who had unsuccessfully spent half his life as a lawyer in Dublin, and who, inheriting little of his predecessor's amiable character, soon showed himself a foe to her and her husband, professedly on account of her marriage with a Roman Catholic. He did not appear to their visit, shortly after his arrival in their neighbourhood, and he never condescended to return it. The affliction experienced by his sensitive sister, from his conduct, entailed upon her a premature accouchement, in which, giving birth to a lifeless babe, she unexpectedly died. The event was matter of triumph rather than of sorrow to her unnatural brother. For, in the first place, totally unguarded against the sudden result, she had died intestate; in the next place, he discovered that her private marriage had been celebrated by a Roman Catholic priest, consequently could not, according to law, hold good; and again, could not give to her nominal husband any right to her property, upon which both had hitherto lived, and which was now the sole means of existence to Shamus's father.

The lawyer speedily set to work upon these points, and with little difficulty succeeded in supplying for Shamus's recollections a day of trouble, already noticed. In fact, his father and he, now without a shilling, took refuge in a distant cabin, where, by the sweat of his parent's brow, as a labourer in the fields, the ill-fated hero of this story was scantily fed and clothed, until maturer years enabled him to relieve the old man's hand of the spade and sickle, and in turn labour for their common wants.

Shamus, becoming a little prosperous in the world, rented a few acres adjacent to his cabin and – married. The increase of his fields did not quite keep pace with the increases of his cares, in the persons of newcomers, for whose well being he was bound to provide. His ray of success in life soon became overclouded, by the calls of the landlord and the tithe-proctor. In truth, three years after his marriage, he received a notice which it were vain to oppose, to quit both his farm and his cabin, and leave his few articles of furniture behind.

At this juncture his father was bedridden, and his wife advanced in her third pregnancy. He put on his hat, walked to the door, fixed his eyes upon the ruins of an old abbey which stood on the slope of an opposite hill, and formed his plan for present measures. By the next evening he had constructed a wattled shed, covered with rushes and leaves, against a gable in the interior of the ruin. Clearing away the nettles and other rank weeds enclosed by his new house, he discovered a long slab on which was carved a cross and letters illegible to his eye; this he made his hearthstone. To furnish the abode, he fetched two large stones, as seats for his wife and himself, shook straw in either corner, and laid in a bundle of twigs. Then he went to the cabin that was no longer his, sent on his wife and two children to the abbey, followed with his father on his back, and laid him upon one of the straw couches. Two days afterwards the old man was a corpse. From his pauper funeral we now see Shamus returning, and to such a home does he bend his heavy steps.

If to know that the enemy of his father and mother did not thrive on the spoils of his oppression could have yielded Shamus any consolation in his lot, he had long ago become aware of circumstances calculated to give this negative comfort. His maternal uncle enjoyed, indeed, his newly acquired property only a few years after it came into his possession. Partly on account of his cruelty to his relations, partly from a meanness and vulgarity of character, which soon displayed itself in his novel situation, and which, it was believed, had previously kept him in the lowest walks of his profession as a Dublin attorney, he found himself neglected and shunned by the gentry of his neighbourhood. To grow richer than anyone who thus insulted him, to blazon abroad reports of his wealth, and to watch opportunities of using it to their injury, became the means of revenge adopted by the parvenu. His legitimate income not promising a rapid accomplishment of this plan, he ventured, using precautions that seemingly set suspicion at defiance, to engage in smuggling adventures on a large scale, for which his proximity to the coast afforded a local opportunity. Notwithstanding all his pettifogging cleverness, the ex-attorney was detected, however, in his illegal traffic, and fined to an amount which swept away half his real property. Driven to desperation by the publicity of his failure, as well as by the failure itself, he tried another grand effort to retrieve his fortune; was again surprised by the revenue officers; in a personal struggle with them, at the head of his band, killed one of their boys; immediately absconded from Ireland; for the last twenty years had not been authentically heard of; but, it was believed, lived under an assumed name in London, deriving an obscure existence from some mean pursuit, of which the very nature enabled him to gratify propensities to drunkenness and other vices, learned during his first career in life.

All this Shamus knew, though only from report, inasmuch as his uncle had exiled himself while he was yet a child, and without previously having become known to the eyes of the nephew he had so much injured. But if Shamus occasionally drew a bitter and almost savage gratification from the downfall of his inhuman persecutor, no recurrence to the past could alleviate the misery of his present situation. He passed under one of the capacious open arches of the old abbey, and then entered his squalid shed reared against its wall, his heart as shattered and as trodden down as the ruins around him. No words of greeting ensued between him and his equally hopeless wife, as she sat on the straw of her bed, rocking to sleep, with feeble and mournful cries, her youngest infant. He silently lighted a fire of withered twigs on his ready-furnished hearthstone; put to roast among their embers a few potatoes which he had begged during the day; divided them between her and her crying children; and as the moon, rising high in the heavens, warned him that night asserted her full empire over the departed day, Shamus sunk down upon the couch from which his father's mortal remains had lately been borne, supperless himself, and dinnerless, too, but not hungry; at least not conscious or recollecting that he was.

His wife and little ones soon slept soundly, but Shamus lay for hours inaccessible to nature's claims for sleep as well as for food. From where he lay he could see, through the open front of his shed, out into the ruins abroad. After much abstraction of his own thoughts, the silence, the extent, and the peculiar desolation of the scene, almost spiritualised by the magic effect of alternate moonshine and darkness, of objects and of their parts, at last diverted his mind, though not to relieve it. He remembered distinctly, for the first time, where he was – an intruder among the dwellings of the dead; he called to mind, too, that the present was their hour for revealing themselves among the remote loneliness and obscurity of their crumbling and intricate abode. As his eye fixed upon a distant stream of cold light or of blank shadow, either the wavering of some feathery herbage from the walls, or the flitting of some night bird over the roofless aisle, made motion which went and came during the instant of his alarmed start, or else some disembodied sleeper around had challenged and evaded his vision, so rapidly as to baffle even the accompaniment of thought. Shamus would, however, recur, during these entrancing aberrations, to his more real causes for terror; and he knew not, and to this day cannot distinctly tell whether he waked or slept, when a new circumstance absorbed his attention. The moon struck fully, under his propped roof, upon the carved slab he had appropriated as a hearthstone, and turning his eye to the spot, he saw the semblance of a man advanced in years, though not very old, standing motionless, and very steadfastly regarding him; the still face of the figure shone like marble in the nightbeam, without giving any idea of the solidity of that material; the long and deep shadows thrown by the forehead over the eyes, left those unusually expressive features vague and uncertain. Upon the head was a close-fitting black cap, the dress was a loose-sleeved, plaited garment of white, descending to the ground, and faced and otherwise checked with black, and girded round the loins; exactly the costume which Shamus had often studied in a little framed and glazed print, hung up in the sacristy of the humble chapel recently built in the neighbourhood of the ruin, by a few descendants of the great religious fraternity to whom, in its day of pride, the abbey had belonged. As he returned very inquisitively, though, as he avers, not now in alarm, the fixed gaze of his midnight visitor, a voice reached him, and he heard these strange words: 'Shamus Dempsey, go to London Bridge, and you will be a rich man.'

'How will that come about, your reverence?' cried Shamus, jumping up from the straw.

But the figure was gone; and he stumbling among the black embers on the remarkable place where it had stood, he fell prostrate, experiencing a change of sensation and of observance of objects around, which might be explained by supposing a transition from a sleeping to a waking state of mind.

The rest of the night he slept little, thinking of the advice he had received, and of the mysterious personage who gave it. But he resolved to say nothing about his vision, particularly to his wife, lest, in her present state of health, the frightful story might distress her; and, as to his own conduct respecting it, he determined to be guided by the future – in fact, he would wait to see if his counsellor came again. He did come again, appearing in the same spot at the same hour of the night, and wearing the same dress, though not the same expression of feature; for the shadowy brows now slightly frowned, and a little severity mingled with the former steadfastness of look.

'Shamus Dempsey, why have you not gone to London Bridge, and your wife so near the time when she will want what you are to get by going there? Remember this is my second warning.'

'Musha, your reverence, an' what am I to do on Lunnon Bridge?'

Again he rose to approach the figure; again it eluded him. Again a change occurred in the quality of the interest with which he regarded the admonition of his visitor. Again he passed a day of doubt as to the propriety of undertaking what seemed to him little less than a journey to the world's end, without a penny in his pocket, and upon the eve of his wife's accouchement, merely in obedience to a recommendation which, according to his creed, was not yet sufficiently strongly given, even were it under any circumstances to be adopted. For Shamus had often heard, and firmly believed, that a dream or a vision, instructing one how to procure riches, ought to be experienced three times before it became entitled to attention.

He lay down, however, half hoping that his vision might thus recommend itself to his notice. It did so.

'Shamus Dempsey,' said the figure, looking more angry than ever, 'you have not yet gone to London Bridge, although I hear your wife crying out to bid you go. And, remember, this is my third warning.'

'Why, then, tundher-an-ouns, your reverence, just stop and tell me' –

Ere he could utter another word the holy visitant disappeared, in a real passion at Shamus's qualified curse; and at the same moment, his confused senses recognised the voice of his wife, sending up from her straw pallet the cries that betoken a mother's distant travail. Exchanging a few words with her, he hurried away, professedly to call up, at her cabin window, an old crone who sometimes attended the very poorest women in Nance Dempsey's situation.

'Hurry to her, Noreen, acuishla, and do the best it's the will of God to let you do. And tell her from me, Noreen,' – he stopped, drawing in his lip, and clutching his cudgel hard.

'Shamus, what ails you, avick?' asked old Noreen; 'what ails you, to make the tears run down in the grey o' the morning?'

'Tell her from me,' continued Shamus, 'that it's from the bottom o' the heart I'll pray, morning and evening, and fresh and fasting, maybe, to give her a good time of it; and to show her a face on the poor child that's coming, likelier than the two that God sent afore it. And that I'll be thinking o' picturing it to my own mind, though I'll never see it far away.'

'Musha, Shamus, what are you speaking of?'

'No matter, Noreen, only God be wid you, and wid her, and wid the weenocks; and tell her what I bid you. More-be-token, tell her that poor Shamus quits her in her throuble, with more love from the heart out than he had for her the first day we came together; and I'll come back to her, at any rate, sooner or later, richer or poorer, or as bare as I went; and maybe not so bare either. But God only knows. The top o' the morning to you, Noreen, and don't let her want the mouthful o' praties while I'm on my thravels. For this' – added Shamus, as he bounded off to the consternation of old Noreen – 'this is the very morning and the very minute that, if I mind the dhrame at all at all, I ought to mind it; ay, without ever turning back to get a look from her, that 'ud kill the heart in my body entirely.'

Without much previous knowledge of the road he was to take, Shamus walked and begged his way along the coast to the town where he might hope to embark for England. Here, the captain of a merchantman agreed to let him work his passage to Bristol, whence he again walked and begged into London.

Without taking rest or food, Shamus proceeded to London Bridge, often put out of his course by wrong directions, and as often by forgetting and misconceiving true ones. It was with old London Bridge that Shamus had to do (not the old one last pulled down, but its more reverend predecessor), which, at that time, was lined at either side by quaintly fashioned houses, mostly occupied by shopkeepers, so that the space between presented, perhaps, the greatest thoroughfare then known in the Queen of Citics. And at about two o'clock in the afternoon, barefooted, ragged, fevered, and agitated, Shamus mingled with the turbid human stream, that roared and chafed over the, as restless and as evanescent, stream which buffeted the arches of old London Bridge. In a situation so novel to him, so much more extraordinary in the reality than his anticipation could have fancied, the poor and friendless stranger felt overwhelmed. A sense of forlornness, of insignificance, and of terror, seized upon his faculties. From the store, or the sneers, or the jostle of the iron-nerved crowd, he shrank with glances of wild timidity, and with a heart as wildly timid as were his looks. For some time he stood or staggered about, unable to collect his thoughts, or to bring to mind what was his business there. But when Shamus became able to refer to the motive of his pauper journey, from his native solitudes into the thick of such a scene, it was no wonder that the zeal of superstition totally subsided amid the astounding truths he witnessed. In fact, the bewildered simpleton now regarded his dream as the merest chimera. Hastily escaping from the thoroughfare, he sought out some wretched place of repose suited to his wretched condition, and there mooned himself asleep, in half accusations at the thought of poor Nance at home, and in utter despair of all his future prospects.

At daybreak the next morning he awoke, a little less agitated, but still with no hope. He was able, however, to resolve upon the best course of conduct now left open to him; and he arranged immediately to retrace his steps to Ireland, as soon as he should have begged sufficient alms to speed him a mile on the road. With this intent he hastily issued forth, preferring to challenge the notice of chance passengers, even at the early hour of dawn, than to venture again in the middle of the day, among the dreaded crowds of the vast city. Very few, indeed, were the passers-by whom Shamus met during his straggling and stealthy walk through the streets, and those of a description little able or willing to afford a halfpenny to his humbled, whining suit, and to his spasmed lip and watery eye. In what direction he went Shamus did not know; but at last he found himself entering upon the scene of his yesterday's terror. Now, however, it presented nothing to renew its former impression. The shops at the sides of the bridge were closed, and the occasional stragglers of either sex who came along inspired Shamus, little as he knew of a great city, with aversion rather than with dread. In the quietness and security of his present position, Shamus was both courageous and weak enough again to summon up his dream.

'Come,' he said, 'since I *am* on Lunnon Bridge, I'll walk over every stone of it, and see what good that will do.'

He valiantly gained the far end. Here one house, of all that stood upon the bridge, began to be opened; it was a public house, and, by a sidelong glance as he passed, Shamus thought that, in the person of a red-cheeked, red-nosed, sunk-eyed, elderly man, who took down the window-shutters, he recognised the proprietor. This person looked at Shamus, in return, with peculiar scrutiny. The wanderer liked neither his regards nor the expression of his countenance, and quickened his steps onward until he cleared the bridge.

'But I'll walk it over at the other side, now,' he bethought, after allowing the publican time to finish opening his house, and retire out of view.

But, repassing the house, the man still appeared, leaning against his door-jamb, and as if waiting for Shamus's return, whom, upon this second occasion, he eyed more attentively than before.

'Sorrow's in him,' thought Shamus, 'have I two heads on me, that I'm such a sight to him? But who cares about his pair of ferret-eyes? I'll thrudge down the middle stone of it, at any rate!'

Accordingly he again walked towards the public house, keeping the middle of the bridge.

'Good-morrow, friend,' said the publican, as Shamus a third time passed his door.

'Sarvant kindly, sir,' answered Shamus, respectfully pulling down the brim of his hat, and increasing his pace.

'An early hour you choose for a morning walk,' continued his new acquaintance.

'Brave and early, faix, sir,' said Shamus, still hurrying off.

'Stop a bit,' resumed the publican. Shamus stood still. 'I see you're a countryman of mine – an Irishman; I'd know one of you at a look, though I'm a long time out of the country. And you're not very well off on London Bridge this morning, either.'

'No, indeed, sir,' replied Shamus, beginning to doubt his skill in physiognomy, at the stranger's kind address; 'but as badly off as a body 'ud wish to be.'

'Come over to look for the work?'

'Nien, sir; but come out this morning to beg a ha'penny, to send me a bit of the road home.'

'Well, here's a silver sixpence without asking. And you'd better sit on the bench by the door here, and eat a crust and a cut of cheese, and drink a drop of good ale, to break your fast.'

With profuse thanks, Shamus accepted this kind invitation; blaming himself at heart for having allowed his opinion of the charitable publican to be guided by the expression of the man's features. 'Handsome is that handsome does,' was Shamus's self-correcting reflection.

While eating his bread and cheese, and drinking his strong ale, they conversed freely together, and Shamus's heart opened more and more to his benefactor. The publican repeatedly asked him what had brought him to London; and though half out of prudence, and half out of shame, the dreamer at first evaded the question, he felt it at last impossible to refuse a candid answer to his generous friend.

'Why, then, sir, only I am such a big fool for telling it to you, it's what brought me to Lunnon Bridge was a quare dhrame I had at home in Ireland, that tould me just to come here, and I'd find a pot of goold'; for such was the interpretation given by Shamus to the vague admonition of his visionary counsellor.

His companion burst into a loud laugh, saying after it – 'Pho, pho, man, don't be so silly as to put faith in nonsensical dreams of that kind. Many a one like it I have had, if I would bother my head with them. Why, within the last ten days, while you were dreaming of finding a pot of gold on London Bridge, I was dreaming of finding a pot of gold in Ireland.'

'Ullaloo, and were you, sir?' asked Shamus, laying down his empty pint.

'Ay, indeed; night after night, an old friar with a pale face, and dressed all in white and black, and a black scullcap on his head, came to me in a dream, and bid me go to Ireland, to a certain spot in a certain county that I know very well, and under the slab of his tomb, that has a cross and some old Romish letters on it, in an old abbey I often saw before now, I'd find a treasure that would make me a rich man all the days of my life.'

'Musha, sir,' asked Shamus, scarce able prudently to control his agitation, 'and did he tell you that the treasure lay buried there ever so long under the open sky and the ould walls?'

'No; but he told me I was to find the slab covered in by a shed, that a poor man had lately built inside the abbey for himself and his family.'

'Whoo, by the powers!' shouted Shamus, at last thrown off his guard by the surpassing joy derived from this intelligence, as well as by the effects of the ale; and, at the same time, he jumped up, cutting caper with his legs, and flourishing his shillelah.

'Why, what's the matter with you?' asked his friend, glancing at him a frowning and misgiving look.

'We ax pardon, sir,' Shamus rallied his prudence. 'An' sure sorrow a thing is the matter wid me, only the dhrop, I believe, made me do it, as it ever and always does, good luck to it for the same. An' isn't what we were spaking about the biggest raumaush [nonsense] undher the sun, sir? Only it's the laste bit in the world quare to me, how you'd have the dhrame about your own country, that you didn't see for so many years, sir – for twenty long years, I think you said, sir?' Shamus had now a new object in putting his sly question.

'If I said so, I forgot,' answered the publican, his suspicions of

Shamus at an end. 'But it is about twenty years, indeed, since I left Ireland.'

'And by your speech, sir, and your dacency, I'll engage you were in a good way in the poor place, afore you left it?'

'You guess correctly, friend.' (The publican gave way to vanity). 'Before misfortunes came over me, I possessed, along with a good hundred acres besides, the very ground that the old ruin I saw in the foolish dream I told you stands upon.'

'An' so did my curse-o'-God's uncle,' thought Shamus, his heart's blood beginning to boil, though, with a great effort, he kept himself seemingly cool. 'And this is the man fornent me, if he answers another word I'll ax him. Faix, sir, and sure that makes your dhrame quarer than ever; and the ground the ould abbey is on, sir, and the good acres round it, did you say they lay somewhere in the poor county myself came from?'

'What county is that, friend?' demanded the publican again with a studious frown.

'The ould County Monaghan, sure, sir,' replied Shamus, very deliberately.

'No, but the county of Clare,' answered his companion.

'Was it?' screamed Shamus, again springing up. The cherished hatred of twenty years imprudently bursting out, his uncle lay stretched at his feet, after a renewed flourish of his cudgel. 'And do you know what you are telling it to this morning? Did you ever hear that the sisther you kilt, left a bit of a *gorsoon* behind her, that one day or other might overhear you? Ay,' he continued, keeping down the struggling man, '*it is* poor Shamus Dempsey that's kneeling by you; ay, and that has more to tell you. The shed built over the old friar's tombstone was built by the hands you feel on your throttle, and that tombstone is his hearthstone; and' – continued Shamus, beginning to bind the prostrate man with a rope, snatched from a bench near them – 'while you lie here awhile, an' no one to help you, in the cool of the morning, I'll just take a start of you on the road home, to lift the flag and get the threasure; and follow me if you dare! You know there's good money bid for your head in Ireland – so here goes. Yes, faith and wid this – *this* to help me on the way!' He snatched up a heavy purse which had fallen from his uncle's pocket in the struggle. 'And sure, there's neither hurt nor harm in getting back a little of a body's own from you. A bright good-morning, uncle dear!'

Shamus dragged his manacled relative into the shop, quickly shut to and locked the door, flung the key over the house into the Thames, and the next instant was running at headlong speed.

He was not so deficient in the calculations of common sense as to think himself yet out of his uncle's power. It appeared, indeed, pretty certain, that neither for the violence done to his person, nor for the purse appropriated by his nephew, the outlawed murderer would raise a hue and cry after one who, aware of his identity, could deliver him up to the laws of his country. But Shamus felt certain that it would be a race between him and his uncle for the treasure that lay under the friar's tombstone. His simple nature supplied no stronger motive for a pursuit on the part of a man whose life now lay in the breath of his mouth. Full of his conviction, however, Shamus saw he had not a moment to lose until the roof of his shed in the old abbey again sheltered him. So, freely making use of his uncle's guineas, he purchased a strong horse in the outskirts of London, and to the surprise, if not under heavy suspicions of the vendor, set off at a gallop upon the road by which he had the day before gained the great metropolis.

A ship was ready to sail at Bristol for Ireland; but, to Shamus's discomfort, she waited for a wind. He got aboard, however, and in the darksome and squalid hold often knelt down and, with clasped hands and panting breast, petitioned Heaven for a favourable breeze. But from morning until evening the wind remained as he had found it, and Shamus despaired. His uncle, meantime, might have reached some other port, and embarked for their country. In the depth of his anguish he heard a brisk bustle upon deck, clambered up to investigate its cause, and found the ship's sails already half unfurled to a wind that promised to bear him to his native shores by the next morning. The last light of day yet lingered in the heavens: he glanced, now under way, to the quay of Bristol. A group who had been watching the departure of the vessel, turned round to note the approach to them of a man who ran furiously towards the place where they stood, pointing after her, and evidently speaking with vehemence, although no words reached Shamus's ear. Neither was his eye sure of this person's features, but his heart read them distinctly. A boat shot from the quay; the man stood up in it, and its rowers made a signal.

Shamus stepped to the gangway, as if preparing to hurl his pursuer into the sea. The captain took a speaking-trumpet, and informing the boat that he could not stop an instant, advised her to wait for another merchantman, which would sail in an hour. And during and after his speech his vessel plowed cheerily on, making as much way as she was adapted to accomplish.

Shamus's bosom felt lightened of its immediate terror, but not freed of apprehension for the future. The ship that was to sail in an hour haunted his thoughts: he did not leave the deck, and, although the night proved very dark, his anxious eyes were never turned from the English coast. Unusual fatigue and want of sleep now and then overpowered him, and his senses swam in a wild and snatching slumber; but from this he would start, carrying out and clinging to the cordage, as the feverish dream of an instant presented him with the swelling canvas of a fast sailing ship, which came suddenly bursting through the gloom of midnight, alongside of his own. Morning dawned, really to unveil to him the object of his fears following almost in the wake of her rival. He glanced in the opposite direction, and beheld the shores of Ireland; in another hour he jumped upon them; but his enemy's face watched him from the deck of the companion vessel, now not more than a few ropes' lengths distant.

Shamus mounted a second good horse, and spurred towards home. Often did he look back, but without seeing any cause for increased alarm. As yet, however, the road had been level and winding, and therefore could not allow him to span much of it at a glance. After noon, it ascended a high and lengthened hill, surrounded by wastes of bog. As he gained the summit of this hill, and again looked back, a horseman appeared, sweeping to its foot. Shamus galloped at full speed down the now quickly falling road; then along its level continuation for about a mile; and then up another eminence, more lengthened, though not so steep as the former; and from it still he looked back, and caught the figure of the horseman breaking over the line of the hill he had passed. For hours such was the character of the chase; until the road narrowed and began to wind amid an uncultivated and uninhabited mountain wilderness. Here Shamus's horse tripped and fell; the rider, little injured, assisted him to his legs, and, with lash and spur, reurged him to pursue his course. The animal went forward in a last effort, and, for still another span of time well befriended his rider. A rocky valley, through which both had been galloping, now opened at its further end, presenting to Shamus's eye, in the distance, the sloping ground, and the ruin which, with is mouldering walls, encircled his poor home; and the setting sun streamed golden rays through the windows and rents of the old abbey.

The fugitive gave a weak cry of joy, and lashed his beast again. The cry seemed to be answered by a shout; and a second time, after a wild plunge, the horse fell, now throwing Shamus off with a force that left him stunned. And yet he heard the hoofs of another horse come thundering down the rocky way; and, while he made a faint effort to rise on his hands and look at his pursuer, the horse and horseman were very near, and the voice of his uncle cried, 'Stand!' at the same time that the speaker fired a pistol, of which the ball struck a stone at Shamus's foot. The next moment his uncle, having left his saddle, stood over him, presenting a second pistol, and he spoke in a low but distinct voice.

'Spawn of a beggar! This is not merely for the chance of riches given by our dreams, though it seems, in the teeth of all I ever thought, that the devil tells truth at last. No, nor it is not quite for the blow; but it is to close the lips that, with a single word, can kill me. You die, to let me live!'

'Help!' aspirated Shamus's heart, turning itself to Heaven; 'help me but now, for the sake of the goold either, but for the sake of them that will be left on the wild world widout me; for them help me, great God!'

Hitherto his weakness and confusion had left him passive. Before his uncle spoke the last words, his silent prayer was offered, and Shamus had jumped upon his assailant. They struggled, and dragged each other down. Shamus felt the muzzle of the pistol at his breast; heard it snap – but only snap; he seized and mastered it, and once more the uncle was at the mercy of his nephew. Shamus's hand was raised to deal a good blow; but he checked himself, and addressed the almost senseless ears of his captive.

'No; you're my mother's blood, and a son of hers will never draw it from your heart; but I can make sure of you again – stop a bit.'

He ran to his own prostrate horse, took off its bridle and its saddle-girth, and with both secured his uncle's limbs, beyond all possibility of the struggler being able to escape from their control.

'There,' resumed Shamus, 'lie there till we have time to send an ould friend to see you, that, I'll go bail, will take good care of your four bones. And do you know where I'm going now? You tould me, on Lunnon Bridge, that you knew that, at least' – pointing to the abbey – 'ay, and the quare ould hearthstone that's to be found in it. And so, look at this, uncle, honey' – he vaulted upon his relation's horse – 'I'm just goin' to lift it off o' the barrel-pot full of good ould goold, and you have only to cry halves, and you'll get it, as sure as that the big divvle is in the town you came from.'

Nance Dempsey was nursing her new-born babe, sitting up in her straw, and doing very well after her late illness, when old Noreen tottered in from the front of the ruin, to tell her that 'the body they were just speaking about was driving up the hill mad, like as if 'twas his own sprit in great troble.' And the listener had not recovered from her surprise, when Shamus ran into the shed, flung himself kneeling by her side, caught her in his arms, then seized her infant, covered it with kisses, and then, roughly throwing it in her lap, turned to the fireplace, raised one of the rocky seats lying near it, poised the ponderous mass over the hearthstone, and shivered into pieces, with one crash, that solid barrier between him and his visionary world of wealth.

'It's cracked he is, out an' out, of a certainty,' said Nance, looking terrified at her husband.

'Nothing else am I,' shouted Shamus, after groping under the broken slab; 'an', for a token, get along with yourself out of this, owld gran!'

He started up and seized her by the shoulder. Noreen remonstrated. He stooped for a stone; she ran; he pursued her to the arches of the ruin. She stopped halfway down the descent. He pelted her with clods to the bottom, and along a good piece of her road homewards; and then danced back into his wife's presence.

'Now, Nance,' he cried, 'now that we're by ourselves, what noise is this like?'

'And he took out han'fuls after han'fuls of the ould goold, afore her face, my dear,' added the original narrator of this story.

'An' after the gaugers and their crony, Ould Nick, ran off with the uncle of him, Nance and he, and the childer, lived together in their father's and mother's house; and if they didn't live and die happy, I wish that you and I may.'

SHERIDAN LE FANU

The Spectre Lovers

There lived some fifteen years since in a small and ruinous house,
little better than a hovel, an old woman who was reported to have
considerably exceeded her eightieth year, and who rejoiced in the
name of Alice, or popularly, Ally Moran. Her society was not much
courted, for she was neither rich, nor, as the reader may suppose,
beautiful. In addition to a lean cur and cat she had one human
companion, her grandson, Peter Brien, whom, with laudable good-
nature, she had supported from the period of his orphanage down to
that of my story, which finds him in his twentieth year. Peter was
a good-natured slob of a fellow much more addicted to wrestling,
dancing, and lovemaking, than to hard work, and fonder of whiskey
punch than good advice. His grandmother had a high opinion of
his accomplishments, which indeed was but natural, and also of his
genius, for Peter had of late years begun to apply his mind to politics;
and as it was plain that he had a mortal hatred of honest labour, his
grandmother predicted, like a true fortune-teller, that he was born to
marry an heiress, and Peter himself (who had no mind to forego his
freedom even on such terms) that he was destined to find a pot of
gold. Upon one point both agreed, that being unfitted by the peculiar
bias of his genius for work, he was to acquire the immense fortune to
which his merits entitled him by means of a pure run of good luck.
This solution of Peter's future had the double effect of reconciling
both himself and his grandmother to his idle courses, and also of
maintaining that even flow of hilarious spirits which made him everywhere welcome, and which was in truth the natural result of his consciousness of approaching affluence.

It happened one night that Peter had enjoyed himself to a very late hour with two or three choice spirits near Palmerstown. They had talked politics and love, sung songs, and told stories, and, above all, had swallowed, in the chastened disguise of punch, at least a pint of good whiskey, every man.

It was considerably past one o'clock when Peter bid his companions goodbye, with a sigh and a hiccough, and lighting his pipe set forth on his solitary homeward way.

The bridge of Chapelizod was pretty nearly the midway point of his night march, and from one cause or another his progress was rather slow, and it was past two o'clock by the time he found himself leaning over its old battlements, and looking up the river, over whose winding current and wooded banks the soft moonlight was falling.

The cold breeze that blew lightly down the stream was grateful to him. It cooled his throbbing head, and he drank it in at his hot lips. The scene, too, had, without his being well sensible of it, a secret fascination. The village was sunk in the profoundest slumber, not a mortal stirring, not a sound afloat, a soft haze covered it all, and the fairy moonlight hovered over the entire landscape.

In a state between rumination and rapture, Peter continued to lean over the battlements of the old bridge, and as he did so he saw, or fancied he saw, emerging one after another along the river bank in the little gardens and enclosures in the rear of the street of Chapelizod, the queerest little whitewashed huts and cabins he had ever seen there before. They had not been there that evening when he passed the bridge on the way to his merry tryst. But the most remarkable thing about it was the odd way in which these quaint little cabins showed themselves. First he saw one or two of them just with the corner of his eye, and when he looked full at them, strange to say, they faded away and disappeared. Then another and another came in view, but all in the same coy way, just appearing and gone again before he could well fix his gaze upon them; in a little while, however, they began to bear a fuller gaze, and he found, as it seemed to himself, that he was able by an effort of attention to fix the vision for a longer and a longer time, and when they waxed faint and nearly vanished, he had the power of recalling them into light and substance, until at last their vacillating indistinctness became less and less, and they assumed a permanent place in the moonlit landscape.

'Be the hokey,' said Peter, lost in amazement, and dropping his pipe into the river unconsciously, 'them is the quarist bits iv mud cabins I ever seen, growing up like musharoons in the dew of an evening, and poppin' up here and down again there, and up again in another place, like so many white rabbits in a warren; and there they stand at last as firm and fast as if they were there from the Deluge; bedad it's enough to make a man a'most believe in the fairies.'

This latter was a large concession from Peter, who was a bit of a free-thinker, and spoke contemptuously in his ordinary conversation of that class of agencies.

Having treated himself to a long last stare at these mysterious fabrics, Peter prepared to pursue his homeward way; having crossed the bridge and passed the mill, he arrived at the corner of the main street of the little town, and casting a careless look up the Dublin road, his eye was arrested by a most unexpected spectacle.

This was no other than a column of foot-soldiers, marching with perfect regularity towards the village, and headed by an officer on horseback. They were at the far side of the turnpike, which was closed; but much to his perplexity he perceived that they marched on through it without appearing to sustain the least check from that barrier.

On they came at a slow march; and what was most singular in the matter was that they were drawing several cannons along with them; some held ropes, others spoked the wheels, and others again marched in front of the guns and behind them, with muskets shouldered, giving a stately character of parade and regularity to this, as it seemed to Peter, most unmilitary procedure.

It was owning either to some temporary defect in Peter's vision, or to some illusion attendant upon mist and moonlight, or perhaps to some other cause, that the whole procession had a certain waving and vapoury character which perplexed and tasked his eyes not a little. It was like the pictured pageant of a phantasmagoria reflected upon smoke. It was as if every breath disturbed it; sometimes it was blurred, sometimes obliterated; now here, now there. Sometimes, while the upper part was quite distinct, the legs of the column would nearly fade away or vanish outright, and then again they would come out into clear relief, marching on with measured tread, while the cocked hats and shoulders grew, as it were, transparent, and all but disappeared.

Notwithstanding these strange optical fluctuations however, the column continued steadily to advance. Peter crossed the street from the corner near the old bridge, running on tiptoe, and with his body stooped to avoid observation, and took up a position upon the raised footpath in the shadow of the houses, where, as the soldiers kept the middle of the road, he calculated that he might, himself undetected, see them distinctly enough as they passed.

'What the div – , what on airth,' he muttered, checking the irreligious ejaculation with which he was about to start, for certain queer misgivings were hovering about his heart, notwithstanding the factitious courage of the whiskey bottle. 'What on airth is the manin' of all this? Is it the French that's landed at last to give us a hand and help us in airnest to this blessed repale? If it is not them, I simply ask who the d—l, I mane who on airth are they, for such sogers as them I never seen before in my born days?'

By this time the foremost of them were quite near, and truth to say they were the queerest soldiers he had ever seen in the course of his life. They wore long gaiters and leather breeches, three-cornered hats, bound with silver lace, long blue coats, with scarlet facings and linings, which latter were shown by a fastening which held together the two opposite corners of the skirt behind; and in front the breasts were in like manner connected at a single point, where and below which they sloped back, disclosing a long-flapped waistcoat of snowy whiteness; they had very large, long cross-belts, and wore enormous pouches of white leather hung extraordinarily low, and on each of which a little silver star was glittering. But what struck him as most grotesque and outlandish in their costume was their extraordinary display of shirt-frill in front, and of ruffle about their wrists, and the strange manner in which their hair was frizzled out and powdered under their hats, and clubbed up into great rolls behind. But one of the party was mounted. He rode a tall white horse with high action and arching neck; he had a snow-white feather in his three-cornered hat, and his coat was shimmering all over with a profusion of silver lace. From these circum-stances Peter concluded that he must be the commander of the detachment, and examined him as he passed attentively. He was a slight, tall man, whose legs did not half fill his leather breeches, and he appeared to be at the wrong side of sixty. He had a shrunken, weather-beaten, mulberry-coloured face, carried a large black patch over one eye, and turned neither to the right nor to the left, but rode on at the head of his men, with a grim, military inflexibility.

The countenances of these soldiers, officers as well as men, seemed all full of trouble, and, so to speak, scared and wild. He watched in vain for a single contented or comely face. They had, one and all, a melancholy and hang-dog look; and as they passed by, Peter fancied that the air grew cold and thrilling.

He had seated himself upon a stone bench, from which, staring with all his might, he gazed upon the grotesque and noiseless procession as it filed by him. Noiseless it was; he could neither hear the jingle of accoutrements, the tread of feet, nor the rumble of the wheels; and when the old colonel turned his horse a little, and made as though he were giving the word of command, and a trumpeter, with a swollen blue nose and white feather fringe round his hat, who was walking beside him, turned about and put his bugle to his lips, still Peter heard nothing, although it was plain the sound had reached the soldiers, for they instantly changed their front to three abreast.

'Botheration!' muttered Peter, 'is it deaf I'm growing?'

But that could not be, for he heard the sighing of the breeze and the rush of the neighbouring Liffey plain enough.

'Well,' said he, in the same cautious key, 'by the piper, this bangs Banagher fairly! It's either the Frinch army that's in it, come to take the town iv Chapelizod by surprise, an' makin' no noise for feard iv wakenin' the inhabitants; or else it's – it's – what it's – somethin' else. But, tundher-an-ouns, what's gone wid Fitzpatrick's shop across the way?'

The brown, dingy stone building at the opposite side of the street looked newer and cleaner that he had been used to see it; the front door of it stood open, and a sentry, in the same grotesque uniform, with shouldered musket, was pacing noiselessly to and fro before it. At the angle of this building, in like manner, a wide gate (of which Peter had no recollection whatever) stood open, before which, also, a similar sentry was gliding, and into this gateway the whole column gradually passed, and Peter finally lost sight of it.

'I'm not asleep; I'm not dhramin',' said he, rubbing his eyes, and stamping slightly on the pavement, to assure himself that he was wide awake. 'It is a quare business, whatever it is; an' it's not alone that, but everything about the town looks strange to me. There's Tresham's house new painted, bedad, an' them flowers in the windies! An' Delany's house, too, that had not a whole pane of glass in it this morning, and scarce a slate on the roof of it! It is not possible it's what it's dhrunk I am. Sure there's the big tree, and not a leaf of it changed since I passed, and the stars overhead, all night. I don't think it is in my eyes it is.'

And so looking about him, and every moment finding or fancying new food for wonder, he walked along the pavement, intending, without further delay, to make his way home.

But his adventures for the night were not concluded. He had nearly reached the angle of the short lane that leads up to the church, when for the first time he perceived that an officer, in the uniform he had just seen, was walking before, only a few yards in advance of him.

The officer was walking along at an easy, swinging gait, and carried his sword under his arm, and was looking down on the pavement with an air of reverie.

In the very fact that he seemed unconscious of Peter's presence, and disposed to keep his reflections to himself, there was something reassuring. Besides, the reader must please to remember that our hero had a *quantum sufficit* of good punch before his adventure commenced, and was thus fortified against those qualms and terrors under which, in a more reasonable state of mind, he might not impossibly have sunk.

The idea of the French invasion revived in full power in Peter's fuddled imagination, as he pursued the nonchalant swagger of the officer.

'Be the powers iv Moll Kelly, I'll ax him what it is,' said Peter, with a sudden accession of rashness. 'He may tell me or not, as he plases, but he can't be offinded, anyhow.'

With this reflection having inspired himself, Peter cleared his voice and began: 'Captain!' said he, 'I ax your pardon, captain, an' maybe you'd be so condescindin' to my ignorance as to tell me, if it's plasin' to yer honour, whether your honour is not a Frinchman, if it's plasin' to you.'

This he asked, not thinking that, had it been as he suspected, not one word of his question in all probability would have been intelligible to the person he addressed. He was, however, understood, for the officer answered him in English, at the same time slackening his pace and moving a little to the side of the pathway, as if to invite his interrogator to take his place beside him.

'No; I am an Irishman,' he answered.

'I humbly thank you honour,' said Peter, drawing nearer – for the affability and the nativity of the officer encouraged him – 'but maybe your honour is in the service of the King of France?'

'I serve the same King as you do,' he answered, with a sorrowful significance which Peter did not comprehend at the time, and, interrogating in turn, he asked, 'But what calls you forth at this hour of the day?'

'The *day*, your honour! – the night, you mane.'

'It was always our way to turn night into day, and we keep to it still,' remarked the soldier. 'But, no matter, come up here to my house; I have a job for you, if you wish to earn some money easily. I live here.'

As he said this, he beckoned authoritatively to Peter, who followed almost mechanically at his heels, and they turned up a little lane near the old Roman Catholic chapel, at the end of which stood, in Peter's time, the ruins of a tall, stonebuilt house.

Like everything else in the town, it had suffered a metamorphosis. The stained and ragged walls were now erect, perfect, and covered with pebble-dash; windowpanes glittered coldly in every window; the green hall-door had a bright brass knocker on it. Peter did not know whether to believe his previous or his present impressions; seeing is believing, and Peter could not dispute the reality of the scene. All the records of his memory seemed but the images of a tipsy dream. In a trance of astonishment and perplexity, therefore, he submitted himself to the chances of his adventure.

The door opened, the officer beckoned with a melancholy air of authority to Peter, and entered. Our hero followed him into a sort of hall, which was very dark, but he was guided by the steps of the soldier, and, in silence, they ascended the stairs. The moonlight, which shone in at the lobbies, showed an old, dark wainscoting, and a heavy oak banister. They passed by closed doors at different landing-places, but all was dark and silent as, indeed, became that late hour of the night.

Now they ascended to the topmost floor. The captain paused for a minute at the nearest door, and, with a heavy groan, pushing it open, entered the room. Peter remained at the threshold. A slight female form in a sort of loose white robe, and with a great deal of dark hair hanging loosely about her, was standing in the middle of the floor, with her back towards them.

The soldier stopped short before he reached her, and said, in a voice of great anguish, 'Still the same, sweet bird – sweet bird! still the same.' Whereupon, she turned suddenly and threw her arms about the neck of the officer, with a gesture of fondness and despair, and her frame was agitated as if by a burst of sobs. He held her close to his breast in silence; and honest Peter felt a strange terror creep over him, as he witnessed these mysterious sorrows and endearments.

'Tonight, tonight – and then ten years more – ten long years – another ten years.'

The officer and the lady seemed to speak these words together: here voice mingled with his in a musical and fearful wail, like a distant summer wind, in the dead hour of night wandering through ruins. Then he heard the officer say alone, in a voice of anguish: 'Upon me be it all, for ever, sweet birdie, upon me.'

And again they seemed to mourn together in the same soft and desolate wail, like sounds of grief heard from a great distance.

Peter was thrilled with horror, but he was also under a strange fascination; and an intense and dreadful curiosity held him fast.

The moon was shining obliquely into the room, and through the window Peter saw the familiar slopes of the Park, sleeping mistily under its shimmer. He could also see the furniture of the room with tolerable distinctness – the old balloon-backed chairs, a four-post bed in a sort of recess and a rack against the wall, from which hung some military clothes and accoutrements; and the sight of all these homely objects reassured him somewhat, and he could not help feeling unspeakably curious to see the face of the girl whose long hair was streaming over the officer's epaulet.

Peter, accordingly, coughed, at first slightly, and afterward more loudly, to recall her from her reverie of grief: and, apparently, he succeeded; for she turned round, as did her companion, and both, standing hand in hand, gazed upon him fixedly. He thought he had never seen such large, strange eyes in all his life; and their gaze seemed to chill the very air around him, and arrest the pulses of his heart. An eternity of misery and remorse was in the shadowy faces that looked upon him.

If Peter had taken less whiskey by a single thimbleful, it is probable that he would have lost heart altogether before these figures, which seemed every moment to assume a more marked and fearful, though hardly definable, contrast to ordinary human shapes.

'What is it you want with me?' he stammered.

'To bring my lost treasure to the churchyard,' replied the lady, in a silvery voice of more than mortal desolation.

The word 'treasure' revived the resolution of Peter, although a cold sweat was covering him, and his hair was bristling with horror; he believed, however, that he was on the brink of fortune, if he could but command nerve to brave the interview to its close.

'And where,' he gasped, 'is it hid – where will I find it?'

They both pointed to the sill of the window, through which the moon was shining at the far end of the room, and the soldier said: 'Under that stone.'

Peter drew a long breath, and wiped the cold dew from his face, preparatory to passing to the window, where he expected to secure the reward of his protracted terrors. But looking steadfastly at the window, he saw the faint image of a new-born child sitting upon the sill in the moonlight, with its little arms stretched toward him, and a smile so heavenly as he never beheld before.

At sight of this, strange to say, his heart entirely failed him; he looked on the figures that stood near, and beheld them gazing on the infantine form with a smile so guilty and distorted, that he felt as if he were entering alive among the scenery of hell, and shuddering, he cried in an irrepressible agony of horror: 'I'll have nothing to say with you, and nothing to do with you: I don't know what yez are or what yez want iv me, but let me go this minute, every one of yez, in the name of God.'

With these words there came a strange rumbling and sighing about Peter's ears; he lost sight of everything, and felt that peculiar and not unpleasant sensation of falling softly, that sometimes supervenes in sleep, ending in a dull shock. After that he had neither dream nor consciousness till he wakened, chill and stiff, stretched between two piles of old rubbish, among the black and roofless walls of the ruined house.

We need hardly mention that the village had put on its wonted air of neglect and decay, or that Peter looked around him in vain for traces of those novelties which had so puzzled and distracted him upon the previous night.

'Ay, ay,' said his grandmother, removing her pipe, as he ended his description of the view from the bridge, 'sure enough I remember myself, when I was a slip of a girl, these little white cabins among the gardens by the river side. The artillery sogers that was married, or had not room in the barracks, used to be in them, but they're all gone long ago.'

'The Lord be merciful to us!' she resumed, when he had described the military procession, 'it's often I seen the regiment marchin' into the town, jist as you saw it last night, acushla. Oh, voch, but it makes my heart sore to think iv them days; they were pleasant times, sure enough; but is not it terrible, avick, to think it's what it was the ghost of the regiment you seen? The Lord betune us an' harm, for it was nothing else, as sure as I'm sittin' here.'

When he mentioned the peculiar physiognomy and figure of the old officer who rode at the head of the regiment: '*That*,' said the old crone, dogmatically, 'was ould Colonel Grimshaw, the Lord presarve us! he's buried in the churchyard iv Chapelizod, and well I remember him, when I was a young thing, an' a cross ould floggin' fellow he was wid the men, an' a devil's boy among the girls – rest his soul!'

'Amen!' said Peter; 'it's often I read his tombstone myself; but he's a long time dead.'

'Sure, I tell you he died when I was no more nor a slip iv a girl – the Lord betune us and harm!'

'I'm afeard it is what I'm not long for this world myself, afther seeing such as that,' said Peter, fearfully.

'Nonsinse, avourneen,' retorted his grandmother, indignantly, though she had herself misgivings on the subject; 'sure there was Phil Doolan, the ferryman, that seen black Ann Scanlan in his own boat, and what harm ever kem of it?'

Peter proceeded with his narrative, but when he came to the description of the house, in which his adventure had had so sinister a conclusion, the old woman was at fault.

'I know the house and the ould walls well, an' I can remember the time there was a roof on it, and the doors an' windows in it, but it had a bad name about being haunted, but by who, or for what, I forget entirely.'

'Did you ever hear was there gold or silver there?' he enquired.

'No, no, avick, don't be thinking about the likes; take a fool's advice, and never go next or near them ugly black walls again the longest day you have to live; an' I'd take my davy, it's what it's the same word the priest himself I'd be afther sayin' to you if you wor to ax his raverence consarnin' it, for it's plain to be seen it was nothing good you seen there, and there's neither luck nor grace about it.'

Peter's adventure made no little noise in the neighbourhood, as the reader may well suppose; and a few evenings after it, being on an errand to old Major Vandeleur, who lived in a snug old-fashioned house, close by the river, under a perfect bower of ancient trees, he was called on to relate the story in the parlour.

The Major was, as I have said, on old man; he was small, lean, and upright, with a mahogany complexion, and a wooden inflexibility of face; he was a man, besides, of few words, and if *he* was old, it follows plainly that his mother was older still. Nobody could guess or tell *how* old, but it was admitted that her own generation had long passed away, and that she had not a competitor left. She had French blood in her veins, and although she did not retain her charms quite so well as Niñon de l'Enclos, she was in full possession of all her mental activity, and talked quite enough for herself and the Major.

'So, Peter,' she said, 'you have seen the dear, old Royal Irish again in the streets of Chapelizod. Make him a tumbler of punch, Frank; and Peter, sit down, and while you take it let us have the story.'

Peter accordingly, seated near the door, with a tumbler of the nectarian stimulant steaming beside him, proceeded with marvellous courage, considering they had no light but the uncertain glare of the fire, to relate with minute particularity his awful adventure. The old lady listened at first with a smile of good-natured incredulity; her cross-examination touching the drinking-bout at Palmerstown had been teasing, but as the narrative proceeded she became attentive, and at length absorbed, and once or twice she uttered ejaculations of pity or awe. When it was over, the old lady looked with a somewhat sad and stern abstraction on the table, patting her cat assiduously meanwhile, and then suddenly looking upon here son, the Major, she said: 'Frank, as sure as I live he has seen the wicked Captain Devereux.'

The Major uttered an inarticulate expression of wonder.

'The house was precisely that he has described. I have told you the story often, as I heard it from your dear grandmother, about the poor young lady he ruined, and the dreadful suspicion about the little baby. *She*, poor thing, died in that house heartbroken, and you know he was shot shortly after in a duel.'

This was the only light that Peter ever received respecting his adventure. It was supposed, however, that he still clung to the hope that treasure of some sort was hidden about the old house, for he was often seen lurking about its walls, and at last his fate overtook him, poor fellow, in the pursuit; for climbing near the summit one day, his holding gave way, and he fell upon the hard uneven ground, fracturing a leg and a rib, and after a short interval died, and he, like the other heroes, lies buried in the little churchyard of Chapelizod.

THOMAS CROFTON CROKER

The Haunted Cellar

There are few people who have not heard of the Mac Carthys – one of the real old Irish families, with the true Milesian blood running in their veins as thick as buttermilk. Many were the clans of this family in the south; as the Mac Carthymore – and the Mac Carthy-reagh – and the Mac Carthy of Muskerry; and all of them were noted for their hospitality to strangers, gentle and simple.

But not one of that name, or of any other, exceeded Justin Mac Carthy, of Ballinacarthy, at putting plenty to eat and drink upon his table; and there was a right hearty welcome for everyone who should share it with him. Many a wine cellar would be ashamed of the name if that at Ballinacarthy was the proper pattern for one. Large as that cellar was, it was crowded with bins of wine, and long rows of pipes, and hogsheads, and casks, that it would take more time to count than any sober man could spare in such a place, with plenty to drink about him, and a hearty welcome to do so.

There are many, no doubt, who will think that the butler would have little to complain of in such a house; and the whole country round would have agreed with them, if a man could be found to remain as Mr MacCarthy's butler for any length of time worth speaking of; yet not one who had been in his service gave him a bad word.

'We have no fault,' they would say, 'to find with the master, and if he could but get anyone to fetch his wine from the cellar, we might everyone of us have grown grey in the house and have lived quiet and contented enough in his service until the end of our days.'

' 'Tis a queer thing that, surely,' thought young Jack Leary, a lad who had been brought up from a mere child in the stables of Ballina-carthy to assist in taking care of the horses, and had occasionally lent a hand in the butler's pantry: – ' 'Tis a mighty queer thing, surely, that

one man after another cannot content himself with the best place in
the house of a good master, but that everyone of them must quit, all
through the means, as they say, of the wine cellar. If the master, long
life to him! would but make me his butler, I warrant never the word
more would be heard of grumbling at his bidding to go to the wine
cellar.'

Young Leary, accordingly, watched for what he conceived to be a
favourable opportunity of presenting himself to the notice of his master.

A few mornings after, Mr Mac Carthy went into his stableyard
rather earlier than usual, and called loudly for the groom to saddle his
horse, as he intended going out with the hounds. But there was no
groom to answer, and young Jack Leary led Rainbow out of the stable.

'Where is William?' enquired Mr Mac Carthy.

'Sir?' said Jack; and Mr Mac Carthy repeated the question.

'Is it William, please your honour?' returned Jack; 'why, then, to
tell the truth, he had just *one* drop too much last night.'

'Where did he get it?' said Mr Mac Carthy; 'for since Thomas went
away the key of the wine cellar has been in my pocket, and I have been
obliged to fetch what was drunk myself.'

'Sorrow a know I know,' said Leary, 'unless the cook might have
given him the *least taste* in life of whiskey. But,' continued he, performing a low bow by seizing with his right hand a lock of hair, and
pulling down his head by it, while his left leg, which had been put
forward, was scraped back against the ground, 'may I make so bold as
just to ask your honour one question?'

'Speak out, Jack,' said Mr Mac Carthy.

'Why, then, does your honour want a butler?'

'Can you recommend me one,' returned his master, with the smile
of good-humour upon his countenance, 'and one who will not be
afraid of going to my wine cellar?'

'Is the wine cellar all the matter?' said young Leary; 'devil a doubt I
have of myself then for that.'

'So you mean to offer me your services in the capacity of butler?'
said Mr Mac Carthy, with some surprise.

'Exactly so,' answered Leary, now for the first time looking up from
the ground.

'Well, I believe you to be a good lad, and have no objection to give
you a trial.'

'Long may your honour reign over us, and the Lord spare you to us!' ejaculated Leary, with another national bow, as his master rode off; and he continued for some time to gaze after him with a vacant stare, which slowly and gradually assumed a look of importance.

'Jack Leary,' said he, at length, 'Jack – is it Jack?' in a tone of wonder; 'faith, 'tis not Jack now, but Mr John, the butler;' and with an air of becoming consequence he strided out of the stableyard towards the kitchen.

It is of little purport to my story, although it may afford an instructive lesson to the reader, to depict the sudden transition of nobody into somebody. Jack's former stable companion, a poor super-annuated hound named Bran, who had been accustomed to receive many an affectionate pat on the head, was spurned from him with a kick and an 'Out of the way, sirrah.' Indeed, poor Jack's memory seemed sadly affected by this sudden change of situation. What established the point beyond all doubt was his almost forgetting the pretty face of Peggy, the kitchen wench, whose heart he had assailed but the preceding week by the offer of purchasing a gold ring for the fourth finger of her right hand, and a lusty imprint of good will upon her lips.

When Mr Mac Carthy returned from hunting, he sent for Jack Leary – so he still continued to call his new butler. 'Jack,' said he, 'I believe you are a trustworthy lad, and here are the keys of my cellar. I have asked the gentlemen with whom I hunted today to dine with me, and I hope they may be satisfied at the way in which you will wait on them at table; but, above all, let there be no want of wine after dinner.'

Mr John having a tolerably quick eye for such things, and being naturally a handy lad, spread his cloth accordingly, laid his plates and knives and forks in the same manner be had seen his predecessors in office perform these mysteries, and really, for the first time, got through attendance on dinner very well.

It must not be forgotten, however, that it was at the house of an Irish country squire, who was entertaining a company of booted and spurred fox-hunters, not very particular about what are considered matters of infinite importance under other circumstances and in other societies.

For instance, few of Mr Mac Carthy's guests (though all excellent and worthy men in their way) cared much whether the punch produced after soup was made of Jamaica or Antigua rum; some even would not have been inclined to question the correctness of good old Irish whiskey; and, with the exception of their liberal host himself, everyone in company preferred the port which Mr Mac Carthy put on his table to the less ardent flavour of claret – a choice rather at variance with modern sentiment.

It was waxing near midnight, when Mr Mac Carthy rung the bell three times. This was a signal for more wine; and Jack proceeded to the cellar to procure a fresh supply, but it must be confessed not without some little hesitation.

The luxury of ice was then unknown in the south of Ireland; but the superiority of cool wine had been acknowledged by all men of sound judgment and true taste.

The grandfather of Mr Mac Carthy, who had built the mansion of Ballinacarthy upon the site of an old castle which had belonged to his ancestors, was fully aware of this important fact; and in the construction of his magnificent wine cellar had availed himself of a deep vault, excavated out of the solid rock in former times as a place of retreat and security. The descent to this vault was by a flight of steep stone stairs, and here and there in the wall were narrow passages – I ought rather to call them crevices; and also certain projections, which cast deep shadows, and looked very frightful when anyone went down the cellar stairs with a single light: indeed, two lights did not much improve the matter, for though the breadth of the shadows became less, the narrow crevices remained as dark and darker than ever.

Summoning up all his resolution, down went the new butler, bearing in his right hand a lantern and the key of the cellar, and in his left a basket, which he considered sufficiently capacious to contain an adequate stock for the remainder of the evening: he arrived at the door without any interruption whatever; but when he put the key, which was of an ancient and clumsy kind – for it was before the days of Bramah's patent – and turned it in the lock, he thought he heard a strange kind of laughing within the cellar, to which some empty bottle that stood upon the floor outside vibrated so violently that they struck against each other: in this he could not be mistaken, although he may have been deceived in the laugh, for the bottles were just at his feet, and he saw them in motion.

Leary paused for a moment, and looked about him with becoming caution. He then boldly seized the handle of the key, and turned it with all his strength in the lock, as if he doubted his own power of doing so; and the door flew open with a most tremendous crash, that if the house had not been built upon the solid rock would have shook it from the foundation.

To recount what the poor fellow saw would be impossible, for he seems not to have known very clearly himself: but what he told the cook the next morning was, that he heard a roaring and bellowing like a mad bull, and that all the pipes and hogsheads and casks in the cellar went rocking backwards and forwards with so much force that he thought everyone would have been staved in, and that he should have been drowned or smothered in wine.

When Leary recovered, he made his way back as well as he could to the dining room, where he found his master and the company very impatient for his return.

'What kept you?' said Mr Mac Carthy in an angry voice; 'and where is the wine ? I rung for it half an hour since.'

'The wine is in the cellar, I hope, sir,' said Jack, trembling violently; 'I hope 'tis not all lost.'

'What do you mean, fool?' exclaimed Mr Mac Carthy in a still more angry tone: 'why did you not fetch some with you?'

Jack looked wildly about him, and only uttered a deep groan.

'Gentlemen,' said Mr Mac Carthy to his guests, 'this is too much. When I next see you to dinner, I hope it will be in another house, for it is impossible I can remain longer in this, where a man has no command over his own wine cellar, and cannot get a butler to do his duty. I have long thought of moving from Ballinacarthy; and I am now determined, with the blessing of God, to leave it tomorrow. But wine shall you have were I to go myself to the cellar for it.' So saying, he rose from table, took the key and lantern from his half-stupified servant, who regarded him with a look of vacancy, and descended the narrow stairs, already described, which led to his cellar.

When he arrived at the door, which he found open, he thought he heard a noise, as if of rats or mice scrambling over the casks, and on advancing perceived a little figure, about six inches in height, seated astride upon the pipe of the oldest port in the place, and bearing a spigot upon his shoulder. Raising the lantern, Mr Mac Carthy con-templated the little fellow with wonder: he wore a red nightcap on his head; before him was a short leather apron, which now, from his attitude, fell rather on one side; and he had stockings of a light blue colour, so long as nearly to cover the entire of his legs; with shoes, having huge silver buckles in them, and with high heels (perhaps out of vanity to make him appear taller). His face was like a withered winter apple; and his nose, which was of a bright crimson colour, about the tip wore a delicate purple bloom, like that of a plum; yet his eyes twinkled 'like those mites of candied dew in moony nights – ' and his mouth twitched up at one side with an arch grin.

'Ha, scoundrel!' exclaimed Mr Mac Carthy, 'have I found you at last? disturber of my cellar – what are you doing there?'

'Sure, and master,' returned the little fellow, looking up at him with one eye, and with the other throwing a sly glance towards the spigot on his shoulder, 'a'n't we going to move tomorrow? and sure you would not leave your own little Cluricaune Naggeneen behind you?'

'Oh!' thought Mr Mac Carthy, 'if you are to follow me, master Naggeneen, I don't see much use in quitting Ballinacarthy.' So filling with wine the basket which young Leary in his fright had left behind him, and locking the cellar door, he rejoined his guests.

For some years after Mr Mac Carthy had always to fetch the wine for his table himself, as the little Cluricaune Naggeneen seemed to feel a personal respect towards him. Notwithstanding the labour of these journeys, the worthy lord of Ballinacarthy lived in his paternal mansion to a good round age, and was famous to the last for the excellence of his wine, and conviviality of his company; but at the time of his death, the same conviviality had nearly emptied his wine cellar; and as it was never so well filled again, nor so often visited, the revels of master Naggeneen became less celebrated, and are now only spoken of among the legendary lore of the country. It is even said that the poor little fellow took the declension of the cellar so to heart, that he became negligent and careless of himself, and that he has been sometimes seen going about with hardly a *skreed* to cover him.

THOMAS CROFTON CROKER

Legend of Bottle Hill

It was in the good days when the little people, most impudently called
fairies, were more frequently seen than they are in these unbelieving
times, that a farmer, named Mick Purcell, rented a few acres of barren
ground in the neighbourhood of the once celebrated preceptory of
Mourne, situated about three miles from Mallow, and thirteen from
'the beautiful city called Cork.' Mick had a wife and family. They all
did what they could, and that was but little, for the poor man had no
child grown up big enough to help him in his work; and all the poor
woman could do was to mind the children, and to milk the one cow,
and to boil the potatoes, and carry the eggs to market to Mallow; but
with all they could do, 'twas hard enough on them to pay the rent.
Well, they did manage it for a good while; but at last came a bad year,
and the little grain of oats was all spoiled, and the chickens died of the
pip, and the pig got the measles, – she was sold in Mallow and brought
almost nothing; and poor Mick found that he hadn't enough to half
pay his rent, and two gales were due.

'Why, then, Molly,' says he, 'what'll we do?'

'Wisha, then, mavournene, what would you do but take the cow to
the fair of Cork and sell her?' says she; 'and Monday is fair day, and so
you must go tomorrow, that the poor beast may be rested *again* the
fair.'

'And what'll we do when she's gone?' says Mick, sorrowfully.

'Never a know I know, Mick; but sure God won't leave us without
Him, Mick; and you know how good He was to us when poor little
Billy was sick, and we had nothing at all for him to take, – that good
doctor gentleman at Ballydahin come riding and asking for a drink of
milk; and how he gave us two shillings; and how he sent the things and

bottles for the child, and gave me my breakfast when I went over to ask a question, so he did; and how he come to see Billy, and never left off his goodness till he was quite well?'

'Oh! you are always that way, Molly, and I believe you are right after all, so I won't be sorry for selling the cow; but I'll go tomorrow, and you must put a needle and thread through my coat, for you know 'tis ripped under the arm.'

Molly told him he should have everything right; and about twelve o'clock next day he left her, getting a charge not to sell his cow except for the highest penny. Mick promised to mind it, and went his way along the road. He drove his cow slowly through the little stream which crosses it, and runs under the old walls of Mourne. As he passed he glanced his eye upon the towers and one of the old elder trees, which were only then little bits of switches.

'Oh, then, if I only had half of the money that's buried in you, 'tisn't driving this poor cow I'd be now! Why, then, isn't it too bad that it should be there covered over with earth, and many a one besides me wanting? Well if it's God's will, I'll have some money myself coming back.'

So saying he moved on after his beast. 'Twas a fine day, and the sun shone brightly on the walls of the old abbey as he passed under them. He then crossed an extensive mountain tract, and after six long miles he came to the top of that hill – Bottle-hill 'tis called now, but that was not the name of it then, and just there a man overtook him. 'Good morning,' says he. 'Good morning, kindly,' says Mick, looking at the stranger, who was a little man, you'd almost call him a dwarf, only he wasn't quite so little neither: he had a bit of an old wrinkled, yellow face, for all the world like a dried cauliflower, only he had a sharp little nose, and red eyes, and white hair, and his lips were not red, but all his face was one colour, and his eyes never were quiet, but looking at everything, and although they were red they made Mick feel quite cold when he looked at them. In truth, he did not much like the little man's company; and he couldn't see one bit of his legs nor his body, for though the day was warm, he was all wrapped up in a big great coat. Mick drove his cow something faster, but the little man kept up with him. Mick didn't know how he walked, for he was almost afraid to look at him, and to cross himself, for fear the old man would be angry. Yet he thought his fellow-traveller did not seem to walk like other men, nor to put one foot before the other, but to glide over the rough road – and rough enough it was – like a shadow, without noise and without effort. Mick's heart trembled within him, and he said a prayer to himself, wishing he hadn't come out that day, or that he was on Fair-hill, or that he hadn't the cow to mind, that he might run away from the bad thing – when, in the midst of his fears, he was again addressed by his companion.

'Where are you going with the cow, honest man?'

'To the fair of Cork, then,' says Mick, trembling at the shrill and piercing tones of the voice.

'Are you going to sell her?' said the stranger.

'Why, then, what else am I going for but to sell her?'

'Will you sell her to me?'

Mick started – he was afraid to have anything to do with the little man, and he was more afraid to say no.

'What'll you give for her?' at last says he.

'I'll tell you what, I'll give you this bottle,' says the little one, pulling a bottle from under his coat.

Mick looked at him and the bottle, and, in spite of his terror, he could not help bursting into a loud fit of laughter.

'Laugh if you will,' said the little man, 'but I tell you this bottle is better for you than all the money you will get for the cow in Cork – ay, than ten thousand times as much.'

Mick laughed again. 'Why then,' says he, 'do you think I am such a fool as to give my good cow for a bottle – and an empty one, too? Indeed, then, I won't.'

'You had better give me the cow, and take the bottle – you'll not be sorry for it.'

'Why, then, and what would Molly say? I'd never hear the end of it; and how would I pay the rent? and what should we all do without a penny of money.'

'I tell you this bottle is better to you than money; take it, and give me the cow. I ask you for the last time, Mick Purcell.'

Mick started.

'How does he know my name?' thought he.

The stranger proceeded: 'Mick Purcell, I know you, and I have regard for you; therefore do as I warn you, or you may be sorry for it. How do you know but your cow will die before you go to Cork?'

Mick was going to say 'God forbid!' but the little man went on (and he was too attentive to say anything to stop him; for Mick was a very civil man, and he knew better than to interrupt a gentleman, and that's what many people, that hold their heads higher, don't mind now).

'And how do you know but there will be much cattle at the fair, and you will get a bad price, or maybe you might be robbed when you are coming home? but what need I talk more to you, when you are determined to throw away your luck, Mick Purcell.'

'Oh! no, I would not throw away my luck, sir,' said Mick; 'and if I was sure the bottle was as good as you say, though I never liked an empty bottle, although I had drank the contents of it, I'd give you the cow in the name –'

'Never mind names,' said the stranger, but give me the cow; I would not tell you a lie. Here, take the bottle, and when you go home do what I direct exactly.'

Mick hesitated.

'Well, then goodbye, I can stay no longer: once more, take it, and be rich; refuse it, and beg for your life, and see your children in poverty, and your wife dying for want – that will happen to you, Mick Purcell!' said the little man with a malicious grin, which made him look ten times more ugly than ever.

'Maybe, 'tis true,' said Mick, still hesitating: he did not know what to do – he could hardly help believing the old man, and at length, in a fit of desperation, he seized the bottle. 'Take the cow,' said he, 'and if you are telling a lie, the curse of the poor will be on you.'

'I care neither for your curses nor your blessings, but I have spoken truth, Mick Purcell, and that you will find tonight, if you do what I tell you.'

'And what's that?' says Mick.

'When you go home, never mind if your wife is angry, but be quiet yourself, and make her sweep the room clean, set the table out right, and spread a clean cloth over it; then put the bottle on the ground, saying these words: "Bottle, do your duty", and you will see the end of it.'

'And is this all?' says Mick.

'No more,' said the stranger, 'Goodbye, Mick Purcell – you are a rich man.'

'God grant it!' said Mick, as the old man moved after the cow, and Mick retraced the road towards his cabin: but he could not help turning back his head, to look after the purchaser of his cow, who was nowhere to be seen.

'Lord between us and harm!' said Mick. 'He can't belong to this earth; but where is the cow?' She too was gone, and Mick went homeward muttering prayers, and holding fast the bottle.

'And what would I do if it broke?' thought he. 'Oh! but I'll take care of that;' so he put it into his bosom, and went on anxious to prove his bottle, and doubting of the reception he should meet from his wife; balancing his anxieties with his expectation, his fears with his hopes, he reached home in the evening, and surprised his wife, sitting over the turf fire in the big chimney.

'Oh! Mick, are you come back? Sure you weren't at Cork all the way What has happened to you? Where is the cow? Did you sell her? How much money did you get for her? What news have you? Tell us everything about it?'

'Why then, Molly, if you'll give me time, I'll tell you all about it. If you want to know where the cow is, 'tisn't Mick can tell you, for the never a know does he know where she is now.

'Oh! then, you sold her; and where's the money?'

'Arrah! stop awhile, Molly, and I'll tell you all about it.'

'But what is that bottle under your waistcoat ?' said Molly, spying its neck sticking out. 'Why, then, be easy now, can't you,' says Mick, 'till I tell it to you;' and putting the bottle on the table, 'That's all I got for the cow.'

His poor wife was thunderstruck. 'All you got! and what good is that, Mick? Oh! I never thought you were such a fool; and what'll we do for the rent, and what – '

'Now, Molly,' says Mick, 'can't you hearken to reason? Didn't I tell you how the old man, or whatsomever he was, met me, – no, he did not meet me neither, but he was there with me – on the big hill, and how he made me sell him the cow, and told me the bottle was the only thing for me?'

'Yes, indeed, the only thing for you, you fool!' said Molly, seizing the bottle to hurl it at her poor husband's head; but Mick caught it and quietly for he minded the old man's advice; loosened his wife's grasp, and placed the bottle again in his bosom. Poor Molly sat down crying, while Mick told her his story, with many a crossing and blessing between him and harm. His wife could not help believing him, particularly as she had as much faith in fairies as she had in the priest, who indeed never discouraged her belief in the fairies; may be, he didn't know she believed in them, and may be, he believed in them himself. She got up, however, without saying one word, and began to sweep the earthen floor with a bunch of heath; then she tidied up everything, and put out the long table, and spread the clean cloth, for she had only one, upon it, and Mick, placing the bottle on the ground, looked at it, and said, 'Bottle, do your duty.'

'Look there! look there, mammy!' said his chubby eldest son, a boy about five years old – 'look there! look there!' and he sprang to his mother's side, as two tiny little fellows rose like light from the bottle, and in an instant covered the table with dishes and plates of gold and silver, full of the finest victuals that ever were seen, and when all was done went into the bottle again. Mick and his wife looked at everything with astonishment they had never seen such plates and dishes before, and didn't think they could ever admire them enough; the very sight almost took away their appetites; but at length Molly said, 'Come and sit down, Mick, and try and eat a bit: sure you ought to be hungry after such a good day's work.'

'Why, then, the man told no lie about the bottle.' Mick sat down, after putting the children to the table; and they made a hearty meal, though they couldn't taste half the dishes. 'Now,' says Molly, 'I wonder will those two good little gentlemen carry away these fine things again?' They waited, but no one came; so Molly put up the dishes and plates very carefully, saying, 'Why, then, Mick, that was no lie sure enough: but you'll be a rich man yet, Mick Purcell.'

Mick and his wife and children went to their bed, not to sleep, but to settle about selling the fine things they did not want, and to take more land. Mick went to Cork and sold his plate, and bought a horse and cart, and began to show that he was making money; and they did all they could to keep the bottle a secret; but for all that, their landlord found it out, for he came to Mick one day, and asked him where he got all his money – sure it was not by the farm; and he bothered him so much, that at last Mick told him of the bottle.

His landlord offered him a deal of money for it, but Mick would not give it, till at last he offered to give him all his farm for ever: so Mick, who was very rich, thought he'd never want any more money, and gave him the bottle: but Mick was mistaken – he and his family spent money as if there was no end of it; and to make the story short, they became poorer and poorer, till at last they had nothing left but one cow; and Mick once more drove his cow before him to sell her at Cork fair, hoping to meet the old man and get another bottle. It was hardly daybreak when he left home, and he walked on at a good pace till he reached the big hill: the mists were sleeping in the valleys and curling like smoke wreaths upon the brown heath around him. The sun rose on his left, and just at his feet a lark sprang from its grassy couch and poured fourth its joyous matin song, ascending into the clear blue sky,

'Till its form like a speck in the airiness blending,
And thrilling with music, was melting in light.'

Mick crossed himself, listening as he advanced to the sweet song of the lark, but thinking, notwithstanding, all the time of the little old man; when, just as he reached the summit of the hill, and cast his eyes over the extensive prospect before and around him, he was startled and rejoiced by the same well-known voice: 'Well, Mick Purcell, I told you you would be a rich man.'

'Indeed, then, sure enough I was, that's no lie for you, sir. Good morning to you, but it is not rich I am now – but have you another bottle, for I want it now as much as I did long ago; so if you have it, sir, here is the cow for it.'

'And here is the bottle,' said the old man, smiling; 'you know what to do with it.'

'Oh! then, sure I do, as good right I have.'

'Well, farewell for ever, Mick Purcell: I told you you would be a rich man.'

'And goodbye to you, sir,' said Mick, as he turned back; 'and good luck to you, and good luck to the big hill – it wants a name, Bottle-hill – goodbye, sir, goodbye': so Mick walked back as fast as he could, never looking after the white-faced little gentleman and the cow, so anxious was he to bring home the bottle. Well, he arrived with it safely enough, and called out as soon as he saw Molly, 'Oh! sure I've another bottle!'

'Arrah! then, have you? why, then, you're a lucky man, Mick Purcell, that's what you are.'

In an instant she put everything right; and Mick, looking at his bottle, exultingly cried out, 'Bottle, do your duty.' In a twinkling, two great stout men with big cudgels issued from the bottle (I do not know how they got room in it), and belaboured poor Mick and his wife and all his family, till they lay on the floor, when in they went again. Mick, as soon as he recovered, got up and looked about him; he thought and thought, and at last he took up his wife and his children; and, leaving them to recover as well as they could, he took the bottle under his coat and went to his landlord, who had a great company: he got a servant to tell him he wanted to speak to him, and at last he came out to Mick.

'Well, what do you want now?'

'Nothing, sir, only I have another bottle.'

'Oh! ho! is it as good as the first?'

'Yes, sir, and better; if you like I will show it to you before all the ladies and gentlemen.'

'Come along, then.' So saying, Mick was brought into the great hall, where he saw his old bottle standing high up on a shelf: 'Ah! ha!' says he to himself, 'maybe I won't have you by and by.'

'Now,' says his landlord, 'show us your bottle.' Mick set it on the floor, and uttered the words: in a moment the landlord was tumbling on the floor; ladies and gentlemen, servants and all, were running, and roaring, and sprawling, and kicking, and shrieking. Wine cups and salvers were knocked about in every direction, until the landlord called out, 'Stop those two devils, Mick Purcell, or I'll have you hanged.'

'They never shall stop,' said Mick, 'till I get my own bottle that I see up there at top of that shelf.'

'Give it down to him, give it down to him, before we are all killed!' says the landlord.

Mick put his bottle in his bosom: in jumped the two men into the new bottle, and he carried them home. I need not lengthen my story by telling how he got richer than ever, how his son married his landlord's only daughter, and how he and his wife died when they were very old, and how some of the servants, fighting at their wake, broke the bottles; but still the hill has the name upon it; ay, and so 'twill be always Bottle-hill to the end of the world, and so it ought, for it is a strange story.

PATRICK KENNEDY

The Ghosts and the Game of Football

❧❧

There was once a poor widow woman's son that was going to look for service, and one winter's evening he came to a strong farmer's house, and this house was very near an old castle. 'God save all here,' says he, when he got inside the door. 'God save you kindly,' says the farmer. 'Come to the fire.' 'Could you give me a night's lodging?' says the boy.

'That we will, and welcome, if you will only sleep in a comfortable room in the old castle above there; and you must have a fire and candlelight, and whatever you like to drink; and if you're alive in the morning I'll give you ten guineas.' 'Sure. I'll be 'live enough if you send no one to kill me.' 'I'll send no one to kill you, you may depend. The place is haunted ever since my father died, and three or four people that slept in the same room were found dead next morning. If you can banish the spirits I'll give you a good farm and my daughter, so that you like one another well enough to be married.' 'Never say't twice. I've a middling safe conscience, and don't fear any evil spirit that ever smelled of brimstone.'

Well and good, the boy got his supper, and then they went up with him to the old castle, and showed him into a large kitchen, with a roaring fire in the grate, and a table, with a bottle and glass, and tumbler on it, and the kettle ready on the hob. They bade him good-night and Godspeed, and went off as if they didn't think their heels were half swift enough. 'Well,' says he to himself, 'if there's any danger, this prayer-book will be usefuller than either the glass or tumbler.' So he kneeled down and read a good many prayers, and then sat by the fire, and waited to see what would happen. In about a quarter of an hour, he heard something bumping along the floor overhead till it came to a hole in the ceiling. There it stopped, and cried out, 'I'll fall, I'll fall.' 'Fall away,' says Jack, and down came a pair of legs on the kitchen floor. They walked to one end of the room, and there they stood, and Jack's hair had like to stand upright on his head along with them. Then another crackling and whacking came to the hole, and the same words passed between the thing above and Jack, and down came a man's body, and went and stood upon the legs. Then comes the head and shoulders, till the whole man, with buckles in his shoes and knee-breeches, and a big flapped waistcoat and a three-cocked hat, was standing in one corner of the room. Not to take up your time for nothing, two more men, more old-fashioned dressed than the first, were soon standing in two other corners. Jack was a little cowed at first; but found his courage growing stronger every moment, and what would you have of it, the three old gentle-men began to kick a *puckeen* [football] as fast as they could, the man in the three-cocked hat playing again' the other two.

'Fair play is bonny play,' says Jack, as bold as he could; but the terror was on him, and the words came out as if he was frightened in his sleep; 'so I'll help *you*, sir.' Well and good, he joined the sport, and kicked away till his shirt was ringing wet, savin' your presence, and the ball flying from one end of the room to the other like thunder, and still not a word was exchanged. At last the day began to break, and poor Jack was dead beat, and he thought, by the way the three ghosts began to look at himself and themselves, that they wished him to speak.

So, says he, 'Gentlemen, as the sport is nearly over, and I done my best to please you, would you tell a body what is the reason of your coming here night after night, and how could I give you rest, if it is rest you want?' 'Them is the wisest words,' says the ghost with the three-cocked hat, 'you ever said in your life. Some of those that came before you found courage enough to take a part in our game, but no one had *misnach* [energy] enough to speak to us. I am the father of the good man of the next house, that man in the left corner is my father, and the man on my right is my grandfather. From father to son we were too fond of money. We lent it at ten times the honest interest it was worth; we never paid a debt we could get over, and almost starved our tenants and labourers.

'Here,' says he, lugging a large drawer out of the wall; 'here is the gold and notes that we put together, and we were not honestly entitled to the one half of it; and here,' says he, opening another drawer, 'are bills and memorandums that'll show who were wronged, and who are entitled to get a great deal paid back to them. Tell my son to saddle two of his best horses for himself and yourself, and keep riding day and night, till every man and woman we ever wronged be rightified. When that is done, come here again some night; and if you don't hear or see anything, we'll be at rest, and you may marry my granddaughter as soon as you please.'

Just as he said these words, Jack could see the wall through his body, and when he winked to clear his sight, the kitchen was as empty as a noggin turned upside down. At that very moment the farmer and his daughter lifted the latch, and both fell on their knees when they saw Jack alive. He soon told them everything that happened, and for three days and nights did the farmer and himself ride about, till there wasn't a single wronged person left without being paid to the last farthing.

The next night Jack spent in the kitchen he fell asleep before he was after sitting a quarter of an hour at the fire, and in his sleep he thought he saw three white birds flying up to heaven from the steeple of the next church.

Jack got the daughter for his wife, and they lived comfortably in the old castle; and if ever he was tempted to hoard up gold, or keep for a minute a guinea or a shilling from the man that earned it through the nose, he bethought him of the ghosts and the game of football.

JEREMIAH CURTIN

The Blood-Drawing Ghost

❧❧❧

There was a young man in the parish of Drimoleague, county Cork, who was courting three girls at one time, and he didn't know which of them would he take; they had equal fortunes, and any of the three was as pleasing to him as any other.

One day when he was coming home from the fair with his two sisters, the sisters began: 'Well, John,' said one of them, 'why don't you get married? Why don't you take either Mary, or Peggy, or Kate?'

'I can't tell you that,' said John, 'till I find which of them has the best wish for me.'

'How will you know?' asked the other.

'I will tell you that as soon as any person will die in the parish.'

In three weeks' time from that day an old man died. John went to the wake and then to the funeral. While they were burying the corpse in the graveyard, John stood near a tomb which was next to the grave, and when all were going away, after burying the old man, he remained standing a while by himself, as if thinking of something; then he put his blackthorn stick on top of the tomb, stood a while longer, and on going from the graveyard left the stick behind him. He went home and ate his supper. After supper John went to a neighbour's house where young people used to meet of an evening, and the three girls happened to be there that time. John was very quiet, so that everyone noticed him.

'What is troubling you this evening, John?' asked one of the girls.

'Oh, I am sorry for my beautiful blackthorn,' said he.

'Did you lose it?'

'I did not,' said John; 'but I left it on the top of the tomb next to the grave of the man who was buried today and whichever of you three will go for it is the woman I'll marry. Well, Mary, will you go for my stick?' asked he.

'Faith, then, I will not,' said Mary.

'Well, Peggy, will you go?'

'If I were without a man forever,' said Peggy, 'I wouldn't go.'

'Well, Kate,' said he to the third, 'will you go for my stick? If you go I'll marry you.'

'Stand to your word,' said Kate, 'and I'll bring the stick.'

'Believe me, that I will,' said John.

Kate left the company behind her, and went for the stick. The graveyard was three miles away and the walk was a long one. Kate came to the place at last and made out the tomb by the fresh grave. When she had her hand on the blackthorn, a voice called from the tomb: 'Leave the stick where it is and open this tomb for me.'

Kate began to tremble and was greatly in dread, but something was forcing her to open the tomb – she couldn't help herself.

'Take the lid off now,' said the dead man when Kate had the door open and was inside in the tomb, 'and take me out of this – take me on your back.'

Afraid to refuse, she took the lid from the coffin, raised the dead man on her back, and walked on in the way he directed. She walked about the distance of a mile. The load, being very heavy, was near breaking her back and killing her. She walked half a mile farther and came to a village; the houses were at the side of the road.

'Take me to the first house,' said the dead man.

She took him.

'Oh, we cannot go in here,' said he, when they came near. 'The people have clean water inside, and they have holy water, too. Take me to the next house.'

She went to the next house.

'We cannot go in there,' said he, when she stopped in front of the door. 'They have clean water, and there is holy water as well.'

She went to the third house.

'Go in here,' said the dead man. 'There is neither clean water nor holy water in this place; we can stop in it.'

They went in.

'Bring a chair now and put me sitting at the side of the fire. Then find me something to eat and to drink.'

She placed him in a chair by the hearth, searched the house, found a dish of oatmeal and brought it. 'I have nothing to give you to drink but dirty water,' said she.

'Bring me a dish and a razor.'

She brought the dish and the razor.

'Come, now,' said he, 'to the room above.'

They went up to the room, where three young men, sons of the man of the house, were sleeping in bed, and Kate had to hold the dish while the dead man was drawing their blood.

'Let the father and mother have that,' said he, 'in return for the dirty water,' meaning that if there was clean water in the house he wouldn't have taken the blood of the young men.

He closed their wounds in the way that there was no sign of a cut on them. 'Mix this now with the meal, get a dish of it for yourself and another for me.'

She got two plates and put the oatmeal in it after mixing it, and brought two spoons. Kate wore a handkerchief on her head; she put this under her neck and tied it; she was pretending to eat, but she was putting the food to hide in the handkerchief till her plate was empty.

'Have you your share eaten?' asked the dead man.

'I have,' answered Kate.

'I'll have mine finished this minute,' said he, and soon after he gave her the empty dish. She put the dishes back in the dresser and didn't mind washing them. 'Come, now,' said he, 'and take me back to the place where you found me.'

'Oh, how can I take you back; you are too great a load; 'twas killing me you were when I brought you.' She was in dread of going from the house again.

'You are stronger after that food than what you were in coming; take me back to my grave.'

She went against her will. She rolled up the food inside the handkerchief. There was a deep hole in the wall of the kitchen by the door, where the bar was slipped in when they barred the door; into this hole she put the handkerchief. In going back she shortened the road by going through a big field at command of the dead man. When they were at the top of the field she asked, was there any cure for those young men whose blood was drawn?

'There is no cure,' said he, 'except one. If any of that food had been spared, three bits of it in each young man's mouth would bring them to life again, and they'd never know of their death.'

'Then,' said Kate in her own mind, 'that cure is to be had.'

'Do you see this field?' asked the dead man.

'I do.'

'Well, there is as much gold buried in it as would make rich people of all who belong to you. Do you see the three *leachtans* [piles of small stones]? Underneath each pile of them is a pot of gold.'

The dead man looked around for a while; then Kate went on, without stopping, till she came to the wall of the graveyard, and just then they heard the cock crow.

'The cock is crowing,' said Kate; 'it's time for me to be going home.'

'It is not time yet,' said the dead man; 'that is a bastard cock.'

A moment after that another cock crowed. 'There the cocks are crowing a second time,' said she.

'No,' said the dead man, 'that is a bastard cock again; that's no right bird.' They came to the mouth of the tomb and a cock crowed the third time.

'Well,' said the girl, 'that must be the right cock.'

'Ah, my girl, that cock has saved your life for you. But for him I would have you with me in the grave for evermore, and if I knew this cock would crow before I was in the grave you wouldn't have the knowledge you have now of the field and the gold. Put me into the coffin where you found me. Take your time and settle me well. I cannot meddle with you now, and 'tis sorry I am to part with you.'

'Will you tell me who you are?' asked Kate.

'Have you ever heard your father or mother mention a man called Edward Derrihy or his son Michael?'

'It's often I heard tell of them,' replied the girl.

'Well, Edward Derrihy was my father; I am Michael. That blackthorn that you came for tonight to this graveyard was the lucky stick for you, but if you had any thought of the danger that was before you, you wouldn't be here. Settle me carefully and close the tomb well behind you.'

She placed him in the coffin carefully, closed the door behind her, took the blackthorn stick, and away home with Kate. The night was far spent when she came. She was tired, and it's good reason the girl had. She thrust the stick into the thatch above the door of the house and rapped. Her sister rose up and opened the door.

'Where did you spend the night?' asked the sister. 'Mother will kill you in the morning for spending the whole night from home.'

'Go to bed,' answered Kate, 'and never mind me.'

They went to bed, and Kate fell asleep the minute she touched the bed, she was that tired after the night.

When the father and mother of the three young men rose next morning, and there was no sign of their sons, the mother went to the room to call them, and there she found the three dead. She began to screech and wring her hands. She ran to the road screaming and wailing. All the neighbours crowded around to know what trouble was on her. She told them her three sons were lying dead in their bed after the night. Very soon the report spread in every direction. When Kate's father and mother heard it they hurried off to the house of the dead men. When they came home Kate was still in bed; the mother took a stick and began to beat the girl for being out all the night and in bed all the day.

'Get up now, you lazy stump of a girl,' said she, 'and go to the wake-house; your neighbour's three sons are dead.'

Kate took no notice of this. 'I am very tired and sick,' said she. 'You'd better spare me and give me a drink.'

The mother gave her a drink of milk and a bite to eat, and in the middle of the day she rose up.

' 'Tis a shame for you not to be at the wake-house yet,' said the mother; 'hurry over now.'

When Kate reached the house, there was a great crowd of people before her and great wailing. She did not cry, but was looking on. The father was as if wild, going up and down the house wringing his hands.

'Be quiet,' said Kate. 'Control yourself.'

'How can I do that, my dear girl, and my three fine sons lying dead in the house?'

'What would you give,' asked Kate, 'to the person who would bring life to them again?'

'Don't be vexing me,' said the father.

'It's neither vexing you I am nor trifling,' said Kate. 'I can put the life in them again.'

'If it was true that you could do that, I would give you all that I have inside the house and outside as well.'

'All I want from you,' said Kate, 'is the eldest son to marry and *Gort na Leachtan* [the field of the stone heaps] as fortune.'

'My dear, you will have that from me with the greatest blessing.'

'Give me the field in writing, from yourself, whether the son will marry me or not.'

He gave her the field in his handwriting. She told all who were inside in the wake house to go outside the door, every man and woman of them. Some were laughing at her and more were crying, thinking it was mad she was. She bolted the door inside, and went to the place where she left the handkerchief, found it, and put three bites of the oatmeal and the blood in the mouth of each young man, and as soon as she did that the three got their natural colour, and they looked like men sleeping. She opened the door, then called on all to come inside, and told the father to go and wake his sons.

He called each one by name, and as they woke they seemed very tired after their night's rest; they put on their clothes, and were greatly surprised to see all the people around. 'How is this?' asked the eldest brother.

'Don't you know of anything that came over you in the night?' asked the father.

'We do not,' said the sons. 'We remember nothing at all since we fell asleep last evening.'

The father then told them everything, but they could not believe it. Kate went away home and told her father and mother of her night's journey to and from the graveyard, and said that she would soon tell them more.

That day she met John.

'Did you bring the stick?' asked he.

'Find your own stick,' said she, 'and never speak to me again in your life.'

In a week's time she went to the house of the three young men, and said to the father, 'I have come for what you promised me.'

'You'll get that with my blessing,' said the father. He called the eldest son aside then and asked would he marry Kate, their neighbour's daughter. 'I will,' said the son. Three days after that the two were married and had a fine wedding. For three weeks they enjoyed a pleasant life without toil or trouble; then Kate said, 'This will not do for us; we must be working. Come with me tomorrow and I'll give yourself and brothers plenty to do, and my own father and brothers as well.'

She took them next day to one of the stone heaps in *Gort na Leachtan*. 'Throw these stones to one side,' said she.

They thought that she was losing her senses, but she told them that they'd soon see for themselves what she was doing. They went to work and kept at it till they had six feet deep of a hole dug; then they met with a flat stone three feet square and an iron hook in the middle of it.

'Sure there must be something underneath this,' said the men. They lifted the flag, and under it was a pot of gold. All were very happy then. 'There is more gold yet in the place,' said Kate. 'Come, now, to the other heap.' They removed that heap, dug down, and found another pot of gold. They removed the third pile and found a third pot full of gold. On the side of the third pot was an inscription, and they could not make out what it was. After emptying it, they placed the pot by the side of the door.

About a month later a poor scholar walked the way, and as he was going in at the door he saw the old pot and the letters on the side of it. He began to study the letters.

'You must be a good scholar if you can read what's on that pot,' said the young man.

'I can,' said the poor scholar, 'and here it is for you. There is a deal more at the south side of each pot.'

The young man said nothing, but putting his hand in his pocket, gave the poor scholar a good day's hire. When he was gone, they went to work and found a deal more of gold at the south side of each stone heap. They were very happy then and very rich, and bought several farms and built fine houses, and it was supposed by all of them in the latter end that it was Derrihy's money that was buried under the *leachtans*, but they could give no correct account of that, and sure why need they care? When they died, they left property to make their children rich to the seventh generation.

JEREMIAH CURTIN

St Martin's Eve

In Iveragh, not very far from the town of Cahirciveen, there lived a farmer named James Shea with his wife and three children, two sons and a daughter. The man was peaceable, honest, and very charitable to the poor, but his wife was hard hearted, never giving even a drink of milk to a needy person. Her younger son was as bad in every way as herself, and whatever the mother did he always agreed with her and was on her side.

This was before the roads and cars were in the Kerry Mountains. The only way of travelling in those days, when a man didn't walk, was to ride sitting on a straw saddle, and the only way to take anything to market was on horseback in creels.

It happened, at any rate, that James Shea was going in the beginning of November to Cork with two firkins of butter, and what troubled him most was the fear that he'd not be home on St Martin's night to do honour to the saint. For never had he let that night pass without drawing blood in honour of the saint. To make sure, he called the elder son and said, 'if I am not at the house on St Martin's night, kill the big sheep that is running with the cows.'

Shea went away to Cork with the butter, but could not be home in time. The elder son went out on St Martin's eve, when he saw that his father was not coming, and drove the sheep into the house.

'What are you doing, you fool, with that sheep?' asked the mother.

'Sure, I'm going to kill it. Didn't you hear my father tell me that there was never a St Martin's night but he drew blood, and do you want to have the house disgraced?'

At this the mother made sport of him and said: 'Drive out the sheep and I'll give you something else to kill by and by.'

So the boy let the sheep out, thinking the mother would kill a goose.

He sat down and waited for the mother to give him whatever she had to kill. It wasn't long till she came in, bringing a big tomcat they had, and the same cat was in the house nine or ten years.

'Here,' said she, 'you can kill this beast and draw its blood. We'll have it cooked when your father comes home.'

The boy was very angry and spoke up to the mother: 'Sure the house is disgraced for ever,' said he, 'and it will not be easy for you to satisfy my father when he comes.'

He didn't kill the cat, you may be sure; and neither he nor his sister ate a bite of supper, and they were crying and fretting over the disgrace all the evening.

That very night the house caught fire and burned down; nothing was left but the four walls. The mother and younger son were burned to death, but the elder son and his sister escaped by some miracle. They went to a neighbour's house, and were there till the father came on the following evening. When he found the house destroyed and the wife and younger son dead he mourned and lamented. But when the other son told him what the mother did on St Martin's eve, he cried out: 'Ah, it was the wrath of God that fell on my house; if I had stopped at home till after St Martin's night, all would be safe and well with me now.'

James Shea went to the priest on the following morning, and asked would it be good or lucky for him to rebuild the house.

'Indeed,' said the priest, 'there is no harm in putting a roof on the walls and repairing them if you will have Mass celebrated in the house before you go to live in it. If you do that all will be well with you.'

[Shea spoke to the priest because people are opposed to repairing or rebuilding a burnt house, and especially if any person has been burned in it.]

Well, James Shea put a roof on the house, repaired it, and had Mass celebrated inside. That evening as Shea was sitting down to supper what should he see but his wife coming in the door to him. He thought she wasn't dead at all. 'Ah, Mary,' said he, ' 'tis not so bad as they told me. Sure, I thought it is dead you were. Oh, then you are welcome home; come and sit down here; the supper is just ready.'

She didn't answer a word, but looked him straight in the face and walked on to the room at the other end of the house. He jumped up, thinking it's sick the woman was, and followed her to the room to help her. He shut the door after him. As he was not coming back for a long time the son thought at last that he'd go and ask the father why he wasn't eating his supper. When he went into the room he saw no sign of his mother, saw nothing in the place but two legs from the knees down. He screamed out for his sister and she came.

'Oh, merciful God!' screamed the sister.

'Those are my father's legs!' cried the brother, 'and Mary, don't you know the stockings, sure you knitted them yourself, and don't I know the brogues very well?'

They called in the neighbours, and, to the terror of them all, they saw nothing but the two legs and feet of James Shea.

There was a wake over the remains that night, and the next day they buried the two legs. Some people advised the boy and girl never to sleep a night in the house, that their mother's soul was lost, and that was why she came and ate up the father, and she would eat themselves as well.

The two now started to walk the world, not caring much where they were going if only they escaped the mother. They stopped the first night at a farmer's house not far from Killarney. After supper a bed was made down for them by the fire, in the corner, and they lay there. About the middle of the night a great noise was heard outside, and the woman of the house called to her boys and servants to get up and go to the cow-house to know why the cows were striving to kill one another. Her own son rose first. When he and the two servant boys went out they saw the ghost of a woman, and she in chains. She made at them, and wasn't long killing the three.

Not seeing the boys come in, the farmer and his wife rose up, sprinkled holy water around the house, blessed themselves and went out, and there they saw the ghost in blue blazes and chains around her. In a coop outside by himself was a March cock. [A cock hatched in March from a cock and hen hatched in March.]

He flew down from his perch and crowed twelve times. That moment the ghost disappeared.

Now the neighbours were roused, and the news flew around that the three boys were killed. The brother and sister didn't say a word to anyone, but, rising up early, started on their journey, begging God's protection as they went. They never stopped nor stayed till they came to Rathmore, near Cork, and, going to a farmhouse, the boy asked for lodgings in God's name.

'I will give you lodgings in His name,' said the farmer's wife.

She brought warm water for the two to wash their hands and feet, for they were tired and dusty. After supper a bed was put down for them, and about the same hour as the night before there was a great noise outside.

'Rise up and go out,' said the farmer's wife, 'some of the cows must be untied.'

'I'll not go out at this hour of the night, if they are untied itself,' said the man, 'I'll stay where I am, if they kill one another, for it isn't safe to go out till the cock crows; after cockcrow I'll go out.'

'That's true for you,' said the farmer's wife, 'and, upon my word, before coming to bed, I forget to sprinkle holy water in the room, and to bless myself.'

So taking the bottle hanging near the bed, she sprinkled the water around the room and toward the threshold, and made the sign of the cross. The man didn't go out until cockcrow. The brother and sister went away early, and travelled all day. Coming evening they met a pleasant-looking man who stood before them in the road.

'You seem to be strangers,' said he, 'and where are you going?'

'We are strangers,' said the boy, 'and we don't know where to go.'

'You need go no farther. I know you well, your home is in Iveragh. I am St Martin, sent from the Lord to protect you and your sister. You were going to draw the blood of a sheep in my honour, but your mother and brother made sport of you, and your mother wouldn't let you do what your father told you. You see what has come to them; they are lost for ever, both of them. Your father is saved in heaven, for he was a good man. Your mother will be here soon, and I'll put her in the way that she'll never trouble you again.'

Taking a rod from his bosom and dipping it in a vial of holy water he drew a circle around the brother and sister. Soon they heard their mother coming, and then they saw her with chains on her, and the rattling was terrible, and flames were rising from her. She came to where they stood, and said: 'Bad luck to you both for being the cause of my misery.'

'God forbid that,' said St Martin. 'It isn't they are the cause, but yourself, for you were always bad. You would not honour me, and now you must suffer for it.'

He pulled out a book and began to read, and after he read a few minutes he told her to depart and not be seen in Ireland again till the day of judgment. She rose in the air in flames of fire, and with such a noise that you'd think all the thunders of heaven were roaring and all the houses and walls in the kingdom were tumbling to the ground.

The brother and sister went on their knees and thanked St Martin. He blessed them and told them to rise, and, taking a little tablecloth out of his bosom, he said to the brother: 'Take this cloth with you and keep it in secret. Let no one know that you have it. If you or your sister are in need go to your room, close the door behind you and bolt it. Spread out the cloth then, and plenty of everything to eat and drink will come to you. Keep the cloth with you always; it belongs to both of you. Now go home and live in the house that your father built, and let the priest come and celebrate Monday Mass in it, and live the life that your father lived before you.'

The two came home, and brother and sister lived a good life. They married, and when either was in need that one had the cloth to fall back on, and their grandchildren are living yet in Iveragh. And this is truth, every word of it, and it's often I heard my poor grandmother tell this story, the Almighty God rest her soul, and she was the woman that wouldn't tell a lie. She knew James Shea and his wife very well.

WILLIAM MAGINN

A Vision of Purgatory

❧

The churchyard of Inistubber is as lonely a one as you would wish to
see on a summer's day or avoid on a winter's night. It is situated in a
narrow valley, at the bottom of three low, barren, miserable hills, on
which there is nothing green to meet the eye – tree or shrub, grass or
weed. The country beyond these hills is pleasant and smiling: rich
fields of corn, fair clumps of oaks, sparkling streams of water, houses
beautifully dotting the scenery, which gently undulates round and
round as far as the eye can reach; but once across the north side of
Inistubber Hill, and you look down upon desolation. There is nothing
to see but, down in the hollow, the solitary churchyard with its broken
wall, and the long lank grass growing over the gravestones, mocking
with its melancholy verdure the barrenness of the rest of the landscape. It is a sad thing to reflect that the only green spot in the
prospect springs from the grave!

Under the east window is a mouldering vault of the de Lacys, a
branch of a family descended from one of the conquerors of Ireland;
and there they are buried when the allotted time calls them to the
tomb. On these occasions a numerous cavalcade, formed from the
adjoining districts in all the pomp and circumstance of woe, is wont to
fill the deserted churchyard, and the slumbering echoes are awakened
to the voice of prayer and wailing, and charged with the sigh that
marks the heart bursting with grief, or the laugh escaping from the
bosom mirth-making under the cloak of mourning. Which of these
feelings was predominant when Sir Theodore de Lacy died is not
written in history; nor is it necessary to enquire. He had lived a jolly,
thoughtless life, rising early for the hunt, and retiring late from the

bottle; a good-humoured bachelor who took no care about the management of his household, provided that the hounds were in order for his going out, and the table ready on his coming in; as for the rest, an easy landlord, a quiet master, a lenient magistrate (except to poachers), and a very excellent foreman of a grand jury. He died one evening while laughing at a story which he had heard regularly thrice a week for the last fifteen years of his life; and his spirit mingled with the claret.

In former times, when the De Lacys were buried, there was a grand breakfast, and all the party rode over to the church to see the last rites paid. The keeners lamented; the country people had a wake before the funeral and a dinner after it – and there was an end. But with the march of mind came trouble and vexation. A man has nowadays no certainty of quietness in his coffin – unless it be a patent one. He is laid down in the grave and, the next morning, finds himself called up to demonstrate and interesting fact! No one, I believe, admires this ceremony; and it is not to be wondered at that Sir Theodore de Lacy held it in especial horror. 'I'd like,' he said one evening, 'to catch one of the thieves coming after me when I'm dead. By the God of War, I'd break every bone in his body! But,' he added with a sigh, 'as I suppose I'll not be able to take my own part then, upon you I leave it, Larry Sweeney, to watch me three days and three nights after they plant me under the sod. There's Doctor Dickenson there – I see the fellow looking at me. Fill your glass, doctor: here's your health! And shoot him, Larry (do you hear?), shoot the doctor like a cock if he ever comes stirring up my poor old bones from their roost of Inistubber.'

'Why, then,' Larry answered, accepting the glass which followed this command, 'long life to both your honours; and it's that I would like to be putting a bullet into Dr Dickenson – Heaven between him and harm! – for wanting your honour away, as if you was a horse's head, to a bonfire. There's nothing, I 'shure you, gintlemin, poor as I am, that would give me greater pleasure.'

'We feel obliged, Larry,' said Sir Theodore, 'for your good wishes.'

'Is it I pull you out of the grave, indeed?' continued the whipper-in (for such he was); 'I'd let nobody pull your honour out of any place, saving 'twas Purgatory; and out of that I'd pull you myself, if I saw you going *there*.'

'I am of opinion, Larry,' said Dr Dickenson, 'you'd turn tail if you saw Sir Theodore on that road. You might go farther and fare worse, you know.'

'Turn tail!' replied Larry. 'It's I that wouldn't – I appale to St Patrick himself over beyond' – pointing to a picture of the Prime Saint of Ireland which hung in gilt daubery behind his master's chair, right opposite to him.

To Larry's horror and astonishment the picture, fixing its eyes upon him, winked with the most knowing air, as if acknowledging the appeal.

'What makes you turn so white, then, at the very thought?' said the doctor, interpreting the visible consternation on our hero in his own way.

'Noting particular,' answered Larry; 'but a wakeness has come strong over me, gintlemin; and, if you have no objection, I'd like to go into the air for a bit.'

Leave was of course granted, and Larry retired amid the laughter of the guests; but, as he retreated, he could not avoid casting a glance on the awful picture; and again the saint winked, with a most malicious smile. It was impossible to endure the repeated infliction, and Larry rushed down the stairs in an agony of fright and amazement.

'Maybe,' thought he, 'it might be my own eyes that wasn't quite steady – or the flame of the candle. But no! He winked at me as plain as ever I winked at Judy Donaghue of a May morning. What he manes by it I can't say; but there's no use of thinking about it; no, nor of talking neither, for who'd believe me if I tould them of it?'

The next evening Sir Theodore died, as has been mentioned, and in due time thereafter was buried, according to the custom of the family, by torchlight in the churchyard of Inistubber. All was fitly performed; and although Dickenson had no design upon the jovial knight – and, if he had not, there was nobody within fifteen miles that could be suspected of such an outrage – yet Larry Sweeney was determined to make good his promise of watching his master. 'I'd think little of telling a lie to him, by the way of no harm, when he was alive,' said he, wiping his eyes as soon as the last of the train had departed, leaving him with a single companion in the lonely cemetery; 'but now that he's dead – God rest his soul! – I'd scorn it. So Jack Kinaley, as behoves my first cousin's son, stay you with me here this blessed night, for betune you and I it ain't lucky to stay by one's self in this ruinated old rookery, where ghosts (God help us!) is as thick as bottles in Sir Theodore's cellar.'

'Never you mind that, Larry,' said Kinaley, a discharged soldier who had been through all the campaigns of the Peninsula: 'never mind, I say, such botherations. Hain't I lain in bivouack on the field at Salamanca, and Tallawora, and the Pyrumnees, and many another place beside, when there was dead corpses lying about in piles, and there was no more ghosts than knee buckles in a ridgemint of Highlanders. Here! Let me prime them pieces, and hand us over the bottle. We'll stay snug under this east window, for the wind's coming down the hill and I defy – '

'None of that bould talk, Jack,' said his cousin. 'As for what ye saw in foreign parts, of dead men killed a-fighting, sure that's nothing to the dead – God rest 'em! – that's here. There, you see, they had company, one with the other, and, being killed fresh-like that morning, had no heart to stir; but here, faith! 'tis a horse of another colour.'

'Maybe it is,' said Jack; 'but the night's coming on; so I'll turn in. Wake me if you see anything; and, after I've got my two hours' rest, I'll relieve you.'

With these words the soldier turned on his side under shelter of a grave, and, as his libations had been rather copious during the day, it was not long before he gave audible testimony that the dread of supernatural visitants had had no effect in disturbing the event current of his fancy.

Although Larry had not opposed the proposition of his kinsman, yet he felt by no means at ease. He put in practice all the usually recommended nostrums for keeping away unpleasant thoughts. He whistled; but the echo sounded so sad and dismal that he did not venture to repeat the experiment. He sang; but, when no more than five notes had passed his lips, he found it impossible to get out a sixth, for the chorus reverberated from the ruinous walls was destruction to all earthly harmony. He cleared his throat; he hummed, he stamped; he endeavoured to walk. All would not do. He wished sincerely that Sir Theodore had gone to Heaven – he dared not suggest even to himself, just then, the existence of any other region – without leaving on him the perilous task of guarding his mortal remains in so desperate a place. Flesh and blood could hardly resist it! Even the preternatural snoring of Jack Kinaley added to the horrors of his position; and, if his application to the spirituous soother of grief beside him was frequent, it is more to be deplored on the score of morality than wondered at on the score of metaphysics. He who censures our hero too severely has never watched the body of a dead baronet in the churchyard of Inistubber at midnight. 'If it was a common, decent, quite, well-behaved churchyard a'self,' thought Larry half aloud, 'but when 'tis a place like this forsaken ould berrin' ground, which is noted for villainy – '

'For what, Larry?' enquired a gentleman stepping out of a niche which contained the only statue time had spared. It was the figure of St Colman, to whom the church was dedicated. Larry had been looking at the figure as it shone forth in ebon and ivory in the light and shadow of the now high-careering moon.

'For what, Larry?' said the gentleman; 'for what do you say the church is noted?'

'For nothing at all, please your honour,' replied Larry, 'except the height of gentility.'

The stranger was about four feet high, dressed in what might be called glowing garments if, in spite of their form, their rigidity did not deprive them of all claim to such an appellation. He wore an antique mitre upon his head; his hands were folded upon his breast; and over his right shoulder rested a pastoral crook. There was a solemn expression in his countenance, and his eye might truly be called stony. His beard could not well be said to wave upon his bosom; but it lay upon it in ample profusion, stiffer than that of a Jew on a frosty morning after mist. In short, as Larry soon discovered to his horror on looking up at the niche, it was no other than St Colman himself, who had stepped forth indignant, in all probability, at the stigma cast by the watcher of the dead on the churchyard of which his saintship was patron.

He smiled with a grisly solemnity – just such a smile as you might imagine would play round the lips of a milestone (if it had any) – at the recantation so quickly volunteered by Larry. 'Well,' said he, 'Lawrence Sweeney – '

'How well the old rogue,' thought Larry, 'knows my name!'

'Since you profess yourself such an admirer of the merits of the churchyard of Inistubber, get up and follow me, till I show you the civilities of the place, for I'm master here, and must do the honours.'

'Willingly would I go with your worship,' replied our friend; 'but you see here I am engaged to Sir Theodore, who, though a good master, was a mighty passionate man when everything was not done as he ordered it, and I am feared to stir.'

'Sir Theodore,' said the saint, 'will not blame you for following me. I assure you he will not.'

'But then – ' said Larry.

'Follow me!' cried the saint in a hollow voice; and, casting upon him his stony eye, drew poor Larry after him, as the bridal guest was drawn by the lapidary glance of the Ancient Mariner, or, as Larry himself afterwards expressed it, 'as a jaw-tooth is wrinched out of an ould woman with a pair of pincers.'

The saint strode before him in silence, not in the least incommoded by the stones and rubbish which at every step sadly contributed to the discomfiture of Larry's shins, who followed his marble conductor into a low vault situated at the west end of the church. In accomplishing this, poor Larry contrived to bestow upon his head an additional organ, the utility of which he was not craniologist enough to discover.

The path lay through coffins piled up on each side of the way in various degrees of decomposition; and excepting that the solid footsteps of the saintly guide, as they smote heavily on the floor of stone, broke the deadly silence, all was still. Stumbling and staggering along, directed only by the casual glimpse of light afforded by the moon where it broke through the dilapidated roof of the vault and served to discover only sights of woe, Larry followed. He soon felt that he was descending, and could not help wondering at the length of the journey. He began to entertain the most unpleasant suspicions as to the character of his conductor; but what could he do? Flight was out of the question, and to think of resistance was absurd. 'Needs must, they say,' thought he to himself, 'when the Devil drives. I see it's much the same when a saint leads.'

At last the dolorous march had an end; and, not a little to Larry's amazement, he found that his guide had brought him to the gate of a lofty hall before which a silver lamp, filled with naphtha, 'yielded light as from a sky.' From within loud sounds of merriment were ringing; and it was evident, from the jocular harmony and the tinkling of glasses, that some subterranean catch-club was not idly employed over the bottle.

'Who's there?' said a porter, roughly responding to the knock of St Colman.

'Be so good,' said the saint mildly, 'my very good fellow, as to open the door without further questions, or I'll break your head. I'm bringing a gentleman here on a visit, whose business is pressing.'

'Maybe so,' thought Larry; 'but what that business may be is more than I can tell.'

The porter sulkily complied with the order, after having apparently communicated the intelligence that a stranger was at hand; for a deep silence immediately followed the tipsy clamour, and Larry, sticking close to his guide, whom he now looked upon almost as a friend when compared with these underground revellers to whom he was about to be introduced, followed him through a spacious vestibule, which gradually sloped into a low-arched room where the company was assembled.

And a strange-looking company it was. Seated round a long table were three and twenty grave and venerable personages, bearded, mitred, stoled and croziered – all living statues of stone, like the saint who had walked out of his niche. On the drapery before them were figured the images of the sun, moon and stars – the inexplicable bear – the mystic temple built by the hand of Hiram – and other symbols of which the uninitiated know nothing. The square, the line, the trowel were not wanting, and the hammer was lying in front of the chair. Labour, however, was over, and, the time for refreshment having arrived, each of the stony brotherhood had a flagon before him; and when we mention that the saints were Irish, and that St Patrick in person was in the chair, it is not to be wondered at that the mitres, in some instances, hung rather loosely on the side of the heads of some of the canonised compotators. Among the company were found St Senanus of Limerick, St Declan of Ardmore, St Canice of Kilkenny, St Finbar of Cork, St Michan of Dublin. St Brandon of Kerry, St Fachnan of Ross, and others of that holy brotherhood. A vacant place, which completed the four-and-twentieth, was kept for St Colman, who, as everybody knows, is of Cloyne; and he, having taken his seat, addressed the President to inform him that he had brought the man.

The man (Larry himself) was awestruck with the company in which he so unexpectedly found himself, and trembled all over when, on the notice of his guide, the eight-and forty eyes of stone were turned directly upon himself.

'You have just nicked the night to a shaving, Larry,' said St Patrick. 'This is our chapter night, and myself and brethren are here assembled on merry occasion! – You know who I am?'

'God bless you riverince!' said Larry, it's I that do well. Often did I see your picture hanging over the door of places where it is' – lowering his voice – 'pleasanter to be than here, buried under an ould church.'

'You may as well say it out, Larry,' said St Patrick. 'And don't think I'm going to be angry with you about it, for I was once flesh and blood myself. But you remember the other night saying that you would think nothing of pulling your master out of Purgatory if you could get at him there, and appealing to me to stand by your words.'

'Y–e–e–s,' said Larry most mournfully, for he recollected the significant look he had received from the picture.

'And,' continued St Patrick, 'you remember also that I gave you a wink, which, you know, is as good any day as a nod – at least, to a blink horse.'

'I'm sure your Riverince,' said Larry with a beating heart, 'is too much of a gintleman to hold a poor man hard to every word he may say of an evening; and therefore – '

'I was thinking so,' said the saint. 'I guessed you'd prove a poltroon when put to the push. What do you think, my brethren, I should do to this fellow?'

A hollow sound burst from the bosoms of the unanimous assembly. The verdict was short but decisive: 'Knock out his brains!'

And, in order to suit the action to the word, the whole four-and-twenty rose at once, and, with their immovable eyes fixed firmly on the face of our hero – who, horror-struck with the sight as he was, could not close his – they began to glide slowly but regularly towards him, bending their line into the form of a crescent so as to environ him on all sides. In vain he fled to the door; its massive folds resisted mortal might. In vain he cast his eyes around in quest of a loophole of retreat – there was none. Closer and closer pressed on the slowly-moving phalanx, and the uplifted croziers threatened soon to put their sentence into execution. Supplication was all that remained – and Larry sank upon his knees.

'Ah then!' said he, 'gintlemin and ancient ould saints as you are, don't kill the father of a large small family who never did hurt to you or yours. Sure, if 'tis your will that I should go to – no matter who, for there's no use in naming his name – might I not as well make up my mind to go there alive and well, stout and hearty, and able to face him, as with my head knocked into bits, as if I had been after a fair or a patthren?'

'You say right,' said St Patrick, checking with a motion of his crozier the advancing assailants, who thereupon returned to their seats. 'I'm glad to see you coming to reason. Prepare for your journey.'

'And how, please your saintship, am I to go?' asked Larry.

'Why,' said St Patrick, 'as Colman here has guided you so far, he may guide you further. But as the journey is into foreign parts, where you aren't likely to be known, you had better take this letter of introduction, which may be of use to you.'

'And here, also Lawrence,' said a Dublin saint (perhaps Michan), 'take you this box also, and make use of it as he to whom you speak shall suggest.'

'Take a hold, and a firm one,' said St Colma, 'Lawrence, of my cassock, and we'll start.'

'All right behind?' cried St Patrick.

'All right!' was the reply.

In an instant vault, table, saints, bell, church faded into air; a rustling hiss of wings was all that was heard, and Larry felt his cheek swept by a current, as if a covey of birds of enormous size were passing him. [It was in all probability the flight of the saints returning to Heaven; but on that point nothing certain has reached us up to the present time of writing.] He had not a long time to wonder at the phenomenon, for he himself soon began to soar, dangling in mid-sky to the skirt of the cassock of his sainted guide. Earth, and all that appertains thereto, speedily passed from his eyes, and they were alone in the midst of circumfused ether, glowing with a sunless light. Above, in immense distance, was fixed the firmament, fastened up with bright stars, fencing around the world with its azure wall. They fled far before any distinguishable object met their eyes. At length a long white streak, shining like silver in the moonbeam, was visible to their sight.

'That,' said St Colman, 'is the Limbo which adjoins the earth, and is the highway for ghosts departing the world. It is called in Milton, a book which I suppose, Larry, you never have read –'

'And how could I, please your worship,' said Larry, 'seein' I don't know a B from a bull's foot?'

'Well, it is called in Milton the 'Paradise of Fools'; and, if it were indeed peopled by all of that tribe who leave the world, it would contain the best company that ever figured on the earth. To the north you see a bright speck?'

'I do.'

'That marks the upward path – narrow and hard to find. To the south you may see a darksome road – broad, smooth, and easy of descent. That is the lower way. It is thronged with the great ones of the world; you may see their figures in the gloom. Those who are soaring upwards are wrapped in the flood of light flowing perpetually from that single spot, and you cannot see them. The silver path on which we enter is the Limbo. Here I part with you. You are to give your letter to the first person you meet. Do your best; be courageous, but observe particularly that you profane no holy name, or I will not answer for the consequences.'

His guide had scarcely vanished when Larry heard the tinkling of a bell in the distance; and, turning his eyes in the quarter whence it proceeded, he saw a grave-looking man in black, with eyes of fire, driving before him a host of ghosts with a switch, as you see turkeys driven on the western road at the approach of Christmas. They were on the highway to Purgatory.

The ghosts were shivering in the thin air, which pinched them severely now that they had lost the covering of their bodies. Among the group Larry recognised his old mastser, by the same means that Ulysses, Aeneas, and others recognised the bodiless forms of their friends in the regions of Acheron.

'What brings a living person,' said the man in black, 'on this pathway? I shall make legal capture of you, Larry Sweeney, for trespassing. You have no business here.'

'I have come,' said Larry, plucking up courage, 'to bring your honour's glory a letter from a company of gintlemin with whom I had the pleasure of spending the evening underneath the ould church of Inistubber.'

'A letter?' said the man in black. 'Where is it?'

'Here, my lord,' said Larry.

'Ho!' cried the black gentleman on opening it; 'I know the handwriting. It won't do, however, my lad; – I see they want to throw dust in my eyes.'

'Whew!' thought Larry. 'That's the very thing. 'Tis for that the ould Dublin boy gave me the box. I'd lay a tenpenny to a brass farthing that it's filled with Lundyfoot.'

Opening the box, therefore, he flung its contents right into the fiery eyes of the man in black, while he was still occupied in reading the letter; – and the experiment was successful.

'Curses! Tche – tche – tche – Curses on it!' exclaimed he, clapping his hands before he eyes, and sneezing most lustily.

'Run, you villains, run,' cried Larry to the ghosts; 'run, you villains, now that his eyes are off you. O master, master! Sir Theodore, jewel! Run to the right-hand side, make for the bright speck, and God give you luck!'

He had forgotten his injunction. The moment the word was uttered he felt the silvery ground sliding from under him; and with the swiftness of thought he found himself on the flat of his back, under the very niche of the old church wall whence he had started, dizzy and confused with the measureless tumble. The emancipated ghosts floated in all directions, emitting their shrill and stridulous cries in the gleaming expanse. Some were again gathered by their old conductor; some, scudding about at random, took the right-hand path, others the left. Into which of them Sir Theodore struck is not recorded; but, as he had heard the direction, let us hope he made the proper choice.

Larry had not much time given him to recover from his fall, for almost in an instant he heard an angry snorting rapidly approaching; and, looking up, whom should he see but the gentleman in black, with eyes gleaming more furiously than ever, and his horns (for in his haste he had let his hat fall) relieved in strong shadow against the moon? Up started Larry; – away ran his pursuer after him. The safest refuge was, of course, the church. Thither ran our hero,

As darts the dolphin from the shark,
Or the deer before the hounds;

and after him – fiercer than the shark, swifter than the hounds – fled the black gentleman. The church is cleared, the chancel entered; and the hot breath of his pursuer glows upon the outstretched neck of Larry. Escape is impossible, the extended talons of the fiend have clutched him by the hair.

'You are mine!' cried the demon. 'If I have lost any of my flock, I have at least got you!'

'O St Patrick!' exclaimed our hero in horror. 'O St Patrick, have mercy upon me, and save me!'

'I tell you what, Cousin Larry,' said Kinaley, chucking him up from behind a gravestone where he had fallen; 'all the St Patricks that ever were born would not have saved you from ould Tom Picton if he caught you sleeping on your post as I've caught you now. By the world of an ould soldier he'd have had the provost-marshal upon you, and I'd not give twopence for the loan of your life. And then, too, I see you have drunk every drop in the bottle. What can you say for yourself?'

'Nothing at all,' said Larry, scratching his head, 'but it was an unlucky dream, and I'm glad it's over.'

GERALD GRIFFIN

The Brown Man

❦

In a lonely cabin, in a lonely glen, on the shores of a lonely lough in one of the most lonesome districts of west Munster, lived a lone woman named Guare. She had a beautiful girl, a daughter named Nora. Their cabin was the only one within three miles round them every way. As to their mode of living, it was simple enough, for all they had was one little garden of white cabbage, and they had eaten that down to a few heads between them, a sorry prospect in a place where even a handful of *prishoc* weed was not to be had without sowing it.

It was a very fine morning in those parts, for it was only snowing and hailing, when Nora and her mother were sitting at the door of their little cottage, and laying out plans for the next day's dinner. On a sudden, a strange horseman rode up to the door. He was strange in more ways than one. He was dressed in brown, his hair was brown, his eyes were brown, his boots were brown, he rode a brown horse, and he was followed by a brown dog.

'I'm come to marry you, Nora Guare,' said the Brown Man.

'Ax my mother fusht, if you plaise, sir,' said Nora, dropping him a curtsy.

'You'll not refuse, ma'am,' said the Brown Man to the old mother, 'I have money enough, and I'll make you daughter a lady, with servants at her call, and all manner of fine doings about her.' And so saying, he flung a purse of gold into the widow's lap.

'Why then the heavens speed you and her together, take her away with you, and make much of her,' said the old mother, quite bewildered with all the money.

'Agh, agh,' said the Brown Man, as he placed her on his horse behind him without more ado. 'Are you all ready now?'

'I am!' said the bride. The horse snorted, and the dog barked, and almost before the word was out of her mouth, they were all whisked away out of sight. After travelling a day and a night, faster than the wind itself, the Brown Man pulled up his horse in the middle of the Mangerton mountain, in one of the most lonesome places that eye ever looked on.

'Here is my estate,' said the Brown Man.

'A'then, is it this wild bog you call an estate?' said the bride.

'Come in, wife; this is my palace,' said the bridegroom.

'What! a clay-hovel, worse than my mother's!'

They dismounted, and the horse and the dog disappeared in an instant, with a horrible noise, which the girl did not know whether to call snorting, barking, or laughing.

'Are you hungry?' said the Brown Man. 'If so, there is your dinner.'

'A handful of raw white-eyes [potatoes] and a grain of salt!'

'And when you are sleepy, here is you bed,' he continued, pointing to a little straw in a corner, at sight of which Nora's limbs shivered and trembled again. It may be easily supposed that she did not make a very hearty dinner that evening, nor did here husband either.

In the dead of the night, when the clock of Muckross Abbey had just tolled one, a low neighing at the door and a soft barking at the window were heard. Nora feigned sleep. The Brown Man passed his hand over her eyes and face. She snored. 'I'm coming,' said he, and he arose gently from her side. In half an hour after she felt him by her side again. He was cold as ice.

The next night the same summons came. The Brown Man rose. The wife feigned sleep. He returned, cold. The morning came.

The next night came. The bell tolled at Muckross, and was heard across the lakes. The Brown Man rose again, and passed a light before the eyes of the feigning sleeper. None slumber so sound as they who *will* not wake. Her heart trembled, but her frame was quiet and firm. A voice at the door summoned the husband.

'You are very long coming. The earth is tossed up, and I am hungry. Hurry! Hurry! Hurry! if you would not lose all.'

'I'm coming!' said the Brown Man. Nora rose and followed instantly. She beheld him at a distance winding through a lane of frost-nipped sallow trees. He often paused and looked back, and once or twice retraced his steps to within a few yards of the tree, behind which she had shrunk. The moonlight, cutting the shadow close and dark about her, afforded the best concealment. He again proceeded, and she followed. In a few minutes the reached they old Abbey of Muckross. With a sickening heart she saw him enter the churchyard. The wind rushed through the huge yew tree and startled her. She mustered courage enough, however, to reach the gate of the churchyard and look in. The Brown Man, the horse, and the dog, were there seated by an open grave, eating something and glancing their brown, fiery eyes about in every direction. The moonlight shone full on them and her. Looking down towards here shadow on the earth, she started with horror to observe it move, although she was herself perfectly still. It waved its black arms, and motioned her back. What the feasters said, she understood not, but she seemed still fixed in the spot. She looked once more on her shadow; it raised one hand, and pointed the way to the lane; then slowly rising from the ground, and confronting her, it walked rapidly off in that direction. She followed as quickly as might be.

She was scarcely in her straw, when the door creaked behind, and her husband entered. He lay down by her side and started.

'Uf! Uf!' said she, pretending to be just awakened, 'how cold you are, my love!'

'Cold, inagh? Indeed you're not very warm yourself, my dear, I'm thinking.'

'Little admiration I shouldn't be warm, and you laving me alone this way at night, till my blood is snow broth, no less.'

'Umph!' said the Brown Man, as he passed his arm round her waist. 'Ha! your heart is beating fast?'

'Little admiration it should. I am not well, indeed. Them praties and salt don't agree with me at all.'

'Umph!' said the Brown Man.

The next morning as they were sitting at the breakfast table together. Nora plucked up a heart and asked leave to go to see her mother. The Brown Man, who ate nothing, looked at her in a way that made her think he knew all. She felt her spirit die away within her.

'If you only want to see your mother,' said he, 'there is no occasion for your going home. I will bring her to you here. I didn't marry you to be keeping you gadding.'

The Brown Man then went out and whistled for his dog and his horse. They both came; and in a very few minutes they pulled up at the old widow's cabin-door.

The poor woman was very glad to see her son-in-law, though she did not know what could bring him so soon.

'Your daughter sends her love to you, mother,' says the Brown Man, the villain, 'and she'd be obliged to you for a *loand* of a *shoot* of your best clothes, as she's going to give a grand party, and the dress-maker has disappointed her.'

'To be sure and welcome,' said the mother; and making up a bundle of clothes, she put them into his hands.

'Whogh! whogh!' said the horse as they drove off, 'that was well done. Are we to have a mail of her?'

'Easy, ma-coppuleen, and you'll get your 'nough before night,' said the Brown Man, 'and you likewise, my little dog.'

'Boh!' cried the dog, 'I'm in no hurry – I hunted down a doe this morning that was fed with milk from the horns of the moon.'

Often in the course of that day did Nora Guare go to the door, and cast her eye over the weary flat before it, to discern, if possible, the distant figures of her bridegroom and mother. The dusk of the second evening found her alone in the desolate cot. She listened to every sound. At length the door opened, and an old woman, dressed in a new jock, and leaning on a staff, entered the hut. 'O mother, are you come?' said Nora, and was about to rush into her arms, when the old woman stopped her.

'Whisht! whisht! my child! – I only stepped in before the man to know how you like him? Speak softly, in dread he'd hear you – he's turning the horse loose, in the swamp, abroad, over.'

'O mother, mother! such a story!'

'Whisht! easy again – how does he use you?'

'Sarrow worse. That straw my bed, and them white-eyes – and bad ones they are – all my diet. And 'tisn't that same, only – '

'Whisht! easy, again! He'll hear you, maybe – Well?'

'I'd be easy enough only for his own doings. Listen, mother. The fusht night, I came about twelve o'clock – '

'Easy, speak easy, eroo!'

'He got up at the call of the horse and the dog, and out a good hour. He ate nothing next day. The second night, and the second day, it was the same story. The third – '

'Husht! husht! Well, the third night?'

'The third night I said I'd watch him. Mother, don't hold my hand so hard . . . He got up, and I got up after him . . . Oh, don't laugh, mother, for 'tis frightful . . . I followed him to Muckross churchyard . . . Mother, mother, you hurt my hand . . . I looked in at the gate – there was great moonlight three, and I could see everything as plain as day.'

'Well, darling – husht! softly! What did you see?'

'My husband by the grave, and the horse . . . Turn your head aside, mother, for your breath is very hot . . . and the dog and they eating. – Ah, you are not my mother!' shrieked the miserable girl, as the Brown Man flung off his disguise, and stood before her, grinning worse than a blacksmith's face through a horse-collar. He just looked at her one moment, and then darted his long fingers into her bosom, from which the red blood spouted in so many streams. She was very soon out of all pain, and a merry supper the horse, the dog, and the Brown Man had that night, by all accounts.

GERALD GRIFFIN

The Dilemma of Phadrig

✦

'There's no use in talken about it, Phadrig. I know an' feel that all's
over wit me. My pains are all gone, to be sure – but in place o' that,
there's a weight like a quern stone down upon my heart, an I feel it
blackenen within me. All I have to say is – think o' your own Mauria
when she's gone, an be kind to poor Patcy.'

'Ah, darlen, don't talk that way – there's hope yet – what'll I do,
what'll the child do without you?'

'Phadrig, there's noan. I'm goen fast, an if you have any regard for
me, you won't say anything that'll bring the thoughts o' you an him
between me an the thoughts o' heaven, for that's what I must think of
now. And if you marry again –'

'Oh, Mauria, honey, will you kill me entirely? Is it *I'll* marry again?'

' – If it be a thing you should marry again,' Mauria resumed,
without taking any notice of her husband's interruption, 'you'll bear
in mind that the best mother that ever walked the ground will love
her own above another's. It stands with raisin an nature. The gander
abroad will pull a strange goslen out of his own flock; and you know
yourself, we could never get the bracket hen to sit upon Nelly
O'Leary's chickens, do what we could. Everything loves its own.
Then, Phadrig, if you see the floury potaties – an the top o' the
milk – an the warm seat be the hob – an the biggest bit o' meat on a
Sunday goen away Hom Patcy – you'll think o' your poor Mauria, an
do her part by him; just quietly, and softly, and without blamen the
woman – for it is only what's nait'rel, an what many a stepmother
does without thinking o' themselves. An above all things, Phadrig,
take care to make him mind his books and his religion, to keep out o'
bad company, an study his readin-made-aisy, and that's the way he'll

be a blessing an a comfort to you in your old days, as I once thought he would be to me in mine.'

Here her husband renewed his promises in a tone of deep affliction.

'An now for yourself, Phadrig. Remember the charge that's upon you, and don't be goen out venturen your life in a little canvas canoe, on the bad autumn days, at Ballybunion; nor wit foolish boys at the Glin and Tarbert fairs' – an don't be so wake-minded as to be trusten to card-drawers, an fairy doctors, an the like; for it's the last word the priest said to me was, that you were too superstitious, and that's a great shame an a heavy sin. But tee you! Phadrig, dear, there's that rogue of a pig at the potaties over – '

Phadrig turned out the grunting intruder, bolted the hurdle-door, and returned to the bedside of his expiring helpmate. That tidy house-keeper, however, exhausted by the exertion which she had made to preserve, from the mastication of the swinish tusk, the fair produce of her husband's conacre of white-eyes, had fallen back on the pillow and breathed her last.

Great was the grief of the widowed Phadrig for her loss – great were the lamentations of her female friends at the evening wake – and great was the jug of whisky-punch which the mourners imbibed at the mouth, in order to supply the loss of fluid which was expended from the eyes. According to the usual cottage etiquette, the mother of the deceased, who acted as mistress of the ceremonies, occupied a capacious hay-bottomed chair near the fireplace – from which she only rose when courtesy called on her to join each of her female acquaintances as they arrived, in the death-wail which (as in politeness bound) they poured forth over the pale piece of earth that lay coffined in the centre of the room. This mark of attention, however, the old lady was observed to omit with regard to one of the fair guests – a round-faced, middle-aged woman, called Milly Rue – or Red Milly, probably because her head might have furnished a solution of the popular conundrum, 'Why is a red-haired lady like a sentinel on his post?'

The fair Milly, however, did not appear to resent this slight, which was occasional (so the whisper went among the guests) by the fact that she had been an old and neglected love of the new widower. All the fiery ingredients of Milly's constitution appeared to be comprehended in her glowing ringlets – and those, report says, were as ardent in hue as their owner was calm and regulated in her temper. It would be a cold

morning, indeed, that a sight of Milly's head would not warm you –
and a hot fit of anger which a few tones of her kind and wrath-
disarming voice would not cool. She dropped, after she had concluded
her 'cry', a conciliating curtsey to the sullen old lady, took an
unobtrusive seat at the foot of the bed, talked of the 'notable' qualities
of the deceased, and was particularly attentive to the flaxen-headed
little Patcy, whom she held in her lap during the whole night, cross-
examining him in his reading and multiplication, and presenting him,
at parting, in token of her satisfaction at his proficiency, with a copy of
The Seven Champions of Christendom, with a fine marble cover and
pictures. Milly acted in this instance under the advice of a prudent
mother, who exhorted her, 'whenever she thought o' maken presents,
that way, not to be layen her money out in cakes or gingerbread, or
things that would be ett off at wanst, an no more about them or the
giver – but to give a strong toy, or a book, or somethen that would
last, and bring her to mind now and then, so as then when a person 'ud
ask where they got that, or who geve it, they'd say, "from Milly Rue",
or "Milly geve it, we're obleest to her", an' be talken an thinken of her
when she'd be away.'

To curb in my tale, which may otherwise become restive and
unmanageable – Milly's deep affliction and generous sympathy made
a serious impression on the mind of the widower, who more than
all was touched by that singularly accidental attachment which she
seemed to have conceived for little Patcy. Nothing would be farther
from his own wishes than any design of a second time changing his
condition; but he felt that it would be going a grievous wrong to the
memory of his first wife if he neglected this opportunity of providing
her favourite Patcy with a protector, so well calculated to supply her
place. He demurred a little on the score of true love, and the violence
which he was about to do his own constant heart – but like the bluff
King Henry, his conscience – 'aye – his conscience', – touched him,
and the issue was that a roaring wedding shook the walls which had
echoed to the wail of death within the few preceding months.

Milly Rue not only supplied the place of a mother to young Patcy,
but presented him in the course of a few years with two merry play-
fellows, a brother and a sister. To do her handsome justice, too, poor
Mauria's anticipations were completely disproved by her conduct, and
it would have been impossible for a stranger to have detected the

stepson of the house from any shade of undue partiality in the mother. The harmony in which they dwelt was unbroken by any accident for many years.

The first shock which burst in with a sudden violence upon their happiness was one of a direful nature. Disease, that pale and hungry fiend who haunts alike the abodes of wealth and of penury; who brushes away with his baleful wing the bloom from beauty's cheek, and the balm of slumber from the pillow of age; who troubles the hope of the young mother with dreams of ghastliness and gloom, and fears that come suddenly, she knows not why nor whence; who sheds his poisonous dews alike on the heart that is buoyant and the heart that is broken; this stern and conquering demon scorned not to knock, one summer morning, at the door of Phadrig's cow-house, and to lay his iron fingers upon a fine milch-cow, a sheeted-stripper which constituted (to use his own emphatic phrase) the poor farmer's 'substance', and to which he might have applied the well-known lines which run nearly as follows:

> She's straight in her back, and thin in her tail;
> She's fine in her horn, and good at the pail;
> She's calm in her eyes, and soft in her skin;
> She's a grazier's without, and a butcher's within.

All the 'cures' in the pharmacopoeia of the village apothecary were expended on the poor animal, without any beneficial effect; and Phadrig, after many conscientious qualms about the dying words of his first wife, resolved to have recourse to that infallible refuge in such cases – a fairy doctor.

He said nothing to the afflicted Milly about his intentions, but slipped out of the cottage in the afternoon, hurried to the Shannon side near Money Point, unmoored his light canvas-built canoe, seated himself in the frail vessel, and fixing his paddles on the *towl-pin*, sped away over the calm face of the waters towards the isle of Scattery, where the renowned Crohoore-na-Ooona, or Connor-of-the-Sheep, the Mohammed of the cottages, at this time took up his residence. This mysterious personage, whose prophecies are still commented on among the cottage circles with looks of deep awe and wonder, was much revered by his contemporaries as a man 'who had seen a dale'; of what nature those sights or visions were was intimated by a mysterious look, and a solemn nod of the head.

In a little time, Phadrig ran his little canoe aground on the sandy beach of Scattery, and, drawing her above high-water mark, proceeded to the humble dwelling of the gifted sheep-shearer with feelings of profound fear and anxiety. He passed the lofty round tower – the ruined grave of St Senanus, in the centre of the little isle – the mouldering church, on which the eye of the poring antiquary may still discern the sculptured image of the two-headed monster, with which cottage tradition says the saint sustained so fierce a conflict on landing in the islet – and which the translator of Odranus has vividly described as 'a dragon, with his forepart covered with huge bristles, standing on end like those of a boar; his mouth gaping wide open with a double row of crooked, sharp tusks, and with such openings that his entrails might be seen; his back like a round island, full of scales and shells; his legs short and hairy, with such steely talons, that the pebble-stones, as he ran along them, sparkled – parching the way wherever he went, and making the sea boil about him where he dived – such was his excessive fiery heat.' Phadrig's knees shook beneath him when he remembered this awful description – and thought of the legends of Lough Dhoola, on the summit of Mount Callon, to which the hideous animal was banished by the saint, to fast on a trout and a half per diem to the end of time; and where, to this day, the neighbouring fishermen declare that, in dragging the lake with their nets, they find the half trout as regularly divided in the centre as if it were done with a knife and scale.

While Phadrig remained with mouth and eyes almost as wide open as those of the sculptured image of the monster which had fascinated him to the spot, a sudden crash among the stones and dock-weed in an opposite corner of the ruin made him start and yellow as if the original were about to quit Lough Dhoola on parole of honour, and use him as a relish after the trout and a half. The noise was occasioned by a little rotund personage, who had sprung from the mouldering wall, and now stood gazing fixedly on the terrified Phadrig, who continued returning that steady glance with a half-frightened, half-crying face – one hand fast clenched upon his breast, and the other extended, with an action of avoidance and deprecation. The person of the stranger was stout and short, rendered still more so by a stoop, which might almost have been taken for a hump – his arms hung forward from his shoulders, like those of a long-armed ape – his hair was grey and bushy, like that of a wanderoo – and his sullen grey eye seemed to be inflamed with ill-humour – his feet were bare and as broad as a camel's – and a leathern girdle buckling round his waist secured a tattered grey frieze riding-coat, and held an enormous pair of shears, which might have clipped off a man's head as readily, perhaps, as a lock of wool. This last article of costume afforded a sufficient indication to Phadrig that he stood in the presence of the awful object of his search.

'Well! an who are *you?*' growled the sheep-shearer, after surveying Phadrig attentively for some moments.

The first gruff sound of his voice made the latter renew his start and roar for fright; after which, composing his terrors as well as he might, he replied, in the words of Autolycus, 'I am only a poor fellow, sir.'

'Well! an what's your business with me?'

'A cure, sir, I wanted for her. A cow o' mine that's very bad inwardly, an we can do nothen for her; and I thought maybe you'd know what is it ail'ded her – an prevail on *them*' (this word was pronounced with an emphasis of deep meaning) 'to leave her to uz.'

'Huth!' the sheep-shearer thundered out, in a tone that made poor Phadrig jump six feet backwards with a fresh yell, 'do you dare to spake of *them* before me. Go along! you villyan o' the airth, an wait for me outside the church, an I'll tell you all about it there; but, first – do you think I can get the *gentlemen* to do anything for me *gratish* – without offeren 'em a trate or a haip'-orth?'

'If their honours wouldn't think two tin-pennies and a fi'penny bit too little – It's all I'm worth in the wide world.'

'Well! we'll see what they'll say to it. Give it here to me. Go now – be off with yourself – if you don't want to have 'em all a-top o' you in a minnit.'

This last hint made our hero scamper over the stones like a startled fawn; nor did he think himself safe until he reached the spot where he had left his canoe, and where he expected the coming of the sheep-shearer; conscience-struck by the breach of his promise to his dying Mauria, and in a state of agonising anxiety with respect to the loving patient in the cow-house.

He was soon after rejoined by Connor-of-the-Sheep.

'There is one way,' said he, 'of saving your cow – but you must lose one of your childer if you wish to save it.'

'O Heaven presarve uz, sir, how is that, if you plase?'

'You must go home,' says the sheep-shearer, 'and say nothen to anybody, but fix in your mind which o' your three childer you'll give for the cow; and when you do that, look in his eyes, and he'll sneeze, an don't you bless him, for the world. Then look in his eyes again, an he'll sneeze again, an still don't think o' blessen him, by any mains. The third time you'll look in his eyes he'll sneeze a third time – an if you don't bless him the third time, he'll die – and your cow will live.'

'An this is the only cure you have to gi' me?' exclaimed Phadrig, his indignation at the moment overcoming his natural timidity.

'The only cure. It was by a dale to do I could prevail on them to let you make the choice itself.'

Phadrig declared stoutly against this decree, and even threw out some hints that he would try whether or no Shaun Lauther, or Strong John, a young rival of the sheep-shearing fairy doctor, might be able to make a better bargain for him with the 'gentlemen.'

'Shaun Lauther!' exclaimed Connor-of-the-Sheep, in high anger – 'Do you compare me to a man that never seen any more than your-self? – that never saw so much as the skirt of a dead man's shroud in the moonlight – or heard as much as the moanen of a sowlth [Bodiless spirit] in an old graveyard? Do you know me? Ask them that do – and they'll tell you how often I'm called up in the night, and kep posten over bog an mountain, till I'm ready to drop down with the sleep – while few voices are heard, I'll be bail, at Shaun Lauther's windey – a little knollidge given him in his drames. It is then that I get mine. Didn't I say before the king o' France was beheaded that a blow would be struck wit an axe in that place, that the sound of it would be heard all over Europe? An wasn't it true? Didn't I hear the shots that were fired at Gibaralthur, an tell it over in Dooly's forge, that the place was relieved that day? – an didn't the news come afterwards in a month's time that I toult nothen but the truth?'

Phadrig had nothing to say in answer to this overwhelming list of interrogatories but to apologise for his want of credulity, and to express himself perfectly satisfied.

With a heavy heart he put forth in his canoe upon the water and prepared to return. It was already twilight, and as he glided along the peaceful shores he ruminated mournfully within his mind on the course which he should pursue. The loss of the cow would be, he considered, almost equivalent to total ruin – and the loss of any one of his lovely children was a probability which he could hardly bear to dwell on for a moment. Still it behoved him to weigh the matter well. Which of them now – supposing it possible that he could think of sacrificing any – which of them would he select for the purpose? The choice was a hard one. There was little Mauria, a fair-haired, blue-eyed little girl – but he could not, for an instant, think of losing her, as she happened to be named after his first wife; her brother, little Shamus, was the least useful of the three, but he was the youngest – 'the child of his old age – a little one!' His heart bled at the idea; he would lose the cow, the pig along with it, before he would harm a hair of the darling infant's head. He thought of Patcy – and he shuddered and leaned heavier on his oars, as if to flee away from the horrible doubt which stole into his heart with that name. It must be one of the three, or the cow was lost forever. The two first-mentioned he certainly would not lose – and Patcy; Again he bade the fiend begone, and trembling in every limb, made the canoe speed rapidly over the tide in the direction of his home.

He drew the little vessel ashore and proceeded towards his cabin. They had been waiting supper for him, and he learned with renewed anxiety that the object of his solicitude, the milch-cow, had rather fallen away than improved in her condition during his absence. He sat down in sorrowful silence with his wife and children to their humble supper of potatoes and thick milk.

He gazed intently on the features of each of the young innocents as they took their places on the suggan chairs that flanked the board. Little Mauria and her brother Shamus looked fresh, mirthful, and blooming from their noisy play in the adjoining paddock, while their elder brother, who had spent the day at school, wore – or seemed, to the distempered mind of his father, to wear a look of sullenness and chagrin. He was thinner, too, than most boys of his age – a circum-stance which Phadrig had never remarked before. It might be the first indications of his poor mother's disease, consumption, that were beginning to declare themselves in his constitution; and if so, his doom was already sealed – and whether the cow died or not, Patcy was certain to be lost. Still the father could not bring his mind to resolve on any settled course, and their meal proceeded in silence.

Suddenly the latch of the door was lifted by some person outside, and a neighbour entered to inform Phadrig that the agent to his landlord had arrived in the adjacent village for the purpose of driving matters to extremity against all those tenants who remained in arrears. At the same moment, too, a low moan of anguish from the cow outside announced the access of a fresh paroxysm of her distemper, which it was very evident the poor animal could never come through in safety.

In an agony of distress and horror the distracted father laid his clenched fingers on the table, and looked fixedly in the eyes of the unsuspecting Patcy. The child sneezed, and Phadrig closed his lips hard, for fear a blessing might escape him. The child at the same time, he observed, looked paler than before.

Fearful lest the remorse which began to awake within his heart might oversway his resolution, and prevent the accomplishment of his unnatural design, he looked hurriedly a second time into the eyes of the little victim. Again the latter sneezed, and again the father, using a violent effort, restrained the blessing which was struggling at his heart. The poor child drooped his head upon his bosom, and letting the untasted food fall from his hand, looked so pale and mournful as to remind his murderer of the look which his mother wore in dying.

It was long – very long – before the heart-struck parent could prevail on himself to complete the sacrifice. The visitor departed; and the first beams of a full moon began to supplant the faint and lingering twilight which was fast fading in the west. The dead of the night drew on before the family rose from their silent and comfortless meal. The agonies of the devoted animal now drew rapidly to a close, and Phadrig still remained tortured by remorse on the one hand, and by selfish anxiety on the other.

A sudden sound of anguish from the cow-house made him start from his seat. A third time he fixed his eyes on those of his child – a third time the boy sneezed – but here the charm was broken.

Milly Rue, looking with surprise and tenderness on the fainting boy, said, 'Why, then, Heaven bless you, child! – It must be a cold you caught, you're sneezen so often.'

At that very second, and in a moan of agony, the crew expired; and at the same moment, a low and plaintive voice outside the door was heard, exclaiming, 'And Heaven bless you, Milly! and the Almighty bless you, and spare you a long time over your children!'

Phadrig staggered back against the wall – his blood froze in his veins – his face grew white as death – his teeth chattered – his eyes stared – his hair moved upon his brow, and the chilling damp of terror exuded over all his frame. He recognised the voice of his first wife; and her pale, cold eye met his at that moment, as her shade flitted by the window in the thin moonlight, and darted on him a glance of mournful reproach. He covered his eyes with his hands, and sunk, senseless, into a chair, while the affrighted Milly and Patcy, who at once assumed his glowing health and vigour, hastened to his assistance. They had all heard the voice, but no one saw the shade nor recognised the tone excepting the conscience-smitten Phadraig.

SHAN F. BULLOCK

Th' Ould Boy

❧❧❧

Below in the kitchen, the plebeians were making merry with quip and crank, pipe and glass, as they sat round the walls and here and there over the floor in the warmth of the great peat fire; their laughter and chatter (subdued though it was, or tried to be) was heard distinctly above in the little parlour, where, round a well-spread table, sat a select company – the *élite* of the wake, you might say – gravely stirring their tea, eating their ham, discoursing on the merits and virtues (now, many of them, first brought to light) of the man who ofttimes had made merry at that very table, and now lay stark and lonely in a room beyond the kitchen.

'Ay, ay,' sobbed the widow from her place behind the teacups; 'it's God's truth; he was the generous heart an' the tender. Och, the heart av a child!'

The spoons clinked dolefully round the cups; the men solemnly wagged their heads; the women sniffed and, to conquer emotion, tried buttered toast.

'How often, here in this very room,' the widow went on, 'did I hear him spake the word. Ay, ay! An' 'twas the great gift o' prayer he had. Ay, ye all know it.'

'Ay, ay,' went the voices; 'we do, we do; 'twas powerful, powerful!'

'An' now he's tuk from us – tuk, tuk,' cried the widow; 'gone an' left us to struggle alone wi' Satan. Ah, dear, dear!'

The men were bent over their plates, the women biting their lips; it was blessed relief when the hard, level voice of Red John went out through the doleful assembly.

'It's truth ye say, ma'am,' said John; 'an' may your man be safe in glory (*Amen – Amen*, went the voices). But for yourself, have no fear o'

Satan an' all his works: next time he makes bold to struggle wi' ye, just ax him if he remembers Red John: that'll settle him.'

With one accord, all eyes were raised and turned wonderingly towards the bottom of the table, where, one hand thrust carelessly into his waistcoat pocket, the other idly playing with his knife, sat Red John: a big man, he was, red-headed, and with a strong, impassive face.

'You're all wonderin'?' he went on, raising his eyes. 'Well, ye needn't. I say to ye all once more: next time Satan tries strugglin', just mention me: that'll finish him.'

Swiftly vanished sorrow and dole; the men found their big, coarse voices; the women pocketed their handkerchiefs: all, even the widow herself, called on John to explain.

'Ye mean to say ye never heard?' asked John. 'No? Well, well. Such is life; an' meself has told the story a score o' times. No odds. Here ye are. An' mind,' he added, shaking his finger, 'no inter-ruptions, an' no sayin' I'm a liar when I'm done . . . Of course, ma'am; of course I'll wait a minute in welcome; an' just ax them down there to keep their bulls' voices quiet. Ye know,' he went on, as the widow went out for a moment (carrying tobacco, or a bottle, or something, for the plebeians in the kitchen), 'it'll nivir do to let the poor thing fret. Och, no; an' there's nothin' like a story to keep the heart from care . . . Back again, ma'am? Well, then, 'twas like this.

'One day – ay, years ago – word came to me that Long Bob was runnin' a brewin' o' potten. Now, when Long Bob brews, I'm off; for let him use treacle, or malt, or whatever he chooses, there's no man these parts (an' I've interviewed a few) can make stuff to grip our tongue like he can. No matter. Soon as I heard word, off I went, for I wanted no dregs; an' after a three-mile pull in the cot at last came to a wee island out in the lake, and there, in the middle o' the scrub an' the stones, was me darlint Still firin' away; an' round it a party o' – Well, never mind, there was more than *one* there I knew, an' all made me welcome. Ah, 'twas great stuff that; with a whiff off it like the middle o' a haystack, an' not a bite in a gallon of it . . . Och, och, ma'am, *is* there anything behind ye there in the press? Sure a toothful'd send the words *flowin'* out o' me . . . That's right, that's right. *Hurroo!* Now, now, only a toothful I said, ma'am; well, so be it. I'll do me endeavours.

'Well,' Red John went on, when the company had drunk the widow's health and wished her long life, 'I pass by all that happened there, just sayin' that we had great times, an' that when about dusk I set out for home I held a tidy sup besides the two lemonade bottles full in me tail pocket. It was cowld night, an' ye know it's lonesome work draggin' a cot about a lake: so I'll not deny but mebbe I *did* wet me lips once or twice on the way; an' I'll acknowledge straight that when I landed it took more than a drop to take the stiffness out o' me joints. But mark me, ma'am, an'all o' ye, ye mus'n't run away wi' the notion that I was fuddled; I held me share, but I was as steady on me pins when I stepped out home as I am the night, an' as clear in the head as yourself, ma'am; long life to ye an' your very good health . . . "Me smilin' little Cruiskeen lawn, lawn, lawn!" sang John in chorus with the plebeians in the kitchen, beating time with his tumbler on the table – "Me smilin' lit–tle Crui–skeen lawn!"

' 'Twas about eleven o'clock – more or less I'll not say as I'm strivin' for the truth, when I got home. Mary an' the childer were all in bed, an' there was a glimmer in the lamp, an' a pot o' porridge waitin' for me over a snug fire; so down I sits an' makes me supper; then lights the pipe and was goin' over (meanin' to make meself comfortable) to hang me coat on the back o' the door when, badness to me, if I didn't catch sight o' the neck o' a bottle stickin' out o' the tail pocket. "Och, och," says I, scratchin' me head, "but it's the sore temptation, och, och! I wonder now would a wee sup hurt one?" An' afore I could make up me mind, the cork was out o' the bottle an' with some o' the poteen in a mug I was over by the dresser liftin' a sup o' water out of a can that stood on the floor.

'Now you'll attend to this, ma'am, an' the rest o' ye; for it's here the fun begins an' it's here I'll be truthfuller than ever. Just as I was stoopin' to get the water, there was a shakin' in the house, an' a blue flash that kind o' dazzled me; an' with that I turns round sharp – when, lo and behold ye, there, sittin' by the fire, wi' his legs crossed an' him lookin' straight at me, was as fine a lookin' gentleman as ever I clapped eyes on. All dressed in black he was, wi' a big cloak fallin' to the ground, an' a top hat, if ye please; an' his hair black, an' his face shaved, an' sorrow a smell o' jewellery on his person. Arrah, Lord save us, thinks I to meself, who are ye at all, an' where did ye come from? An', somehow, the way he saw there that cool, an' the *divilish* way he looked at me set me shakin'; if it hadn't been for the cup in the mug I'd ha' dropped on the floor. But the poteen gave me courage; an' wi' that I minded me manners an' spakes out.

' "Good evenin', Sir," says I; "it's pretty late ye'll be?" He looked straight at me, keepin' his legs crossed, an' not one word he answered. Then, thinkin', maybe, he was hard o' hearin' I spakes again.

' "Good evenin', sir," says I; "is it missed your way ye have the night?"

'But sorrow a word; there he sat in the chair – just as ye are yourself, ma'am, beggin' pardon an' meanin' no comparisons; an' never moved hand or foot or budged a lip. So I scratched me head an' cast about what I was to do; for I couldn't keep standin' there like a fool, an I was afraid to move. What in glory, thinks I, am I to do? Than all of a sudden the thought struck me; an' round I turns to the coat hangin' on the back o' the door, an' takes th' other lemonade bottle out o' the pocket.

' "Axin' your pardon, sir," says I, "but if it's not makin' bold, could I offer ye the least taste just to keep the raw from your bones?"

'Not a word he answered; but, thinks I, there's a twinkle in your eye, me boy, that looks as if you'd be partial to a drop; an' ye all know a nod's as good as a wink to a blind horse. So, keepin' an eye on him over me shoulder, I turned an' got another mug off the dresser, an' mixin' a tidy dose I went across the floor an' offered it t' him. Like a lamb, sirs, he took it; gulped it down an' smacked his lips on the last drop. But see here, ma'am; may I never see light if the draught didn't turn into blue blazes in his throat. Ye laugh? Well, don't then, if it isn't at your own ignorance. Laugh! troth most o' ye'll see worse than that after ye die.' And John winked over his glass at the company.

'Well, thunder an' turf, thinks I to meself, what kind of a customer is this? Sure if he'd be sociable even it'd not be so bad. Howsomede'er, thinks I, I'll make meself at home by me own fire; an' down I plops on a stool fornenst him, pulls out the cutty, fills it, an' lights up. After a couple o' whiffs I wipes the shank on me coat an' offers it to him.

' "Mebbe you'd like a draw?" says I, holdin' the cutty to him across the hearth; "people these parts say it goes well wi' poteen."

'He reached out an' tuk it, knocked the ashes off it, an' put it in his mouth. May death have me, ma'am, if the sight didn't parch me tongue! Every whiff o' him was a blue strame o' fire; an' ye could see blue blazes dancin' over the pipe; an' the eyes o' him glared like a cat's in the dark. An' he never moved a limb; just sat there as unconcerned as ever in his black suit, movin' his lips an' whiffin' out them infernal blue strames.

' "Ah, great powers!" says I; "what are ye at all, at all? Why are ye here? Why are ye here?"

'An' with that, for I was frightened powerful, I tumbled off the stool, an' with an odious clatter went rash among the pots an' pot-hooks. An' the next thing I hears is Mary gettin' out o' bed in the room above an' liftin' the latch to come an' see what was up.

'She drew back immediately she seen someone wi' me – by good luck the gentleman had his back to her; an' in a minute or two down she comes in her petticoats – savin' your presence, ladies all – an' wid a shawl round her shoulders.

' "What's the matter, John?" says she, kind o' frightened like, an' standin' behind the boy-o, sittin' there like a graven image smokin' away.

' "Nothin'," says I.

' "But I was woke out o' me sleep wi' a shockin' clatter?" says she.

' "Ye were," says I, "right enough. I stumbled over the pot there."

' "You're late?" says she.

' "I am," says I.

' "What kep' ye," says she.

' "Aw, nothin' particular," says I. "Just made a *kaley* or two. The gentleman there lost his way in the bog, an' he's warmin' himself before he starts out again."

'All the time we were discoorsin', I was winkin' at Mary to spake to the boy-o; for I thought it powerful *un*genteel to stand there wi'out addressin' him. At last, she comes round, an' drops a curtsy, an' says she, in a haltin' kind o' way, not a bit like Mary's usual style o' talkin', for, as ye all know, she's blessed wi' the gift of the gab: ' "Savin' your presence, sir," says she, "for appearin' in these duds afore ye; but – I – was loth – to wait – long – for I was afraid somethin' bad had ha–happened when I heard – heard – "

'Not another word could she get out; I could see her eyes openin' wide, an her jaw droppin', an' she fell a-tremblin'. For the boy-o just riz his eyes 'n looked at her; kept them hard on her, an' never moved a muscle, nor spoke a word, nor stopped puffin' blue blazes out o' me ould cutty.

'All of a sudden Mary turns to me, white as a corpse, an' says she:
' "God in Heaven! John Graham, who's this? An' what's goin' to
happen to us at all?'

'I couldn't answer; an' I thought Mary was goin' into a fit.

' "Look at the mouth o' him," shouts she, "blue flames comin' out
o' it! An' his nose! An' look at his eyes! Aw, God help us!" – an' she lets
a screech; *"look at his feet! Cloots – cloots! It's the devil himself!"*

'An' with that she tears from the kitchen up into her room an' bolts
the door.

I was fair flabbergasted. What could I do? Thinks I, what brings th'
ould boy to my fireside? I rubs me head an' looks hard at him; then
gets up, an' creepin' to the table empties the lemonade bottle down
me throat.

'Boys, but poteen's the darlin' stuff; it put a new heart in me; an'
cleared me head; an' made me feel fit to fight twenty devils.

'Off I peels me waistcoat; tucks up me shirtsleeves, an' spits on me
hands: then up I steps to Mister Divil.

' "Ye ould ragamuffin," says I, an' whacks me fists in his face, "what
brings ye roamin' like a roarin' lion to decent Prodestan' houses? Did
ye ever hear tell o' Red John Graham," says I, "that hits man or devil
like the kick o' a horse? Look at the face o' him, then,' an' I glares
straight at him; 'look at him," says I, "ye tarnation ould scarecrow; look
an' tremble, Mister Beelzebub! Ye're in the wrong house the night, ye
flamin' ould tinker ye!" says I. "Your kind isn't here, Apollyon. I'm
Red John, me boy, that fears neither man nor devil. Let me at your
face," says I – an' from the bedroom comes Mary's voice shoutin':
"Hurroo, John! Pelt the ould vagabond. Pepper him, John." "I will, Mary," I
shouts; *"I will.* Come out. Stand up. Give me three minutes at your
wizened countenance till I leave ye a laughin' stock for your own
angels."

'Then I made a grab,' shouted John, knocking his chair over as he
jumped up, and upsetting his tumbler as he made a false clutch at his
neighbour's hair. I made a grab at the head o' him just like that.

' *"Come out!"* roars I. *"Come out an' be kilt!"* An' with the word I fell
on me head in the corner over an empty chair.'

'Gone?' cried the widow. 'He was gone?'

'Ay,' answered John; 'when I came to there was no one there but
Mary, flingin' water over me an' roarin' *meila murther.*'

'Prime,' went up the voices. 'It's prime. Bully for you, John. Tight boy, John.' Then, from halfway down the table, came the voice of a sceptic.

'Well,' it said, 'in me own experience I've known poteen do *quare* things; but never before this night did I hold it responsible for makin' a man the biggest liar at a wake. Is there no one else? Och, is there no one else? Can no one tell a sober lie for a change?'

John leant over the table towards the sceptic. 'Young man,' he said, 'ye call me a lair, an' ye say I was drunk. Your years, an' the house we're in, I'll excuse ye this time; but never again, mind. An' if you, or any other person here, repeats such things, I'll take ye home an' prove me words by sittin' ye in the very chair th' ould boy sat in: an' I'll give ye the wiggin' I meant for him into the bargain.'

LETITIA MACLINTOCK

Far Darrig in Donegal

Pat Diver, the tinker, was a man well accustomed to a wandering life, and to strange shelters; he had shared the beggar's blanket in smoky cabins; he had crouched beside the still in many a nook and corner where poteen was made on the wild Innishowen mountains; he had even slept on the bare heather, or on the ditch, with no roof over him but the vault of heaven; yet were all his nights of adventure tame and commonplace when compared with one especial night.

During the day preceding that night, he had mended all the kettles and saucepans in Moville and Greencastle, and was on his way to Culdaff, when night overtook him on a lonely mountain road.

He knocked at one door after another asking for a night's lodging, while he jingled the halfpence in his pocket, but was everywhere refused.

Where was the boasted hospitality of Innishowen, which he had never before known to fail? It was of no use to be able to pay when the people seemed so churlish. Thus thinking, he made his way toward a light a little further on, and knocked at another cabin door.

An old man and woman were seated one at each side of the fire.

'Will you be pleased to give me a night's lodging, sir?' asked Pat respectfully.

'Can you tell a story?' returned the old man.

'No, then, sir, I canna say I'm good at storytelling' replied the puzzled tinker.

'Then you maun just gang further, for none but them that can tell a story will get in here.'

This reply was made in so decided a tone that Pat did not attempt to repeat his appeal, but turned away reluctantly to resume his weary journey.

'A story, indeed,' muttered he. 'Auld wives fables to please the weans!'

As he took up his bundle of tinkering implements, he observed a barn standing rather behind the dwelling house, and, aided by the rising moon, he made his way toward it.

It was a clean, roomy barn, with a piled-up heap of straw in one corner. Here was a shelter not to be despised; so Pat crept under the straw, and was soon asleep.

He could not have slept very long when he was awakened by the tramp of feet, and, peeping cautiously through a crevice in his straw covering, he saw four immensely tall men enter the barn, dragging a body, which they threw roughly upon the floor.

They next lighted a fire in the middle of the barn, and fastened the corpse by the feet with a great rope to a beam in the roof. One of them then began to turn it slowly before the fire. 'Come on,' said he, addressing a gigantic fellow, the tallest of the four – 'I'm tired; you be to tak' your turn.'

'Faix an' troth, I'll no turn him,' replied the big man. 'There's Pat Diver in under the straw, why wouldn't he tak' his turn?'

With hideous clamour the four men called the wretched Pat, who, seeing there was no escape, thought it was his wisest plan to come forth as he was bidden.

'Now, Pat,' said they, 'you'll turn the corpse, but if you let him burn you'll be tied up there and roasted in his place.'

Pat's hair stood on end, and the cold perspiration poured from his forehead, but there was nothing for it but to perform his dreadful task.

Seeing him fairly embarked in it, the tall men went away.

Soon, however, the flames rose so high as to singe the rope, and the corpse fell with a great thud upon the fire, scattering the ashes and embers, and extracting a howl of anguish from the miserable cook, who rushed to the door, and ran for his life.

He ran on until he was ready to drop with fatigue, when, seeing a drain overgrown with tall, rank grass, he thought he would creep in there and lie hidden till morning.

But he was not many minutes in the drain before he heard the heavy tramping again, and the four men came up with their burthen, which they laid down on the edge of the drain.

'I'm tired,' said one, to the giant; 'it's your turn to carry him a piece now.'

'Faix and troth, I'll no carry him,' replied he, 'but there's Pat Diver in the drain, why wouldn't he come out and tak' his turn?'

'Come out, Pat, come out,' roared all the men, and Pat, almost dead with fright, crept out.

He staggered on under the weight of the corpse until he reached Kiltown Abbey, a ruin festooned with ivy, where the brown owl hooted all night long, and the forgotten dead slept around the walls under dense, matted tangles of brambles and ben-weed.

No one ever buried there now, but Pat's tall companions turned into the wild graveyard, and began digging a grave.

Pat, seeing them thus engaged, thought he might once more try to escape, and climbed up into a hawthorn tree in the fence, hoping to be hidden in the boughs.

'I'm tired,' said the man who was digging the grave; 'here, take the spade,' addressing the big man, 'it's your turn.'

'Faix an' troth, it's no my turn,' replied he, as before. 'There's Pat Diver in the tree, why wouldn't he come down and tak' his turn?'

Pat came down to take the spade, but just then the cocks in the little farmyards and cabins round the abbey began to crow, and the men looked at one another.

'We must go,' said they, 'and well is it for you, Pat Diver, that the cocks crowed, for if they had not, you'd just ha' been bundled into that grave with the corpse.'

Two months passed, and Pat had wandered far and wide over the county Donegal, when he chanced to arrive at Raphoe during a fair.

Among the crowd that filled the Diamond he came suddenly on the big man.

'How are you, Pat Diver?' said he, bending down to look into the tinker's face.

'You've the advantage of me, sir, for I havna' the pleasure of knowing you,' faltered Pat.

'Do you not know me, Pat?' Whisper – 'When you go back to Innishowen, you'll have a story to tell!'

LETITIA MACLINTOCK

Jamie Freel and the Young Lady

꧁꧂

Down in Fannet, in time gone by, lived Jamie Freel and his mother. Jamie was the widow's sole support; his strong arm worked for her untiringly, and as each Saturday night came round he poured his wages into her lap, thanking her dutifully for the halfpence which she returned him for tobacco.

He was extolled by his neighbours as the best son ever known or heard of. But he had neighbours of whose opinion he was ignorant – neighbours who lived pretty close to him, whom he had never seen, who are, indeed, rarely seen by mortals, except on May Eves and Halloweens.

An old ruined castle, about a quarter of a mile from his cabin, was said to be the abode of the 'wee folk'. Every Halloween were the ancient windows lighted up, and passers-by saw little figures flitting to and fro inside the building, while they heard the music of flutes and pipes.

It was well known that fairy revels took place; but nobody had the courage to intrude on them.

Jamie had often watched the little figures from a distance, and listened to the charming music, wondering what the inside of the castle was like; but one Halloween he got up, and took his cap, saying to his mother, 'I'm awa to the castle to seek my fortune.'

'What!' cried she. 'Would you venture there – you that's the widow's one son? Dinna be sae venturesome and foolitch, Jamie! They'll kill you, an' then what'll come o' me?'

'Never fear, mother; nae harm'll happen me, but I maun gae.'

He set out, and, as he crossed the potato field, came in sight of the castle, whose windows were ablaze with light that seemed to turn the russet leaves, still clinging to the crab tree branches, into gold.

Halting in the grove at one side of the ruin, he listened to the elfin revelry, and the laughter and singing made him all the more determined to proceed.

Numbers of little people, the largest about the size of a child of five years old, were dancing to the music of flutes and fiddles, while others drank and feasted.

'Welcome, Jamie Freel! welcome, welcome, Jamie!' cried the company, perceiving their visitor. The word 'Welcome' was caught up and repeated by every voice in the castle.

Time flew, and Jamie was enjoying himself very much, when his hosts said, 'We're going to ride to Dublin tonight to steal a young lady. Will you come too, Jamie Freel?'

'Ay, that I will,' cried the rash youth, thirsting for adventure.

A troop of horses stood at the door. Jamie mounted, and his steed rose with him into the air. He was presently flying over his mother's cottage, surrounded by the elfin troop, and on and on they went, over bold mountains, over little hills, over the deep Lough Swilley, over towns and cottages, where people were burning nuts and eating apples and keeping merry Halloween. It seemed to Jamie that they flew all round Ireland before they got to Dublin.

'This is Derry,' said the fairies, flying over the cathedral spire; and what was said by one voice was repeated by all the rest, till fifty little voices were crying out, 'Derry! Derry! Derry!'

In like manner was Jamie informed as they passed over each town on the route, and at length he heard the silvery voices cry, 'Dublin! Dublin!'

It was no mean dwelling that was to be honoured by the fairy visit, but one of the finest houses in Stephen's Green.

The troop dismounted near a window, and Jamie saw a beautiful face on a pillow in a splendid bed. He saw the young lady lifted and carried away, while the stick which was dropped in her place on the bed took her exact form.

The lady was placed before one rider and carried a short way, then given to another, and the names of the towns were cried out as before.

They were approaching home. Jamie heard 'Rathmullan', 'Milford', 'Tamney', and then he knew they were near his own house.

'You've all had your turn at carrying the young lady,' said he. 'Why wouldn't I get her for a wee piece?'

'Ay, Jamie,' replied they pleasantly, 'you may take your turn at carrying her, to be sure.'

Holding his prize very tightly he dropped down near his mother's door.

'Jamie Freel! Jamie Freel! is that the way you treat us?' cried they, and they, too, dropped down near the door.

Jamie held fast, though he knew not what he was holding, for the little folk turned the lady into all sorts of strange shapes. At one moment she was a black dog, barking and trying to bite; at another a glowing bar of iron, which yet had no heat; then again a sack of wool.

But still Jamie held her, and the baffled elves were turning away when a tiny woman, the smallest of the party, exclaimed, 'Jamie Freel has her awa frae us, but he sall nae hae gude of her, for I'll mak' her deaf and dumb,' and she threw something over the young girl.

While they rode off, disappointed, Jamie Freel lifted the latch and went in.

'Jamie, man!' cried his mother, 'you've been awa all night. What have they done to you?'

'Naething bad, mother; I hae the very best o' gude luck. Here's a beautiful young lady I hae brought you for company.'

'Bless us and save us!' exclaimed the mother; and for some minutes she was so astonished she could not think of anything else to say.

Jamie told the story of the night's adventure, ending by saying, 'Surely you wouldna have allowed me to let her gang with them to be lost for ever?'

'But a *lady*, Jamie! How can a lady eat we'er [our] poor diet and live in we're poor way? I ax you that, you foolitch fellow!'

'Well, mother, sure it's better for her to be here nor yonder,' said he pointed in the direction of the castle.

Meanwhile, the deaf and dumb girl shivered in her light clothing, stepping close to the humble turf fire.

'Poor crathur, she's quare and handsome! Nae wonder they set their hearts on her,' said the old woman, gazing at their guest with pity and admiration. 'We maun dress her first; but what in the name o' fortune, has I fit for the likes o' her to wear?'

She went to her press in 'the room' and took out her Sunday gown of brown drugget. She then opened a drawer and drew forth a pair of white stockings, a long snowy garment of fine linen, and a cap, her 'dead dress,' as she called it.

These articles of attire had long been ready for a certain triste ceremony, in which she would someday fill the chief part, and only saw the light occasionally when they were hung out to air; but she was willing to give even these to the fair trembling visitor, who was turning in dumb sorrow and wonder from her to Jamie, and from Jamie back to her.

The poor girl suffered herself to be dressed, and then sat down on a 'creepie' in the chimney corner and buried her face in her hands.

'What'll we do to keep us a lady like thou?' cried the old woman.

'I'll work for you both, mother,' replied the son.

'An' how could a lady live on we're poor diet?' she repeated.

'I'll work for her,' was all Jamie's answer.

He kept his word. The young lady was very sad for a long time, and tears stole down her cheeks many an evening, while the old woman spun by the fire and Jamie made salmon nets, an accomplishment acquired by him in hopes of adding to the comfort of his guest.

But she was always gentle, and tried to smile when she perceived them looking at her; and by degrees she adapted herself to their ways and mode of life. It was not very long before she began to feed the pig, mash potatoes and meal for the fowls, and knit blue worsted socks.

So a year passed and Halloween came round again. 'Mother,' said Jamie, taking down his cap, 'I'm off to the ould castle to seek my fortune.'

'Are you mad, Jamie?' cried his mother in terror; 'sure they'll kill you this time for what you done on them last year.'

Jamie made light of her fears and went his way.

As he reached the crab tree he saw bright lights in the castle windows as before, and heard loud talking. Creeping under the window he heard the wee folk say, 'That was a poor trick Jamie Freel played us this night last year, when he stole the nice young lady from us.'

'Ay,' said the tiny woman, 'an' I punished him for it, for there she sits a dumb image by the hearth, but he does na' know that three drops out o' this glass that I hold in my hand wad gie her her hearing and her speech back again.'

Jamie's heart beat fast as he entered the hall. Again he was greeted by a chorus of welcomes from the company – 'Here comes Jamie Freel! Welcome, welcome, Jamie!'

As soon as the tumult subsided the little woman said, 'You be to drink our health, Jamie, out o' this glass in my hand.'

Jamie snatched the glass from her and darted to the door. He never knew how he reached his cabin, but he arrived there breathless and sank on a stove by the fire.

'You're kilt, surely, this time, my poor boy,' said his mother.

'No, indeed, better luck than ever this time!' and he gave the lady three drops of the liquid that still remained at the bottom of the glass, notwithstanding his mad race over the potato field.

The lady began to speak, and her first words were words of thanks to Jamie.

The three inmates of the cabin had so much to say to one another that, long after cockcrow, when the fairy music had quite ceased, they were talking round the fire.

'Jamie,' said the lady, 'be pleased to get me paper and pen and ink that I may write to my father and tell him what has become of me.'

She wrote, but weeks passed and she received no answer. Again and again she wrote, and still no answer.

At length she said, 'You must come with me to Dublin, Jamie, to find my father.'

'I hae no money to hire a car for you,' he answered; 'an' how can you travel to Dublin on your foot?'

But she implored him so much that he consented to set out with her and walk all the way from Fannet to Dublin. It was not as easy as the fairy journey; but at last they rang the bell at the door of the house in Stephen's Green.

'Tell my father that his daughter is here,' said she to the servant who opened the door.

'The gentleman that lives here has no daughter, my girl. He had one, but she died better nor a year ago.'

'Do you not know me, Sullivan?'

'No, poor girl, I do not.'

'Let me see the gentleman. I only ask to see him.'

'Well, that's not much to ax. We'll see what can be done.'

In a few moments the lady's father came to the door.

'How care you call me your father?' cried the old gentleman angrily. 'You are an impostor. I have no daughter.'

'Look in my face, father, and surely you'll remember me.'

'My daughter is dead and buried. She died a long, long time ago.' The old gentleman's voice changed from anger to sorrow. 'You can go,' he concluded.

'Stop, dear father, till you look at this ring on my finger. Look at your name and mine engraved on it.'

'It certainly is my daughter's ring, but I do not know how you came by it. I fear in no honest way.'

'Call my mother – she will be sure to know me,' said the poor girl, who by this time was weeping bitterly.

'My poor wife is beginning to forget her sorrow. She seldom speaks of her daughter now. Why should I renew her grief by reminding her of her loss?'

But the young lady persevered till at last the mother was sent for.

'Mother,' she began, when the old lady came to the door, 'don't you know your daughter?'

'I have no daughter. My daughter died, and was buried a long, long time ago.'

'Only look in my face and surely you'll know me.'

The old lady shook her head.

'You have all forgotten me; but look at this mole on my neck. Surely, mother, you know me now?'

'Yes, yes,' said the mother, 'my Gracie had a mole on her neck like that; but then I saw her in her coffin, and saw the lid shut down upon her.'

It became Jamie's turn to speak, and he gave the history of the fairy journey, of the theft of the young lady, of the figure he had seen laid in its place, of her life with his mother in Fannet, of last Halloween, and of the three drops that had released her from her enchantments.

She took up the story when he paused and told how kind the mother and son had been to her.

The parents could not make enough of Jamie. They treated him with every distinction, and when he expressed his wish to return to Fannet, said they did not know what to do to express their gratitude.

But an awkward complication arose. The daughter would not let him go without her. 'If Jamie goes, I'll go, too,' she said. 'He saved me from the fairies, and has worked for me ever since. If it had not been for him, dear father and mother, you would never have seen me again. If he goes, I'll go, too.'

This being her resolution, the old gentleman said that Jamie should become his son-in-law. The mother was brought from Fannet in a coach-and-four, and there was a splendid wedding.

They all lived together in the grand Dublin house, and Jamie was heir to untold wealth at his father-in-law's death.

JAMES BERRY

The Adventures of Foranan O'Fergus, the Physician

❧

About the beginning of the seventeenth century there dwelt near the village of Borus a man named Foranan O'Fergus, and the little green toonagh or hillock where he lived, located between Borus and Forigil at the foot of the brown hill of Cuck-a-Kishawn, is called even to this day Auththie Foranan, which means the place of Foranan's house; surely O'Fergus must have left his footprints deeply imprinted on the sands of time when the name of the glen in which he lived is handed down to posterity.

This old man was a medical doctor, for the O'Ferguses were for at least five hundred years the acknowledged hereditary physicians of the Western Owls of the O'Malleys. They were all skilled leeches, for they had to undergo a rigid course of training from their fathers who kept a careful record of all the cures each effected during his lifetime, together with notes of how he treated the various cases of different maladies which came to his notice and which he cured, as well as the peculiar cases in which he was not able to effect a cure. These valuable records were written by hand, generally in Irish, and sometimes in Latin, for the art of printing was not in vogue in those days in the far West. The reader can see from the foregoing that the O'Ferguses weren't quacks, but were learned physicians. They were a small tribe or clan and don't seem to have been a prolific race, but they were far-famed, the males for their fine, masculine physique and florid complexions, the females for their beauty and feminine grace and winsome ways.

In the days I write about, the great valley which environs the little town of Louisburgh in West Mayo was all covered by a primeval forest so dense that if a man mounted a tree branch at Fairy Hill on the seashore at Bunowen, he could travel from branch to branch without touching the ground until he reached Glan Bawn, a distance of at least six miles. The grandparents of the present writer saw it in the state I have described when they were children. How it was denuded of its timber in such a short period is astonishing to me, but it can be accounted for by the fact that the invaders, the Brownes, the Binghams and the Palmers, cut down the woods in which the rightful owners, whom they called Rapparees, were concealed, for well they knew their lives were in danger until the woods were cut down.

On a certain day in summer, Foranan O'Fergus received two urgent calls, one from the bleak, storm-swept village of Cloonthie, some distance West of the charming vale of Cloonlara, where a man lay dangerously sick, and the other to visit three young men who lived in a little ravine called Dereen-an-Albanagh, on the banks of Killary Bay, about a mile or two distant from its mouth, and who had been grievously wounded in a very peculiar manner. When Foranan had breakfast, he began to prepare to set out. He took down his Bireath or Baret cap, a Celtic headgear which resembled a Turkish turban; as usual he blessed himself by making the sign of the cross before he placed the cap on his head.

Next he took down his skean dhu which hung on its scabbard on the wall of his bedchamber and he hung it on his right hip, for in those days no man dared go abroad without it for the woods were infested with wild hogs, wolves, and enormous wildcats. He put on his kothamore or Celtic cloak, the most becoming garment I have ever seen on the back of a tall, well-shaped man. I dare say this garment is now extinct, for I haven't seen one in over sixty years. O'Fergus next caught hold of his Kleagh alpeen or alpinstock, a pole about six feet long, sharpened on one end, which our ancestors used for hill climbing. He called to his side Flann, his great wolfhound, blue-coloured, coarse-haired and brown-eyed. He was thoroughly equipped for the journey as he crossed his threshold and disappeared through the wild woods. His wife, who had De Danann blood in her veins and who retained some of their superstitions, caught a live coal with the tongs and cast it on the floor in a peculiar manner. If the tongs when cast opened wide it boded good, but if the tongs did not open to the full extent, this boded evil. She cast the coal skilfully, but the tongs didn't open, and her heart sank within her, for well she knew by the unlucky omen that the partner of her joys and sorrows would encounter many dangers before she clasped him again to her white, throbbing bosom.

Foranan held on his way towards the West and soon issued from the woods at Tully. He crossed the river with his faithful Flann by his side, climbed Run-na-hallya and traversed the great moor called Ru-na-goppal; soon he reached Furmoyle, once the happy hunting ground of the far-famed Fena of Erin. He continued on through Carra-an-Iska and the charming vale of Cloonlara, and soon reached Cloonthie where he entered the humble home of Roger O'Toole who lay on his death bed. When he entered the dark, rude cabin, many of the old men of the village followed him, for they wished to salute their hereditary physician.

The doctor examined the wounded man, and then turned towards the villagers to ask, 'This man must have got a fall from some tremendous height or cliff, so pray tell me, Toby Stanton, how did it happen, for his spine is broken, and he has but three days to live.' 'Musha, doctor,' said Stanton, 'he did get a great fall, and it was all his own fault for he would not be advised by us, for although a small man he was always headstrong and contrary, and now this is the end of it and I often told him so, for he would fight with his nails, and yet he was a good neighbour, the crathereen.'

'About two months ago,' he continued, 'O'Toole sent his fine mare grazing on the wild mountains of Mweelrea, and his son went out to see her each Sunday, and she was coming on fine. Last Sunday when the boy went to see her, she was dead in Lugatharee on the shore of Doolough, at the foot of the great cliff, cast down by the eagles. There she lay on the broad of her back and with her neck broken, so the son returned weeping and told his father. The father got into a rage and swore he would have it out with the eagles. The next morning he took down his skean dhu and hung it on his hip; next he took a brown flannel quilt which he rolled up and placed under his arm, and he set out for Doolough, some five miles distant from his home. We followed him, for we knew something terrible was going to take place.

'When we reached the Glan Cullin on the western shore of the lake, we saw the dead mare in the deep, dark glen of Lugatharee, at the foot of the great cliff. We lay in ambush under the wide, spreading holly trees while O'Toole went on towards the dead animal. He drew his skean and ripped her open as she lay on her back. He removed the entrails and hid them, and then he wrapped the old quilt around him and lay down in the cavity of the carcass. Suddenly a strange thing happened, and the climax came sooner than we had expected, for two great eagles floated down from the cliff and alighted on the carrion. O'Toole stretched forth his right hand and took hold of the leg of one of the eagles above the talons, while with his left hand he caught the other eagle in a similar manner. The sacred monsters arose with a scream and took wing, carrying O'Toole with them, for the brave little Celt held on to them like grim death.

'There was a strong wind blowing which helped them to soar aloft towards their home in the terrible precipice. O'Toole must have realised his terrible position as he hung in the air between heaven and earth, for well he knew they would tear him to pieces or cast him headlong into the dark chasm. When they had raised him a hundred feet in the air, he loosened his grip and fell with a great crash on his back on the soft morass. We rushed towards him, but we found him stark dead, so we cut down some roan saplings which grew among the holly in the glen, and of these we made a rude litter on which we carried him home with much grief. When we reached home, we found to our astonishment that he had life in him and could take a sup, and it was then, doctor, that we sent for you,' concluded Stanton. 'Well now,' said Foranan, 'send for your parish priest, Father David Lyons, to anoint him and prepare him for eternity, for he has only three days to live.' 'We will send for him, but it's hard to locate him,' said Stanton, 'for you know he has no house or home of his own, and never had.' 'I know that,' said Foranan.

Father David Lyons was born in the village of Killadoon, midway between Killary Bay and the present town of Louisburgh. When he was twenty years old, he went to Spain and entered the College of Salamanca where he remained until he was ordained a priest, and then he returned to Ireland to be appointed by the Archbishop of Tuam as parish priest of Kilgeever, his native parish. He never had a curate, for although he was a small man, he possessed more than one man's share of strength and vigour. While he was in Spain he never met a man fit to wrestle him, nor did he ever meet one in Connacht fit to wrestle him either. Until the day of his death he never had a house or home, but went about from village to village, sleeping in the houses of the country people, on some straw in a corner of the kitchen, for he didn't know at what moment he might have to spring up and rush to the mountains for safety, for the priest hunters were abroad in the land in those days. He never accepted dues, save what should go to the bishop; he never had a farthing in his pocket, or in a box or a trunk, for he never had a box or trunk.

He always wore a body coat, vest, and breeches of black frieze, a strong pair of brogues over which he wore a pair of knitted spatters, all of which he got from the people, but although he was dressed in this humble garb, when he took out his stole, and kissed it, and placed it around his neck, he could dry up the Red Sea or bring down Manna from heaven. He lived to be a great age, and he was vigorous to the last. He died in his native village, and he lies slumbering in a nameless grave in Killeen in the charming vale of Cloonlara, where perhaps his slumbers are as serene and tranquil as those of any canon or other dignitary of the Church who might leave eight or ten thousand pounds behind him to some worthless relatives who may never offer up a prayer for the repose of the soul of the benefactor who left them the windfall.

Leaving Roger O'Toole to the ministrations of Father David Lyons, Foranan departed and set out for the banks of the Killary, and as the shades of evening were beginning to descend he reached his destination and entered the dark, rude cabin of Ulick Burke, whose three stalwart sons were greviously wounded and disfigured, for each of them had lost half a nose. Foranan stood in the cabin, spellbound and appalled. 'How in the world did this happen, pray tell me at once,' he said. 'Oh no, not until you have partaken of some refreshments,' answered the old man, 'for it is a long and sad story.' The old woman got up and handed him a noggin of boiled new milk sweetened with honey, into which was poured two glasses of poteen or iska baha, and when he had taken this strengthening beverage, he sat down to dinner.

At the conclusion of the meal, the oldest son began to relate his sad story. 'About a week ago,' he said, 'I went to bed just after saying the Rosary, and I fell into a tranquil sleep, but about the dead hour of the night a Naugh stood at my bedside.' [To enlighten the present-day reader who may not know what a Naugh is, let it be said that it is a friendly kind of ghost of whom the peasantry were not afraid, for the Naugh came to tell the sleeper where he would find a hidden treasure.] 'The Naugh stood at my bedside and said to me, Go to the lake of Althor which lies beneath the northern bank of the rugged hill of Derrygoriv. There you will see a firm turf bank, and when you reach the centre of this bank, stretch on your stomach and look beneath you into the lake. There you will see about two feet of the bogdale tree which is embedded in the bog protruding into the water; look closely at it, and then you will see a pot hung by a pothook on it, just as if it hung over a fire. The pot is filled to the cosheen with gold, but around the cosheen you will see coiled an enormous serpent which is nothing more or less than the spirit of the dead miser who hoarded up this gold. Then insert your gaff under the pothooks, lift up the pot and with all speed run towards the stream which divides two townlands; jump across it with the pot, the spell will be broken, and the gold is yours.

'The Naugh came to my bedside the second and third nights, repeating the same advice, so on the next morning I took a strong gaff with me and set out for the lake. When I reached it, I made for the northern bank and began to investigate in order to locate the pot. Sure enough, I saw it hanging on the beam some six feel below the surface. Then I stretched on my stomach in order to catch hold of the pothooks with the gaff and lift up the pot, and then the serpent looked up at me with her terrible green eyes, and at once I became fascinated and helpless as an infant. Nor could I move hand or foot, but kept looking at it spellbound until it stiffened itself, reached up and deliberately bit off half my nose and disfigured me for life. Then my two other brothers attempted to lift the pot, but each was fascinated and spellbound, so each of them also lost half a nose.' 'Well,' said the doctor, 'I am unable to furnish you with new ones; all I can do is to give you some ointment which will soon heal the wounds. Just rub it on like Vaseline, or Zam Buck, and in a few days you will be all right.'

The next morning, Foranan arose early and determined to climb the western brow of the great mountain in order to take a short cut to his home in the East. He didn't need to climb to its apex, but only to the table land beneath the great cone. Even this climb was a task which would have deterred Hannibal in his best days, but the doctor was bound that he would surmount all obstacles and achieve his goal. He caught hold of his kleagh alpeen or climbing pole and began to climb the southern side of the great mountain of Mweelrea which bulges out and overhangs the waters of deep Killary Bay, for he had learned climbing since his earliest youth, and he had a nerve as strong and a step as firm and sure as that of an Alpine Ibex, and as he climbed his ever-faithful Flann kept close beside him. When he had climbed some fifteen hundred feet, he reached the plateau or table land which stretched away from South to North, the whole breadth of the hill, as vast and undulating as an American prairie. He held on his way towards the North.

When he had traversed about two-thirds of the table land, he came to a lake which tradition states is inhabited by a fiend, or by many fiends. This lake is called Lough Cum, or the lake of the hound, and it is supposed to have the most beautiful gravely shores of any lake in Ireland. Tradition says that if a man stood on the shore and challenged the lake to send up a champion to fight him, the lake would produce a champion. Or if a man called upon the lake to send up a dog to fight his dog, the lake would send up a black hound which would rend his dog.

Foranan did a deed of folly which he had cause to regret until the day of his death, for in order to test the legend, he called on the lake to send up a hound to fight Flann. No sooner had he uttered the words than the great black hound arose out of the lake and the fight began. It lasted from noonday until the sun was fast waning towards the West, and Flann was torn and wounded in many places, and his life was fast ebbing away. Then the lake hound caught him by the throat and sprang into the lake with the wolfhound's thrashing form, never to rise again. Foranan smote his breast, realising that with his inquisitiveness and folly he had lost his ever-faithful friend, a friend who so often hazarded his life in order to save his master, and now he was gone forever, the true and brave Flann.

With despair in his heart, Foranan fled down the deep declivity of the mountain, leaving that lake of demons far above him. He reached the lowlands between Doogan Hill and the little hamlet of Shraugh Rusky, six miles across the level moors from his home. He began to traverse the vast moor which stretches northward from Glankeen and Derryfeach and trends downward towards the village of Lachta,

Shraugh-na-lusid, and Shraugh-na-cliha. When he reached the centre of the moor he encountered a lake, a portion of which was overgrown with tall bulrushes, while the other portion was covered with beautiful white water lilies which glinted and sparkled in the summer evening sunshine. When he drew near the eastern shore of the lake, above which grew a shrubbery of sally, hazel and yew trees, he saw a sight which appalled him, a wild hog running towards him. It was a sow who had just farrowed a litter of young ones, and who had heard his footsteps long before he had seen her, and now he knew his end had come. Oh, if he had Flann, the brave and fearless Flann would rend and tear her to pieces, but Flann was lost through his own fault.

He stood there unarmed and defenceless. It is true he had his knife, but well he knew he was no match for the sow at close quarters, for she would rend him with her horrible tusks. He signed himself with the cross and bade farewell to hope, although he was no craven, but an intrepid, dauntless man. He determined to fight to the death with the weapon he carried. He took hold of his climbing pole with both hands, as you would a spear or lance. It was of wild mountain holly, as firm and hard as iron, and sharp-pointed on one end. When the rabid monster drew near him, open-mouthed, he drove his alpinstock with all his strength and vigour into her mouth and it went through her neck behind the ear. He drew out the weapon suddenly, and the sow's lifeblood gushed forth in torrents from the wounds. She fell with a great splash into the lake below and sank forever, and from that day to ours the lake is called Lough-na-Muicka, or the lake of the pig.

Foranan looked up with gratitude to heaven for his escape from a cruel death by the skin of his teeth, and then resumed his journey. He soon reached Shraugh-na-lusid and crossed the great river which could well be named the little Nile, for from its source beneath the great mountain of Curwock at Sachta it winds its way through fertile plains until it discharges its waters into Clew Bay at Bunowen. When he crossed the river, night had set in, that is, if a midsummer's night should be called night: 'For the sun loves to pause, with so fond a delay, that the night only draws a thin veil o'er the day'.

However, the witching hour of the night had come, and the evil one was abroad seeking whom he might devour. When Foranan drew near his home, he met a sluggish mountain stream in which there was no ford. All pedestrians passing that way had to leap across the river. Just as the doctor reached the proper spot for jumping, some huge, dark object stood on the opposite bank, barring his progress. Foranan went along the stream until he found another spot where he could jump, but again the great beast confronted him. Again he retreated to the proper place for jumping, but the great beast lurked on the other side. He tried several spots, but always with the same result. Then Foranan knew that this was a fiend who sought to exhaust him in order that he would perish on the bleak moor.

Determined to fight once more for his life, Foranan took off his baret cap and blessed himself. He drew his skean dhu out of its sheath, made the sign of the cross on the blade, and then with the bound of an enraged panther, he sprang across the stream and buried his skean dhu to the hilt in the vitals of the demon. A voice croaked forth from the huge, hairy body, imploring, 'Good man, draw out your knife and give another stab.' 'Oh no,' answered Foranan, 'one stab is sufficient, for tradition says that if a man draws his knife out of a demon, the fiend will then slay him.' He left his skean dhu in the vitals of the demon and turned away. When he knocked at his door and his wife cast it open, she saw that his eyes were closed, and she realised that he had encountered a fiend, so she led him by the hand to a straw armchair beside the fire. From the saltbox which hung on the wall above his head she administered to him three pinches of salt in the name of the Trinity. Her husband opened his eyes, the danger of fainting now being removed. He was safe home.

WILLIAM CARLETON

Moll Roe's Marriage or the Pudding Bewitched

❧❧❧

It is utterly impossible for anyone but an Irishman fully to comprehend the extravagance to which the spirit of Irish humour is often carried, and that even in circumstances which one would suppose it ought least to be expected. In other countries the house of death is in reality the house of mourning, and so indeed it is also in Ireland, where domestic grief is felt with a power that reaches to the uttermost depths of the heart. But then in Ireland this very fullness of sorrow, unlike that which is manifested elsewhere, is accompanied by so many incongruous associations, apparently incompatible with, or rather altogether opposed to, the idea of affliction, that strangers, when assured of such an anomalous admixture of feelings, can scarcely bring themselves to believe in their existence. I have said that in Ireland the house of death is without doubt the house of mourning; but I must not conceal the additional fact, that it is also, in consequence of the calamity which has occurred, the house of fun, and of fun, too, so broad, grotesque, and extravagant, that in no other condition of society, even in Ireland, is there anything to be found like it. This, no doubt, may appear a rather startling assertion, but it is quite true.

And now many of my sagacious readers will at once set about accounting for such a singular combination of mad mirth and profound sorrow. Let them, however, spare their metaphysics, for I will save them a long process of reasoning on the subject, by stating, that all this clatter of laughter and comic uproar proceeds from a principle that does honour to Paddy's heart – I mean sympathy with those whom the death of some dear relative has thrown into affliction. Indeed no people sympathise more deeply with each other than the Irish, or enter more fully into the spirit that prevails, whether it be one of joy or sorrow. The reason, then, why the neighbours and acquaintances of the deceased flock at night to hold Wakes – the merriest of all merry meetings – frequently in the very house where he or she lies dead, is simply that the sense of the bereavement may be mitigated by the light-hearted amusements which are enacted before their eyes. The temperament of the Irish, however, is strongly susceptible of the extremes of mirth and sorrow, and our national heart is capable of being moved by the two impulses almost at the same moment. Many a time I have seen a widow sitting over the dead body of an affectionate husband, midst her desolate orphans, so completely borne away by the irresistible fun of some antic wag, who acted as Master of the Revels, that she has been forced into a fit of laughter that brought other tears than those of sorrow to her eyes. Often has the father – the features of the pious and chaste mother of his children composed into the mournful stillness of death before him – been, in the same manner, carried into a fit of immoderate mirth on witnessing the inimitable drolleries exhibited in 'Boxing the Connaughtman', or the convulsive fun of the 'Screw-pin Dance'. The legends and tales and stories that are told at Irish wakes all bear the impress of this mad extravagance; and it is because I am now about to relate one of them, that I have deemed it expedient to introduce it to my readers by this short but necessary preface. Those who peruse it are not to imagine that I am gravely writing it in my study; but that, on the contrary, they are sitting in the chimney-corner, at an Irish wake, and that some droll *Senachie*, his face lit up into an expression of broad farcical humour, is proceeding somewhat as follows.

'Moll Roe Rafferty was the son – daughter I mane – of ould Jack Rafferty, who was remarkable for a habit he had of always wearing his head undher his hat; but indeed the same family was a quare one, as everybody knew that was acquainted wid them. It was said of them – but whether it was thrue or not I won't undhertake to say, for 'fraid I'd tell a lie – that whenever they didn't wear shoes or boots, they always went barefooted; but I hard afterwards that this was disputed, so rather than say anything to injure their caracther, I'll let that pass. Now, ould Jack Rafferty had two sons, Paddy and Molly – but! what are you all laughing at? – I mane a son and daughter, and it was generally believed among the neighbours, that they were brother and sister, which you know might be thrue or it might not; but that's a thing that, wid the help o' goodness, we have nothing to say to. Throth there was many ugly things put out on them that I don't wish to repate, such as that neither Jack nor his son Paddy ever walked a perch widout puttin' one foot afore the other, like a salmon; an' I know that it was whispered about, that whenever Moll Roe slep', she had an out of the way custom of keepin' her eyes shut. If she did, however, God forgive her – the loss was her own; for sure we all know that when one comes to shut their eyes they can't see as far before them as another.

'Moll Roe was a fine young bouncin' girl, large and lavish, wid a purty head o' hair on her like scarlet, that bein' one of the raisons why she was called Roe or Red; her arms an' cheeks were much the colour of the hair, an' her saddle nose was the purtiest thing of its kind that ever was on a face. Her fists – for, thank goodness, she was well sarved wid them too – had a strong simularity to two thumpin' turnips, reddened by the sun; an' to keep all right and tight, she had a temper as fiery as her head – for, indeed, it was well known that all the Raffertys were *warm*-hearted. Howandiver, it appears that God gives nothing in vain, and of course the same fists, big and red as they were, if all that is said about them is thrue, were not so much given to her for ornament as use. At laist, takin' them in connection wid her lively temper, we have it upon good authority, that there was no danger of their getting blue-moulded for want of practice. She had a twist, too, in one of her eyes that was very becomin' in its way, and made her poor husband, when she got him, take it into his head that she could see round a corner. She found him out in many quare things, widout doubt; but whether it was owin' to that or not I wouldn't undertake to say, *for fraid I'd tell a lie*.

'Well, begad, anyhow, it was Moll Roe that was the *dilsy*; and as they say that marriages does be *sometimes* made in heaven, so did it happen that there was a nate vagabone in the neighbourhood, just as much overburdened wid beauty as herself, and he was named Gusty Gillespie. Gusty, the Lord guard us, was what they call a black-mouth Prosbytarian, and wouldn't keep Christmas day, the blagard, except what they call 'ould style.' Gusty was rather good-lookin' when seen in the dark, as well as Moll herself; and indeed it was purty well known that – accordin' as the talk went – it was in nightly meetings that they had an opportunity of becomin' detached to one another. They quensequence was, that in due time both families began to talk very seriously as to what was to be done. Moll's brother, Pawdien O'Rafferty, gave Gusty the best of two choices. What they were it's not worth spaikin about; but at any rate one of them was a poser, an' as Gusty knew his man, he soon came to his senses. Accordingly everything was deranged for their marriage, and it was appointed that they should be spliced by the Reverend Samuel M'Shuttle, the Prosbytarian parson, on the following Sunday.

'Now this was the first marriage that had happened for a long time in the neighbourhood betune a black mouth an' a Catholic, an' of coorse there was strong objections on both sides aginst it; an' begad, only for one thing it would never a tuck place at all. At any rate, faix, there was one of the bride's uncles, ould Harry Connolly, a fairy man, who could cure all complaints wid a secret he had, and as he didn't wish to see his niece marrid upon such a fellow, he fought bitterly against the match. All Moll's friends, however, stood up for the marriage barrin' him, an' of course the Sunday was appointed, as I said, that they were to be dovetailed together.

'Well, the day arrived, and Moll as became her went to mass, and Gusty to meeting, afther which they were to join one another in Jack Rafferty's, where the priest, Father M'Sorley, was to slip up afther mass, to take his dinner wid them, and to keep Misther M'Shuttle, who was to marry them, company. Nobody remained at home but ould Jack Rafferty an' his wife, who stopped to dress the dinner, for to tell the truth it was to be a great let out entirely. Maybe, if all was known, too, that Father M'Sorley was to give them a cast of his office over an' above the Ministher, in regard that Moll's friends weren't altogether satisfied at the kind of marriage which M'Shuttle could give them. The sorrow may care about that – splice here – splice there – all I can say is, that when Mrs Rafferty was goin' to tie up a big bad pudden, in walks Harry Connolly, the fairy-man, in a rage, and shouts out, – 'Blood and blunderbushes, what are yez here for?"

' "Arra why, Harry? Why avick?"

' "Why, the sun's in the suds and the moon in the high Horicks;

there's a clipstick comin' an, an' there you're both as unconsarned as if it was about to rain mether. Go out and cross yourselves three times in the name o' the four Mandromarvins, for as prophecy says: Fill the pot, Eddy supernaculum – a blazing star's a rare spectaculum. Go out both of you and look at the sun, I say, an' ye'll see the condition he's in – off!"

'Begad, sure enough, Jack gave a bounce to the door, an' his wife leaped like a two year ould, till they were both got on a stile beside the house to see what was wrong in the sky.

' "Arra, what is it, Jack," said she, 'can you see anything?"

' "No," says he, "sorra the full o' my eye of anything I can spy, barrin' the sun himself, that's not visible in regard of the clouds. God guard us! I doubt there's something to happen."

' "If there wasn't, Jack, what 'ud put Harry that knows so much, in the state he's in?"

' "I doubt it's this marriage," said Jack: "betune ourselves, it's not over and above religious for Moll to marry a black-mouth, an' only for – , but it can't be helped now, though you see, the divil a taste o' the sun is willin' to show his face upon it."

' "As to that," says the wife, winkin' wid both her eyes, "if Gusty's satisfied with Moll, it's enough. I know who'll carry the whip hand, anyhow; but in the mane time let us ax Harry 'ithin what ails the sun."

'Well, they accordingly went in an' put the question to him.

' "Harry, what's wrong, ahagur? What is it now, for if anybody alive knows, 'tis yourself?"

' "Ah!" said Harry, screwin' his mouth with a kind of a dry smile, "the sun has a hard twist o' the cholic; but never mind that, I tell you you'll have a merrier weddin' than you think, that's all"; and havin' said this he put on his hat and left the house.

'Now Harry's answer relieved them very much, and so, afther calling to him to be back for the dinner, Jack sat down to take a shough o' the pipe, and the wife lost no time in tying up the pudden and puttin' it in the pot to be boiled.

'In this way things went on well enough for a while, Jack smokin' away, an' the wife cookin' an' dhressin' at the rate of a hunt. At last Jack, while sittin', as I said, contentedly at the fire, thought he could persave an odd dancin' kind of motion in the pot, that puzzled him a good deal.

' "Katty," said he, "what the dickens is in this pot on the fire?"

' "Nerra thing but the big pudden. Why do you ax?" says she.

' "Why," said he, "if ever a pot took it into its head to dance a jig, and this did. Thunder and sparables, look at it!"

'Begad, it was true enough; there was the pot bobbin' up an' down and from side to side, jiggin' it away as merry as a grig; an' it was quite aisy to see that it wasn't the pot itself, but what was inside of it, that brought about the hornpipe.

' "Be the hole o' my coat," shouted Jack, "there's something alive in it, or it would never cut such capers!"

' "Be the vestment, there is, Jack; something sthrange entirely has got into it. Wirra, man alive, what's to be done?"

'Jist as she spoke, the pot seemed to cut the buckle in prime style, and afther a spring that 'ud shame a dancin'-masther, off flew the lid, and out bounced the pudden itself, hoppin', as nimble as a pea on a drumhead, about the floor. Jack blessed himself, and Katty crossed herself. Jack shouted, and Katty screamed. "In the name of the nine Evangils,' said he, 'keep your distance, no one here injured you!"

'The pudden, however, made a set at him, and Jack lepped first on a chair and then on the kitchen table to avoid it. It then danced towards Katty who was now repatin' her pather an' avys at the top of her voice, while the cunnin' thief of a pudden was hoppin' and jiggen it round her, as if it was amused at her distress.

' "If I could get the pitchfork," said Jack, "I'd dale wid it – by goxty I'd thry its mettle."

' "No, no," shouted Katty thinkin there was a fairy in it, "let us spake it fair. Who knows what harm it might do? Aisy now," said she to the pudden, "aisy, dear; don't harm honest people that never meant to offend you. It wasn't us – no, in throth, it was ould Harry Connolly that bewitched you; persue him if you wish, but spare a woman like me; for, whisper, dear, I'm not in a condition to be frightened – throth I'm not."

'The pudden, bedad, seemed to take her at her word, and danced away from her towards Jack, who, like the wife, believin' there was a fairy in it, an' that spakin' it fair was the best plan, thought he would give it a soft word as well as her.

' "Plase your honour," said Jack, "she only spaiks the truth. You don't know what harm you might do her; an', upon my voracity, we both feels much oblaiged to your honour for your quietness. Faith, it's quite clear that if you weren't a gentlemanly pudden all out, you'd act otherwise. Ould Harry, the dam' rogue, is your mark; he's jist gone down the road there, and if you go fast you'll overtake him. Be me song, your dancin'-masther did his duty anyhow. Thank your honour! God speed you, an' may you never meet wid a priest, parson, or alderman in your thravels!"

'Jist as Jack spoke the pudden appeared to take the hint, for it quietly hopped out, and as the house was directly on the road side, turned down towards the bridge, the very way that ould Harry went. It was very natural of coorse that Jack and Katty should go out to see how it intended to thravel: and, as the day was Sunday, it was but natural, too, that a greater number of people than usual were passin' the road. This was a fact. And when Jack and his wife were seen followin' the pudden, the whole neighbourhood was soon up and afther it.

' "Jack Rafferty, what is it?" Katty, ahagur, will you tell us what it manes?'

' "Why," replied Katty, "be the vestments, it's my big pudden that's bewitched, an' it's now hot-foot pursuin' – here she stopped, not wishin' to mention her brother's name, – "someone or other that surely put *pistrogues* [put it under fairy influence] an it."

'This was enough; Jack now seein' that he had assistance, found his courage comin' back to him, so says he to Katty, "Go home," says he, "an' lose no time in makin' another pudden as good, an' here's Paddy Scanlan's wife, Bridget, says she'll let you boil it on her fire, as you'll wan't our own to dress the rest o' the dinner; and Paddy himself will lend me a pitchfork, for divle resave the morsel of the same pudden will escape till I let the wind out of it, now that I've the neighbours to back an' support me," says Jack.

'This was agreed to, and Katty went back to prepare a fresh pudden, while Jack an' half the townland pursued the other wid spades, graips, pitchforks, scythes, flails, and all possible description of instruments. On the pudden went, however, at the rate of about six Irish miles an hour, an' divle sich a chase ever was seen. Catholics, Prodestans, an' Prosbytarians were all afther it, armed as I said, an' bad end to the thing but its own activity could save it. Here it made a hop, and there a prod was made at it; but off it went, an' someone as aiger to get a slice at it on the other side, got the prod instead of the pudden. Big Frank Farrell, the miller of Ballyboulteen, got a prod backwards that brought a hullabaloo out of him you might hear at the other end of the parish. One got a slice of the sythe, another a whack of a flail, a third a rap of a spade that made him look nine ways at wanst.

' "Where is it goin'?" asked one.

' "It's goin to mass," replied a second. "Then it's a Catholic pudden," exclaimed a third – "down wid it." "No," said a fourth, "it's above superstition; my life for you, it's on it's way to Meeting. Three cheers for it, if it turns to Carntaul. "Prod the sowl out of it, if it's a Prodestan," shouted the others; "if it turns to the left, slice it into pancakes: we'll have no Prodestan puddens here."

'Begod, by this time the people were on the point of beginnin' to have a regular fight about it, when, very fortunately, it took a short turn down a little by-lane that led towards the Methodist praichin'-house, an' in an instant all parties were in an uproar against it as a Methodist pudden. "It's a Wesleyan," shouted several voices, "an' by this an' by that into a Methodist chapel it won't put a foot today, or we'll lose a fall. Let the wind out of it. Come, boys, where's your pitchforks?"

'The divle purshue the one of them, however, ever could touch the pudden, an' jist when they thought they had it up against the gavel of the Methodist chapel, bedad it gave them the slip, and hops over to the left, clane into the river, and sails away before all their eyes as light as an eggshell.

'Now, it so happened, that a little below this place, the demesne-wall of Colonel Bragshaw was built up to the very edge of the river on each side of its banks; and so findin' there was a stop put to their pursuit of it, they went home again, every man, woman, and child of them puzzled to think what the pudden was at all – whether Catholic, Prodestan, Prosbytarian, or Methodist – what it meant, or where it was goin'! Had Jack Rafferty an' his wife been willin' to let out the opinion they held about Harry Connolly betwitchin' it, there is no doubt but poor Harry might be badly trated by the crowd when their blood was up. They had some sense enough, howandiver, to keep that to themselves, for Harry, bein' an' ould bachelor, was a kind friend to the Raffertys. So, of coorse, there was all kinds of talk about it – some guessin' this, and some guessin' that – one party sayin' the pudden was of their side, another party denyin' it, an' insistin' it belonged to them, an' so on.

'In the mane time, Katty Rafferty, for 'fraid the dinner might come short, went home and made another pudden much about the same size as the one that had escaped, and bringin' it over to their next neighbour, Paddy Scanlan's, it was put into a pot and placed on the fire to boil, hopin' that it might be done in time, espishilly as they were to have the priest an' the ministher, and that both loved a warm slice of a good pudden as well as e'er a pair of gintlemen in Europe.

'Anyhow, the day passed; Moll and Gusty were made man an' wife, an' no two could be more lovin'. Their friends that had been asked to the weddin' were saunterin' about in pleasant little groups till dinner time, chattin' an' laughin', but, above all things, sthrivin' to account for the figaries of the pudden, for, to tell the truth, its adventures had now gone through the whole parish.

'Well, at any rate, dinner-time was dhrawin' near, and Paddy Scanlan was sittin' comfortably wid his wife at the fire, the pudden boilen before their eyes, when in walks Harry Connolly, in a flutter, shoutin' – "Blood and blunderbushes, what are yez here for?"

' "Arra, why Harry – why, avick?" said Mrs Scanlan.

' "Why," said Harry, "the sun's in the suds an' the moon in the high Horicks. Here's a clipstick comin' an, an' there you sit as unconsarned as if it was about to rain mether! Go out an' cross yourselves three times in the name of the four Mandromarvins, for, as the prophecy says: – Fill the pot, Eddy, supernaculum – a blazin' star's rare spectaculum. Go out both of you, an' look at the sun, I say, and ye'll see the condition he's in – off!"

' "Ay, but, Harry, what's that rowled up in the tail of your cotamore [big coat]?"

' "Out wid yez," said Harry; "cross yourselves three times in the name of the four Mandromarvins, an' pray aginst the clipstick – the sky's fallen'."

'Begad it was hard to say whether Paddy or the wife got out first, they were so much alarmed by Harry's wild thin face, an' piercin' eyes; so out they went to see what was wondherful in the sky, an' kep' lookin' an' lookin' in every direction, but divle a thing was to be seen, barrin' the sun shinin' down with great good humour, an' not a single cloud in the sky.

'Paddy an' the wife now came in laughin', to scould Harry, who, no doubt, was a great wag, in his way, when he wished. "Musha bad scran to you, Harry – ." They had time to say no more, howandiver, for, as they were goin' into the door, they met him comin' out of it wid a reek of smoke out of his tail like a limekiln.

' "Harry," shouted Bridget, "my sowl to glory, but the tail of your cothamore's a-fire – you'll be burned. Don't you see the smoke that's out of it?"

' "Cross yourselves three times," said Harry, widout stoppin', or even lookin' behind him – "corss yourselves three times in the name of the four Mandromarvins, for, as the prophecy says: – Fill the pot, Eddy – " They could hear no more, for Harry appeared to feel like a man that carried something a great deal hotter than he wished, as anyone might see by the liveliness of his motions, and the quare faces he was forced to make as he went along.

' "What the dickens is he carryin' in the skirts of his big coat," asked Paddy.

' "My sowl to happiness, but maybe he has stole the pudden," said Bridget, "for its known that many a sthrange thing he does."

'They immediately examined the pot, but found that the pudden was there as safe as tuppence, an' this puzzled them the more, to think that what it was he could be carryin' about wid him in the manner he did. But little they knew what he had done while they were sky gazin'.

'Well, anyhow, the day passed and the dinner was ready, an' no doubt but a fine gatherin' there was to partake of it. The priest and the Prosbytarian ministher had met the Methodist praicher – a divilish stretch of an appetite he had, in troth – on their way to Jack Rafferty's, an' as they knew they could take the liberty, why they insisted on his dinin' wid them; for afther all, begad, in thim times the clargy of all descriptions lived on the best footin' among one another, not all as one as now, – but no matther. Well, they had nearly finished their dinner, when Jack Rafferty himself axed Katty for the pudden; but jist as he spoke, in it came as big as a mess-pot.

' "Gintlemen," said he, "I hope none of you will refuse tastin' a bit of Katty's pudden; I don't mane the dancin' one that took to its travels today, but a good solid fellow that she med since."

' "To be sure we won't," replied the priest; "so, Jack, put a thrifle on them three plates at your right hand, and send them over here to the clargy, an' maybe," he said laughin' – for he was a droll good-humoured man – "maybe, Jack, we won't set you a proper example."

' "Wid a heart an' a half, yer reverence an' gintlemen; in throth, it's not a bad example ever any of you set us at the likes, or ever will set us, I'll go bail. An' sure I only wish it was betther fare I had for you; but we're humble people, gintlemen, and so you can't expect to meet here what you would in higher places."

' "Betther a male of herbs," said the Methodist praicher, "where pace is – " He had time to go no farther, however, for, much to his amazement, the priest and the ministher, started up from the table jist as he was goin' to swallow the first spoonful of the pudden, and before you could say Jack Robinson, started away at a lively jig down the floor.

'At this moment a neighbour's son came runnin' in an' tould them that the parson was comin' to see the new-married couple, an' wish them all happiness; an' the words were scarcely out of his mouth when he made his appearance. What to think he knew not, when he saw the priest an' ministher footing it away at the rate of a weddin'. He had very little time, however, to think, for, before he could sit down, up starts the Methodist praicher, and clappin' his two fists in his sides, chimes in in great style along wid them.

' "Jack Rafferty," says he – and, by the way, Jack was his tenant – "what the dickens does all this mane?" says he; "I'm amazed!"

' "The divle a particle o' me can tell you," says Jack; "but will your reverence jist taste a morsel o' pudden merely that the young couple may boast that you ait at their weddin', for sure if you wouldn't, who would?"

' "Well," says he, "to gratify them I will; so just a morsel. But, Jack, this bates Banagher," says he again, puttin' the spoonful o'pudden into his mouth, "has there been dhrink here?"

' "Oh, the divle a *spudh*," says Jack, "for although there's plinty in the house, faith, it appears the gintlemen wouldn't wait for it. Unless they took it elsewhere, I can make nothin' of this."

'He had scarcely spoken, when the parson, who was an active man, cut a caper a yard high, an' before you could bless yourself, the four clargy were hard at work dancin', as if for a wager. Begad, it would be impossible for me to tell you the state the whole meetin' was in when they seen this. Some were hoarse wid laughin'; some turned up their eyes wid wondher; many thought them mad, an' others thought they had turned up their little fingers a thrifle too often.

' "Be goxty, it's a burnin shame," said one, "to see four clargy in sich a state at this early hour!" "Thundher an' ounze, what's over them at all?" says others; "why, one would think they're bewitched. Holy Moses, look at the caper the Methodist cuts! An' Father M'Sorley! *Honam an dioual*! who would think he could handle his feet at such a rate! Be this an' be that, he cuts the buckle, and docs the treblin step aiquil to Paddy Horaghan, the dancin'-masther himself! An' see! Bad cess to the morsel of the ministher an' the parson that's not hard at *Pease upon a trencher*, an' it of a Sunday too! Whirroo, gintlemen, the fun's in yez afther all – whish! more power to yez."

'The sorra's own fun they had, an' no wondher; but judge of what they felt, when all at once they saw ould Jack Rafferty himself bouncin' in among them, an' footin it away like the best o' them. Bedad no play could come up to it, an' nothin' could be heard but laughin', shouts of encouragement, and clappin' of hands like mad. Now the minute Jack Rafferty left the chair where he had been carvin' the pudden, ould Harry Cannolly comes over and claps himself down in his place, in ordher to send it round, of course; an' he was scarcely sated, when who should make his appearance but Barney Hartigan, the piper. Barney, by the way, had been sent for early in the day; but bein' from home when the message for him went, he couldn't come any sooner.

' "Begorra," said Barney, "you're airly at the work, gintlemen! Oh, blessed Phadrig! – the clargy too! *Honam an dioual*, what does this mane? But, divle may care, yez shan't want the music while there's a blast in the pipes, anyhow!" So sayin' he gave them *Jig Polthogue*, an' after that *Kiss my Lady*, in his best style.

'In the meantime the fun went on thick an' threefold, for it must be remimbered that Harry, the ould knave, was at the pudden; an' maybe he didn't sarve it about in double quick time too. The first he helped was the bride, and, before you could say chopstick, she was at it hard an' fast before the Methodist praicher, who immediately quit Father M'Sorley, and gave a jolly spring before her that threw them into convulsions. Harry liked this, and made up his mind soon to find partners for the rest; so he accordingly sent the pudden about like lightnin'; an' to make a long story short, barrin' the pipe an' himself, there wasn't a pair o' heels in the house but was as busy at the dancin' as if their lives depinded on it.

' "Barney," says Harry, "jist taste a morsel o' this pudden, divle the sich a bully of a pudden ever you ett; here, you sowl! thry a snig of it – it's beautiful."

' "To be sure I will," says Barney, "I'm not the boy to refuse a good thing; but, Harry, be quick, for you know my hands is engaged; an' it would be a thousand pities not to keep them in music, an' they so well inclined. Thank you, Harry; begad that is a famous pudden; but blood an' turnips, what's this for!"

'The word was scarcely out of his mouth when he bounced up, pipes an' all, an' dashed into the middle of them. "Hurroo, your sowls, let us make a night of it! The Ballyboulteen boys for ever! Go it, your reverence – turn your partner – heel an' toe, minister. Good! Well done again. – Whish! Hurroo! Here's for Ballyboulteen, an' the sky over it!"

'Bad luck to sich a set ever was seen together in this world, or will again, I suppose. The worst, however, wasn't come yet, for jist as they were in the very heat and fury of the dance, what do you think comes hoppin' in among them but another pudden, as nimble an' as merry as the first! That was enough; they all had heard of – the clergy among the rest – an' most o' them had seen, the other pudden, and knew that there must be either the divle or a fairy in it sure enough. Well as I said, in it comes to the thick o' them; but the very appearance of it was enough. Off the four clergy danced, and off the whole weddiners danced after them, everyone makin' the best of their way home; but divle a sowl of them able to break out of the step, if they were to be hanged for it. Throth it wouldn't lave a laugh in you to see the priest an' the parson dancin' down the road on their way home together, and the ministher and Methodist praicher cuttin' the buckle as they went along in the opposite direction. To make short work of it, they all danced home at last, wid scarce a puff of wind in them; the bride and bridegroom danced away to bed; an' now, boys, come an' let us dance the *Horo Lheig* in the barn 'idout. But you see, boys, before we go, an' in ordher that I may make everything plain, I had as good tell you, that Harry, in crossing the bridge of Ballyboulteen, a couple of miles below Squire Bragshaw's demesne-wall, saw the puddin floatin down the river – the truth is he was waitin' for it; but be this as it may, he took it out, for the wather had made it as clane as a new pin, and tuckin' it up in the tail of his big coat, contrived as you all guess, I suppose, to change it while Paddy Scanlan an' the wife were examinin' the sky; an' for the other, he contrived to bewitch it in the same manner, by gettin' a fairy to go into it, for, indeed, it was purty well known that the same Harry was hand an' glove wid the good people. Others will tell you that it was half a pound of quicksilver he put into it; but that doesn't stand to raison. At any rate, boys, I have tould you the adventures of the Mad Pudden of Ballyboulteen; but I don't wish to tell you many other things about it that happened – *for fraid I' tell a lie.*'

[This superstition of the dancing or bewitched pudding has not, so far as I have been able to ascertain, ever been given to the public before. The singular tendency to saltation is attributed to two causes, both of which are introduced in the tale. Some will insist that a fairy-man or fairy-woman has the power to bewitch a pudding by putting a fairy into it; whilst others maintain that a competent portion of quicksilver will make it dance over half the parish.]

WILLIAM CARLETON

The Three Wishes

❦

In ancient times there lived a man called Billy Dawson, and he was known to be a great rogue. They say he was descended from the family of the Dawsons, which was the reason, I suppose, of his carrying their name upon him.

Billy, in his youthful days, was the best hand at doing nothing in all Europe; devil a mortal could come next or near him at idleness; and, in consequence of his great practice that way, you may be sure that if any man could make a fortune by it he would have done it.

Billy was the only son of his father, barring two daughters, but they have nothing to do with the story I'm telling you. Indeed it was kind father and grandfather for Billy to be handy at the knavery as well as the idleness, for it was well known that not one of their blood ever did an honest act, except with a roguish intention. In short, they were altogether a *dacent* connection and a credit to the name. As for Billy, all the villainy of the family, both plain and ornamental, came down to him by way of legacy, for it so happened that the father, in spite of all his cleverness, had nothing but his roguery to *lave* him.

Billy, to do him justice, improved the fortune he got. Every day advanced him farther into dishonesty and poverty, until, at the long run, he was acknowledged on all hands to be the completest swindler and the poorest vagabond in the whole parish.

Billy's father, in his young days, had often been forced to acknowledge the inconvenience of not having a trade, in consequence of some nice point in law, called the 'Vagrant Act,' that sometimes troubled him. On this account he made up his mind to give Bill an occupation, and he accordingly bound him to a blacksmith; but whether Bill was to *live* or *die* by *forgery* was a puzzle to his father – though the neighbours said that *both* was most likely. At all events, he was put apprentice to a smith for seven years, and a hard card his master had to play in managing him. He took the proper method, however, for Bill was so lazy and roguish that it would vex a saint to keep him in order.

'Bill,' says his master to him one day that he had been sunning himself about the ditches, instead of minding his business, 'Bill, my boy, I'm vexed to the heart to see you in such a bad state of health. You're very ill with that complaint called an *all-overness*; however,' says he, 'I think I can cure you. Nothing will bring you about but three or four sound doses every day of a medicine called "the oil o' the hazel". Take the first dose now,' says he, and he immediately banged him with a hazel cudgel until Bill's bones ached for a week afterward.

'If you were my son,' said his master, 'I tell you that, as long as I could get a piece of advice growing convenient in the hedges, I'd have you a different youth from what you are. If working was a sin, Bill, not an innocenter boy ever broke bread than you would be. Good people's scarce, you think; but however that may be, I throw it out as a hint, that you must take your medicine till you're cured, whenever you happen to get unwell in the same way.'

From this out he kept Bill's nose to the grinding stone, and whenever his complaint returned he never failed to give him a hearty dose for his improvement.

In the course of time, however, Bill was his own man and his own master, but it would puzzle a saint to know whether the master or the man was the more precious youth in the eyes of the world.

He immediately married a wife, and devil a doubt of it, but if *he* kept *her* in whiskey and sugar, *she* kept *him* in hot water. Bill drank and she drank; Bill fought and she fought; Bill was idle and she was idle; Bill whacked her and she whacked Bill. If Bill gave her one black eye, she gave him another, *just to keep herself in countenance*. Never was there a blessed pair so well met, and a beautiful sight it was to see them both at breakfast time, blinking at each other across the potato basket, Bill with his right eye black, and she with her left.

In short, they were the talk of the whole town; and to see Bill of a morning staggering home drunk, his shirt sleeves rolled up on his smutted arms, his breast open, and an old tattered leather apron, with one corner tucked up under his belt, singing one minute and fighting with his wife the next – she, reeling beside him with a discoloured eye, as aforesaid, a dirty ragged cap on one side of her head, a pair of Bill's old slippers on her feet, a squalling child on her arm – now cuffing and dragging Bill, and again kissing and hugging him! Yes, it was a pleasant picture to see this loving pair in such a state!

This might do for a while, but it could not last. They were idle, drunken, and ill conducted; and it was not to be supposed that they would get a farthing candle on their words. They were, of course, *druv* to great straits; and faith, they soon found that their fighting and drinking and idleness made them the laughing sport of the neighbours; but neither brought food to their *childhre*, put a coat upon their backs, nor satisfied their landlord when he came to look for his own. Still, the never a one of Bill but was a funny fellow with strangers, though, as we said, the greatest rogue unhanged.

One day he was standing against his own anvil, completely in a brown study – being brought to his wit's end how to make out a breakfast for the family. The wife was scolding and cursing in the house, and the naked creatures of children squalling about her knees for food. Bill was fairly at an amplush, and knew not where or how to turn himself, when a poor, withered old beggar came into the forge, tottering on his staff. A long white beard fell from his chin, and he looked as thin and hungry that you might blow him, one would think, over the house. Bill at this moment had been brought to his senses by distress, and his heart had a touch of pity toward the old man, for, on looking at him a second time, he clearly saw starvation and sorrow in his face.

'God save you, honest man!' said Bill.

The old man gave a sigh, and raising himself with great pain on his staff, he looked at Bill in a very beseeching way.

'Musha. God save you kindly!' says he. 'Maybe you could give a poor, hungry, helpless ould man a mouthful of something to ait? You see yourself I'm not able to work; if I was, I'd scorn to be beholding to anyone.'

'Faith, honest man,' said Bill, 'if you knew who you're speaking to, you'd as soon ask a monkey for a churnstaff as me for either mate or money. There's not a blackguard in the three kingdoms so fairly on the *shaughran* as I am for both the one and the other. The wife within is sending the curses thick and heavy on me, and the *childhre's* playing the cat's melody to keep her in comfort. Take my word for it, poor man, if I had either mate or money I'd help you, for I know particularly well what it is to want them at the present spaking; an empty sack won't stand, neighbour.'

So far Bill told him truth. The good thought was in his heart, because he found himself on a footing with the beggar; and nothing brings down pride, or softens the heart, like feeling what it is to want.

'Why, you are in a worse state than I am,' said the old man; 'you have a family to provide for, and I have only myself to support.

'You may kiss the book on that, my old worthy,' replied Bill; 'but come, what I can do for you I will; plant yourself up here beside the fire, and I'll give it a blast or two of my bellows that will warm the old blood in your body. It's a cold, miserable, snowy day, and a good heat will be of service.'

'Thank you kindly,' said the old man; 'I *am* cold, and a warming at your fire will do me good, sure enough. Oh, but it *is* a bitter, bitter day; God bless it!'

He then sat down, and Bill blew a rousing blast that soon made the stranger edge back from the heat. In a short time he felt quite comfortable, and when the numbness was taken out of his joints, he buttoned himself up and prepared to depart.

'Now,' says he to Bill, 'you hadn't the food to give me, but *what you could you did*. Ask any three wishes you choose, and be they what they may, take my word for it, they shall be granted.'

Now, the truth is, that Bill, though he believed himself a great man in point of 'cuteness, wanted, after all, a full quarter of being square, for there is always a great difference between a wise man and a knave. Bill was so much of a rogue that he could not, for the blood of him, ask an honest wish, but stood scratching his head in a puzzle.

'Three wishes!' said he. 'Why, let me see – did you say *three*?'

'Ay,' replied the stranger, 'three wishes – that was what I said.'

'Well,' said Bill, 'here goes – aha! – let me alone, my old worthy! – faith I'll overreach the parish, if what you say is true. I'll cheat them in dozens, rich and poor, old and young; let me alone, man – I have it here,' and he tapped his forehead with great glee. 'Faith, you're the sort to meet of a frosty morning, when a man wants his breakfast; and I'm sorry that I have neither money nor credit to get a bottle of whiskey, that we might take our morning together.'

'Well, but let us hear the wishes,' said the old man; 'my time is short, and I cannot stay much longer.'

'Do you see this sledge hammer?' said Bill, 'I wish, in the first place, that whoever takes it up in their hands may never be able to lay it down till I give them lave; and that whoever begins to sledge with it may never stop sledging till it's my pleasure to release him.

'Secondly – I have an armchair, and I wish that whoever sits down in it may never rise out of it till they have my consent.

'And, thirdly – that whatever money I put into my purse, nobody may have power to take it out of it but myself!'

'You Devil's rip!' says the old man in a passion, shaking his staff across Bill's nose. 'Why did you not ask something that would sarve you both here and hereafter? Sure it's as common as the market cross, that there's not a vagabone in His Majesty's dominions stands more in need of both.'

'Oh! by the elevens,' said Bill, 'I forgot that altogether! Maybe you'd be civil enough to let me change one of them? The sorra purtier wish ever was made than I'll make, if only you'll give me another chance at it.'

'Get out, you reprobate,' said the old fellow, still in a passion. 'Your day of grace is past. Little you knew who was speaking to you all this time. I'm St Moroky, you blackguard, and I gave you an opportunity of doing something for yourself and your family; but you neglected it, and now your fate is cast, you dirty, bog-trotting profligate. Sure, it's well known what you are! Aren't you a byword in everybody's mouth, you and your scold of a wife? By this and by that, if ever you happen to come across me again, I'll send you to where you won't freeze, you villain!'

He then gave Bill a rap of his cudgel over the head and laid him at his length beside the bellows, kicked a broken coal scuttle out of his way, and left the forge in a fury.

When Billy recovered himself from the effects of the blow and began to think on what had happened, he could have quartered himself with vexation for not asking great wealth as one of the wishes at least; but now the die was cast on him, and he could only make the most of the three he pitched upon.

He now bethought him how he might turn them to the best account, and here his cunning came to his aid. He began by sending for his wealthiest neighbours on pretence of business, and when he got them under his roof he offered them the armchair to sit down in. He now had them safe, nor could all the art of man relieve them except worthy Bill was willing. Bill's plan was to make the best bargain he could before he released his prisoners; and let him alone for knowing how to make their purses bleed. There wasn't a wealthy man in the country he did not fleece. The parson of the parish bled heavily; so did the lawyer; and a rich attorney, who had retired from practice, swore that the Court of Chancery itself was paradise compared to Bill's chair.

This was all very good for a time. The fame of his chair, however, soon spread; so did that of his sledge. In a short time neither man, woman, nor child would darken his door; all avoided him and his fixtures as they would a spring gun or mantrap. Bill, so long as he fleeced his neighbours, never wrought a hand's turn; so that when his money was out he found himself as badly off as ever. In addition to all this, his character was fifty times worse than before, for it was the general belief that he had dealings with the old boy. Nothing now could exceed his misery, distress, and ill temper. The wife and he and their children all fought among one another. Everybody hated them, cursed them, and avoided them. The people thought they were acquainted with more than Christian people ought to know. This, of course, came to Bill's ears, and it vexed him very much.

One day he was walking about the fields, thinking of how he could raise the wind once more; the day was dark, and he found himself, before he stopped, in the bottom of a lonely glen covered by great bushes that grew on each side. 'Well,' thought he, when every other means of raising money failed him, 'it's reported that I'm in league with the old boy, and as it's a folly to have the name of the connection without the profit, I'm ready to make a bargain with him any day – so,' said he, raising his voice, 'Nick, you sinner, if you be convenient and willing why stand out here; show your best leg – here's your man.'

The words were hardly out of his mouth when a dark, sober-looking old gentleman, not unlike a lawyer, walked up to him. Bill looked at the foot and saw the hoof. 'Morrow, Nick,' says Bill.

'Morrow, Bill,' says Nick. 'Well, Bill, what's the news?'

'Devil a much myself hears of late,' says Bill; 'is there anything *fresh* below?'

'I can't exactly say, Bill; I spend little of my time down now; the Tories are in office, and my hands are consequently too full of business here to pay much attention to anything else.'

'A fine place this, sir,' says Bill, 'to take a constitutional walk in; when I want an appetite I often come this way myself – hem! *High* feeding is very bad without exercise.'

'High feeding! Come, come, Bill, you know you didn't taste a morsel these four-and-twenty hours.'

'You know that's a bounce, Nick. I ate a breakfast this morning that would put a stone of flesh on you, if you only smelt at it.'

'No matter; this is not to the purpose. What's that you were muttering to yourself a while ago? If you want to come to the brunt, here I'm for you.'

'Nick,' said Bill, 'you're complate; you want nothing barring a pair of Brian O'Lynn's breeches.'

Bill, in fact, was bent on making his companion open the bargain, because he had often heard that, in that case, with proper care on his own part, he might defeat him in the long run. The other, however, was his match.

'What was the nature of Brian's garment?' enquired Nick.

'Why, you know the song,' said Bill:

> Brian O'Lynn had no breeches to wear,
> So he got a sheep's skin for to make him a pair;
> With the fleshy side out and the woolly side in,
> 'They'll be pleasant and cool,' says Brian O'Lynn.

'A cool pare would sarve you, Nick.'

'You're mighty waggish today, Misther Dawson.'

'And good right I have,' said Bill; 'I'm a man snug and well to do in the world; have lots of money, plenty of good eating and drinking, and what more need a man wish for?'

'True,' said the other; 'in the meantime it's rather odd that so respectable a man should not have six inches of unbroken cloth in his apparel. You're as naked a tatterdemalion as I ever laid my eyes on; in full dress for a party of scarecrows, William?'

'That's my own fancy, Nick; I don't work at my trade like a gentleman. This is my forge dress, you know.'

'Well, but what did you summon me here for?' said the other; 'you may as well speak out, I tell you, for, my good friend, unless you do, I shan't. Smell that.'

'I smell more than that,' said Bill; 'and by the way, I'll thank you to give me the windy side of you – curse all sulphur, I say. There, that's what I call an improvement in my condition. But as you *are* so stiff,' says Bill, 'why, the short and long of it is – that – ahem – you see I'm – tut – sure you know I have a thriving trade of my own, and that if I like I needn't be at a loss; but in the meantime I'm rather in a kind of a so – so – don't you *take*?'

And Bill winked knowingly, hoping to trick him into the first proposal.

'You must speak aboveboard, my friend,' says the other. 'I'm a man of few words, blunt and honest. If you have anything to say, be plain. Don't think I can be losing my time with such a pitiful rascal as you are.'

'Well,' says Bill. 'I want money, then, and am ready to come into terms. What have you to say to that, Nick?'

'Let me see – let me look at you,' says his companion, turning him about. 'Now, Bill, in the first place, are you not as finished a scarecrow as ever stood upon two legs?'

'I play second fiddle to you there again,' says Bill.

'There you stand, with the blackguards' coat of arms quartered under your eye, and – '

'Don't make little of *black*guards,' said Bill, 'nor spake disparagingly of your *own* crest.'

'Why, what would you bring, you brazen rascal, if you were fairly put up at auction?'

'Faith, I'd bring more bidders than you would,' said Bill, 'if you were to go off at auction tomorrow. I tell you they should bid *downward* to come to your value, Nicholas. We have no coin *small* enough to purchase you.'

'Well, no matter,' said Nick. 'If you are willing to be mine at the expiration of seven years, I will give you more money than ever the rascally breed of you was worth.'

'Done!' said Bill. 'But no disparagement to my family, in the meantime; so down with the hard cash, and don't be a *neger*.'

The money was accordingly paid down; but as nobody was present, except the giver and receiver, the amount of what Bill got was never known.

'Won't you give me a luck penny?' said the old gentleman.

'Tut,' said Billy, 'so prosperous an old fellow as you cannot want it;

however, bad luck to you, with all my heart! and it's rubbing grease to a fat pig to say so. Be off now, or I'll commit suicide on you. Your absence is a cordial to most people, you infernal old profligate. You have injured my morals even for the short time you have been with me, for I don't find myself so virtuous as I was.'

'Is that your gratitude, Billy?'

'Is it gratitude *you* speak of, man? I wonder you don't blush when you name it. However, when you come again, if you bring a third eye in your head you will see what I mane, Nicholas, *ahagur*.'

The old gentleman, as Bill spoke, hopped across the ditch on his way to *Downing* street, where of late 'tis thought he possesses much influence.

Bill now began by degrees to show off, but still wrought a little at his trade to blindfold the neighbours. In a very short time, however, he became a great man. So long indeed as he was a poor rascal, no decent person would speak to him; even the proud servingmen at the 'big house' would turn up their noses at him. And he well deserved to be made little of by others, because he was mean enough to make little of himself. But when it was seen and known that he had oceans of money, it was wonderful to think, although he was *now* a greater blackguard than ever, how those who despised him before began to come round him and court his company. Bill, however, had neither sense nor spirit to make those sunshiny friends know their distance; not he – instead of that he was proud to be seen in decent company, and so long as the money lasted, it was, 'hail fellow well met' between himself and every fair-faced *spunger* who had a horse under him, a decent coat to his back, and a good appetite to eat his dinners. With riches and all, Bill was the same man still; but, somehow or other, there is a great difference between a rich profligate and a poor one, and Bill found it so to his cost in *both* cases.

Before half the seven years was passed, Bill had his carriage and his equipages; was hand and glove with my Lord This, and my Lord That; kept hounds and hunters; was the first sportsman at the Curragh; patronised every boxing ruffian he could pick up; and betted night and day on cards, dice, and horses. Bill, in short, *should* be a blood, and except he did all this, he could not presume to mingle with the fashionable bloods of his time.

It's an old proverb, however, that 'what is got over the Devil's back is sure to go off under it,' and in Bill's case this proved true. In short, the old boy himself could not supply him with money so fast as he made it fly; it was 'come easy, go easy,' with Bill, and so sign was on it, before he came within two years of his time he found his purse empty.

And now came the value of his summer friends to be known. When it was discovered that the cash was no longer flush with him – that stud, and carriage, and hounds were going to the hammer – whish! off they went, friends, relations, pot companions, dinner caters, black-legs, and all, like a flock of crows that had smelled gunpowder. Down Bill soon went, week after week and day after day, until at last he was obliged to put on the leather apron and take to the hammer again; and not only that, for as no experience could make him wise, he once more began his taproom brawls, his quarrels with Judy, and took to his 'high feeding' at the dry potatoes and salt. Now, too, came the cutting tongues of all who knew him, like razors upon him. Those that he scorned because they were poor and himself rich now paid him back his own with interest; and those that he measured himself with, because they were rich, and who only countenanced him in consequence of his wealth, gave him the hardest word in their cheeks. The Devil mend him! He deserved it all, and more if he had got it.

Bill, however, who was a hardened sinner, never fretted himself down an ounce of flesh by what was said to him or of him. Not he; he cursed, and fought, and swore, and schemed away as usual, taking in everyone he could; and surely none could match him at villainy of all sorts and sizes.

At last the seven years became expired, and Bill was one morning sitting in his forge, sober and hungry, the wife cursing him, and children squalling as before; he was thinking how he might defraud some honest neighbour out of a breakfast to stop their mouths and his own, too, when who walks in to him but old Nick to demand his bargain.

'Morrow, Bill!' says he with a sneer.

'The Devil welcome you!' says Bill. 'But you have a fresh memory.'

'A bargain's a bargain between two *honest* men, any day,' says Satan; 'when I speak of honest men, I mean yourself and *me*, Bill'; and he put his tongue in his cheek to make game of the unfortunate rogue he had come for.

'Nick, my worthy fellow,' said Bill, 'have bowels; you wouldn't do a shabby thing; you wouldn't disgrace your own character by putting more weight upon a falling man. You know what it is to get a *come-down* yourself, my worthy; so just keep your toe in your pump, and walk off with yourself somewhere else. A *cool* walk will sarve you better than my company, Nicholas.'

'Bill, it's no use in shirking,' said his friend; 'your swindling tricks may enable you to cheat others, but you won't cheat *me*, I guess. You want nothing to make you perfect in your way but to travel; and travel you shall under my guidance, Billy. No, no – I'm not to be swindled, my good fellow. I have rather a – a – better opinion of myself, Mr D., than to think that you could outwit one Nicholas Clutie, Esq. – ahem!'

'You may sneer, you sinner,' replied Bill, 'but I tell you that I have outwitted men who could buy and sell you to your face. Despair, you villain, when I tell you that *no attorney* could stand before me.'

Satan's countenance got blank when he heard this; he wriggled and fidgeted about and appeared to be not quite comfortable.

'In that case, then,' says he, 'the sooner I *deceive* you the better; so turn out for the *Low Countries*.'

'Is it come to that in earnest?' said Bill. 'Are you going to act the rascal at the long run?'

' 'Pon honour, Bill.'

'Have patience, then, you sinner, till I finish this horseshoe – it's the last of a set I'm finishing for one of your friend the attorney's horses. And here, Nick, I hate idleness; you know it's the mother of mischief; take this sledge hammer and give a dozen strokes or so, till I get it out of hands, and then here's with you, since it must be so.'

He then gave the bellows a puff that blew half a peck of dust in Clubfoot's face, whipped out the red-hot iron, and set Satan sledging away for bare life.

'Faith,' says Bill to him, when the shoe was finished, 'it's a thousand pities ever the sledge should be out of your hand; the great *Parra Gow* was a child to you at sledging, you're such an able tyke. Now just exercise yourself till I bid the wife and *childhre* goodbye, and then I'm off.'

Out went Bill, of course, without the slightest notion of coming back; no more than Nick had that he could not give up the sledging, and indeed neither could he, but was forced to work away as if he was sledging for a wager. This was just what Bill wanted. He was now compelled to sledge on until it was Bill's pleasure to release him; and so we leave him very industriously employed, while we look after the worthy who outwitted him.

In the meantime Bill broke cover and took to the country at large; wrought a little journey work wherever he could get it, and in this way went from one place to another, till, in the course of a month, he walked back very coolly into his own forge to see how things went on in his absence. There he found Satan in a rage, the perspiration pouring from him in torrents, hammering with might and main upon the naked anvil. Bill calmly leaned back against the wall, placed his hat upon the side of his head, put his hands into his breeches pockets, and began to whistle *Shaun Gow's* hornpipe. At length he says, in a very quiet and good-humoured way: 'Morrow, Nick!'

'Oh!' says Nick, still hammering away. 'Oh! you double-distilled villain (hech!), may the most refined ornamental (hech!) collection of curses that ever was gathered (hech!) into a single nosegay of ill fortune (hech!) shine in the buttonhole of your conscience (hech!) while your name is Bill Dawson! I denounce you (hech!) as a double-milled villain, a finished, hot-pressed knave (hech!), in comparison of whom all the other knaves I ever knew (hech!), attorneys included, are honest men. I brand you (hech!) as the pearl of cheats, a tiptop take-in (hech!). I denounce you, I say again, for the villainous treatment (hech!) I have received at your hands in this most untoward (hech!) and unfortunate transaction between us; for (hech!) unfortunate, in every sense, is he that has anything to do with (hech!) such a prime and finished impostor.'

'You're very warm, Nicky,' says Bill; 'what puts you into a passion, you old sinner? Sure if it's your own will and pleasure to take exercise at my anvil, *I'm* not to be abused for it. Upon my credit, Nicky, you ought to blush for using such blackguard language, so unbecoming your grave character. You cannot say that it was I set you a-hammering at the empty anvil, you profligate.

'However, as you are so very industrious, I simply say it would be a thousand pities to take you from it. Nick, I love industry in my heart, and I always encourage it, so work away; its not often you spend your time so creditably. I'm afraid if you weren't at that you'd be worse employed.'

'Bill, have bowels,' said the operative; 'you wouldn't go to lay more weight on a falling man, you know; you wouldn't disgrace your character by such a piece of iniquity as keeping an inoffensive gentleman, advanced in years, at such an unbecoming and rascally job as this. Generosity's your top virtue, Bill; not but that you have many other excellent ones, as well as that, among which, as you say yourself, I reckon industry; but still it is in generosity you shine. Come, Bill, honour bright, and release me.'

'Name the terms, you profligate.'

'You're above terms, William; a generous fellow like you never thinks of terms.'

'Goodbye, old gentleman!' said Bill very coolly; 'I'll drop in to see you once a month.'

'No, no, Bill, you infern – a – a – . You excellent, worthy, delightful fellow, not so fast; not so fast. Come, name your terms, you sland – My dear Bill, name your terms.'

'Seven years more.'

'I agree; but – '

'And the same supply of cash as before, down on the nail here.'

'Very good; very good. You're rather simple, Bill; rather soft, I must confess. Well, no matter. I shall yet turn the tab – a – hem! You are an exceedingly simple fellow, Bill; still there will come a day, my *dear* Bill – there will come – '

'Do you grumble, you vagrant? Another word, and I double the terms.'

'Mum, William – mum; *tace* is Latin for a candle.'

'Seven years more of grace, and the same measure of the needful that I got before. Ay or no?'

'Of grace, Bill! Ay! ay! ay! There's the cash. I accept the terms. Oh, blood! The rascal – of grace! Bill!'

'Well, now drop the hammer and vanish,' says Billy; 'but what would you think to take this sledge, while you stay, and give me a – Eh! Why in such a hurry?' he added, seeing that Satan withdrew in double-quick time.

'Hollo! Nicholas!' he shouted. 'Come back; you forgot something!' And when the old gentleman looked behind him, Billy shook the hammer at him, on which he vanished altogether.

Billy now got into his old courses; and what shows the kind of people the world is made of, he also took up with his old company. When they saw that he had the money once more and was sowing it about him in all directions, they immediately began to find excuses for his former extravagance.

'Say what you will,' said one, 'Bill Dawson's a spirited fellow and bleeds like a prince.'

'He's a hospitable man in his own house, or out of it, as ever lived,' said another.

'His only fault is,' observed a third, 'that he is, if anything, too generous, and doesn't know the value of money; his fault's on the right side, however.'

'He has the spunk in him,' said a fourth; 'keeps a capital table, prime wines, and a standing welcome for his friends.'

'Why,' said a fifth, 'if he doesn't enjoy his money while he lives, he won't when he's dead; so more power to him, and a wider throat to his purse.'

Indeed, the very persons who were cramming themselves at his expense despised him at heart. They knew very well, however, how to take him on the weak side. Praise his generosity, and he would do anything; call him a man of spirit, and you might fleece him to his face. Sometimes he would toss a purse of guineas to this knave, another to that flatterer, a third to a bully, and a fourth to some broken-down rake – and all to convince them that he was a sterling friend – a man of mettle and liberality. But never was he known to help a virtuous and struggling family – to assist the widow or the fatherless, or to do any other act that was truly useful. It is to be supposed the reason of this was that as he spent it, as most of the world do, in the service of the Devil, by whose aid he got it, he was prevented from turning it to a good account. Between you and me, dear reader, there are more persons acting after Bill's fashion in the same world than you dream about.

When his money was out again, his friends played him the same rascally game once more. No sooner did his poverty become plain than the knaves began to be troubled with small fits of modesty, such as an unwillingness to come to his place when there was no longer anything to be got there. A kind of virgin bashfulness prevented them from speaking to him when they saw him getting out on the wrong side of his clothes. Many of them would turn away from him in the prettiest and most delicate manner when they thought he wanted to borrow money from them – all for fear of putting him to the blush for asking it. Others again, when they saw him coming toward their houses about dinner hour, would become so confused, from mere gratitude, as to think themselves in another place; and their servants, seized, as it were, with the same feeling, would tell Bill that their masters were 'not at home.'

At length, after travelling the same villainous round as before, Bill was compelled to betake himself, as the last remedy, to the forge; in other words, he found that there is, after all, nothing in this world that a man can rely on so firmly and surely as his own industry. Bill, however, wanted the organ of common sense, for his experience – and it was sharp enough to leave an impression – ran off him like water off a duck.

He took to his employment sorely against his grain, but he had now no choice. He must either work or starve, and starvation is like a great doctor – nobody tries it till every other remedy fails them. Bill had been twice rich; twice a gentleman among blackguards, but always a blackguard among gentlemen, for no wealth or acquaintance with decent society could rub the rust of his native vulgarity off him. He was now a common blinking sot in his forge; a drunken bully in the taproom, cursing and browbeating everyone as well as his wife; boasting of how much money he had spent in his day; swaggering about the high doings he carried on; telling stories about himself and Lord This at the Curragh; the dinners he gave – how much they cost him – and attempting to extort credit upon the strength of his former wealth. He was too ignorant, however, to know that he was publishing his own disgrace and that it was a mean-spirited thing to be proud of what ought to make him blush through a deal board nine inches thick.

He was one morning industriously engaged in a quarrel with his wife, who, with a three-legged stool in her hand, appeared to mistake his head for his own anvil; he, in the meantime, paid his addresses to her with his leather apron, when who steps in to jog his memory about the little agreement that was between them but old Nick. The wife, it seems, in spite of all her exertions to the contrary, was getting the worst of it; and Sir Nicholas, willing to appear a gentleman of great gallantry, thought he could not do less than take up the lady's quarrel, particularly as Bill had laid her in a sleeping posture. Now Satan

thought this too bad, and as he felt himself under many obligations to
the sex, he determined to defend one of them on the present occasion;
so as Judy rose, he turned upon the husband and floored him by a
clever facer.

'You unmanly villain,' said he, 'is this the way you treat your wife?
'Pon honour Bill, I'll chastise you on the spot. I could not stand by, a
spectator of such ungentlemanly conduct, without giving up all claim
to gallant – ' Whack! The word was divided in his mouth by the blow
of a churnstaff from Judy, who no sooner saw Bill struck than she
nailed Satan, who 'fell' once more.

'What, you villain! That's for striking my husband like a murderer
behind his back,' said Judy, and she suited the action to the word.
'That's for interfering between man and wife. Would you murder the
poor man before my face, eh? If he bates me, you shabby dog you,
who has a better right? I'm sure it's nothing out of your pocket. Must
you have your finger in every pie?'

This was anything but *idle* talk, for at every word she gave him a
remembrance, hot and heavy. Nicholas backed, danced, and hopped;
she advanced, still drubbing him with great perseverance, till at length
he fell into the redoubtable armchair, which stood exactly behind him.
Bill, who had been putting in two blows for Judy's one, seeing that his
enemy was safe, now got between the Devil and his wife, *a situation
that few will be disposed to envy him.*

'Tenderness, Judy,' said the husband; 'I hate cruelty. Go put the
tongs in the fire, and make them red-hot. Nicholas, you have a nose,'
said he.

Satan began to rise but was rather surprised to find that he could
not budge.

'Nicholas,' says Bill, 'how is your pulse? You don't look well; that is
to say, you look worse than usual.'

The other attempted to rise but found it a mistake.

'I'll thank you to come along,' said Bill. 'I have a fancy to travel
under your guidance, and we'll take the *Low Countries* in our way,
won't we? Get to your legs, you sinner; you know a bargain's a bargain
between two *honest* men, Nicholas, meaning *yourself* and *me*. Judy, are
the tongs hot?'

Satan's face was worth looking at as he turned his eyes from the
husband to the wife and then fastened them on the tongs, now nearly

at a furnace heat in the fire, conscious at the same time that he could not move out of the chair.

'Billy,' said he, 'you won't forget that I rewarded you generously the last time I saw you, in the way of business.'

'Faith, Nicholas, it fails me to remember any generosity I ever showed you. Don't be womanish. I simply want to see what kind of stuff your nose is made of and whether it will stretch like a rogue's conscience. If it does we will flatter it up the chimly with red-hot tongs, and when this old hat is fixed on the top of it, let us alone for a weathercock.'

'Have a *fellow-feeling*, Mr Dawson; you know we ought not to dispute. Drop the matter, and I give you the next seven years.'

'We know all that,' says Billy, opening the red-hot tongs very coolly.

'Mr Dawson,' said Satan, 'if you cannot remember my friendship to yourself, don't forget how often I stood your father's friend, your grandfather's friend, and the friend of all your relations up to the tenth generation. I intended, also, to stand by your children after you, so long as the name of Dawson – and a respectable one it is – might last.'

'Don't be blushing, Nick,' says Bill; 'you are too modest; that was ever your failing; hold up your head, there's money bid for you. I'll give you such a nose, my good friend, that you will have to keep an outrider before you, to carry the end of it on his shoulder.'

'Mr Dawson, I pledge my honour to raise your children in the world as high as they can go, no matter whether they desire it or not.'

'That's very kind of you,' says the other, 'and I'll do as much for your nose.'

He gripped it as he spoke, and the old boy immediately sung out; Bill pulled, and the nose went with him like a piece of warm wax. He then transferred the tongs to Judy, got a ladder, resumed the tongs, ascended the chimney, and tugged stoutly at the nose until he got it five feet above the roof. He then fixed the hat upon the top of it and came down.

'There's a weathercock,' said Billy; 'I defy Ireland to show such a beauty. Faith, Nick, it would make the purtiest steeple for a church in all Europe, and the old hat fits it to a shaving.'

In this state, with his nose twisted up the chimney, Satan sat for some time, experiencing the novelty of what might be termed a peculiar sensation. At last the worthy husband and wife began to relent.

'I think,' said Bill, 'that we have made the most of the nose, as well as the joke; I believe, Judy, it's long enough.'

'What is?' says Judy.

'Why, the joke,' said the husband.

'Faith, and I think so is the nose,' said Judy.

'What do you say yourself, Satan?' said Bill.

'Nothing at all, William,' said the other; 'but that – ha! ha! – it's a good joke – an excellent joke, and a goodly nose, too, as it *stands*. You were always a gentlemanly man, Bill, and did things with a grace; still, if I might give an opinion on such a trifle – '

'It's no trifle at all,' says Bill, 'if you spake of the nose.'

'Very well, it is not,' says the other; 'still, I am decidedly of opinion that if you could shorten both the joke and the nose without further violence, you would lay me under very heavy obligations, which I shall be ready to acknowledge and *repay* as I ought.'

'Come,' said Bill, 'shell out once more, and be off for seven years. As much as you came down with the last time, and vanish.'

The words were scarcely spoken, when the money was at his feet and Satan invisible. Nothing could surpass the mirth of Bill and his wife at the result of this adventure. They laughed till they fell down on the floor.

It is useless to go over the same ground again. Bill was still incorrigible. The money went as the Devil's money always goes. Bill caroused and squandered but could never turn a penny of it to a good purpose. In this way year after year went, till the seventh was closed and Bill's hour come. He was now, and had been for some time past, as miserable a knave as ever. Not a shilling had he, nor a shilling's worth, with the exception of his forge, his cabin, and a few articles of crazy furniture. In this state he was standing in his forge as before, straining his ingenuity how to make out a breakfast, when Satan came to look after him. The old gentleman was sorely puzzled how to get at him. He kept skulking and sneaking about the forge for some time, till he saw that Bill hadn't a cross to bless himself with. He immediately changed himself into a guinea and lay in an open place where he knew Bill would see him. 'If,' said he. 'I once get into his possession, I can manage him.' The honest smith took the bait, for it was well gilded; he clutched the guinea, put it into his purse, and closed it up. 'Ho! Ho!' shouted the Devil out of the purse. 'You're caught, Bill; I've secured you at last, you knave you. Why don't you despair you villain, when you think of what's before you?'

'Why, you unlucky ould dog,' said Bill, 'is it there you are? Will you always drive your head into every loophole that's set for you? Faith, Nick *achora*, I never had you bagged till now.'

Satan then began to tug and struggle with a view of getting out of the purse, but in vain.

'Mr Dawson,' said he, 'we understand each other. I'll give the seven years additional and the cash on the nail.'

'Be aisey, Nicholas. You know the weight of the hammer, that's enough. It's not a whipping with feathers you're going to get, anyhow. Just be aisey.'

'Mr Dawson, I grant I'm not your match. Release me, and I double the case. I was merely trying your temper when I took the shape of a guinea.'

'Faith and I'll try yours before I lave it, I've a notion.' He immediately commenced with the sledge, and Satan sang out with a considerable want of firmness. 'Am I heavy enough!' said Bill.

'Lighter, lighter, William, if you love me. I haven't been well latterly, Mr Dawson – I have been delicate – my health, in short, is in a very precarious state, Mr Dawson.'

'I can believe *that*,' said Bill, 'and it will be more so before I have done with you. Am I doing it right?'

'Bill,' said Nick, 'is this gentlemanly treatment in your own respectable shop? Do you think, if you dropped into my little place, that I'd act this rascally part toward you? Have you no compunction?'

'I know,' replied Bill, sledging away with vehemence, 'that you're notorious for giving your friends a *warm* welcome. Devil an ould youth more so; but you must be daling in bad coin, must you? However, good or bad, you're in for a sweat now, you sinner. Am I doin' it purty?'

'Lovely, William – but, if possible, a little more delicate.'

'Oh, how delicate you are! Maybe a cup o' tay would sarve you, or a little small gruel to compose your stomach?'

'Mr Dawson,' said the gentleman in the purse, 'hold your hand and let us understand one another. I have a proposal to make.'

'Hear the sinner anyhow,' said the wife.

'Name your own sum,' said Satan, 'only set me free.'

'No, the sorra may take the toe you'll budge till you let Bill off,' said the wife; 'hould him hard, Bill, barrin' he sets you clear of your engagement.

'There it is, my posy,' said Bill; 'that's the condition. If you don't give *me up*, here's at you once more – and you must double the cash you gave the last time, too. So, if you're of that opinion, say *ay* – leave the cash and be off.'

The money appeared in a glittering heap before Bill, upon which he exclaimed, 'The *ay* has it, you dog. Take to your pumps now, and fair weather after you, you vagrant; but, Nicholas – Nick – here, here – ' The other looked back and saw Bill, with a broad grin upon him, shaking the purse at him. 'Nicholas, come back,' said he. 'I'm short a guinea.' Nick shook his fist and disappeared.

It would be useless to stop now, merely to inform our readers that Bill was beyond improvement. In short, he once more took to his old habits and lived on exactly in the same manner as before. He had two sons – one as great a blackguard as himself, and who was also named after him; the other was a well-conducted, virtuous young man called James, who left his father and, having relied upon his own industry and honest perseverance in life, arrived afterward to great wealth and built the town called Castle Dawson, which is so called from its founder until this day.

Bill, at length, in spite of all his wealth, was obliged, as he himself said, 'to travel' – in other words, he fell asleep one day and forgot to awaken; or, in still plainer terms, he died.

Now, it is usual, when a man dies, to close the history of his life and adventures at once; but with our hero this cannot be the case. The moment Bill departed he very naturally bent his steps toward the residence of St Moroky, as being, in his opinion, likely to lead him toward the snuggest berth he could readily make out. On arriving, he gave a very humble kind of a knock, and St Moroky appeared.

'God save your Reverence!' said Bill, very submissively.

'Be off; there's no admittance here for so poor a youth as you are,' said St Moroky.

He was now so cold and fatigued that he cared like where he went, provided only, as he said himself, 'he could rest his bones and get an air of the fire.' Accordingly, after arriving at a large black gate, he knocked, as before, and was told he would get *instant* admittance the moment he gave his name.

'Billy Dawson,' he replied.

'Off, instantly,' said the porter to his companions, 'and let His Majesty know that the rascal he dreads so much is here at the gate.'

Such a racket and tumult were never heard as the very mention of Billy Dawson created.

In the meantime, his old acquaintance came running toward the gate with such haste and consternation that his tail was several times nearly tripping up his heels.

'Don't admit that rascal,' he shouted; 'bar the gate – make every chain and lock the bolt fast – I won't be safe – and I won't stay here, nor none of us need stay here, if he gets in – my bones are sore yet after him. No, no – begone, you villain – you'll get no entrance here – I know you too well.'

Bill could not help giving a broad, malicious grin at Satan, and, putting his nose through the bars, he exclaimed, 'Ha! you ould dog, I have you afraid of me at last, have I?'

He had scarcely uttered the words, when his foe, who stood inside, instantly tweaked him by the nose, and Bill felt as if he had been gripped by the same red-hot tongs with which he himself had formerly tweaked the nose of Nicholas.

Bill then departed but soon found that in consequence of the inflammable materials which strong drink had thrown into his nose, that organ immediately took fire, and, indeed, to tell the truth, kept burning night and day, winter and summer, without ever once going out from that hour to this.

Such was the sad fate of Billy Dawson, who has been walking without stop or stay, from place to place, ever since; and in consequence of the flame on his nose, and his beard being tangled like a wisp of hay, he has been christened by the country folk Will-o'-the-Wisp, while, as it were, to show the mischief of his disposition, the circulating knave, knowing that he must seek the coldest bogs and quagmires in order to cool his nose, seizes upon that opportunity of misleading the unthinking and tipsy night travellers from their way, just that he may have the satisfaction of still taking in as many as possible.

BRAM STOKER

The Judge's House

❧❧❧

When the time for his examination drew near Malcolm Malcolmson made up his mind to go somewhere to read by himself. He feared the attractions of the seaside, and also he feared completely rural isolation, for of old he knew its charms, and so he determined to find some unpretentious little town where there would be nothing to distract him. He refrained from asking suggestions from any of his friends, for he argued that each would recommend some place of which he had knowledge, and where he had already acquaintances. As Malcolmson wished to avoid friends he had no wish to encumber himself with the attention of friends' friends, and so he determined to look out for a place for himself. He packed a portmanteau with some clothes and all the books he required, and then took ticket for the first name on the local timetable which he did not know.

When at the end of three hours' journey he alighted at Benchurch, he felt satisfied that he had so far obliterated his tracks as to be sure of having a peaceful opportunity of pursuing his studies. He went straight to the one inn which the sleepy little place contained, and put up for the night. Benchurch was a market town, and once in three weeks was crowded to excess, but for the remainder of the twenty-one days it was as attractive as a desert. Malcolmson looked around the day after his arrival to try to find quarters more isolated than even so quiet an inn as the Good Traveller afforded. There was only one place which took his fancy, and it certainly satisfied his wildest ideas regarding quiet; in fact, quiet was not the proper word to apply to it – desolation was the only term conveying any suitable idea of its isolation. It was an old rambling, heavy-built house of the Jacobean style, with heavy gables and windows, unusually small, and set higher than was customary in such houses, and was surrounded with a high brick wall massively built. Indeed, on examination, it looked more like a fortified house than an ordinary dwelling. But all these things pleased Malcolmson. 'Here,' he thought, 'is the very spot I have been looking for, and if I can only get opportunity of using it I shall be happy.' His joy was increased when he realised beyond doubt that it was not at present inhabited.

From the post-office he got the name of the agent, who was rarely surprised at the application to rent a part of the old house. Mr Carnford, the local lawyer and agent, was a genial old gentleman, and frankly confessed his delight at anyone being willing to live in the house.

'To tell you the truth,' said he, 'I should be only too happy, on behalf of the owners, to let anyone have the house rent free for a term of years if only to accustom the people here to see it inhabited. It has been so long empty that some kind of absurd prejudice has grown up about it, and this can be best put down by its occupation – if only,' he added with a sly glance at Malcolmson, 'by a scholar like yourself, who wants its quiet for a time.'

Malcolmson thought it needless to ask the agent about the 'absurd prejudice'; he knew he would get more information, if he should require it, on that subject from other quarters. He paid his three months' rent, got a receipt, and the name of an old woman who would probably undertake to 'do' for him, and came away with the keys in his pocket. He then went to the landlady of the inn, who was a cheerful and most kindly person, and asked her advice as to such stores and provisions as he would be likely to require. She threw up her hands in amazement when he told her where he was going to settle himself.

'Not in the Judge's House!' she said and grew pale as she spoke. He explained the locality of the house, saying that he did not know its name. When he had finished, she answered: 'Aye, sure enough – sure enough the very place. It is the Judge's House sure enough.' He asked her to tell him about the place, why so called, and what there was against it. She told him that it was so called locally because it had been many years before – how long she could not say, as she was herself from another part of the country, but she thought it must have been a hundred years or more – the abode of a judge who was held in great terror on account of his harsh sentences and his hostility to prisoners at Assizes. As to what there was against the house itself she could not tell. She had often asked, but no one could inform her; but there was a general feeling that there was *something*, and for her own part she would not take all the money in Drinkwater's Bank and stay in the house an hour by herself. Then she apologised to Malcolmson for her disturbing talk.

'It is too bad of me, sir, and you – and a young gentleman, too – if you will pardon me saying it, going to live there all alone. If you were my boy – and you'll excuse me for saying it – you wouldn't sleep there a night, not if I had to go there myself and pull the big alarm bell that's on the roof!' The good creature was so manifestly in earnest, and was so kindly in her intentions, that Malcolmson, although amused, was touched. He told her kindly how much he appreciated her interest in him, and added: 'But, my dear Mrs Witham, indeed you need not be concerned about me! A man who is reading for the Mathematical Tripos has too much to think of to be disturbed by any of these mysterious "somethings", and his work is of too exact and prosaic a kind to allow of his having any corner in his mind for mysteries of any kind. Harmonical Progression, Permutations and Combinations, and Elliptic Functions have sufficient mysteries for me!' Mrs Witham kindly undertook to see after his commissions, and he went himself to look for the old woman who had been recommended to him. When he returned to the Judge's House with her, after an interval of a couple of hours, he found Mrs Witham herself waiting with several men and boys carrying parcels, and an upholsterer's man with a bed in a cart, for she said, though tables and chairs might be all very well, a bed that hadn't been aired for maybe fifty years was not proper for young ones to lie on. She was evidently curious to see the inside of the house; and though manifestly so afraid of the 'somethings' that at the slightest sound she clutched on to Malcolmson, whom she never left for a moment, went over the whole place.

After his examination of the house, Malcolmson decided to take up his abode in the great dining-room, which was big enough to serve for all his requirements; and Mrs Witham, with the aid of the char-woman, Mrs Dempster, proceeded to arrange matters. When the hampers were brought in and unpacked, Malcolmson saw that with much kind forethought she had sent from her own kitchen sufficient provisions to last for a few days. Before going she expressed all sorts of kind wishes; and at the door turned and said: 'And perhaps, sir, as the room is big and drafty it might be well to have one of those big screens put round your bed at night – though, truth to tell, I would die myself if I were to be so shut in with all kinds of – of "things" that put their heads round the sides, or over the top, and look on me!' The image which she had called up was too much for her nerves, and she fled incontinently.

Mrs Dempster sniffed in a superior manner as the landlady disappeared, and remarked that for her own part she wasn't afraid of all the bogies in the kingdom.

'I'll tell you what it is, sir,' she said, 'bogies is all kinds and sorts of things – except bogies! Rats and mice, and beetles; and creaky doors, and loose slates, and broken panes, and stiff drawer handles, that stay out when you pull them and then fall down in the middle of the night. Look at the wainscot of the room! It is old – hundreds of years old! Do you think there's no rats and beetles there! And do you imagine, sir, that you won't see none of them? Rats is bogies, I tell you, and bogies is rats; and don't you get to think anything else!'

'Mrs Dempster,' said Malcolmson gravely, making her a polite bow, 'you know more than a Senior Wrangler! And let me say, that, as a mark of esteem for your indubitable soundness of head and heart, I shall, when I go, give you possession of this house, and let you stay here by yourself for the last two months of my tenancy, for four weeks will serve my purpose.'

'Thank you kindly, sir!' she answered, 'but I couldn't sleep away from home a night. I am in Greenhow's Charity, and if I slept a night away from my rooms I should lose all I have got to live on. The rules is very strict; and there's too many watching for a vacancy for me to run any risks in the matter. Only for that, sir, I'd gladly come here and attend on you altogether during your stay.'

'My good woman,' said Malcolmson hastily, 'I have come here on a purpose to obtain solitude; and believe me that I am grateful to the late Greenhow for having organised his admirable charity – whatever it is – that I am perforce denied the opportunity of suffering from such a form of temptation! St Anthony himself could not be more rigid on the point!'

The old woman laughed harshly. 'Ah, you young gentlemen,' she said, 'you don't fear for naught; and belike you'll get all the solitude you want here.' She set to work with her cleaning; and by nightfall, when Malcolmson returned from his walk – he always had one of his books to study as he walked – he found the room swept and tidied, a fire burning on the old hearth, the lamp lit, and the table spread for supper with Mrs Witham's excellent fare. 'This is comfort, indeed,' he said, as he rubbed his hands.

When he had finished his supper, and lifted the tray to the other end of the great oak dining-table, he got out his books again, put fresh wood on the fire, trimmed his lamp, and set himself down to a spell of real hard work. He went on without a pause till about eleven o'clock, when he knocked off for a bit to fix his fire and lamp and to make himself a cup of tea. He had always been a tea-drinker, and during his college life had sat late at work and had taken tea late. The rest was a great luxury to him, and he enjoyed it with a sense of delicious, voluptuous ease. The renewed fire leaped and sparkled, and threw quaint shadows through the great old room; and as he sipped his hot tea he revelled in the sense of isolation from his kind. Then it was that he began to notice for the first time what a noise the rats were making.

'Surely,' he thought, 'they cannot have been at it all the time I was reading. Had they been, I must have noticed it!' Presently, when the noise increased, he satisfied himself that it was really new. It was evident that at first the rats had been frightened at the presence of a stranger, and the light of fire and lamp; but that as the time went on they had grown bolder and were now disporting themselves as was their wont.

How busy they were! and hark to the strange noises! Up and down behind the old wainscot, over the ceiling and under the floor they raced, and gnawed, and scratched! Malcolmson smiled to himself as he recalled to mind the saying of Mrs Dempster, 'Bogies is rats, and rats is bogies!' The tea began to have its effect of intellectual and nervous stimulus, he saw with joy another long spell of work to be done before the night was past, and in the sense of security which it gave him, he allowed himself the luxury of a good look round the room. He took his lamp in one hand, and went all round, wondering that so quaint and beautiful an old house had been so long neglected. The carving of the oak on the panels of the wainscot was fine, and on and round the doors and windows it was beautiful and of rare merit. There were some old pictures on the walls, but they were coated so thick with dust and dirt that he could not distinguish any detail of them, though he held his lamp as high as he could over his head. Here and there as he went round he saw some crack or hole blocked for a moment by the face of a rat with its bright eyes glittering in the light, but in an instant it was gone, and a squeak and a scamper followed. The thing that most struck him, however, was the rope of the great alarm bell on the roof, which hung down in a corner of the room on the right-hand side of the fireplace. He pulled up close to the hearth a great high-backed carved oak chair, and sat down to his last cup of tea. When this was done he made up the fire, and went back to his work, sitting at the corner of the table, having the fire to his left. For a little while the rats disturbed him somewhat with their perpetual scampering, but he got accustomed to the noise as one does to the ticking of the clock or to the roar of moving water; and he became so immersed in his work that everything in the world, except the problem which he was trying to solve, passed away from him.

He suddenly looked up, his problem was still unsolved, and there was in the air that sense of the hour before the dawn, which is so dread to doubtful life. The noise of the rats had ceased. Indeed it seemed to him that it must have ceased but lately and that it was the sudden cessation which had disturbed him. The fire had fallen low, but still it threw out a deep red glow. As he looked he started in spite of his *sang froid*.

There on the great high-backed carved oak chair by the right side of the fireplace sat an enormous rat, steadily glaring at him with baleful eyes. He made a motion to it as though to hunt it away, but it did not stir. Then he made the motion of throwing something. Still it did not stir, but showed its great white teeth angrily, and its cruel eyes shone in the lamplight with an added vindictiveness.

Malcolmson felt amazed, and seizing the poker from the hearth ran at it to kill it. Before, however, he could strike it, the rat, with a squeak that sounded like the concentration of hate, jumped upon the floor, and, running up the rope of the alarm bell, disappeared in the darkness beyond the range of the green-shaded lamp. Instantly, strange to say, the noisy scampering of the rats in the wainscot began again.

By this time Malcolmson's mind was quite off the problem; and as a shrill cockcrow outside told him of the approach of morning, he went to bed and to sleep.

He slept so sound that he was not even waked by Mrs Dempster coming in to make up his room. It was only when she had tided up the place and got his breakfast ready and tapped on the screen which closed in his bed that he woke. He was a little tired still after his night's hard work, but a strong cup of tea soon freshened him up and, taking his book, he went out for his morning walk, bringing with him a few sandwiches lest he should not care to return till dinner time. He found a quiet walk between high elms some way outside the town, and here he spent the greater part of the day studying his Laplace. On his return he looked in to see Mrs Witham and to thank her for her kindness. When she saw him coming through the diamond-paned bay window of her sanctum, she came out to meet him and asked him in. She looked at him searchingly and shook her head as she said: 'You must not overdo it, sir. You are paler this morning than you should be. Too late hours and too hard work on the brain isn't good for any man! But tell me, sir, how did you pass the night? Well, I hope? But, my heart! sir, I was glad when Mrs Dempster told me this morning that you were all right and sleeping sound when she went in.'

'Oh, I was all right,' he answered smiling; 'the "somethings" didn't worry me, as yet. Only the rats; and they had a circus, I tell you, all over the place. There was one wicked looking old devil that sat up on my own chair by the fire and wouldn't go till I took the poker to him, and then he ran up the rope of the alarm bell and got to somewhere up the wall or the ceiling – I couldn't see where, it was so dark.'

'Mercy on us,' said Mrs Witham, 'an old devil, and sitting on a chair by the fireside! Take care, sir! take care! There's many a true word spoken in jest.'

'How do you mean? 'Pon my word I don't understand.'

'An old devil! The old devil, perhaps. There! sir, you needn't laugh,' for Malcolmson had broken into a hearty peal. 'You young folks think it easy to laugh at things that makes older ones shudder. Never mind, sir! never mind. Please God, you'll laugh all the time. It's what I wish you myself!' and the good lady beamed all over in sympathy with his enjoyment, her fears gone for a moment.

'Oh, forgive me!' said Malcolmson presently. 'Don't think me rude, but the idea was too much for me – that the old devil himself was on the chair last night!' And at the thought he laughed again. Then he went home to dinner.

This evening the scampering of the rats began earlier; indeed it had been going on before his arrival, and only ceased whilst his presence by its freshness disturbed them. After dinner he sat by the fire for a while and had a smoke; and then, having cleared his table, began to work as before. Tonight the rats disturbed him more than they had done on the previous night. How they scampered up and down and under and over! How they squeaked, and scratched, and gnawed! How they, getting bolder by degrees, came to the mouths of their holes and to the chinks and cracks and crannies in the wainscoting till their eyes shone like tiny lamps as the firelight rose and fell. But to him, now doubtless accustomed to them, their eyes were not wicked; only their playfulness touched him. Sometimes the boldest of them made sallies out on the floor or along the mouldings of the wainscot. Now and again as they disturbed him Malcolmson made a sound to frighten them, smiting the table with his hand or giving a fierce 'Hsh, hsh,' so that they fled straightway to their holes.

And so the early part of the night wore on; and despite the noise Malcolmson got more and more immersed in his work.

All at once he stopped, as on the previous night, being overcome by a sudden sense of silence. There was not the faintest sound of gnaw, or scratch, or squeak. The silence was as of the grave. He remembered the odd occurrence of the previous night, and instinctively he looked at the chair standing close by the fireside. And then a very odd sensation thrilled through him.

There, on the great old high-backed carved oak chair beside the fireplace sat the same enormous rat, steadily glaring at him with baleful eyes.

Instinctively he took the nearest thing to his hand, a book of logarithms, and flung it at it. The book was badly aimed and the rat did not stir, so again the poker performance of the previous night was repeated; and again the rat, being closely pursued, fled up the rope of the alarm bell. Strangely, too, the departure of this rat was instantly followed by the renewal of the noise made by the general rat community. On this occasion, as on the previous one, Malcolmson could not see at what part of the room the rat disappeared, for the green shade of his lamp left the upper part of the room in darkness, and the fire had burned low.

On looking at his watch he found it was close on midnight and, not sorry for the *divertissement*, he made up his fire and made himself his nightly pot of tea. He had got through a good spell of work, and thought himself entitled to a cigarette; and so he sat on the great carved oak chair before the fire and enjoyed it. Whilst smoking he began to think that he would like to know where the rat disappeared to, for he had certain ideas for the morrow not entirely disconnected with a rat trap. Accordingly he lit another lamp and placed it so that it would shine well into the right-hand corner of the wall by the fireplace. Then he got all the books he had with him, and placed them handy to throw at the vermin. Finally he lifted the rope of the alarm bell and placed the end of it on the table, fixing the extreme end under the lamp. As he handled it he could not help noticing how pliable it was, especially for so strong a rope, and one not in use. 'You could hang a man with it,' he thought to himself. When his preparations were made he looked around, and said complacently: 'There now, my friend, I think we shall learn something of you this time!' He began his work again, and though as before somewhat disturbed at first by the noise of the rats, soon lost himself in his proposition and problems.

Again he was called to his immediate surroundings suddenly. This time it might not have been the sudden silence only which took his attention; there was a slight movement of the rope, and the lamp moved. Without stirring, he looked to see if his pile of books was within range, and then cast his eye along the rope. As he looked he saw the great rat drop from the rope on the oak armchair and sit there glaring at him. He raised a book in his right hand, and taking careful aim, flung it at the rat. The latter, with a quick movement, sprang aside and dodged the missile. He then took another book, and a third, and flung them one after another at the rat, but each time unsuccessfully. At last, as he stood with a book poised in his hand to throw, the rat squeaked and seemed afraid. This made Malcolmson more than ever eager to strike, and the book flew and struck the rat a resounding blow. It gave a terrified squeak, and turning on his pursuer a look of terrible malevolence, ran up the chair-back and made a great jump to the rope of the alarm bell and ran up it like lightning. The lamp rocked under the sudden strain, but it was a heavy one and did not topple over. Malcolmson kept his eyes on the rat, and saw it by the light of the second lamp leap to a moulding of the wainscot and disappear through a hole in one of the great pictures which hung on the wall, obscured and invisible through its coating of dirt and dust.

'I shall look up my friend's habitation in the morning,' said the student, as he went over to collect his books. 'The third picture from the fireplace; I shall not forget.' He picked up the books one by one, commenting on them as he lifted them. *Conic Sections* he does not mind, nor *Cycloidal Oscillations*, nor the *Principia*, nor *Quaternions*, nor *Thermodynamics*. Now for a book that fetched him!' Malcolmson took it up and looked at it. As he did so he started, and a sudden pallor overspread his face. He looked round uneasily and shivered slightly, as he murmured to himself: 'The Bible my mother gave me! What an odd coincidence.' He sat down to work again, and the rats in the wainscot renewed their gambols. They did not disturb him, however; somehow their presence gave him a sense of companionship. But he could not attend to his work, and after striving to master the subject on which he was engaged, gave it up in despair, and went to bed as the first streak of dawn stole in through the eastern window.

He slept heavily but uneasily, and dreamed much; and when Mrs Dempster woke him late in the morning he seemed ill at ease, and for a few minutes did not seem to realise exactly where he was. His first request rather surprised the servant.

'Mrs Dempster, when I am out today I wish you would get the steps and dust or wash those pictures – specially that one the third from the fireplace – I want to see what they are.'

Late in the afternoon Malcolmson worked at his books in the shaded walk, and the cheerfulness of the previous day came back to him as the day wore on, and he found that his reading was progressing well. He had worked out to a satisfactory conclusion all the problems which had as yet baffled him, and it was in a state of jubilation that he paid a visit to Mrs Witham at the Good Traveller. He found a stranger in the cozy sitting-room with the landlady, who was introduced to him as Dr Thornhill. She was not quite at ease, and this, combined with the doctor's plunging at once into a series of questions, made Malcolmson come to the conclusion that his presence was not an accident, so without preliminary he said: 'Dr Thornhill, I shall with pleasure answer you any question you may choose to ask me if you will answer me one question first.'

The doctor seemed surprised, but he smiled and answered at once, 'Done! What is it?'

'Did Mrs Witham ask you to come here and see me and advise me?'

Dr Thornhill for a moment was taken aback, and Mrs Witham got fiery red and turned away; but the doctor was a frank and ready man, and he answered at once and openly: 'She did, but she didn't intend you to know it. I suppose it was my clumsy haste that made you suspect. She told me that she did not like the idea of your being in that house all by yourself, and that she thought you took too much strong tea. In fact, she wants me to advise you if possible to give up the tea and the very late hours. I was a keen student in my time, so I suppose I may take the liberty of a college man, and without offence, advise you not quite as a stranger.'

Malcolmson with a bright smile held out his hand. 'Shake! as they say in America,' he said. 'I must thank you for your kindness and Mrs Witham too, and your kindness deserves a return on my part. I promise to take no more strong tea – no tea at all till you let me – and I shall go to bed tonight at one o'clock at latest. Will that do?'

'Capital,' said the doctor. 'Now tell us all that you noticed in the old house,' and so Malcolmson then and there told in minute detail all that had happened in the last two nights. He was interrupted every now and then by some exclamation from Mrs Witham, till finally when he told of the episode of the Bible the landlady's pent-up emotions found vent in a shriek; and it was not till a stiff glass of brandy and water had been administered that she grew composed again. Dr Thornhill listened with a face of growing gravity, and when the narrative was complete and Mrs Witham had been restored, he asked: 'The rat always went up the rope of the alarm bell?'

'I suppose you know,' said the doctor after a pause, 'what the rope is?'

'It is,' said the doctor slowly, 'the very rope which the hangman used for all the victims of the judge's judicial rancour!' Here he was interrupted by another scream from Mrs Witham, and steps had to be taken for her recovery. Malcolmson having looked at his watch, and found that it was close to his dinner hour, had gone home before her complete recovery.

When Mrs Witham was herself again she almost assailed the doctor with angry questions as to what he meant by putting such horrible ideas into the poor young man's mind. 'He has quite enough there already to upset him,' she added. Dr Thornhill replied: 'My dear madam, I had a distinct purpose in it! I wanted to draw his attention to the bell rope, and to fix it there. It may be that he is in a highly overwrought state, and has been studying too much, although I am bound to say that he seems as sound and healthy a young man, mentally and bodily, as ever I saw – but then the rats – and that suggestion of the devil.' The doctor shook his head and went on. 'I would have offered to go and stay the first night with him but that I felt sure it would have been a cause of offence. He may get in the night some strange fright or hallucination and if he does I want him to pull that rope. All alone as he is, it will give us warning, and we may reach him in time to be of service. I shall be sitting up pretty late tonight and shall keep my ears open. Do not be alarmed if Benchurch gets a surprise before morning.'

'Oh, doctor, what do you mean? What do you mean?'

'I mean this; that possibly – nay, more probably – we shall hear the great alarm bell from the Judge's House tonight,' and the doctor made about as effective an exit as could be thought of.

When Malcolmson arrived home he found that it was a little after his usual time, and Mrs Dempster had gone away – the rules of Greenhow's Charity were not to be neglected. He was glad to see that the place was bright and tidy with a cheerful fire and a well-trimmed lamp. The evening was colder than might have been expected in April, and a heavy wind was blowing with such rapidly-increasing strength that there was every promise of a storm during the night. For a few minutes after his entrance the noise of the rats ceased; but so soon as they became accustomed to his presence they began again. He was glad to hear them, for he felt once more the feeling of companionship in their noise, and his mind ran back to the strange fact that they only ceased to manifest themselves when that other – the great rat with the baleful eyes – came upon the scene. The reading-lamp only was lit and its green shade kept the ceiling and the upper part of the room in darkness, so that the cheerful light from the hearth spreading over the floor and shining on the white cloth laid over the end of the table was warm and cheery. Malcolmson sat down to his dinner with a good appetite and a buoyant spirit. After his dinner and a cigarette he sat steadily down to work, determined not to let anything disturb him, for he remembered his promise to the doctor, and made up his mind to make the best of the time at his disposal.

For an hour or so he worked all right, and then his thoughts began to wander from his books. The actual circumstances around him, the calls on his physical attention, and his nervous susceptibility were not to be denied. By this time the wind had become a gale, and the gale a storm. The old house, solid though it was, seemed to shake to its foundations, and the storm roared and raged through its many chimneys and its queer old gables, producing strange, unearthly sounds in the empty rooms and corridors. Even the great alarm bell on the roof must have felt the force of the wind, for the rope rose and fell slightly, as though the bell were moved a little from time to time, and the limber rope fell on the oak floor with a hard and hollow sound.

As Malcolmson listened to it he bethought himself of the doctor's words, 'It is the rope which the hangman used for the victims of the judge's judicial rancour,' and he went over to the corner of the fireplace and took it in his hand to look at it. There seemed a sort of deadly interest in it, and as he stood there he lost himself for a moment in speculation as to who these victims were, and the grim wish of the judge to have such a ghastly relic ever under his eyes. As he stood there the swaying of the bell on the roof still lifted the rope now and again; but presently there came a new sensation – a sort of tremor in the rope, as though something was moving along it.

Looking up instinctively Malcolmson saw the great rat coming slowly down towards him, glaring at him steadily. He dropped the rope and started back with a muttered curse, and the rat turning ran up the rope again and disappeared, and at the same instant Malcolmson became conscious that the noise of the other rats, which had ceased for a while, began again.

All this set him thinking, and it occurred to him that he had not investigated the lair of the rat or looked at the pictures, as he had intended. He lit the other lamp without the shade, and, holding it up, went and stood opposite the third picture from the fireplace on the right-hand side where he had seen the rat disappear on the previous night.

At the first glance he started back so suddenly that he almost dropped the lamp, and a deadly pallor overspread his face. His knees shook, and heavy drops of sweat came on his forehead, and he trembled like an aspen. But he was young and plucky, and pulled himself together, and after the pause of a few seconds stepped forward again, raised the lamp, and examined the picture which had been dusted and washed, and now stood out clearly.

It was of a judge dressed in his robes of scarlet and ermine. His face was strong and merciless, evil, crafty, and vindictive, with a sensual mouth, hooked nose of ruddy colour, and shaped like the beak of a bird of prey. The rest of the face was of a cadaverous colour. The eyes were of peculiar brilliance and with a terribly malignant expression. As he looked at them, Malcolmson grew cold, for he saw there the very counterpart of the eyes of the great rat. The lamp almost fell from his hand, he saw the rat with its baleful eyes peering out through the hole in the corner of the picture, and noted the sudden cessation of the noise of the other rats. However, he pulled himself together, and went on with his examination of the picture.

The judge was seated in a great high-backed carved oak chair, on the right-hand side of a great stone fireplace where, in the corner, a rope hung down from the ceiling, its end lying coiled on the floor. With a feeling of something like horror, Malcolmson recognised the scene of the room as it stood, and gazed around him in an awestruck manner as though he expected to find some strange presence behind him. Then he looked over to the corner of the fireplace – and with a loud cry he let the lamp fall from his hand.

There, in the judge's armchair, with the rope hanging behind, sat the rat with the judge's baleful eyes, now intensified and with a fiendish leer. Save for the howling of the storm without there was silence.

The fallen lamp recalled Malcolmson to himself. Fortunately it was of metal, and so the oil was not spilt. However, the practical need of attending to it settled at once his nervous apprehensions. When he had turned it out, he wiped his brow and thought for a moment.

'This will not do,' he said to himself. 'If I go on like this I shall become a crazy fool. This must stop! I promised the doctor I would not take tea. Faith, he was pretty right! My nerves must have been getting into a queer state. Funny I did not notice it. I never felt better in my life. However, it is all right now, and I shall not be such a fool again.'

Then he mixed himself a good stiff glass of brandy and water and resolutely sat down to his work.

It was nearly an hour later when he looked up from his book, disturbed by the sudden stillness. Without, the wind howled and roared louder then ever, and the rain drove in sheets against the windows, beating like hail on the glass; but within there was no sound whatever save the echo of the wind as it roared in the great chimney, and now and then a hiss as a few raindrops found their way down the chimney in a lull of the storm. The fire had fallen low and had ceased to flame, though it threw out a red glow. Malcolmson listened attentively, and presently heard a thin, squeaking noise, very faint. It came from the corner of the room where the rope hung down, and he thought it was the creaking of the rope on the floor as the swaying of the bell raised and lowered it. Looking up, however, he saw in the dim light the great rat clinging to the rope and gnawing it. The rope was already nearly gnawed through – he could see the lighter colour where the strands were laid bare. As he looked the job was completed, and the severed end of the rope fell clattering on the oaken floor, whilst for an instant the great rat remained like a knob or tassel at the end of the rope, which now began to sway to and fro. Malcolmson felt for a moment another pang of terror as he thought that now the possibility of calling the outer world to his assistance was cut off, but an intense anger took its place, and seizing the book he was reading he hurled it at the rat. The blow was well aimed, but before the missile could reach him the rat dropped off and struck the floor with a soft thud. Malcolmson instantly rushed over towards him, but it darted away and disappeared in the darkness of the shadows of the room. Malcolmson felt that his work was over for the night, and determined then and there to vary the monotony of the proceedings by a hunt for the rat, and took off the green shade of the lamp so as to insure a wider spreading light. As he did so the gloom of the upper part of the room was relieved, and in the new flood of light, great by comparison with the previous darkness, the pictures on the wall stood out boldly. From where he stood, Malcolmson saw right opposite to him the third picture on the wall from the right of the fireplace. He rubbed his eyes in surprise, and then a great fear began to come upon him.

In the centre of the picture was a great irregular patch of brown canvas, as fresh as when it was stretched on the frame. The background was as before, with chair and chimney-corner and rope, but the figure of the judge had disappeared.

Malcolmson, almost in a chill of horror, turned slowly round, and then he began to shake and tremble like a man in a palsy. His strength seemed to have left him, and he was incapable of action or movement, hardly even of thought. He could only see and hear.

There, on the great high-backed carved oak chair sat the judge in his robes of scarlet and ermine, with his baleful eyes glaring vindictively, and a smile of triumph on the resolute, cruel mouth, as he lifted with his hands a *black cap*. Malcolmson felt as if the blood was running from his heart, as one does in moments of prolonged suspense. There was a ringing in his ears. Without, he could hear the roar and howl of the tempest, and through it, swept on the storm, came the striking of midnight by the great chimes in the marketplace. He stood for a space of time that seemed to him endless still as a statue, and with wide-open, horror-struck eyes, breathless. As the clock struck, so the smile of triumph on the judge's face intensified, and at the last stroke of midnight he placed the black cap on his head.

Slowly and deliberately the judge rose from his chair and picked up the piece of the rope of the alarm bell which lay on the floor, drew it through his hands as if he enjoyed its touch, and then deliberately began to knot one end of it, fashioning it into a noose. This he tightened and tested with his foot, pulling hard at it till he was satisfied and then making a running noose of it, which he held in his hand. Then he began to move along the table on the opposite side to Malcolmson keeping his eyes on him until he had passed him, when with a quick movement he stood in front of the door. Malcolmson then began to feel that he was trapped, and tried to think of what he should do. There was some fascination in the judge's eyes, which he never took off him, and he had, perforce, to look. He saw the judge approach – still keeping between him and the door – and raise the noose and throw it towards him as if to entangle him. With a great effort he made a quick movement to one side, and saw the rope fall beside him, and heard it strike the oaken floor. Again the judge raised the noose and tried to ensnare him, ever keeping his baleful eyes fixed on him, and each time by a mighty effort the student just managed to evade it. So this went on for many times, the judge seeming never discouraged nor discomposed at failure, but playing as a cat does with a mouse. At last in despair, which had reached its climax, Malcolmson cast a quick glance round him. The lamp seemed to have blazed up, and there was a fairly good light in the room. At the many rat-holes and in the chinks and crannies of the wainscot he saw the rats' eyes; and this aspect, that was purely physical, gave him a gleam of comfort. He looked round and saw that the rope of the great alarm bell was laden with rats. Every inch of it was covered with them, and more and more were pouring through the small circular hole in the ceiling whence it emerged, so that with their weight the bell was beginning to sway.

Hark! it had swayed till the clapper had touched the bell. The sound was but a tiny one, but the bell was only beginning to sway, and it would increase.

At the sound the judge, who had been keeping his eyes fixed on Malcolmson, looked up, and a scowl of diabolical anger overspread his face. His eyes fairly glowed like hot coals, and he stamped his foot with a sound that seemed to make the house shake. A dreadful peal of thunder broke overhead as he raised the rope again, whilst the rats kept running up and down the rope as though working against time. This time, instead of throwing it, he drew close to his victim, and held open the noose as he approached. As he came closer there seemed something paralysing in his very presence, and Malcolmson stood rigid as a corpse. He felt the judge's icy fingers touch his throat as he adjusted the rope. The noose tightened – tightened. Then the judge, taking the rigid form of the student in his arms, carried him over and placed him standing in the oak chair, and stepping up beside him, put his hand up and caught the end of the swaying rope of the alarm bell. As he raised his hand the rats fled squeaking, and disappeared through the hole in the ceiling. Taking the end of the noose which was round Malcolmson's neck he tied it to the hanging-bell rope, and then descending pulled away the chair.

*   *   *

When the alarm bell of the Judge's House began to sound, a crowd soon assembled. Lights and torches of various kinds appeared, and soon a silent crowd was hurrying to the spot. They knocked loudly at the door, but there was no reply. Then they burst in the door, and poured into the great dining room, the doctor at the head.

There at the end of the rope of the great alarm bell hung the body of the student, and on the face of the judge in the picture was a malignant smile.

FRANCIS MARION CRAWFORD

The Dead Smile

❧❦❧

I

Sir Hugh Ockram Smiled as he sat by the open window of his study, in the late August afternoon, and just then a curiously yellow cloud obscured the low sun, and the clear summer light turned lurid, as if it had been suddenly poisoned and polluted by the foul vapours of a plague. Sir Hugh's face seemed, at best, to be made of fine parchment drawn skintight over a wooden mask, in which two eyes were sunk out of sight, and peered from far within through crevices under the slanting, wrinkled lids, alive and watchful like two toads in their holes, side by side and exactly alike. But as the light changed, then a little yellow glare flashed in each. Nurse Macdonald said once that when Sir Hugh smiled he saw the faces of two women in hell – two dead women he had betrayed. (Nurse Macdonald was a hundred years old.) And the smile widened, stretching the pale lips across the discoloured teeth in an expression of profound self-satisfaction, blended with the most unforgiving hatred and contempt for the human soul. The hideous disease of which he was dying had touched his brain. His son stood beside him, tall, white, and delicate as an angel in a primitive picture, and though there was deep distress in his violet eyes as he looked at his father's face, he felt the shadow of that sickening smile stealing across his own lips and parting them and drawing them against his will. And it was like a bad dream, for he tried not to smile and smiled the more. Beside him, strangely like him in her wan, angelic beauty, with the same shadowy golden hair, the same sad violet eyes, the same luminously pale face, Evelyn Warburton rested one hand upon his arm. And as she looked into her uncle's eyes, and could not turn her own away, she knew that the deathly smile was hovering on her own red lips, drawing them tightly across her little teeth, while two bright tears ran down her cheeks to her mouth, and dropped from the upper to the lower lip while she smiled – and the smile was like the shadow of death and the seal of damnation upon her pure, young face.

'Of course,' said Sir Hugh very slowly, and still looking out at the trees, 'if you have made up your mind to be married, I cannot hinder you, and I don't suppose you attach the smallest importance to my consent – '

'Father!' exclaimed Gabriel reproachfully.

'No, I do not deceive myself,' continued the old man, smiling terribly. 'You will marry when I am dead, though there is a very good reason why you had better not – why you had better not,' he repeated very emphatically, and he slowly turned his toad eyes upon the lovers.

'What reason?' asked Evelyn in a frightened voice.

'Never mind the reason, my dear. You will marry just as if it did not exist.' There was a long pause. 'Two gone,' he said, his voice lowering strangely, 'and two more will be four – all together – for ever and ever, burning, burning, burning bright.'

At the last words his head sank slowly back, and the little glare of the toad eyes disappeared under the swollen lids, and the lurid cloud passed from the westering sun, so that the earth was green again and the light pure. Sir Hugh had fallen asleep, as he often did in his last illness, even while speaking.

Gabriel Ockram drew Evelyn away, and from the study they went out into the dim hall, softly closing the door behind them, and each audibly drew breath, as though some sudden danger had been passed. They laid their hands each in the other's and their strangely-alike eyes met in a long look, in which love and perfect understanding were darkened by the secret terror of an unknown thing. Their pale faces reflected each other's fear.

'It is his secret,' said Evelyn at last. 'He will never tell us what it is.'

'If he dies with it,' answered Gabriel, 'let it be on his own head!'

'On his head!' echoed the dim hall. It was a strange echo, and some were frightened by it, for they said that if it were a real echo it should repeat everything and not give back a phrase here and there, now speaking, now silent. But Nurse Macdonald said that the great hall would never echo a prayer when an Ockram was to die, though it would give back curses ten for one.

'On his head!' it repeated quite softly, and Evelyn started and looked round.

'It is only the echo.' said Gabriel, leading her away.

They went out into the late afternoon light, and sat upon a stone seat behind the chapel, which was built across the end of the east wing. It was very still, not a breath stirred, and there was no sound near them. Only far off in the park a songbird was whistling the high prelude to the evening chorus.

'It is very lonely here,' said Evelyn, taking Gabriel's hand nervously, and speaking as if she dreaded to disturb the silence. 'If it were dark, I should be afraid.'

'Of what? Of me?' Gabriel's sad eyes turned to her.

'Oh no! How could I be afraid of you? But of the old Ockrams – they say they are just under our feet here in the north vault outside the chapel, all in their shrouds, with no coffins, as they used to bury them.'

'As they always will – as they will bury my father, and me. They say an Ockram will not lie in a coffin.'

'But it cannot be true – these are fairy tales – ghost stories!' Evelyn nestled nearer to her companion, grasping his hand more tightly, and the sun began to go down.

'Of course. But there is a story of old Sir Vernon, who was beheaded for treason under James II. The family brought his body back from the scaffold in an iron coffin with heavy locks, and they put it in the north vault. But ever afterwards, whenever the vault was opened to bury another of the family, they found the coffin wide open, and the body standing upright against the wall, and the head rolled away in a corner, smiling at it.'

'As Uncle Hugh smiles?' Evelyn shivered.

'Yes, I suppose so,' answered Gabriel, thoughtfully. 'Of course I never saw it, and the vault has not been opened for thirty years – none of us have died since then.'

'And if – if Uncle Hugh dies – shall you – ' Evelyn stopped, and her beautiful thin face was quite white.

'Yes. I shall see him laid there too – with his secret, whatever it is.' Gabriel sighed and pressed the girl's little hand.

'I do not like to think of it,' she said unsteadily. 'O Gabriel, what can the secret be? He said we had better not marry – not that he forbade it – but he said it so strangely, and he smiled – ugh!' Her small white teeth chattered with fear, and she looked over her shoulder while drawing still closer to Gabriel. 'And, somehow, I felt it in my own face – '

'So did I,' answered Gabriel in a low, nervous voice. 'Nurse Macdonald – ' He stopped abruptly.

'What? What did she say?'

'Oh – nothing. She has told me things – they would frighten you, dear. Come, it is growing chilly.' He rose, but Evelyn held his hand in both of hers, still sitting and looking up into his face.

'But we shall be married, just the same – Gabriel! Say that we shall!'

'Of course, darling – of course. But while my father is so very ill it is impossible – '

'O Gabriel, Gabriel dear! I wish we were married now!' cried Evelyn in sudden distress. 'I know that something will prevent it and keep us apart.'

'Nothing shall!'

'Nothing?'

'Nothing human,' said Gabriel Ockram, as she drew him down to her.

And their faces, that were so strangely alike, met and touched – and Gabriel knew that the kiss had a marvellous savour of evil, but on Evelyn's lips it was like the cool breath of a sweet and mortal fear. And neither of them understood, for they were innocent and young. Yet she drew him to her by her lightest touch, as a sensitive plant shivers and waves its thin leaves, and bends and closes softly upon what it wants, and he let himself be drawn to her willingly, as he would if her touch had been deadly and poisonous; for she strangely loved that half voluptuous breath of fear and he passionately desired the nameless evil something that lurked in her maiden lips.

'It is as if we loved in a strange dream,' she said.

'I fear the waking,' he murmured.

'We shall not wake, dear – when the dream is over it will have already turned into death, so softly that we shall not know it. But until then – '

She paused, and her eyes sought his, and their faces slowly came nearer. It was as if they had thoughts in their red lips that foresaw and foreknew the deep kiss of each other.

'Until then – ' she said again, very low, and her mouth was nearer to his.

'Dream – till then,' murmured his breath.

2

Nurse Macdonald was a hundred years old. She used to sleep sitting all bent together in a great old leathern armchair with wings, her feet in a bag footstool lined with sheepskin, and many warm blankets wrapped about her, even in summer. Beside her a little lamp always burned at night by an old silver cup, in which there was something to drink.

Her face was very wrinkled, but the wrinkles were so small and fine and near together that they made shadows instead of lines. Two thin locks of hair, that was turning from white to a smoky yellow again, were drawn over her temples from under her starched white cap. Every now and then she woke, and her eyelids were drawn up in tiny folds like little pink silk curtains, and her queer blue eyes looked straight before her through doors and walls and worlds to a far place beyond. Then she slept again, and her hands lay one upon the other on the edge of the blanket; the thumbs had grown longer than the fingers with age, and the joints shone in the low lamplight like polished crab-apples.

It was nearly one o'clock in the night, and the summer breeze was blowing the ivy branch against the panes of the window with a hushing caress. In the small room beyond, with the door ajar, the girl-maid who took care of Nurse Macdonald was fast asleep. All was very quiet. The old woman breathed regularly, and her in-drawn lips trembled each time as the breath went out, and her eyes were shut.

But outside the closed window there was a face, and violet eyes were looking steadily at the ancient sleeper, for it was like the face of Evelyn Warburton, though there were eighty feet from the sill of the window to the foot of the tower. Yet the cheeks were thinner than Evelyn's, and as white as a gleam, and her eyes stared, and the lips were not red with life, they were dead and painted with new blood.

Slowly Nurse Macdonald's wrinkled eyelids folded themselves back, and she looked straight at the face at the window while one might count ten.

'Is it time?' she asked in her little old, faraway voice.

While she looked the face at the window changed, for the eyes opened wider and wider till the white glared all round the bright violet, and the bloody lips opened over gleaming teeth, and stretched and widened and stretched again, and the shadowy golden hair rose and streamed against the window in the night breeze. And in answer to Nurse Macdonald's question came the sound that freezes the living flesh.

That low moaning voice that rises suddenly, like the scream of a storm, from a moan to a wail, from a wail to a howl, from a howl to the fear-shriek of the tortured dead – he who has heard knows, and he can bear witness that the cry of the banshee is an evil cry to hear alone in the deep night. When it was over and the face was gone, Nurse Macdonald shook a little in her great chair, and still she looked at the black square of the window, but there was nothing more there, nothing but the night, and the whispering ivy branch. She turned her head to the door that was ajar, and there stood the girl in her white gown, her teeth chattering with fright.

'It is time, child.' said Nurse Macdonald. 'I must go to him, for it is the end.'

She rose slowly, leaning her withered hands upon the arms of the chair, and the girl brought her a woollen gown and a great mantle, and her crutch-stick, and made her ready. But very often the girl looked at the window and was unjointed with fear, and often Nurse Macdonald shook her head and said words which the maid could not understand.

'It was like the face of Miss Evelyn,' said the girl at last, trembling.

But the ancient woman looked up sharply and angrily, and her queer blue eyes glared. She held herself by the arm of the great chair with her left hand, and lifted up her crutch-stick to strike the maid with all her might. But she did not.

'You are a good girl,' she said, 'but you are a fool. Pray for wit, child, pray for wit – or else find service in another house than Ockram Hall. Bring the lamp and help me under my left arm.'

The crutch-stick clacked on the wooden floor, and the low heels of the woman's slippers clappered after her in slow triplets as Nurse

Macdonald got toward the door. And down the stairs each step she took was a labour in itself, and by the clacking noise the waking servants knew that she was coming, very long before they saw her.

No one was sleeping now, and there were lights and whisperings and pale faces in the corridors near Sir Hugh's bedroom, and now someone went in, and now someone came out, but everyone made way for Nurse Macdonald, who had nursed Sir Hugh's father more than eighty years ago.

The light was soft and clear in the room. There stood Gabriel Ockram by his father's bedside, and there knelt Evelyn Warburton, her hair lying like a golden shadow down her shoulders, and her hands clasped nervously together. And opposite Gabriel, a nurse was trying to make Sir Hugh drink. But he would not, and though his lips were parted, his teeth were set. He was very, very thin and yellow now, and his eyes caught the light sideways and were as yellow coals.

'Do not torment him,' said Nurse Macdonald to the woman who held the cup. 'Let me speak to him, for his hour is come.'

'Let her speak to him,' said Gabriel in a dull voice.

So the ancient woman leaned to the pillow and laid the feather-weight of her withered hand, that was like a brown moth, upon Sir Hugh's yellow fingers, and she spoke to him earnestly, while only Gabriel and Evelyn were left in the room to hear.

'Hugh Ockram,' she said, 'this is the end of your life; and as I saw you born, and saw your father born before you, I am come to see you die. Hugh Ockram, will you tell me the truth?'

The dying man recognised the little faraway voice he had known all his life, and he very slowly turned his yellow face to Nurse Macdonald; but he said nothing. Then she spoke again.

'Hugh Ockram, you will never see the daylight again. Will you tell the truth?'

His toad-like eyes were not dull yet. They fastened themselves on her face.

'What do you want of me?' he asked, and each word struck hollow on the last. 'I have no secrets. I have lived a good life.'

Nurse Macdonald laughed – a tiny, cracked laugh, that made her old head bob and tremble a little, as if her neck were on a steel spring. But Sir Hugh's eyes grew red, and his pale lips began to twist.

'Let me die in peace,' he said slowly.

But Nurse Macdonald shook her head, and her brown, mothlike hand left his and fluttered to his forehead.

'By the mother that bore you and died of grief for the sins you did, tell me the truth!'

Sir Hugh's lips tightened on his discoloured teeth.

'Not on earth,' he answered slowly.

'By the wife who bore your son and died heartbroken, tell me the truth!'

'Neither to you in life, nor to her in eternal death.'

His lips writhed, as if the words were coals between them, and a great drop of sweat rolled across the parchment of his forehead. Gabriel Ockram bit his hand as he watched his father die. But Nurse Macdonald spoke a third time.

'By the woman whom you betrayed, and who waits for you this night, Hugh Ockram, tell me the truth!'

'It is too late. Let me die in peace.'

The writhing lips began to smile across the set yellow teeth, and the toad eyes glowed like evil jewels in his head.

'There is time,' said the ancient woman. 'Tell me the name of Evelyn Warburton's father. Then I will let you die in peace.'

Evelyn started back, kneeling as she was, and stared at Nurse Macdonald, and then at her uncle.

'The name of Evelyn's father?' he repeated slowly, while the awful smile spread upon his dying face.

The light was growing strangely dim in the great room. As Evelyn looked, Nurse Macdonald's crooked shadow on the wall grew gigantic. Sir Hugh's breath came thick, rattling in his throat, as death crept in like a snake and choked it back. Evelyn prayed aloud, high and clear.

Then something rapped at the window, and she felt her hair rise upon her head in a cool breeze, as she looked around in spite of herself. And when she saw her own white face looking in at the window, and her own eyes staring at her through the glass, wide and fearful, and her own hair streaming against the pane, and her own lips dashed with blood. She rose slowly from the floor and stood rigid for one moment, till she screamed once and fell back into Gabriel's arms. But the shriek that answered hers was the fear-shriek of the tormented corpse, out of which the soul cannot pass for shame of deadly sins, though the devils fight in it with corruption, each for their due share.

Sir Hugh Ockram sat upright in his deathbed, and saw and cried aloud: 'Evelyn!' His harsh voice broke and rattled in his chest as he sank down. But still Nurse Macdonald tortured him, for there was a little life left in him still.

'You have seen the mother as she waits for you, Hugh Ockram. Who was this girl Evelyn's father? What was his name?'

For the last time the dreadful smile came upon the twisted lips, very slowly, very surely now, and the toad eyes glared red, and the parchment face glowed a little in the flickering light. For the last time words came.

'They know it in hell.'

Then the glowing eyes went out quickly, the yellow face turned waxen pale, and a great shiver ran through the thin body as Hugh Ockram died.

But in death he still smiled, for he knew his secret and kept it still, on the other side, and he would take it with him, to lie with him for ever in the north vault of the chapel where the Ockrams lie uncoffined in their shrouds – all but one. Though he was dead, he smiled, for he had kept his treasure of evil truth to the end, and there was none left to tell the name he had spoken, but there was all the evil he had not undone left to bear fruit.

As they watched – Nurse Macdonald and Gabriel, who held Evelyn still unconscious in his arms while he looked at the father – they felt the dead smile crawling along their own lips – the ancient crone and the youth with the angel's face. Then they shivered a little, and both looked at Evelyn as she lay with her head on his shoulder, and, though she was very beautiful, the same sickening smile was twisting her mouth too, and it was like the foreshadowing of a great evil which they could not understand.

But by and by they carried Evelyn out, and she opened her eyes and the smile was gone. From far away in the great house the sound of weeping and crooning came up the stairs and echoed along the dismal corridors, for the women had begun to mourn the dead master, after the Irish fashion, and the hall had echoes of its own all that night, like the far-off wail of the banshee among forest trees.

When the time was come they took Sir Hugh in his winding-sheet on a trestle bier, and bore him to the chapel and through the iron door and down the long descent to the north vault, with tapers, to lay him by his father. And two men went in first to prepare the place and came back staggering like drunken men, and white, leaving their lights behind them.

But Gabriel Ockram was not afraid, for he knew. And he went in alone and saw that the body of Sir Vernon Ockram was leaning upright against the stone wall, and that his head lay on the ground near by with the face turned up, and the dried leathern lips smiled horribly at the dried-up corpse, while the iron coffin, lined with black velvet, stood open on the floor.

Then Gabriel took the thing in his hands, for it was very light, being quite dried by the air of the vault, and those who peeped in from the door saw him lay it in the coffin again, and it rustled a little, like a bundle of reeds, and sounded hollow as it touched the sides and the bottom. He also placed the head upon the shoulders and shut down the lid, which fell to with a rusty spring that snapped.

After that they laid Sir Hugh beside his father, with the trestle bier on which they had brought him, and they went back to the chapel.

But when they saw one another's faces, master and men, they were all smiling with the dead smile of the corpse they had left in the vault, so that they could not bear to look at one another until it had faded away.

3

Gabriel Ockram became Sir Gabriel, inheriting the baronetcy with the half-ruined fortune left by his father, and still Evelyn Warburton lived at Ockram Hall, in the south room that had been hers ever since she could remember anything. She could not go away, for there were no relatives to whom she could have gone, and besides there seemed to be no reason why she should not stay. The world would never trouble itself to care what the Ockrams did on their Irish estates, as it was long since the Ockrams had asked anything of the world.

So Sir Gabriel took his father's place at the dark old table in the dining room, and Evelyn sat opposite to him, until such time as their mourning should be over, and they might be married at last. And meanwhile their lives went on as before, since Sir Hugh had been a hopeless invalid during the last year of his life, and they had seen him but once a day for a little while, spending most of their time together in a strangely perfect companionship.

But though the late summer saddened into autumn, and autumn darkened into winter, and storm followed storm, and rain poured on rain through the short days and the long nights, yet Ockram Hall seemed less gloomy since Sir Hugh had been laid in the north vault beside his father. And at Christmastide Evelyn decked the great hall with holly and green boughs, and huge fires blazed on every hearth. Then the tenants were all bidden to a New Year's dinner, and they ate and drank well, while Sir Gabriel sat at the head of the table. Evelyn came in when the port wine was brought, and the most respected of the tenants made a speech to propose her health.

It was long, he said, since there had been a Lady Ockram. Sir Gabriel shaded his eyes with his hand and looked down at the table, but a faint colour came into Evelyn's transparent cheeks. But, said the grey-haired farmer, it was longer still since there had been a Lady Ockram so fair as the next was to be, and he gave the health of Evelyn Warburton.

Then the tenants all stood up and shouted for her, and Sir Gabriel stood up likewise, beside Evelyn. And when the men gave the last and loudest cheer of all, there was a voice not theirs, above them all, higher, fiercer, louder – a scream not earthly, shrieking for the bride of Ockram Hall. And the holly and the green boughs over the great chimney piece shook and slowly waved as if a cool breeze were blowing over them. But the men turned very pale, and many of them sat down their glasses, but others let them fall upon the floor for fear. And looking into one another's faces, they were all smiling strangely, a dead smile, like dead Sir Hugh's. One cried out words in Irish, and the fear of death was suddenly upon them all so that they fled in panic, falling over one another like wild beasts in the burning forest, when the thick smoke runs along the flame, and the tables were overset, and drinking glasses and bottles were broken in heaps, and the dark red wine crawled like blood upon the polished floor.

Sir Gabriel and Evelyn stood alone at the head of the table before the wreck of the feast, not daring to turn to see each other, for each knew that the other smiled. But his right arm held her and his left hand clasped her right as they stared before them, and but for the shadows of her hair one might not have told their two faces apart. They listened long, but the cry came not again, and the dead smile faded from their lips, while each remembered that Sir Hugh Ockram lay in the north vault, smiling in his winding-sheet, in the dark, because he had died with his secret.

So ended the tenants' New Year's dinner. But from that time on Sir Gabriel grew more and more silent, and his face grew even paler and thinner than before. Often without warning and without words, he would rise from his seat, as if something moved him against his will, and he would go out into the rain or the sunshine to the north side of the chapel, and sit on the stone bench, staring at the ground as if he could see through it, and through the vault below, and through the white winding-sheet in the dark, to the dead smile that would not die.

Always when he went out in that way Evelyn came out presently and sat beside him. Once, too, as in summer, their beautiful faces came suddenly near, and their lids drooped, and their red lips were almost joined together. But as their eyes met, they grew wide and wild, so that the white showed in a ring all round the deep violet, and their teeth chattered, and their hands were like hands of corpses, each in the other's for the terror of what was under their feet, and of what they knew but could not see.

Once, also, Evelyn found Sir Gabriel in the Chapel alone, standing before the iron door that led down to the place of death, and in his hand there was the key to the door, but he had not put it in the lock. Evelyn drew him away, shivering, for she had also been driven in waking dreams to see that terrible thing again, and to find out whether it had changed since it had lain there.

'I'm going mad,' said Sir Gabriel, covering his eyes with his hand as he went with her. 'I see it in my sleep, I see it when I am awake – it draws me to it, day and night – and unless I see it I shall die!'

'I know,' answered Evelyn, 'I know. It is as if threads were spun from it, like a spider's, drawing us down to it.' She was silent for a moment, and then she stared violently and grasped his arm with a man's strength, and almost screamed the words she spoke. 'But we must not go there!' she cried. 'We must not go!'

Sir Gabriel's eyes were half shut, and he was not moved by the agony on her face.

'I shall die unless I see it again,' he said, in a quiet voice not like his own. And all that day and that evening he scarcely spoke, thinking of it, always thinking, while Evelyn Warburton quivered from head to foot with a terror she had never known.

She went alone, on a grey winter's morning, to Nurse Macdonald's room in the tower, and sat down beside the great leathern easy chair, laying her thin white hand upon the withered fingers.

'Nurse,' she said, 'what was it that Uncle Hugh should have told you, that night before he died? It must have been an awful secret – and yet, though you asked him, I feel somehow that you know it, and that you know why he used to smile so dreadfully.'

The old woman's head moved slowly from side to side.

'I can only guess – I shall never know,' she answered slowly in her cracked little voice.

'But what do you guess? Who am I? Why did you ask who my father was? You know I am Colonel Warburton's daughter, and my mother was Lady Ockram's sister, so that Gabriel and I are cousins. My father was killed in Afghanistan. What secret can there be?'

'I do not know. I can only guess.'

'Guess what?' asked Evelyn imploringly, and pressing the soft withered hands, as she leaned forward. But Nurse Macdonald's wrinkled lids dropped suddenly over her queer blue eyes, and her lips shook a little with her breath as if she were asleep.

Evelyn waited. By the fire the Irish maid was knitting fast, and the needles clicked like three or four clocks ticking against each other. And the real clock on the wall solemnly ticked alone, checking off the seconds of the woman who was a hundred years old, and had not many days left. Outside the ivy branch beat the window in the wintry blast, as it had beaten against the glass a hundred years ago.

Then as Evelyn sat there she felt again the waking of a horrible desire – the sickening wish to go down, down to the thing in the north vault, and to open the winding-sheet, and see whether it had changed, and she held Nurse Macdonald's hands as if to keep herself in her place and fight against the appalling attraction of the evil dead.

But the old cat that kept Nurse Macdonald's feet warm, lying always on the bag footstool, got up and stretched itself, and looked up into Evelyn's eyes, while its back arched, and its tail thickened and bristled, and its ugly pink lips drew back in a devilish grin, showing its sharp teeth. Evelyn stared at it, half fascinated by its ugliness. Then the creature suddenly put out one paw with all its claws spread, and spat at the girl, and all at once the grinning cat was like the smiling corpse far down below, so that Evelyn shivered down to her small feet and covered her face with her free hand lest Nurse Macdonald should wake and see the dead smile there, for she could feel it.

The old woman had already opened her eyes again, and she touched her cat with the end of her crutch-stick, whereupon its back went down and its tail shrunk, and it sidled back to its place in the bag footstool. But its yellow eyes looked up sideways at Evelyn, between the slits of its lids.

'What is it that you guess, Nurse?' asked the young girl again.

'A bad thing – a wicked thing. But I dare not tell you, lest it might not be true, and the very thought should blast your life. For if I guess right, he meant that you should not know, and that you two should marry, and pay for his old sin with your souls.'

'He used to tell us that we ought not to marry –'

'Yes – he told you that, perhaps – but it was as if a man put poisoned meat before a starving beast, and said "do not eat", but never raised his hand to take the meat away. And if he told you that you should not marry, it was because he hoped you would, for of all men living or dead, Hugh Ockram was the falsest man that ever told a cowardly lie and the cruelest that ever hurt a weak woman, and the worst that ever loved a sin.'

'But Gabriel and I love each other,' said Evelyn very sadly.

Nurse Macdonald's old eyes looked far away, at sights seen long ago, and that rose in the grey winter air amid the mists of an ancient youth.

'If you love, you can die together,' she said very slowly. 'Why should you live, if it is true? I am a hundred years old. What has life given me? The beginning is fire, the end is a heap of ashes, and between the end and the beginning lies all the pain in the world. Let me sleep, since I cannot die.'

Then the old woman's eyes closed again, and her head sank a little lower upon her breast.

So Evelyn went away and left her asleep, with the cat asleep on the bag footstool; and the young girl tried to forget Nurse Macdonald's words, but she could not, for she heard them over and over again in the wind, and behind her on the stairs. And as she grew sick with fear of the frightful unknown evil to which her soul was bound, she felt a bodily something pressing her, and pushing her, and forcing her on, and from the other side she felt threads that drew her mysteriously, and when she shut her eyes, she saw in the chapel behind the altar the low iron door through which she must pass to go to the thing.

And as she lay awake at night, she drew the sheet over her face, lest she should see shadows on the wall beckoning her, and the sound of her own warm breath made whisperings in her ears, while she held the mattress with her hands to keep from getting up and going to the chapel. It would have been easier if there had not been a way thither through the library, by a door which was never locked. It would be fearfully easy to take her candle and go softly through the sleeping house. And the key of the vault lay under the altar behind a stone that turned. She knew that little secret. She could go alone and see.

But when she thought of it, she felt her hair rise on her head, and first she shivered so that the bed shook, and then the horror went through her in a cold thrill that was agony again, like a myriads of icy needles boring into her nerves.

4

The old clock in Nurse Macdonald's tower struck midnight. From her room she could hear the creaking chains and weights in their box in the corner of the staircase, and overheard the jarring of the rusty lever that lifted the hammer. She had heard it all her life. It struck eleven strokes clearly and then came the twelfth, with a dull half-stroke, as though the hammer were too weary to go on, and had fallen asleep against the bell.

The old cat got up from the bag footstool and stretched itself, and Nurse Macdonald opened her ancient eyes and looked slowly round the room by the dim light of the night lamp. She touched the cat with her crutch-stick and it lay down upon her feet. She drank a few drops from her cup and went to sleep again.

But downstairs Sir Gabriel sat straight up as the clock struck, for he had dreamed a fearful dream of horror, and his heart stood still, till he awoke at its stopping, and it beat again furiously with his breath, like a wild thing set free. No Ockram had ever known fear waking, but sometimes it came to Sir Gabriel in his sleep.

He pressed his hands on his temples as he sat up in bed, and his hands were icy cold, but his head was hot. The dream faded far, and in its place there came the sick twisting of his lips in the dark that would have been a smile. Far off, Evelyn Warburton dreamed that the dead smile was on her mouth, and awoke, starting with a little moan, her face in her hands shivering.

But Sir Gabriel struck a light and got up and began to walk up and down his great room. It was midnight, and he had barely slept an hour, and in the north of Ireland the winter nights are long.

'I shall go mad,' he said to himself, holding his forehead. He knew that it was true. For weeks and months the possession of the thing had grown upon him like a disease, till he could think of nothing without thinking first of that. And now all at once it outgrew his strength, and he knew that he must be its instrument or lose his mind – that he must do the deed he hated and feared if he could fear anything, or that something would snap in his brain and divide him from life while he was yet alive. He took the candlestick in his hand, the old-fashioned heavy candlestick that had always been used by the head of the house. He did not think of dressing, but went as he was, in his silk night-clothes and his slippers, and he opened the door. Everything was very still in the great old house. He shut the door behind him and walked noiselessly on the carpet through the long corridor. A cool breeze blew over his shoulder and blew the flame of his candle straight out from him. Instinctively he stopped and looked round, but all was still, and the upright flame burned steadily. He walked on, and instantly a strong draft was behind him, almost extinguishing the light. It seemed to blow him on his way, ceasing whenever he turned, coming again when he went on – invisible, icy.

Down the great staircase to the echoing hall he went, seeing nothing but the flame of the candle standing away from him over the guttering wax, while the cold wind blew over his shoulder and through his hair. On he passed through the open door into the library, dark with old books and carved bookcases, on through the door in the shelves, with painted shelves on it, and the imitated backs of books, so that one needed to know where to find it – and it shut itself after him with a soft click. He entered the low-arched passage, and though the door was shut behind him and fitted tightly in its frame, still the cold breeze blew the flame forward as he walked. And he was not afraid, but his face was very pale, and his eyes were wide and bright, looking before him, seeing already in the dark air the picture of the thing beyond. But in the chapel he stood still, his hand on the little turning stone tablet in the back of the stone altar. On the tablet were engraved the words, '*Clavis sepulchri Clarissimorum Dominorum De Ockram*' – ('the key to the vault of the most illustrious lord of Ockram'). Sir Gabriel paused and listened. He fancied that he heard a sound far off in the great house where all had been so still, but it did not come again. Yet he waited at the last, and looked at the low iron door. Beyond it, down the long descent, lay his father uncoffined, six months dead, corrupt, terrible in his clinging shroud. The strangely preserving air of the vault could not yet have done its work completely. But on the thing's ghastly features, with their half-dried, open eyes, there would still be the frightful smile with which the man had died – the smile that haunted.

As the thought crossed Sir Gabriel's mind, he felt his lips writhing, and he struck his own mouth in wrath with the back of his hand so fiercely that a drop of blood ran down his chin and another, and more, falling back in the gloom upon the chapel pavement. But still his bruised lips twisted themselves. He turned the tablet by the simple secret. It needed no safer fastening, for had each Ockram been confined in pure gold, and had the door been wide, there was not a man in Tyrone brave enough to go down to the place, saving Gabriel Ockram himself, with his angel's face and his thin, white hands, and his sad unflinching eyes. He took the great gold key and set it into the lock of the iron door, and the heavy, rattling noise echoed down the descent beyond like footsteps, as if a watcher had stood behind the iron and were running away within, with heavy dead feet. And though he was standing still, the cool wind was from behind him, and blew the flame of the candle against the iron panel. He turned the key.

Sir Gabriel saw that his candle was short. There were new ones on the altar, with long candlesticks, and he lit one and left his own burning on the floor. As he set it down on the pavement his lip began to bleed again, and another drop fell upon the stones.

He drew the iron door open and pushed it back against the chapel wall, so that it should not shut of itself while he was within, and the horrible draft of the sepulchre came up out of the depths in his face, foul and dark. He went in, but though the fetid air met him, yet the flame of the tall candle was blown straight from him against the wind while he walked down the easy incline with steady steps, his loose slippers slapping the pavement as he trod.

He shaded the candle with his hand, and his fingers seemed to be made of wax and blood as the light shone through them. And in spite of him the unearthly draft forced the flame forward, till it was blue over the black wick, and it seemed as if it must go out. But he went straight on, with shining eyes.

The downward passage was wide, and he could not always see the walls by the struggling light, but he knew when he was in the place of death by the larger, drearier echo of his steps in the greater space and by the sensation of a distant blank wall. He stood still, almost enclosing the flame of the candle in the hollow of his hand. He could see a little, for his eyes were growing used to the gloom. Shadowy forms were outlined in the dimness, where the biers of the Ockrams stood crowded together, side by side, each with its straight, shrouded corpse, strangely preserved by the dry air, like the empty shell that the locust sheds in summer. And a few steps before him he saw clearly the dark shape of headless Sir Vernon's iron coffin, and he knew that nearest to it lay the thing he sought.

He was as brave as any of those dead men had been, and they were his fathers, and he knew that sooner or later he should lie there himself, beside Sir Hugh, slowly drying to a parchment shell. But he was still alive, and he closed his eyes a moment, and three great drops stood on his forehead.

Then he looked again, and by the whiteness of the winding sheet he knew his father's corpse, for all the others were brown with age; and, moreover, the flame of the candle was blown towards it. He made four steps till he reached it, and suddenly the light burned straight and high, shedding a dazzling yellow glare upon the fine linen that was all white, save over the face, and where the joined hands were laid on the breast. And at those places ugly stains had spread, darkened with outlines of the features and of the tight-clasped fingers. There was a frightful stench of drying death.

As Sir Gabriel looked down, something stirred behind him, softly at first, then more noisily, and something fell to the stone floor with a dull thud and rolled up to his feet; he started back, and saw a withered head lying almost face upward on the pavement, grinning at him. He felt the cold sweat standing on his face, and his heart beat painfully.

For the first time in all his life that evil thing which men call fear was getting hold of him, checking his heart strings as a cruel driver checks a quivering horse, clawing at his backbone with icy hands, lifting his hair with freezing breath climbing up and gathering in his midriff with leaden weight.

Yet presently he bit his lip and bent down, holding the candle in one hand, to lift the shroud back from the head of the corpse with the other. Slowly he lifted it.

Then it clove to the half-dried skin of the face, and his hand shook as if someone had struck him on the elbow, but half in fear and half in anger at himself, he pulled it, so that it came away with a little ripping sound. He caught his breath as he held it, not yet throwing it back, and not yet looking. The horror was working in him, and he felt that old Vernon Ockram was standing up in his iron coffin, headless, yet watching him with the stump of his severed neck.

While he held his breath he felt the dead smile twisting his lips. In sudden wrath at his own misery, he tossed the death-stained linen backward, and looked at last. He ground his teeth lest he should shriek aloud.

There it was, the thing that haunted him, that haunted Evelyn Warburton, that was like a blight on all that came near him.

The dead face was blotched with dark stains, and the thin, grey hair was matted about the discoloured forehead. The sunken lids were half open, and the candle light gleamed on something foul where the toad eyes had lived.

But yet the dead thing smiled, as it had smiled in life; the ghastly lips were parted and drawn wide and tight upon the wolfish teeth, cursing still, and still defying hell to do its worst – defying, cursing, and always and for ever smiling alone in the dark.

Sir Gabriel opened the winding-sheet where the hands were, and the blackened, withered fingers were closed upon something stained and mottled. Shivering from head to foot, but fighting like a man in agony for his life, he tried to take the package from the dead man's hold. But as he pulled at it the claw-like fingers seemed to close more tightly, and when he pulled harder the shrunken hands and arms rose from the corpse with a horrible look of life following his motion – then as he wrenched the sealed packet loose at last, the hands fell back into their place still folded.

He set down the candle on the edge of the bier to break the seals from the stout paper. And, kneeling on one knee, to get a better light, he read what was within, written long ago in Sir Hugh's queer hand.

He was no longer afraid.

He read how Sir Hugh had written it all down that it might perchance be a witness of evil and of his hatred; how he had loved Evelyn Warburton, his wife's sister; and how his wife had died of a broken heart with his curse upon her, and how Warburton and he had fought side by side in Afghanistan, and Warburton had fallen; but Ockram had brought his comrade's wife back a full year later, and little Evelyn, her child, had been born in Ockram Hall. And next, how he had wearied of the mother, and she had died like her sister with his curse on her. And then, how Evelyn had been brought up as his niece, and how he had trusted that his son Gabriel and his daughter, innocent and unknowing, might love and marry, and the souls of the women he had betrayed might suffer another anguish before eternity was out. And, last of all, he hoped that someday, when nothing could be undone, the two might find his writing and live on, not daring to tell the truth for their children's sake and the world's word, as man and wife.

This he read, kneeling beside the corpse in the north vault, by the light of the altar candle; and when he had read it all, he thanked God aloud that he had found the secret in time. But when he rose to his feet and looked down at the dead face it was changed, and the smile was gone from it for ever, and the jaw had fallen a little, and the tired dead lips were relaxed. And then there was a breath behind him and close to him, not cold like that which had blown the flame of the candle as he came, but warm and human. He turned suddenly.

There she stood, all in white, with her shadowy golden hair – for she had risen from her bed and had followed him noiselessly, and had found him reading, and had herself read over his shoulder. He started violently when he saw her, for his nerves were unstrung – and then he cried out her name in the still place of death: 'Evelyn!'

'My brother!' she answered, softly and tenderly, putting out both hands to meet his.

OSCAR WILDE

The Canterville Ghost

A Hylo-Idealistic Romance

❧❧❧

CHAPTER I

When Mr Hiram B. Otis, the American Minister, bought Canterville Chase, everyone told him he was doing a very foolish thing, as there was no doubt at all that the place was haunted. Indeed, Lord Canterville himself, who was a man of the most punctilious honour, had felt it his duty to mention the fact to Mr Otis when they came to discuss terms.

'We have not cared to live in the place ourselves,' said Lord Canterville, 'since my grandaunt, the Dowager Duchess of Bolton, was frightened into a fit, from which she never really recovered, by two skeleton hands being placed on her shoulders as she was dressing for dinner, and I feel bound to tell you, Mr Otis, that the ghost has been seen by several living members of my family, as well as by the rector of the parish, the Reverend Augustus Dampier, who is a Fellow of King's College, Cambridge. After the unfortunate accident to the Duchess, none of our younger servants would stay with us, and Lady Canterville often got very little sleep at night, in consequence of the mysterious noises that came from the corridor and the library.'

'My Lord,' answered the minister, 'I will take the furniture and the ghost at a valuation. I come from a modern country, where we have everything that money can buy; and with all our spry young fellows painting the Old World red, and carrying off your best actresses and prima-donnas, I reckon that if there were such a thing as a ghost in Europe, we'd have it at home in a very short time in one of our public museums, or on the road as a show.'

'I fear that the ghost exists,' said Lord Canterville, smiling, 'though it may have resisted the overtures of your enterprising impresarios. It has been well known for three centuries, since 1584 in fact, and always makes its appearance before the death of any member of our family.'

'Well, so does the family doctor for that matter, Lord Canterville. But there is no such thing, sir, as a ghost, and I guess the laws of nature are not going to be suspended for the British aristocracy.'

'You are certainly very natural in America,' answered Lord Canterville, who did not quite understand Mr Otis's last observation, 'and if you don't mind a ghost in the house, it is all right. Only you must remember I warned you.'

A few weeks after this, the purchase was completed, and at the close of the season the minister and his family went down to Canterville Chase. Mrs Otis, who, as Miss Lucretia R. Tappan, of West 53rd Street, had been a celebrated New York belle, was now a very handsome, middle-aged woman, with fine eyes and a superb profile. Many American ladies on leaving their native land adopt an appearance of chronic ill-health, under the impression that it is a form of European refinement, but Mrs Otis had never fallen into this error. She had a magnificent constitution, and a really wonderful amount of animal spirits. Indeed, in many respects, she was quite English, and was an excellent example of the fact that we have really everything in common with America nowadays, except, of course, language. Her eldest son, christened Washington by his parents in a moment of patriotism, which he never ceased to regret, was a fair-haired, rather good-looking young man, who had qualified himself for American diplomacy by leading the German at the Newport Casino for three successive seasons, and even in London was well known as an excellent dancer. Gardenias and the peerage were his only weaknesses. Otherwise he was extremely sensible. Miss Virginia E. Otis was a little girl of fifteen, lithe and lovely as a fawn, and with a fine freedom in her large blue eyes. She was a wonderful amazon, and had once raced old Lord Bilton on her pony twice round the park, winning by a length and a half, just in front of the Achilles statue, to the huge delight of the young Duke of Cheshire, who proposed for her on the spot, and was sent back to Eton that very night by his guardians, in floods of tears. After Virginia came the twins, who were usually called 'the Stars and Stripes', as they were always getting swished. They were delightful boys, and with the exception of the worthy minister, the only true republicans of the family.

As Canterville Chase is seven miles from Ascot, the nearest railway station, Mr Otis had telegraphed for a waggonette to meet them, and they started on their drive in high spirits. It was a lovely July evening, and the air was delicate with the scent of the pine woods. Now and then they heard a woodpigeon brooding over its own sweet voice, or saw, deep in the rustling fern, the burnished breast of the pheasant. Little squirrels peered at them from the beech trees as they went by, and the rabbits scudded away through the brushwood and over the mossy knolls, with their white tails in the air. As they entered the avenue of Canterville Chase, however, the sky became suddenly overcast with clouds, a curious stillness seemed to hold the atmosphere, a great flight of rooks passed silently over their heads, and, before they reached the house, some big drops of rain had fallen.

Standing on the steps to receive them was an old woman, neatly dressed in black silk, with a white cap and apron. This was Mrs Umney, the housekeeper, whom Mrs Otis, at Lady Canterville's earnest request, had consented to keep on in her former position. She made them each a low curtsey as they alighted and said, in a quaint, old-fashioned manner, 'I bid you welcome to Canterville Chase.' Following her, they passed through the fine Tudor hall into the library, a long, low room, panelled in black oak, at the end of which was a large stained-glass window. Here they found tea laid out for them, and, after taking off their wraps, they sat down and began to look round, while Mrs Umney waited on them.

Suddenly Mrs Otis caught sight of a dull red stain on the floor just by the fireplace and, quite unconscious of what it really signified, said to Mrs Umney, 'I am afraid something has been spilt there.'

'Yes, madam,' replied the old housekeeper in a low voice, 'blood has been spilt on that spot.'

'How horrid,' cried Mrs Otis; 'I don't at all care for bloodstains in a sitting-room. It must be removed at once.'

The old woman smiled, and answered in the same low, mysterious voice, 'It is the blood of Lady Eleanore de Canterville, who was murdered on that very spot by her own husband, Sir Simon de Canterville, in 1575. Sir Simon survived her nine years, and disappeared suddenly under very mysterious circumstances. His body has never been discovered, but his guilty spirit still haunts the Chase. The bloodstain has been much admired by tourists and others, and cannot be removed.'

'That is all nonsense,' cried Washington Otis; 'Pinkerton's Champion Stain Remover and Paragon Detergent will clean it up in no time,' and before the terrified housekeeper could interfere he had fallen upon his knees, and was rapidly scouring the floor with a small stick of what looked like a black cosmetic. In a few moments no trace of the bloodstain could be seen.

'I knew Pinkerton would do it,' he exclaimed triumphantly, as he looked round at his admiring family; but no sooner had he said these words than a terrible flash of lightning lit up the sombre room, a fearful peal of thunder made them all start to their feet, and Mrs Umney fainted.

'What a monstrous climate!' said the American Minister calmly, as he lit a long cheroot. 'I guess the old country is so over-populated that they have not enough decent weather for everybody. I have always been of opinion that emigration is the only thing for England.'

'My dear Hiram,' cried Mrs Otis, 'what can we do with a woman who faints?'

'Charge it to her like breakages,' answered the minister; 'she won't faint after that;' and in a few moments Mrs Umney certainly came to. There was no doubt, however, that she was extremely upset, and she sternly warned Mr Otis to beware of some trouble coming to the house.

'I have seen things with my own eyes, sir,' she said, 'that would make any Christian's hair stand on end, and many and many a night I have not closed my eyes in sleep for the awful things that are done here.' Mr Otis, however, and his wife warmly assured the honest soul that they were not afraid of ghosts, and, after invoking the blessings of Providence on her new master and mistress, and making arrangements for an increase of salary, the old housekeeper tottered off to her own room.

The storm raged fiercely all that night, but nothing of particular note occurred. The next morning, however, when they came down to breakfast, they found the terrible stain of blood once again on the floor. 'I don't think it can be the fault of the Paragon Detergent,' said Washington, 'for I have tried it with everything. It must be the ghost.' He accordingly rubbed out the stain a second time, but the second morning it appeared again. The third morning also it was there, though the library had been locked up at night by Mr Otis himself, and the key carried upstairs. The whole family were now quite interested; Mr Otis began to suspect that he had been too dogmatic in his denial of the existence of ghosts, Mrs Otis expressed her intention of joining the Psychical Society, and Washington prepared a long letter to Messrs Myers and Podmore on the subject of the Permanence of Sanguineous Stains when connected with Crime. That night all doubts about the objective existence of phantasmata were removed for ever.

The day had been warm and sunny; and, in the cool of the evening, the whole family went out for a drive. They did not return home till nine o'clock, when they had a light supper. The conversation in no way turned upon ghosts, so there were not even those primary conditions of receptive expectation which so often precede the presentation of psychical phenomena. The subjects discussed, as I have since learned from Mr Otis, were merely such as form the ordinary conversation of cultured Americans of the better class, such as the immense superiority of Miss Fanny Davenport over Sarah Bernhardt as an actress; the difficulty of obtaining green corn, buckwheat cakes and hominy, even in the best English houses; the importance of Boston in the development of the world-soul; the advantages of the baggage-check system in railway travelling; and the sweetness of the New York accent as compared to the London drawl. No mention at all was made of the supernatural, nor was Sir Simon de Canterville alluded to in anyway. At eleven o'clock the family retired, and by half-past all the lights were out. Some time after, Mr Otis was awakened by a curious noise in the corridor, outside his room. It sounded like the clank of metal, and seemed to be coming nearer every moment. He got up at once, struck a match, and looked at the time. It was exactly one o'clock. He was quite calm, and felt his pulse, which was not at all feverish. The strange noise still continued, and with it he heard distinctly the sound of foot-steps. He put on his slippers, took a small oblong phial out of his dressing-case, and opened the door. Right in front of him he saw, in the wan moonlight, an old man of terrible aspect. His eyes were as red burning coals; long grey hair fell over his shoulders in matted coils; his garments, which were of antique cut, were soiled and ragged, and from his wrists and ankles hung heavy manacles and rusty gyves.

'My dear sir,' said Mr Otis, 'I really must insist on your oiling those chains, and have brought you for that purpose a small bottle of the Tammany Rising Sun Lubricator. It is said to be completely efficacious upon one application, and there are several testimonials to that effect on the wrapper from some of our most eminent native divines. I shall leave it here for you by the bedroom candles, and will be happy to supply you with more should you require it.' With these words the United States Minister laid the bottle down on a marble table, and, closing his door, retired to rest.

For a moment the Canterville ghost stood quite motionless in natural indignation; then, dashing the bottle violently upon the polished floor, he fled down the corridor, uttering hollow groans, and emitting a ghastly green light. Just, however, as he reached the top of the great oak staircase, a door was flung open, two little white-robed figures appeared, and a large pillow whizzed past his head! There was evidently no time to be lost, so, hastily adopting the Fourth Dimension of Space as a means of escape, he vanished through the wainscoting, and the house became quite quiet.

On reaching a small secret chamber in the left wing, he leaned up against a moonbeam to recover his breath, and began to try and realise his position. Never, in a brilliant and uninterrupted career of three hundred years, had he been so grossly insulted. He thought of the Dowager Duchess, whom he had frightened into a fit as she stood before the glass in her lace and diamonds; of the four housemaids, who had gone off into hysterics when he merely grinned at them through the curtains of one of the spare bedrooms; of the rector of the parish, whose candle he had blown out as he was coming late one night from the library, and who had been under the care of Sir William Gull ever since, a perfect martyr to nervous disorders; and of old Madame de Tremouillac, who, having wakened up one morning early and seen a skeleton seated in an armchair by the fire reading her diary, had been confined to her bed for six weeks with an attack of brain fever, and, on her recovery, had become reconciled to the church, and broken off her connection with that notorious sceptic Monsieur de Voltaire. He remembered the terrible night when the wicked Lord Canterville was found choking in his dressing-room, with the knave of diamonds halfway down his throat, and confessed, just before he died, that he had cheated Charles James Fox out of £50,000 at Crockford's by means of that very card, and swore that the ghost had made him swallow it. All his great achievements came back to him again, from the butler who had shot himself in the pantry because he had seen a green hand tapping at the window pane, to the beautiful Lady Stut-field, who was always obliged to wear a black velvet band round her throat to hide the mark of five fingers burnt upon her white skin, and who drowned herself at last in the carp-pond at the end of the King's Walk. With the enthusiastic egotism of the true artist he went over his most celebrated performances, and smiled bitterly to himself as he recalled to mind his last appearance as 'Red Ruben, or the Strangled Babe', his début as 'Gaunt Gibeon, the Bloodsucker of Bexley Moor', and the furore he had excited one lovely June evening by merely playing ninepins with his own bones upon the lawn-tennis ground. And after all this, some wretched modern Americans were to come and offer him the Rising Sun Lubricator, and throw pillows at his head! It was quite unbearable. Besides, no ghosts in history had ever been treated in this manner. Accordingly, he determined to have vengeance, and remained till daylight in an attitude of deep thought.

CHAPTER 3

The next morning when the Otis family met at breakfast, they discussed the ghost at some length. The United States Minister was naturally a little annoyed to find that his present had not been accepted. 'I have no wish,' he said, 'to do the ghost any personal injury, and I must say that, considering the length of time he has been in the house, I don't think it is at all polite to throw pillows at him' – a very just remark, at which, I am sorry to say, the twins burst into shouts of laughter. 'Upon the other hand,' he continued, 'if he really declines to use the Rising Sun Lubricator, we shall have to take his chains from him. It would be quite impossible to sleep, with such a noise going on outside the bedrooms.'

For the rest of the week, however, they were undisturbed, the only thing that excited any attention being the continual renewal of the bloodstain on the library floor. This certainly was very strange, as the door was always locked at night by Mr Otis, and the windows kept closely barred. The chameleon-like colour, also, of the stain excited a good deal of comment. Some mornings it was a dull (almost Indian) red, then it would be vermilion, then a rich purple, and once when they came down for family prayers, according to the simple rites of the Free American Reformed Episcopalian Church, they found it a bright emerald-green. These kaleidoscopic changes naturally amused the party very much, and bets on the subject were freely made every evening. The only person who did not enter into the joke was little Virginia, who, for some unexplained reason, was always a good deal distressed at the sight of the bloodstain, and very nearly cried the morning it was emerald-green.

The second appearance of the ghost was on Sunday night. Shortly after they had gone to bed they were suddenly alarmed by a fearful crash in the hall. Rushing downstairs, they found that a large suit of old armour had become detached from its stand, and had fallen on the stone floor, while, seated in a high-backed chair, was the Canterville ghost, rubbing his knees with an expression of acute agony on his face. The twins, having brought their peashooters with them, at once discharged two pellets on him, with that accuracy of aim which can only be attained by long and careful practice on a writing-master, while the United States Minister covered him with his revolver, and called upon him, in accordance with Californian etiquette, to hold up his hands! The ghost started up with a wild shriek of rage, and swept through them like a mist, extinguishing Washington Otis's candle as he passed, and so leaving them all in total darkness. On reaching the top of the staircase he recovered himself, and determined to give his celebrated peal of demoniac laughter. This he had on more than one occasion found extremely useful. It was said to have turned Lord Raker's wig grey in a single night, and had certainly made three of Lady Canterville's French governesses give warning before their month was up. He accordingly laughed his most horrible laugh, till the old vaulted roof rang and rang again, but hardly had the fearful echo died away when a door opened, and Mrs Otis came out in a light blue dressing-gown. 'I am afraid you are far from well,' she said, 'and have brought you a bottle of Dr Dobell's tincture. If it is indigestion, you will find it a most excellent remedy.' The ghost glared at her in fury, and began at once to make preparations for turning himself into a large black dog, an accomplishment for which he was justly renowned, and to which the family doctor always attributed the permanent idiocy of Lord Canterville's uncle, the Hon. Thomas Horton. The sound of approaching footsteps, however, made him hesitate in his fell purpose, so he contented himself with becoming faintly phosphorescent, and vanished with a deep churchyard groan, just as the twins had come up to him.

On reaching his room he entirely broke down, and became a prey to the most violent agitation. The vulgarity of the twins, and the gross materialism of Mrs Otis, were naturally extremely annoying, but what really distressed him most was that he had been unable to wear the suit of mail. He had hoped that even modern Americans would be thrilled by the sight of a Spectre In Armour, if for no more sensible reason, at least out of respect for their national poet Longfellow, over whose graceful and attractive poetry he himself had whiled away many a weary hour when the Cantervilles were up in town. Besides, it was his own suit. He had worn it with great success at the Kenilworth tournament, and had been highly complimented on it by no less a person than the Virgin Queen herself. Yet when he had put it on, he had been completely overpowered by the weight of the huge breastplate and steel casque, and had fallen heavily on the stone pavement, barking both his knees severely, and bruising the knuckles of his right hand.

For some days after this he was extremely ill, and hardly stirred out of his room at all, except to keep the bloodstain in proper repair. However, by taking great care of himself, he recovered, and resolved to make a third attempt to frighten the United States Minister and his family. He selected Friday, the 17th of August, for his appearance, and spent most of that day in looking over his wardrobe, ultimately deciding in favour of a large slouched hat with a red feather, a winding-sheet frilled at the wrists and neck, and a rusty dagger. Towards evening a violent storm of rain came on, and the wind was so high that all the windows and doors in the old house shook and rattled. In fact, it was just such weather as he loved. His plan of action was this. He was to make his way quietly to Washington Otis's room, gibber at him from the foot of the bed, and stab himself three times in the throat to the sound of slow music. He bore Washington a special grudge, being quite aware that it was he who was in the habit of removing the famous Canterville bloodstain, by means of Pinkerton's Paragon Detergent. Having reduced the reckless and foolhardy youth to a condition of abject terror, he was then to proceed to the room occupied by the United States Minister and his wife, and there to place a clammy hand on Mrs Otis's forehead, while he hissed into her trembling husband's ear the awful secrets of the charnel-house. With regard to little Virginia, he had not quite made up his mind. She had never insulted him in any way, and was pretty and gentle. A few hollow groans from the wardrobe, he thought, would be more than sufficient, or, if that failed to wake her, he might grabble at the counterpane with palsy-twitching fingers. As for the twins, he was quite determined to teach them a lesson. The first thing to be done was, of course, to sit upon their chests, so as to produce the stifling sensation of nightmare. Then, as their beds were quite close to each other, to stand between them in the form of a green, icy-cold corpse, till they became paralysed with fear, and, finally, to throw off the winding-sheet, and crawl round the room, with white bleached bones and one rolling eyeball, in the character of 'Dumb Daniel, or the Suicide's Skeleton', a role in which he had on more than one occasion produced a great effect, and which he considered quite equal to his famous part of 'Martin the Maniac, or the Masked Mystery'.

At half-past ten he heard the family going to bed. For some time he was disturbed by wild shrieks of laughter from the twins, who, with the light-hearted gaiety of schoolboys, were evidently amusing themselves before they retired to rest, but at a quarter past eleven all was still, and, as midnight sounded, he sallied forth. The owl beat against the window panes, the raven croaked from the old yew tree, and the wind wandered moaning round the house like a lost soul; but the Otis family slept unconscious of their doom, and high above the rain and storm he could hear the steady snoring of the Minister for the United States. He stepped stealthily out of the wainscoting, with an evil smile on his cruel, wrinkled mouth, and the moon hid her face in a cloud as he stole past the great oriel window, where his own arms and those of his murdered wife were blazoned in azure and gold. On and on he glided, like an evil shadow, the very darkness seeming to loathe him as he passed. Once he thought he heard something call, and stopped; but it was only the baying of a dog from the Red Farm, and he went on, muttering strange sixteenth-century curses, and ever and anon brandishing the rusty dagger in the midnight air. Finally he reached the corner of the passage that led to luckless Washington's room. For a moment he paused there, the wind blowing his long grey locks about his head, and twisting into grotesque and fantastic folds the nameless horror of the dead man's shroud. Then the clock struck the quarter, and he felt the time was come. He chuckled to himself, and turned the corner; but no sooner had he done so, than, with a piteous wail of terror, he fell back, and hid his blanched face in his long, bony hands. Right in front of him was standing a horrible spectre, motionless as a carven image, and monstrous as a madman's dream! Its head was bald and burnished; its face round, and fat, and white; and hideous laughter seemed to have writhed its features into an eternal grin. From the eyes streamed rays of scarlet light, the mouth was a wide well of fire, and a hideous garment, like to his own, swathed with its silent snows the Titan form. On its breast was a placard with strange writing in antique characters, some scroll of shame it seemed, some record of wild sins, some awful calendar of crime, and, with its right hand, it bore aloft a falchion of gleaming steel.

Never having seen a ghost before, he naturally was terribly frightened, and, after a second hasty glance at the awful phantom, he fled back to his room, tripping up in his long winding-sheet as he sped down the corridor, and finally dropping the rusty dagger into the minister's jackboots, where it was found in the morning by the butler. Once in the privacy of his own apartment, he flung himself down on a small pallet-bed, and hid his face under the clothes. After a time, however, the brave old Canterville spirit asserted itself, and he determined to go and speak to the other ghost as soon as it was daylight. Accordingly, just as the dawn was touching the hills with silver, he returned towards the spot where he had first laid eyes on the grisly phantom, feeling that, after all, two ghosts were better than one, and that, by the aid of his new friend, he might safely grapple with the twins. On reaching the spot, however, a terrible sight met his gaze. Something had evidently happened to the spectre, for the light had entirely faded from its hollow eyes, the gleaming falchion had fallen from its hand, and it was leaning up against the wall in a strained and uncomfortable attitude. He rushed forward and seized it in his arms, when, to his horror, the head slipped off and rolled on the floor, the body assumed a recumbent posture, and he found himself clasping a white dimity bed-curtain, with a sweeping-brush, a kitchen cleaver, and a hollow turnip lying at his feet! Unable to understand this curious transformation, he clutched the placard with feverish haste, and there, in the grey morning light, he read these fearful words:

> The Otis Ghoste
> Ye Onlie True and Originale Spook
> Beware of Ye Imitations
> All others are Counterfeite

The whole thing flashed across him. He had been tricked, foiled and outwitted! The old Canterville look came into his eyes; he ground his toothless gums together; and, raising his withered hands high above his head, swore, according to the picturesque phraseology of the antique school, that when Chanticleer had sounded twice his merry horn, deeds of blood would be wrought, and Murder walk abroad with silent feet.

Hardly had he finished this awful oath when, from the red-tiled roof of a distant homestead, a cock crew. He laughed a long, low, bitter laugh, and waited. Hour after hour he waited, but the cock, for some strange reason, did not crow again. Finally, at half-past seven, the arrival of the housemaids made him give up his fearful vigil, and he stalked back to his room, thinking of his vain hope and baffled purpose. There he consulted several books of ancient chivalry, of which he was exceedingly fond, and found that, on every occasion on which his oath had been used, Chanticleer had always crowed a second time. 'Perdition seize the naughty fowl,' he muttered. 'I have seen the day when, with my stout spear, I would have run him through the gorge, and made him crow for me as 'twere in death!' He then retired to a comfortable lead coffin, and stayed there till evening.

The next day the ghost was very weak and tired. The terrible excitement of the last four weeks was beginning to have its effect. His nerves were completely shattered, and he started at the slightest noise. For five days he kept his room, and at last made up his mind to give up the point of the bloodstain on the library floor. If the Otis family did not want it, they clearly did not deserve it. They were evidently people on a low, material plane of existence, and quite incapable of appreciating the symbolic value of sensuous phenomena. The question of phantasmic apparitions, and the development of astral bodies, was of course quite a different matter, and really not under his control. It was his solemn duty to appear in the corridor once a week, and to gibber from the large oriel window on the first and third Wednesday in every month, and he did not see how he could honourably escape from his obligations. It is quite true that his life had been very evil, but, upon the other hand, he was most conscientious in all things connected with the supernatural. For the next three Saturdays, accordingly, he traversed the corridor as usual between midnight and three o'clock, taking every possible precaution against being either heard or seen. He removed his boots, trod as lightly as possible on the old worm-eaten boards, wore a large black velvet cloak, and was careful to use the Rising Sun Lubricator for oiling his chains. I am bound to acknowledge that it was with a good deal of difficulty that he brought himself to adopt this last mode of protection. However, one night, while the family were at dinner, he slipped into Mr Otis's bedroom and carried off the bottle. He felt a little humiliated at first, but afterwards was sensible enough to see that there was a great deal to be said for the invention, and, to a certain degree, it served his purpose. Still, in spite of everything, he was not left unmolested. Strings were continually being stretched across the corridor, over which he tripped in the dark, and on one occasion, while dressed for the part of 'Black Isaac, or the Huntsman of Hogley Woods', he met with a severe fall, through treading on a butter-slide, which the twins had constructed from the entrance of the Tapestry Chamber to the top of the oak staircase. This last insult so enraged him, that he resolved to make one final effort to assert his dignity and social position, and determined to visit the insolent young Etonians the next night in his celebrated character of 'Reckless Rupert, or the Headless Earl'.

He had not appeared in this disguise for more than seventy years; in fact, not since he had so frightened pretty Lady Barbara Modish by means of it, that she suddenly broke off her engagement with the present Lord Canterville's grandfather, and ran away to Gretna Green with handsome Jack Castleton, declaring that nothing in the world would induce her to marry into a family that allowed such a horrible phantom to walk up and down the terrace at twilight. Poor Jack was afterwards shot in a duel by Lord Canterville on Wandsworth Common, and Lady Barbara died of a broken heart at Tunbridge Wells before the year was out, so, in every way, it had been a great success. It was, however, an extremely difficult 'make-up', if I may use such a theatrical expression in connection with one of the greatest mysteries of the supernatural, or, to employ a more scientific term, the higher-natural world, and it took him fully three hours to make his preparations. At last everything was ready, and he was very pleased with his appearance. The big leather riding-boots that went with the dress were just a little too large for him, and he could only find one of the two horse-pistols, but, on the whole, he was quite satisfied, and at a quarter past one he glided out of the wainscoting and crept down the corridor. On reaching the room occupied by the twins, which I should mention was called the Blue Bedchamber, on account of the colour of its hangings, he found the door just ajar. Wishing to make an effective entrance, he flung it wide open, when a heavy jug of water fell right down on him, wetting him to the skin, and just missing his left shoulder by a couple of inches. At the same moment he heard stifled shrieks of laughter proceeding from the four-post bed. The shock to his nervous system was so great that he fled back to his room as hard as he could go, and the next day he was laid up with a severe cold. The only thing that at all consoled him in the whole affair was the fact that he had not brought his head with him, for, had he done so, the consequences might have been very serious.

He now gave up all hope of ever frightening this rude American family, and contented himself, as a rule, with creeping about the passages in list slippers, with a thick red muffler round his throat for fear of draughts, and a small arquebuse, in case he should be attacked by the twins. The final blow he received occurred on the 19th of September. He had gone downstairs to the great entrance-hall, feeling sure that there, at any rate, he would be quite unmolested, and was amusing himself by making satirical remarks on the large Saroni photographs of the United States Minister and his wife, which had now taken the place of the Canterville family pictures. He was simply but neatly clad in a long shroud, spotted with churchyard mould, had tied up his jaw with a strip of yellow linen, and carried a small lantern and a sexton's spade. In fact, he was dressed for the character of 'Jonas the Graveless, or the Corpse-Snatcher of Chertsey Barn', one of his most remarkable impersonations, and one which the Cantervilles had every reason to remember, as it was the real origin of their quarrel with their neighbour, Lord Rufford. It was about a quarter past two o'clock in the morning, and, as far as he could ascertain, no one was stirring. As he was strolling towards the library, however, to see if there were any traces left of the bloodstain, suddenly there leaped out on him from a dark corner two figures, who waved their arms wildly above their heads, and shrieked out 'boo!' in his ear.

Seized with a panic, which, under the circumstances, was only natural, he rushed for the staircase, but found Washington Otis waiting for him there with the big garden-syringe; and being thus hemmed in by his enemies on every side, and driven almost to bay, he vanished into the great iron stove which, fortunately for him, was not lit, and had to make his way home through the flues and chimneys, arriving at his own room in a terrible state of dirt, disorder and despair.

After this he was not seen again on any nocturnal expedition. The twins lay in wait for him on several occasions, and strewed the passages with nutshells every night to the great annoyance of their parents and the servants, but it was of no avail. It was quite evident that his feelings were so wounded that he would not appear. Mr Otis consequently resumed his great work on the history of the Democratic Party, on which he had been engaged for some years; Mrs Otis organised a wonderful clam bake, which amazed the whole county; the boys took to lacrosse, euchre, poker, and other American national games; and Virginia rode about the lanes on her pony, accompanied by the young Duke of Cheshire, who had come to spend the last week of his holidays at Canterville Chase. It was generally assumed that the ghost had gone away, and, in fact, Mr Otis wrote a letter to that effect to Lord Canterville, who, in reply, expressed his great pleasure at the news, and sent his best congratulations to the minister's worthy wife.

The Otises, however, were deceived, for the ghost was still in the house, and though now almost an invalid, was by no means ready to let matters rest, particularly as he heard that among the guests was the young Duke of Cheshire, whose granduncle, Lord Francis Stilton, had once bet a hundred guineas with Colonel Carbury that he would play dice with the Canterville ghost, and was found the next morning lying on the floor of the cardroom in such a helpless paralytic state, that though he lived on to a great age, he was never able to say anything again but 'Double Sixes'. The story was well known at the time, though, of course, out of respect for the feelings of the two noble families, every attempt was made to hush it up; and a full account of all the circumstances connected with it will be found in the third volume of Lord Tattle's *Recollections of the Prince Regent and his Friends*. The ghost, then, was naturally very anxious to show that he had not lost his influence over the Stiltons, with whom, indeed, he was distantly connected, his own first cousin having been married *en secondes noces* to the Sieur de Bulkeley, from whom, as everyone knows, the Dukes of Cheshire are lineally descended. Accordingly, he made arrangements for appearing to Virginia's little lover in his celebrated impersonation of 'The Vampire Monk, or the Bloodless Benedictine', a performance so horrible that when old Lady Startup saw it, which she did on one fatal New Year's Eve, in the year 1764, she went off into the most piercing shrieks, which culminated in violent apoplexy, and died in three days, after disinheriting the Cantervilles, who were her nearest relations, and leaving all her money to her London apothecary. At the last moment, however, his terror of the twins prevented his leaving his room, and the little Duke slept in peace under the great feathered canopy in the Royal Bedchamber, and dreamed of Virginia.

A few days after this, Virginia and her curly-haired cavalier went out riding on Brockley meadows, where she tore her habit so badly in getting through a hedge, that, on her return home, she made up her mind to go up by the back staircase so as not to be seen. As she was running past the Tapestry Chamber, the door of which happened to be open, she fancied she saw someone inside, and thinking it was her mother's maid, who sometimes used to bring her work there, looked in to ask her to mend her habit. To her immense surprise, however, it was the Canterville Ghost himself! He was sitting by the window, watching the ruined gold of the yellowing trees fly through the air, and the red leaves dancing madly down the long avenue. His head was leaning on his hand, and his whole attitude was one of extreme depression. Indeed, so forlorn, and so much out of repair did he look, that little Virginia, whose first idea had been to run away and lock herself in her room, was filled with pity, and determined to try and comfort him. So light was her footfall, and so deep his melancholy, that he was not aware of her presence till she spoke to him.

'I am so sorry for you,' she said, 'but my brothers are going back to Eton tomorrow, and then, if you behave yourself, no one will annoy you.'

'It is absurd asking me to behave myself,' he answered, looking round in astonishment at the pretty little girl who had ventured to address him, 'quite absurd. I must rattle my chains, and groan through keyholes, and walk about at night, if that is what you mean. It is my only reason for existing.'

'It is no reason at all for existing, and you know you have been very wicked. Mrs Umney told us, the first day we arrived here, that you had killed your wife.'

'Well, I quite admit it,' said the Ghost petulantly, 'but it was a purely family matter, and concerned no one else.'

'It is very wrong to kill anyone,' said Virginia, who at times had a sweet Puritan gravity, caught from some old New England ancestor.

'Oh, I hate the cheap severity of abstract ethics! My wife was very plain, never had my ruffs properly starched, and knew nothing about cookery. Why, there was a buck I had shot in Hogley Woods, a magnificent pricket, and do you know how she had it sent up to table? However, it is no matter now, for it is all over, and I don't think it was very nice of her brothers to starve me to death, though I did kill her.'

'Starve you to death? Oh, Mr Ghost, I mean Sir Simon, are you hungry? I have a sandwich in my case. Would you like it?'

'No, thank you, I never eat anything now; but it is very kind of you, all the same, and you are much nicer than the rest of your horrid, rude, vulgar, dishonest family.'

'Stop!' cried Virginia, stamping her foot, 'it is you who are rude, and horrid, and vulgar, and as for dishonesty, you know you stole the paints out of my box to try and furbish up that ridiculous bloodstain in the library. First you took all my reds, including the vermilion, and I couldn't do any more sunsets, then you took the emerald-green and the chrome-yellow, and finally I had nothing left but indigo and Chinese white, and could only do moonlight scenes, which are always depressing to look at, and not at all easy to paint. I never told on you, though I was very much annoyed, and it was most ridiculous, the whole thing; for who ever heard of emerald-green blood?'

'Well, really,' said the Ghost, rather meekly, 'what was I to do? It is a very difficult thing to get real blood nowadays, and as your brother began it all with his Paragon Detergent, I certainly saw no reason why I should not have your paints. As for colour, that is always a matter of taste: the Cantervilles have blue blood, for instance, the very bluest in England; but I know you Americans don't care for things of this kind.'

'You know nothing about it, and the best thing you can do is to emigrate and improve your mind. My father will be only too happy to give you a free passage, and though there is a heavy duty on spirits of every kind, there will be no difficulty about the Custom House, as the officers are all Democrats. Once in New York, you are sure to be a great success. I know lots of people there who would give a hundred thousand dollars to have a grandfather, and much more than that to have a family Ghost.'

'I don't think I should like America.'

'I suppose because we have no ruins and no curiosities,' said Virginia satirically.

'No ruins! No curiosities!' answered the Ghost; 'you have your navy and your manners.'

'Good-evening; I will go and ask papa to get the twins an extra week's holiday.'

'Please don't go, Miss Virginia,' he cried; 'I am so lonely and so unhappy, and I really don't know what to do. I want to go to sleep and I cannot.'

'That's quite absurd! You have merely to go to bed and blow out the candle. It is very difficult sometimes to keep awake, especially at church, but there is no difficulty at all about sleeping. Why, even babies know how to do that, and they are not very clever.'

'I have not slept for three hundred years,' he said sadly, and Virginia's beautiful blue eyes opened in wonder; 'for three hundred years I have not slept, and I am so tired.'

Virginia grew quite grave, and her little lips trembled like rose-leaves. She came towards him, and kneeling down at his side, looked up into his old withered face.

'Poor, poor Ghost,' she murmured; 'have you no place where you can sleep?'

'Far away beyond the pine woods,' he answered, in a low dreamy voice, 'there is a little garden. There the grass grows long and deep, there are the great white stars of the hemlock flower, there the nightingale sings all night long. All night long he sings, and the cold, crystal moon looks down, and the yew tree spreads out its giant arms over the sleepers.'

Virginia's eyes grew dim with tears, and she hid her face in her hands.

'You mean the Garden of Death,' she whispered.

'Yes, Death. Death must be so beautiful. To lie in the soft brown earth, with the grasses waving above one's head, and listen to silence. To have no yesterday, and no tomorrow. To forget time, to forgive life, to be at peace. You can help me. You can open for me the portals of Death's house, for Love is always with you, and Love is stronger than Death is.'

Virginia trembled, a cold shudder ran through her, and for a few moments there was silence. She felt as if she was in a terrible dream.

Then the Ghost spoke again, and his voice sounded like the sighing of the wind.

'Have you ever read the old prophecy on the library window?'

'Oh, often,' cried the little girl, looking up; 'I know it quite well. It is painted in curious black letters, and it is difficult to read. There are only six lines:

> 'When a golden girl can win
> Prayer from out the lips of sin,
> When the barren almond bears,
> And a little child gives away its tears,
> Then shall all the house be still
> And peace come to Canterville.

But I don't know what they mean.'

'They mean,' he said sadly, 'that you must weep for me for my sins, because I have no tears, and pray with me for my soul, because I have no faith, and then, if you have always been sweet, and good, and gentle, the Angel of Death will have mercy on me. You will see fearful shapes in darkness, and wicked voices will whisper in your ear, but they will not harm you, for against the purity of a little child the powers of hell cannot prevail.'

Virginia made no answer, and the Ghost wrung his hands in wild despair as he looked down at her bowed golden head. Suddenly she stood up, very pale, and with a strange light in her eyes. 'I am not afraid,' she said firmly, 'and I will ask the Angel to have mercy on you.'

He rose from his seat with a faint cry of joy, and taking her hand bent over it with old-fashioned grace and kissed it. His fingers were as cold as ice, and his lips burned like fire, but Virginia did not falter, as he led her across the dusky room. On the faded green tapestry were broidered little huntsmen. They blew their tasselled horns and with their tiny hands waved to her to go back. 'Go back! little Virginia,' they cried, 'go back!' but the Ghost clutched her hand more tightly, and she shut her eyes against them. Horrible animals with lizard tails, and goggle eyes, blinked at her from the carven chimney-piece, and murmured 'Beware! little Virginia, beware! we may never see you again,' but the Ghost glided on more swiftly, and Virginia did not listen. When they reached the end of the room he stopped, and muttered some words she could not understand. She opened her eyes, and saw the wall slowly fading away like a mist, and a great black cavern in front of her. A bitter cold wind swept round them, and she felt something pulling at her dress. 'Quick, quick,' cried the Ghost, 'or it will be too late,' and, in a moment, the wainscoting had closed behind them, and the Tapestry Chamber was empty.

About ten minutes later, the bell rang for tea, and, as Virginia did not come down, Mrs Otis sent up one of the footmen to tell her. After a little time he returned and said that he could not find Miss Virginia anywhere. As she was in the habit of going out to the garden every evening to get flowers for the dinner-table, Mrs Otis was not at all alarmed at first, but when six o'clock struck, and Virginia did not appear, she became really agitated, and sent the boys out to look for her, while she herself and Mr Otis searched every room in the house. At half-past six the boys came back and said that they could find no trace of their sister anywhere. They were all now in the greatest state of excitement, and did not know what to do, when Mr Otis suddenly remembered that, some few days before, he had given a band of gypsies permission to camp in the park. He accordingly at once set off for Blackfell Hollow, where he knew they were, accompanied by his eldest son and two of the farm-servants. The little Duke of Cheshire, who was perfectly frantic with anxiety, begged hard to be allowed to go too, but Mr Otis would not allow him, as he was afraid there might be a scuffle. On arriving at the spot, however, he found that the gypsies had gone, and it was evident that their departure had been rather sudden, as the fire was still burning, and some plates were lying on the grass. Having sent off Washington and the two men to scour the district, he ran home, and despatched telegrams to all the police inspectors in the county, telling them to look out for a little girl who had been kidnapped by tramps or gypsies. He then ordered his horse to be brought round, and, after insisting on his wife and the three boys sitting down to dinner, rode off down the Ascot Road with a groom. He had hardly, however, gone a couple of miles when he heard some-body galloping after him, and, looking round, saw the little Duke coming up on his pony, with his face very flushed and no hat. 'I'm awfully sorry, Mr Otis,' gasped out the boy, 'but I can't eat any dinner as long as Virginia is lost. Please, don't be angry with me; if you had let us be engaged last year, there would never have been all this trouble. You won't send me back, will you? I can't go! I won't go!'

The minister could not help smiling at the handsome young

scapegrace, and was a good deal touched at his devotion to Virginia, so leaning down from his horse, he patted him kindly on the shoulders, and said, 'Well, Cecil, if you won't go back I suppose you must come with me, but I must get you a hat at Ascot.'

'Oh, bother my hat! I want Virginia!' cried the little Duke, laughing, and they galloped on to the railway station. There Mr Otis enquired of the station-master if anyone answering the description of Virginia had been seen on the platform, but could get no news of her. The station-master, however, wired up and down the line, and assured him that a strict watch would be kept for her, and, after having bought a hat for the little Duke from a linen-draper, who was just putting up his shutters, Mr Otis rode off to Bexley, a village about four miles away, which he was told was a well-known haunt of the gypsies, as there was a large common next to it. Here they roused up the rural policeman, but could get no information from him, and, after riding all over the common, they turned their horses' heads homewards and reached the Chase about eleven o'clock, dead-tired and almost heartbroken. They found Washington and the twins waiting for them at the gatehouse with lanterns, as the avenue was very dark. Not the slightest trace of Virginia had been discovered. The gypsies had been caught on Brockley meadows, but she was not with them, and they had explained their sudden departure by saying that they had mistaken the date of Chorton Fair, and had gone off in a hurry for fear they might be late. Indeed, they had been quite distressed at hearing of Virginia's disappearance, as they were very grateful to Mr Otis for having allowed them to camp in his park, and four of their number had stayed behind to help in the search. The carp-pond had been dragged, and the whole Chase thoroughly gone over, but without any result. It was evident that, for that night at any rate, Virginia was lost to them; and it was in a state of the deepest depression that Mr Otis and the boys walked up to the house, the groom following behind with the two horses and the pony. In the hall they found a group of frightened servants, and lying on a sofa in the library was poor Mrs Otis, almost out of her mind with terror and anxiety, and having her forehead bathed with eau-de-Cologne by the old housekeeper. Mr Otis at once insisted on her having something to eat, and ordered up supper for the whole party. It was a melancholy meal, as hardly anyone spoke, and even the twins were awestruck and subdued, as they were very fond of their sister. When they had finished, Mr Otis, in spite of the entreaties of the little Duke, ordered them all to bed, saying that nothing more could be done that night, and that he would telegraph in the morning to Scotland Yard for some detectives to be sent down immediately. Just as they were passing out of the dining-room, midnight began to boom from the clock tower, and when the last stroke sounded they heard a crash and a sudden shrill cry; a dreadful peal of thunder shook the house, a strain of unearthly music floated through the air, a panel at the top of the staircase flew back with a loud noise, and out on the landing, looking very pale and white, with a little casket in her hand, stepped Virginia. In a moment they had all rushed up to her. Mrs Otis clasped her passionately in her arms, the Duke smothered her with violent kisses, and the twins executed a wild war-dance round the group.

'Good heavens! child, where have you been?' said Mr Otis, rather angrily, thinking that she had been playing some foolish trick on them. 'Cecil and I have been riding all over the country looking for you, and your mother has been frightened to death. You must never play these practical jokes any more.'

'Except on the Ghost! Except on the Ghost!' shrieked the twins, as they capered about.

'My own darling, thank God you are found; you must never leave my side again,' murmured Mrs Otis, as she kissed the trembling child, and smoothed the tangled gold of her hair.

'Papa,' said Virginia quietly, 'I have been with the Ghost. He is dead, and you must come and see him. He had been very wicked, but he was really sorry for all that he had done, and he gave me this box of beautiful jewels before he died.'

The whole family gazed at her in mute amazement, but she was quite grave and serious; and, turning round, she led them through the opening in the wainscoting down a narrow secret corridor, Washington following with a lighted candle, which he had caught up from the table. Finally, they came to a great oak door, studded with rusty nails. When Virginia touched it, it swung back on its heavy hinges, and they found themselves in a little low room, with a vaulted ceiling, and one tiny grated window. Imbedded in the wall was a huge iron ring, and chained to it was a gaunt skeleton, that was stretched out at full length on the stone floor, and seemed to be trying to grasp with its long fleshless fingers an old-fashioned trencher and ewer, that were placed just out of its reach. The jug had evidently been once filled with water, as it was covered inside with green mould. There was nothing on the trencher but a pile of dust. Virginia knelt down beside the skeleton, and, folding her little hands together, began to pray silently, while the rest of the party looked on in wonder at the terrible tragedy whose secret was now disclosed to them.

'Hallo!' suddenly exclaimed one of the twins, who had been looking out of the window to try and discover in what wing of the house the room was situated. 'Hallo! the old withered almond tree has blossomed. I can see the flowers quite plainly in the moonlight.'

'God has forgiven him,' said Virginia gravely, as she rose to her feet, and a beautiful light seemed to illumine her face.

'What an angel you are!' cried the young Duke, and he put his arm round her neck and kissed her.

CHAPTER 7

Four days after these curious incidents a funeral started from Canterville Chase at about eleven o'clock at night. The hearse was drawn by eight black horses, each of which carried on its head a great tuft of nodding ostrich-plumes, and the leaden coffin was covered by a rich purple pall, on which was embroidered in gold the Canterville coat-of-arms. By the side of the hearse and the coaches walked the servants with lighted torches, and the whole procession was wonderfully impressive. Lord Canterville was the chief mourner, having come up specially from Wales to attend the funeral, and sat in the first carriage along with little Virginia. Then came the United States Minister and his wife, then Washington and the three boys, and in the last carriage was Mrs Umney. It was generally felt that, as she had been frightened by the ghost for more than fifty years of her life, she had the right to see the last of him. A deep grave had been dug in the corner of the churchyard, just under the old yew tree, and the service was read in the most impressive manner by the Reverend Augustus Dampier. When the ceremony was over, the servants, according to an old custom observed in the Canterville family, extinguished their torches, and, as the coffin was being lowered into the grave, Virginia stepped forward and laid on it a large cross made of white and pink almond-blossoms. As she did so, the moon came out from behind a cloud, and flooded with its silent silver the little churchyard, and from a distant copse a nightingale began to sing. She thought of the ghost's description of the Garden of Death, her eyes became dim with tears, and she hardly spoke a word during the drive home.

The next morning, before Lord Canterville went up to town, Mr Otis had an interview with him on the subject of the jewels the ghost had given to Virginia. They were perfectly magnificent, especially a certain ruby necklace with old Venetian setting, which was really a superb specimen of sixteenth-century work, and their value was so great that Mr Otis felt considerable scruples about allowing his daughter to accept them.

'My lord,' he said, 'I know that in this country mortmain is held to apply to trinkets as well as to land, and it is quite clear to me that these jewels are, or should be, heirlooms in your family. I must beg you, accordingly, to take them to London with you, and to regard them simply as a portion of your property which has been restored to you under certain strange conditions. As for my daughter, she is merely a child, and has as yet, I am glad to say, but little interest in such appurtenances of idle luxury. I am also informed by Mrs Otis, who, I may say, is no mean authority upon art – having had the privilege of spending several winters in Boston when she was a girl – that these gems are of great monetary worth, and if offered for sale would fetch a tall price. Under these circumstances, Lord Canterville, I feel sure that you will recognise how impossible it would be for me to allow them to remain in the possession of any member of my family; and, indeed, all such vain gauds and toys, however suitable or necessary to the dignity of the British aristocracy, would be completely out of place among those who have been brought up on the severe, and I believe immortal, principles of republican simplicity. Perhaps I should mention that Virginia is very anxious that you should allow her to retain the box as a memento of your unfortunate but misguided ancestor. As it is extremely old, and consequently a good deal out of repair, you may perhaps think fit to comply with her request. For my own part, I confess I am a good deal surprised to find a child of mine expressing sympathy with mediaevalism in any form, and can only account for it by the fact that Virginia was born in one of your London suburbs shortly after Mrs Otis had returned from a trip to Athens.'

Lord Canterville listened very gravely to the worthy minister's speech, pulling his grey moustache now and then to hide an involuntary smile, and when Mr Otis had ended, he shook him cordially by the hand, and said, 'My dear sir, your charming little daughter rendered my unlucky ancestor, Sir Simon, a very important service, and I and my family are much indebted to her for her marvellous courage and pluck. The jewels are clearly hers, and, egad, I believe that if I were heartless enough to take them from her, the wicked old fellow would be out of his grave in a fortnight, leading me the devil of a life. As for their being heirlooms, nothing is an heirloom that is not so mentioned in a will or legal document, and the existence of these jewels has been quite unknown. I assure you I have no more claim on them than your butler, and when Miss Virginia grows up I dare say she will be pleased to have pretty things to wear. Besides, you forget, Mr Otis, that you took the furniture and the ghost at a valuation, and anything that belonged to the ghost passed at once into your possession, as, whatever activity Sir Simon may have shown in the corridor at night, in point of law he was really dead, and you acquired his property by purchase.'

Mr Otis was a good deal distressed at Lord Canterville's refusal, and begged him to reconsider his decision, but the good-natured peer was quite firm, and finally induced the minister to allow his daughter to retain the present the ghost had given her, and when, in the spring of 1890, the young Duchess of Cheshire was presented at the Queen's first drawing-room on the occasion of her marriage, her jewels were the universal theme of admiration. For Virginia received the coronet, which is the reward of all good little American girls, and was married to her boy-lover as soon as he came of age. They were both so charming, and they loved each other so much, that everyone was delighted at the match, except the old Marchioness of Dumbleton, who had tried to catch the Duke for one of her seven unmarried daughters, and had given no less than three expensive dinner-parties for that purpose, and, strange to say, Mr Otis himself. Mr Otis was extremely fond of the young Duke personally, but, theoretically, he objected to titles, and, to use his own words, 'was not without apprehension lest, amid the enervating influences of a pleasure-loving aristocracy, the true principles of republican simplicity should be forgotten'. His objections, however, were completely overruled, and I believe that when he walked up the aisle of St George's, Hanover Square, with his daughter leaning on his arm, there was not a prouder man in the whole length and breadth of England.

The Duke and Duchess, after the honeymoon was over, went down to Canterville Chase, and on the day after their arrival they walked over in the afternoon to the lonely churchyard by the pine woods. There had been a great deal of difficulty at first about the inscription on Sir Simon's tombstone, but finally it had been decided to engrave on it simply the initials of the old gentleman's name, and the verse from the library window. The Duchess had brought with her some lovely roses, which she strewed upon the grave, and after they had stood by it for some time they strolled into the ruined chancel of the old abbey. There the Duchess sat down on a fallen pillar, while her husband lay at her feet smoking a cigarette and looking up at her beautiful eyes. Suddenly he threw his cigarette away, took hold of her hand, and said to her, 'Virginia, a wife should have no secrets from her husband.'

'Dear Cecil! I have no secrets from you.'

'Yes, you have,' he answered, smiling, 'you have never told me what happened to you when you were locked up with the ghost.'

'I have never told anyone, Cecil,' said Virginia gravely.

'I know that, but you might tell me.'

'Please don't ask me, Cecil, I cannot tell you. Poor Sir Simon! I owe him a great deal. Yes, don't laugh, Cecil, I really do. He made me see what Life is, and what Death signifies, and why Love is stronger than both.'

The Duke rose and kissed his wife lovingly.

'You can have your secret as long as I have your heart,' he murmured.

'You have always had that, Cecil.'

'And you will tell our children someday, won't you?'

Virginia blushed.

CHARLOTTE RIDDELL

Hertford O'Donnell's Warning

❦

Many a year, before chloroform was thought of, there lived in an old rambling house, in Gerrard Street, Soho, a clever Irishman called Hertford O'Donnell.

After Hertford O'Donnell he was entitled to write, MRCS for he had studied hard to gain this distinction, and the older surgeons at Guy's (his hospital) considered him one of the most rising operators of the day.

Having said chloroform was unknown at the time this story opens, it will strike my readers that, if Hertford O'Donnell were a rising and successful operator in those days, of necessity he combined within himself a larger number of striking qualities than are by any means necessary to form a successful operator in these.

There was more than mere hand skill, more than even thorough knowledge of his profession, then needful for the man, who, dealing with conscious subjects, essayed to rid them of some of the diseases to which flesh is heir. There was greater courage required in the manipulator of old than is altogether essential at present. Then, as now, a thorough mastery of his instruments, a steady hand, a keen eye, a quick dexterity were indispensable to a good operator; but, added to all these things, there formerly required a pulse which knew no quickening, a mental strength which never faltered, a ready power of adaptation in unexpected circumstances, fertility of resource in difficult cases, and a brave front under all emergencies.

If I refrain from adding that a hard as well as a courageous heart was an important item in the program, it is only out of deference to general opinion, which, among other strange delusions, clings to the belief that courage and hardness are antagonistic qualities.

Hertford O'Donnell, however, was hard as steel. He understood his work, and he did it thoroughly; but he cared no more for quivering nerves and shrinking muscles, for screams of agony, for faces white with pain, and teeth clenched in the extremity of anguish, than he did for the stony countenances of the dead, which so often in the dissecting room appalled younger and less experienced men.

He had no sentiment, and he had no sympathy. The human body was to him merely an ingenious piece of mechanism, which it was at once a pleasure and a profit to understand. Precisely as Brunel loved the Thames Tunnel, or any other singular engineering feat, so O'Donnell loved a patient on whom he had operated successfully, more especially if the ailment possessed by the patient were of a rare and difficult character.

And for this reason he was much liked by all who came under his hands, since patients are apt to mistake a surgeon's interest in their cases for interest in themselves; and it was gratifying to John Dicks, plasterer, and Timothy Regan, labourer, to be the happy possessors of remarkable diseases, which produced a cordial understanding between them and the handsome Irishman.

If he had been hard and cool at the moment of hacking them to pieces, that was all forgotten or remembered only as a virtue, when, after being discharged from hospital like soldiers who have served in a severe campaign, they met Mr O'Donnell in the street, and were accosted by that rising individual just as though he considered himself nobody.

He had a royal memory, this stranger in a strange land, both for faces and cases; and like the rest of his countrymen, he never felt it beneath his dignity to talk cordially to corduroy and fustian.

In London, as at Calgillan, he never held back his tongue from speaking a cheery or a kindly word. His manners were pliable enough, if his heart were not; and the porters, and the patients, and the nurses, and the students at Guy's were all pleased to see Hertford O'Donnell.

Rain, hail, sunshine, it was all the same; there was a life and a brightness about the man which communicated itself to those with whom he came in contact. Let the mud in the Borough be a foot deep or the London fog as thick as pea soup, Mr O'Donnell never lost his temper, never muttered a surly reply to the gatekeeper's salutation, but spoke out blithely and cheerfully to his pupils and his patients, to the sick and to the well, to those below and to those above him.

And yet, spite of all these good qualities, spite of his handsome face, his fine figure, his easy address, and his unquestionable skill as an operator, the dons, who acknowledged his talent, shook their heads gravely when two or three of them in private and solemn conclave talked confidentially of their younger brother.

If there were many things in his favour, there were more in his disfavour. He was Irish – not merely by the accident of birth, which might have been forgiven, since a man cannot be held accountable for such caprices of Nature, but by every other accident and design which is objectionable to the orthodox and respectable and representative English mind.

In speech, appearance, manner, taste, modes of expression, habits of life, Hertford O'Donnell was Irish. To the core of his heart he loved the island which he declared he never meant to re-visit; and among the English he moved to all intents and purposes a foreigner, who was resolved, so said the great prophets at Guy's, to rush to destruction as fast as he could, and let no man hinder him.

'He means to go the whole length of his tether,' observed one of the ancient wiseacres to another; which speech implied a conviction that Hertford O'Donnell, having sold himself to the Evil One, had determined to dive the full length of his rope into wickedness before being pulled to that shore where even wickedness is negative – where there are no mad carouses, no wild, sinful excitements, nothing but impotent wailing and gnashing of teeth.

A reckless, graceless, clever, wicked devil – going to his natural home as fast as in London anyone possibly speeds thither; this was the opinion his superiors held of the man who lived all alone with a housekeeper and her husband (who acted as butler) in his big house near Soho.

Gerrard Street – made famous by De Quincey – was not then an utterly shady and forgotten locality; carriage-patients found their way to the rising young surgeon – some great personages thought it not beneath them to fee an individual whose consulting rooms were situated on what was even then considered the wrong side of Regent Street. He was making money, and he was spending it; he was over head and ears in debt – useless, vulgar debt – senselessly contracted, never bravely faced. He had lived at an awful pace ever since he came to London, a pace which only a man who hopes and expects to die young can ever travel.

Life was good, was it? Death, was he a child, or a woman, or a coward, to be afraid of that hereafter? God knew all about the trifle which had upset his coach, better than the dons at Guy's.

Hertford O'Donnell understood the world pretty thoroughly, and the ways thereof were to him as roads often traversed; therefore, when he said that at the Day of Judgment he felt certain he should come off as well as many of those who censured him, it may be assumed, that, although his views of post-mortem punishment were vague, unsatisfactory and infidel, still his information as to the peccadilloes of his neighbours was such as consoled himself.

And yet, living all alone in the old house near Soho Square, grave thoughts would intrude into the surgeon's mind – thoughts which were, so to say, italicised by peremptory letters, and still more peremptory visits from people who wanted money.

Although he had many acquaintances he had no single friend, and accordingly these thoughts were received and brooded over in solitude – in those hours when, after returning from dinner, or supper, or congenial carouse, he sat in his dreary rooms, smoking his pipe and considering means and ways, chances and certainties.

In good truth he had started in London with some vague idea that as his life in it would not be of long continuance, the pace at which he elected to travel could be little consequence; but the years since his first entry into the Metropolis were now piled one on the top of another, his youth was behind him, his chances of longevity, spite of the way he had striven to injure his constitution, quite as good as ever. He had come to that period in existence, to that narrow strip to tableland, whence the ascent of youth and the descent of age are equally discernible – when, simply because he has lived for so many years, it strikes a man as possible he may have to live for just as many more, with the ability for hard work gone, with the boon companions scattered, with the capacity for enjoying convivial meetings a mere memory, with small means perhaps, with no bright hopes, with the pomp and the circumstance and the fairy carriages, and the glamour which youth flings over earthly objects, faded away like the pageant of yesterday, while the dreary ceremony of living has to be gone through today and tomorrow and the morrow after, as though the gay cavalcade and the martial music, and the glittering helmets and the prancing steeds were still accompanying the wayfarer to his journey's end.

Ah! my friends, there comes a moment when we must all leave the coach, with its four bright bays, its pleasant outside freight, its cheery company, its guard who blows the horn so merrily through villages and along lonely country roads.

Long before we reach that final stage, where the black business claims us for its own special property, we have to bid goodbye to all easy, thoughtless journeying, and betake ourselves, with what zest we may, to traversing the common of reality. There is no royal road across it that ever I heard of. From the king on his throne to the labourer who vaguely imagines what manner of being a king is, we have all to tramp across that desert at one period of our lives, at all events; and that period usually is when, as I have said, a man starts to find the hopes, and the strength, and the buoyancy of youth left behind, while years and years of life lie stretching out before him.

The coach he has travelled by drops him here. There is no appeal, there is no help; therefore, let him take off his hat and wish the new passengers good speed, without either envy or repining.

Behold, he has had his turn, and let whosoever will mount on the box-seat of life again, and tip the coachman and handle the ribbons – he shall take that pleasant journey no more, no more forever.

Even supposing a man's springtime to have been a cold and ungenial one, with bitter easterly winds and nipping frosts biting the buds and retarding the blossoms, still it was spring for all that – spring with the young green leaves sprouting forth, with the flowers unfolding tenderly, with the songs of the birds and the rush of waters, with the summer before and the autumn afar off, and winter remote as death and eternity, but when once the trees have donned their summer foliage, when the pure white blossoms have disappeared, and the gorgeous red and orange and purple blaze of many-coloured flowers fills the gardens, then if there come a wet, dreary day, the idea of autumn and winter is not so difficult to realise. When once twelve o'clock is reached, the evening and night become facts, not possibilities; and it was of the afternoon, and the evening, and the night, Hertford O'Donnell sat thinking on the Christmas Eve, when I crave permission to introduce him to my readers.

A good-looking man ladies considered him. A tall, dark-complectioned, black-haired, straight-limbed, deeply divinely blue-eyed fellow, with a soft voice, with a pleasant brogue, who had ridden like a centaur over the loose stone walls in Connemara, who had danced all night at the Dublin balls, who had walked across the Bennebeola Mountains, gun in hand, day after day, without weariness, who had fished in every one of the hundred lakes you can behold from the top of that mountain near the Recess Hotel, who had led a mad, wild life in Trinity College, and a wilder, perhaps, while 'studying for a doctor' – as the Irish phrase goes – in Edinburgh, and who, after the death of his eldest brother left him free to return to Calgillan, and pursue the usual utterly useless, utterly purposeless, utterly pleasant life of an Irish gentleman possessed of health, birth, and expectations, suddenly kicked over the paternal traces, bade adieu to Calgillan Castle and the blandishments of a certain beautiful Miss Clifden, beloved of his mother, and laid out to be his wife, walked down the avenue without even so much company as a gossoon to carry his carpetbag, shook the dust from his feet at the lodge gates, and took his seat on the coach, never once looking back at Calgillan, where his favourite mare was standing in the stable, his greyhounds chasing one another round the home paddock, his gun at half-cock in his dressing-room and his fishing-tackle all in order and ready for use.

He had not kissed his mother, or asked for his father's blessing; he left Miss Clifden, arrayed in her brand-new riding-habit, without a word of affection or regret; he had spoken no syllable of farewell to any servant about the place; only when the old woman at the lodge bade him good-morning and God-blessed his handsome face, he recommended her bitterly to look at it well for she would never see it more.

Twelve years and a half had passed since then, without either Miss Clifden or any other one of the Calgillan people having set eyes on Master Hertford's handsome face.

He had kept his vow to himself; he had not written home; he had not been indebted to mother or father for even a tenpenny-piece during the whole of that time; he had lived without friends; and he had lived without God – so far as God ever lets a man live without him.

One thing only he felt to be needful – money; money to keep him when the evil days of sickness, or age, or loss of practice came upon him. Though a spendthrift, he was not a simpleton; around him he saw men, who, having started with fairer prospects than his own, were, nevertheless, reduced to indigence; and he knew that what had happened to others might happen to himself.

An unlucky cut, slipping on a piece of orange-peel in the street, the merest accident imaginable, is sufficient to change opulence to beggary in the life's program of an individual, whose income depends on eye, on nerve, on hand; and, besides the consciousness of this fact, Hertford O'Donnell knew that beyond a certain point in his profession, progress was not easy.

It did not depend quite on the strength of his own bow and shield whether he counted his earnings by hundreds or thousands. Work may achieve competence; but mere work cannot, in a profession, at all events, compass fortune.

He looked around him, and he perceived that the majority of great men – great and wealthy – had been indebted for their elevation, more to the accident of birth, patronage, connection, or marriage, than to personal ability.

Personal ability, no doubt, they possessed; but then, little Jones, who lived in Frith Street, and who could barely keep himself and his wife and family, had ability, too, only he lacked the concomitants of success.

He wanted something or someone to puff him into notoriety – a brother at Court – a lord's leg to mend – a rich wife to give him prestige in Society; and in his absence of this something or someone, he had grown grey-haired and fainthearted while labouring for a world which utterly despises its most obsequious servants.

'Clatter along the streets with a pair of fine horses, snub the middle classes, and drive over the commonalty – that is the way to compass wealth and popularity in England,' said Hertford O'Donnell, bitterly; and as the man desired wealth and popularity, he sat before his fire, with a foot on each hob, and a short pipe in his mouth, considering how he might best obtain the means to clatter along the streets in his carriage, and splash plebeians with mud from his wheels like the best.

In Dublin he could, by means of his name and connection, have done well; but then he was not in Dublin, neither did he want to be. The bitterest memories of his life were inseparable from the very name of the Green Island, and he had no desire to return to it.

Besides, in Dublin, heiresses are not quite so plentiful as in London;

and an heiress, Hertford O'Donnell had decided, would do more for him then years of steady work.

A rich wife could clear him of debt, introduce him to fashionable practice, afford him that measure of social respectability which a medical bachelor invariably lacks, deliver him from the loneliness of Gerrard Street, and the domination of Mr and Mrs Coles.

To most men, deliberately bartering away their independence for money seems so prosaic a business that they strive to gloss it over even to themselves, and to assign every reason for their choice, save that which is really the influencing one.

Not so, however, with Hertford O'Donnell. He sat beside the fire scoffing over his proposed bargain – thinking of the lady's age, her money bags, her desirable house in town, her seat in the country, her snobbishness, her folly.

'It could be a fitting ending,' he sneered, 'and why I did not settle the matter tonight passes my comprehension. I am not a fool, to be frightened with old women's tales; and yet I must have turned white. I felt I did, and she asked me whether I were ill. And then to think of my being such an idiot as to ask her if she had heard anything like a cry, as though she would be likely to hear that, she with her poor parvenu blood, which I often imagine must have been mixed with some of her father's strong pickling vinegar. What a deuce could I have been dreaming about? I wonder what it really was.' And Hertford O'Donnell pushed his hair back off his forehead, and took another draught from the too familiar tumbler, which was placed conveniently on the chimney-piece.

'After expressly making up my mind to propose, too!' he mentally continued. 'Could it have been conscience – that myth, which some-body, who knew nothing about the matter, said, "Makes cowards of us all"? I don't believe in conscience; and even if there be such a thing capable of being developed by sentiment and cultivation, why should it trouble me? I have no intention of wronging Miss Janice Price Ingot, not the least. Honestly and fairly I shall marry her; honestly and fairly I shall act by her. An old wife is not exactly an ornamental article of furniture in a man's house; and I do not know that the fact of her being well gilded makes her look any handsomer. But she shall have no cause for complaint; and I will go and dine with her tomorrow, and settle the matter.'

Having arrived at which resolution, Mr O'Donnell arose, kicked down the fire – burning hollow – with the heel of his boot, knocked the ashes out of his pipe, emptied his tumbler, and bethought him it was time to go to bed. He was not in the habit of taking his rest so early as a quarter to twelve o'clock; but he felt unusually weary – tired mentally and bodily – and lonely beyond all power of expression.

'The fair Janet would be better than this,' he said, half aloud; and then, with a start and a shiver, and a blanched face, he turned sharply round, while a low, sobbing, wailing cry echoed mournfully through the room. No form of words could give an idea of the sound. The plaintiveness of the Aeolian harp – that plaintiveness which so soon affects and lowers the highest spirits – would have seemed wildly gay in comparison with the sadness of the cry which seemed floating in the air. As the summer wind comes and goes among the trees, so that mournful wail came and went – came and went. It came in a rush of sound, like a gradual crescendo managed by a skilful musician, and died away in a lingering note, so gently that the listener could scarcely tell the exact moment when it faded into utter silence.

I say faded, for it disappeared as the coastline disappears in the twilight, and there was total stillness in the apartment.

Then, for the first time, Hertford O'Donnell looked at his dog, and beholding the creature crouched into a corner beside the fireplace, called upon him to come out.

His voice sounded strange even to himself, and apparently the dog thought so too, for he made no effort to obey the summons.

'Come here, sir,' his master repeated, and then the animal came crawling reluctantly forward with his hair on end, his eyes almost starting from his head, trembling violently, as the surgeon, who caressed him, felt.

'So you heard it, Brian?' he said to the dog. 'And so your ears are sharper than Miss Ingot's, old fellow. It's a mighty queer thing to think of, being favoured with a visit from a Banshee in Gerrard Street; and as the lady has travelled so far, I only wish I knew whether there is any sort of refreshment she would like to take after her long journey.'

He spoke loudly, and with a certain mocking defiance, seeming to think the phantom he addressed would reply; but when he stopped at the end of his sentence, no sound came through the stillness. There was a dead silence in the room – a silence broken only by the falling of cinders on the hearth and the breathing of his dog.

'If my visitor would tell me,' he proceeded, for whom this lamentation is being made, whether for myself, or for some member of my illustrious family, I should feel immensely obliged. It seems too much honour for a poor surgeon to have such attention paid him. Good Heavens! What is that?' he exclaimed, as a ring, loud and peremptory, woke all the echoes in the house, and brought his housekeeper, in a state of distressing dishabille, 'out of her warm bed,' as she subsequently stated, to the head of the staircase.

Across the hall Hertford O'Donnell strode, relieved at the prospect of speaking to any living being. He took no precaution of putting up the chain, but flung the door wide. A dozen burglars would have proved welcome in comparison with that ghostly intruder he had been interviewing; therefore, as has been said, he threw the door wide, admitting a rush of wet, cold air, which made poor Mrs Coles' few remaining teeth chatter in her head.

'Who is there? What do you want?' asked the surgeon, seeing no person, and hearing no voice. 'Who is there? Why the devil can't you speak?'

When even this polite exhortation failed to elicit an answer, he passed out into the night and looked up the street and down the street, to see nothing but the driving rain and the blinking lights.

'If this goes on much longer I shall soon think I must be either mad or drunk,' he muttered, as he re-entered the house and locked and bolted the door once more.

'Lord's sake! What is the matter, sir?' asked Mrs Coles, from the upper flight, careful only to reveal the borders of her nightcap to Mr O'Donnell's admiring gaze. 'Is anybody killed? Have you to go out, sir?'

'It was only a runaway rig,' he answered, trying to reassure himself with an explanation he did not in his heart believe.

'Runaway – I'd run away them!' murmured Mrs Coles, as she retired to the conjugal couch, where Coles was, to quote her own expression, 'snoring like a pig through it all.'

Almost immediately afterwards she heard her master ascend the stairs and close his bedroom door.

'Madam will surely be too much of a gentlewoman to intrude here,' thought the surgeon, scoffing even at his own fears; but when he lay down he did not put out his light, and made Brian leap up and crouch on the coverlet beside him.

The man was fairly frightened, and would have thought it no discredit to his manhood to acknowledge as much. He was not afraid of death, he was not afraid of trouble, he was not afraid of danger; but he was afraid of the Banshee; and as he lay with his hand on the dog's head, he recalled the many stories he had been told concerning this family retainer in the days of his youth.

He had not thought about her for years and years. Never before had he heard her voice himself. When his brother died she had not thought it necessary to travel up to Dublin and give him notice of the impending catastrophe. 'If she had, I would have gone down to Calgillan, and perhaps saved his life,' considered the surgeon. 'I wonder who this is for? If for me, that will settle my debts and my marriage. If I could be quite certain it was either of the old people, I would start tomorrow.'

Then vaguely his mind wandered on to think of every Banshee story he had ever heard in his life. About the beautiful lady with the wreath of flowers, who sat on the rocks below Red Castle, in the Country Antrim, crying till one of the sons died for love of her; about the Round Chamber at Dunluce, which was swept clean by the Banshee every night; about the bed in a certain great house in Ireland, which was slept in constantly, although no human being ever passed in or out after dark; about that General Officer who, the night before Waterloo, said to a friend, 'I have heard the Banshee, and shall not come off the field alive tomorrow; break the news gently to poor Carry'; and who, nevertheless, coming safe off the field, had subsequently news about poor Carry broken tenderly and pitifully to him; about the lad, who, aloft in the rigging, hearing through the night a sobbing and wailing coming over the waters, went down to the captain and told him he was afraid they were somehow out of their reckoning, just in time to save the ship, which, when morning broke, they found but for his warning would have been on the rocks. It was blowing great guns, and the sea was all in a fret and turmoil, and they could sometimes see in the trough of the waves, as down a valley, the cruel black reefs they had escaped.

On deck the captain stood speaking to the boy who had saved them, and asking how he knew of their danger; and when the lad told him, the captain laughed, and said her ladyship had been outwitted that time.

But the boy answered, with a grave shake of his head, that the warning was either for him or his, and that if he got safe to port there would be bad tidings waiting for him from home; whereupon the captain bade him go below, and get some brandy and lie down.

He got the brandy, and he lay down, but he never rose again; and when the storm abated – when a great calm succeeded to the previous tempest – there was a very solemn funeral at sea; and on their arrival at Liverpool the captain took a journey to Ireland to tell a widowed mother how her only son died, and to bear his few effects to the poor desolate soul.

And Hertford O'Donnell thought again about his own father riding full-chase across country, and hearing, as he galloped by a clump of plantation, something like a sobbing and wailing. The hounds were in full cry, but he still felt, as he afterwards expressed it, that there was something among those trees he could not pass; and so he jumped off his horse, and hung the reins over the branch of a Scotch fir, and beat the cover well, but not a thing could he find in it.

Then, for the first time in his life, Miles O'Donnell turned his horse's head from the hunt, and, within a mile of Calgillan, met a man running to tell him his brother's gun had burst, and injured him mortally.

And he remembered the story also, of how Mary O'Donnell, his great aunt, being married to a young Englishman, heard the Banshee as she sat one evening waiting for his return; and of how she, thinking the bridge by which he often came home unsafe for horse and man, went out in a great panic, to meet and entreat him to go round by the main road for her sake. Sir Edward was riding along in the moonlight, making straight for the bridge, when he beheld a figure dressed all in white crossing it. Then there was a crash, and the figure disappeared.

The lady was rescued and brought back to the hall; but next morning there were two dead bodies within its walls – those of Lady Eyreton and her stillborn son.

Quicker than I write them, these memories chased one another through Hertford O'Donnell's brain; and there was one more terrible memory than any, which would recur to him, concerning an Irish nobleman who, seated alone in his great town house in London, heard the Banshee, and rushed out to get rid of the phantom, which wailed in his ear, nevertheless, as he strode down Piccadilly. And then the surgeon remembered how that nobleman went with a friend to the opera, feeling sure that there no Banshee, unless shed had a box, could find admittance, until suddenly he heard her singing up among the highest part of the scenery, with a terrible mournfulness, and a pathos which made the prima donna's tenderest notes seem harsh by comparison.

As he came out, some quarrel arose between him and a famous fire-eater, against whom he stumbled; and the result was that the next afternoon there was a new Lord, for he was killed in a duel with Captain Bravo.

Memories like these are not the most enlivening possible; they are apt to make a man fanciful, and nervous, and wakeful; but as time ran on, Hertford O'Donnell fell asleep, with his candle still burning, and Brian's cold nose pressed against his hand.

He dreamt of his mother's family – the Hertfords of Artingbury, Yorkshire, far-off relatives of Lord Hertford – so far off that even Mrs O'Donnell held no clue to the genealogical maze.

He thought he was at Artingbury, fishing; that it was a misty summer morning, and the fish rising beautifully. In his dreams he hooked one after another, and the boy who was with him threw them into the basket.

At last there was one more difficult to land than the others; and the boy, in his eagerness to watch the sport, drew nearer and nearer to the bank, while the fisher, intent on his prey, failed to notice his companions' danger.

Suddenly there was a cry, a splash, and the boy disappeared from sight.

Next instance he rose again, however, and then, for the first time, Hertford O'Donnell saw his face.

It was one he knew well.

In a moment he plunged into the water, and struck out for the lad. He had him by the hair, he was turning to bring him back to land, when the stream suddenly changed into a wide, wild, shoreless sea, where the billows were chasing one another with a mad demoniac mirth.

For a while O'Donnell kept the lad and himself afloat. They were swept under the waves, and came up again, only to see larger waves rushing towards them; but through all, the surgeon never loosened his hold, until a tremendous billow, engulfing them both, tore the boy from his grasp.

With the horror of his dream upon him he awoke to hear a voice quite distinctly: 'Go to the hospital – go at once!'

The surgeon started up in bed, rubbing his eyes, and looked around. The candle was flickering faintly in its socket. Brian, with his ears pricked forward, had raised his head at his master's sudden movement.

Everything was quiet, but still those words were ringing in his ear: 'Go to the hospital – go at once!'

The tremendous peal of the bell overnight, and this sentence, seemed to be simultaneous.

That he was wanted at Guy's – wanted imperatively – came to O'Donnell like an inspiration. Neither sense nor reason had anything to do with the conviction that roused him out of bed, and made him dress as speedily as possible, and grope his way down the staircase, Brian following.

He opened the front door, and passed out into the darkness. The rain was over, and the stars were shining as he pursued his way down Newport Market, and thence, winding in and out in a southeasterly direction, through Lincoln's Inn Fields and Old Square to Chancery Lane, whence he proceeded to St Paul's.

Along the deserted streets he resolutely continued his walk. He did not know what he was going to Guy's for. Some instinct was urging him on, and he neither strove to combat nor control it. Only once did the thought of turning back cross his mind, and that was at the archway leading into Old Square. There he had paused for a moment, asking himself whether he were not gone stark, staring mad; but Guy's seemed preferable to the haunted house in Gerrard Street, and he walked resolutely on, determined to say, if any surprise were expressed at his appearance, that he had been sent for.

Sent for? – yea, truly; but by whom?

On through Cannot Street; on over London Bridge, where the lights flickered in the river, and the sullen splash of the water flowing beneath the arches, washing the stone piers, could be heard, now the human din was hushed and lulled to sleep. On, thinking of many things: of the days of his youth; of his dead brother; of his father's heavily encumbered estate; of the fortune his mother had vowed she would leave to some charity rather than to him, if he refused to marry according to her choice; of his wild life in London; of the terrible cry he had heard overnight – that unearthly wail which he could not drive from his memory even when he entered Guy's, and confronted the porter, who said: 'You have been sent for, sir; did you meet the messenger?'

Like one in a dream, Hertford O'Donnell heard him; like one in a dream, also, he asked what was the matter.

'Bad accident, sir; fire; feel off a balcony – unsafe – old building. Mother and child – a son; child with compound fracture of thigh.'

This, the joint information of porter and house-surgeon, mingled together, and made a boom in Mr O'Donnell's ears like the sound of the sea breaking on a shingly shore.

Only one sentence he understood properly – 'Immediate amputation necessary.' At this point he grew cool; he was the careful, cautious, successful surgeon, in a moment.

'The child you say?' he answered. 'Let me see him.'

The Guy's Hospital of today may be different to the Guy's Hertford O'Donnell knew so well. Railways have, I believe, swept away the old operation room; railways may have changed the position of the former accident ward, to reach which, in the days of which I am writing, the two surgeons had to pass a staircase leading to the upper stories.

On the lower step of this staircase, partially in shadow, Hertford O'Donnell beheld, as he came forward, an old woman seated.

An old woman with streaming grey hair, with attenuated arms, with head bowed forward, with scanty clothing, with bare feet; who never looked up at their approach, but sat unnoticing, shaking her head and wringing her hands in an extremity of despair.

'Who is that?' asked Mr O'Donnell, almost involuntarily.

'Who is what?' demanded his companion.

'That – that woman,' was the reply.

'What woman?'

'There – are you blind? – seated on the bottom step of the staircase. What is she doing?' persisted Mr O'Donnell.

'There is no woman near us,' his companion answered, looking at the rising surgeon very much as though he suspected him of seeing double.

'No woman!' scoffed Hertford. 'Do you expect me to disbelieve the evidence of my own eyes?' and he walked up to the figure, meaning to touch it.

But as he assayed to do so, the woman seemed to rise in the air and float away, with her arms stretched high up over her head, uttering such a wail of pain, and agony, and distress, as caused the Irishman's blood to curdle.

'My God! Did you hear that?' he said to his companion.

'What?' was the reply.

Then, although he knew the sound had fallen on deaf ears, he answered: 'The wail of the Banshee! Some of my people are doomed!'

'I trust not,' answered the house-surgeon, who had an idea, nevertheless, that Hertford O'Donnell's Banshee lived in a whisky bottle, and would at some remote day make an end to the rising and clever operator.

With nerves utterly shaken, Mr O'Donnell walked forward to the accident ward. There with his face shaded from the light, lay his patient – a young boy, with a compound fracture of the thing.

In that ward, in the face of actual danger or pain capable of relief, the surgeon had never known faltering or fear; and now he carefully examined the injury, felt the pulse, enquired as to the treatment pursued, and ordered the sufferer to be carried to the operation room.

While he was looking out his instruments he heard the boy lying on the table murmur faintly: 'Tell her not to cry so – tell her not to cry.'

'What is he talking about?' Hertford O'Donnell enquired.

'The nurse says he has been speaking about some woman crying ever since he came in – his mother, most likely,' answered one of the attendants.

'He is delirious then?' observed the surgeon.

'No, sir,' pleaded the boy, excitedly, 'no; it is that woman – that woman with the grey hair. I saw her looking from the upper window before the balcony gave way. She has never left me since, and she won't be quiet, wringing her hands and crying.'

'Can you see her now?' Hertford O'Donnell enquired, stepping to the side of the table. 'Point out where she is.'

Then the lad stretched forth a feeble finger in the direction of the door, where clearly, as he had seen her seated on the stairs, the surgeon saw a woman standing – a woman with grey hair and scanty clothing, and upstretched arms and bare feet.

'A word with you, sir,' O'Donnell said to the house-surgeon, drawing him back from the table. 'I cannot perform this operation: send for some other person. I am ill; I am incapable.'

'But,' pleaded the other, 'there is no time to get anyone else. We sent for Mr West, before we troubled you, but he was out of town, and all the rest of the surgeons live so far away. Mortification may set in at any moment and – .'

'Do you think you require to teach me my business?' was the reply. 'I know the boy's life hangs on a thread, and that is the very reason I cannot operate. I am not fit for it. I tell you I have seen tonight that which unnerves me utterly. My hand is not steady. Send for someone else without delay. Say I am ill – dead! – what you please. Heavens! There she is again, right over the boy! Do you hear her?' and Hertford O'Donnell fell fainting on the floor.

How long he lay in that deathlike swoon I cannot say; but when he returned to consciousness, the principal physician of Guy's was standing beside him in the cold grey light of the Christmas morning.

'The boy?' murmured O'Donnell, faintly.

'Now, my dear fellow, kept yourself quiet,' was the reply.

'The boy?' he repeated, irritably. 'Who operated?'

'No one,' Dr Lanson answered. 'It would have been useless cruelty. Mortification had set in and – '

Hertford O'Donnell turned his face to the wall, and his friend could not see it.

'Do not distress yourself,' went on the physician, kindly. 'Allington says he could not have survived the operation in any case. He was quite delirious from the first, raving about a woman with grey hair and – '

'I know,' Hertford O'Donnell interrupted; 'and the boy had a mother, they told me, or I dreamt it.'

'Yes, she was bruised and shaken, but not seriously injured.'

'Has she blue eyes and fair hair – fair hair all rippling and wavy? Is she white as a lily, with just a faint flush of colour in her cheek? Is she young and trusting and innocent? No; I am wandering. She must be nearly thirty now. Go, for God's sake, and tell me if you can find a woman you could imagine having once been a girl such as I describe.'

'Irish?' asked the doctor; and O'Donnell made a gesture of assent.

'It is she then,' was the reply, 'a woman with the face of an angle.'

'A woman who should have been my wife,' the surgeon answered; 'whose child was my son.'

'Lord help you!' ejaculated the doctor. Then Hertford O'Donnell raised himself from the sofa where they had laid him, and told his companion the story of his life – how there had been a bitter feud between his people and her people – how they were divided by old animosities and by difference of religion – how they had met by stealth, and exchanged rings and vows, all for naught – how is family had insulted hers, so that her father, wishful for her to marry a kinsman of his own, bore her off to a faraway land, and made her write him a letter of eternal farewell – how his own parents had kept all knowledge of the quarrel from him till she was utterly beyond his reach – how they had vowed to discard him unless he agreed to marry according to their wishes – how he left home, and came to London, and sought his fortune. All this Hertford O'Donnell repeated; and when he had finished, the bells were ringing for morning service – ringing loudly, ringing joyfully, 'Peace on earth, goodwill towards men.'

But there was little peace that morning for Hertford O'Donnell. He had to look on the face of his dead son, wherein he beheld, as though reflected, the face of the boy in this dream.

Afterwards, stealthily he followed his friend, and beheld, with her eyes closed, her cheeks pale and pinched, her hair thinner but still falling like a veil over her, the love of his youth, the only woman he had ever loved devotedly and unselfishly.

There is little space left here to tell of how the two met at last – of how the stone of the years seemed suddenly rolled away from the tomb of their past, and their youth arose and returned to them, even amid their tears.

She had been true to him, through persecution, through contumely, through kindness, which was more trying; through shame, and grief, and poverty, she had been loyal to the lover of her youth; and before the New Year dawned there came a letter from Calgillan, saying that the Banshee's wail had been heard there, and praying Hertford, if he were still alive, to let bygones be bygones, in consideration of the long years of estrangement – the anguish and remorse of his afflicted parents.

More than that. Hertford O'Donnell, if a reckless man, was

honourable; and so, on the Christmas Day when he was to have proposed for Miss Ingot, he went to that lady, and told her how he had wooed and won, in the years of his youth, one who after many days was miraculously restored to him; and from the hour in which he took her into his confidence, he never thought her either vulgar or foolish, but rather he paid homage to the woman who, when she had heard the whole tale repeated, said, simply 'Ask her to come to me till you can claim her – and God bless you both!'

CHARLOTTE RIDDELL

The Last of Squire Ennismore

❧❧❧

'Did I see it myself? No, sir; I did not see it; and my father before me did not see it; nor his father before him, and he was Phil Regan, just the same as myself. But it is true, for all that; just as true as that you are looking at the very place where the whole thing happened. My great-grandfather (and he did not die till he was ninety-eight) used to tell, many and many's the time, how he met the stranger, night after night, walking lonesome-like about the sands where most of the wreckage came ashore.'

'And the old house, then, stood behind that belt of Scotch firs?'

'Yes; and a fine house it was, too. Hearing so much talk about it when a boy, my father said, made him often feel as if he knew every room in the building, though it had all fallen to ruin before he was born. None of the family ever lived in it after the squire went away. Nobody else could be got to stop in the place. There used to be awful noises, as if something was being pitched from the top of the great staircase down in to the hall; and then there would be a sound as if a hundred people were clinking glasses and talking all together at once. And then it seemed as if barrels were rolling in the cellars; and there would be screeches, and howls, and laughing, fit to make your blood run cold. They say there is gold hid away in the cellars; but not one has ever ventured to find it. The very children won't come here to play; and when the men are ploughing the field behind, nothing will make them stay in it, once the day begins to change. When the night is coming on, and the tide creeps in on the sand, more than one thinks he has seen mighty queer things on the shore.'

'But what is it really they think they see? When I asked my landlord to tell me the story from beginning to end, he said he could not remember it; and, at any rate, the whole rigmarole was nonsense, put together to please strangers.'

'And what is he but a stranger himself? And how should he know the doings of real quality like the Ennismores? For they were gentry, every one of them – good old stock; and as for wickedness, you might have searched Ireland through and not found their match. It is a sure thing, though, that if Riley can't tell you the story, I can; for, as I said, my own people were in it, of a manner of speaking. So, if your honour will rest yourself off your feet, on that bit of a bank, I'll set down my creel and give you the whole pedigree of how Squire Ennismore went away from Ardwinsagh.'

It was a lovely day, in the early part of June; and, as the Englishman cast himself on a low ridge of sand, he looked over Ardwinsagh Bay with a feeling of ineffable content. To his left lay the Purple Headland; to his right, a long range of breakers, that went straight out into the Atlantic till they were lost from sight; in front lay the Bay of Ardwinsagh, with its bluish-green water sparkling in the summer sunlight, and here and there breaking over some sunken rock, against which the waves spent themselves in foam.

'You see how the current's set, Sir? That is what makes it dangerous for them as doesn't know the coast, to bathe here at any time, or walk when the tide is flowing. Look how the sea is creeping in now, like a racehorse at the finish. It leaves that tongue of sand bars to the last, and then, before you could look round, it has you up to the middle. That is why I made bold to speak to you; for it is not alone on the account of Squire Ennismore the bay has a bad name. But it is about him and the old house you want to hear. The last mortal being that tried to live in it, my great-grandfather said, was a creature, by name Molly Leary; and she had neither kith nor kin, and begged for her bite and sup, sheltering herself at night in a turf cabin she had built at the back of a ditch. You may be sure she thought herself a made woman when the agent said, "Yes: she might try if she could stop in the house; there was peat and bog-wood," he told her, "and half a crown a week for the winter, and a golden guinea once Easter came," when the house was to be put in order for the family; and his wife gave Molly some warm clothes and a blanket or two; and she was well set up.

'You may be sure she didn't choose the worst room to sleep in; and for a while all went quiet, till one night she was wakened by feeling the bedstead lifted by the four corners and shaken like a carpet. It was a heavy four-post bedstead, with a solid top: and her life seemed to go out of her with the fear. If it had been a ship in a storm off the Headland, it couldn't have pitched worse and then, all of a sudden, it was dropped with such a bang as nearly drove the heart into her mouth.

'But that, she said, was nothing to the screaming and laughing, and hustling and rushing that filled the house. If a hundred people had been running hard along the passages and tumbling downstairs, they could not have made greater noise.

'Molly never was able to tell how she got clear of the place; but a man coming late home from Ballycloyne Fair found the creature crouched under the old thorn there, with very little on her – saving your honour's presence. She had a bad fever, and talked about strange things, and never was the same woman after.'

'But what was the beginning of all this? When did the house first get the name of being haunted?'

'After the old Squire went away: that was what I purposed telling you. He did not come here to live regularly till he had got well on in years. He was near seventy at the time I am talking about; but he held himself as upright as ever, and rode as hard as the youngest; and could have drunk a whole roomful under the table, and walked up to bed as unconcerned as you please at the dead of the night.

'He was a terrible man. You couldn't lay your tongue to a wickedness he had not been in the forefront of – drinking, duelling, gambling – all manner of sins had been meat and drink to him since he was a boy almost. But at last he did something in London so bad, so beyond the beyonds, that he thought he had best come home and live among people who did not know so much about his goings on as the English. It was said that he wanted to try and stay in this world for ever; and that he had got some secret drops that kept him well and hearty. There was something wonderful queer about him, anyhow.

'He could hold foot with the youngest; and he was strong, and had a fine fresh colour in his face; and his eyes were like a hawk's; and there was not a break in his voice – and him near upon three-score and ten!

'At last and at long last it came to be the March before he was seventy – the worst March ever known in all these parts – such blowing, sleeting, snowing, had not been experienced in the memory of man;

when one blusterous night some foreign vessel went to bits on the Purple Headland. They say it was an awful sound to hear the death-cry that went up high above the noise of the wind; and it was as bad a sight to see the shore there strewed with corpses of all sorts and sizes, from the little cabin-boy to the grizzled seaman.

'They never knew who they were or where they came from, but some of the men had crosses, and beads, and suchlike, so the priest said they belonged to him, and they were all buried deeply and decently in the chapel graveyard.

'There was not much wreckage of value drifted on shore. Most of what is lost about the Head stays there; but one thing did come into the bay – a puncheon of brandy.

'The Squire claimed it; it was his right to have all that came on his land, and he owned this seashore from the Head to the breakers – every foot – so, in course, he had the brandy; and there was sore ill will because he gave his men nothing, not even a glass of whiskey.

'Well, to make a long story short, that was the most wonderful liquor anybody ever tasted. The gentry came from far and near to take share, and it was cards and dice, and drinking and storytelling night after night – week in, week out. Even on Sundays, God forgive them! The officers would drive over from Ballycloyne, and sit emptying tumbler after tumbler till Monday morning came, for it made beautiful punch.

'But all at once people quit coming – a word went round that the liquor was not all it ought to be. Nobody could say what ailed it, but it got about that in some way men found it did not suit them.

'For one thing, they were losing money very fast.

'They could not make head against the Squire's luck, and a hint was dropped the puncheon ought to have been towed out to sea, and sunk in fifty fathoms of water.

'It was getting to the end of April, and fine, warm weather for the time of year, when first one and then another, and then another still, began to take notice of a stranger who walked the shore alone at night. He was a dark man, the same colour as the drowned crew lying in the chapel graveyard, and had rings in his ears, and wore a strange kind of hat, and cut wonderful antics as he walked, and had an ambling sort of gait, curious to look at. Many tried to talk to him, but he only shook his head; so, as nobody could make out where he came from or what he wanted, they made sure he was the spirit of some poor wretch who was tossing about the Head, longing for a snug corner in holy ground.

'The priest went and tried to get some sense out of him.

' "Is it Christian burial you're wanting?" asked his reverence; but the creature only shook his head.

' "Is it word sent to the wives and daughters you've left orphans and widows, you'd like?" But no; it wasn't that.

' "Is it for sin committed you're doomed to walk this way? Would masses comfort ye? There's a heathen," said his reverence; "Did you ever hear tell of a Christian that shook his head when masses were mentioned?"

' "Perhaps he doesn't understand English, Father," says one of the officers who was there; "Try him with Latin."

'No sooner said than done. The priest started off with such a string of aves and paters that the stranger fairly took to his heels and ran.

' "He is an evil spirit," explained the priest, when he stopped, tired out, "and I have exorcised him."

'But next night my gentleman was back again, as unconcerned as ever.

' "And he'll just have to stay," said his reverence, "For I've got lumbago in the small of my back, and pains in all my joints – never to speak of a hoarseness with standing there shouting; and I don't believe he understood a sentence I said."

'Well, this went on for a while, and people got that frightened of the man, or appearance of a man, they would not go near the sand; till in the end, Squire Ennismore, who had always scoffed at the talk, took it into his head he would go down one night, and see into the rights of the matter. He, maybe, was feeling lonesome, because, as I told your honour before, people had left off coming to the house, and there was nobody for him to drink with.

'Out he goes, then, bold as brass; and there were a few followed him. The man came forward at sight of the Squire and took off his hat with a foreign flourish. Not to be behind in civility, the Squire lifted his.

' "I have come, sir," he said, speaking very loud, to try to make him understand, "to know if you are looking for anything, and whether I can assist you to find it.'

'The man looked at the Squire as if he had taken the greatest liking to him, and took off his hat again.

' "Is it the vessel that was wrecked you are distressed about?"

'There came no answer, only a mournful shake of the head.

' "Well, *I* haven't your ship, you know; it went all to bits months ago; and, as for the sailors, they are snug and sound enough in consecrated ground."

'The man stood and looked at the Squire with a queer sort of smile on his face.

' "What *do* you want?" asked Mr Ennismore in a bit of a passion. "If anything belonging to you went down with the vessel, it's about the Head you ought to be looking for it, not here – unless, indeed, it's after the brandy you're fretting!"

'Now, the Squire had tried him in English and French, and was now speaking a language you'd have thought nobody could understand; but, faith, it seemed natural as kissing to the stranger.

' "Oh! That's where you are from, is it?" said the Squire. "Why couldn't you have told me so at once? I can't give you the brandy, because it mostly is drunk; but come along, and you shall have as stiff a glass of punch as ever crossed your lips." And without more to-do off they went, as sociable as you please, jabbering together in some outlandish tongue that made moderate folks' jaws ache to hear it.

'That was the first night they conversed together, but it wasn't the last. The stranger must have been the height of good company, for the Squire never tired of him. Every evening, regularly, he came up to the house, always dressed the same, always smiling and polite, and then the Squire called for brandy and hot water, and they drank and played cards till cockcrow, talking and laughing into the small hours.

'This went on for weeks and weeks, nobody knowing where the man came from, or where he went; only two things the old housekeeper did know – that the puncheon was nearly empty, and that the Squire's flesh was wasting off him; and she felt so uneasy she went to the priest, but he could give her no manner of comfort.

'She got so concerned at last that she felt bound to listen at the dining-room door; but they always talked in that foreign gibberish, and whether it was blessing or cursing they were at she couldn't tell.

'Well, the upshot of it came one night in July – on the eve of the Squire's birthday – there wasn't a drop of spirit left in the puncheon – no, not as much as would drown a fly. They had drunk the whole lot clean up – and the old woman stood trembling, expecting every minute to hear the bell ring for more brandy, for where was she to get more if they wanted any?

'All at once the Squire and the stranger came out into the hall. It was a full moon, and light as day.

' "I'll go home with you tonight by way of a change," says the Squire.

' "Will you so?" asked the other.

' "That I will," answered the Squire.

' "It is your own choice, you know."

' "Yes; it is my own choice; let us go."

'So they went. And the housekeeper ran up to the window on the great staircase and watched the way they took. Her niece lived there as housemaid, and she came and watched, too; and, after a while, the butler as well. They all turned their faces this way, and looked after their master walking beside the strange man along these very sands. Well, they saw them walk on, and on, and on, and on, till the water took them to their knees, and then to their waists, and then to their armpits, and then to their throats and their heads; but long before that the women and the butler were running out on the shore as fast as they could, shouting for help.'

'Well?' said the Englishman.

'Living or dead, Squire Ennismore never came back again. Next morning, when the tides ebbed again, one walking over the sand saw the print of a cloven foot – that he tracked to the water's edge. Then everybody knew where the Squire had gone, and with whom.'

'And no more search was made?'

'Where would have been the use searching?'

'Not much, I suppose. It's a strange story, anyhow.'

'But true, your honour – every word of it.'

'Oh! I have no doubt of that,' was the satisfactory reply.

DOUGLAS HYDE

Teig O'Kane and the Corpse

❧

There was once a grown-up lad in the County Leitrim, and he was strong and lively, and the son of a rich farmer. His father had plenty of money, and he did not spare it on the son. Accordingly, when the boy grew up he liked sport better than work, and, as his father had no other children, he loved this one so much that he allowed him to do in everything just as it pleased himself. He was very extravagant, and he used to scatter the gold money as another person would scatter the white. He was seldom to be found at home, but if there was a fair, or a race, or a gathering within ten miles of him, you were dead certain to find him there. And he seldom spent a night in his father's house, but he used to be always out rambling, and, like Shawn Bwee long ago, there was: 'grádh gach cailin i mbrollach a léine, the love of every girl in the breast of his shirt,' and it's many's the kiss he got and he gave, for he was very handsome, and there wasn't a girl in the country but would fall in love with him, only for him to fasten his two eyes on her, and it was for that someone made this *rann* on him:

> Look at the rogue, it's for kisses he's rambling,
> It isn't much wonder, for that was his way;
> He's like an old hedgehog, at night he'll be scrambling
> From this place to that, but he'll sleep in the day.

At last he became very wild and unruly. He wasn't to be seen day or night in his father's house, but always rambling or going on his *Kailee* (night visit) from place to place and from house to house, so that the old people used to shake their heads and say to one another, 'It's easy seen what will happen to the land when the old man dies; his son will run through it in a year, and it won't stand him that long itself.'

He used to be always gambling and card-playing and drinking, but his father never minded his bad habits, and never punished him. But it happened one day that the old man was told that the son had ruined the character of a girl in the neighbourhood, and he was greatly angry, and he called the son to him, and said to him, quietly and sensibly – 'Avic,' says he, 'you know I loved you greatly up to this, and I never stopped you from doing your choice thing whatever it was, and I kept plenty of money with you, and I always hoped to leave you the house and land, and all I had after myself would be gone; but I heard a story of you today that has disgusted me with you. I cannot tell you the grief that I felt when I heard such a thing of you, and I tell you now plainly that unless you marry that girl I'll leave house and land and everything to my brother's son. I never could leave it to anyone who would make so bad a use of it as you do yourself, deceiving women and coaxing girls. Settle with yourself now whether you'll marry that girl and get my land as a fortune with her, or refuse to marry her and give up all that was coming to you; and tell me in the morning which of the two things you have chosen.'

'Och! *Domnoo Sheery*! father, you wouldn't say that to me, and I such a good son as I am. Who told you I wouldn't marry the girl?' says he.

But his father was gone, and the lad knew well enough that he would keep his word too; and he was greatly troubled in his mind, for as quiet and as kind as the father was, he never went back on a word that he had once said, and there wasn't another man in the country who was harder to bend than he was.

The boy did not know rightly what to do. He was in love with the girl indeed, and he hoped to marry her sometime or other, but he would much sooner have remained another while as he was, and follow on at his old tricks – drinking, sporting, and playing cards; and, along with that, he was angry that his father should order him to marry, and should threaten him if he did not do it.

'Isn't my father a great fool,' says he to himself. 'I was ready enough, and only too anxious, to marry Mary; and now since he threatened me, faith I've a great mind to let it go another while.'

His mind was so much excited that he remained between two notions as to what he should do. He walked out into the night at last to cool his heated blood, and went on to the road. He lit a pipe, and as the night

was fine he walked and walked on, until the quick pace made him begin
to forget his trouble. The night was bright, and the moon half full.
There was not a breath of wind blowing, and the air was calm and mild.
He walked on for nearly three hours, when he suddenly remembered
that it was late in the night, and time for him to turn. 'Musha! I think I
forgot myself,' says he; 'it must be near twelve o'clock now.'

The word was hardly out of his mouth, when he heard the sound of
many voices, and the trampling of feet on the road before him. 'I don't
know who can be out so late at night as this, and on such a lonely
road,' said he to himself.

He stood listening, and he heard the voices of many people talking,
but he could not understand what they were saying. 'Oh, wirra!' says
he, 'I'm afraid. It's not Irish or English they have; it can't be they're
Frenchmen!' He went on a couple of yards further, and he saw well
enough by the light of the moon a band of little people coming towards
him, and they were carrying something big and heavy with them. 'Oh,
murder!' says he to himself, 'sure it can't be that they're the good
people that's in it!' Every *rib* of hair that was on his head stood up, and
there fell a shaking on his bones, for he saw that they were coming to
him fast.

He looked at them again, and perceived that there were about
twenty little men in it, and there was not a man at all of them higher
than about three feet or three feet and a half, and some of them were
grey, and seemed very old. He looked again, but he could not make
out what was the heavy thing they were carrying until they came up
to him, and then they all stood round about him. They threw the
heavy thing down on the road, and he saw on the spot that it was a
dead body.

He became as cold as the Death, and there was not a drop of blood
running in his veins when an old little grey *maneen* came up to him
and said, 'Isn't it lucky we met you, Teig O'Kane?'

Poor Teig could not bring out a word at all, nor open his lips, if he
were to get the world for it, and so he gave no answer.

'Teig O'Kane,' said the little grey man again, 'isn't it timely you
met us?'

Teig could not answer him.

'Teig O'Kane,' says he, 'the third time, isn't it lucky and timely that
we met you?'

But Teig remained silent, for he was afraid to return an answer, and his tongue was as if it was tied to the roof of his mouth.

The little grey man turned to his companions, and there was joy in his bright little eye. 'And now,' says he, 'Teig O'Kane hasn't a word, we can do with him what we please. Teig, Teig,' says he, 'you're living a bad life, and we can make a slave of you now, and you cannot withstand us, for there's no use in trying to go against us. Lift that corpse.'

Teig was so frightened that he was only able to utter the two words, 'I wont't'; for as frightened as he was he was obstinate and stiff, the same as ever.

'Teig O'Kane won't lift the corpse,' said the little *maneen* with a wicked little laugh, for all the world like the breaking of a *lock* of dry *kippeens*, and with a little harsh voice like the striking of a cracked bell. 'Teig O'Kane won't lift the corpse – make him lift it'; and before the word was out of his mouth they had all gathered round poor Teig, and they all talking and laughing through each other.

Teig tried to run from them, but they followed him, and a man of them stretched out his foot before him as he ran, so that Teig was thrown in a heap on the road. Then before he could rise up the fairies caught him, some by the hands and some by the feet, and they held him tight, in a way that he could not stir, with his face against the ground. Six or seven of them raised the body then, and pulled it over to him, and left it down on his back. The breast of the corpse was squeezed against Teig's back and shoulders, and the arms of the corpse were thrown around Teig's neck. Then they stood back from him a couple of yards, and let him get up. He rose, foaming at the mouth and cursing, and he shook himself, thinking to throw the corpse off his back. But his fear and his wonder were great when he found that the two arms had a tight hold round his own neck, and that the two legs were squeezing his hips firmly, and that, however strongly he tried, he could not throw it off, any more than a horse can throw off its saddle. He was terribly frightened then, and he thought he was lost. 'Ochone! for ever,' said he to himself, 'it's the bad life I'm leading that has given the good people this power over me. I promise to God and Mary, Peter and Paul, Patrick and Bridget, that I'll mend my ways for as long as I have to live, if I come clear out of this danger – and I'll marry the girl.'

The little grey man came up to him again, and said he to him, 'Now, Teig*een*,' says he, 'you didn't lift the body when I told you to lift it, and see how you were made to lift it; perhaps when I tell you to bury it, you won't bury it until you're made to bury it!'

'Anything at all that I can do for your honour,' said Teig, 'I'll do it,' for he was getting sense already, and if it had not been for the great fear that was on him, he never would have let that civil word slip out of his mouth.

The little man laughed a sort of laugh again. 'You're getting quiet now, Teig,' says he. 'I'll go bail but you'll be quiet enough before I'm done with you. Listen to me now, Teig O'Kane, and if you don't obey me in all I'm telling you to do, you'll repent it. You must carry with you this corpse that is on your back to Teampoll-Démus, and you must bring it into the church with you, and make a grave for it in the very middle of the church, and you must raise up the flags and put them down again the very same way, and you must carry the clay out of the church and leave the place as it was when you came, so that no one could know that there had been anything changed. But that's not all. Maybe that the body won't be allowed to be buried in that church; perhaps some other man has the bed, and, if so, it's likely he won't share it with this one. If you don't get leave to bury it in Teampoll-Démus, you must carry it to Carrick-fhad-vic-Orus, and bury it in the churchyard there; and if you don't get it into that place, take it with you to Teampoll Ronan; and if that churchyard is closed on you, take it to Imlogue-Fada; and if you're not able to bury it there, you've no more to do than to take it to Kill-Breedya, and you can bury it there without hindrance. I cannot tell you what one on those churches is the one where you will have leave to bury that corpse under the clay, but I know that it will be allowed you to bury him at some church or other of them. If you do this work rightly, we will be thankful to you, and you will have no cause to grieve; but if you are slow or lazy, believe me we shall take satisfaction of you.'

When the grey little man had done speaking, his comrades laughed and clapped their hands together. 'Glic! Glic! Hwee! Hwee!' they all cried; 'go on, go on, you have eight hours before you till daybreak, and if you haven't this man buried before the sun rises, you're lost.' They struck a fist and a foot behind on him, and drove him on in the road. He was obliged to walk, and to walk fast, for they gave him no rest.

He thought himself that there was not a wet path, or a dirty *boreen*, or a crooked contrary road in the whole county, that he had not walked that night. The night was at times very dark, and whenever there would come a cloud across the moon he could see nothing, and then he used often to fall. Sometimes he was hurt, and sometimes he escaped, but he was obliged always to rise on the moment and to hurry on. Sometimes the moon would break out clearly, and then he would look behind him and see the little people following at his back. And he heard them speaking amongst themselves, talking and crying out, and screaming like a flock of seagulls; and if he was to save his soul he never understood as much as one word of what they were saying.

He did not know how far he had walked, when at last one of them cried out to him, 'Stop here!' He stood, and they all gathered round him.

'Do you see those withered trees over there?' says the old boy to him again. 'Teampoll-Démus is among those trees, and you must go in there by yourself, for we cannot follow you or go with you. We must remain here. Go on boldly.'

Teig looked from him, and he saw a high wall that was in places half broken down, and an old grey church on the inside of the wall, and about a dozen withered old trees scattered here and there round it. There was neither leaf nor twig on any of them, but their bare crooked branches were stretched out like the arms of an angry man when he threatens. He had no help for it, but was obliged to go forward. He was a couple of hundred yards from the church, but he walked on, and never looked behind him until he came to the gate of the churchyard. The old gate was thrown down, and he had no difficulty in entering. He turned then to see if any of the little people were following him, but there came a cloud over the moon, and the night became so dark that he could see nothing. He went into the churchyard, and he walked up the old grassy pathway leading to the church. When he reached the door, he found it locked. The door was large and strong, and he did not know what to do. At last he drew out his knife with difficulty, and stuck it in the wood to try if it were not rotten, but it was not.

'Now,' said he to himself, 'I have no more to do; the door is shut, and I can't open it.'

Before the words were rightly shaped in his own mind, a voice in his ear said to him, 'Search for the key on the top of the door, or on the wall.'

He started. 'Who is that speaking to me?' he cried, turning round; but he saw no one. The voice said in his ear again, 'Search for the key on the top of the door, or on the wall.'

'What's that?' said he, and the sweat running from his forehead; 'who spoke to me?'

'It's I, the corpse, that spoke to you!' said the voice.

'Can you talk?' said Teig.

'Now and again,' said the corpse.

Teig searched for the key, and he found it on the top of the wall. He was too much frightened to say any more, but he opened the door wide, and as quickly as he could, and he went in, with the corpse on his back. It was as dark as pitch inside, and poor Teig began to shake and tremble.

'Light the candle,' said the corpse.

Teig put his hand in his pocket, as well as he was able, and drew out a flint and steel. He struck a spark out of it, and lit a burnt rag he had in his pocket. He blew it until it made a flame, and he looked round him. The church was very ancient, and part of the wall was broken down. The windows were blown in or cracked, and the timbers of the seats were rotten. There were six or seven old iron candlesticks left there still, and in one of these candlesticks Teig found the stump of an old candle, and he lit it. He was still looking round him in the strange and horrid place in which he found himself, when the cold corpse whispered in his ear, 'Bury me now, bury me now; there is a spade and turn the ground.' Teig looked from him, and he saw a spade lying beside the altar. He took it up, and he placed the blade under a flag that was in the middle of the aisle, and leaning all his weight on the handle of the spade, he raised it. When the first flag was raised it was not hard to raise the others near it, and he moved three or four of them out of their places. The clay that was under them was soft and easy to dig, but he had not thrown up more than three or four shovelfuls when he felt the iron touch something soft like flesh. He threw up three or four more shovelfuls from around it, and then he saw that it was another body that was buried in the same place.

'I am afraid I'll never be allowed to bury the two bodies in the same hole,' said Teig, in his own mind. 'You corpse, there on my back,' says he, 'will you be satisfied if I bury you down here?' But the corpse never answered him a word.

'That's a good sign,' said Teig to himself. 'Maybe he's getting quiet,' and he thrust the spade down in the earth again. Perhaps he hurt the flesh of the other body, for the dead man that was buried there stood up in the grave, and shouted an awful shout. 'Hoo! Hoo!! Hoo!!! Go! go!! go!!! or you're a dead, dead, dead man!' And then he fell back in the grave again. Teig said afterwards, that of all the wonderful things he saw that night, that was the most awful to him. His hair stood upright on his head like the bristles of a pig, the cold sweat ran off his face, and then came a tremor over all his bones, until he thought that he must fall.

But after a while he became bolder, when he saw that the second corpse remained lying quietly there, and he threw in the clay on it again, and he smoothed it overhead, and he laid down the flags carefully as they had been before. 'It can't be that he'll rise up any more,' said he.

He went down the aisle a little further, and drew near to the door, and began raising the flags again, looking for another bed for the corpse on his back. He took up three or four flags and put them aside, and then he dug the clay. He was not long digging until he laid bare an old woman without a thread upon her but her shirt. She was more lively than the first corpse, for he had scarcely taken any of the clay away from about her, when she sat up and began to cry, 'Ho, you *bodach* (clown)! Ha, you *bodach*! Where has he been that he got no bed?'

Poor Teig drew back, and when she found that she was getting no answer, she closed her eyes gently, lost her vigour, and fell back quietly and slowly under the clay. Teig did to her as he had done to the man – he threw the clay back on her, and left the flags down overhead.

He began digging again near the door, but before he had thrown up more than a couple of shovelfuls, he noticed a man's hand laid bare by the spade. 'By my soul, I'll go no further, then,' said he to himself; 'what use is it for me?' And he threw the clay in again on it, and settled the flags as they had been before.

He left the church then, and his heart was heavy enough, but he shut the door and locked it, and left the key where he found it. He sat

down on a tombstone that was near the door, and began thinking. He
was in great doubt what he should do. He laid his face between his two
hands, and cried for grief and fatigue, since he was dead certain at this
time that he never would come home alive. He made another attempt
to loosen the hands of the corpse that were squeezed round his neck,
but they were as tight as if they were clamped; and the more he tried
to loosen them, the tighter they squeezed him. He was going to sit
down once more, when the cold, horrid lips of the dead man said to
him, 'Carrick-fhad-vic-Orus,' and he remembered the command of
the good people to bring the corpse with him to that place if he should
be unable to bury it where he had been.

He rose up, and looked about him. 'I don't know the way,' he said.

As soon as he had uttered the word, the corpse stretched out
suddenly its left hand that had been tightened round his neck, and
kept it pointing out, showing him the road he ought to follow. Teig
went in the direction that the fingers were stretched, and passed out
of the churchyard. He found himself on an old rutty, stony road, and
he stood still again, not knowing where to turn. The corpse stretched
out its bony hand a second time, and pointed out to him another
road – not the road by which he had come when approaching the old
church. Teig followed that road, and whenever he came to a path or
road meeting it, the corpse always stretched out its hand and pointed
with its fingers, showing him the way he was to take.

Many was the crossroad he turned down, and many was the crooked
boreen he walked, until he saw from him an old burying-ground at last,
beside the road, but there was neither church nor chapel nor any
other building in it. The corpse sequeezed him tightly, and he stood.
'Bury me, bury me in the burying-ground,' said the voice.

Teig drew over towards the old burying-place, and he was not
more than about twenty yards from it, when, raising his eyes, he saw
hundreds and hundreds of ghosts – men, women, and children –
sitting on the top of the wall round about, or standing on the inside of
it, or running backwards and forwards, and pointing at him, while he
could see their mouths opening and shutting as if they were speaking,
though he heard no word, nor any sound amongst them at all.

He was afraid to go forward, so he stood where he was, and the
moment he stood, all the ghosts became quiet, and ceased moving.
Then Teig understood that it was trying to keep him from going in,

that they were. He walked a couple of yards forwards, and immediately the whole crowd rushed together towards the spot to which he was moving, and they stood so thickly together that it seemed to him that he never could break through them, even though he had a mind to try. But he had no mind to try it. He went back broken and dispirited, and when he had gone a couple of hundred yards from the burying-ground, he stood again, for he did not know what way he was to go. He heard the voice of the corpse in his ear, saying 'Teampoll-Ronan,' and the skinny hand was stretched out again, pointing him out the road.

As tired as he was, he had to walk, and the road was neither short nor even. The night was darker than ever, and it was difficult to make his way. Many was the toss he got, and many a bruise they left on his body. At last he saw Teampoll-Ronan from him in the distance, standing in the middle of the burying-ground. He moved over towards it, and thought he was all right and safe, when he saw no ghosts nor anything else on the wall, and he thought he would never be hindered now from leaving his load off him at last. He moved over to the gate, but as he was passing in, he tripped on the threshold. Before he could recover himself, something that he could not see seized him by the neck, by the hands, and by the feet, and bruised him, and shook him, and chocked him, until he was nearly dead; and at last he was lifted up, and carried more than a hundred yards from that place, and then thrown down in an old dyke, with the corpse still clinging to him.

He rose up, bruised and sore, but feared to go near the place again, for he had seen nothing the time he was thrown down and carried away.

'You corpse, up on my back?' said he, 'shall I go over again to the churchyard?' – but the corpse never answered him.

'That's a sign you don't wish me to try it again,' said Teig.

He was now in great doubt as to what he ought to do, when the corpse spoke in his ear, and said, 'Imlogue-Fada.'

'Oh, murder!' said Teig, 'must I bring you there? If you keep me long walking like this, I tell you I'll fall under you.'

He went on, however, in the direction the corpse pointed out to him. He could not have told, himself, how long he had been going, when the dead man behind suddenly squeezed him, and said, 'There!'

Teig looked from him, and he saw a little low wall, that was so broken down in places that it was no wall at all. It was in a great wide field, in from the road; and only for three or four great stones at the corners, that were more like rocks than stones, there was nothing to show that there was either graveyard or burying-ground there.

'Is this Imlogue-Fada? Shall I bury you here?' said Teig.

'Yes,' said the voice.

'But I see no grave or gravestone, only this pile of stones,' said Teig.

The corpse did not answer, but stretched out its long fleshless hand to show Teig the direction in which he was to go. Teig went on accordingly, but he was greatly terrified, for he remembered what had happened to him at the last place. He went on, 'with his heart in his mouth,' as he said himself afterwards; but when he came to within fifteen or twenty yards of the little low square wall, there broke out a flash of lightning, bright yellow and red, with blue streaks in it, and went round about the wall in one course, and it swept by as fast as the swallow in the clouds, and the longer Teig remained looking at it the faster it went, till at last it became like a bright ring of flame round the old graveyard, which no one could pass without being burnt by it. Teig never saw, from the time he was born, and never saw afterwards, so wonderful or so splendid a sight as that was. Round went the flame, white and yellow and blue sparks leaping out from it as it went, and although at first it had been no more than a thin, narrow line, it increased slowly until it was at last a great broad band, and it was continually getting broader and higher, and throwing out more brilliant sparks, till there was never a colour on the ridge of the earth that was not to be seen in that fire; and lightning never shone and flame never flamed that was so shining and so bright as that.

Teig was amazed; he was half dead with fatigue, and he had no courage left to approach the wall. There fell a mist over his eyes, and there came a *soorawn* in his head, and he was obliged to sit down upon a great stone to recover himself. He could see nothing but the light, and he could hear nothing but the whirr of it as it shot round the paddock faster than a flash of lightning.

As he sat there on the stone, the voice whispered once more in his ear, 'Kill-Breedya'; and the dead man squeezed him so tightly that he cried out. He rose again, sick, tired, and trembling, and went forward as he was directed. The wind was cold, and the road was bad, and the load upon his back was heavy, and the night was dark, and he himself was nearly worn out, and if he had very much farther to go he must have fallen dead under his burden.

At last the corpse stretched out its hand, and said to him, 'Bury me there.'

'This is the last burying-place,' said Teig in his own mind; 'and the little grey man said I'd be allowed to bury him in some of them, so it must be this; it can't be but they'll let him in here.'

The first faint streak of the ring of day was appearing in the east, and the clouds were beginning to catch fire, but it was darker than ever, for the moon was set, and there were no stars.

'Make haste, make baste!' said the corpse; and Teig hurried forward as well as he could to the graveyard, which was a little place on a bare hill, with only a few graves in it. He walked boldly in through the open gate, and nothing touched him, nor did he either hear or see anything. He came to the middle of the ground, and then stood up and looked round him for a spade or shovel to make a grave. As he was turning round and searching, he suddenly perceived what startled him greatly – a newly-dug grave right before him. He moved over to it, and looked down, and there at the bottom he saw a black coffin. He clambered down into the hole and lifted the lid, and found that (as he thought it would be) the coffin was empty. He had hardly mounted up out of the hole, and was standing on the brink, when the corpse, which had clung to him for more than eight hours, suddenly relaxed its hold of his neck, and loosened its shins from round his hips, and sank down with a plop into the open coffin.

Teig fell down on his two knees at the brink of the grave, and gave thanks to God. He made no delay then, but pressed down the coffin lid in its place, and threw in the clay over it with his two hands, and when the grave was filled up, he stamped and leaped on it with his feet, until it was firm and hard, and then he left the place.

The sun was fast rising as he finished his work, and the first thing he did was to return to the road, and look out for a house to rest himself in. He found an inn at last; and lay down upon a bed there, and slept till night. Then he rose up and ate a little, and fell asleep again till morning. When he awoke in the morning he hired a horse and rode home. He was more than twenty-six miles from home where he was, and he had come all that way with the dead body on his back in one night.

All the people at his own home thought that he must have left the country, and they rejoiced greatly when they saw him come back.

Everyone began asking him where he had been, but he would not tell anyone except his father.

He was a changed man from that day. He never drank too much; he never lost his money over cards; and especially he would not take the world and be out late by himself of a dark night.

He was not a fortnight at home until he married Mary, the girl he had been in love with, and it's at their wedding the sport was, and it's he was the happy man from that day forward, and it's all I wish that we may be as happy as he was.

GLOSSARY – *Rann*, a stanza; *kailee (céilidhe)*, a visit in the evenings; *wirra (a mhuire)*, 'Oh, Mary!' an exclamation like the French *dame*; rib, a single hair (in Irish, *ribe*); *a lock (glac)*, a bundle or wisp, or a little share of anything; *kippeen (cipín)*, a rod or twig; *boreen (bóitrín)*, a lane; *bodach*, a clown; *soorawn (suarán)*, vertigo. *Avic (a Mhic)* = my son, or rather, Oh, son. *Mic* is the vocative of *Mac*.

DANIEL CORKERY

The Eyes of the Dead

❧

I

If he had not put it off for three year Johns Spillane's homecoming
would have been that of a famous man. Bonfires would have been
lighted on the hilltops of Rossamara, and the ships passing by, twenty
miles out, would have wondered what they meant.

Three years ago, the *Western Star*, an Atlantic liner, one night tore
her iron plates to pieces against the cliff-like face of an iceberg, and
in less than an hour sank in the waters. Of the seven hundred and
eighty-nine human souls aboard her one only had been saved, John
Spillance, able seaman, of Rossamara in the country of Cork. The
name of the little fishing village, his own name, his picture, were in all
the papers of the world, it seemed, not only because he alone had
escaped, but by reason of the manner of that escape. He had clung to
a drift of wreckage, must have lost consciousness for more than a
whole day, floated then about on the ocean for a second day, for a
second night, and had arrived at the threshold of another dreadful
night when he was rescued. A fog was coming down on the waters. It
frightened him more than the darkness. He raised a shout. He kept
on shouting. When safe in the arms of his rescuers his breathy, almost
inaudible voice was still forcing out some cry which they interpreted
as Help! Help!

That was what had struck the imagination of men – the half-insane
figure sending his cry over the waste of waters, the fog thickening,
and the night falling. Although the whole world had read also of the
groping rescue ship, of Spillane's bursts of hysterical laughter, of his
inability to tell his story until he had slept eighteen hours on end,

what remained in the memory was the lonely figure sending his cry over the sea.

And then, almost before his picture had disappeared from the papers, he had lost himself in the great cities of the States. To Rossamara no world had come from himself, nor for a long time from any acquaintance; but then, when about a year had gone by, his sister or mother as they went up the road to Mass of a Sunday might be stopped and informed in a whispering voice that John had been seen in Chicago, or, it might be, in New York, or Boston, or San Francisco, or indeed anywhere. And from the meagreness of the messages it was known, with only too much certainty, that he had not, in exchanging sea for land, bettered his lot. If once again his people had happened on such empty tidings of him, one knew it by their bowed and stilly attitude in the little church as the light whisper of the Mass rose and fell about them.

When three years had gone by he lifted the latch of his mother's house one October evening and stood awkwardly in the middle of the floor. It was nightfall and not a soul had seen him break down from the ridge and cross the roadway. He had come secretly from the ends of the earth.

And before he was an hour in their midst he rose up impatiently, timidly, and stole into his bed.

'I don't want any light,' he said, and as his mother left him there in the dark, she heard him yield his whole being to a sigh of thankfulness. Before that he had told them he felt tired, a natural thing, since he had tramped fifteen miles from the railway station in Skibbereen. But day followed day without his showing any desire to rise from the bedclothes and go abroad among the people. He had had enough of the sea, it seemed; enough too of the great cities of the States. He was a pity, the neighbours said; and the few of them who from time to time caught glimpses of him, reported him as not yet having lost the scared look that the ocean had left on him. His hair was grey or nearly grey, they said, and, swept back fiercely from his forehead, a fashion strange to the place, seemed to pull his eyes open, to keep them wide open, as he looked at you. His moustache also was grey, they said, and his cheeks were grey too, sunken and dark with shadows. Yet his mother and sister, the only others in the house, were glad to have him back with them; at any rate, they said, they knew where he was.

They found nothing wrong with him. Of speech neither he nor they ever had had the gift; and as day followed day, and week week, the same few phrases would carry them through the day and into the silence of night. In the beginning they had thought it natural to speak with him about the wreck; soon, however, they came to know that it was a subject for which he had no welcome. In the beginning also, they had thought to rouse him by bringing the neighbour to his bedside, but such visits instead of cheering him only left him sunken in silence, almost in despair. The priest came to see him once in a while, and advise the mother and sister, Mary her name was, to treat him as normally as they could, letting on that his useless presence was no affliction to them nor even a burden. In time John Spillane was accepted by all as one of those unseen ones, or seldom-seen ones, who are to be found in every village in the word – the bedridden, the struck-down, the aged – forgotten of all except the few faithful creatures who bring the cup to the bedside of a morning, and open the curtains to let in the sun.

2

In the nearest house, distant a quarter-mile from them, lived Tom Leane. In the old days before John Spillane went to sea, Tom had been his companion, and now of a night-time he would drop in if he had any story worth telling or if, on the day following, he chanced to be going back to Skibbereen, where he might buy the Spillanes such goods as they needed, or sell a pig for them, slipping it in among his own. He was a quiet creature, married, and struggling to bring up the little family that was thickening about him. In the Spillanes' he would, dragging at the pipe, sit on the settle, and quietly gossip with the old woman while Mary moved about on the flags putting the household gear tidy for the night. But all three of them, as they kept up the simple talk, were never unaware of the silent listener in the lower room. Of that room the door was kept open; but no lamp was lighted within it; no lamp indeed was needed, for a shaft of light from the kitchen struck into it showing one or two of the religious pictures on the wall and giving sufficient light to move about in. Sometimes the conversation would drift away from the neighbourly doings, for even to Rossamara tidings from the great world abroad would sometimes come; in the middle of such gossip, however, a sudden thought would strike Tom Leane, and, raising his voice, he would blurt out: 'But sure 'tis foolish for the like of me to be talking about these far-off places, and that man inside after travelling the world, over and thither.' The man inside, however, would give no sign whatever whether their gossip had been wise or foolish. They might hear the bed creak, as if he had turned with impatience at their mention of his very presence.

There had been a spell of stormy weather, it was now the middle of February, and for the last five days at twilight the gale seemed always to set in for a night of it. Although there was scarcely a house around that part of the southwest Irish coast that had not some one of its members, husband or brother or son, living on the sea, sailoring abroad or fishing the home waters or those of the Isle of Man – in no other house was the strain of a spell of disastrous weather so noticeable in the faces of its inmates. The old woman, withdrawn into herself, would handle her beads all day long, her voice every now and then raising itself, in forgetfulness, to a sort of moan not unlike the wind's upon which the younger woman would chide her with a 'Sh! sh!' and bend vigorously upon her work to keep bitterness from her thoughts. At such a time she might enter her brother's room and find him raised on his elbow in the bed, listening to the howling winds, scared it seemed, his eyes fixed and wide open. He would drink the warm milk she had brought him, and hand the vessel back without a word. And in the selfsame attitude she would leave him.

The fifth night instead of growing in loudness and fierceness the wind died away somewhat. It became fitful, promising the end of the storm; and before long they could distinguish between the continuous groaning and pounding of the sea and the sudden shout the dying tempest would fling among the treetops and the rocks. They were thankful to note such signs of relief; the daughter became more active, and the mother put by her beads. In the midst of a sudden sally of the wind's the latch was raised, and Tom Leane gave them greeting. His face was rosy and glowing under his sou'wester; his eyes were sparkling from the sting of the salty gusts. To see him, so sane, so healthy, was to them like a blessing. 'How is it with ye?' he said, cheerily, closing the door to.

'Good, then, good, then,' they answered him, and the mother rose almost as if she would take him by the hand. The reply meant that nothing unforeseen had befallen them. He understood as much. He shook a silent head in the direction of the listener's room, a look of enquiry in his eyes, and this look Mary answered with a sort of hopeless upswing of her face. Things had not improved in the lower room.

The wind died away, more and more; and after some time streamed by with a shrill steady undersong; all through, however, the crashing of the sea on the jagged rocks beneath kept up an unceasing clamour. Tom had a whole budget of news for them. Finny's barn had been stripped of its roof; a window in the chapel had been blown in; and Largy's store of fodder had been shredded in the wind; it littered all the bushes to the east. There were rumours of a wreck somewhere; but it was too soon yet to know what damage the sea had done in its five days' madness. The news he had brought them did not matter; what mattered was his company, the knitting of their half-distraught household once again to humankind. Even when at last he stood up to go, their spirits did not droop, so great had been the restoration.

'We're finished with it for a while anyhow,' Tom said, rising for home.

'We are, we are; and who knows, it mightn't be after doing all the damage we think.'

He shut the door behind him. The two women had turned towards the fire when they thought they again heard his voice outside. They wondered at the sound; they listened for his footsteps. Still staring at the closed door, once more they heard his voice. This time they were sure. The door reopened, and he backed in, as one does from an unexpected slap of rain in the face. The light struck outwards, and they saw a white face advancing. Some anxiety, some uncertainty, in Tom's attitude as he backed away from that advancing face, invaded them so that they too became afraid. They saw the stranger also hesitating, looking down his own limbs. His clothes were dripping; they were clung in about him. He was bare headed. When he raised his face again, his look was full of apology. His features were large and flat, and grey as a stone. Every now and then a spasm went through them, and they wondered what it meant. His clab of a mouth hung open; his unshaven chin trembled. Tom spoke to him: 'You'd better come in; but 'tis many another house would suit you better than this.'

They heard a husky, scarce-audible voice reply: 'A doghouse would do, or a stable.' Bravely enough he made an effort to smile.

'Oh, 'tisn't that at all. But come in, come in.' He stepped in slowly and heavily, again glancing down his limbs. The water running from his clothes spread in a black pool on the flags. The young woman began to touch him with her finger tips as with some instinctive sympathy, yet could not think, it seemed, what was best to be done. The mother, however, vigorously set the fire-wheel at work, and Tom built up the fire with bog-timber and turf. The stranger meanwhile stood as if half-dazed. At last, as Mary with a candle in her hand stood pulling out dry clothes from a press, he blurted out in the same husky voice, Welsh in accent: 'I think I'm the only one!'

They understood the significance of the words, but it seemed wrong to do so.

'What is it you're saying?' Mary said, but one would not have recognised the voice for hers, it was so toneless. He raised a heavy sailor's hand in an awkward taproom gesture: 'The others, they're gone, all of them.'

The spasm again crossed his homely features, and his hand fell. He bowed his head. A coldness went through them. They stared at him. He might have thought them inhuman. But Mary suddenly pulled herself together, leaping at him almost: 'Sh! Sh!' she said, 'speak low, speak low, low,' and as she spoke, all earnestness, she towed him first in the direction of the fire, and then away from it, haphazardly it seemed. She turned from him and whispered to Tom: 'Look, take him up into the loft, and he can change his clothes. Take these with you, and the candle, the candle.' And she reached him the candle eagerly. Tom led the stranger up the stairs, it was more like a ladder, and the two of them disappeared into the loft. The old woman whispered: 'What was it he said?'

' 'Tis how his ship is sunk.'

'Did he says he was the only one?'

'He said that.'

'Did himself hear him?' She nodded towards her son's room.

'No, didn't you see me pulling him away from it? But he'll hear him now. Isn't it a wonder Tom Wouldn't walk easy on the boards!'

No answer from the old woman. She had deliberately seated herself in her accustomed place at the fire, and now moaned out: 'Aren't we in a cruel way, not knowing how he'd take a thing!'

'Am I better tell him there's a poor seaman after coming in on us?'

'Do you hear them above! Do you hear them!'

In the loft the men's feet were loud on the boards. The voice they were half-expecting to hear they then heard break in on the clatter of the boots above: 'Mother! Mother!'

'Yes, child, yes.'

'Who's aloft? Who's going around like that, or is it dreaming I am?'

The sounds from above were certainly like what one hears in a ship. They thought of this, but they also felt something terrible in that voice they had been waiting for: they hardly knew it for the voice of the man they had been listening to for five months.

'Go in and tell him the truth,' the mother whispered. 'Who are we to know what's right to be done. Let God have the doing of it.' She threw her hands in the air.

Mary went in to her brother, and her limbs were weak and cold. The old woman remained seated at the fire, swung round from it, her eyes towards her son's room, fixed, as the head itself was fixed, in the tension of anxiety.

After a few minutes Mary emerged with a strange alertness upon her: 'He's rising! He's getting up! 'Tis his place, he says. He's quite good.' She meant he seemed bright and well. The mother said: 'We'll take no notice of him, only just as if he was always with us.'

'Yes.'

They were glad then to hear the two men in the loft groping for the stair head. The kettle began to splutter in the boil, and Mary busied herself with the table and tea cups.

The sailor came down, all smiles in his ill-fitting, haphazard clothes. He looked so overjoyed one might think he would presently burst into song.

'The fire is good,' he said. 'It puts life in one. And the dry clothes too. My word, I'm thankful to you, good people; I'm thankful to you.' He shook hands with them all effusively.

'Sit down now; drink up the tea.'

'I can't figure it out; less than two hours ago, out there . . . As he spoke he raised his hand towards the little porthole of a window, looking at them with his eyes staring. 'Don't be thinking of anything, but drink up the hot tea,' Mary said.

He nodded and set to eat with vigour. Yet suddenly he would stop, as if he were ashamed of it, turn half-round and look at them with beaming eyes, look from one to the other and back again; and they affably would nod back at him. 'Excuse me, people,' he would say, 'excuse me.' He had not the gift of speech, and his too-full heart could not declare itself. To make him feel at his ease, Tom Leane sat down away from him, and the women began to find something to do about the room. Then there were only little sounds in the room: the breaking of the eggs, the turning of the fire-wheel, the wind going by. The door of the lower room opened silently, so silently that none of them heard it, and before they were aware, the son of the house, with his clothes flung on loosely, was standing awkwardly in the middle of the floor, looking down on the back of the sailorman bent above the table. 'This is my son,' the mother thought of saying. 'He was after going to bed when you came in.'

The Welshman leaped to his feet, and impulsively, yet without many words, shook John Spillane by the hand, thanking him and all the household. As he seated himself again at the table John made his way silently towards the settle from which, across the room, he could see the sailor as he bent over his meal.

The stranger put the cup away from him, he could take no more; and Tom Leane and the womenfolk tried to keep him in talk, avoiding, as by some mutual understanding, the mention of what he had come through. The eyes of the son of the house were all the time fiercely buried in him. There came a moment's silence in the general chatter, a moment it seemed impossible to fill, and the sailorman swung his chair half-round from the table, a spoon held in his hand lightly: 'I can't figure it out. I can't nohow figure it out. Here I am, fed full like a prize beast; and warm – Oh, but I'm thankful – and all my mates,' with the spoon he was pointing towards the sea – 'white, and cold like dead fish! I can't figure it out.'

To their astonishment a voice travelled across the room from the settle.

'Is it how ye struck?'

'Struck! Three times we struck! We struck last night, about this time last night. And off we went in a puff! Fine, we said. We struck again. 'Twas just coming light. And off again. But when we struck the third time, 'twas like that!' He clapped his hands together; 'She went in matchwood! 'Twas dark. Why, it can't be two hours since!'

'She went to pieces?' the same voice questioned him.

'The *Nan Tidy* went to pieces, sir! No one knew what had happened or where he was. 'Twas too sudden. I found myself clung about a snag of rock. I hugged it.'

He stood up, hoisted as from within.

'Is it you that was on the look-out?'

'Me! We'd all been on the look-out for three days. My word, yes, three days. We were stupefied with it!'

They were looking at him as he spoke, and they saw the shiver again cross his features; the strength and warmth that the food and comfort had given him fell from him, and he became in an instant the half-drowned man who had stepped in to them that night with the clothes sagging about his limbs, ' 'Twas bad, clinging to that rock, with them all gone! 'Twas lonely! Do you know, I was so frightened I couldn't call out.' John Spillane stood up, slowly, as if he too were being hoisted from within.

'Were they looking at you?'

'Who?'

'The rest of them. The eyes of them.'

'No,' the voice had dropped, 'no, I didn't think of that!' The two of them stared as if fascinated by each other.

'You didn't!' It seemed that John Spillane had lost the purpose of his questioning. His voice was thin and weak; but he was still staring with unmoving, puzzled eyes at the stranger's face. The abashed creature before him suddenly seemed to gain as much eagerness as he had lost:

his words were hot with anxiety to express himself adequately: 'But now, isn't it curious, as I sat there, there at that table, I thought somehow they would walk in, that it would be right for them, somehow, to walk in, all of them!'

His words, his eager lowered voice, brought in the darkness outside, its vastness, its terror. They seemed in the midst of an unsubstantial world. They feared that the latch would lift, yet dared not glance at it, lest that should invite the lifting. But it was all one to the son of the house, he appeared to have gone away into some mood of his own; his eyes were glaring, not looking at anything or anyone close at hand. With an instinctive groping for comfort, they all, except him, began to stir, to find some little homely task to do: Mary Handled the tea ware, and Tom his pipe, when a rumbling voice, very indistinct, stilled them all again. Words, phrases, began to reach them – that a man's eyes will close and he on the lookout, close in spite of himself, that it wasn't fair, it wasn't fair, it wasn't fair! And lost in his agony, he began to glide through them, explaining, excusing the terror that was in him: 'All round. Staring at me. Blaming me. A sea of them. Far, far! Without a word out of them, only their eyes in the darkness, pale like candles!'

Transfixed, they glared at him, at his round-shouldered sailor's back disappearing again into his den of refuge. They could not hear his voice any more, they were afraid to follow him.

A. E. COPPARD

The Gollan

There was once a peasant named Goose who had worked his back crooked with never a thank-ye from providence or man, and he had a son, Gosling, whom the neighbours called the Gollan for short. The Gollan was an obedient child and strong, though not by nature very willing. He was so obedient that he would do without question whatever anybody told him to do. One day he was bringing his mother three eggs in a basket and he met a rude boy.

'Hoi,' called the rude boy, 'are those eggs the bouncing eggs?'

'Are they?' enquired the Gollan.

'Try one and see,' the rude boy said.

The Gollan took one of the eggs from the basket and dropped it to the ground, and it broke.

'Haw!' complained the rude one, 'you did not do it properly. How could an egg bounce if you dropped it so? You must throw it hard and it will fly back into your hand like a bird.'

So the Gollan took another and dashed it to the ground and waited. But the egg only lay spilled at his feet.

'No, no, no! Stupid fellow!' the rude boy cried. 'Look. Throw the other one up in the air high as you can and all three will bounce back into your basket.'

So the Gollan threw the last egg up on high, but it only dropped beside the others and all lay in a slop of ruins.

'Oh dear! What will my mother say? Oh dear!' wept the Gollan.

The rude boy merely put his thumb to his nose and ran off upon his proper business, laughing.

The Gollan grew up a great powerful fellow, and whatever anyone told him to do, it might be simple, it might be hard, he did it without repining, which shows that he had a kind heart anyway, though he had little enough inclination to work; indeed he had no wish to at all.

One day his father said to him: 'My son, you are full of strength and vigour, you are the prop of my old age and the apple of my two eyes. Take now these five and twenty pigs and go you to market and dispose of them. Beware of false dealing, and you may hear wonders.'

'What wonders should I hear?'

'Mum,' said his father, 'is the word. Say nothing and scare nobody.'

He gave him two noggins of ale and off went the Gollan. And it was a queer half and half day, however, but full of colour. There were poppies in the green corn, charlock in the Swedes, and weak sunlight in the opaline sky. He tried to drive the pigs but they had their minds set upon some other matters and would not go where they should because of distractions and interruptions. There was the green corn, there were the swedes, and there were heifers in the lane, lambs afield, and hens in every hedge, so before he had gone a mile the pigs were all astray.

'I don't care where those pigs go,' then said the Gollan to himself. 'I don't trouble about those pigs as long as I have my strength and vigour.' So he lay down under a nut hazel-bush and was soon sleeping.

In the course of time – long or short makes no odds – he heard someone whistling shrilly, and waking up he looked about him to the right hand and to the left and soon saw a person caught hard and fast in a catchpole, a little plump man with a red beard and bright buckled shoes.

'Well met, friend!' the little man called out. 'Pray release me from this trap and I will make your fortune.' So the Gollan went and put out all his strength and vigour, with a heave and a hawk and a crash, until he had drawn the little plump man out of the trap and set him free.

'Thanks, friend,' said the leprechaun – for he was that and no less, not like any man you ever read about. 'You have done me a kind service. Ask any reward you will and I will give it.'

'Sir,' said the Gollan, 'there is no matter about that. I am the prop of my father's age and the apple of his two eyes. I have strength and vigour with which I work for what I need.'

'Unhappy is that man,' the leprechaun answered, 'who serves his need and not his choice. You have strength and vigour, but how do you use it?'

The Gollan drew himself up proudly: 'I can crack rocks and hew trees.'

'Well, then,' replied the other, 'crack on, and hew.'

'Alas,' the Gollan explained, 'I have four fingers and a thumb on one hand, four fingers and a thumb on the other, all of them able – but not one of them willing.' And he confided to the leprechaun that it was his doom and distress to be at the beck and call of everyone because of his strength and vigour, and he with no heart to refuse to do a deed required of him.

'That cannot be endured. I can easily remedy it,' said the leprechaun. 'I will make you invisible to mankind, except only when you are asleep. Nobody will be able to see you when you are awake and walking, therefore they will not be able to give you a task of any kind.'

So he made the Gollan invisible there and then, and no one saw the Gollan any more, save his parents when he was sleeping, and his life became a bed or roses and a bower of bliss. Where is the Gollan? – people would say. But though they knew he was thereabout they could not set eyes on him and they could not find him. If the Gollan were only with us – they would say – he would do this tiresome labour, he would do it well. But as he was no longer visible to them they could not catch him and they could not ask him. The Gollan would be about in the sunlight day after day doing nothing at all, and got so blown up with pride that he thought: 'I am invisible, no one can task me in my strength and vigour. I am king of all the unseen world, and that is as good as twenty of these other kings. I live as I choose, and I take my need as I want it.'

But though it was all very grand to be invisible the Gollan soon found out that there was small blessing in it. He could be seen by none save when he slept, but the truth is neither could he see anybody – man, woman, or child. No one could hear him, but then he himself could hear no one – man, woman, or child. It was the same way with smelling, touching and tasting. Animals and birds he could see, and he could talk to them, but they were so hard of understanding that he might as well have conversed with a monument or a door. Sure, he had kept his wits but he had lost his five senses, and that is cruel fortune.

After a while his heart grew weary for the sight of his friends and the talk and sounds of people, he was tired of seeing animals and birds only, so he went to a hawk he knew that had the most piercing gaze, and said: 'Friend, lend me your two eyes for a while and I will pawn you my own for their safe return.'

'Will I? Will I?' mused the hawk.

'You will!' the Gollan sternly said.

So they exchanged, but the Gollan was greatly deceived by these hawk eyes. He went about wearing them far and near, and he saw thousands of mice and birds and moles, but those eyes never set their gaze on a single human creature, good, bad, or medium. What was worse, rascally things, they never seemed to want to! The farther he wandered the more sure it became that those eyes were merely looking out for moles and voles and suchlike. He saw nothing else except a jackass with fine upstanding ears straying in a bethistled waste whom he accosted: 'Friend, lend me your two ears for a while. I will pawn you my own for their safe return.'

'Will you? Won't you?' mused the ass.

'I will,' declared the Gollan, for he longed to hear human speech again, or a song to cheer him.

So they exchanged. But the Gollan was more deceived and bewildered than ever, for he never caught the sound of any pleasant human talk. What he heard was only an ass's bald portion, vile oaths, denunciations, and abuse. And although it all rushed into one ear and quickly fell out of the other, it was not good hearing at all; it was not satisfactory. When he heard a pig grunting not far off he hastened to the pig, saying: 'Friend, lend me your nose. I will pawn you mine for its safe return.'

'Ask me no more,' said the pig, surveying him with a rueful smile as he suffered the Gollan to make the exchange.

But something kept the Gollan from smelling anything save what a pig may smell. Instead of flowers, the odour of fruit, or the cook's oven, the swinish nostrils delighted only in the vapours of swill and offal and ordure. Surely – thought the Gollan – it is better to be invisible and senseless than to live thus. So he tried no further, but gave back the eyes, the ears, and the nose and received his pledges again.

Now at that time the king of the land was much put about by the reason of a little pond that lay in front of his palace. It was a meager patch of water and no ways good.

'If only this were a lake,' sighed the king, 'a great lake of blue water with neat waves and my ships upon it and my swans roving and my snipe calling and my fish going to and fro, my realm would be a great realm and the envy of the whole world.'

And one day, as he was wandering and wondering what he could do about this, he came upon the Gollan lying on a green bank drowsing and dreaming. Of course when the king set eyes on him, he saw him and knew him.

'Hoi, Gollan!' the king roared at him. 'Stretch out that water for me!' Just like that. The Gollan woke up and at once became invisible again, but he was so startled at being roared at that without thinking, just absent-mindedly, he stretched out the water of the king's pond and there and then it became a fine large lake with neat waves and ships and swans and suchlike, beautiful – though when he learned the right of it the Gollan was crabby and vexed, 'I am the king of the unseen world, and that's as good as any twenty of these other kings.' Still, he could not alter it back again. Whatever he did had to stay as it was once done: it could neither be changed nor improved.

However, by the reason of his fine new lake and ships the king's realm became the envy of all other nations, who began to strive after it after it and attack it. The king was not much of a one for martial dispositions and so the whole of his country was soon beleaguered and the people put to miserable extravagances.

Now although the Gollan could not directly see or hear anything of this, yet one way and another he came to know something of the misfortune, and then he was worn to a tatter with rage and fury by the reason he was such a great one for the patriotism. And he was powerless to help now his five senses were gone from him.

'O, what sort of a game is this,' he thought, 'now the world is in ruins and I have no more senses than a ghost or a stone! I had the heart of an ass when I took that red-haired villain out of his trap and had his reward. Reward! Take it back! Take it back, you palavering old crow of a catchpole! You have cramped me tight and hauled me to a grave. Take it back, you!'

'Well met, friend,' a voice replied, and there was the old leprechaun bowing before him. 'Your wish is granted.'

True it was. They were standing beside a field of corn ripe and ready, waving and sighing it was. The Gollan could hear once more, he could touch, taste, and smell again, and he could see his own royal king as clear as print on a page of history hurrying down the road towards them.

'What else can I do for you?' asked the little red-haired man.

'I fancy,' said the Gollan, jerking his thumb towards the king, 'he is running to ask me for a large great army.'

'You shall have that,' said the leprechaun, vanishing away at the king's approach.

'Gollan,' the king says, 'I want a large great army.'

'Yes, Sir,' says the Gollan. 'Will you have the grenadiers, the bombardiers, or men of the broadsword?'

He said he would have the bombardiers.

Well, the Gollan made a pass of his hand over that field of corn, and the standing stalks at once began to whistle and sway sideways. Before you could blink a lash there they were, 50,000 men and noblemen, all marking time, all dressed to glory with great helmets and eager for battle.

'Gollan,' says the king, 'will you undertake the command of this my noble army?'

'I will that, Sir.'

'Lead on, then,' says the king, and 'may the blood of calamity never splash upon one single rib of the whole lot of you.'

Which, it is good to say, it never did. The Gollan then marched them straightway to battle by the shore of the lake.

'Get ready now,' cried General Gollan, 'here comes the artillery with their big guns!'

The bombardiers began to prepare themselves and first gave a blast on their trumpets, but the enemy got ready sooner and fired off a blast on all their culverins, mortars, and whatnot. Ah, what a roar they let out of that huge and fatal cannonade! It would have frightened the trunk of a tree out of its own bark, and at the mere sound of it every man of General Gollan's army toppled to the earth like corn that is cut, never to rise again.

'What is it and all!' cried the distracted Gollan. 'Is this another joke of that palavering old crow of a catchpole? By the soul of my aunty!' he exclaimed, as he surveyed his exposed position amid all those fallen bombardiers, so neat, so gallant, so untimely dead, 'By the soul of my aunty I think I'd rather be invisible now!'

In a twink he was invisible once more, and his five senses gone again; but none of his friends ever had time to enquire what became of him because the conquering general painfully exterminated them all.

Unseen, unknown, the good Gollan lived on for many years in great privation, and when he at last came to die (though nobody knew even about that) he had grown mercifully wise and wrote his own epitaph – though nobody ever saw it: 'To choose was my need, but need brooks no choosing'.

GEORGE MOORE

A Play-House in the Waste

❧❧❧

'It's a closed mouth that can hold a good story,' as the saying goes, and very soon it got about that Father MacTurnan had written to Rome saying he was willing to take a wife to his bosom for patriotic reasons, if the Pope would relieve him of his vow of celibacy. And many phrases and words from his letter (translated by whom – by the Bishop or Father Meehan? – nobody ever knew) were related over the Dublin firesides, till at last out of the talk a tall gaunt man emerged, in an old overcoat, green from weather and wear, the tails of it flapping as he rode his bicycle through the great waste bog that lies between Belmullet and Crossmolina. His name! We liked it. It appealed to our imagination. MacTurnan! It conveyed something from afar like Hamlet or Don Quixote. He seemed as near and as far from us as they, till Pat Comer, one of the organisers of the IAOS, came in and said, after listening to the talk that was going round:

'Is it of the priest that rides in the great Mayo bog you are speaking? If it is, you haven't got the story rightly.' As he told us the story, so it is printed in this book. And we sat wondering greatly, for we seemed to see a soul on its way to heaven. But round a fire there is always one who cannot get off the subject of women and blasphemy – a papist generally he is; and it was Quinn that evening who kept plaguing us with jokes, whether it would be a fat girl or a thin that the priest would choose if the Pope gave him leave to marry, until at last, losing all patience with him, I bade him be silent, and asked Pat Comer to tell us if the Priest was meditating a new plan for Ireland's salvation. 'For a mind like his,' I said, 'would not stand still and problems such as ours waiting to be solved.'

'You're wrong there! He thinks no more of Ireland, and neither reads nor plans, but knits stockings ever since the wind took his playhouse away.'

'Took his playhouse away!' said several.

'And why would he be building a playhouse,' somebody asked, 'and he living in a waste?'

'A queer idea, surely!' said another. 'A playhouse in the waste!'

'Yes, a queer idea,' said Pat, 'but a true one all the same, for I have seen it with my own eyes – or the ruins of it – and not later back than three weeks ago, when I was staying with the priest himself. You know the road, all of you – how it straggles from Foxford through the bog alongside of bog holes deep enough to drown one, and into which the jarvey and myself seemed in great likelihood of pitching, for the car went down into great ruts, and the horse was shying from one side of the road to the other, and at nothing so far as we could see.'

'There's nothing to be afeared of, yer honour; only once was he near leaving the road, the day before Christmas, and I driving the doctor. It was here he saw it – a white thing gliding – and the wheel of the car must have gone within an inch of the bog hole.'

'And the doctor. Did he see it?' I said.

'He saw it too, and so scared was he that the hair rose up and went through his cap.'

'Did the jarvey laugh when he said that?' we asked Pat Comer; and Pat answered: 'Not he! Them fellows just speak as the words come to them without thinking. Let me get on with my story. We drove on for about a mile, and it was to stop him from clicking his tongue at the horse that I asked him if the bog was Father MacTurnan's parish.'

'Every mile of it, sir,' he said, 'every mile of it, and we do be seeing him buttoned up in his old coat riding along the roads on his bicycle going to sick calls.'

'Do you often be coming this road?' says I.

'Not very often, sir. No one lives here except the poor people, and the priest and the doctor. Faith! there isn't a poorer parish in Ireland, and everyone of them would have been dead long ago if it had not been for Father James.'

'And how does he help them?'

'Isn't he always writing letters to the Government asking for relief works? Do you see those bits of roads?'

'Where do those roads lead to?'

'Nowhere. Them roads stops in the middle of the bog when the money is out.'

'But,' I said, 'surely it would be better if the money were spent upon permanent improvements – on drainage, for instance.'

The jarvey didn't answer; he called to his horse, and not being able to stand the clicking of his tongue, I kept on about the drainage.

'There's no fall, sir.'

'And the bog is too big,' I added, in hope of encouraging conversation.

'Faith it is, sir.'

'But we aren't very far from the sea, are we?'

'About a couple of miles.'

'Well then,' I said, 'couldn't a harbour be made?'

'They were thinking about that, but there's no depth of water, and everyone's against emigration now.'

'Ah! the harbour would encourage emigration.'

'So it would, your honour.'

'But is there no talk about home industries, weaving, lacemaking?'

'I won't say that.'

'But has it been tried?'

'The candle do be burning in the priest's window till one in the morning, and he sitting up thinking of plans to keep the people at home. Now, do ye see that house, sir, fornint my whip at the top of the hill? Well, that's the playhouse he built.'

'A playhouse?'

'Yes, yer honour. Father James hoped the people might come from Dublin to see it, for no play like it had ever been acted in Ireland before, sir!'

'And was the play performed?'

'No, yer honour. The priest had been learning them all the summer, but the autumn was on them before they had got it by rote, and a wind came and blew down one of the walls.'

'And couldn't Father MacTurnan get the money to build it up?'

'Sure, he might have got the money, but where'd be the use when there was no luck in it?'

'And who were to act the play?'

'The girls and the boys in the parish, and the prettiest girl in all the parish was to play Good Deeds.'

'So it was a miracle play,' I said.

'Do you see that man? It's the priest coming out of Tom Burke's cabin, and I warrant he do be bringing him the Sacrament, and he having the holy oils with him, for Tom won't pass the day; we had the worst news of him last night.'

'And I can tell you,' said Pat Comer, dropping his story for a moment and looking round the circle, 'it was a sad story the jarvey told me. He told it well, for I can see the one-roomed hovel full or peat smoke, the black iron pot with traces of the yellow stirabout in it on the hearth, and the sick man on the pallet bed, and the priest by his side mumbling prayers together. Faith! these jarveys can tell a story– none better.'

'As well as yourself, Pat,' one of us said. And Pat began to tell of the miles of bog on either side of the straggling road, of the hilltop to the left, with the playhouse showing against the dark and changing clouds; of a woman in a red petticoat, a handkerchief tied round her head, who had flung down her spade the moment she caught sight of the car, of the man who appeared on the brow and blew a horn. 'For she mistook us for bailiffs,' said Pat, 'and two little sheep hardly bigger than geese were driven away.'

'A playhouse in the waste for these people,' I was saying to myself all the time, till my meditations were interrupted by the jarvey telling that the rocky river we crossed was called the Greyhound – a not inappropriate name, for it ran swiftly . . . Away down the long road a white cottage appeared, and the jarvey said to me, 'That is the priest's house.' It stood on the hillside some little way from the road, and all the way to the door I wondered how his days passed in the great loneliness of the bog.

'His reverence isn't at home, yer honour – he's gone to attend a sick call.'

'Yes, I know – Tom Burke.'

'And is Tom better, Mike?'

'The devil a bether he'll be this side of Jordan,' the jarvey answered, and the housekeeper showed me into the priest's parlour. It was lined with books, and I looked forward to a pleasant chat when we had finished our business. At that time I was on a relief committee, and the people were starving in the poor parts of the country.

'I think he'll be back in about an hour's time, yer honour.' But the priest seemed to be detained longer than his housekeeper expected, and the moaning of the wind round the cottage reminded me of the small white thing the horse and the doctor had seen gliding along the road. 'The priest knows the story – he will tell me,' I said, and piled more turf on the fire – fine sods of hard black turf they were, and well do I remember seeing them melting away. But all of a sudden my eyes closed. I couldn't have been asleep more than a few minutes when it seemed to me a great crowd of men and women had gathered about the house, and a moment after the door was flung open, and a tall, gaunt man faced me.

'I've just come,' he said, 'from a deathbed, and they that have followed me aren't far from death if we don't succeed in getting help.' I don't know how I can tell you of the crowd I saw round the house that day. We are accustomed to see poor people in towns cowering under arches, but it is more pitiful to see people starving in the fields on the mountain side. I don't know why it should be so, but it is. But I call to mind two men in ragged trousers and shirts as ragged, with brown beards on faces yellow with famine; and the words of one of them are not easily forgotten: 'The white sun of Heaven doesn't shine upon two poorer men than upon this man and myself.' I can tell you I didn't envy the priest his job, living all his life in the waste listening to tales of starvation, looking into famished faces. There were some women among them, kept back by the men, who wanted to get their word in first. They seemed to like to talk about their misery . . . and I said: 'They are tired of seeing each other. I am a spectacle, a show, an amusement for them. I don't know if you can catch my meaning?'

'I think I do,' Father James answered. And I asked him to come for a walk up the hill and show me the playhouse.

Again he hesitated, and I said: 'You must come, Father MacTurnan, for a walk. You must forget the misfortunes of those people for a while.' He yielded, and we spoke of the excellence of the road under our feet, and he told me that when he conceived the idea of a play-house, he had already succeeded in persuading the inspector to agree that the road they were making should go to the top of the hill. 'The policy of the Government,' he said, 'from the first was that relief works should benefit nobody except the workers, and it is sometimes very difficult to think out a project for work that will be perfectly useless. Arches have been built on the top of hills, and roads that lead nowhere. A strange sight to the stranger a road must be that stops suddenly in the middle of a bog. One wonders at first how a Government could be so foolish, but when one thinks of it, it is easy to understand that the Government doesn't wish to spend money on works that will benefit a class. But the road that leads nowhere is difficult to make, even though starving men are employed upon it; for a man to work well there must be an end in view, and I can tell you it is difficult to bring even starving men to engage on a road that leads nowhere. If I'd told everything I am telling you to the inspector, he wouldn't have agreed to let the road run to the top of the hill; but I said to him: 'The road leads nowhere; as well let it end at the top of the hill as down in the valley.' So I got the money for my road and some money for my playhouse, for of course the playhouse was as useless as the road; a playhouse in the waste can neither interest of benefit anybody! But there was an idea at the back of my mind all the time that when the road and the playhouse were finished, I might be able to induce the Government to build a harbour?'

'But the harbour would be of use.'

'Of very little,' he answered. 'For the harbour to be of use a great deal for dredging would have to be done.'

'And the Government needn't undertake the dredging. How very ingenious! I suppose you often come here to read your breviary?'

'During the building of the playhouse I often used to be up here, and during the rehearsals I was here every day.'

'If there was a rehearsal,' I said to myself, 'there must have been a play.' And I affected interest in the grey shallow sea and the erosion of the low-lying land – a salt marsh filled with pools.

'I thought once,' said the priest, 'that if the play were a great success, a line of flat-bottomed steamers might be built.'

'Sitting here in the quiet evenings,' I said to myself, 'reading his breviary, dreaming of a line of steamships crowded with visitors! He has been reading about the Oberammergau performances.' So that was his game – the road, the playhouse, the harbour – and I agreed with him that no one would have dared to predict that visitors would have come from all sides of Europe to see a few peasants performing a miracle play in the Tyrol.

'Come,' I said, 'into the playhouse and let me see how you built it.'

Half a wall and some of the roof had fallen, and the rubble had not been cleared away, and I said: 'It will cost many pounds to repair the damage, but having gone so far you should give the play a chance.'

'I don't think it would be advisable,' he muttered, half to himself, half to me.

As you may well imagine, I was anxious to hear if he had discovered any aptitude for acting among the girls and the boys who lived in the cabins.

'I think' he answered me, 'that the play would have been fairly acted; I think that, with a little practice, we might have done as well as they did at Oberammergau.'

An odd man, more willing to discuss the play that he had chosen than the talents of those who were going to perform it, and he told me that it had been written in the fourteenth century in Latin, and that he had translated it into Irish.

I asked him if it would have been possible to organise an excursion from Dublin – 'Oberammergau in the West.'

'I used to think so. But it is eight miles from Rathowen, and the road is a bad one, and when they got here there would be no place for them to stay; they would have to go all the way back again, and that would be sixteen miles.'

'Yet you did well, Father James, to build the playhouse, for the people could work better while they thought they were accomplishing something. Let me start a subscription for you in Dublin.'

'I don't think that it would be possible – '

'Not for me to get fifty pounds?'

'You might get the money, but I don't think we could ever get a performance of the play.'

'And why not?' I said.

'You see, the wind came and blew down the wall. The people are very pious; I think they felt that the time they spent rehearsing might have been better spent. The playhouse disturbed them in their ideas. They hear Mass on Sundays, and there are the Sacraments, and they remember they have to die. It used to seem to me a very sad thing to see all the people going to America; the poor Celt disappearing in America, leaving his own country, leaving his language, and very often his religion.'

'And does it no longer seem to you sad that such a thing should happen?'

'No, not if it is the will of God. God has specially chosen the Irish race to convert the world. No race has provided so many missionaries, no race has preached the Gospel more frequently to the heathen; and once we realise that we have to die, and very soon, and that the Catholic Church is the only true Church, our ideas about race and nationality fade from us. We are here, not to make life successful and triumphant, but to gain heaven. That is the truth, and it is to the honour of the Irish people that they have been selected by God to preach the truth, even though they lose their nationality in preaching it. I do not except you to accept these opinions. I know that you think very differently, but living here I have learned to acquiesce in the will of God.'

He stopped speaking suddenly, like one ashamed of having expressed himself too openly, and soon after we were met by a number of peasants, and the priest's attention was engaged; the inspector of the relief works had to speak to him; and I didn't see him again until dinner-time.

'You have given them hope,' he said.

This was gratifying to hear, and the priest sat listening while I told him of the looms already established in different parts of the country. We talked about half an hour, and then, like one who suddenly remembers, the priest got up and fetched his knitting.

'Do you knit every evening?'

'I have got into the way of knitting lately – it passes the time.'

'But do you never read?' I asked, and my eyes went towards the bookshelves.

'I used to read a great deal. But there wasn't a woman in the parish that could turn a heel properly, so I had to learn to knit.'

'Do you like knitting better than reading?' I asked, feeling ashamed of my curiosity.

'I have constantly to attend sick calls, and if one is absorbed in a book one doesn't like to put it aside.'

'I see you have two volumes of miracle plays!'

'Yes, and that's another danger: a book begets all kinds of ideas and notions into one's head. The idea of that playhouse came out of those books.'

'But,' I said, 'you don't think that God sent the storm because He didn't wish a play to be performed?'

'One cannot judge God's designs. Whether God sent the storm or whether it was accident must remain a matter for conjecture; but it is not a matter of conjecture that one is doing certain good by devoting oneself to one's daily task, getting the Government to start new relief works, establishing schools for weaving. The people are entirely dependent upon me, and when I'm attending to their wants I know I'm doing right'.

The playhouse interested me more than the priest's ideas of right and wrong, and I tried to get him back to get him back to it; but the subject seemed a painful one, and I said to myself: 'The jarvey will tell me all about it tomorrow. I can rely on him to fin out the whole story from the housekeeper in the kitchen.' And sure enough, we hadn't got to the Greyhound River before he was leaning across the well of the car talking to me and asking if the priest was thinking of putting up the wall of the playhouse.

'The wall of the playhouse?' I said.

'Yes, yer honour. Didn't I see both of you going up the hill in the evening time?'

'I don't think we shall ever see a play in the playhouse.'

'Why would we, since it was God that sent the wind that blew it down?'

'How do you know it was God that sent the wind? It might have been the devil himself, or somebody's curse.'

'Sure it is of Mrs Sheridan you do be thinking, yer honour, and of her daughter – she that was to be playing Good Deeds in the play, yer honour; and wasn't she wake coming home from the learning of the play? And when the signs of her wakeness began to show, the widow Sheridan took a halter off the cow and tied Margaret to the wall, and she was in the stable till the child was born. Then didn't her mother take a bit of string and tie it round the child's throat, and bury it near the playhouse; and it was three nights after that the storm rose, and the child pulled the thatch out of the roof.'

'But did she murder the child?'

'Sorra wan of me knows. She sent for the priest when she was dying, and told him what she had done.'

'But the priest wouldn't tell what he heard in the confessional,' I said.

'Mrs Sheridan didn't die that night; not till the end of the week, and the neighbours heard her talking of the child she had buried, and then they all knew what the white thing was they had seen by the roadside. The night the priest left her he saw the white thing standing in front of him, and if he hadn't been a priest he'd have dropped down dead; so he took some water from the bog hole and dashed it over it, saying, "I baptise thee in the name of the Father, and of the Son, and of the Holy Ghost!" '

The driver told his story like one saying his prayers, and he seemed to have forgotten that he had a listener.

'It must have been a great shock to the priest.'

'Faith it was, sir, to meet an unbaptised child on the roadside, and that child the only bastard that was ever born in the parish – so Tom Mulhare says, and he's the oldest man in the county.'

'I was altogether a very queer idea – this playhouse.'

'It was indeed, sir, a quare idea, but you see he's quare man. He has been always thinking of something to do good, and it is said that he thinks too much. Father James is a very quare man, your honour'

ROSA MULHOLLAND

The Ghost at the Rath

Many may disbelieve this story, yet there are some still living who can remember hearing, when children, of the events which it details, and of the strange sensation which their publicity excited. The tale, in its present form, is copied, by permission, from a memoir written by the chief actor in the romance, and preserved as a sort of heirloom in the family whom it concerns.

In the year —, I, John Thunder, Captain in the — Regiment, having passed many years abroad following my profession, received notice that I had become owner of certain properties which I had never thought to inherit. I set off for my native land, arrived in Dublin, found that my good fortune was real, and at once began to look about me for old friends. The first I met with, quite by accident, was curly-headed Frank O'Brien, who had been at school with me, though I was ten years his senior. He was curly-headed still, and handsome, as he had promised to be, but careworn and poor. During an evening spent at his chambers I drew all his history from him. He was a briefless barrister. As a man he was not more talented than he had been as a boy. Hard work and anxiety had not brought him success, only broken his health and soured his mind. He was in love, and he could not marry. I soon knew all about Mary Leonard, his fiancée, whom he had met at a house in the country somewhere, in which she was governess. They had now been engaged for two years – she active and hopeful, he sick and despondent. From the letters of hers which he showed me, I thought she was worth all the devotion he felt for her. I considered a good deal about what could be done for Frank, but I could not easily hit upon a plan to assist him. For ten chances you have of helping a sharp man, you have not two for a dull one.

In the meantime my friend must regain his health, and a change of air and scene was necessary. I urged him to make a voyage of discovery to the Rath, an old house and park which had come into my possession as portion of my recently acquired estates. I had never been to the place myself but it had once been the residence of Sir Luke Thunder, of generous memory, and I knew that it was furnished, and provided with a caretaker. I pressed him to leave Dublin at once, and promised to follow him as soon as I found it possible to do so.

So Frank went down to the Rath. The place was two hundred miles away; he was a stranger there, and far from well. When the first week came to an end, and I had heard nothing from him, I did not like the silence; when a fortnight had passed, and still not a word to say he was alive, I felt decidedly uncomfortable; and when the third week of his absence arrived at Saturday without bringing me news, I found myself whizzing through a part of the country I had never travelled before, in the same train in which I had seen Frank seated at our parting.

I reached D—, and, shouldering my knapsack, walked right into the heart of a lovely woody country. Following the directions I had received, I made my way to a lonely road, on which I met not a soul, and which seemed cut out of the heart of a forest, so closely were the trees ranked on either side, and so dense was the twilight made by the meeting and intertwining of the thick branches overhead. In these shades I came upon a gate, like a gate run to seed, with tall, thin, brick pillars, brandishing long grasses from their heads, and spotted with a melancholy crust of creeping moss. I jangled a cracked bell, and an old man appeared from the thickets within, stared at me, then admitted me with a rusty key. I breathed freely on hearing that my friend was well and to be seen. I presented a letter to the old man, having a fancy not to avow myself.

I found my friend walking up and down the alleys of a neglected orchard, with the lichened branches tangled above his head, and ripe apples rotting about his feel. His hands were locked behind his back, and his heard was set on one side, listening to the singing of a bird. I never had seen him look so well; yet there was a vacancy about his whole air which I did not like. He did not seem at all surprised to see me, asked had he really not written to me; thought he had; was so comfortable that he had forgotten everything else. He fancied he had only been there about three days; could not imagine how the time had passed. He seemed to talk wildly, and this, coupled with the unusual happy placidity of his manner, confounded me. The place knew him, he told me confidentially; the place belonged to him, or should; the birds sang him this, the very trees bent before him as he passed, the air whispered him that he had been long expected, and should be poor no more. Wrestling with my judgement ere it might pronounce him mad, I followed him indoors. The Rath was no ordinary old country-house. The acres around it were so wildly overgrown that it was hard to decide which had been pleasure-ground and where the thickets had begun. The plan of the house was fine, with mullioned windows, and here and there a fleck of stained glass flinging back the challenge of an angry sunset. The vast rooms were full of a dusky glare from the sky as I strolled through them in the twilight. The antique furniture had many a blood-red stain on the abrupt notches of its dark carvings; the dusty mirrors flared back at the windows, while the faded curtains produced streaks of uncertain colour from the depths of their sullen foldings.

Dinner was laid for us in the library, a long wainscoted room, with an enormous fire roaring up the chimney, sending a dancing light over the dingy titles of long unopened books. The old man who had unlocked the fate for me served us at table, and, after drawing the dusty curtains, and furnishing us with a plentiful supply of fuel and wine, left us. His clanking hobnailed shoes went echoing away in the distance over the unmatted tiles of the vacant hall till a door closed with a resounding clang very far away, letting us know that we were shut up together for the night in this vast, mouldy, oppressive old house.

I felt as if I could scarcely breathe in it. I could not eat with my usual appetite. The air of the place seemed heavy and tainted. I grew sick and restless. The very wine tasted badly, as if it had been drugged. I had a strange feeling that I had been in the house before, and that something evil had happened to me in it. Yet such could not be the case. What puzzled me most was, that I should feel dissatisfied at seeing Frank looking so well, and eating so heartily. A little time before I should have been glad to suffer something to see him as he looked now; and yet not quite as he looked now. There was a drowsy contentment about him which I could not understand. He did not talk of his work, or of any wish to return to it. He seemed to have no thought of anything but the delight of hanging about that old house, which had certainly cast a spell over him.

About midnight he seized a light, and proposed retiring to our rooms. 'I have such delightful dreams in this place,' he said. He volunteered, as we issued into the hall, to take me upstairs and show me the upper regions of his paradise. I said, 'Not tonight.' I felt a strange creeping sensation as I looked up the vast black staircase, wide enough for a coach to drive down, and at the heavy darkness bending over it like a curse, while our lamps made drips of light down the first two or three gloomy steps. Our bedrooms were on the ground floor, and stood opposite on another off a passage which led to a garden. Into mine Frank conducted me, and left me for his own.

The uneasy feeling which I have described did not go from me with him, and I felt a restlessness amounting to pain when left alone in my chamber. Efforts had evidently been made to render the room habitable, but there was a something antagonistic to sleep in every angle of its many crooked corners. I kicked chairs out of their prim order along the wall, and banged things about here and there; finally, thinking that a good night's rest was the best cure for an inexplicably disturbed frame of mind, I undressed as quickly as possible, and laid my head on my pillow under a canopy, like the wings of a gigantic bird of prey wheeling above me ready to pounce.

But I could not sleep. The wind grumbled in the chimney, and the boughs swished in the garden outside; and between these noises I thought I heard sounds coming from the interior of the old house, where all should have been still as the dead down in their vaults. I could not make out what these sounds were. Sometimes I thought I heard feet running about, sometimes I could have sworn there were double knocks, tremendous tantarararas at the great hall door. Sometimes I heard the clashing of dishes, the echo of voices calling, and the dragging about of furniture. Whilst I sat up in bed trying to account for these noises, my door suddenly flew open, a bright light streamed in from the passage without, and a powdered servant in an elaborate livery of antique pattern stood holding the handle of the door in his hand, and bowing low to me in the bed.

'Her ladyship, my mistress, desires your presence in the drawing-room, sir.'

This was announced in the measured tone of a well-trained

domestic. Then with another bow he retired, the door closed, and I was left in the dark to determine whether I had not suddenly awakened from a tantalising dream. In spite of my very wakeful sensations, I believe I should have endeavoured to convince myself that I had been sleeping, but that I perceived light shining under my door, and through the keyhole, from the passage. I got up, lit my lamp, and dressed myself as hastily as I was able.

I opened my door, and the passage down which a short time before I had almost groped my way, with my lamp blinking in the dense foggy darkness, was now illuminated with a light as bright as gas. I walked along it quickly, looking right and left to see whence the glare proceeded. Arriving at the hall, I found it also blazing with light, and filled with perfume. Groups of choice plants, heavy with blossoms, made it look like a garden. The mosaic floor was strewn with costly mats. Soft colours and gilding shone from the walls, and canvases that had been black gave forth faces of men and women looking brightly from their burnished frames. Servants were running about, the dining-room and drawing-room doors were opening and shutting, and as I looked through each I saw vistas of light and colour, the moving of brilliant crowds, the waving of feathers, and glancing of brilliant dresses and uniforms. A festive hum reached me with a drowsy subdued sound, as if I were listening with stuffed ears. Standing aside by an orange tree, I gave up speculating on what this might be, and concentrated all my powers on observation.

Wheels were heard suddenly, and a resounding knock banged at the door till it seemed that the very rooks in the chimneys must be startled out of their nests. The door flew open, a flaming of lanterns was seen outside, and a dazzling lady came up the steps and swept into the hall. When she held up her cloth of silver train, I could see the diamonds that twinkled on her feet. Her bosom was covered with roses, and there was a red light in her eyes like the reflection from a hundred glowing fires. Her black hair went coiling about her head, and couched among the braids lay a jewel not unlike the head of a snake. She was flashing and glowing the gems and flowers. Her beauty and brilliance made me dizzy. Then came faintness in the air, as if her breath had poisoned it. A whirl of storm came in with her, and rushed up the staircase like a moan. The plants shuddered and shed their blossoms, and all the lights is grew dim a moment, then flared up again.

Now the drawing-room door opened, and a gentleman came out with a young girl learning on his arm. He was a fine-looking, middle-aged gentleman, with a mild countenance.

The girl was a slender creature, with golden hair and a pale face. She was dressed in pure white, with a large ruby like a drop of blood at her throat. They advanced together to receive the lady who had arrived. The gentleman offered his arm to the stranger, and the girl who was displaced for her fell back, and walked behind them with a downcast air. I felt irresistibly impelled to follow them, and passed with them into the drawing-room. Never had I mixed in a finer, gayer crowd. The costumes were rich and of an old-fashioned pattern. Dancing was going forward with spirit – minuets and country dances. The stately gentleman was evidently the host, and moved among the company, introducing the magnificent lady right and left. He led her to the head of the room presently, and they mixed in the dance. The arrogance of her manner and the fascination of her beauty were wonderful.

I cannot attempt to describe the strange manner in which I was in this company, and yet not of it. I seemed to view all I beheld through some fine and subtle medium. I saw clearly, yet I felt that it was not with my ordinary naked eyesight. I can compare it to nothing but looking at a scene through a piece of smoked or coloured glass. And just in the same way (as I have said before) all sounds seemed to reach me as if I were listening with ears imperfectly stuffed. No one present took any notice of me. I spoke to several, and they made no reply – did not even turn their eyes upon me, nor show in any way that they heard me. I planted myself straight in the way of a fine fellow in a general's uniform, but he, swerving neither to right nor left by an inch, kept on his way, as though I were a streak of mist, and left me behind him. Everyone I touched eluded me somehow. Substantial as they all looked, I could not contrive to lay my hand on anything that felt like solid flesh. Two or three times I felt a momentary relief from the oppressive sensations which distracted me, when I firmly believed I saw Frank's head at some distance among the crowd, now in one room and now in another, and again in the conservatory, which was hung with lamps, and filled with people walking about among the flowers. But, whenever I approached, he had vanished. At last I came upon him, sitting by himself on a couch behind a curtain watching the dancers. I laid my hand upon his shoulder. Here was something substantial at last. He did not look up; he seemed aware neither of my touch not my speech. I looked in his staring eyes, and found that he was sound asleep. I could not wake him.

Curiosity would not let me remain by his side. I again mixed with the crowd, and found the stately host still leading about the magnificent lady. No one seemed to notice that the golden-haired girl was sitting weeping in a corner; no one but the beauty in the silver train, who sometimes glanced at her contemptuously. Whilst I watched her distress a group came between me and her, and I wandered into another room, where, as though I had turned from one picture of her to look at another, I beheld her dancing gaily, in the full glee of Sir Roger de Coverley, with a fine-looking youth, who was more plainly dressed than any other person in the room. Never was a better-matched pair to look at. Down the middle they danced, hand in hand, his face full of tenderness, hers beaming with joy, right and left bowing and curtseying, parted and meeting again, smiling and whispering; but over the heads of smaller women there were the fierce eyes of the magnificent beauty scowling at them. Then again the crowd shifted around me, and this scene was lost.

For some time I could see no trace of the golden-haired girl in any of the rooms. I looked for her in vain, till at last I caught a glimpse of her standing smiling in a doorway with her finger lifted, beckoning. At whom? Could it be at me? Her eyes were fixed on mine. I hastened into the hall, and caught sight of her white dress passing up the wide black staircase from which I had shrunk some hours earlier. I followed her, she keeping some steps in advance. It was intensely dark, but by the gleaming of her gown I was able to trace her flying figure. Where we went I knew not, up how many stairs, down how many passages, till we arrived at a low-roofed large room with sloping roof and queer windows where there was a dim light, like the sanctuary light in a deserted church. Here, when I entered, the golden head was glimmering over something which I presently discerned to be a cradle wrapped round with white curtains, and with a few fresh flowers fastened up on the hood of it, as if to catch a baby's eye. The fair sweet face looked up at me with a glow of pride on it, smiling with happy dimples. The white hands unfolded the curtains, and stripped back the coverlet. Then, suddenly there went a rushing moan all round the weird room, that seemed like a gust of wind forcing in through the crannies, and shaking the jingling old windows in their sockets. The cradle was an empty one. The girl fell back with a look of horror on her pale face that I shall never forget, then, flinging her arms above her head, she dashed from the room.

I followed her as fast as I was able, but the wild white figure was too swift for me. I had lost her before I reached the bottom of the staircase. I searched for her, first in one room, then in another, neither could I see her foe (as I already believed to be), the lady of the silver train. At length I found myself in a small anteroom, where a lamp was expiring on the table. A window was open, close by it the golden-haired girl was lying sobbing in a chair, while the magnificent lady was bending over her as if soothingly, and offering her something to drink in a goblet. The moon was rising behind the two figures. The shuddering light of the lamp was flickering over the girl's bright head, the rich embossing of the golden cup, the lady's silver robes, and, I thought, the jewelled eyes of the serpent looked out from her bending head. As I watched, the girl raised her face and drank, then suddenly dashed the goblet away; while a cry such as I never heard but once, and shiver to remember, rose to the very roof of the old house, and the clear sharp word '*Poisoned!*' rang and reverberated from hall and chamber in a thousand echoes, like the clash of a peal of bells. The girl dashed herself from the open window, leaving the cry clamouring behind her. I heard the violent opening of doors and running of feet, but I waited for nothing more. Maddened by what I had witnessed, I would have felled the murderess, but she glided unhurt from under my vain blow. I sprang from the window after the wretched white figure. I saw it flying on before me with a speed I could not overtake. I ran till I was dizzy. I called like a madman, and heard the owls croaking back to me. The moon grew huge and bright, the trees grew out before it like the bushy heads of giants, the river lay keen and shining like a long unsheathed sword, couching for deadly work among the rushes. The white figure shimmered and vanished, glittered brightly on before me, shimmered and vanished again, shimmered, staggered, fell, and disappeared in the river. Of what she was, phantom or reality, I thought not at the moment; she had the semblance of a human being going to destruction, and I had the frenzied impulse to save her. I rushed forward with one last effort, struck my foot against the root of a tree, and was dashed to the ground. I remember a crash, momentary pain and confusion; then nothing more.

When my senses returned, the red clouds of the dawn were shining in the river beside me. I arose to my feet, and found that, though much bruised, I was otherwise unhurt. I busied my mind in recalling the strange circumstances which had brought me to that place in the dead of the night. The recollection of all I had witnessed was vividly present to my mind. I took my way slowly to the house, almost expecting to see the marks of wheels and other indications of last night's revel, but the rank grass that covered the gravel was uncrushed, not a blade disturbed, not a stone displaced. I shook one of the drawing-room windows till I shook off the old rusty hasp inside, flung up the creaking sash, and entered. Where were the brilliant draperies and carpets, the soft gilding, the vases teeming with flowers, the thousand sweet odours of the night before? Not a trace of them; no, nor even a ragged cobweb swept away, nor a stiff chair moved an inch from its melancholy place, nor the face of a mirror relieved from one speck of its obscuring dust!

Coming back into the open air, I met the old man from the gate walking up one of the weedy paths. He eyed me meaningly from head to foot, but I gave him good-morrow cheerfully.

'You see I am poking about early,' I said.

'I' faith, sir,' said he, 'an' ye look like a man that had been pokin' about *all night*.'

'How so?' said I.

'Why, ye see, sir,' said he, 'I'm used to 't, an' I can read it in yer face like prent. Some sees one thing an' some another, an' some only feels an' hears. The poor jintleman inside, *he* says nothin', but he has beautyful dhrames. An' for the Lord's sake, sir, take him out o' this, for I've seen him wandherin' about like a ghost himself in the heart of the night, an' him that sound sleepin' that I couldn't wake him!'

*   *   *

At breakfast I said nothing to Frank of my strange adventures. He had rested well, he said, and boasted of his enchanting dreams. I asked him to describe them, when he grew perplexed and annoyed. He remembered nothing, but that his spirit had been delightfully entertained whilst his body reposed. I now felt a curiosity to go through the old house, and was not surprised, on pushing open a door at the end of a remote mouldy passage, to enter the identical chamber into which I had followed the pale-faced girl when she beckoned me out of the drawing-room. There were the low brooding roof and slanting walls, the short wide latticed windows to which the noonday sun was trying to pierce through a forest of leaves. The hangings rotting with age shook like dreary banners at the opening of the door, and there in the middle of the room was the cradle; only the curtains that had been white were blackened with dirt, and laced and overlaced with cobwebs. I parted the curtains, bringing down a shower of dust upon the floor, and saw lying upon the pillow, within, a child's tiny shoe, and a toy. I need not describe the rest of the house. It was vast and rambling, and, as far as furniture and decorations were concerned, the wreck of grandeur.

Having strange subject for meditation, I walked alone in the orchard that evening. This orchard sloped towards the river I have mentioned before. The trees were old and stunted, and the branches tangled overhead. The ripe apples were rolling in the long bleached grass. A row of taller trees, sycamores and chestnuts, straggled along by the river's edge, ferns and tall weeds grew round and amongst them, and between their trunks, and behind the rifts in the foliage, the water was seen to flow. Walking up and down one of the paths I alternately faced these trees and turned my back upon them. Once when coming towards them I chanced to lift my glance, started, drew my hands across my eyes, looked again, and finally stood still gazing in much astonishment. I saw distinctly the figure of a lady standing by one of the trees, bending low towards the grass. Her face was a little turned away, her dress a bluish-white, her mantle a dun-brown colour. She held a spade in her hand, and her foot was upon it, as if she were in the act of digging. I gazed at her for some time, vainly trying to guess at whom she might be, then I advanced towards her. As I approached, the outlines of her figure broke up and disappeared, and I found that she was only an illusion presented to me by the curious accidental grouping of the lines of two trees which had shaped the space between them into the semblance of the form I have described. A patch of the flowing water had been her robe, a piece of russet moorland her cloak. The spade was an awkward young shoot slanting up from the root of one of the trees. I stepped back and tried to piece her out again bit by bit, but could not succeed. That night I did not feel at all inclined to return to my dismal chamber, and lie awaiting such another summons as I had once received. When Frank bade me good-night, I heaped fresh coals on the fire, took down from the shelves a book, from which I lifted the dust in layers with my penknife, and, dragging an armchair close to the hearth, tried to make myself as comfortable as might be. I am a strong, robust man, very unimaginative, and little troubled with affections of the nerves, but I confess that my feelings were not enviable, sitting thus alone in that queer old house, with last night's strange pantomime still vividly present to my memory. In spite of my efforts at coolness, I was excited by the prospect of what yet might be in store for me before morning. But these feelings passed away as the night wore on, and I nodded asleep over my book.

I was startled by the sound of a brisk light step walking overhead. Wide awake at once, I sat up and listened. The ceiling was low, but I could not call to mind what room it was that lay above the library in which I sat. Presently I heard the same step upon the stairs, and the loud sharp rustling of a silk dress sweeping against the banisters. The step paused at the library door, and then there was silence. I got up, and with all the courage I could summon seized a light, and opened the door; but there was nothing in the hall but the usual heavy darkness and damp mouldy air. I confess I felt more uncomfortable at that moment than I had done at any time during the preceding night. All the visions that had then appeared to me had produced nothing like the horror of thus feeling a supernatural presence which my eyes were not permitted to behold.

I returned to the library, and passed the night there. Next day I sought for the room above it in which I had heard the footsteps, but could discover no entrance to any such room. Its windows, indeed, I counted from the outside, though they were so overgrown with ivy I could hardly discern them, but in the interior of the house I could find no door to the chamber. I asked Frank about it, but he knew and cared nothing on the subject; I asked the old man at the lodge, and he shook his head.

'Och!' he said, 'don't ask about that room. The door's built up, and flesh and blood have no consarn wid it. It was *her own* room.'

'Whose own?' I asked.

'Ould Lady Thunder's. An' whist, sir! *that's her grave!*'

'What do you mean?' I said. 'Are you out of your mind?'

He laughed queerly, drew nearer, and lowered his voice. 'Nobody has asked about the room these years but yourself,' he said. 'Nobody misses it goin' over the house. My grandfather was an old retainer o' the Thunder family, my father was in the service too, an' I was born myself before the ould lady died. Yon was her room, an' she left her eternal curse on her family if so be they didn't lave her coffin there. *She* wasn't goin' undher the ground to the worms. So there it was left, an' they built up the door. God love ye, sir, an' don't go near it. I wouldn't have told you, only I know ye've seen plenty about already, an' ye have the look o' one that'd be ferretin' things out, savin' yer presence.'

He looked at me knowingly, but I gave him no information, only thanked him for putting me on my guard. I could scarcely credit what he told me about the room; but my curiosity was excited regarding it. I made up my mind that day to try and induce Frank to quit the place on the morrow. I felt more and more convinced that the atmosphere was not healthful for his mind, whatever it might be for his body. The sooner we left the spot the better for us both; but the remaining night which I had to pass there I resolved on devoting to the exploring of the walled-up chamber. What impelled me to this resolve I do not know. The undertaking was not a pleasant one, and I should hardly have ventured on it had I been forced to remain much longer at the Rath. But I knew there was little chance of sleep for me in that house, and I thought I might as well go and seek for my adventures as sit waiting for them to come for me, as I had done the night before. I felt a relish for my enterprise, and expected the night with satisfaction. I did not say anything of my intention either to Frank or the old man at the lodge. I did not want to make a fuss, and have my doings talked of all over the country. I may as well mention here that again, on this evening, when walking in the orchard, I saw the figure of the lady digging between the trees. And again I saw that this figure was an illusive appearance; that the water was her gown, and the moorland her cloak, and a willow in the distance her tresses.

As soon as the night was pretty far advanced, I placed a ladder against the window which was least covered over with the ivy, and mounted it, having provided myself with a dark lantern. The moon rose full behind some trees that stood like a black bank against the horizon, and glimmered on the panes as I ripped away branches and leaves with a knife, and shook the old crazy casement open. The sashes were rotten, and the fastenings easily gave way. I placed my lantern on a bench within, and was soon standing beside it in the chamber. The air was insufferably close and mouldy, and I flung the window open to the widest, and beat the bowering ivy still further back from about it, so as to let the fresh air of heaven blow into the place. I then took my lantern in hand, and began to look about me.

The room was vast and double; a velvet curtain hung between me and an inner chamber. The darkness was thick and irksome, and the scanty light of my lantern only tantalised me. My eyes fell on some tall spectral-looking candelabra furnished with wax candles, which, though black with age, still bore the marks of having been guttered by a draught that had blown on them fifty years ago. I lighted these; they burned up with a ghastly flickering, and the apartment, with its fittings, was revealed to me. These latter had been splendid in the days of their freshness: the appointments the rest of the house were mean in comparison. The ceiling was painted with fine allegorical figures, also spaces of the walls between the dim mirrors and the sumptuous hangings of crimson velvet, with their tarnished golden tassels and fringes. The carpet still felt luxurious to the tread, and the dust could not altogether obliterate the elaborate fancy of its flowery design. There were gorgeous cabinets laden with curiosities, wonderfully carved chairs, rare vases, and antique glasses of every description, under some of which lay little heaps of dust which had once no doubt been blooming flowers. There was a table laden with books of poetry and science, drawings and drawing materials, which showed that the occupant of the room had been a person of mind. There was also a writing-table scattered over with yellow papers, and a work-table at a window, on which lay reels, a thimble, and a piece of what had once been white muslin, but was now saffron colour, sewn with gold thread, a rusty needle sticking in it. This and the pen lying on the inkstand, the paperknife between the leaves of a book, the loose sketches shaken out by the side of a portfolio, and the ashes of a fire on the wide mildewed hearth-place, all suggested that the owner of this retreat had been snatched from it without warning, and that whoever had thought proper to build up the doors, had also thought proper to touch nothing that had belonged to her.

Having surveyed all these things, I entered the inner room, which was a bedroom. The furniture of this was in keeping with that of the other chamber. I saw dimly a bed enveloped in lace, and a dressing-table fancifully garnished and draped. Here I espied more candelabra, and going forward to set the lights burning, I stumbled against something. I turned the blaze of my lantern on this something, and started with a sudden thrill of horror. It was a large stone coffin.

I own that I felt very strangely for the next few minutes. When I had recovered the shock, I set the wax candles burning, and took a better survey of this odd burial-place. A wardrobe stood open, and I saw dresses hanging within. A gown lay upon a chair, as if just thrown off, and a pair of dainty slippers were beside it. The toilet-table looked as if only used yesterday, judging by the litter that covered it; hair-brushes lying this way and that way, essence-bottles with the stoppers out, paint pots uncovered, a ring here, a wreath of artificial flowers there, and in front of tall that the coffin, the tarnished Cupids that bore the mirror between their hands smirking down at it with a grim complacency.

On the corner of this table was a small golden salver, holding a plate of some black mouldered food, an antique decanter filled with wine, a glass, and a phial with some thick black liquid, uncorked. I felt weak and sick with the atmosphere of the place, and I seized the decanter, wiped the dust from it with my handkerchief, tasted, found that the wine was good, and drank a moderate draught. Immediately it was swallowed I felt a horrid giddiness, and sank upon the coffin. A raging pain was in my head and a sense of suffocation in my chest. After a few intolerable moments I felt better, but the heavy air pressed on me stiflingly, and I rushed from this inner room into the larger and outer chamber. Here a blast of cool air revived me, and I saw that the place was changed.

A dozen other candelabra besides those I had lighted were flaming round the walls, the hearth was all ruddy with a blazing fire, everything that had been dim was bright, the lustre had returned to the gilding, the flowers bloomed in the vases. A lady was sitting before the hearth in a low armchair. Her light loose gown swept about her on the carpet, her black hair fell round her to her knees, and into it her hands were thrust as she leaned her forehead upon them, and stared between them into the fire. I had scarcely time to observe her attitude when she turned her head quickly towards me, and I recognised the handsome face of the magnificent lady who had played such a sinister part in the strange scenes that had been enacted before me two nights ago. I saw something dark looming behind her chair, but I thought it was only her shadow thrown backward by the firelight.

She arose and came to meet me, and I recoiled from her. There was something horridly fixed and hollow in her gaze, and filmy in the stirring of her garments. The shadow, as she moved, grew more firm and distinct in outline, and followed her like a servant where she went.

She crossed half of the room, then beckoned me, and sat down at the writing-table. The shadow waited beside her, adjusted her paper, placed the ink-bottle near her and the pen between her fingers. I felt impelled to approach her, and to take my place at her left shoulder, so as to be able to see what she might write. The shadow stood motionless at her other hand. As I became accustomed to the shadow's presence he grew more visibly loathsome and hideous. He was quite distinct from the lady, and moved independently of her with long ugly limbs. She hesitated about beginning to write, and he made a wild gesture with his arm, which brought her hand quickly to the paper, and her pen began to move at once. I needed not to bend and scrutinise in order to read. Every words as it was forming flashed before me like a meteor.

'I am the spirit of Madeline, Lady Thunder, who lived and died in this house, and whose coffin stands in yonder room among the vanities in which I delighted. I am constrained to make my confession to you, John Thunder, who are the present owner of the estates of your family.'

Here the hand trembled and stopped writing. But the shadow made a threatening gesture, and the hand fluttered on.

'I was beautiful, poor, and ambitious, and when I entered this house first on the night of a ball given by Sir Luke Thunder, I determined to become its mistress. His daughter, Mary Thunder, was the only obstacle in my way. She divined my intention, and stood between me and her father. She was a gentle, delicate girl, and no match for me. I pushed her aside, and became Lady Thunder. After that I hated her, and made her dread me. I had gained the object of my ambition, but I was jealous of the influence possessed by her over her father, and I revenged myself by crushing the joy out her young life. In this I defeated my own purpose. She eloped with a young man who was devoted to her, though poor, and beneath her in station. Her father was indignant at first, and my malice was satisfied; but as time passed on I had no children, and she had a son, soon after whose birth her husband died. Then her father took her back to his heart, and the boy was his idol and heir.'

Again the hand stopped writing, the ghostly head drooped, and the whole figure was convulsed. But the shadow gesticulated fiercely, and, cowering under its menace, the wretched spirit went on: 'I caused the child to be stolen away. I thought I had done it cunningly, but she tracked the crime home to me. She came and accused me of it, and in the desperation of my terror at discovery, I gave her poison to drink. She rushed from me and from the house in frenzy, and in her mortal anguish fell in the river. People thought she had gone mad from grief for her child, and committed suicide. I only knew the horrible truth. Sorrow brought an illness upon her father, of which he died. Up to the day of his death he dad search made for the child. Believing that it was alive, and must be found, he willed all his property to it, his rightful heir, and to its heirs for ever. I buried the deeds under a tree in the orchard, and forged a will, in which all was bequeathed to me during my lifetime. I enjoyed my state and grandeur till the day of my death, which came upon me miserably, and, after that, my husband's possessions went to a distant relation of his family. Nothing more was heard of the fate of the child two was stolen; but he lived and married, and his daughter now toils for her bread – his daughter, who is the rightful owner of all that is said to belong to you, John Thunder. I tell you this that you may devote yourself to the task of discovering this wronged girl, and giving up to her that which you are unlawfully possessed of. Under the thirteenth tree standing on the brink of the river at the foot of the orchard you will find buried the genuine will of Sir Luke Thunder. When you have found and read it, do justice, as you value your soul. In order that you may know the grandchild of Mary Thunder when you find her, you shall behold her in a vision – '

The last words grew dim before me; the light faded away, and all the place was in darkness, except one spot on the opposite wall. On this spot the light glimmered softly, and against the brightness the outlines of a figure appeared, faintly at first, but, growing firm and distinct, became filled in and rounded at last to the perfect semblance of life. The figure was that of a young girl in a plain black dress, with a

bright, happy face, and pale gold hair softly banded on her fair forehead. She might have been the twin-sister of the pale-faced girl whom
I had seen bending over the cradle two nights ago; but her healthier,
gladder, and prettier sister. When I had gazed on her some moments,
the vision faded away as it had come; the last vestige of the brightness
died out upon the wall, and I found myself once more in total darkness. Stunned for a time by the sudden changes, I stood watching for
the return of the lights and figures; but in vain. By and by my eyes grew
accustomed to the obscurity, and I saw the sky glimmering behind the
little window which I had left open. I could soon discern the writing-
table beside me, and possessed myself of the slips of loose paper which
lay upon it. I then made my way to the window. The first streaks
of dawn were in the sky as I descended my ladder, and I thanked
God that I breathed the fresh morning air once more, and heard the
cheering sound of the cocks crowing.

*   *   *

All thought of acting immediately upon last night's strange revelations,
almost all memory of them, was for the time banished from my mind
by the unexpected trouble of the next few days. That morning I found
an alarming change in Frank. Feeling sure that he was going to be ill, I
engaged a lodging in a cottage in the neighbourhood, whither we
removed before nightfall, leaving the accursed Rath behind us. Before
midnight he was in the delirium of a raging fever.

I thought it right to let his poor little fiancée know his state, and
wrote to her, trying to alarm her no more than was necessary. On the
evening of the third day after my latter went I was sitting by Frank's
bedside, when an unusual bustle outside aroused my curiosity, and
going into the cottage kitchen I saw a figure standing in the firelight
which seemed a third appearance of that vision of the pale-faced
golden-haired girl which was now thoroughly imprinted on my
memory – a third, with all the woe of the first and all the beauty of the
second. But this was a living, breathing apparition. She was throwing
off her bonnet and shawl, and stood there at home in a moment in her
plain black dress. I drew my hand across my eyes to make sure that they
did not deceive me. I had beheld so many supernatural visions lately
that it seemed as thought I could scarcely believe in the reality of
anything till I had touched it.

'Oh, sir,' said the visitor, 'I am Mary Leonard, and are you poor Frank's friend? Oh, sir, we are all the world to one another, and I could not let him die without coming to see him!'

And here the poor little traveller burst into tears. I cheered her as well as I could, telling her that Frank would soon, I trusted, be out of all danger. She told me that she had thrown up her situation in order to come and nurse him. I said we had got a more experienced nurse than she could be, and then I gave her to the care of our landlady, a motherly countrywoman. After that I went back to Frank's bedside, nor left it for long till he was convalescent. The fever had swept away all that strangeness in this manner which had afflicted me, and he was quite himself again.

There was a joyful meeting of the lovers. The more I saw of Mary Leonard's bright face the more thoroughly was I convinced that she was the living counterpart of the vision I had seen in the burial chamber. I made enquiries as to her birth, and her father's history, and found that she was indeed the grandchild of that Mary Thunder whose history had been so strangely related to me, and the rightful heiress of all those properties which for a few months only had been mine. Under the tree in the orchard, the thirteenth, and that by which I had seen the lady digging, were found the buried deeds which had been described to me. I made an immediate transfer of property, whereupon some others who thought they had a chance of being my heirs disputed the matter with me, and went to law. Thus the affair has gained publicity, and become a nine days' wonder. Many things have been in my favour, however: the proving of Mary's birth and of Sir Luke's will, the identification of Lady Thunder's handwriting on the slips of paper which I had brought from the burial chamber; also other matters which a search in that chamber brought to light. I triumphed, and I now go abroad, leaving Frank and his Many made happy by the possession of what could only have been a burden to me.

So the manuscript ends. Major Thunder fell in battle a few years after the adventure it relates. Frank O'Brien's grandchildren hear of him with gratitude and awe. The Rath has been long since totally dismantled and left to go to ruin.

FORREST REID

Courage

୨୧୨

When the children came to stay with their grandfather, young Michael Aherne, walking with the others from the station to the rectory, noticed the high grey wall that lined one side of the long, sleepy lane, and wondered what lay beyond it. For above his head, over the tops of the mossy stones, trees stretched green arms that beckoned to him, and threw black shadows on the white, dusty road. His four brothers and sisters, stepping demurely beside tall, rustling Aunt Caroline, left him lagging behind, and, when a white bird fluttered out for a moment into the sunlight, they did not even see it. Michael called to them, and eight eyes turned straightaway to the trees, but were too late. So he trotted on and took fat, tried Barbara's place by Aunt Caroline.

'Does anybody live there?' he asked; but Aunt Caroline shook her head. The house, whose chimneys he presently caught a glimpse of through the trees, had been empty for years and years; the people to whom it belonged lived somewhere else.

Michael learned more than this from Rebecca, the cook, who told him that the house was empty because it was haunted. Long ago a lady lived there, but she had been very wicked and very unhappy, poor thing, and even now could find no rest in her grave . . .

*   *   *

It was on an afternoon when he was all alone that Michael set out to explore the stream running past the foot of the rectory garden. He would follow it, he thought, wherever it led him; follow it just as his father, far away in wild places, had followed mighty rivers into the heart of the forest. The long, sweet, green grass brushed against his legs, and a white cow, with a buttercup hanging from the corner of her mouth, gazed at him in mild amazement as he flew past. He kept to the meadow side, and on the opposite bank the leaning trees made little magic caves tapestried with green. Black flies darted restlessly about, and every now and again he heard strange splashes – splashes of birds, of fish; the splash of a rat; and once the heavy, floundering splash of the cow herself, plunging into the water up to her knees. He watched her tramp through the sword-shaped leaves of a bed of irises, while the rich black mud oozed up between patches of bright green weed. A score of birds made a quaint chorus of trills and peeps, chuckles and whistles; a wren, like a tiny winged mouse, flitted about the ivy-covered bole of a hollow elm. Then Michael came unexpectedly to the end of his journey, for an iron gate was swung here right across the stream, and on either side of it, as far as he could see, stretched a high grey wall.

He paused. The gate was padlocked, and its spiked bars were so narrow that to climb it would not be easy. Suddenly a white bird rose out of the burning green and gold of the trees, and for a moment, in the sunlight, it was the whitest thing in the world. The it flew back again into the mysterious shadow, and Michael stood breathless.

He knew now where he was, knew that this wall must be a continuation of the wall in the lane. The stooping trees leaned down as if to catch him in their arms. He looked at the padlock on the gate and saw that it was half eaten by rust. He took off his shoes and stockings. Stringing them about his neck, he waded through the water and with a stone struck the padlock once, twice – twice only, for at the second blow the lock dropped into the stream, with a dull splash. Michael tugged at the rusty bolt, and in a moment or two the gate was open. On the other side he clambered up the bank to put on his shoes, and it was then that, as he glanced behind him, he saw the gate swing slowly back in silence.

That was all, yet it somehow startled him, and he had a fantastic impression that he had not been meant to see it. 'Of course it must have moved of its own weight,' he told himself, but it gave him an uneasy feeling as of someone following stealthily on his footsteps, and he remembered Rebecca's story.

Before him was a dark, moss-grown path, like the narrow aisle of a huge cathedral whose pillars were the over-arching trees. It seemed to lead on through an endless green stillness, and he stood dreaming on the outermost fringe, wondering, doubting, not very eager to explore further.

He walked on, and the noise of the stream died away behind him, like the last warning murmur of the friendly world outside. Suddenly, turning at an abrupt angle, he came upon the house. It lay beyond what had once been a lawn, and the grass, coarse and matted, grew right up to the doorsteps, which were green, with gaping apertures between the stones. Ugly, lived stains, lines of dark moss and lichen, crept over the red bricks; and the shutters and blinds looked as if they had been closed for ever. Then Michael's heart gave a jump, for at that moment an uneasy puff of wind stirred one of the lower shutters, which flapped back with a dismal rattle.

He stood there while he might have counted a hundred, on the verge of flight, poised between curiosity and fear. At length curiosity, the spirit of adventure, triumphed, and he advanced to a closer inspection. With his nose pressed to the pane, he gazed into a large dark room, across which lay a band of sunlight, thin as a stretched ribbon. He gave the window a tentative push, and, to his surprise, it yielded. Had there been another visitor here? he wondered. For he saw that the latch was not broken, must have been drawn back from within, or forced, very skilfully, in some way that had left no mark upon the woodwork. He made these reflections and then, screwing up his courage, stepped across the sill.

Once inside, he had a curious sense of relief. He could somehow *feel* that the house was empty, that not even the ghost of a ghost lingered there. With this certainty, everything dropped consolingly, yet half disappointingly, back into the commonplace, and he became conscious that outside it was broad daylight, and that ghost stories were nothing more than a kind of fairytale. He opened the other shutters, letting the rich afternoon light pour in. Though the house had been empty for so long, it smelt sweet and fresh, and not a speck of dust was visible anywhere. He drew his fingers over the top of one of the little tables, but so clean was it that might have been polished that morning. He touched the faded silks and curtains, and sniffed at faintly smelling china jars. Over the wide carved chimney-piece hung a picture of a lady, very young and beautiful. She was sitting in a chair, and beside her stood a tall, delicate boy of Michael's own age. One of the boy's hands rested on the lady's shoulder, and the other held a gilt-clasped book. Michael, gazing at them, easily saw that they were mother and son. The lady seemed to him infinitely lovely, and presently she made him think of his own mother, and with that he began to feel homesick, and all kinds of memories returned to him. They were dim and shadowy, and, as he stood there dreaming, it seemed to him that somehow his mother was bound up with this other lady – he could not tell how – and at last he turned away, wishing that he had not looked at the picture. He drew from his pocket the letter he had received that morning. His mother was better; she would soon be quite well again. Yesterday she had been out driving for more than an hour, she told him, and today she felt a little tired, which was why her letter must be rather short . . . And he remembered, remembered through a sense of menacing trouble only half realised during those days of uneasy waiting in the silent rooms at home; only half realised even at the actual moment of goodbye – remembered that last glimpse of her face, smiling, smiling so beautifully and bravely . . .

He went out into the hall and unbarred and flung wide the front door, before ascending to the upper storeys. He found many curious things, but, above all, in one large room, he discovered a whole store of toys – soldiers, puzzles, books, a bow and arrows, a musical box with a little silver key lying beside it. He wound it up, and a gay, sweet melody tinkled out into the silence, thin and fragile, losing itself in the empty vastness of that still house, like the flicker of a taper in a cave.

He opened a door leading into a second room, a bedroom, and, sitting down in the window-seat, began to turn the pages of an old illuminated volume he found there, full of strange pictures of saints and martyrs, all glowing in gold and bright colours, yet somehow sinister, disquieting. It was with a start that, as he looked up, he noticed how dark it had become indoors. The pattern had faded out of the chintz bed curtains, and he could no longer see clearly into the further corners of the room. It was from these corners that the darkness seemed to be stealing out, like a thin smoke, spreading slowly over everything. Then a strange fancy came to him, and it seemed to him that he had lived in this house for years and years, and that all his other life was but a dream. It was so dark now that the bed curtains were like pale shadows, and outside, over the trees, the moon was growing brighter. He must go home . . .

He sat motionless, trying to realise what had happened, listening, listening, for it was as if the secret, hidden heart of the house had begun very faintly to beat. Faintly at first, a mere stirring of the vacant atmosphere, yet, as the minutes passed, it gathered strength, and with this consciousness of awakening life a fear came also. He listened in the darkness, and though he could hear nothing, he had a vivid sense that he was no longer alone. Whatever had dwelt here before had come back, was perhaps even now creeping up the stairs. A sickening, stupefying dread paralysed him. It had not come for him, he told himself – whatever it was. It wanted to avoid him, and perhaps he could get downstairs without meeting it. Then it flashed across his mind, radiantly, savingly, that if he had not seen it by now it was only because it *was* avoiding him. He sprang to his feet and opened the door – not the door leading to the other room, but one giving on the landing.

Outside, the great well of the staircase was like a yawning pit of blackness. His heart thumped as he stood clutching at the wall. With shut eyes, lest he should see something he had no desire to see, he took two steps forward and gripped the balusters. Then, with eyes still tightly shut, he ran quickly down – quickly, recklessly, as if a fire were at his heels.

Down in the hall, the open door showed as a dim silver-grey square, and he ran to it, but the instant he passed the threshold his panic left him. A fear remained, but it was no longer blind and brutal. It was as if a voice had spoken to him, and, as he stood there, a sense that everything swayed in a balance, that everything depended upon what he did next, swept over him. He looked up at the dark, dreadful staircase. Nothing had pursued him, and he knew now that nothing *would* pursue him. Whatever was there was not there for that purpose, and if he were to see it he must go in search of it. But if he left it? If he left it now, he knew that he should leave something else as well. In forsaking one he should forsake both; in losing one he should lose both. Another spirit at this moment was close to him, and it was the spirit of his mother, who, invisible, seemed to hold his hand keep him there upon the step. But why – why? He could only tell that she *wanted* him to stay: but of that he was certain. If he were a coward she would know. It would be impossible to hide it from her. She might forgive him – she would forgive him – but it could never be the same again. He steadied himself against the side of the porch. The cold moonlight washed through the dim hall, and turned to a glimmering greyness the lowest flight of stairs. With sobbing breath and wide eyes he retraced his steps, but at the foot of the stairs he stopped once more. The greyness ended at the first landing; beyond that, an impenetrable blackness led to those awful upper storeys. He put his foot on the lowest stair, and slowly, step by step, he mounted, clutching the balusters. He did not pause on the landing, but walked on into the darkness, which seemed to close about his slight figure like the heavy wings of a monstrous tomb.

On the uppermost landing of all, the open doors allowed a faint light to penetrate. He entered the room of the toys and stood beside the table. The beating of the blood in his ears almost deafened him. 'If only it would come now!' he prayed, for he felt that he could not tolerate the strain of waiting. But nothing came; there was neither sight nor sound. At length he made his final effort, and crossing to the door, which was now closed, turned the handle. For a moment the room seemed empty, and he was conscious of a sudden, an immense relief. Then, close by the window-seat, in the dim twilight, he perceived something. He stood still, while a deathly coldness descended upon him. At first hardly more than a shadow, a thickening of the darkness, what he gazed upon made no movement, and so long as it remained thus, with head mercifully lowered, he felt that he could bear it. But the suspense tortured him, and presently a faint moan of anguish rose from his dry lips. With that, the grey, marred face, the face he dreaded to see, was slowly lifted. He tried to close his eyes, but could not. He felt himself sinking to the ground, and clutched at the doorpost for support. Then suddenly he seemed to know that it, too, this – this thing – was afraid, and that what it feared was his fear. He saw the torment, the doubt and despair, that glowed in the smoky dimness of those hollowed, dreadful eyes. How changed was this lady from the bright, beautiful lady of the picture! He felt a pity for her, and as his compassion grew his fear diminished. He watched her move slowly towards him – nearer, nearer – only now there was something else that mingled with his dread, battling with it, overcoming it; and when at last she held out her arms to him, held them wide in a supreme, soundless appeal, he knew that it had conquered. He came forward and lifted his face to hers. At the same instant she bent down over him and seemed to draw him to her. An icy coldness, as of a dense mist, enfolded him, and he felt and saw no more . . .

*   *   *

When he opened his eyes the moon was shining upon him, and he knew at once that he was alone. He knew, moreover, that he was now free to go. But the house no longer held any terror for him, and, as he scrambled to his feet, he felt a strange happiness that was very quiet, and a little like that he used to feel when, after he had gone up to bed, he lay growing sleepier and sleepier, while he listened to his mother singing. He must go home, but he would not go for a minute or two yet. He moved his hand, and it struck against a box of matches lying on a table. He had not known they were there, but now he lighted the tall candles on the chimney-piece, and as he did so he became more vividly aware of what he had felt dimly ever since he had opened his eyes. Some subtle atmospheric change had come about, though in what it consisted he could not at once tell. It was like a hush in the air, the strange hush which comes with the falling of snow. But how could there be snow in August? and, moreover, this was within the house, not outside. He lifted one of the candlesticks and saw that a delicate powder of dust had gathered upon it. He looked down at his own clothes – they, too, were covered with that same thin powder. Then he knew what was happening. The dust of years had begun to fall again; silently, slowly, like a soft and continuous caress, laying every-thing in the house to sleep.

Dawn was breaking when, with a candle in either hand, he descended the broad, whitening staircase. As he passed out into the garden he saw lanterns approaching, and knew they had come to look for him. They were very kind, very gentle with him, and it was not till the next day that he learned of the telegram which had come in his absence.

DOROTHY MACARDLE

The Prisoner

❧❧

It was on an evening late in May that Liam Daly startled us by strolling into Una's room, a thin, laughing shadow of the boy we had known at home. We had imagined him a helpless convalescent still in Ireland and welcomed him as if he had risen from the dead. For a while there was nothing but clamourous question and answer, raillery, revelry and the telling of news; his thirty-eight days' hunger-strike had already become a theme of whimsical wit; but once or twice as he talked his face sobered and he hesitated, gazing at me with a pondering burdened look.

'He holds me with his glittering eye!' I complained at last. He laughed.

'Actually,' he said, 'you're right. There *is* a story I have to tell – sometime, somewhere, and if you'll listen, I couldn't do better than to tell it here and now.'

He had found an eager audience, but his grace face quieted us and it was in an intent silence that he told his inexplicable tale.

'You'll say it was a dream,' he began, 'and I hope you'll be right; I could never make up my mind; it happened in the gaol. You know Kilmainham?' He smiled at Larry who nodded. 'The gloomiest prison in Ireland, I suppose – goodness knows how old. When the strike started I was in a punishment cell, a "noisome dungeon", right enough, complete with rats and all, dark always, and dead quiet; none of the others were in that wing. It amounted to solitary confinement, of course, and on hunger-strike that's bad, the trouble is to keep a hold of your mind.

'I think it was about the thirtieth day I began to be afraid – afraid of going queer. It's not a pretty story, all this,' he broke off, looking remorsefully at Una, 'but I'd like you to understand – I want to know what you think.

'They'd given up bringing in food and the doctor didn't trouble himself overmuch with me; sometimes a warder would look through the peep-hole and shout a remark; but most of the day and all night I was alone.

'The worst was losing the sense of time; you've no idea how that torments you. I'd doze and wake up and not know whether a day or only an hour had gone; I'd think sometimes it was the fiftieth day, maybe, and we'd surely be out soon; then I'd think it was the thirtieth still; then a crazy notion would come that there was no such thing as time in prison at all; I don't know how to explain – I used to think that time went past outside like a stream, moving on, but in prison you were in a kind of whirlpool – time going round and round with you, so that you'd never come to anything, even death, only back again to yesterday and round to today and back to yesterday again. I got terrified, then, of going mad; I began talking and chattering to myself, trying to keep myself company, and that only made me worse because I found I couldn't stop – something seemed to have got into my brain and to be talking – talking hideous, blasphemous things, and I couldn't stop it. I thought I was turning into that – Ah, there's no describing it!

'At times I'd fight my way out of it and pray. I knew, at those times, that the blaspheming thing wasn't myself; I thought 'twas a foul spirit, some old criminal maybe, that had died in that cell. Then the fear would come on me that if I died insane he'd take possession of me and I'd get lost in Hell. I gave up praying for everything except the one thing, then – that I'd die before I went mad. One living soul to take to would have saved me; when the doctor came I'd all I could do to keep from crying out to him not to leave me alone; but I'd just sense enough left to hold on while he was there.

'The solitude and the darkness were like one – the one enemy – you couldn't hear and you couldn't see. At times it was pitch black; I'd think I was in my coffin then and the silence trying to smother me. Then I'd seem to float up and away – to lose my body, and then wake up suddenly in a cold sweat, my heart drumming with the shock. The darkness and I were two things hating one another, striving to destroy one another – it closing on me, crushing me, stifling the life out of my brain – I trying to pierce it, trying to see – My God, it was awful!

'One black night the climax came. I thought I was dying and that 'twas a race between madness and death. I was striving to keep my mind clear till my heart would stop, prying to go sane to God. And the darkness was against me – the darkness, thick and powerful and black. I said to myself that if I could pierce that, if I could make myself see – see anything, I'd not go mad. I put out all the strength I had, striving to see the window or the peep-hole or the crucifix on the wall, and failed. I knew there was a little iron seat clamped into the wall in the corner opposite the bed. I willed, with a desperate, frenzied intensity, to see that; and I did see it at last. And when I saw it all the fear and strain died away in me, because I saw that I was not alone.

'He was sitting there quite still, a limp, despairing figure, his head bowed, his hands hanging between his knees; for a long time I waited, then I was able to see better and I saw that he was a boy – fair-haired, white-faced, quite young, and there were fetters on his feet. I can tell you, my heart went out to him, in pity and thankfulness and love.

'After a while he moved, lifted up his head and stared at me – the most piteous look I have ever seen.

'He was a young lad with thin, starved features and deep eye-sockets like a skull's; he looked, then bowed his head down hopelessly again, not saying a word. But I knew that his whole torment was the need to speak, to tell something; I got quite strong and calm, watching him, waiting for him to speak.

'I waited a long while, and that dizzy sense of time working in a circle took me, the circles getting larger and larger, like eddies in a pool, again. At last he looked up and rested his eyes beseechingly on me as if imploring me to be patient; I understood; I had conquered the dark – he had to break through the silence – I knew it was very hard.

'I saw his lips move and at last I heard him – a thin, weak whisper came to me: "Listen – listen – for the love of God!"

'I looked at him, waiting; I didn't speak; it would have scared him. He leaned forward, swaying, his eyes fixed, not on mine, but on some awful vision of their own; the eyes of a soul in purgatory, glazed with pain.

' "Listen, listen!" I heard, "the truth! You must tell it – it must be remembered; it must be written down!"

' "I will tell it," I said, very gently, "I will tell it if I live."

' "Live, live, and tell it!" he said, moaningly and then, then he began. I can't repeat his words, all broken, shuddering phrases; he talked as if to himself only – I'll remember as best I can.

' "My mother, my mother!" he kept moaning, and "the name of shame!" "They'll put the name of shame on us," he said, "and my mother that is so proud – so proud she never let a tear fall, though they murdered my father before her eyes! Listen to me!" He seemed in an anguish of haste and fear, striving to tell me before we'd be lost again. "Listen! Would I do it to save my life? God knows I wouldn't, and I won't! But they'll say I did it! They'll say it to her. They'll be pouring out their lies through Ireland and I cold in my grave!"

'His thin body was shaken with anguish; I didn't know what to do for him. At last I said, "Sure, no one'll believe their lies."

' "My Lord won't believe it!" he said vehemently. "Didn't he send me up and down with messages to his lady? Would he do that if he didn't know I loved him – know I could go to any death?"

' " 'Twas in the Duke's Lawn they caught me," he went on. " 'Twas on Sunday last and they're starving me ever since; trying night and day they are to make me tell them what house he's in – and God knows I could tell them! I could tell!"

'I knew well the dread that was on him. I said, "There's no fear," and he looked at me a little quieter then.

' "They beat me," he went on. "They half strangled me in the Castle Yard and then they threw me in here. Listen to me! Are you listening?" he kept imploring. "I'll not have time to tell you all!"

' "Yesterday one of the redcoats came to me – an officer, I suppose, and he told me my Lord will be caught. Some lad that took his last message sold him . . . He's going to Moira House in the morning, disguised; they'll waylay him – attack him in the street. They say there'll be a fight – and sure I know there will – and he'll be alone; they'll kill him. He laughed, the devil – telling me that! He laughed, I tell you, because I cried.

' "A priest came in to me then – a priest! My God, he was a fiend! He came in to me in the dead of night, when I was lying shivering and sobbing for my Lord. He sat and talked to me in a soft voice – I thought at first he was kind. Listen till I tell you! Listen till you hear all! He told me I could save my Lord's Life. They'd go quietly to his house and take him; there'd be no fighting and he'd not be hurt. I'd only have to say where his lodging was. My God, I stood up and cursed him! He, a priest! God forgive me if he was."

' "He was no priest," I said, trying to quiet him. "That's an old tale."

' "He went out then," the poor boy went on, talking feverishly, against time. "And a man I'd seen at the Castle came in, a man with a narrow face and a black cloak. The priest was with him and he began talking to me again, the other listening, but I didn't mind him or answer him at all. He asked me wasn't my mother a poor widow, and wasn't I her only son. Wouldn't I do well to take her to America, he said, out of the hurt and harm, and make a warm home for her, where she could end her days in peace. I could earn the right to it, he said – good money, and the passage out, and wasn't it my duty as a son. The face of my mother came before me – the proud, sweet look she has, like a queen; I minded the loving voice of her and she saying, 'I gave your father for Ireland and I'd give you.' My God, my God, what were they but fiends? What will I do, what will I do at all?"

'He was in an agony, twisting his thin hands.

' "You'll die and leave her her pride in you," I said.

'Then, in broken gasps he told me the rest.

' "The Castle man – he was tall, he stood over me – he said, 'You'll tell us what we want to know.' "

' "I'll die first," I said to him and he smiled. He had thin, twisted lips – and he said, "You'll hang in the morning like a dog."

' "Like an Irishman, please God," I said.

' "He went mad at that and shook his first in my face and talked sharp and wicked through his teeth. O my God! I went down on my knees to him, I asked him in God's holy name! How will I bear it? How will I bear it at all?"

'He was overwhelmed with woe and terror; he bowed his head and trembled from head to foot.

' "They'll hang me in the morning," he gasped, looking at me haggardly. "And they'll take him and they'll tell him I informed. The black priest'll go to my mother – he said it! Himself said it! He'll tell her I informed! It will be the death blow on her heart – worse than death! 'Twill be written in the books of Ireland to the end of time. They'll cast the word of shame on my grave."

'I never saw a creature in such pain – it would break your heart. I put out all the strength I had and swore an oath to him. I swore that if

I lived I'd give out the truth, get it told and written through Ireland. I don't know if he heard; he looked at me wearily, exhausted, and sighed and leaned his head back against the wall.

'I was tired out and half conscious only, but there was a thing I was wanting to ask. For a while I couldn't remember what it was, then I remembered again and asked it: "Tell me, what is your name?"

'I could hardly see him. The darkness had taken him again, and the silence; his voice was very far off and faint.

' "I forget," it said. "I have forgotten. I can't remember my name."

'It was quite dark then. I believe I fainted. I was unconscious when I was released.'

* * *

Max Barry broke the puzzled silence with a wondering exclamation: 'Lord Edward! More than a hundred years!'

'Poor wretch!' laughed the irrepressible Frank. 'In Kilmainham since ninety-eight!'

'Ninety-eight?' Larry looked up quickly. 'You weren't in the hospital were you, Liam? I was. You know it used to be the condemned cell. There's a name carved on the window-sill, and a date in ninety-eight – I can't – I can't remember the name.'

'Was there anyone accused, Max?' Una asked. 'Any record of a boy?'

Max frowned: 'Not that I remember – but so many were suspect – it's likely enough – poor boy!'

'I never could find out,' said Liam. 'Of course I wasn't far off delirium. It may have been hallucination or a dream.'

I did not believe he believed that and looked at him. He smiled.

'I want you to write it for me,' he pleaded quietly. 'I promised, you see.'

SHERIDAN LE FANU

The Watcher

It is now more than fifty years since the occurrences which I am about to relate caused a strange sensation in the gay society of Dublin. The fashionable world, however, is no recorder of traditions; the memory of selfishness seldom reaches far; and the events which occasionally disturb the polite monotony of its pleasant and heartless progress, however stamped with the characters of misery and horror, scarcely outlive the gossip of a season, and (except, perhaps, in the remem– brance of a few more directly interested in the consequences of the catastrophe) are in a little time lost to the recollection of all. The appetite for scandal, or for horror, has been sated; the incident can yield no more of interest or novelty; curiosity, frustrated by impenetrable mystery, gives over the pursuit in despair; the tale has ceased to be new, grows stale and flat; and so, in a few years, enquiry subsides into indifference.

Somewhere about the year 1794, the younger brother of a certain baronet, whom I shall call Sir James Barton, returned to Dublin. He had served in the navy with some distinction, having commanded one of his Majesty's frigates during the greater part of the American war. Captain Barton was now apparently some two or three-and-forty years of age. He was an intelligent and agreeable companion, when he chose it, though generally reserved, and occasionally even moody. In society, however, he deported himself as a man of the world and a gentleman. He had not contracted any of the noisy brusqueness sometimes acquired at sea, on the contrary, his manners were remarkably easy, quiet, and even polished. He was in person about the middle size, and somewhat strongly formed; his coun-tenance was marked with the lines of thought, and on the whole

wore an expression of gravity and even of melancholy. Being, however, as we have said, a man of perfect breeding, as well as of affluent
circumstances and good family, he had, of course, ready access to the
best society of the metropolis, without the necessity of any other
credentials. In his personal habits Captain Barton was economical.
He occupied lodgings in one of the then fashionable streets in the
south side of the town, kept but one horse and one servant, and
though a reputed free-thinker, he lived an orderly and moral life,
indulging neither in gaming, drinking, nor any other vicious pursuit,
living very much to himself, without forming any intimacies, or
choosing any companions, and appearing to mix in gay society rather
for the sake of its bustle and distraction, than for any opportunities
which it offered of interchanging either thoughts or feelings with its
votaries. Barton was therefore pronounced a saving, prudent, unsocial
sort of a fellow, who bid fair to maintain his celibacy alike against
stratagem and assault, and was likely to live to a good old age, die rich
and leave his money to a hospital.

It was soon apparent, however, that the nature of Captain Bartons
plans had been totally misconceived. A young lady, whom we shall
call Miss Montague, was at this time introduced into the fashionable
world of Dublin by her aunt, the Dowager Lady Rochdale. Miss
Montague was decidedly pretty and accomplished, and having some
natural cleverness, and a great deal of gaiety, became for a while
the reigning toast. Her popularity, however, gained her, for a time,
nothing more than that unsubstantial admiration which, however
pleasant as an incense to vanity is by no means necessarily antecedent
to matrimony, for, unhappily for the young lady in question, it was
an understood thing, that, beyond her personal attractions, she had
no kind of earthly provision. Such being the state of affairs, it will
readily be believed that no little surprise was consequent upon the
appearance of Captain Barton as the avowed lover of the penniless
Miss Montague.

His suit prospered, as might have been expected, and in a short
time it was confidentially communicated by old Lady Rochdale to
each of her hundred and fifty particular friends in succession, that
Captain Barton had actually tendered proposals of marriage, with
her approbation, to her niece, Miss Montague, who had, moreover,
accepted the offer of his hand, conditionally upon the consent of her

father, who was then upon his homeward voyage from India, and expected in two or three months at furthest. About his consent there could be no doubt. The delay, therefore, was one merely of form; they were looked upon as absolutely engaged, and Lady Rochdale, with a vigour of old-fashioned decorum with which her niece would, no doubt, gladly have dispensed, withdrew her thenceforward from all further participation in the gaieties of the town. Captain Barton was a constant visitor as well as a frequent guest at the house, and was permitted all the privileges and intimacy which a betrothed suitor is usually accorded. Such was the relation of parties, when the mysterious circumstances which darken this narrative with inexplicable melancholy first began to unfold themselves.

Lady Rochdale resided in a handsome mansion at the north side of Dublin, and Captain Bartons lodgings, as we have already said, were situated at the south. The distance intervening was considerable, and it was Captain Barton's habit generally to walk home without an attendant, as often as he passed the evening with the old lady and her fair charge. His shortest way in such nocturnal walks lay, for a considerable space, through a line of streets which had as yet been merely laid out, and little more than the foundations of the houses constructed. One night, shortly after his engagement with Miss Montague had commenced, he happened to remain usually late, in company only with her and Lady Rochdale. The conversation had turned upon the evidences of revelation, which he had disputed with the callous scepticism of a confirmed infidel. What were called 'French principles' had, in those days, found their way a good deal into fashionable society, especially that portion of it which professed allegiance to Whiggism, and neither the old lady nor her charge was so perfectly free from the taint as to look upon Captain Barton's views as any serious objection to the proposed union. The discussion had degenerated into one upon the supernatural and the marvellous, in which he had pursued precisely the same line of argument and ridicule. In all this, it is but true to state, Captain Barton was guilty of no affectation; the doctrines upon which he insisted were, in reality, but too truly the basis of his own fixed belief, if so it might be called; and perhaps not the least strange of the many strange circumstances connected with this narrative, was the fact that the subject of the fearful influences we are about to describe was himself, from the deliberate conviction of years, an utter disbeliever in what are usually termed preternatural agencies.

It was considerably past midnight when Mr Barton took his leave, and set out upon his solitary walk homeward. He rapidly reached the lonely road, with its unfinished dwarf walls tracing the foundations of the projected rows of houses on either side. The moon was shining mistily, and its imperfect light made the road he trod but additionally dreary; that utter silence, which has in it something indefinably exciting, reigned there, and made the sound of his steps, which alone broke it, unnaturally loud and distinct. He had proceeded thus some way, when on a sudden he heard other footsteps, pattering at a measured pace, and, as it seemed, about two score steps behind him. The suspicion of being dogged is at all times unpleasant; it is, however, especially so in a spot so desolate and lonely: and this suspicion became so strong in the mind of Captain Barton, that he abruptly turned about to confront his pursuers, but, though there was quite sufficient moonlight to disclose any object upon the road he had traversed, no form of any kind was visible.

The steps he had heard could not have been the reverberation of his own, for he stamped his foot upon the ground, and walked briskly up and down, in the vain attempt to wake an echo. Though by no means a fanciful person, he was at last compelled to charge the sounds upon his imagination, and treat them as an illusion. Thus satisfying himself, he resumed his walk, and before he had proceeded a dozen paces, the mysterious footfalls were again audible from behind, and this time, as if with the special design of showing that the sounds were not the responses of an echo, the steps sometimes slackened nearly to a halt, and sometimes hurried for six or eight strides to a run, and again abated to a walk.

Captain Barton, as before, turned suddenly round, and with the same result; no object was visible above the deserted level of the road. He walked back over the same ground, determined that, whatever might have been the cause of the sounds which had so disconcerted him, it should not escape his search; the endeavour, however, was unrewarded. In spite of all his scepticism, he felt something like a superstitious fear stealing fast upon him, and, with these unwonted and uncomfortable sensations, he once more turned and pursued his way. There was no repetition of these haunting sounds, until he had reached the point where he had last stopped to retrace his steps. Here they were resumed, and with sudden starts of running, which threatened to bring the unseen pursuer close up to the alarmed pedestrian. Captain Barton arrested his course as formerly; the unaccountable nature of the occurrence filled him with vague and almost horrible sensations, and, yielding to the excitement he felt gaining upon him, he shouted, sternly, 'Who goes there?'

The sound of one's own voice, thus exerted, in utter solitude, and followed by total silence, has in it something unpleasantly exciting, and he felt a degree of nervousness which, perhaps, from no cause had he ever known before. To the very end of this solitary street the steps pursued him, and it required a strong effort of stubborn pride on his part to resist the impulse that prompted him every moment to run for safety at the top of his speed. It was not until he had reached his lodging, and sat by his own fireside, that he felt sufficiently reassured to arrange and reconsider in his own mind the occurrences which had so discomposed him: so little a matter, after all, is sufficient to upset the pride of scepticism, and vindicate the old simple laws of nature within us.

Mr Barton was next morning sitting at a late breakfast, reflecting upon the incidents of the previous night, with more of inquisitiveness than awe – so speedily do gloomy impressions upon the fancy disappear under the cheerful influences of day – when a letter just delivered by the postman was placed upon the table before him. There was nothing remarkable in the address of this missive, except that it was written in a hand which he did not know – perhaps it was disguised – for the tall narrow characters were sloped backward; and with the self-inflicted suspense which we so often see practised in such cases, he puzzled over the inscription for a full minute before he broke the seal. When he did so, he read the following words, written in the same hand:

Mr Barton, late captain of the *Dolphin*, is warned of *danger*. He will do wisely to avoid – Street – (here the locality of his last night's adventure was named) – if he walks there as usual, he will meet with something bad. Let him take warning, once for all, for he has good reason to dread

THE WATCHER.

Captain Barton read and re-read this strange effusion; in every light

and in every direction he turned it over and over. He examined the
paper on which it was written, and closely scrutinised the handwriting.
Defeated here, he turned to the seal; it was nothing but a patch of
wax, upon which the accidental impression of a coarse thumb was
imperfectly visible. There was not the slightest mark, no clue or
indication of any kind, to lead him to even a guess as to its possible
origin. The writers object seemed a friendly one, and yet he subscribed
himself as one whom he had 'good reason to dread'. Altogether, the
letter, its author, and its real purpose, were to him an inexplicable
puzzle, and one, moreover, unpleasantly suggestive, in his mind, of
associations connected with the last night's adventure.

In obedience to some feeling – perhaps of pride – Mr Barton did not
communicate, even to his intended bride, the occurrences which we
have just detailed. Trifling as they might appear, they had in reality
most disagreeably affected his imagination, and he cared not to
disclose, even to the young lady in question, what she might possibly
look upon as evidences of weakness. The letter might very well be but
a hoax, and the mysterious footfall but a delusion of his fancy. But
although he affected to treat the whole affair as unworthy of a thought,
it yet haunted him pertinaciously, tormenting him with perplexing
doubts, and depressing him with undefined apprehensions. Certain it
is, that for a considerable time afterwards he carefully avoided the
street indicated in the letter as the scene of danger.

It was not until about a week after the receipt of the letter which I
have transcribed, that anything further occurred to remind Captain
Barton of its contents, or to counteract the gradual disappearance
from his mind of the disagreeable impressions which he had then
received. He was returning one night, after the interval I have stated,
from the theatre, which was then situated in Crow Street, and having
there handed Miss Montague and Lady Rochdale into their carriage,
he loitered for some time with two or three acquaintances. With
these, however, he parted close to the College, and pursued his
way alone. It was now about one o'clock, and the streets were quite
deserted. During the whole of his walk with the companions from
whom he had just parted, he had been at times painfully aware of the
sound of steps, as it seemed, dogging them on their way. Once or
twice he had looked back, in the uneasy anticipation that he was again
about to experience the same mysterious annoyances which had so

much disconcerted him a week before, and earnestly hoping that he might *see* some form from whom the sounds might naturally proceed. But the street was deserted; no form was visible. Proceeding now quite alone upon his homeward way, he grew really nervous and uncomfortable, as he became sensible, with increased distinctness, of the well-known and now absolutely dreaded sounds.

By the side of the dead wall which bounded the College Park, the sounds followed, recommencing almost simultaneously with his own steps. The same unequal pace, sometimes slow, sometimes, for a score yards or so, quickened to a run, was audible from behind him. Again and again he turned, quickly and stealthily he glanced over his shoulder almost at every half-dozen steps; but no one was visible. The horrors of this intangible and unseen persecution became gradually all but intolerable; and when at last he reached his home his nerves were strung to such a pitch of excitement that he could not rest, and did not attempt even to lie down until after the daylight had broken.

He was awakened by a knock at his chamber-door, and his servant entering, handed him several letters which had just been received by the early post. One among them instantly arrested his attention; a single glance at the direction aroused him thoroughly. He at once recognised its character, and read as follows:

> You may as well think, Captain Barton, to escape from your own shadow as from me; do what you may, I will see you as often as I please, and you shall see me, for I do not want to hide myself, as you fancy. Do not let it trouble your rest, Captain Barton; for, with a *good conscience*, what need you fear from the eye of
>
> THE WATCHER?

It is scarcely necessary to dwell upon the feelings elicited by a perusal of this strange communication. Captain Barton was observed to be unusually absent and out of spirits for several days afterwards; but no one divined the cause. Whatever he might think as to the phantom steps which followed him, there could be no possible illusion about the letters he had received; and, to say the least of it, their immediate sequence upon the mysterious sounds which had haunted him was an odd coincidence. The whole circumstance, in his own mind, was vaguely and instinctively connected with certain passages in his past life, which, of all others, he hated to remember.

It so happened that just about this time, in addition to his approaching nuptials, Captain Barton had fortunately, perhaps, for himself, some business of an engrossing kind connected with the adjustment of a large and long-litigated claim upon certain properties. The hurry and excitement of business had its natural effect in gradually dispelling the marked gloom which had for a time occasionally oppressed him, and in a little while his spirits had entirely resumed their accustomed tone.

During all this period, however, he was occasionally dismayed by indistinct and half-heard repetitions of the same annoyance, and that in lonely places, in the day time as well as after nightfall. These renewals of the strange impressions from which he had suffered so much were, however, desultory and faint, insomuch that often he really could not, to his own satisfaction, distinguish between them and the mere suggestions of an excited imagination. One evening he walked down to the House of Commons with a Mr Norcott, a Member. As they walked down together he was observed to become absent and silent, and to a degree so marked as scarcely to consist with good breeding; and this, in one who was obviously in all his habits so perfectly a gentleman, seemed to argue the pressure of some urgent and absorbing anxiety. It was afterwards known that, during the whole of that walk, he had heard the well-known footsteps dogging him as he proceeded. This, however, was the last time he suffered from this phase of the persecution of which he was already the anxious victim. A new and a very different one was about to be presented.

Of the new series of impressions which were afterwards gradually to work out his destiny, that evening disclosed the first; and but for its relation to the train of events which followed, the incident would scarcely have been remembered by anyone. As they were walking in at the passage, a man (of whom his friend could afterwards remember only that he was short in stature, looked like a foreigner, and wore a kind of travelling-cap) walked very rapidly, and, as if under some fierce excitement, directly towards them, muttering to himself fast and vehemently the while. This odd-looking person proceeded straight toward Barton, who was foremost, and halted, regarding him for a moment or two with a look of menace and fury almost maniacal; and then turning about as abruptly, he walked before them at the same agitated pace, and disappeared by a side passage. Norcott distinctly remembered being a good deal shocked at the countenance and bearing of this man, which indeed irresistibly impressed him with an undefined sense of danger, such as he never felt before or since from the presence of anything human; but these sensations were far from amounting to anything so disconcerting as to flurry or excite him – he had seen only a singularly evil countenance, agitated, as it seemed, with the excitement of madness. He was absolutely astonished, however, at the effect of this apparition upon Captain Barton. He knew him to be a man of proved courage and coolness in real danger, a circumstance which made his conduct upon this occasion the more conspicuously odd. He recoiled a step or two as the stranger advanced, and clutched his companions arm in silence, with a spasm of agony or terror; and then, as the figure disappeared, shoving him roughly back, he followed it for a few paces, stopped in great disorder, and sat down upon a form. A countenance more ghastly and haggard it was impossible to fancy.

'For God's sake, Barton, what is the matter?' said Norcott, really alarmed at his friend's appearance. 'You're not hurt, are you? nor unwell? What is it?'

'What did he say? I did not hear it. What was it?' asked Barton, wholly disregarding the question.

'Tut, tut, nonsense!' said Norcott, greatly surprised; 'who cares what the fellow said? You are unwell, Barton, decidedly unwell; let me call a coach.'

'Unwell! Yes, no, not exactly unwell,' he said, evidently making an effort to recover his self-possession; 'but, to say the truth, I am fatigued, a little overworked, and perhaps over anxious. You know I have been in Chancery, and the winding up of a suit is always a nervous affair. I have felt uncomfortable all this evening; but I am better now. Come, come, shall we go on?'

'No, no. Take my advice, Barton, and go home; you really do need rest; you are looking absolutely ill. I really do insist on your allowing me to see you home,' replied his companion.

It was obvious that Barton was not himself disinclined to be persuaded. He accordingly took his leave, politely declining his friend's offered escort. Notwithstanding the few commonplace regrets which Norcott had expressed, it was plain that he was just as little deceived as

Barton himself by the extempore plea of illness with which he had accounted for the strange exhibition, and that he even then suspected some lurking mystery in the matter.

Norcott called next day at Bartons lodgings, to enquire for him, and learned from the servant that he had not left his room since his return the night before; but that he was not seriously indisposed, and hoped to be out again in a few days. That evening he sent for Dr Richards, then in large and fashionable practice in Dublin, and their interview was, it is said, an odd one.

He entered into a detail of his own symptoms in an abstracted and desultory kind of way, which seemed to argue a strange want of interest in his own cure, and, at all events, made it manifest that there was some topic engaging his mind of more engrossing importance than his present ailment. He complained of occasional palpitations, and headache. Dr Richards asked him, among other questions, whether there was any irritating circumstance or anxiety to account for it. This he denied quickly and peevishly; and the physician thereupon declared his opinion, that there was nothing amiss except some slight derangement of the digestion, for which he accordingly wrote a prescription, and was about to withdraw, when Mr Barton, with the air of a man who suddenly recollects a topic which had nearly escaped him, recalled him.

'I beg your pardon, doctor, but I had really almost forgot; will you permit me to ask you two or three medical questions? – rather odd ones, perhaps, but as a wager depends upon their solution, you will, I hope, excuse my unreasonableness.'

The physician readily undertook to satisfy the enquirer.

Barton seemed to have some difficulty about opening the proposed interrogatories, for he was silent for a minute, then walked to his bookcase and returned as he had gone; at last he sat down, and said: 'You'll think them very childish questions, but I can't recover my wager without a decision; so I must put them. I want to know first about lockjaw. If a man actually has had that complaint, and appears to have died of it – so that in fact a physician of average skill pronounces him actually dead – may he, after all, recover?'

Dr Richards smiled, and shook his head.

'But – but a blunder may be made,' resumed Barton. 'Suppose an ignorant pretender to medical skill; may *he* be so deceived by any stage of the complaint, as to mistake what is only a part of the progress of the disease, for death itself?'

'No one who had ever seen death,' answered he, 'could mistake it in the case of lockjaw.'

Barton mused for a few minutes. 'I am going to ask you a question, perhaps still more childish; but first tell me, are not the regulations of foreign hospitals, such as those of, let us say, Lisbon, very lax and bungling? May not all kinds of blunders and slips occur in their entries of names, and so forth?'

Dr Richards professed his inability to answer that query.

'Well, then, doctor, here is the last of my questions. You will probably laugh at it; but it must out nevertheless. Is there any disease, in all the range of human maladies, which would have the effect of perceptibly contracting the stature, and the whole frame – causing the man to shrink in all his proportions, and yet to preserve his exact resemblance to himself in every particular – with the one exception, his height and bulk; *any* disease, mark, no matter how rare, how little believed in, generally, which could possibly result in producing such an effect?'

The physician replied with a smile, and a very decided negative.

'Tell me, then,' said Barton, abruptly, 'if a man be in reasonable fear of assault from a lunatic who is at large, can he not procure a warrant for his arrest and detention?'

'Really, that is more a lawyer's question than one in my way,' replied Dr Richards; 'but I believe, on applying to a magistrate, such a course would be directed.'

The physician then took his leave; but, just as he reached the hall-door, remembered that he had left his cane upstairs, and returned. His reappearance was awkward, for a piece of paper, which he recognised as his own prescription, was slowly burning upon the fire, and Barton sitting close by with an expression of settled gloom and dismay. Dr Richards had too much tact to appear to observe what presented itself; but he had seen quite enough to assure him that the mind, and not the body, of Captain Barton was in reality the seat of his sufferings.

A few days afterwards, the following advertisement appeared in the Dublin newspapers:

If Sylvester Yelland, formerly a foremast man on board his Majesty's frigate *Dolphin*, or his nearest of kin, will apply to Mr Robery Smith, solicitor, at his office, Dame Street, he or they may hear of something greatly to his or their advantage. Admission may be had at any hour up to twelve o'clock at night for the next fortnight, should parties desire to avoid observation; and the strictest secrecy, as to all communications intended to be confidential, shall be honourably observed.

The *Dolphin*, as we have mentioned, was the vessel which Captain Barton had commanded; and this circumstance, connected with the extraordinary exertions made by the circulation of handbills, etc., as well as by repeated advertisements, to secure for this strange notice the utmost possible publicity, suggested to Dr Richards the idea that Captain Barton's extreme uneasiness was somehow connected with the individual to whom the advertisement was addressed, and he himself the author of it. This, however, it is needless to add, was no more than a conjecture. No information whatsoever, as to the real purpose of the advertisement itself, was divulged by the agent, nor yet any hint as to who his employer might be.

Mr Barton, although he had latterly begun to earn for himself the character of a hypochondriac, was yet very far from deserving it. Though by no means lively, he had yet, naturally, what are termed 'even spirits,' and was not subject to continual depressions. He soon, therefore, began to return to his former habits; and one of the earliest symptoms of this healthier tone of spirits was his appearing at a grand dinner of the Freemasons, of which worthy fraternity he was himself a brother. Barton, who had been at first gloomy and abstracted, drank much more freely than was his wont – possibly with the purpose of dispelling his own secret anxieties – and under the influence of good wine, and pleasant company, became gradually (unlike his usual self) talkative, and even noisy. It was under this unwonted excitement that he left his company at about half-past ten o'clock; and as conviviality is a strong incentive to gallantry, it occurred to him to proceed forthwith to Lady Rochdale's, and pass the remainder of the evening with her and his destined bride.

Accordingly, he was soon at — Street, and chatting gaily with the ladies. It is not to be supposed that Captain Barton had exceeded the limits which propriety prescribes to good fellowship; he had merely taken enough of wine to raise his spirits, without, however, in the least degree unsteadying his mind, or affecting his manners. With this undue elevation of spirits had supervened an entire oblivion or contempt of those undefined apprehensions which had for so long weighed upon his mind, and to a certain extent estranged him from society; but as the night wore away, and his artificial gaiety began to flag, these painful feelings gradually intruded themselves again, and he grew abstracted and anxious as heretofore. He took his leave at length, with an unpleasant foreboding of some coming mischief, and with a mind haunted with a thousand mysterious apprehensions, such as, even while he acutely felt their pressure, he, nevertheless, inwardly strove, or affected to contemn.

It was his proud defiance of what he considered to be his own weakness which prompted him upon this occasion to the course which brought about the adventure which we are now about to relate. Mr Barton might have easily called a coach, but he was conscious that his strong inclination to do so proceeded from no cause other than what he desperately persisted in representing to himself to be his own superstitious tremors. He might also have returned home by a rout different from that against which he had been warned by his mysterious correspondent; but for the same reason he dismissed this idea also, and with a dogged and half desperate resolution to force matters to a crisis of some kind,, to see if there were any reality in the causes of his former suffering, and if not, satisfactorily to bring their delusiveness to the proof, he determined to follow precisely the course which he had trodden upon the night so painfully memorable in his own mind as that on which his strange persecution had commenced. Though, sooth to say, the pilot who for the first time steers his vessel under the muzzles of a hostile battery never felt his resolution more severely tasked than did Captain Barton, as he breathlessly pursued this solitary path; a path which, in spite of every effort of scepticism and reason, he felt to be, as respected *him*, infested by a malignant influence.

He pursued his way steadily and rapidly, scarcely breathing from intensity of suspense; he, however, was troubled by no renewal of the dreaded footsteps, and was beginning to feel a return of confidence, as, more than three-fourths of the way being accomplished with impunity, he approached the long line of twinkling oil lamps which indicated the frequented streets. This feeling of self-congratulation was, however, but momentary. The report of a musket at some two hundred yards behind him, and the whistle of a bullet close to his head, disagreeably and startlingly dispelled it. His first impulse was to retrace his steps in pursuit of the assassin; but the road on either side was, as we have said, embarrassed by the foundations of a street, beyond which extended waste fields, full of rubbish and neglected lime and brick kilns, and all now as utterly silent as though no sound had ever disturbed their dark and unsightly solitude. The futility of attempting, single-handed, under such circumstances, a search for the murderer, was apparent, especially as no further sound whatever was audible to direct his pursuit.

With the tumultuous sensations of one whose life had just been exposed to a murderous attempt, and whose escape has been the narrowest possible, Captain Barton turned, and without, however, quickening his pace actually to a run, hurriedly pursued his way. He had turned, as we have said, after a pause of a few seconds, and had just commenced his rapid retreat, when on a sudden he met the well-remembered little man in the fur cap. The encounter was but momentary. The figure was walking at the same exaggerated pace, and with the same strange air of menace as before; and as it passed him, he thought he heard it say, in a furious whisper, 'Still alive, still alive!'

The state of Mr Barton's spirits began now to work a corresponding alteration in his health and looks, and to such a degree that it was impossible that the change should escape general remark. For some reasons, known but to himself, he took no step whatsoever to bring the attempt upon his life, which he had so narrowly escaped, under the notice of the authorities; on the contrary, he kept it jealously to himself; and it was not for many weeks after the occurrence that he mentioned it, and then in strict confidence to a gentleman, the torments of his mind having at last compelled him to consult a friend.

Spite of his blue devils, however, poor Barton, having no satisfactory reason to render to the public for any undue remissness in the attentions which his relation to Miss Montague required, was obliged to exert himself, and present to the world a confident and cheerful bearing. The true source of his sufferings, and every circumstance connected with them, he guarded with a reserve so jealous, that it seemed dictated by at least a suspicion that the origin of his strange persecution was known to himself, and that it was of a nature which, upon his own account, he could not or dare not disclose.

The mind thus turned in upon itself, and constantly occupied with a haunting anxiety which it dared not reveal, or confide to any human breast, became daily more excited; and, of course, more vividly impressible, by a system of attack which operated through the nervous system; and in this state he was destined to sustain, with increasing frequency, the stealthy visitations of that apparition, which from the first had seemed to possess so unearthly and terrible a hold upon his imagination.

*   *   *

It was about this time that Captain Barton called upon the then celebrated preacher, Dr Macklin, with whom he had a slight acquaintance; and an extraordinary conversation ensued. The divine was seated in his chambers in college, surrounded with works upon his favourite pursuit and deep in theology, when Barton was announced. There was something at once embarrassed and excited in his manner, which, along with his wan and haggard countenance, impressed the student with the unpleasant consciousness that his visitor must have recently suffered terribly indeed to account for an alteration so striking, so shocking.

After the usual interchange of polite greeting, and a few common-place remarks, Captain Barton, who obviously perceived the surprise which his visit had excited, and which Dr Macklin was unable wholly to conceal, interrupted a brief pause by remarking – 'This is a strange call, Dr Macklin, perhaps scarcely warranted by an acquaintance so slight as mine with you. I should not, under ordinary circumstances, have ventured to disturb you, but my visit is neither an idle nor impertinent intrusion. I am sure you will not so account it, when – '

Dr Macklin interrupted him with assurances, such as good breeding suggested, and Barton resumed: 'I am come to task your patience by asking your advice. When I say your patience, I might, indeed, say more; I might have said your humanity, your compassion; for I have been, and am a great sufferer.'

'My dear sir,' replied the churchman, 'it will, indeed, afford me infinite gratification if I can give you comfort in any distress of mind, but – but – '

'I know what you would say,' resumed Barton, quickly. 'I am an unbeliever, and, therefore, incapable of deriving help from religion, but don't take that for granted. At least you must not assume that, however unsettled my convictions may be, I do not feel a deep, a very deep, interest in the subject. Circumstances have lately forced it upon my attention in such a way as to compel me to review the whole question in a more candid and teachable spirit, I believe, than I ever studied it in before.'

'Your difficulties, I take it for granted, refer to the evidences of revelation,' suggested the clergyman.

'Why – no – yes; in fact I am ashamed to say I have not considered even my objections sufficiently to state them connectedly but – but there is one subject on which I feel a peculiar interest.'

He paused again, and Dr Macklin pressed him to proceed.

'The fact is,' said Barton, 'whatever may be my uncertainty as to the authenticity of what we are taught to call revelation, of one fact I am deeply and horribly convinced: that there does exist beyond this a spiritual world – a system whose workings are generally in mercy hidden from us – a system which may be, and which is sometimes, partially and terribly revealed. I am sure, I know,' continued Barton, with increasing excitement, 'there is a God – a dreadful God – and that retribution follows guilt. In ways, the most mysterious and stupendous; by agencies, the most inexplicable and terrific; there is a spiritual system – great Heavens, how frightfully I have been convinced – a system malignant, and inexorable, and omnipotent, under whose persecutions I am, and have been, suffering the torments of the damned! – yes, sir – yes – the fires and frenzy of hell'

As Barton continued, his agitation became so vehement that the divine was shocked and even alarmed. The wild and excited rapidity with which he spoke, and, above all, the indefinable horror which stamped his features, afforded a contrast to his ordinary cool and unimpassioned self-possession, striking and painful in the last degree.

'My dear sir,' said Dr Macklin, after a brief pause, 'I fear you have been suffering much, indeed; but I venture to predict that the depression under which you labour will be found to originate in purely physical causes, and that with a change of air and the aid of a few tonics, your spirits will return, and the tone of your mind be once more cheerful and tranquil as heretofore. There was, after all, more truth than we are quite willing to admit in the classic theories which assigned the undue predominance of any one affection of the mind to the undue action or torpidity of one or other of our bodily organs. Believe me, that a little attention to diet, exercise, and the other essentials of health, under competent direction, will make you as much yourself as you can wish.'

'Dr Macklin,' said Barton, with something like a shudder, 'I *cannot* delude myself with such a hope. I have no hope to cling to but one, and that is, that by some other spiritual agency more potent than that which tortures me, *it* may be combated, and I delivered. If this may not be, I am lost – now and for ever lost.'

'But, Mr Barton, you must remember,' urged his companion, 'that others have suffered as you have done, and – '

'No, no, no,' interrupted he with irritability; 'no, sir, I am not a credulous – far from a superstitious man. I have been, perhaps, too much the reverse – too sceptical, too slow of belief; but unless I were one whom no amount of evidence could convince, unless I were to condemn the repeated, the *perpetual* evidence of my own senses, I am now – now at last constrained to believe I have no escape from the conviction, the overwhelming certainty, that I am haunted and dogged, go where I may, by – by a Demon.'

There was an almost preternatural energy of horror in Barton's face, as, with its damp and deathlike lineaments turned towards his companion, he thus delivered himself.

'God help you, my poor friend' said Dr Macklin, much shocked. 'God help you for, indeed, you *are* a sufferer, however your sufferings may have been caused.'

'Ay, ay, God help me,' echoed Barton sternly; 'but *will* He help me? will He help me?'

'Pray to Him; pray in an humble and trusting spirit,' said he.

'Pray, pray,' echoed he again; 'I can't pray; I could as easily move a mountain by an effort of my will. I have not belief enough to pray; there is something within me that will not pray. You prescribe impossibilities – literal impossibilities.'

'You will not find it so, if you will but try,' said Dr Macklin.

'Try! I *have* tried, and the attempt only fills me with confusion and terror. I have tried in vain, and more than in vain. The awful, unutterable idea of eternity and infinity oppresses and maddens my brain, whenever my mind approaches the contemplation of the Creator I recoil from the effort, scared, confounded, terrified. I tell you, Dr Macklin, if I am to be saved, it must be by other means. The idea of the Creator is to me intolerable; my mind cannot support it.'

'Say, then, my dear sir,' urged he, 'say how you would have me serve you. What you would learn of me. What can I do or say to relieve you?'

'Listen to me first,' replied Captain Barton, with a subdued air, and an evident effort to suppress his excitement; 'listen to me while I detail the circumstances of the terrible persecution under which my life has become all but intolerable – a persecution which has made me fear *death* and the world beyond the grave as much as I have grown to hate existence.'

Barton then proceeded to relate the circumstances which we have already detailed, and then continued: 'This has now become habitual – an accustomed thing. I do not mean the actual seeing him in the flesh; thank God, *that* at least is not permitted daily Thank God, from the unutterable horrors of that visitation I have been mercifully allowed intervals of repose, though none of security; but from the consciousness that a malignant spirit is following and watching me wherever I go, I have never, for a single instant, a temporary respite: I am pursued with blasphemies, cries of despair, and appalling hatred; I hear those dreadful sounds called after me as I turn the corners of streets; they come in the night-time while I sit in my chamber alone; they haunt me everywhere, charging me with hideous crimes, and – great God – threatening me with coming vengeance and eternal misery! Hush do you hear *that?*' he cried, with a horrible smile of triumph. 'There – there, will that convince you?'

The clergyman felt the chillness of horror irresistibly steal over him, while, during the wail of a sudden gust of wind, he heard, or fancied he heard, the half articulate sounds of rage and derision mingling in their sough.

'Well, what do you think of *that?*' at length Barton cried, drawing a long breath through his teeth

'I hear the wind,' said Dr Macklin; 'what should I think of it? What is there remarkable about it?'

'The prince of the powers of the air,' muttered Barton, with a shudder.

'Tut, tut my dear sir!' said the student, with an effort to reassure himself; for though it was broad daylight, there was nevertheless something disagreeably contagious in the nervous excitement under which his visitor so obviously suffered 'You must not give way to those wild fancies: you must resist those impulses of the imagination.'

'Ay, ay; "resist the devil, and he will flee from thee," ' said Barton, in the same tone; 'but *how* resist him? Ay, there it is: there is the rub. What – *what* am I to do? What *can* I do?'

'My dear sir, this is fancy,' said the man of folios 'you are your own tormentor.'

'No, no, sir; fancy has no part in it,' answered Barton, somewhat sternly. 'Fancy, forsooth! Was it that made *you*, as well as me, hear, but this moment, those appalling accents of hell? Fancy, indeed! No, no.'

'But you have seen this person frequently,' said the ecclesiastic; 'why have you not accosted or secured him? Is it not somewhat precipitate, to say no more, to assume, as you have done, the existence of preternatural agency, when, after all, everything may be easily accountable, if only proper means were taken to sift the matter.'

'There are circumstances connected with this – this *appearance*,' said Barton, 'which it were needless to disclose, but which to *me* are proofs of its horrible and unearthly nature. I know that the being who haunts me is not *man*. I say I *know* this; I could prove it to your own conviction.' He paused for a minute, and then added, 'And as to accosting it, I dare not – I could not. When I see it I am powerless; I stand in the gaze of death, in the triumphant presence of preter-human power and malignity; my strength, and faculties, and memory all forsake me. Oh, God! I fear, sir, you know not what you speak of. Mercy, mercy heaven have pity on me.'

He leaned his elbow on the table, and passed his hand across his eyes, as if to exclude some image of horror, muttering the last words of the sentence he had just concluded, again and again.

'Dr Macklin,' he said, abruptly raising himself, and looking full upon the clergyman with an imploring eye, 'I know you will do for me whatever may be done. You know now fully the circumstances and the nature of the mysterious agency of which I am the victim. I tell you I cannot help myself; I cannot hope to escape; I am utterly passive. I conjure you, then, to weigh my case well, and if anything may be done for me by vicarious supplication, by the intercession of the good, or by any aid or influence whatsoever, I implore of you, I adjure you in the name of the Most High, give me the benefit of that influence, deliver me from the body of this death! Strive for me; pity me! I know you will; you cannot refuse this; it is the purpose and object of my visit. Send me away with some hope, however little – some faint hope of ultimate deliverance, and I will nerve myself to endure, from hour to hour, the hideous dream into which my existence is transformed.'

Dr Macklin assured him that all he could do was to pray earnestly for him, and that so much he would not fail to do. They parted with a hurried and melancholy valediction. Barton hastened to the carriage which awaited him at the door, drew the blinds, and drove away, while Dr Macklin returned to his chamber, to ruminate at leisure upon the strange interview which had just interrupted his studies.

It was not to be expected that Captain Barton's changed and eccentric habits should long escape remark and discussion. Various were the theories suggested to account for it. Some attributed the alteration to the pressure of secret pecuniary embarrassments; others to a repugnance to fulfil an engagement into which he was presumed to have too precipitately entered; and others, again, to the supposed incipiency of mental disease, which latter, indeed, was the most plausible, as well as the most generally received, of the hypotheses circulated in the gossip of the day.

From the very commencement of this change, at first so gradual in its advances, Miss Montague had, of course, been aware of it. The intimacy involved in their peculiar relation, as well as the near interest which it inspired, afforded, in her case, alike opportunity and motive for the successful exercise of that keen and penetrating observation peculiar to the sex. His visits became, at length, so interrupted, and his manner, while they lasted, so abstracted, strange, and agitated, that Lady Rochdale, after hinting her anxiety and her suspicions more than once, at length distinctly stated her anxiety, and pressed for an explanation. The explanation was given, and although its nature at first relieved the worst solicitudes of the old lady and her niece, yet the circumstances which attended it, and the really dreadful consequences which it obviously threatened as regarded the spirits, and, indeed, the reason, of the now wretched man who made the strange declaration, were enough, upon a little reflection, to fill their minds with perturbation and alarm.

General Montague, the young lady's father, at length arrived. He had himself slightly known Barton, some ten or twelve years previously, and being aware of his fortune and connections, was disposed to regard him as an unexceptionable and indeed a most desirable match for his daughter. He laughed at the story of Barton's supernatural visitations, and lost not a moment in calling upon his intended son-in-law.

'My dear Barton,' he continued gaily, after a little conversation, 'my sister tells me that you are a victim to blue devils in quite a new and original shape.'

Barton changed countenance, and sighed profoundly.

'Come, come; I protest this will never do,' continued the general; 'you are more like a man on his way to the gallows than to the altar. These devils have made quite a saint of you.'

Barton made an effort to change the conversation.

'No, no, it won't do,' said his visitor, laughing; 'I am resolved to say out what I have to say about this magnificent mock mystery of yours. Come, you must not be angry; but, really, it is too bad to see you, at your time of life, absolutely frightened into good behaviour, like a naughty child, by a bugaboo, and, as far as I can learn, a very particularly contemptible one. Seriously, though, my dear Barton, I have been a good deal annoyed at what they tell me; but, at the same time, thoroughly convinced that there is nothing in the matter that may not be cleared up, with just a little attention and management, within a week at furthest.'

'Ah, general, you do not know – ' he began.

'Yes, but I do know quite enough to warrant my confidence,' interrupted the soldier. 'I know that all your annoyance proceeds from the occasional appearance of a certain little man in a cap and a greatcoat, with a red vest and bad countenance, who follows you about, and pops upon you at the corners of lanes, and throws you into ague fits. Now, my dear fellow, I'll make it my business to *catch* this mischievous little mountebank, and either beat him into a jelly with my own hands, or have him whipped through the town at the cart's tail.'

'If *you* knew what I know,' said Barton, with gloomy agitation, 'you would speak very differently. Don't imagine that I am so weak and foolish as to assume, without proof the most overwhelming, the conclusion to which I have been forced. The proofs are here, locked up here.' As he spoke, he tapped upon his breast, and with an anxious sigh continued to walk up and down the room.

'Well, well, Barton,' said his visitor, 'I'll wager a rump and a dozen I collar the ghost, and convince yourself before many days are over.'

He was running on in the same strain when he was suddenly arrested, and not a little shocked, by observing Barton, who had approached the window, stagger slowly back, like one who had received a stunning blow – his arm feebly extended towards the street, his face and his very lips white as ashes – while he uttered, 'There – there – there!'

General Montague started mechanically to his feet, and, from the window of the drawing-room, saw a figure corresponding, as well as his hurry would permit him to discern, with the description of the person whose appearance so constantly and dreadfully disturbed the repose of his friend. The figure was just turning from the rails of the area upon which it had been leaning, and without waiting to see more, the old gentleman snatched his cane and hat, and rushed down the stairs and into the street, in the furious hope of securing the person, and punishing the audacity of the mysterious stranger. He looked around him, but in vain, for any trace of the form he had himself distinctly beheld. He ran breathlessly to the nearest corner, expecting to see from thence the retreating figure, but no such form was visible. Back and forward, from crossing to crossing, he ran at fault, and it was not until the curious gaze and laughing countenances of the passers-by reminded him of the absurdity of his pursuit, that he checked his hurried pace, lowered his walking-cane from the menacing altitude which he had mechanically given it, adjusted his hat, and walked composedly back again, inwardly vexed and flurried. He found Barton pale and trembling in every joint; they both remained silent, though under emotions very different. At last Barton whispered, 'You saw it?'

'It! – him – someone – you mean – to be sure I did,' replied Montague, testily. 'But where is the good or the harm of seeing him? The fellow runs like a lamplighter. I wanted to *catch* him, but he had stolen away before I could reach the hall door. However, it is no great matter; next time, I dare say, I'll do better; and, egad, if I once come within reach of him. I'll introduce his shoulders to the weight of my cane, in a way to make him cry *peccavi*.'

Notwithstanding General Montague's undertakings and exhortations, however, Barton continued to suffer from the selfsame unexplained cause. Go how, when, or where he would. He was still constantly dogged or confronted by the hateful being who had established over him so dreadful and mysterious an influence; nowhere, and at no time, was he secure against the odious appearance which haunted him with such diabolical perseverance. His depression, misery, and excitement became more settled and alarming every day, and the mental agonies that ceaselessly preyed upon him began at last so sensibly to affect his general health, that Lady Rochdale and General Montague succeeded (without, indeed, much difficulty) in persuading him to try a short tour on the Continent, in the hope that an entire change of scene would, at all events, have the effect of breaking through the influences of local association, which the more sceptical of his friends assumed to be by no means inoperative in suggesting and perpetuating what they conceived to be a mere form of nervous illusion. General Montague, moreover, was persuaded that the figure which haunted his intended son-in-law was by no means the creation of his own imagination, but, on the contrary, a substantial form of flesh and blood, animated by a spiteful and obstinate resolution, perhaps with some murderous object in perspective, to watch and follow the unfortunate gentleman. Even this hypothesis was not a very pleasant one; yet it was plain that if Barton could once be convinced that there was nothing preternatural in the phenomenon, which he had hitherto regarded in that light, the affair would lose all its terrors in his eyes, and wholly cease to exercise upon his health and spirits the baneful influence which it had hitherto done. He therefore reasoned, that if the annoyance were actually escaped from by mere change of scene, it obviously could not have originated in any supernatural agency.

Yielding to their persuasions, Barton left Dublin for England, accompanied by General Montague. They posted rapidly to London, and thence to Dover, whence they took the packet with a fair wind for Calais. The general's confidence in the result of the expedition on Barton's spirits had risen day by day since their departure from the shores of Ireland; for, to the inexpressible relief and delight of the latter, he had not, since then, so much as even once fancied a repetition of those impressions which had, when at home, drawn him gradually down to the very abyss of horror and despair. This exemption from what he had begun to regard as the inevitable condition of his existence, and the sense of security which began to pervade his mind, were inexpressibly delightful; and in the exultation of what he considered his deliverance, he indulged in a thousand happy anticipations for a future into which so lately he had hardly dared to look. In short, both he and his companion secretly congratulated themselves upon the termination of that persecution which had been to its immediate victim a source of such unspeakable agony.

It was a beautiful day, and a crowd of idlers stood upon the jetty to receive the packet, and enjoy the bustle of the new arrivals. Montague walked a few paces in advance of his friend, and as he made his way through the crowd, a little man touched his arm, and said to him, in a broad provincial *patois*: 'Monsieur is walking too fast; he will lose his sick comrade in the throng, for, by my faith, the poor gentleman seems to be fainting.'

Montague turned quickly, and observed that Barton did indeed look deadly pale. He hastened to his side.

'My poor fellow, are you ill?' he asked anxiously.

The question was unheeded, and twice repeated, ere Barton stammered: 'I saw him – by —, I saw him!'

'*Him*! – who? – where? – when did you see him? – where is he?' cried Montague, looking around him.

'I saw him – but he is gone,' repeated Barton, faintly.

'But where – where? For God's sake, speak,' urged Montague, vehemently.

'It is but this moment – *here*,' said he.

'But what did he look like? – what had he on? – what did he wear? – quick, quick,' urged his excited companion, ready to dart among the crowd, and collar the delinquent on the spot.

'He touched your arm – he spoke to you – he pointed to me. God be merciful to me, there is no escape!' said Barton, in the low, subdued tones of intense despair.

Montague had already bustled away in all the flurry of mingled hope and indignation; but though the singular *personnel* of the stranger who had accosted him was vividly and perfectly impressed upon his recollection, he failed to discover among the crowd even the slightest resemblance to him. After a fruitless search, in which he enlisted the services of several of the bystanders, who aided all the more zealously as they believed he had been robbed, he at length, out of breath and baffled, gave over the attempt.

'Ah, my friend, it won't do,' said Barton, with the faint voice and bewildered, ghastly look of one who had been stunned by some mortal shock; 'there is no use in contending with it; whatever it is, the dreadful association between me and it is now established; I shall never escape – never, never!'

'Nonsense, nonsense, my dear fellow; don't talk so,' said Montague, with something at once of irritation and dismay; 'you must not; never mind, I say – never mind, we'll jockey the scoundrel yet.'

It was, however, but lost labour to endeavour henceforward to inspire Barton with one ray of hope; he became utterly desponding. This intangible and, as it seemed, utterly inadequate influence was fast destroying his energies of intellect, character, and health. His first object was now to return to Ireland, there, as he believed, and now almost hoped, speedily to die.

To Ireland, accordingly, he came, and one of the first faces he saw upon the shore was again that of his implacable and dreaded persecutor. Barton seemed at last to have lost not only all enjoyment and every hope in existence, but all independence of will besides. He now submitted himself passively to the management of the friends most nearly interested in his welfare. With the apathy of entire despair, he implicitly assented to whatever measures they suggested and advised; and, as a last resource, it was determined to remove him to a house of Lady Rochdale's in the neighbourhood of Clontarf, where, with the advice of his medical attendant (who persisted in his opinion that the whole train of impressions resulted merely from some nervous derangement) it was resolved that he was to confine himself strictly to the house, and to make use only of those apartments which commanded a view of an enclosed yard, the gates of which were to be kept jealously locked. These precautions would at least secure him against the casual appearance of any living form which his excited imagination might possibly confound with the spectre which, as it was contended, his fancy recognised in every figure that bore even a distant or general resemblance to the traits with which he had at first invested it. A month or six weeks' absolute seclusion under these conditions, it was hoped, might, by interrupting the series of these terrible impressions, gradually dispel the predisposing apprehension, and effectually break up the associations which had confirmed the supposed disease, and rendered recovery hopeless. Cheerful society and that of his friends was to be constantly supplied, and on the whole, very sanguine expectations were indulged in, that under this treatment the obstinate hypochondria of the patient might at length give way.

Accompanied, therefore, by Lady Rochdale, General Montague, and his daughter – his own affianced bride – poor Barton, himself never daring to cherish a hope of his ultimate emancipation from the strange horrors under which his life was literally wasting away, took possession of the apartments whose situation protected him against the dreadful intrusions from which he shrank with such unutterable terror.

After a little time, a steady persistence in this system began to manifest its results in a very marked though gradual improvement alike in the health and spirits of the invalid. Not, indeed, that anything at all approaching to complete recovery was yet discernible. On the contrary, to those who had not seen him since the commencement of his strange sufferings, such an alteration would have been apparent as might well have shocked them. The improvement, however, such as it was, was welcomed with gratitude and delight, especially by the poor young lady, whom her attachment to him, as well as her now singularly painful position, consequent on his mysterious and protracted illness, rendered an object of pity scarcely one degree less to be commiserated than himself.

A week passed – a fortnight – a month – and yet no recurrence of the hated visitation had agitated and terrified him as before. The treatment had, so far, been followed by complete success. The chain of association had been broken. The constant pressure upon the over-tasked spirits had been removed, and, under these comparatively favourable circumstances, the sense of social community with the world about him, and something of human interest, if not of enjoyment, began to reanimate his mind.

It was about this time that Lady Rochdale, who, like most old ladies of the day, was deep in family receipts, and a great pretender to medical science, being engaged in the concoction of certain unpalatable mixtures of marvellous virtue, despatched her own maid to the kitchen garden with a list of herbs which were there to be carefully culled and brought back to her for the purpose stated. The hand-maiden, however, returned with her task scarce half-completed, and a good deal flurried and alarmed. Her mode for accounting for

her precipitate retreat and evident agitation was odd, and to the old
lady unpleasantly startling.

It appeared that she had repaired to the kitchen garden, pursuant to
her mistress's directions, and had there begun to make the specified
selection among the rank and neglected herbs which crowded one
corner of the enclosure, and while engaged in this pleasant labour she
carelessly sang a fragment of an old song, as she said, 'to keep herself
company.' She was, however, interrupted by a sort of mocking echo of
the air she was singing; and looking up, she saw through the old thorn
hedge, which surrounded the garden, a singularly ill-looking, little
man, whose countenance wore the stamp of menace and malignity,
standing close to her at the other side of the hawthorn screen. She
described herself as utterly unable to move or speak, while he charged
her with a message for Captain Barton, the substance of which she
distinctly remembered to have been to the effect that he, Captain
Barton, must come abroad as usual, and show himself to his friends
out of doors, or else prepare for a visit in his own chamber. On
concluding this brief message, the stranger had, with a threatening
air, got down into the outer ditch, and seizing the hawthorn stems in
his hands, seemed on the point of climbing through the fence, a feat
which might have been accomplished without much difficulty. Without, of course, awaiting this result, the girl, throwing down her
treasures of thyme and rosemary, had turned and run, with the
swiftness of terror, to the house. Lady Rochdale commanded her, on
pain of instant dismissal, to observe an absolute silence respecting all
that portion of the incident which related to Captain Barton; and, at
the same time, directed instant search to be made by her men in the
garden and fields adjacent. This measure, however, was attended with
the usual unsuccess, and filled with fearful and indefinable misgivings,
Lady Rochdale communicated the incident to her brother. The story,
however, until long afterwards, went no further, and of course it
was jealously guarded from Barton, who continued to mend, though
slowly and imperfectly.

Barton now began to walk occasionally in the courtyard which
we have mentioned, and which, being surrounded by a high wall,
commanded no view beyond its own extent. Here he, therefore,
considered himself perfectly secure; and, but for a careless violation
of orders by one of the grooms, he might have enjoyed, at least for

some time longer, his much-prized immunity. Opening upon the public road, this yard was entered by a wooden gate, with a wicket in it, which was further defended by an iron gate upon the outside. Strict orders had been given to keep them carefully locked; but, in spite of these, it had happened that one day, as Barton was slowly pacing this narrow enclosure, in his accustomed walk, and reaching the further extremity, was turning to retrace his steps, he saw the boarded wicket ajar, and the face of his tormentor immovably looking at him through the iron bars. For a few seconds he stood riveted to the earth, breathless and bloodless, in the fascination of that dreaded gaze, and then fell helplessly upon the pavement.

There was he found a few minutes afterwards, and conveyed to his room, the apartment which he was never afterwards to leave alive. Henceforward, a marked and unaccountable change was observable in the tone of his mind. Captain Barton was now no longer the excited and despairing man he had been before; a strange alteration had passed upon him, an unearthly tranquillity reigned in his mind; it was the anticipated stillness of the grave.

'Montague, my friend, this struggle is nearly ended now,' he said, tranquilly, but with a look of fixed and fearful awe. 'I have, at last, some comfort from that world of spirits, from which my *punishment* has come. I know now that my sufferings will be soon over.'

Montague pressed him to speak on.

'Yes,' said he, in a softened voice, 'my punishment is nearly ended. From sorrow perhaps I shall never, in time or eternity, escape; but my *agony* is almost over. Comfort has been revealed to me, and what remains of my allotted struggle I will bear with submission, even with hope.'

'I am glad to hear you speak so tranquilly, my dear fellow,' said Montague; 'peace and cheerfulness of mind are all you need to make you what you were.'

'No, no, I never can be that,' said he, mournfully. 'I am no longer fit for life. I am soon to die: I do not shrink from death as I did. I am to see *him* but once again, and then all is ended.'

'He said so, then?' suggested Montague.

'*He?*' No, no; good tidings could scarcely come through him; and these were good and welcome and they came so solemnly and sweetly, with unutterable love and melancholy, such as I could not, without saying more than is needful or fitting, of other long-past scenes and persons, fully explain to you.' As Barton said this he shed tears.

'Come, come,' said Montague, mistaking the source of his emotions, 'you must not give way. What is it, after all, but a pack of dreams and nonsense; or, at worst, the practices of a scheming rascal that enjoys his power of playing upon your nerves, and loves to exert it; a sneaking vagabond that owes you a grudge, and pays it off this way, not daring to try a more manly one.'

'A grudge, indeed, he owes me; you say rightly,' said Barton, with a sullen shudder; 'a grudge as you call it. Oh, God! when the justice of heaven permits the Evil One to carry out a scheme of vengeance, when its execution is committed to the lost and frightful victim of sin, who owes his own ruin to the man, the very man, whom he is commissioned to pursue; then, indeed, the torments and terrors of hell are anticipated on earth. But heaven has dealt mercifully with me: hope has opened to me at last; and if death could come without the dreadful sight I am doomed to see, I would gladly close my eyes this moment upon the world. But though death is welcome, I shrink with an agony you cannot understand; a maddening agony, an actual frenzy of terror, from the last encounter with that – that DEMON, who has drawn me thus to the verge of the chasm, and who is himself to plunge me down. I am to see him again, once more, but under circumstances unutterably more terrific than ever.'

As Barton thus spoke, he trembled so violently that Montague was really alarmed at the extremity of his sudden agitation, and hastened to lead him back to the topic which had before seemed to exert so tranquillising an effect upon his mind.

'It was not a dream,' he said, after a time; 'I was in a different state, I felt differently and strangely; and yet it was all as real, as clear and vivid, as what I now see and hear; it was a reality.'

'And what *did* you see and hear?' urged his companion.

'When I awakened from the swoon I fell into on seeing *him*,' said Barton, continuing, as if he had not heard the question, 'it was slowly, very slowly; I was reclining by the margin of a broad lake, surrounded by misty hills, and a soft, melancholy, rose-coloured light illuminated it all. It was indescribably sad and lonely, and yet more beautiful than any earthly scene. My head was leaning on the lap of a girl, and she was singing a strange and wondrous song, that told, I known not how, whether by words or harmony, of all my life, all that is past, and all that is still to come. And with the song the old feelings that I thought had perished within me came back, and tears flowed from my eyes, partly for the song and its mysterious beauty, and partly for the unearthly sweetness of her voice; yet I know the voice, oh! how well; and I was spellbound as I listened and looked at the strange and solitary scene, without stirring, almost without breathing, and, alas, alas! alas! without turning my eyes toward the face that I knew was near me, so sweetly powerful was the enchantment that held me. And so, slowly and softly, the song and scene grew fainter, and ever fainter, to my senses, till all was dark and still again. And then I wakened to this world, as you saw, comforted, for I knew that I was forgiven much.' Barton wept again long and bitterly.

From this time, as we have said, the prevailing tone of his mind was one of profound and tranquil melancholy. This, however, was not without its interruptions. He was thoroughly impressed with the conviction that he was to experience another and a final visitation, illimitably transcending in horror all he had before experienced. From this anticipated and unknown agony he often shrunk in such paroxysms of abject terror and distraction, as filled the whole household with dismay and superstitious panic. Even those among them who affected to discredit the supposition of preternatural agency in the matter, were often in their secret souls visited during the darkness and solitude of night with qualms and apprehensions which they would not have readily confessed; and none of them attempted to dissuade Barton from the resolution on which he now systematically acted, of shutting himself up in his own apartment. The window-blinds of this room were kept jealously down; and his own man was seldom out of his presence, day or night, his bed being placed in the same chamber.

This man was an attached and respectable servant; and his duties, in addition to those ordinarily imposed upon *valets*, but which Barton's independent habits generally dispensed with, were to attend carefully to the simple precautions by means of which his master hoped to exclude the dreaded intrusion of the 'Watcher,' as the strange letter he had at first received had designated his persecutor. And, in addition to attending to these arrangements, which consisted merely in anticipating the possibility of his master's being, through any unscreened window or opened door, exposed to the dreaded influence, the valet was never to suffer him to be for one moment alone: total solitude, even for a minute, had become to him now almost as intolerable as the idea of going abroad into the public ways; it was an instinctive anticipation of what was coming.

It is needless to say, that, under these mysterious and horrible circumstances, no steps were taken toward the fulfilment of that engagement into which he had entered. There was quite disparity enough in point of years, and indeed of habits, between the young lady and Captain Barton, to have precluded anything like very vehement or romantic attachment on her part. Though grieved and anxious, therefore, she was very far from being heart-broken; a circumstance which, for the sentimental purposes of our tale, is much to be deplored. But truth must be told, especially in a narrative whose chief, if not only, pretensions to interest consist in a rigid adherence to facts, or what are so reported to have been.

Miss Montague, nevertheless, devoted much of her time to a patient but fruitless attempt to cheer the unhappy invalid. She read for him, and conversed with him; but it was apparent that whatever exertions he made, the endeavour to escape from the one constant and ever-present fear that preyed upon him was utterly and miserably unavailing.

Young ladies, as all the world knows, are much given to the cultivation of pets; and among those who shared the favour of Miss Montague was a fine old owl, which the gardener, who caught him napping among the ivy of a ruined stable, had dutifully presented to that young lady.

The caprice which regulates such preferences was manifested in the extravagant favour with which this grim and ill-favoured bird was at once distinguished by his mistress; and, trifling as this whimsical circumstance may seem, I am forced to mention it, inasmuch as it is connected, oddly enough, with the concluding scene of the story. Barton, so far from sharing in this liking for the new favourite, regarded it from the first with an antipathy as violent as it was utterly unaccountable. Its very vicinity was insupportable to him. He seemed to hate and dread it with a vehemence absolutely laughable, and to those who have never witnessed the exhibition of antipathies of this kind, his dread would seem all but incredible.

With these few words of preliminary explanation, I shall proceed to state the particulars of the last scene in this strange series of incidents.

It was almost two o'clock one winter's night, and Barton was, as usual at that hour, in his bed; the servant we have mentioned occupied a smaller bed in the same room, and a candle was burning. The man was on a sudden aroused by his master, who said: 'I can't get it out of my head that that accursed bird has escaped somehow, and is lurking in some corner of the room. I have been dreaming of him. Get up, Smith, and look about; search for him. Such hateful dreams!'

The servant rose, and examined the chamber, and while engaged in so doing, he heard the well-known sound, more like a long-drawn gasp than a hiss, with which these birds from their secret haunts affright the quiet of the night. This ghostly indication of its proximity, for the sound proceeded from the passage upon which Barton's chamber-door opened, determined the search of the servant, who, opening the door, proceeded a step or two forward for the purpose of driving the bird away. He had, however, hardly entered the lobby, when the door behind him slowly swung to under the impulse, as it seemed, of some gentle current of air; but as immediately over the door there was a kind of window, intended in the daytime to aid in lighting the passage, and through which the rays of the candle were then issuing, the valet could see quite enough for his purpose. As he advanced he heard his master (who, lying in a well-curtained bed had not, as it seemed, perceived his exit from the room) call him by name, and direct him to place the candle on the table by his bed. The servant, who was now some way in the long passage, did not like to raise his voice for the purpose of replying, lest he should startle the sleeping inmates of the house, began to walk hurriedly and softly back again, when, to his amazement, he heard a voice in the interior of the chamber answering calmly, and the man actually saw, through the window which over-topped the door, that the light was slowly shifting, as if carried across the chamber in answer to his master's call. Palsied by a feeling akin to terror, yet not unmingled with a horrible curiosity, he stood breathless and listening at the threshold, unable to summon resolution to push open the door and enter. Then came a rustling of the curtains, and a sound like that of one who in a low voice hushes a child to rest, in the midst of which he heard Barton say, in a tone of stifled horror – 'Oh, God – oh, my God!' and repeat the same exclamation several times. Then ensued a silence, which again was broken by the same strange soothing sound; and at last there burst forth, in one swelling peal, a yell of agony so appalling and hideous, that, under some impulse of ungovernable horror, the man rushed to the door, and with his whole strength strove to force it open. Whether it was that, in his agitation, he had himself but imperfectly turned the handle, or that the door was really secured upon the inside, he failed to effect an entrance; and as he tugged and pushed, yell after yell rang louder and wilder through the chamber, accompanied all the while by the same hushing sounds. Actually freezing with terror, and scarce knowing what he did, the man turned and ran down the passage, wringing his hands in the extremity of horror and irresolution. At the stair-head he was encountered by General Montague, scared and eager, and just as they met the fearful sounds had ceased.

'What is it? – who – where is your master?' said Montague, with the incoherence of extreme agitation. 'Has anything – for God's sake, is anything wrong?'

'Lord have mercy on us, it's all over,' said the man, staring wildly towards his master's chamber. 'He's dead, sir; I'm sure he's dead.'

Without waiting for enquiry or explanation, Montague, closely followed by the servant, hurried to the chamber-door, turned the handle, and pushed it open. As the door yielded to his pressure, the ill-omened bird of which the servant had been in search, uttering its spectral warning, started suddenly from the far side of the bed, and flying through the doorway close over their heads, and extinguishing, in its passage, the candle which Montague carried, crashed through the skylight that overlooked the lobby, and sailed away into the darkness of the outer space.

'There it is, God bless us!' whispered the man, after a breathless pause.

'Curse that bird!' muttered the general, startled by the suddenness of the apparition, and unable to conceal his discomposure.

'The candle was moved,' said the man, after another breathless pause; 'see, they put it by the bed!'

'Draw the curtains, fellow, and don't stand gaping there,' whispered Montague, sternly.

The man hesitated.

'Hold this, then,' said Montague, impatiently, thrusting the candle-stick into the servant's hand; and himself advancing to the bedside, he drew the curtains apart. The light of the candle, which was still burning at the bedside, fell upon a figure huddled together, and half upright, at the head of the bed. It seemed as though it had shrunk back as far as the solid panelling would allow, and the hands were still clutched in the bedclothes.

'Barton, Barton, Barton!' cried the general, with a strange mixture of awe and vehemence.

He took the candle, and held it so that it shone full upon his face. The features were fixed, stern and white; the jaw was fallen, and the sightless eyes, still open, gazed vacantly forward toward the front of the bed.

'God Almighty, he's dead!' muttered the general, as he looked upon this fearful spectacle. They both continued to gaze upon it in silence for a minute or more. 'And cold, too,' said Montague, withdrawing his hand from that of the dead man.

'And see, see; may I never have life, sir,' added the man, after another pause, with a shudder, 'but there was something else on the bed with him! Look there – look there; see that, sir!'

As the man thus spoke, he pointed to a deep indenture, as if caused by a heavy pressure, near the foot of the bed.

Montague was silent.

'Come, sir, come away, for God's sake!' whispered the man, drawing close up to him, and holding fast by his arm while he glanced fearfully round; 'what good can be done here now? – come away, for God's sake!'

At this moment they heard the steps of more than one approaching, and Montague, hastily desiring the servant to arrest their progress, endeavoured to loose the rigid grip with which the fingers of the dead man were clutched in the bedclothes, and drew, as well as he was able, the awful figure into a reclining posture. Then closing the curtains carefully upon it, he hastened himself to meet those who were approaching.

*   *   *

It is needless to follow the personages so slightly connected with this narrative into the events of their after lives; it is enough for us to remark that no clue to the solution of these mysterious occurrences was ever afterwards discovered; and so long an interval having now passed, it is scarcely to be expected that time can throw any new light upon their inexplicable obscurity. Until the secrets of the earth shall be no longer hidden, these transactions must remain shrouded in mystery.

The only occurrence in Captain Barton's former life to which reference was ever made, as having any possible connection with the sufferings with which his existence closed, and which he himself seemed to regard as working out a retribution for some grievous sin of his past life, was a circumstance which not for several years after his death was brought to light. The nature of this disclosure was painful to his relatives and discreditable to his memory.

It appeared, then, that some eight years before Captain Barton's final return to Dublin, he had formed, in the town of Plymouth, a guilty attachment, the object of which was the daughter of one of the ship's crew under his command. The father had visited the frailty of his unhappy child with extreme harshness, and even brutality, and it was said that she had died heart-broken. Presuming upon Barton's implication in her guilt, this man had conducted himself towards him with marked insolence, and Barton resented this – and what he resented with still more exasperated bitterness, his treatment of the unfortunate girl – by a systematic exercise of those terrible and arbitrary severities with which the regulations of the navy arm those who are responsible for its discipline. The man had at length made his escape, while the vessel was in port at Lisbon, but died, as it was said, in an hospital in that town, of the wounds inflicted in one of his recent and sanguinary punishments.

Whether these circumstances in reality bear or not upon the occurrences of Barton's afterlife, it is of course impossible to say. It seems, however, more than probable that they were, at least in his own mind, closely associated with them. But however the truth may be as to the origin and motives of this mysterious persecution, there can be no doubt that, with respect to the agencies by which it was accomplished, absolute and impenetrable mystery is like to prevail until the day of doom.

SHERIDAN LE FANU

Passage in the Secret History of an Irish Countess

The following paper is written in a female hand, and was no doubt communicated to my much regretted friend by the lady whose early history it serves to illustrate, the Countess D—. She is no more – she long since died, a childless and a widowed wife, and, as her letter sadly predicts, none survive to whom the publication of this narrative can prove 'injurious, or even painful'. Strange! two powerful and wealthy families, that in which she was born, and that into which she had married, are utterly extinct.

To those who know anything of the history of Irish families, as they were less than a century ago, the facts which immediately follow will at once suggest the names of the principal actors; and to others their publication would be useless – to us, possibly, if not probably injurious. I have therefore altered such of the names as might, if stated, get us into difficulty; others, belonging to minor characters in the strange story, I have left untouched.

MY DEAR FRIEND – You have asked me to furnish you with a detail of the strange events which marked my early history, and I have, without hesitation, applied myself to the task, knowing that, while I live, a kind consideration for my feelings will prevent you giving publicity to the statement; and conscious that, when I am no more, there will not survive one to whom the narrative can prove injurious, or even painful.

My mother died when I was quite an infant, and of her I have no recollection, even the faintest. By her death, my education and habits were left solely to the guidance of my surviving parent; and, so far as a stern attention to my religious instruction, and an active anxiety evinced by his procuring for me the best masters to perfect me in those accomplishments which my station and wealth might seem to require, could avail, he amply discharged the task.

My father was what is called an oddity, and his treatment of me, though uniformly kind, flowed less from affection and tenderness than from a sense of obligation and duty. Indeed, I seldom even spoke to him except at meal-times, and then his manner was silent and abrupt; his leisure hours, which were many, were passed either in his study or in solitary walks; in short, he seemed to take no further interest in my happiness or improvement than a conscientious regard to the discharge of his own duty would seem to claim.

Shortly before my birth, a circumstance had occurred which had contributed much to form and to confirm my father's secluded habits – it was the fact that a suspicion of murder had fallen upon his younger brother, a suspicion not sufficiently definite to lead to an indictment, yet strong enough to ruin him in public opinion.

This disgraceful and dreadful doubt cast upon the family name my father felt deeply and bitterly, and not the less so that he himself was thoroughly convinced of his brother's innocence. The sincerity and strength of this impression he shortly afterwards proved in a manner which produced the dark events which follow. Before, however, I enter upon the statement of them, I ought to relate the circumstances which had awakened the suspicion inasmuch as they are in themselves somewhat curious, and, in their effects, most intimately connected with my after history.

My uncle, Sir Arthur T—n, was a gay and extravagant man, and, among other vices, was ruinously addicted to gambling; this unfortunate propensity, even after his fortune had suffered so severely as to render inevitable a reduction in his expenses by no means inconsiderable, nevertheless continued to actuate him, almost to the exclusion of all other pursuits. He was a proud, or rather a vain man, and could not bear to make the diminution of his income a matter of gratulation and triumph to those with whom he had hitherto competed; and the consequence was that he frequented no longer the expensive haunts of dissipation, and retired from the gay world, leaving his coterie to discover his reasons as best they might.

He did not, however, forego his favourite vice, for, though he could not worship his divinity in the costly temples where it was formerly his wont to take his stand, yet he found it very possible to bring about him a sufficient number of the votaries of chance to answer all his ends. The consequence was that Carrickleigh, which was the name of my uncle's residence, was never without one or more of such reckless visitors.

It happened that upon one occasion he was visited by one Hugh Tisdall – a gentleman of loose habits but of considerable wealth – who had, in early youth, travelled with my uncle upon the Continent. The period of his visit was winter, and, consequently, the house was nearly deserted except by its regular inmates; Mr Tisdall was therefore highly acceptable, particularly as my uncle was aware that his visitor's tastes accorded exactly with his own.

Both parties seemed determined to avail themselves of their suitability during the brief stay which Mr Tisdall had promised; the consequence was that they shut themselves up in Sir Arthur's private room for nearly all the day and the greater part of the night, during the space of nearly a week. At the end of this period the servant having one morning, as usual, knocked at Mr Tisdall's bedroom door repeatedly, received no answer, and, upon attempting to enter, found that it was locked. This appeared suspicious, and the inmates of the house having been alarmed, the door was forced open, and, on proceeding to the bed, they found the body of its occupant perfectly lifeless, and hanging halfway out, the head downwards, and near the floor. One deep wound had been inflicted upon the temple, apparently with some blunt instrument, which had penetrated the brain; and another blow less effective, probably the first aimed, had grazed the head, removing some of the scalp, but leaving the skull untouched. The door had been double-locked upon the inside, in evidence of which the key still lay where it had been placed in the lock.

The window, though not secured on the interior, was closed – a circumstance not a little puzzling, as it afforded the only other mode of escape from the room; it looked out, too, upon a kind of courtyard, round which the old buildings stood, formerly accessible by a narrow doorway and passage lying in the oldest side of the quadrangle, but which had since been built up, so as to preclude all ingress or egress. The room was also upon the second storey, and the height of the window considerable. Near the bed were found a pair of razors belonging to the murdered man, one of them upon the ground and both of them open. The weapon which had inflicted the mortal wound was not to be found in the room, nor were any footsteps or other traces of the murderer discoverable.

At the suggestion of Sir Arthur himself, a coroner was instantly summoned to attend, and an inquest was held; nothing, however, in any degree conclusive was elicited. The walls, ceiling, and floor of the room were carefully examined, in order to ascertain whether they contained a trap-door or other concealed mode of entrance – but no such thing appeared.

Such was the minuteness of investigation employed that although the grate had contained a large fire during the night, they proceeded to examine even the very chimney, in order to discover whether escape by it were possible; but this attempt, too, was fruitless, for the chimney, built in the old fashion, rose in a perfectly perpendicular line from the hearth to a height of nearly fourteen feet above the roof, affording in its interior scarcely the possibility of ascent, the flue being smoothly plastered, and sloping towards the top like an inverted funnel. Even if the summit of the chimney were attained, it promised, owing to its great height, but a precarious descent upon the sharp and steep-ridged roof. The ashes, too, which lay in the grate, and the soot, as far as it could be seen, were undisturbed, a circumstance almost conclusive.

Sir Arthur was of course examined; his evidence was given with a clearness and unreserve which seemed calculated to silence all suspicion. He stated that up to the day and night immediately preceding the catastrophe, he had lost to a heavy amount, but that, at their last sitting, he had not only won back his original loss, but upwards of four thousand pounds in addition; in evidence of which he produced an acknowledgment of debt to that amount in the handwriting of the deceased, and bearing the date of the fatal night. He had mentioned the circumstance to his lady, and in presence of some of the domestics; which statement was supported by their respective evidence.

One of the jury shrewdly observed that the circumstance of Mr Tisdall's having sustained so heavy a loss might have suggested to some ill-minded persons, accidentally hearing it, the plan of robbing him, after having murdered him, in such a manner as might make it appear that he had committed suicide; a supposition which was strongly supported by the razors having been found thus displaced, and removed from their case. Two persons had probably been engaged in the attempt, one watching by the sleeping man, and ready to strike him in case of his awakening suddenly, while the other was procuring the razors and employed in inflicting the fatal gash so as to make it appear to have been the act of the murdered man himself. It was said that while the juror was making this suggestion Sir Arthur changed colour.

Nothing, however, like legal evidence appeared against him, and the consequence was that the verdict was found against a person or persons unknown; and for some time the matter was suffered to rest, until, after about five months, my father received a letter from a person signing himself Andrew Collis, and representing himself to be the cousin of the deceased. This letter stated that Sir Arthur was likely to incur not merely suspicion, but personal risk, unless he could account for certain circumstances connected with the recent murder, and contained a copy of a letter written by the deceased, and bearing date – the day of the week, and of the month – upon the night the deed of blood had been perpetrated. Tisdall's note ran as follows:

DEAR COLLIS – I have had sharp work with Sir Arthur; he tried some of his stale tricks, but soon found that *I* was Yorkshire too; it would not do – you understand me. We went to the work like good ones, head, heart and soul; and, in fact, since I came here, I have lost no time. I am rather fagged, but I am sure to be well paid for my hardship I never want sleep so long as I can have the music of a dice-box, and wherewithal to pay the piper. As I told you, he tried some of his queer turns, but I foiled him like a man, and, in return, gave him more than he could relish of the genuine *dead knowledge*.

In short, I have plucked the old baronet as never baronet was plucked before; I have scarce left him the stump of a quill; I have got promissory notes in his hand to the amount of – if you like round numbers, say, thirty thousand pounds, safely deposited in my portable strong-box, alias double-clasped pocket-book. I leave this ruinous old rat-hole early on tomorrow, for two reasons – first, I do not want to play with Sir Arthur deeper than I think his security, that is, his money, or his money's worth, would warrant; and, secondly, because I am safer a hundred miles from Sir Arthur than in the house with him. Look you, my worthy, I tell you this between ourselves – I may be wrong, but, by G—, I am as sure as that I am now living, that Sir A— attempted to poison me last night. So much for old friendship on both sides!

When I won the last stake, a heavy one enough, my friend leant his forehead upon his hands, and you'll laugh when I tell you that his head literally smoked like a hot dumpling. I do not know whether his agitation was produced by the plan which he had against me, or by his having lost so heavily – though it must be allowed that he had reason to be a little funked, whichever way his thoughts went; but he pulled the bell, and ordered two bottles of champagne. While the fellow was bringing them he drew out a promissory note to the full amount, which he signed, and, as the man came in with the bottles and glasses, he desired him to be off; he filled out a glass for me, and, while he thought my eyes were off, for I was putting up his note at the time, he dropped something slyly into it, no doubt to sweeten it; but I saw it all, and when he handed it to me, I said, with an emphasis which he might or might not understand: 'There is some sediment in this; I'll not drink it.'

'Is there?' said he, and at the same time snatched it from my hand and threw it into the fire. What do you think of that? have I not a tender chicken to manage? Win or lose, I will not play beyond five thousand tonight, and tomorrow sees me safe out of the reach of Sir Arthur's champagne. So, all things considered, I think you must allow that you are not the last who have found a knowing boy in

Yours to command,

HUGH TISDALL

Of the authenticity of this document I never heard my father express a doubt; and I am satisfied that, owing to his strong conviction in favour of his brother, he would not have admitted it without sufficient enquiry, inasmuch as it tended to confirm the suspicions which already existed to his prejudice.

Now, the only point in this letter which made strongly against my uncle was the mention of the 'double-clasped pocketbook' as the receptacle of the papers likely to involve him, for this pocketbook was not forthcoming, nor anywhere to be found, nor had any papers referring to his gaming transactions been found upon the dead man.

However, whatever might have been the original intention of this Collis, neither my uncle nor my father ever heard more of him; but he published the letter in Faulkner's Newspaper, which was shortly afterwards made the vehicle of a much more mysterious attack. The passage in that periodical to which I allude appeared about four years afterwards, and while the fatal occurrence was still fresh in public recollection. It commenced by a rambling preface, stating that 'a *certain person* whom *certain* persons thought to be dead, was not so, but living, and in full possession of his memory, and moreover ready and able to make *great* delinquents tremble.' It then went on to describe the murder, without, however, mentioning names; and in doing so, it entered into minute and circumstantial particulars of which none by an *eye-witness* could have been possessed, and by implications almost too unequivocal to be regarded in the light of insinuation, to involve the '*titled gambler*' in the guilt of the transaction.

My father at once urged Sir Arthur to proceed against the paper in an action of libel; but he would not hear of it, nor consent to my father's taking any legal steps whatever in the matter. My father, however, wrote in a threatening tone to Faulkner, demanding a surrender of the author of the obnoxious article. The answer to this application is still in my possession, and is penned in an apologetic tone: it states that the manuscript had been handed in, paid for, and inserted as an advertisement, without sufficient enquiry, or any knowledge as to whom it referred.

No step, however, was taken to clear my uncle's character in the judgment of the public; and as he immediately sold a small property, the application of the proceeds of which was known to none, he was said to have disposed of it to enable himself to buy off the threatened information. However the truth might have been, it is certain that no charges respecting the mysterious murder were afterwards publicly made against my uncle, and, as far as external disturbances were concerned, he enjoyed henceforward perfect security and quiet.

A deep and lasting impression, however, had been made upon the public mind, and Sir Arthur T—n was no longer visited or noticed by the gentry and aristocracy of the county, whose attention and courtesies he had hitherto received. He accordingly affected to despise these enjoyments which he could not procure, and shunned even that society which he might have commanded.

This is all that I need recapitulate of my uncle's history, and I now recur to my own. Although my father had never, within my recollection, visited, or been visited by, my uncle, each being of sedentary, procrastinating, and secluded habits, and their respective residences being very far apart – the one lying in the county of Galway, the other in that of Cork – he was strongly attached to his brother, and evinced his affection by an active correspondence, and by deeply and proudly resenting that neglect which had marked Sir Arthur as unfit to mix in society.

When I was about eighteen years of age, my father, whose health had been gradually declining, died, leaving me in heart wretched and desolate, and, owing to his previous seclusion, with few acquaintances, and almost no friends.

The provisions of his will were curious, and when I had sufficiently come to myself to listen to or comprehend them, surprised me not a little: all his vast property was left to me, and to the heirs of my body, for ever; and, in default of such heirs, it was to go after my death to my uncle, Sir Arthur, without any entail.

At the same time, the will appointed him my guardian, desiring that I might be received within his house, and reside with his family, and under his care, during the term of my minority; and in consideration of the increased expense consequent upon such an arrangement, a handsome annuity was allotted to him during the term of my proposed residence.

The object of this last provision I at once understood: my father desired, by making it the direct, apparent interest of Sir Arthur that I should die without issue, while at the same time placing me wholly in his power, to prove to the world how great and unshaken was his confidence in his brother's innocence and honour, and also to afford him an opportunity of showing that this mark of confidence was not unworthily bestowed.

It was a strange, perhaps an idle scheme; but as I had been always brought up in the habit of considering my uncle as a deeply-injured man, and had been taught, almost as a part of my religion, to regard him as the very soul of honour, I felt no further uneasiness respecting the arrangement than that likely to result to a timid girl of secluded habits from the immediate prospect of taking up her abode for the first time in her life among total strangers. Previous to leaving my home, which I felt I should do with a heavy heart, I received a most tender and affectionate letter from my uncle, calculated, if anything could do so, to remove the bitterness of parting from scenes familiar and dear from my earliest childhood, and in some degree to reconcile me to the change.

It was during a fine autumn that I approached the old domain of Carrickleigh. I shall not soon forget the impression of sadness and of gloom which all that I saw produced upon my mind; the sunbeams were falling with a rich and melancholy tint upon the fine old trees, which stood in lordly groups, casting their long, sweeping shadows over rock and sward. There was an air of desolation and decay about the spot, which amounted almost to desolation; the symptoms of this increased in number as we approached the building itself, near which the ground had been originally more artificially and carefully cultivated than elsewhere, and the neglect consequently more immediately and strikingly betrayed itself.

As we proceeded, the road wound near the beds of what had been formerly two fishponds – now nothing more than stagnant swamps, overgrown with rank weeds, and here and there encroached upon by the straggling underwood. The avenue itself was much broken, and in many places the stones were almost concealed by grass and nettles; the loose stone walls which had here and there intersected the broad park were, in many places, broken down, so as no longer to answer their original purpose as fences; piers were now and then to be seen, but the gates were gone. And, to add to the general air of dilapidation, some huge trunks were lying scattered through the venerable old trees, either the work of the winter storms, or perhaps the victims of some extensive but desultory scheme of denudation, which the projector had not capital or perseverance to carry into full effect.

After the carriage had travelled a mile of this avenue, we reached the summit of rather an abrupt eminence, one of the many which added to the picturesqueness, if not to the convenience of this rude passage. From the top of this ridge the grey walls of Carrickleigh were visible, rising at a small distance in front, and darkened by the hoary wood which crowded around them. It was a quadrangular building of considerable extent, and the front which lay towards us, and in which the great entrance was placed, bore unequivocal marks of antiquity; the timeworn, solemn aspect of the old building, the ruinous and deserted appearance of the whole place, and the associations which connected it with a dark page in the history of my family, combined to depress spirits already predisposed for the reception of sombre and dejecting impressions.

When the carriage drew up in the grass-grown courtyard before the hall door, two lazy-looking men, whose appearance well accorded with that of the place which they tenanted, alarmed by the obstreperous barking of a great chained dog, ran out from some half-ruinous out-houses, and took charge of the horses; the hall door stood open, and I entered a gloomy and imperfectly lighted apartment, and found no one within. However, I had not long to wait in this awkward predicament, for before my luggage had been deposited in the house - indeed, before I had well removed my cloak and other wraps, so as to enable me to look around - a young girl ran lightly into the hall, and kissing me heartily, and somewhat boisterously, exclaimed: 'My dear cousin, my dear Margaret, I am so delighted, so out of breath. We did not expect you till ten o'clock; my father is somewhere about the place; he must be close at hand. James, Corney - run out and tell your master - my brother is seldom at home, at least at any reasonable hour - you must be so tired, so fatigued, let me show you to your room. See that Lady Margaret's luggage is all brought up, you must lie down and rest yourself. Deborah, bring some coffee - Up these stairs! We are so delighted to see you, you cannot think how lonely I have been. How steep these stairs are, are they not? I am so glad you are come; I could hardly bring myself to believe that you were really coming; how good of you, dear Lady Margaret.'

There was real good nature and delight in my cousin's greeting, and a kind of constitutional confidence of manner which placed me at once at ease, and made me feel immediately upon terms of intimacy with her. The room into which she ushered me, although partaking in the general air of decay which pervaded the mansion and all about it, had nevertheless been fitted up with evident attention to comfort, and even with some dingy attempt at luxury; but what pleased me most was that it opened, by a second door, upon a lobby which communicated with my fair cousin's apartment; a circumstances which divested the room, in my eyes, of the air of solitude and sadness which would otherwise have characterised it, to a degree almost painful to one so dejected in spirits as I was.

After such arrangements as I found necessary were completed, we both went down to the parlour, a large wainscoted room, hung round with grim old portraits, and, as I was not sorry to see, containing in its ample grate a large and cheerful fire. Here my cousin had leisure to talk more at ease; and from her I learned something of the manners and the habits of the two remaining members of her family, whom I had not yet seen.

On my arrival I had known nothing of the family among whom I was come to reside, except that it consisted of three individuals, my uncle, and his son and daughter, Lady T—n having been long dead. In addition to this very scanty stock of information, I shortly learned from my communicative companion that my uncle was, as I had suspected, completely reserved in his habits, and besides that, having been so far back as she could well recollect, always rather strict (as reformed rakes frequently become), he had latterly been growing more gloomily and sternly religious than heretofore.

Her account of her brother was far less favourable, though she did not say anything directly to his disadvantage. From all that I could gather from her, I was led to suppose that he was a specimen of the idle, coarse-mannered, profligate, low-minded 'squirearchy' – a result which might naturally have flowed from the circumstance of his being, as it were, outlawed from society, and driven for companionship to grades below his own; enjoying, too, the dangerous prerogative of spending much money.

However, you may easily suppose that I found nothing in my cousin's communication fully to bear me out in so very decided a conclusion.

I awaited the arrival of my uncle, which was every moment to be expected, with feelings half of alarm, half of curiosity – a sensation which I have often since experienced, though to a less degree, when upon the point of standing for the first time in the presence of one of whom I have long been in the habit of hearing or thinking with interest.

It was, therefore, with some little perturbation that I heard, first a light bustle at the outer door, then a slow step traverse the hall, and finally witnessed the door open, and my uncle enter the room. He was a striking-looking man; from peculiarities both of person and of garb, the whole effect of his appearance amounted to extreme singularity. He was tall, and when young his figure must have been strikingly elegant; as it was, however, its effect was marred by a very decided stoop. His dress was of a sober colour, and in fashion anterior to anything which I could remember. It was, however, handsome, and by no means carelessly put on. But what completed the singularity of his appearance was his uncut white hair, which hung in long, but not at all neglected curls, even so far as his shoulders, and which combined with his regularly classic features and fine dark eyes, to bestow upon him an air of venerable dignity and pride which I have never seen equalled elsewhere. I rose as he entered, and met him about the middle of the room; he kissed my cheek and both my hands, saying: 'You are most welcome, dear child, as welcome as the command of this poor place and all that it contains can make you. I am most rejoiced to see you – truly rejoiced. I trust that you are not much fatigued – pray be seated again.' He led me to my chair, and continued: 'I am glad to perceive you have made acquaintance with Emily already; I see, in your being thus brought together, the foundation of a lasting friendship. You are both innocent, and both young. God bless you – God bless you, and make you all that I could wish!'

He raised his eyes, and remained for a few moments silent, as if in secret prayer. I felt that it was impossible that this man, with feelings so quick, so warm, so tender, could be the wretch that public opinion had represented him to be. I was more than ever convinced of his innocence.

His manner was, or appeared to me, most fascinating; there was a mingled kindness and courtesy in it which seemed to speak benevolence itself. It was a manner which I felt cold art could never have taught; it owed most of its charm to its appearing to emanate directly from the heart; it must be a genuine index of the owner's mind. So I thought.

My uncle having given me fully to understand that I was most welcome, and might command whatever was his own, pressed me to take some refreshment; and on my refusing, he observed that previously to bidding me good-night, he had one duty further to perform, one in whose observance he was convinced I would cheerfully acquiesce.

He then proceeded to read a chapter from the Bible; after which he took his leave with the same affectionate kindness with which he had greeted me, having repeated his desire that I should consider everything in his house as altogether at my disposal. It is needless to say that I was much pleased with my uncle – it was impossible to avoid being so; and I could not help saying to myself, if such a man as this is not safe from the assaults of slander, who is? I felt much happier than I had done since my father's death, and enjoyed that night the first refreshing sleep which had visited me since that event.

My curiosity respecting my male cousin did not long remain unsatisfied – he appeared the next day at dinner. His manners, though not so coarse as I had expected, were exceedingly disagreeable; there was an assurance and a forwardness for which I was not prepared; there was less of the vulgarity of manner, and almost more of that of the mind, than I had anticipated. I felt quite uncomfortable in his presence; there was just that confidence in his look and tone which would read encouragement even in mere toleration; and I felt more disgusted and annoyed at the coarse and extravagant compliments which he was pleased from time to time to pay me, than perhaps the extent of the atrocity might fully have warranted. It was, however, one consolation that he did not often appear, being much engrossed by pursuits about which I neither knew nor cared anything; but when he did appear, his attentions, either with a view to his amusement or to some more serious advantage, were so obviously and perseveringly directed to me, that young and inexperienced as I was, even *I* could not be ignorant of his preference. I felt more provoked by this odious persecution than I can express, and discouraged him with so much vigour, that I employed even rudeness to convince him his assiduities were unwelcome; but all in vain.

This had gone on for nearly a twelvemonth, to my infinite annoyance, when one day as I was sitting at some needlework with my companion Emily, as was my habit, in the parlour, the door opened, and my cousin Edward entered the room. There was something, I thought, odd in his manner; a kind of struggle between shame and impudence – a kind of flurry and ambiguity which made him appear, if possible, more than ordinarily disagreeable.

'Your servant, ladies,' he said, seating himself at the same time; 'sorry to spoil your tête-à-tête, but never mind! I'll only take Emily's place for a minute or two; and then we part for a while, fair cousin. Emily, my father wants you in the corner turret. No shilly-shally; he's in a hurry.' She hesitated. 'Be off – tramp, march!' he exclaimed, in a tone which the poor girl dared not disobey.

She left the room, and Edward followed her to the door. He stood there for a minute or two, as if reflecting what he should say, perhaps satisfying himself that no one was within hearing in the hall.

At length he turned about, having closed the door, as if carelessly, with his foot; and advancing slowly, as if in deep thought, he took his seat at the side of the table opposite to mine.

There was a brief interval of silence, after which he said: 'I imagine that you have a shrewd suspicion of the object of my early visit; but I suppose I must go into particulars. Must I?'

'I have no conception,' I replied, 'what your object may be.'

'Well, well,' said he, becoming more at his ease as he proceeded, 'it may be told in a few words. You know that it is totally impossible – quite out of the question – that an offhand young fellow like me, and a good-looking girl like yourself, could meet continually, as you and I have done, without an attachment – a liking growing up on one side or other; in short, I think I have let you know as plain as if I spoke it, that I have been in love with you almost from the first time I saw you.'

He paused; but I was too much horrified to speak. He interpreted my silence favourably.

'I can tell you,' he continued, 'I'm reckoned rather hard to please, and very hard to *hit*. I can't say when I was taken with a girl before; so you see fortune reserved me – '

Here the odious wretch wound his arm round my waist. The action at once restored me to utterance, and with the most indignant vehemence I released myself from his hold, and at the same time said: 'I have not been insensible, sir, of your most disagreeable attentions – they have long been a source of much annoyance to me; and you must be aware that I have marked my disapprobation – my disgust – as unequivocally as I possibly could, without actual indelicacy.'

I paused, almost out of breath from the rapidity with which I had spoken; and, without giving him time to renew the conversation, I hastily quitted the room, leaving him in a paroxysm of rage and mortification.

As I ascended the stairs, I heard him open the parlour-door with violence, and take two or three rapid strides in the direction in which I was moving. I was now much frightened, and ran the whole way until I reached my room; and having locked the door, I listened breathlessly, but heard no sound. This relieved me for the present; but so much had I been overcome by the agitation and annoyance attendant upon the scene which I had just gone through, that when Emily knocked at my door, I was weeping in strong hysterics.

You will readily conceive my distress, when you reflect upon my strong dislike to my cousin Edward, combined with my youth and extreme inexperience. Any proposal of such a nature must have agitated me; but that it should have come from the man whom of all others I most loathed and abhorred, and to whom I had, as clearly as manner could do it, expressed the state of my feelings, was almost too overwhelming to be borne. It was a calamity, too, in which I could not claim the sympathy of my cousin Emily, which had always been extended to me in my minor grievances. Still I hoped that it might not be unattended with good; for I thought that one inevitable and most welcome consequence would result from this painful *eclaircissement*, in the discontinuance of my cousin's odious persecution.

When I arose next morning, it was with the fervent hope that I might never again behold the face, or even hear the name, of my cousin Edward but such a consummation, though devoutly to be wished, was hardly likely to occur. The painful impressions of yesterday were too vivid to be at once erased; and I could not help feeling some dim foreboding of coming annoyance and evil.

To expect on my suitor's part anything like delicacy or consideration for me was out of the question. I saw that he had set his heart upon my property, and that he was not likely easily to forego such an acquisition – possessing what might have been considered opportunities and facilities almost to compel my compliance.

I now keenly felt the unreasonableness of my father's conduct in placing me to reside with a family of all whose members, with one exception, he was wholly ignorant, and I bitterly felt the helplessness of my situation. I determined, however, in case of my cousin's persevering in his addresses, to lay all the particulars before my uncle (although he had never in kindness or intimacy gone a step beyond our first interview), and to throw myself upon his hospitality and his sense of honour for protection against a repetition of such scenes.

My cousin's conduct may appear to have been an inadequate cause for such serious uneasiness; but my alarm was caused neither by his acts nor words, but entirely by his manner, which was strange and even intimidating to excess. At the beginning of yesterday's interview there was a sort of bullying swagger in his air, which towards the close gave place to the brutal vehemence of an undisguised ruffian – a transition which had tempted me into a belief that he might seek even forcibly to extort from me a consent to his wishes, or by means still more horrible, of which I scarcely dared to trust myself to think, to possess himself of my property.

I was early next day summoned to attend my uncle in his private room, which lay in a corner turret of the old building; and thither I accordingly went, wondering all the way what this unusual measure might prelude. When I entered the room, he did not rise in his usual courteous way to greet me, but simply pointed to a chair opposite to his own. This boded nothing agreeable. I sat down, however, silently waiting until he should open the conversation.

'Lady Margaret,' at length he said, in a tone of greater sternness than I had thought him capable of using, 'I have hitherto spoken to you as a friend, but I have not forgotten that I am also your guardian, and that my authority as such gives me a right to control your conduct. I shall put a question to you, and I expect and will demand a plain, direct answer. Have I rightly been informed that you have contemptuously rejected the suit and hand of my son Edward?'

I stammered forth with a good deal of trepidation: 'I believe – that is, I have, sir, rejected my cousin's proposals; and my coldness and discouragement might have convinced him that I had determined to do so.'

'Madam,' replied he, with suppressed, but, as it appeared to me, intense anger, 'I have lived long enough to know that coldness and discouragement, and such terms, form the common cant of a worthless coquette. You know to the full, as well as I, that *coldness and discouragement* may be so exhibited as to convince their object that he is neither distasteful nor indifferent to the person who wears this manner. You know, too, none better, that an affected neglect, when skilfully managed, is amongst the most formidable of the engines which artful beauty can employ. I tell you, madam, that having, without one word spoken in discouragement, permitted my son's most marked attentions for a twelvemonth or more, you have no right to dismiss him with no further explanation than demurely telling him that you had always looked coldly upon him; and neither your wealth nor your *ladyship*' (there was an emphasis of scorn on the word, which would have become Sir Giles Overreach himself) 'can warrant you in treating with contempt the affectionate regard of an honest heart.'

I was too much shocked at this undisguised attempt to bully me into an acquiescence in the interested and unprincipled plan for their own aggrandisement, which I now perceived my uncle and his son to have deliberately entered into, at once to find strength or collectedness to frame an answer to what he had said. At length I replied, with some firmness: 'In all that you have just now said, sir, you have grossly misstated my conduct and motives. Your information must have been most incorrect as far as it regards my conduct towards my cousin; my manner towards him could have conveyed nothing but dislike; and if anything could have added to the strong aversion which I have long felt towards him, it would be his attempting thus to trick and frighten me into a marriage which he knows to be revolting to me, and which is sought by him only as a means for securing to himself whatever property is mine.'

As I said this, I fixed my eyes upon those of my uncle, but he was too old in the world's ways to falter beneath the gaze of more searching eyes than mine; he simply said: 'Are you acquainted with the provisions of your father's will?'

I answered in the affirmative; and he continued: 'Then you must be aware that if my son Edward were – which God forbid – the unprincipled, reckless man you pretend to think him' – (here he spoke very slowly, as if he intended that every word which escaped him should be registered in my memory, while at the same time the expression of his countenance underwent a gradual but horrible change and the eyes which he fixed upon me became so darkly vivid, that I almost lost sight of everything else) – 'if he were what you have described him, think you, girl, he could find no briefer means than wedding contracts to gain his ends? 'twas but to gripe your slender neck until the breath had stopped, and lands, and lakes, and all were his.'

I stood staring at him for many minutes after he had ceased to speak, fascinated by the terrible serpent-like gaze, until he continued with a welcome change of countenance: 'I will not speak again to you upon this topic until one month has passed. You shall have time to consider the relative advantages of the two courses which are open to you. I should be sorry to hurry you to a decision. I am satisfied with having stated my feelings upon the subject, and pointed out to you the path of duty. Remember this day month – not one word sooner.'

He then rose, and I left the room, much agitated and exhausted.

This interview, all the circumstances attending it, but most particularly the formidable expression of my uncle's countenance while he talked, though hypothetically, of murder, combined to arouse all my worst suspicions of him. I dreaded to look upon the face that had so recently worn the appalling livery of guilt and malignity. I regarded it with the mingled fear and loathing with which one looks upon an object which has tortured them in a nightmare.

In a few days after the interview, the particulars of which I have just related, I found a note upon my toilet-table, and on opening it I read as follows:

> My dear Lady Margaret – You will be perhaps surprised to see a strange face in your room today. I have dismissed your Irish maid, and secured a French one to wait upon you – a step rendered necessary by my proposing shortly to visit the Continent, with all my family.
>
>   Your faithful guardian,
>
>   Arthur T—n

On enquiry, I found that my faithful attendant was actually gone, and far on her way to the town of Galway; and in her stead there appeared a tall, raw-boned, ill-looking, elderly Frenchwoman, whose sullen and presuming manners seemed to imply that her vocation had never before been that of a lady's maid. I could not help regarding her as a creature of my uncle's, and therefore to be dreaded, even had she been in no other way suspicious.

Days and weeks passed away without any, even a momentary doubt upon my part, as to the course to be pursued by me. The allotted period had at length elapsed; the day arrived on which I was to communicate my decision to my uncle. Although my resolution had never for a moment wavered, I could not shake off the dread of the approaching colloquy; and my heart sank within me as I heard the expected summons.

I had not seen my cousin Edward since the occurrence of the grand *eclaircissement*; he must have studiously avoided me – I suppose from policy, it could not have been from delicacy. I was prepared for a terrific burst of fury from my uncle, as soon as I should make known my determination; and I not unreasonably feared that some act of violence or of intimidation would next be resorted to.

Filled with these dreary forebodings, I fearfully opened the study door, and the next minute I stood in my uncle's presence. He received me with a politeness which I dreaded, as arguing a favourable anticipation respecting the answer which I was to give; and after some slight delay, he began by saying: 'It will be a relief to both of us, I believe, to bring this conversation as soon as possible to an issue. You will excuse me, then, my dear niece, for speaking with an abruptness which, under other circumstances, would be unpardonable. You have, I am certain, given the subject of our last interview fair and serious consideration; and I trust that you are now prepared with candour to lay your answer before me. A few words will suffice – we perfectly understand one another.'

He paused, and I, though feeling that I stood upon a mine which might in an instant explode, nevertheless answered with perfect composure: 'I must now, sir, make the same reply which I did upon the last occasion, and I reiterate the declaration which I then made, than I never can nor will, while life and reason remain, consent to a union with my cousin Edward.'

This announcement wrought no apparent change in Sir Arthur, except that he became deadly, almost lividly pale. He seemed lost in dark thought for a minute, and then with a slight effort said: 'You have answered me honestly and directly; and you say your resolution is unchangeable. Well, would it had been otherwise – would it had been otherwise; but be it as it is, I am satisfied.'

He gave me his hand – it was cold and damp as death; under an assumed calmness, it was evident that he was fearfully agitated. He continued to hold my hand with an almost painful pressure, while, as if unconsciously, seeming to forget my presence, he muttered: 'Strange, strange, strange, indeed! fatuity, helpless fatuity!' there was here a long pause. 'Madness indeed to strain a cable that is rotten to the very heart – it must break – and then – all goes.'

There was again a pause of some minutes, after which, suddenly changing his voice and manner to one of wakeful alacrity, he exclaimed: 'Margaret, my son Edward shall plague you no more. He leaves this country on tomorrow for France – he shall speak no more upon this subject – never, never more – whatever events depended upon your answer must now take their own course; but, as for this fruitless proposal, it has been tried enough; it can be repeated no more.'

At these words he coldly suffered my hand to drop, as if to express his total abandonment of all his projected schemes of alliance; and certainly the action, with the accompanying words, produced upon my mind a more solemn and depressing effect than I believed possible to have been caused by the course which I had determined to pursue; it struck upon my heart with an awe and heaviness which *will* accompany the accomplishment of an important and irrevocable act, even though no doubt or scruple remains to make it possible that the agent should wish it undone.

'Well,' said my uncle, after a little time, 'we now cease to speak upon this topic, never to resume it again. Remember you shall have no further uneasiness from Edward; he leaves Ireland for France on tomorrow; this will be a relief to you. May I depend upon your honour that no word touching the subject of this interview shall ever escape you?'

I gave him the desired assurance; he said: 'It is well – I am satisfied; we have nothing more, I believe, to say upon either side, and my presence must be a restraint upon you, I shall therefore bid you farewell.'

I then left the apartment, scarcely knowing what to think of the strange interview which had just taken place.

On the next day my uncle took occasion to tell me that Edward had actually sailed, if his intention had not been interfered with by adverse circumstances; and two days subsequently he actually produced a letter from his son, written, as it said, on board, and despatched while the ship was getting under weigh. This was a great satisfaction to me and as being likely to prove so, it was no doubt communicated to me by Sir Arthur.

During all this trying period, I had found infinite consolation in the society and sympathy of my dear cousin Emily. I never in afterlife formed a friendship so close, so fervent, and upon which, in all its progress, I could look back with feelings of such unalloyed pleasure, upon whose termination I must ever dwell with so deep, yet so unembittered regret. In cheerful converse with her I soon recovered my spirits considerably, and passed my time agreeably enough, although still in the strictest seclusion.

Matters went on sufficiently smooth, although I could not help sometimes feeling a momentary, but horrible uncertainty respecting my uncle's character; which was not altogether unwarranted by the circumstances of the two trying interviews whose particulars I have just detailed. The unpleasant impression which these conferences were calculated to leave upon my mind was fast wearing away, when there occurred a circumstance, slight indeed in itself, but calculated irresistibly to awaken all my worst suspicions, and to overwhelm me again with anxiety and terror.

I had one day left the house with my cousin Emily, in order to take a ramble of considerable length, for the purpose of sketching some favourite views, and we had walked about half a mile, when I perceived that we had forgotten our drawing materials, the absence of which would have defeated the object of our walk. Laughing at our own thoughtlessness, we returned to the house, and leaving Emily without, I ran upstairs to procure the drawing-books and pencils, which lay in my bedroom.

As I ran up the stairs I was met by the tall, ill-looking Frenchwoman, evidently a good deal flurried.

'Que veut, madame?' said she, with a more decided effort to be polite than I had ever known her make before.

'No, no – no matter,' said I, hastily running by her in the direction of my room.

'Madame,' cried she, in a high key, 'restez ici, s'il vous plait; votre chambre n'est pas faite – your room is not ready for your reception yet.'

I continued to move on without heeding her. She was some way behind me, and feeling that she could not otherwise prevent my entrance, for I was now upon the very lobby, she made a desperate attempt to seize hold of my person: she succeeded in grasping the end of my shawl, which she drew from my shoulders; but slipping at the same time upon the polished oak floor, she fell at full length upon the boards.

A little frightened as well as angry at the rudeness of this strange woman, I hastily pushed open the door of my room, at which I now stood, in order to escape from her; but great was my amazement on entering to find the apartment occupied.

The window was open, and beside it stood two male figures; they appeared to be examining the fastenings of the casement, and their backs were turned towards the door. One of them was my uncle; they both turned on my entrance, as if startled. The stranger was booted and cloaked, and wore a heavy broad-leafed hat over his brows. He turned but for a moment, and averted his face; but I had seen enough to convince me that he was no other than my cousin Edward. My uncle had some iron instrument in his hand, which he hastily concealed behind his back; and, coming towards me, said something as if in an explanatory tone; but I was too much shocked and confounded to understand what it might be. He said something about 'repairs – window-frames – cold, and safety.'

I did not wait, however, to ask or to receive explanations, but hastily left the room. As I went down the stairs I thought I heard the voice of the French woman in all the shrill volubility of excuse, which was met, however, by suppressed but vehement imprecations, or what seemed to me to be such, in which the voice of my cousin Edward distinctly mingled.

I joined my cousin Emily quite out of breath. I need not say that my head was too full of other things to think much of drawing for that day. I imparted to her frankly the cause of my alarms, but at the same time as gently as I could; and with tears she promised vigilance, and devotion, and love. I never had reason for a moment to repent the unreserved confidence which I then reposed in her. She was no less surprised than I at the unexpected appearance of her brother, whose departure for France neither of us had for a moment doubted, but which was now proved by his actual presence to be nothing more than an imposture, practised, I feared, for no good end.

The situation in which I had found my uncle had removed completely all my doubts as to his designs. I magnified suspicions into certainties, and dreaded night after night that I should be murdered in my bed. The nervousness produced by sleepless nights and days of anxious fears increased the horrors of my situation to such a degree, that I at length wrote a letter to a Mr Jefferies, an old and faithful friend of my father's, and perfectly acquainted with all his affairs, praying him, for God's sake, to relieve me from my present terrible situation, and communicating without reserve the nature and grounds of my suspicions.

This letter I kept sealed and directed for two or three days always about my person – for discovery would have been ruinous – in expectation of an opportunity which might be safely trusted, whereby to have it placed in the post-office. As neither Emily nor I was permitted to pass beyond the precincts of the demesne itself, which was surrounded by high walls formed of dry stone, the difficulty of procuring such an opportunity was greatly enhanced.

At this time Emily had a short conversation with her father, which she reported to me instantly.

After some indifferent matter, he had asked her whether she and I were upon good terms, and whether I was unreserved in my disposition. She answered in the affirmative; and he then enquired whether I had been much surprised to find him in my chamber on the other day. She answered that I had been both surprised and amused.

'And what did she think of George Wilson's appearance?'

'Who?' enquired she.

'Oh, the architect,' he answered, 'who is to contract for the repairs of the house; he is accounted a handsome fellow.'

'She could not see his face,' said Emily, 'and she was in such a hurry to escape that she scarcely noticed him.'

Sir Arthur appeared satisfied, and the conversation ended.

This slight conversation, repeated accurately to me by Emily, had the effect of confirming, if indeed anything was required to do so, all that I had before believed as to Edward's actual presence; and I naturally became, if possible, more anxious than ever to despatch the letter to Mr Jefferies. An opportunity at length occurred.

As Emily and I were walking one day near the gate of the demesne, a man from the village happened to be passing down the avenue from the house; the spot was secluded, and as this person was not connected by service with those whose observation I dreaded, I committed the letter to his keeping, with strict injunctions that he should put it without delay into the receiver of the town post-office; at the same time I added a suitable gratuity, and the man, having made many protestations of punctuality, was soon out of sight.

He was hardly gone when I began to doubt my discretion in having trusted this person; but I had no better or safer means of despatching the letter, and I was not warranted in suspecting him of such wanton dishonesty as an inclination to tamper with it; but I could not be quite satisfied of its safety until I had received an answer, which could not arrive for a few days. Before I did, however, an event occurred which a little surprised me.

I was sitting in my bedroom early in the day, reading by myself, when I heard a knock at the door.

'Come in,' said I; and my uncle entered the room.

'Will you excuse me?' said he. 'I sought you in the parlour, and thence I have come here. I desire to say a word with you. I trust that you have hitherto found my conduct to you such as that of a guardian towards his ward should be.'

I dared not withhold my assent.

'And,' he continued, 'I trust that you have not found me harsh or unjust, and that you have perceived, my dear niece, that I have sought to make this poor place as agreeable to you as may be.'

I assented again; and he put his hand in his pocket, whence he drew a folded paper, and dashing it upon the table with startling emphasis, he said: 'Did you write that letter?'

The sudden and fearful alteration of his voice, manner, and face, but, more than all, the unexpected production of my letter to Mr Jefferies, which I at once recognised, so confounded and terrified me that I felt almost choking.

I could not utter a word.

'Did you write that letter?' he repeated, with slow and intense emphasis. 'You did, liar and hypocrite! You dared to write this foul and infamous libel; but it shall be your last. Men will universally believe you mad, if I choose to call for an enquiry. I can make you appear so. The suspicions expressed in this letter are the hallucinations and alarms of moping lunacy. I have defeated your first attempt, madam; and by the holy God, if ever you make another, chains, straw, darkness, and the keeper's whip shall be your lasting portion!'

With these astounding words he left the room, leaving me almost fainting.

I was now almost reduced to despair; my last cast had failed; I had no course left but that of eloping secretly from the castle and placing myself under the protection of the nearest magistrate. I felt if this were not done, and speedily, that I should be *murdered*.

No one, from mere description, can have an idea of the unmitigated horror of my situation – a helpless, weak, inexperienced girl, placed under the power and wholly at the mercy of evil men, and feeling that she had it not in her power to escape for a moment from the malignant influences under which she was probably fated to fall; and with a consciousness that if violence, if murder were designed, her dying shriek would be lost in void space; no human being would be near to aid her, no human interposition could deliver her.

I had seen Edward but once during his visit, and, as I did not meet with him again, I began to think that he must have taken his departure – a conviction which was to a certain degree satisfactory, as I regarded his absence is indicating the removal of immediate danger.

Emily also arrived circuitously at the same conclusion, and not without good grounds, for she managed indirectly to learn that Edward's black horse had actually been for a day and part of a night in the castle stables, just at the time of her brother's supposed visit. The horse had gone and, as she argued, the rider must have departed with it.

This point being so far settled, I felt a little less uncomfortable; when, being one day alone in my bedroom, I happened to look out from the window, and, to my unutterable horror, I beheld, peering through an opposite casement, my cousin Edward's face. Had I seen the evil one himself in bodily shape, I could not have experienced a more sickening revulsion.

I was too much appalled to move at once from the window, but I did so soon enough to avoid his eye. He was looking fixedly into the narrow quadrangle upon which the window opened. I shrank back unperceived, to pass the rest of the day in terror and despair. I went to my room early that night, but I was too miserable to sleep.

At about twelve o'clock, feeling very nervous, I determined to call my cousin Emily, who slept, you will remember, in the next room, which communicated with mine by a second door. By this private entrance I found my way into her chamber, and without difficulty persuaded her to return to my room and sleep with me. We accordingly lay down together, she undressed, and I with my clothes on, for I was every moment walking up and down the room, and felt too nervous and miserable to think of rest or comfort.

Emily was soon fast asleep, and I lay awake, fervently longing for the first pale gleam of morning; reckoning every stroke of the old clock with an impatience which made every hour appear like six.

It must have been about one o'clock when I thought I heard a slight noise at the partition-door between Emily's room and mine, as if caused by somebody turning the key in the lock. I held my breath, and the same sound was repeated at the second door of my room – that which opened upon the lobby – the sound was here distinctly caused by the revolution of the bolt in the lock, and it was followed by a slight pressure upon the door itself, as if to ascertain the security of the lock.

The person, whoever it might be, was probably satisfied, for I heard the old boards of the lobby creak and strain, as if under the weight of somebody moving cautiously over them. My sense of hearing became unnaturally, almost painfully acute. I suppose my imagination added distinctness to sounds vague in themselves. I thought that I could actually hear the breathing of the person who was slowly returning down the lobby. At the head of the staircase there appeared to occur a pause; and I could distinctly hear two or three sentences hastily whispered; the steps then descended the stairs with apparently less caution. I now ventured to walk quickly and lightly to the lobby door, and attempted to open it; it was indeed fast locked upon the outside, as was also the other.

I now felt that the dreadful hour was come; but one desperate expedient remained – it was to awaken Emily, and by our united strength to attempt to force the partition-door, which was slighter than the other, and through this to pass to the lower part of the house, whence it might be possible to escape to the grounds, and forth to the village.

I returned to the bedside and shook Emily, but in vain. Nothing that I could do availed to produce from her more than a few incoherent words – it was a deathlike sleep. She had certainly drunk of some narcotic, as had I probably also, spite of all the caution with which I had examined everything presented to us to eat or drink.

I now attempted, with as little noise as possible, to force first one door, then the other; but all in vain. I believe no strength could have effected my object, for both doors opened inwards. I therefore collected whatever movables I could carry thither, and piled them against the doors, so as to assist me in whatever attempts I should make to resist the entrance of those without. I then returned to the bed and endeavoured again, but fruitlessly, to awaken my cousin. It was not sleep, it was torpor, lethargy, death. I knelt down and prayed with an agony of earnestness; and then seating myself upon the bed, I awaited my fate with a kind of terrible tranquillity.

I heard a faint clanking sound from the narrow court which I have already mentioned, as if caused by the scraping of some iron instrument against stones or rubbish. I at first determined not to disturb the calmness which I now felt by uselessly watching the proceedings of those who sought my life; but as the sounds continued, the horrible curiosity which I felt overcame every other emotion, and I determined, at all hazards, to gratify it. I therefore crawled upon my knees to the window, so as to let the smallest portion of my head appear above the sill.

The moon was shining with an uncertain radiance upon the antique grey buildings, and obliquely upon the narrow court beneath, one side of which was therefore clearly illuminated, while the other was lost in obscurity; the sharp outlines of the old gables, with their nodding clusters of ivy, being at first alone visible.

Whoever or whatever occasioned the noise which had excited my curiosity, was concealed under the shadow of the dark side of the quadrangle. I placed my hand over my eyes to shade them from the moonlight, which was so bright as to be almost dazzling, and, peering into the darkness, I first dimly, but afterwards gradually almost with full distinctness, beheld the form of a man engaged in digging what appeared to be a rude hole close under the wall. Some implements, probably a shovel and pickaxe, lay beside him, and to these he every now and then applied himself as the nature of the ground required. He pursued his task rapidly, and with as little noise as possible.

'So,' thought I, as, shovelful after shovelful, the dislodged rubbish mounted into a heap, 'they are digging the grave in which, before two hours pass, I must lie, a cold, mangled corpse. I am *theirs* – I cannot escape.'

I felt as if my reason was leaving me. I started to my feet, and in mere despair I applied myself again to each of the two doors alternately. I strained every nerve and sinew, but I might as well have attempted, with my single strength, to force the building itself from its foundation. I threw myself madly upon the ground, and clasped my hands over my eyes as if to shut out the horrible images which crowded upon me.

The paroxysm passed away. I prayed once more, with the bitter, agonised fervour of one who feels that the hour of death is present and inevitable. When I arose, I went once more to the window and looked out, just in time to see a shadowy figure glide stealthily along the wall. The task was finished. The catastrophe of the tragedy must soon be accomplished.

I determined now to defend my life to the last; and that I might be able to do so with some effect, I searched the room for something which might serve as a weapon; but either through accident, or from an anticipation of such a possibility, everything which might have been made available for such a purpose had been carefully removed. I must then die tamely, and without an effort to defend myself.

A thought suddenly struck me – might it not be possible to escape through the door, which the assassin must open in order to enter the room? I resolved to make the attempt. I felt assured that the door through which ingress to the room would be effected was that which opened upon the lobby. It was the more direct way, besides being, for obvious reasons, less liable to interruption than the other. I resolved, then, to place myself behind a projection of the wall, whose shadow would serve fully to conceal me, and when the door should be opened, and before they should have discovered the identity of the occupant of the bed, to creep noiselessly from the room, and then to trust to Providence for escape.

In order to facilitate this scheme, I removed all the lumber which I had heaped against the door; and I had nearly completed my arrangements, when I perceived the room suddenly darkened by the close approach of some shadowy object to the window. On turning my eyes in that direction, I observed at the top of the casement, as if suspended from above, first the feet, then the legs, then the body, and at length the whole figure of a man present himself. It was Edward T—n.

He appeared to be guiding his descent so as to bring his feet upon the centre of the stone block which occupied the lower part of the window; and, having secured his footing upon this, he kneeled down and began to gaze into the room. As the moon was gleaming into the chamber, and the bed curtains were drawn, he was able to distinguish the bed itself and its contents. He appeared satisfied with his scrutiny, for he looked up and made a sign with his hand, upon which the rope by which his descent had been effected was slackened from above, and he proceeded to disengage it from his waist; this accomplished, he applied his hands to the window-frame, which must have been ingeniously contrived for the purpose, for, with apparently no resistance, the whole frame, containing casement and all, slipped from its position in the wall, and was by him lowered into the room.

The cold night wind waved the bed-curtains, and he paused for a moment; all was still again, and he stepped in upon the floor of the room. He held in his hand what appeared to be a steel instrument, shaped something like a hammer, but larger and sharper at the extremities. This he held rather behind him, while, with three long, tiptoe strides, he brought himself to the bedside.

I felt that the discovery must now be made, and held my breath in momentary expectation of the execration in which he would vent his surprise and disappointment. I closed my eyes – there was a pause, but it was a short one. I heard two dull blows, given in rapid succession: a quivering sigh, and the long-drawn, heavy breathing of the sleeper was for ever suspended. I unclosed my eyes, and saw the murderer fling the quilt across the head of his victim: he then, with the instrument of death still in his hand, proceeded to the lobby door, upon which he tapped sharply twice or thrice. A quick step was then heard approaching, and a voice whispered something from without. Edward answered, with a kind of chuckle, 'Her ladyship is past complaining; unlock the door, in the devil's name, unless you're afraid to come in, and help me to lift the body out of the window.'

The key was turned in the lock – the door opened, and my uncle entered the room.

I have told you already that I had placed myself under the shade of a projection of the wall, close to the door. I had instinctively shrunk down, cowering towards the ground, on the entrance of Edward through the window. When my uncle entered the room, he and his son both stood so very close to me that his hand was every moment upon the point of touching my face. I held my breath, and remained motionless as death.

'You had no interruption from the next room?' said my uncle.

'No,' was the brief reply.

'Secure the jewels, Ned; the French harpy must not lay her claws upon them. You're a steady hand, by G—! not much blood – eh?'

'Not twenty drops,' replied his son, 'and those on the quilt.'

'I'm glad it's over,' whispered my uncle again. 'We must lift the – the *thing* through the window and lay the rubbish over it.'

They then turned to the bedside, and, winding the bedclothes round the body, carried it between them slowly to the window, and, exchanging a few brief words with someone below, they shoved it over the window-sill, and I heard it fall heavily on the ground underneath.

'I'll take the jewels,' said my uncle; 'there are two caskets in the lower drawer.'

He proceeded, with an accuracy which, had I been more at ease, would have furnished me with matter of astonishment, to lay his hand upon the very spot where my jewels lay; and having possessed himself of them, he called to his son: 'Is the rope made fast above?'

'I'm not a fool – to be sure it is,' replied he.

They then lowered themselves from the window. I now rose lightly and cautiously, scarcely daring to breathe, from my place of concealment, and was creeping towards the door, when I heard my cousin's voice, in a sharp whisper, exclaim: 'Scramble up again! G— d d—n you, you've forgot to lock the room-door!' and I perceived, by the straining of the rope which hung from above, that the mandate was instantly obeyed.

Not a second was to be lost. I passed through the door, which was only closed, and moved as rapidly as I could, consistently with stillness, along the lobby. Before I had gone many yards, I heard the door through which I had just passed double-locked on the inside. I glided down the stairs in terror, lest, at every corner, I should meet the murderer or one of his accomplices.

I reached the hall, and listened for a moment, to ascertain whether all was silent around; no sound was audible. The parlour windows opened on the park, and through one of them I might, I thought, easily effect my escape. Accordingly, I hastily entered; but, to my consternation, a candle was burning in the room, and by its light I saw a figure seated at the dinner-table, upon which lay glasses, bottles, and the other accompaniments of a drinking-party. Two or three chairs were placed about the table irregularly, as if hastily abandoned by their occupants.

A single glance satisfied me that the figure was that of my French attendant. She was fast asleep, having probably drunk deeply. There was something malignant and ghastly in the calmness of this bad woman's features, dimly illuminated as they were by the flickering blaze of the candle. A knife lay upon the table, and the terrible thought struck me – 'Should I kill this sleeping accomplice, and thus secure my retreat?'

Nothing could be easier – it was but to draw the blade across her throat – the work of a second. An instant's pause, however, corrected me. 'No,' thought I, 'the God who has conducted me thus far through the valley of the shadow of death, will not abandon me now. I will fall into their hands, or I will escape hence, but it shall be free from the stain of blood. His will be done!'

I felt a confidence arising from this reflection, an assurance of protection which I cannot describe. There was no other means of escape, so I advanced, with a firm step and collected mind, to the window. I noiselessly withdrew the bars and unclosed the shutters – I pushed open the casement, and, without waiting to look behind me, I ran with my utmost speed, scarcely feeling the ground under me, down the avenue, taking care to keep upon the grass which bordered it.

I did not for a moment slacken my speed, and I had now gained the centre point between the park-gate and the mansion-house. Here the avenue made a wider circuit, and in order to avoid delay, I directed my way across the smooth sward round which the pathway wound, intending, at the opposite side of the flat, at a point which I distinguished by a group of old birch trees, to enter again upon the beaten track, which was from thence tolerably direct to the gate.

I had, with my utmost speed, got about halfway across this broad flat, when the rapid treading of a horse's hoofs struck upon my ear. My heart swelled in my bosom as though I would smother. The clattering of galloping hoofs approached – I was pursued – they were now upon the sward on which I was running – there was not a bush or a bramble to shelter me – and, as if to render escape altogether desperate, the moon, which had hitherto been obscured, at this moment shone forth with a broad clear light, which made every object distinctly visible.

The sounds were now close behind me. I felt my knees bending under me, with the sensation which torments one in dreams. I reeled – I stumbled – I fell – and at the same instant the cause of my alarm wheeled past me at full gallop. It was one of the young fillies which pastured loose about the park, whose frolics had thus all but maddened me with terror. I scrambled to my feet, and rushed on with weak but rapid steps, my sportive companion still galloping round and round me with many a frisk and fling, until, at length, more dead than alive, I reached the avenue-gate, and crossed the stile, I scarce knew how.

I ran through the village, in which all was silent as the grave, until my progress was arrested by the hoarse voice of a sentinel, who cried, 'Who goes there?' I felt that I was now safe. I turned in the direction of the voice, and fell fainting at the soldier's feet. When I came to myself, I was sitting in a miserable hovel, surrounded by strange faces, all bespeaking curiosity and compassion.

Many soldiers were in it also: indeed, as I afterwards found, it was employed as a guardroom by a detachment of troops quartered for that night in the town. In a few words I informed their officer of the circumstances which had occurred, describing also the appearance of the persons engaged in the murder; and he, without loss of time, proceeded to the mansion-house of Carrickleigh, taking with him a party of his men. But the villains had discovered their mistake, and had effected their escape before the arrival of the military.

The Frenchwoman was, however, arrested in the neighbourhood upon the next day. She was tried and condemned upon the ensuing assizes; and previous to her execution, confessed that '*she had a hand in making Hugh Tisdall's bed.*' She had been a housekeeper in the castle at the time, and a kind of *chère amie* of my uncle's. She was, in reality, able to speak English like a native, but had exclusively used the French language, I suppose, to facilitate her disguise. She died the same hardened wretch she had lived, confessing her crimes only, as she alleged, that her doing so might involve Sir Arthur T—n, the great author of her guilt and misery, and whom she now regarded with unmitigated detestation.

With the particulars of Sir Arthur's and his son's escape, as far as they are known, you are acquainted. You are also in possession of their after fate – the terrible, the tremendous retribution which, after long delays of many years, finally overtook and crushed them. Wonderful and inscrutable are the dealings of God with His creatures.

Deep and fervent as must always be my gratitude to Heaven for my deliverance, effected by a chain of providential occurrences, the failing of a single link of which must have ensured my destruction, I was long before I could look back upon it with other feelings than those of bitterness, almost of agony. The only being that had ever really loved me, my nearest and dearest friend, ever ready to sympathise, to counsel, and to assist – the gayest, the gentlest, the warmest heart; the only creature on earth that cared for me – *her* life had been the price of my deliverance; and I then uttered the wish, which no event of my long and sorrowful life has taught me to recall, that she had been spared, and that, in her stead, *I* were mouldering in the grave, forgotten and at rest.

SHERIDAN LE FANU

Strange Event in the Life of
Schalken the Painter

❧

You will no doubt be surprised, my dear friend, at the subject of the following narrative. What had I to do with Schalken, or Schalken with me? He had returned to his native land, and was probably dead and buried before I was born; I never visited Holland, nor spoke with a native of that country. So much I believe you already know. I must, then, give you my authority, and state to you frankly the ground upon which rests the credibility of the strange story which I am about to lay before you.

I was acquainted, in my early days, with a Captain Vandael, whose father had served King William in the Low Countries, and also in my own unhappy land during the Irish campaigns. I know not how it happened that I liked this man's society, spite of his politics and religion: but so it was; and it was by means of the free intercourse to which our intimacy gives rise that I became possessed of the curious tale which you are about to hear.

I had often been struck, while visiting Vandael, by a remarkable picture, in which, though no *connoisseur* myself, I could not fail to discern some very strong peculiarities, particularly in the distribution of light and shade, as also a certain oddity in the design itself, which interested my curiosity. It represented the interior of what might be a chamber in some antique religious building – the foreground was occupied by a female figure, arrayed in a species of white robe, part of which was arranged so as to form a veil. The dress, however, was not strictly that of any religious order. In its hand the figure bore a lamp, by whose light alone the form and face were illuminated; the features were marked by an arch smile, such as pretty women wear when engaged in successfully practising some roguish trick; in the background, and (excepting where the dim red light of an expiring fire serves to define the form) totally in the shade, stood the figure of a man equipped in the old fashion, with doublet and so forth, in an attitude of alarm, his hand being placed upon the hilt of his sword, which he appeared to be in the act of drawing.

'There are some pictures,' said I to my friend, 'which impress one, I know not how, with a conviction that they represent not the mere ideal shapes and combinations which have floated through the imagination of the artist, but scenes, faces, and situations which have actually existed. When I look upon that picture, something assures me that I behold the representation of a reality.'

Vandael smiled, and, fixing his eyes upon the painting musingly, he said: 'Your fancy has not deceived you, my good friend, for that picture is the record, and I believe a faithful one, of a remarkable and mysterious occurrence. It was painted by Schalken, and contains, in the face of the female figure which occupies the most prominent place in the design, an accurate portrait of Rose Velderkaust, the niece of Gerard Douw, the first and, I believe, the only love of Godfrey Schalken. My father knew the painter well, and from Schalken himself he learned the story of the mysterious drama, one scene of which the picture has embodied. This painting, which is accounted a fine specimen of Schalken's style, was bequeathed to my father by the artist's will, and, as you have observed, is a very striking and interesting production.'

I had only to request Vandael to tell the story of the painting in order to be gratified; and thus it is that I am enabled to submit to you a faithful recital of what I heard myself, leaving you to reject or to allow the evidence upon which the truth of the tradition depends – with this one assurance, that Schalken was an honest, blunt Dutchman, and, I believe, wholly incapable of committing a flight of imagination; and further, that Vandael, from whom I heard the story, appeared firmly convinced of its truth.

There are few forms upon which the mantle of mystery and romance could seem to hang more ungracefully than upon that of the uncouth and clownish Schalken – the Dutch boor – the rude and dogged, but most cunning worker in oils, whose pieces delight the initiated of the present day almost as much as his manner disgusted the refined of his own; and yet this man, so rude, so dogged, so slovenly, I had almost said so savage in mien and manner, during his after successes, had been selected by the capricious goddess, in his early life, to figure as the hero of a romance by no means devoid of interest or of mystery.

Who can tell how meet he may have been in his young days to play the part of the lover or of the hero? who can say that in early life he had been the same harsh, unlicked, and rugged boor that, in his maturer age, he proved? or how far the neglected rudeness which afterwards marked his air, and garb, and manners, may not have been the growth of that reckless apathy not unfrequently produced by bitter misfortunes and disappointments in early life?

These questions can never now be answered.

We must content ourselves, then, with a plain statement of facts, leaving matters of speculation to those who like them.

When Schalken studied under the immortal Gerard Douw, he was a young man; and in spite of the phlegmatic constitution and excitable manner which he shared, we believe, with his countrymen, he was not incapable of deep and vivid impressions, for it is an established fact that the young painter looked with considerable interest upon the beautiful niece of his wealthy master.

Rose Velderkaust was very young, having, at the period of which we speak, not yet attained her seventeenth year; and, if tradition speaks truth, she possessed all the soft dimpling charms of the fair, light-haired Flemish maidens. Schalken had not studied long in the school of Gerard Douw when he felt this interest deepening into something of a keener and intenser feeling than was quite consistent with the tranquillity of his honest Dutch heart; and at the same time he perceived, or thought he perceived, flattering symptoms of a reciprocal attachment, and this was quite sufficient to determine whatever indecision he might have heretofore experienced, and to lead him to devote exclusively to her every hope and feeling of his heart. In short, he was as much in love as a Dutchman could be. He was not long in making his passion known to the pretty maiden herself, and his declaration was followed by a corresponding con-fession upon her part.

Schalken, howbeit, was a poor man, and he possessed no counter-balancing advantages of birth or position to induce the old man to consent to a union which must involve his niece and ward in the strugglings and difficulties of a young and nearly friendless artist. He was, therefore, to wait until time had furnished him with opportunity, and accident with success; and then, if his labours were found sufficiently lucrative, it was to be hoped that his proposals might at least be listened to by her jealous guardian. Months passed away, and, cheered by the smiles of the little Rose, Schalken's labours were redoubled, and with such effect and improvement as reasonably to promise the realisation of his hopes, and no contemptible eminence in his art, before many years should have elapsed.

The even course of this cheering prosperity was, unfortunately, destined to experience a sudden and formidable interruption, and that, too, in a manner so strange and mysterious as to baffle all investigation, and throw upon the events themselves a shadow of almost supernatural horror.

Schalken had one evening remained in the master's studio considerably longer than his more volatile companions, who had gladly availed themselves of the excuse which the dusk of evening afforded to withdraw from their several tasks, in order to finish a day of labour in the jollity and conviviality of the tavern.

But Schalken worked for improvement, or rather for love. Besides, he was now engaged merely in sketching a design, an operation which, unlike that of colouring, might be continued as long as there was light sufficient to distinguish between canvas and charcoal. He had not then, nor, indeed, until long after, discovered the peculiar powers of his pencil; and he was engaged in composing a group of extremely roguish-looking and grotesque imps and demons, who were inflicting various ingenious torments upon a perspiring and pot-bellied St Anthony, who reclined in the midst of them, apparently in the last stage of drunkenness.

The young artist, however, though incapable of executing, or even of appreciating, anything of true sublimity, had nevertheless discernment enough to prevent his being by any means satisfied with his work; and many were the patient erasures and corrections which the limbs and features of saint and devil underwent, yet all without producing in their new arrangement anything of improvement or increased effect.

The large, old-fashioned room was silent, and, with the exception of himself, quite deserted by its usual inmates. An hour had passed – nearly two – without any improved result. Daylight had already declined, and twilight was fast giving way to the darkness of night. The patience of the young man was exhausted, and he stood before his unfinished production, absorbed in no very pleasing ruminations, one hand buried in the folds of his long dark hair, and the other holding the piece of charcoal which had so ill executed its office, and which he now rubbed, without much regard to the sable streaks which it produced, with irritable pressure upon his ample Flemish inexpressibles.

'Pshaw!' said the young man aloud, 'would that picture, devils, saint, and all, were where they should be – in hell!'

A short, sudden laugh, uttered startlingly close to his ear, instantly responded to the ejaculation.

The artist turned sharply round, and now for the first time became aware that his labours had been overlooked by a stranger.

Within about a yard and a half, and rather behind him, there stood what was, or appeared to be, the figure of an elderly man: he wore a short cloak, and broad-brimmed hat with a conical crown, and in his hand, which was protected with a heavy, gauntlet-shaped glove, he carried a long ebony walking-stick, surmounted with what appeared, as it glittered dimly in the twilight to be a massive head of gold; and upon his breast, through the folds of the cloak, there shone the links of a rich chain of the same metal.

The room was so obscure that nothing further of the appearance of the figure could be ascertained, and the face was altogether overshadowed by the heavy flap of the beaver which overhung it, so that no feature could be clearly discerned. A quantity of dark hair escaped from beneath this sombre hat, a circumstance which, connected with the firm, upright carriage of the intruder, proved that his years could not exceed threescore or thereabouts.

There was an air of gravity and importance about the garb of this person, and something indescribably odd – I might say awful – in the perfect, stonelike movelessness of the figure, that effectually checked the testy comment which had at once risen to the lips of the irritated artist. He therefore, as soon as he had sufficiently recovered the surprise, asked the stranger, civilly, to be seated, and desired to know if he had any message to leave for his master.

'Tell Gerard Douw,' said the unknown, without altering his attitude in the smallest degree, 'that Mynher Vanderhausen, of Rotterdam, desires to speak with him tomorrow evening at this hour, and, if he please, in this room, upon matters of weight; that is all. Good-night.'

The stranger, having finished this message, turned abruptly, and, with a quick but silent step quitted the room before Schalken had time to say a word in reply.

The young man felt a curiosity to see in what direction the burgher of Rotterdam would turn on quitting the studio, and for that purpose he went directly to the window which commanded the door.

A lobby of considerable extent intervened between the inner door of the painter's room and the street entrance, so that Schalken occupied the post of observation before the old man could possibly have reached the street.

He watched in vain, however. There was no other mode of exit.

Had the old man vanished, or was he lurking about the recesses of the lobby for some bad purpose? This last suggestion filled the mind of Schalken with a vague horror, which was so unaccountably intense as to make him alike afraid to remain in the room alone and reluctant to pass through the lobby.

However, with an effort which appeared very disproportioned to the occasion, he summoned resolution to leave the room, and, having double-locked the door, and thrust the key in his pocket, without looking at the right or left, he traversed the passage which had so recently, perhaps still, contained the person of his mysterious visitant, scarcely venturing to breathe till he had arrived in the open street.

'Mynher Vanderhausen,' said Gerard Douw, within himself, as the appointed hour approached; 'Mynher Vanderhausen, of Rotterdam! I never heard of the man till yesterday. What can he want of me? A portrait, perhaps, to be painted; or a younger son or a poor relation to be apprenticed; or a collection to be valued; or – pshaw! there's no one in Rotterdam to leave me a legacy. Well, whatever the business may be, we shall soon know it all.'

It was now the close of day, and every easel, except that of Schalken, was deserted. Gerard Douw was pacing the apartment with the restless step of impatient expectation, every now and then humming a passage from a piece of music which he was himself composing for, though no great proficient, he admired the art; sometimes pausing to glance over the work of one of his absent pupils, but more frequently placing himself at the window, from whence he might observe the passengers who threaded the obscure by-street in which his studio was placed.

'Said you not, Godfrey,' exclaimed Douw, after a long and fruitless gaze from his post of observation, and turning to Schalken – 'said you not the hour of appointment was at about seven by the clock of the Stadhouse?'

'It had just told seven when I first saw him, sir,' answered the student.

'The hour is close at hand, then,' said the master, consulting a horologe as large and as round as a full-grown orange. 'Mynher Vanderhausen, from Rotterdam – is it not so?'

'Such was the name.'

'And an elderly man, richly clad?' continued Douw.

'As well as I might see,' replied his pupil. 'He could not be young, nor yet very old neither, and his dress was rich and grave, as might become a citizen of wealth and consideration.'

At this moment the sonorous boom of the Stadhouse clock told, stroke after stroke, the hour of seven; the eyes of both master and student were directed to the door; and it was not until the last peal of the old bell had ceased to vibrate, that Douw exclaimed: 'So, so; we shall have his worship presently – that is, if he means to keep his hour; if not, thou mayst wait for him, Godfrey, if you court the acquaintance of a capricious burgomaster. As for me, I think our old Leyden contains a sufficiency of such commodities, without an importation from Rotterdam.'

Schalken laughed, as in duty bound; and, after a pause of some minutes, Douw suddenly exclaimed: 'What if it should all prove a jest, a piece of mummery got up by Vankarp, or some such worthy! I wish you had run all risks, and cudgelled the old burgomaster, stadholder, or whatever else he may be, soundly. I would wager a dozen of Rhenish, his worship would have pleaded old acquaintance before the third application.'

'Here he comes, sir,' said Schalken, in a low, admonitory tone; and instantly, upon turning towards the door, Gerard Douw observed the same figure which had, on the day before, so unexpectedly greeted the vision of his pupil Schalken.

There was something in the air and mien of the figure which at once satisfied the painter that there was no mummery in the case, and that he really stood in the presence of a man of worship; and so, without hesitation, he doffed his cap, and courteously saluting the stranger, requested him to be seated.

The visitor waved his hand slightly, as if in acknowledgment of the courtesy, but remained standing.

'I have the honour to see Mynher Vanderhausen, of Rotterdam?' said Gerard Douw.

'The same,' was the laconic reply.

'I understood your worship desires to speak with me,' continued Douw, 'and I am here by appointment to wait your commands.'

'Is that a man of trust?' said Vanderhausen, turning towards Schalken, who stood at a little distance behind his master.

'Certainly,' replied Gerard.

'Then let him take this box and get the nearest jeweller or goldsmith to value its contents, and let him return hither with a certificate of the valuation.'

At the same time he placed a small case, about nine inches square, in the hands of Gerard Douw, who was as much amazed at its weight as at the strange abruptness with which it was handed to him.

In accordance with the wishes of the stranger, he delivered it into the hands of Schalken, and repeating *his* directions, despatched him upon the mission.

Schalken disposed his precious charge securely beneath the folds of his cloak, and rapidly traversing two or three narrow streets, he stopped at a corner house, the lower part of which was then occupied by the shop of Jewish goldsmith.

Schalken entered the shop, and calling the little Hebrew into the obscurity of its back recesses, he proceeded to lay before him Van–derhausen's packet.

On being examined by the light of a lamp, it appeared entirely cased with lead, the outer surface of which was much scraped and soiled, and nearly white with age. This was with difficulty partially removed, and disclosed beneath a box of some dark and singularly hard wood; this, too, was forced, and after the removal of two or three folds of linen, its contents proved to be a mass of golden ingots, close packed, and, as the Jew declared, of the most perfect quality.

Every ingot underwent the scrutiny of the little Jew, who seemed to feel an epicurean delight in touching and testing these morsels of the glorious metal; and each one of them was replaced in the box with the exclamation: '*Mein Gott*, how very perfect! not one grain of alloy – beautiful, beautiful!'

The task was at length finished, and the Jew certified under his hand that the value of the ingots submitted to his examination amounted to many thousand rix-dollars.

With the desired document in his bosom, and the rich box of gold carefully pressed under his arm, and concealed by his cloak, he retraced his way, and, entering the studio, found his master and the stranger in close conference.

Schalken had no sooner left the room, in order to execute the commission he had taken in charge, than Vanderhausen addressed Gerard Douw in the following terms: 'I may not tarry with you tonight more than a few minutes, and so I shall briefly tell you the matter upon which I come. You visited the town of Rotterdam some four months ago, and then I saw in the church of : Lawrence your niece, Rose Velderkaust. I desire to marry her, and if I satisfy you as to the fact that I am very wealthy – more wealthy than any husband you could dream of for her – I expect that you will forward my views to the utmost of your authority. If you approve my proposal, you must close with it at once, for I cannot command time enough to wait for calculations and delays.'

Gerard Douw was, perhaps, as much astonished as anyone could be by the very unexpected nature of Mynher Vanderhausen's communication; but he did not give vent to any unseemly expression of surprise. In addition to the motives supplied by prudence and politeness, the painter experienced a kind of chill and oppressive sensation – a feeling like that which is supposed to affect a man who is placed unconsciously in immediate contact with something to which he has a natural antipathy – an undefined horror and dread – while standing in the presence of the eccentric stranger, which made him very unwilling to say anything that might reasonably prove offensive.

'I have no doubt,' said Gerard, after two or three prefatory hems, 'that the connection which you propose would prove alike advantageous and honourable to my niece; but you must be aware that she has a will of her own, and may not acquiesce in what *we* may design for her advantage.'

'Do not seek to deceive me, Sir Painter,' said Vanderhausen; 'you are her guardian – she is your ward. She is mine if *you* like to make her so.'

The man of Rotterdam moved forward a little as he spoke, and Gerard Douw, he scarce knew why, inwardly prayed for the speedy return of Schalken.

'I desire,' said the mysterious gentleman, 'to place in your hands at once an evidence of my wealth, and a security for my liberal dealing with your niece. The lad will return in a minute or two with a sum in value five times the fortune which she has a right to expect from a husband. This shall lie in your hands, together with her dowry, and you may apply the united sum as suits her interest best; it shall be all exclusively hers while she lives. Is that liberal?'

Douw assented, and inwardly thought that fortune had been extraordinarily kind to his niece. The stranger, he deemed, must be most wealthy and generous, and such an offer was not to be despised, though made by a humourist, and one of no very prepossessing presence.

Rose had no very high pretensions, for she was almost without dowry; indeed, altogether so, excepting so far as the deficiency had been supplied by the generosity of her uncle. Neither had she any right to raise any scruples against the match on the score of birth, for her own origin was by no means elevated; and as to other objections, Gerard resolved, and, indeed, by the usages of the time was warranted in resolving, not to listen to them for a moment.

'Sir,' said he, addressing the stranger, 'your offer is most liberal, and whatever hesitation I may feel in closing with it immediately, arises solely from my not having the honour of knowing anything of your family or station. Upon these points you can, of course, satisfy me without difficulty?'

'As to my respectability,' said the stranger, drily, 'you must take that for granted at present; pester me with no enquiries; you can discover nothing more about me than I choose to make known. You shall have sufficient security for my respectability – my word, if you are honourable: if you are sordid, my gold.'

'A testy old gentleman,' thought Douw; 'he must have his own way. But, all things considered, I am justified in giving my niece to him. Were she my own daughter, I would do the like by her. I will not pledge myself unnecessarily, however.'

'You will not pledge yourself unnecessarily,' said Vanderhausen, strangely uttering the very words which had just floated through the mind of his companion; 'but you will do so if it *is* necessary, I presume; and I will show you that I consider it indispensable. If the gold I mean to leave in your hands satisfies you, and if you desire that my proposal shall not be at once withdrawn, you must, before I leave this room, write your name to this engagement.'

Having thus spoken, he placed a paper in the hands of Gerard, the contents of which expressed an engagement entered into by Gerard Douw, to give to Wilken Vanderhausen, of Rotterdam, in marriage, Rose Velderkaust, and so forth, within one week of the date hereof.

While the painter was employed in reading this covenant, Schalken, as we have stated, entered the studio, and having delivered the box and the valuation of the Jew into the hands of the stranger, he was about to retire, when Vanderhausen called to him to wait; and, presenting the case and the certificate to Gerard Douw, he waited in silence until he had satisfied himself by an inspection of both as to the value of the pledge left in his hands. At length he said: 'Are you content?'

The painter said 'he would fain have another day to consider.'

'Not an hour,' said the suitor, coolly.

'Well, then,' said Douw, 'I am content; it is a bargain.'

'Then sign at once,' said Vanderhausen; 'I am weary.'

At the same time he produced a small case of writing materials, and Gerard signed the important document.

'Let this youth witness the covenant,' said the old man; and Godfrey Schalken unconsciously signed the instrument which bestowed upon another that hand which he had so long regarded as the object and reward of all his labours.

The compact being thus completed, the strange visitor folded up the paper, and stowed it safely in an inner pocket.

'I will visit you tomorrow night, at nine of the clock, at your house, Gerard Douw, and will see the subject of our contract. Farewell.' And so saying, Wilken Vanderhausen moved stiffly, but rapidly out of the room.

Schalken, eager to resolve his doubts, had placed himself by the window in order to watch the street entrance; but the experiment served only to support his suspicions, for the old man did not issue from the door. This was very strange, very odd, very fearful. He and his master returned together, and talked but little on the way, for each had his own subjects of reflection, of anxiety, and of hope.

Schalken, however, did not know the ruin which threatened his cherished schemes.

Gerard Douw knew nothing of the attachment which had sprung up between his pupil and his niece; and even if he had, it is doubtful whether he would have regarded its existence as any serious obstruction to the wishes of Mynher Vanderhausen.

Marriages were then and there matters of traffic and calculation; and it would have appeared as absurd in the eyes of the guardian to make a mutual attachment an essential element in a contract of marriage, as it would have been to draw up his bonds and receipts in the language of chivalrous romance.

The painter, however, did not communicate to his niece the important step which he had taken in her behalf, and his resolution arose not from any anticipation of opposition on her part, but solely from a ludicrous consciousness that if his ward were, as she very naturally might do, to ask him to describe the appearance of the bridegroom whom he destined for her, he would be forced to confess that he had not seen his face, and, if called upon, would find it impossible to identify him.

Upon the next day, Gerard Douw having dined, called his niece to him, and having scanned her person with an air of satisfaction, he took her hand, and looking upon her pretty, innocent face with a smile of kindness, he said: 'Rose, my girl, that face of yours will make your fortune.' Rose blushed and smiled. 'Such faces and such tempers seldom go together, and, when they do, the compound is a love-potion which few heads or hearts can resist. Trust me, thou wilt soon be a bride, girl. But this is trifling, and I am pressed for time, so make ready the large room by eight o'clock tonight, and give directions for supper at nine. I expect a friend tonight; and observe me, child, do thou trick thyself out handsomely. I would not have him think us poor or sluttish.'

With these words he left the chamber, and took his way to the room to which we have already had occasion to introduce our readers – that in which his pupils worked.

When the evening closed in, Gerard called Schalken, who was about to take his departure to his obscure and comfortless lodgings, and asked him to come home and sup with Rose and Vanderhausen.

The invitation was of course accepted, and Gerard Douw and his pupil soon found themselves in the handsome and somewhat antique-looking room which had been prepared for the reception of the stranger.

A cheerful wood-fire blazed in the capacious hearth; a little at one side an old-fashioned table, with richly-carved legs, was placed – destined, no doubt, to receive the supper, for which preparations were going forward; and ranged with exact regularity stood the tall-backed chairs whose ungracefulness was more than counterbalanced by their comfort.

The little party, consisting of Rose, her uncle, and the artist, awaited the arrival of the expected visitor with considerable impatience.

Nine o'clock at length came, and with it a summons at the street-door, which, being speedily answered, was followed by a slow and emphatic tread upon the staircase; the steps moved heavily across the lobby, the door of the room in which the party which we have described were assembled slowly opened, and there entered a figure which startled, almost appalled, the phlegmatic Dutchmen, and nearly made Rose scream with affright; it was the form, and arrayed in the garb, of Mynher Vanderhausen; the air, the gait, the height was the same, but the features had never been seen by any of the party before.

The stranger stopped at the door of the room, and displayed his form and face completely. He wore a dark coloured cloth cloak, which was short and full, not falling quite to the knees; his legs were cased in dark purple silk stockings, and his shoes were adorned with roses of the same colour. The opening of the cloak in front showed the undersuit to consist of some very dark, perhaps sable material, and his hands were enclosed in a pair of heavy leather gloves which ran up considerably above the wrist, in the manner of a gauntlet. In one hand he carried his walking-stick and his hat, which he had removed, and the other hung heavily by his side. A quantity of grizzled hair descended in long tresses from his head, and its folds rested upon the plaits of a stiff ruff, which effectually concealed his neck.

So far all was well; but the face! – all the flesh of the face was coloured with the bluish leaden hue which is sometimes produced by the operation of metallic medicines administered in excessive quantities; the eyes were enormous, and the white appeared both above and below the iris, which gave to them an expression of insanity, which was heightened by their glassy fixedness; the nose was well enough, but the mouth was writhed considerably to one side, where it opened in order to give egress to two long, discoloured fangs, which projected from the upper jaw, far below the lower lip; the hue of the lips themselves bore the usual relation to that of the face, and was consequently nearly black. The character of the face was malignant, even satanic, to the last degree; and, indeed, such a combination of horror could hardly be accounted for, except by supposing the corpse of some atrocious malefactor, which had long hung blackening upon the gibbet, to have at length become the habitation of a demon – the frightful sport of satanic possession.

It was remarkable that the worshipful stranger suffered as little as possible of his flesh to appear, and that during his visit he did not once remove his gloves.

Having stood for some moments at the door, Gerard Douw at length found breath and collectedness to bid him welcome, and, with a mute inclination of the head, the stranger stepped forward into the room.

There was something indescribably odd, even horrible about all his motions, something undefinable, something unnatural, unhuman – it was as if the limbs were guided and directed by a spirit unused to the management of bodily machinery.

The stranger said hardly anything during his visit, which did not exceed half an hour; and the host himself could scarcely muster courage enough to utter the few necessary salutations and courtesies: and, indeed, such was the nervous terror which the presence of Vanderhausen inspired, that very little would have made all his entertainers fly bellowing from the room.

They had not so far lost all self-possession, however, as to fail to observe two strange peculiarities of their visitor.

During his stay he did not once suffer his eyelids to close, nor even to move in the slightest degree; and further, there was deathlike stillness in his whole person, owing to the total absence of the heaving motion of the chest caused by the process of respiration.

These two peculiarities, though when told they may appear trifling, produced a very striking and unpleasant effect when seen and observed. Vanderhausen at length relieved the painter of Leyden of his inauspicious presence; and with no small gratification the little party heard the street door close after him.

'Dear uncle,' said Rose, 'what a frightful man! I would not see him again for the wealth of the States!'

'Tush, foolish girl!' said Douw, whose sensations were anything but comfortable. 'A man may be as ugly as the devil, and yet if his heart and actions are good, he is worth all the pretty-faced, perfumed puppies that walk the Mall. Rose, my girl, it is very true he has not thy pretty face, but I know him to be wealthy and liberal; and were he ten times more ugly – '

'Which is inconceivable,' observed Rose.

'These two virtues would be sufficient,' continued her uncle, 'to counterbalance all his deformity; and if not of power sufficient actually to alter the shape of the features, at least of efficacy enough to prevent one thinking them amiss.'

'Do you know, uncle,' said Rose, 'when I saw him standing at the door, I could not get it out of my head that I saw the old, painted, wooden figure that used to frighten me so much in the church of St Laurence at Rotterdam.'

Gerard laughed, though he could not help inwardly acknowledging the justness of the comparison. He was resolved, however, as far as he could, to check his niece's inclination to ridicule the ugliness of her intended bridegroom, although he was not a little pleased to observe that she appeared totally exempt from that mysterious dread of the stranger, which, he could not disguise it from himself, considerably affected him, as it also did his pupil Godfrey Schalken.

Early on the next day there arrived from various quarters of the town, rich presents of silks, velvets, jewellery, and so forth, for Rose; and also a packet directed to Gerard Douw, which, on being opened, was found to contain a contract of marriage, formally drawn up, between Wilken Vanderhausen of the Boom-quay, in Rotterdam, and Rose Velderkaust of Leyden, niece to Gerard Douw, master in the art of painting, also of the same city; and containing engagements on the part of Vanderhausen to make settlements upon his bride far more splendid than he had before led her guardian to believe likely, and which were to be secured to her use in the most unexceptionable manner possible – the money being placed in the hands of Gerard Douw himself.

I have no sentimental scenes to describe, no cruelty of guardians or magnanimity of wards, or agonies of lovers. The record I have to make is one of sordidness, levity, and interest. In less than a week after the first interview which we have just described, the contract of marriage was fulfilled, and Schalken saw the prize which he would have risked anything to secure, carried off triumphantly by his formidable rival.

For two or three days he absented himself from the school; he then returned and worked, if with less cheerfulness, with far more dogged resolution than before; the dream of love had given place to that of ambition.

Months passed away, and, contrary to his expectation, and, indeed, to the direct promise of the parties, Gerard Douw heard nothing of his niece or her worshipful spouse. The interest of the money, which was to have been demanded in quarterly sums, lay unclaimed in his hands. He began to grow extremely uneasy.

Mynher Vanderhausen's direction in Rotterdam he was fully possessed of. After some irresolution he finally determined to journey thither – a trifling undertaking, and easily accomplished – and thus to satisfy himself of the safety and comfort of his ward, for whom he entertained an honest and strong affection.

His search was in vain, however. No one in Rotterdam had ever heard of Mynher Vanderhausen.

Gerard Douw left not a house in the Boom-quay untried; but all in vain. No one could give him any information whatever touching the object of his enquiry; and he was obliged to return to Leyden, nothing wiser than when he had left it.

On his arrival he hastened to the establishment from which Vanderhausen had hired the lumbering, though, considering the times, most luxurious vehicle which the bridal party had employed to convey them to Rotterdam. From the driver of this machine he learned, that having proceeded by slow stages, they had late in the evening approached Rotterdam; but that before they entered the city, and while yet nearly a mile from it, a small party of men, soberly clad, and after the old fashion, with peaked beards and moustaches, standing in the centre of the road, obstructed the further progress of the carriage. The driver reined in his horses, much fearing, from the obscurity of the hour, and the loneliness of the road, that some mischief was intended.

His fears were, however, somewhat allayed by his observing that these strange men carried a large litter, of an antique shape, and which they immediately set down upon the pavement, whereupon the bridegroom, having opened the coach-door from within, descended, and having assisted his bride to do likewise, led her, weeping bitterly and wringing her hands, to the litter, which they both entered. It was then raised by the men who surrounded it, and speedily carried towards the city, and before it had proceeded many yards the darkness concealed it from the view of the Dutch chariot.

In the inside of the vehicle he found a purse, whose contents more than thrice paid the hire of the carriage and man. He saw and could tell nothing more of Mynher Vanderhausen and his beautiful lady. This mystery was a source of deep anxiety and almost of grief to Gerard Douw.

There was evidently fraud in the dealing of Vanderhausen with him, though for what purpose committed he could not imagine. He greatly doubted how far it was possible for a man possessing in his countenance so strong an evidence of the presence of the most demoniac feelings to be in reality anything but a villain; and every day that passed without his hearing from or of his niece, instead of inducing him to forget his fears, tended more and more to intensify them.

The loss of his niece's cheerful society tended also to depress his spirits; and in order to dispel this despondency, which often crept upon his mind after his daily employment was over, he was wont frequently to prevail upon Schalken to accompany him home, and by his presence to dispel, in some degree, the gloom of his otherwise solitary supper.

One evening, the painter and his pupil were sitting by the fire, having accomplished a comfortable supper. They had yielded to that silent pensiveness sometimes induced by the process of digestion, when their reflections were disturbed by a loud sound at the street-door, as if occasioned by some person rushing forcibly and repeatedly against it. A domestic had run without delay to ascertain the cause of the disturbance, and they heard him twice or thrice interrogate the applicant for admission, but without producing an answer or any cessation of the sounds.

They heard him then open the hall door, and immediately there followed a light and rapid tread upon the staircase. Schalken laid his hand on his sword, and advanced towards the door. It opened before he reached it, and Rose rushed into the room. She looked wild and haggard, and pale with exhaustion and terror; but her dress surprised them as much even as her unexpected appearance. It consisted of a kind of white woollen wrapper, made close about the neck, and descending to the very ground. It was much deranged and travel-soiled. The poor creature had hardly entered the chamber when she fell senseless on the floor. With some difficulty they succeeded in reviving her, and on recovering her senses she instantly exclaimed, in a tone of eager, terrified impatience: 'Wine, wine, quickly, or I'm lost!'

Much alarmed at the strange agitation in which the call was made, they at once administered to her wishes, and she drank some wine with a haste and eagerness which surprised him. She had hardly swallowed it, when she exclaimed with the same urgency: 'Food, food, at once, or I perish!'

A considerable fragment of a roast joint was upon the table, and Schalken immediately proceeded to cut some, but he was anticipated; for no sooner had she become aware of its presence than she darted at it with the rapacity of a vulture, and, seizing it in her hands, she tore off the flesh with her teeth and swallowed it.

When the paroxysm of hunger had been a little appeased, she appeared suddenly to become aware how strange her conduct had been, or it may have been that other more agitating thoughts recurred to her mind, for she began to weep bitterly, and to wring her hands.

'Oh! send for a minister of God,' said she; 'I am not safe till he comes; send for him speedily.'

Gerard Douw despatched a messenger instantly, and prevailed on his niece to allow him to surrender his bedchamber to her use; he also persuaded her to retire to it at once and to rest; her consent was extorted upon the condition that they would not leave her for a moment.

'Oh that the holy man were here!' she said; 'he can deliver me. The dead and the living can never be one – God has forbidden it.'

With these mysterious words she surrendered herself to their guidance, and they proceeded to the chamber which Gerard Douw had assigned to her use.

'Do not – do not leave me for a moment,' said she. 'I am lost for ever if you do.'

Gerard Douw's chamber was approached through a spacious apartment, which they were now about to enter. Gerard Douw and

Schalken each carried a wax candle, so that sufficient degree of light was cast upon all surrounding objects. They were now entering the large chamber, which, as I have said, communicated with Douw's apartment, when Rose suddenly stopped, and, in a whisper which seemed to thrill with horror, she said: 'O God! he is here – he is here! See, see – there he goes!'

She pointed towards the door of the inner room, and Schalken thought he saw a shadowy and ill-defined form gliding into that apartment. He drew his sword, and raising the candle so as to throw its light with increased distinctness upon the objects in the room, he entered the chamber into which the figure had glided. No figure was there – nothing but the furniture which belonged to the room, and yet he could not be deceived as to the fact that something had moved before them into the chamber.

A sickening dread came upon him, and the cold perspiration broke out in heavy drops upon his forehead; nor was he more composed when he heard the increased urgency, the agony of entreaty, with which Rose implored them not to leave her for a moment.

'I saw him,' said she. 'He's here! I cannot be deceived – I know him. He's by me – he's with me – he's in the room. Then, for God's sake, as you would save, do not stir from beside me!'

They at length prevailed upon her to lie down upon the bed, where she continued to urge them to stay by her. She frequently uttered incoherent sentences, repeating again and again, 'The dead and the living cannot be one – God has forbidden it!' and then again, 'Rest to the wakeful – sleep to the sleepwalkers.'

These and such mysterious and broken sentences she continued to utter until the clergyman arrived.

Gerard Douw began to fear, naturally enough, that the poor girl, owing to terror or ill-treatment, had become deranged; and he half suspected, by the suddenness of her appearance, and the unseasonableness of the hour, and, above all, from the wildness and terror of her manner, that she had made her escape from some place of confinement for lunatics, and was in immediate fear of pursuit. He resolved to summon medical advice as soon as the mind of his niece had been in some measure set at rest by the offices of the clergyman whose attendance she had so earnestly desired; and until this object had been attained, he did not venture to put any questions to her, which might possibly, by reviving painful or horrible recollections, increase her agitation.

The clergyman soon arrived – a man of ascetic countenance – and venerable age – one whom Gerard Douw respected much, forasmuch as he was a veteran polemic, though one, perhaps, more dreaded as a combatant than beloved as a Christian – of pure morality, subtle brain, and frozen heart. He entered the chamber which communicated with that in which Rose reclined, and immediately on his arrival she requested him to pray for her, as for one who lay in the hands of Satan, and who could hope for deliverance only from Heaven.

That our readers may distinctly understand all the circumstances of the event which we were about imperfectly to describe, it is necessary to state the relative positions of the parties who were engaged in it. The old clergyman and Schalken were in the anteroom of which we have already spoken; Rose lay in the inner chamber, the door of which was open; and by the side of the bed, at her urgent desire, stood her guardian; a candle burned in the bedchamber, and three were lighted in the outer apartment.

The old man now cleared his voice, as if about to commence; but before he had time to begin, a sudden gust of air blew out the candle which served to illuminate the room in which the poor girl lay, and she with hurried alarm, exclaimed: 'Godfrey, bring in another candle; the darkness is unsafe.'

Gerard Douw, forgetting for the moment her repeated injunctions in the immediate impulse, stepped from the bedchamber into the other, in order to supply what she desired.

'O God! do not go, dear uncle!' shrieked the unhappy girl; and at the same time she sprang from the bed and darted after him, in order, by her grasp, to detain him.

But the warning came too late, for scarcely had he passed the threshold, and hardly had his niece had time to utter the startling exclamation, when the door which divided the two rooms closed violently after him, as if swung to by a strong blast of wind.

Schalken and he both rushed to the door, but their united and desperate efforts could not avail so much as to shake it.

Shriek after shriek burst from the inner chamber, with all the piercing loudness of despairing terror. Schalken and Douw applied every energy and strained every nerve to force open the door; but all in vain.

There was no sound of struggling from within, but the screams seemed to increase in loudness, and at the same time they heard the bolts of the latticed window withdrawn, and the window itself grated upon the sill as if thrown open.

One last shriek, so long and piercing and agonised as to be scarcely human, swelled from the room, and suddenly there followed a deathlike silence.

A light step was heard crossing the floor, as if from the bed to the window; and almost at the same instant the door gave way, and yielding to the pressure of the external applicants, they were nearly precipitated into the room. It was empty. The window was open, and Schalken sprang to a chair and gazed out upon the street and at the canal below. He saw no form, but he beheld, or thought he beheld, the waters of the broad canal beneath settling ring after ring in heavy circular ripples, as if a moment before disturbed by the immersion of some large and heavy mass.

No trace of Rose was ever after discovered, nor was anything certain respecting her mysterious wooer detected or even suspected; no clue whereby to trace the intricacies of the labyrinth, and to arrive at a distinct conclusion was to be found. But an incident occurred, which, though it will not be received by our rational readers as at all approaching to evidence upon the matter, nevertheless produced a strong and a lasting impression upon the mind of Schalken.

Many years after the events which we had detailed, Schalken, then remotely situated, received an intimation of his father's death, and of his intended burial upon a fixed day in the church of Rotterdam. It was necessary that a very considerable journey should be performed by the funeral procession, which, as it will readily be believed, was not very numerously attended. Schalken with difficulty arrived in Rotterdam late in the day upon which the funeral was appointed to take place. The procession had not then arrived. Evening closed in, and still it did not appear.

Schalken strolled down to the church – he found it open; notice of the arrival of the funeral had been given, and the vault in which the body was to be laid had been opened. The official who corresponds to our sexton, on seeing a well-dressed gentleman, whose object was to attend the expected funeral, pacing the aisle of the church, hospitably invited him to share with him the comforts of a blazing wood fire, which as was his custom in winter time upon such occasions, he had kindled on the hearth of a chamber which communicated by a flight of steps with the vault below.

In this chamber Schalken and his entertainer seated themselves; and the sexton, after some fruitless attempts to engage his guest in conversation, was obliged to apply himself to his tobacco-pipe and can to solace his solitude.

In spite of his grief and cares, the fatigues of a rapid journey of nearly forty hours gradually overcame the mind and body of Godfrey Schalken, and he sank into a deep sleep, from which he was awakened by someone shaking him gently by the shoulder. He first thought that the old sexton had called him, but *he* was no longer in the room.

He roused himself, and as soon as he could clearly see what was around him, he perceived a female form, clothed in a kind of light robe of muslin, part of which was so disposed as to act as a veil, and in her hand she carried a lamp. She was moving rather away from him, and towards the flight of steps which conducted towards the vaults.

Schalken felt a vague alarm at the sight of this figure, and at the same time an irresistible impulse to follow its guidance. He followed it towards the vaults, but when it reached the head of the stairs, he paused; the figure paused also, and turning gently round, displayed, by the light of the lamp it carried, the face and features of his first love, Rose Velderkaust. There was nothing horrible, or even sad, in the countenance. On the contrary, it wore the same arch smile which used to enchant the artist long before in his happy days.

A feeling of awe and of interest, too intense to be resisted, prompted him to follow the spectre, if spectre it were. She descended the stairs – he followed; and, turning to the left, through a narrow passage she led him, to his infinite surprise, into what appeared to be an old-fashioned Dutch apartment, such as the pictures of Gerard Douw have served to immortalise.

Abundance of costly antique furniture was disposed about the room, and in one corner stood a four-post bed, with heavy black cloth curtains around it. The figure frequently turned towards him with the same arch smile; and when she came to the side of the bed, she drew the curtains, and by the light of the lamp which she held towards its contents, she disclosed to the horror-stricken painter, sitting bolt upright in the bed, the livid and demoniac form of Vanderhausen. Schalken had hardly seen him when he fell senseless upon the floor, where he lay until discovered, on the next morning, by persons employed in closing the passages into the vaults. He was lying in a cell of considerable size, which had not been disturbed for a long time, and he had fallen beside a large coffin which was supported upon small stone pillars, a security against the attacks of vermin.

To his dying day Schalken was satisfied of the reality of the vision which he had witnessed, and he has left behind him a curious evidence of the impression which it wrought upon his fancy, in a painting executed shortly after the event we have narrated, and which is valuable as exhibiting not only the peculiarities which have made Schalken's pictures sought after, but even more so as presenting a portrait, as close and faithful as one taken from memory can be, of his early love, Rose Velderkaust, whose mysterious fate must ever remain matter of speculation.

The picture represents a chamber of antique masonry, such as might be found in most old cathedrals, and is lighted faintly by a lamp carried in the hand of a female figure, such as we have above attempted to describe; and in the background, and to the left of him who examines the painting, there stands the form of a man apparently aroused from sleep, and by his attitude, his hand being laid upon his sword, exhibiting considerable alarm; this last figure is illuminated only by the expiring glare of a wood or charcoal fire.

The whole production exhibits a beautiful specimen of that artful and singular distribution of light and shade which has rendered the name of Schalken immortal among the artists of his country. This tale is traditionary, and the reader will easily perceive, by our studiously omitting to heighten many points of the narrative, when a little additional colouring might have added effect to the recital, that we have desired to lay before him, not a figment of the brain, but a curious tradition connected with, and belonging to, the biography of a famous artist.

SHERIDAN LE FANU

The Fortunes of Sir Robert Ardagh

In the south of Ireland, and on the borders of the country of Limerick, there lies a district of two or three miles in length, which is rendered interesting by the fact that it is one of the very few spots throughout this country in which some vestiges of aboriginal forests still remain. It has little or none of the lordly character of the American forest, for the axe has felled its oldest and its grandest trees; but in the close wood which survives live all the wild and pleasing peculiarities of nature: its complete irregularity, its vistas, in whose perspective the quiet cattle are browsing; its refreshing glades, where the grey rocks arise from amid the nodding fern; the silvery shafts of the old birch trees; the knotted trunks of the hoary oak, the grotesque but graceful branches which never shed their honours under the tyrant pruning-hook the soft green sward; the chequered light and shade; the wild luxuriant weeds; the lichen and the moss – all are beautiful alike in the green freshness of spring or in the sadness and sere of autumn. Their beauty is of that kind which makes the heart full with joy – appealing to the affections with a power which belongs to nature only. This wood runs up, from below the base, to the ridge of a long line of irregular hills, having perhaps, in primitive times, formed but the skirting of some mighty forest which occupied the level below. But now, alas! whither have we drifted? whither has the tide of civilisation borne us? It has passed over a land unprepared for it – it has left nakedness behind it; we have lost our forests, but our marauders remain; we have destroyed all that is picturesque, while we have retained everything that is revolting in barbarism.

Through the midst of this woodland there runs a deep gully or glen, where the stillness of the scene is broken in upon by the brawling of a mountain-stream, which, however, in the winter season, swells into a rapid and formidable torrent. There is one point at which the glen becomes extremely deep and narrow; the sides descend to the depth of some hundred feet, and are so steep as to be nearly perpendicular. The wild trees which have taken root in the crannies and chasms of the rock are so intersected and entangled, that one can with difficulty catch a glimpse of the stream which wheels, flashes, and foams below, as if exulting in the surrounding silence and solitude.

This spot was not unwisely chosen, as a point of no ordinary strength, for the erection of a massive square tower or keep, one side of which rises as if in continuation of the precipitous cliff on which it is based. Originally, the only mode of ingress was by a narrow portal in the very wall which overtopped the precipice, opening upon a ledge of rock which afforded a precarious pathway, cautiously intersected, however, by a deep trench cut out with great labour in the living rock; so that, in its pristine state, and before the introduction of artillery into the art of war, this tower might have been pronounced, and that not presumptuously, impregnable.

The progress of improvement and the increasing security of the times had, however, tempted its successive proprietors, if not to adorn, at least to enlarge their premises, and about the middle of the last century, when the castle was last inhabited, the original square tower formed but a small part of the edifice.

The castle, and a wide tract of the surrounding country, had from time immemorial belonged to a family which, for distinctness, we shall call by the name of Ardagh; and owing to the associations which, in Ireland, almost always attach to scenes which have long witnessed alike the exercise of stern feudal authority, and of that savage hospitality which distinguished the good old times, this building has become the subject and the scene of many wild and extraordinary traditions. One of them I have been enabled, by a personal acquaintance with an eye-witness of the events, to trace to its origin and yet it is hard to say whether the events which I am about to record appear more strange and improbable as seen through the distorting medium of tradition, or in the appalling dimness of uncertainty which surrounds the reality.

Tradition says that, sometime in the last century, Sir Robert Ardagh, a young man, and the last heir of that family, went abroad and served in foreign armies and that, having acquired considerable honour and emolument, he settled at Castle Ardagh, the building we have just now attempted to describe. He was what the country people call a *dark* man that is, he was considered morose, reserved, and ill-tempered and, as it was supposed from the utter solitude of his life, was upon no terms of cordiality with the other members of his family.

The only occasion upon which he broke through the solitary monotony of his life was during the continuance of the racing season, and immediately subsequent to it; at which time he was to be seen among the busiest upon the course, betting deeply and unhesitatingly, and invariably with success. Sir Robert was, however, too well known as a man of honour, and of too high a family, to be suspected of any unfair dealing. He was, moreover, a soldier, and a man of intrepid as well as of a haughty character and no one cared to hazard a surmise, the consequences of which would be felt most probably by its originator only.

Gossip, however, was not silent; it was remarked that Sir Robert never appeared at the race-ground, which was the only place of public resort which he frequented, except in company with a certain strange-looking person, who was never seen elsewhere, or under other circumstances. It was remarked, too, that this man, whose relation to Sir Robert was never distinctly ascertained, was the only person to whom he seemed to speak unnecessarily; it was observed that while with the country gentry he exchanged no further communication than what was unavoidable in arranging his sporting transactions, with this person he would converse earnestly and frequently. Tradition asserts that, to enhance the curiosity which this unaccountable and exclusive preference excited, the stranger possessed some striking and unpleasant peculiarities of person and of garb – though it is not stated, however, what these were – but they, in conjunction with Sir Robert's secluded habits and extraordinary run of luck – a success which was supposed to result from the suggestions and immediate advice of the unknown – were sufficient to warrant report in pronouncing that there was something *queer* in the wind, and in surmising that Sir Robert was playing a fearful and a hazardous game, and that, in short, his strange companion was little better than the Devil himself.

Years rolled quietly away, and nothing very novel occurred in the arrangements of Castle Ardagh, excepting that Sir Robert parted with his odd companion, but as nobody could tell whence he came, so nobody could say whither he had gone. Sir Robert's habits, however, underwent no consequent change; he continued regularly to frequent the race meetings, without mixing at all in the convivialities of the gentry, and immediately afterwards to relapse into the secluded monotony of his ordinary life.

It was said that he had accumulated vast sums of money – and, as his bets were always successful and always large, such must have been the case. He did not suffer the acquisition of wealth, however, to influence his hospitality or his housekeeping – he neither purchased land, nor extended his establishment and his mode of enjoying his money must have been altogether that of the miser – consisting merely in the pleasure of touching and telling his gold, and in the consciousness of wealth.

Sir Robert's temper, so far from improving, became more than ever gloomy and morose. He sometimes carried the indulgence of his evil dispositions to such a height that it bordered upon insanity. During these paroxysms he would neither eat, drink, nor sleep. On such occasions he insisted on perfect privacy, even from the intrusion of his most trusted servants; his voice was frequently heard, sometimes in earnest supplication, sometimes raised, as if in loud and angry altercation with some unknown visitant. Sometimes he would for hours together walk to and fro throughout the long oak-wainscoted apartment which he generally occupied, with wild gesticulations and agitated pace, in the manner of one who has been roused to a state of unnatural excitement by some sudden and appalling intimation.

These paroxysms of apparent lunacy were so frightful, that during their continuance even his oldest and most faithful domestics dared not approach him; consequently his hours of agony were never intruded upon, and the mysterious causes of his sufferings appeared likely to remain hidden for ever.

On one occasion a fit of this kind continued for an unusual time; the ordinary term of their duration – about two days – had been long past, and the old servant who generally waited upon Sir Robert after these visitations, having in vain listened for the well-known tinkle of his master's hand bell, began to feel extremely anxious; he feared that his master might have died from sheer exhaustion, or perhaps put an end to his on existence during his miserable depression. These fears at length became so strong, that having in vain urged some of his brother servants to accompany him, he determined to go up alone, and himself see whether any accident had befallen Sir Robert.

He traversed the several passages which conducted from the new to the more ancient parts of the mansion, and having arrived in the old hall of the castle, the utter silence of the hour – for it was very late in the night – the idea of the nature of the enterprise in which he was engaging himself, a sensation of remoteness from anything like human companionship, but, more than all, the vivid but undefined anticipation of something horrible, came upon him with such oppressive weight that he hesitated as to whether he should proceed. Real uneasiness, however, respecting the fate of his master, for who he felt that kind of attachment which the force of habitual intercourse not unfrequently engenders respecting objects not in themselves amiable, and also a latent unwillingness to expose his weakness to the ridicule of his fellow-servants, combined to overcome his reluctance; and he had just placed his foot upon the first step of the staircase which conducted his master's chamber, when his attention was arrested by low but distinct knocking at the hall-door. Not, perhaps, very sorry at finding thus an excuse even for deferring his intended expedition, he placed the candle upon a stone block which lay in the hall and approached the door, uncertain whether his ears had not deceived him. This doubt was justified by the circumstance that the hall entrance had been for nearly fifty years disused as a mode of ingress to the castle. The situation of this gate also, which we have endeavoured to describe, opening upon a narrow ledge of rock which overhangs a perilous cliff, rendered it at all times, but particularly at night, a dangerous entrance. This shelving platform of rock, which formed the only avenue to the door, was divided, as I have already stated, by a broad chasm, the planks across which had long disappeared, by decay or otherwise; so that it seemed at least highly improbable that any man could have found his way across the passage in safety to the door, more particularly on a night like this, of singular darkness. The old man, therefore, listened attentively, to ascertain whether the first application should be followed by another. He had not long to wait. The same low but singularly distinct knocking was repeated; so low that it seemed as if the applicant had employed no harder or heavier instrument than his hand, and yet, despite the immense thickness of the door, with such strength that the sound was distinctly audible.

The knock was repeated a third time, without any increase of loudness; and the old man, obeying an impulse for which to his dying hour he could never account, proceeded to remove, one by one, the three great oaken bars which secured the door. Time and damp had effectually corroded the iron chambers of the lock, so that it afforded little resistance. With some effort, as he believed, assisted from without, the old servant succeeded in opening the door; and a low, square-built figure, apparently that of a man wrapped in a large black cloak, entered the hall. The servant could not see much of this visitor with any distinctness; his dress appeared foreign, the skirt of his ample cloak was thrown over one shoulder; he wore a large felt hat, with a very heavy leaf, from under which escaped what appeared to be a mass of long sooty-black hair his feet were cased in heavy riding-boots. Such were the few particulars which the servant had time and light to observe. The stranger desired him to let his master know instantly that a friend had come, by appointment, to settle some business with him. The servant hesitated, but a slight motion on the part of his visitor, as if to possess himself of the candle, determined him; so, taking it in his hand, he ascended the castle stairs, leaving the guest in the hall.

On reaching the apartment which opened upon the oak chamber he was surprised to observe the door of that room partly open, and the room itself lit up. He paused, but there was no sound; he looked in, and saw Sir Robert, his head and the upper part of his body reclining on a table, upon which two candles burned; his arms were stretched forward on either side, and perfectly motionless; it appeared that, having been sitting at the table, he had thus sunk forward, either dead or in a swoon. There was no sound of breathing; all was silent, except the sharp ticking of a watch, which lay beside the lamp. The servant coughed twice or thrice, but with no effect; his fears now almost amounted to certainty, and he was approaching the table on which his master partly lay, to satisfy himself of his death, when Sir Robert slowly raised his head, and, throwing himself back in his chair, fixed his eyes in a ghastly and uncertain gaze upon his attendant. At length he said, slowly and painfully, as if he dreaded the answer: 'In God's name, what are you?'

'Sir,' said the servant, 'a strange gentleman wants to see you below.'

At this intimation Sir Robert, starting to his feet and tossing his arms wildly upwards, uttered a shriek of such appalling and despairing terror that it was almost too fearful for human endurance; and long after the sound had ceased it seemed to the terrified imagination of the old servant to roll through the deserted passages in bursts of unnatural laughter. After a few moments Sir Robert said: 'Can't you send him away? Why does he come so soon? O Merciful Powers! let him leave me for an hour; a little time. I can't see him now; try to get him away. You see I can't go down now I have not strength. O God! O God! let him come back in an hour it is not long to wait. He cannot lose anything by it; nothing, nothing, nothing. Tell him that! Say anything to him.'

The servant went down. In his own words, he did not feel the stairs under him till he got to the hall. The figure stood exactly as he had left it. He delivered his master's message as coherently as he could. The stranger replied in a careless tone: 'If Sir Robert will not come down to me; I must go up to him.'

The man returned, and to his surprise he found his master much more composed in manner. He listened to the message, and though the cold perspiration rose in drops upon his forehead faster than he could wipe it away, his manner had lost the dreadful agitation which had marked it before. He rose feebly, and casting a last look of agony behind him, passed from the room to the lobby, where he signed to his attendant not to follow him. The man moved as far as the head of the staircase, from whence he had a tolerably distinct view of the hall, which was imperfectly lighted by the candle he had left there.

He saw his master reel, rather than walk, down the stairs, clinging all the way to the banisters. He walked on, as if about to sink every moment from weakness. The figure advanced as if to meet him, and in passing struck down the light. The servant could see no more; but there was a sound of struggling, renewed at intervals with silent but fearful energy. It was evident, however, that the parties were approaching the door, for he heard the solid oak sound twice or thrice, as the feet of the combatants, in shuffling hither and thither over the floor, struck upon it. After a slight pause, he heard the door thrown open with such violence that the leaf seemed to strike the side-wall of the hall, for it was so dark without that this could only be surmised by the sound. The struggle was renewed with an agony and intenseness of energy that betrayed itself in deep-drawn gasps. One desperate effort, which terminated in the breaking of some part of the door, producing a sound as if the doorpost was wrenched from its position, was followed by another wrestle, evidently upon the narrow ledge which ran outside the door, overtopping the precipice. This proved to be the final struggle; it was followed by a crashing sound as if some heavy body had fallen over, and was rushing down the precipice through the light boughs that crossed near the top. All then became still as the grave, except when the moan of the night-wind sighed up the wooded glen.

The old servant had not nerve to return through the hall, and to him the darkness seemed all but endless; but morning at length came, and with it the disclosure of the events of the night. Near the door, upon the ground, lay Sir Robert's sword-belt, which had given way in the scuffle. A huge splinter from the massive doorpost had been wrenched off by an almost superhuman effort – one which nothing but the gripe of a despairing man could have severed – and on the rocks outside were left the marks of the slipping and sliding of feet.

At the foot of the precipice, not immediately under the castle, but dragged some way up the glen, were found the remains of Sir Robert, with hardly a vestige of a limb or feature left distinguishable. The right hand, however, was uninjured, and in its fingers were clutched, with the fixedness of death, a long lock of coarse sooty hair – the only direct circumstantial evidence of the presence of a second person.

SHERIDAN LE FANU

The Dream

Dreams! What age, or what country of the world, has not felt and acknowledged the mystery of their origin and end? I have thought not a little upon the subject, seeing it is one which has been often forced upon my attention, and sometimes strangely enough; and yet I have never arrived at anything which at all appeared a satisfactory conclusion. It does appear that a mental phenomenon so extraordinary cannot be wholly without its use. We know, indeed, that in the olden times it has been made the organ of communication between the Deity and His creatures; and when a dream produces upon a mind, to all appearance hopelessly reprobate and depraved, an effect so powerful and so lasting as to break down the inveterate habits, and to reform the life of an abandoned sinner, we see in the result, in the reformation of morals which appeared incorrigible, in the reclamation of a human soul which seemed to be irretrievably lost, something more than could be produced by a mere chimera of the slumbering fancy, something more than could arise from the capricious images of a terrified imagination. And while Reason rejects as absurd the superstition which will read a prophecy in every dream, she may, without violence to herself, recognise, even in the wildest and most incongruous of the wanderings of a slumbering intellect, the evidences and the fragments of a language which may be spoken, which *has* been spoken, to terrify, to warn and to command. We have reason to believe too, by the promptness of action which in the age of the prophets followed all intimations of this kind, and by the strength of conviction and strange permanence of the effects resulting from certain dreams in latter times – which effects we ourselves may have witnessed – that when this medium of communication has been employed by the Deity, the evidences of His presence have been unequivocal. My thoughts were directed to this subject in a manner to leave a lasting impression upon my mind, by the events which I shall now relate, the statement of which, however extraordinary, is nevertheless accurate.

About the year 17—, having been appointed to the living of C—, I rented a small house in the town which bears the same name: one morning in the month of November, I was awakened before my usual time by my servant, who bustled into my bedroom for the purpose of announcing a sick call. As the Catholic Church holds her last rites to be totally indispensable to the safety of the departing sinner, no conscientious clergyman can afford a moment's unnecessary delay, and in little more than five minutes I stood ready, cloaked and booted for the road, in the small front parlour in which the messenger, who was to act as my guide, awaited my coming. I found a poor little girl crying piteously near the door, and after some slight difficulty I ascertained that her father was either dead or just dying.

'And what may be your father's name, my poor child?' said I. She held down her head as if ashamed. I repeated the question, and the wretched little creature burst into floods of tears still more bitter than she had shed before. At length, almost angered by conduct which appeared to me so unreasonable, I began to lose patience, and I said rather harshly: 'If you will not tell me the name of the person to whom you would lead me, your silence can arise from no good motive, and I might be justified in refusing to go with you at all.'

'Oh, don't say that – don't say that!' cried she. 'Oh, sir, it was that I was afeard of when I would not tell you – I was afeard, when you heard his name, you would not come with me; but it is no use hidin' it now – it's Pat Connell, the carpenter, your honour.'

She looked in my face with the most earnest anxiety, as if her very existence depended upon what she should read there. I relieved the child at once. The name, indeed, was most unpleasantly familiar to me; but, however fruitless my visits and advice might have been at another time, the present was too fearful an occasion to suffer my doubts of their utility, or my reluctance to re-attempting what appeared a hopeless task, to weigh even against the lightest chance that a consciousness of his imminent danger might produce in him a more docile and tractable disposition. Accordingly I told the child to lead

the way, and followed her in silence. She hurried rapidly through the
long narrow street which forms the great thoroughfare of the town.
The darkness of the hour, rendered still deeper by the close approach
of the old-fashioned houses, which lowered in tall obscurity on either
side of the way; the damp, dreary chill which renders the advance of
morning peculiarly cheerless, combined with the object of my walk –
to visit the deathbed of a presumptuous sinner, to endeavour, almost
against my own conviction, to infuse a hope into the heart of a dying
reprobate – a drunkard but too probably perishing under the
consequences of some mad fit of intoxication; all these circumstances
served to enhance the gloom and solemnity of my feelings, as I silently
followed my little guide, who with quick steps traversed the uneven
pavement of the Main Street. After a walk of about five minutes, she
turned off into a narrow lane, of that obscure and comfortless class
which is to be found in almost all small old-fashioned towns, chill,
without ventilation, reeking with all manner of offensive effluvia, and
lined by dingy, smoky, sickly and pent-up buildings, frequently not
only in a wretched but in a dangerous condition.

'Your father has changed his abode since I last visited him, and, I
am afraid, much for the worse,' said I.

'Indeed he has, sir; but we must not complain,' replied she. 'We
have to thank God that we have lodging and food, though it's poor
enough, it is, your honour.'

Poor child! thought I. How many an older head might learn
wisdom from thee – how many a luxurious philosopher, who is skilled
to preach but not to suffer, might not thy patient words put to the
blush! The manner and language of my companion were alike above
her years and station; and, indeed, in all cases in which the cares and
sorrows of life have anticipated their usual date, and have fallen,
as they sometimes do, with melancholy prematurity to the lot of
childhood, I have observed the result to have proved uniformly the
same. A young mind, to which joy and indulgence have been strangers,
and to which suffering and self-denial have been familiarised from the
first, acquires a solidity and an elevation which no other discipline
could have bestowed, and which, in the present case, communicated a
striking but mournful peculiarity to the manners, even to the voice, of
the child. We paused before a narrow, crazy door, which she opened
by means of a latch, and we forthwith began to ascend the steep and

broken stairs which led to the sick man's room.

As we mounted flight after flight towards the garret-floor, I heard more and more distinctly the hurried talking of many voices. I could also distinguish the low sobbing of a female. On arriving upon the uppermost lobby, these sounds became fully audible.

'This way, your honour,' said my little conductress; at the same time, pushing open a door of patched and half-rotten plank, she admitted me into the squalid chamber of death and misery. But one candle, held in the fingers of a scared and haggard-looking child, was burning in the room, and that so dim that all was twilight or darkness except within its immediate influence. The general obscurity, however, served to throw into prominent and startling relief the deathbed and its occupant. The light fell with horrible clearness upon the blue and swollen features of the drunkard. I did not think it possible that a human countenance could look so terrific. The lips were black and drawn apart; the teeth were firmly set; the eyes a little unclosed, and nothing but the whites appearing. Every feature was fixed and livid, and the whole face wore a ghastly and rigid expression of despairing terror such as I never saw equalled. His hands were crossed upon his breast, and firmly clenched while, as if to add to the corpse-like effect of the whole, some white cloths, dipped in water, were wound about the forehead and temples.

As soon as I could remove my eyes from this horrible spectacle, I observed my friend Dr D—, one of the most humane of a humane profession, standing by the bedside. He had been attempting, but unsuccessfully, to bleed the patient, and had now applied his finger to the pulse.

'Is there any hope?' I enquired in a whisper.

A shake of the head was the reply. There was a pause, while he continued to hold the wrist; but he waited in vain for the throb of life – it was not there: and when he let go the hand, it fell stiffly back into its former position upon the other.

'The man is dead,' said the physician, as he turned from the bed where the terrible figure lay.

Dead! thought I, scarcely venturing to look upon the tremendous and revolting spectacle. Dead! without an hour for repentance, even a moment for reflection. Dead! without the rites which even the best should have. Was there a hope for him? The glaring eyeball, the grinning mouth, the distorted brow – that unutterable look in which a painter would have sought to embody the fixed despair of the nethermost hell – These were my answer.

The poor wife sat at a little distance, crying as if her heart would break – the younger children clustered round the bed, looking with wondering curiosity upon the form of death, never seen before.

When the first tumult of uncontrollable sorrow had passed away, availing myself of the solemnity and impressiveness of the scene, I desired the heart-stricken family to accompany me in prayer, and all knelt down while I solemnly and fervently repeated some of those prayers which appeared most applicable to the occasion. I employed myself thus in a manner which I trusted was not unprofitable, at least to the living, for about ten minutes; and having accomplished my task, I was the first to arise.

I looked upon the poor, sobbing, helpless creatures who knelt so humbly around me, and my heart bled for them. With a natural transition I turned my eyes from them to the bed in which the body lay; and, great God! what was the revulsion, the horror which I experienced on seeing the corpse-like, terrific thing seated half upright before me. The white cloths which had been wound about the head had now partly slipped from their position, and were hanging in grotesque festoons about the face and shoulders, while the distorted eyes leered from amid them: 'A sight to dream of, not to tell.'

I stood actually riveted to the spot. The figure nodded its head and lifted its arm, I thought, with a menacing gesture. A thousand confused and horrible thoughts at once rushed upon my mind. I had often read that the body of a presumptuous sinner, who, during life, had been the willing creature of every satanic impulse, had been known, after the human tenant had deserted it, to become the horrible sport of demoniac possession.

I was roused by the piercing scream of the mother, who now, for the first time perceived the change which had taken place. She rushed towards the bed, but, stunned by the shock and overcome by the conflict of violent emotions, before she reached it she fell prostrate upon the floor.

I am perfectly convinced that had I not been startled from the torpidity of horror in which I was bound by some powerful and arousing stimulant, I should have gazed upon this unearthly apparition until I had fairly lost my senses. As it was, however, the spell was broken – superstition gave way to reason: the man whom all believed to have been actually dead was living!

Dr D— was instantly standing by the bedside, and upon examination he found that a sudden and copious flow of blood had taken place from the wound which the lancet had left; and this, no doubt, had effected his sudden and almost preternatural restoration to an existence from which all thought he had been for ever removed. The man was still speechless, but he seemed to understand the physician when he forbade his repeating the painful and fruitless attempts which he made to articulate, and he at once resigned himself quietly into his hands.

I left the patient with leeches upon his temples, and bleeding freely, apparently with little of the drowsiness which accompanies, apoplexy. Indeed, Dr D— told me that he had never before witnessed a seizure which seemed to combine the symptoms of so many kinds, and yet which belonged to none of the recognised classes; it certainly was not apoplexy, catalepsy, nor *delirium tremens*, and yet it seemed, in some degree, to partake of the properties of all. It was strange, but stranger things are coming.

During two or three days Dr D— would not allow his patient to converse in a manner which could excite or exhaust him, with anyone; he suffered him merely as briefly as possible to express his immediate wants. And it was not until the fourth day after my early visit, the particulars of which I have just detailed, that it was thought expedient that I should see him, and then only because it appeared that his extreme importunity and impatience to meet me were likely to retard his recovery more than the mere exhaustion attendant upon a short conversation could possibly do. Perhaps, too, my friend entertained some hope that if by holy confession his patient's bosom were eased of the perilous stuff which no doubt oppressed it, his recovery would be more assured and rapid. It was then, as I have said, upon the fourth day after my first professional call, that I found myself once more in the dreary chamber of want and sickness.

The man was in bed, and appeared low and restless. On my entering the room he raised himself in the bed, and muttered, twice or thrice,

'Thank God! thank God!'

I signed to those of his family who stood by to leave the room, and took a chair beside the bed. So soon as we were alone, he said, rather doggedly: 'There's no use in telling me of the sinfulness of bad ways – I know it all. I know where they lead to – I have seen everything about it with my own eyesight, as plain as I see you.' He rolled himself in the bed, as if to hide his face in the clothes; and then suddenly raising himself, he exclaimed with startling vehemence, 'Look, sir! there is no use in mincing the matter: I'm blasted with the fires of hell; I have been in hell. What do you think of that? In hell – I'm lost for ever – I have not a chance. I am damned already – damned – damned!'

The end of this sentence he actually shouted. His vehemence was perfectly terrific; he threw himself back, and laughed, and sobbed hysterically. I poured some water into a teacup, and gave it to him. After he had swallowed it, I told him if he had anything to communicate, to do so as briefly as he could, and in a manner as little agitating to himself as possible; threatening at the same time, though I had no intention of doing so, to leave him at once in case he again gave way to such passionate excitement.

'It's only foolishness,' he continued, 'for me to try to thank you for coming to such a villain as myself at all. It's no use for me to wish good to you, or to bless you; for such as me has no blessings to give.'

I told him that I had but done my duty, and urged him to proceed to the matter which weighed upon his mind. He then spoke nearly as follows: 'I came in drunk on Friday night last, and got to my bed here; I don't remember how. Sometime in the night it seemed to me I wakened, and feeling uneasy in myself, I got up out of the bed. I wanted the fresh air; but I would not make a noise to open the window, for fear I'd waken the crathurs. It was very dark and trouble-some to find the door but at last I did get it, and I groped my way out, and went down as easy as I could. I felt quite sober, and I counted the steps one after another, as I was going down, that I might not stumble at the bottom.

'When I came to the first landing-place – God be about us always! – the floor of it sunk under me, and I went down – down – down, till the senses almost left me. I do not know how long I was falling, but it seemed to me a great while. When I came rightly to myself at last, I was sitting near the top of a great table; and I could not see the end of it, if it had any, it was so far off. And there was men beyond reckoning sitting down all along by it, at each side, as far as I could see at all. I did not know at first was it in the open air; but there was a close smothering feel in it that was not natural. And there was a kind of light that my eyesight never saw before, red and unsteady; and I did not see for a long time where it was coming from, until I looked straight up, and then I seen that it came from great balls of blood-coloured fire that were rolling high overhead with a sort of rushing, trembling sound, and I perceived that they shone on the ribs of a great roof of rock that was arched overhead instead of the sky. When I seen this, scarce knowing what I did, I got up, and I said, "I have no right to be here; I must go." And the man that was sitting at my left hand only smiled, and said, "Sit down again; you can *never* leave this place." And his voice was weaker than any child's voice I ever heard and when he was done speaking he smiled again.

'Then I spoke out very loud and bold, and I said, "In the name of God, let me out of this bad place." And there was a great man that I did not see before, sitting at the end of the table that I was near; and he was taller than twelve men, and his face was very proud and terrible to look at. And he stood up and stretched out his hand before him; and when he stood up, all that was there, great and small, bowed down with a sighing sound; and a dread came on my heart, and he looked at me, and I could not speak. I felt I was his own, to do what he liked with, for I knew at once who he was; and he said, "If you promise to return, you may depart for a season; and the voice he spoke with was terrible and mournful, and the echoes of it went rolling and swelling down the endless cave, and mixing with the trembling of the fire overhead; so that when he sat down there was a sound after him, all through the place, like the roaring of a furnace. And I said, with all the strength I had, 'I promise to come back – in God's name let me go!"

'And with that I lost the sight and the hearing of all that was there, and when my senses came to me again, I was sitting in the bed with the blood all over me, and you and the rest praying around the room.'

Here he paused, and wiped away the chill drops which hung upon his forehead.

I remained silent for some moments. The vision which he had just described struck my imagination not a little, for this was long before Vathek and the 'Hall of Eblis' had delighted the world; and the description which he gave had, as I received it, all the attractions of novelty beside the impressiveness which always belongs to the narration of an *eyewitness*, whether in the body or in the spirit, of the scenes which he describes. There was something, too, in the stern horror with which the man related these things, and in the incongruity of his description with the vulgarly received notions of the great place of punishment, and of its presiding spirit, which struck my mind with awe, almost with fear. At length he said, with an expression of horrible, imploring earnestness, which I shall never forget: 'Well, sir, is there any hope; is there any chance at all? or is my soul pledged and promised away for ever? is it gone out of my power? must I go back to the place?'

In answering him, I had no easy task to perform; for however clear might be my internal conviction of the groundlessness of his fears, and however strong my scepticism respecting the reality of what he had described, I nevertheless felt that his impression to the contrary, and his humility and terror resulting from it, might be made available as no mean engines in the work of his conversation from profligacy, and of his restoration to decent habits and to religious feeling.

I therefore told him that he was to regard his dream rather in the light of a warning than in that of a prophecy; that our salvation depended not upon the word or deed of a moment, but upon the habits of a life; that if he at once discarded his idle companions and evil habits, and firmly adhered to a sober, industrious, and religious course of life, the powers of darkness might claim his soul in vain, for that there were higher and firmer pledges than human tongue could utter, which promised salvation to him who should repent and lead a new life.

I left him much comforted, and with a promise to return upon the next day. I did so, and found him much more cheerful, and without any remains of the dogged sullenness which I suppose had arisen from his despair. His promises of amendment were given in that tone of deliberate earnestness which belongs to deep and solemn determination and it was with no small delight that I observed, after repeated visits, that his good resolutions, so far from failing, did but gather strength by time; and when I saw that man shake off the idle and debauched companions whose society had for years formed alike his amusement and his ruin, and revive his long-discarded habits of industry and sobriety, I said within myself, There is something more in all this than the operation of an idle dream.

One day, some time after his perfect restoration to health, I was surprised, on ascending the stairs for the purpose of visiting this man, to find him busily employed in nailing down some planks upon the landing-place, through which, at the commencement of his mysterious vision, it seemed to him that he had sunk. I perceived at once that he was strengthening the floor with a view to securing himself against such a catastrophe, and could scarcely forbear a smile as I bid 'God bless his work.'

He perceived my thoughts, I suppose, for he immediately said: 'I can never pass over that floor without trembling. I'd leave this house if I could, but I can't find another lodging in the town so cheap, and I'll not take a better till I've paid off all my debts, please God; but I could not be easy in my mind till I made it as safe as I could. You'll hardly believe me, your honour, that while I'm working, maybe a mile away, my heart is in a flutter the whole way back, with the bare thoughts of the two little steps I have to walk upon this bit of a floor. So it's no wonder, sir, I'd try to make it sound and firm with any idle timber I have.'

I applauded his resolution to pay off his debts, and the steadiness with which he perused his plans of conscientious economy, and passed on.

Many months elapsed, and still there appeared no alteration in his resolutions of amendment. He was a good workman, and with his better habits he recovered his former extensive and profitable employment. Everything seemed to promise comfort and respectability. I have little more to add, and that shall be told quickly. I had one evening met Pat Connell, as he returned from his work, and as usual, after a mutual, and on his side respectful salutation, I spoke a few words of encouragement and approval. I left him industrious, active, healthy – when next I saw him, not three days after, he was a corpse.

The circumstances which marked the event of his death were somewhat strange – I might say fearful. The unfortunate man had accidentally met an old friend just returned, after a long absence; and in a moment of excitement, forgetting everything in the warmth of his joy, he yielded to his urgent invitation to accompany him into a public-house, which lay close by the spot where the encounter had taken place. Connell, however, previously to entering the room, had announced his determination to take nothing more than the strictest temperance would warrant.

But oh! who can describe the inveterate tenacity with which a drunkard's habits cling to him through life? He may repent, he may reform, he may look with actual abhorrence upon his past profligacy; but amid all this reformation and compunction, who can tell the moment in which the base and ruinous propensity may not recur, triumphing over resolution, remorse, shame, everything, and prostrating its victim once more in all that is destructive and revolting in that fatal vice?

The wretched man left the place in a state of utter intoxication. He was brought home nearly insensible, and placed in his bed. The younger part of the family retired to rest much after their usual hour; but the poor wife remained up sitting by the fire, too much grieved and shocked at the occurrence of what she had so little expected, to settle to rest. Fatigue, however, at length overcame her, and she sank gradually into an uneasy slumber. She could not tell how long she had remained in this state; but when she awakened, and immediately on opening her eyes, she perceived by the faint red light of the smouldering turf embers, two persons, one of whom she recognised as her husband, noiselessly gliding out of the room.

'Pat, darling, where are you going?' said she.

There was no answer – the door closed after them but in a moment she was startled and terrified by a loud and heavy crash, as if some ponderous body had been hurled down the stair.

Much alarmed, she started up, and going to the head of the staircase, she called repeatedly upon her husband, but in vain.

She returned to the room, and with the assistance of her daughter, whom I had occasion to mention before, she succeeded in finding and lighting a candle, with which she hurried again to the head of the staircase.

At the bottom lay what seemed to be a bundle of clothes, heaped together, motionless, lifeless – it was her husband. In going down the stairs, for what purpose can never now be known, he had fallen helplessly and violently to the bottom, and coming head foremost, the spine of the neck had been dislocated by the shock, and instant death must have ensued.

The body lay upon that landing-place to which his dream had referred.

It is scarcely worth endeavouring to clear up a single point in a narrative where all is mystery; yet I could not help suspecting that the second figure which had been seen in the room by Connell's wife on the night of his death might have been no other than his own shadow.

I suggested this solution of the difficulty; but she told me that the unknown person had been considerably in advance of her husband, and on reaching the door, had turned back as if to communicate something to his companion.

It was, then, a mystery.

Was the dream verified? – whither had the disembodied spirit sped? who can say? We know not. But I left the house of death that day in a state of horror which I could not describe. It seemed to me that I was scarce awake. I heard and saw everything as if under the spell of a nightmare. The coincidence was terrible.

SHERIDAN LE FANU

A Chapter in the History of a Tyrone Family

☙❧

In the following narrative I have endeavoured to give as nearly as possible the *ipsissima verba* of the valued friend from whom I received it, conscious that any aberration from *her* mode of telling the tale of her own life would at once impair its accuracy and its effect.

Would that, with her words, I could also bring before you her animated gesture, the expressive countenance, the solemn and thrilling air and accent with which she related the dark passages in her strange story; and, above all, that I could communicate the impressive consciousness that the narrator had seen with her own eyes, and personally acted in the scenes which she described. These accompaniments, taken with the additional circumstance that she who told the tale was one far too deeply and sadly impressed with religious principle to misrepresent or fabricate what she repeated as fact, gave to the tale a depth of interest which the recording of the events themselves could hardly have produced.

I became acquainted with the lady from whose lips I heard this narrative nearly twenty years since, and the story struck my fancy so much that I committed it to paper while it was still fresh in my mind; and should its perusal afford you entertainment for a listless half-hour, my labour shall not have been bestowed in vain.

I find that I have taken the story down as she told it, in the first person, and perhaps this is as it should be.

She began as follows: My maiden name was Richardson, the designation of a family of some distinction in the county of Tyrone. I was the younger of two daughters, and we were the only children. There was a difference in our ages of nearly six years, so that I did not, in my childhood, enjoy that close companionship which sisterhood, in other circumstances, necessarily involves; and while I was still a child, my sister was married.

The person upon whom she bestowed her hand was a Mr Carew, a gentleman of property and consideration in the north of England.

I remember well the eventful day of the wedding; the thronging carriages, the noisy menials, the loud laughter, the merry faces, and the gay dresses. Such sights were then new to me, and harmonised ill with the sorrowful feelings with which I regarded the event which was to separate me from a sister whose tenderness alone had hitherto more than supplied all that I wanted in my mother's affection.

The day soon arrived which was to remove the happy couple from Ashtown House. The carriage stood at the hall-door, and my poor sister kissed me again and again, telling me that I should see her soon.

The carriage drove away, and I gazed after it until my eyes filled with tears, and, returning slowly to my chamber, I wept more bitterly and, so to speak, more desolately, than ever I had wept before.

My father had never seemed to love or to take an interest in me. He had desired a son, and I think he never thoroughly forgave me my unfortunate sex.

My having come into the world at all as his child he regarded as a kind of fraudulent intrusion; and as his antipathy to me had its origin in an imperfection of mine too radical for removal, I never even hoped to stand high in his good graces.

My mother was, I dare say, as fond of me as she was of anyone; but she was a woman of a masculine and a worldly cast of mind. She had no tenderness or sympathy for the weaknesses, or even for the affections, of woman's nature, and her demeanour towards me was peremptory, and often even harsh.

It is not to be supposed, then, that I found in the society of my parents much to supply the loss of my sister. About a year after her marriage, we received letters from Mr Carew, containing accounts of my sister's health, which, though not actually alarming, were calculated to make us seriously uneasy. The symptoms most dwelt upon were loss of appetite, and a cough.

The letters concluded by intimating that he would avail himself of my father and mother's repeated invitation to spend some time at Ashtown, particularly as the physician who had been consulted as to my sister's health had strongly advised a removal to her native air.

There were added repeated assurances that nothing serious was apprehended, as it was supposed that a deranged state of the liver was the only source of the symptoms which at first had seemed to intimate consumption.

In accordance with this announcement, my sister and Mr Carew arrived in Dublin, where one of my father's carriages awaited them, in readiness to start upon whatever day or hour they might choose for their departure.

It was arranged that Mr Carew was, as soon as the day upon which they were to leave Dublin was definitely fixed, to write to my father, who intended that the two last stages should be performed by his own horses, upon whose speed and safety far more reliance might be placed than upon those of the ordinary post-horses, which were at that time, almost without exception, of the very worst order. The journey, one of about ninety miles, was to be divided; the larger portion being reserved for the second day.

On Sunday a letter reached us, stating that the party would leave Dublin on Monday, and in due course reach Ashtown upon Tuesday evening.

Tuesday came: the evening closed in, and yet no carriage: darkness came on, and still no sign of our expected visitors.

Hour after hour passed away, and it was now past twelve; the night was remarkably calm, scarce a breath stirring, so that any sound, such as that produced by the rapid movement of a vehicle, would have been audible at a considerable distance. For some such sound I was feverishly listening.

It was, however, my father's rule to close the house at nightfall, and the window-shutters being fastened, I was unable to reconnoitre the avenue as I would have wished. It was nearly one o'clock, and we began almost to despair of seeing them upon that night, when I thought I distinguished the sound of wheels, but so remote and faint as to make me at first very uncertain. The noise approached; it became louder and clearer; it stopped for a moment.

I now heard the shrill screaming of the rusty iron, as the avenue gate revolved on its hinges; again came the sound of wheels in rapid motion.

'It is they,' said I, starting up 'the carriage is in the avenue.'

We all stood for a few moments breathlessly listening. On thundered the vehicle with the speed of the whirlwind; crack went the whip, and clatter went the wheels, as it rattled over the uneven pavement of the court. A general and furious barking from all the dogs about the house hailed its arrival.

We hurried to the hall in time to hear the steps let down with the sharp clanging noise peculiar to the operation, and the hum of voices exerted in the bustle of arrival. The hall door was now thrown open, and we all stepped forth to greet our visitors.

The court was perfectly empty; the moon was shining broadly and brightly upon all around; nothing was to be seen but the tall trees with their long spectral shadows, now wet with the dews of midnight.

We stood gazing from right to left as if suddenly awakened from a dream; the dogs walked suspiciously, growling and snuffling about the court, and by totally and suddenly ceasing their former loud barking, expressed the predominance of fear.

We stared one upon another in perplexity and dismay, and I think I never beheld more pale faces assembled. By my father's directions, we looked about to find anything which might indicate or account for the noise which we had heard; but no such thing was to be seen – even the mire which lay upon the avenue was undisturbed. We returned to the house, more panic-stricken than I can describe.

On the next day, we learned by a messenger, who had ridden hard the greater part of the night, that my sister was dead On Sunday evening she had retired to bed rather unwell, and on Monday her indisposition declared itself unequivocally to be malignant fever. She became hourly worse, and, on Tuesday night, a little after midnight, she expired.

I mention this circumstance, because it was one upon which a thousand wild and fantastical reports were founded, though one would have thought that the truth scarcely required to be improved upon; and again, because it produced a strong and lasting effect upon my spirits, and indeed, I am inclined to think, upon my character.

I was, for several years after this occurrence, long after the violence of my grief subsided, so wretchedly low-spirited and nervous, that I could scarcely be said to live; and during this time, habits of indecision, arising out of a listless acquiescence in the will of others, a fear of encountering even the slightest opposition, and a disposition to shrink from what are commonly called amusements, grew upon me so strongly, that I have scarcely even yet altogether overcome them.

We saw nothing more of Mr Carew. He returned to England as soon as the melancholy rites attendant upon the event which I have just mentioned were performed; and not being altogether inconsolable, he married again within two years; after which, owing to the remoteness of our relative situations, and other circumstances, we gradually lost sight of him.

I was now an only child; and, as my elder sister had died without issue, it was evident that, in the ordinary course of things, my father's property, which was altogether in his power, would go to me; and the consequence was, that before I was fourteen, Ashtown House was besieged by a host of suitors. However, whether it was that I was too young, or that none of the aspirants to my hand stood sufficiently high in rank or wealth, I was suffered by both parents to do exactly as I pleased; and well was it for me, as I afterwards found, that fortune, or rather Providence, had so ordained it, that I had not suffered my affections to become in any degree engaged, for my mother would never have suffered any silly fancy of mine, as she was in the habit of styling an attachment, to stand in the way of her ambitious views – views which she was determined to carry into effect in defiance of every obstacle, and in order to accomplish which she would not have hesitated to sacrifice anything so unreasonable and contemptible as a girlish passion.

When I reached the age of sixteen, my mother's plans began to develop themselves; and, at her suggestion, we moved to Dublin to sojourn for the winter, in order that no time might be lost in disposing of me to the best advantage.

I had been too long accustomed to consider myself as of no importance whatever, to believe for a moment that I was in reality the cause of all the bustle and preparation which surrounded me; and being thus relieved from the pain which a consciousness of my real situation would have inflicted, I journeyed towards the capital with a feeling of total indifference.

My father's wealth and connection had established him in the best society, and consequently, upon our arrival in the metropolis, we commanded whatever enjoyment or advantages its gaieties afforded.

The tumult and novelty of the scenes in which I was involved did not fail considerably to amuse me, and my mind gradually recovered its tone, which was naturally cheerful.

It was almost immediately known and reported that I was an heiress, and of course my attractions were pretty generally acknowledged.

Among the many gentlemen whom it was my fortune to please, one, ere long, established himself in my mother's good graces, to the exclusion of all less important aspirants. However, I had not understood or even remarked his attentions, nor in the slightest degree suspected his or my mother's plans respecting me, when I was made aware of them rather abruptly by my mother herself.

We had attended a splendid ball, given by Lord M— at his residence in Stephen's Green, and I was, with the assistance of my waiting-maid, employed in rapidly divesting myself of the rich ornaments which, in profuseness and value, could scarcely have found their equals in any private family in Ireland.

I had thrown myself into a lounging-chair beside the fire, listless and exhausted after the fatigues of the evening, when I was aroused from the reverie into which I had fallen by the sound of footsteps approaching my chamber, and my mother entered.

'Fanny, my dear,' said she, in her softest tone, 'I wish to say a word or two with you before I go to rest. You are not fatigued, love, I hope?'

'No, no, madam, I thank you,' said I, rising at the same time from my seat, with the formal respect so little practised now.

'Sit down, my dear,' said she, placing herself upon a chair beside me; 'I must chat with you for a quarter of an hour or so. Saunders' (to the maid), 'you may leave the room; do not close the room door, but shut that of the lobby.'

This precaution against curious ears having been taken as directed, my mother proceeded: 'You have observed, I should suppose, my dearest Fanny – indeed, you *must* have observed Lord Glenfallen's marked attentions to you?'

'I assure you, madam – ' I began.

'Well, well, that is all right,' interrupted my mother. 'Of course, you must be modest upon the matter; but listen to me for a few moments, my love, and I will prove to your satisfaction that your modesty is quite unnecessary in this case. You have done better than we could have hoped, at least, so very soon. Lord Glenfallen is in love with you. I give you joy of your conquest;' and, saying this, my mother kissed my forehead.

'In love with me!' I exclaimed in unfeigned astonishment.

'Yes, in love with you,' repeated my mother; 'devotedly, distractedly in love with you. Why, my dear, what is there wonderful in it? Look in the glass, and look at these,' she continued, pointing, with a smile, to the jewels which I had just removed from my person, and which now lay in a glittering heap upon the table.

'May there not – ' said I, hesitating between confusion and real alarm, 'is it not possible that some mistake may be at the bottom of all this?'

'Mistake, dearest! none,' said my mother. 'None; none in the world. Judge for yourself; read this, my love.' And she placed in my hand a letter, addressed to herself, the seal of which was broken. I read it through with no small surprise. After some very fine complimentary flourishes upon my beauty and perfections, as also upon the antiquity and high reputation of our family, it went on to make a formal proposal of marriage, to be communicated or not to me at present, as my mother should deem expedient; and the letter wound up by a request that the writer might be permitted, upon our return to Ashtown House, which was soon to take place, as the spring was now tolerably advanced, to visit us for a few days, in case his suit was approved.

'Well, well, my dear,' said my mother, impatiently; 'do you know who Lord Glenfallen is?'

'I do, madam,' said I, rather timidly; for I dreaded an altercation with my mother.

'Well, dear, and what frightens you?' continued she. 'Are you afraid of a title? What has he done to alarm you? He is neither old nor ugly.'

I was silent, though I might have said, 'He is neither young nor handsome.'

'My dear Fanny,' continued my mother, 'in sober seriousness, you have been most fortunate in engaging the affections of a nobleman such as Lord Glenfallen, young and wealthy, with first-rate – yes, acknowledged *first-rate* abilities, and of a family whose influence is not exceeded by that of any in Ireland. Of course, you see the offer in the same light that I do – indeed, I think you *must*.'

This was uttered in no very dubious tone. I was so much astonished by the suddenness of the whole communication, that I literally did not know what to say.

'You are not in love?' said my mother, turning sharply, and fixing her dark eyes upon me with severe scrutiny.

'No, madam,' said I, promptly horrified – what young lady would not have been? – at such a query.

'I'm glad to hear it,' said my mother, drily. 'Once, nearly twenty years ago, a friend of mine consulted me as to how he should deal with a daughter who had made what they call a love-match – beggared herself, and disgraced her family; and I said, without hesitation, take no care for her, but cast her off. Such punishment I awarded for an offence committed against the reputation of a family not my own; and what I advised respecting the child of another, with full as small compunction I would *do* with mine. I cannot conceive anything more unreasonable or intolerable than that the fortune and the character of a family should be marred by the idle caprices of a girl.'

She spoke this with great severity, and paused as if she expected some observation from me.

I, however, said nothing.

'But I need not explain to you, my dear Fanny,' she continued, 'my views upon this subject; you have always known them well, and I have never yet had reason to believe you are likely to offend me voluntarily, or to abuse or neglect any of those advantages which reason and duty tell you should be improved. Come hither, my dear; kiss me, and do not look so frightened. Well, now, about this letter – you need not answer it yet; of course, you must be allowed time to make up your mind. In the meantime, I will write to his lordship to give him my permission to visit us at Ashtown. Good-night, my love.'

And thus ended one of the most disagreeable, not to say astounding, conversations I had ever had. It would not be easy to describe exactly what were my feelings towards Lord Glenfallen; – whatever might have been my mother's suspicions, my heart was perfectly disengaged – and hitherto, although I had not been made in the slightest degree acquainted with his real views, I had liked him very much as an agreeable, well-informed man, whom I was always glad to meet in society. He had served in the navy in early life, and the polish which his manners received in his after intercourse with courts and cities had not served to obliterate that frankness of manner which belongs proverbially to the sailor.

Whether this apparent candour went deeper than the outward bearing, I was yet to learn. However, there was no doubt that, as far as I had seen of Lord Glenfallen, he was, though perhaps not so young as might have been desired in a lover, a singularly pleasing man; and whatever feeling unfavourable to him had found its way into my mind, arose altogether from the dread, not an unreasonable one, that constraint might be practised upon my inclinations. I reflected, however, that Lord Glenfallen was a wealthy man, and one highly thought of; and although I could never expect to love him in the romantic sense of the term, yet I had no doubt but that, all things considered, I might be more happy with him than I could hope to be at home.

When next I met him it was with no small embarrassment; his tact and good breeding, however, soon reassured me, and effectually prevented my awkwardness being remarked upon. And I had the satisfaction of leaving Dublin for the country with the full conviction that nobody, not even those most intimate with me, even suspected the fact of Lord Glenfallen's having made me a formal proposal.

This was to me a very serious subject of self-gratification, for, besides my instinctive dread of becoming the topic of the speculations of gossip, I felt that if the situation which I occupied in relation to him were made publicly known, I should stand committed in a manner which would scarcely leave me the power of retraction.

The period at which Lord Glenfallen had arranged to visit Ashtown House was now fast approaching, and it became my mother's wish to form me thoroughly to her will, and to obtain my consent to the proposed marriage before his arrival, so that all things might proceed smoothly, without apparent opposition or objection upon my part. Whatever objections, therefore, I had entertained were to be subdued; whatever disposition to resistance I had exhibited or had been supposed to feel, were to be completely eradicated before he made his appearance; and my mother addressed herself to the task with a decision and energy against which even the barriers her imagination had created could hardly have stood.

If she had, however, expected any determined opposition from me, she was agreeably disappointed. My heart was perfectly free, and all my feelings of liking and preference were in favour of Lord Glenfallen; and I well knew that in case I refused to dispose of myself as I was desired, my mother had alike the power and the will to render my existence as utterly miserable as even the most ill-assorted marriage could possibly have made it.

You will remember, my good friend, that I was very young and very completely under the control of my parents, both of whom, my mother particularly, were unscrupulously determined in matters of this kind, and willing, when voluntary obedience on the part of those within their power was withheld, to compel a forced acquiescence by an unsparing use of all the engines of the most stern and rigorous domestic discipline.

All these combined, not unnaturally induced me to resolve upon yielding at once, and without useless opposition, to what appeared almost to be my fate.

The appointed time was come, and my now accepted suitor arrived; he was in high spirits, and, if possible, more entertaining than ever.

I was not, however, quite in the mood to enjoy his sprightliness; but whatever I wanted in gaiety was amply made up in the triumphant and gracious good-humour of my mother, whose smiles of benevolence and exultation were showered around as bountifully as the summer sunshine.

I will not weary you with unnecessary details. Let it suffice to say, that I was married to Lord Glenfallen with all the attendant pomp and circumstance of wealth, rank, and grandeur. According to the usage of the times, now humanely reformed, the ceremony was made, until long past midnight, the season of wild, uproarious, and promiscuous feasting and revelry.

Of all this I have a painfully vivid recollection, and particularly of the little annoyances inflicted upon me by the dull and coarse jokes of the wits and wags who abound in all such places, and upon all such occasions.

I was not sorry when, after a few days, Lord Glenfallen's carriage appeared at the door to convey us both from Ashtown for any change would have been a relief from the irksomeness of ceremonial and formality which the visits received in honour of my newly-acquired titles hourly entailed upon me.

It was arranged that we were to proceed to Cahergillagh, one of the Glenfallen estates, lying, however, in a southern county; so that, owing to the difficulty of the roads at the time; a tedious journey of three days intervened.

I set forth with my noble companion, followed by the regrets of some, and by the envy of many; though God knows I little deserved the latter. The three days of travel were now almost spent, when passing the brow of a wild heathy hill, the domain of Cahergillagh opened suddenly upon our view.

It formed a striking and a beautiful scene. A lake of considerable extent stretching away towards the west, and reflecting from its broad, smooth waters the rich glow of the setting sun, was overhung by steep hills, covered by a rich mantle of velvet sward, broken here and there by the grey front of some old rock, and exhibiting on their shelving sides and on their slopes and hollows every variety of light and shade. A thick wood of dwarf oak, birch, and hazel skirted these hills, and clothed the shores of the lake, running out in rich luxuriance upon every promontory, and spreading upward considerably upon the side of the hills.

'There lies the enchanted castle,' said Lord Glenfallen, pointing towards a considerable level space intervening between two of the picturesque hills which rose dimly around the lake.

This little plain was chiefly occupied by the same low, wild wood which covered the other parts of the domain; but towards the centre, a mass of taller and statelier forest trees stood darkly grouped together, and among them stood an ancient square tower, with many buildings of a humbler character, forming together the manor-house, or, as it was more usually called, the Court of Cahergillagh.

As we approached the level upon which the mansion stood, the winding road gave us many glimpses of the timeworn castle and its surrounding buildings; and seen as it was through the long vistas of the fine old trees, and with the rich glow of evening upon it, I have seldom beheld an object more picturesquely striking.

I was glad to perceive, too, that here and there the blue curling smoke ascended from stacks of chimneys now hidden by the rich, dark ivy which, in a great measure, covered the building. Other indications of comfort made themselves manifest as we approached; and indeed, though the place was evidently one of considerable antiquity, it had nothing whatever of the gloom of decay about it.

'You must not, my love,' said Lord Glenfallen, 'imagine this place worse than it is. I have no taste for antiquity – at least I should not choose a house to reside in because it is old. Indeed, I do not recollect that I was even so romantic as to overcome my aversion to rats and rheumatism, those faithful attendants upon your noble relics of feudalism; and I much prefer a snug, modern, unmysterious bedroom, with well-aired sheets, to the waving tapestry, mildewed cushions, and all the other interesting appliances of romance. However, though I cannot promise you all the discomfort generally belonging to an old castle, you will find legends and ghostly lore enough to claim your respect; and if old Martha be still to the fore, as I trust she is, you will soon have a supernatural and appropriate anecdote for every closet and corner of the mansion. But here we are – so, without more ado, welcome to Cahergillagh!'

We now entered the hall of the castle, and while the domestics were employed in conveying our trunks and other luggage which we had brought with us for immediate use, to the apartments which Lord Glenfallen had selected for himself and me, I went with him into a spacious sitting-room, wainscoted with finely-polished black oak, and hung round with the portraits of various worthies of the Glenfallen family.

This room looked out upon an extensive level covered with the softest green sward, and irregularly bounded by the wild wood I have before mentioned, through the leafy arcade formed by whose boughs and trunks the level beams of the setting sun were pouring. In the distance a group of dairymaids were plying their task, which they accompanied throughout with snatches of Irish songs which, mellowed by the distance, floated not unpleasingly to the ear; and beside them sat or lay, with all the grave importance of conscious protection, six or seven large dogs of various kinds. Farther in the distance, and through the cloisters of the arching wood, two or three ragged urchins were employed in driving such stray kine as had wandered farther than the rest to join their fellows.

As I looked upon the scene which I have described, a feeling of tranquillity and happiness came upon me, which I have never experienced in so strong a degree; and so strange to me was the sensation that my eyes filled with tears.

Lord Glenfallen mistook the cause of my emotion, and taking me kindly and tenderly by the hand, he said: 'Do not suppose, my love, that it is my intention to *settle* here. Whenever you desire to leave this, you have only to let me know your wish, and it shall be complied with; so I must entreat of you not to suffer any circumstances which I can control to give you one moment's uneasiness. But here is old Martha; you must be introduced to her, one of the heirlooms of our family.'

A hale, good-humoured, erect old woman was Martha, and an agreeable contrast to the grim, decrepid hag which my fancy had conjured up, as the depository of all the horrible tales in which I doubted not this old place was most fruitful.

She welcomed me and her master with a profusion of gratulations, alternately kissing our hands and apologising for the liberty; until at length Lord Glenfallen put an end to this somewhat fatiguing ceremonial by requesting her to conduct me to my chamber, if it were prepared for my reception.

I followed Martha up an old-fashioned oak staircase into a long, dim passage, at the end of which lay the door which communicated with the apartments which had been selected for our use; here the old woman stopped, and respectfully requested me to proceed.

I accordingly opened the door, and was about to enter, when something like a mass of black tapestry, as it appeared, disturbed by my sudden approach, fell from above the door, so as completely to screen the aperture; the startling unexpectedness of the occurrence, and the rustling noise which the drapery made in its descent, caused me involuntarily to step two or three paces backward. I turned, smiling and half-ashamed, to the old servant, and said: 'You see what a coward I am.'

The woman looked puzzled, and, without saying any more, I was about to draw aside the curtain and enter the room, when, upon turning to do so, I was surprised to find that nothing whatever interposed to obstruct the passage.

I went into the room, followed by the servant-woman, and was amazed to find that it, like the one below, was wainscoted, and that nothing like drapery was to be found near the door.

'Where is it?' said I; 'what has become of it?'

'What does your ladyship wish to know?' said the old woman.

'Where is the black curtain that fell across the door, when I attempted first to come to my chamber?' answered I.

'The cross of Christ about us!' said the old woman, turning suddenly pale.

'What is the matter, my good friend?' said I; 'you seem frightened.'

'Oh no your ladyship,' said the old woman, endeavouring to conceal her agitation; but in vain, for tottering towards a chair, she sank into it, looking so deadly pale and horror-struck that I thought every moment she would faint.

'Merciful God, keep us from harm and danger!' muttered she at length.

'What can have terrified you so?' said I, beginning to fear that she had seen something more than had met my eye. 'You appear ill, my poor woman!'

'Nothing, nothing, my lady,' said she, rising. 'I beg your ladyship's pardon for making so bold. May the great God defend us from misfortune!'

'Martha,' said I, 'something has frightened you very much, and I insist on knowing what it is; your keeping me in the dark upon the subject will make me much more uneasy than anything you could tell me. I desire you, therefore, to let me know what agitates you; I command you to tell me.'

'Your ladyship said you saw a black curtain falling across the door when you were coming into the room,' said the old woman.

'I did,' said I; 'but though the whole thing appears somewhat strange, I cannot see anything in the matter to agitate you so excessively.'

'It's for no good you saw that, my lady,' said the crone; 'something terrible is coming. It's a sign, my lady – a sign that never fails.'

'Explain, explain what you mean, my good woman,' said I, in spite of myself, catching more than I could account for, of her superstitious terror.

'Whenever something – something *bad* is going to happen to the Glenfallen family, someone that belongs to them sees a black handkerchief or curtain just waved or falling before their faces. I saw it myself,' continued she, lowering her voice, 'when I was only a little girl, and I'll never forget it. I often heard of it before, though I never saw it till then, nor since, praised be God. But I was going into Lady Jane's room to waken her in the morning; and sure enough when I got first to the bed and began to draw the curtain, something dark was waved across the division, but only for a moment; and when I saw rightly into the bed, there she was lying cold and dead, God be merciful to me! So, my lady, there is small blame to me to be daunted when anyone of the family sees it for it's many the story I heard of it, though I saw it but once.'

I was not of a superstitious turn of mind, yet I could not resist a feeling of awe very nearly allied to the fear which my companion had so unreservedly expressed; and when you consider my situation, the loneliness, antiquity, and gloom of the place, you will allow that the weakness was not without excuse.

In spite of old Martha's boding predictions, however, time flowed on in an unruffled course. One little incident, however, though trifling in itself, I must relate, as it serves to make what follows more intelligible.

Upon the day after my arrival, Lord Glenfallen of course desired to make me acquainted with the house and domain; and accordingly we set forth upon our ramble. When returning, he became for some time silent and moody, a state so unusual with him as considerably to excite my surprise.

I endeavoured by observations and questions to arouse him – but in vain. At length, as we approached the house, he said, as if speaking to himself: ' 'Twere madness – madness – madness,' repeating the words bitterly; 'sure and speedy ruin.'

There was here a long pause; and at length, turning sharply towards me, in a tone very unlike that in which he had hither- to addressed me, he said: 'Do you think it possible that a woman can keep a secret?'

'I am sure,' said I, 'that women are very much belied upon the score of talkativeness, and that I may answer your question with the same directness with which you put it – I reply that I *do* think a woman can keep a secret.'

'But I do not,' said he, drily.

We walked on in silence for a time. I was much astonished at his unwonted abruptness – I had almost said rudeness.

After a considerable pause he seemed to recollect himself, and with an effort resuming his sprightly manner, he said: 'Well, well, the next thing to keeping a secret well is not to desire to possess one; talkativeness and curiosity generally go together. Now I shall make test of you, in the first place, respecting the latter of these qualities. I shall be your *Bluebeard* – tush, why do I trifle thus? Listen to me, my dear Fanny; I speak now in solemn earnest. What I desire is intimately, inseparably connected with your happiness and honour as well as my own; and your compliance with my request will not be difficult. It will impose upon you a very trifling restraint during your sojourn here, which certain events which have occurred since our arrival have determined me shall not be a long one. You must promise me, upon your sacred honour, that you will visit *only* that part of the castle which can be reached from the front entrance, leaving the back entrance and the part of the building commanded immediately by it to the menials, as also the small garden whose high wall you see yonder; and never at any time seek to pry or peep into them, nor to open the door which communicates from the front part of the house through the corridor with the back. I do not urge this in jest or in caprice, but from a solemn conviction that danger and mischief will be the certain consequences of your not observing what I prescribe. I cannot explain myself further at present. Promise me, then, these things, as you hope for peace here and for mercy hereafter.'

I did make the promise as desired; and he appeared relieved; his manner recovered all its gaiety and elasticity: but the recollection of the strange scene which I have just described dwelt painfully upon my mind.

More than a month passed away without any occurrence worth recording; but I was not destined to leave Cahergillagh without further adventure. One day, intending to enjoy the pleasant sunshine in a ramble through the woods, I ran up to my room to procure my hat and cloak. Upon entering the chamber I was surprised and somewhat startled to find it occupied. Beside the fireplace, and nearly opposite the door, seated in a large, old-fashioned elbow-chair, was placed the figure of a lady. She appeared to be nearer fifty than forty, and was dressed suitably to her age, in a handsome suit of flowered silk; she had a profusion of trinkets and jewellery about her person, and many rings upon her fingers. But although very rich, her dress was not gaudy or in ill taste. But what was remarkable in the lady was, that although her features were handsome, and upon the whole pleasing, the pupil of each eye was dimmed with the whiteness of cataract, and she was evidently stone-blind. I was for some seconds so surprised at this unaccountable apparition, that I could not find words to address her.

'Madam,' said I, 'there must be some mistake here – this is my bedchamber.'

'Marry come up,' said the lady, sharply; '*your* chamber! Where is Lord Glenfallen?'

'He is below, madam,' replied I; 'and I am convinced he will be not a little surprised to find you here.'

'I do not think he will,' said she, 'with your good leave; talk of what you know something about. Tell him I want him. Why does the minx dilly-dally so?'

In spite of the awe which this grim lady inspired, there was something in her air of confident superiority which, when I considered our relative situations, was not a little irritating.

'Do you know, madam, to whom you speak?' said I.

'I neither know nor care,' said she; 'but I presume that you are someone about the house, so again I desire you, if you wish to continue here, to bring your master hither forthwith.'

'I must tell you, madam,' said I, 'that I am Lady Glenfallen.'

'What's that?' said the stranger, rapidly.

'I say, madam,' I repeated, approaching her that I might be more distinctly heard, 'that I am Lady Glenfallen.'

'It's a lie, you trull!' cried she, in an accent which made me start, and at the same time, springing forward, she seized me in her grasp, and shook me violently, repeating, 'It's a lie – it's a lie!' with a rapidity and vehemence which swelled every vain of her face. The violence of her action, and the fury which convulsed her face, effectually terrified me, and disengaged myself from her grasp, I screamed as loud as I could for help. The blind woman continued to pour out a torrent of abuse upon me, foaming at the mouth with rage, and impotently shaking her clenched fist towards me.

I heard Lord Glenfallen's step upon the stairs, and I instantly ran out; as I passed him I perceived that he was deadly pale, and just caught the words: 'I hope that demon has not hurt you?'

I made some answer, I forget what, and he entered the chamber, the door of which he locked upon the inside. What passed within I know not; but I heard the voices of the two speakers raise in loud and angry altercation.

I thought I heard the shrill accents of the woman repeat the words, 'Let her look to herself;' but I could not be quite sure. This short sentence, however, was, to my alarmed imagination, pregnant with fearful meaning.

The storm at length subsided, though not until after a conference of more than two long hours. Lord Glenfallen then returned, pale and agitated.

'That unfortunate woman,' said he, 'is out of her mind. I dare say she treated you to some of her ravings; but you need not dread any further interruption from her: I have brought her so far to reason. She did not hurt you, I trust.'

'No, no,' said I; 'but she terrified me beyond measure.'

'Well,' said he, 'she is likely to behave better for the future; and I dare swear that neither you nor she would desire, after what has passed, to meet again.'

This occurrence, so startling and unpleasant, so involved in mystery, and giving rise to so many painful surmises, afforded me no very agreeable food for rumination.

All attempts on my part to arrive at the truth were baffled; Lord Glenfallen evaded all my enquiries, and at length peremptorily forbade any further allusion to the matter. I was thus obliged to rest satisfied with what I had actually seen, and to trust to time to resolve the perplexities in which the whole transaction had involved me.

Lord Glenfallen's temper and spirits gradually underwent a complete and most painful change; he became silent and abstracted, his manner to me was abrupt and often harsh, some grievous anxiety seemed ever present to his mind; and under its influence his spirits sank and his temper became soured.

I soon perceived that his gaiety was rather that which the stir and excitement of society produce, than the result of a healthy habit of mind; every day confirmed me in the opinion, that the considerate good-nature which I had so much admired in him was little more than a mere manner; and to my infinite grief and surprise, the gay, kind, open-hearted nobleman who had for months followed and flattered me, was rapidly assuming the form of a gloomy, morose, and singularly selfish man. This was a bitter discovery, and I strove to conceal it from myself as long as I could; but the truth was not to be denied, and I was forced to believe that my husband no longer loved me, and that he was at little pains to conceal the alteration in his sentiments.

One morning after breakfast, Lord Glenfallen had been for some time walking silently up and down the room, buried in his moody reflections, when pausing suddenly, and turning towards me, he exclaimed: 'I have it – I have it! We must go abroad, and stay there too; and if that does not answer, why – why, we must try some more effectual expedient. Lady Glenfallen, I have become involved in heavy embarrassments. A wife, you know, must share the fortunes of her husband, for better for worse; but I will waive my right if you prefer remaining here – here at Cahergillagh. For I would not have you seen elsewhere without the state to which your rank entitles you; besides, it would break your poor mother's heart,' he added, with sneering gravity. 'So make up your mind – Cahergillagh or France. I will start if possible in a week, so determine between this and then.'

He left the room, and in a few moments I saw him ride past the window, followed by a mounted servant. He had directed a domestic to inform me that he should not be back until the next day.

I was in very great doubt as to what course of conduct I should pursue as to accompanying him in the continental tour so suddenly determined upon. I felt that it would be a hazard too great to encounter; for at Cahergillagh I had always the consciousness to sustain me, that if his temper at any time led him into violent or unwarrantable treatment of me, I had a remedy within reach, in the protection and support of my own family, from all useful and effective communication with whom, if once in France, I should be entirely debarred.

As to remaining at Cahergillagh in solitude, and, for aught I knew, exposed to hidden dangers, it appeared to me scarcely less objectionable than the former proposition; and yet I feared that with one or other I must comply, unless I was prepared to come to an actual breach with Lord Glenfallen. Full of these unpleasing doubts and perplexities, I retired to rest.

I was wakened, after having slept uneasily for some hours, by some person shaking me rudely by the shoulder; a small lamp burned in my room, and by its light, to my horror and amazement, I discovered that my visitant was the selfsame blind old lady who had so terrified me a few weeks before.

I started up in the bed, with a view to ring the bell, and alarm the domestics; but she instantly anticipated me by saying: 'Do not be frightened, silly girl! If I had wished to harm you, I could have done it while you were sleeping; I need not have wakened you. Listen to me, now, attentively and fearlessly, for what I have to say interests you to the full as much as it does me. Tell me here, in the presence of God, did Lord Glenfallen marry you – *actually marry* you? Speak the truth, woman.'

'As surely as I live and speak,' I replied, 'did Lord Glenfallen marry me, in presence of more than a hundred witnesses.'

'Well,' continued she, 'he should have told you *then*, before you married him, that he had a wife living – that I am his wife. I feel you tremble – tush! do not be frightened. I do not mean to harm you. Mark me now – you are *not* his wife. When I make my story known you will be so neither in the eye of God nor of man. You must leave this house upon tomorrow. Let the world know that your husband has another wife living; go you into retirement, and leave him to justice, which will surely overtake him. If you remain in this house after tomorrow, you will reap the bitter fruits of your sin.'

So saying, she quitted the room, leaving me very little disposed to sleep.

Here was food for my very worst and most terrible suspicions; still there was not enough to remove all doubt. I had no proof of the truth of this woman's statement.

Taken by itself, there was nothing to induce me to attach weight to it; but when I viewed it in connection with the extraordinary mystery of some of Lord Glenfallen's proceedings, his strange anxiety to exclude me from certain portions of the mansion, doubtless lest I should encounter this person – the strong influence, nay, command which she possessed over him, a circumstance clearly established by the very fact of her residing in the very place where, of all others, he should least have desired to find her – her thus acting, and continuing to act in direct contradiction to his wishes; when, I say, I viewed her disclosure in connection with all these circumstances, I could not help feeling that there was at least a fearful verisimilitude in the allegations which she had made.

Still I was not satisfied, nor nearly so. Young minds have a reluctance almost insurmountable to believing, upon anything short of unquestionable proof, the existence of premeditated guilt in anyone whom they have ever trusted; and in support of this feeling I was assured that if the assertion of Lord Glenfallen, which nothing in this woman's manner had led me to disbelieve, were true, namely that her mind was unsound, the whole fabric of my doubts and fears must fall to the ground.

I determined to state to Lord Glenfallen freely and accurately the substance of the communication which I had just heard, and in his words and looks to seek for its proof or refutation. Full of these thoughts, I remained wakeful and excited all night, every moment fancying that I heard the step or saw the figure of my recent visitor, towards whom I felt a species of horror and dread which I can hardly describe.

There was something in her face, though her features had evidently been handsome, and were not, at first sight, unpleasing, which, upon a nearer inspection, seemed to indicate the habitual prevalence and indulgence of evil passions, and a power of expressing mere animal anger with an intenseness that I have seldom seen equalled, and to which an almost unearthly effect was given by the convulsive quivering of the sightless eyes.

You may easily suppose that it was no very pleasing reflection to me to consider that, whenever caprice might induce her to return, I was within the reach of this violent and, for aught I knew, insane woman, who had, upon that very night, spoken to me in a tone of menace, of which her mere words, divested of the manner and look with which she uttered them, can convey but a faint idea.

Will you believe me when I tell you that I was actually afraid to leave my bed in order to secure the door, lest I should again encounter the dreadful object lurking in some corner or peeping from behind the window-curtains, so very a child was I in my fears?

The morning came, and with it Lord Glenfallen. I knew not, and indeed I cared not, where he might have been; my thoughts were wholly engrossed by the terrible fears and suspicions which my last night's conference had suggested to me. He was, as usual, gloomy and abstracted, and I feared in no very fitting mood to hear what I had to say with patience, whether the charges were true or false.

I was, however, determined not to suffer the opportunity to pass, or Lord Glenfallen to leave the room, until, at all hazards, I had unburdened my mind.

'My lord,' said I, after a long silence, summoning up all my firmness, 'my lord, I wish to say a few words to you upon a matter of very great importance, of very deep concernment to you and to me.'

I fixed my eyes upon him to discern, if possible, whether the announcement caused him any uneasiness; but no symptom of any such feeling was perceptible.

'Well, my dear,' said he, 'this is no doubt a very grave preface, and portends, I have no doubt, something extraordinary. Pray let us have it without more ado.'

He took a chair, and seated himself nearly opposite to me.

'My lord,' said I, 'I have seen the person who alarmed me so much a short time since, the blind lady, again, upon last night.' His face, upon which my eyes were fixed, turned pale; he hesitated for a moment, and then said: 'And did you, pray, madam, so totally forget or spurn my express command, as to enter that portion of the house from which your promise, I might say your oath, excluded you? Answer me that!' he added fiercely.

'My lord,' said I, 'I have neither forgotten your *commands*, since such they were, nor disobeyed them. I was, last night, wakened from my sleep, as I lay in my own chamber, and accosted by the person whom I have mentioned. How she found access to the room I cannot pretend to say.'

'Ha! this must be looked to,' said he, half reflectively. 'And pray,' added he quickly, while in turn he fixed his eyes upon me, 'what did this person say? since some comment upon her communication forms, no doubt, the sequel to your preface.'

'Your lordship is not mistaken,' said I; 'her statement was so extraordinary that I could not think of withholding it from you. She told me, my lord, that you had a wife living at the time you married me, and that she was that wife.'

Lord Glenfallen became ashy pale, almost livid; he made two or three efforts to clear his voice to speak, but in vain, and turning suddenly from me, he walked to the window. The horror and dismay which, in the olden time, overwhelmed the woman of Endor when her spells unexpectedly conjured the dead into her presence, were but types of what I felt when thus presented with what appeared to be almost unequivocal evidence of the guilt whose existence I had before so strongly doubted.

There was a silence of some moments, during which it were hard to conjecture whether I or my companion suffered most.

Lord Glenfallen soon recovered his self-command; he returned to the table, again sat down, and said: 'What you have told me has so astonished me, has unfolded such a tissue of motiveless guilt, and in a quarter from which I had so little reason to look for ingratitude or treachery, that your announcement almost deprived me of speech; the person in question, however, has one excuse, her mind is, as I told you before, unsettled. You should have remembered that, and hesitated to receive as unexceptionable evidence against the honour of your husband, the ravings of a lunatic. I now tell you that this is the last time I shall speak to you upon this subject, and, in the presence of the God who is to judge me, and as I hope for mercy in the day of judgment, I swear that the charge thus brought against me is utterly false, unfounded, and ridiculous. I defy the world in any point to taint my honour; and, as I have never taken the opinion of madmen touching your character or morals, I think it but fair to require that you will evince a like tenderness for me; and now, once for all, never again dare to repeat to me your insulting suspicions, or the clumsy and infamous calumnies of fools. I shall instantly let the worthy lady who contrived this somewhat original device understand fully my opinion upon the matter. Good morning.'

And with these words he left me again in doubt, and involved in all the horrors of the most agonising suspense.

I had reason to think that Lord Glenfallen wreaked his vengeance upon the author of the strange story which I had heard, with a violence which was not satisfied with mere words for old Martha, with whom I was a great favourite, while attending me in my room, told me that she feared her master had ill-used the poor blind Dutchwoman, for that she had heard her scream as if the very life were leaving her, but added a request that I should not speak of what she had told me to anyone, particularly to the master.

'How do you know that she is a Dutchwoman?' enquired I, anxious to learn anything whatever that might throw a light upon the history of this person, who seemed to have resolved to mix herself up in my fortunes.

'Why, my lady,' answered Martha, 'the master often calls her the Dutch hag, and other names you would not like to hear, and I am sure she is neither English nor Irish; for, whenever they talk together, they speak some queer foreign lingo, and fast enough, I'll be bound. But I ought not to talk about her at all; it might be as much as my place is worth to mention her, only you saw her first yourself, so there can be no great harm in speaking of her now.'

'How long has this lady been here?' continued I.

'She came early on the morning after your ladyship's arrival,' answered she; 'but do not ask me any more, for the master would think nothing of turning me out of doors for daring to speak of her at all, much less to *you*, my lady.'

I did not like to press the poor woman further, for her reluctance to speak on this topic was evident and strong.

You will readily believe that upon the very slight grounds which my information afforded, contradicted as it was by the solemn oath of my husband, and derived from what was, at best, a very questionable source, I could not take any very decisive measures whatever; and as to the menace of the strange woman who had thus unaccountably twice intruded herself into my chamber, although, at the moment, it occasioned me some uneasiness, it was not, even in my eyes, sufficiently formidable to induce my departure from Cahergillagh.

A few nights after the scene which I have just mentioned, Lord Glenfallen having, as usual, retired early to his study, I was left alone in the parlour to amuse myself as best I might.

It was not strange that my thoughts should often recur to the agitating scenes in which I had recently taken a part.

The subject of my reflections, the solitude, the silence, and the lateness of the hour, as also the depression of spirits to which I had of late been a constant prey, tended to produce that nervous excitement which places us wholly at the mercy of the imagination.

In order to calm my spirits I was endeavouring to direct my thoughts into some more pleasing channel, when I heard, or thought I heard, uttered within a few yards of me, in an odd, half-sneering tone, the words: 'There is blood upon your ladyship's throat.'

So vivid was the impression that I started to my feet, and involuntarily placed my hand upon my neck.

I looked around the room for the speaker, but in vain.

I went then to the room-door, which I opened, and peered into the passage, nearly faint with horror lest some leering shapeless thing should greet me upon the threshold.

When I had gazed long enough to assure myself that no strange object was within sight,

'I have been too much of a rake lately; I am racking out my nerves,' said I, speaking aloud, with a view to reassure myself.

I rang the bell, and, attended by old Martha, I retired to settle for the night.

While the servant was – as was her custom – arranging the lamp which I have already stated always burned during the night in my chamber, I was employed in undressing, and, in doing so, I had recourse to a large looking-glass which occupied a considerable portion of the wall in which it was fixed, rising from the ground to a height of about six feet; this mirror filled the space of a large panel in the wainscoting opposite the foot of the bed.

I had hardly been before it for the lapse of a minute when something like a black pall was slowly waved between me and it.

'Oh, God! there it is,' I exclaimed, wildly. 'I have seen it again, Martha – the black cloth.'

'God be merciful to us, then!' answered she, tremulously crossing herself. 'Some misfortune is over us.'

'No, no, Martha,' said I, almost instantly recovering my collectedness; for, although of a nervous temperament, I had never been superstitious. 'I do not believe in omens. You know I saw, or fancied I saw, this thing before, and nothing followed.'

'The Dutch lady came the next morning,' replied she.

'But surely her coming scarcely deserved such a dreadful warning,' I replied.

'She is a strange woman, my lady,' said Martha; 'and she is not *gone* yet – mark my words.'

'Well, well, Martha,' said I, 'I have not wit enough to change your opinions, nor inclination to alter mine; so I will talk no more of the matter. Good-night,' and so I was left to my reflections.

After lying for about an hour awake, I at length fell into a kind of doze; but my imagination was very busy, for I was startled from this unrefreshing sleep by fancying that I heard a voice close to my face exclaim as before: 'There is blood upon your ladyship's throat.'

The words were instantly followed by a loud burst of laughter.

Quaking with horror, I awakened, and heard my husband enter the room. Even this was a relief.

Scared as I was, however, by the tricks which my imagination had played me, I preferred remaining silent, and pretending to sleep, to attempting to engage my husband in conversation, for I well knew that his mood was such, that his words would not, in all probability, convey anything that had not better be unsaid and unheard.

Lord Glenfallen went into his dressing-room, which lay upon the right-hand side of the bed. The door lying open, I could see him by himself, at full length upon a sofa, and, in about half an hour, I became aware, by his deep and regularly drawn respiration, that he was fast asleep.

When slumber refuses to visit one, there is something peculiarly irritating, not to the temper, but to the nerves, in the consciousness that someone is in your immediate presence, actually enjoying the boon which you are seeking in vain; at least, I have always found it so, and never more than upon the present occasion.

A thousand annoying imaginations harassed and excited me; every object which I looked upon, though ever so familiar, seemed to have acquired a strange phantomlike character, the varying shadows thrown by the flickering of the lamplight seemed shaping themselves into grotesque and unearthly forms, and whenever my eyes wandered to the sleeping figure of my husband, his features appeared to undergo the strangest and most demoniacal contortions.

Hour after hour was told by the old clock, and each succeeding one found me, if possible, less inclined to sleep than its predecessor.

It was now considerably past three; my eyes, in their involuntary wanderings, happened to alight upon the large mirror which was, as I have said, fixed in the wall opposite the foot of the bed. A view of it was commanded from where I lay, through the curtains. As I gazed fixedly upon it, I thought I perceived the broad sheet of glass shifting its position in relation to the bed; I riveted my eyes upon it with intense scrutiny; it was no deception, the mirror, as if acting of its own impulse, moved slowly aside, and disclosed a dark aperture in the wall, nearly as large as an ordinary door; a figure evidently stood in this, but the light was too dim to define it accurately.

It stepped cautiously into the chamber, and with so little noise, that had I not actually seen it, I do not think I should have been aware of its presence. It was arrayed in a kind of woollen nightdress, and a white handkerchief or cloth was bound tightly about the head; I had no difficulty, spite of the strangeness of the attire, in recognising the blind woman whom I so much dreaded.

She stooped down, bringing her head nearly to the ground, and in that attitude she remained motionless for some moments, no doubt in order to ascertain if any suspicious sounds were stirring.

She was apparently satisfied by her observations, for she immediately recommended her silent progress towards a ponderous mahogany dressing-table of my husband's. When she had reached it, she paused again, and appeared to listen attentively for some minutes; she then noiselessly opened one of the drawers, from which, having groped for some time, she took something, which I soon perceived to be a case of razors. She opened it, and tried the edge of each of the two instruments upon the skin of her hand; she quickly selected one, which she fixed firmly in her grasp. She now stooped down as before, and having listened for a time, she, with the hand that was disengaged, groped her way into the dressing-room where Lord Glenfallen lay fast asleep.

I was fixed as if in the tremendous spell of a nightmare. I could not stir even a finger; I could not lift my voice; I could not even breathe; and though I expected every moment to see the sleeping man murdered, I could not even close my eyes to shut out the horrible spectacle which I had not the power to avert.

I saw the woman approach the sleeping figure, she laid the un-occupied hand lightly along his clothes, and having thus ascertained his identity, she, after a brief interval, turned back and again entered my chamber; here she bent down again to listen.

I had now not a doubt but that the razor was intended for my throat; yet the terrific fascination which had locked all my powers so long, still continued to bind me fast.

I felt that my life depended upon the slightest ordinary exertion, and yet I could not stir one joint from the position in which I lay, nor even make noise enough to waken Lord Glenfallen.

The murderous woman now, with long, silent steps, approached the bed; my very heart seemed turning to ice; her left hand, that which was disengaged, was upon the pillow; she gradually slid it forward towards my head, and in an instant, with the speed of lightning, it was clutched in my hair, while, with the other hand, she dashed the razor at my throat.

A slight inaccuracy saved me from instant death; the blow fell short, the point of the razor grazing my throat. In a moment, I know not how, I found myself at the other side of the bed, uttering shriek after shriek; the wretch was however determined, if possible, to murder me.

Scrambling along by the curtains, she rushed round the bed towards me; I seized the handle of the door to make my escape. It was, however, fastened. At all events, I could not open it. From the mere instinct of recoiling terror, I shrunk back into a corner. She was now within a yard of me. Her hand was upon my face.

I closed my eyes fast, expecting never to open them again, when a blow, inflicted from behind by a strong arm, stretched the monster senseless at my feet. At the same moment the door opened, and several domestics, alarmed by my cries, entered the apartment.

I do not recollect what followed, for I fainted. One swoon succeeded another, so long and deathlike, that my life was considered very doubtful.

At about ten o'clock however, I sank into a deep and refreshing sleep, from which I was awakened at about two, that I might swear my deposition before a magistrate, who attended for that purpose.

I accordingly did so, as did also Lord Glenfallen, and the woman was fully committed to stand her trial at the ensuing assizes.

I shall never forget the scene which the examination of the blind woman and of the other parties afforded.

She was brought into the room in the custody of two servants. She wore a kind of flannel wrapper, which had not been changed since the night before. It was torn and soiled, and here and there smeared with blood, which had flowed in large quantities from a wound in her head. The white handkerchief had fallen off in the scuffle, and her grizzled hair fell in masses about her wild and deadly pale countenance.

She appeared perfectly composed, however, and the only regret she expressed throughout, was at not having succeeded in her attempt, the object of which she did not pretend to conceal.

On being asked her name, she called herself the Countess Glenfallen, and refused to give any other title.

'The woman's name is Flora Van-Kemp,' said Lord Glenfallen.

'It *was*, it *was*, you perjured traitor and cheat!' screamed the woman; and then there followed a volley of words in some foreign language. 'Is there a magistrate here?' she resumed; 'I am Lord Glenfallen's wife – I'll prove it – write down my words. I am willing to be hanged or burned, so *he* meets his deserts. I did try to kill that doll of his; but it was he who put it into my head to do it – two wives were too many; I was to murder her, or she was to hang me: listen to all I have to say.'

Here Lord Glenfallen interrupted.

'I think, sir,' said he, addressing the magistrate 'that we had better proceed to business; this unhappy woman's furious recriminations but waste our time. If she refuses to answer your questions, you had better, I presume, take my depositions.'

'And are you going to swear away my life, you black-perjured murderer?' shrieked the woman. 'Sir, sir, sir, you must hear me,' she continued, addressing the magistrate; 'I can convict him – he bid me murder that girl, and then, when I failed, he came behind me, and struck me down, and now he wants to swear away my life. Take down all I say.'

'If it is your intention,' said the magistrate, 'to confess the crime with which you stand charged, you may, upon producing sufficient evidence, criminate whom you please.'

'Evidence! – I have no evidence but myself,' said the woman. 'I will swear it all – write down my testimony – write it down, I say – we shall hang side by side, my brave lord – all your own handy-work, my gentle husband!'

This was followed by a low, insolent, and sneering laugh, which, from one in her situation, was sufficiently horrible.

'I will not at present hear anything,' replied he, 'but distinct answers to the questions which I shall put to you upon this matter.'

'Then you shall hear nothing,' replied she sullenly, and no inducement or intimidation could bring her to speak again.

Lord Glenfallen's deposition and mine were then given, as also those of the servants who had entered the room at the moment of my rescue.

The magistrate then intimated that she was committed, and must proceed directly to gaol, whither she was brought in a carriage of Lord Glenfallen's, for his lordship was naturally by no means indifferent to the effect which her vehement accusations against himself might produce, if uttered before every chance hearer whom she might meet with between Cahergillagh and the place of confinement whither she was despatched.

During the time which intervened between the committal and the trial of the prisoner, Lord Glenfallen seemed to suffer agonies of mind which baffled all description; he hardly ever slept, and when he did, his slumbers seemed but the instruments of new tortures, and his waking hours were, if possible exceeded in intensity of terror by the dreams which disturbed his sleep.

Lord Glenfallen rested, if to lie in the mere attitude of repose were to do so, in his dressing-room, and thus I had an opportunity of witnessing, far oftener than I wished it, the fearful workings of his mind. His agony often broke out into such fearful paroxysms that delirium and total loss of reason appeared to be impending. He frequently spoke of flying from the country, and bringing with him all the witnesses of the appalling scene upon which the prosecution was founded; then, again, he would fiercely lament that the blow which he had inflicted had not ended at all.

The assizes arrived, however, and upon the day appointed Lord Glenfallen and I attended in order to give our evidence.

The cause was called on, and the prisoner appeared at the bar.

Great curiosity and interest were felt respecting the trial, so that the court was crowded to excess.

The prisoner, however, without appearing to take the trouble of listening to the indictment, pleaded guilty, and no representations on the part of the court availed to induce her to retract her plea.

After much time had been wasted in a fruitless attempt to prevail upon her to reconsider her words, the court proceeded, according to the usual form, to pass sentence.

This having been done, the prisoner was about to be removed, when she said, in a low, distinct voice: 'A word – a word, my lord! – Is Lord Glenfallen here in the court?'

On being told that he was, she raised her voice to a tone of loud menace, and continued: 'Hardress, Earl of Glenfallen, I accuse you here in this court of justice of two crimes – first, that you married a second wife while the first was living; and again, that you prompted me to the murder, for attempting which I am to die. Secure him – chain him – bring him here!'

There was a laugh through the court at these words, which were naturally treated by the judge as a violent extemporary recrimination, and the woman was desired to be silent.

'You won't take him, then?' she said; 'you won't try him? You'll let him go free?'

It was intimated by the court that he would certainly be allowed 'to go free,' and she was ordered again to be removed.

Before, however, the mandate was executed, she threw her arms wildly into the air, and uttered one piercing shriek so full of preternatural rage and despair, that it might fitly have ushered a soul into those realms where hope can come no more.

The sound still rang in my ears, months after the voice that had uttered it was for ever silent.

The wretched woman was executed in accordance with the sentence which had been pronounced.

For some time after this event, Lord Glenfallen appeared, if possible, to suffer more than he had done before, and altogethcr his language, which often amounted to half confessions of the guilt imputed to him, and all the circumstances connected with the late occurrences, formed a mass of evidence so convincing that I wrote to my father, detailing the grounds of my fears, and imploring him to come to Cahergillagh without delay, in order to remove me from my husband's control, previously to taking legal steps for a final separation.

Circumstanced as I was, my existence was little short of intolerable, for, besides the fearful suspicions which attached to my husband, I plainly perceived that if Lord Glenfallen were not relieved, and that speedily, insanity must supervene. I therefore expected my father's arrival, or at least a letter to announce it, with indescribable impatience.

About a week after the execution had taken place, Lord Glenfallen one morning met me with an unusually sprightly air.

'Fanny,' said he, 'I have it now for the first time in my power to explain to your satisfaction everything which has hitherto appeared suspicious or mysterious in my conduct. After breakfast come with me to my study, and I shall, I hope, make all things clear.'

This invitation afforded me more real pleasure than I had experienced for months. Something had certainly occurred to tranquillise my husband's mind in no ordinary degree, and I thought it by no means impossible that he would, in the proposed interview, prove himself the most injured and innocent of men.

Full of this hope, I repaired to his study at the appointed hour. He was writing busily when I entered the room, and just raising his eyes, he requested me to be seated.

I took a chair as he desired, and remained silently awaiting his leisure, while he finished, folded, directed, and sealed his letter. Laying it then upon the table with the address downward, he said,

'My dearest Fanny, I know I must have appeared very strange to you and very unkind – often even cruel. Before the end of this week I will show you the necessity of my conduct – how impossible it was that I should have seemed otherwise. I am conscious that many acts of mine must have inevitably given rise to painful suspicions – suspicions which, indeed, upon one occasion, you very properly communicated to me. I have got two letters from a quarter which commands respect, containing information as to the course by which I may be enabled to prove the negative of all the crimes which even the most credulous suspicion could lay to my charge. I expected a third by this morning's post, containing documents which will set the matter for ever at rest, but owing, no doubt, to some neglect, or perhaps to some difficulty in collecting the papers, some inevitable delay, it has not come to hand this morning, according to my expectation. I was finishing one to the very same quarter when you came in, and if a sound rousing be worth anything, I think I shall have a special messenger before two days have passed. I have been anxiously considering with myself, as to whether I had better imperfectly clear up your doubts by submitting to your inspection the two letters which I have already received, or wait till I can triumphantly vindicate myself by the production of the documents which I have already mentioned, and I have, I think, not unnaturally decided upon the latter course. However, there is a person in the next room whose testimony is not without its value – excuse me for one moment.'

So saying, he arose and went to the door of a closet which opened from the study; this he unlocked, and half opening the door, he said, 'It is only I,' and then slipped into the room, and carefully closed and locked the door behind him.

I immediately heard his voice in animated conversation. My curiosity upon the subject of the letter was naturally great, so, smothering any little scruples which I might have felt, I resolved to look at the address of the letter which lay, as my husband had left it, with its face upon the table. I accordingly drew it over to me, and turned up the direction.

For two or three moments I could scarce believe my eyes, but there could be no mistake – in large characters were traced the words. 'To the Archangel Gabriel in Heaven.'

I had scarcely returned the letter to its original position, and in some degree recovered the shock which this unequivocal proof of insanity produced, when the closet door was unlocked, and Lord Glenfallen re-entered the study, carefully closing and locking the door again upon the outside.

'Whom have you there?' enquired I, making a strong effort to appear calm.

'Perhaps,' said he, musingly, 'you might have some objection to seeing her, at least for a time.'

'Who is it?' repeated I.

'Why,' said he, 'I see no use in hiding it – the blind Dutch-woman. I have been with her the whole morning. She is very anxious to get out of that closet; but you know she is odd, she is scarcely to be trusted.'

A heavy gust of wind shook the door at this moment with a sound as if something more substantial were pushing against it.

'Ha, ha, ha! – do you hear her?' said he, with an obstreperous burst of laughter.

The wind died away in a long howl, and Lord Glenfallen, suddenly checking his merriment, shrugged his shoulders, and muttered: 'Poor devil, she has been hardly used.'

'We had better not tease her at present with questions,' said I, in as unconcerned a tone as I could assume, although I felt every moment as if I should faint.

'Humph! may be so,' said he. 'Well, come back in an hour or two, or when you please, and you will find us here.'

He again unlocked the door, and entered with the same precautions which he had adopted before, locking the door upon the inside; and as I hurried from the room, I heard his voice again exerted as if in eager parley.

I can hardly describe my emotions; my hopes had been raised to the highest, and now, in an instant, all was gone; the dreadful consummation was accomplished – the fearful retribution had fallen upon the guilty man – the mind was destroyed, the power to repent was gone.

The agony of the hours which followed what I would still call my awful interview with Lord Glenfallen, I cannot describe; my solitude was, however, broken in upon by Martha, who came to inform me of the arrival of a gentleman, who expected me in the parlour.

I accordingly descended, and, to my great joy, found my father seated by the fire.

This expedition upon his part was easily accounted for: my communications had touched the honour of the family. I speedily informed him of the dreadful malady which had fallen upon the wretched man.

My father suggested the necessity of placing some person to watch him, to prevent his injuring himself or others.

I rang the bell, and desired that one Edward Cooke, an attached servant of the family, should be sent to me.

I told him distinctly and briefly the nature of the service required of him, and, attended by him, my father and I proceeded at once to the study. The door of the inner room was still closed, and everything in the outer chamber remained in the same order in which I had left it.

We then advanced to the closet-door, at which we knocked, but without receiving any answer.

We next tried to open the door, but in vain; it was locked upon the inside. We knocked more loudly, but in vain.

Seriously alarmed, I desired the servant to force the door, which was, after several violent efforts, accomplished, and we entered the closet.

Lord Glenfallen was lying on his face upon a sofa.

'Hush!' said I; 'he is asleep.' We paused for a moment.

'He is too still for that,' said my father.

We all of us felt a strong reluctance to approach the figure.

'Edward,' said I, 'try whether your master sleeps.'

The servant approached the sofa where Lord Glenfallen lay. He leant his ear towards the head of the recumbent figure, to ascertain whether the sound of breathing was audible. He turned towards us, and said: 'My lady, you had better not wait here; I am sure he is dead!'

'Let me see the face,' said I, terribly agitated; 'you *may* be mistaken.'

The man then, in obedience to my command, turned the body round, and, gracious God! what a sight met my view.

The whole breast of the shirt, with its lace frill, was drenched with his blood, as was the couch underneath the spot where he lay.

The head hung back, as it seemed, almost severed from the body by a frightful gash, which yawned across the throat. The razor which had inflicted the wound was found under his body.

All, then, was over; I was never to learn the history in whose termination I had been so deeply and so tragically involved.

The severe discipline which my mind had undergone was not

bestowed in vain. I directed my thoughts and my hopes to that place where there is no more sin, nor danger, nor sorrow.

Thus ends a brief tale whose prominent incidents many will recognise as having marked the history of a distinguished family; and though it refers to a somewhat distant date, we shall be found not to have taken, upon that account, any liberties with the facts.

CECIL FRANCES ALEXANDER

The Legend of Stumpie's Brae

Heard ye no'tell of the Stumpie's Brae*?
Sit down, sit down, young friend,
I'll make your flesh to creep today,
And your hair to stan' on end.

Young man, it's hard to strive wi' sin,
And the hardest strife of a'
Is where the greed o' gain creeps in,
And drives God's grace awa'.

Oh, it's quick to do, but it's lang to rue,
When the punishment comes at last,
And we would give the world to undo
The deed that's done and past.

Over yon strip of meadow land,
And over the burnie bright,
Dinna ye mark the fir trees stand,
Around yon gable white?

I mind it weel, in my younger days
The story yet was rife:
There dwelt within that lonely place
A farmer man and his wife.

---

* This ballad embodies an actual legend attached to a lonely spot on the border
of the county of Donegal. The *language* of the ballad is the peculiar semi-
Scottish dialect spoken in the north of Ireland.

They sat together all alone,
One blessed autumn night,
When the trees without, and hedge, and stone,
Were white in the sweet moonlight.

The boys and girls were gone down all
A wee to the blacksmith's wake;
There pass'd ane on by the window small,
And guv the door a shake.

The man he up and open'd the door –
When he had spoken a bit,
A pedlar men stepp'd into the floor,
Down he tumbled the pack he bore,
Right heavy pack was it.

'Gude save us a',' says the wife, wi' a smile,
'But yours is a thrivin' trade.' –
'Ay, ay, I've wander'd mony a mile,
And plenty have I made.'

The man sat on by the dull fire flame,
When the pedlar went to rest;
Close to his ear the Devil came,
And slipp'd intil his breast.

He look'd at his wife by the dim fire light,
And she was as bad as he –
'Could we no' murder thon man the night?' –
'Ay, could we, ready,' quo' she.

He took the pickaxe without a word,
Whence it stood, ahint the door;
As he pass'd in, the sleeper stirr'd,
That never waken'd more.

'He's dead!' says the auld man, coming back –
'What o' the corp, my dear?'

'We'll bury him snug in his ain bit pack,
Never ye mind for the loss of the sack,
I've ta'en out a' the gear.'

'The pack's owre short by twa gude span
'What'll we do?' quo' he –
'Oh, you're a doited, unthoughtfu' man,
We'll cut him off at the knee.'

They shorten'd the corp, and they pack'd him tight,
Wi' his legs in a pickle hay;
Over the burn, in the sweet moonlight,
They carried him till this brae.

They shovell'd a hole right speedily,
They laid him in on his back –
'A right pair are ye,' quo' the PEDLAR, quo' he,
Sitting bolt upright in the pack.

'Ye think ye've laid me snugly here,
And none shall know my station;
But I'll hant ye far, and I'll hant ye near,
Father and son, wi' terror and fear,
To the nineteenth generation.'

The twa were sittin' the vera next night,
When the dog began to cower,
And they knew, by the pale blue fire light,
That the Evil One had power.

It had stricken nine, just nine o' the clock –
The hour when the man lay dead;
There came to the outer door a knock,
And a heavy, heavy tread.

The old man's head swam round and round,
The woman's blood 'gan freeze,
For it was not like a natural sound,

But like someone stumping o'er the ground
An the banes of his twa bare knees.

And through the door, like a sough of air,
And stump, stump, round the twa,
Wi' his bloody head, and his knee banes bare –
They'd maist ha'e died of awe!

The wife's black locks ere morn grew white,
They say, as the mountain snaws;
The man was as straight as a staff that night,
But he stoop'd when the morning rose.

Still, year and day, as the clock struck NINE,
The hour when they did the sin,
The wee bit dog began to whine,
And the ghaist came clattering in.

Ae night there was a fearful flood –
Three days the skies had pour'd;
And white wi' foam, and black wi' mud,
The burn in fury roar'd.

Quo' she – 'Gude man, ye need na turn
Sae pale in the dim fire light;
The Stumpie canna cross the burn,
He'll no' be here the night.

'For it's o'er the bank, and it's o'er the linn,
And it's up to the meadow ridge – '
'Ay,' quo' the Stumpie hirpling in,
And he gied the wife a slap on the chin,
'But I cam' round by the bridge!'

And stump, stump, stump, to his plays again,
And o'er the stools and chairs;
Ye'd surely hae thought ten women and men
Were dancing there in pairs.

They sold their gear, and over the sea
To a foreign land they went,
Over the sea – but wha can flee
His appointed punishment?

The ship swam over the water clear,
Wi' the help o' the eastern breeze;
But the vera first sound in guilty fear,
O'er the wide, smooth deck, that fell on their ear
Was the tapping o' them twa knees.

In the woods of wild America
Their weary feet they set;
But Stumpie was there the first, they say,
And he haunted them on to their dying day,
And he follows their children yet.

I haud ye, never the voice of blood
Call'd from the earth in vain;
And never has crime won worldly good,
But it brought its after-pain.

This is the story o' Stumpie's Brae,
And the murderers' fearfu' fate:
Young man, your face is turn'd that way,
Ye'll be ganging the night that gate.

Ye'll ken it weel, through the few fir trees,
The house where they wont to dwell;
Gin ye meet ane there, as daylight flees,
Stumping about on the banes of his knees,
It'll jist be Stumpie himsel'.

TRADITIONAL

Daniel Crowley and the Ghosts

There lived a man in Cork whose name was Daniel Crowley. He was a coffin-maker by trade, and had a deal of coffins laid by, so that his apprentice might sell them when himself was not at home.

A messenger came to Daniel Crowley's shop one day and told him that there was a man dead at the end of the town, and to send up a coffin for him, or to make one.

Daniel Crowley took down a coffin, put it on a donkey cart, drove to the wake house, went in and told the people of the house that the coffin was there for them. The corpse was laid out on a table in a room next to the kitchen. Five or six women were keeping watch around it; many people were in the kitchen. Daniel Crowley was asked to sit down and commence to shorten the night: that is, to tell stories, amuse himself and others. A tumbler of punch was brought, and he promised to do the best he could.

He began to tell stories and shorten the night. A second glass of punch was brought to him, and he went on telling tales. There was a man at the wake who sang a song: after him another was found, and then another. Then the people asked Daniel Crowley to sing, and he did. The song that he sang was of another nation. He sang about the good people, the fairies. The song pleased the company, they desired him to sing again, and he did not refuse.

Daniel Crowley pleased the company so much with his two songs that a woman who had three daughters wanted to make a match for one of them and get Daniel Crowley as a husband for her. Crowley was a bachelor, well on in years, and had never thought of marrying.

The mother spoke of the match to a woman sitting next to her. The woman shook her head, but the mother said: 'If he takes one of my daughters I'll be glad, for he has money laid by. Do you go and speak to him, but say nothing of me at first.'

The woman went to Daniel Crowley then, and told him that she had a fine, beautiful girl in view, and that now was his time to get a good wife; he'd never have such a chance again.

Crowley rose up in great anger. 'There isn't a woman wearing clothes that I'd marry,' said he. 'There isn't a woman born that could bring me to make two halves of my loaf for her.'

The mother was insulted now and forget herself. She began to abuse Crowley.

'Bad luck to you, you hairy little scoundrel,' said she, 'you might be a grandfather to my child. You are not fit to clean the shoes on her feet. You have only dead people for company day and night; 'tis by them you make your living.'

'Oh, then,' said Daniel Crowley, 'I'd prefer the dead to the living any day if all the living were like you. Besides, I have nothing against the dead. I am getting employment by them and not by the living, for 'tis the dead that want coffins.'

'Bad luck to you, 'tis with the dead you ought to be and not with the living; 'twould be fitter for you to go out of this altogether and go to your dead people.'

'I'd go if I knew how to go to them,' said Crowley.

'Why not invite them to supper?' retorted the woman.

He rose up then, went out, and called: 'Men, women, children, soldiers, sailors, all people that I have ever made coffins for, I invite you tonight to my house, and I'll spend what is needed in giving a feast.'

The people who were watching the dead man on the table saw him smile when he heard the invitation. They ran out of the room in a fright and out of the kitchen, and Daniel Crowley hurried away to his shop as fast as ever his donkey could carry him. On the way he came to a public-house and, going in, bought a pint bottle of whiskey, put it in his pocket, and drove on.

The workshop was locked and the shutters down when he left that evening, but when he came near he saw that all the windows were shining with light, and he was in dread that the building was burning or that robbers were in it. When right there Crowley slipped into a corner of the building opposite, to know could he see what was happening, and soon he saw crowds of men, women, and children walking toward his shop and going in, but none coming out. He was hiding some time when a man tapped him on the shoulder and asked, 'Is it here you are, and we waiting for you? 'Tis a shame to treat company this way. Come now.'

Crowley went with the man to the shop, and as he passed the threshold he saw a great gathering of people. Some were neighbours, people he had known in the past. All were dancing, singing, amusing themselves. He was not long looking on when a man came up to him and said: 'You seem not to know me, Daniel Crowley.'

'I don't know you,' said Crowley. 'How could I?'

'You might then, and you ought to know me, for I am the first man you made a coffin for, and 'twas I gave you the first start in business.'

Soon another came up, a lame man: 'Do you know me, Daniel Crowley?'

'I do not.'

'I am your cousin, and it isn't long since I died.'

'Oh, now I know you well, for you are lame. In God's name,' said Crowley to the cousin, 'how am I to get these people out o' this. What time is it?'

''Tis early yet, it's hardly eleven o'clock, man.'

Crowley wondered that it was so early.

'Receive them kindly,' said the cousin; 'be good to them, make merriment as you can.'

'I have no money with me to get food or drink for them; 'tis night now, and all places are closed,' answered Crowley.

'Well, do the best you can,' said the cousin.

The fun and dancing went on, and while Daniel Crowley was looking around, examining everything, he saw a woman in the far-off comer. She took no part in the amusement, but seemed very shy in herself.

'Why is that woman so shy – she seems to be afraid?' asked he of the cousin. 'And why doesn't she dance and make merry like others?'

'Oh, 'tis not long since she died, and you gave the coffin, as she had no means of paying for it. She is in dread you'll ask her for the money, or let the company know that she didn't pay,' said the cousin.

The best dancer they had was a piper by the name of John Reardon from the city of Cork. The fiddler was one John Healy. Healy brought no fiddle with him, but he made one, and the way he made it was to take off what flesh he had on his body. He rubbed up and down on his own ribs, each rib having a different note, and he made the loveliest music that Daniel Crowley had ever heard. After that the whole company followed his example. All threw off what flesh they had on them and began to dance jigs and hornpipes in their bare bones. When by chance they struck against one another in dancing, you'd think it was Brandon Mountain that was sinking Mount Eagle, with the noise that was in it.

Daniel Crowley plucked up all his courage to know could he live through the night, but still he thought daylight would never come. There was one man, John Sullivan, that he noticed especially. This man had married twice in his life, and with him came the two women. Crowley saw him taking out the second wife to dance a breakdown, and the two danced so well that the company were delighted, and all the skeletons had their mouths open, laughing. He danced and knocked so much merriment out of them all that his first wife, who was at the end of the house, became jealous and very mad altogether. She ran down to where he was and told him she had a better right to dance with him than the second wife; 'That's not the truth for you,' said the second wife, 'I have a better right than you. When he married me you were a dead woman and he was free, and, besides, I'm a better dancer than what you are, and I will dance with him whether you like it or not.'

'Hold your tongue!' screamed the first wife. 'Sure, you couldn't come to this feast tonight at all but for the loan of another woman's shinbones.'

Sullivan looked at his two wives and asked the second one: 'Isn't it your own shinbones you have?'

'No, they are borrowed. I borrowed a neighbouring woman's shins from her, and 'tis those I have with me tonight.'

'Who is the owner of the shinbones you have under you?' asked the husband.

'They belong to one Catherine Murray. She hadn't a very good name in life.'

'But why didn't you come on your own feet?'

'Oh, I wasn't good myself in life, and I was put under a penalty, and the penalty is that whenever there is a feast or a ball I cannot go to it unless I am able to borrow a pair of shins.'

Sullivan was raging when he found that the shinbones he had been dancing with belonged to a third woman, and she not the best, and he gave a slap to the wife that sent her spinning into a corner.

The woman had relations among the skeletons present, and they were angry when they saw the man strike their friend. 'We'll never let that go with him,' said they. 'We must knock satisfaction out of Sullivan!'

The woman's friends rose up, and, as there were no clubs or weapons, they pulled off their left arms and began to slash and strike with them in terrible fashion. There was an awful battle in one minute.

While this was going on Daniel Crowley was standing below at the end of the room, cold and hungry, not knowing but he'd be killed. As Sullivan was trying to dodge the blows sent against him, he got as far as Daniel Crowley and stepped on his toe without knowing it; Crowley got vexed and gave Sullivan a blow with his fist that drove the head from him and sent it flying to the opposite corner.

When Sullivan saw his head flying off from the blow, he ran, and, catching it, aimed a blow at Daniel Crowley with the head, and aimed so truly that he knocked him under the bench; then, having him at a disadvantage, Sullivan hurried to the bench and began to strangle him. He squeezed his throat and held him so firmly between the bench and the floor that the man lost his senses and couldn't remember a thing more.

When Daniel Crowley came to himself in the morning, his apprentice found him stretched under the bench with an empty bottle under his arm. He was bruised and pounded. His throat was sore where Sullivan had squeezed it; he didn't know how the company broke up, nor when his guests went away.

TRADITIONAL

John Reardon and the Sister Ghosts

Once there was a farmer, a widower, Tom Reardon, who lived near Castlemain. He had an only son, a fine strong boy, who was almost a man, and the boy's name was John. This farmer married a second time, and the stepmother hated the boy and gave him neither rest nor peace. She was turning the father's mind against the son, till at last the farmer resolved to put the son in a place where a ghost was, and this ghost never let any man go without killing him.

One day the father sent the son to the forge with some chains belonging to a plough; he would have two horses ploughing next day.

The boy took the chains to the forge; and it was nearly evening when the father sent him, and the forge was four miles away.

The smith had much work and he hadn't the chains mended till close on to midnight. The smith had two sons, and they didn't wish to let John go, but he said he must go, for he had promised to be home and the father would kill him if he stayed away. They stood before him in the door, but he went in spite of them.

When two miles from the forge a ghost rose up before John, a woman; she attacked him and they fought for two hours, when he put the plough chain round her. She could do nothing then, because what belongs to a plough is blessed. He fastened the chain and dragged the ghost home with him, and told her to go to the bedroom and give the father and stepmother a rough handling, not to spare them.

The ghost beat them till the father cried for mercy, and said if he lived till morning he'd leave the place, and that the wife was the cause of putting John in the way to be killed.

John put food on the table and told the ghost to sit down and eat for herself, but she refused and said he must take her back to the very spot where he found her. John was willing to do that, and he went with her. She told him to come to that place on the following night, that there was a sister of hers, a ghost, a deal more determined and stronger than what herself was.

John told her that maybe the two of them would attack and kill him. She said that they would not, that she wanted his help against the sister, and that he would not be sorry for helping her. He told her he would come, and when he was leaving her she said not to forget the plough chains.

Next morning the father was going to leave the house, but the wife persuaded him to stay. 'That ghost will never walk the way again,' said she. John went the following night, and the ghost was waiting before him on the spot where he fought with her. They walked on together two miles by a different road, and halted. They were talking in that place a while when the sister came and attacked John Reardon, and they were fighting two hours and she was getting the better of the boy, when the first sister put the plough chains around her. He pulled her home with the chains, and the first sister walked along behind them. When John came to the house, he opened the door, and when the father saw the two ghosts he said that if morning overtook him alive he'd leave the son everything, the farm and the house.

The son told the second ghost to go down and give a good turn to the stepmother; 'Let her have a few strong knocks,' said he.

The second ghost barely left life in the stepmother. John had food on the table, but they would not take a bite, and the second sister said he must take her back to the very spot where he met her first. He said he would. She told him that he was the bravest man that ever stood before her, and that she would not threaten him again in the world, and told him to come the next night. He said he would not, for the two might attack and get the better of him. They promised they would not attack, but would help him, for it was to get the upper hand of the youngest and strongest of the sisters that they wanted him, and that he must bring the plough chains, for without them they could do nothing.

He agreed to go if they would give their word not to harm him. They said they would give their word and would help him the best they could.

The next day, when the father was going to leave the place, the wife would not let him. 'Stay where you are,' she said, 'they'll never trouble us again.'

John went the third night, and, when he came, the two sisters were before him, and they walked till they travelled four miles then told him to stop on the green grass at one side and not to be on the road.

They weren't waiting long when the third sister came, and red lightning flashing from her mouth. She went at John, and with the first blow that she gave him put him on his knees. He rose with the help of the two sisters, and for three hours they fought, and the youngest sister was getting the better of the boy when the two others threw the chains around her. The boy dragged her away home with him then, and, when the stepmother saw the three sisters coming, herself and John's father were terrified and they died of fright, the two of them

John put food on the table and told the sisters to come and eat, but they refused, and the youngest told him that he must take her to the spot where he fought with her. All four went to that place, and at parting they promised never to harm him and to put him in the way that he would never need to do a day's work, nor his children after him, if he had any. The eldest sister told him to come on the following night, and to bring a spade with him; she would tell him, she said, her whole history from first to last.

He went, and what she told him was this: Long ago her father was one of the richest men in all Ireland; her mother died when the three sisters were very young, and ten or twelve years after the father died, and left the care of all the wealth and treasures in the castle to herself, telling her to make three equal parts of it, and to let herself and each of the other two sisters have one of those parts. But she was in love with a young man unknown to her father, and one night when the two sisters were fast asleep, and she thought if she killed them she would have the whole fortune for herself and her husband, she took a knife and cut their throats, and when she had them killed she got sorry and did the same to herself. The sentence put on them was that none of the three was to have rest or peace till some man without fear would come and conquer them, and John was the first to attempt this.

She took him then to her father's castle – only the ruins of it were standing, no roof and only some of the walls, and showed where all the riches and treasures were. John, to make sure, took his spade and dug away, dug with what strength was in him, and just before daybreak he came to the treasure. That moment the three sisters left good health with him, turned into three doves, and flew away.

He had riches enough for himself and for seven generations after him.

The Witch Hare

About the commencement of the last century there lived in the vicinity of the once famous village of Aghavoe a wealthy farmer, named Bryan Costigan. This man kept an extensive dairy and a great many milch cows and every year made considerable sums by the sale of milk and butter. The luxuriance of the pasture lands in this neighbourhood has always been proverbial; and, consequently, Bryan's cows were the finest and most productive in the country, and his milk and butter the richest and sweetest, and brought the highest price at every market at which he ordered these articles for sale.

Things continued to go on thus prosperously with Bryan Costigan, when, one season all at once, he found his cattle declining in appearance, and his dairy almost entirely profitless. Bryan, at first, attributed this change to the weather, or some such cause, but soon found or fancied reasons to assign it to a far different source. The cows, without any visible disorder, daily declined, and were scarcely able to crawl about on their pasture; many of them, instead of milk, gave nothing but blood; and the scanty quantity of milk which some of them continued to supply was so bitter that even the pigs would not drink it; while the butter which it produced was of such a bad quality, and stunk so horribly, that the very dogs would not eat it. Bryan applied for remedies to all the quacks and 'fairy-women' in the country – but in vain. Many of the imposters declared that the mysterious malady in his cattle went beyond *their* skill; while others, although they found no difficulty in tracing it to superhuman agency, declared that they had no control in the matter, as the charm under the influence of which his property was made away with, was too powerful to be dissolved by anything less than the special interposition of Divine Providence. The poor farmer became almost distracted; he saw ruin staring him in the face; yet what was he to do? Sell his cattle and purchase others! No; that was out of the question, as they looked so miserable and emaciated that no one would even take them as a present, while it was also impossible to sell to a butcher, as the flesh of one which he killed for his own family was as black as a coal, and stunk like any putrid carrion.

The unfortunate man was thus completely bewildered. He knew not what to do; he became moody and stupid; his sleep forsook him by night, and all day he wandered about the fields, among his 'fairy-stricken' cattle like a maniac.

Affairs continued in this plight, when one very sultry evening in the latter days of July, Bryan Costigan's wife was sitting at her own door, spinning at her wheel, in a very gloomy and agitated state of mind. Happening to look down the narrow green lane which led from the high road to her cabin, she espied a little old woman barefoot, and enveloped in an old scarlet cloak, approaching slowly, with the aid of a crutch which she carried in one hand, and a cane or walking-stick in the other. The farmer's wife felt glad at seeing the odd-looking stranger; she smiled, and yet she knew not why, as she neared the house. A vague and indefinable feeling of pleasure crowded on her imagination; and, as the old woman gained the threshold, she bade her 'welcome' with a warmth which plainly told that her lips gave utterance but to the genuine feelings of her heart.

'God bless this good house and all belonging to it,' said the stranger as she entered.

'God save you kindly, and you are welcome, whoever you are,' replied Mrs Costigan.

'Hem, I thought so,' said the old woman with a significant grin. 'I thought so, or I wouldn't trouble you.'

The farmer's wife ran, and placed a chair near the fire for the stranger, but she refused, and sat on the ground near where Mrs Costigan had been spinning. Mrs Costigan had now time to survey the old hag's person minutely. She appeared of great age; her countenance was extremely ugly and repulsive; her skin was rough and deeply embrowned as if from long exposure to the effects of some tropical climate; her forehead was low, narrow, and indented with a thousand wrinkles; her long grey hair fell in matted elf-locks from beneath a white linen skull cap; her eyes were bleared, bloodsotten, and obliquely set in their sockets, and her voice was croaking, tremulous, and, at times, partially inarticulate. As she squatted on the floor, she looked round the house with an inquisitive gaze; she peered pryingly from corner to corner, with an earnestness of look, as if she had the faculty, like the Argonaut of old, to see through the very depths of the earth, while Mrs C. kept watching her motions with mingled feelings of curiosity, awe, and pleasure.

'Mrs,' said the old woman, at length breaking silence, 'I am dry with the heat of the day; can you give me a drink?'

'Alas!' replied the farmer's wife, 'I have no drink to offer you except water, else you would have no occasion to ask me for it.'

'Are you not the owner of the cattle I see yonder?' said the old hag, with a tone of voice and manner of gesticulation which plainly indicated her foreknowledge of the fact.

Mrs Costigan replied in the affirmative, and briefly related to her every circumstance connected with the affair, while the old woman still remained silent, but shook her grey head repeatedly and still continued gazing round the house with an air of importance and self-sufficiency.

When Mrs C. had ended, the old hag remained a while as if in a deep reverie; at length she said: 'Have you any of the milk in the house?'

'I have,' replied the other.

'Show me some of it.'

She filled a jug from a vessel and handed it to the old sybil, who smelled it, then tasted it, and spat out what she had taken on the floor.

'Where is your husband?' she asked.

'Out in the fields,' was the reply.

'I must see him.'

A messenger was despatched for Bryan, who shortly after made his appearance.

'Neighbour,' said the stranger, 'your wife informs me that your cattle are going against you this season.'

'She informs you right,' said Bryan.

'And why have you not sought a cure?'

'A cure!' re-echoed the man; 'why, woman, I have sought cures until I was heartbroken, and all in vain; they get worse every day.'

'What will you give me if I cure them for you?'

'Anything in our power,' replied Bryan and his wife, both speaking joyfully, and with a breath.

'All I will ask from you is a silver sixpence, and that you will do everything which I will bid you,' said she.

The farmer and his wife seemed astonished at the moderation of her demand. They offered her a large sum of money.

'No,' said she, 'I don't want your money; I am no cheat, and I would not even take sixpence, but that I can do nothing till I handle some of your silver.'

The sixpence was immediately given her, and the most implicit obedience promised to her injunctions by both Bryan and his wife, who already began to regard the old beldame as their tutelary angel.

The hag pulled off a black silk ribbon or filet which encircled her head inside her cap, and gave it to Bryan, saying: 'Go, now, and the first cow you touch with this ribbon, turn her into the yard, but be sure you don't touch the second, nor speak a word until you return; be also careful not to let the ribbon touch the ground, for, if you do, all is over.'

Bryan took the talismanic ribbon and soon returned, driving a red cow before him.

The old hag went out, and, approaching the cow, commenced pulling hairs out of her tail, at the same time singing some verse in the Irish language, in a low, wild, and unconnected strain. The cow appeared restive and uneasy, but the old witch still continued her mysterious chant until she had the ninth hair extracted. She then ordered the cow to be drove back to her pasture, and again entered the house.

'Go, now,' said she to the woman, 'and bring me some milk from every cow in your possession.'

She went, and soon returned with a large pail filled with a frightful-looking mixture of milk, blood, and corrupt matter. The old woman got it into the churn, and made preparations for churning.

'Now,' she said, 'you both must churn, make fast the door and windows, and let there be no light but from the fire; do not open your lips until I desire you, and by observing my direction, I make no doubt but, ere the sun goes down, we will find out the infernal villain who is robbing you.'

Bryan secured the doors and windows, and commenced churning.

The old sorceress sat down by a blazing fire which had been specially lighted for the occasion, and commenced singing the same wild song which she had sung at the pulling of the cow hairs, and after a little time she cast one of the nine hairs into the fire, still singing her mysterious strain, and watching, with intense interest, the witching process.

A loud cry, as if from a female in distress, was now heard approaching the house; the old witch discontinued her incantations, and listened attentively. The crying voice approached the door.

'Open the door quickly,' shouted the charmer.

Bryan unbarred the door, and all three rushed out the yard, when they heard the same cry down the *boreheen*, but could see nothing.

'It is all over,' shouted the old witch; 'something has gone amiss, and our charm for the present is ineffectual.'

They now turned back quite crestfallen, when, as they were entering the door, the sybil cast her eyes downward, and perceiving a piece of horseshoe nailed on the threshold, she vociferated: 'Here I have it; no wonder our charm was abortive. The person that was crying abroad is the villain who has your cattle bewitched; I brought her to the house, but she was not able to come to the door on account of that horseshoe. Remove it instantly, and we will try our luck again.'

Bryan removed the horseshoe from the doorway, and by the hag's directions placed it on the floor under the churn, having previously reddened it in the fire.

They again resumed their manual operations. Bryan and his wife began to churn, and the witch again to sing her strange verses, and casting her cow hairs into the fire until she had them all nearly exhausted. Her countenance now began to exhibit evident traces of vexation and disappointment. She got quite pale, her teeth gnashed, her hand trembled, and as she cast the ninth and last hair into the fire, her person exhibited more the appearance of a female demon than of a human being.

Once more the cry was heard, and an aged red-haired woman was seen approaching the house quickly.

'Ho, ho!' roared the sorceress, 'I knew it would be so; my charm has succeeded; my expectations are realised, and here she comes, the villain who has destroyed you.'

'What are we to do now?' asked Bryan.

'Say nothing to her,' said the hag; 'give her whatever she demands, and leave the rest to me.'

The woman advanced screeching vehemently, and Bryan went out to meet her. She was a neighbour, and she said that one of her best cows was drowning in a pool of water – that there was no one at home but herself, and she implored Bryan to go rescue the cow from destruction.

Bryan accompanied her without hesitation; and having rescued the cow from her perilous situation, was back again in a quarter of an hour.

It was now sunset, and Mrs Costigan set about preparing supper.

During supper they reverted to the singular transactions of the day. The old witch uttered many a fiendish laugh at the success of her incantations, and enquired who was the woman whom they had so curiously discovered.

Bryan satisfied her in every particular. She was the wife of a neighbouring farmer; her name was Rachel Higgins; and she had been long suspected to be on familiar terms with the spirit of darkness. She had five or six cows; but it was observed by her sapient neighbours that she sold more butter every year than other farmers' wives who had twenty. Bryan had, from the commencement of the decline in his cattle, suspected her for being the aggressor, but as he had no proof, he held his peace.

'Well,' said the old beldame, with a grim smile, 'it is not enough that we have merely discovered the robber; all is in vain if we do not take steps to punish her for the past, as well as to prevent her inroads for the future.'

'And how will that be done?' said Bryan.

'I will tell you; as soon as the hour of twelve o'clock arrives tonight, do you go to the pasture, and take a couple of swift-running dogs with you; conceal yourself in some place convenient to the cattle; watch them carefully; and if you see anything, whether man or beast, approach the cows, set on the dogs, and if possible make them draw the blood of the intruder; then *all* will be accomplished. If nothing approaches before sunrise, you may return, and we will try something else.'

Convenient there lived the cowherd of a neighbouring squire. He was a hardy, courageous young man, and always kept a pair of very ferocious bulldogs. To him Bryan applied for assistance, and he cheerfully agreed to accompany him, and, moreover, proposed to fetch a couple of his master's best greyhounds, as his own dogs, although extremely fierce and bloodthirsty, could not be relied on for swiftness. He promised Bryan to be with him before twelve o'clock, and they parted.

Bryan did not seek sleep that night; he sat up anxiously awaiting the midnight hour. It arrived at last, and his friend, the herdsman, true to his promise, came at the time appointed. After some further admonitions from the *Collough*, they departed. Having arrived at the field, they consulted as to the best position they could choose for concealment. At last they pitched on a small brake of fern, situated at the extremity of the field, adjacent to the boundary ditch, which was thickly studded with large, old white-thorn bushes. Here they crouched themselves, and made the dogs, four in number, lie down beside them, eagerly expecting the appearance of their as yet unknown and mysterious visitor.

Here Bryan and his comrade continued a considerable time in nervous anxiety, still nothing approached, and it became manifest that morning was at hand; they were beginning to grow impatient, and were talking of returning home, when on a sudden they heard a rushing sound behind them, as if proceeding from something endeavouring to force a passage through the thick hedge in their rear. They looked in that direction, and judge of their astonishment, when they perceived a large hare in the act of springing from the ditch, and leaping on the ground quite near them. They were now convinced that this was the object which they had so impatiently expected, and they were resolved to watch her motions narrowly.

After arriving to the ground, she remained motionless for a few moments, looking around her sharply. She then began to skip and jump in a playful manner, now advancing at a smart pace toward the cows and again retreating precipitately, but still drawing nearer and nearer at each sally. At length she advanced up to the next cow, and sucked her for a moment; then on to the next, and so respectively to every cow on the field – the cows all the time lowing loudly, and appearing extremely frightened and agitated. Bryan, from the moment the hare commenced sucking the first, was with difficulty restrained from attacking her; but his more sagacious companion suggested to him that it was better to wait until she would have done, as she would then be much heavier, and more unable to effect her escape than at present. And so the issue proved; for being now done sucking them all, her belly appeared enormously distended, and she made her exit slowly and apparently with difficulty. She advanced toward the hedge where she had entered, and as she arrived just at the clump of ferns where her foes were couched, they started up with a fierce yell, and hallooed the dogs upon her path.

The hare started off at a brisk pace, squirting up the milk she had sucked from her mouth and nostrils, and the dogs making after her rapidly. Rachel Higgins's cabin appeared, through the grey of the morning twilight, at a little distance; and it was evident that puss seemed bent on gaining it, although she made a considerable circuit through the fields in the rear. Bryan and his comrade, however, had their thoughts, and made toward the cabin by the shortest route, and had just arrived as the hare came up panting and almost exhausted, and the dogs at her very scut. She ran round the house, evidently confused and disappointed at the presence of the men, but at length made for the door. In the bottom of the door was a small, semicircular aperture, resembling those cut in fowl-house doors for the ingress and egress of poultry. To gain this hole, puss now made a last and desperate effort, and had succeeded in forcing her head and shoulders through it, when the foremost of the dogs made a spring and seized her violently by the haunch. She uttered a loud and piercing scream, and struggled desperately to free herself from his grip, and at last succeeded, but not until she left a piece of her rump in his teeth. The men now burst open the door; a bright turf fire blazed on the hearth, and the whole floor was streaming with blood. No hare, however, could be found, and the men were more than ever convinced that it was old Rachel, who had, by the assistance of some demon, assumed the form of the hare, and they now determined to have her if she were over the earth. They entered the bedroom, and heard some smothered groaning, as if proceeding from someone in extreme agony. They went to the corner of the room from whence the moans proceeded, and there, beneath a bundle of freshly-cut rushes, found the form of Rachel Higgins, writhing in the most excruciating agony, and almost smothered in a pool of blood. The men were astounded; they addressed the wretched old woman, but she either could not, or would not, answer them. Her wound still bled copiously; her tortures appeared to increase, and it was evident that she was dying. The aroused family thronged around her with cries and lamentations; she did not seem to heed them, she got worse and worse, and her piercing yells fell awfully on the ears of the bystanders. At length she expired, and her corpse exhibited a most appalling spectacle, even before the spirit had well departed.

Bryan and his friend returned home. The old hag had been previously aware of the fate of Rachel Higgins, but it was not known by what means she acquired her supernatural knowledge. She was delighted at the issue of her mysterious operations. Bryan pressed her much to accept of some remuneration for her services, but she utterly rejected such proposals. She remained a few days at his house, and at length took her leave and departed, no one knew whither.

Old Rachel's remains were interred that night in the neighbouring churchyard. Her fate soon became generally known, and her family, ashamed to remain in their native village, disposed of their property, and quitted the country forever. The story, however, is still fresh in the memory of the surrounding villagers; and often, it is said, amid the grey haze of a summer twilight, may the ghost of Rachel Higgins, in the form of a hare, be seen scudding over her favourite and well-remembered haunts.

TRADITIONAL

Donald and His Neighbours

❧❧

Hudden and Dudden and Donald O'Nery were near neighbours in the barony of Balinconlig, and plowed with three bullocks; but the two former, envying the present prosperity of the latter, determined to kill his bullock, to prevent his farm from being properly cultivated and laboured, that going back in the world he might be induced to sell his lands, which they meant to get possession of. Poor Donald, finding his bullock killed, immediately skinned it, and throwing the skin over his shoulder, with the fleshy side out, set off to the next town with it, to dispose of it to the best of his advantage. Going along the road a magpie flew on the top of the hide, and began picking it, chattering all the time. The bird had been taught to speak, and imitate the human voice, and Donald, thinking he understood some words it was saying, put round his hand and caught hold of it. Having got possession of it, he put it under his greatcoat, and so went on to town. Having sold the hide, he went into an inn to take a dram, and following the landlady into the cellar, he gave the bird a squeeze which made it chatter some broken accents that surprised her very much. 'What is that I hear?' said she to Donald. 'I think it is talk and yet I do not understand.' 'Indeed,' said Donald, 'it is a bird I have that tells me everything, and I always carry it with me to know when there is any danger. 'Faith,' says he, 'it says you have far better liquor than you are giving me.' 'That is strange,' said she, going to another cask of better quality, and asking him if he would sell the bird. 'I will,' said Donald, 'if I get enough for it.' 'I will fill your hat with silver if you leave it with me.' Donald was glad to hear the news, and taking the silver, set off, rejoicing at his good luck. He had not been long at home until he met with Hudden and Dudden. 'Mr,' said he, 'you thought you had done me a bad turn, but you could not have done me a better; for look here, what I have got for the hide,' showing them a hatful of silver; 'you never saw such a demand for hides in your life as there is at present.' Hudden and Dudden that very night killed their bullocks, and set out the next morning to sell their hides. On coming to the place they went through all the merchants, but could only get a trifle for them; at last they had to take what they could get, and came home in a great rage, and vowing revenge on poor Donald. He had a pretty good guess how matters would turn out, and he being under the kitchen window, he was afraid they would rob him, or perhaps kill him when asleep, and on that account when he was going to bed he left his old mother in his place, and lay down in her bed, which was in the other side of the house, and they taking the old woman for Donald, choked her in her bed, but he making some noise, they had to retreat, and leave the money behind them, which grieved them very much. However by daybreak, Donald got his mother on his back, and carried her to town. Stopping at a well, he fixed his mother with her staff, as if she was stooping for a drink, and then went into a public house convenient and called for a dram. 'I wish,' said he to a woman that stood near him, 'you would tell my mother to come in; she is at yon well trying to get a drink, and she is hard of hearing; if she does not observe you, give her a little shake and tell her that I want her.' The woman called her several times, but she seemed to take no notice; at length she went to her and shook her by the arm, but when she let her go again, she tumbled on her head into the well, and, as the woman thought, was drowned. She, in her great surprise and fear at the accident, told Donald what had happened. 'O mercy,' said he, 'what is this?' He ran and pulled her out of the well, weeping and lamenting all the time, and acting in such a manner that you would imagine that he had lost his senses. The woman, on the other hand, was far worse than Donald, for his grief was only feigned, but she imagined herself to be the cause of the old woman's death. The inhabitants of the town, hearing what had happened, agreed to make Donald up a good sum of money for his loss, as the accident happened in their place, and Donald brought a greater sum home with him than he got for the magpie. They buried Donald's mother, and as soon as he saw Hudden and Dudden he showed them the last purse of money he had got. 'You thought to kill me last night,' said he, 'but it was good for me it happened on my mother, for I got all that purse for her to make gunpowder.'

That very night Hudden and Dudden killed their mothers, and the next morning set off with them to town. On coming to the town with their burthen on their sacks, they went up and down crying, 'Who will buy old wives for gunpowder?' so that everyone laughed at them, and the boys at last clotted them out of the place. They then saw the cheat, and vowed revenge on Donald, buried the old women, and set off in pursuit of him. Coming to his house, they found him sitting at his breakfast, and seizing him, put him in a sack, and went to drown him in a river at some distance. As they were going along the highway they raised a hare, which they saw had but three feet, and throwing off the sack, ran after her, thinking by her appearance she would be easily taken. In their absence there came a drover that way, and hearing Donald singing in the sack, wondered greatly what could be the matter. 'What is the reason,' said he, 'that you are singing, and you confined?' 'Oh, I am going to heaven,' said Donald, 'and in a short time I expect to be free from trouble.' 'O dear,' said the drover, 'what will I give you if you let me to your place?' 'Indeed, I do not know,' said he, 'it would take a good sum.' 'I have not much money,' said the drover, 'but I have twenty head of fine cattle, which I will give you to exchange places with me.' 'Well,' says Donald, 'I do not care if I should loose the sack, and I will come out.' In a moment the drover liberated him, and went into the sack himself, and Donald drove home the fine heifers, and left them in his pasture. Hudden and Dudden, having caught the hare, returned, and getting the sack on one of their backs, carried Donald, as they thought, to the river and threw him in, where he immediately sank. They then marched home, intending to take immediate possession of Donald's property, but how great was their surprise when they found him safe at home before them with such a fine herd of cattle, whereas they knew he had none before. 'Donald,' said they, 'what is all this? We thought you were drowned, and yet you are here before us.' 'Ah!' said he, 'if I had but help along with me when you threw me in, it would have been the best job ever I met with, for of all the sight of cattle and gold that ever was seen is there, and no one to own them, but I was not able to manage more than what you see, and I could show you the spot where you might get hundreds.' They both swore they would be his friend, and Donald accordingly led them to a very deep part of the river, and lifted up a stone. 'Now,' said he, 'Watch this,' throwing it into the stream; 'there is the very place, and go in, one of you first, and if you want help, you have nothing to do but call.' Hudden jumping in, and sinking to the bottom, rose up again, and making a bubbling noise, as those do that are drowning, attempted to speak, but could not. 'What is that he is saying now?' says Dudden 'Faith,' says Donald, 'he is calling for help; don't you hear him?' 'Stand about,' said he, running back, 'till I leap in. I know how to do it better than any of you.' Dudden, to have the advantage of him, jumped in off the bank, and was drowned along with Hudden, and this was the end of Hudden and Dudden.

PATRICK KENNEDY

Hairy Rouchy

❧

There was once a widow woman, as often there was, and she had three daughters. The eldest and the second eldest were as handsome as the moon and the evening star, but the youngest was all covered with hair, and her face was as brown as a berry, and they called her Hairy Rouchy. She lighted the fire in the morning, cooked the food, and made the beds, while her sisters would be stringing flowers on a hank, or looking at themselves in the glass, or sitting with their hands across. 'No one will ever come to marry us in this lonesome place,' said the eldest, one day; 'so you and I,' said she to the second sister, 'may as well go seek our fortune.' 'That's the best word you ever spoke,' said the other. 'Bake our cake and kill our cock, mother, and away we go.' Well, so she did. 'And now, girls,' said she, 'which will you have, half this with my blessing, or the whole of it with my curse?' 'Curse or no curse, mother, the whole of it is little enough.'

Well, they set off, and says Hairy Rouchy to her mother when they got to the end of the lane, 'Mother, give me your blessing, and a quarter of the griddle cake, I must go after these girls, for I fear ill luck is in their road.' She gave her blessing and the whole of the cake, and she went off running, and soon overtook them. 'Here's Hairy Rouchy,' says the eldest, 'she'll make a show of us. We'll tie her to this big stone.' So they tied her to the big stone and went their way, but when they were a quarter of a mile further, there she was three perches behind them. Well, they were vexed enough, and the next clamp of turf they passed, they made her lie down, and piled every sod of it over her.

When they were a quarter of a mile further they looked back again, and there was the girl three perches behind them, and weren't they mad! To make a long story short, they fastened her in a pound, and they put the tying of the three smalls on her, and fastened her to a tree. The next quarter of a mile she was up by their side, and at last they were tired, and let her walk behind them.

Well, they walked and they walked till they were tired, and till the greyness of night came round them, and they saw a light at a distance. When they came up, what was it but a giant's house, and great sharp teeth were in the heads of himself, and his wife, and his three daughters. Well, they got lodging, and when sleep time was coming they were put into one bed, and the giant's daughters' bed touched the head of theirs. Well becomes my brave Hairy Rouchy, when the giant's daughters were asleep, she took off the hair necklaces from her own neck and the necks of her sisters, and put them on the giant's daughters' necks, and she put their gold and silver and diamond necklaces on the necks of her sisters and herself, and then watched to see what would happen.

The giant and his wife were sitting by the fire, and says he, 'Won't these girls make a fine meat pie for us tomorrow.' 'Won't they,' says she, and she smacked her lips, 'but I'll have some trouble singeing that hairy one.' 'They are all asleep now,' says he, and he called in his red-headed *giolla* [servant]. 'Go and put them strangers out of pain,' says he. 'But how'll I know them from your daughters,' says the giolla. 'Very easy, they have only hair necklaces round their necks.'

Well, you may all guess what happened. So the night faded away, and the morning came, and what did the giant see at the flight of darkness, when the gate was opened by the cowboy, but Hairy Rouchy walking out through it after her two sisters. Down the stairs he came, five at a time, and out of the bawn he flew, and *magh go bragh* with him after the girls. The eldest screamed out, and the second eldest screamed out, but the youngest took one under each arm, and if she didn't lay leg to ground, you may call me a storyteller. She ran like the wind, and the giant ran like the north wind; the sparks of fire he struck out of the stones hit her on the back, and the sparks of fire she struck out of the stones scorched his face. At last they came near the wide and deep river that divided his land from the land of the King of Spain, and into that land he daren't pass. Over the wide deep river went Hairy Rouchy with a high, very active bound, and after her went the giant. His heels touched the bank, and back into the water went his head and body. He dragged himself out on his own side, and sat down on the bank, and looked across, and this is what he said: 'You're there, Hairy Rouchy,' says he. 'No thanks to you for it,' says she. 'You got my three daughters killed,' says he. 'It was to save our own lives,' says she. 'When will you come to see me again,' says he. 'When I have business,' says she. 'Divel be in your road,' says he. 'It's better pray than curse,' says she.

The three girls went on till they came to the King of Spain's castle, where they were well entertained, and the King's eldest son and the eldest sister fell in love with one another, and the second son and the second sister fell in love with one another, and poor Hairy Rouchy fell in love with the youngest son, but he didn't fall in love with her.

Well, the next day, when they were at breakfast, says the King to her, 'Good was your deed at the giant's house, and if you only bring me the talking golden quilt that's covering himself and his wife, my eldest son may marry your eldest sister.' 'I'll try, says she, 'worse than lose I can't.'

So that night, when the giant and his wife were fast asleep, the quilt felt a hand pulling it off the bed. 'Who are you?' says the quilt. 'Mishe' [myself], says the girl, and she pulled away. 'Waken, master,' says the quilt, 'someone is taking me away.' 'And who's taking you away?' says he. 'It's mische that's doing it,' says the quilt. 'Then let mishe stop his tricks, and not be disturbing us.' 'But I tell you, mishe is carrying me off.' 'If mishe says another word, I'll get up and throw him in the fire.' So the poor quilt had nothing to do but hold its tongue.

'But,' says the giant's wife, after a few minutes, 'maybe the divel bewitched the quilt to walk off with itself.' 'Faith and maybe so,' says the giant; 'I'll get up and look.' So he searched the room, and the stairs, and the hall, and the bawn, and the bawn gate was open, '*Mile mollachd*,' says he; 'Hairy Rouchy was here,' and to the road he took. But when he was on the hill she was in the hollow, and when he was in the hollow she was on the hill, and when he came to the hither side of the river she was on the thither. 'You're there, Hairy Rouchy,' says he. 'No thanks to you,' says she. 'You took away my speaking golden quilt,' says he. 'It was to get my eldest sister married,' says she. 'When will you come back?' 'Divel be in your road,' says he. 'It's better pray than curse,' says she; and the same night the speaking golden quilt was covering the Kind and Queen of Spain.

Well, the wedding was made, but there was little notice taken of poor Hairy Rouchy, and she spent a good part of the day talking to a poor travelling woman that she often relieved at home and that was come by accident as far as Spain.

So the next day, when they were at breakfast again, says the King, 'Hairy Rouchy, if you bring me tomorrow morning, the *chloive solais* [sword of light] that hangs at the giant's bed's head, my second son will marry your second sister.' 'I'll make the trial,' says she; 'worse than lose I can't.'

Well, the next night the giant's wife was boiling his big pot of gruel, and Hairy Rouchy was sitting by the chimbly on the straws that covered the ridge pole, and dropping fistfuls of salt into the pot. 'You put too much salt in this porridge,' says the giant to his wife, when he was supping it. 'I'm sure I didn't put in more than four spoonfuls,' says she. 'Well, well, that was the right size; still it tastes mortial salty.'

When he was in bed he cries out, 'Wife, I'll be a piece of cured bacon before morning if I don't get a drink.' 'Oh, then, purshuin to the sup of water in the house,' says she. 'Well, call up the giolla out of the settle, and let him bring a pailful from the well.' So, the giolla got up in a bad humour, scratching his head, and went to the door with the pail in his hand. There was Hairy Rouchy by the jamb, and maybe she didn't dash fistfuls of sand and salt into his eyes. 'Oh, master, master,' says he, 'the sky is as black as your hat, and it's pelting hail-stones on me; I'll never find the well.' 'Here you *onshuch*, take the sword of light, and it will show you the way.'

So he took the *chloive solais*, and made his way to the well, and while he was filling the pail he laid the sword on the ground. That was all the girl wanted. She snatched it up, waved it round her head, and the light flashed over hills and hollows. 'If you're not into the house like a shot,' says she, 'I'll send your head half a mile away.' The poor giolla was only too glad to get off, and she was soon flying like the wind to the river, and the giant hot foot after her. When she was in the hollow he was on the hill . . .

'You're a very good girl, indeed,' says the King of Spain to Hairy Rouchy, the morning after the second marriage. 'You deserve a reward. So bring me the giant's *puckawn* [a goat-sprite] with the golden bells round his neck as soon as you like, and you must get my youngest son for a husband.' 'But maybe he won't have me,' says she. 'Indeed an' I will,' says the prince; 'so good a sister can't make a bad wife.' 'But I'm all hairy and brown,' says she. 'That's no sin,' says the prince.

Sure enough, the night after, she was hard and fast in the giant's outhouse, stuffing the puckawn's bells with the marrow of the elder; and when she thought the job was well finished she was leading him out. She had a band on his mouth, but when my brave puck found he couldn't bawl, he took to rear and kick like a puck as he was. Out came the elder marrow from three of the bells, and the sound that came from them was enough to waken the dead. She drove him at his full speed before her, but after came the giant like a storm. She could escape him if she liked, but she would not return without puck, and bedad she was soon pinned and brought back to the giant's big kitchen. There was his wife and the giolla, and if he wasn't proud to show them his prisoner there's not a glove in Wexford.

'Now, ma'am,' says he to her, 'I have you safe after all the mischief you done me. If I was in your power what would you do to me?' 'Oh, wouldn't I tie you up to the ceiling in a sack, you ould tyrant, and go myself and giolla to the wood, cut big clubs, and break every bone in your body one after another. Then if there was any life left in you, we'd make a fire of the green boughs underneath, and stifle the little that was left out of you.' 'The very thing I'll do with you,' says he.

So he put her in a sack, tied her up to the beam that went across the kitchen, and went off with the giolla to the wood to cut down the clubs and green branches, leaving his wife to watch the prisoner. She expected to hear crying and sobbing from out of the sack, but the girl did nothing but shout and laugh. 'Is it mad, you are,' says she, 'and death so near you?' 'Death indeed. Why, the bottom of the sack is full of diamonds, and pearls, and guineas, and there is the finest views all round me you ever see – castles, and lawns, and lakes, and the finest flowers.' 'Is it lies you're telling?' 'Oh, dickens a lie. If I'd let you up, but I won't, you'd see and feel it all.'

But the giant's wife over-persuaded her, and when she was loosened, and got the other into the sack, she tied her hard and fast, ran to the outhouse, threw a rope round the puckawn's neck, and he and she were soon racing like the wind toward the river. The giant and the giolla were soon back, and he wondered where his wife could be. But he saw the sack still full, and the two began to whack it like so many blacksmiths. 'Oh, Lord,' says the poor woman, 'it's myself that's here.'

But she roared out, 'Ah, sure, I'm your wife, don't kill me for goodness sake.' 'Be the laws,' says the giolla, 'it's the mistress. Oh, bad luck to you, Hairy Rouchy; this is your doing. Run and catch her, master, while I take the poor mistress down, and see what I can do for her.' Off went the big fellow like a *bowarra*, but when he came to this side of the river, panting and puffing, there was the girl and his darling puckawn on the other side, and she ready to burst her sides with the laughing.

'You're there, my damsel,' 'No thanks, etc.' So the scolding match went on to the end and then says he, 'If you were in my place and I in yours now, what would you do?' 'I'd stoop down and drink the river dry to get at you.' But she didn't stop to see whether he was fool enough to take her advice, but led her goat to the palace. Oh, wasn't there great joy and clapping of hands when the golden bells were heard a-ringing up the avenue, and into the big bawn. She didn't mind how anyone looked but the youngest prince; and though he didn't appear very rejoiced, there was a kind of smile in his face, and she was satisfied.

Well, the next morning, when they were all setting out to the church, and the bridegroom was mounted on his horse, and the bride getting into the coach, she asked him for leave to take the poor travelling woman in along with her. 'It's a queer request,' says he, 'but do as you like; you must have some reason for it.' Well, when all were dismounting or getting out of their coaches, he went to open the door for his bride, and the sight almost left his eyes; for there sitting fornent him was the most beautiful young woman he ever beheld. She had the same kind innocent look that belonged to Hairy Rouchy, but she had also the finest colour in her face, and neck, and hands, and her hair, instead of the tangled brake it used to be, was nicely plaited and curled, and was the finest dark brown in the world.

Glad enough she was to see the joy and surprise in his face, and if they were not the happy bride and bridegroom I never saw one. When they were talking by themselves, she told him that an enchantment was laid on her when she was a child, and she was always to remain the fright she was, till someone would marry her for the sake of her disposition. The travelling woman was her guardian fairy in disguise. There were two unhappy marriages and one happy one in the King of Spain's family, and I'll let everyone here guess which was which.

THOMAS CROFTON CROCKER

The Legend of Knockgrafton

There was once a poor man who lived in the fertile glen of Aherlow, at the foot of the gloomy Galtee mountains, and he had a great hump on his back: he looked just as if his body had been rolled up and placed upon his shoulders; and his head was pressed down with the weight so much that his chin, when the was sitting, used to rest upon his knees for support. The country people were rather shy of meeting him in any lonesome place, for though, poor creature, he was as harmless and as inoffensive as a new-born infant, yet his deformity was so great that he scarcely appeared to be a human creature, and some ill-minded persons had set strange stories about him afloat. He was said to have a great knowledge of herbs and charms; but certain it was that he had a mighty skilful hand in plaiting straws and rushes into hats and baskets, which was the way he made his livelihood.

Lusmore, for that was the nickname put upon him by reason of his always wearing a sprig of the fairy cap, or lusmore (the foxglove), in his little straw hat, would ever get a higher penny for his plaited work than anyone else, and perhaps that was the reason why someone, out of envy, had circulated the strange stories about him. Be that as it may, it happened that he was returning one evening from the pretty town of Cahir toward Cappagh, and as little Lusmore walked very slowly, on account of the great hump upon his back, it was quite dark when he came to the old moat of Knockgrafton, which stood on the right-hand side of his road.

Tired and weary was he, and no ways comfortable in his own mind at thinking how much farther he had to travel, and that he should be walking all the night; so he sat down under the moat to rest himself, and began looking mournfully enough upon the moon, which, 'Rising in clouded majesty, at length Apparent Queen, unveil'd her peerless light, And o'er the dark her silver mantle threw.'

Presently there rose a wild strain of unearthly melody upon the ear of little Lusmore; he listened, and he thought that he had never heard such ravishing music before. It was like the sound of many voices, each mingling and blending with the other so strangely that they seemed to be one, though all singing different strains, and the words of the song were these: '*Da Luan, Da Mort, Da Luan, Da Mort, Da Luan, Da Mort.*' There would be a moment's pause, and then the round of melody went on again.

Lusmore listened attentively, scarcely drawing his breath lest he might lose the slightest note. He now plainly perceived that the singing was within the moat; and though at first it had charmed him so much, he began to get tired of hearing the same round sung over and over so often without any change; so availing himself of the pause when '*Da Luan, Da Mort*', had been sung three times, he took up the tune, and raised it with the words '*agus Da Dardeen*', and then went on singing with the voices inside of the moat, '*Da Luan, Da Mort*', finishing the melody, when the pause again came, with '*agus Da Dardeen*'. [The words *La Luan, Da Mort agus Da Dardeen* are Irish for 'Monday, Tuesday, and Wednesday too.']

The fairies within Knockgrafton, for the song was a fairy melody, when they heard this addition to the tune, were so much delighted that, with instant resolve, it was determined to bring the mortal among them, whose musical skill so far exceeded theirs, and little Lusmore was conveyed into their company with the eddying speed of a whirlwind.

Glorious to behold was the sight that burst upon him as he came down through the moat, twirling round and round, with the lightness of a straw, to the sweetest music that kept time to his motion. The greatest honour was then paid him, for he was put above all the musicians, and he had servants tending upon him, and everything to his heart's content, and a hearty welcome to all; and, in short, he was made as much of as if he had been the first man in the land.

Presently Lusmore saw a great consultation going forward among the fairies, and, notwithstanding all their civility, he felt very much frightened, until one stepping out from the rest came up to him and said:

'Lusmore! Lusmore!
Doubt not, nor deplore,
For the hump which you bore
On your back is no more;
Look down on the floor,
And view it, Lusmore! Lusmore!'

When these words were said poor little Lusmore felt himself so light, and so happy, that he thought he could have bounded at one jump over the moon, like the cow in the history of the cat and the fiddle; and he saw, with inexpressible pleasure, his hump tumble down upon the ground from his shoulders. He then tried to lift up his head, and he did so with becoming caution, fearing that he might knock it against the ceiling of the grand hall, where he was; he looked round and round again with the greatest wonder and delight upon everything, which appeared more and more beautiful; and, over-powered at beholding such a resplendent scene, his head grew dizzy, and his eyesight became dim. At last he fell into a sound sleep, and when he awoke he found that it was broad daylight, the sun shining brightly, and the birds singing sweetly; and that he was lying just at the foot of the moat of Knockgrafton, with the cows and sheep grazing peacefully round about him. The first thing Lusmore did, after saying his prayers, was to put his hand behind to feel for his hump, but no sign of one was there on his back, and he looked at himself with great pride, for he had now become a well-shaped, dapper little fellow, and more than that, found himself in a full suit of new clothes, which he concluded the fairies had made for him.

Toward Cappagh he went, stepping out as lightly, and springing up at every step as if he had been all his life dancing-master. Not a creature who met Lusmore knew him without his hump, and he had a great work to persuade everyone that he was the same man – in truth he was not, so far as the outward appearances went.

Of course it was not long before the story of Lusmore's hump got about, and a great wonder was made of it. Through the country, for miles round, it was the talk of everyone, high and low.

One morning, as Lusmore was sitting contented enough at his cabin door, up came an old woman to him and asked him if he could direct her to Cappagh.

'I need give you no directions, my good woman,' said Lusmore, 'for this is Cappagh; and whom may you want here?'

'I have come,' said the woman, 'out of Decie's country, in the country of Waterford, looking after one Lusmore, who, I have heard tell, had his hump taken off by the fairies; for there is a son of a gossip of mine who has got a hump on him that will be his death; and maybe, if he could use the same charm as Lusmore the hump may be taken off him. And now I have told you the reason of my coming so far: 'tis to find out about this charm, if I can.'

Lusmore, who was ever a good-natured little fellow, told the woman all the particulars, how he had raised the tune for the fairies at Knockgrafton, how his hump had been removed from his shoulders, and how he had got a new suit of clothes into the bargain.

The woman thanked him very much, and then went away quite happy and easy in her own mind. When she came back to her gossip's house, in the county of Waterford, she told her everything that Lusmore had said and they put the little humpbacked man, who was a peevish and cunning creature from his birth, upon a car, and took him all the way across the county. It was a long journey, but they did not care for that, so the hump was taken from off him; and they brought him, just at nightfall, and left him under the old moat of Knockgrafton.

Jack Madden, for that was the humpy man's name, had not been sitting there long when he heard the tune going on within the moat much sweeter than before; for the fairies were singing it the way Lusmore had settled their music for them, and the song was going on: *'Da Luan, Da Mort, Da Luan, Da Mort, Da Luan, Da Mort, agus Da Dardeen'*, without ever stopping. Jack Madden, who was in a great hurry to get quit of his hump, never thought of waiting until the fairies had done, or watching for a fit opportunity to raise the tune higher again than Lusmore had; so having heard them sing it over seven times without stopping, out he bawls, never minding the time or the humour of the tune, or how he could bring his words in properly, *'agus Da Dardeen, agus Da Hena'*, thinking that if one day was good, two were better; and that if Lusmore had one new suit of clothes given him, he should have two. [*Da Hena* is Thursday.]

No sooner had the words passed his lips than he was taken up and whisked into the moat with prodigious force; and the fairies came crowding round about him with great anger, screeching and screaming, and roaring out: 'Who spoiled our tune? Who spoiled our tune?' and one stepped up to him above all the rest, and said:

> 'Jack Madden, Jack Madden
> Your words come so bad in
> The tune we felt glad in;
> This castle you're had in,
> That your life we may sadden;
> Here's two humps for Jack Madden!'

And twenty of the strongest fairies brought Lusmore's hump, and put it down upon poor Jack's back, over his own, where it became fixed as firmly as if it was nailed on with twelve-penny nails, by the best carpenter that ever drove one. Out of their castle they then kicked him; and in the morning, when Jack Madden's mother and her gossip came to look after their little man, they found him half dead, lying at the foot of the moat, with the other hump upon his back. Well to be sure, how they did look at each other! but they were afraid to say anything, lest a hump might be put upon their own shoulders. Home they brought the unlucky Jack Madden with them, as downcast in their hearts and their looks as ever two gossips were; and what through the weight of his other hump, and the long journey, he died soon after, leaving, they say, his heavy curse to anyone who would go to listen to fairy tunes again.

THOMAS CROFTON CROKER

Daniel O'Rourke

People may have heard of the renowned adventures of Daniel O'Rourke, but how few are there who know that the cause of all his perils, above and below, was neither more nor less than his having slept under the walls of the Pooka's tower. I knew the man well. He lived at the bottom of Hungry Hill, just at the right-hand side of the road as you go toward Bantry. An old man was he, at the time he told me the story, with grey hair and red nose; and it was on the 25th of June, 1813, that I heard it from his own lips, as he sat smoking his pipe under the old poplar tree, on as fine an evening as ever shone from the sky. I was going to visit the caves in Dursey Island, having spent the morning at Glengariff.

'I am often *axed* to tell it, sir,' said he, 'so that this is not the first time. The master's son, you see, had come from beyond foreign parts in France and Spain, as young gentlemen used to go before Buonaparte or any such was heard of; and sure enough there was a dinner given to all the people on the ground, gentle and simple, high and low, rich and poor. The *ould* gentlemen were the gentlemen after all, saving your honour's presence. They'd swear at a body a little, to be sure, and, maybe, give one a cut of a whip now and then, but we were no losers by it in the end; and they were so easy and civil, and kept such rattling houses, and thousands of welcomes; and there was no grinding for rent, and there was hardly a tenant on the estate that did not taste of his landlord's bounty often and often in a year; but now it's another thing. No matter for that, sir, for I'd better be telling you my story.

'Well, we had everything of the best, and plenty of it; and we ate, and we drank and we danced, and the young master by the same token danced with Peggy Barry, from the *Bohereen* – a lovely young couple they were, though they are both low enough now. To make a long story short, I got, as a body may say, the same thing as tipsy almost, for I can't remember ever at all, no ways, how it was I left the place; only I did leave it, that's certain. Well, I thought for all that, in myself, I'd just step to Molly Cronohan's, the fairy woman, to speak a word about the bracket heifer that was bewitched; and so as I was crossing the stepping-stones of the ford of Ballyashenogh, and as looking up at the stars and blessing myself – for why? it was Lady-day – I missed my foot, and souse I fell into the water. "Death alive!" thought I, "I'll be drowned now!" However, I began swimming, swimming, swimming away for the dear life, till at last I got ashore, somehow or other, but never the one of me can tell how, upon a *dissolute* island.

'I wandered and wandered about there, without knowing where I wandered, until at last I got into a big bog. The moon was shining as bright as day, or your fair lady's eyes, sir (with the pardon for mentioning her), and I looked east and west, and north and south, and every way, and nothing did I see but bog, bog, bog – I could never find out how I got into it; and my heart grew cold with fear, for sure and certain I was that it would be my *berrin* place. So I sat down upon a stone which, as good luck would have it, was close by me, and I began to scratch my head, and sing the *Ullagone* – when all of a sudden the moon grew black, and I looked up, and saw something for all the world as if it was moving down between me and it, and I could not tell what it was. Down it came with a pounce, and looked at me full in the face; and what was it but an eagle? as fine a one as ever flew from the kingdom of Kerry. So he looked at me in the face, and says he to me, "Daniel O'Rourke," says he, "how do you do?" "Very well, I thank you, sir," says I; "I hope you're well"; wondering out of my senses all the time how an eagle came to speak like a Christian. "What brings you here, Dan?" says he. "Nothing at all, sir," says I; "only I wish I was safe home again." "Is it out of the island you want to go, Dan?" says he. " 'Tis, sir," says I: so I up and told him how I had taken a drop too much, and fell into the water; how I swam to the island; and how I got into the bog and did not know my way out of it. "Dan," says he, after a minute's thought, "though it is very improper for you to get drunk on Lady-day, yet as you are a decent, sober man, who 'tends mass well and never flings stones at me or mine, nor cries out after us in the fields – my life for yours," says he; "so get up on my back, and grip me well for fear you'd fall off, and I'll fly you out of the bog." "I am afraid," says I, "your honour's making game of me; for who ever heard of riding horseback on an eagle before?" " 'Pon the honour of a gentleman," says he, putting his right foot on his breast, "I am quite in earnest: and so now either take my offer or starve in the bog – besides, I see that your weight is sinking the stone."

'It was true enough as he said, for I found the stone every minute going from under me. I had no choice; so thinks I to myself, faint heart never won fair lady, and this is fair persuadance. "I thank your honour," says I, "for the loan of your civility; and I'll take your kind offer."

'I therefore mounted upon the back of the eagle, and held him tight enough by the throat, and up he flew in the air like a lark. Little I knew the trick he was going to serve me. Up – up – up, God knows how far up he flew. "Why then," said I to him – thinking he did not know the right road home – very civilly, because why? I was in his power entirely; "sir," says I, "please your honour's glory, and with humble submission to your better judgment, if you'd fly down a bit, you're now just over my cabin, and I could be put down there, and many thanks to your worship."

' "*Arrah*, Dan," said he, "do you think me a fool? Look down the next field, and don't you see two men and a gun? By my word it would be no joke to be shot this way, to oblige a drunken blackguard that I picked up off of a *could* stone in a bog." "Bother you," said I to myself, but I did not speak out, for where was the use? Well, sir, up he kept flying, flying, and I asking him every minute to fly down, and all to no use. "Where in the world are you going, sir?" says I to him. "Hold your tongue, Dan," says he: "mind your own business, and don't be interfering with the business of other people." "Faith, this is my business, I think," says I. "Be quiet, Dan," says he: so I said no more.

'At last where should we come to, but to the moon itself. Now you can't see it from this, but there is, or there was in my time, a reaping-hook sticking out of the side of the moon, this way (drawing the figure thus, Ω, on the ground with the end of his stick).

' "Dan," said the eagle, "I'm tired with this long fly; I had no notion 'twas so far." "And my lord, sir,' said I, "who in the world *axed* you to fly so far – was it I? Did not I beg and pray and beseech you to stop half an hour ago?" "There's no use talking, Dan," said he; "I'm tired bad enough, so you must get off, and sit down on the moon until I rest myself." "Is it sit down on the moon?" said I, "is it upon that little round thing, then? why, then, sure I'd fall off in a minute, and be *kilt* and spilt and smashed all to bits; you are a vile deceiver – so you are." "Not at all, Dan, said he; "you can catch fast hold of the reaping-hook that's sticking out of the side of the moon, and 'twill keep you up." "I won't then," said I. "Maybe not," said he, quite quiet. "If you don't, my man, I shall just give you a shake, and one slap of my wing, and send you down to the ground, where every bone in your body will be smashed as small as a drop of dew on a cabbage-leaf in the morning." "Why, then, I'm in a fine way," said I to myself, "ever to have come along with the likes of you;" and so giving him a hearty curse in Irish, for fear he'd know what I said, I got off his back with a heavy heart, took hold of the reaping hook, and sat down upon the moon, and a mighty cold seat it was, I can tell you that.

'When he had me there fairly landed, he turned about on me, and said: "Good morning to you, Daniel O'Rourke," said he; 'I think I've nicked you fairly now. You robbed my nest last year' ('twas true enough for him, but how he found it out is hard to say), "and in return you are freely welcome to cool your heels dangling upon the moon like a cockthrow."

' "Is that all, and is this the way you leave me, you brute, you," says I. "You ugly, unnatural *baste*, and is this the way you serve me at last? Bad luck to yourself, with your hook'd nose, and to all your breed, you blackguard." 'Twas all to no manner of use; he spread out his great big wings, burst out a-laughing, and flew away like lightning. I bawled after him to stop; but I might have called and bawled for ever, without his minding me. Away he went, and I never saw him from that day to this sorrow fly away with him! You may be sure I was in a disconsolate condition, and kept roaring out for the bare grief, when all at once a door opened right in the middle of the moon, creaking on its hinges as if it had not been opened for a month before, I suppose they never thought of greasing 'em, and out there walks – who do you think, but the man in the moon himself? I knew him by his bush.

' "Good-morrow to you, Daniel O'Rourke," said he; "how do you do?" "Very well, thank your honour," said I. "I hope your honour's well." "What brought you here, Dan?" said he. So I told him how I was a little overtaken in liquor at the master's, and how I was cast on a dissolute island, and how I lost my way in the bog, and how the thief of an eagle promised to fly me out of it and how, instead of that, he had fled me up to the moon.

' "Dan," said the man in the moon, taking a pinch of snuff when I was done, "you must not stay here." "Indeed, sir," says I, " 'tis much against my will I'm here at all; but how am I to go back?" "That's your business," said he; "Dan, mine is to tell you that here you must not stay; so be off in less than no time." "I'm doing no harm," says I, "only holding on hard by the reaping-hook, lest I fall off." "That's what you must not do, Dan," says he. "Pray, sir," say I, "may I ask how many you are in family, that you would not give a poor traveller lodging: I'm sure 'tis not so often you're troubled with strangers coming to see you, for 'tis a long way." "I'm by myself, Dan," says he; "but you'd better let go the reaping-hook." "Faith, and with your leave," says I, "I'll not let go the grip, and the more you bid me, the more I won't let go; – so I will." "You had better, Dan," says he again. "why, then, my little fellow," says I, taking the whole weight of him with my eye from head to foot, "there are two words to that bargain; and I'll not budge, but you may if you like." "We'll see how that is to be," says he; and back he went, giving the door such a great bang after him (for it was plain he was huffed) that I thought the moon and all would fall down with it.

'Well, I was preparing myself to try strength with him, when back again he comes, with the kitchen cleaver in his hand, and, without saying a word, he gives two bangs to the handle of the reaping-hook that was keeping me up, and *whap*! it came in two. "Good-morning to you, Dan," says the spiteful little old blackguard, when he saw me cleanly falling down with a bit of the handle in my hand; I thank you for your visit and fair weather after you, Daniel.' I had not time to make answer to him, for I was tumbling over and over and rolling and rolling, at the rate of a fox-hunt. "God help me!" says I, "but this is a pretty pickle for a decent man to be seen in at this time of night: I am now sold fairly." The word was not out of my mouth when, *whiz*! what should fly by close to my ear but a flock of wild geese, all the way from my own bog of Ballyasheenogh, else how should they know *me*? The *ould* gander, who was their general, turning about his head, cried out to me, "Is that you, Dan?" "The same," said I, not a bit daunted now at what he said, for I was by this time used to all kinds of *bedevilment*, and, besides, I knew him of ould. "Good-morrow to you," says he,

"Daniel O'Rourke; how are you in health this morning?" "Very well, sir," says I, "I thank you kindly," drawing my breath, for I was mightily in want of some. "I hope your honour's the same." "I think 'tis falling you are, Daniel," says he. "You may say that, sir," says I. "And where are you going all the way so fast?" said the gander. So I told him how I had taken the drop, and how I came on the island, and how I lost my way in the bog, and how the thief of an eagle flew me up to the moon, and how the man in the moon turned me out. "Dan," said he, "I'll save you: put out your hand and catch me by the leg, and I'll fly you home." "Sweet is your hand in a pitcher of honey, my jewel," says I, though all the time I thought within myself that I don't much trust you; but there was no help, so I caught the gander by the leg, and away I and the other geese flew after him fast as hops.

'We flew, and we flew, and we flew, until we came right over the wide ocean. I knew it well, for I saw Cape Clear to my right hand, sticking up out of the water. "Ah, my lord,' said I to the goose, for I thought it best to keep a civil tongue in my head anyway, "fly to land if you please." "It is impossible, you see, Dan"; said he, "for a while, because you see we are going to Arabia." "To Arabia!" said I; "that's surely some place in foreign parts, far away. Oh! Mr Goose: why then, to be sure, I'm a man to be pitied among you." "Whist, whist, you fool," said he, "hold your tongue; I tell you Arabia is a very decent sort of place, as like West Carbery as one egg is like another, only there is a little more sand there."

'Just as we were talking, a ship hove in sight, scudding so beautiful before the wind. "Ah! then, sir," said I, "will you drop me on the ship, if you please?" "We are not fair over it," said he; "if I dropped you now you would go splash into the sea." "I would not," says I; "I know better than that, for it is just clean under us, so let me drop now at once."

' "If you must, you must," said he; "there, take your way"; and he opened his claw, and faith he was right – sure enough I came down plump into the very bottom of the salt sea! Down to the very bottom I went, and I gave myself up then forever, when a whale walked up to me, scratching himself after his night's sleep, and looked me full in the face, and never the word did he say, but lifting up his tail, he splashed me all over again with the cold salt water till there wasn't a dry stitch upon my whole carcass! and I heard somebody saying – 'twas a voice I knew, too – "Get up, you drunken brute, off o' that," and with that I woke up and there was Judy with a tub full of water, which she was splashing all over me for, rest her soul! though she was a good wife, she never could bear to see me in drink, and had a bitter hand of her own.

' "Get up," said she again: "and of all places in the parish would no place *sarve* your turn to lie down upon but under the *ould* walls of Carrigapooka? an *uneasy* resting I am sure you had of it." And sure enough I had: for I was fairly bothered out of my senses with eagles, and men of the moons, and flying ganders, and whales, driving me through bogs, and up to the moon, and down to the bottom of the green ocean. If I was in drink ten times over, long would it be before I'd lie down in the same spot again, I know that.'

D. R. MᶜANALLY, JR

About the Fairies

❧

The Oriental luxuriance of the Irish mythology is nowhere more conspicuously displayed than when dealing with the history, habits, characteristics, and pranks of the 'good people'. According to the most reliable of the rural 'fairy-men', a race now nearly extinct, the fairies were once angels, so numerous as to have formed a large heaven. When Satan sinned and drew throngs of the heavenly host with him into open rebellion, a large number of the less warlike spirits stood aloof from the contest that followed, fearing the consequences, and not caring to take sides till the issue of the conflict was determined. Upon the defeat and expulsion of the rebellious angels, those who had remained neutral were punished by banishment from heaven, but their offence being only one of omission, they were not consigned to the pit with Satan and his followers, but were sent to earth where they still remain, not without hope that on the last day they may be pardoned and readmitted to Paradise. They are thus on their good behaviour, but having power to do infinite harm, they are much feared, and spoken of either in a whisper or aloud, as the 'good people'.

Unlike leprechauns, who are not considered fit associates for reputable fairies, the good people are not solitary, but quite sociable, and always live in large societies, the members of which pursue the cooperative plan of labour and enjoyment, owning all their property, the kind and amount of which are somewhat indefinite, in common, and uniting their efforts to accomplish any desired object, whether of work or play. They travel in large bands, and although their parties are never seen in the daytime, there is little difficulty in ascertaining their line of march, for, 'sure they make the terriblest little cloud o' dust iver raised, an' not a bit o' wind in it at all', so that a fairy migration is sometimes the talk of the country. 'Though, be nacher, they're not the length av yer finger, they can make thimselves the bigness av a tower when it plazes thim, an' av that ugliness that ye'd faint wid the looks o' thim, as knowin' they can shtrike ye dead on the shpot or change ye into a dog, or a pig, or a unicorn, or anny other dirthy baste they plaze.'

As a matter of fact, however, the fairies are by no means so numerous at present as they were formerly, a recent historian remarking that the National Schools and societies of Father Mathew are rapidly driving the fairies out of the country, for 'they hate larnin' an' wisdom an' are lovers av nacher entirely'.

In a few remote districts, where the schools are not yet well esta blished, the good people are still found, and their doings are narrated with a childlike faith in the power of these first inhabitants of Ireland, for it seems to be agreed that they were in the country long before the coming either of the Irishman or of his Sassenagh oppressor.

The bodies of the fairies are not composed of flesh and bones, but of an ethereal substance, the nature of which is not determined. 'Ye can see thimselves as plain as the nose on yer face, an' can see through thim like it was a mist.' They have the power of vanishing from human sight when they please, and the fact that the air is sometimes full of them inspires the respect entertained for them by the peasantry. Sometimes they are heard without being seen, and when they travel through the air, as they often do, are known by a humming noise similar to that made by a swarm of bees. Whether or not they have wings is uncertain. Barney Murphy, of Kerry, thought they had; for several seen by him a number of years ago seemed to have long, semi-transparent pinions, 'like thim that grows on a dhraggin-fly'. Barney's neighbours, however, contradicted him by stoutly denying the good people the attribute of wings, and intimated that at the time Barney saw the fairies he was too drunk to distinguish a pair of wings from a pair of legs, so this branch of the subject must remain in doubt.

With regard to their dress, the testimony is undisputed. Young lady fairies wear pure white robes and usually allow their hair to flow loosely over their shoulders; while fairy matrons bind up their tresses in a coil on the top or back of the head, also surrounding the temples with a golden band. Young gentlemen elves wear green jackets, with white breeches and stockings; and when a fairy of either sex has need of a cap or head-covering, the flower of the foxglove is brought into requisition.

Male fairies are perfect in all military exercises, for, like the other inhabitants of Ireland, fairies are divided into factions, the objects of contention not, in most cases, being definitely known. In Kerry, a number of years ago, there was a great battle among the fairies, one party inhabiting a rath or sepulchral mound, the other an unused and lonely graveyard. Paddy O'Donohue was the sole witness of this encounter, the narrative being in his own words.

'I was lyin' be the road, bein' on me way home an' tired wid the walkin'. A bright moon was out that night, an' I heard a noise like a million av sogers, thrampin' on the road, so I riz me an' looked, an' the way was full av little men, the length o' me hand, wid grane coats on, an' all in rows like wan o' the ridgmints; aitch wid a pike on his showlder an' a shield on his arrum. Wan was in front, beway he was the ginral, walkin' wid his chin up as proud as a paycock. Jagers, but I was skairt an' prayed fasther than iver I did in me life, for it was too clost to me entirely they wor for comfort or convaynience aither. But they all went by, sorra the wan o' thim turnin' his head to raygard me at all, Glory be to God for that same; so they left me. Afther they were clane gone by, I had curiosity for to see phat they were afther, so I folly'd thim, a good bit aff, an' ready to jump an' run like a hare at the laste noise, for I was afeared if they caught me at it, they'd make a pig o' me at wanst or change me into a baste complately. They marched into the field bechuxt the graveyard an' the rath, an' there was another army there wid red coats, from the graveyard, an' the two armies had the biggest fight ye iver seen, the granes agin the reds. Afther lookin' on a bit, I got axcited, for the granes were batin' the reds like blazes, an' I up an' give a whilloo an' called out, "At 'em agin! Don't lave wan o' the blaggards!" An' wid that word, the sight left me eyes an' I remimber no more till mornin', an' there was I, layin' on the road where I seen thim, as shtiff as a crutch.'

The homes of the fairies are commonly in raths, tumuli of the pagan days of Ireland, and, on this account, raths are much dreaded, and after sundown are avoided by the peasantry. Attempts have been made to remove some of these raths, but the unwillingness of the peasants to engage in the work, no matter what inducements may be offered in compensation, has generally resulted in the abandonment of the undertaking. On one of the islands in the Upper Lake of Killarney there is a rath, and the proprietor, finding it occupied too much ground, resolved to have it levelled to increase the arable surface of the field. The work was begun, but one morning, in the early dawn, as the labourers were crossing the lake on their way to the island, they saw a procession of about two hundred persons, habited like monks, leave the island and proceed to the mainland, followed, as the workmen thought, by a long line of small, shining figures. The phenomenon was perhaps genuine, for the mirage is by no means an uncommon appearance in some parts of Ireland, but work on the rath was at once indefinitely postponed. Besides raths, old castles, deserted graveyards, ruined churches, secluded glens in the mountains, springs, lakes, and caves all are the homes and resorts of fairies, as is very well known on the west coast.

The better class of fairies are fond of human society and often act as guardians to those they love. In parts of Donegal and Galway they are believed to receive the souls of the dying and escort them to the gates of heaven, not, however, being allowed to enter with them. On this account, fairies love graves and graveyards, having often been seen walking to and fro among the grassy mounds. There are, indeed, some accounts of faction fights among the fairy bands at or shortly after a funeral, the question in dispute being whether the soul of the departed belonged to one or the other faction.

The amusements of the fairies consist of music, dancing, and ball-playing. In music their skill exceeds that of men, while their dancing is perfect, the only drawback being the fact that it blights the grass, 'fairy-rings' of dead grass, apparently caused by a peculiar fungous growth, being common in Ireland. Although their musical instruments are few, the fairies use these few with wonderful skill. Near Colooney, in Sligo, there is a 'knowledgeable woman', whose grandmother's aunt once witnessed a fairy ball, the music for which was furnished by an orchestra which the management had no doubt been at great pains and expense to secure and instruct.

'It was the cutest sight alive. There was a place for thim to shtand on, an' a wondherful big fiddle av the size ye cud slape in it, that was played be a monsthrous frog, an' two little fiddles, that two kittens fiddled on, an' two big drums, baten be cats, an' two trumpets, played be fat pigs. All round the fairies were dancin' like angels, the fireflies givin' thim light to see by, an' the moonbames shinin' on the lake, for it was be the shore it was, an' if ye don't belave it, the glen's still there, that they call the fairy glen to this blessed day.'

The fairies do much singing, seldom, however, save in chorus, and their songs were formerly more frequently heard than at present. Even now a belated peasant, who has been at a wake, or is coming home from a fair, in passing a rath will sometimes hear the soft strains of their voices in the distance, and will hurry away lest they discover his presence and be angry at the intrusion on their privacy. When in unusually good spirits they will sometimes admit a mortal to their revels, but if he speaks, the scene at once vanishes, he becomes insensible, and generally finds himself by the roadside the next morning, 'wid that degray av pains in his arrums an' legs an' back, that if sixteen thousand divils were afther him, he cudn't stir a toe to save the sowl av him, that's phat the fairies do be pinchin' an' punchin' him for comin' on them an' shpakin' out loud.'

Kindly disposed fairies often take great pleasure in assisting those who treat them with proper respect, and as the favours always take a practical form, there is sometimes a business value in the show of reverence for them. There was Barney Noonan, of the County Leitrim, for instance, 'An' sorra a betther boy was in the county than Barney. He'd work as reg'lar as a pump, an' liked a bit av divarshun as well as anybody when he'd time for it, that wasn't aften, to be sure, but small blame to him, for he wasn't rich be no manner o' manes. He'd a power av ragard av the good people, an' when he wint be the rath beyant his field, he'd pull aff his caubeen an' take the dudheen out av his mouth, as p'lite as a dancin' masther, an' say, "God save ye, ladies an' gintlemen," that the good people always heard though they niver showed thimselves to him. He'd a bit o' bog, that the hay was on, an' afther cuttin' it, he left it for to dhry, an' the sun come out beautiful an' in a day or so the hay was as dhry as powdher an' ready to put away.

'So Barney was goin' to put it up, but, it bein' the day av the fair, he thought he'd take the calf an' sell it, an' so he did, an' comin' up wid the boys, he stayed over his time, bein' hindhered wid dhrinkin' an' dancin' an' palaverin' at the gurls, so it was afther dark when he got home an' the night as black as a crow, the clouds gatherin' on the tops av the mountains like avil sper'ts an' crapin' down into the glens like disthroyin' angels, an' the wind howlin' like tin thousand Banshees, but Barney didn't mind it all wan copper, bein' glorified wid the dhrink he'd had. So the hay niver enthered the head av him, but in he wint an' tumbled in bed an' was shnorin' like a horse in two minnits, for he was a bach'ler, God bless him, an' had no wife to gosther him an' ax him where he'd been, an' phat he'd been at, an' make him tell a hundred lies about not gettin' home afore. So it came on to thunder an' lighten like as all the avil daymons in the univarse were fightin' wid cannons in the shky, an' by an' by there was a clap loud enough to shplit ye skull an' Barney woke up.

' "Tattheration to me," says he to himself, "it's goin' for to rain an' me hay on the ground. Phat'll I do?" says he.

'So he rowled over on the bed an' looked out av a crack for to see if it was raley rainin'. An there was the biggest crowd he iver seen av little men an' wimmin. They'd built a row o' fires from the cow-house to the bog an' were comin' in a shtring like the cow goin' home, aitch wan wid his two arrums full o' hay. Some were in the cow-house, resayvin' the hay; some were in the field, rakin' the hay together; an' some were shtandin' wid their hands in their pockets beways they were the bosses, tellin' the rest for to make haste. An' so they did, for every wan run like he was after goin' for the docther, an' brought a load an' hurried back for more.

'Barney looked through the crack at thim a crossin' himself ivery minnit wid admiration for the shpeed they had. "God be good to me," says he to himself, " 'tis not ivery gossoon in Leitrim that's got hay-makers like thim," only he never spake a work out loud, for he knew very well the good people 'udn't like it. So they brought in all the hay an' put it in the house an' thin let the fires go out an' made another big fire in front o' the dure, an' begun to dance round it wid the swatest music Barney iver heard.

'Now be this time he'd got up an' feelin' aisey in his mind about the hay, begun to be very merry. He looked on through the dure at thim dancin', an' by an' by they brought out a jug wid little tumblers and begun to drink summat that they poured out o' the jug. If Barney had the sense av a herrin', he'd a kept shtill an' let thim dhrink their fill widout openin' the big mouth av him, bein' that he was as full as a goose himself an' naded no more; but when he seen the jug an' the tumblers an' the fairies drinkin' away wid all their mights, he got mad an' bellered out like a bull, "Arra–a–a–h now, ye little attomies, is it dhrinkin' ye are, an' never givin' a sup to a thirsty mortial that always thrates yez as well as he knows how," and immedjitly the fairies, an' the fire, an' the jug all wint out av his sight, an' he to bed agin in a timper. While he was layin' there, he thought he heard talkin' an' a cugger-mugger goin' on, but when he peeped out agin, sorra a thing did he see but the black night an' the rain comin' down an' aitch dhrop the full av a wather-noggin. So he wint to slape, continted that the hay was in, but not plazed that the good people'ud be pigs entirely, to be afther dhrinkin' undher his eyes an' not offer thim a taste, no, not so much as a shmell at the jug.

'In the mornin' up he gets an' out for to look at the hay an' see if the fairies put it in right, for he says, "It's a job they're not used to." So he looked in the cow-house an' thought the eyes'ud lave him when there wasn't a shtraw in the house at all. "Holy Moses," says he, "phat have they done wid it?" an' he couldn't consave phat had gone wid the hay. So he looked in the field an' it was all there; bad luck to the bit av it had the fairies left in the house at all, but when he shouted at thim, they got tarin' mad an' took all the hay back agin to the bog, puttin' every shtraw where Barney laid it, an' it was as wet as a drownded cat. But it was a lesson to him he niver forgot, an' I go bail that the next time the fairies help him in wid his hay he'll kape shtill an' let thim dhrink thimselves to death if they plaze widout sayin' a word.'

The good people have the family relations of husband and wife, parent and child, and although it is darkly hinted by some that fairy husbands and wives have as many little disagreements as are found in mortal households, 'for, sure a woman's tongue is longer than a man's patience' and 'a husband is bound for to be gosthered day in an' day out, for a woman's jaw is sharpened on the divil's grindshtone,' yet opinions unfavourable to married happiness among the fairies are not generally received. On the contrary, it is believed that married life in fairy circles is regulated on the basis of the absolute submission of the wife to the husband. As this point was elucidated by a Donegal woman, 'They're wan, that's the husband an' the wife, but he's more the wan than she is.'

The love of children is one of the most prominent traits of fairy character, but as it manifests itself by stealing beautiful babes, replacing them by young leprechauns, the fairies are much dreaded by west coast mothers, and many precautions are much dreaded by west coast mothers, and many precautions are taken against the elves. Thefts of this kind now rarely occur, but once they were common, as 'in thim owld times ye cud see tin fairies where there isn't wan now, be razon o' thim lavin' the counthry'.

A notable case of baby stealing occurred in the family of Termon Magrath, who had a castle, now in picturesque ruins, on the shore of Lough Erne, in the Country Donegal. The narrator of the incident was 'a knowledgable woman', who dwelt in an apology for a cabin, a thatched shed placed against the precipitous side of the glen almost beneath the castle. The wretched shelter was nearly concealed from view by the overhanging branches of a large tree and by thick under-growth, and seemed unfit for a pigpen, but, though her surroundings were poor beyond description, 'Owld Meg', in the language of one of her neighbours, 'knew a dale av fairies an' witches an' could kape thim from a babby betther than anny woman that iver dhrew the breath av life.' A bit of tobacco to enable her to take a 'dhraw o' the pipe, an' that warms me heart to the whole worruld,' brought forth the story.

'It's a manny year ago, that Termon Magrath wint, wid all his army, to the war in the County Tyrone, an' while he was gone the babby was born an' they called her Eva. She was her mother's first, so she felt moighty onaisey in her mind about her's knowin' that the good people do be always afther the first wan that comes, an' more whin it's a girl that's in it, that they thry to stale harder than they do a boy, bekase av belavin' they're aisier fur to rare, though it's mesilf that doesn't belave that same, fur wan girl makes more throuble than tin boys an' isn't a haporth more good.

'So whin the babby was born they sent afther an owld struckawn av a widdy that set up for a wise woman, that knew no more o' doctherin' than a pig av Paradise, but they thought she could kape away the fairies, that's a job that takes no ind av knowledge in thim that thries it. But the poor owld woman did the best she knew how, an' so, God be good to her, she wasn't to be blamed fur that, but it's the likes av her that do shame thim that's larned in such things, fur they make people think all wise wimmin as ignerant as hersilf. So she made the sign o' the crass on the babby's face wid ashes, an' towld thim to bit aff its nails and not cut thim till nine weeks, an' held a burnin' candle afore its eyes, so it'ud do the deeds av light an' not av darkness, an' mixed sugar an' salt an' oil, an' give it to her, that her life'ud be swate an' long presarved an' go smooth, but the owld widdy forgot wan thing. She didn't put a lucky shamrock, that's got four leaves, in a gospel an' tie it 'round the babby's neck wid a t'read pulled out av her gown, an' not mindin' this, all the rest was no good at all. No more did she tell the mother not to take her eyes aff the child till the ninth day; afther that the fairies cudn't take it.

'So the nurse tuk the babby in the next room an' laid it on the bed, an' wint away for a minnit, but thinkin' she heard it cry, back she come an' there was the babby, bedclothes an' all just goin' through the flure, bein' dhrawn be the fairies. The nurse scraiched an' caught the clothes an' the maid helped her, so that the two o' thim pulled wid all their mights an' got the bedclothes up agin, but while the child was out o' sight, the fairies changed it an' put a fairy child in its place, but the nurse didn't know phat the fairies done, no more did the owld struckawn, that shows she was an ignerant woman entirely. But the fairies tuk Eva away undher the lake where they trated her beautiful. Every night they gev her a dance, wid the loveliest music that was iver heard, wid big drums an' little drums, an' fiddles an' pipes an' thrumpets, fur such a band the good people do have when they give a dance.

'So she grew an' the quane said she should have a husband among the fairies, but she fell in love wid an owld leprechaun, an' the quane, to sarcumvint her, let her walk on the shore o' the lake where she met Darby O'Hoolighan an' loved him an' married him be the quane's consint. The quane towld her to tell him if he shtruck her three blows widout a razon, she'd lave him an' come back to the fairies. The quane gev her a power av riches, shape an' pigs widout number an' more oxen than ye cud count in a week. So she an' Darby lived together as happy as two doves, an' she hadn't as much care as a blind piper's dog, morebetoken, they had two boys, good lookin' like their mother an' shtrong as their father.

'Wan day, afther they'd been marred siventeen year, she an' Darby were goin' to a weddin', an' she was shlow, so Darby towld her fur to harry an' gev her a slap on the shouldher wid the palm av his hand, so she begun to cry. He axed her phat ailed he an' she towld him he'd shtruck her the first av the three blows. So he was mighty sorry an' said he'd be careful, but it wasn't more than a year after, when he was taichin' wan o' the boys to use a shtick, that she got behind him an' got hit wid the shillaly. That was the second blow, an' made her lose her timper, an' they had a rale quarl. So he got mad, sayin' that nayther o' thim blows ought to be counted, bein' they both come be accident. So he flung the shtick agin the wall, "Divil take the shtick," says he, an' went out quick, an' the shtick fell back from the wall an' hit her an the head. "That's the third," says she, an' she kissed her sons an' walked out. Thin she called the cows in the field an' they left grazin' an' folly'd her; she called the oxen in the shtalls an' they quit atin' an' come out; an' she shpoke to the calf that was hangin' in the yard, that they'd killed that mornin' an' it got down an' come along. The lamb that was killed the day afore, it come; an' the pigs that were salted an' thim hangin' up to dhry, they come, all afther her in a shtring. Thin she called to her things in the house, an' the chairs walked out, an' the tables, an' the chist av drawers, an' the boxes, all o' thim put out legs like bastes an' come along, wid the pots an' pans, an' gridiron, an' buckets, an' noggins, an' kish, lavin' the house as bare as a 'victed tinant's, an' all afther her to the lake, where they wint undher an' dis–appeared, an' haven't been seen be man or mortial to this blessed day.

'Now, there's thim that says the shtory aint thrue, fur, says they, how'ud a woman do such a thrick as go aff that a way an' take ivery thing she had, just bekase av her husband hittin' her be accident thim three times. But thim that says it forgits that she was a young wan, aven if she did have thim boys I was afther tellin' ye av, an' faith, it's no lie I'm sayin', that it's not in the power av the angels o' God to be knowin' phat a young wan'ull be doin'. Afther they get owld, an' do be losin' their taythe, an' their beauty goes, thin they're sober an' get over thim notions; but it takes a dale av time to make an owld wan out av a young wan.

'But she didn't forget the boys she'd left, an' wanst in a while she'd come to the aidge av the lake whin they were clost be the bank an' spake wid thim, fur aven, if she was half a fairy, she'd the mother's heart that the good God put in her bosom; an' wan time they seen her wid a little attomy av a man alang wid her, that was a leprechaun, as they knewn be the look av him, an' that makes me belave that the rale rayzon av her lavin' her husband was to get back to the owld leprechaun she was in love wid afore she was marr'd to Darby O'Hoolighan.'

D. R. McANALLY, JR

Satan as a Sculptor

꙳

Near one of the fishing villages which abound on the Clare coast, a narrow valley runs back from the sea into the mountains, opening between two precipices that, ages ago, were rent asunder by the forces of nature. On entering the valley by the road leading from the seashore, nothing can be seen but barren cliffs and craggy heights, covered here and there by patches of the moss peculiar to the country. After making some progress, the gorge narrows, the moss becomes denser on the overhanging rocks; trees, growing out of clefts in the precipices, unite their branches above the chasm, and shroud the depths, so that, save an hour or two at noon, the rays of the sun do not penetrate to the crystal brook, rippling along at the bottom over its bed of moss-covered pebbles, – now flashing white as it leaps down a declivity, now hiding itself under the overreaching ferns, now coming again into the light, but always hurrying on as though eager to escape from the dark, gloomy retreat, and, for a moment, enjoy the sunshine of the wider valley beyond before losing its life in the sea.

At a narrow turn in the valley and immediately over the spot where the brook has its origin in a spring bursting out of a crevice in the rock and falling into a circular well partly scooped out, partly built up for the reception of the sparkling water, a cliff rises perpendicularly to the height of fifty feet, surmounted, after a break in the strata, by another, perhaps twenty feet higher, the upper portion being curiously wrought by nature's chisel into the shape of a human countenance. The forehead is shelving, the eyebrows heavy and menacing; the nose large and hooked like the beak of a hawk; the upper lip short, the chin prominent and pointed, while a thick growth of ferns in the shelter of the crag forming the nose gives the impression of a small moustache and goatee. Above the forehead a mass of tangled undergrowth and ferns bears a strong resemblance to an Oriental turban. An eye is plainly indicated by a bit of light-coloured stone, and altogether the face has a sinister leer, that, in an ignorant age, might easily inspire the fears of a superstitious people.

On a level with the chin and to the right of the face is the mouth of a cave, reached by a path up the hillside, rude steps in the rock rendering easier the steep ascent. The cave can be entered only by stooping, but inside a room nearly seven feet high and about twelve feet square presents itself. Undoubtedly the cave was once the abode of an anchorite, for on each side of the entrance a Latin cross is deeply carved in the rock, while within, at the further side, and opposite the door, a block of stone four feet high was left for an altar. Above it, a shrine is hollowed out of the stone wall, and over the cavity is another cross, surmounted by the mystic I.H.S.

The legend of the cave was told by an old 'wise woman' of the neighbourhood with a minuteness of detail that rendered the narrative more tedious than graphic. A devout believer in the truth of her own story, she told it with wonderful earnestness, combining fluency of speech with the intonations of oratory.

' 'Tis the cave av the saint, but phat saint I'm not rightly sartain. Some say it was St Patrick himself, but 'tis I don't belave that same. More say it was the blessed St Kevin, him that done owld King O'Toole out av his land in the bargain he made fur curin' his goose, but that's not thrue aither, an' it's my consate they're right that say it was St Tigernach, the same that built the big Abbey av Clones in Monaghan. His Riverince, Father Murphy, says that same, an' sorra a wan has a chance av knowin' betther than him.

'An' the big head on the rock there is the divil's face that the saint made him put there, the time the blessed man was too shmart fur hi whin the Avil Wan thried to do him.

'A quare owld shtory it is, an' the quol'ty that come down here on the coast laugh if it's towld thim, an' say it's a t'underin' big lie that's in it, bekase they don't undhershtand it, but if men belaved nothin' they didn't undhershtand, it's a short craydo they'd have. But I was afther tellin', St Tigernach lived in the cave, it bein' him an' no other; morebetoken, he was a good man an' shrewder than a fox. He made the cave fur himself an' lived there, an' ivery day he'd say tin thousand paters, an' five thousand aves, an' a thousand craydos, an' thin go out among the poor. There wasn't manny poor thin in Ireland, Glory be to God, fur the times was betther thin, but phat there was looked up to the saint, fur he was as good as a cupboard to thim, an' whin he begged fur the poor, sorra a man'ud get from him till he'd given him a copper or more, fur he'd shtick like a constable to ye till he'd get his money. An' all that were parshecuted, an' the hungry, an' naked, and God's poor, wint to the saint like a child to its mother an' towld him the whole o'their heart.

'While the blessed saint lived here, over acrass the hill an' beyant the peat-bog there was a hedger an' ditcher named O'Connor. He was only a poor labourin' man, an' the owld woman helped him, while his girl, be the name o' Kathleen, tinded the house, fur I must tell ye, they kept a boord in the corner beways av a bar an' a jug wid potheen that they sowld to thim that passed, fur it was afore the days av the gaugers, bad cess to thim, an' ivery man dhrunk phat he plazed widout payin' a pinny to the govermint. So O'Connor made the potheen himself an' Kathleen sowld it to the turf-cutters, an' mighty little did they buy, bekase they'd no money. She was a fine girl, wid a pair av eyes that'ud dint the hearts av owld an' young, an' wid a dacint gown fur the week an' a clane wan fur the Sunday, an' just such a girl as'ud make an owld felly feel himself young agin. Sorra the taste av divilmint was there in the girl at all, fur she was good as the sunshine in winther an' as innycent as a shpring lamb, an' wint to church an' did her jooty reglar.

'She was afther fallin' in love wid a young felly that done ditchin' an' they were to be marr'd whin he got his house done an' his father gev him a cow. He wasn't rich be no manes, but as fur feelin' poverty, he never dhreamt o' such a thing, fur he'd the love o' Kathleen an' thought it a forchune.

'In thim thimes the castle at the foot o' the hill was kept be a lord, that wid roomytisms an' panes in his jints was laid on his bed all the time, and the son av him, Lord Robert, was the worst man to be runnin' afther girls iver seen in the County Clare. He was the dandy among thim an' broke the hearts o' thim right an' lift like he was shnappin' twigs undher his feet. Manny a wan he desaved an' let go to the gods, as they did at wanst, fur whin the divil gets his foot on a woman's neck, she niver lifts her head agin.

'Wan day, Lord Robert's father's roomytism got the betther av him an' laid him out, an' they gev him an iligant wake an' berryin', an' while they were at the grave Lord Robert looked up an' seen Kathleen shtandin' among the people an' wondhered who she was. So he come into the eshtate an' got a stable full av horses an' dogs, an' did a power o' huntin', an' as he was a sojer, he'd a shwarm av throopers at the cassel, all the like av himself. But not long afther the berryin', Lord Robert was huntin' in the hills, an' he come down towards the bog an' seen O'Connor's cabin, an' says to his man, "Bedad, I wondher if they've a dhrop to shpare here, I'm mortial dhry." So in they wint, an' axed an' got thim their dhrink, an' thin he set the wicked eyes av him on the girl an' at wanst remimbered her.

'   "It's a mighty fine girl ye are," says he to Kathleen, "thin, an' fit fur the house av a prince."

'   "None o' yer deluderhin' talk to me, sorr," says Kathleen to him. "I know ye, an' it's no good I know av ye, says she to him. 'T was the good girl she was an' as firm as a landlord in a bad year when she thought there was anny avil intinded."

'So he wint away that time an' come agin an' agin when he was huntin' an' always had some impidince to say at her. She towld her parrents av it, an' though they didn't like it at all, they wasn't afeared fur the girl, an' he'd spind more in wan dhrinkin' than they'd take in in a week, so they were not sorry to see him come, but ivery time he come he wint away more detarmined to have the girl, an' whin he found he cudn't get her be fair manes he shwore he'd do it be foul. So wanst, whin she'd been cowlder to him than common an' wouldn't have a prisint he brought her, he says to her, "Begob, I'll bring ye to terms. If ye won't accept me prisints, I'll make ye bend yer will widout prisints," an' he wint away. She got frighted, an' whin she saw Tim Maccarty, she towld him av Lord Robert an' phat he said. Well, it made Tim mighty mad. "Tatther an' agers," says he, "be the powers, I'll break every bone in his body if he lays a finger on yer showlder; but, fur all that, whin Tim got to thinkin', he got skairt av Kathleen."

'   "Sure," says he to himself, "ain't wimmin like glass jugs, that'll break wid the laste touch? I'll marry her immejitly an' take out av Clare into Kerry," says he, "an' let him dare to come afther her there," says he, for he knew that if Lord Robert came into the Kerry mountains, the boys'ud crack his shkull wid the same compuncshusness that they'd have to an egg shell. So he left aff the job an' convaynienced himself to go to Kathleen that night an' tell her his belafe.

' "Am n't I afeared fur ye, me darlin'," says he, "and wouldn't I dhrowned me in the say if anny harm'ud come to ye, so I think we'd betther be married at wanst."

'So Kathleen consinted an' made a bundle av her Sunday gown, an' they shtarted fur the saint's cave, that bein' the nearest place they cud be marr'd at, an' being' marr'd be him was like bein' marr'd be a priest.

'So they wint alang the road to where the footpath laves it be the oak tree, then up the path an' through the boreen to where Misther Dawson's black mare broke her leg jumpin' the hedge, an' whin they rached that shpot they heard a noise on the road behint thim an' stud be the hedge, peepin' through to have a look at it an' see phat it was. An' there was Lord Robert an' a dozen av his bad min, wid their waypons an' the armour on thim shinin' in the moonlight. It was ridin' to O'Connor's they were, an' whin Tim an' Kathleen set their eyes on thim, they seen they'd made a narrer eshcape.

'Howandiver, as soon as Lord Robert an' his min were out o' sight, they ran wid all their shpeed, an' lavin' the path where Dennis Murphy fell into the shtrame lasht winter comin' back from Blanigan's wake whin he'd had too much, they tuk the rise o' the hill, an' that was a mishtake. If they'd kep be the hedge an' 'round be the footbridge, then up the footway the other side o' the brook an' ferninst the mill, they'd have kep out o' sight, an' been safe enough; but as they were crassin' the hill, wan av Robert's min saw thim, fur it was afther the girl he was sure enough, an' whin he found from her father her an' Tim were gone, they rode aff here an' there sarchin' afther thim. Whin the sojer shpied thim on the top o' the hill, he blew his thrumpet, an' here come all the rest shtreelin' along on the run, round the hill as fast as their bastes'ud take thim, fur they guessed where the two'ud be goin'. An' Katleen an' Tim come tumblin' down the shlope, an' bad luck to the minnit they'd to shpare whin they got into the cave before there was the whole gang, wid their horses puffin', an' their armours rattlin' like a pedler's tins.

'The saint was on a pile av shtraw in the corner, shnorin' away out av his blessed nose, fur it was as sound aslape as a pig he was, bein' tired entirely wid a big day's job, an' didn't wake up wid their comin' in. So Lord Robert an' his min left their horse below an' climbed up an' looked in, but cud see nothin' be razon av the darkness.

' "Arrah now," says he, "Kathleen, come along out o' that now, fur I've got ye safe an' sound."

'They answered him niver a word, but he heard a noise that was the saint turnin' over on his beed bein' onaisey in his slape.

' "Come along out o' that," he repaited; "an' you, Tim Maccarty, if ye come out, ye may go back to yer ditchin', but if ye wait fur me to fetch ye, the crows'ull be atin' ye at sunrise. Shtrike a light," says he. So they did, an' looked in an' saw Tim an' Kathleen, wan on aitch side o' the althar, holdin' wid all their mights to the crass that was on it.

' "Dhrag thim out av it," says Lord Robert, an' the min went in, but afore they come near thim, St Tigernach shtopped shnorin', bein' wakened wid the light an' jabberin', an' shtud up on the flure.

' "Howld on now," says the blessed saint, "phat's the matther here? Phat's all this murtherin' noise about?" says he.

'Lord Robert's min all dhrew back, for there was a power o' fear av the saint in the county, an' Lord Robert undhertuk to axplain that the girl was a sarvint av his that run away wid that thafe av a ditcher, but St Tigernach seen through the whole thrick at wanst.

' "Lave aff," says he. "Don't offer fur to thrape thim lies on me. Pack aff wid yer murtherers, or it's the curse ye'll get afore ye can count yer fingers," an' wid that all the min went out, an' Lord Robert afther thim, an' all he cud say 'udn't pervail on the sojers to go back afther the girl.

' "No, yer Anner," says they to him; "we ate yer Anner's mate, an' dhrink yer Anner's dhrink, an' 'ull do yer Anner's biddin' in all that's right. We're parfectly willin' to wait till mornin' an' murther the ditcher an' shtale the girl whin they come out an' get away from the saint, but he musn't find it out. It's riskin' too much. Begorra, we've got sowls to save," says they, so they all got on their horses an' shtarted back to the cassel.

'Lord Robert folly'd thim a bit, but the avil heart av him was so set on Kathleen that he cudn't bear the thought av lettin' her go. So whin he got to the turn av the road, "T'underation," says he, " 'tis the wooden head that's set on me showldhers, that I didn't think av the witch afore."

'Ye see, in the break av the mountains beyant the mill, where the rath is, there was in thim times the cabin av a great witch. 'T was a dale av avil she done the County Clare wid shtorms an' rainy sayzons an' cows lavin' aff their milk, an' she'd a been dhrownded long afore, but fur fear av the divil, her masther, that was at her elbow, whinever she'd crook her finger. So to her Lord Robert wint, an' gev a rap on the dure, an' in. There she sat wid a row av black cats on aitch side, an' the full av a shkillet av sarpints a-shtewin' on the fire. He knew her well, fur she'd done jobs fur him afore, so he made bowld to shtate his arriant widout so much as sayin' good-day to ye. The owld fagot made a charm to call her masther, an' that minnit he was shtandin' be her side, bowin' an' schrapin' an' shmilin' like a gintleman come to tay. He an' Lord Robert fell to an' had a power av discoorse on the bargain, fur Robert was a sharp wan an' wanted the conthract onsartain-like, hopin' to chate the divil at the end, as we all do, be the help av God, while Satan thried to make it shtronger than a tinant's lace. Afther a dale av palatherin', they aggrade that the divil was to do all that Lord Robert axed him fur twinty years, an' then to have him sowl an' body; but if he failed, there was an end av the bargain. But there was a long face on the owld felly whin the first thing he was bid to do was to bring Kathleen out o' the cave an' carry her to the cassel.

‘ "By Jayminny," says Satan, "it's no aisey job fur to be takin' her from the power av a great sant like him,' a-scratchin' his head. 'But come on, we'll thry."

'So the three av thim mounted on the wan horse, Lord Robert in the saddle, the divil behind, an' the witch in front av him, an' away like the wind to the cave. Whin they got to the turn o' the hill, they got aff an' hid in the bushes bechune the cave an' the shpring, bekase, as Satan axplained to Lord Robert, ivery night, just at midnight, the saint wint to get him a dhrink av wather, bein' dhry wid the devotions, an' 'ud bring the full av a bucket back wid him.

‘ "We'll shtop him be the shpring," says the divil, wid the witch, "an' you an' me'ull shtale the girl while he's talkin'.''

'So while the clock was shtrikin' fur twilve, out come the saint wid the wather-bucket an' shtarted to the shpring. Whin he got there an' was takin' his dhrink, up comes the witch an' begins tellin' him av a son she had (she was purtindin', ye ondhershtand, an' lyin' to him) that was as lazy as a car-horse an' as much in the way as a sore thumb, an' axin' the saint's advice phat to do wid him, while Satan an' Lord

Robert ran into the cave. The divil picked up Kathleen in his arrums, but he darn't have done that same, only she was on the other side av the cave an' away from the althar, but Tim was shtandin' by it, an' shtarted out wid her kickin' an' schraichin'. Tim ran to grip him, but Satan tossed him back like a ball an' he fell on the flure.

' "Howld on till I shtick him," says Lord Robert, pullin' out his soord.

' "Come on, ye bosthoon," says Satan to him. "Sure the saint'ull be on us if we don't get away quick," an' bedad, as he said thim words, the dure opened, an' in come St Tigernach wid a bucket av wather on his arrum an' in a hurry, fur he misthrusted something.

' "God's presince be about us," says the blessed saint, whin he saw the divil, an' the turkey-bumps begun to raise on his blessed back an' the shweat a-comin' o his face, fur he knewn Satan well enough, an' consaved the owld felly had come fur himself be razon av a bit o' mate he ate that day, it bein' av a Friday; axceptin' he didn't ate the mate but only tasted it an' then spit it out agin to settle a quarl bechune a butcher an' a woman that bought the mate an' said it was bad, only he was afeared Satan didn't see him when he sput it out agin. "God's presince be about us," says the saint, a-crossin' himself as fast as he cud. In a minnit though, he seen it wasn't him, but Kathleen, that was in it, an' let go the wather an' caught the blessed crass that was hangin' on him wid his right hand an' gripped Satan be the throat wid his lift, a-pushin' the crass in his face.

'The divil dhropped Kathleen like it was a bag av male she was, an' she rolled over an' over on the flure like a worrum till she raiched the althar an' stuck to it as tight as the bark on a tree. An' a fine thing it was to see the inimy av our sowls a-lyin' there trimblin', wid the saint's fut on his neck.

' "Glory be to God," says the saint. "Lie you there till I make an example av ye," says he, an' turned to look fur Lord Robert, bekase he knewn the two o' thim'ud be in it. But the Sassenagh naded no invitation to be walkin' aff wid himself, but whin he seen phat come to the divil, he run away wid all the legs he had, an' the witch wid him, an' Tim after thim wid a whoop an' a fishtful av shtones. But they left him complately an' got away disconsarted, an' Tim come back.

' "Raise up," says St Tigernach to the divil, "an' shtand in the corner," makin' the blessed sign on the ground afore him. "I'm after marryin' these two at wanst, widout fee or license, an' you shall be the witness."

'So he married thim there, while the divil looked on. Faix, it's no lie I'm tellin' ye; it's not the onliest marryin' the divil's been at, but he's not aften seen at thim when he's in as low sper'ts as he was at that. But it was so that they were married wid Satan fur a witness, an' some says the saint thransported thim to Kerry through the air, but 'tisn't meself that belaves that same, but that they walked to Kilrush an' wint to Kerry in a fisherman's boat.

'Afther they'd shtarted, the saint turns to Satan an' says, "No more av yer thricks wid them two, me fine felly, fur I mane to give you a job that'll kape ye out av mischief fur wan time at laste," fur he was mightily vexed wid him a-comin' that-a-way right into his cave the same as if the place belonged to him.

' "Go you to work," says he, "an' put yer face on the rock over the shpring, so that as long as the mountain shtands min can come an' see phat sort av a dirthy lookin' baste ye are."

'So Satan wint out an' looked up at the rock, shmilin', as fur to say that was not great matther, an' whin the blessed man seen the grin that was on him, he says, "None av yer inchantmints will I have at all, at all. It's honest work ye'll do, an' be the same token, here's me own hammer an' chisel that ye'll take," an' wid that the divil looked mighty sarious, an' left aff grinnin' for he parsaived the clift was granite.

' "Sure it's jokin' yer Riverince is," says he, "ye don't mane it. Sorra the harder bit av shtone bechuxt this an' Donegal," an' it was thrue for him, fur he knew the coast well.

' "Bad luck to the taste av a lie's in it," says the saint. "So take yer waypons an' go at it, owld Buck-an'-Whye, fur the sooner ye begin, the quicker ye'll be done, an' the shtone won't soften be yer watin'. Mind ye kape a civil tongue in yer head while ye're at the job, or it'll be a holiday to the wan I'll find ye," says he, lookin' at him very fierce.

'So wid great displazemint, Satan tuk the hammer an' chisel, an' climbed up an' wint to work a cuttin' his own face on the shtone, an' it was as hard as iron it was, an whin he'd hit it a couple av cracks, he shtopped an' shuck his head an' thin scratched over his year wid the chisel an' looked round at the saint as fur to say somethin', but the blessed saint looked at him agin so fayroshus, that he made no raimark at all, but turned back to the clift quick an' begun to hammer away in airnest till the shweat shtud on his haythenish face like the dhrops on a wather-jug.

'On the next day, Lord Robert thought he'd call the owld Inimy, an' remind him that, bein' as he'd failed to get Kathleen, their bargain was aff. So he made the charm Satan gev him, but he didn't come fur anny thrial he'd make.

' "Bad scran to the Imp," says he. "Sure he must be mighty busy or maybe he's forgot entirely."

'So he out an' wint to see the witch, but she wasn't in, an' while he was waitin' for her, bein' not far away from the saint's cave, he thought he'd have a peep, an' see if Tim an' Kathleen were shtill there. So he crawled over the top o' the hill beyant the cave like the sarpint that he was, an' whin he come down a little, he seen the owld Pooka on the clift, wid the hammer in wan hand an' the chisel in the other a poundin' away at the rock an' hangin' on be his tail to a tree. Lord Robert thought the eyes'ud lave his head, fur he seen it was the divil sure enough, but he cudn't rightly make out phat he was doin'. So he crawled down till he seen, an' thin, when he undhershtood, he riz an' come an' took a sate on a big shtone ferninst the clift, a shlappin' his legs wid his hands, an' roarin' an' the wather bilin' out av his eyes wid laughin'.

' "Hilloo Nickey," says he, when he'd got his breath agin an' cud shpake. "Is it yerself that's in it?" Mind the impidince av him, shpakin' that familiar to the inimy av our sowls, but faix, he'd a tongue like a jews harp, an' cud use it too.

' "Kape from me," says Satan to him agin, as crass as two shticks, an' widout turnin' his head fur to raigard him. "Lave me! Begorra, I'll wipe the clift aff wid yer carkidge if ye come anny closter," says he.

' "A–a–a–h, woorroo, now. Aisey, ye desayvin' owld blaggard," says Lord Robert, as bowld as a ram, fur he knewn that Satan daren't lave the job to come at him. "Will ye kape yer timper? Sure ye haven't the manners av a goat; to be shpakin' to a gintleman like that. I've just come to tell ye that bein' ye failed, our bargain's aff," says he.

' "Out wid ye," says the divil, turnin' half round an' howldin' be wan hand to the big shtone nose he'd just done, an' shakin' the other fist wid the chisel in it at Lord Robert. "D' ye think I want to be aggervated wid the likes av ye, ye whey-faced shpalpeen, an' me losin' the whole day, an' business pressin' at this saison, an' breakin' me back on the job, an' me fingers sore wid the chisel, an' me tail shkinned wid howldin' on? Bad luck to the shtone, it's harder than a Scotchman's head, it is, so it is," says he, turnin' back agin when he seen the saint at the dure av the cave. An' thin he begun a peckin' away at the clift fur dear life, shwearin' to himself, so the saint cudn't hear him, every time he give his knuckles an onlucky crack wid the hammer.

' "Ye're not worth the throuble," says he to Lord Robert; he was that full av rage he cudn't howld in. "It's a paltherin' gossoon I was fur thriflin' wid ye whin I was sure ave ye annyhow."

' "Yer a liar," says Lord Robert, "ye desaivin' nagurly Haythen. If ye was sure o' me phat did ye want to make a bargain fur?"

' "Yer another," says Satan. "Isn't a sparrer in yer hand betther than a goose on a shtring?"

'So they were goin' on wid the blaggardin' match, whin the blessed saint, that come out whin he heard thim begin, an' thin set on the dure a-watchin', to see that owld Nick didn't schamp the job, interfared.

' "Howld yer pace, Satan, an' kape at yer work," says he. "An' for you, ye blatherin', milk-faced villin, wid the heart as black as a crow, walk aff wid ye an' go down on yer hard hearted onbelavin' knees, or it's no good'ull come o' ye." An' so he did.

'Do I belave the shtory? Troth, I dunno. It's quare things happened in them owld days, an' there's the face on the clift as ugly as the divil cud be an' the hammer an' chisel are in the church an' phat betther proof cud ye ax?

'Phat come av the lovers? No more do I know that, barrin' they grew owld an' shtayed poor an' forgot the shpringtime av youth in the winter av age, but if they lived a hunderd years, they niver forgot the marryin' in the saint's cave, wid the black face av the Avil Wan lookin' on from the dark corner.'

HERMINIE KAVANAGH

Darby O'Gill and the Leprechaun

The news that Darby O'Gill had spint six months with the Good People spread fast and far and wide.

At fair or hurlin' or market he would be backed be a crowd agin some convaynient wall and there for hours men, women, and childher, with jaws dhroppin' and eyes bulgin'd, stand ferninst him listening to half-frightened questions or to bould, mystarious answers.

Alway, though, one bit of wise adwise inded his discoorse: 'Nayther make nor moil nor meddle with the fairies,' Darby'd say. 'If you're going along the lonely boreen at night and you hear, from some fairy fort, a sound of fiddles, or of piping, or of sweet woices singing, or of little feet pattherin' in the dance, don't turn your head, but say your prayers an' hould on your way. The pleasures the Good People'll share with you have a sore sorrow hid in them, an' the gifts they'll offer are only made to break hearts with.'

Things went this a-way till one day in the market, over among the cows, Maurteen Cavanaugh, the schoolmasther – a cross-faced, argifying ould man he was – conthradicted Darby pint blank. 'Stay a bit,' says Maurteen, catching Darby by the coat-collar. 'You forget about the little fairy cobbler, the leprechaun,' he says. 'You can't deny that to catch the leprechaun is great luck entirely. If one only fix the glance of his eye on the cobbler, that look makes the fairy a presner – one can do anything with him as long as a human look covers the little lad and he'll give the favours of three wishes to buy his freedom,' says Maurteen.

At that Darby, smiling high and knowledgeable, made answer over the heads of the crowd.

'God help your sinse, honest man!' he says. 'Around the favours of thim same three wishes is a bog of thricks an' cajolories and conditions that'll defayt the wisest.

'First of all, if the look be taken from the little cobbler for as much as the wink of an eye, he's gone forever,' he says. 'Man alive, even when he does grant the favours of the three wishes, you're not safe, for, if you tell anyone you've seen the leprechaun, the favours melt like snow, or if you make a fourth wish that day – whiff! they turn to smoke. Take my advice – nayther make nor moil nor meddle with the fairies.'

'Thrue for ye,' spoke up long Pether McCarthy, siding in with Darby. 'Didn't Barney McBride, on his way to early mass one May morning, catch the fairy cobbler sewing an' workin' away under a hedge. "Have a pinch of snuff, Barney agra," says the leprechaun, handing up the little snuffbox. But, mind ye, when my poor Barney bint to take a thumb an' finger full, what did the little villain do but fling the box, snuff and all, into Barney's face. An' thin, whilst the poor lad was winkin' and blinkin', the leprechaun gave one leap and was lost in the reeds.

'Thin, again, there was Peggy O'Rourke, who captured him fair an' square in a hawthorn-bush. In spite of his wiles she wrung from him the favours of the three wishes. Knowing, of course, that if she towld of what had happened to her the spell was broken and the wishes wouldn't come thrue, she hurried home, aching and longing to in some way find from her husband Andy what wishes she'd make.

'Throwing open her own door, she said, "What would ye wish for most in the world, Andy dear? Tell me an' your wish'll come thrue," says she. A peddler was crying his wares out in the lane. "Lanterns, tin lanterns!" cried the peddler. "I wish I had one of thim lanterns," says Andy, careless, and bendin' over to get a coal for his pipe, when, lo and behold, there was the lantern in his hand.

'Well, so vexed was Peggy that one of her fine wishes should be wasted on a palthry tin lantern, that she lost all patience with him. "Why thin, bad scran to you!" says she – not mindin' her own words – "I wish the lantern was fastened to the ind of your nose!"

'The word wasn't well out of her mouth till the lantern *was* hung swinging from the ind of Andy's nose in a way that the wit of man couldn't loosen. It took the third and last of Peggy's wishes to relayse Andy.'

'Look at that, now!' cried a dozen voices from the admiring crowd. 'Darby said so from the first.'

Well, after a time people used to come from miles around to see Darby and sit under the sthraw-stack beside the stable to adwise with our hayro about their most important business – what was the best time for the settin' of hins, or what was good to cure colic in childher, an' things like that.

Any man so parsecuted with admiration an' hayrofication might aisily feel his chest swell out a bit, so it's no wondher that Darby set himself up for a knowledgeable man.

He took to talkin' slow an' shuttin' one eye whin he listened, and he walked with a knowledgeable twist to his chowlders. He grew monsthrously fond of fairs and public gatherings where people made much of him, and he lost every ounce of liking he ever had for hard worruk.

Things wint on with him in this way from bad to worse, and where it would have inded no man knows, if one unlucky morning he hadn't rayfused to bring in a creel of turf his wife Bridget had axed him to fetch her. The unfortunate man said it was no work for the likes of him.

The last word was still on Darby's lips whin he rayalised his mistake, an' he'd have given the world to have the sayin' back again.

For a minute you could have heard a pin dhrop. Bridget, instead of being in a hurry to begin at him, was crool dayliberate. She planted herself in the door, her two fists on her hips, an' her lips shut.

The look Julius Sayser'd trow at a servant-girl he'd caught stealing sugar from the rile cupboard was the glance she waved up and down from Darby's toes to his head, and from his head to his brogues agin.

Thin she began an' talked steady as a fall of hail that has now an' then a bit of lightning an' tunder mixed in it.

The knowledgeable man stood purtendin' to brush his hat and tryin' to look brave, but the heart inside of him was meltin' like butther.

Bridget began aisily be carelessly mentioning a few of Darby's best known wakenesses. Afther that she took up some of them not so well known, being ones Darby himself had sayrious doubts about having at all. But on these last she was more savare than on the first. Through it all he daren't say a word – he only smiled lofty and bitther.

'Twas but natural next for Bridget to explain what a poor crachure her husband was the day she got him, an what she might have been if she had married ayther one of the six others who had axed her. The step for her was a little one, thin, to the shortcomings and misfortunes of his blood relations, which she follyed back to the blaggardisms of his fourth cousin, Phelim McFadden.

Even in his misery poor Darby couldn't but marvel at her wondherful memory.

By the time she began talking of her own family, and especially about her Aunt Honoria O'Shaughnessy, who had once shook hands with a Bishop, and who in the rebellion of '98 had turn a brick at a Lord Liftenant, whin he was riding by, Darby was as wilted and as forlorn-looking as a roosther caught out in the winther rain.

He lost more pride in those few minutes than it had taken months to gather an' hoard. It kept falling in great drops from his forehead.

Just as Bridget was lading up to what Father Cassidy calls a pur-roar-ration – that being the part of your wife's discoorse whin, after telling you all she's done for you, and all she's stood from your relaytions, she breaks down and cries, and so smothers you entirely – just as she was coming to that, I say, Darby scrooged his caubeen down on his head, stuck his fingers in his two ears, and, making one grand rush through the door, bolted as fast as his legs could carry him down the road toward Sleive-na-mon Mountains.

Bridget stood on the step looking afther him, too surprised for a word. With his fingers still in his ears, so that he couldn't hear her commands to turn back, he ran without stopping till he came to the willow tree near Joey Hooligan's forge. There he slowed down to fill his lungs with the fresh, sweet air.

'Twas one of those warm-hearted, laughing autumn days which steals for a while the bonnet and shawl of the May. The sun, from a sky of feathery whiteness, laned over, telling jokes to the worruld, an' the goold harvest-fields and purple hills, lasy and continted, laughed back at the sun. Even the blackbird flying over the haw tree looked down an' sang to those below, 'God save all here'; an' the linnet from her bough answered back quick an' sweet, 'God save you kindly, sir!'

With such pleasant sight and sounds an' twitterings at every side, our hayro didn't feel the time passing till he was on top of the first hill of the Sleive-na-mon Mountains, which, as everyone knows, is called the Pig's Head.

It wasn't quite lonesome enough on the Pig's Head, so our hayro plunged into the walley an' climbed the second mountain – the Divil's Pillow where 'twas lonesome and desarted enough to shuit anyone.

Beneath the shade of a tree, for the days was warm, he set himself down in the long, sweet grass, lit his pipe, and let his mind go free. But, as he did, his thoughts rose together like a flock of frightened, angry pheasants, an' whirred back to the owdacious things Bridget had said about his relations.

Wasn't she the mendageous, humbrageous woman, he thought, to say such things about as illegant stock, as the O'Gills and the O'Gradys?

Why, Wullum O'Gill, Darby's uncle, at that minute, was head butler at Castle Brophy, and was known far an' wide as being one of the foinest scholars an' as having the most beautiful pair of legs in all Ireland!

This same Wullum O'Gill had tould Bridget in Darby's own hearing, on a day when the three were going through the great picture-gallery at Castle Brophy, that the O'Gills at one time had been Kings in Ireland.

Darby never since could raymember whether this time was before the flood or afther the flood. Bridget said it was durin' the flood, but surely that sayin' was nonsinse.

Howsumever, Darby knew his Uncle Wullum was right, for he often felt in himself the signs of greatness. And now as he sat alone on the grass, he said out loud: 'If I had me rights I'd be doing nothing all day long but sittin' on a throne, an' playin' games of forty-five with the Lord Liftenant an' some of me generals. There never was a lord that likes good ating or dhrinking betther nor I, or who hates worse to get up airly in the morning. That last disloike I'm tould is a great sign entirely of gentle blood the worruld over,' says he.

As for the wife's people, the O'Hagans an' the O'Shaughnessys, well – they were no great shakes, he said to himself, at laste so far as looks were concerned. All the handsomeness in Darby's childher came from his own side of the family. Even Father Cassidy said the childher took afther the O'Gills.

'If I were rich,' said Darby, to a lazy ould bumble-bee who was droning an' tumbling in front of him, 'I'd have a castle like Castle Brophy, with a great picture-gallery in it. On one wall I'd put the picture of the O'Gills and the O'Gradys, and on the wall ferninst them I'd have the O'Hagans an' the O'Shaughnessys.'

At that ideah his heart bubbled in a new and fierce deloight. 'Bridget's people,' he says agin, scowling at the bee, 'would look four times as common as they raylly are, whin they were compared in that way with my own relations. An' whenever Bridget got rampageous I'd take her in and show her the difference betwixt the two clans, just to punish her, so I would.'

How long the lad sat that way warming the cowld thoughts of his heart with drowsy, pleasant dhrames an' misty longings he don't rightly know, whin – tack, tack, tack, tack, came the busy sound of a little hammer from the other side of a fallen oak.

'Be jingo!' he says to himself with a start, ' 'tis the leprechaun that's in it.'

In a second he was on his hands an' knees, the tails of his coat flung across his back, an' he crawling softly toward the sound of the hammer. Quiet as a mouse he lifted himself up on the mossy log to look over, and there before his two popping eyes was a sight of wondheration.

Sitting on a white stone an' working away like fury, hammering pegs into a little red shoe, half the size of your thumb, was a bald-headed ould cobbler of about twice the hoight of your hand. On the top of a round, snub nose was perched a pair of horn-rimmed spectacles, an' a narrow fringe of iron-grey whuskers grew undher his stubby chin. The brown leather apron he wore was so long that it covered his green knee-breeches an' almost hid the knitted grey stockings.

The leprechaun – for it was he indade – as he worked, mumbled an' mutthered in great discontent: 'Oh, haven't I the hard, hard luck,' he said. 'I'll never have thim done in time for her to dance in tonight. So, thin, I'll be kilt entirely,' says he. 'Was there ever another quane of the fairies as wearing on shoes an' brogues an' dancin' slippers? Haven't I the – ' Looking up, he saw Darby.

'The top of the day to you, dacint man!' says the cobbler, jumpin' up. Giving a sharp cry, he pinted quick at Darby's stomach. 'But, wirra, wirra, what's that wooly, ugly thing you have crawling an' creepin' on your weskit?' he said, purtendin' to be all excited.

'Sorra thing on my weskit,' answered Darby, cool as ice, 'or anywhere else that'll make me take my two bright eyes off'n you – not for a second,' says he.

'Well! Well! will you look at that, now?' laughed the cobbler.

'Mark how quick an' handy he took me up! Will you have a pinch of snuff, clever man?' he axed, houlding up the little box.

'Is it the same snuff you gave Barney McBride a while ago?' axed Darby, sarcastic. 'Lave off your foolishness,' says our hayro, growin' fierce, 'and grant me at once the favours of the three wishes, or I'll have you smoking like a herring in my own chimney before nightfall,' says he.

At that the leprechaun, seeing that he but wasted time on so knowledgeable a man as Darby O'Gill, surrendhered, and granted the favours of the three wishes.

'What is it you ask?' says the cobbler, himself turning on a sudden very sour an' sullen.

'First an' foremost,' says Darby, 'I want a home of my ansisthers, an' it must be a castle like Castle Brophy, with pictures of my kith an' kin on the wall, and then facing them pictures of my wife Bridget's kith an' kin on the other wall.'

'That favour I give ye, that wish I grant ye,' says the fairy, making the shape of a castle on the ground with his awl.

'What next?' he grunted.

'I want goold enough for me an' my generations to enjoy in grandeur the place forever.'

'Always the goold,' sneered the little man, bending to dhraw with his awl on the turf the shape of a purse.

'Now for your third and last wish. Have a care!'

'I want the castle set on this hill – the Divils Pillow – where we two stand,' says Darby. Then sweeping with his arm, he says, 'I want the land about to be my demesne.'

The leprechaun stuck his awl on the ground. 'That wish I give you, that wish I grant you,' he says. With that he straightened himself up, and grinning most aggravaytin' the while, he looked Darby over from top to toe. 'You're a foine, knowledgeable man, but have a care of the fourth wish!' says he.

Bekase there was more of a challenge than friendly warning in what the small lad said, Darby snapped his fingers at him an' cried: 'Have no fear, little man! If I got all Ireland ground for making a fourth wish, however small, before midnight I'd not make it. I'm going home now to fetch Bridget an' the childher, and the only fear or unaisiness I have is that you'll not keep your word, so as to have the castle here ready before us when I come back.'

'Oho! I'm not to be thrusted, amn't I?' screeched the little lad, flaring into a blazing passion. He jumped upon the log that was betwixt them, and with one fist behind his back shook the other at Darby.

'You ignorant, suspicious-minded blaggard!' says he. 'How dare the likes of you say the likes of that to the likes of me!' cried the cobbler. 'I'd have you to know,' he says, 'that I had a repitation for truth an' voracity ayquil if not shuperior to the best, before you were born!' he shouted. 'I'll take no high talk from a man that's afraid to give words to his own wife if whin she's in a tantrum!' says the leprechaun.

'It's aisy to know you're not a married man,' says Darby, mighty scornful, 'bekase if you –'

The lad stopped short, forgetting what he was going to say in his surprise an' aggaytation, for the far side of the mountain was waving up an' down before his eyes like a great green blanket that is being shook by two women, while at the same time high spots of turf on the hillside toppled sidewise to level themselves up with the low places. The enchantment had already begun to make things ready for the castle. A dozen foine trees that stood in a little grove bent their heads quickly together, and thin by some inwisible hand they were plucked up by the roots an' dhropped aside much the same as a man might grasp a handful of weeds an' fling them from his garden.

The ground under the knowledgeable man's feet began to rumble an' heave. He waited for no more. With a cry that was half of gladness an' half of fear, he turned on his heel an' started on a run down into the walley, leaving the little cobbler standing on the log, shouting abuse after him an' ballyraggin' him as he ran.

So excited was Darby that, going up the Pig's Head, he was nearly run over by a crowd of great brown building stones which were moving down slow an' ordherly like a flock of driven sheep – but they moved without so much as bruising a blade of grass or bendin' a twig, as they came.

Only once, and that at the top of the Pig's Head, he trew a look back.

The Divil's Pillow was in a great commotion; a whirlwind was sweeping over it – whether of dust or of mist he couldn't tell.

Afther this, Darby never looked back again or to the right or the left of him, but kept straight on till he found himself, panting and pufflng, at his own kitchen door. 'Twas tin minutes before he could spake, but at last, whin he tould Bridget to make ready herself and the childher to go up to the Divil's Pillow with him, for once in her life that raymarkable woman, without axing, How comes it so, What rayson have you, or Why should I do it, set to work washing the childer's faces.

Maybe she dabbed a little more soap in their eyes than was needful, for 'twas a habit she had; though this time if she did, not a whimper broke from the little hayros. For the matther of that, not one word, good, bad or indifferent, did herself spake till the whole family were trudging down the lane two by two, marching like sojers.

As they came near the first hill along its sides the evening twilight turned from purple to brown, and at the top of the Pig's Head the darkness of a black night swooped suddenly down on them. Darby hurried on a step or two ahead, an' resting his hand upon the large rock that crowns the hill, looked anxiously over to the Divil's Pillow. Although he was ready for something foine, yet the greatness of the foineness that met his gaze knocked the breath out of him.

Across the deep walley, and on top of the second mountain, he saw lined against the evening sky the roof of an imminse castle, with towers an' parrypets an' battlements. Undher the towers a thousand sullen windows glowed red in the black walls. Castle Brophy couldn't hould a candle to it.

'Behold!' says Darby, flinging out his arm, and turning to his wife, who had just come up – 'behold the castle of my ansisthers who were my forefathers!'

'How,' says Bridget, quick and scornful – 'how could your aunt's sisters be your four fathers?'

What Darby was going to say to her he don't just raymember, for at that instant from the right-hand side of the mountain came a cracking of whips, a rattling of wheels, an' the rush of horses, and, lo and behold! a great dark coach with flashing lamps, and drawn by four coal-black horses, dashed up the hill and stopped beside them. Two shadowy men were on the driver's box.

'Is this Lord Darby O'Gill?' axed one of them, in a deep, muffled woice. Before Darby could reply, Bridget took the words out of his mouth.

'It is!' she cried, in a kind of a half cheer, 'an' Lady O'Gill an' the childher.'

'Then hurry up!' says the coachman. 'Your supper's gettin' cowld.'

Without waiting for anyone Bridget flung open the carriage door, an' pushin' Darby aside jumped in among the cushions. Darby, his heart sizzlin' with vexation at her audaciousness, lifted in one after another the childher, and then got in himself.

He couldn't undherstand at all the change in his wife, for she had always been the odherliest, modestist woman in the parish.

Well, he'd no sooner shut the door than crack went the whip, the horses gave a spring, the carriage jumped, and down the hill they went. For fastness there was never another carriage-ride like that before nor since. Darby hildt tight with both hands to the window, his face pressed against the glass. He couldn't tell whether the horses were only flying or whether the coach was falling down the hill into the walley. By the hollow feeling in his stomach he thought they were falling. He was striving to think of some prayers when there came a terrible jolt which sint his two heels against the roof an' his head betwixt the cushions. As he righted himself the wheels began to grate on a graveled road, an' plainly they were dashing up the side of the second mountain.

Even so, they couldn't have gone far whin the carriage dhrew up in a flurry, an' he saw through the gloom a high iron gate being slowly opened.

'Pass on,' said a voice from somewhere in the shadows; 'their supper's getting cowld.'

As they flew undher the great archway, Darby had a glimpse of the thing which had opened the gate, and had said their supper was getting cowld. It was standing on its hind legs – in the darkness he couldn't be quite sure as to its shape, but it was ayther a Bear or a Loin.

His mind was in a pondher about this when, with a swirl an' a bump, the carriage stopped another time, an' now it stood before a broad flight of stone steps which led up to the main door of the castle. Darby, half afraid, peering out through the darkness, saw a square of light high above him which came from the open hall door. Three sarvants in livery stood waiting on the thrashol.

'Make haste, make haste!' says one, in a doleful voice; 'their supper's gettin' cowld.'

Hearing these words, Bridget imagetly bounced out, an' was halfway up the steps before Darby could ketch her an' hould her till the childher came up.

'I never in all my life saw her so owdacious,' he says, half cryin', an' linkin' her arm to keep her back, an' thin, with the childher following two by two, according to size, the whole family payraded up the steps, till Darby, with a gasp of deloight, stopped on the thrashol of a splendid hall. From a high ceiling hung great flags from every nation an' domination, which swung and swayed in the dazzlin' light. Two lines of men and maid servants dhressed in silks an' satins an' brocades, stood facing aich other, bowing an' smiling an' wavin' their hands in welcome. The two lines stretched down to the goold stairway at the far ind of the hall. For half of one minute Darby, every eye in his head as big as a tay-cup, stood hesitaytin'. Thin he said, 'Why should it flutther me? Arrah, ain't it all mine? Aren't all these people in me pay? I'll engage it's a pritty penny all this grandeur is costing me to keep up this minute.' He trew out his chist. 'Come on, Bridget!' he says; 'let's go into the home of my ansisthers.'

Howandever, scarcely had he stepped into the beautiful place whin two pipers with their pipes, two fiddlers with their fiddles, two flute-players with their flutes, an' they dhressed in scarlet an' goold, stepped out in front of him, and thus to maylodius music the family proudly marched down the hall, climbed up the goolden stairway at its ind, an' thin turned to enter the biggest room Darby had ever seen.

Something in his sowl whuspered that this was the picture-gallery.

'Be the powers of Pewther!' says the knowledgeable man to himself, 'I wouldn't be in Bridget's place this minute for a hatful of money! Wait, oh just wait, till she has to compare her own relations with my own foine people! I know how she'll feel, but I wondher what she'll say,' he says.

The thought that all the unjust things, all the unraysonable things Bridget had said about his kith an' kin were just going to be disproved and turned against herself, made him proud an' almost happy.

But wirrasthrue! He should have raymembered his own adwise not to make nor moil nor meddle with the fairies, for here he was to get the first hard welt from the little leprechaun.

It was the picture-gallery sure enough, but how terribly different everything was from what the poor lad expected. There on the left wall, grand an' noble, shone the pictures of Bridget's people. Of all the well-dressed, handsome, proud-appearing persons in the whole worruld, the O'Hagans an' the O'Shaughnessys would compare with the best. This was a hard enough crack, though a crushinger knock was to come. Ferninst them on the right wall glowered the O'Gills and the O'Gradys, and of all the ragged, sheep-stealing, hangdog-looking villains one ever saw in jail or out of jail, it was Darby's kindred.

The place of honour on the right wall was given to Darby's fourth cousin, Phelem McFadden, an' he was painted with a pair of handcuffs on him. Wullum O'Gill had a squint in his right eye, and his thin legs bowed like hoops on a barrel.

If you have ever at night been groping your way through a dark room, and got a sudden, hard bump on the forehead from the edge of the door, you can undherstand the feelings of the knowledgeable man.

'Take that picture out!' he said, hoarsely, as soon as he could speak. 'An' will someone kindly inthrojuice me to the man who med it? Bekase,' he says, 'I intend to take his life! There was never a crass-eyed O'Gill since the world began,' says he.

Think of his horror an' surprise whin he saw the left eye of Wullum O'Gill twist itself slowly over toward his nose and squint worse than the right eye.

Purtending not to see this, an' hoping no one else did, Darby fiercely led the way over to the other wall.

Fronting him stood the handsome picture of Honoria O'Shaughnessy, an' she dhressed in a shuit of tin clothes like the knights of ould used to wear – armour I think they calls it.

She hildt a spear in her hand with a little flag on the blade, an' her smile was proud and high.

'Take that likeness out, too,' says Darby, very spiteful; 'that's not a dacint shuit of clothes for any woman to wear!'

The next minute you might have knocked him down with a feather, for the picture of Honoria O'Shaughnessy opened its mouth an' stuck out its tongue at him.

'The supper's getting cowld, the supper's getting cowld!' someone cried at the other ind of the picture gallery. Two big doors were swung open, an' glad enough was our poor hayro to folly the musicianers down to the room where the ating an' drinking were to be thransacted.

This was a little room with lots of looking-glasses, and it was bright with a thousand candles, and white with the shining-ist marble. On the table was biled beef an' reddishes an' carrots an' roast mutton an' all kinds of important ating an' drinking. Beside there stood fruits an' sweets an' – but, sure, what is the use in talkin'?

A high-backed chair stood ready for aich of the family, an' 'twas a lovely sight to see them all whin they were sitting there – Darby at the head, Bridget at the foot, the childher – the poor little paythriarchs – sitting bolt upright on aich side, with a bewigged and befrilled serving-man standing haughty behind every chair.

The atin' and dhrinkin' would have begun at once – in throth there was already a bit of biled beef on Darby's plate – only that he spied a little silver bell beside him. Sure, 'twas one like those the quality keep to ring whin they want more hot wather for their punch, but it puzzled the knowledgeable man, and 'twas the beginning of his misfortune.

'I wondher,' he thought, 'if 'tis here for the same raison as the bell is at the Curragh races – do they ring this one so that all at the table will start ating and dhrinking fair, an' no one will have the advantage, or is it,' he says to himself agin, 'to ring whin the head of the house thinks everyone has had enough. Haven't the quality quare ways! I'll be a long time learning them,' he says.

He sat silent and puzzling an' staring at the biled beef on his plate, afeard to start in without ringing the bell, an' dhreadin' to risk ringing it. The grand sarvants towered cowldly on every side, their chins tilted, but they kep' throwing over their chowlders glances so scornful and haughty that Darby shivered at the thought of showing any un-cultivaytion.

While our hayro sat thus in unaisy contimplation an' smouldherin' mortification an' flurried hesitaytion, a powdhered head was poked over his chowlder, and a soft, beguiling voice said, 'Is there anything else you'd wish for?'

The foolish lad twisted in his chair, opened his mouth to spake, and gave a look at the bell; shame rushed to his cheeks, he picked up a bit of the biled beef on his fork, an' to consale his turpitaytion gave the misfortunit answer: 'I'd wish for a pinch of salt, if you plaze,' says he.

'Twas no sooner said than came the crash. Oh, tunderation an' murdheration, what a roaring crash it was! The lights winked out together at a breath an' left a pitchy, throbbing darkness. Overhead and to the sides was a roaring, smashing, crunching noise, like the ocean's madness when the winthry storm breaks agin the Kerry shore, an' in that roar was mingled the tearing and the splitting of the walls and the fading of the chimneys. But through all this confusion could be heard the shrill, laughing woice of the leprechaun. 'The clever man med his fourth grand wish' it howled.

Darby – a thousand wild woices screaming an' mocking above him – was on his back kicking and squirming and striving to get up, but some load hilt him down, an' something bound his eyes shut.

'Are you kilt, Bridget asthore?' he cried; 'Where are the childher?' he says.

Instead of answer there suddenly flashed a fierce an' angry silence, an' its quickness frightened the lad more than all the wild confusion before.

'Twas a full minute before he dared to open his eyes to face the horrors which he felt were standing about him; but when courage enough to look came, all he saw was the night-covered mountain, a purple sky, and a thin, new moon, with one trembling goold star a hand's space above its bosom.

Darby struggled to his feet. Not a stone of the castle was left, not a sod of turf but what was in its ould place; every sign of the little cobbler's work had melted like April snow. The very trees Darby had seen pulled up by the roots that same afternoon now stood a waving blur below the new moon, an' a nightingale was singing in their branches. A cricket chirped lonesomely on the same fallen log which had hidden the leprechaun.

'Bridget! Bridget!' Darby called agin an' agin. Only a sleepy owl on a distant hill answered.

A shivering thought jumped into the boy's bewildered sowl – maybe the leprechaun had stolen Bridget an' the childher.

The poor man turned, and for the last time darted down into the night-filled walley.

Not a pool in the road he waited to go around, not a ditch in his path he didn't leap over, but ran as he never ran before till he raiched his own front door.

His heart stood still as he peeped through the window. There were the childher croodled around Bridget, who sat with the youngest asleep in her lap before the fire, rocking back an' forth, an' she crooning a happy, continted baby-song.

Tears of gladness crept into Darby's eyes as he looked in upon her. 'God bless her!' he says to himself. 'She's the flower of the O'Hagans and the O'Shaughnessys, and she's a proud feather in the caps of the O'Gills and the O'Gradys.'

'Twas well he had this happy thought to cheer him as he lifted the door-latch, for the manest of all the little cobbler's spiteful thricks waited in the house to meet Darby – nayther Bridget nor the childher raymembered a single thing of all that had happened to them during the day. They were willing to make their happydavitts that they had been no farther than their own petatie-patch since morning.

D. R. MᶜANALLY, JR

The Defeat of the Widows

When superstitions have not yet been banished from any other part of the world it is not wonderful that they should still be found in the country districts of Ireland, rural life being especially favourable to the perpetuation of old ways of living and modes of thought, since in an agricultural district less change takes place in a century than may, in a city, be observed in a single decade. Country people preserve their old legends with their antique styles of apparel, and thus the relics of the pagan ages of Ireland have come down from father to son, altered and adapted to the changes in the country and its population. Thus, for instance, the old-fashioned witch is no longer found in any part of Ireland, her memory lingering only as a tradition, but her modern successor is frequently met with, and in many parishes a retired hovel in a secluded lane is a favourite resort of the neighbouring peasants, for it is the home of the Pishogue, or wise woman, who collects herbs, and, in her way, doctors her patients sometimes with simple medicinal remedies, sometimes with charms, according to their gullibility and the nature of their ailments.

Not far from Ballinahinch, a fishing village on Birterbuy Bay, in the County Galway, and in the most lonely valley of the neighbourhood, there dwells one of these wise women who supplant the ancient witches. The hovel which shelters her bears every indication of wretched poverty; the floor is mud, the smoke escapes through a hole in the thatch in default of a chimney; the bed is a scanty heap of straw in the corner, and two rude shelves, bearing a small assortment of cracked jars and broken bottles, constitute Moll's stock in trade.

The misery of her household surroundings, however, furnished to the minds of her patients no argument against the efficiency of her remedies, Moll being commonly believed to have 'a power av goold,' though no one had ever see any portion thereof. But with all her reputed riches she had no fear of robbers, for 'she could aisily do for thim did they but come as many as the shtraws in the thatch,' and would-be robbers, no doubt understanding that fact, prudently consulted their own safety by staying away from the vicinity of her cabin.

'Owld Moll,' as she was known, was a power in the parish, and her help was sought in many emergencies. Did a cow go dry, Moll knew the reason and might possibly remove the spell; if a baby fell ill, Moll had an explanation of its ailment, and could tell at a glance whether the little one was or was not affected by the evil of a secret enemy. If a pig was stolen, she was shrewd in her conjectures as to the direction its wrathful owner must take in the search. But her forte lay in bringing about love-matches. Many were the charms at her command for this purpose, and equally numerous the successes with which she was accredited. Some particulars of her doings in this direction were furnished by Jerry Magwire, a jolly car-man of Galway, who had himself been benefited by her services.

'Sure I was married meself be her manes,' stated Jerry, 'an' this is the way it was. Forty-nine years ago come next Mickelmas, I was a good-lookin' young felly, wid a nate cabin on the road from Ballinasloe to Ballinamore, havin' a fine car an' a mare an' her colt, that was as good as two horses whin the colt grew up. I was afther payin' coort to Dora O'Callighan, that was the dawther av Misther O'Callighan that lived in the County Galway, an', be the same token, was a fine man. In thim times I used be comin' over here twict or three times a year wid a bagman, commercial thraveller, you'd call him, an' I heard say av Owld Moll, an' she wasn't owld thin, an' the next time I come, I wint to her an' got an inchantmint. Faix, some av it is gone from me, but I mind that I was to change me garthers, an' tie on me thumb a bit o' bark she gev me, an' go to the churchyard on Halloween, an' take the first chilla-ca-pooka (snail) I found on a tombshtone, an' begob, it was that same job that was like to be the death o' me, it bein' dark an' I bendin' to look clost, a hare jumped in me face from undher the shtone. "Jagers," says I, an' me fallin' on me back on the airth an' the life lavin' me. "Presince o' God be about me," says I, for I knewn the inchantmint wasn't right, no more I oughtn't to be at it, but the hare was skairt like meself an' run, an' I found the shnail an' run too wid the shweat pourin' aff me face in shtrames.

'So I put the shnail in a plate that I covered wid another, an' av the Sunday, I opened it fur to see phat letters it writ, an' bad luck to the wan o' thim cud I rade at all, fur in thim days I cudn't tell A from any other letther. I tuk the plate to Misther O'Callighan, fur he was a fine scholar an' cud rade both books an' writin', an' axed him phat the letters was.

' "A–a–ah, ye ignerant gommoch," says he to me, "yer head's as empty as a drum. Sure here's no writin' at all, only marks that the shnail's afther makin' an' it crawlin' on the plate."

'So I explained the inchantmint to him, an' he looked a little closter, an' thin jumped wid shurprise.

' "Oh," says he. "Is that thrue?" says he. "Ye must axqueeze me, Misther Magwire. Sure the shnails doesn't write a good hand, an' I'm an owld man an' me eyes dim, but I see it betther now. Faith, the first letter's a D," says he, an' thin he shtudied awhile. "An' the next is a O, an' thin there's a C," says he, "only the D an' the C is bigger than the O, an' that's all the letters there is," says he.

' "An' phat does thim letters shpell?" says I, bekase I didn't know.

' "Ah, bad scran to 'em," says he; "there's thim cows in me field agin," says he. "Ax Dora, here she comes," an' away he wint as she come in, an' I axed her phat D.O.C. shpelt; an' she towld me her name, an' I go bail she was surprised to find the shnail had writ thim letters on the plate, so we marr'd the next Sunday.

'But Owld Moll is a knowledgeable woman an' has a power av shpells an' charms. There's Tim Gallagher, him as dhrives the public car out o' Galway, he's bought his luck av her be the month, fur nigh on twenty year, barin' wan month, that he forgot, an' that time he shpilt his load in the ditch an' kilt a horse, bein' too dhrunk to dhrive.

'Whin me dawther Dora, that was named afther her mother, was ill afther she'd been to the dance, whin O'Hoolighan's Peggy was married to Paddy Noonan (she danced too hard in the cabin an' come home in the rain), me owld woman wint to Moll an' found that Dora had been cast wid an avil eye. So she gev her a tay to dhrink an' a charm to wear agin it, an' afther she'd dhrunk the tay an' put on the charm the faver lift her, an' she was well entirely.

'Sure Moll towld me wan magpie manes sorrow, two manes luck, three manes a weddin', an' four manes death; an' didn't I see four o' thim the day o' the fair in Ennis whin O'Dougherty was laid out? An' whin O'Riley cut his arrum wid a billhook, an' the blood was runnin', didn't she tie a shtring on the arrum an' dip a raven's feather into the blood av a black cat's tail, an' shtop the bleedin'? An' didn't she bid me take care o' meself the day I met a red-headed woman afore dinner, an' it wasn't six months till I met the woman in the mornin', it a-rainin' an' ivery dhrop the full o' yer hat, an' me topcoat at home, an' that same night was I tuk wid the roomytics an' didn't shtir a toe fur a fortnight. Faix, she's an owld wan is Moll; phat she can't do it n't worth thryin'. If she goes fur to make a match, all the fathers in Ireland cudn't purvint it, an' it's no use o' their settin' theirselves agin her, fur her head's as long as a summer day an' as hard as a shillalee.

'Did iver ye hear how she got a husband for owld Miss Rooney, the same that married Misther Dooley that kapes the Aygle Inn in Lisdoon Varna, an' tuk him clane away from the Widdy Mulligan an' two more widdy's that were comin' down upon him like kites on a young rabbit?

'Well, it's a mighty improvin' shtory, fur it shows that widdys can be baten whin they're afther a husband, that some doesn't belave, but they do say it takes a witch, the divil, an' an owld maid to do it, an' some think that all o' thim isn't aiquel to a widdy, aven if there's three o' thim an' but wan av her.

'The razon av it is this. Widdy wimmin are like lobsthers, whin they wanst ketch holt, begob, they've no consate av lettin' go at all, but will shtick to ye tighter than a toenail, till ye've aither to marry thim or murther thim, that's the wan thing in the end; fur if ye marry thim ye're talked to death, an' if ye murther thim ye're only dacintly hanged out o' the front dure o' the jail. Whin they're afther a husband, they're as busy as owld Nick, an' as much in airnest as a dog in purshoot av a flea. More-be-token, they're always lookin' fur the proper man, an' if they see wan that they think will shuit, bedad, they go afther him as strait as an arrer, an' if he doesn't take the alarum an' run like a shape-thief, the widdy'ull have him afore the althar an' married fast an' tight while he'd be sayin'a craydo.

'They know so much be wan axpayrience av marryin', that, barrin' it's a widdy man that's in it, an' he nows as much as thimselves, they'll do for him at wanst, bekase it's well undhershtood that a bach'ler, aither young or owld, has as much show av outshtrappin' a widdy as a mouse agin a weasel.

'Now, this Misther Dooley was an owld bach'ler, nigh on five an' thirty, an' about fifteen years ago, come next Advint, he come from Cork wid a bit o' money, an' tuk the farm beyant Misther McCoole's on the lift as ye come out o' Galway. He wasn't a bad lookin' felly, an' liked the ladics, an' the first time he was in chapel afther takin' the farm, aitch widdy an' owld maid set the two eyes av her on him, an' the Widdy Mulligan says to herself, says she, "Faix, that's just the man to take the place av me dear Dinnis," fur, ye see the widdy's always do spake that-a-way av their husbands, a-givin' them the good word after they're dead, so as to make up fur the tonge lashin's they give 'em whin they're alive. It's quare, so it is, phat widdys are like. Whin ye see a widdy at the wake schraimin' fit to shplit yer head wid the noise, an' flingin' herself acrass the grave at the berryin' like it was a bag o'male she was, an' thin spakin' all the time av "me poor dear hushband", I go bail they lived together as paceful as a barrel full o' cats an' dogs; no more is it sorrow that's in it, but raimorse that's tarin' at her, an' the shquailin' an' kickin' is beways av a pinnance fur the gostherin' she done him whin he was livin', fur the more there's in a jug, the less noise it makes runnin' out, an' whin ye've a heavy load to carry, ye nade all yer breath, an' so have none to waste tellin' how it's breakin' yer back.

'So it was wid the Widdy Mulligan, that kept the Shamrock Inn, for her Dinnis was a little ottomy av a gossoon, an' her the full av a dure, an' the arrum on her like a smith an' the fut like a leg o' mutton. Och, she was big enough thin, but she's a horse entirely now, wid the walk av a duck, an' the cheeks av her shakin' like a bowl av shtirabout whin she goes. Her poor Dinnis darn't say his sowl belonged to him, but was conthrolled be her, an' they do say his last words were, "I'll have pace", that was phat he niver had afther he married her, fur she was wan that'ud be shmilin' an' shmilin' an' the tongue av her like a razer. She'd a good bit o' property in the inn, siven beds in the house fur thravellers, an' six childher, the oldest nigh on to twelve, an' from him on down in reg'lar steps like thim in front o' the coorthouse.

'Now, a bit up the shtrate from the Shamrock there was a little shop kept be Missis O'Donnell, the widdy av Tim O'Donnell, that died o' bein' mortified in his legs that broke be his fallin' aff his horse wan night whin he was comin' back from Athlone, where he'd been to a fair. Missis O'Donnell was a wapin' widdy, that's got eyes like a hydrant, where ye can turn on the wather whin ye plaze. Begorra, thim's the widdys that'ull do fur anny man, fur no more can ye tell phat's in their minds be lookin' at their faces than phat kind av close they've got on be lookin' at their shadders, an' whin they corner a man that's tinder-hearted, an' give a shy look at him up out o' their eyes, an' thin look down an' sind two or three dhrops o' wather from undher their eye-lashers, the only salvation fur him is to get up an' run like it was a bag o' gun-powdher she was. So Missis O'Donnell, whin she seen Misther Dooley, tuk the same notion into her head that the Widdy Mulligan did, fur she'd two childher, a boy an' a gurrul, that were growin' up, an' the shop wasn't payin' well.

'There was another widdy in it, the Widdy McMurthry, that afther-wards married a sargeant av the polis, an' lives in Limerick. She was wan o' thim frishky widdy's that shtruts an' wears fine close an' puts on more airs than a paycock. She was a fine-lookin' woman thim times, an' had money in plinty that she got be marryin' McMurthry, that was owld enough to be a father to her an' died o' dhrinkin' too much whishkey at first, an' thin too much sulphur-wather at Lisdoon Varna to set him right agin. She was always ready wid an answer to ye, fur it was quick witted she was, wid slathers o' talk that didn't mane annything, an' a giggle that she didn't nade to hunt fur whin she wanted it to make a show wid. An' she'd a dawther that was a fine child, about siventeen, a good dale like her mother.

'Now, Misther Dooley has a kind heart in his body fur wimmin in gineral, an' as he liked a bit o' chaff wid thim on all occashuns, he wasn't long in gettin' acquainted wid all the wimmin o' the parish, an' was well liked be thim, an', be the same token, wasn't be the men, fur men, be nacher, doesn't like a woman's man anny more than wimmin like a man's woman. But, afther a bit, he begun to centhre himself on the three widdys, an' sorra the day' ud go by whin he come to town but phat he'd give wan or another o' thim a pace av his comp'ny that was very plazin' to thim. Bedad, he done that same very well, for he made a round av it for to kape thim in suspince. He'd set in the ale room o' the Shamrock an hour in the afthernoon an' chat wid the Widdy Mulligan as she was sarvin' the dhrink, an' shtop in the Widdy

O'Donnell's shop as he was goin' by, to get a thrifle or a bit av shwates an' give to her childher beways av a complimint, an' thin go to Missis McMurthry's to tay, an' so got on well wid thim all. An' it's me belafe he'd be doin' that same to this blessed day only that the widdys begun to be pressin' as not likin' fur to wait any longer. Fur, mind ye, a widdy's not like a young wan that'll wait fur ye to spake an' if ye don't do it, 'ull go on foriver, or till she gets tired av waitin' an' takes some wan else that does spake, widout sayin' a word to ye at all; but the widdy'ull be hintin' an' hintin', an' her hints'ull be as shtrong as a donkey's kick, so that the head o' ye has to be harder than a pavin'-shtone if ye don't undhershtand, an' ye've got to have more impidince than a monkey if ye don't spake up an' say something about marryin'.

'Well, as I was afther sayin', the widdys begun to be pressin' him clost: the Widdy Mulligan tellin' him how good her business was an' phat a savin' there'd be if a farm an' a public were put together; the Widdy O'Donnell a-lookin' at him out av her tears an' sighin' an' tellin' him how lonely he must be out on a farm an' nobody but a man wid him in the house, fur she was lonesome in town, an' it wasn't natheral at all, so it wasn't, fur aither man or woman to be alone; an' the Widdy McMurthry a palatherin' to him that if he'd a fine, good-lookin' woman that loved him, he'd be a betther man an' a changed man entirely. So they wint on, the widdys a-comin' at him, an' he thryin' to kape wid thim all, as he might have knewn he couldn't do (barrin' he married the three o' thim like a Turk), until aitch wan got to undhershtand, be phat he said to her, that he was goin' to marry her, an' the minnit they got this in their heads, aitch begged him that he'd shtay away from the other two, fur aitch knew he wint to see thim all. By jayminy, it bothered him thin, fur he liked to talk to thim all aiquelly, an' didn't want to confine his agrayable comp'ny to anny wan o' thim. So he got out av it thish-a-way. He promised the Widdy McMurthry that he'd not go to the Shamrock more than wanst in the week, nor into the Widdy O'Donnell's barrin' he naded salt fur his cow; an' said to the Widdy Mulligan that he'd not more than spake to Missis O'Donnell whin he wint in, an' that he'd go no more at all to Missis McMurthry's; an' he towld Missis O'Donnell that whin he wint to the Shamrock he'd get his sup an' thin lave at wanst, an' not go to the Widdy McMurthry's axceptin' whin his horse wanted to be shod, the blacksmith's bein' ferninst her dure that it'ud be convaynient fur him to wait at. So he shmiled wid himself thinkin' he'd done thim complately, an' made up his mind that whin his pitaties were dug he'd give up the farm an' get over into Country Clare, away from the widdys.

'But thim that think widdys are fools are desaved entirely, an' so was Misther Dooley, fur instead av his troubles bein' inded, begob, they were just begun. Ivery time he wint into the Shamrock Missis O'Donnell heard av it an' raymonshtrated wid him, an' 'ud cry at him beways it was dhrinkin' himself to death he was; afther lavin' the Shamrock, the Widdy Mulligan'ud set wan av her boys to watch him up the strate an' see if he shtopped in the shop. Av coorse he cudn't go by, an' whin he come agin, the Widdy Mulligan'ud gosther him about it, an' thin he'd promise not to do it agin. No more cud he go in the Widdy O'Donnell's shop widout meetin' Missis McMurthry's dawther that was always shtreelin' on the strate, an' thin her mother'ud say to him it was a power o' salt his cow was atin', an' the Widdy O'Donnell towld him his horse must be an axpensive baste fur to nade so much shooin'.

'Thin he'd tell thim a lot o' lies that they purtinded to belave an' didn't, bekase they're such desavers thimselves that it isn't aisey fur to do thim, but Dooley begun to think if it got anny hotter fur him he'd lave the pitaties to the widdys to divide bechune thim as a raytribution fur the loss av himself, an' go to Clare widout delay.

'While he'd this bother on him he got to know owld Miss Rooney, that lived wid her mother an' father on the farm next but wan to his own, but on the other side o' the way, an' the manes be which he got to know her was this. Wan mornin', whin Dooley's man, Paddy, wint to milk the cow, bad scran to the dhrop she'd to shpare, an' he pullin' an' pullin', like it was ringin' the chapel bell he was, an' she kickin', an' no milk comin', faix not as much as'ud blind the eye av a midge. So he wint an' towld Misther Dooley.

' "I can get no milk," says he. "Begorra the cow's as dhry as a fiddler's troat," says he.

' "Musha, thin," says Misther Dooley, "it's the lazy omadhawn ye are. I don't belave it. Can ye milk at all?" says he.

' "I can," says Paddy, "as well as a calf," says he. "But phat's the use ov pullin'? Ye'd get the same quantity from a rope," says he.

'So Dooley wint out an' thried himself an' didn't get as much as a shmell of milk.

' "Phat's the matther wid the baste?" says he, "an' her on the grass from sun to sun."

' "Be jakers," says Paddy, "it's my consate that she's bewitched."

' "It's thrue fur ye," says Dooley, as the like was aften knewn. "Go you to Misther Rooney's wid the pail an' get milk fur the calf, an' ax if there's a Pishogue hereabouts."

'So Paddy wint an' come back sayin' that the young lady towld him there was.

' "So there's a young lady in it," thinks Dooley. Faix, the love av coortin' was shtrong on him. "Did ye ax her how to raich the woman?"

' "Bedad, I didn't. I forgot," says Paddy.

' "That's yerself entirely," says Dooley to him agin. "I'd bether thrust me arriants to a four-legged jackass as to wan wid two. He'd go twict as fast an' remimber as much. I'll go meself," says he, only wantin' an axcuse, an' so he did. He found Miss Rooney thried to be plazin', an' it bein' convainient, he wint agin, an' so it was ivery day whin he'd go fur the calf's milk he'd have a chat wid her, an' sometimes come over in the avenin', bekase it wasn't healthy fur him in town just thin.

'But he wint to Owld Moll about the cow, an' the charm she gev him soon made the baste all right agin, but, be that time, he'd got used to goin' to Rooney's an' liked it betther than the town, bekase whinever he wint to town he had to make so many axcuses he was afeared the widdys'ud ketch him in a lie.

'So he shtayed at home most times and wint over to Rooney's the rest, fur it wasn't a bad job at all, though she was about one an' forty, an' had give up the fight fur a husband an' so saiced strugglin'. As long as they've anny hope, owld maids are the most praypostherous craythers alive, fur they' ll fit thimselves wid the thrappin's av a young gurrul an' look as onaisey in thim as a boy wid his father's britches on. But whin they've consinted to the sitiwation an' saiced to struggle, thin they begin to be happy an' enjoy life a bit, but there's no aise in the worruld fur thim till thin. Now Miss Rooney had gev up the contist an' plasthered her hair down on aitch side av her face so smooth ye'd shwear it was ironed it was, an' begun to take the worruld aisey.

'But there's thim that says an owld maid niver does give up her hope, only lets on to be continted so as to lay in amboosh fur anny onsuspishus man that happens to shtray along, an' faix, it looks that-a-way from phat I'm goin' to tell ye, bekase as soon as Misther Dooley begun to come over an' palather his fine talk to her an' say shwate things, thin she up an' begins shtrugglin' harder nor iver, bekase it was afther she'd let go, an' comin' onexpected-like she thought it was a dispinsation av Providence, whin rayly it was only an accident it was, beways av Dooley's cow goin' dhry an' the calf too young to lave suckin' an' ate grass.

'Annyhow, wan day, afther Misther Dooley had talked purty nice the avenin' afore, she put an her cloak, an' wint to Owld Moll an' in an' shut the dure.

' "Now, Moll," she says to the owld cuillean, "it's a long time since I've been to ye, barrin' the time the goat was lost, fur, sure, I lost me confidince in ye. Ye failed me twict, wanst whin John McCune forgot me whin he wint to Derry an' thin come back an' married that Mary O'Niel, the impidint young shtrap, wid the air av her as red as a glowin' coal; an' wanst whin Misther McFinnigan walked aff from me an' married the Widdy Bryan. Now ye must do yer besht, fur I'm thinkin' that, wid a little industhry, I cud get Misther Dooley, the same that the town widdys is so flusthrated wid."

' "An' does he come to see ye, at all?" says Moll.

' "Faith he does, an' onless I'm mishtaken is mightily plazed wid his comp'ny whin it's me that's in it," says Miss Rooney.

' "An' phat widdys is in it," says Moll, as she didn't know, bekase sorra a step did the widdys go to her wid their love doin's, as they naded no help, an' cud thransact thim affairs thimselves as long as their tongues held out.

'So Miss Rooney towld her, an' Moll shuk her head. "Jagers," says she, "I'm afeared yer goose is cooked if all thim widdys is after him. I won't thry," says she.

'But Miss Rooney was as much in airnest as the widdys, troth, I'm thinkin', more, bekase she was fairly aitchin' fur a husband now she'd got her mind on it.

' "Sure, Moll," says she, "ye wouldn't desart me now an' it me last show. Thim widdys can marry who they plaze, bad scran to 'em, but if Misther Dooley gets from me, divil fly wid the husband I'll get at all, at all," beginnin' to cry.

'So, afther a dale av palatherin', Moll consinted to thry, bein' it was the third time Miss Rooney had been to her, besides, she wanted to save her charackther for a knowledgeable woman. So she aggrade to do her best, an' gev her a little bag to carry wid 'erbs in it, an' writ some words on two bits av paper an' the same in Latin. It was an awful charm, no more do I remimber it, fur it was niver towld me, nor to anny wan else, fur it was too dreadful to say axceptin' in Latin an' in a whisper fur fear the avil sper'ts'ud hear it, that don't undhershtand thim dape langwidges.

' "Now, darlint," says owld Moll, a-givin' her wan, "take you this charm an' kape it on you an' the bag besides, an' ye must manage so as this other paper'ull be on Misther Dooley, an' if it fails an he don't marry ye I'll give ye back yer money an' charge ye nothing at all," says she.

'So Miss Rooney tuk the charms an' paid Owld Moll one pound five, an' was to give her fifteen shillins more afther she was married to Dooley.

'She wint home, bothered entirely how she'd get the charm on Dooley, an' the avenin' come, an' he wid it, an' shtill she didn't know. So he set an' talked an' talked, an' by an' he dhrunk up the rest av the whiskey an' wather in his glass an' got up to go.

' "Why, Misther Dooley," says she, bein' all at wanst shtruck be an idee. "Was iver the like seen av yer coat?" says she. "Sure it's tore in the back. Sit you down agin wan minnit an' I'll mend it afore ye can light yer pipe. Take it aff," says she.

' "Axqueeze me," says Dooley. "I may be a bigger fool than I look, or I may look a bigger fool than I am, but I know enough to kape the coat on me back whin I'm wid a lady," says he.

' "Then take a sate an' I'll sow it on ye," says she to him agin, so he set down afore the fire, an' she, wid a pair av shizzors an' a nadle, wint behind him an' at the coat. 'T was a sharp thrick av her, bekase she took the shizzors, an' whin she was lettin' on to cut aff the t'reads that she said were hangin', she ripped the collar an' shlipped in the bit o' paper, an' sowed it up as nate as a samesthress in less than no time.

' "It's much beholden to ye I am," say Dooley, risin' wid his pipe lit. "An' it's a happy man I'd be if I'd a young woman av yer size to do the like to me ivery day."

' "Glory be to God," says Miss Rooney to herself, fur she thought the charm was beginnin' to work. But she says to him, "Oh, it's talkin' ye are. A fine man like you can marry who he plazes."

'So Dooley wint home, an' she, think' the business as good as done, towld her mother that night she was to marry Misther Dooley. The owld lady cudn't contain herself or the saycret aither, so the next mornin' towld it to her sister, an' she to her dawther that wint to school wid Missis McMurthry's gurrul. Av coorse the young wan cudn't howld her jaw anny more than the owld wans, an' up an' towld the widdy's dawther an' she her mother an' the rest o' the town, so be the next day every wan knew that Dooley was goin' to marry Miss Rooney: that shows, if ye want to shpread a bit o' news wid a quickness aiquel to the tellygraph, ye've only to tell it to wan woman as a saycret.

'Well, me dear, the noise the widdys made'ud shtun a dhrummer. Dooley hadn't been in town fur a week, an' widdys bein' nacherly suspishus, they misthrusted that somethin' was wrong, but divil a wan o' thim thought he'd do such an onmannerly thrick as that. But they all belaved it, bekase widdys judge iverybody be themselves, so they were mighty mad.

'The Widdy McMurthry was first to hear the news, as her dawther towld her, an' she riz in a fury. "Oh the owdashus villin," says she; "to think av him comin' her an' me listenin' at him that was lyin' fasther than a horse'ud throt. But I'll have justice, so I will, an' see if there's a law for a lone widdy. I'll go to the judge, fur, I forgot to tell ye, it was jail delivery an' the coort was settin' an' the judge down from Dublin wid a wig on him the size av a bar'l.

'Whin they towld Missis O'Donnell, she bust out cryin' an' says, "Sure it can't be thrue. It isn't in him to desave a poor widdy wid only two childer, an' me thrustin' on him' so she wint into the back room an' laid on the bed.

'But whin the Widdy Mulligan learned it, they thought she'd take a fit, the face av her got so red an' she chokin' wid rage. "Tatther an' agers," says she. "If I only had that vagabone here five minnits, it's a long day it'ud be afore he'd desave another tinder-hearted faymale."

' "Oh, be aisey," says wan to her, "faix, you're not the onliest wan that's in it. Sure there's the Widdy O'Donnell an' Missis McMurthry that he's desaved aiquelly wid yerself."

' "Is that thrue?" says she; "by this an' by that I'll see thim an' we'll go to the judge an' have him in the prision. Sure the Quane's a widdy herself an' knows how it feels, an' her judge'ull take the part av widdys that's misconshtrewed be a nagurly blaggard like owld Dooley. Bad luck to the seed, breed, an' generation av him. I cud mop up the flure wid him, the divil roast him, an' if I lay me hands on him, I'll do it," says she, an' so she would; an' a blessin it was to Misther Dooley he was not in town just thin, but at home, diggin' pitaties as fast as he cud, an' chucklin' to himself how he'd send the pitaties to town be Paddy, an' himself go to Clare an' get away from the whole tribe av widdys an' owld maids.

'So the Widdy Mulligan wint afther the Widdy O'Donnell an' tuk her along, an' they towld thim av the Widdy McMurthry an' how she was done be him, an they got her too, fur they all said, "Sure we wouldn't marry him fur him, but only want to see him punished fur misconshtructing phat we said to him an' lying to us." Be this time half the town was ready an' aiger to go wid thim to the coort, an' so they did, an' in, wid the offishers thryin' to kape thim out, an' the wimmin shovin' in, an' all their frinds wid 'em, an' the shur'f callin' out "Ordher in the coort", an' the judge lookin' over his shpectacles at thim.

' "Phat's this at all?" says the judge, wid a solemnious voice. "Is it a riat it is, or a faymale convulsion?" – whin he seen all the wimmin. "Phat's the matther?" says he, an' wid that all the wimmin begun at wanst, so as the noise av thim was aiquel to a 'viction.

' "Marcy o' God," says the judge, "phat's in the faymales at all? Are they dishtracted entirely, or bewitched, or only dhrunk?" says he.

' "We're crazy wid graif, yer Lordshap," they schraimed at him at wanst. "It's justice we want agin the uppresser."

' "Phat's the uppresser been a-doin'?" axed the judge.

' "Disthroyin' our pace, an' that av our families," they said to him.

' "Who is the oppresser?" he axed.

' "Owld Dooley," they all shouted at him at the wan time, like it was biddin' at an auction they were.

'So at first the judge cudn't undhershtand at all, till some wan whishpered the truth to him an' thin he scrotched his chin wid a pen.

' "Is it a man fur to marry all thim widdys? Be me wig, he's a bowld wan. Go an' fetch him," he says to a consthable. "Be sated, ladies, an' ye'll have justice," he says to the widdys, very p'lite. "Turn out thim other blaggards," he says to the shur'f, an' away wint the polisman afther Dooley.

'He found him at home, wid his coat aff, an' him an' Paddy diggin' away at the pitaties for dear life, bekase he wanted to get thim done.

' "Misther Dooley," says the consthable to him, "ye're me prish'ner. Come along, ye must go wid me at wanst."

'At first, Dooley was surprised in that degray he thought the life'ud lave him, as the consthable come up behind him on the quiet, so as to give him no show to run away.

' "Phat for?" says Dooley to him, whin he'd got his wind agin.

' "Faix, I'm not sartain," says the polisman, that wasn't a bad felly; "but I belave it's along o' thim widdys that are so fond o' ye. The three o' thim's in the coort an' all the faymales in town, an' the judge sint me afther ye, an' ye must come at wanst, so make ready to go immejitly."

' "Don't go wid him," says Paddy, wid his sleeves rowled up an' spitting in his hands. "Lave me at him," says he, but Dooley wouldn't, bekase he was a paceable man. But he wasn't anxshus to go to the coort at all; begob, he'd all the coortin' he naded, but bein' there was no help fur it, he got his coat, the same that Miss Rooney sowed the charm in, an' shtarted wid the consthable.

'Now, it was that mornin' that owld Rooney was in town, thryin' to sell a goat he had, that gev him no end o' throuble be losin' itself part of the time an' the rest be jumpin' on the thatch an' stickin' its feet through. But he cudn't sell it, as ivery wan knew the bast as well as himself, an' so he was sober, that wasn't common wid him. Whin he seen the widdys an' the other wimmin wid thim shtravigerin' through the strate on the way to the coort an' heard the phillaloo they were afther makin', he axed phat the matther was. So they towld him, an' says he, "Be the powers, if it's a question av makin' him marry some wan, me dawther has an inthrust in the matther," so he dhropped the goat's shtring an' shtarted home in a lamplighter's throt to fetch her, an' got there about the time the polisman nabbed Dooley.

' "There, they're afther goin' now," says he to her. "Make haste, or we'll lose thim," an' aff they run, she wid her charm an' he widout his coat, grippin' a shillalee in his fisht, an' caught up wid Paddy that was follerin' the polisman an' Dooley.

'So they jogged along, comfortable enough, the polisman an' Dooley in the lade, afther thim owld Rooney an' Paddy, blaggardin' the consthable ivery fut o' the way, an' offerin' fur to bate him so as he wouldn't know himself be lookin' in the glass, an' Miss Rooney in the rare, wondherin' if the charm'ud work right. But Dooley didn't let a word out av his jaw, as knowin' he'd nade all his breath afther gettin' into the coort.

'At the rise o' the hill the pursesshun was met be about a hunderd o' the town boys that come out fur to view thim, an' that yelled at Dooley how the widdys were waitin' to tare him in paces, an' that he was as good as a dead man a'ready, so he was; an' whin they got into town, all the men jined the show, roarin' wid laughter an' shoutin' at Dooley that the judge cudn't do anny more than hang him at wanst, an' to shtand it like a hayro, bekase they'd all be at the hangin' an' come to the wake besides an' have a tundherin' big time. But he answered thim niver a word, so they all wint on to the coort, an' in, bringin' the other half o' the town wid 'em, the faymale half bein' there kapin' comp'ny wid the widdys.

'The minnit they come nie the dure, all the widdys an' wimmin begun in wan breath to make raimarks on thim.

' "A–a–a–ah, the hang-dog face he has," says Missis McMurthry. "Sure hasn't he the look av a shape-thief on the road to the gallus?"

' "See the haythen vagabone," says the Widdy Mulligan. "If I had me tin fingers on him for five minnits, it's all the satiswhackshun I'd ax. Bad cess to the hair I'd lave on the head av him or in his whushkers aither."

'But the Widdy O'Donnell only cried, an' all the wimmin turned their noses up whin they seen Miss Rooney comin' in.

' "Look at that owld thing," says they. "Phat a power av impidince! Mind the consate av her to be comin' here wid him. Sure she hasn't the shame av a shtone monkey," says they av her.

' "Silence in the coort," says the shur'f. "Stop that laughin' be the dure. Git along down out o' thim windys," says he to the mob that Dooley an' the consthable brought wid thim.

' "Misther Dooley," says the judge, "I'm axed to b'lave ye're thryin' to marry four wimmin at wanst, three av the same aforeshed bein' widdys an' the other wan not. Is it thrue, or do ye plade not guilty?" says he.

' "It's not thrue, yer Lordshap," says Dooley, shpakin' up, bekase he seen he was in for it an' put on a bowld face. "Thim widdys is crazy to get a husband, an' misconsayved the manin' o' me words," says he, an' that minnit you'd think a faymale lunattic ashylum broke loose in the coort.

'They all gabbled at wanst like a field av crows. They said he was a haythen, a Toork, a vulgar shpalpeen, a lyin' blaggard, a uppresser av the widdy, a robber av the orphin, he was worse than a nagur, he was, so he was, an' they niver thought av belavin' him, nor av marryin' him aither till he axed thim, an' so on.

'The judge was a married man himself an' knewn it was no use thryin' to shtop the gostherin', for it was a joke av him to say that the differ bechuxt a woman an' a book was you cud shut up a book, so he let thim go on till they were spint an' out o' breath an' shtopped o' thimselves like an owld clock that's run down.

' "The sintince av this coort, Misther Dooley, is, that ye marry wan av 'em an' make compinsation to the other wans in a paycoonyary way be payin' thim siven poun' aitch."

' "Have marcy, yer Lordshap," says Dooley, bekase he seen himself shtripped av all he had. "Make it five poun', an' that's more than I've got in money."

' "Siven pound, not a haporth less," says the judge. "if ye haven't the money ye can pay it in projuice. An' make yer chice bechune the wimmin who ye'll marry, as it's married ye'll be this blessed day, bekase ye've gone too long a'ready," says the judge, very starn, an' thin the widdys all got quite, an' begun to be sorry they gev him so many hard names.

' "Is it wan o' the widdy's must I marry?" says Dooley, axin' the judge, an' the charm in his coller beginnin' to work hard an' remind him av Miss Rooney, that was settin' on wan side, trimblin'.

' "Tare an' 'ouns," says the judge. "Bad luck to ye, ye onmannerly idjit," as he was gettin' vexed wid Dooley, that was shtandin', acrotchin' the head av him like he was thryin' to encourage his brains. "Wasn't it wan o' the wimmin that I tould ye to take?" says he.

' "If that's phat yer Lordshap syas, axin' yer pardin an' not mis-doubtin' ye, if it's plazin' to ye, bedad, I'll take the owld maid, bekase thim widdys have got a sight av young wans, an' childer are like toothpicks, ivery man wants his own an' not another felly's." But he had another razon that he towld to me afther; says he, "If I've got to have a famly, be jakers, I want to have the raisin' av it meself," an' my blessin' on him for that same.

'But whin he was spakin' an' said he'd take Miss Rooney, wid that word she fainted away fur dead, an' was carried out o' the coort be her father an' Paddy.

'So it was settled, an' as Dooley didn't have the money, the widdys aggrade to take their pay some other way. The Widdy Mulligan tuk the pitaties he was diggin' whin the polisman gripped him, as she said they'd kape the inn all winter. The Widdy McMurthry got his hay, which come convaynient, bekase her brother kep post horses an' tuk the hay av her at two shillins undher the market. Missis O'Donnell got the cow that made all the throuble be goin' dhry at the wrong time, an' bein' it was a good cow was vally'd at tin poun' so she geve him three poun', an' was to sind him the calf whin it was weaned. So the widdys were all paid for bein' wounded in their hearts be Misther Dooley, an' a good bargain they made av it, bekase a widdy's affections are like garden weeds, the more ye thrample thim the fasther they grow.

'Misther Dooley got Miss Rooney, an' she a husband, fur they pulled her out av her faint wid a bucket o' wather, an' the last gossoon in town wint from the coort to the chapel wid Miss Rooney an Misther Dooley, the latther crassin' himself ivery minnit an' blessin' God ivery step he tuk that it wasn't the jail he was goin' to, an' they were married there wid a roarin' crowd waitin' in the strate fur to show thim home. But they sarcumvinted thim, bekase they wint out the back way an' through Father O'Donohue's garden, an' so home, lavin' the mob howlin' before the chapel dure like wild Ingines.

'An' that's the way the owld maid defated three widdys, that isn't often done, no more would she have done it but for owld Moll an' the charm in Dooley's coat. But he's very well plazed, an' that I know, for afther me first wife died, her I was tellin' ye av, I got the roomytics in me back like tin t'ousand divils clawin' at me backbone, an' I made me mind up that I'd get another wife, bekase I wanted me back rubbed, sence it'ull be chaper, says I, to marry some wan to rub it than to pay a boy to do that same. So I was lookin' roun' an' met Misther Dooley an' spake av it to him, an' good luk it'ud have been if I'd tuk his advice, but I didn't, bein' surrounded be a widdy afther, that's rubbed me back well fur me only wid a shtick. But says he to me, "Take you my advice Misther Magwire, an' whin ye marry, get you an owld maid, if there's wan to be had in the counthry. Gurruls is flighty an' axpectin' too much av ye, an' widdys is greedy buzzards as ye've seen by my axpayriences, but owld maids is humble, an' thankful for gettin' a husband at all, God bless 'em, so they shtrive to plaze an' do as ye bid thim widout grumblin' or axin' throublesome questions." '

D. R. McANALLY, JR

The Henpecked Giant

No locality of Ireland is fuller of strange bits of fanciful legend than the neighbourhood of the Giant's Causeway. For miles along the coast the geological strata resemble that of the Causeway, and the gradual disintegration of the stone has wrought many peculiar and picturesque effects among the basaltic pillars, while each natural novelty has woven round it a tissue of traditions and legends, some appropriate, others forced, others ridiculous misapplications of commonplace tales. Here, a long straight row of columns known as the 'Giant's Organ', and tradition pictures the scene when the giants of old, with their gigantic families, sat on the Causeway and listened to the music; there, a group of isolated pillars is called the 'Giant's Chimneys', since they once furnished an exit for the smoke of the gigantic kitchen. A solitary pillar, surrounded by the crumbling remains of others, bears a distant resemblance to a seated female figure, the 'Giant's Bride', who slew her husband and attempted to flee, but was overtaken by the power of a magician, who changed her into stone as she was seated by the shore, waiting for the boat that was to carry her away. Further on, a cluster of columns forms the 'Giant's Pulpit', where a presumably outspoken gigantic preacher denounced the sins of a gigantic audience. The Causeway itself, according to legend, formerly extended to Scotland, being originally constructed by Finn Maccool and his friends, this notable giant having invited Benandoner, a Scotch giant of much celebrity, to come over and fight him. The invitation was accepted, and Maccool, out of politeness, built the Causeway the whole distance, the big Scotchman thus walking over dry-shod to receive his beating.

Some distance from the mainland is found the Ladies' Wishing Chair, composed of blocks in the Great Causeway, wishes made while seated here being certain of realisation. To the west of the Wishing Chair a solitary pillar rises from the sea, the 'Grey Man's Love'. Look to the mainland, and the mountain presents a deep, narrow cleft, with perpendicular sides, the 'Grey Man's Path'. Out in the sea, but unfortunately not often in sight, is the 'Grey Man's Isle', at present inhabited only by the Grey Man himself. As the island, however, appears but once in seventeen years, and the Grey Man is never seen save on the eve of some awful calamity, visitors to the Causeway have a very slight chance of seeing either island or man. There can be no doubt though of the existence of both, for everybody knows he was one of the greatest of the giants during his natural lifetime, nor could any better evidence be asked than the facts that his sweetheart, turned into stone, still stands in sight of the Causeway; the precipice, from which she flung herself into the sea, is still known by the name of the 'Lovers' Leap'; and the path he made through the mountain is still used by him when he leaves his island and comes on shore.

It is not surprising that so important a personage as the Grey Man should be the central figure of many legends, and indeed over him the story-makers seem to have had vigorous competition, for thirty or forty narratives are current in the neighbourhood concerning him and the principal events of his life. So great a collection of legendary lore on one topic rendered the choice of a single tradition which should fairly cover the subject a matter of no little difficulty. As sometimes happens in grave undertakings, the issue was determined by accident. A chance boat excursion led to the acquaintance of Mr Barney O'Toole, a fisherman, and conversation developed the fact that this gentleman was thoroughly posted in the local legends, and was also the possessor of a critical faculty which enabled him to differentiate between the probable and the improbable, and thus to settle the historical value of a tradition. In his way, he was also a philosopher, having evidently given much thought to social issues, and expressing his conclusions thereupon with the ease and freedom of a master mind.

Upon being informed of the variety and amount of legendary material collected about the Grey Man and his doings, Barney unhesitatingly pronounced the entire assortment worthless, and condemned all the gathered treasures as the creations of petty intellects, which could not get out of the beaten track, but sought in the supernatural a reason for and explanation of every fact that seemed at variance with the routine of daily experience. In his opinion, the Grey Man is never seen at all in our day and generation, having been gathered to his fathers ages ago; nor is there any enchanted island; to use his own language, 'all thim shtories bein' made be thim blaggard guides that set up av a night shtringin' out laigends for to enthertain the quol'ty.'

'Now, av yer Anner wants to hear it, I can tell ye the thrue shtory av the Grey Man, no more is there anny thing wondherful in it, but it's just as I had it from me grandfather, that towld it to the childher for to entertain thim.

'It's very well beknownst that in thim owld days there were gionts in plinty hereabouts, but they didn't make the Causeway at all, for that's a work o' nacher, axceptin' the Grey Man's Path, that I'm goin' to tell ye av. But ivery wan knows that there were gionts, bekase if there wasn't, how cud we know o' thim at all, but wan thing's sartain, they were just like us, axceptin' in the matther o' size, for wan ov thim'ud make a dozen like the men that live now.

'Among the gionts that lived about the Causeway there was wan, a young giont named Finn O'Goolighan, that was the biggest av his kind, an' none o' them cud hide in a kish. So Finn, for the size av him, was a livin' terror. His little finger was the size av yer Anner's arrum, an' his wrist as big as yer leg, an' so he wint, bigger an' bigger. Whin he walked he carried an oak tree for a shtick, ye cud crawl into wan av his shoes, an' his caubeen'ud cover a boat. But he was a good-humoured young felly wid a laugh that'ud deefen ye, an' a plazin' word for all he met, so as if ye run acrass him in the road, he'd give ye "good morrow kindly", so as ye'd feel the betther av it all day. He'd work an' he'd play an' do aither wid all the might that was in him. Av a week day you'd see him in the field or on the shore from sun to sun as busy as a hen wid a dozen chicks; an' av a fair-day or av a Sunday, there he'd be, palatherin' at the girls, an' dancin' jigs that he done wid extrame nateness, or havin' a bout wid a shtick on some other felly's head, an' indade, at that he was so clever that it was a delight for to see him, for he'd crack a giont's shkull that was as hard as a pot wid wan blow an' all the pleasure in life. So he got to be four or five an' twenty an' not his betther in the County Antrim.

'Wan fine day, his father, Bryan O'Goolighan, that was as big a giont as himself, says to him, says he, "Finn, me Laddybuck, I'm thinkin' ye'll want to be gettin' marr'd."

' "Not me," says Finn.

' "An' why not?" says his father.

' "I've no consate av it," says Finn.

' "Ye'd be the betther av it," says his father.

' "Faix, I'm not sure o' that," says Finn; "gettin' marr'd is like turnin' a corner, ye don't know phat ye're goin' to see," says he.

' "Thrue for ye,' says owld Bryan, for he'd had axpayrience himself, "but if ye'd a purty woman to make the stir-about for ye av a mornin' wid her won white hands, an' to watch out o' the dure for ye in the avenin,' an' put on a sod o' turf whin she sees ye comin', ye'd be a betther man," says he.

' "Bedad, it's not aisey for to conthravene that same,' says Finn, "barrin' I mightn't git wan like that. Wimmin is like angels," says he. "There's two kinds av 'em, an' the wan hat shmiles like a dhrame o' heaven afore she's marr'd, is the wan that gits to be a tarin' divil afther her market's made an' she's got a husband."

'Ye see Finn was a mighty smart young felly, if he was a giont, but his father didn't give up hope av gettin' him marr'd, for owld folks that's been through a dale o' throuble that-a-way always thries to get the young wans into the same thrap, beways, says they, av taichin' them to larn something. But Bryan was a wise owld giont, an' knewn, as the Bible says, there's time enough for all things. So he quit him, an' that night he spake wid the owld woman an' left it wid her, as knowin' that whin it's a matther o' marryin', a woman is more knowledgable an' can do more to bring on that sort o' mis'ry in wan day than a man can in all the years God gives him.

'Now, in ordher that ye see the pint, I'm undher the needcessity av axplainin' to yer Anner that Finn didn't be no manes have the hathred at wimmin that he purtinded, for indade he liked them purty well, but he thought he undhershtood thim well enough to know that the more ye talk swate to thim, the more they don't like it, barrin' the're fools, that sometimes happens. So whin he talked wid 'em or about thim, he spake o' thim shuperskillious, lettin' on to despise the lasht wan o' thim, that was a takin' way he had, for wimmin love thimselves a dale bether than ye'd think, unless yer Anner's marr'd an' knows, an' that Finn knew, so he always said o' thim the manest things he cud get out av his head, an' that made thim think av him, that was phat he wanted. They purtinded to hate him for it, but he didn't mind that, for he knewn it was only talk, an' there wasn't wan o' thim that wouldn't give the lasht tooth out av her jaw to have him for a husband.

'Well, as I was sayin', afther owld Bryan give Finn up, his mother tuk him in hand, throwin' a hint at him wanst in a while, sighin' to him how glad she'd be to have a young lady giont for a dawther, an' dhroppin' a word about phat an iligant girl Burthey O'Ghallaghy was, that was the dawther av wan o' the naburs, that she got Finn, unbeknownst to himself, to be thinkin' about Burthey. She was a fine young lady giont, about tin feet high, as broad as a cassel dure, but she was good size for Finn, as ye know be phat I said av him. So when Finn's mother see him takin' her home from church afther benediction, an' the nabers towld her how they obsarved him lanin' on O'Ghallaghy's wall an' Burthey lightin' his pipe wid a coal, she thought to herself, "fair an' aisey goes far in a day," an' made her mind up that Finn'ud marry Burthey. An' so, belike, he'd a' done, if he hadn't gone over, wan onlucky day, to the village beyant, where the common people like you an' me lived.

'When he got there, in he wint to the inn to get him his dhrink, for it's a mishtake to think that thim gionts were all blood-suckin' blaggards as the Causeway guides say, but, barrin' they were in dhrink, were as paceable as rabbits. So when Finn wint in, he says, "God save ye," to thim settin', an' gev the table a big crack wid his shillaylah as for to say he wanted his glass. But instead o' the owld granny that used for to fetch him his potheen, out shteps a nate little woman wid hair an' eyes as black as a crow an' two lips on her as red as a cherry an' a quick sharp way like a cat in a hurry.

' "An' who are you, me Dear?" says Finn, lookin' up.

' "I'm the new barmaid, Sorr, av it's plazin' to ye," says she, makin' a curchey, an' lookin' shtrait in his face.

' "It is plazin'," says Finn. " 'tis I that's glad to be sarved be wan like you. Only," says he, "I know be the look o' yer eye ye've a timper."

' "Dade I have," says she, talkin' back at him, "an' ye'd betther not wake it."

'Finn had more to say an' so did she, that I won't throuble yer Anner wid, but when he got his fill av dhrink an' said all he'd in his head, an' she kep' aven wid him at ivery pint, he wint away mightily plazed. The next Sunday but wan he was back agin, an' the Sunday afther, an' afther that agin. By an' by, he'd come over in the avenin' afther the work was done, an' lane on the bar or set on the table, talkin' wid the barmaid, for she was as sharp as a thornbush, an' sorra a word Finn'ud say to her in impidince or anny other way, but she'd give him his answer afore he cud get his mouth shut.

'Now, be this time, Finn's mother had made up her mind that Finn'ud marry Burthey, an' so she sent for the matchmaker, an' they talked it all over, an' Finn's father seen Burthey's father, an' they settled phat Burthey'ud get an' phat Finn was to have, an' were come to an agraymint about the match, onbeknownst to Finn, bekase it was in thim days like it is now, the matches bein' made be the owld people, an' all the young wans did was to go an' be marr'd an' make the best av it. Afther all, maybe that's as good a way as anny, for whin ye've got all the throuble on yer back ye can stagger undher, there's not a haporth o' differ whether ye got undher it yerself or whether it was put on ye, an' so it is wid gettin' marr'd, at laste so I'm towld.

'Annyhow, Finn's mother was busy wid preparin' for th weddin' whin she heard how Finn was afther puttin' in his time at the village. ' "Sure that won't do," she says to herself; "he ought to know betther than to be spendin' ivery rap he's got in dhrink an' gostherin' at that black-eyed huzzy, an' he to be marr'd to the best girl in the county." So that night, when Finn come in, she spake fair an' soft to him that he'd give up goin' to the inn, an' get ready for to be marr'd at wanst. An' that did well enough till she got to the marryin', when Finn riz up aff his sate, an' shut his taith so hard he bruk his pipestem to smithereens.

' "Say no more, mother," he says to her. "Burthey's good enough, but I wouldn't marry her if she was made av goold. Begob, she's too big. I want no hogs'ead av a girl like her," says he. "If I'm to be marr'd, I want a little woman. They're betther o' their size, an' it don't take so much to buy gowns for thim, naither do they ate so much," says he.

' "A-a-ah, baithershin," says his mother to him; "phat d'ye mane be talkin' that-a-way, an' me workin' me fingers to the bone clanin' the house for ye, an' relavn' ye av all the coortin' so as ye'd not be bothered in the laste wid it."

' "Shmall thanks to ye," says Finn, 'sure isn't the coortin' the best share o' the job?'

' "Don't ye mane to marry her?" says his mother.

' "Divil a toe will I go wid her," says Finn.

' "Out, ye onmannerly young blaggard, I'd tell ye to go to the divil, but ye're on the way fast enough, an' bad luck to the fut I'll shtir to halt ye. Only I'm sorry for Burthey," says she, "wid her new gown made. When her brother comes back, begob 'tis he that'll be the death av ye immedjitly afther he dhrops his two eyes on ye."

' "Aisey now," says Finn, "if he opens his big mouth at me, I'll make him wondher why he wasn't born deef an' dumb," says he, an' so he would, for all that he was so paceable.

'Afther that, phat was his mother to do but lave aff an' go to bed, that she done, givin' Finn all the talk in her head an' a million curses besides, for she was mightily vexed at bein' bate that way an' was in a divil av a timper along o' the house-clanin', that always puts wimmin into a shtate av mind.

'So the next day the news was towld, an' Finn got to be a holy show for the nabers, bekase av not marryin' Burthey an' wantin' the barmaid. They were afeared to say annything to himself about it, for he'd an arm on him the thick o' yer waist, an' no wan wanted to see how well he cud use it, but they'd whisper afther him, an' whin he wint along the road, they'd pint afther him, an' by an' by a giont like himself, an uncle av him towld him he'd betther lave the counthry, an' so he thought he'd do an' made ready for to shtart.

'But poor Burthey pined wid shame an' grief at the loss av him, for she loved im wid all the heart she had, an' that was purty big. So she fell aff her weight, till from the size av a hogs'ead she got no bigger round than a barrel an' was like to die. But all the time she kept on hopin' that he'd come to her, but whin she heard for sartain he was goin' to lave the counthry she let go an' jumped aff that clift into the say an' committed shooicide an' drownded herself. She wasn't turned into a pillar at all, that's wan o' thim guides' lies; she just drownded like anybody that fell into the wather would, an' was found afther an' berrid be the fishermen, an' a hard job av it they had, for she weighed a ton. But they called the place the Lovers' Lape, bekase she jumped from it, an' lovin' Finn the way she did, the lape she tuk made the place be called afther her an' that's razon enough.

'Finn was showbogher enough afore, but afther that he seen it was no use thryin' for to live in Ireland at all, so he got the barmaid, that was aiquel to goin' wid him, the more that ivery wan was agin him, that's beway o' the conthrariness av wimmin, that are always ready for to do annything ye don't want thim to do, an' wint to Scotland an' wasn't heard av for a long time.

'About twelve years afther, there was a great talk that Finn had got back from Scotland wid his wife an' had taken the farm over be the village, the first on the left as ye go down the mountain. At first there was no end av the fuss that was, for Burthey's frinds hadn't forgotten, but it all come to talk, so Finn settled down quite enough an' wint to work. But he was an althercd man. His hair an' beard were grey as a badger, so they called him the Grey Man, an' he'd a look on him like a shapestalin' dog. Everybody wondhered, but they didn't wondher long, for it was aisely persaived he had cause enough, for the tongue o' Missis Finn wint like a stame-ingine, kapin' so far ahead av her branes that she'd have to shtop an' say "an'–uh, an'–uh," to give the latther time for to ketch up. Jagers, but she was the woman for to talk an' schold an' clack away till ye'd want to die to be rid av her. When she was young she was a purty nice girl, but as she got owlder her nose got sharp, her lips were as thin as the aidge av a sickle, an' her chin was as pinted as the bow av a boat. The way she managed Finn was beautiful to see, for he was that afeared av her tongue that he darn't say his sowl belonged to him when she was by.

'When he got up airly in the mornin', she'd ax, 'Now phat are ye raisin' up so soon for, an' me just closin' me eyes in slape?' an' if he'd lay abed, she'd tell him to "get along out o' that now, ye big gossoon; if it wasn't for me ye'd do nothin' at all but slape like a pig." If he'd go out, she'd gosther him about where he was goin' an' phat he meant to do when he got there; if he shtayed at home, she'd raymark that he done nothin' but set in the cabin like a boss o' shtraw. When he thried for to plaze her, she'd grumble at him bekase he did 't thry sooner; when he let her be, she'd fall into a fury an' shtorm till his hair shtud up like it was bewitched it was.

'She'd more thricks than a showman's dog. If scholdin' didn't do for Finn, she'd cry at him, an' had tin childher that she larned to cry at him too, an' when she begun, the tin o' thim'ud set up a yell that'ud deefen a thrumpeter, so Finn'ud give in.

'She cud fall ill on tin minnits notice, an' if Finn was obsthreperous in that degray that she cudn't do him no other way, she'd let on her head ached fit to shplit, so she'd go to bed an' shtay there till she'd got him undher her thumb agin. So she knew just where to find him whin she wanted him; that wimmin undhershtand, for there's more divilmint in wan woman's head about gettin' phat she wants than in tin men's bodies.

'Sure, if iver anybody had raison to remimber the ould song, 'When I was single,' it was Finn.

'So, ye see, Finn, the Grey Man, was afther havin' the divil's own time, an' that was beways av a mishtake he made about marryin'. He thought it was wan o' thim goold bands the quol'ty ladies wear on their arrums, but he found it was a handcuff it was. Sure wimmin are quare craythers. Ye think life wid wan o' thim is like a sunshiny day an' it's nothing but drizzle an' fog from dawn to dark, an' it's my belafe that Misther O'Day wasn't far wrong when he said wimmin are like the owld gun he had in the house an' that wint aff an the shly wan day an' killed the footman. "Sure it looked innycent enough," says he, "but it was loaded all the same an' only waitin' for an axcuse to go aff at some wan, an' that's like a woman, so it is," he'd say, an' ivery wan'ud laugh when he towld that joke, for he was the landlord, "That's like a woman, for she's not to be thrusted avin when she's dead." "

'But it's me own belafe that the most sarious mishtake av Finn's was in marryin' a little woman. There's thim that says all wimmin is a mishtake be nacher, but there's a big differ bechuxt a little woman an' a big wan, the little wans have sowls too big for their bodies, so are always lookin' out for a big man to marry, an' the bigger he is, the betther they like him, as knowin' they can manage him all the aisier. So it was wid Finn an' his little wife, for be hook an' be crook she rejuiced him in that obejince that if she towld him for to go an' shtand on his head in the corner, he'd do it wid the rish av his life, bekase he'd wanted to die an' go to heaven as he heard the priest say there was no marryin' there, an' though he didn't dare to hint it, he belaved in his sowl that the rayzon was the wimmin didn't get that far.

'Afther they'd been living here about a year, Finn thought he'd fish a bit an' so help along, considherin' he'd a big family an' none o' the childher owld enough for to work. So he got a boat an' did purty well an' his wife used to come acrass the hill to the shore to help him wid the catch. But it was far up an' down agin an' she'd get tired wid climbin' the hill an' jawing at Finn on the way.

'So wan day as they were comin' home, they passed a cabin an' there was the man that lived there, that was only a ditcher, a workin' away on the side av the hill down the path to the shpring wid a crowbar, movin' a big shtone, an' the shweat rollin' in shtrames aff his face.

' "God save ye," says Finn to him.

'God save ye kindly," says he to Finn.

' "It's a bizzy man ye are," says Finn.

' "Thrue for ye," says the ditcher. "It's along o' the owld woman. 'The way to the shpring is too stape an' shtoney,' says she to me, an' sure, I'm afther makin' it aisey for her."

' "Ye're the kind av a man to have," says Missis Finn, shpakin' up. "Sure all wimmin isn't blessed like your wife," says she, lookin' at Finn, who let on to laugh when he wanted to shwear. They had some more discoorse, thin Finn an' his wife wint on, but it put a big notion into her head. If the bogthrotter, that was only a little ottommy, 'ud go to work like that an' make an aisey path for his owld woman to the shpring, phat's the rayzon Finn cudn't fall to an' dig a path through the mountains, so she cud go to the say an' to the church on the shore widout breakin' her back climbin' up an' then agin climbin' down. 'T was the biggest consate iver in the head av her, an' she wasn't wan o' thim that'ud let it cool aff for the want o' talkin' about it, so she up an' towld it to Finn, an' got afther him to do it. Finn wasn't aiger for to thry, bekase it was Satan's own job, so he held out agin all her scholdin' an' beggin' an' cryin'. Then she got sick on him, wid her headache, an' wint to bed, an' whin Finn was about she'd wondher out loud phat she was iver born for an' why she cudn't die. Then she'd pray, so as Finn'ud hear her, to all the saints to watch over her big gossoon av a husband an' not forget him just bekase he was a baste, an' if Finn'ud thry to quiet her, she'd pray all the louder, an' tell him it didn't matther, she was dyin' an' 'ud soon be rid av him an' his brutal ways, so as Finn got half crazy wid her an' was ready to do annything in the worruld for to get her quiet.

'Afther about a week av this thratemint, Finn give in an' wint to work wid a pick an' shpade on the Grey Man's Path. But thim that says he made it in wan night is ignerant, for I belave it tuk him a month at laste; if not more. So that's the thrue shtory av the Grey Man's Path, as me grandfather towld it, an' shows that a giont's size isn't a taste av help to him in a contist wid a woman's jaw.

'But to be fair wid her, I belave the onliest fault Finn's wife had was, she was possist be the divil, an' there's thim that thinks that's enough. I mind me av a young felly wan time tatt was in love, an' so to be axcused, that wished he'd a hunderd tongues so to do justice to his swateheart. So after that he marr'd her, an' whin they'd been marr'd a while an' she'd got him undher her fisht, says they to him, "An' how about yer hunderd tongues?" "Begorra," says he to thim agin, "wid a hunderd I'd get along betther av coorse than wid wan, but to be ayquel to the waggin' av her jaw I'd nade a hunderd t'ousand."

'So it's a consate I have that Missis Finn was not a haporth worse nor the rest o' thim, an' that's phat me grandfather said too, that had been marr'd twict, an' so knewn phat he was talkin' about. An' whin he towld the shtory av the Grey Man, he'd always end it wid a bit av poethry:

> 'The first rib did bring in ruin
> As the rest have since been doin';
> Some be wan way, some another,
> Woman shtill is mischief's mother.
>
> 'Be she good or be she avil,
> Be she saint or be she divil,
> Shtill unaisey is his life
> That is marr'd wid a wife.'

D. R. MᶜANALLY, JR

The Leprechaun

❧❧❧

Every mythology has its good and evil spirits which are objects of adoration and subjects of terror, and often both classes are worshipped from opposite motives; the good, that the worshipper may receive benefit; the evil, that he may escape harm. Sometimes good deities are so benevolent that they are neglected, superstitious fear directing all devotion towards the evil spirits to propitiate them and avert the calamities they are ever ready to bring upon the human race; sometimes the malevolent deities have so little power that the prayer of the pious is offered up to the good spirits that they may pour out still further favours, for man is a worshipping being, and will prostrate himself with equal fervour before the altar whether the deity be good or bad.

Midway, however, between the good and evil beings of all mythologies there is often one whose qualities are mixed; not wholly good nor entirely evil, but balanced between the two, sometimes doing a generous action, then descending to a petty meanness, but never rising to nobility of character nor sinking to the depths of depravity; good from whim, and mischievous from caprice.

Such a being is the leprechaun of Ireland, a relic of the pagan mythology of that country. By birth the leprechaun is of low descent, his father being an evil spirit and his mother a degenerate fairy; by nature he is a mischief-maker, the Puck of the Emerald Isle. He is of diminutive size, about three feet high, and is dressed in a little red jacket or roundabout, with red breeches buckled at the knee, grey or black stockings, and a hat, cocked in the style of a century ago, over a little, old, withered face. Round his neck is an Elizabethan ruff, and frills of lace are at his wrists. On the wild west coast, where the

Atlantic winds bring almost constant rains, he dispenses with ruff and frills and wears a frieze overcoat over his pretty red suit, so that, unless on the lookout for the cocked hat, 'ye might pass a leprechaun on the road and never know it's himself that's in it at all.'

In Clare and Galway, the favourite amusement of the leprechaun is riding a sheep or goat, or even a dog, when the other animals are not available, and if the sheep look weary in the morning or the dog is muddy and worn out with fatigue, the peasant understands that the local leprechaun has been going on some errand that lay at a greater distance than he cared to travel on foot. Aside from riding the sheep and dogs almost to death, the leprechaun is credited with much small mischief about the house. Sometimes he will make the pot boil over and put out the fire, then again he will make it impossible for the pot to boil at all. He will steal the bacon-flitch, or empty the potatokish, or fling the baby down on the floor, or occasionally will throw the few poor articles of furniture about the room with a strength and vigour altogether disproportioned to his diminutive size. But his mischievous pranks seldom go further than to drink up all the milk or despoil the proprietor's bottle of its poteen, sometimes, in sportiveness, filling the bottle with water, or, when very angry, leading the fire up to the thatch, and then startling the inmates of the cabin with his laugh as they rise, frightened, to put out the flames.

To offset these troublesome attributes, the leprechaun is very domestic, and sometimes attaches himself to a family, always of the 'rale owld shtock', accompanying its representatives from the castle to the cabin and never deserting them unless driven away by some act of insolence or negligence, 'for, though he likes good atin', he wants phat he gets to come wid an open hand, an' 'ud laver take the half av a pratee that's freely given than the whole av a quail that's begrudged him.' But what he eats must be specially intended for him, an instance being cited by a Clare peasant of a leprechaun that deserted an Irish family, because, on one occasion, the dog having left a portion of his food, it was set by for the leprechaun. 'Jakers, 't was as mad as a little wasp he was, an' all that night they heard him workin' away in the cellar as busy as a nailer an' a sound like a catheract av wather goin' widout sayein'. In the mornin' they wint to see phat he'd been at, but he was gone, an' whin they come to thry for the wine, bad loock to the dhrop he'd left, but all was gone from ivory cask an' bottle, and they were filled wid say-wather, beways av rayvinge o' phat they done him.'

In different country districts the leprechaun has different names. In the northern counties he is the logheryman; in Tipperary, he is the lurigadawne; in Kerry, the luricawne; in Monaghan, the cluricawne. The dress also varies. The logheryman wears the uniform of some British infantry regiments, a red coat and white breeches, but instead of a cap, he wears a broad-brimmed, high, pointed hat, and after doing some trick more than usually mischievous, his favourite position is to poise himself on the extreme point of his hat, standing at the top of a wall or on a house, feet in the air, then laugh heartily and disappear. The lurigadawne wears an antique slashed jacket of red, with peaks all round and a jockey cap, also sporting a sword, which he uses as a magic wand. The luricawne is a fat, pursy little fellow whose jolly round face rivals in redness the cutaway jacket he wears, that always has seven rows of seven buttons in each row, though what use they are has never been determined, since his jacket is never buttoned, nor, indeed, can it be, but falls away from a shirt invariably white as the snow. When in full dress he wears a helmet several sizes too large for him, but, in general, prudently discards this article of headgear as having a tendency to render him conspicuous in a country where helmets are obsolete, and wraps his head in a handkerchief that he ties over his ears.

The cluricawne of Monaghan is a little dandy, being gorgeously arrayed in a swallow-tailed evening coat of red with green vest, white breeches, black stockings, and shoes that 'fur the shine av 'em 'ud shame a lookin'-glass'. His hat is a long cone without a brim, and is usually set jauntily on one side of his curly head. When greatly provoked, he will sometimes take vengeance by suddenly ducking and poking the sharp point of his hat into the eye of the offender. Such conduct is, however, exceptional, as he commonly contents himself with soundly abusing those at whom he has taken offence, the objects of his anger hearing his voice but seeing nothing of his person.

One of the most marked peculiarities of the leprechaun family is their intense hatred of schools and schoolmasters, arising, perhaps, from the ridicule of them by teachers, who affect to disbelieve in the existence of the leprechaun and thus insult him, for 'it's very well beknownst, that unless ye belave in him an' thrate him well, he'll lave an' come back no more.' He does not even like to remain in the neighbourhood where a national school has been established, and as such schools are now numerous in Ireland, the leprechauns are becoming scarce. 'Wan gineration of taichers is enough for thim, bekase the families where the little fellys live forgit to set thim out the bit an' sup, an' so they lave.' The few that remain must have a hard time keeping soul and body together for nowhere do they now receive any attention at meal-times, nor is the anxiety to see one by any means so great as in the childhood of men still living. Then, to catch a leprechaun was certain fortune to him who had the wit to hold the mischief-maker a captive until demands for wealth were complied with.

'Mind ye,' said a Kerry peasant, 'the onliest time ye can ketch the little vagabone is whin he's settin' down, an' he niver sets down axceptin' whin his brogues want mendin'. He runs about so much he wears thim out, an' whin he feels his feet on the ground, down he sets undher a hidge or behind a wall, or in the grass, an' takes thim aff an' mends thim. Thin comes you by, as quiet as a cat an' sees him there, that ye can aisily, be his red coat, an' you shlippin' up on him, catches him in yer arrums.

' "Give up yer goold," says you.
' "Begob, I've no goold," says he.
' "Then outs wid yer magic purse," says you.
'But it's like pullin' a hat full av taith to get aither purse or goold av him. He's got goold be the ton, an' can tell ye where ye can put yer finger on it, but he wont, till ye make him, an' that ye must do be no aisey manes. Some cuts aff his wind be chokin' him, an' some bates him, but don't for the life o' ye take yer eyes aff him, fur if ye do, he's aff like a flash an' the same man niver sees him agin, an' that's how it was wid Michael O'Dougherty.

'He was afther lookin' for wan nigh a year, fur he wanted to get married an' hadn't any money, so he thought the aisiest was to ketch a luricawne. So he was lookin' an' watchin' an' the fellys makin' fun av him all the time. Wan night he was comin' back afore day from a wake he'd been at, an' on the way home he laid undher the hidge an' shlept awhile, thin riz an' walked on. So as he was walkin', he seen a luricawne in the grass be the road a-mendin' his brogues. So he shlipped up an' got him fast enough, an' thin made him tell him where was his goold. The luricawne tuk him to nigh the place in the break o' the hills an' was goin' fur to show him, when all at wanst Mike heard the most outprobrious scraich over the head av him that'ud make the hairs av ye shtand up like a mad cat's tail.

' "The saints defind me," says he, "phat's that?" an' he looked up from the luricawne that he was carryin' in his arrums. That minnit the little attomy wint out av his sight, fur he looked away from it an' it was gone, but he heard it laugh when it wint an' he niver got the goold but died poor, as me father knows, an' he a boy when it happened.'

Although the leprechauns are skilful in evading curious eyes, and, when taken, are shrewd in escaping from their captors, their tricks are sometimes all in vain, and after resorting to every device in their power, they are occasionally compelled to yield up their hidden stores, one instance of which was narrated by a Galway peasant.

'It was Paddy Donnelly av Connemara. He was always hard at work as far as anny wan seen, an' bad luck to the day he'd miss, barrin' Sundays. When all'ud go to the fair, sorra a fut he'd shtir to go near it, no more did a dhrop av dhrink crass his lips. When they'd ax him why he didn't take divarshun, he'd laugh an' tell thim his field was divarshun enough fur him, an' by an' by he got rich, so they knewn that when they were at the fair or wakes or shports, it was lookin' fur a leprechaun he was an' not workin', an' he got wan too, fur how else cud he get rich at all.'

And so it must have been, in spite of the denials of Paddy Donnelly, though, to do him justice, he stoutly affirmed that his small property was acquired by industry, economy, and temperance. But according to the opinions of his neighbours, 'bad scran to him 't was as greedy as a pig he was, fur he knewn where the goold was, an' wanted it all fur himself, an' so lied about it like the leprechauns, that's known to be the biggest liars in the world.'

The leprechaun is an old bachelor elf who successfully resists all efforts of scheming fairy mammas to marry him to young and beautiful fairies, persisting in single blessedness even in exile from his kind, being driven off as a punishment for his heterodoxy on matrimonial subjects. This is one explanation of the fact that leprechauns are always seen alone, though other authorities make the leprechaun solitary by preference, he having learned the hollowness of fairy friendship and the deceitfulness of fairy femininity, and left the society of his kind in disgust at its lack of sincerity.

It must be admitted that the latter explanation seems the more reasonable, since whenever the leprechaun has been captured and forced to engage in conversation with his captor he displayed conversational powers that showed an ability to please, and as woman kind, even among fairy circles, are, according to an Irish proverb, 'aisily caught be an oily tongue', the presumption is against the expulsion of the leprechaun and in favour of his voluntary retirement.

However this may be, one thing is certain to the minds of all wise women and fairy-men, that he is the 'thrickiest little divil that iver wore a brogue', whereof abundant proof is given. There was Tim O'Donovan, of Kerry, who captured a leprechaun and forced him to disclose the spot where the 'pot o' goold' was concealed. Tim was going to make the little rogue dig up the money for him, but, on the leprechaun advancing the plea that he had no spade, released him, marking the spot by driving a stick into the ground and placing his hat on it. Returning the next morning with a spade, the spot pointed out by the 'little ottomy av a desaver' being in the centre of a large bog, he found, to his unutterable disgust, that the leprechaun was too smart for him, for in every direction innumerable sticks rose out of the bog, each bearing aloft an old 'caubeen' so closely resembling his own that poor Tim, after long search, was forced to admit himself baffled and give up the gold that, on the evening before, had been fairly within his grasp, if 'he'd only had the brains in his shkull to make the leprechaun dig it for him, shpade or no shpade.'

Even when caught, therefore, the captor must outwit the captive, and the wily little rascal, having a thousand devices, generally gets away without giving up a penny, and sometimes succeeds in bringing the eager fortune hunter to grief, a notable instance of which was the case of Dennis O'Bryan, of Tipperary, as narrated by an old woman of Crusheen.

'It's well beknownst that the leprechaun has a purse that's got the charmed shillin'. Only wan shillin', but the wondher av the purse is this: No matther how often ye take out a shillin' from it, the purse is niver empty at all, but whin ye put yer finger in agin, ye always find wan there, fur the purse fills up when ye take wan from it, so ye may shtand all day countin' out the shillin's an' they comin', that's a thrick av the good peoples an' be magic.

'Now Dinnis was a young blaggard that was always afther peepin' about undher the hidge fur to ketch a leprechaun, though they do say that thim that doesn't sarch afther thim see thim oftener that thim that does, but Dinnis made his mind up that if there was wan in the counthry, he'd have him, fur he hated work worse than sin, an' did be settin' in a shebeen day in an' out till you'd think he'd grow on the sate. So wan day he was comin' home, an' he seen something red over in the corner o' the field, an' in he goes, as quiet as a mouse, an' up on the leprechaun an' grips him be the collar an' down's him on the ground.

' "Arrah, now, ye ugly little vagbone," says he, "I've got ye at last. Now give up yer goold, or by jakers I'll choke the life out av yer pin-squazin' carkidge, ye owld cobbler, ye," says he, shakin' him fit to make his head dhrop aff.

'The leprechaun begged, and scritched, an' cried, an' said he wasn't a rale leprechaun that was in it, but a young wan that hadn't anny goold, but Dinnis wouldn't let go av him, an' at last the leprechaun said he'd take him to the pot ov goold that was hid be the say, in a glen in Clare. Dinnis didn't want to go so far, bein' afeared the leprechawn'ud get away, an' he thought the divilish baste was afther lyin' to him, bekase he knewn there was goold closter than that, an' so he was chokin' him that his eyes stood out till ye cud knock 'em aff wid a shtick, an' the leprechaun axed him would he lave go if he'd give him the magic purse. Dinnis thought he'd betther do it, fur he was mortially afeared the oudacious little villin'ud do him so thrick an' get away, so he tuk the purse, afther lookin' at it to make sure it was red shilk, an' had the shillin' in it, but the minnit he tuk his two eyes aff the leprechaun, away wint the rogue wid a laugh that Dinnis didn't like at all.

'But he was feelin' very comfortable be razon av gettin' the purse, an' says to himself, "Begorra, 'tis mesilf that'll ate the full av me waistband fur wan time, an' dhrink till a stame-ingine can't squaze wan dhrop more down me neck," says he, and aff he goes like a quarther-horse fur Miss Clooney's sheebeen, that's where he used fur to go. In he goes, an' there was Paddy Grogan, an' Tim O'Donovan, an' Mike Conathey, an' Bryan Flaherty, an' a shtring more av 'om settin' on the table, an' he pulls up a sate an' down he sets, a-callin' to Miss Clooney to bring her best.

' "Where's yer money?" says she to him, fur he didn't use to have none barrin' a tuppence or so.

' "Do you have no fear," says he, "fur the money," says he, "ye pinny-schrapin' owld shkeleton," this was beways av a shot at her, fur it was the size av a load o' hay she was, an' weighed a ton. "Do you bring yer best," says he. "I'm a gintleman av forchune, bad loock to the job o' work I'll do till the life laves me. Come, jintlemin, dhrink at my axpinse." An' so they did an' more than wanst, an' afther four or five guns apace, Dinnis ordhered dinner fur thim all, but Miss Clooney towld him sorra the bit or sup more'ud crass the lips av him till he paid fur that he had. So out he pulls the magic purse fur to pay, an' to show it thim an' towld thim phat it was an' where he got it.

' "And was it the leprechaun gev it ye?" says they.

' "It was," says Dinnis, "an' the varchew av this purse is sich, that if ye take shillin's out av it be the handful all day long, they'll be comin' in a shtrame like whishkey out av a jug," says he, pullin' out wan.

'And thin, me jewel, he put in his fingers afther another, but it wasn't there, for the leprechaun made a ijit av him, an' instid o' givin' him the right purse, gev him wan just like it, so as onless ye looked clost, ye cudn't make out the differ betune thim. But the face on Dinnis was a holy show when he seen the leprechaun had done him, an' he wid only a shillin', an' half a crown av dhrink down the troats av thim.

' "To the divil wid you an' yer leprechauns, an' purses, an' magic shillin's," schreamed Miss Clooney, belavin', an' small blame to her that's, that it was lyin' to her he was. "Ye're a thafe, so ye are, dhrinkin' up me dhrink, wid a lie on yer lips about the purse, an' insultin' me into the bargain," says she, thinkin' how he called her a shkeleton, an' her a load fur a waggin. "Yer impidince bates owld Nick, so it does," says she; so she up an' hits him a power av a crack on the head wid a bottle; an' the other felly's, a thinkin' sure that it was a lie he was afther tellin' them, an' he laving thim to pay fur the dhrink he'd had, got on him an' belted him out av the face it was nigh on to dead he was. Then a consthable comes along an' hears the phillaloo they did be makin' an' comes in.

' "Tatther an' agers," says he, "lave aff. I command the pace. Phat's the matther here?"

'So they towld him an' he consayved that Dinnis shtole the purse an' tuk him be the collar.

' "Lave go," says Dinnis. "Sure phat's the harrum o' getting the purse av a leprechaun?"

' "None at all," says the polisman, "av ye projuice the leprechaun an' make him teshtify he gev it ye an' that ye haven't been burglarious an' sacrumvinted another man's money," says he.

'But Dinnis cudn't do it, so the cunsthable tumbled him into the jail. From that he wint to corrt an' got thirty days at hard labour, that he niver done in this life afore, an' afther he got out, he said he'd left lookin' for leprechauns, fur they were too shmart fur him entirely, an' it's thrue fur him, bekase I belave they were.'

THOMAS CROFTON CROKER

Master and Man

❧❧

Billy Mac Daniel was once as likely a young man as ever shook his brogue at a patron [a festival held in honour of some patron saint], emptied a quart or handled a shillelagh; fearing for nothing but the want of drink; caring for nothing but who should pay for it; and thinking of nothing but how to make fun over it; drunk or sober, a word and a blow was ever the way with Billy Mac Daniel; and a mighty easy way it is of either getting into or of ending a dispute. More is the pity that, through the means of his thinking, and fearing, and caring for nothing, this same Billy Mac Daniel fell into bad company; for surely the good people are the worst of all company anyone could come across.

It so happened that Billy was going home one clear frosty night not long after Christmas; the moon was round and bright; but although it was as fine a night as heart could wish for, he felt pinched with cold. 'By my word,' chattered Billy, 'a drop of good liquor would be no bad thing to keep a man's soul from freezing in him; and I wish I had a full measure of the best.'

'Never wish it twice, Billy,' said a little man in a three-cornered hat, bound all about with gold lace, and with great silver buckles in his shoes, so big that it a wonder how he could carry them, and he held out a glass as big as himself, filled with as good liquor as eye ever looked on or lip tasted.

'Success, my little fellow,' said Billy Mac Daniel nothing daunted, though well he knew the little man to belong to the *good people*; 'here's your health, anyway, and thank you kindly; no matter who pays for the drink'; and he took the glass and drained it to the very bottom without ever taking a second breath to it.

'Success,' said the little man; 'and you're heartily welcome, Billy; but don't think to cheat me as you have done others – out with your purse and pay me like a gentleman.'

'Is it I pay you?' said Billy; 'could I not just take you up and put you in my pocket as easily as a blackberry?'

'Billy Mac Daniel,' said the little man, getting very angry, 'you shall be my servant for seven years and a day, and that is the way I will be paid; so make ready to follow me.'

When Billy heard this he began to be very sorry for having used such bold words toward the little man; and he felt himself, yet could not tell how, obliged to follow the little man the livelong night about the country, up and down, and over hedge and ditch, and through bog and brake, without any rest.

When morning began to dawn the little man turned round to him and said, 'You may now go home, Billy, but on your peril don't fail to meet me in the Fort-field tonight; or if you do it may be the worse for you in the long run. If I find you a good servant, you will find me an indulgent master.'

Home went Billy Mac Daniel; and though he was tired and weary enough, never a wink of sleep could he get for thinking of the little man; but he was afraid not to do his bidding, so up he got in the evening, and away he went to the Fort-field. He was not long there before the little man came towards him and said, 'Billy, I want to go a long journey tonight; so saddle one of my horses, and you may saddle another for yourself, as you are to go along with me, and may be tired after your walk last night.'

Billy thought this very considerate of his master, and thanked him accordingly: 'But,' said he, 'if I may be so bold, sir, I would ask which is the way to your stable, for never a thing do I see but the fort here, and the old thorn tree in the corner of the field, and the stream running at the bottom of the hill, with the bit of bog over against us.'

'Ask no questions, Billy,' said the little man, 'but go over to that bit of bog, and bring me two of the strongest rushes you can find.'

Billy did accordingly, wondering what the little man would be at; and he picked two of the stoutest rushes he could find, with a little bunch of brown blossom stuck at the side of each, and brought them back to his master.

'Get up, Billy,' said the little man, taking one of the rushes from him and striding across it.

'Where shall I get up, please your honour?' said Billy.

'Why, upon horseback, like me, to be sure,' said the little man.

'Is it after making a fool of me you'd be,' said Billy, 'bidding me get a horseback upon that bit of a rush? Maybe you want to persuade me that the rush I pulled but a while ago out of the bog over there is a horse?'

'Up! up! and no words,' said the little man, looking very angry; 'the best horse you ever rode was but a fool to it.' So Billy, thinking all this was in joke, and fearing to vex his master, straddled across the rush. 'Borram! Borram! Borram!' cried the little man three times (which, in English, means to become great), and Billy did the same after him; presently the rushes swelled up into fine horses, and away they went full speed; but Billy, who had put the rush between his legs, without much minding how he did it, found himself sitting on horseback the wrong way, which was rather awkward, with his face to the horse's tail; and so quickly had his steed started off with him that he had no power to turn round, and there was therefore nothing for it but to hold on by the tail.

At last they came to their journey's end, and stopped at the gate of a fine house. 'Now, Billy,' said the little man, 'do as you see me do, and follow me close; but as you did not know your horse's head from his tail, mind that your own head does not spin round until you can't tell whether you are standing on it or your heels; for remember that old liquor, though able to make a cat speak, can make a man dumb.'

The little man then said some queer kind of words, out of which Billy could make no meaning; but he contrived to say them after him for all that; and in they both went through the keyhole of the door, and through one keyhole after another, until they got into the wine-cellar, which was well stored with all kinds of wine.

The little man fell to drinking as hard as he could, and Billy noway disliking the example, did the same. 'The best of masters are you, surely,' said Billy to him; 'no matter who is the next; and well pleased will I be with your service if you continue to give me plenty to drink.'

'I have made no bargain with you,' said the little man, 'and will make none; but up and follow me.' Away they went, through keyhole after keyhole; and each mounting upon the rush which he left at the hall door, scampered off, kicking the clouds before them like snowballs, as soon as the words, 'Borram, Borram, Borram,' had passed their lips.

When they came back to the Fort-field the little man dismissed Billy, bidding him to be there the next night at the same hour. Thus did they go on, night after night, shaping their course one night here, and another night there; sometimes north, and sometimes east, and sometimes south, until there was not a gentleman's wine-cellar in all Ireland they had not visited, and could tell the flavour of every wine in it as well, ay, better than the butler himself.

One night when Billy Mac Daniel met the little man as usual in the Fort-field, and was going to the bog to fetch the horses for their journey, his master said to him, 'Billy, I shall want another horse tonight, for maybe we may bring back more company than we take.' So Billy, who now knew better than to question any order given to him by his master, brought a third rush, much wondering who it might be that would travel back in their company, and whether he was about to have a fellow-servant. 'If I have,' thought Billy, 'he shall go and fetch the horses from the bog every night; for I don't see why I am not, every inch of me, as good a gentleman as my master.'

Well, away they went, Billy leading the third horse, and never stopped until they came to a snug farmer's house, in the county Limerick, close under the old castle of Carrigogunniel, that was built, they say, by the great Brian Boru. Within the house there was great carousing going forward, and the little man stopped outside for some time to listen; then turning round all of a sudden, said, 'Billy, I will be a thousand years old tomorrow!'

'God bless us, sir,' said Billy; 'will you?'

'Don't say these words again, Billy,' said the little old man, 'or you will be my ruin forever. Now Billy, as I will be a thousand years in the world tomorrow, I think it is full time for me to get married.'

'I think so too, without any kind of doubt at all,' said Billy, 'if ever you mean to marry.'

'And to that purpose,' said the little man, 'have I come all the way to Carrigogunniel; for in this house, this very night, is young Darby Riley going to be married to Bridget Rooney; and as she is a tall and comely girl, and has come of decent people, I think of marrying her myself, and taking her off with me.'

'And what will Darby Riley say to that?' said Billy.

'Silence' said the little man, putting on a mighty severe look; 'I did not bring you here with me to ask questions,' and without holding further argument, he began saying the queer words which had the power of passing him through the keyhole as free as air, and which Billy thought himself mighty clever to be able to say after him.

In they both went; and for the better viewing the company, the little man perched himself up as nimbly as a cock-sparrow upon one of the big beams which went across the house over all their heads, and Billy did the same upon another facing him; but not being much accustomed to roosting in such a place, his legs hung down as untidy as may be, and it was quite clear he had not taken pattern after the way in which the little man had bundled himself up together. If the little man had been a tailor all his life, he could not have sat more contentedly upon his haunches.

There they were, both master and man, looking down upon the fun that was going forward; and under them were the priest and piper, and the father of Darby Riley, with Darby's two brothers and his uncle's son; and there were both the father and the mother of Bridget Rooney, and proud enough the old couple were that night of their daughter, as good right they had; and her four sisters, with brand-new ribbons in their caps, and her three brothers all looking as clean and as clever as any three boys in Munster, and there were uncles and aunts, and gossips and cousins enough besides to make a full house of it; and plenty was there to eat and drink on the table for everyone of them, if they had been double the number.

Now it happened, just as Mrs Rooney had helped his reverence to the first cut of the pig's head which was placed before her, beautifully bolstered up with white savoys, that the bride gave a sneeze, which made everyone at the table start, but not a soul said 'and bless us'. All thinking that the priest would have done so, as he ought if he had done his duty, no one wished to take the word out of his mouth, which, unfortunately, was preoccupied with pig's head and greens. And after a moment's pause the fun and merriment of the bridal feast went on without the pious benediction.

Of this circumstance both Billy and his master were no inattentive spectators from their exalted stations. 'Ha!' exclaimed the little man, throwing one leg from under him with a joyous flourish, and his eye twinkled with a strange light, while his eyebrows became elevated into the curvature of Gothic arches; 'Ha!' said he, leering down at the bride, and then up at Billy, 'I have half of her now, surely. Let her sneeze but twice more, and she is mine, in spite of priest, mass-book, and Darby Riley.'

Again the fair Bridget sneezed; but it was so gently, and she blushed so much, that few except the little man took, or seemed to take, any notice; and no one thought of saying 'God bless us.'

Billy all this time regarded the poor girl with a most rueful expression of countenance; for he could not help thinking what a terrible thing it was for a nice young girl of nineteen, with large blue eyes, transparent skin, and dimpled cheeks, suffused with health and joy, to be obliged to marry an ugly little bit of a man, who was a thousand years old, barring a day.

At this critical moment the bride gave a third sneeze, and Billy roared out with all his might, 'God save us!' Whether this exclamation resulted from his soliloquy, or from the mere force of habit, he never could tell exactly himself; but no sooner was it uttered than the little man, his face glowing with rage and disappointment, sprung from the beam on which he had perched himself, and shrieking out in the shrill voice of a cracked bagpipe, 'I discharge you from my service, Billy Mac Daniel – take *that* for your wages,' gave poor Billy a most furious kick in the back, which sent his unfortunate servant sprawling upon his face and hands right in the middle of the supper table.

If Billy was astonished, how much more so was everyone of the company into which he was thrown with so little ceremony. But when they heard his story, Father Cooney laid down his knife and fork, and married the young couple out of hand with all speed; and Billy Mac Daniel danced the Rinka at their wedding, and plenty he did drink at it too, which was what he thought more of than dancing.

D. R. McANALLY, JR

How the Lakes were Made

❧❧❧

Among the weird legends of the Irish peasantry is found a class of stories peculiar both in the nature of the subject and in the character of the tradition. From the dawn of history, and even before, the island has been crowded with inhabitants, and as the centres of population changed, towns and cities were deserted and fell into ruins. Although no longer inhabited, their sites are by no means unknown or forgotten, but in many localities where now appear only irregular heaps of earth and stones to which the archeologist sometimes finds difficulty in attributing an artificial origin there linger among the common people tales of the city that once stood on the spot; of its walls, its castles, its palaces, its temples, and the pompous worship of the deities there adored. Just as, in Palestine, the identification of Bible localities has, in many instances, been made complete by the preservation among the Bedouins of the Scriptural names, so, in Ireland, the cities of pagan times are now being located through the traditions of the humble tillers of the soil, who transmit from father to son the place-names handed down for untold generations.

Instances are so abundant as to defy enumeration, but a most notable one is Tara, the greatest as it was the holiest city of pagan Ireland. Now it is a group of irregular mounds that the casual observer would readily mistake for natural hills, but for ages the name clung to the place until at last the attention of antiquaries was attracted, interest was roused, investigation made, excavation begun, and the site of Tara made a certainty.

Not all ancient Irish cities, however, escaped the hand of time as well as Tara, for there are geological indications of great natural convulsions in the island at a date comparatively recent, and not a few of the Irish lakes, whose name is legion, were formed by depression or upheaval, almost within the period of written history. A fertile valley traversed by a stream, a populous city by the little river, an earthquake-upheaval lower down the watercourse, closing the exist from the valley, a rising and spreading of the water, an exodus of the inhabitants, such has undoubtedly been the history of Lough Derg and Lough Ree, which are but reservoirs in the course of the River Shannon, while the upper and lower Erne lakes are likewise simply expansions of the river Erne. Lough Neag had a similar origin, the same being also true of Loughs Allen and Key. The Killarney Lakes give indisputable evidence of the manner in which they were formed, being enlargements of the Laune, and Loughs Carra and Mask, in Mayo, are believed to have a subterranean outlet to Lough Carrib, the neighbourhood of all three testifying in the strongest possible manner to the sudden closing of the natural outlet for the contributing streams.

The towns which at one time stood on ground now covered by the waters of these lakes were not forgotten. The story of their fate was told by one generation to another, but in course of ages the natural cause, well known to the unfortunates at the time of the calamity, was lost to view, and the story of the disaster began to assume supernatural features. The destruction of the city became sudden; the inhabitants perished in their dwellings; and, as a motive for so signal an event was necessary, it was found in the punishment of duty neglected or crime committed.

Lough Allen is a small body of water in the County Leitrim, and on its shores, partly covered by the waves, are several evidences of human habitation, indications that the waters at present are much higher than formerly. Among the peasants in the neighbourhood there is a legend that the little valley once contained a village. In the public square there was a fountain guarded by spirits, fairies, elves, and leprechauns, who objected to the building of the town in that locality, but upon an agreement between themselves and the first settlers permitted the erection of the houses on condition that the fountain be covered with an elegant stone structure, the basin into which the water flowed from the spring to be protected by a cover never to be left open, under pain of the town's destruction, 'the good people being that nate an' clane that they didn't want the laste speck av dust in the wather they drunk.'

So a decree was issued, by the head man of the town, that the cover be always closed by those resorting to the fountain for water, and that due heed might be taken, children, boys under age, and unmarried women, were forbidden under any circumstances to raise the lid of the basin.

For many years things went on well, the fairies and the townspeople sharing alike the benefits of the fountain, till, on one unlucky day, preparations for a wedding were going on in a house close by, and the mother of the bride stood in urgent need of a bucket of water. Not being able to bring it herself, the alleged reason being 'she was scholdin' the house in ordher,' she commanded her daughter, the bride expectant, to go in her stead.

The latter objected, urging the edict of the headman already mentioned, but was overcome, partly by her mother's argument, that 'the good people know ye're the same as married now that the banns are cried', but principally by the more potent consideration, 'Av ye havn't that wather here in a wink, I'll not lave a whole bone in yer body, ye lazy young shtrap, an' me breaking me back wid the work', she took the bucket and proceeded to the fountain with the determination to get the water and 'shlip out agin afore the good people'ud find her out'. Had she adhered to this resolution, all would have been well, as the fairies would have doubtless overlooked this infraction of the city ordinance. But as she was filling the pail, her lover came in. Of course the two at once began to talk of the all-important subject, and having never before taken water from the fountain, she turned away, forgetting to close the cover of the well. In an instant, a stream, resistless in force, burst forth, and though all the married women of the town ran to put down the cover, their efforts were in vain, the flood grew mightier, the village was submerged, and, with two exceptions, all the inhabitants were drowned. The girl and her lover violated poetic justice by escaping; for, seeing the mischief they had done, they were the first to run away, witnessed the destruction of the town from a neighbouring hill, and were afterwards married, the narrator of this incident coming to the sensible conclusion that 'it was too bad entirely that the wans that got away were the wans that, be rights, ought to be droonded first'.

Upper Lough Erne has a legend, in all important particulars identical with that of Lough Allen, the catastrophe being, however, in the former case brought about by the carelessness of a woman who left her baby at home when she went after water and hearing it scream, 'as aven the best babies do be doin', God bless 'em, for no betther rayson than to lishen at thimselves,' she hurried back, forgetting to cover the well, with a consequent calamity like that which followed similar forgetfulness at Lough Allen.

In the County Mayo is found Lough Conn, once, according to local storytellers, the site of a village built within and around the enclosure of a castle. The lord of the castle, being fond of fish, determined to make a fishpond, and as the spot selected for the excavation was covered by the cabins of his poorest tenants, he ordered all the occupants to be turned out forthwith, an order at once carried out 'wid process-sarvers, an' bailiffs, an' consthables, an' sogers, an' polis, an' the people all shtandin' 'round'. One of the evicted knelt on the ground and cursed the chief with 'all the seed, breed and gineration av 'im,' and prayed 'that the throut-pond'ud be the death av 'im.' The prayer was speedily answered, for no sooner was the water turned into the newly-made pond, than an overflow resulted; the valley was filled; the waves climbed the walls of the castle, nor ceased to rise till they had swept the chief from the highest tower, where 'he was down an his hard hearted knees, sayin' his baids as fast as he cud, an' bawlin' at all the saints aither to bring him a boat or taiche him how to swim quick.' Regard for the unfortunate tenants, however, prevented any interference by the saints thus vigorously and practically supplicated, so the chief was drowned and went, as the storyteller concluded, to a locality where he 'naded more wather than he'd left behind him, an' had the comp'ny av a shwarm av other landlords that turned out the poor to shtarve.'

Lough Gara, in Sligo, flows over a once thriving little town, the City of Peace, destroyed by an overflow on account of the lack of charity for strangers. A poor widow entered it one night leading a child on each side and carrying a baby at her breast. She asked alms and shelter, but in vain; from door to door she went, but the customary Irish hospitality, so abundant alike to the deserving and to the unworthy, was lacking. At the end of the village 'she begun to scraich, yer Anner, wid that strength you'd think she'd shplit her troat. 'At this provocation, all the inhabitants at once ran to ascertain the reason of so unusual a noise, upon which, when they were gathered 'round her, the woman pronounced the curse of the widow and orphan on the people and their town. They laughed at her and returned home, but that night, the brook running through the village became a torrent, the outlet was closed, the waters rose, and 'ivery wan o' them oncharitable blaggards wor drownded, while they wor aslape. Bad cess to the lie that's in it, for, sure there's the lake to this blessed day.'

In County Antrim there lies Lough Neag, one of the largest and most beautiful bodies of water on the island. The waters of the lake are transparently blue, and even small pebbles on the bottom can be seen at a considerable depth. Near the southern end, a survey of the bottom disclosed hewn stones laid in order, and careful observations have traced the regular walls of a structure of considerable dimensions. Tradition says it was a castle, surrounded by the usual village, and accounts for its destruction by the lake in this wise. In ancient times, the castle was owned by an Irish chief named Shane O'Donovan, noted for his bad traits of character, being merciless in war, tyrannical in peace, feared by his neighbours, hated by his dependents, and detested by everybody for his inhospitality and want of charity. His castle then stood by the bank of the lake, on an elevated promontory, almost an island, being joined to the mainland by a narrow isthmus, very little above the water level.

By chance there came into that part of Ireland an angel who had been sent from heaven to observe the people and note their piety. In the garb and likeness of a man, weary and footsore with travel, the angel spied the castle from the hills above the lake, came down, and boldly applied for a night's lodging. Not only was his request refused, 'but the oncivil Shane O'Donovan set an his dogs fur to bite him.' The angel turned away, but no sooner had he left the castle gate than the villagers ran 'round him and a contest ensued as to which of them should entertain the traveller. He made his choice, going to the house of a cobbler who was 'that poor that he'd but the wan pitatee, and when he wanted another he broke wan in two'. The heavenly visitor shared the cobbler's potato and slept on the cobbler's floor, 'puttin' his feet into the fire to kape thim warrum', but at daylight he rose, and calling the inhabitants of the village, led them out, across the isthmus to a hill near by, and bid them look back. They did so, beholding the castle and promontory separated from the mainland and beginning to subside into the lake. Slowly, almost imperceptibly, the castle sank, while the waters rose around, but stood like a wall on every side of the castle, not wetting a stone from turret to foundation. At length the wall of water was higher than the battlements, the angel waved his hand, the waves rushed over the castle and its sleeping inmates, and the O'Donovan inhospitality was punished. The angel pointed to a spot near by, told the villagers to build and prosper there; then, as the awe-stricken peasants kneeled before him, his clothing became white and shining, wings appeared on his shoulders, he rose into the air and vanished from their sight.

Of somewhat different origin is the pretty Lough Derryclare, in Connemara, south of the Joyce Country. The ferocious O'Flahertys frequented this region in past ages, and, with the exception of Oliver Cromwell, no historical name is better known in the west of Ireland than O'Flaherty. One of this doughty race was, it seems, a model of wickedness. 'He was as proud as a horse wid a wooden leg, an' so bad, that, savin' yer presince, the divil himself was ashamed av him.' This O'Flaherty had sent a party to devastate a neighbouring village, but as the men did not return promptly, he started with a troop of horse in the direction they had taken. On the way he was passing through a deep ravine at the bottom of which flowed a tiny brook, when he met his returning troops, and questioning them as to the thoroughness with which their bloody work had been done, found, to his great wrath, that they had spared the church and those who took refuge in its sacred precincts.

'May God drownd me where I shtand,' said he, 'if I don't shlay thim all an the althar,' and no doubt he would have done so, but the moment the words passed his lips, the rivulet became a seething torrent, drowned him and his men, and the lake was formed over the spot where they stood when the curse was pronounced. 'An' sometimes, they say, that when the lake is quite shtill, ye may hear the groans av the lost sowls chained at the bottom.'

The fairies are responsible for at least two of the Irish lakes, Lough Key and the Upper Lough Killarney. The former is an enlargement of the River Boyle, a tributary of the Shannon, and is situated in Roscommon. At a low stage of water, ruins can be discerned at the bottom of the river, and are reported to be those of a city whose inhabitants injudiciously attempted to swindle the 'good people' in a land bargain. The city was built, it seems, by permission of the fairies, the understanding being that all raths were to be left undisturbed. For a long time the agreement was respected, fairies and mortals living side by side, and neither class interfering with the other. But, as the necessity for more arable land became evident, it was determined by the townspeople to level several raths and mounds that interfered with certain fields and boundary lines. The dangers of such a course were plainly pointed out by the local 'fairy-man,' and all the 'knowledgeable women' lifted their voices against it, but in vain; down the raths must come and down they came, to the consternation of the knowing ones, who predicted no end of evil from so flagrant a violation of the treaty with the fairies.

The night after the demolition of the raths, one of the townsmen was coming through the gorge below the city, when, 'Millia, murther, there wor more than a hundherd t'ousand little men in grane jackets bringin' shtones an' airth an' buildin' a wall acrass the glen. Begob, I go bail but he was the skairt man when he seen phat they done, an' run home wid all the legs he had an' got his owld woman an' the childher. When she axed him phat he was afther, he towld her to howld her whisht or he'd pull the tongue out av her an' to come along an' not spake a word. So they got to the top o' the hill an then they seen the wathers swapin' an the city an' niver a sowl was there left o' thim that wor in it. So the good people had their rayvinge, an' the like o' that makes men careful wid raths, not to displaze their betthers, for there's no sayin' phat they'll do.'

The Upper Killarney lake was created by the fairy queen of Kerry to punish her lover, the young Prince O'Donohue. She was greatly fascinated by him, and, for a time, he was as devoted to her as woman's heart could wish. But things changed, for, in the language of the boatman, who told the legend, 'whin a woman loves a man, she's satisfied wid wan, but whin a man loves a woman, belike he's not contint wid twenty av her, an' so was it wid O'Donohue.' No doubt, however, he loved the fairy queen as long as he could, but in time tiring of her, 'he concluded to marry a foine lady, and when the quane rayproached him wid forgittin' her, at first he said it wasn't so, an' whin she proved it an him, faith he'd not a word left in his jaw. So afther a dale o' blasthogue bechuxt thim, he got as mad as Paddy Monagan's dog when they cut his tail aff, an' towld her he wanted no more av her, an' she towld him agin for to go an' marry his red-headed gurrul, "but mark ye," says she to him, "ye shall niver resave her into yer cassel." No more did he, for the night o' the weddin', while they were all dhrinkin' till they were ready to burst, in comes the waither an' says, "Here's the wather," says he. "Wather," says O'Donohue, "we want no wather tonight. Dhrink away." "But the wather's risin'," says the waither. "Arrah, ye Bladdherang," says O'Donohue, "phat d' ye mane be inthrudin' an agrayble frinds an such an outspishus occasion wid yer presince? Be aff, or be the powdhers o' war I'll wather ye," says he, risin' up for to shlay the waither. But wan av his gintlemin whuspered the thruth in his year an' towld him to run. So he did an' got away just in time, for the cassel was half full o' wather whin he left it. But the quane didn't want to kill him, so he got away an' built another cassel an the hill beyant where he lived wid his bride.'

Still another origin for the Irish lakes is found in Mayo, where Lough Carra is attributed to a certain 'giont', by name unknown, who formerly dwelt in the neighbourhood, and, with one exception, found everything necessary for comfort and convenience. He was a cleanly 'giont', and desirous of performing his ablutions regularly and thoroughly. The streams in the neighbourhood were ill adapted to his use, for when he entered any one of them for bathing purposes 'bad scran to the wan that'ud take him in furder than to the knees.' Obviously this was not deep enough, so one day when unusually in need of a bath and driven desperate by the inadequacy of the means, 'he spit an his han's an' went to work an' made Lough Carra. "Bedad," says he, "I'll have a wash now,' an' so he did," and doubtless enjoyed it, for the lake is deep and the water clear and pure.

Just below Lough Carra is Lough Mask, a large lake between Mayo and Galway. Concerning its origin, traditionary authorities differ, some maintain that the lake was the work of fairies, others holding that it was scooped out by a rival of the cleanly gigantic party already mentioned, a theory apparently confirmed by the fact that it has no visible outlet, though several streams pour into it, its waters, it is believed, escaping by a subterranean channel to Lough Corrib, thence to the sea. Sundry unbelievers, however, stoutly assert a conviction that 'it's so be nacher entirely an' thim that says it's not is ignerant gommochs that don't know,' and in the face of determined scepticism the question of the origin of the lake must remain unsettled.

Thus far, indeed, it is painful to be compelled to state that scarcely one of the narratives of this chapter passes undisputed among the veracious tradition-mongers of Ireland. Like most other countries in this practical, poetry-decrying age, the Emerald Isle has scientists and sceptics, and among the peasants are found many men who have no hesitation in proclaiming their disbelief in 'thim owld shtories,' and who even openly affirm that 'laigends about fairies an' giants is all lies complately.' In the face of this growing tendency towards materialism and the disposition to find in natural causes an explanation of wonderful events, it is pleasant to be able to conclude this chapter with an undisputed account of the origin of Lough Ree in the River Shannon, the accuracy of the information being in every particular guaranteed by a boatman on the Shannon, 'a respectable man,' who solemnly asseverated 'Sure, that's no laigend, but the blessed truth as I'm livin' this minnit, for I'd sooner cut out me tongue be the root than desave yer Anner, when every wan knows there's not a taste av a lie in it at all.'

'When the blessed St Pathrick was goin' through Ireland from wan end to the other buildin' churches, an' Father Malone says he built three hundherd an' sixty foive, that's a good manny, he come to Roscommon be the way av Athlone, where ye saw the big barracks an' the sojers. So he passed through Athlone, the counthry bein' full o' haythens entirely an' not av Crissans, and went up the Shannon, kapin' the river on his right hand, an' come to a big peat bog, that's where the lake is now. There were more than a thousand poor omadhawns av haythens a-diggin' the peat, an' the blessed saint convarted thim at wanst afore he'd shtir a toe to go anny furder. Then he built thim a church an the hill be the bog, an' gev thim a holy man fur a priest be the name o' Caruck, that I b'lave is a saint too or lasteways ought to be fur phat he done. So St Pathrick left thim wid the priest, givin' him great power on the divil an' avil sper'ts, and towld him to build a priest's house as soon as he cud. So the blessed Caruck begged an' begged as long as he got anny money, an' whin he'd the last ha'penny he cud shtart, he begun the priest's house fur to kape monks in.

'But the divil was watchin' him ivery minnit, fur it made the owld felly tarin' mad to see himself bate out o' the face that-a-way in the country where he'd been masther so long, an' he determined he'd spile the job. So wan night, he goes to the bottom o' the bog, an' begins dammin' the shtrame, from wan side to the other, layin' the shtones shtrong an' tight, an' the wather begins a risin an the bog. Now it happened that the blessed Caruck wasn't aslape as Satan thought, but up an' about, for he misthrusted that the Owld Wan was dodgin' round like a wayzel, an' was an the watch fur him. So when the blessed man saw the wather risin' on the bog an' not a taste o' rain fallin', "Phat's this?" says he. "Sure it's some o' Satan's deludherin'."

'So down he goes bechuxt the hills an' kapin' from the river, an' comes up below where the divil was workin' away pilin' on the airth an' shtones. So he comes craipin' up on him an' when he got purty clost, he riz an' says, 'Hilloo, Nayber!' Now Belzebub was like to dhrop on the ground wid fright at the look av him, he was that astonished. But there was no gettin' away, so he shtopped on the job, wiped the shweat aff his face, an' says, "Hilloo yerself."

' "Ye're at yer owld thricks," says the blessed Caruck.

' "Shmall blame to me, that's," says Belzebub, "wid yer churches an' saints an' convartin' thim haythens, ye're shpiling me business entirely. Sure, haven't I got to airn me bread?" says he, spakin' up as bowld as a cock, and axcusin' himself.

'At first the blessed Caruck was goin' to be rough wid him for shtrivin' to interfare wid the church an' the priest's house be risin' the wather on thim, but that minnit the moon shone out as bright as day an' he looked back an' there was the beautifulest lake he iver set his blessed eyes on, an' the church wid its towers riz above it like a fairy cassel in a dhrame, an' he clasped his hands wid delight. So Satan looked too an' was mortefied to death wid invy when he seen how he bate himself at his own game.

'So the blessed Caruck twold Belzebub to lave the dam where it was, an' then, thinkin' av the poor bog-throtters that 'ud nade the turf, he ordhered him beways av a punishmint, to dig all the turf there was in the bog an' pile it up on the hill to dhry.

' "Don't you lave as much as a speck av it undher wather," says he to him, "or as sure as I'm a saint I'll make ye repint it to the end of' yer snakin' life," says he, an' thin stud on the bank an' watched the Owld Deludher while he brought out the turf in loads on his back, an' ivery load as big as the church, till the hape av sods was as high as a mountain. So he got it done be mornin', an' glad enough was the divil to have the job aff his hands, fur he was as wet as a goose in May an' as tired as a pedler's donkey. So the blessed Caruck towld him to take himself aff an' not come back: that he was mighty well plazed to do.

'That's the way the lake come to be here, an' the blessed Caruck come well out o' that job, fur he sold the turf an' built a big house on the shore wid the money, an' chated the divil besides, Glory be to God, when the Owld Wan was thryin' his best fur to sarcumvint a saint.'

D. R. M^CANALLY, JR

Taming the Pooka

The west and northwest coast of Ireland shows many remarkable geological formations, but, excepting the Giant's Causeway, no more striking spectacle is presented than that to the south of Galway Bay. From the sea, the mountains rise in terraces like gigantic stairs, the layers of stone being apparently harder and denser on the upper surfaces than beneath, so the lower portion of each layer, disintegrating first, is washed away by the rains and a clearly defined step is formed. These terraces are generally about twenty feet high, and of a breadth, varying with the situation and exposure, of from ten to fifty feet.

The highway from Ennis to Ballyvaughn, a fishing village opposite Galway, winds, by a circuitous course, through these freaks of nature, and, on the long descent from the high land to the sea level, passes the most conspicuous of the neighbouring mountains, the Corkscrew Hill. The general shape of the mountain is conical, the terraces composing it are of wonderful regularity from the base to the peak, and the strata being sharply upturned from the horizontal, the impression given is that of a broad road carved out of the sides of the mountain and winding by an easy ascent to the summit.

' 'Tis the Pooka's Path they call it,' said the car-man. 'Phat's the Pooka? Well, that's not aisy to say. It's an avil sper't that does be always in mischief, but sure it niver does sarious harrum axceptin' to thim that desarves it, or thim that shpakes av it disrespictful. I never seen it, Glory be to God, but there's thim that has, and be the same token, they do say that it looks like the finest black horse that iver wore shoes. But it isn't a horse at all at all, for no horse 'ud have eyes av fire, or be breathin' flames av blue wid a shmell o' sulfur, savin' yer presince, or a shnort like thunder, and no mortial horse'ud take the lapes it does, or go as fur widout gettin' tired. Sure when it give Tim O'Bryan the ride it give him, it wint from Gort to Athlone wid wan jump, an' the next it tuk he was in Mullingyar, and the next was in Dublin, and back agin be way av Kilkenny an' Limerick, an' niver turned a hair. How far is that? Faith I dunno, but it's a power av distance, an' clane acrost Ireland an' back. He knew it was the Pooka bekase it shpake to him like a Christian mortial, only it isn't agrayable in its language an' 'ull niver give ye a dacint word afther ye're on its back, an' sometimes not before aither.

'Sure Dennis O'Rourke was after comin' home wan night, it was only a boy I was, but I mind him tellin' the shtory, an' it was at a fair in Galway he'd been. He'd been havin' a sup, some says more, but whin he come to the rath, and jist beyant where the fairies dance and ferninst the wall where the polisman was shot last winther, he fell in the ditch, quite spint and tired complately. It wasn't the length as much as the wideness av the road was in it, fur he was goin' from wan side to the other an' it was too much fur him entirely. So he laid shtill fur a bit and thin thried fur to get up, but his legs wor light and his head was heavy, an' whin he attempted to get his feet an the road 't was his head that was an it, bekase his legs cudn't balance it. Well, he laid there and was bet entirely, an' while he was studyin' how he'd raise, he heard the throttin' av a horse on the road. " 'Tis meself 'ull get the lift now," says he, and laid waitin', and up comes the Pooka. Whin Dennis seen him, begob, he kivered his face wid his hands and turned on the breast av him, and roared wid fright like a bull.

' "Arrah thin, ye snakin' blaggard," says the Pooka, mighty short, "lave aff yer bawlin' or I'll kick ye to the ind av next week," says he to him.

'But Dennis was scairt, an' bellered louder than afore, so the Pooka, wid his hoof, give him crack on the back that knocked the wind out av him.

' "Will ye lave aff," says the Pooka, "or will I give ye another, ye roarin' dough-face?"

'Dennis left aff blubberin' so the Pooka got his timper back.

' "Shtand up, ye guzzlin' sarpint," says the Pooka, "I'll give ye a ride."

' "Plaze yer honour," says Dennis, "I can't. Sure I've not been afther drinkin' at all, but shmokin' too much an' atin', an' it's sick I am, and not ontoxicated."

' "Och, ye dhrunken buzzard," says the Pooka, "Don't offer fur to desave me," liftin' up his hoof agin, an' givin' his tail a swish that sounded like the noise av a catheract, "Didn't I thrack ye for two miles be yer breath," says he, "An' you shmellin' like a potheen fact'ry," says he, "an' the nose on yer face as red as a turkey-cock's. Get up, or I'll lift ye," says he, jumpin' up an' cracking his hind fut like he was doin' a jig.

'Dennis did his best, an' the Pooka helped him wid a grip o' the teeth on his collar.

' "Pick up yer caubeen," says the Pooka, "an' climb up. I'll give ye such a ride as ye niver dhramed av."

' "Ef it's plazin' to yer honour," says Dennis, "I'd laver walk. Ridin' makes me dizzy," says he.

' " 'Tis not plazin'," says the Pooka, "will ye get up or will I kick the shtuffin' out av yer cowardly carkidge," says he, turnin' round an' flourishin' his heels in Dennis' face.

'Poor Dennis thried, but he cudn't, so the Pooka tuk him to the wall an' give him a lift an it, an' whin Dennis was mounted, an' had a tight howld on the mane, the first lep he give was down the rock there, a thousand feet into the field ye see, thin up agin, an' over the mountain, an' into the say, an' out agin, from the top av the waves to the top av the mountain, an' afther the poor soggarth av a ditcher was nigh on to dead, the Pooka come back here wid him an' dhropped him in the ditch where he found him, an' blowed in his face to put him to slape, so lavin' him. An' they found Dennis in the mornin' an' carried him home, no more cud he walk for a fortnight be razon av the wakeness av his bones fur the ride he'd had.

'But sure, the Pooka's a different baste entirely to phat he was afore King Bryan Boru tamed him. Niver heard av him? Well, he was the king av Munster an' all Ireland an' tamed the Pooka wanst fur all on the Corkschrew Hill ferninst ye.

'Ye see, in the owld days, the counthry was full av avil sper'ts, an' fairies an' witches, an' divils entirely, and the harrum they done was onsaycin', for they wore always comin' an' goin', like Mulligan's blanket, an' widout so much as sayin', by yer lave. The fairies'ud be dancin' on the grass every night be the light av the moon, an' stalin' away the childhre, an' many's the wan they tuk that niver come back. The owld rath on the hill beyant was full av the dead, an' afther nightfall they'd come from their graves an' walk in a long line wan afther another to the owld church in the valley where they'd go in an' stay till cockcrow, thin they'd come out agin an' back to the rath. Sorra a parish widout a witch, an' some nights they'd have a great enthertainmint on the Corkschrew Hill, an' you'd see thim, wid shnakes on their arrums an' necks an' ears, be way av jewels, an' the eyes av dead men in their hair, comin' for miles an' miles, some ridin' through the air on shticks an' bats an' owls, an' some walkin', an' more on Pookas an' horses wid wings that'ud come up in line to the top av the hill, like the cabs at the dure o' the theayter, an' lave thim there an' hurry aff to bring more.

'Sometimes the Owld Inimy, Satan himself, 'ud be there at the enthertainmint, comin' an a monsthrous dhraggin, wid grane shcales an' eyes like the lightnin' in the heavens, an' a roarin' fiery mouth like a limekiln. It was the great day thin, for they do say all the witches brought their rayports at thim saysons fur to show him phat they done.

'Some'ud tell how they shtopped the wather in a spring, an' incon-vanienced the nabers, more'ud show how they dhried the cow's milk, an' made her kick the pail, an' they'd all laugh like to shplit. Some had blighted the corn, more had brought the rains on the harvest. Some towld how their enchantmints made the childhre fall ill, some said how they set the thatch on fire, more towld how they shtole the eggs, or spiled the crame in the churn, or bewitched the butther so it 'udn't come, or led the shape into the bog. But that wasn't all.

'Wan'ud have the head av a man murthered be her manes, an' wid it the hand av him hung fur the murther; wan'ud bring the knife she'd scuttled a boat wid an' pint in the say to where the corpses laid av the fishermen she'd dhrownded; wan'ud carry on her breast the child she'd shtolen an' meant to bring up in avil, an' another wan'ud show the little white body av a babby she'd smothered in its slape. And the corpse-candles'ud tell how they desaved the thraveller, bringin' him to the river, an' the avil sper'ts'ud say how they dhrew him in an' down to the bottom in his sins an' thin to the pit wid him. An' owld Belzebub'ud listen to all av thim, wid a rayporther, like thim that's afther takin' down the spaches at a Lague meetin', be his side, a-writing phat they said, so as whin they come to be paid, it 'udn't be forgotten.

'Thim wor the times fur the Pookas too, fur they had power over thim that wint forth afther night, axceptin' it was on an arriant av marcy they were. But sorra a sinner that hadn't been to his juty reglar'ud iver see the light av day agin afther meetin' a Pooka thin, for the baste'ud aither kick him to shmithereens where he stud, or lift him on his back wid his teeth an' jump into the say wid him, thin dive, lavin' him to dhrownd, or shpring over a clift wid him an' tumble him to the bottom a bleedin' corpse. But wasn't there the howls av joy whin a Pooka'ud catch a sinner unbeknownst, an' fetch him on the Corkschrew wan o' the nights Satan was there. Och, God defind us, phat a sight it was. They made a ring wid the corpse-candles, while the witches tore him limb from limb, an' the fiends drunk his blood in red-hot iron noggins wid shrieks o' laughter to smother his schreams, an' the Pookas jumped on his body an' thrampled it into the ground, an' the timpest'ud whishle a chune, an' the mountains about'ud kape time, an' the Pookas, an' witches, an' sper'ts av avil, an' corpse-candles, an' bodies o' the dead, an' divils, 'ud all jig together round the rock where owld Belzebub'ud set shmilin', as fur to say he'd ax no betther divarshun. God's presince be wid us, it makes me crape to think av it.

'Well, as I was afther sayin', in the time av King Bryan, the Pookas done a dale o' harrum, but as thim that they murthered wor dhrunken bastes that wor in the shebeens in the day an' in the ditch be night, an' wasn't missed whin the Pookas tuk them, the King paid no attintion, an' small blame to him that's.

'But wan night, the queen's babby fell ill, an' the king says to his man, says he, "Here, Riley, get you up an' on the white mare an' go fur the docther."

' "Musha thin," says Riley, an' the king's counthry house was in the break o' the hills, so Riley'ud pass the rath an' the Corkschrew on the way afther the docther; "Musha thin," says he, aisey and on the quiet, "it's mesilf that doesn't want that same job."

'So he says to the king, "Won't it do in the mornin'?"

' "It will not," says the king to him. "Up, ye lazy beggar, atin' me bread, an' the life lavin' me child."

'So he wint, wid great shlowness, tuk the white mare, an' aff, an' that was the last seen o' him or the mare aither, fur the Pooka tuk 'em.

Sorra a taste av a lie's in it, for thim that said they seen him in Cork two days afther, thrading aff the white mare, was desaved be the sper'ts, that made it seem to be him whin it wasn't that they've a thrick o'doin'.

'Well, the babby got well agin, bekase the docther didn't get there, so the king left botherin' afther it and begun to wondher about Riley an' the white mare, and sarched fur thim but didn't find thim. An' thin he knewn that they was gone entirely, bekase, ye see, the Pooka didn't lave as much as a hair o' the mare's tail.

' "Wurra thin," says he, "is it horses that the Pooka'ull be stalin'? Bad cess to its impidince! This'ull niver do. Sure we'll be ruinated entirely," says he.

'Mind ye now, it's my consate from phat he said, that the king wasn't consarned much about Riley, fur he knewn that he cud get more Irishmen whin he wanted thim, but phat he meant to say was that if the Pooka tuk to horse-stalin', he'd be ruinated entirely, so he would, for where'ud he get another white mare? So it was a mighty sarious question an' he retired widin himself in the coort wid a big book that he had that towld saycrets. He'd a sight av larnin', had the king, aquel to a school-masther, an' a head that'ud sarcumvint a fox.

'So he read an' read as fast as he cud, an' afther readin' widout shtoppin', barrin' fur the bit av' sup, fur siven days an' nights, he come out, an' whin they axed him cud he bate the Pooka now, he said niver a word, axceptin' a wink wid his eye, as fur to say he had him.

'So that day he was in the fields an' along be the hedges an' ditches from sunrise to sunset, collection' the matarials av a dose dur the Pooka, but phat he got, faith, I dunno, no more does any wan, fur he never said, but kep the saycret to himself an' didn't say it aven to the quane, fur he knewn that saycrets run through a woman like wather in a ditch. But there was wan thing about it that he cudn't help tellin', fur he wanted it but cudn't get it widout help, an' that was three hairs from the Pooka's tail, axceptin' which the charm 'udn't work. So he towld a man he had, he'd give him no end av goold if he'd get thim fur him, but the felly pulled aff his caubeen an' scrotched his head an' says, "Faix, yer honour, I dunno phat'll be the good to me av the goold if the Pooka gets a crack at me carkidge wid his hind heels," an' he wudn't undhertake the job on no wages, so the king begun to be afeared that his loaf was dough.

'But it happen'd av the Friday, this bein' av a Chewsday, that the Pooka caught a sailor that hadn't been on land only long enough to get bilin' dhrunk, an' got him on his back, so jumped over the clift wid him lavin' him dead enough, I go bail. Whin they come to sarch the sailor to see phat he had in his pockets, they found three long hairs round the third button av his topcoat. So they tuk thim to the king tellin' him where they got thim, an' he was greatly rejiced, bekase now he belaved he had the Pooka sure enough, so he ended his inchantmint.

'But as the avenin' come, he riz a doubt in the mind av him thish-a-way. Ev the three hairs wor out av the Pooka's tail, the charm'ud be good enough, but if they wasn't, an' was from his mane inshtead, or from a horse inshtead av a Pooka, the charm 'udn't work an' the Pooka'ud get atop av him wid all the feet he had at wanst an' be the death av him immejitly. So this nate and outprobrious argymint shtruck the king wid great force an' fur a bit, he was onaisey. But wid a little sarcumvintion, he got round it, for he confist an' had absolu-tion so as he'd be ready, thin he towld wan av the sarvints to come in an' tell him afther supper, that there was a poor widdy in the boreen beyant the Corkschrew that wanted help that night, that it'ud be an arriant av marcy he'd be on, an' so safe agin the Pooka if the charm didn't howld.

' "Sure, phat'll be the good o' that?" says the man, "It'ull be a lie, an' won't work."

' "Do you be aisey in yer mind," says the king to him agin, "do as yer towld an' don't argy, for that's a pint av mettyfisics," says he, faix it was a dale av deep larnin' he had, "that's a pint av mettyfisics an' the more ye argy on thim subjics, the less ye know," says he, an' it's thrue fur him. "Besides, aven if it's a lie, it'll desave the Pooka, that's no mettyfishian, an' it's my belafe that the end is good enough for the manes," says he, a-thinking av the white mare.

'So, afther supper, as the king was settin' afore the fire, an' had the charm in his pocket, the sarvint come in and towld him about the widdy.

' "Begob," says the king, like he was surprised, so as to desave the Pooka complately, "Ev that's thrue, I must go relave her at wants." So he riz an' put on sojer boots, wid shpurs on 'em a fut acrost, an' tuk a long whip in his hand, for fear, he said, the widdy'ud have dogs, thin

wint to his chist an' tuk his owld stockin' an' got a suv'rin out av it, –
Och, 't was the shly wan he was, to do everything so well, – an' wint
out wid his right fut first, an' the shpurs a-rattlin' as he walked.

'He come acrost the yard, an' up the hill beyant you an' round the
corner, but seen nothin' at all. Thin up the fut path round the
Corkscrew n' met niver a sowl but a dog that he cast a shtone at. But
he did 't go out av the road to the widdy's, for he was afeared that if he
met the Pooka an' he caught him in a lie, not bein' in the road to
where he said he was goin', it'ud be all over wid him. So he walked up
an' down bechuxt the owld church below there an' the rath on the hill,
an' jist as the clock was shtrikin' fur twelve, he heard a horse in front
av him, as he was walkin' down, so he turned an' wint the other way,
gettin' his charm ready, an' the Pooka come up afther him.

' "The top o' the mornin' to yer honour," says the Pooka, as perlite
as a Frinchman, for he seen be his close that the king wasn't a common
blaggard like us, but was wan o' the rale quolity.

' "Me sarvice to ye," says the king to him agin, as bowld as a ram,
an' whin the Pooka heard him shpake, he got perliter than iver, an'
made a low bow an shcrape wid his fut, thin they wint on together an'
fell into discoorse.

' " 'Tis a black night for thravelin'," says the Pooka.

' "Indade it is," says the king, "it's not me that'ud be out in it, if it
wasn't a case o' needcessity. I'm on an arriant av charity," says he.

' "That's rale good o' ye," says the Pooka to him, "and if I may make
bowld to ax, phat's the needcessity?"

' " 'Tis to relave a widdy-woman," says the king.

' "Oho," says the Pooka, a-throwin' back his head laughin' wid
great plazin' ness an' nudgin' the king wid his leg on the arrum,
beways that it was a joke it was bekase the king said it was to relave a
widdy he was goin'. "Oho," says the Pooka, " 'tis mesilf that's glad to
be in the comp'ny av an iligint jintleman that's on so plazin' an arriant
av marcy," says he. "An' how owld is the widdy-woman?" says he,
bustin' wid the horrid laugh he had.

' "Musha thin," says the king, gettin' red in the face an' not likin'
the joke the laste bit, for jist betune us, they do say that afore he
married the quane, he was the laddy-buck wid the wimmin, an' the
quane's maid towld the cook, that towld the footman, that said to the
gardener, that towld the nabers that many's the night the poor king

was as wide awake as a hare from sun to sun wid the quane a-gostherin'
at him about that same. More betoken, there was a widdy in it, that
was as sharp as a rat-thrap an' surrounded him whin he was young an'
hadn't as much sinse as a goose, an' was like to marry him at wanst in
shpite av all his relations, as widdys unhershtand how to do. So it's my
consate that it wasn't dacint for the Pooka to be afther laughin' that-a-
way, an' shows that avil sper'ts is dirthy blaggards that can't talk wid
jintlemin. "Musha," thin, says the king, bekase the Pooka's laughin'
wasn't agrayable to listen to, "I don't know that same, fur I niver seen
her, but, be jagers, I belave she's a hundherd, an' as ugly as Belzebub,
an' whin her owld man was alive, they tell me she had a timper like a
gandher, an' was as aisey to manage as an armful o' cats," says he. "But
she's in want, an' I'm afther bringin' her a suv'rin," says he.

'Well, the Pooka sayced his laughin', fur he seen the king was very
vexed, an' says to him, "And if it's plazin', where does she live?"

' "At the ind o' the boreen beyant the Corkschrew," says the king,
very short.

' "Begob, that's a good bit," says the Pooka.

' "Faix, it's thrue for ye," says the king, "more betoken, it's up hill
ivery fut o' the way, an' me back is bruk entirely wid the stapeness,"
says he, be way av a hint he'd like a ride.

' "Will yer honour get upon me back," says the Pooka. "Sure I'm
afther goin' that-a-way, an' yu don't mind gettin' a lift?" says he, a-
fallin' like the stupid baste he was, into the thrap the king had made
fur him.

' "Thanks," says the king, "I b'lave not. I've no bridle nor saddle,"
says he, "besides, it's the shpring o' the year, an' I'm afeared ye're
sheddin', an' yer hair'ull come aff an' spile me new britches," says he,
lettin' on to make axcuse.

' "Have no fear," says the Pooka. "Sure I niver drop me hair. It's no
ordinary garron av a horse I am, but a most oncommon baste that's
used to the quolity," says he.

' "Yer spache shows that," says the king, the clever man that he was,
to be perlit that-a-way to a Pooka, that's known to be a divil out-en-
out, "but ye must exqueeze me this avenin' bekase, d'ye mind, the
road's full o' shtones an' monsthrous stape, an' ye look so young, I'm
afeared ye'll shtumble an' give me a fall," says he.

' "Arrah thin," says the Pooka, "it's thrue fur yer honour, I do look young," an' he begun to prance on the road givin' himself airs like an owld widdy man afther wantin' a young woman, "but me age is owlder than ye'd suppoge. How owld'ud ye say I was," says he, shmilin'.

' "Begorra, divil a bit know I," says the king, "but if it's agrayble to ye, I'll look in yer mouth an' give ye an answer," says he.

'So the Pooka come up to him fair an' soft an' stratched his mouth like as he thought the king was wantin' fur to climb in, an' the king put his hand on his jaw like as he was goin' to see the teeth he had: and thin, that minnit he shlipped the three hairs round the Pooka's jaw, an' whin he done that, he dhrew thim tight, an' said the charm crossin' himself the while, an' immejitly the hairs wor cords av stale, an' held the Pooka tight, be way av a bridle.

' "Arra–a–a–h, how, ye bloody baste av a murtherin' divil ye," says the king, pullin' out his big whip that he had consaled in this topcoat, an' giving the Pooka a crack wid it undher his stummick, "I'll give ye a ride ye won't forgit in a hurry," says he, "ye black Turk av a four-legged nagur an' you shtaling me white mare," says he, hittin' him agin.

' "Oh my," says the Pooka, as he felt the grip av the iron on his jaw an' knewn he was undher an inchantmint, "Oh my, phat's this at all," rubbin' his breast wid his hind heel, where the whip had hit him, an' thin jumpin' wid his fore feet out to cotch the air an' thryin' fur to break away. "Sure I'm ruined, I am, so I am," says he.

' "It's thrue fur ye," says the king, "begoo it's the wan thrue thing ye iver said," says he, a-jumpin' on his back, an' givin' him the whip an' the two shpurs wid all his might.

'Now I forgot to tell ye that whin the king made his inchantmint, it was good fur siven miles round, and the Pooka knewn that same as well as the king an' so he shtarted like a cunshtable was afther him, but the king was afeared to let him go far, thinkin' he'd do the siven miles in a jiffy an' the inchantmint'ud be broken like a rotten shtring, so he turned him up the Corkschrew.

' "I'll give ye all the axercise ye want," says he, "in thravellin' round this hill," an' round an' round they wint, the king shtickin' the big shpurs in him every jump an' crakin' him wid the whip till his sides run blood in shtrames like a mill race, an' his schreams av pain wor heard all over the worruld so that the king av France opened his windy and axed the polisman why he didn't shtop the fightin' in the shtrate.

Round an' round an' about the Corkschrew wint the king, a-lashin' the Pooka, till his feet made the path ye see on the hill bekase he wint so often.

'And whin mornin' come, the Pooka axed the king phat he'd let him go fur, an' the king was gettin' tired an' towld him that he must niver shtale another horse, an' never kill another man, barrin' furrin blaggards that wasn't Irish, an' whin he give a man a ride, he must bring him back to the shpot where he got him an' lave him there. So the Pooka consinted, Glory be to God, an' got aff, an' that's the way he was tamed, an' axplains how it was that Dennis O'Rourke was left be the Pooka in the ditch jist where he found him.'

'More betoken, the Pooka's an althered baste every way, fur now he dhrops his hair like a common horse, and it's often found shtrickin' to the hedges where he jumped over, an' they do say he doesn't shmell half as shtrong o' sulfur as he used, nor the fire out o' his nose isn't so bright. But all the king did fur him 'udn't taiche him to be civil in his spache, an' whin he meets ye in the way, he spakes just as much like a blaggard as ever. An' it's out av divilment entirely he does it, bekase he can be perlite as ye know be phat I towld ye av him sayin' to the king, an' that proves phat I said to ye that avil sper'ts can't larn rale good manners, no matther how hard they thry.

'But the fright he got never left him, an' so he kapes out av the highways an' thravels be the futpaths, an' so isn't often seen. An' it's my belafe that he can do no harrum at all to thim that fears God, an' there's thim that says he niver shows himself nor meddles wid man nor mortial barrin' they're in dhrink, an' mebbe there's something in that too, fur it doesn't take much dhrink to make a man see a good dale.'

D. R. MᶜANALLY, JR

The Sexton of Cashel

❧❦❧

All over Ireland, from Cork to Belfast, from Dublin to Galway, are scattered the ruins of churches, abbeys, and ecclesiastical buildings, the relics of a country once rich, prosperous and populous. These ruins raise their castellated walls and towers, noble even in decay, sometimes in the midst of a village, crowded with the miserably poor; sometimes on a mountain, in every direction commanding magnificent prospects; sometimes on an island in one of the lakes, which, like emeralds in a setting of deeper green, gem the surface of the rural landscape and contribute to increase the beauty of scenery not surpassed in the world.

Ages ago the voice of prayer and the song of praise ceased to ascend from these sacred edifices, and they are now visited only by strangers, guides, and parties of humble peasants, the foremost bearing on their shoulders the remains of a companion to be laid within the hallowed enclosure, for although the church is in ruins, the ground in and about it is still holy and in service when pious hands lay away in the bosom of earth the bodies of those who have borne the last burden, shed the last tear, and succumbed to the last enemy. But among all the pitiable spectacles presented in this unhappy country, none is better calculated to inspire sad reflections than a rural graveyard. The walls of the ruined church tower on high, with massive cornice and pointed window; within stand monuments and tombs of the Irish great; kings, princes, and archbishops lie together, while about the hallowed edifice are huddled the graves of the poor; here, sinking so as to be indistinguishable from the sod; there, rising in new-made proportions; yonder marked with a wooden cross, or a round stick, the branch of a tree rudely trimmed, but significant as the only token bitter poverty could furnish of undying love; while over all the graves, alike of the high born and of the lowly, the weeds and nettles grow.

'Sure there's no saxton, Sorr,' said car-man Jerry Magwire, in answer to a question, 'We dig the graves ourselves whin we put them away, an' sometimes there's a fight in the place whin two berryin's meet. Why is that? Faith, it's not for us to be talkin' o' them deep subjects widout respĭct, but it's the belafe that the last wan berrid must be carryin' wather all the time to the sowls in Purgathory till the next wan comes to take the place av him. So, ye mind, when two berryin's happen to meet, aitch party is shtrivin' to be done foorst, an' wan thries to make the other lave aff, an' thin they have it. Troth, Irishmen are too handy wid their fishts entirely, it's a weak pint wid 'em. But it's a sad sight, so it is, to see the graves wid the nettles on thim an' the walls all tumblin'. It isn't every owld church that has a caretaker like him of Cashel. Bedad, he was betther nor a flock av goats to banish the weeds.

'Who was he? Faith, I niver saw him but the wan time, an' thin I had only a shot at him as he was turnin' a corner, for it was as I was lavin' Cormac's chapel the time I wint to Cashel on a pinance, bekase av a little throuble on me mind along av a pig that wasn't mine, but got mixed wid mine whin I was afther killin' it. But, as I observed, it was only a shot at him I had, for it wasn't aften that he was seen in the daytime, but done all his work in the night, an' it isn't me that'ud be climbin' the Rock av Cashel afther the sun'ud go to slape. Not that there's avil sper'ts there, for none that's bad can set fut on that holy ground day or night, but I'm not afther wantin' to meet a sper't av any kind, even if it's good, for how can ye tell about thim. Sure aven the blessed saints have been desaved, an' it's not for a sinner like me to be settin' up for to know more than thimselves. But it was the long, bent body that he had, like he'd a burdhen on his back, as they say, God be good to him, he had on his sowl, an' the great, blue eyes lookin' out as if he was gazin' on the other worruld. No, I didn't run down the rock, but I didn't walk aither, but jist bechuxt the two, wid a sharp eye round the corners that I passed. No more do I belave there was harrum in him, but, God's prisence be about us, ye can't tell.

'He was a man o' Clare be the name av Paddy O'Sullivan, an' lived on the highway betune Crusheen an' Ennis, an' they do say that whin he was a lad, there wasn't a finer to be seen in the County; a tall, shtrappin' young felly wid an eye like a bay'net, an' a fisht like a shmith, an' the fut an' leg av him'ud turn the hearts o' half the wimmin in the parish. An' they was all afther him, like they always do be whin a man is good lookin', sure I've had a little o' that same exparience mesilf. Ye needn't shmile. I know me head has no more hair on it than an egg, an' I think me last tooth'ull come out tomorrer, bad cess to the day, but they do say that forty years ago, I cud have me pick av the gurruls, an' mebbe they're mishtaken an' mebbe not. But I was sayin', the gurruls were afther Paddy like rats afther chaze, an' sorra wan o' thim but whin she spied him on the road, 'ud shlip behind the hedge to shmooth her locks a bit an' set the shawl shtraight on her head. An' whin there was a bit av a dance, niver a boy'ud get a chance till Paddy made his chice to dance wid, an' sorra a good word the rest o' the gurruls'ud give that same. Och, the tongues that wimmin have! Sure they're sharper nor a draggin's tooth. Faith, I know that well too, for I married two o' them an' larned a deal too afther doin' it, an' axin' yer pardon, it's my belafe that if min knewn as much before marryin' as afther, bedad, the owld maid population'ud be greatly incrased.

'Howandiver, afther a bit, Paddy left carin' for thim all, that, in my consate, is a moighty safe way, and begun to look afther wan. Her name was Nora O'Moore, an' she was as clever a gurrul as'ud be found bechuxt Limerick an' Galway. She was kind o' resarved like, wid a face as pale as a shroud, an' hair as black as a crow, an' eyes that looked at ye an' never seen ye. No more did she talk much, an' whin Paddy'ud be sayin' his fine spaches, she'd listen wid her eyes cast down, an' whin she'd had enough av his palaver, she'd jist look at him an' somehow Paddy felt that his p'liteness wasn't the thing to work wid. He cudn't undhershtand her, an' bedad, many's the man that's caught be not undhershtandin' thim. There's rivers that's quiet on top bekase they're deep, an' more that's quiet bekase they're not deep enough to make a ripple, but phat's the differ if ye can't sound thim, an' whin a woman's quiet, begorra, it's not aisy to say if she's deep or shallow. But Nora was a deep wan, an' as good as iver drew a breath. She thought a dale av Paddy, only she'd be torn limb from limb afore she'd let him know it till he confist first. Well, my dear, paddy wint on, at firsht it was only purtindin' he was, an' whin he found she cudn't be tuk wid his chaff, he got in airnest, an' afore he knewn it, he was dead in love wid Nora, an' had as much show for gettin' out agin as a shape in a bog, an' sorra a bit did he know at all at all, whether she cared a traneen for him. It's funny entirely that whin a man thinks a woman is afther him, he's aff like a hare, but if she doesn't car a rap, begob, he'll give the nose aff his face to get her. So it was wid paddy an' Nora, axceptin' that Paddy didn't know that Nora wanted him as much as he wanted her.

'So, wan night, whin he was bringin' her from a dance that they'd been at, he said to her that he loved her betther than life an' towld her would she marry him, an' she axed was it jokin' or in airnest he was, an' he said cud she doubt it whin he loved her wid all the veins av his heart, an' she trimbled, turnin' paler than iver, an' thin blushin' rosy red for joy an' towld him yes, an' he kissed her, an' they both thought the throuble was all over foreiver. It's a way thim lovers has,, an' they must be axcused, bekase it's the same wid thim all.

'But it wann't at all, fur Nora had an owld squireen av a father, that was as full av maneness as eggs is av mate. Sure he was the divil entirely at home, an' niver left off wid the crassness that was in im. The timper av him was spiled be rason o' losing his bit o' money wid cards an' racin', an' like some min, he tuk it out wid his wife an' dawther. There was only the three o' thim in it, an' they do say that whin he was crazy wid dhrink, he'd bate thim right an' lift, an' turn thim out o' the cabin into the night, niver heeding, the baste, phat'ud come to thim. But they niver said a word thimselves, an' the nabers only larned av it be seein' thim.

'Well. Whin O'Moore was towld that Paddy was kapin' comp'ny wid Nora, an' the latther an' her mother towld him she wanted fur to marry Paddy, thw owld felly got tarin' mad, fur he was as proud as a paycock, an' though he'd nothin' himself, he riz agin the match, an' all the poor mother an' Nora cud say 'udn't sthir him.

' "Sure I've nothin' agin him," he'd say, "barrin' he's as poor as a fiddler, an' I want Nora to make a good match."

'Now the owld felly had a match in his mind fur Nora, a lad from Tipperary, whose father was a farmer there, an' had a shmart bit av land wid no end av shape grazin' on it, an' the Tipperary boy wasn't bad at all, only as shtupid as a donkey, an' whin he'd come to see Nora, bad cess to the word he'd to say, only look at her a bit an' thin fall aslape an' knock his head agin the wall. But he wanted her, an' his father an' O'Moore put their heads together over a glass an' aggrade that the young wans'ud be married.

' "Sure I don't love him a bit, father," Nora'ud say.

' "Be aff wid yer nonsinse," he'd say to her. "Phat does it matther about love, whin he's got more nor a hundred shape. Sure I wudn't give the wool av thim fur all the love in Clare," says he, an' wid that the argymint'ud end.

'So Nora towld paddy an' Paddy said he'd not give her up for all the men in Tipperary or all the shape in Ireland, an' it was aggrade that in wan way or another, they'd be married in spite av owld O'Moore, though Nora hated to do it, bekase, as I was afther tellin' ye, she was a good gurrul, an' wint to mass an' to her duty reg'lar. But like the angel that she was, she towld her mother an' the owld lady was agrayble, an' so Nora consinted.

'But O'Moore was shrewder than a fox whin he was sober, an' that was whin he'd no money to shpend in dhrink, an' this being' wan o' thim times, he watched Nora an' begun to suspicion somethin'. So he made belave that everything was right an' the next time that Murphy, that bein' the name o' the Tipperary farmer, came, the two owld fellys settled it that O'Moore an' Nora'ud come to Tipperary av the Winsday afther, that bein' the day o' the fair in Ennis that they knew Paddy'ud be at, an' whin they got to Tipperary, they'd marry Nora an' young Murphy at wanst. So owld Murphy was to sind the car afther thim an' everything was made sure. So, av the Winsday, towards noon, says owld O'Moore to Nora: ' "Be in a hurry now, me child, an' make yersel' as fine as ye can, an' Murphy's car'ull be here to take us to the fair."

'Nora didn't want to go, for Paddy was comin' out in the afthernoon, misthrustin' that owld O'Moore'ud be at the fair. But O'Moore only towld her to make hast wid hersilf or they'd be late, an' she did. So the car came, wid a boy dhriving, an' owld O'Moore axed the boy if he wanted to go to the fair, so that Nora cudn't hear him, an' the boy said yes, an' O'Moore towld him to go an' he'd dhrive an' bring him back tomorrer. So the boy wint away, an' O'Moore an' Nora got up an' shtrated. Whin they came to the crass-road, O'Moore tuk the road to Tipperary.

' "Sure father, ye're wrong," says Nora, "that's not the way."

' "No more is it," said the owld desayver, "but I'm afther wantin' to see a frind o' mine over here a bit an' we'll come round to the Ennis road on the other side," says he.

'So Nora thought no more av it, but whin they wint on an' on, widout shtoppin' at all, she begun to be disquisitive agin.

' "Father, is it to Ennis or not ye're takin' me," says she.

'Now, be this time, they'd got on a good bit, an' the owld villin seen it was no use thryin' to desave her any longer.

' "I'm not," says he, "but it's to Tipperary ye're goin', where ye're to be married to Misther Murphy this blessed day, so ye are, an' make no throuble about it aither, or it'll be the worse for ye," says he, lookin' moighty black.

'Well, at first Nora thought her heart'ud shtand still. 'Sure, Father dear, ye don't mane it, ye cudn't be so cruel. It's like a blighted tree I'd be, wid that man,' an' she thried to jump aff the car, but her father held her wid a grip av stale.

' "Kape still," says he wid his teeth closed like a vise. "If ye crass me, I'm like to murdher ye. It's me only escape from prison, for I'm in debt an' Murphy'ull help me," says he. "Sure," says he, saftenin' a bit as he seen the white face an' great pleadin' eyes, "Sure ye'll be happy enough wid Murphy. He loves ye, an' ye can love him, an' besides, think o' the shape."

'But Nora sat there, a poor dumb thing, wid her eyes lookin' deeper than iver wid the misery that was in thim. An' from that minit, she didn't spake a word, but all her sowl was determined that she'd die afore she'd marry Murphy, but how she'd get out av it she didn't know at all, but watched her chance to run.

'Now it happened that owld O'Moore, bein' disturbed in his mind, mistuk the way, an' whin he come to the crass-roads, wan to Tipperary an' wan to Cashel, he tuk the wan for the other, an' whin the horse thried to go home to Tipperary, he wudn't let him, but pulled him into the Cashel road. Faix, he might have knewn that if he'd let the baste alone, he'd take him right, fur horses knows a deal more than ye'd think. That horse o' mine is only a common garron av a baste, but he tuk me from Ballyvaughn to Lisdoon Varna wan night whin it was so dark that ye cudn't find yer nose, an' wint be the rath in a gallop, like he'd seen the good people. But niver mind, I'll tell ye the shtory sometime, only I was thinkin' O'Moore might have knewn betther.

'But they tuk the Cashel road an' wint on as fast as they cud, for it was afthernoon an' gettin' late. An' O'Moore kept lookin' about an' wonderin' that he didn't know the counthry, though he'd niver been to Tipperary but wanst, an' afther a while, he gev up that he was lost entirely. No more wud he ax the people on the road, but gev thim "God save ye" very short, for he was afeared Nora might make throuble. An' by an' by, it come on to rain, an' whin they turned the corner av a hill, he seen the Rock o' Cashel wid the churches onit, an' thin he stopped.

' "Phat's this at all," says he. "Faix, if that isn't Cashel I'll ate it, an' we've come out o' the way altogether."

'Nora answered him niver a word, an' he shtarted to turn round, but whin he looked at the horse, the poor baste was knocked up entirely.

' "We'll go on to Cashel," says he, "an' find a shebeen, an' go back in the mornin'. It's hard luck we're afther havin'," says he.

'So they wint on, an' jist afore they got to the Rock, they seen a nate lodgin' house be the road an' wint in. He left Nora to sit be the fire, while he wint to feed the horse, an' whin he come back in a minit, he looked for her, but faith, she'd given him the shlip an' was gone complately.

' "Where is me dawther?" says he.

' "Faith, I dunno," says the maid. "She walked out av the dure on the minit," says she.

'Owld O'Moore run, an' Satan an' none but himself turned him in the way she was afther takin.' God be good to thim, no wan iver knewn phat tuk place, but whin they wint wid a lanthern to sarch fur thim whin they didn't raturn, they found the marks o' their feet on the road to the strame. Halfway down the path they picked up Nora's shawl that was torn an' flung on the ground an' fut marks in plenty they found, as if he had caught her an' thried to howld her an' cudn't, an' on the marks wint to the high bank av the strame, that was a torrent be razon av the rain. An' there they ended wid a big slice o' the bank fallen in, an' the sarchers crassed thimselves wid fright an wint back an' prayed for the repose av their sowls.

'The next day they found thim, a good Irish mile down the strame, owld O'Moore wid wan hand howlding her gown an' the other wan grippin' her collar an' the clothes half torn aff her poor cowld corpse, her hands stratched out afore her, wid the desperation in her heart to get away, an' her white face wid the great eyes an' the light gone out av thim, the poor craythur, God give her rest, an' so to us all.

'They laid thim dacintly, wid candles an' all, an' the wake that they

had was shuparb, fur the shtory was towld in all the counthry, wid
the vartues av Nora; an' the O'Brian's come from Ennis, an' the
O'Moore's from Crusheen, an' the Murphy's an' their frinds from
Tipperary, an' more from Clonmel. There was a power av atin' an'
slathers av dhrink fur thim that wanted it, fur, d' ye mind, thim of
Cashel thried fur to show the rale Irish hoshpitality bekase O'Moore
an' Nora were sint there to die an' they thought it was their juty to
thrate thim well. An' all the County Clare an' Tipperary was at the
berryin', an' they had three keeners, the best that iver was, wan from
Ennis, wan from Tipperary, an' wan from Limerick, so that the
praises av Nora wint on day an' night till the berryin' was done. An'
they made Nora's grave in Cormac's Chapel just front o' the Archbishop's tomb in the wall an' berried her first, an' tuk O'Moore as far
from her as they cud get him, an' put his grave as clost be the wall as
they cud go fur the shtones an' jist ferninst the big gate on the left
hand side, an' berried him last, an' sorra the good word they had fur
him aither.

'Poor Paddy wint nayther to the wake nor to the berryin', fur afther
they towld him the news, he sat as wan in a dhrame, no more cud they
rouse him. He'd go to his work very quite, an' niver shpake a word.
An' so it was, about a fortnight afther, he says to his mother, says he,
"Mother I seen Nora last night an' she stood be me side an' laid her
hand on me brow, an' says 'Come to Cashel, Paddy dear, an' be wid
me.' " An' his mother was frighted entirely, for she parsaved he was
wrong in his head. She thried to aise his mind, but the next night he
disappeared. They folly'd him to Cashel, but he dodged an' kept from
thim complately whin they come an' so they left him. In the day he'd
hide an' slape, an' afther night, Nora's sper't'ud mate him an' walk
wid him up an' down the shtones av the Chapel an' undher the arches
av the Cathaydral, an' he cared fur her grave, an' bekase she was
berried there, fur the gravs av all thim that shlept on the Rock. No
more had he any frinds, but thim o' Cashel'ud lave pitaties an' bread
where he'd see it an' so he lived. Fur sixty wan years was he on the
Rock an' never left it, but he'd sometimes show himself in the day
whin there was a berryin', an' say, "Ye've brought me another frind,"
an' help in the work, an' never was there a graveyard kept like that
o' Cashel.

'When he got owld, an' where he cud look into the other worruld,

Nora came ivery night an' brought more wid her, sper'ts av kings an' bishops that rest on Cashel, an' there's thim that's seen the owld man walkin' in Cormac's Chapel, Nora holdin' him up an' him discoorsin' wid the mighty dead. They found him wan day, cowld an' shtill, on Nora's grave, an' laid him be her side, God rest his sowl, an' there he slapes today, God be good to him.

'They said he was only a poor owld innocent, but all is aqualised, an' thim that's despised sometimes have betther comp'ny among the angels than that of mortials.'

JOSEPH JACOBS

The Field of Boliauns

One fine day in harvest – it was indeed Ladyday in harvest, that everybody knows to be one of the greatest holidays in the year – Tom Fitzpatrick was taking a ramble through the ground, and went along the sunny side of a hedge; when all of a sudden he heard a clacking sort of noise a little before him in the hedge. 'Dear me,' said Tom, 'but isn't it surprising to hear the stonechatters singing so late in the season?' So Tom stole on, going on the tops of his toes to try if he could get a sight of what was making the noise, to see if he was right in his guess. The noise stopped; but as Tom looked sharply through the bushes, what should he see in a nook of the hedge but a brown pitcher, that might hold about a gallon and a half of liquor; and by and by a little wee teeny tiny bit of an old man, with a little *motty* of a cocked hat stuck upon the top of his head, a deeshy daushy leather apron hanging before him, pulled out a little wooden stool, and stood up upon it, and dipped a little piggin into the pitcher, and took out the full of it, and put it beside the stool, and then sat down under the pitcher, and began to work at putting a heel-piece on a bit of a brogue just fit for himself. 'Well, by the powers,' said Tom to himself, 'I often heard tell of the Lepracauns, and, to tell God's truth, I never rightly believed in them – but here's one of them in real earnest. If I go knowingly to work, I'm a made man. They say a body must never take their eyes off them, or they'll escape.'

Tom now stole on a little further, with his eye fixed on the little man just as a cat does with a mouse. So when he got up quite close to him, 'God bless your work, neighbour,' said Tom.

The little man raised up his head, and 'Thank you kindly,' said he.

'I wonder you'd be working on the holiday!' said Tom.

'That's my own business, not yours,' was the reply.

'Well, maybe you'd be civil enough to tell us what you've got in the pitcher there?' said Tom.

'That I will with pleasure,' said he; 'it's good beer.'

'Beer!' said Tom. 'Thunder and fire! where did you get it?'

'Where did I get it, is it? Why, I made it. And what do you think I made it of?'

'Devil a one of me knows,' said Tom; 'but of malt, I suppose, what else?'

'There you're out. I made it of heath.'

'Of heath!' said Tom, bursting out laughing; 'sure you don't think me to be such a fool as to believe that?'

'Do as you please,' said he, 'but what I tell you is the truth. Did you never hear tell of the Danes?'

'Well, what about them?' said Tom.

'Why, when they were here they taught us to make beer out of the heath, and the secret's in my family ever since.'

'Will you give a body a taste of your beer?' said Tom.

'I'll tell you what it is, young man, it would be fitter for you to be looking after your father's property than to be bothering decent quiet people with your foolish questions. There now, while you're idling away your time here, there's the cows have broke into the oats, and are knocking the corn all about.'

Tom was taken so by surprise with this that he was just on the very point of turning round when he recollected himself; so, afraid that the like might happen again, he made a grab at the Lepracaun, and caught him up in his hand; but in his hurry he overset the pitcher, and spilled all the beer, so that he could not get a taste of it to tell what sort it was. He then swore that he would kill him if he did not show him where his money was. Tom looked so wicked and so bloody-minded that the little man was quite frightened; so says he, 'Come along with me a couple of fields off, and I'll show you a crock of gold.'

So they went, and Tom held the Lepracaun fast in his hand, and never took his eyes from off him, though they had to cross hedges and ditches, and a crooked bit of bog, till at last they came to a great field all full of boliauns, and the Lepracaun pointed to a big boliaun, and says he, 'Dig under that boliaun, and you'll get the great crock all full of guineas.'

Tom in his hurry had never thought of bringing a spade with him, so he made up his mind to run home and fetch one; and that he might know the place again he took off one of his red garters, and tied it round the boliaun.

Then he said to the Lepracaun, 'Swear ye'll not take that garter away from that boliaun.' And the Lepracaun swore right away not to touch it.

'I suppose,' said the Lepracaun, very civilly, 'you have no further occasion for me?'

'No,' says Tom; 'you may go away now, if you please, and God speed you, and may good luck attend you wherever you go.'

'Well, goodbye to you, Tom Fitzpatrick,' said the Lepracaun; 'and much good might it do you when you get it.'

So Tom ran for dear life, till he came home and got a spade, and then away with him, as hard as he could go, back to the field of boliauns; but when he got there, lo and behold! not a boliaun in the field but had a red garter, the very model of his own, tied about it; and as to digging up the whole field, that was all nonsense, for there were more than forty good Irish acres in it. So Tom came home again with his spade on his shoulder, a little cooler than he went, and many's the hearty curse he gave the Lepracaun every time he thought of the neat turn he had served him.